John Mitford

The Works of John Dryden

Vol. II

SALZWASSER
VERLAG

John Mitford

The Works of John Dryden

Vol. II

Reprint of the original, first published in 1859.

1st Edition 2022 | ISBN: 978-3-37513-403-7

Verlag (Publisher): Salzwasser Verlag GmbH, Zeilweg 44, 60439 Frankfurt, Deutschland
Vertretungsberechtigt (Authorized to represent): E. Roepke, Zeilweg 44, 60439 Frankfurt, Deutschland
Druck (Print): Books on Demand GmbH, In de Tarpen 42, 22848 Norderstedt, Deutschland

THE

WORKS OF JOHN DRYDEN,

IN VERSE AND PROSE,

WITH A LIFE,

BY REV. JOHN MITFORD.

IN TWO VOLUMES.

VOL. II.

NEW YORK:
HARPER & BROTHERS, PUBLISHERS,
329 & 331 PEARL STREET,
FRANKLIN SQUARE.
1859.

CONTENTS.

VOL. II.

CONTENTS.

TO

THE RIGHT HONOURABLE

PHILIP,

EARL OF CHESTERFIELD, &c.*

MY LORD,

I CANNOT begin my address to your lordship better than in the words of Virgil:

> ——Quod optanti divûm promittere nemo
> Auderet, volvenda dies, en, attulit ultro.

Seven years together I have concealed the longing which I had to appear before you: a time as tedious as Æneas passed in his wandering voyage, before he reached the promised Italy. But I considered, that nothing which my meanness could produce was worthy of your patronage. At last this happy occasion offered, of presenting to you the best poem of the best poet. If I balked this opportunity, I was in despair of finding such another; and, if I took it, I was still uncertain whether you would vouchsafe to accept it from my hands. It was a bold venture which I made, in desiring your permission to lay my unworthy labours at your feet. But my rashness has succeeded beyond my hopes; and you have been pleased not to suffer an old man to go discontented out of the world, for want of that protection, of which he had been so long ambitious. I have known a gentleman in disgrace, and not daring to appear before King Charles the Second, though he much desired it: at length he took the confidence to attend a fair lady to the court, and told his majesty, that, under her protection, he had presumed to wait on him. With the same humble confidence, I present myself before your lordship, and, attending on Virgil, hope a gracious reception. The gentleman succeeded, because the powerful lady was his friend; but I have too much injured my great author, to expect he should intercede for me. I would have translated him; but, according to the literal French and Italian phrases, I fear I have *traduced* him. It is the fault of many a well-meaning man, to be officious in a wrong place, and do a prejudice where he had endeavoured to do a service. Virgil wrote his Georgics in the full strength and vigour of his age, when his judgment was at the height, and before his fancy was declining. He had (according to our homely saying) his full swing at this poem, beginning it about the age of thirty-five, and scarce concluding it before he arrived at forty. It is observed, both of him and Horace, (and I believe it will hold in all great poets,) that, though they wrote before with a certain heat of genius which inspired them, yet that heat was not perfectly digested. There is required a continuance of warmth, to ripen the best and noblest fruits. Thus Horace, in his First and Second Book of Odes, was still rising, but came not to his meridian till the Third; after which, his judgment was an overpoise to his imagination: he grew too cautious to be bold enough; for he descended in his Fourth by slow degrees, and, in his Satires and Epistles, was more a philosopher and a critic than a poet. In the beginning of summer, the days are almost at a stand, with little variation of length or shortness, because at that time the diurnal motion of the sun partakes more of a right line than of a spiral. The same is the method of nature in the frame of man. He seems at forty to be fully in his summer tropic; somewhat before, and

* Philip Stanhope, second Earl of Chesterfield, born in 1634. He was a man of considerable talent and political activity; was active in forwarding the Restoration; and enjoyed at the court of Charles II several offices, but was now retired. He died in 1713.

somewhat after, he finds in his soul but small increases or decays. From fifty to three-score, the balance generally holds even, in our colder climates: for he loses not much in fancy; and judgment, which is the effect of observation, still increases. His succeeding years afford him little more than the stubble of his own harvest: yet, if his constitution be healthful, his mind may still retain a decent vigour; and the gleanings of that Ephraim, in comparison with others, will surpass the vintage of Abiezer. I have called this somewhere, by a bold metaphor, a green old age; but Virgil has given me his authority for the figure—

Jam senior; sed cruda Deo, viridisque senectus.

Among those few who enjoy the advantage of a latter spring, your lordship is a rare example; who, being now arrived at your great climacteric, yet give no proof of the least decay of your excellent judgment and comprehension of all things which are within the compass of human understanding. Your conversation is as easy as it is instructive; and I could never observe the least vanity, or the least assuming, in any thing you said, but a natural unaffected modesty, full of good sense, and well digested; a clearness of notion, expressed in ready and unstudied words. No man has complained, or even can, that you have discoursed too long on any subject; for you leave us in an eagerness of learning more; pleased with what we hear, but not satisfied, because you will not speak so much as we could wish. I dare not excuse your lordship from this fault; for, though it is none in you, it is one to all who have the happiness of being known to you. I must confess, the critics make it one of Virgil's beauties, that, having said what he thought convenient, he always left somewhat for the imagination of his readers to supply; that they might gratify their fancies, by finding more in what he had written, than at first they could; and think they had added to his thought, when it was all there beforehand, and he only saved himself the expense of words. However it was, I never went from your lordship, but with a longing to return, or without a hearty curse to him who invented ceremonies in the world, and put me on the necessity of withdrawing, when it was my interest, as well as my desire, to have given you a much longer trouble. I cannot imagine, (if your lordship will give me leave to speak my thoughts,) but you have had a more than ordinary vigour in your youth; for too much of heat is required at first, that there may not too little be left at last. A prodigal fire is only capable of large remains; and yours, my lord, still burns the clearer in declining. The blaze is not so fierce as at the first; but the smoke is wholly vanished; and your friends, who stand about you, are not only sensible of a cheerful warmth, but are kept at an awful distance by its force. In my small observations of mankind, I have ever found, that such as are not rather too full of spirit when they are young, degenerate to dulness in their age. Sobriety in our riper years is the effect of a well-concocted warmth: but, where the principles are only phlegm, what can be expected from the waterish matter, but an insipid manhood, and a stupid old infancy—discretion in leading-strings, and a confirmed ignorance on crutches? Virgil, in his Third Georgic, when he describes a colt, who promises a courser for the race, or for the field of battle, shows him the first to pass the bridge, which trembles under him, and to stem the torrent of the flood. His beginnings must be in rashness—a noble fault; but time and experience will correct that error, and tame it into a deliberate and well-weighed courage, which knows both to be cautious and to dare, as occasion offers. Your lordship is a man of honour, not only so unstained, but so unquestioned, that you are the living standard of that heroic virtue; so truly such, that if I would flatter you, I could not. It takes not from you, that you were born with principles of generosity and probity; but it adds to you, that you have cultivated nature, and made those principles the rule and measure of all your actions. The world knows this, without my telling; yet poets have a right of recording it to all posterity:

Dignum laude virum Musa vetat mori.

Epaminondas, Lucullus, and the two first Cæsars, were not esteemed the worse commanders, for having made philosophy and the liberal arts their study. Cicero might have been their equal, but that he wanted courage. To have both these virtues, and to have improved them both with a softness of manners and a sweetness of conversation—few of our nobility can fill that character. One there is, and so conspicuous by his own light, that he needs not

Digito monstrari, et dicier, "Hic est!"

To be nobly born, and of an ancient family, is in the extremes of fortune, either good or bad; for virtue and descent are no inheritance. A long series of ancestors shows the native with great advantage at the first; but, if he any way degenerate from his line, the least spot is visible on ermine. But, to preserve this whiteness in its original purity, you, my lord, have, like that ermine, forsaken the common track of busi-

ease, which is not always clean: you have chosen for yourself a private greatness, and will not be polluted with ambition. It has been observed in former times, that none have been so greedy of employments, and of managing the public, as they who have least deserved their stations. But such only merit to be called patriots, under whom we see their country flourish. I have laughed sometimes, (for who would always be a Heraclitus?) when I have reflected on those men, who from time to time have shot themselves into the world. I have seen many successions of them; some bolting out upon the stage with vast applause, and others hissed off, and quitting it with disgrace. But, while they were in action, I have constantly observed, that they seemed desirous to retreat from business: greatness, they said, was nauseous, and a crowd was troublesome: a quiet privacy was their ambition. Some few of them, I believe, said this in earnest, and were making a provision against future want, that they might enjoy their age with ease. They saw the happiness of a private life, and promised to themselves a blessing, which every day it was in their power to possess. But they deferred it, and lingered still at court, because they thought they had not yet enough to make them happy: they would have more, and laid in, to make their solitude luxurious: — a wretched philosophy, which Epicurus never taught them in his garden. They loved the prospect of this quiet in reversion, but were not willing to have it in possession: they would first be old, and make as sure of health and life, as if both of them were at their dispose. But put them to the necessity of a present choice, and they preferred continuance in power; like the wretch who called Death to his assistance, but refused him when he came. The great Scipio was not of their opinion, who indeed sought honours in his youth, and endured the fatigues with which he purchased them. He served his country when it was in need of his courage and conduct, till he thought it was time to serve himself; but dismounted from the saddle when he found the beast which bore him began to grow restiff and ungovernable. But your lordship has given us a better example of moderation. You saw betimes, that ingratitude is not confined to commonwealths; and therefore, though you were formed alike for the greatest of civil employments and military commands, yet you pushed not your fortune to rise in either, but contented yourself with being capable, as much as any whosoever, of defending your country with your sword, or assisting it with your counsel, when you were called.* For the rest, the respect and love which was paid you, not only in the province where you live, but generally by all who had the happiness to know you, was a wise exchange for the honours of the court—a place of forgetfulness, at the best, for well-deservers. It is necessary, for the polishing of manners, to have breathed that air; but it is infectious, even to the best morals, to live always in it. It is a dangerous commerce, where an honest man is sure at the first of being cheated, and he recovers not his' losses, but by learning to cheat others. The undermining smile becomes at length habitual; and the drift of his plausible conversation is only to flatter one, that he may betray another. Yet it is good to have been a looker on, without venturing to play; that a man may know false dice another time, though he never means to use them. I commend not him who never knew a court, but him who forsakes it because he knows it. A young man deserves no praise, who, out of melancholy zeal, leaves the world before he has well tried it, and runs headlong into religion. He who carries a maidenhead into a cloister, is sometimes apt to lose it there, and to repent of his repentance. He only is like to endure austerities, who has already found the inconvenience of pleasures: for almost every man will be making experiments in one part or another of his life; and the danger is the less when we are young; for, having tried it early, we shall not be apt to repeat it afterwards. Your lordship therefore may properly be said to have chosen a retreat, and not to have chosen it till you had maturely weighed the advantages of rising higher, with the hazards of the fall.

Res, non parta labore, sed relicta,

was thought by a poet to be one of the requisites to a happy life. Why should a reasonable man put it into the power of Fortune to make him miserable, when his ancestors have taken care to release him from her? Let him venture, says Horace, *qui zonam perdidit*. He, who has nothing, plays securely; for he may win, and cannot be poorer if he loses: but he who is born to a plentiful estate, and is ambitious of offices at court, sets a stake to Fortune, which she can seldom answer. If he gains nothing, he loses all, or part of what was once his own, and, if he gets, he cannot be certain but he may refund.

* Dryden's praise, though often hyperbolical, is always founded on some circumstances appropriate to its object. Lord Chesterfield, who had enjoyed offices of honour at the court of Charles II., now lived in retirement at an elegant villa, according to Mr. Malone, near Twickenham.

In short, however he succeeds, it is covetousness that induced him first to play; and covetousness is the undoubted sign of ill sense at bottom. The odds are against him, that he loses; and one loss may be of more consequence to him than all his former winnings. It is like the present war of the Christians against the Turks; every year they gain a victory, and by that a town; but, if they are once defeated, they lose a province at a blow, and endanger the safety of the whole empire. You, my lord, enjoy your quiet in a garden, where you have not only the leisure of thinking, but the pleasure to think of nothing which can discompose your mind. A good conscience is a port which is land-locked on every side, and where no winds can possibly invade, no tempests can arise. There a man may stand upon the shore, and not only see his own image, but that of his Maker, clearly reflected from the undisturbed and silent waters. Reason was intended for a blessing; and such it is to men of honour and integrity, who desire no more than what they are able to give themselves; like the happy old Corycian, whom my author describes in his Fourth Georgic, whose fruits and sallads, on which he lived contented, were all of his own growth, and his own plantation. Virgil seems to think, that the blessings of a country life are not complete without an improvement of knowledge by contemplation and reading.

> O fortunatos nimium, sua si bona nôrint,
> Agricolas!

It is but half possession, not to understand that happiness which we possess. A foundation of good sense, and a cultivation of learning, are required to give a seasoning to retirement, and make us taste the blessing. God has bestowed on your lordship the first of these; and you have bestowed on yourself the second. Eden was not made for beasts, though they were suffered to live in it, but for their master, who studied God in the works of his creation. Neither could the devil have been happy there with all his knowledge; for he wanted innocence to make him so. He brought envy, malice, and ambition, into Paradise, which soured to him the sweetness of the place. Wherever inordinate affections are, 'tis hell. Such only can enjoy the country, who are capable of thinking when they are there, and have left the passions behind them in the town. Then they are prepared for solitude; and, in that solitude, is prepared for them,

> Et secura quies, et nescia fallere vita.

As I began this Dedication with a verse of Virgil, so I conclude it with another.

The continuance of your health, to enjoy that happiness which you so well deserve, and which you have provided for yourself, is the sincere and earnest wish of

Your lordship's
Most devoted
And most obedient servant
JOHN DRYDEN.

AN

ESSAY ON THE GEORGICS.

BY

MR. ADDISON.*

VIRGIL may be reckoned the first who introduced three new kinds of poetry among the Romans, which he copied after three the greatest masters of Greece. Theocritus and Homer have still disputed for the advantage over him in Pastoral and Heroics; but I think all are unanimous in giving him the precedence to Hesiod in his "Georgics." The truth of it is, the sweetness and rusticity of a Pastoral cannot be so well expressed in any other tongue as in the Greek, when rightly mixed and qualified with the Doric dialect; nor can the majesty of a Heroic poem anywhere appear so well as in this language, which has a natural greatness in it, and can be often rendered more deep and sonorous by the pronunciation of the Ionians. But, in the middle style, where the writers in both tongues are on a level, we see how far Virgil has excelled all who have written in the same way with him.

There has been abundance of criticism spent on Virgil's "Pastorals" and "Æneis;" but the "Georgics" are a subject which none of the critics have sufficiently taken into their consideration; most of them passing it over in silence, or casting it under the same head with pastoral: a division by no means proper, unless we suppose the style of a husbandman ought to be imitated in a Georgic, as that of a shepherd is in a Pastoral. But, though the scene of both these poems lies in the same place, the speakers in them are of a quite different character, since the precepts of husbandry are not to be delivered with the simplicity of a ploughman, but with the address of a poet. No rules, therefore, that relate to pastoral, can any way affect the Georgics, which fall under that class of poetry which consists in giving plain and direct instructions to the reader; whether they be moral duties, as those of Theognis and Pythagoras, or philosophical speculations, as those of Aratus and Lucretius, or rules of practice, as those of Hesiod and Virgil. Among these different kinds of subjects, that which the Georgic goes upon, is, I think, the meanest and least improving, but the most pleasing and delightful. Precepts of morality, besides the natural corruption of our tempers, which makes us averse to them, are so abstracted from ideas of sense, that they seldom give an opportunity for those beautiful descriptions and images which are the spirit and life of poetry. Natural philosophy has indeed sensible objects to work upon; but then it often puzzles the reader with the intricacy of its notions, and perplexes him with the multitude of its disputes. But this kind of poetry I am now speaking of addresses itself wholly to the imagination: it is altogether conversant among the fields and woods, and has the most delightful part of nature for its province. It raises in our minds a pleasing variety of scenes and land-

* Addison had already distinguished himself as a man of letters, and as an admirer of Dryden, by a copy of verses addressed to our author, and by a translation of the Fourth Book of the Georgics, exclusive of the story of Aristaeus. This last performance is liberally commended by Dryden in the Postscript to Virgil. The following Essay, which has been much admired for judicious criticism contained in elegant language, was sent by him to our author, but without permission to prefix the writer's name. This circumstance led Tickell to throw some reflection on Dryden, as if he had meant to assume to himself the merit of the composition. This charge was refuted by Steele, in a letter to Congreve, prefixed to an edition of the comedy of "The Drummer," in 1722, who proves, that the Essay was the same paper which Dryden calls the Preface to the Georgics, and which he acknowledges to have been sent by a friend, whose name he was not at liberty to make public. See the article *Addison* in the "Biographia Britannica."

scapes, whilst it teaches us, and makes the driest of its precepts look like a description. *A Georgic, therefore, is some part of the science of husbandry put into a pleasing dress, and set off with all the beauties and embellishments of poetry.* Now, since this science of husbandry is of a very large extent, the poet shows his skill in singling out such precepts to proceed on, as are useful, and at the same time most capable of ornament. Virgil was so well acquainted with this secret, that, to set off his Georgics, he has run into a set of precepts, which are almost foreign to his subject, in that beautiful account he gives us of the signs in nature, which precede the changes of the weather.

And, if there be so much art in the choice of fit precepts, there is much more required in the treating of them, that they may fall in after each other by a natural unforced method, and show themselves in the best and most advantageous light. They should all be so finely wrought together in the same piece, that no coarse seam may discover where they join; as, in a curious brede of needlework, one colour falls away by such just degrees, and another rises so insensibly, that we see the variety, without being able to distinguish the total vanishing of the one from the first appearance of the other. Nor is it sufficient to range and dispose this body of precepts into a clear and easy method, unless they are delivered to us in the most pleasing and agreeable manner: for there are several ways of conveying the same truth to the mind of man; and to choose the pleasantest of these ways is that which chiefly distinguishes poetry from prose, and makes Virgil's rules of husbandry pleasanter to read than Varro's. Where the prose-writer tells us plainly what ought to be done, the poet often conceals the precept in a description, and represents his countryman performing the action in which he would instruct his reader. Where the one sets out, as fully and distinctly as he can, all the parts of the truth which he would communicate to us, the other singles out the most pleasing circumstance of this truth, and so conveys the whole in a more diverting manner to the understanding. I shall give one instance, out of a multitude of this nature, that might be found in the Georgics, where the reader may see the different ways Virgil has taken to express the same thing, and how much pleasanter every manner of expression is, than the plain and direct mention of it would have been. It is in the Second Georgic, where he tells us what trees will bear grafting on each other:

Et sæpe alterius ramos impune videmus
Vertere in alterius, mutatamque insita mala
Ferre pyrum, et prunis lapidosa rubescere corna
——Steriles platani malos gessere valentes;
Castaneæ fagus, ornusque incanuit albo
Flore pyri; *glandemque sues fregere sub ulmis.*
——————Nec longum tempus; et ingens
Exiit ad cœlum ramis felicibus arbos;
Miraturque novas frondes, et non sua poma.

Here, we see, the poet considered all the effects of this union between trees of different kinds, and took notice of that effect which had the most surprise, and by consequence the most delight in it, to express the capacity that was in them of being thus united. This way of writing is everywhere much in use among the poets, and is particularly practised by Virgil, who loves to suggest a truth indirectly, and, without giving us a full and open view of it, to let us see just so much as will naturally lead the imagination into all the parts that lie concealed. This is wonderfully diverting to the understanding, thus to receive a precept, that enters, as it were, through a by-way, and to apprehend an idea that draws a whole train after it. For here the mind, which is always delighted with its own discoveries, only takes the hint from the poet, and seems to work out the rest by the strength of her own faculties.

But, since the inculcating precept upon precept will at length prove tiresome to the reader, if he meets with no other entertainment,—the poet must take care not to encumber his poem with too much business, but sometimes to relieve the subject with a moral reflection, or let it rest a while for the sake of a pleasant and pertinent digression. Nor is it sufficient to run out into beautiful and diverting digressions, (as it is generally thought,) unless they are brought in aptly, and are something of a piece with the main design of the Georgic: for they ought to have a remote alliance at least to the subject, that so the whole poem may be more uniform and agreeable in all its parts. We should never quite lose sight of the country, though we are sometimes entertained with a distant prospect of it. Of this nature are Virgil's descriptions of the origin of agriculture, of the fruitfulness of Italy, of a country life, and the like, which are not brought in by force, but naturally rise out of the principal argument and design of the poem. I know no one digression in the Georgics that may seem to contradict this observation, besides that in the latter end of the first book, where the poet launches out into a discourse of the battle of Pharsalia, and the actions of Augustus: but it is worth while to consider how admirably he has turned the course of his narration into its proper channel, and made his husbandman concerned even in what relates to the battle, in those inimitable lines:

Scilicet et tempus veniet, cum finibus illis
Agricola, incurvo terram molitus aratro,
Exesa inveniet scabra rubigine pila,
Aut gravibus rastris galeas pulsabit inanes,
Grandiaque effossis mirabitur ossa sepulcris.

And afterwards, speaking of Augustus's actions, he still remembers, that agriculture ought to be some way hinted at throughout the whole poem:

Non ullus aratro
Dignus honos: squalent abductis arva colonis;
Et curvæ rigidum falces conflantur in ensem.

We now come to the style which is proper to a Georgic; and indeed this is the part on which the poet must lay out all his strength, that his words may be warm and glowing, and that every thing he describes may immediately present itself, and rise up to the reader's view. He ought, in particular, to be careful of not letting his subject debase his style, and betray him into a meanness of expression, but everywhere to keep up his verse in all the pomp of numbers, and dignity of words.

I think nothing, which is a phrase or saying in common talk, should be admitted into a serious poem; because it takes off from the solemnity of the expression, and gives it too great a turn of familiarity. Much less ought the low phrases and terms of art, that are adapted to husbandry, have any place in such a work as the Georgic, which is not to appear in the natural simplicity and nakedness of its subject, but in the pleasantest dress that poetry can bestow on it. Thus Virgil, to deviate from the common form of words, would not make use of *tempore*, but *sidere*, in his first verse, and everywhere else abounds with metaphors, Grecisms, and circumlocutions, to give his verse the greater pomp, and preserve it from sinking into a plebeian style. And herein consists Virgil's master-piece, who has not only excelled all other poets, but even himself, in the language of his Georgics, where we receive more strong and lively ideas of things from his words, than we could have done from the objects themselves; and find our imaginations more affected by his descriptions, than they would have been by the very sight of what he describes.

I shall now, after this short scheme of rules, consider the different success that Hesiod and Virgil have met with in this kind of poetry, which may give us some farther notion of the excellence of the Georgics. To begin with Hesiod:—If we may guess at his character from his writings, he had much more of the husbandman than the poet in his temper: he was wonderfully grave, discreet, and frugal: he lived altogether in the country, and was probably, for his great prudence, the oracle of the neighbourhood. These principles of good husbandry ran through his works, and directed him to the choice of tillage and merchandise, for the subject of that which is the most celebrated of them. He is everywhere bent on instruction, avoids all manner of digressions, and does not stir out of the field once in the whole Georgic. His method, in describing month after month, with its proper seasons and employments, is too grave and simple; it takes off from the surprise and variety of the poem, and makes the whole look but like a modern almanac in verse. The reader is carried through a course of weather, and may beforehand guess whether he is to meet with snow or rain, clouds or sunshine, in the next description. His descriptions, indeed, have abundance of nature in them; but then it is nature in her simplicity and undress. Thus, when he speaks of January,—"The wild beasts," says he, "run shivering through the woods, with their heads stooping to the ground, and their tails clapped between their legs; the goats and oxen are almost flayed with cold: but it is not so bad with the sheep, because they have a thick coat of wool about them. The old men too are bitterly pinched with the weather: but the young girls feel nothing of it, who sit at home with their mothers by a warm fireside." Thus does the old gentleman give himself up to a loose kind of tattle, rather than endeavour after a just poetical description. Nor has he shown more of art or judgment in the precepts he has given us, which are sown so very thick, that they clog the poem too much, and are often so minute and full of circumstances, that they weaken and unnerve his verse. But, after all, we are beholden to him for the first rough sketch of a Georgic; where we may still discover something venerable in the antiqueness of the work: but, if we would see the design enlarged, the figures reformed, the colouring laid on, and the whole piece finished, we must expect it from a greater master's hand.

Virgil has drawn out the rules of tillage and planting into two books, which Hesiod has despatched in half a one; but has so raised the natural rudeness and simplicity of his subject with such a significancy of expression, such a pomp of verse, such variety of transitions, and such a solemn air in his reflections, that, if we look on both poets together, we see in one the plainness of a downright countryman, and, in the other, something of a rustic majesty, like that of a Roman dictator at the ploughtail. He delivers the meanest of his precepts with a kind of grandeur: he breaks the clods, and tosses the dung about, with an air of gracefulness. His prognostications of the weather are taken out of Aratus, where we may see how judiciously he has picked out those that are most proper for his husbandman's observation; how he has enforced the expression, and heightened the images, which he found in the original.

The second book has more wit in it, and a greater boldness in its metaphors, than any of the rest. The poet, with a great beauty, applies oblivion, ignorance, wonder, desire, and the like, to his trees. The last Georgic has, indeed, as many metaphors, but not so daring as this; for human thoughts and passions may be more naturally ascribed to a bee, than to an inanimate plant. He who reads over the pleasures of a country life, as they are described by Virgil in the latter end of this book, can scarce be of Virgil's mind in preferring even the life of a philosopher to it.

We may, I think, read the poet's clime in his description; for he seems to have been in a sweat at the writing of it:

> ——O! qui me gelidis in vallibus Hœmi
> Sistat, et ingenti ramorum protegat umbra—

and is everywhere mentioning, among his chief pleasures, the coolness of his shades and rivers, vales and grottoes, which a more northern poet would have omitted, for the description of a sunny hill and fireside.

The Third Georgic seems to be the most laboured of them all: there is a wonderful vigour and spirit in the description of the horse and chariot race. The force of love is represented in noble instances, and very sublime expressions. The Scythian winter-piece appears so very cold and bleak to the eye, that a man can scarce look on it without shivering. The murrain, at the end, has all the expressiveness that words can give. It was here that the poet strained hard to outdo Lucretius in the description of his Plague: and, if the reader would see what success he had, he may find it at large in Scaliger.

But Virgil seems nowhere so well pleased, as when he is got among his Bees in the Fourth Georgic; and ennobles the actions of so trivial a creature, with metaphors drawn from the most important concerns of mankind. His verses are not in a greater noise and hurry in the battles of Æneas and Turnus, than in the engagement of two swarms. And as, in his Æneis, he compares the labours of his Trojans to those of bees and pismires, here he compares the labours of the bees to those of the Cyclops. In short, the last Georgic was a good prelude to the Æneis, and very well showed what the poet could do in the description of what was really great, by his describing the mock grandeur of an insect with so good a grace. There is more pleasantness in the little platform of a garden, which he gives us about the middle of this book, than in all the spacious walks and water-works of Rapin. The speech of Proteus, at the end, can never be enough admired, and was indeed very fit to conclude so divine a work.

After this particular account of the beauties in the Georgics, I should, in the next place, endeavour to point out its imperfections, if it has any. But, though I think there are some few parts in it that are not so beautiful as the rest, I shall not presume to name them, as rather suspecting my own judgment, than I can believe a fault to be in that poem, which lay so long under Virgil's correction, and had his last hand put to it. The First Georgic was probably burlesqued in the author's lifetime; for we still find in the scholiasts a verse that ridicules part of a line translated from Hesiod—*Nudus ara, sere nudus:* And we may easily guess at the judgment of this extraordinary critic, whoever he was, from his censuring this particular precept. We may be sure Virgil would not have translated it from Hesiod, had he not discovered some beauty in it; and indeed the beauty of it is, what I have before observed to be frequently met with in Virgil, the delivering the precept so indirectly, and singling out the particular circumstance of sowing and ploughing naked, to suggest to us, that these employments are proper only in the hot season of the year.

I shall not here compare the style of the Georgics with that of Lucretius, (which the reader may see already done in the preface to the second volume of Miscellany Poems,) but shall conclude this poem to be the most complete, elaborate, and finished piece of all antiquity. The Æneis, indeed, is of a nobler kind; but the Georgic is more perfect in its kind. The Æneis has a greater variety of beauties in it; but those of the Georgic are more exquisite. In short, the Georgic has all the perfection that can be expected in a poem written by the greatest poet in the flower of his age, when his invention was ready, his imagination warm, his judgment settled, and all his faculties in their full vigour and maturity.

THE POEMS OF DRYDEN.

TRANSLATIONS FROM VIRGIL.

PASTORAL I.

OR,

TITYRUS AND MELIBŒUS.

ARGUMENT

The occasion of the first pastoral was this. When Augustus had settled himself in the Roman empire, that he might reward his veteran troops for their past service, he distributed among them all the lands that lay about Cremona and Mantua; turning out the right owners for having sided with his enemies. Virgil was a sufferer among the rest; who afterwards recovered his estate by Mæcenas's intercession, and, as an instance of his gratitude, composed the following pastoral, where he sets out his own good fortune in the person of Tityrus, and the calamities of his Mantuan neighbours in the character of Melibœus.

MELIBŒUS.

Beneath the shade which beechen boughs diffuse,
You, Tityrus, entertain your sylvan muse.
Round the wide world in banishment we roam,
Forc'd from our pleasing fields and native home;
While, stretch'd at ease, you sing your happy loves,
And Amaryllis fills the shady groves.

TITYRUS.

These blessings, friend, a deity bestow'd;
For never can I deem him less than God.
The tender firstlings of my woolly breed
Shall on his holy altar often bleed.
He gave me kine to graze the flow'ry plain,
And to my pipe renew'd the rural strain.

MELIBŒUS.

I envy not your fortune but admire,
That, while the raging sword and wasteful fire
Destroy the wretched neighbourhood around,
No hostile arms approach your happy ground.
Far diff'rent is my fate: my feeble goats
With pains I drive from their forsaken cotes.
And this, you see, I scarcely drag along,
Who, yeaning, on the rocks has left her young;
The hope and promise of my failing fold.
My loss, by dire portents the gods foretold;
For, had I not been blind, I might have seen:—
Yon riven oak, the fairest of the green,
And the hoarse raven, on the blasted bough,
By croaking from the left, presaged the coming blow,
But tell me, Tityrus, what heavenly pow'r
Preserv'd your fortune in that fatal hour?

TITYRUS.

Fool that I was, I thought imperial Rome
Like Mantua, where on market days we come,
And thither drive our tender lambs from home.
So kids and whelps their sires and dams express;
And so the great I measur'd by the less.
But country towns, compar'd with her, appear
Like shrubs, when lofty cypresses are near.

MELIBŒUS.

What great occasion call'd you hence to Rome?

TITYRUS.

Freedom, which came at length, tho' slow to come.
Nor did my search of liberty begin,
Till my black hairs were chang'd upon my chin;
Nor Amaryllis would vouchsafe a look,
Till Galatea's meaner bonds I broke
Till then a helpless, hopeless, homely swain,
I sought not freedom, nor aspired to gain:
Though many a victim from my folds was bought,
And many a cheese to country markets brought,
Yet all the little that I got, I spent,
And still returned as empty as I went.

MELIBŒUS.

We stood amaz'd to see your mistress mourn,
Unknowing that she pin'd for your return:
We wonder'd why she kept her fruit so long,
For whom so late th' ungather'd apples hung.
But now the wonder ceases, since I see
She kept them only, Tityrus, for thee.
For thee the bubbling springs appear'd to mourn,
And whisp'ring pines made vows for thy return

TITYRUS.

What should I do?—While here I was enchain'd
No glimpse of godlike liberty remain'd;

Nor could I hope, in any place but there,
To find a god so present to my pray'r.
There first the youth of heavenly birth I view'd,
For whom our monthly victims are renew'd.
He heard my vows, and graciously decreed
My grounds to be restor'd, my former flocks to feed.

MELIBŒUS.

O fortunate old man! whose farm remains—
For you sufficient—and requires your pains;
Though rushes overspread the neighb'ring plains,
Though here the marshy grounds approach your fields,
And there the soil a stony harvest yields.
Your teeming ewes shall no strange meadows try,
Nor fear a rot from tainted company,
Behold! yon bord'ring fence of sallow trees
Is fraught with flow'rs, the flow'rs are fraught with bees.
The busy bees, with a soft murmuring strain,
Invite to gentle sleep the lab'ring swain.
While, from the neighb'ring rock, with rural songs,
The pruner's voice the pleasing dream prolongs,
Stock-doves and turtles tell their am'rous pain,
And from the lofty elms, of love complain.

TITYRUS.

Th' inhabitants of seas and skies shall change,
And fish on shore, and stags in air shall range,
The banish'd Parthian dwell on Arar's brink,
And the blue German shall the Tigris drink,
Ere I, forsaking gratitude and truth,
Forget the figure of that godlike youth.

MELIBŒUS.

But we must beg our bread in climes unknown,
Beneath the scorching or the freezing zone:
And some to far Oaxis shall be sold,
Or try the Libyan heat, or Scythian cold;
The rest among the Britons be confin'd;
A race of men from all the world disjoin'd.
O! must the wretched exiles ever mourn,
Nor, after length of rolling years, return?
Are we condemn'd by fate's unjust decree,
No more our houses and our homes to see?
Or shall we mount again the rural throne,
And rule the country kingdoms once our own;
Did we for these barbarians plant and sow?
On these, on these, our happy fields bestow?
Good heaven! what dire effects from civil discord flow!
Now let me graft my pears, and prune the vine;
The fruit is theirs, the labour only mine.
Farewell, my pastures, my paternal stock,
My fruitful fields, and my more fruitful flock!
No more, my goats, shall I behold you climb
The steepy cliffs, or crop the flow'ry thyme!
No more extended in the grot below,
Shall see you browsing on the mountain's brow
The prickly shrubs; and after on the bare,
Leap down the deep abyss, and hang in air.
No more my sheep shall sip the morning dew;
No more my song shall please the rural crew:
Adieu my tuneful pipe! and all the world, adieu!

TITYRUS.

This night, at least, with me forget your care,
Chestnuts, and curds, and cream shall be your fare:
The carpet-ground shall be with leaves o'erspread;
And boughs shall weave a cov'ring for your head.
For see, yon sunny hill the shade extends;
And curling smoke from cottages ascends.

PASTORAL II.

OR,

ALEXIS.

ARGUMENT.

The commentators can by no means agree on the person of Alexis, but are all of opinion that some beautiful youth is meant by him, to whom Virgil here makes love, in Corydon's language and simplicity. His way of courtship is wholly pastoral; he complains of the boy's coyness; recommends himself for his beauty and skill in piping; invites the youth into the country, where he promises him the diversions of the place, with a suitable present of nuts and apples. But when he finds nothing will prevail, he resolves to quit his troublesome amour, and betake himself again to his former business.

Young Corydon th' unhappy shepherd swain,
The fair Alexis lov'd, but lov'd in vain;
And underneath the beechen shade, alone,
Thus to the woods and mountains made his moan:
Is this, unkind Alexis, my reward?
And must I die unpitied and unheard?
Now the green lizard in the grove is laid;
The sheep enjoy the coolness of the shade,
And Thestylis wild thyme and garlic beats
For harvest hinds, o'erspent with toil and heats;
While in the scorching sun I trace in vain
Thy flying footsteps o'er the burning plain.
The creaking locusts with my voice conspire,
They fried with heat, and I with fierce desire.
How much more easy was it to sustain
Proud Amaryllis, and her haughty reign,
The scorns of young Menalcas, once my care,
Though he was black, and thou art heavenly fair.
Trust not too much to that enchanting face!
Beauty's a charm; but soon the charm will pass.
White lilies lie neglected on the plain,
While dusky hyacinths for use remain.
My passion is thy scorn; nor wilt thou know
What wealth I have, what gifts I can bestow;
What stores my dairies and my folds contain—
A thousand lambs that wander on the plain;

New milk, that, all the winter, never fails
And, all the summer, overflows the pails.
Amphion sung not sweeter to his herd,
When summon'd stones the Theban turrets rear'd.
Nor am I so deform'd; for, late I stood
Upon the margin of the briny flood:
The winds were still: and, if the glass be true,
With Daphnis I may vie, though judg'd by you.
O leave the noisy town: O come and see
Our country cots, and live content with me!
To wound the flying deer, and from their cotes
With me to drive a-field the browsing goats;
To pipe and sing, and, in our country strain,
To copy or perhaps contend with Pan.
Pan taught to join with wax unequal reeds;
Pan loves the shepherds, and their flocks he feeds.
Nor scorn the pipe: Amyntas, to be taught,
With all his kisses would my skill have bought.
Of seven smooth joints, a mellow pipe I have,
Which, with his dying breath, Damœtas gave,
And said, "this, Corydon, I leave to thee;
For only thou deserv'st it after me."
His eyes Amyntas durst not upward lift;
For much he grudg'd the praise, but more the gift.
Besides, two kids, that in the valley stray'd,
I found by chance, and to my fold convey'd,
They drain two bagging udders ev'ry day;
And these shall be companions of thy play:
Both fleck'd with white, the true Arcadian stain,
Which Thestylis had often begg'd in vain:
And she shall have them, if again she sues,
Since you the giver and the gift refuse.
Come to my longing arms, my lovely care!
And take the presents which thy nymphs prepare.
White lilies in full canisters they bring,
With all the glories of the purple spring.
The daughters of the flood have search'd the mead
For violets pale, and cropp'd the poppy's head,
The short narcissus and fair daffodil,
Pansies to please the sight, and cassia sweet to smell;
And set soft hyacinths with iron-blue,
To shade marsh marigolds of shining hue;
Some bound in order, others loosely strew'd,
To dress thy bow'r, and trim thy new abode.
Myself will search our planted grounds at home,
For downy peaches and the glossy plum:
And thrash the chestnuts in the neighb'ring grove,
Such as my Amaryllis us'd to love.
The laurel and the myrtle sweets agree;
And both in nosegays shall be bound for thee.
Ah, Corydon! ah poor unhappy swain!
Alexis will thy homely gifts disdain:
Nor, should'st thou offer all thy little store,
Will rich Iolas yield, but offer more.
What have I done, to name that wealthy swain?
So powerful are his presents, mine so mean!
The boar amidst my crystal streams I bring,
And southern winds to blast my flowery spring.
Ah cruel creature! whom dost thou despise?
The gods, to live in woods, have left the skies;
And godlike Paris, in the Idæan grove,
To Priam's wealth prefer'd Œnone's love.
In cities which she built, let Pallas reign;
Tow'rs are for gods, but forests for the swain.
The greedy lioness the wolf pursues,
The wolf the kid, the wanton kid the browse;
Alexis, thou art chas'd by Corydon:
All follow sev'ral games, and each his own.
See, from afar the fields no longer smoke;
The sweating steers, unharness'd from the yoke
Bring, as in triumph, back the crooked plough;
The shadows lengthen as the sun goes low;
Cool breezes now the raging heats remove:
Ah, cruel heav'n! that made no cure for love!
I wish for balmy sleep, but wish in vain:
Love has no bounds in pleasure, or in pain.
What frenzy, shepherd, has thy soul possess'd?
Thy vineyard lies half prun'd and half undress'd
Quench, Corydon, thy long unanswered fire!
Mind what the common wants of life require,
On willow twigs employ thy weaving care;
And find an easier love, though not so fair.

PASTORAL III.

OR,

PALÆMON.

MENALCAS, DAMŒTAS, PALÆMON

ARGUMENT.

Damœtas and Manaclas, after some smart strokes of country raillery, resolve to try who has the most skill at song; and accordingly make their neighbour Palæmon judge of their performances; who, after a full hearing of both parties, declares himself unfit for the decision of so weighty a controversy and leaves the victory undetermined.

MENALCAS.

Ho, swain! what shepherd owns those ragged sheep?

DAMŒTAS.

Ægon's they are: he gave them me to keep.

MENALCAS.

Unhappy sheep of an unhappy swain!
While he Neæra courts, but courts in vain,

And fears that I the damsel shall obtain,
Thou, varlet, dost thy master's gains devour;
Thou milk'st his ewes and often twice an hour;
Of grass and fodder thou defraud'st the dams,
And of their mother's dugs the starving lambs.

DAMŒTAS.

Good words young catamite, at least to men;
We know who did your business, how, and, when:
And in what chapel too you play'd your prize,
And what the gods observ'd with leering eyes—
The nymphs were kind and laugh'd: and there your safety lies.

MENALCAS.

Yes, when I cropt the hedges of the leys,
Cut Micon's tender vines, and stole the stays:

DAMŒTAS.

Or rather, when, beneath yon ancient oak,
The bow of Daphnis, and the shafts, you broke,
When the fair boy receiv'd the gift of right;
And, but for mischief, you had died for spite.

MENALCAS.

What nonsense would the fool thy master prate,
When thou, his knave, canst talk at such a rate!
Did I not see you, rascal, did I not,
When you lay snug to snap young Damon's goat?
His mongrel bark'd: I ran to his relief,
And cried, "There, there he goes! stop, stop the thief!"
Discover'd, and defeated of your prey,
You skulk'd behind the fence, and sneak'd away.

DAMŒTAS.

An honest man may freely take his own:
The goat was mine, by singing fairly won.
A solemn match was made: he lost the prize.
Ask Damon, ask, if he the debt denies.
I think he dares not: If he does, he lies.

MENALCAS.

Thou sing with him, thou booby!—Never pipe
Was so profan'd to touch that blubber'd lip.
Dunce at the best! in streets but scarce allow'd
To tickle, on thy straw, the stupid crowd.

DAMŒTAS

To bring it to the trial, will you dare
Our pipes, our skill, our voices, to compare?
My brinded heifer to the stake I lay:
Two thriving calves she suckles twice a day,
And twice, besides her beestings, never fail
To store the dairy with a brimming pail.
Now back your singing with an equal stake.

MENALCAS.

That should be seen, if I had one to make.
You know too well I feed my father's flock:
What can I wager from the common stock?
A stepdame too I have, a cursed she,
Who rules my hen-peck'd sire, and orders me;
Both number twice a day the milky dams
And once she takes the tale of all the lambs.
But, since you will be mad, and since you may
Suspect my courage, if I should not lay,
The pawn I proffer shall be full as good:
Two bowls I have, well turn'd, of beechen wood:
Both by divine Alcimedon were made:
To neither of them yet the lip is laid.
The lids are ivy: grapes in clusters lurk
Beneath the carving of the curious work.
Two figures on the sides emboss'd appear—
Conon, and, what's his name, who made the sphere,
And show'd the seasons of the sliding year,
Instructed in his trade the lab'ring swain,
And when to reap, and when to sow the grain?

DAMŒTAS.

And I have two, to match your pair, at home;
The wood the same; from the same hand they come,
(The kimbo handles seem with bear's-foot carv'd)
And never yet to table have been serv'd;
Where Orpheus on his lyre laments his love,
With beasts encompass'd and a dancing grove,
But these, nor all the proffers you can make,
Are worth the heifer which I set to stake.

MENALCAS.

No more delays, vain boaster, but begin!
I prophesy beforehand, I shall win:
Palæmon shall be judge how ill you rhyme.
I'll teach you how to brag another time.

DAMŒTAS.

Rhymer, come on! and do the worst you can.
I fear not you, nor yet a better man.
With silence, neighbour, and attention, wait:
For 'tis a business of a high debate.

PALÆMON.

Sing then: the shade affords a proper place;
The trees are cloth'd with leaves, the fields with grass;
The blossoms blow; the birds on bushes sing;
And nature has accomplish'd all the spring.
The challenge to Damœtas shall belong:
Menalcas shall sustain his under-song:
Each in his turn, your tuneful numbers bring:
By turns the tuneful Muses love to sing.

DAMŒTAS.

From the great father of the gods above
My Muse begins; for all is full of Jove;
To Jove the care of heav'n and earth belongs;
My flocks he blesses, and he loves my songs.

MENALCAS.

Me Phœbus loves; for he my Muse inspires;
And, in her songs, the warmth he gave, requires.
For him, the god of shepherds and their sheep,
My blushing hyacinths and my bays I keep.

DAMŒTAS.

My Phyllis me with pelted apples plies:
Then tripping to the wood the wanton hies,
And wishes to be seen before she flies.

MENALCAS.

But fair Amyntas comes unask'd to me,
And offers love, and sits upon my knee.
Not Delia to my dogs is known so well as he.

DAMŒTAS.

To the dear mistress of my love-sick mind,
Her swain a pretty present has design'd:
I saw two stock-doves billing, and ere long
Will take the nest; and hers shall be the
young.

MENALCAS.

Ten ruddy wildings in the wood I found,
And stood on tip-toes, reaching from the ground:
I sent Amyntas all my present store;
And will, to-morrow, send as many more.

DAMŒTAS.

The lovely maid lay panting in my arms;
And all she said and did was full of charms.
Winds! on your wings to heav'n her accents
bear;
Such words as heav'n alone is fit to hear.

MENALCAS.

Ah! what avails it me, my love's delight,
To call you mine, when absent from my sight?
I hold the nets, while you pursue the prey;
And must not share the dangers of the day.

DAMŒTAS.

I keep my birthday: send my Phyllis home;
At shearing-time, Iolas you may come.

MENALCAS.

With Phyllis I am more in grace than you:
Her sorrow did my parting steps pursue:
"Adieu, my dear!" she said, "a long adieu!"

DAMŒTAS.

The nightly wolf is baneful to the fold,
Storms to the wheat, to buds the bitter cold;
But, from my frowning fair, more ills I find,
Than from the wolves, and storms, and winter-
wind.

MENALCAS.

The kids with pleasure browse the bushy plain;
The showers are grateful to the swelling grain;
To teeming ewes the sallow's tender tree;
But, more than all the world, my love to me.

DAMŒTAS.

Pollio my rural verse vouchsafes to read:
A heifer, Muses, for your patron breed.

MENALCAS.

My Pollio writes himself:—a bull he bred,
With spurning heels, and with a butting head.

DAMŒTAS.

Who Pollio loves, and who his Muse admires,
Let Pollio's fortune crown his full desires.
Let myrrh instead of thorn his fences fill,
And show'rs of honey from his oaks distil.

MENALCAS.

Who hates not living Bavius, let him be [thee!
(Dead Mævius!) damn'd to love thy works and
The same ill taste of sense would serve to join
Dog-foxes in the yoke, and shear the swine

DAMŒTAS. [spring,

Ye boys, who pluck the flow'rs, and spoil the
Beware the secret snake that shoots a sting.

MENALCAS.

Graze not too near the banks, my jolly sheep:
The ground is false; the running streams are
deep:
See, they have caught the father of the flock,
Who dries his fleece upon the neighb'ring rock

DAMŒTAS.

From rivers drive the kids, and sling your hook:
Anon I'll wash them in the shallow brook.

MENALCAS.

To fold, my flock!—when milk is dried with
heat,
In vain the milk-maid tugs an empty teat.

DAMŒTAS.

How lank my bulls from plenteous pasture come!
But love, that drains the herd, destroys the
groom.

MENALCAS.

My flocks are free from love, yet look so thin,
Their bones are barely cover'd with their skin.
What magic has bewitch'd the woolly dams,
And what ill eyes beheld the tender lambs?

DAMŒTAS.

Say, where the round of heav'n, which all con-
tains,
To three short ells on earth our sight restrains:
Tell that, and raise a Phœbus for thy pains.

MENALCAS.

Nay tell me first, in what new region springs
A flow'r, that bears inscrib'd the names of
kings;
And thou shalt gain a present as divine
As Phœbus' self: for Phyllis shall be thine.

PALÆMON.

So nice a diff'rence in your singing lies,
That both have won, or both deserv'd the prize.
Rest equal happy both; and all who prove
The bitter sweets, and pleasing pains of love.
Now dam the ditches, and the floods restrain:
Their moisture has already drench'd the plain.

PASTORAL IV.

OR,

POLLIO.

ARGUMENT.

The Poet celebrates the birthday of Saloninus, the son of Pollio, born in the consulship of his father, after the taking of Salonæ, a city in Dalmatia. Many of the verses are translated from one of the Sibyls, who prophesied of our Saviour's birth.

SICILIAN Muse, begin a loftier strain.
Tho' lowly shrubs, and trees that shade the plain,
Delight not all; Sicilian Muse, prepare
To make the vocal woods deserve a consul's care.
The last great age, foretold by sacred rhymes,
Renews its finish'd course: Saturnian times
Roll round again; and mighty years, begun
From their first orb in radiant circles run.
The base degen'rate iron offspring ends;
A golden progeny from heaven descends.
O chaste Lucina! speed the mother's pains;
And haste the glorious birth! thy own Apollo reigns!
The lovely boy, with his auspicious face,
Shall Pollio's consulship and triumph grace:
Majestic months set out (with him) to their appointed race.
The father banish'd virtue shall restore;
And crimes shall threat the guilty world no more.
The son shall lead the life of gods, and be
By gods and heroes seen, and gods and heroes see.
The jarring nations he in peace shall bind,
And with paternal virtues rule mankind.
Unbidden earth shall wreathing ivy bring,
And fragrant herbs (the promises of spring,)
As her first off'rings to her infant king.
The goats with strutting dugs shall homeward speed,
And lowing herds secure from lions feed.
His cradle shall with rising flow'rs be crown'd:
The serpent's brood shall die: the sacred ground
Shall weeds and pois'nous plants refuse to bear;
Each common bush shall Syrian roses wear.
But when heroic verse his youth shall raise,
And form it to hereditary praise,
Unlabour'd harvests shall the fields adorn,
And cluster'd grapes shall blush on every thorn;
The knotted oaks shall showers of honey weep;
And thro' the matted grass the liquid gold shall creep.
Yet, of old fraud some footsteps shall remain:
The merchant still shall plough the deep for gain:
Great cities shall with walls be compass'd round;
And sharpen'd shares shall vex the fruitful ground;
Another Tiphys shall new seas explore;
Another Argo land the chiefs upon th' Iberian shore;
Another Helen other wars create,
And great Achilles urge the Trojan fate
But, when to ripen'd manhood he shall grow,
The greedy sailor shall the seas forego:
No keel shall cut the waves for foreign ware
For every soil shall every product bear.
The lab'ring hind his oxen shall disjoin:
No plough shall hurt the glebe, no pruning-hook the vine;
Nor wool shall in dissembled colour shine;
But the luxurious father of the fold
With native purple, and unborrow'd gold,
Beneath his pompous fleece shall proudly sweat,
And under Tyrian robes the lamb shall bleat.
The Fates, when they this happy web have spun,
Shall bless the sacred clue, and bid it smoothly run.
Mature in years, to ready honours move,
O, of celestial seed! O, foster-son of Jove!
See, lab'ring Nature calls thee to sustain
The nodding frame of heav'n, and earth, and main!
See to their base restor'd, earth, seas, and air;
And joyful ages, from behind, in crowding ranks appear.
To sing thy praise, would heav'n my breath prolong,
Infusing spirits worthy such a song,
Not Thracian Orpheus should transcend my lays,
Nor Linus crown'd with never fading bays;
Though each his heav'nly parent should inspire;
The Muse instruct the voice, and Phœbus tune the lyre.
Should Pan contend in verse, and thou my theme,
Arcadian judges should their god condemn.
Begin, auspicious boy! to cast about
Thy infant eyes, and, with a smile, thy mother single out.
Thy mother well deserves that short delight.
The nauseous qualms of ten long months and travail to requite.
Then smile! the frowning infant's doom is read;
No god shall crown the board, nor goddess bless the bed.

PASTORAL V.

OR,

DAPHNIS.

ARGUMENT.

Mopsus and Menalcas, two very expert shepherds at a song, begin one by consent to the memory of Daphnis, who is supposed by the best critics o

PASTORAL V.

represent Julius Cæsar. Mopsus laments his death; Menalcas proclaims his divinity; the whole eclogue consisting of an elegy and an apotheosis.

MENALCAS.

Since on the downs our flocks together feed,
And since my voice can match your tuneful reed,
Why sit we not beneath the grateful shade,
Which hazels, intermix'd with elms, have made?

MOPSUS.

Whether you please that sylvan scene to take,
Where whistling winds uncertain shadows make;
Or will you to the cooler cave succeed,
Whose mouth the curling vines have overspread?

MENALCAS.

Your merit and your years command the choice:
Amyntas only rivals you in voice.

MOPSUS.

What will not that presuming shepherd dare,
Who thinks his voice with Phœbus may compare?

MENALCAS.

Begin you first: if either Alcon's praise,
Or dying Phillis, have inspir'd your lays;
If her you mourn, or Codrus you commend,
Begin; and Tityrus your flocks shall tend.

MOPSUS.

Or shall I rather the sad verse repeat,
Which on the beech's bark I lately writ?
I writ, and sung betwixt. Now bring the swain
Whose voice you boast, and let him try the strain.

MENALCAS.

Such as the shrub to the tall olive shows,
Or the pale sallow of the blushing rose;
Such is his voice, if I can judge aright,
Compar'd to thine in sweetness and in height.

MOPSUS.

No more, but sit, and hear the promis'd lay:
The gloomy grotto makes a doubtful day.
The nymphs about the breathless body wait
Of Daphnis, and lament his cruel fate.
The trees and floods were witness to their tears:
At length the rumour reach'd his mother's ears.
The wretched parent, with a pious haste,
Came running, and his lifeless limbs embrac'd.
She sigh'd, she sobb'd; and furious with despair,
She rent her garments, and she tore her hair,
Accusing all the gods, and ev'ry star.
The swains forgot their sheep, nor near the brink
Of running waters brought their herds to drink.
The thirsty cattle, of themselves, abstain'd
From water, and their grassy fare disdain'd.
The death of Daphnis woods and hills deplore;
They cast the sound to Libya's desert shore;
The Libyan lions hear, and hearing roar.
Fierce tigers Daphnis taught the yoke to bear,
And first with curling ivy dress'd the spear.
Daphnis did rites to Bacchus first ordain,
And holy revels for his reeling train.
As vines the trees, as grapes the vines adorn,
As bulls the herds, and fields the yellow corn;
So bright a splendour, so divine a grace,
The glorious Daphnis cast on his illustrious race.
When envious Fate the godlike Daphnis took,
Our guardian gods the fields and plains forsook:
Pales no longer swell'd the teeming grain,
Nor Phœbus fed his oxen on the plain:
No fruitful crop the sickly fields return;
But oats and darnel choke the rising corn.
And where the vales with violets once were crown'd
Now knotty burns and thorns disgrace the ground.
Come, shepherds, come, and strew with leaves the plain;
Such fun'ral rites your Daphnis did ordain.
With cypress boughs the crystal fountains hide,
And softly let the running waters glide.
A lasting monument to Daphnis raise,
With this inscription to record his praise;
"Daphnis, the fields' delight, the shepherds' love,
Renown'd on earth, and deifi'd above;
Whose flock excell'd the fairest on the plains,
But less than he himself surpass'd the swains."

MENALCAS.

O heav'nly poet! such thy verse appears,
So sweet, so charming to my ravish'd ears,
As to the weary swain with cares opprest,
Beneath the sylvan shade, refreshing rest;
As to the fev'rish traveller, when first
He finds a crystal stream to quench his thirst.
In singing, as in piping, you excel;
And scarce your master could perform so well.
O fortunate young man! at least your lays
Are next to his, and claim the second praise.
Such as they are, my rural songs I join,
To raise our Daphnis to the pow'rs divine;
For Daphnis was so good, to love whate'er was mine.

MOPSUS.

How is my soul with such a promise rais'd!
For both the boy was worthy to be prais'd,
And Stimicon has often made me long
To hear, like him, so soft, so sweet a song.

MENALCAS.

Daphnis, the guest of heaven, with wond'ring eyes
Views, in the milky way, the starry skies,
And far beneath him, from the shining sphere,
Beholds the moving clouds, and rolling year.

For this with cheerful cries the woods resound,
The purple spring arrays the varied ground,
The nymphs and shepherds dance, and Pan himself is crown'd.
The wolf no longer prowls for nightly spoils,
Nor birds the springes fear, nor stags the toils;
For Daphnis reigns above, and deals from thence
His mother's milder beams, and peaceful influence.
The mountain-tops unshorn, the rocks rejoice;
The lowly shrubs partake of human voice.
Assenting Nature, with a gracious nod,
Proclaims him, and salutes the new-admitted god.
Be still propitious, every good be thine!
Behold! four hallow'd altars we design;
And two to thee, and two to Phœbus rise;
On both is offer'd annual sacrifice.
The holy priests, at each returning year,
Two bowls of milk and two of oil shall bear;
And I myself the guests with friendly bowls will cheer.
Two goblets will I crown with sparkling wine,
The gen'rous vintage of the Chian vine:
These will I pour to thee, and make the nectar thine.
In winter shall the genial feast be made
Before the fire; by summer in the shade,
Damœtas shall perform the rites divine;
And Lyctian Ægon in the song shall join.
Alphesibœus, tripping, shall advance,
And mimic satyrs in his antic dance,
When to the nymphs our annual rites we pay,
And when our fields with victims we survey—
While savage boars delight in shady woods,
And finny fish inhabit in the floods—
While bees on thyme, and locusts feed on dew—
Thy grateful swains these honours shall renew.
Such honours as we pay to pow'rs divine,
To Bacchus and to Ceres, shall be thine.
Such annual honours shall be given; and thou
Shalt hear, and shalt condemn thy suppliants to their vow.

MOPSUS.

What present, worth thy verse, can Mopsus find?
Not the soft whispers of the southern wind,
That play through trembling trees, delight me more
Nor murmuring billows on the sounding shore;
Nor winding streams that through the valley glide,
And the scarce cover'd pebbles gently chide.

MENALCAS.

Receive you first this tuneful pipe, the same
That play'd my Corydon's unhappy flame;
The same that sung Neæra's conqu'ring eyes,
And, had the judge been just, had won the prize.

MOPSUS.

Accept from me this sheep-hook in exchange;
The handle brass; the knobs in equal range,
Antigenes, with kisses, often tried
To beg this present, in his beauty's pride
When youth and love are hard to be denied:
But what I could refuse to his request,
Is yours unask'd; for you deserve it best.

PASTORAL VI.

OR,

SILENUS.

ARGUMENT.

Two young shepherds, Chromis and Mnasylus having been often promised a song by Silenus chance to catch him asleep in this pastoral; where they bind him hand and foot, and then claim his promise. Silenus, finding they would be put off no longer, begins his song, in which he describes the formation of the universe, and the original of animals, according to the Epicurean philosophy; and then runs through the most surprising transformations which have happened in Nature since her birth. This pastoral was designed as a compliment to Syron the Epicurean, who instructed Virgil and Varus in the principles of that philosophy. Silenus acts as tutor, Chromis and Mnasylus as the two pupils.

I FIRST transferr'd to Rome Sicilian strains;
Nor blush'd the Doric Muse to dwell on Mantuan plains.
But when I tried her tender voice, too young,
And fighting kings and bloody battles sung,
Apollo check'd my pride, and bade me feed
My fatt'ning flocks, nor dare beyond the reed.
Admonish'd thus, while every pen prepares
To write thy praises, Varus, and thy wars,
My past'ral Muse her humble tribute brings;
And yet not wholly uninspir'd she sings:
For all who read, and, reading, not disdain
These rural poems, and their lowly strain,
The name of Varus, oft inscrib'd shall see
In ev'ry grove, and ev'ry vocal tree;
And all the sylvan reign shall sing of thee:
Thy name, to Phœbus and the muses known,
Shall in the front of ev'ry page be shown;
For, he who sings thy praise secures his own.
Proceed, my Muse!—Two Satyrs on th ground,
Stretch'd at his ease, their sire Silenus found.
Doz'd with his fumes, and heavy with his load,
They found him snoring in his dark abode,
And seiz'd with youthful arms the drunken god
His rosy wreath was dropt not long before,
Borne by the tide of wine, and floating on the floor.

His empty can, with ears half worn away,
Was hung on high, to boast the triumph of the day.
Invaded thus, for want of better bands,
His garland they unstring, and bind his hands,
For, by the fraudful god deluded long,
They now resolve to have their promis'd song;
Ægle came in, to make their party good—
The fairest Naïs of the neighb'ring flood—
And, while he stares around with stupid eyes,
His brows with berries, and his temples, dies.
He finds the fraud, and with a smile demands,
On what design the boys had bound his hands.
"Loose me," he cried; "'t was impudence to find
A sleeping god; 't is sacrilege to bind.
To you the promis'd poem I will pay;
The nymph shall be rewarded in her way."
He rais'd his voice, and soon a num'rous throng
Of tripping Satyrs crowded to the song;
And sylvan Fauns, and savage beasts, advanc'd;
And nodding forests to the numbers danc'd.
Not by Hæmonian hills the Thracian bard,
Nor awful Phœbus was on Pindus heard
With deeper silence, or with more regard.
He sung the secret seeds of Nature's frame;
How seas, and earth, and air, and active flame,
Fell through the mighty void, and, in their fall,
Were blindly gather'd in this goodly ball.
The tender soil, then stiff'ning by degrees,
Shut from the bounded earth the bounding seas.
Then earth and ocean, various forms disclose;
And a new sun to the new world arose;
And mists, condens'd to clouds, obscure the sky;
And clouds, dissolv'd, the thirsty ground supply.
The rising trees the lofty mountains grace:
The lofty mountains feed the savage race,
Yet few, and strangers, in th' unpeopled place.
From thence the birth of man the song pursu'd,
And how the world was lost, and how renew'd:
The reign of Saturn, and the golden age;
Prometheus' theft, and Jove's avenging rage;
The cries of Argonauts for Hylas drown'd,
With whose repeated name the shores resound;
Then mourns the madness of the Cretan queen:
Happy for her if herds had never been.
What fury, wretched woman, seiz'd thy breast?
The maids of Argus (though with rage possess'd,
Their imitated lowings fill'd the grove,)
Yet shunn'd the guilt of thy prepost'rous love,
Nor sought the youthful husband of the herd,
Tho' lab'ring yokes on their own necks they fear'd,
And felt for budding horns on their smooth foreheads rear'd.
Ah, wretched queen! you range the pathless wood,
While on a flow'ry bank he chews the cud,
Or sleeps in shades, or through the forest roves,
And roars with anguish for his absent loves.
"Ye nymphs, with toils his forest-walk surround,
And trace his wand'ring footsteps on the ground.
But, ah! perhaps my passion he disdains,
And courts the milky mothers of the plains.
We search th' ungrateful fugitive abroad,
While they at home sustain his happy load."
He sung the lover's fraud; the longing maid,
With golden fruit, like all the sex, betray'd;
The sisters mourning for their brother's loss;
Their bodies hid in barks, and furr'd with moss;
How each a rising alder now appears,
And o'er the Po distils her gummy tears:
Then sung, how Gallus, by a Muse's hand,
Was led and welcom'd to the sacred strand;
The senate rising to salute their guest,
And Linus thus their gratitude express'd:
"Receive this present, by the Muses made,
The pipe on which th' Ascræan pastor play'd;
With which of old he charm'd the savage train,
And call'd the mountain ashes to the plain.
Sing thou, on this, thy Phœbus, and the wood
Where once his fane of Parian marble stood:
On this his ancient oracles rehearse;
And with new numbers grace the god of verse."
Why should I sing the double Scylla's fate?
The first by love transform'd, the last by hate—
A beauteous maid above; but magic arts
With barking dogs deform'd her nether parts:
What vengeance on the passing fleet she pour'd,
The master frighted, and the mates devour'd.
Then ravish'd Philomel the song exprest;
The crime reveal'd; the sisters' cruel feast;
And how in fields the lapwing Tereus reigns,
The warbling nightingale in woods complains:
While Procne makes on chimney-tops her moan,
And hovers o'er the palace once her own.
Whatever songs besides the Delphian god
Had taught the laurels, and the Spartan flood
Silenus sung: the vales his voice rebound,
And carry to the skies the sacred sound.
And now the setting sun had warn'd the swain
To call his counted cattle from the plain:
Yet still th' unwearied sire pursues the tuneful strain.
Till, unperceiv'd, the heavens with stars were hung,
And sudden night surpris'd the yet unfinish'd song.

PASTORAL VII.

OR,

MELIBŒUS.

ARGUMENT.

Melibœus here gives us the relation of a sharp poetical contest between Thyrsis and Corydon, at which he and Daphnis were present; who both declared for Corydon.

Beneath a holm, repair'd two jolly swains,
(Their sheep and goats together graz'd the plains)
Both young Arcadians, both alike inspir'd
To sing, and answer as the song requir'd.
Daphnis, as umpire, took the middle seat;
And fortune thither led my weary feet.
For, while I fenc'd my myrtles from the cold,
The father of my flock had wander'd from the fold.
Of Daphnis I inquir'd: he smiling said,
"Dismiss your fear," and pointed where he fed
"And if no greater cares disturb your mind,
Sit here with us in covert of the wind.
Your lowing heifers, of their own accord,
At wat'ring time, will seek the neighbouring ford.
Here wanton Mincius winds along the meads,
And shades his happy banks with bending reeds.
And see, from yon old oak that meets the skies,
How black the clouds of swarming bees arise."
What should I do? nor was Alcippi nigh,
Nor absent Phillis could my care supply,
To house, and feed by hand my weaning lambs,
And drain the strutting udders of their dams.
Great was the strife betwixt the singing swains:
And I preferr'd my pleasure to my gains.
Alternate rhyme the ready champion chose:
These Corydon rehears'd, and Thyrsis those.

CORYDON.

Ye muses, ever fair and ever young,
Assist my numbers and inspire my song.
With all my Codrus, O! inspire my breast;
For Codrus, after Phœbus, sings the best.
Or, if my wishes have presum'd too high,
And stretch'd their bounds beyond mortality,
The praise of artful numbers I resign,
And hang my pipe upon the sacred pine.

THYRSIS.

Arcadian swains, your youthful poet crown
With ivy-wreaths, though surly Codrus frown.
Or, if he blast my muse with envious praise,
Then fence my brows with amulets of bays.
Lest his ill arts or his malicious tongue
Should poison, or bewitch my growing song.

CORYDON.

These branches of a stag, this tusky boar
(The first essay of arms untried before)
Young Micon offers, Delia, to thy shrine.
But, speed his hunting with thy pow'r divine;
Thy statue then of Parian stone shall stand;
Thy legs in buskins with a purple band.

THYRSIS.

This bowl of milk, these cakes, (our country fare)
For thee, Priapus, yearly we prepare,
Because a little garden is thy care.
But, if the falling lambs increase my fold,
Thy marble statue shall be turn'd to gold.

CORYDON.

Fair Galatea, with thy silver feet,
O, whiter than the swan, and more than Hybla sweet!
Tall as a poplar, taper as the pole!
Come, charm thy shepherd, and restore my soul.
Come, when my lated sheep at night return;
And crown the silent hours, and stop the rosy morn.

THYRSIS.

May I become as abject in thy sight
As sea-weed on the shore, and black as night;
Rough as a burr; deform'd like him who chaws
Sardinian herbage to contract his jaws;
Such and so monstrous let thy swain appear,
If one day's absence looks not like a year.
Hence from the field, for shame! the flock deserves
No better feeding while the shepherd starves.

CORYDON.

Ye mossy springs, inviting easy sleep,
Ye trees, whose leafy shades those mossy fountains keep.
Defend my flock! The summer heats are near,
And blossoms on the swelling vines appear.

THYRSIS.

With heapy fires our cheerful hearth is crown'd,
And firs for torches in the woods abound:
We fear not more the winds and wintry cold,
Than streams the banks, or wolves the bleating fold.

CORYDON.

Our woods with juniper and chestnuts crown'd,
With falling fruits and berries paint the ground;
And lavish nature laughs, and strews her stores around.
But, if Alexis from our mountains fly,
E'en running rivers leave their channels dry.

THYRSIS.

Parch'd are the plains, and frying is the field,
Nor with'ring vines their juicy vintage yield,
But, if returning Phyllis bless the plain,
The grass revives; the woods are green again;
And Jove descends in showers of kindly rain.

CORYDON.

The poplar is by great Alcides worn;
The brows of Phœbus his own bays adorn;
The branching vine the jolly Bacchus loves;
The Cyprian queen delights in myrtle groves;
With hazel Phyllis crowns her flowing hair;
And, while she loves that common wreath to wear,
Nor bays, nor myrtle boughs, with hazel shall compare.

THYRSIS.

The tow'ring ash is fairest in the woods;
In gardens, pines, and poplars by the floods;
But, if my Lucidas will ease my pains,
And often visit our forsaken plains,
To him the tow'ring ash shall yield in woods,
In gardens, pines, and poplars by the floods.

MELIBŒUS.

These rhymes I did to memory commend,
When vanquish'd Thyrsis did in vain contend;
Since when 'tis Corydon among the swains,
Young Corydon without a rival reigns.

PASTORAL VIII.

OR

PHARMACEUTRIA.

ARGUMENT.

This pastoral contains the songs of Damon and Alphesibœus. The first of them bewails the loss of his mistress, and repines at the success of his rival Mopsus. The other repeats the charms of some enchantress, who endeavoured by her spells and magic to make Daphnis in love with her.

THE mournful muse of two despairing swains,
The love rejected and the lovers' pains;
To which the savage lynxes list'ning stood;
The rivers stood in heaps, and stopp'd the running flood;
The hungry herd their needful food refuse—
Of two despairing swains, I sing the mournful muse.

Great Pollio! thou, for whom thy Rome prepares
The ready triumph of thy finish'd wars,
Whether Timavus or th' Illyrian coast,
Whatever land or sea, thy presence boast;
Is there an hour in fate reserved for me,
To sing thy deeds in numbers worthy thee?
In numbers like to thine, could I rehearse,
Thy lofty tragic scenes, thy labour'd verse,
The world another Sophocles in thee,
Another Homer should behold in me
Amidst thy laurels let this ivy twine:
Thine was my earliest muse, my latest shall be thine.

Scarce from the world the shades of night withdrew,
Scarce were the flocks refresh'd with morning dew,
When Damon, stretch'd beneath an olive shade,
And wildly staring upwards, thus inveigh'd
Against the conscious gods, and curs'd the maid:
"Star of the morning, why dost thou delay?
Come, Lucifer, drive on the lagging day,
While I my Nisa's perjur'd faith deplore—
Witness, ye pow'rs by whom she falsely swore
The gods, alas! are witnesses in vain:
Yet shall my dying breath to heaven complain.
Begin with me, my flute, the sweet Mænalian strain.

"The pines of Mænalus, the vocal grove,
Are ever full of verse and full of love:
They hear the hinds, they hear their god complain,
Who suffer'd not the reeds to rise in vain.
Begin with me, my flute, the sweet Mænalian strain.

"Mopsus triumphs; he weds the willing fair.
When such is Nisa's choice, what lover can despair?
Now griffons join with mares; another age
Shall see the hound and hind their thirst assuage,
Promiscuous at the spring. Prepare the lights
O Mopsus! and perform the bridal rites.
Scatter thy nuts among the scrambling boys:
Thine is the night, and thine the nuptial joys.
For thee the sun declines: O happy swain!
Begin with me, my flute, the sweet Mænalian strain.

"O Nisa! justly to thy choice condemn'd!
Whom hast thou taken, whom hast thou contemn'd?
For him, thou hast refus'd my browzing herd,
Scorn'd my thick eye-brows, and my shaggy beard.
Unhappy Damon sighs and sings in vain,
While Nisa thinks no god regards a lover's pain,
Begin with me, my flute, the sweet Mænalian strain.

"I view'd thee first, (how fatal was the view!)
And led thee where the ruddy wildings grew,
High on the planted hedge, and wet with morning dew.
Then scarce the bending branches I could win;
The callow down began to clothe my chin.
I saw, I perish'd, yet indulg'd my pain.
Begin with me, my flute, the sweet Mænalian strain.

"I know thee, love! in deserts thou wert bred,
And at the dugs of savage tigers fed;

Alien of birth, usurper of the plains!
Begin with me, my flute, the sweet Mænalian strains.
"Relentless love the cruel mother led,
The blood of her unhappy babes to shed:
Love lent the sword; the mother struck the blow;
Inhuman she, but more inhuman thou:
Alien of birth, usurper of the plains!
Begin with me, my flute, the sweet Mænalian strains.
"Old doting Nature, change thy course anew;
And let the trembling lamb the wolf pursue.
Let oaks now glitter with Hesperian fruit,
And purple daffodils from alder shoot;
Fat amber let the tamarisk distil,
And hooting owls contend with swans in skill;
Hoarse Tityrus strive with Orpheus in the woods,
And challenge fam'd Arion on the floods.
Or, oh, let Nature cease, and Chaos reign!
Begin with me, my flute, the sweet Mænalian strain.
"Let earth be sea, and let the whelming tide
The lifeless limbs of luckless Damon hide:
Farewell, ye secret woods and shady groves,
Haunts of my youth, and conscious of my loves!
From yon high cliff I plunge into the main:
Take the last present of thy dying swain:
And cease, my silent flute, the sweet Mænalian strain."

Now take your turns, ye Muses, to rehearse
His friend's complaints, and mighty magic verse.
"Bring running water; bind those altars round
With fillets, and with vervain strew the ground:
Make fat with frankincense the sacred fires,
To reinflame my Daphnis with desires.
'Tis done: we want but verse.—Restore, my charms,
My ling'ring Daphnis to my longing arms.
"Pale Phœbe, drawn by verse, from heav'n descends;
And Circe chang'd with charms Ulysses' friends.
Verse breaks the ground, and penetrates the brake,
And in the winding cavern splits the snake.
Verse fires the frozen veins.—Restore, my charms,
My ling'ring Daphnis to my longing arms.
"Around his waxen image first I wind
Three woollen fillets, of three colours join'd;
Thrice bind about his thrice devoted head,
Which round the sacred altar thrice is led.
Unequal numbers please the gods.—My charms,
Restore my Daphnis to my longing arms.
"Knit with three knots the fillets: knit them strait;
Then say, 'These knots to love I consecrate.'
Haste, Amaryllis, haste!—Restore, my charms,
My lovely Daphnis to my longing arms.
"As fire this figure hardens, made of clay,
And this of wax with fire consumes away;
Such let the soul of cruel Daphnis be—
Hard to the rest of women, soft to me.
Crumble the sacred mole of salt and corn:
Next in the fire the bays with brimstone burn:
And, while it crackles in the sulphur, say,
''Tis I for Daphnis burn; thus Daphnis burn away!
This laurel is his fate.'—Restore, my charms,
My lovely Daphnis to my longing arms.
"As when the raging heifer, through the grove,
Stung with desire, pursues her wand'ring love;
Faint at the last, she seeks the weedy pools,
To quench her thirst, and on the rushes rolls,
Careless of night, unmindful to return;
Such fruitless fires perfidious Daphnis burn,
While I so scorn his love!—Restore, my charms,
My ling'ring Daphnis to my longing arms.
"These garments once were his, and left to me,
The pledges of his promis'd loyalty,
Which underneath my threshold I bestow.
These pawns, O sacred earth! to me my Daphnis owe,
As these were his, so mine is he.—My charms,
Restore their ling'ring lord to my deluded arms.
"These pois'nous plants, for magic use design'd,
(The noblest and the best of all the baneful kind)
Old Mœris brought me from the Pontic strand,
And cull'd the mischief of a bounteous land.
Smear'd with these pow'rful juices, on the plain,
He howls, a wolf among the hungry train;
And oft the mighty necromancer boasts,
With these, to call from tombs the stalking ghosts,
And from the roots to tear the standing corn,
Which, whirl'd aloft, to distant fields is borne:
Such is the strength of spell. Restore, my charms,
My ling'ring Daphnis to my longing arms.
"Bear out these ashes: cast them in the brook;
Cast backwards o'er your head; nor turn your look:
Since neither gods nor godlike verse can move,
Break out, ye smother'd fires, and kindle smother'd love.
Exert your utmost pow'r, my ling'ring charms;
And force my Daphnis to my longing arms.

"See, while my last endeavours I delay,
The waking ashes rise, and round our altars play!
Run to the threshold, Amaryllis—hark!
Our Hylax opens, and begins to bark.
Good heav'n! may lovers what they wish believe?
Or dream their wishes, and those dreams deceive?
No more! my Daphnis comes! no more, my charms!
He comes, he runs, he leaps, to my desiring arms."

PASTORAL IX.

OR,

LYCIDAS AND MŒRIS.

ARGUMENT.

When Virgil, by the favour of Augustus, had recovered his patrimony near Mantua, and went in hope to take possession, he was in danger to be slain by Arius the centurion, to whom those lands were assigned by the emperor, in reward of his service against Brutus and Cassius. This pastoral therefore is filled with complaints of this hard usage; and the persons introduced are the bailiff of Virgil, Mœris, and his friend Lycidas.

LYCIDAS.

Ho, Mœris! whither on thy way so fast?
This leads to town.

MŒRIS.

O Lycidas! at last
The time is come, I never thought to see,
(Strange revolutions for my farm and me!)
When the grim captain in a surly tone
Cries out, "Pack up, ye rascals, and be gone."
Kick'd out, we set the best face on't we could,
And these two kids, t' appease his angry mood,
I bear,—of which the Furies give him good!

LYCIDAS.

Your country friends were told another tale—
That from the sloping mountain to the vale,
And dodder'd oak, and all the banks along,
Menalcas sav'd his fortune with a song.

MŒRIS.

Such was the news, indeed; but songs and rhymes
Prevail as much in these hard iron times,
As would a plump of trembling fowl, that rise
Against an eagle sousing from the skies.
And had not Phœbus warn'd me, by the croak
Of an old raven from a hollow oak,
To shun debate, Menalcas had been slain,
And Mœris not surviv'd him, to complain.

LYCIDAS.

Now heaven defend! could barbarous rage induce
The brutal son of Mars t' insult the sacred Muse?
Who then should sing the nymphs? or who rehearse
The waters gliding in a smoother verse?
Of Amaryllis praise that heavenly lay,
That shorten'd, as we went, our tedious way—
"O Tityrus, tend my herd, and see them fed;
To morning pastures, ev'ning waters, led;
And 'ware the Libyan ridgil's butting head."

MŒRIS.

Or what unfinish'd he to Varus read—
"Thy name, O Varus, (if the kinder pow'rs
Preserve our plains, and shield the Mantuan tow'rs,
Obnoxious by Cremona's neighbouring crime)
The wings of swans and stronger-pinion'd rhyme,
Shall raise aloft, and soaring bear above—
Th' immortal gift of gratitude to Jove."

LYCIDAS.

Sing on, sing on: for I can ne'er be cloy'd.
So may thy swarms the baleful yew avoid:
So may thy cows their burden'd bags distend,
And trees to goats their willing branches bend.
Mean as I am, yet have the Muses made
Me free, a member of the tuneful trade:
At least the shepherds seem to like my lays;
But I discern their flatt'ry from their praise:
I nor to Cinna's ears, nor Varus', dare aspire,
But gabble, like a goose amidst the swan-like choir.

MŒRIS

'T is what I have been conning in my mind;
Nor are thy verses of a vulgar kind.
"Come, Galatea! come! the seas forsake?
What pleasures can the tides with their hoarse murmurs make?
See, on the shore inhabits purple spring;
Where nightingales their love-sick ditty sing:
See, meads with purling streams, with flow'rs the ground,
The grottoes cool with shady poplars crown'd,
And creeping vines on arbours weav'd around.
Come then, and leave the waves' tumultuous roar;
Let the wild surges vainly beat the shore."

LYCIDAS.

Or that sweet song I heard with such delight;
The same you sung alone one starry night.
The tune I still retain, but not the words.

MŒRIS.

"Why, Daphnis, dost thou search in old records,
To know the seasons when the stars arise?
See, Cæsar's lamp is lighted in the skies—
The star, whose rays the blushing grapes adorn,
And swell the kindly rip'ning ears of corn.
Under this influence graft the tender shoot;
Thy children's children shall enjoy the fruit."

The rest I have forgot, for cares and time
Change all things, and untune my soul to rhyme.
I could have once sung down a summer's sun:
But now the chime of poetry is done:
My voice grows hoarse, I feel the notes decay;
As if the wolves had seen me first to-day.
But these, and more than I to mind can bring,
Menalcas has not yet forgot to sing.

LYCIDAS.

Thy faint excuses but inflame me more:
And now the waves roll silent to the shore;
Hush'd winds the topmost branches scarcely bend,
As if thy tuneful song they did attend:
Already we have half our way o'ercome
Far off I can discern Bianor's tomb,
Here, where the lab'rer's hands have form'd a bow'r
Of wreathing trees, in singing waste an hour.
Rest here thy weary limbs; thy kids lay down:
We've day before us yet to reach the town
Or if, ere night, the gathering clouds we fear,
A song will help the beating storm to bear.
And that thou mayst not be too late abroad,
Sing, and I'll ease thy shoulders of thy load.

MŒRIS.

Cease to request me; let us mind our way:
Another song requires another day.
When good Menalcas comes, if he rejoice,
And find a friend at court, I'll find a voice.

PASTORAL X.

OR,

GALLUS.

ARGUMENT.

Gallus, a great patron of Virgil, and an excellent poet, was very deeply in love with one Cytheris, whom he calls Lycoris, and who had forsaken him for the company of a soldier. The poet therefore supposes his friend Gallus retired, in his height of melancholy, into the solitudes of Arcadia, (the celebrated scene of pastorals,) where he represents him in a very languishing condition, with all the rural deities about him, pitying his hard usage, and condoling his misfortune.

THY sacred succour, Arethusa, bring,
To crown my labour, ('tis the last I sing,)
Which proud Lycoris may with pity view:
The muse is mournful, though the numbers few,
Refuse me not a verse, to grief and Gallus due.
So may thy silver streams beneath the tide,
Unmix'd with briny seas, securely glide.
Sing then my Gallus, and his hopeless vows;
Sing while my cattle crop the tender browse.
The vocal grove shall answer to the sound,
And echo, from the vales, the tuneful voice rebound.
What lawns or woods withheld you from his aid,
Ye nymphs, when Gallus was to love betray'd,
To love, unpitied by the cruel maid?
Not steepy Pindus could retard your course,
Nor cleft Parnassus, nor the Aonian source:
Nothing that owns the Muses, could suspend
Your aid to Gallus:—Gallus is their friend.
For him the lofty laurel stands in tears,
And hung with humid pearls the lowly shrub appears.
Mænalian pines the godlike swain bemoan,
When spread beneath a rock, he sigh'd alone,
And cold Lycæus wept from ev'ry dropping stone.
The sheep suround their shepherd, as he lies.
Blush not, sweet poet, nor the name despise:
Along the streams, his flock Adonis fed;
And yet the queen of beauty blest his bed.
The swains and tardy neatherds came, and last
Menalcas, wet with beating winter mast.
Wond'ring they ask'd from whence arose thy flame.
Yet more amaz'd, thy own Apollo came.
Flush'd were his cheeks, and glowing were his eyes:
"Is she thy care? is she thy care?" he cries,
"Thy false Lycoris flies thy love and thee,
And for thy rival tempts the raging sea,
The forms of horrid war, and heav'n's inclemency."
Silvanus came: his brows a country crown
Of fennel, and of nodding lilies, drown.
Great Pan arriv'd; and we beheld him too,
His cheeks and temples of vermilion hue.
"Why, Gallus, this immod'rate grief?" he cried.
"Think'st thou that love with tears is satisfied?
The meads are sooner drunk with morning dews,
The bees with flow'ry shrubs, the goats with browse."
Unmov'd, and with dejected eyes, he mourn'd:
He paus'd, and then these broken words return'd:
"'Tis past; and pity gives me no relief:
But you, Arcadian swains, shall sing my grief,
And on your hills my last complaints renew:
So sad a song is only worthy you.
How light would lie the turf upon my breast,
If you my suff'rings in your songs exprest!
Ah! that your birth and bus'ness had been mine—
To pen the sheep, and press the swelling vine.
Had Phyllis or Amyntas caus'd my pain,
Or any nymph or shepherd on the plain,
(Tho' Phyllis brown, tho' black Amyntas were,
Are violets not sweet, because not fair?)

Beneath the sallows and the shady vine,
My loves had mix'd their pliant limbs with mine:
Phyllis with myrtle wreaths had crown'd my hair,
And soft Amyntas sung away my care.
Come, see what pleasures in our plains abound;
The woods, the fountains, and the flow'ry ground.
As you are beauteous, were you half so true,
Here could I live, and love, and die with only you.
Now I to fighting fields am sent afar,
And strive in winter camps with toils of war;
While you, (alas, that I should find it so!)
To shun my sight your native soil forego,
And climb the frozen Alps, and tread th' eternal snow.
Ye frosts and snows, her tender body spare!
Those are not limbs for icicles to tear.
For me, the wilds and deserts are my choice;
The Muses once my care, my once harmonious voice.
There will I sing, forsaken and alone:
The rocks and hollow caves shall echo to my moan.
The rind of ev'ry plant her name shall know;
And, as the rind extends, the love shall grow.
Then on Arcadian mountains will I chase
(Mix'd with the woodland nymphs) the savage race;
Nor cold shall hinder me, with horns and hounds
To tread the thickets, or to leap the mounds.
And now methinks o'er steepy rocks I go,
And rush through sounding woods, and bend the Parthian bow;
As if with sports my suff'rings I should ease,
Or by my pains the god of love appease.
My frenzy changes: I delight no more
On mountain tops to chase the tusky boar:
No game but hopeless love my thoughts pursue:
Once more, ye nymphs, and songs, and sounding woods, adieu!
Love alters not for us his hard decrees,
Not though beneath the Thracian clime we freeze,
Or Italy's indulgent heav'n forego,
And in mid-winter tread Sithonian snow;
Or, when the barks of elms are scorch'd, we keep
On Meroe's burning plains the Libyan sheep.
In hell, and earth, and seas, and heav'n above,
Love conquers all; and we must yield to love."
My Muses, here your sacred raptures end:
The verse was what I ow'd my suff'ring friend.
This while I sung, my sorrows I deceiv'd,
And bending osiers into baskets weav'd.
The song, because inspir'd by you, shall shine;
And Gallus will approve, because 'tis mine—
Gallus, for whom my holy flames renew,
Each hour, and ev'ry moment rise in view:
As alders, in the spring, their boles extend,
And heave so fiercely, that the bark they rend,
Now let us rise: for hoarseness oft invades
The singer's voice, who sings beneath the shades.
From juniper unwholsome dews distil,
That blast the sooty corn, the withering herbage kill.
Away, my goats, away! for you have brows'd your fill.

GEORGICS.

GEORGIC I.

ARGUMENT.

The poet, in the beginning of this book, propounds the general design of each Georgic: and, after a solemn invocation of all the gods who are any way related to his subject, he addresses himself in particular to Augustus, whom he compliments with divinity; and after strikes into his business. He shows the different kinds of tillage proper to different soils, traces out the orignal of agriculture, gives a catalogue of the husbandman's tools, specifies the employments peculiar to each season, describes the changes of the weather, with the signs in heaven and earth that forebode them; instances many of the prodigies that happened near the time of Julius Cæsar's death; and shuts up all with a supplication to the gods for the safety of Augustus, and the preservation of Rome.

What makes a plenteous harvest, when to turn
The fruitful soil, and when to sow the corn;
The care of sheep, of oxen, and of kine;
And how to raise on elms the teeming vine;
The birth and genius of the frugal bee,
I sing, Mæcenas, and I sing to thee.
Ye deities! who fields and plains protect,
Who rule the seasons, and the year direct,
Bacchus and fost'ring Ceres, pow'rs divine,
Who gave us corn for mast, for water, wine—
Ye Fauns, propitious to the rural swains,
Ye nymphs that haunt the mountains and the plains,
Join in my work, and to my numbers bring
Your needful succour; for your gifts I sing.
And thou, whose trident struck the teeming earth,
And made a passage for the courser's birth;

And thou, for whom the Cean shore sustains
The milky herds, that graze the flow'ry plains;
And thou, the shepherds' tutelary god,
Leave, for a while, O Pan, thy lov'd abode;
And, if Arcadian fleeces be thy care,
From fields and mountains to my song repair.
Inventor, Pallas, of the fatt'ning oil,
Thou founder of the plough and ploughman's toil:
And thou, whose hands the shroud-like cypress rear;
Come, all ye gods and goddesses, that wear
The rural honours, and increase the year;
You, who supply the ground with seeds of grain;
And you, who swell those seeds with kindly rain;
And chiefly thou, whose undetermin'd state
Is yet the bus'ness of the gods, debate,
Whether in after-times, to be declar'd,
The patron of the world, and Rome's peculiar guard.
Or o'er the fruits and seasons to preside,
And the round circuit of the year to guide—
Pow'rful of blessings, which thou strew'st around,
And with thy goddess mother's myrtle crown'd.
Or wilt thou, Cæsar, choose the wat'ry reign
To smooth the surges and correct the main?
Then mariners, in storms, to thee shall pray;
E'en utmost Thule shall thy pow'r obey;
And Neptune shall resign the fasces of the sea.
The wat'ry virgins for thy bed shall strive,
And Tethys all her waves in dowry give.
Or wilt thou bless our summers with thy rays,
And, seated near the Balance, poise the days
Where, in the void of heav'n, a space is free,
Betwixt the Scorpion and the Maid for thee?
The Scorpion, ready to receive thy laws,
Yields half his region, and contracts his claws.
Whatever part of heav'n thou shalt obtain,
(For let not hell presume of such a reign;
Nor let so dire a thirst of empire move
Thy mind, to leave thy kindred gods above;
Though Greece admires Elysium's blest retreat,
Though Proserpine affects her silent seat,
And, importun'd by Ceres to remove,
Prefers the fields below to those above)
Be thou propitious, Cæsar! guide my course,
And to my bold endeavours add thy force:
Pity the poet's and the ploughman's cares;
Int'rest thy greatness in our mean affairs,
And use thyself betimes to hear and grant our pray'rs.
While yet the spring is young, while earth unbinds
Her frozen bosom to the western winds;
While mountain snows dissolve against the sun,
And streams, yet new, from precipices run;
E'en in this early dawning of the year,
Produce the plough, and yoke the sturdy steer,
And goad him till he groans beneath his toil,
Till the bright share is buried in the soil.
That crop rewards the greedy peasant's pains,
Which twice the sun, and twice the cold sustains,
And bursts the crowded barns with more than promis'd gains.
But, ere we stir the yet unbroken ground,
The various course of seasons must be found;
The weather and the setting of the winds,
The culture suiting to the sev'ral kinds
Of seeds and plants, and what will thrive and rise,
And what the genius of the soil denies.
This ground with Bacchus, that with Ceres, suits:
That other loads the trees with happy fruits:
A fourth, with grass unbidden, decks the ground.
Thus Tmolus is with yellow saffron crown'd:
India black ebon and white iv'ry bears;
And soft Idume weeps her od'rous tears.
Thus Pontus sends her beaver stones from far,
And naked Spaniards temper steel for war:
Epirus, for th' Elean chariot, breeds
(In hopes of palms) a race of running steeds.
This is th' orig'nal contract; these the laws
Impos'd by Nature, and by Nature's cause,
On sundry places, when Deucalion hurl'd
His mother's entrails on the desert world;
Whence men, a hard laborious kind, were born.
Then borrow part of winter for thy corn;
And early, with thy team, the glebe in furrows turn;
That, while the turf lies open and unbound,
Succeeding suns may bake the mellow ground.
But, if the soil be barren, only scar
The surface, and but lightly print the share,
When cold Arcturus rises with the sun:
Lest wicked weeds the corn should overrun
In wat'ry soils; or lest the barren sand
Should suck the moisture from the thirsty land
Both these unhappy soils the swain forbears,
And keeps a sabbath of alternate years,
That the spent earth may gather heart again,
And, better'd by cessation, bear the grain.
At least where vetches, pulse, and tares, have stood,
And stalks of lupines grew (a stubborn wood,)
Th' ensuing season, in return, may bear
The bearded product of the golden year:
For flax and oats will burn the tender field,
And sleepy poppies harmful harvest yield.
But sweet vicissitudes of rest and toil
Make easy labour and renew the soil,
Yet sprinkle sordid ashes all around,
And load with fatt'ning dung the fallow ground.

Thus change of seeds for meagre soils is best;
And earth manur'd, not idle, though at rest.
Long practice has a sure improvement found
With kindled fires to burn the barren ground
When the light stubble, to the flames resign'd
Is driv'n along, and crackles in the wind.
Whether from hence the hollow womb of earth
Is warm'd with secret strength for better birth;
Or, when the latent vice is cur'd by fire,
Redundant humours through the pores expire;
Or that the warmth distends the chinks, and makes [takes;
New breathings, whence new nourishment she
Or that the heat the gaping ground constrains;
New knits the surface, and new strings the veins;
Lest soaking show'rs should pierce her secret seat,
Or freezing Boreas chill her genial heat,
Or scorching suns too violently beat.
Nor is the profit small the peasant makes,
Who smooths with harrows, or who pound with rakes,
The crumbling clods: nor Ceres from on high
Regards his labours with a grudging eye,
Nor his, who ploughs across the furrow'd grounds,
And on the back of earth inflicts new wounds;
For he, with frequent exercise, commands
Th' unwilling soil, and tames the stubborn lands.
Ye swains, invoke the pow'rs who rule the sky
For a moist summer and a winter dry;
For winter drought rewards the peasant's pain,
And broods indulgent on the buried grain.
Hence Mysia boasts her harvests, and the tops
Of Gargarus admired their happy crops.
When first the soil receives the fruitful seed,
Make no delay, but cover it with speed:
So fenc'd from cold the pliant furrows break,
Before the surly clod resists the rake;
And call the floods from high, to rush amain
With pregnant streams, to swell the teeming grain.
Then, when the fiery suns too fiercely play,
And shrivell'd herbs on with'ring stems decay,
The wary ploughman, on the mountain's brow,
Undams his wat'ry stores—huge torrents flow,
And, rattling down the rocks, large moisture yield,
Temp'ring the thirsty fever of the field—
And, lest the stem, too feeble for the freight,
Should scarce sustain the head's unwieldly weight,
Sends in his feeding flocks betimes, t' invade
The rising bulk of the luxuriant blade,
Ere yet th' aspiring offspring of the grain
O'ertops the ridges of the furrow'd plain;
And drains the standing waters, when they yield
Too large a bev'rage to the drunken field:
But most in autumn, and the show'ry spring,
When dubious months uncertain weather bring
When fountains open, when impetuous rain
Swells hasty brooks, and pours upon the plain;
When earth with slime and mud is cover'd o'er
Or hollow places spew their wat'ry store.
Nor yet the ploughman, nor the lab'ring steer,
Sustain alone the hazards of the year:
But glutton geese, and the Strymonian crane,
With foreign troops invade the tender grain;
And tow'ring weeds malignant shadows yield;
And spreading succ'ry chokes the rising field.
The sire of gods and men, with hard decrees,
Forbids our plenty to be bought with ease,
And wills that mortal men, inur'd to toil,
Should exercise, with pains, the grudging soil;
Himself invented first the shining share
And whetted human industry by care;
Himself did handicrafts and arts ordain,
Nor suffer'd sloth to rust his active reign.
Ere this, no peasant vex'd the peaceful ground,
Which only turfs and greens for altars found:
No fences parted fields, nor marks nor bounds
Distinguish'd acres of litigious grounds:
But all was common, and the fruitful earth
Was free to give her unexacted birth.
Jove added venom to the viper's brood,
And swell'd, with raging storms, the peaceful flood;
Commission'd hungry wolves t' infest the fold,
And shook from oaken leaves the liquid gold;
Remov'd from human reach the cheerful fire,
And from the rivers bade the vine retire;
That studious need might useful arts explore;
From furrow'd fields to reap the foodful store,
And force the veins of clashing flints t' expire,
The lurking seeds of their celestial fire.
Then first on seas the hollow'd alder swam;
Then sailors quarter'd heav'n, and found a name
For ev'ry fix'd and ev'ry wand'ring star—
The Pleiads, Hyads, and the Northern Car.
Then toils for beasts, and lime for birds, were found,
And deep-mouth'd dogs did forest-walks surround;
And casting-nets were spread in shallow brooks
Drags in the deep, and baits were hung on hooks.
Then saws were tooth'd, and sounding axes made;
(For, wedges first did yielding wood invade)
And various arts in order did succeed,
(What cannot endless labour, urg'd by need?)
First Ceres taught the ground with grain to sow,
And arm'd with iron shares the crooked plough
When now Dodonian oaks no more supplied
Their mast, and trees their forest-fruits denied.

Soon was his labour doubled to the swain,
And blasting mildews blacken'd all his grain:
Though thistles chok'd the fields, and kill'd the corn,
And an unthrifty crop of weeds was born:
Then burs and brambles, an unbidden crew
Of graceless guests th' unhappy field subdue;
And oats unblest, and darnel domineers,
And shoots its head above the shining ears;
So that, unless the land with daily care
Is exercis'd, and, with an iron war
Of rakes and harrows, the proud foes expell'd,
And birds with clamours frighted from the field;
Unless the boughs are lopp'd that shade the plain
And heav'n invok'd with vows for fruitful rain—
On others' crops you may with envy look,
And shake for food the long-abandon'd oak.
Nor must we pass untold what arms they wield,
Who labour tillage and the furrow'd field;
Without whose aid the ground her corn denies,
And nothing can be sown, and nothing rise—
The crooked plough, the share, the tow'ring height
Of wagons and the cart's unwieldly weight,
The sled, the tumbril, hurdles, and the flail,
The fan of Bacchus, with the flying sail—
These all must be prepar'd if ploughmen hope
The promis'd blessing of a bounteous crop.
Young elms, with early force, in copses bow,
Fit for the figure of the crooked plough.
Of eight feet long a fasten'd beam prepare:
On either side the head, produce an ear;
And sink a socket for the shining share.
Of beech the plough-tail and the bending yoke,
Or softer linden harden'd in the smoke.
I could be long in precepts; but I fear
So mean a subject might offend your ear.
Delve of convenient depth your threshing floor:
With temper'd clay, then fill and face it o'er;
And let the weighty roller run the round,
To smooth the surface of th' unequal ground;
Lest, crack'd with summer heats, the flooring flies,
Or sinks, and through the crannies weeds arise:
For sundry foes the rural realm surround:
The field-mouse builds her garner under ground
For gather'd grain: the blind laborious mole
In winding mazes works her hidden hole:
In hollow caverns vermin make abode—
The hissing serpent, and the swel'ing toad:
The corn devouring weasel here abides,
And the wise ant her wintry store provides.
  Mark well the flow'ring almonds in the wood:
If od'rous blooms the bearing branches load,
The glebe will answer to the sylvan reign;
Great heats will follow, and large crops of grain.
But, if a wood of leaves o'ershade the tree
Such and so barren will thy harvest be:
In vain the hind shall vex the threshing-floor
For empty chaff and straw will be thy store.
Some steep their seed, and some in caldrons boil,
With vig'rous nitre and with lees of oil,
O'er gentle fires, th' exub'rant juice to drain,
And swell the flatt'ring husks with fruitful grain.
Yet, the success is not for years assur'd,
Though chosen is the seed, and fully cur'd,
Unless the peasant, with his annual pain,
Renews his choice, and culls the largest grain.
Thus all below, whether by Nature's curse,
Or Fate's decree, degen'rate still to worse.
So the boat's brawny crew the current stem,
And, slow advancing, struggle with the stream.
But, if they slack their hands, or cease to strive,
Then down the flood with headlong haste they drive.
  Nor must the ploughman less observe the skies,
When the Kids, Dragon, and Arcturus rise,
Then sailors homeward bent, who cut their way
Thro' Helle's stormy straits, and oyster-breeding sea.
But, when Astrea's balance, hung on high,
Betwixt the nights and days divides the sky,
Then yoke your oxen, sow your winter grain,
Till cold December comes with driving rain.
Linseed and fruitful poppy bury warm,
In a dry season, and prevent the storm.
Sow beans and clover in a rotten soil,
And millet rising from your annual toil,
When with his golden horns, in full career
The bull beats down the barriers of the year,
And Argo and the dog forsake the northern sphere.
  But if your care to wheat alone extend,
Let Maia with her sisters first descend.
And the bright Gnossian diadem downward bend,
Before you trust in earth your future hope;
Or else expect a listless lazy crop.
Some swains have sown before; but most have found
A husky harvest from the grudging ground.
Vile vetches would you sow, or lentils lean,
The growth of Egypt, or the kidney bean,
Begin when the slow Wagoner descends;
Nor cease your sowing till midwinter ends.
For this, through twelve bright signs Apollo guides
The year, and earth in sev'ral climes divides.
Five girdles bind the skies: the torrid zone
Glows with the passing and repassing sun:

Far on the right and left, th' extremes of heav'n
To frosts and snows and bitter blasts are giv'n:
Betwixt the midst and these, the gods assign'd
Two habitable seats for human kind,
And 'cross their limits, cut a sloping way,
Which the twelve signs in beauteous order sway. [rise
Two poles turn round the globe; one seen to
O'er Scythian hills, and one in Libyan skies;
The first sublime in heav'n, the last is whirl'd
Below the regions of the nether world,
Around our pole the spiry Dragon glides,
And like a winding stream, the Bears divides—
The less and greater, who by Fate's decree
Abhor to dive beneath the northern sea.
There, as they say, perpetual night is found
In silence brooding on th' unhappy ground:
Or, when Aurora leaves our northern sphere
She lights the downward heav'n, and rises there;
And, when on us she breathes the living light,
Red Vesper kindles there the tapers of the night.
From hence uncertain seasons we may know:
And when to reap the grain, and when to sow;
Or when to fell the furzes: when 't is meet
To spread the flying canvass for the fleet.
Observe what stars arise or disappear;
And the four quarters of the rolling year.
But, when cold weather and continu'd rain
The lab'ring husband in his house restrain,
Let him forecast his work with timely care:
Which else is huddled, when the skies are fair:
Then let him mark the sheep, or whet the shining share,
Or hollow trees for boats, or number o'er
His sacks, or measure his increasing store,
Or sharpen stakes, or head the forks, or twine
The sallow twigs to tie the straggling vine;
Or wicker baskets weave, or air the corn,
Or grinded grain betwixt two marbles turn.
No laws, divine or human, can restrain,
From necessary works the lab'ring swain.
E'en holy days and feasts permission yield
To float the meadows, or to fence the field,
To fire the brambles, snare the birds, and steep
In wholesome waterfalls the woolly sheep.
And oft the drudging ass is driven, with toil,
To neighb'ring towns with apples and with oil;
Returning, late and laden, home with gain
Of barter'd pitch, and handmills for the grain.
The lucky days, in each revolving moon,
For labour choose: the fifth be sure to shun;
That gave the Furies and pale Pluto birth,
And arm'd against the skies, the sons of earth.
With mountains pil'd on mountains, thrice they strove
To scale the steepy battlements of Jove;
And thrice his lightning and red thunder play'd,
And their demolish'd work in ruin laid.
The sev'nth is, next the tenth, the best to join
Young oxen to the yoke, and plant the vine.
Then, weavers, stretch your stays upon the weft.
The ninth is good for travel, bad for theft.
Some works in dead of night are better done,
Or when the morning dew prevents the sun.
Parch'd meads and stubble mow by Phœbe's light,
Which both require the coolness of the night;
For, moisture then abounds, and pearly rains
Descend in silence to refresh the plains.
The wife and husband equally conspire
To work by night, and rake the winter fire:
He sharpens torches in the glim'ring room;
She shoots the flying shuttle through the loom,
Or boils in kettles must of wine, and skims,
With leaves, the dregs that overflow the brims,
And, till the watchful cock awakes the day,
She sings to drive the tedious hours away.
But, in warm weather, when the skies are clear,
By daylight reap the product of the year;
And in the sun your golden grain display,
And thresh it out and winnow it by day.
Plough naked, swain, and naked sow the land;
For lazy winter numbs the lab'ring hand.
In genial winter, swains enjoy their store,
Forget their hardships, and recruit for more.
The farmer to full bowls invites his friends,
And, what he got with pains, with pleasure spends.
So sailors, when escap'd from stormy seas,
First crown their vessels, then indulge their ease.
Yet that's the proper time to thresh the wood
For mast of oak, your father's homely food;
To gather laurel-berries, and the spoil
Of bloody myrtles, and to press your oil:
For stalking cranes to set the guileful snare;
T' inclose the stags in toils, and hunt the hare;
With Balearic slings, or Gnossian bow,
To persecute from far the flying doe,
Then, when the fleecy skies new clothe the wood,
And cakes of rustling ice come rolling down the flood.

Now sing we stormy stars, when autumn weighs
The year, and adds to nights, and shortens days,
And suns declining shine with feeble rays:
What cares must then attend the toiling swain,
Or when the low'ring spring, with lavish rain,
Beats down the slender stem and bearded grain,
While yet the head is green, or, lightly swell'd
With milky moisture, overlooks the field.
E'en when the farmer, now secure of fear,
Sends in the swains to spoil the finish'd year,

E'en while the reaper fills his greedy hands,
And binds the golden sheaves in brittle bands,
Oft have I seen a sudden storm arise,
From all the warring winds that sweep the skies:
The heavy harvest from the root is torn,
And whirl'd aloft the lighter stubble borne:
With such a force the flying rack is driv'n,
And such a winter wears the face of heav'n.
And oft whole sheets descend of sluicy rain,
Suck'd by the spongy clouds from off the main:
The lofty skies, at once come pouring down,
The promis'd crop, and golden labours drown.
The dikes are fill'd; and, with a roaring sound,
The rising rivers float the nether ground;
And rocks the bellowing voice of boiling seas rebound.
The father of the gods his glory shrouds,
Involv'd in tempests, and a night of clouds;
And, from the middle darkness flashing out,
By fits he deals his fiery bolts about.
Earth feels the motions of her angry god;
Her entrails tremble, and her mountains nod;
And flying beasts in forests seek abode:
Deep horror seizes ev'ry human breast;
Their pride is humbled, and their fear confess'd,
While he from high his rolling thunder throws,
And fires the mountains with repeated blows:
The rocks are from their old foundations rent;
The winds redouble, and the rains augment:
The waves on heaps are dash'd against the shore;
And now the woods, and now the billows, roar.
In fear of this, observe the starry signs,
Where Saturn houses, and where Hermes joins.
But first to heav'n thy due devotions pay,
And annual gifts on Ceres' altar lay.
When winter's rage abates, when cheerful hours
Awake the spring, the spring awakes the flow'rs,
On the green turf thy careless limbs display,
And celebrate the mighty Mother's day:
For then the hills with pleasing shades are crown'd,
And sleeps are sweeter on the silken ground:
With milder beams the sun serenely shines:
Fat are the lambs, and luscious are the wines.
Let ev'ry swain adore her pow'r divine,
And milk and honey mix with sparkling wine:
Let all the choir of clowns attend the show,
In long procession, shouting as they go
Invoking her to bless their yearly stores,
Invoking plenty to their crowded floors.
Thus in the spring, and thus in summer's heat,
Before the sickles touch the rip'ning wheat,
On Ceres call; and let the lab'ring hind
With oaken wreaths his hollow temples bind:
On Ceres let him call, and Ceres praise,
With uncouth dances, and with country lays.
And that by certain signs we may presage
Of heats and rains, and wind's impetuous rage,
The sov'reign of the heav'ns has set on high
The moon, to mark the changes of the sky;
When southern blasts should cease, and when the swain
Should near their fold his feeding flocks restrain.
For, ere the rising winds begin to roar,
The working seas advance to wash the shore:
Soft whispers run along the leafy woods;
And mountains whistle to the murm'ring floods.
E'en then the doubtful billows scarce abstain
From the toss'd vessel on the troubled main;
When crying cormorants forsake the sea,
And, stretching to the covert, wing their way;
When sportful coots run skimming o'er the strand;
When watchful herons leave their wat'ry stand,
And, mounting upward with erected flight,
Gain on the skies, and soar above the sight.
And oft, before tempestuous winds arise,
The seeming stars fall headlong from the skies,
And, shooting through the darkness, gild the night
With sweeping glories, and long trails of light;
And chaff with eddy-winds is whirl'd around,
And dancing leaves are lifted from the ground;
And floating feathers on the waters play.
But, when the winged thunder takes his way
From the cold north, and east and west engage,
And at their frontiers meet with equal rage,
The clouds are crush'd: a glut of gather'd rain
The hollow ditches fills, and floats the plain;
And sailors furl their dropping sheets amain.
Wet weather seldom hurts the most unwise;
So plain the signs, such prophets are the skies.
The wary crane foresees it first, and sails
Above the storm, and leaves the lowly vales:
The cow looks up, and from afar can find
The change of heaven, and snuffs it in the wind:
The swallow skims the river's wat'ry face:
The frogs renew the croaks of their loquacious race:
The careful ant her secret cell forsakes,
And drags her eggs along the narrow tracks:
At either horn the rainbow drinks the flood:
Huge flocks of rising rooks forsake their food,
And, crying, seek the shelter of the wood.
Besides, the sev'ral sorts of wat'ry fowls,
That swim the seas or haunt the standing pools,
The swans that sail along the silver flood,
And dive with stretching necks to search their food,
Then lave their backs with sprinkling dews in vain,
And stem the stream to meet the promis'd rain.

The crow with clam'rous cries the show'r demands,
And single stalks along the desert sands.
The nightly virgin, while her wheel she plies
Foresees the storm impending in the skies,
When sparkling lamps their sputt'ring light advance,
And in the sockets oily bubbles dance.
Then, after showers, 'tis easy to descry
Returning suns and a serener sky:
The stars shine smarter; and the moon adorns,
As with unborrow'd beams, her sharpen'd horns.
The filmy gossamer now flits no more,
Nor halcyons bask on the short sunny shore:
Their litter is not toss'd by sows unclean;
But a blue droughty mist descends upon the plain;
And owls, that mark the setting sun, declare
A star-light evening, and a morning fair.
Tow'ring aloft avenging Nisus flies,
While, dar'd, below the guilty Scylla lies.
Wherever frighted Scylla flies away
Swift Nisus follows, and pursues his prey:
Where injured Nisus takes his airy course,
Thence trembling Scylla flies, and shuns his force,
This punishment pursues th' unhappy maid,
And thus the purple hair is dearly paid:
Then, thrice the ravens rend the liquid air,
And croaking notes proclaim the settled fair.
Then round their airy palaces they fly,
To greet the sun; and, seiz'd with secret joy,
When storms are overblown, with food repair
To their forsaken nests, and callow care.
Not that I think their breasts with heav'nly souls
Inspir'd, as man, who destiny controls.
But with the changeful temper of the skies,
As rains condense, and sunshine rarifies,
So turn the species in their alter'd minds,
Compos'd by calms and discompos'd by winds:
From hence proceeds the bird's harmonious voice;
From hence the cows exult, and frisking lambs rejoice.
Observe the daily circle of the sun,
And the short year of each revolving moon:
By them thou shalt foresee the following day;
Nor shall a starry night thy hopes betray.
When first the moon appears, if then she shrouds
Her silver crescent tipp'd with sable clouds,
Conclude she bodes a tempest on the main,
And brews for fields impetuous floods of rain.
Or, if her face with fiery flushing glow,
Expect the rattling winds aloft to blow.
But, four nights old, (for that's the surest sign)
With sharpen'd horns if glorious then she shine,
Next day, nor only that, but all the moon,
'Till her revolving race be wholly run,
Are void of tempests, both by land and sea,
And sailors in the port their promis'd vow shall pay.
Above the rest, the sun who never lies,
Foretells the change of weather in the skies.
For, if he rise unwilling to his race,
Clouds on his brow, and spots upon his face,
Or if through mists he shoots his sullen beams,
Frugal of light, in loose and straggling streams,
Suspect a drizzling day, with southern rain,
Fatal to fruits and flocks, and promis'd grain.
Or, if Aurora, with half open'd eyes,
And a pale sickly cheek, salute the skies
How shall the vine, with tender leaves, defend
Her teeming clusters, when the storms descend
When ridgy roofs and tiles can scarce avail
To bar the ruin of the rattling hail?
But more than all, the setting sun survey,
When down the steep of heav'n he drives the day:
For oft we find him finishing his race,
With various colours erring on his face.
If fiery red his glowing globe descends,
High winds and furious tempests he portends;
But, if his cheeks are swoln with livid blue,
He bodes wet weather by his wat'ry hue:
If dusky spots are varied on his brow,
And streak'd with red, a troubled colour show,
That sullen mixture shall at once declare
Winds, rain, and storms, and elemental war.
What desp'rate madman then would venture o'er
The frith, or haul his cables from the shore?
But, if with purple rays he brings the light,
And a pure heav'n reigns to quiet night,
No rising winds, or falling storms are nigh;
But northern breezes through the forests fly,
And drive the rack, and purge the ruffled sky.
Th' unerring sun by certain signs declares
What the late ev'n or early morn prepares,
And when the south projects a stormy day,
And when the clearing north will puff the clouds away.
The sun reveals the secrets of the sky;
And who dares give the source of light the lie?
The change of empires often he declares,
Fierce tumults, hidden treasons, open wars.
He first the fate of Cæsar did foretell,
And pitied Rome, when Rome in Cæsar fell;
In iron clouds conceal'd the public light;
And impious mortals fear'd eternal night.
Nor was the fact foretold by him alone:
Nature herself stood forth and seconded the sun.
Earth, air, and seas, with prodigies were sign'd;
And birds obscene, and howling dogs, divin'd.

What rocks did Ætna's bellowing mouth expire
From her torn entrails! and what floods of fire!
What clanks were heard, in German skies afar,
Of arms and armies, rushing to the war!
Dire earthquakes rent the solid Alps below,
And from their summits shook th' eternal snow,
Pale spectres in the close of night were seen;
And voices heard of more than mortal men,
In silent groves: dumb sheep and oxen spoke;
And streams ran backward, and their beds forsook:
The yawning earth disclos'd th' abyss of hell:
The weeping statues did the wars foretell;
And holy sweat from brazen idols fell.
Then, rising in his might, the king of floods
Rush'd through the forest, tore the lofty woods,
And, rolling onward, with a sweepy sway,
Bore houses, herds, and lab'ring hinds away,
Blood sprang from wells; wolves howl'd in towns by night,
And boiling victims did the priests affright.
Such peals of thunder never pour'd from high,
Nor forky light'nings flash'd from such a sullen sky.
Red meteors ran across the etherial space;
Stars disappear'd, and comets took their place.
For this th' Emathian plains once more were strew'd
With Roman bodies, and just heav'n thought good
To fatten twice those fields with Roman blood.
Then, after length of time, the lab'ring swains,
Who turn the turfs of those unhappy plains,
Shall rusty piles from the plough'd furrows take,
And over empty helmets pass the rake—
Amaz'd at antique titles on the stones,
And mighty relics of gigantic bones
Ye home-born deities of mortal birth!
Thou father Romulus, and mother Earth,
Goddess unmov'd! whose guardian arms extend,
O'er Tuscan Tiber's course, and Roman tow'rs defend;
With youthful Cæsar your joint pow'rs engage,
Nor hinder him to save the sinking age.
O! let the blood, already spilt, atone
For the past crimes of curst Laomedon!
Heav'n wants thee there: and long the gods, we know,
Have grudg'd thee, Cæsar, to the world below,
Where fraud and rapine right and wrong confound,
Where impious arms from ev'ry part resound,
And monstrous crimes in ev'ry shape are crown'd.
The peaceful peasant to the wars is press'd;
The fields lie fallow in inglorious rest;
The plain no pasture to the flock affords;
The crooked scythes are straighten'd into swords;
And there Euphrates her soft offspring arms,
And here the Rhine rebellows with alarms;
The neighb'ring cities range on several sides,
Perfidious Mars long plighted leagues divides,
And o'er the wasted world in triumph rides.
So four fierce coursers, starting to the race,
Scour through the plain, and lengthen every pace;
Nor reins, nor curbs, nor threat'ning cries, they fear,
But force along the trembling charioteer

GEORGIC II.

ARGUMENT.

The subject of the following book is planting; in handling of which argument, the poet shows all the different methods of raising trees, describes their variety, and gives rules for the management of each in particular. He then points out the soils in which the several plants thrive best, and thence takes occasion to run out into the praises of Italy; after which, he gives some directions for discovering the nature of every soil, prescribes rules for dressing of vines, olives, &c. and concludes the Georgic with a panegyric on a country life.

Thus far of tillage, and of heav'nly signs;
Now sing, my Muse, the growth of gen'rous vines,
The shady groves, the woodland progeny,
And the slow product of Minerva's tree.
Great father Bacchus! to my song repair;
For clust'ring grapes are thy peculiar care:
For thee large bunches load the bending vine;
And the last blessings of the year are thine.
To thee his joys the jolly Autumn owes,
When the fermenting juice the vat o'erflows.
Come, strip with me, my god! come drench all o'er
Thy limbs in must of wine, and drink at ev'ry pore.
Some trees their birth to bounteous nature owe;
For some, without the pains of planting, grow.
With osiers thus the banks of brooks abound,
Sprung from the wat'ry genius of the ground.
From the same principles gray willows come
Herculean poplar, and the tender broom
But some, from seeds inclos'd in earth arise;
For thus the mastful chestnut mates the skies.
Hence rise the branching beech and vocal oak,
Where Jove of old oraculously spoke.
Some from the root a rising wo[illegible]
Thus elms, and thus the savage cherry grows:
Thus the green bay, that binds the poet's brows,
Shoots, and is shelter'd by the mother's bo[illegible]

These ways of planting Nature did ordain,
For trees and shrubs, and all the sylvan reign.
Others there are, by late experience found,
Some cut the shoots, and plant in furrow'd ground;
Some cover rooted stalks in deeper mould;
Some, cloven-stakes; and (wondrous to behold!)
Their sharpen'd ends in earth their footing place;
And the dry poles produce a living race;
Some bow their vines, which buried in the plain;
Their tops in distant arches rise again.
Others no root require; the lab'rer cuts
Young slips, and in the soil securely puts.
Ev'n stumps of olives, bar'd of leaves, and dead,
Revive, and oft redeem their wither'd head.
'T is usual now an inmate graff to see
With insolence invade a foreign tree:
Thus pears and quinces from the crabtree come;
And thus the ready cornel bears the plum.
Then let the learned gard'ner mark with care
The kinds of stocks, and what those kinds will bear;
Explore the nature of each sev'ral tree,
And, known, improve with artful industry;
And let no spot of idle earth be found;
But cultivate the genius of the ground:
For open Ismarus will Bacchus please;
Taburnus loves the shade of olive-trees.
The virtues of the sev'ral soils I sing.—
Mæcenas, now thy needful succour bring!
O thou, the better part of my renown,
Inspire thy poet, and thy poem crown:
Embark with me, while I new tracts explore,
With flying sails and breezes from the shore
Not that my song in such a scanty space,
So large a subject fully can embrace—
Not though I were supplied with iron lungs,
A hundred mouths, fill'd with as many tongues:
But steer my vessel with a steady hand,
And coast along the shore in sight of land.
Nor will I tire thy patience with a train
Of preface, or what ancient poets feign.
The trees which of themselves advance in air
Are barren kinds, but strongly built and fair,
Because the vigour of the native earth
Maintains the plant, and makes a manly birth.
Yet these, receiving grafts of other kind,
Or thence transplanted, change their savage mind,
Their wildness lose, and, quitting nature's part,
Obey the rules and discipline of art.
The same do trees, that, sprung from barren roots,
In open fields transplanted bear their fruits.
For, where they grow, the native energy,
Turns all into the substance of the tree,
Starves and destroys the fruit, is only made
For brawny bulk, and for a barren shade.
The plant that shoots from seed, a sullen tree,
At leisure grows, for late posterity,
The gen'rous flavour lost, the fruits decay,
And savage grapes are made the bird's ignoble prey.
Much labour is requir'd in trees, to tame
Their wild disorder, and in ranks reclaim.
Well must the ground be digg'd, and better dress'd,
New soil to make, and meliorate the rest.
Old stakes of olive trees in plants revive
By the same method Paphian myrtles live:
But nobler vines by propagation thrive.
From roots hard hazels, and from scions rise
Tall ash, and taller oak that mates the skies.
Palm, poplar, fir, descending from the steep
Of hills, to try the dangers of the deep.
The thin-leav'd arbute hazel-graffs receives;
And planes huge apples bear, that bore but leaves.
Thus mastful beech the bristly chestnut bears,
And the wild ash is white with blooming pears.
And greedy swine from grafted elms are fed
With falling acorns, that on oaks are bred.
But various are the ways to change the state
Of plants, to bud, to graff, t' inoculate.
For, where the tender rinds of trees disclose
Their shooting gems, a swelling knot there grows:
Just in that space a narrow slit we make,
Then other buds from bearing trees we take
Inserted thus, the wounded rind we close,
In whose moist womb th' admitted infant grows
But, when the smoother bole from knots is free
We make a deep incision in the tree.
And in the solid wood the slip inclose;
The batt'ning bastard shoots again and grows
And in short space the laden boughs arise,
With happy fruit advancing to the skies.
The mother plant admires the leaves unknown
Of alien trees, and apples not her own.
Of vegetable woods are various kinds;
And the same species are of several minds.
Lotes, willows, elms, have different forms allow'd:
So fun'ral cypress, rising like a shroud.
Fat olive trees of sundry sorts appear,
Of sundry shapes: their unctious berries bear.
Radii long olives, orchites round produce,
And bitter pausia, pounded for the juice.
Alcinoüs' orchard various apples bears:
Unlike are burgamots and pounder pears.
Nor our Italian vines produce the shape,
Or taste, or flavour of the Lesbian grape.
The Thasian vines in richer soils abound;
The Mareotic grow in barren ground.

The Psythian grape we dry: Lagean juice
Will stamm'ring tongues and stagg'ring feet produce.
Rath ripe are some, and some of later kind,
Of golden some, and some of purple rind.
How shall I praise the Rhætian grape divine,
Which yet contends not with Falernian wine?
Th' Arminian many a consulship survives,
And longer than the Lydian vintage lives,
Or high Phanæus, king of Chian growth:
But, for large quantities and lasting both,
The less Argitis bears the prize away
The Rhodian, sacred to the solemn day,
In second services is pour'd to Jove,
And best accepted by the gods above.
Nor must Bumástus his old honours lose,
In length and largeness like the dugs of cows.
I pass the rest, whose ev'ry race, and name,
And kinds, are less material to my theme;
Which, who would learn, as soon may tell the sands,
Driv'n by the western wind on Libyan lands;
Or number, when the blust'ring Eurus roars,
The billows beating on Ionian shores.
Nor ev'ry plant on ev'ry soil will grow:
The sallow loves the wat'ry ground and low;
The marshes, alders: Nature seems t' ordain
The rocky cliff for the wild ash's reign;
The baleful yew to northern blasts assigns,
To shores the myrtles, and to mounts the vines.
Regard the extremest cultivated coast,
From hot Arabia to the Scythian frost:
All sorts of trees their sev'ral countries know;
Black ebon only will in India grow,
And od'rous frankincense on the Sabæan bough.
Balm slowly trickles thro' the bleeding veins
Of happy shrubs in Idumæan plains.
The green Egyptian thorn, for med'cine good,
With Æthiops' hoary trees and woolly wood,
Let others tell; and how the Seres spin
Their fleecy forests in a slender twine;
With mighty trunks of trees on Indian shores,
Whose height above the feather'd arrow soars,
Shot from the toughest bow, and, by the brawn
Of expert archers with vast vigour drawn.
Sharp tasted citrons Median climes produce,
(Bitter the rind, but gen'rous is the juice)
A cordial fruit, a present antidote
Against the direful stepdame's deadly draught,
Who, mixing wicked weeds with words impure,
The fate of envied orphans would procure.
Large is the plant, and like a laurel grows,
And, did it not a diff'rent scent disclose,
A laurel were: the fragrant flow'r contemn
The stormy wind, tenacious of their stem.
With this, the Medes to lab'ring age bequeath
New lungs, and cure the sourness of the breath.

But neither Median woods, (a plenteous land)
Fair Ganges, Hermus rolling golden sand,
Nor Bactria, nor the richer Indian fields,
Nor all the gummy stores Arabia yields,
Nor any foreign earth of greater name,
Can with sweet Italy contend in fame.
No bulls, whose nostrils breathe a living flame,
Have turn'd our turf; no teeth of serpents here
Were sown, an arm'd host and iron crop to bear.
But fruitful vines, and the fat olive's freight,
And harvests heavy with their fruitful weight,
Adorn our fields; and on the cheerful green
The grazing flocks and lowing herds are seen.
The warrior horse, here bred, is taught to train:
There flows Clitumnus through the flow'ry plain,
Whose waves, for triumphs after prosp'rous war,
The victim ox, and snowy sheep prepare.
Perpetual spring our happy climate sees:
Twice breed the cattle, and twice bear the trees;
And summer suns recede by slow degrees.
Our land is from the rage of tigers freed,
Nor nourishes the lion's angry seed;
Nor pois'nous aconite is here produc'd,
Or grows unknown, or is, when known, refus'd;
Nor in so vast a length our serpents glide,
Or rais'd on such a spiry volume ride.
Next add our cities of illustrious name,
Their costly labour, and stupendous frame;
Our forts on steepy hills, that far below
See wanton streams in winding valleys flow,
Our twofold seas, that, washing either side,
A rich recruit of foreign stores provide;
Our spacious lakes; thee, Larius, first; and next
Benacus, with tempestuous billows vex'd.
Or shall I praise thy ports, or mention make
Of the vast mound that binds the Lucrine lake?
Or the disdainful sea, that, shut from thence,
Roars round the structure, and invades the fence.
There, where secure the Julian waters glide,
Or where Avernus' jaws admit the Tyrrhene tide?
Our quarries deep in earth, were fam'd of old
For veins of silver, and for ore of gold.
Th' inhabitants themselves their country grace;
Hence rose the Marsian and Sabellian race.
Strong limb'd and stout, and to the wars inclin'd,
And hard Ligurians, a laborious kind,
And Volscians arm'd with iron-headed darts.
Besides—an offspring of undaunted hearts—
The Decii, Marii, great Camillus, came
From hence, and greater Scipio's double name,

And mighty Cæsar, whose victorious arms
To farthest Asia carry fierce alarms,
Avert unwarlike Indians from his Rome,
Triumph abroad, secure our peace at home.
Hail, sweet Saturnian soil! of fruitful grain
Great parent, greater of illustrious men!
For thee my tuneful accents will I raise,
And treat of arts disclos'd in ancient days,
Once more unlock for thee the sacred spring,
And old Ascræan verse in Roman cities sing.
The nature of the sev'ral soils now see
Their strength, their colour, their fertility:
And first for heath, and barren hilly ground,
Where meagre clay and flinty stones abound,
Where the poor soil all succour seems to want—
Yet this suffices the Palladian plant.
Undoubted signs of such a soil are found;
For here wild olive-shoots o'erspread the ground,
And heaps of berries strew the fields around.
But, where the soil, with fatt'ning moisture fill'd,
Is cloth'd with grass, and fruitful to be till'd,
Such as in cheerful vales we view from high,
Which dripping rocks with rolling streams supply,
And feed with ooze; where rising hillocks run
In length; and open to the southern sun;
Where fern succeeds, ungrateful to the plough—
That gentle ground to gen'rous grapes allow.
Strong stocks of vines it will in time produce,
And overflow the vats with friendly juice,
Such as our priests in golden goblets pour
To gods, the givers of the cheerful hour,
Then when the bloated Tuscan blows his horn,
And reeking entrails are in chargers borne.
If herds or fleecy flocks be more thy care,
Or goats that graze the field, and burn it bare,
Then seek Tarentum's lawns, and furthest coast,
Or such a field as hapless Mantua lost,
Where silver swans sail down the wat'ry road,
And graze the floating herbage of the flood.
There crystal streams perpetual tenor keep,
Nor food nor springs are wanting to thy sheep;
For, what the day devours, the nightly dew
Shall to the morn in pearly drops renew.
Fat crumbling earth is fitter for the plough,
Putrid and loose above, and black below;
For ploughing is an imitative toil,
Resembling nature in an easy soil.
No land for seed like this; no fields afford
So large an income to the village lord:
No toilings teams from harvest-labour come
So late at night, so heavy-laden home.
The like of forest land is understood,
From whence the surly ploughman grubs the wood,
Which had for length of ages idle stood.
Then birds forsake the ruins of their seat,
And, flying from their nests, their callow young forget.
The coarse lean gravel, on the mountain-sides,
Scarce dewy bev'rage for the bees provides;
Nor chalk nor crumbling stones, the food of snakes,
That work in hollow earth their winding tracks,
The soil exhaling clouds of subtle dews,
Imbibing moisture which with ease she spews,
Which rusts not iron, and whose mould is clean,
Well cloth'd with cheerful grass, and ever green,
Is good for olives, and aspiring vines,
Embracing husband-elms in am'rous twines;
Is fit for feeding cattle, fit to sow,
And equal to the pasture and the plough.
Such is the soil of fat Campanian fields;
Such large increase the land that joins Vesuvius yields;
And such a country could Acerræ boast,
Till Clanius overflow'd the unhappy coast.
I teach thee next the diff'ring soils to know,
The light for vines, the heavier for the plough.
Choose first a place for such a purpose fit:
There dig the solid earth and sink a pit;
Next fill the hole with its own earth again,
And trample with thy feet and tread it in:
Then, if it rise not to the former height
Of superfice, conclude that soil is light,
A proper ground for pasturage and vines.
But, if the sullen earth, so press'd, repines
Within its native mansion to retire,
And stays without, a heap of heavy mire,
'Tis good for arable, a glebe that asks
Tough teams of oxen, and laborious tasks.
Salt earth and bitter are not fit to sow,
Nor will be tam'd and mended by the plough.
Sweet grapes degen'rate there; and fruits, declin'd
From their first flav'rous taste, renounce their kind.
This truth by sure experiment is tried:
For first an osier colander provide
Of twigs thick wrought (such toiling peasants twine,
When thro' straight passages they strain their wine:)
In this close vessel place that earth accurs'd,
But fill'd brimful with wholesome water first;
Then run it through: the drops will rope around,
And, by the bitter taste, disclose the ground.
The fatter earth by handling we may find,
With ease distinguish'd from the meagre kind
Poor soil will crumble into dust; the rich
Will to the fingers cleave like clammy pitch:
Moist earth produces corn and grass, but both
Too rank and too luxuriant in their growth.
Let not my land so large a promise boast,
Lest the rank ears in length of stem be lost.

The heavier earth is by her weight betray'd.
The lighter in the poising hand is weigh'd.
'Tis easy to distinguish by the sight
The colour of the soil, and black from white.
But the cold ground is difficult to know;
Yet this the plants, that prosper there, will show—
Black ivy, pitch-trees, and the baleful yew.
These rules consider'd well, with early care
The vineyard destin'd for thy vines prepare:
But, long before the planting, dig the ground,
With furrows deep that cast a rising mound.
The clods, expos'd to winter winds, will bake;
For putrid earth will best the vineyards take;
And hoary frosts, after the painful toil
Of delving hinds, will rot the mellow soil.
Some peasants, not t' omit the nicest care,
Of the same soil their nursery prepare,
With that of their plantation; lest the tree,
Translated, should not with the soil agree.
Beside, to plant it as it was, they mark
The heav'ns four quarters on the tender bark,
And to the north or south restore the side,
Which at their birth did heat or cold abide:
So strong is custom; such effects can use
In tender souls of pliant plants produce.
Choose next a province for thy vineyard's reign,
On hills above, or in the lowly plain.
If fertile fields or valleys be thy choice
Plant thick: for bounteous Bacchus will rejoice
In close plantations there: but if the vine
On rising ground be plac'd, or hills supine,
Extend thy loose battalions largely wide,
Op'ning thy ranks and files on either side,
But marshall'd all in order as they stand;
And let no soldier straggle from his band.
As legions in the field their front display
To try the fortune of some doubtful day,
And move to meet their foes with sober pace,
Strict to their figure, though in wider space,
Before the battle joins, while from afar
The field yet glitters with the pomp of war,
And equal Mars, like an impartial lord,
Leaves all to fortune, and the dint of sword—
So let thy vines in intervals be set,
But not their rural discipline forget:
Indulge their width, and add a roomy space,
That their extremest lines may scarce embrace:
Nor this alone to indulge a vain delight,
And make a pleasing prospect for the sight;
But, for the ground itself, this only way,
Can equal vigour to the plants convey,
Which, crowded, want the room, their branches to display.
How deep they must be planted, wouldst thou know?
In shallow furrows vines securely grow.
Not so the rest of plants; for Jove's own tree,
That holds the woods in awful sov'reignty,
Requires a depth of lodging in the ground,
And, next the lower skies, a bed profound:
High as his topmost boughs to heav'n ascend,
So low his roots to hell's dominions tend.
Therefore, nor winds, nor winter's range o'erthrows
His bulky body; but unmov'd he grows:
For length of ages lasts his happy reign;
And lives of mortal man contend in vain.
Full in the midst of his own strength he stands,
Stretching his brawny arms, and leafy hands;
His shade protects the plains; his head the hills commands.
The hurtful hazel in thy vineyard shun;
Nor plant it to receive the setting sun;
Nor break the topmost branches from the tree;
Nor prune, with blunted knife, the progeny.
Root up wild olives from thy labour'd lands;
For sparkling fire, from hind's unwary hands,
Is often scatter'd o'er their unctuous rinds,
And after spread abroad by raging winds:
For first the smould'ring flame the trunk receives;
Ascending thence, it crackles in the leaves;
At length victorious to the top aspires
Involving all the wood in smoky fires;
But most, when driven by winds, the flaming storm
Of the long fires destroys the beauteous form.
In ashes then th' unhappy vineyard lies:
Nor will the blasted plants from ruin rise;
Nor will the wither'd stock be green again;
But the wild olive shoots, and shades th' ungrateful plain.
Be not seduc'd with wisdom's empty shows,
To stir the peaceful ground when Boreas blows.
When winter frosts constrain the field with cold,
The fainty root can take no steady hold.
But, when the golden spring reveals the year,
And the white bird returns, whom serpents fear,
That season deem the best to plant thy vines:
Next that, is when autumnal warmth declines,
Ere heat is quite decay'd or cold begun,
Or Capricorn admits the winter sun.
The spring adorns the woods, renews the leaves:
The womb of earth the genial seed receives:
For then Almighty Jove descends, and pours
Into his buxom bride his fruitful show'rs;
And, mixing his large limbs with hers, he feeds
Her births with kindly juice, and fosters teeming seeds.
Then joyous birds frequent the lonely grove,
And beasts, by nature stung, renew their love.

Then fields the blades of buried corn disclose;
And, while the balmy western spirit blows;
Earth to the breath her bosom dares expose.
With kindly moisture then the plants abound;
The grass securely springs above the ground;
The tender twig shoots upward to the skies,
And on the faith of the new sun relies.
The swerving vines on the tall elms prevail:
Unhurt by southern show'rs or northern hail,
They spread their gems, the genial warmth to share,
And boldly trust their buds in open air.
In this soft season (let me dare to sing)
The world was hatch'd by heaven's imperial king—
In prime of all the year, and holy-days of spring.
Then did the new creation first appear;
Nor other was the tenor of the year,
When laughing heav'n did the great birth attend,
And eastern winds their wintry breath suspend:
Then sheep first saw the sun in open fields;
And savage beasts were sent to stock the wilds;
And golden stars flew up to light the skies;
And man's relentless race from stony quarries rise.
Nor could the tender new creation bear
Th' excessive heats or coldness of the year,
But, chill'd by winter, or by summer fir'd,
The middle temper of the spring requir'd,
When warmth and moisture did at once abound,
And heaven's indulgence brooded on the ground.
For what remains, in depth of earth secure
Thy cover'd plants, and dung with hot manure;
And shells and gravel in the ground enclose;
For through their hollow chinks the water flows,
Which, thus imbib'd, returns in misty dews,
And, steaming up, the rising plant renews.
Some husbandmen, of late have found the way,
A hilly heap of stones above to lay,
And press the plants with shards of potter's clay.
This fence against immod'rate rain they found,
Or, when the Dog-star cleaves the thirsty ground.
Be mindful, when thou hast entomb'd the shoot,
With store of earth around to feed the root;
With iron teeth of rakes and prongs, to move
The crusted earth, and loosen it above.
Then exercise thy sturdy steers to plough
Betwixt thy vines, and teach the feeble row
To mount on reeds, and wands, and, upward led,
On ashen poles to raise their forky head.
On these new crutches let them learn to walk,
Till, swerving upwards with a stronger stalk,
They brave the winds, and, clinging to their guide,
On tops of elms at length triumphant ride.
But, in their tender nonage, while they spread
Their springing leaves, and lift their infant head,
And upward while they shoot in open air,
Indulge their childhood, and the nurslings spare;
Nor exercise thy rage on new-born life:
Nor let thy hand supply the pruning-knife,
And crop luxuriant stragglers, nor be loth
To strip the branches of their leafy growth.
But, when the rooted vines, with steady hold,
Can clasp their elms, then, husbandmen, be bold
To lop the disobedient boughs, that staid
Beyond their ranks; let crooked steel invade
The lawless troops, which discipline disclaim,
And their superfluous growth with rigour tame.
Next, fenc'd with hedges and deep ditches round,
Exclude th' enroaching cattle from thy ground,
While yet the tender gems but just appear,
Unable to sustain th' uncertain year;
Whose leaves are not alone foul winter's prey,
But oft by summer suns are scorch'd away.
And worse than both, become th' unworthy browse
Of buffaloes, salt goats, and hungry cows.
For not December's frost that burns the boughs,
Nor dog-days' parching heat that splits the rocks,
Are half so harmful as the greedy flocks,
Their venom'd bite, and scars indented on the stocks.
For this, the malefactor goat was laid
On Bacchus' altar, and his forfeit paid.
At Athens thus old comedy began,
When round the streets the reeling actors ran,
In country villages, and crossing ways,
Contending for the prizes of their plays;
And, glad with Bacchus, on the grassy soil,
Leap'd o'er the skins of goats besmear'd with oil.
Thus Roman youth, deriv'd from ruin'd Troy,
In rude Saturnian rhymes express their joy:
With taunts, and laughter loud, their audience please,
Deform'd with vizards, cut from barks of trees.
In jolly hymns they praise the god of wine,
Whose earthen images adorn the pine,
And there are hung on high, in honour of the vine.
A madness so devout the vineyard fills:
In hollow valleys and on rising hills,
On whate'er side he turns his honest face,
And dances in the wind, those fields are in his grace.
To Bacchus therefore let us tune our lays,
And in our mother tongue resound his praise.
Thin cakes in chargers, and a guilty goat,
Dragg'd by the horns, be to his altars brought;
Whose offer'd entrails shall his crime reproach,
And drip their fatness from the hazel broach.
To dress thy vines, new labour is requir'd;
Nor must the painful husbandman be tir'd.

For thrice at least, in compass of the year,
Thy vineyard must employ the sturdy steer
To turn the glebe, besides thy daily pain
To break the clods, and make the surface plain,
T' unload the branches, or the leaves to thin,
That suck the vital moisture of the vine.
Thus in a circle runs the peasant's pain,
And the year rolls within itself again.
E'en in the lowest months, when storms have shed
From vines the hairy honours of their head.
Not then the grudging hind his labour ends,
But to the coming year his care extends.
E'en then the naked vine he persecutes;
His pruning knife at once reforms and cuts.
Be first to dig the ground: be first to burn
The branches lopp'd; and first the props return
Into thy house that bore the burden'd vines;
But last to reap the vintage of thy wines.
Twice in the year luxuriant leaves o'ershade
The encumber'd vine; rough brambles twice invade:
Hard labour both!—Commend the large excess
Of spacious vineyards; cultivate the less.
Besides, in woods the shrubs of prickly thorn,
Sallows and reeds on banks of rivers borne,
Remain to cut—for vineyards useful found
To stay thy vines, and fence thy fruitful ground.
Nay, when thy tender trees at length are bound; [free:
When peaceful vines from pruning-hooks are
When husbands have survey'd the last degree,
And utmost files of plants, and order'd ev'ry tree;
E'en when they sing at ease in full content
Insulting o'er the toils they underwent,
Yet still they find a future task remain,
To turn the soil, and break the clods again:
And, after all, their joys are insincere,
While falling rains on ripening grapes they fear.
Quite opposite to these are olives found:
No dressing they require, and dread no wound,
Nor rakes nor harrows need; but fix'd below
Rejoice in open air, and unconcern'dly grow.
The soil itself due nourishment supplies:
Plough but the furrows, and the fruits arise,
Content with small endeavours, till they spring,
Soft peace they figure, and sweet plenty bring:
Then olives plant, and hymns to Pallas sing.
  Thus apple-trees, whose trunks are strong to bear
Their spreading boughs, exert themselves in air,
Want no supply, but stand secure alone,
Not trusting foreign forces, but their own,
Till with the ruddy freight the bending branches groan.
  Thus trees of nature, and each common bush,
Uncultivated thrive, and with red berries blush.
Wild shrubs are shorn for browse: the tow'ring height
Of unctuous trees are torches for the night.
And shall we doubt, (indulging easy sloth,)
To sow, to set, and to reform their growth?
To leave the lofty plants—the lowly kind
Are for the shepherd or the sheep design'd,
E'en humble broom and osiers have their use,
And shade for sheep, and food for flocks produce;
Hedges for corn, and honey for the bees,
Besides the pleasing prospect of the trees.
How goodly looks Cytrous, ever green
With boxen groves! with what delight are seen
Narycian woods of pitch, whose gloomy shade
Seems for retreat of heav'nly Muses made!
But much more pleasing are those fields to see,
That need not ploughs, nor human industry.
E'en cold Caucasian rocks with trees are spread,
And wear green forests on their hilly head.
Though bending from the blast of eastern storms,
Tho' shent their leaves, and shatter'd are their arms,
Yet heav'n their various plants for use designs—
For houses, cedars—and, for shipping, pines—
Cypress provides for spokes and wheels of wains,
And all for keels of ships, that scour the wat'ry plains.
Willows in twigs are fruitful, elms in leaves;
The war, from stubborn myrtle, shafts receives—
From cornels, javelins; and the tougher yew
Receives the bending figure of a bow.
Nor box, nor limes without their use are made,
Smooth grain'd, and proper for the turner's trade:
Which curious hands may carve, and steel with ease invade.
Light alder stems the Po's impetuous tide,
And bees in hollow oaks their honey hide.
Now balance with these gifts, the fumy joys
Of wine, attended with eternal noise.
Wine urg'd to lawless lust the Centaurs' train;
Thro' wine they quarrel'd, and thro' wine were slain.
  O happy, if he knew his happy state,
The swain, who, free from bus'ness and debate
Receives his easy food from Nature's hand,
And just returns of cultivated land!
No palace, with a lofty gate, he wants,
T' admit the tides of early visitants,
With eager eyes devouring as they pass,
The breathing figures of Corinthian brass.
No statues threaten, from high pedestals;
No Persian arras hides his homely walls,

With antic vests, which, through their shady fold,
Betray the streaks of ill-dissembled gold;
He boasts no wool, whose native white is dy'd
With purple poison of Assyrian pride:
No costly drugs of Araby defile,
With foreign scents, the sweetness of his oil:
But easy quiet, a secure retreat,
A harmless life that knows not how to cheat;
With home-bred plenty, the rich owner bless;
And rural pleasures crown his happiness.
Unvex'd with quarrels, undisturb'd with noise,
The country king his peaceful realm enjoys—
Cool grots, and living lakes, the flow'ry pride
Of meads, and streams that through the valley glide,
And shady groves that easy sleep invite,
And, after toilsome days, a soft repose at night.
Wild beasts of nature in his woods abound;
And youth, of labour patient, plough the ground,
Inur'd to hardship, and to homely fare
Nor venerable age is wanting there,
In great examples to the youthful train;
Nor are the gods ador'd with rites profane.
From hence Astræa took her flight; and here
The prints of her departing steps appear.
Ye sacred Muses! with whose beauty fir'd,
My soul is ravish'd, and my brain inspir'd—
Whose priest I am, whose holy fillets wear—
Would you your poet's first petition hear;
Give me the ways of wand'ring stars to know,
The depths of heav'n above, and earth below;
Teach me the various labours of the moon,
And whence proceed th' eclipses of the sun:
Why flowing tides prevail upon the main,
And in what dark recess they shrink again;
What shakes the solid earth; what cause delays
The summer nights, and shortens winter days.
But, if my heavy blood restrain the flight
Of my free soul, aspiring to the height
Of nature, and unclouded fields of light—
My next desire is, void of care and stife,
To lead a soft, secure, inglorious life—
A country cottage near a crystal flood,
A winding valley, and a lofty wood.
Some god conduct me to the sacred shades,
Where Bacchanals are sung by Spartan maids,
Or lift me high to Hæmus' hilly crown,
Or in the plains of Tempe lay me down,
Or lead me to some solitary place,
And cover my retreat from human race.
Happy the man, who, studying Nature's laws,
Through known effects can trace the secret cause—
His mind, possessing in a quiet state,
Fearless of Fortune, and resign'd to Fate!
And happy too is he, who decks the bow'rs
Of Sylvans, and adores the rural pow'rs—
Whose mind, unmov'd, the bribes of courts can see,
Their glitt'ring baits, and purple slavery—
Nor hopes the people's praise, nor fears their frown,
Nor, when contending kindred tear the crown,
Will set up one, or pull another down.
Without concern he hears, but hears from far,
Of tumults, and descents, and distant war;
Nor with a superstitious fear is aw'd,
For what befalls at home, or what abroad.
Nor envies he the rich their heapy store,
Nor his own peace disturbs with pity for the poor.
He feeds on fruits, which, of their own accord
The willing ground and laden trees afford,
From his lov'd home no lucre him can draw;
The senate's mad decrees he never saw;
Nor heard, at bawling bars, corrupted law.
Some to the seas, and some to camps, resort,
And some with impudence invade the court:
In foreign countries, others seek renown;
With wars and taxes, others waste their own,
And houses burn, and household gods deface,
To drink in bowls which glitt'ring gems enchase,
To loll on couches, rich with citron steds,
And lay their guilty limbs on Tyrian beds
This wretch in earth entombs his golden ore,
Hov'ring and brooding on his buried store.
Some patriot fools to pop'lar praise aspire
Of public speeches, which worse fools admire,
While, from both benches, with redoubled sounds,
Th' applause of lords and commoners abounds.
Some, through ambition, or through thirst of gold,
Have slain their brothers, or their country sold,
And, leaving their sweet homes, in exile run
To lands that lie beneath another sun.
The peasant, innocent of all these ills,
With crooked ploughs the fertile fallow tills,
And the round year with daily labour fills:
And hence the country markets are supplied:
Enough remains for houshold charge beside,
His wife and tender children to sustain,
And gratefully to feed his dumb deserving train.
Nor cease his labours till the yellow field
A full return of bearded harvest yield—
A crop so plenteous, as the land to load,
O'ercome the crowded barns, and lodge on ricks abroad.
Thus ev'ry several season is employ'd,
Some spent in toil, and some in ease enjoy'd.
The yeaning ewes prevent the springing year:
The laded boughs their fruits in autumn bear;
'Tis then the vine her liquid harvest yields,
Bak'd in the sunshine of ascending fields.
The winter comes; and then the falling mast
For greedy swine provides a full repast:
Then olives, ground in mills, their fatness boast;
And winter fruits are mellow'd by the frost.

His cares are eas'd with intervals of bliss;
His little children climbing for a kiss,
Welcome their father's late return at night,
His faithful bed is crown'd with chaste delight;
His kine with swelling udders ready stand,
And, lowing for the pail, invite the milker's hand.
His wanton kids, with budding horns prepar'd
Fight harmless battles in his homely yard:
Himself, in rustic pomp, on holy-days,
To rural pow'rs a just oblation pays,
And on the green his careless limbs displays.
The hearth is in the midst: the herdsmen round
The cheerful fire, provoke his health in goblets crown'd.
He calls on Bacchus, and propounds the prize:
The groom his fellow groom at buts defies,
And bends his bow, and levels with his eyes.
Or, stript for wrestling, smears his limbs with oil,
And watches, with a trip, his foe to foil.
Such was the life the frugal Sabines led
So Remus and his brother god were bred,
From whom th' austere Etrurian virtue rose;
And this rude life our homely fathers chose.
Old Rome from such a race deriv'd her birth,
(The seat of empire, and the conquer'd earth)
Which now on sev'n high hills triumphant reigns,
And in that compass all the world contains.
Ere Saturn's rebel son usurp'd the skies,
When beasts were only slain for sacrifice,
While peaceful Crete enjoy'd her ancient lord,
Ere sounding hammers forg'd th' inhuman sword,
Ere hollow drums were beat, before the breath
Of brazen trumpets rung the peals of death,
The good old god his hunger did assuage
With roots and herbs, and gave the golden age.
But, over-labour'd with so long a course,
'Tis time to set at ease the smoking horse.

GEORGIC III.

ARGUMENT.

This book begins with the invocation of some rural deities, and a compliment to Augustus: after which Virgil directs himself to Mæcenas, and enters on his subject. He lays down rules for the breeding and management of horses, oxen, sheep, goats, and dogs; and interweaves several pleasant descriptions of a chariot-race, of the battle of the bulls, of the force of love, and of the Scythian winter. In the latter part of the book, he relates the diseases incident to cattle: and ends with the description of a fatal murrain that formerly raged among the Alps.

THY fields, propitious Pales, I rehearse;
And sing thy pastures in no vulgar verse,
Amphrysian shepherd! the Lycæan woods,
Arcadia's flow'ry plains, and pleasing floods.
All other themes, that careless minds invite,
Are worn with use, unworthy me to write.
Busiris' altars, and the dire decrees
Of hard Eurystheus ev'ry reader sees:
Hylas the boy, Latona's erring isle,
And Pelops' iv'ry shoulder, and his toil
For fair Hippodame, with all the rest
Of Grecian tales, by poets are express'd.
New ways I must attempt, my grov'ling name
To raise aloft, and wing my flight to fame.
I, first of Romans, shall in triumph come
From conquer'd Greece, and bring her trophies home,
With foreign spoils adorn my native place,
And with Idume's palms my Mantua grace.
Of Parian stone a temple will I raise,
Where the slow Mincius through the valley strays,
Where cooling streams invite the flocks to drink,
And reeds defend the winding water's brink.
Full in the midst shall mighty Cæsar stand,
Hold the chief honours, and the dome command.
Then I, conspicuous in my Tyrian gown,
(Submitting to his godhead my renown)
A hundred coursers from the goal will drive:
The rival chariots in the race shall strive.
All Greece shall flock from far, my games to see:
The whorlbat, and the rapid race, shall be
Reserv'd for Cæsar, and ordain'd by me.
Myself, with olive crown'd, the gifts will bear.
E'en now methinks the public shouts I hear,
The passing pageants, and the pomps appear.
I to the temple will conduct the crew,
The sacrifice, and sacrificers view,
From thence return, attended with my train,
Where the proud theatres disclose the scene,
Which interwoven Britons seem to raise,
And show the triumph which their shame displays.
High o'er the gate, in elephant and gold,
The crowd shall Cæsar's Indian war behold:
The Nile shall flow beneath; and, on the side,
His shatter'd ships on brazen pillars ride.
Next him Niphates, with inverted urn,
And dropping sedge, shall his Armenia mourn,
And Asian cities in our triumph borne.
With backward bows the Parthians shall be there,
And, spurring from the fight, confess their fear.
A double wreath shall crown our Cæsar's brows—
Two diff'rent trophies, from two diff'rent foes.
Europe with Afric in his fame shall join;
But neither shore his conquests shall confine.
The Parian marble there shall seem to move
In breathing statues, not unworthy Jove,
Resembling heroes, whose ethereal root
Is Jove himself, and Cæsar is the fruit.

Tros and his race the sculptor shall employ;
And he—the god who built the walls of Troy.
Envy herself at last, grown pale and dumb,
(By Cæsar combatted and overcome)
Shall give her hands, and fear the curling snakes
Of lashing Furies, and the burning lakes;
The pains of famish'd Tantalus shall feel,
And Sisyphus that labours up the hill
The rolling rock in vain; and curst Ixion's wheel.
Meantime we must pursue the sylvan lands,
(Th' abode of nymphs) untouch'd by former hands:
For such, Mæcenas are thy hard commands,
Without thee, nothing lofty can I sing.
Come then, and with thyself, thy genius bring,
With which inspir'd, I brook no dull delay:
Cithæron loudly calls me to my way;
Thy hounds, Tayg'tus, open, and pursue their prey.
High Epidaurus urges on my speed,
Fam'd for his hills, and for his horses' breed:
From hills and dales the cheerful cries rebound;
For Echo hunts along, and propagates the sound.
A time will come, when my maturer muse,
In Cæsar's wars, a nobler theme shall choose,
And through more ages bear my sovereign's praise,
Than have from Tithon past to Cæsar's days.
The gen'rous youth, who studious of the prize,
The race of running coursers multiplies,
Or to the plough the sturdy bullock breeds,
May know that from the dam the worth of each proceeds.
The mother-cow must wear a lowr'ing look,
Sour-headed, strongly neck'd, to bear the yoke.
Her double dew-lap from her chin descends,
And at her knees the pond'rous burden ends.
Long are her sides and large; her limbs are great;
Rough are her ears, and broad her horny feet.
Her colour shining black, but fleck'd with white;
She tosses from the yoke; provokes the fight;
She rises in her gait, is free from fears,
And in her face a bull's resemblance bears:
Her ample forehead with a star is crown'd;
And with her length of tail she sweeps the ground.
The bull's insult at four she may sustain;
But, after ten, from nuptial rites refrain.
Six seasons use, but then release the cow,
Unfit for love, and for the lab'ring plough.
Now while their youth is fill'd with kindly fire,
Submit thy females to the lusty sire:
Watch the quick motions of the frisking tail;
Then serve their fury with the rushing male,
Indulging pleasure lest the breed should fail.
In youth alone, unhappy mortals live;
But, ah! the mighty bliss is fugitive:
Discolour'd sickness, anxious labour, come,
And age, and death's inexorable doom.
Yearly thy herds in vigour will impair,
Recruit and mend them with thy yearly care
Still propagate; for still they fall away:
'Tis prudence to prevent th' entire decay.
Like diligence requires the courser's race
In early choice, and for a longer space.
The colt, that for a stallion is design'd,
By sure presages shows his gen'rous kind:
Of able body, sound of limb and wind;
Upright he walks, on pasterns firm and straight
His motions easy; prancing in his gait;
The first to lead the way, to tempt the flood,
To pass the bridge unknown, nor fear the trembling wood;
Dauntless at empty noises; lofty neck'd;
Shrp-headed, barrel-bellied, broadly back'd;
Brawny his chest, and deep; his colour gray;
For beauty, dappled, or the brightest bay:
Faint white and dun will scarce the rearing pay.
The fiery courser when he hears from far
The sprightly trumpets, and the shouts of war,
Pricks up his ears; and, trembling with delight,
Shifts place, and paws, and hopes the promis'd fight.
On his right shoulder his thick mane reclin'd,
Ruffles at speed, and dances in the wind.
His horny hoofs are jetty black and round;
His chine is double; starting with a bound
He turns the turf, and shakes the solid ground.
Fire from his eyes, clouds from his nostrils flow,
He bears his rider headlong on the foe.
Such was the steed in Grecian poets fam'd,
Proud Cyllarus, by Spartan Pollux tam'd:
Such coursers bore to fight the god of Thrace:
And such, Achilles, was thy warlike race.
In such a shape, grim Saturn did restrain
His heav'nly limbs, and flow'd with a such mane,
When, half surpris'd, and fearing to be seen,
The lecher gallop'd from his jealous queen,
Ran up the ridges of the rocks amain,
And with shrill neighings fill'd the neighb'ring plain.
But, worn with years, when dire diseases come,
Then hide his not ignoble age at home,
In peace t' enjoy his former palms and pains;
And gratefully be kind to his remains.
For, when his blood no youthful spirits move,
He languishes and labours in his love;
And, when the sprightly seed should swiftly come,
Dribbling he drudges, and defrauds the womb.

In vain he burns, like hasty stubble fires,
And in himself, his former self requires.
His age and courage weigh; nor those alone;
But note his father's virtues and his own:
Observe, if he disdains to yield the prize,
Of loss impatient, proud of victories.
Hast thou beheld, when from the goal they start,
The youthful charioteers with heaving heart
Rush to the race; and panting, scarcely bear
Th' extremes of fev'rish hope and chilling fear;
Stoop to the reins, and lash with all their force?
The flying chariot kindles in the course:
And now alow, and now aloft they fly,
As borne through air, and seem to touch the sky.
No stop, no stay: but clouds of sand arise,
Spurn'd, and cast backward on the followers' eyes.
The hindmost blows the foam upon the first:
Such is the love of praise, an honourable thirst.
Bold Ericthonius was the first who join'd
Four horses for the rapid race design'd,
And o'er the dusty wheels presiding sate:
The Lapithæ, to chariots, add the state
Of bits and bridles; taught the steed to bound,
To run the ring, and trace the mazy round;
To stop, to fly, the rules of war to know;
T' obey the rider, and to dare the foe.
To choose a youthful steed with courage fir'd,
To breed him, break him, back him, are requir'd
Experienc'd masters; and in sundry ways,
Their labours equal, and alike their praise.
But, once again, the batter'd horse beware:
The weak old stallion will deceive thy care,
Though famous in his youth for force and speed,
Or was of Argos or Epirian breed,
Or did from Neptune's race, or from himself proceed.
These things premis'd, when now the nuptial time
Approaches for the stately steed to climb,
With food enable him to make his court;
Distend his chine, and pamper him for sport:
Feed him with herbs, whatever thou canst find,
Of gen'rous warmth, and of salacious kind:
Then water him, and (drinking what he can)
Encourage him to thirst again, with bran.
Instructed thus, produce him to the fair,
And join in wedlock to the longing mare.
For, if the sire be faint, or out of case,
He will be copied in his famish'd race,
And sink beneath the pleasing task assign'd
(For all's too little for the craving kind.)
As for the females, with industrious care
Take down their mettle; keep them lean and bare:
When conscious of their past delight, and keen
To take the leap, and prove the sport again,
With scanty measure then supply their food;
And, when athirst, restrain them from the flood;
Their bodies harass; sink them when they run;
And fry their melting marrow in the sun.
Starve them, when barns beneath their burden groan,
And winnow'd chaff by western winds is blown:
For fear the rankness of the swelling womb
Should scant the passage, and confine the room;
Lest the fat furrows should the sense destroy
Of genial lust, and dull the seat of joy.
But let them suck the seed with greedy force,
And close involve the vigour of the horse.
The male has done: thy care must now proceed
To teeming females, and the promis'd breed.
First let them run at large, and never know
The taming yoke, or draw the crooked plough.
Let them not leap the ditch, or swim the flood,
Or lumber o'er the meads, or cross the wood;
But range the forest, by the silver side
Of some cool stream, where Nature shall provide
Green grass, and fatt'ning clover for their fare,
And mossy caverns for their noontide lair,
With rocks above, to shield the sharp nocturnal air.
About th' Alburnian groves, with holly green,
Of winged insects, mighty swarms are seen:
This flying plague (to mark its quality)
Œstros the Grecians call—Asylus, we—
A fierce loud buzzing breeze.—Their stings draw blood,
And drive the cattle gadding through the wood.
Seiz'd with unusual pains, they loudly cry:
Tanagrus hastens thence, and leaves his channel dry.
This curse the jealous Juno did invent,
And first employ'd for Iö's punishment.
To shun this ill, the cunning leach ordains,
In summer's sultry heats (for then it reigns,)
To feed the females ere the sun arise,
Or late at night, when stars adorn the skies.
When she has calv'd, then set the dam asid:
And for the tender progeny provide.
Distinguish all betimes with branding fire,
To note the tribe, the lineage, and the sire;
Whom to reserve for husband for the herd;
Or who shall be to sacrifice preferr'd;
Or whom thou shalt to turn thy glebe allow,
To smooth the furrows, and sustain the plough
The rest, for whom no lot is yet decreed,
May run in pastures, and at pleasure feed.
The calf, by nature and by genius made
To turn the glebe, breed to the rural trade.
Set him betimes to school; and let him be
Instructed there in rules of husbandry,
While yet his youth is flexible and green,
Nor bad examples of the world has seen.

Early begin the stubborn child to break;
For his soft neck, a supple collar make
Of bending osiers; and (with time and care
Inur'd that easy servitude to bear)
Thy flatt'ring method on the youth pursue:
Join'd with his school-fellows by two and two,
Persuade them first to lead an empty wheel,
That scarce the dust can raise, or they can feel:
In length of time produce the lab'ring yoke,
And shining shares, that make the furrow smoke.
Ere the licentious youth be thus restrain'd,
Or moral precepts on their minds have gain'd,
Their wanton appetites not only feed
With delicates of leaves, and marshy weed,
But with thy sickle reap the rankest land,
And minister the blade with bounteous hand:
Nor be with harmful parsimony won
To follow what our homely sires have done,
Who fill'd the pail with beastings of the cow;
But all her udder to the calf allow.
If to the warlike steed thy studies bend,
Or for the prize in chariots to contend,
Near Pisa's flood the rapid wheels to guide,
Or in Olympian groves aloft to ride,
The gen'rous labours of the coursers, first,
Must be with sight of arms and sound of trumpets nurs'd;
Inur'd the groaning axle-tree to bear;
And let him clashing whips in stables hear.
Soothe him with praise, and make him understand
The loud applauses of his master's hand:
This, from his weaning, let him well be taught;
And then betimes, in a soft snaffle wrought,
Before his tender joints with nerves are knit,
Untried in arms, and trembling at the bit.
But when to four full springs his years advance,
Teach him to run the round, with pride to prance,
And (rightly manag'd) equal time to beat,
To turn, to bound and measure, and curvet.
Let him to this, with easy pains, be brought,
And seem to labour, when he labours not.
Thus form'd for speed, he challenges the wind,
And leaves the Scythian arrow far behind:
He scours along the field, with loosen'd reins,
And treads so light, he scarcely prints the plains;
Like Boreas in his race, when rushing forth,
He sweeps the skies, and clears the cloudy north,
The waving harvest bends beneath his blast;
The forest shakes; the groves their honours cast;
He flies aloft, and with impetuous roar
Pursues the foaming surges to the shore.
Thus o'er th' Elean plains, thy well-breath'd horse
Impels the flying car, and wins the course,
Or bred to Belgian wagons, leads the way,
Untir'd at night, and cheerful all the day.
When once he's broken, feed him full and high;
Indulge his growth, and his gaunt sides supply,
Before his training, keep him poor and low;
For his stout stomach with his food will grow:
The pamper'd colt will discipline disdain,
Impatient of the lash, and restiff to the reign.
Wouldst thou their courage and their strength improve?
Too soon they must not feel the stings of love.
Whether the bull or courser be thy care,
Let him not leap the cow, or mount the mare.
The youthful bull must wander in the wood,
Behind the mountain or beyond the flood,
Or in the stall at home his fodder find,
Far from the charms of that alluring kind.
With two fair eyes his mistress burns his breast,
He looks, and languishes, and leaves his rest
Forsakes his food, and pining for the lass,
Is joyless of the grove, and spurns the growing grass.
The soft seducer, with enticing looks,
The bellowing rivals to the fight provokes.
A beauteous heifer in the wood is bred:
The stooping warriors aiming head to head,
Engage their clashing horns: with dreadful sound
The forest rattles, and the rocks rebound.
They fence, they push, and, pushing, loudly roar:
Their dew-laps and their sides are bath'd in gore.
Nor, when the war is over, is it peace;
Nor will the vanquish'd bull his claim release;
But feeding in his breast his ancient fires,
And cursing fate, from his proud foe retires.
Driv'n from his native land to foreign grounds,
He with a gen'rous rage resents his wounds,
His ignominious flight, the victor's boast,
And more than both, the loves, which unreveng'd he lost.
Often he turns his eyes, and with a groan,
Surveys the pleasing kingdoms, once his own,
And therefore to repair his strength he tries,
Hard'ning his limbs with painful exercise;
And rough upon the flinty rock he lies.
On prickly leaves and on sharp herbs he feeds,
Then to the prelude of a war proceeds.
His horns, yet sore, he tries against a tree,
And meditates his absent enemy.
He snuffs the wind; his heels the sand excite
But, when he stands collected in his might,
He roars and promises a more successful fight.
Then, to redeem his honour at a blow
He moves his camp, to meet his careless foe.
Not with more madness, rolling from afar
The spumy waves proclaim the wat'ry war,

And mounting upwards, with a mighty roar,
March onwards, and insult the rocky shore.
They mate the middle region with their height,
And fall no less than with a mountain's weight;
The waters boil, and, belching, from below
Black sands, as from a forceful engine throw.
Thus ev'ry creature, and of ev'ry kind,
The secret joys of sweet coition find.
Not only man's imperial race, but they
That wing the liquid air, or swim the sea,
Or haunt the desert, rush into the flame:
For love is lord of all, and is in all the same.
'Tis with this rage, the mother-lion stung,
Scours o'er the plain, regardless of her young:
Demanding rites of love, she sternly stalks,
And hunts her lover in his lonely walks.
'Tis then the shapeless bear his den forsakes;
In woods, and fields, a wild destruction makes;
Boars whet their tusks; to battle tigers move,
Enrag'd with hunger, more enrag'd with love.
Then wo to him, that, in the desert land
Of Libya, travels o'er the burning sand!
The stallion snuffs the well known scent afar,
And snorts and trembles for the distant mare:
Nor bits nor bridles can his rage restrain;
And rugged rocks are interpos'd in vain:
He makes his way o'er mountains, and contemns
Unruly torrents, and unforded streams.
The bristled boar, who feels the pleasing wound,
New grinds his armed tusks, and digs the ground.
The sleepy lecher shuts his little eyes;
About his churning chaps the frothy bubbles rise:
He rubs his sides against a tree; prepares
And hardens both his shoulders for the wars.
What did the youth, when Love's unerring dart
Transfix'd his liver, and inflam'd his heart?
Alone, by night, his watery way he took:
About him, and above, the billows broke:
The sluices of the sky were open spread;
And rolling thunder rattled o'er his head.
The raging tempest call'd him back in vain,
And ev'ry boding omen of the main:
Nor could his kindred, nor the kindly force
Of weeping parents, change his fatal course;
No, not the dying maid, who must deplore
His floating carcass on the Sestian shore.
I pass the wars that spotted lynxes make
With their fierce rivals for the female's sake,
The howling wolves', the mastiffs' am'rous rage;
When e'en the fearful stag dares for his hind engage.
But, far above the rest, the furious mare,
Barr'd from the male, is frantic with despair:
For, when her pouting vent declares her pain,
She tears the harness, and she rends the rein.
For this, (when Venus gave them rage and pow'r)
Their master's mangled members they devour,
Of love defrauded in their longing hour.
For love, they force through thickets of the wood,
They climb the steepy hills, and stem the flood.
When, at the spring's approach, their marrow burns,
(For with the spring their genial warmth returns)
The mares to cliffs of rugged rocks repair,
And with wide nostrils snuff the western air:
When (wondrous to relate) the parent wind,
Without the stallion propagates the kind.
Then, fir'd with am'rous rage, they take their flight
Thro' plains, and mount the hills' unequal height;
Nor to the north, nor to the rising sun,
Nor southward to the rainy regions, run,
But boring to the west, and hov'ring there,
With gaping mouths they draw prolific air,
With which impregnate, from their groins they shed,
A slimy juice, by false conception bred.
The shepherd knows it well, and calls by name
Hippomanes, to note the mother's flame.
This, gather'd in the planetary hour,
With noxious weeds, and spell'd with words of pow'r,
Dire stepdames in the magic bowl infuse,
And mix, for deadly draughts, the pois'nous juice.
But time is lost, which never will renew,
While we too far the pleasing path pursue,
Surveying nature with too nice a view.
Let this suffice for herds: our following care
Shall woolly flocks and shaggy goats declare.
Nor can I doubt what toil I must bestow,
To raise my subject from a ground so low;
And the mean matter which my theme affords,
T' embellish with magnificence of words.
But the commanding muse my chariot guides,
Which o'er the dubious cliff securely rides:
And pleas'd I am, no beaten road to take,
But first the way to new discov'ries make.
Now, sacred Pales, in a lofty strain
I sing the rural honours of thy reign.
First, with assiduous care, from winter keep,
Well-fodder'd in the stalls, thy tender sheep:
Then spread with straw the bedding of thy fold,
With fern beneath, to 'fend the bitter cold:
That free from gouts thou may'st preserve thy care,
And clear from scabs, produc'd by freezing air.
Next let thy goats officiously be nurs'd,
And led to living streams, to quench their thirst.

Feed them with winter-browse; and, for their lair,
A cote, that opens to the south, prepare;
Where basking in the sunshine they may lie,
And the short remnants of his heat enjoy.
This during winter's drizzly reign be done,
Till the new Ram receives the exalted sun:
For hairy goats of equal profit are
With woolly sheep, and ask an equal care.
'T is true, the fleece, when drunk with Tyrian juice,
Is dearly sold: but not for needful use:
For the salacious goat increases more,
And twice as largely yields her milky store.
The still distended udders never fail,
But, when they seem exhausted, swell the pail.
Meantime the pastor shears their hoary beards,
And eases of their hair the loaden herds.
Their cam'lots, warm in tents, the soldier hold,
And shield the shiv'ring mariner from cold.
On shrubs they browse, and, on the bleaky top
Of rugged hills, the thorny bramble crop.
Attended with their bleating kids, they come
At night, unask'd, and mindful of their home;
And scarce their swelling bags the threshold overcome.
So much the more thy diligence bestow
In depth of winter to defend the snow,
By how much less the tender helpless kind,
For their own ills, can fit provision find.
Then minister the browse with bounteous hand;
And open let thy stacks all winter stand.
But, when the western winds with vital pow'r
Call forth the tender grass and budding flow'r,
Then, at the last, produce in open air
Both flocks; and send them to their summer fare.
Before the sun while Hesperus appears,
First let them sip from herbs the pearly tears
Of morning dews, and after break their fast
On green-sward ground—a cool and grateful taste.
But, when the day's fourth hour has drawn the dews,
And the sun's sultry heat their thirst renews;
When creaking grasshoppers on shrubs complain,
Then lead them to their watering-troughs again.
In summer's heat, some bending valley find,
Clos'd from the sun, but open to the wind;
Or seek some ancient oak, whose arms extend
In ample breadth, thy cattle to defend,
Or solitary grove, or gloomy glade,
To shield them with its venerable shade.
Once more to wat'ring lead; and feed again
When the low sun is sinking to the main,
When rising Cynthia sheds her silver dews,
And the cool evening-breeze the meads renews.
When linnets fill the woods with tuneful sound,
And hollow shores the halcyon's voice rebound.
Why should my muse enlarge on Libyan swains,
Their scatter'd cottages, and ample plains,
Where oft the flocks without a leader stray,
Or through continu'd deserts take their way,
And, feeding, add the length of night to day?
Whole months they wander, grazing as they go;
Nor folds, nor hospitable harbour know.
Such an extent of plains, so vast a space
Of wilds unknown, and of untasted grass,
Allures their eyes; the shepherd last appears,
And with him all his patrimony bears,
His house and household gods, his trade of war,
His bow and quiver, and his trusty cur.
Thus, under heavy arms, the youth of Rome
Their long laborious marches overcome,
Cheerly their tedious travels undergo,
And pitch their sudden camp before the foe.
Not so the Scythian shepherd tends his fold,
Nor he who bears in Thrace the bitter cold,
Nor he who treads the bleak Mæotian strand,
Or where proud Ister rolls his yellow sand.
Early they stall their flocks and herds; for there
No grass the fields, no leaves the forests, wear;
The frozen earth lies buried there, below
A hilly heap, sev'n cubits deep in snow:
And all west allies of stormy Boreas blow.
The sun from far peeps with a sickly face,
Too weak, the clouds and mighty fogs to chase,
When up the skies he shoots his rosy head,
Or in the ruddy ocean seeks his bed.
Swift rivers are with sudden ice constrain'd
And studded wheels are on its back sustain'd,
A hostry now for wagons, which before
Tall ships of burden on its bosom bore.
The brazen caldrons with the frosts are flaw'd;
The garments, stiff with ice, at hearths is thaw'd.
With axes first they cleave the wine; and thence,
By weight, the solid portions they dispense.
From locks uncomb'd, and from the frozen beard,
Long icicles depend, and crackling sounds are heard.
Meantime, perpetual sleet and driving snow
Obscure the skies, and hang on herds below.
The starving cattle perish in their stalls;
Huge oxen stand enclos'd in wintry walls
Of snow congeal'd; whole herds are buried there,
Of mighty stags, and scarce their horns appear.
The dext'rous huntsman wounds not these afar
With shafts or darts, or makes a distant war

With dogs, or pitches toils to stop their flight,
But close engages in unequal fight;
And, while they strive in vain to make their way
Through hills of snow, and pitifully bray,
Assaults with dint of sword, or pointed spears,
And homeward, on his back, the joyful burden bears.
The men to subterranean caves retire,
Secure from cold, and crowd the cheerful fire:
With trunks of elms and oaks the hearth they load,
Nor tempt th' inclemency of heaven abroad.
Their jovial nights in frolics and in play
They pass, to drive the tedious hours away;
And their cold stomachs with crown'd goblets cheer
Of windy cider, and of barmy beer.
Such are the cold Rhipæan race, and such
The savage Scythian, and unwarlike Dutch,
Where skins of beasts the rude barbarians wear,
The spoils of foxes, and the furry bear.
Is wool thy care? Let not thy cattle go
Where bushes are, where burs and thistles grow;
Nor in too rank a pasture let them feed:
Then of the purest white select thy breed:
E'en though a snowy ram thou shalt behold,
Prefer him not in haste, for husband to thy fold:
But search his mouth; and, if a swarthy tongue
Is underneath his humid palate hung,
Reject him, lest he darken all the flock;
And substitute another from thy stock.
'Twas thus, with fleeces milky white, (if we
May trust report) Pan, god of Arcady,
Did bribe thee, Cynthia; nor didst thou disdain,
When call'd in woody shades, to cure a lover's pain.
If milk be thy design, with plenteous hand
Bring clover-grass; and from the marshy land
Salt herbage for the fodd'ring rack provide,
To fill their bags, and swell the milky tide.
These raise their thirst, and to the taste restore
The savour of the salt, on which they fed before.
Some, when the kids their dams too deeply drain,
With gags and muzzles their soft mouths restrain.
Their morning milk the peasants press at night;
Their ev'ning meal before the rising light,
To market bear; or sparingly they steep
With seas'ning salt, and stor'd for winter keep.
Nor, last, forget thy faithful dogs: but feed
With fatt'ning whey the mastiff's gen'rous breed,
And Spartan race, who, for the fold's relief,
Will prosecute with cries the nightly thief,
Repulse the prowling wolf, and hold at bay
The mountain robbers rushing to the prey.
With cries of hounds, thou may'st pursue the fear
Of flying hares, and chase the fallow deer,
Rouse from their desert dens the bristled rage
Of boars; and beamy stags in toils engage.
With smoke of burning cedar scent thy walls,
And fume with stinking galbanum thy stalls,
With that rank odour from thy dwelling-place
To drive the viper's brood and all the venom'd race:
For often, under stalls unmov'd, they lie,
Obscure in shades, and shunning heav'n's broad eye:
And snakes, familiar, to the hearth succeed,
Disclose their eggs, and near the chimney breed—
Whether to roofy houses they repair,
Or sun themselves abroad in open air,
In all abodes of pestilential kind
To sheep and oxen, and the painful hind.
Take, shepherd, take a plant of stubborn oak,
And labour him with many a sturdy stroke,
Or with hard stones demolish from afar
His haughty crest, the seat of all the war;
Invade his hissing throat, and winding spires;
Till, stretch'd in length, th' unfolded foe retires.
He drags his tail, and for his head provides,
And in some secret cranny slowly glides;
But leaves expos'd to blows his back and batter'd sides.
In fair Calabria's woods a snake is bred,
With curling crest, and with advancing head:
Waving he rolls, and makes a winding track
His belly spotted, burnish'd is his back.
While springs are broken, while the southern air,
And dropping heav'ns the moisten'd earth repair,
He lives on standing lakes and trembling bogs,
And fills his maw with fish, or with loquacious frogs:
But when, in muddy pools, the water sinks,
And the chapt earth is furrow'd o'er with chinks,
He leaves the fens, and leaps upon the ground,
And, hissing, rolls his glaring eyes around.
With thirst inflam'd, impatient of the heats,
He rages in the fields, and wide destruction threats.
Oh! let not sleep my closing eyes invade
In open plains, or in the secret shade,
When he, renew'd in all the speckled pride
Of pompous youth, has cast his slough aside,
And in his summer liv'ry rolls along,
Erect, and brandishing his forky tongue,
Leaving his nest, and his imperfect young,
And thoughtless of his eggs, forgets to rear
The hopes of poison for the following year.
The causes and the signs shall next be told,
Of ev'ry sickness that infects the fold.

A scabber tetter on their pelts will stick,
When the raw rain has pierc'd them to the quick,
Or searching frosts have eaten through the skin,
Or burning icicles are lodg'd within:
Or, when the fleece is shorn, if sweat remains
Unwash'd, and soaks into their empty veins;
When their defenceless limbs the brambles tear,
Short of their wool, and naked from the shear.
Good shepherds, after shearing, drench their sheep;
And their flock's father (forc'd from high to leap)
Swims down the stream, and plunges in the deep.
They oint their naked limbs with mother'd oil;
Or, from the founts where living sulphurs boil;
They mix a med'cine to foment their limbs,
With scum that on the molten silver swims;
Fat pitch, and black bitumen, add to these,
Besides the waxen labour of the bees,
And hellebore, and squills deep rooted in the seas.
Receipts abound; but, searching all thy store,
The best is still at hand, to lance the sore,
And cut the head; for, till the core be found,
The secret vice is fed, and gathers ground,
While, making fruitless moan, the shepherd stands,
And, when the lancing knife requires his hands,
Vain help, with idle pray'rs, from heav'n demands.
Deep in their bones when fevers fix their seat,
And rack their limbs, and lick the vital heat.
The ready cure to cool the raging pain
Is underneath the foot to breathe a vein.
This remedy the Scythian shepherds found:
Th' inhabitants of Thracia's hilly ground,
And Gelons, use it, when for drink and food
They mix their curdled milk with horses' blood.
But, where thou seest a single sheep remain
In shades aloof, or couch'd upon the plain,
Or listlessly to crop the tender grass,
Or late to lag behind with truant pace;
Revenge the crime, and take the traitor's head,
Ere in the faultless flock the dire contagion spread.
On winter seas we fewer storms behold,
Than foul diseases that infect the fold.
Nor do those ills on single bodies prey,
But oft'ner bring the nation to decay,
And sweep the present stock and future hope away.
A dire example of this truth appears,
When, after such a length of rolling years,
We see the naked Alps, and thin remains
Of scatter'd cots, and yet unpeopled plains,
Once fill'd with grazing flocks, the shepherds' happy reigns.
Here, from the vicious air and sickly skies,
A plague did on the dumb creation rise:
During th' autumnal heats th' infection grew,
Tame cattle and the beasts of nature slew,
Pois'ning the standing lakes, and pools impure;
Nor was the foodful grass in fields secure.
Strange death! for, when the thirsty fire had drunk
Their vital blood, and the dry nerves were shrunk,
When the contracted limbs were cramp'd, e'en then
A wat'rish humour swell'd and ooz'd again.
Converting into bane the kindly juice,
Ordain'd by Nature for a better use.
The victim ox, that was for altars prest,
Trimm'd with white ribbons, and with garlands drest,
Sunk of himself, without the gods' command,
Preventing the slow sacrificer's hand.
Or, by the holy butcher if he fell,
Th' inspected entrails could no fates foretell:
Nor, laid on altars, did pure flames arise;
But clouds of smould'ring smoke forbade the sacrifice.
Scarcely the knife was redden'd with his gore,
Or the black poison stain'd the sandy floor.
The thriven calves in meads their food forsake,
And render their sweet souls before the plenteous rack.
The fawning dog runs mad; the wheezing swine
With coughs is chok'd, and labours from the chine:
The victor horse, forgetful of his food,
The palm renounces, and abhors the flood.
He paws the ground; and on his hanging ears
A doubtful sweat in clammy drops appears:
Parch'd is his hide, and rugged are his hairs.
Such are the symptoms of the young disease;
But, in time's process, when his pains increase,
He rolls his mournful eyes: he deeply groans
With patient sobbing, and with manly moans.
He heaves for breath; which, from his lungs supplied.
And fetch'd from far, distends his lab'ring side.
To his rough palate his dry tongue succeeds:
And ropy gore he from his nostrils bleeds.
A drench of wine has with success been us'd,
And through a horn the gen'rous juice infus'd,
Which, timely taken, op'd his closing jaws,
But, if too late, the patient's death did cause:
For the too vig'rous dose too fiercely wrought,
And added fury to the strength it brought.
Recruited into rage, he grinds his teeth
In his own flesh. and feels approaching death.
Ye gods, to better fate good men dispose,
And turn that impious error on our foes!
The steer, who to the yoke was bred to bow
(Studious of tillage, and the crooked plough)

Falls down and dies; and, dying, spews a flood
Of foamy madness, mix'd with clotted blood.
The clown, who, cursing Providence, repines,
His mournful fellow from the team disjoins;
With many a groan forsakes his fruitless care,
And in th' unfinish'd furrow leaves the share.
The pining steer no shades of lofty woods,
Nor flow'ry meads, can ease, nor crystal floods
Roll'd from the rock: his flabby flanks decrease;
His eyes are settled in a stupid peace;
His bulk too weighty for his thighs is grown;
And his unwieldly neck hangs drooping down.
Now what avails his well-deserving toil
To turn the glebe, or smooth the rugged soil?
And yet he never supt in solemn state,
(Nor undigested feasts did urge his fate)
Nor day to night luxuriously did join,
Nor surfeited on rich Campanian wine.
Simple his bev'rage, homely was his food,
The wholesome herbage, and the running flood:
No dreadful dreams awak'd him with affright:
His pains by day secur'd his rest at night.
'Twas then that buffaloes, ill pair'd, were seen
To draw the car of Jove's imperial queen,
For want of oxen; and the lab'ring swain
Scratch'd, with a rake, a furrow for his grain,
And cover'd with his hand, the shallow seed again.
He yokes himself, and up the hilly height
With his own shoulders, draws the wagon's weight.
The nightly wolf, that round th' inclosure prowl'd
To leap the fence, now plots not on the fold,
Tam'd with a sharper pain. The fearful doe,
And flying stag, amidst the greyhounds go,
And round the dwellings roam of man, their fiercer foe.
The scaly nations of the sea profound,
Like shipwreck'd carcasses, are driv'n aground,
And mighty phocæ, never seen before
In shallow streams, are stranded on the shore.
The viper dead within her hole is found:
Defenceless was the shelter of the ground.
The water-snake, whom fish and paddocks fed,
With staring scales lies poison'd in his bed:
To birds their native heav'ns contagious prove:
From clouds they fall, and leave their souls above.
Besides, to change their pasture 't is in vain,
Or trust to physic: physic is their bane.
The learned leeches in despair depart,
And shake their heads, desponding of their art.
Tisiphone let loose from under ground,
Majestically pale, now treads the round,
Before her drives Diseases and Affright,
And ev'ry moment rises to the sight,
Aspiring to the skies, encroaching on the light.
The rivers, and their banks, and hills around,
With lowings and with dying bleats resound.
At length, she strikes a universal blow:
To death at once whole herds of cattle go:
Sheep, oxen, horses, fall: and, heap'd on high,
The diff'ring species in confusion lie,
Till, warn'd by frequent ills, the way they found
To lodge their loathsome carrion under ground;
For useless to the currier were their hides;
Nor could their tainted flesh with ocean-tides
Be freed from filth; nor could Vulcanian flame
The stench abolish, or the savour tame.
Nor safely could they shear their fleecy store,
(Made drunk with pois'nous juice, and stiff with gore)
Or touch the web: but, if the vest they wear
Red blisters rising on their paps appear
And flaming carbuncles, and noisome sweat,
And clammy dews, that loathsome lice beget;
'Till the slow-creeping evil eats his way,
Consumes the parching limbs, and makes the life his prey.

GEORGIC IV.

ARGUMENT.

Virgil has taken care to raise the subject of each Georgic. In the first, he has only dead matter on which to work. In the second, he just steps on the world of life, and describes that degree of it which is to be found in vegetables. In the third, he advances to animals: and, in the last, he singles out the bee, which may be reckoned the most sagacious of them, for his subject.

In this Georgic, he shows us what station is most proper for the bees, and when they begin to gather honey: how to call them home when they swarm; and how to part them when they are engaged in battle. From hence he takes occasion to discover their different kinds: and, after an excursion, relates their prudent and politic administration of affairs, and the general diseases that often rage in their hives, with the proper symptoms and remedies of each disease. In the last place he lays down a method of repairing their kind, supposing their whole breed lost; and gives at large the history of its invention.

The gifts of heav'n my following song pursues,
Aerial honey, and ambrosial dews.
Mæcenas, read this other part, that sings
Embattl'd squadrons and advent'rous kings—
A mighty pomp, though made of little things.
Their arms, their arts, their manners, I disclose,
And how they war, and whence the people rose.
Slight is the subject, but the praise not small,
If heav'n assist, and Phœbus hear my call.
First, for thy bees a quiet station find,
And lodge them under covert of the wind;
(For winds, when homeward they return, will drive
The loaded carriers from their evening hive,)
Far from the cows' and goats' insulting crew,
That trample down the flow'rs, and brush the dew.
The painted lizard, and the birds of prey,
Foes of the frugal kind, be far away—

The titmouse, and the pecker's hungry brood,
And Procne, with her bosom stain'd in blood:
These rob the trading citizens, and bear
The trembling captives through the liquid air,
And for their callow young a cruel feast prepare.
But near a living stream their mansion place,
Edg'd round with moss, and tufts of matted grass:
And plant, (the wind's impetuous rage to stop)
Wild olive trees, or palms, before the busy shop;
That when the youthful prince, with proud alarm,
Calls out the venturous colony to swarm—
When first their way through yielding air they wing,
New to the pleasures of their native spring—
The banks of brooks may make a cold retreat
For the raw soldiers from the scalding heat,
And neighb'ring trees with friendly shade invite
The troops, unus'd to long laborious flight.
Then o'er the running stream or standing lake,
A passage for thy weary people make;
With osier floats the standing water strew;
Of massy stones make bridges, if it flow;
That basking in the sun thy bees may lie,
And, resting there their flaggy pinions dry,
When, late returning home, the laden host
By raging winds is wreck'd upon the coast.
Wild thyme and sav'ry set around their cell,
Sweet to the taste, and fragrant to the smell:
Set rows of rosemary with flow'ring stem,
And let the purple vi'lets drink the stream.
Whether thou build the palace of thy bees
With twisted osiers, or with barks of trees,
Make but a narrow mouth; for as the cold
Congeals into a lump the liquid gold,
So 'tis again dissolv'd by summer's heat;
And the sweet labours by extremes defeat.
And therefore not in vain, th' industrous kind
With dauby wax and flow'rs the chinks have lin'd,
And with their stores of gather'd glue, contrive
To stop the vents and crannies of their hive.
Not birdlime, or Idæan pitch, produce
A more tenacious mass of clammy juice.
Nor bees are lodg'd in hives alone, but found
In chambers of their own beneath the ground:
Their vaulted roofs are hung in pumices,
And in the rotten trunks of hollow trees.
But plaster thou the chinky hives with clay,
And leafy branches o'er their lodgings lay:
Nor place them where too deep a water flows,
Or where the yew, their pois'nous neighbour, grows;
Nor roast red crabs, t' offend the niceness of their nose;
Nor near the streaming stench of muddy ground;
Nor hollow rocks that render back the sound,
And double images of voice rebound
For what remains, when golden suns appear,
And under earth have driv'n the winter year,
The winged nation wanders through the skies,
And o'er the plains and shady forests flies:
Then, stooping on the meads and leafy bow'rs,
They skim the floods, and sip the purple flow'rs.
Exalted hence, and drunk with secret joy,
Their young succession all their cares employ:
They breed, they brood, instruct, and educate,
And make provision for the future state:
They work their waxen lodgings in their hives,
They labour honey to sustain their lives.
But when thou seest a swarming cloud arise,
That sweeps aloft, and darkens all the skies,
The motions of their hasty flight attend;
And know, to floods or woods, their airy march they bend.
Then melfoil beat, and honey-suckles pound;
With these alluring savours strew the ground.
And mix with tinkling brass the cymbal's droning sound.
Straight to their ancient cells, recall'd from air,
The reconcil'd deserter's will repair.
But, if intestine broils alarm the hive,
(For two pretenders oft for empire strive)
The vulgar in divided factions jar;
And murm'ring sounds proclaim the civil war.
Inflam'd with ire, and trembling with disdain,
Scarce can their limbs their mighty souls contain.
With shouts, the coward's courage they excite,
And martial clangors call them out to fight:
With hoarse alarms the hollow camp rebounds,
That imitate the trumpets angry sounds:
Then to their common standards they repair;
The nimble horsemen scour the fields of air;
In form of battle drawn, they issue forth,
And ev'ry knight is proud to prove his worth.
Prest for their country's honour, and their kings,
On their sharp beaks they wet their pointed stings,
And exercise their arms, and tremble with their wings.
Full in the midst the haughty monarchs ride;
The trusty guards come up, and close the side;
With shouts the daring foe to battle is defied.
Thus, in the season of unclouded spring,
To war they follow their undaunted king,
Crowd through their gates; and, in the fields of light,
The shocking squadrons meet in mortal fight.
Headlong they fall from high, and wounded wound;
And heaps of slaughter'd soldiers bite the ground.

Hard hailstones lie not thicker on the plain,
Nor shaken oaks such show'rs of acorns rain.
With gorgeous wings, the marks of sovereign sway,
The two contending princes make their way;
Intrepid through the midst of danger go,
Their friends encourage and amaze the foe.
With mighty souls in narrow bodies prest,
They challenge, and encounter breast to breast;
So fix'd on fame, unknowing how to fly,
And obstinately bent to win or die,
That long the doubtful combat they maintain,
Till one prevails—for one can only reign.
Yet all these dreadful deeds, this deadly fray,
A cast of scatter'd dust will soon allay,
And undecided leave the fortune of the day.
When both the chiefs are sunder'd from the fight,
Then to the lawful king restore his right;
And let the wasteful prodigal be slain,
That he, who best deserves, alone may reign.
With ease distinguish'd is the regal race:
One monarch wears an honest open face:
Shap'd to his size, and godlike to behold,
His royal body shines with specks of gold,
And ruddy scales; for empire he design'd,
Is better born, and of a nobler kind.
That other looks like nature in disgrace:
Gaunt are his sides, and sullen is his face,
And like their grizzly prince appear his gloomy race.
Grim, ghastly, rugged, like a thirsty train
That long have travell'd through a desert plain,
And spit from their dry chaps the gather'd dust again.
The better brood, unlike the bastard crew,
Are mark'd with royal streaks of shining hue;
Glitt'ring and ardent though in body less:
From these at pointed seasons, hope to press
Huge heavy honeycombs, of golden juice
Not only sweet, but pure, and fit for use,
T' allay the strength and hardness of the wine,
And with old Bacchus, new metheglin join.
But, when the swarms are eager of their play,
And loathe their empty hives, and idly stray,
Restrain the wanton fugitives, and take
A timely care to bring the truants back,
The task is easy—but to clip the wings
Of their high-flying arbitrary kings.
At their command, the people swarm away:
Confine the tyrant, and the slaves will stay.
Sweet gardens, full of saffron flowers, invite
The wand'ring gluttons, and retard their flight—
Besides the god obscene, who frights away,
With his lath sword, the thieves and birds of prey,
With his own hand, the guardian of the bees,
For slips of pine may search the mountain trees,
And with wild thyme and sav'ry plant the plain,
Till his hard horny fingers ache with pain;
And deck with frutiful trees the fields around,
And with refreshing waters drench the ground.
Now, did I not so near my labours end,
Strike sail, and hast'ning to the harbour tend,
My song to flow'ry gardens might extend—
To teach the vegetable arts to sing,
The Pæstan roses, and their double spring;
How succ'ry drinks the running streams, and how
Green beds of parsley near the river grow;
How cucumbers along the surface creep,
With crooked bodies, and with bellies deep—
The late narcissus, and the winding trail
Of bear's foot, myrtles green, and ivy pale:
For, where with stately tow'rs Tarentum stands,
And deep Galæsus soaks the yellow sands,
I chanc'd an old Corycian swain to know,
Lord of few acres, and those barren too,
Unfit for sheep or vines, and more unfit to sow:
Yet, lab'ring well his little spot of ground,
Some scatt'ring pot-herbs here and there he found,
Which, cultivated with his daily care,
And bruis'd with vervain, were his frugal fare.
Sometimes white lilies did their leaves afford
With wholesome poppy flow'rs, to mend his homely board:
For, late returning home, he supp'd at ease,
And wisely deem'd the wealth of monarchs less:
The little of his own, because his own did please.
To quit his care, he gather'd first of all,
In spring the roses, apples in the fall:
And, when cold winter split the rocks in twain,
And ice the running rivers did restrain,
He stripp'd the bear's-foot of its leafy growth,
And, calling western winds, accus'd the spring of sloth.
He therefore first among the swains was found
To read the product of his labour'd ground,
And squeeze the comb, with golden liquor crown'd.
His limes were first in flow'rs; his lofty pines,
With friendly shade, secur'd his tender vines.
For ev'ry bloom his trees in spring afford,
An autumn apple was by tale restor'd.
He knew to rank his elms in even rows,
For fruit the grafted pear-tree to dispose,
And tame to plums the sourness of the sloes.
With spreading planes he made a cool retreat,
To shade good fellows from the summer's heat,
But, straiten'd in my space, I must forsake
This task, for others afterwards to take.
Describe we next the nature of the bees,
Bestow'd by Jove for secret services,

When, by the tinkling sound of timbrels led,
The king of heav'n in Cretan caves they fed.
Of all the race of animals, alone
The bees have common cities of their own,
And common sons: beneath one law they live,
And with one common stock their traffic drive.
Each has a certain home, a sev'ral stall:
All is the state's; the state provides for all.
Mindful of coming cold, they share the pain,
And hoard, for winter's use, the summer's gain.
Some o'er the public magazines preside;
And some are sent new forage to provide.
These drudge in fields abroad; and those at home
Lay deep foundations for the labour'd comb,
With dew, narcissus-leaves, and clammy gum.
To pitch the waxen flooring some contrive;
Some nurse the future nation of the hive;
Sweet honey some condense; some purge the grout;
The rest, in cells apart, the liquid nectar shut:
All, with united force, combine to drive
The lazy drones from the laborious hive:
With envy stung, they view each others deeds:
With diligence the fragrant work proceeds.
As when the Cyclops, at th' almighty nod,
New thunder hasten for their angry god,
Subdu'd in fire the stubborn metal lies;
One brawny smith the puffing bellows plies,
And draws and blows reciprocating air:
Others to quench the hissing mass prepare:
With lifted arms they order ev'ry blow,
And chime their sounding hammers in a row;
With labour'd anvils Ætna groans below.
Strongly they strike; huge flakes of flames expire:
With tongs they turn the steel, and vex it in the fire.
If little things with great we may compare,
Such are the bees, and such their busy care;
Studious of honey, each in his degree, [bee—
The youthful swain, the grave experienc'd
That in the field; this, in affairs of state
Employ'd at home, abides within the gate,
To fortify the combs, to build the wall,
To prop the ruins, lest the fabric fall:
But, late at night, with weary pinions come
The lab'ring youth, and heavy laden, home.
Plains, meads, and orchards, all the day he plies;
The gleans of yellow thyme distend his thighs:
He spoils the saff'ron flow'rs: he sips the blues
Of vi'lets, wilding blooms, and willow dews.
Their toil is common; common is their sleep;
They shake their wings when morn begins to peep;
Rush through the city gates without delay;
Nor ends their work but with declining day.
Then, having spent the last remains of light,
They give their bodies due repose at night,
When hollow murmurs of their evening bells
Dismiss the sleepy swains, and toll them to their cells.
When once in beds their weary limbs they steep,
No buzzing sounds disturb their golden sleep
'Tis sacred silence all. Nor dare they stray,
When rain is promis'd, or a stormy day;
But near the city walls their wat'ring take,
Nor forage far, but short excursions make.
And as when empty barks on billows float,
With sandy ballast sailors trim the boat;
So bees bear gravel stones, whose poising weight
Steers through the whistling winds their steady flight.
But (what's more strange) their modest appetites,
Averse from Venus, fly the nuptial rites.
No lust enervates their heroic mind,
Nor wastes their strength on wanton womankind;
But in their mouths reside their genial pow'rs:
They gather children from the leaves and flow'rs.
Thus make they kings to fill the regal seat,
And thus their little citizens create,
And waxen cities build, the palaces of state.
And oft on rocks their tender wings they tear,
And sink beneath the burdens which they bear;
Such rage of honey in their bosom beats,
And such a zeal they have for flow'ry sweets.
Thus, though the race of life they quickly run,
Which in the space of sev'n short years is done:
Th' immortal line in sure succession reigns;
The fortune of the family remains;
And grandsires' grandsires the long list contains.
Besides, not Egypt, India, Media, more
With servile awe their idol king adore:
While he survives, in concord and content
The commons live, by no divisions rent:
But the great monarch's death dissolves the government.
All goes to ruin; they themselves contrive
To rob the honey, and subvert the hive.
The king presides, his subjects' toil surveys,
The servile route their careful Cæsar praise:
Him they extol; they worship him alone;
They crowd his levees, and support his throne:
They raise him on their shoulders with a shout;
And, when their sov'reign's quarrel calls them out,
His foes to mortal combat they defy,
And think it honour at his feet to die.
Induc'd by such examples some have taught
That bees have portion of etherial thought—
Endu'd with particles of heavenly fires;
For God the whole created mass inspires.

Through heav'n, and earth, and ocean's depth, he throws
His influence round, and kindles as he goes,
Hence flocks, and herds, and men, and beasts, and fowls,
With breath are quicken'd, and attract their souls;
Hence take the forms his prescience did ordain,
And into him at length resolve again.
No room is left for death: they mount the sky,
And to their own congenial planets fly.
Now, when thou hast decreed to seize their stores,
And by prerogative to break their doors,
With sprinkled water first the city choke,
And then pursue the citizens with smoke.
Two honey-harvests fall in ev'ry year:
First, when the pleasing Pleiades appear,
And, springing upward, spurn the briny seas:
Again, when their affrighted choir surveys
The wat'ry Scorpion mend his pace behind,
With a black train of storms, and winter wind,
They plunge into the deep, and safe protection find.
Prone to revenge, the bees, a wrathful race,
When once provok'd, assault the aggressor's face,
And through the purple veins a passage find;
There fix their stings, and leave their souls behind.
But, if a pinching winter thou foresee
And wouldst preserve thy famish'd family;
With fragrant thyme the city fumigate,
And break the waxen walls to save the state.
For lurking lizards often lodge, by stealth;
Within the suburbs, and purloin their wealth;
And worms, that shun the light, a dark retreat
Have found in combs, and undermin'd the seat;
Or lazy drones, without their share of pain,
In winter-quarters free, devour the gain;
Or wasps infest the camp with loud alarms,
And mix in battle with unequal arms
Or secret moths are there in silence fed;
Or spiders in the vault their snary webs have spread.
The more oppress'd by foes, or famine-pin'd,
The more increase thy care to save the sinking kind:
With greens and flow'rs recruit their empty hives,
And seek fresh forage to sustain their lives.
But, since they share with man one common fate,
In health and sickness, and in turns of state,—
Observe the symptoms. When they fall away,
And languish with insensible decay,
They change their hue; with haggard eyes they stare;
Lean are their looks, and shagged is their hair:
And crowds of dead, that never must return
To their lov'd hives, in decent pomp are borne.
Their friends attend the hearse; the next relations mourn.
The sick, for air, before the portal gasp,
Their feeble legs within each other clasp,
Or idle in their empty hives remain,
Benumb'd with cold, and listless of their gain.
Soft whispers then, and broken sounds, are heard,
As when the woods by gentle winds are stirr'd,
Such stifled noise as the close furnace hides,
Or dying murmurs of departing tides.
This when thou seest galbanean odours use,
And honey in the sickly hive infuse.
Through reeden pipes convey the golden flood,
T' invite the people to their wonted food.
Mix it with thicken'd juice of sodden wines,
And raisins from the grapes of Psythian vines.
To these add pounded galls, and roses dry,
And, with Cecropian thyme, strong-scented centaury.
A flow'r there is, that grows in meadow-ground,
Amellus call'd, and easy to be found;
For, from one root, the rising stem bestows
A wood of leaves, and vi'let purple boughs:
The flow'r itself is glorious to behold,
And shines on altars like refulgent gold—
Sharp to the taste—by shepherds near the stream
Of Mella found; and thence they gave the name.
Boil this restoring root in gen'rous wine,
And set beside the door, the sickly stock to dine.
But, if the lab'ring kind be wholly lost,
And not to be retriev'd with care or cost;
'T is time to touch the precepts of an art
Th' Arcadian master did of old impart;
And how he stock'd his empty hives again,
Renew'd with putrid gore of oxen slain.
An ancient legend I prepare to sing,
And upward follow Fame's immortal spring;
For, where with sevenfold horns mysterious Nile
Surrounds the skirts of Egypt's fruitful isle,
And where in pomp the sunburnt people ride,
On painted barges o'er the teeming tide,
Which, pouring down from Ethiopian lands,
Makes green the soil with slime, and black prolific sands—
That length of region, and large tract of ground,
In this one art a sure relief have found.
First, in a place, by nature close, they build
A narrow flooring, gutter'd, wall'd, and til'd.
In this, four windows are contriv'd, that strike
To the four winds oppos'd, their beams oblique.
A steer of two years old they take, whose head
Now first with burnish'd horns begins to spread:

They stop his nostrils while he strives in vain
To breathe free air, and struggles with his pain.
Knock'd down, he dies: his bowels bruis'd within,
Betray no wound on his unbroken skin.
Extended thus, in this obscene abode
They leave the beast; but first sweet flow'rs are strew'd
Beneath his body, broken boughs and thyme,
And pleasing cassia just renew'd in prime.
This must be done ere spring makes equal day,
When western winds on curling waters play:
Ere painted meads produce their flow'ry crops,
Or swallows twitter on the chimney tops.
The tainted blood, in this close prison pent,
Begins to boil, and through the bones ferment.
Then (wondrous to behold) new creatures rise,
A moving mass at first, and short of thighs;
Till shooting out with legs, and imp'd with wings,
The grubs proceed to bees with pointed stings,
And, more and more affecting air, they try
Their tender pinions, and begin to fly:
At length, like summer storms from spreading clouds,
That burst at once, and pour impetuous floods—
Or flights of arrows from the Parthian bows,
When from afar they gall embattled foes—
With such a tempest through the skies they steer;
And such a form the winged squadrons bear.
What god, O Muse! this useful science taught?
Or by what man's experience was it brought?
Sad Aristæus from fair Tempe fled—
His bees with famine or diseases dead:—
On Peneus' banks he stood, and near his holy head;
And, while his falling tears the stream suppli'd,
Thus mourning to his mother goddess cried:
"Mother Cyrene! mother, whose abode
Is in the depth of this immortal flood!
What boots it, that from Phœbus' loins I spring
The third, by him and thee, from heav'n's high king?
O! where is all thy boasted pity gone,
And promise of the skies to thy deluded son?
Why didst thou me, unhappy me, create,
Odious to gods, and borne to bitter fate?
Whom scarce my sheep, and scarce my painful plough,
The needful aids of human life allow:
So wretched is thy son, so hard a mother thou!
Proceed, inhuman parent, in thy scorn;
Root up my trees; with blights destroy my corn;
My vineyards ruin, and my sheepfolds burn.
Let loose thy rage, let all thy spite be shown;
Since thus thy hate pursues the praises of thy son."
But, from her mossy bow'r below the ground,
His careful mother heard the plaintive sound—
Encompass'd with her sea-green sisters round.
One common work they pli'd; their distaffs full
With carded locks of blue Milesian wool.
Spio, with Drymo brown, and Xantho fair,
And sweet Phyllodoce with long dishevell'd hair,
Cydippe with Lycorias, one a maid,
And one that once had call'd Lucina's aid;
Clio and Beroe, from one father both;
Both girt with gold, and clad in particolour'd cloth;
Opis the meek, and Deiopeia proud:
Nisæa lofty, with Ligea loud;
Thalia joyous, Ephyre the sad,
And Arethusa, once Diana's maid,
But now (her quiver left) to love betray'd.
To these Clymene the sweet theft declares
Of Mars; and Vulcan's unavailing cares;
And all the rapes of gods, and ev'ry love,
From ancient Chaos down to youthful Jove:
Thus while she sings, the sisters turn the wheel,
Empty the woolly rack, and fill the reel.
A mournful sound again the mother hears;
Again the mournful sound invades the sisters' ears.
Starting at once from their green seats, they rise—
Fear in their heart, amazement in their eyes.
But Arethusa, leaping from her bed,
First lifts above the waves her beauteous head,
And, crying from afar, thus to Cyrene said:
"O sister, not with causeless fear possest!
No stranger voice disturbs thy tender breast,
'T is Aristæus, 'tis thy darling son,
Who to his careless mother makes his moan.
Near his paternal stream he sadly stands,
With downcast eyes, wet cheeks, and folded hands.
Upbraiding heav'n from whence his lineage came,
And cruel calls the gods, and cruel thee, by name."
Cyrene, mov'd with love, and seiz'd with fear,
Cries out, "Conduct my son, conduct him here:
'Tis lawful for the youth, deriv'd from gods,
To view the secrets of our deep abodes."
At once she wav'd her hand on either side;
At once the ranks of swelling streams divide.
Two rising heaps of liquid crystal stand,
And leave a space betwixt, of empty sand.
Thus safe receiv'd, the downward track he treads,
Which to his mother's wat'ry palace leads.
With wond'ring eyes he views the secret store
Of lakes, that, pent in hollow caverns, roar;
He hears the crackling sounds of coral woods,
And sees the secret source of subterranean floods;

And where, distinguish'd in their sev'ral cells,
The fount of Phasis, and of Lycus, dwells;
Where swift Enipeus in his bed appears,
And Tyber his majestic forehead rears;
Whence Anio flows, and Hypanis profound
Breaks thro' th' opposing rocks with raging sound;
Where Po first issues from his dark abodes,
And, awful in his cradle, rules the floods:
Two golden horns on his large front he wears,
And his grim face a bull's resemblance bears:
With rapid course he seeks the sacred main,
And fattens, as he runs, the fruitful plain.
Now, to the court arriv'd, th' admiring son
Beholds the vaulted roofs of pory stone,
Now to his mother goddess tells his grief,
Which she with pity hears, and promises relief.
Th' officious nymphs, attending in a ring,
With water drawn from their perpetual spring,
From earthly dregs his body purify,
And rub his temples, with fine towels, dry;
Then load the tables with a lib'ral feast,
And honour with full bowls their friendly guest.
The sacred altars are involv'd in smoke;
And the bright choir their kindred gods invoke.
Two bowls the mother fills with Lydian wine;
Then thus: "Let these be pour'd, with rites divine,
To the great authors of our wat'ry line—
To father Ocean, this; and this," she said,
"Be to the nymphs his sacred sisters paid,
Who rule the wat'ry plains, and hold the woodland shade."
She sprinkled thrice, with wine, the vestal fire;
Thrice to the vaulted roof the flames aspire.
Rais'd with so blest an omen, she begun,
With words like these, to cheer her drooping son:
"In the Carpathian bottom, makes abode
The shepherd of the seas, a prophet and a god.
High o'er the main in wat'ry pomp he rides,
His azure car and finny coursers guides—
Proteus his name.—To his Pallenian port
I see from far the weary god resort.
Him, not alone, we river gods adore,
But aged Nereus hearkens to his lore.
With sure foresight, and with unerring doom,
He sees what is, and was, and is to come.
This Neptune gave him, when he gave to keep
His scaly flocks, that graze the wat'ry deep.
Implore his aid; for Proteus only knows
The secret cause, and cure, of all thy woes.
But first the wily wizard must be caught;
For, unconstrain'd, he nothing tells for nought;
Nor is with pray'rs, or bribes, or flattery bought.
Surprise him first, and with hard fetters bind;
Then all his frauds will vanish into wind.
I will myself conduct thee on thy way,
When next the southing sun inflames the day,
When the dry herbage thirsts for dews in vain,
And sheep, in shades, avoid the parching plain;
Then will I lead thee to his secret seat,
When, weary with his toil, and scorch'd with heat,
The wayward sire frequents his cool retreat.
His eyes with heavy slumber overcast—
With force invade his limbs, and bind him fast.
Thus surely bound, yet be not over bold:
The slipp'ry god will try to loose his hold,
And various forms assume, to cheat thy sight,
And with vain images of beasts affright;
With foamy tusks, he seems a bristly boar,
Or imitates the lion's angy roar;
Breaks out in crackling flames to shun thy snares,
Hisses a dragon, or a tiger stares;
Or with a wild thy caution to betray,
In fleeting streams attempts to slide away.
But thou, the more he varies forms, beware
To strain his fetters with a stricter care,
Till, tiring all his arts, he turns again
To his true shape, in which he first was seen."
This said, with nectar she her son anoints;
Infusing vigour through his mortal joints:
Down from his head the liquid odours ran;
He breath'd of heav'n, and look'd above a man.
Within a mountain's hollow womb, there lies
A large recess conceal'd from human eyes,
Where heaps of billows, driv'n by wind and tide,
In form of war their wat'ry ranks divide,
And their like centries set, without the mouth abide:
A station safe for ships, when tempests roar,
A silent harbour, and a cover'd shore.
Secure within resides the various god,
And draws a rock upon his dark abode.
Hither with silent steps, secure from sight,
The goddess guides her son, and turns him from the light:
Herself, involv'd in clouds, precipitates her flight.
'Twas noon; the sultry Dog-star from the sky
Scorch'd Indian swains; the rivel'd grass was dry;
The sun with flaming arrows pierc'd the flood,
And, darting to the bottom, bak'd the mud;
When weary Proteus, from the briny waves,
Retir'd for shelter to his wonted caves.
His finny flocks about their shepherd play,
And, rolling round him spurt the bitter sea:
Unwieldily they wallow first in ooze,
Then in the shady covert seek repose.
Himself, their herdsman, on the middle mount,
Takes of his muster'd flocks a just account
So, seated on a rock, a shepherd's groom
Surveys his evening flocks returning home,

When lowing calves and bleating lambs, from far,
Provoke the prowling wolf to nightly war.
Th' occasion offers, and the youth complies;
For scarce the weary god had clos'd his eyes,
When, rushing on with shouts, he binds in chains
The drowsy prophet, and his limbs constrains.
He, not unmindful of his usual art,
First in dissembled fire attempts to part:
Then roaring beasts, and running streams, he tries
And wearies all his miracles of lies.
But, having shifted ev'ry form to 'scape,
Convinc'd of conquest, he resum'd his shape,
And thus, at length, in human accent spoke:
"Audacious youth! what madness could provoke
A mortal man t' invade a sleeping god?
What bus'ness brought thee to my dark abode?"
To this th' audacious youth: "Thou know'st full well
My name and bus'ness, god; nor need I tell.
No man can Proteus cheat: but, Proteus, leave
Thy fraudful arts, and do not thou deceive.
Following the gods' command I come t' implore
Thy help, my perish'd people to restore."
The seer, who could not yet his wrath assuage,
Roll'd his green eyes, that sparkled with his rage,
And gnash'd his teeth, and cried, "no vulgar god
Pursues thy crimes, nor with a common rod
Thy great misdeeds have met a due reward,
And Orpheus' dying prayers at length are heard.
For crimes, not his, the lover lost his life,
And at thy hands requires his murder'd wife:
Nor (if the Fates assist not) canst thou 'scape
The just revenge of that intended rape.
To shun thy lawless lust the dying bride,
Unwary, took along the river's side,
Nor at her heels perceiv'd the deadly snake,
That kept the bank, in covert of the brake.
But all her fellow-nymphs the mountains tear
With loud laments, and break the yielding air:
The realms of Mars remurmur all around,
And echoes to th' Athenian shores rebound.
Th' unhappy husband, husband now no more,
Did on his tuneful harp his loss deplore;
And sought his mournful mind with music to restore.
On thee, dear wife, in deserts all alone,
He call'd, sigh'd, sung: his griefs with day begun,
Nor were they finish'd with the setting sun,
E'en to the dark dominions of the night
He took his way, through forests void of light,
And dar'd amidst the trembling ghosts to sing,
And stood before th' inexorable king.
Th' infernal troops like passing shadows glide,
And, list'ning, crowd the sweet musician's side—
(Not flocks of birds when driv'n by storms or night,
Stretch to the forest with so thick a flight)—
Men, matrons, children, and th' unmarried maid,
The mighty hero's more majestic shade,
And youths on funeral piles before their parents laid.
All these Cocytus bounds with squalid reeds,
With muddy ditches, and with deadly weeds;
And baleful Styx encompasses around,
With nine slow circling streams, th' unhappy ground.
E'en from the depths of hell the damn'd advance;
Th' infernal mansions, nodding seem to dance;
The gaping three-mouth'd dog forgets to snarl:
The Furies hearken, and their snakes uncurl;
Ixion seems no more his pain to feel.
But leans attentive on his standing wheel.
All dangers past, at length the lovely bride
In safety goes, with her melodious guide,
Longing the common light again to share,
And draw the vital breath of upper air—
He first; and close behind him follow'd she;
For such was Proserpine's severe decree—
When strong desires th' impatient youth invade,
By little caution and much love betray'd:
A fault, which easy pardon might receive,
Were lovers judges, or could hell forgive.
For, near the confines of etherial light,
And longing for the glimm'ring of a sight,
Th' unwary lover casts his eyes behind,
Forgetful of the law nor master of his mind.
Straight all his hopes exhal'd in empty smoke;
And his long toils were forfeit for a look.
Three flashes of blue lightning gave the sign
Of cov'nants broke; three peals of thunder join.
Then thus the bride: 'what fury seiz'd on thee,
Unhappy man! to lose thyself and me?
Dragg'd back again by cruel destinies,
An iron slumber shuts my swimming eyes.
And now farewell! involv'd in shades of night
For ever I am ravish'd from thy sight.
In vain I reach my feeble hands, to join
In sweet embraces—ah! no longer thine!'
She said; and from his eyes the fleeting fair
Retir'd like subtle smoke dissolv'd in air,
And left the hopeless lover in despair.
In vain, with folding arms, the youth essay'd
To stop her flight, and strain the flying shade:
He prays; he raves; all means in vain he tries,
With rage inflam'd, astonish'd with surprise:
But she return'd no more, to bless his longing eyes.
Nor would th' infernal ferrymen once more,
Be brib'd to waft him to the farther shore.

What should he do, who twice had lost his love?
What notes invent? what new petitions move?
Her soul already was consign'd to fate,
And shiv'ring in the leaky sculler sate.
For sev'n continu'd months, if fame say true,
The wretched swain his sorrow did renew:
By Stryman's freezing streams he sat alone:
The rocks were mov'd to pity with his moan:
Trees bent their heads to hear him sing his wrongs:
Fierce tigers couch'd around, and loll'd their fawning tongues.
So, close in poplar shades, her children gone,
The mother nightingale laments alone,
Whose nest some prying churl had found, and thence,
By stealth, convey'd th' unfeather'd innocence.
But she supplies the night with mournful strains;
And melancholy music fills the plains.
Sad Orpheus thus his tedious hours employs,
Averse from Venus, and from nuptial joys,
Alone he tempts the frozen floods, alone
Th' unhappy climes, where spring was never known;
He mourn'd his wretched wife, in vain restor'd,
And Pluto's unavailing boon deplor'd.
The Thracian matrons—who the youth accus'd
Of love disdain'd, and marriage rites refus'd—
With furies and nocturnal orgies fir'd,
At length against his sacred life conspir'd.
Whom e'en the savage beasts had spar'd, they kill'd,
And strew'd his mangled limbs about the field.
Then, when his head, from his fair shoulders torn,
Wash'd by the waters, was on Hebrus borne,
E'en then his trembling tongue invok'd his bride;
With his last voice, 'Eurydice,' he cried.
'Eurydice,' the rocks and river-banks replied."
This answer Proteus gave; no more he said,
But in the billows plung'd his hoary head;
And, where he leap'd, the waves in circles wide, ly spread.
The nymph return'd her drooping son to cheer,
And bid him banish his superfluous fear:
"For now," said she, "the cause is known, from whence
Thy wo succeeded, and for what offence
The nymphs, companions of th' unhappy maid,
This punishment upon thy crimes have laid;
And sent a plague among thy thriving bees.
With vows and suppliant pray'rs their pow'rs appease;
The soft Napæan race will soon repent
Their anger, and remit the punishment.
The secret in an easy method lies;
Select four brawny bulls for sacrifice,
Which on Lycæus graze without a guide;
Add four fair heifers yet in yoke untried,
For these, four altars in their temple rear,
And then adore the woodland pow'rs with pray'r.
From the slain victims pour the streaming blood,
And leave their bodies in the shady wood:
Nine mornings thence, Lethæan poppy bring,
T' appease the manes of the poet's king:
And, to propitiate his offended bride,
A fatted calf, and a black ewe provide:
This finish'd, to the former woods repair."
His mother's precepts he performs with care;
The temple visits, and adores with pray'r;
Four altars raises; from his herd he culls,
For slaughter, four the fairest of his bulls:
Four heifers from his female store he took,
All fair, and all unknowing of the yoke,
Nine mornings thence, with sacrifice and pray'rs,
The pow'rs aton'd, he to the grove repairs.
Behold a prodigy! for, from within
The broken bowels and the bloated skin,
A buzzing noise of bees his ears alarms:
Straight issue through the sides assembling swarms.
Dark as a cloud, they make a wheeling flight,
Then on a neighb'ring tree, descending, light:
Like a large cluster of black grapes they show,
And make a large dependence from the bough.
Thus have I sung of fields, and flocks, and trees,
And of the waxen work of lab'ring bees;
While mighty Cæsar, thund'ring from afar,
Seeks on Euphrates' banks the spoils of war;
With conq'ring arts asserts his country's cause,
With arts of peace the willing people draws;
On the glad earth the golden age renews,
And his great father's path to heav'n pursues;
While I at Naples pass my peaceful days,
Affecting studies of less noisy praise;
And, bold through youth, beneath the beechen shade,
The lays of shepherds, and their loves have play'd.

THE MOST HONOURABLE

JOHN,

LORD MARQUIS OF NORMANBY, EARL OF MULGRAVE,* &c. AND KNIGHT OF THE MOST NOBLE ORDER OF THE GARTER.

A HEROIC poem, truly such, is undoubtedly the greatest work which the soul of man is capable to perform. The design of it is to form the mind to heroic virtue by example. It is conveyed in verse, that it may delight, while it instructs: the action of it is always one, entire, and great. The least and most trivial episodes, or under-actions, which are interwoven in it, are parts either necessary or convenient to carry on the main design; either so necessary, that, without them, the poem must be imperfect, or so convenient, that no others can be imagined more suitable to the place in which they are. There is nothing to be left void in a firm building; even the cavities ought not to be filled with rubbish, (which is of a perishable kind, destructive to the strength,) but with brick or stone, though of less pieces, yet of the same nature, and fitted to the crannies. Even the least portions of them must be of the epic kind: all things must be grave, majestical, and sublime; nothing of a foreign nature, like the trifling *novels*, which Ariosto,* and others, have inserted in their poems; by which the reader is misled into another sort of pleasure, opposite to that which is designed in an epic poem. One raises the soul, and hardens it to virtue; the other softens it, and unbends it into vice. One conduces to the poet's aim, the completing of his work, which he is driving on, labouring and hastening in every line; the other slackens his pace, diverts him from his way, and locks him up, like a knight-errant, in an enchanted castle, when he should be pursuing his first adventure. Statius, as Bossu has well observed, was ambitious of trying his strength with his master Virgil, as Virgil had before tried his with Homer. The Grecian gave the two Romans an example, in the games which were celebrated at the funerals of Patroclus. Virgil imitated the invention of Homer, but changed the sports. But both the Greek and Latin poet took their occasions from the subject; though to confess the truth, they were both ornamental, or, at best, convenient parts of it, rather than of necessity arising from it. Statius, who, through his whole poem, is noted for want of conduct and judgment, instead of staying, as he might have done, for the death of Capaneus, Hippomedon, Tydeus, or some other of his seven champions, (who are heroes all alike,) or more properly for the tragical end of the two brothers, whose exequies the next successor had leisure to perform when the siege was raised, and in the interval betwixt the poet's first action and his second—went out of his way, as it were on prepense malice, to commit a fault. For he took his opportunity to kill a royal infant by the means of a serpent, (that author of all evil,) to make way for those funeral honours which he intended for him. Now, if this innocent had been of any relation to his Thebais—if he had either furthered or hindered the taking of the town—the poet might have found some sorry excuse, at least, for de-

* The early editions, by an absurd and continued blunder, read Aristotle. Ariosto, and indeed all the heroic Italian poets, Tasso excepted, have chequered their romantic fictions with lighter stories, such as those of Jocondo and of Adonio, in the "Orlando Furioso." But neither Ariosto, nor his predecessors Boiardo and Pulci, ever entertained the idea of writing a regular epic poem after the ancient rules. On the contrary, they often drop the mask in the middle of the romantic wonders which they relate; and plainly show, how very far they are from considering the narrative as serious. It was, therefore, consistent with their plan, to admit such light and frivolous narratives, as might relieve the general gravity of their tale, which resembled an epic poem as little as a melo-drama does a tragedy

* Mulgrave's early and intimate connexion with our author has been often noticed in this edition. In the reign of William III. he remained in a sort of disgrace, from his attachment to the exiled king; yet, in 1694, he was created Marquis of Normanby; in the reign of the queen, he rose still higher; and it is said that the dignities, offices, and influence, which he then enjoyed, were the reward of the ambitious love which he had dared to entertain for that princess, when she was only the Lady Anne, second daughter to the Duke of York.—See *Dryden's Life*; also *Dedication to Aureng-Zebe.*

taining the reader from the promised siege. On these terms, this Capaneus of a poet engaged his two immortal predecessors; and his success was answerable to his enterprise.*

If this economy must be observed in the minutest parts of an epic poem, which, to a common reader, seem to be detached from the body, and almost independent of it; what soul, though sent into the world with great advantages of nature, cultivated with the liberal arts and sciences, conversant with histories of the dead, and enriched with observations on the living, can be sufficient to inform the whole body of so great a work? I touch here but transiently, without any strict method, on some few of those many rules of imitating nature, which Aristotle drew from Homer's Iliads and Odysseys, and which he fitted to the drama; furnishing himself also with observations from the practice of the theatre, when it flourished under Æschylus, Euripides, and Sophocles: for the original of the stage was from the epic poem. Narration, doubtless, preceded acting, and gave laws to it: what at first was told artfully, was, in process of time, represented gracefully to the sight and hearing. These episodes of Homer, which were proper for the stage, the poets amplified each into an action; out of his limbs they formed their bodies; what he had contracted, they enlarged; out of one Hercules, were made infinity of pigmies, yet all indued with human souls; for from him, their great creator, they have each of them the *divinæ particulam auræ*. They flowed from him at first, and are at last resolved into him. Nor were they only animated by him, but their measure and symmetry was owing to him. His one, entire, and great action was copied by them according to the proportions of the drama. If he finished his orb within the year, it sufficed to teach them, that their action being less, and being also less diversified with incidents, their orb, of consequence, must be circumscribed in a less compass, which they reduced within the limits either of a natural or an artificial day; so that, as he taught them to amplify what he had shortened, by the same rule, applied the contrary way, he taught them to shorten what he had amplified. Tragedy is the miniature of human life; an epic poem is the draught at length.† Here, my lord, I must contract also; for before I was aware, I was almost running into a long digression, to prove, that there is no such absolute necessity that the time of a stage action should so strictly be confined to twenty-four hours, as never to exceed them, for which Aristotle contends, and the Grecian stage has practised. Some longer space on some occasions, I think, may be allowed, especially for the English theatre, which requires more variety of incidents than the French. Corneille himself, after long practice, was inclined to think, that the time allotted by the ancients was too short to raise and finish a great action: and better a mechanic rule were stretched or broken, than a great beauty were omitted. To raise, and afterwards to calm the passions—to purge the soul from pride, by the examples of human miseries, which befall the greatest—in few words, to expel arrogance, and introduce compassion, are the great effects of tragedy; great, I must confess, if they were altogether as true as they are pompous. But are habits to be introduced at three hours' warning? are radical diseases so suddenly removed? A mountebank may promise such a cure, but a skilful physician will not undertake it. An epic poem is not in so much haste: it works leisurely; the changes which it makes are slow; but the cure is likely to be more perfect. The effects of tragedy, as

* I quote, from Mr. Malone, Mr. Harte's vindication of Statius; premising, however, that it is far from amounting to an exculpation of that boisterous author, whose works have fallen into oblivion even among scholars, in due proportion to the ripening of poetical taste.

"Mr. Dryden, in his excellent Preface to the Æneid, takes occasion to quarrel with Statius, and calls the present book (the Sixth) 'an ill-timed and injudicious episode.' I wonder so severe a remark could pass from that gentleman, who was an admirer of our author, even to superstition. I own I can scarce forgive myself to contradict so great a poet, and so good a critic: *talium enim virorum ut admiratio maxima, ita censura difficilis*. However, the present case may admit of very alleviating circumstances. It may be replied, in general, that the design of this book was to give a respite to the main action, introducing a mournful, but pleasing variation, from terror to pity. It is also highly probable, that Statius had an eye to the funeral obsequies of Polydore and Anchises, mentioned in the third and fifth books of Virgil. We may also look upon them as a prelude, opening the mind by degrees to receive the horrors of a future war. This is intimated in some measure by the derivation of the word *Archemorus*."—*Note on Mr. Walter Harte's Translation of the Sixth Book of the Thebaid.*

Notwithstanding what Mr. Harte has stated, our author seldom mentions Statius, without reprobating his turgid and bombast style.

† Dryden, as was excellently observed by Sir Samuel Garth, in his "Funeral Eulogy," always thought that species of composition most excellent upon which his labour had been more immediately employed. In the "Essay upon Dramatic Poesy," he had preferred the tragedy to the epic poem, and here he has reversed their station, and rank. I think the principal distinction is noticed below. Tragedy is addressed, as it were, to the eye; and, the whole scene, to be enjoyed, even in perusal, must be supposed present to the observation. But epic poetry is, by its nature, narrative; and, therefore, while it is capable of the beauties of more extended description, and more copious morality, it is excluded from that immediate and energetic appeal to the senses manifested in the drama.

I said, are too violent to be lasting. If it be answered, that, for this reason, tragedies are often to be seen, and the dose to be repeated, this is tacitly to confess, that there is more virtue in one heroic poem than in many tragedies. A man is humbled one day, and his pride returns the next. Chymical medicines are observed to relieve oftener than to cure: for it is the nature of spirits to make swift impressions, out not deep. Galenical decoctions, to which I may properly compare an epic poem, have more of body in them; they work by their substance and their weight. It is one reason of Aristotle's to prove, that tragedy is the more noble, because it turns in a shorter compass: the whole action being circumscribed within the space of four-and-twenty hours. He might prove as well, that a mushroom is to be preferred before a peach, because it shoots up in the compass of a night. A chariot may be driven round a pillar in less space than a large machine, because the bulk is not so great. Is the Moon a more noble planet than Saturn, because she makes her revolution in less than thirty days, and he in little less than thirty years? Both their orbs are in proportion to their several magnitudes; and, consequently, the quickness or slowness of their motion, and the time of their circumvolutions, is no argument of the greater or less perfection. And, besides, what virtue is there in a tragedy, which is not contained in an epic poem, where pride is humbled, virtue rewarded, and vice punished; and those more amply treated, than the narrowness of the drama can admit? The shining quality of an epic hero, his magnanimity, his constancy, his patience, his piety, or whatever characteristical virtue his poet gives him, raises first our admiration. We are naturally prone to imitate what we admire; and frequent acts produce a habit. If the hero's chief quality be vicious, as, for example, the choler and obstinate desire of vengeance in Achilles, yet the moral is instructive: and, besides, we are informed in the very proposition of the Iliads, that this anger was pernicious; that it brought a thousand ills on the Grecian camp. The courage of Achilles is proposed to imitation, not his pride and disobedience to his general, nor his brutal cruelty to his dead enemy, nor the selling his body to his father.* We abhor these actions while we read them; and what we abhor we never imitate. The poet only shows them, like rocks or quicksands, to be shunned.

By this example, the critics have concluded, that it is not necessary the manners of the hero should be virtuous. They are poetically good, if they are of a piece; though, where a character of perfect virtue is set before us, it is more lovely; for there the whole hero is to be imitated. This is the Æneas of our author; this is that idea of perfection in an epic poem, which painters and statuaries have only in their minds, and which no hands are able to express. These are the beauties of a god in a human body. When the picture of Achilles is drawn in tragedy, he is taken with those warts, and moles, and hard features, by those who represent him on the stage, or he is no more Achilles; for his creator, Homer, has so described him. Yet even thus he appears a perfect hero, though an imperfect character of virtue. Horace paints him after Homer, and delivers him to be copied on the stage with all those imperfections.* Therefore they are either not faults in a heroic poem, or faults common to the drama. After all, on the whole merits of the cause, it must be acknowledged, that the epic poem is more for the manners, and tragedy for the passions. The passions, as I have said, are violent; and acute distempers require medicines of a strong and speedy operation. Ill habits of the mind are like chronical diseases, to be corrected by degrees, and cured by alteratives; wherein, though purges are sometimes necessary, yet diet, good air, and moderate exercise, have the greatest part. The matter being thus stated, it will appear, that both sorts of poetry are of use for their proper ends. The stage is more active; the epic poem works at greater leisure, yet is active

* The cant of supposing, that the Iliad contained an obvious and intentional moral, was at this time so established among the critics, that even Dryden durst not shake himself free of it. In all probability, the ancient blind bard only thought of so arranging his splendid tale of Troy divine, that it should arrest the attention of his hearers. Doubtless, an admirable moral may be often extracted from his poem; because it contains an accurate picture of human nature, which can never be truly presented, without conveying a lesson of instruction. But it may shrewdly be suspected, that the moral was as little intended by the author, as it would have been the object of a historian, whose work is equally pregnant with morality, though a detail of facts be only intended. We may be pretty sure, that Homer meant his Achilles, the favourite of the gods, as a character approaching perfection; and if he is cruel, proud, disobedient, and vengeful, I am afraid it was only because these attributes, in a savage state, are deemed as little derogatory from the character of a hero, as dissipation and gallantry are blemishes in that of a modern fine gentleman.

* The opinion of Horace is a confirmation of what is stated above. None of the ancients ventured to impute the rudeness of Homer's characters to the barbarity of the poet's age. The faults which they could not shut their eyes against, must, they thought, have been equally apparent to the bard himself; although, in all probability, he meant, that these very attributes in his heroes should be considered as virtues.

too, when need requires; for dialogue is imitated by the drama, from the more active parts of it. One puts off a fit, like the *quinquina*, and relieves us only for a time; the other roots out the distemper, and gives a healthful habit. The sun enlightens and cheers us, dispels fogs, and warms the ground with his daily beams; but the corn is sowed, increases, is ripened, and is reaped for use in process of time, and in its proper season. I proceed, from the greatness of the action, to the dignity of the actors; I mean to the persons employed in both poems. There likewise tragedy will be seen to borrow from the epopee; and that which borrows is always of less dignity, because it has not of its own. A subject, it is true, may lend to his sovereign; but the act of borrowing makes the king inferior, because he wants, and the subject supplies. And suppose the persons of the drama wholly fabulous, or of the poet's invention, yet heroic poetry gave him the examples of that invention, because it was first, and Homer the common father of the stage. I know not of any one advantage which tragedy can boast above heroic poetry, but that it is represented to the view, as well as read, and instructs in the closet, as well as on the theatre. This is an uncontended excellence, and a chief branch of its prerogative; yet I may be allowed to say, without partiality, that herein the actors share the poet's praise. Your lordship knows some modern tragedies which are beautiful on the stage, and yet I am confident you would not read them. "Tryphon the stationer"* complains, they are seldom asked for in his shop. The poet who flourished in the scene, is damned in the *ruelle*;† nay more, he is not esteemed a good poet by those, who see and hear his extravagancies with delight. They are a sort of stately fustian, and lofty childishness. Nothing but nature can give a sincere pleasure; where that is not imitated, it is grotesque painting; "the fine woman ends in a fish's tail."

I might also add, that many things, which not only please, but are real beauties in the reading, would appear absurd upon the stage; and those not only the *speciosa miracula*, as Horace calls them, of transformations, of Scylla, Antiphates, and the Læstrygons, which cannot be represented even in operas; but the prowess of Achilles or Æneas would appear ridiculous in our dwarf-heroes of the theatre. We can believe they routed armies, in Homer or in Virgil; but *ne Hercules contra duos* in the drama. I forbear to instance in many things, which the stage cannot or ought not to represent; for I have said already more than I intended on this subject, and should fear it might be turned against me, that I plead for the pre-eminence of epic poetry, because I have taken some pains in translating Virgil, if this were the first time that I had delivered my opinion in this dispute. But I have more than once already maintained the rights of my two masters against their rivals of the scene,* even while I wrote tragedies myself, and had no thoughts of this present undertaking. I submit my opinion to your judgment, who are better qualified than any man I know, to decide this controversy. You come, my lord, instructed in the cause, and needed not that I should open it. Your "Essay of Poetry,"† which was published without a name, and of which I was not honoured with the confidence, I read over and over with much delight, and as much instruction, and, without flattering you, or making myself more moral than I am — not without some envy. I was loth to be informed how an epic poem should be written, or how a tragedy should be contrived and managed, in better verse, and with more judgment, than I could teach others. A native of Parnassus, and bred up in the studies of its fundamental laws, may receive new light from his contemporaries; but it is a grudging kind of praise which he gives his benefactors. He is more obliged, than he is willing to acknowledge; there is a tincture of malice in his commendations; for where I own I am taught, I confess my want of knowledge. A judge upon the bench may, out of good nature, or at least interest, encourage the pleadings of a puny counsellor; but he does not willingly commend his brother sergeant at the bar, especially when he controls his law, and exposes that ignorance which is made sacred by his place. I gave the unknown author his due commendation, I must confess; but who can answer for me and for the rest of the poets who heard me read the poem,

* "*Bibliopola Tryphon*," a character twice mentioned by Martial, Epig. lib. iv. 72. xiii. 3. Dryden probably means Tonson.

† A Gallicism for the toilet, at which the ladies of Dryden's time, in imitation of their neighbours of France, were wont to receive visits, and hear recitations and readings.

* Dryden, in the "Essay on Dramatic Poesy," maintains the cause of Shakspeare and Jonson against the French dramatists.

† It appeared first in 1682, and drew the public attention by much sound criticism, expressed in pointed language; although the verse is so untunable and rugged, as to sound very disagreeably to modern ears. Dryden is mentioned with only a qualified degree of respect, and that paid solely to his satirical powers:

> The laureat here may justly claim our praise,
> Crown'd by Mac-Flecnoe with immortal bays;
> Yet once his Pegasus has borne dead weight,
> Rid by some lumpish minister of state.

The last couplet alludes to the "Hind and Panther

whether we should not have been better pleased to have seen our own names at the bottom of the title-page? Perhaps we commended it the more, that we might seem to be above the censure. We are naturally displeased with an unknown critic, as the ladies are with a lampooner, because we are bitten in the dark, and know not where to fasten our revenge. But great excellencies will work their way through all sorts of opposition. I applauded rather out of decency, than affection; and was ambitious, as some yet can witness, to be acquainted with a man, with whom I had the honour to converse, and that almost daily, for so many years together. Heaven knows, if I have heartily forgiven you this deceit. You extorted a praise, which I should willingly have given, had I known you. Nothing had been more easy, than to commend a patron of a long standing. The world would join with me, if the encomiums were just; and, if unjust, would excuse a grateful flatterer. But to come anonymous upon me, and force me to commend you against my interest, was not altogether so fair, give me leave to say, as it was politic; for, by concealing your quality, you might clearly understand how your work succeeded, and that the general approbation was given to your merit, not your titles. Thus, like Apelles, you stood unseen behind your own Venus, and received the praises of the passing multitude; the work was commended, not the author; and I doubt not, this was one of the most pleasing adventures of your life.*

I have detained your lordship longer than I intended in this dispute of preference betwixt the epic poem and the drama, and yet have not formally answered any of the arguments which are brought by Aristotle on the other side, and set in the fairest light by Dacier. But I suppose, without looking on the book, I may have touched on some of the objections; for, in this address to your lordship, I design not a treatise of heroic poetry, but write in a loose epistolary way, somewhat tending to that subject, after the example of Horace, in his First Epistle of the Second Book to Augustus Cæsar, and in that to the Pisos, which we call his "Art of Poetry;" in both of which he observes no method that I can trace, whatever Scaliger the father, or Heinsius, may have seen, or rather think they had seen. I have taken up, laid down, and resumed, as often as I pleased, the same subject; and this loose proceeding I shall use through all this prefatory dedication. Yet all this while I have been sailing with some side-wind or other toward the point I proposed in the beginning,—the greatness and excellency of a heroic poem, with some of the difficulties which attend that work. The comparison, therefore, which I made betwixt the epopee and the tragedy, was not altogether a digression; for it is concluded on all hands, that they are both the master-pieces of human wit.

In the mean time, I may be bold to draw this corollary from what has been already said, that the file of heroic poets is very short; all are not such who have assumed that lofty title in ancient or modern ages, or have been so esteemed by their partial and ignorant admirers.

There have been but one great Ilias, and one Æneis, in so many ages. The next, but the next with a long interval betwixt, was the Jerusalem;* I mean not so much in distance of time, as in excellency. After these three are entered, some lord-chamberlain should be appointed, some critic of authority should be set before the door, to keep out a crowd of little poets, who press for admission, and are not of quality. Mævius would be deafening your lordship's ears with his

Fortunam Priami cantabo, et nobile bellum—

mere fustian, as Horace would tell you, from behind, without pressing forward, and more smoke than fire. Pulci, Boiardo, and Ariosto,† would cry out, "Make room for the Italian poets the descendants of Virgil in a right line:" father Le Moine, with his Saint Louis; and Scuderi with his Alaric, for a godly king and a Gothic conqueror; and Chapelain would take it ill that his *Maid* should be refused a place with Helen and

* Our author mentions elsewhere, "The Essay of Poetry, which I publicly valued before I knew the author of it." Although his lordship's experiment proved thus successful, I may be permitted to hint, that most noble authors may find it rather hazardous.

* Tasso's "Jerusalem Delivered" seems to have been the first heroic poem attempted upon a classical model, after the revival of literature.

† Pulci wrote the "Moragante Maggiore," Boiardo the "Orlando Innamorato," and Ariosto the well-known continuation of that poem, called the "Orlando Furioso." The first two poems, like the "Amadigi," and a number of others in the same taste, are rather to be considered as an improvement upon the old metrical romances, than as attempts at epic poetry. At the same time, these authors do not always expect their readers to receive with gravity the marvels which they narrate; but introduce at every turn some ludicrous image, to show how little they are themselves serious. Although Ariosto is immeasurably distinguished by brilliancy of imagination, and beauty of expression, from the rest of those romancers, yet even his delightful work may be more properly termed a romance of chivalry than an epic poem; a distinction which the Tuscan bard can hardly regret, since it has afforded, throughout Europe, more general delight than all the epics in the world, if we except those of Homer and Virgil.

Lavinia.* Spenser† has a better plea for his "Fairy Queen," had his action been finished, or had been one; and Milton, if the Devil had not been his hero, instead of Adam; if the giant had not foiled the knight, and driven him out of his strong hold, to wander through the world with his lady errant; and if there had not been more machining persons than human in his poem. After these, the rest of our English poets shall not be mentioned. I have that honour for them which I ought to have; but, if they are worthies, they are not to be ranked amongst the three whom I have named, and who are established in their reputation.

Before I quitted the comparison betwixt epic poetry and tragedy, I should have acquainted my judge with one advantage of the former over the latter, which I now casually remember, out of the preface of Ségrais before his translation of the Æneis, or out of Bossu, no matter which: "The style of the heroic poem is, and ought to be, more lofty than that of the drama." The critic is certainly in the right, for the reason already urged; the work of tragedy is on the passions, and in a dialogue; both of them abhor strong metaphors, in which the epopee delights. A poet cannot speak too plainly on the stage: for *volat irrevocabile verbum;* the sense is lost, if it be not taken flying. But what we read alone we have leisure to digest; there an author may beautify his sense by the boldness of his expression, which if we understand not fully at the first, we may dwell upon it, till we find the secret force and excellence. That which cures the manners by alterative physic, as I said before, must proceed by insensible degrees; but that which purges the passions, must do its business all at once, or wholly fail of its effect, at least in the present operation, and without repeated doses. We must beat the iron while it is hot, but we may polish it at leisure. Thus, my lord, you pay the fine of my forgetfulness; and yet the merits of both causes are where they were, and undecided, till you declare whether it be more for the benefit of mankind to have their manners in general corrected, or their pride and hard-heartedness removed.

I must now come closer to my present business, and not think of making more invasive wars abroad, when, like Hannibal, I am called back to the defence of my own country. Virgil is attacked by many enemies; he has a whole confederacy against him; and I must endeavour to defend him as well as I am able. But their principal objections being against his moral, the duration or length of time taken up in the action of the poem, and what they have to urge against the manners of his hero; I shall omit the rest as mere cavils of grammarians; at the worst, but casual slips of a great man's pen, or inconsiderable faults of an admirable poem, which the author had not leisure to review before his death. Macrobius has answered what the ancients could urge against him; and some things I have lately read in Tanneguy le Fèvre, Valois, and another whom I name not, which are scarce worth answering. They begin with the moral of his poem, which I have elsewhere confessed, and still must own, not to be so noble as that of Homer.* But let both be fairly stated; and, without contradicting my first opinion, I can show, that Virgil's was as useful to the Romans of his age, as Homer's was to the Grecians of his, in what time soever he may be supposed to have lived and flourished. Homer's moral was to urge the necessity of union, and of a good understanding betwixt confederate states and princes engaged in a war with a mighty monarch; as also of discipline in an army, and obedience in the several chiefs to the supreme commander of the joint forces. To inculcate this, he sets forth the ruinous effects of discord in the camp of those allies, occasioned by the quarrel betwixt

* "La Pucelle D'Orleans." It will hardly, I hope, be expected, that an editor of Dryden should be deeply read in the French epopee, which of all styles of poetry is the most uniformly stiff and freezing.

† That Spenser's twelve champions, each of whom was to achieve a distinct and separate adventure, could ever have been so brought together, as to entitle the "Fairy Queen" to be called a regular epic, may be justly doubted. I confess I think it probable, that the difficulty of concluding his work was one great cause of its being left unfinished.

Dryden's objection to the "Paradise Lost," is founded on the unhappy termination, which is contrary to the rules of the epopee. Even so it has been disputed, whether a tragedy, which ends happily, is properly and regularly entitled to the name. Yet the story is more completely winded up in the "Paradise Lost," than in the "Iliad," where Troy is left standing, after all the battles which are fought about it. Our reverence for the ancients, in this and many other instances, has been driven to superstitious bigotry.

* In the following comparison, our author assumes, that the "Iliad" was actually written with a view to its moral tendency. But considering the matter fairly, and without prejudice, there is as much reason for supposing, that Shakspeare had a great public purpose to accomplish in every one of his plays, which we know were only written to fill the Bull or the Fortune theatres, as the songs of Homer were recited, minstrel-like, for the supply of his daily wants. But both these gifted men had an intuitive knowledge of human nature, which cannot be justly described, without an evident though undesigned moral pressing itself on the hearers. Virgil's poem, however, had certainly a political, if not a moral purpose; for, while it gratified the nobles of the court of Augustus, by deducing their descent from the followers of Æneas, it tamed their republican spirit, by describing the monarchy of the emperor, not as a usurpation, but an hereditary, though interrupted succession, from the wandering Prince of Troy.

the general and one of the next in office under him. Agamemnon gives the provocation, and Achilles resents the injury Both parties are faulty in the quarrel; and accordingly they are both punished: the aggressor is forced to sue for peace to his inferior on dishonourable conditions: the deserter refuses the satisfaction offered; and his obstinacy costs him his best friend. This works the natural effect of choler, and turns his rage against him by whom he was last affronted, and most sensibly. The greater anger expels the rest; but his character is still preserved. In the mean time the Grecian army receives loss on loss, and is half destroyed by a pestilence into the bargain;

Quidquid delirant reges, plectuntur Achivi.

As the poet, in the first part of the example, had shown the bad effects of discord, so, after the reconcilement, he gives the good effects of unity; for Hector is slain, and then Troy must fall. By this it is probable, that Homer lived when the Median monarchy was grown formidable to the Grecians, and that the joint endeavours of his countrymen were little enough to preserve their common freedom from an encroaching enemy. Such was his moral, which all critics have allowed to be more noble than that of Virgil, though not adapted to the times in which the Roman poet lived. Had Virgil flourished in the age of Ennius, and addressed to Scipio, he had probably taken the same moral, or some other not unlike it: for then the Romans were in as much danger from the Carthaginian commonwealth, as the Grecians were from the Assyrian or Median monarchy. But we are to consider him as writing his poem in a time when the old form of government was subverted, and a new one just established by Octavius Cæsar, in effect by force of arms, but seemingly by the consent of the Roman people. The commonwealth had received a deadly wound in the former civil wars betwixt Marius and Sylla. The commons, while the first prevailed, had almost shaken off the yoke of the nobility; and Marius and Cinna, like the captains of the mob, under the specious pretence of the public good, and of doing justice on the oppressors of their liberty, revenged themselves, without form of law, on their private enemies. Sylla, in his turn, proscribed the heads of the adverse party: he too had nothing but liberty and reformation in his mouth; (for the cause of religion is but a modern motive to rebellion, invented by the Christian priesthood, refining on the heathen;*) Sylla, to be sure, meant no more good to the Roman people than Marius before him, whatever he declared; but sacrificed the lives, and took the estates, of all his enemies, to gratify those who brought him into power. Such was the reformation of the government by both parties. The senate and the commons were the two bases on which it stood; and the two champions of either faction, each, destroyed the foundations of the other side; so the fabric, of consequence, must fall betwixt them, and tyranny must be built upon their ruins. This comes of altering fundamental laws and constitutions—like him, who, being in good health, lodged himself in a physician's house, and was over-persuaded by his landlord to take physic, (of which he died,) for the benefit of his doctor. *Stava ben:* (was written on his monument) *ma, per star meglio, sto quì.*

After the death of those two usurpers, the commonwealth seemed to recover, and held up its head for a little time. But it was all the while in a deep consumption, which is a flattering disease. Pompey, Crassus, and Cæsar had found the sweets of arbitrary power; and each being a check to the other's growth, struck up a false friendship among themselves, and divided the government betwixt them, which none of them was able to assume alone. These were the public spirited men o' their age; that is, patriots for their own interest. The commonwealth looked with a florid countenance in their management, spread in bulk, and all the while was wasting in the vitals. Not to trouble your lordship with the repetition of what you know—after the death of Crassus, Pompey found himself outwitted by Cæsar, broke with him, overpowered him in the senate, and caused many unjust decrees to pass against him. Cæsar, thus injured, and unable to resist the faction of the nobles, which was now uppermost, (for he was a Marian,) had recourse to arms; and his cause was just against Pompey, but not against his country, whose constitution ought to have been sacred to him, and never to have been violated on the account of any private wrong. But he prevailed; and, heaven declaring for him, he became a providential monarch, under the title of perpetual dictator. He being murdered by his own son,* whom I neither dare commend, nor can justly blame, (though Dante, in his *Inferno*, has put him and Cassius, and

* This is one of our author's unseemly and far too frequent sneers at the clerical order, for which he is severely reprehended by Milbourne.

* Here again Milbourne is very clamorous for authority, and exclaims, that it is one of the fundamental laws of Parnassus to write true history. Dryden probably rested upon the scandalous tale, that Cæsar intrigued with Servilia, the mother of Brutus; though it seems more likely, that he applied to his assassin the endearing epithet of *my son* merely as a term of affectionate friendship.

Judas Iscariot betwixt them, into the great devil's mouth,) the commonwealth popped up its head for the third time, under Brutus and Cassius, and then sunk for ever.

Thus the Roman people were grossly gulled twice or thrice over, and as often enslaved, in one century, and under the same pretence of reformation. At last the two battles of Philippi gave the decisive stroke against liberty; and, not long after, the commonwealth was turned into a monarchy, by the conduct and good fortune of Augustus. It it is true, that the despotic power could not have fallen into better hands than those of the first and second Cæsar. Your lordship well knows what obligations Virgil had to the latter of them: he saw, beside, that the commonwealth was lost without resource; the heads of it destroyed: the senate new moulded, grown degenerate, and either bought off, or thrusting their own necks into the yoke, out of fear of being forced. Yet I may safely affirm for our great author, (as men of good sense are generally honest,) that he was still of republican principles in his heart,

Secretosque pios, his dantem jura Catonem.*

I think, I need use no other argument to justify my opinion, than that of this one line, taken from the eighth book of the Æneis. If he had not well studied his patron's temper, it might have ruined him with another prince. But Augustus was not discontented, at least that we can find, that Cato was placed, by his own poet, in Elysium, and there giving laws to the holy souls who deserved to be separated from the vulgar sort of good spirits; for his conscience could not but whisper to the arbitrary monarch, that the kings of Rome were at first elective, and governed not without a senate;—that Romulus was no hereditary prince; and though, after his death, he received divine honours for the good he did on earth, yet he was but a god of their own making;—that the last Tarquin was expelled justly for overt acts of tyranny, and mal-administration; for such are the conditions of an elective kingdom: and I meddle not with others, being, for my own opinion, of Montaigne's principles, that an honest man ought to be contented with that form of government, and with those fundamental constitutions of it, which he received from his ancestors, and under which himself was born; though at the same time he confessed freely, that, if he could have chosen his place of birth, it should have been at Venice—which, for many reasons, I dislike, and am better pleased to have been born an Englishman.

But, to return from my long rambling—I say, that Virgil having maturely weighed the condition of the times in which he lived; that an entire liberty was not to be retrieved; that the present settlement had the prospect of a long continuance in the same family, or those adopted into it; that he held his paternal estate from the bounty of the conqueror, by whom he was likewise enriched, esteemed, and cherished; that this conqueror, though of a bad kind, was the very best of it; that the arts of peace flourished under him; that all men might be happy, if they would be quiet; that, now he was in possession of the whole, yet he shared a great part of his authority with the senate; that he would be chosen into the ancient offices of the commonwealth, and ruled by the power which he derived from them, and prorogued his government from time to time, still, as it were, threatening to dismiss himself from public cares, which he exercised more for the common good, than for any delight he took in greatness:—these things, I say, being considered by the poet, he concluded it to be the interest of his country to be so governed; to infuse an awful respect into the people towards such a prince; by that respect to confirm their obedience to him, and by that obedience to make them happy. This was the moral of his divine poem;*—hon-

* The sense which our author has put on this line, has been warmly disputed; many commentators contending, that the elder Cato, called the Censor, and not Cato of Utica, is the person therein honoured. Pope held the same opinion with our poet, and abandoned it; and Spence, quoted by Mr. Malone, thus expresses himself:—"Virgil represents the blessed in Elysium, and Cato giving laws to them. This agrees best with the character of Cato the Censor. See Plutarch's account of the elder Cato; of his strict judgment and laws; of the statue set up to his honour in the temple of Salus, and of the inscription under it, in his life of that great lawgiver. Seneca speaks as highly of him in that capacity, as of Scipio in the military way: *M. Porcius Censorius, quem tam reipublicæ profuit nasci, quam Scipionem; alter enim cum hostibus nostris bellum, alter cum moribus gessit.* Epist. lxxxvii. If Cato Uticensis could have been placed at all in Elysium by Virgil, (who says, that such as kill themselves are in another part of Hades,) he would, at least, be a very improper person to be set by him in so eminent a situation there."

* This is disputed by the learned Heyne. "De *consilio* quod poeta in Æneide conscribenda secutus sit, et de *fine*, quem propositum habuerit, multa varii comminiscuntur. Nihil quidem magis alienum esse potest ab epico carmine quam *allegoria;* jugulat enim totam ejus vim, rerum et hominum dignitatem attenuat, gratum animi errorem excutit, et æstum inter legendum refrigerat, voluptatemque omnem intercipit. Certatim tamen viri docti argutiis suis Æneæ per somnum nobis eripere, et Augustum submittere allaborarunt. Etiam ex parata nova in Latio sede miseros Trojanos exturbarunt: adumbratum esse, a poeta novum tum Romæ constitutum unius principatum. Simili acumine alii arcana. nescio quæ, dominationis Augusteæ consilia, in Æneide condenda deprehendere sibi visi sunt. Ita

ent in the poet; honourable to the emperor, whom he derives from a divine extraction; and reflecting part of that honour on the Roman people, whom he derives also from the Trojans; and not only profitable, but necessary, to the present age, and likely to be such to their posterity. That it was the received opinion, that the Romans were descended from the Trojans, and Julius Cæsar from Iülus the son of Æneas, was enough for Virgil; though perhaps he thought not so himself, or that Æneas ever was in Italy; which Bochartus manifestly proves. And Homer, where he says that Jupiter hated the house of Priam, and was resolved to transfer the kingdom to the family of Æneas, yet mentions nothing of his leading a colony into a foreign country, and settling there. But that the Romans valued themselves on their Trojan ancestry, is so undoubted a truth, that I need not prove it. Even the seals which we have remaining of Julius Cæsar, which we know to be antique, have the star of Venus over them (though they were all graven after his death,) as a note that he was deified. I doubt not but one reason, why Augustus should be so passionately concerned for the preservation of the Æneïs, which its author had condemned to be burnt, as an imperfect poem, by his last will and testament, was, because it did him a real service, as well as an honour; that a work should not be lost, where his divine original was celebrated in verse, which had the character of immortality stamped upon it.

Neither were the great Roman families, which flourished in his time, less obliged by him than the emperor. Your lordship knows with what address he makes mention of them,* as captains of ships, or leaders in the war; and even some of Italian extraction are not forgotten. These are the single stars which are sprinkled through the Æneïs: but there are whole constellations of them in the Fifth Book. And I could not but take notice, when I translated it, of some favourite families to which he gives the victory and awards the prizes, in the person of his hero, at the funeral games which

Spencius, elegantis ingenii vir, [Polymetis, Dial. iii. p. 17. sqq.] πολιτικὸν epos esse Æneidem sibi persuasum habebat; neque aliud quicquam poetam spectasse, quam ut animis libertatis ereptæ desiderio ægris fomenta admoveret, et novum principem approbaret. Nihil tamen Æneæ personam, fortunam, facta, et fata habere videas, quod ei consilio respondeat; nullus in Æneide populus est liber, qui dominum accipiat; nulla regni seu imperii, monarchiam vocamus, bona videas exposita aut commendata; verbo nihil occurrit, quo libertatis amore contacti animi adduci aut allici possint, ut a bono principe malint tuto regnari quam cum libertatis vano nomine paucorum potentium dominatione vexari. In Juliæ gentis honorem, quæ ab Iulo Æneæ filio originem ducere videri volebat, nonnulla passim suaviter memorari, ad Augusti laudes ingeniose alia inseri, ipsa carminis lectione manifestum sit, et a veteribus quoque Grammaticis jam monitum est locis pluribus; sed, quantam vim ea res ad dominationem Augusti commmendandam habere potuerit, mihi non satis constare lubenter fateor. Neque, si nova Æneæ sedes in Latio divinis humanisque juribus vallata fuerit, quale inde propugnaculum novo Augusti regno partum sit, intelligo; ut adeo, si demonstrari hoc possit, poetæ consilium illud in Æneide condenda propositum fuisse, parum feliciter eum in eo perficiendo et exsequendo versatum videri dicerem.

"In eandem tamen opinionem jam ante Spencium inciderat vir doctus inter Francogallos, [L'Abbé Vatry,] qui inprimis similitudinem inter Æneæ et Augusti personam et fortunam diserte persequitur. Ingeniose eum ludere non neges; et convenit ei cum multis aliis doctis viris, qui opinantur, Augustum sub Æneæ persona esse adumbratum; eo referunt multa alia. Videas nonnullos tam egregie sibi placere in hoc invento, ut undique conquirant et venentur ea, quæ ad Augustum accommodari possint. Sic oris dignitas, (lib. i. 589, *Os humerosque deo*,) cum assentatione in Augustum memorata est. Ignoscenda hæc putem alicui ex media assentatorum turba, qui Æneide lecta unam vel alteram Æneæ laudem ad Augustum traheret, ut Principi palparet. Sed, ut Maro tam dissimiles personas, fortunas, virtutes, et facta ac res gestas, inter se comparare voluerit, mihi quidem, si ejus judicium et elegantiam recte teneo, parum probabile videtur. Sapientior erat poeta, et rei poeticæ intelligentior, quam ut talem cogitationem in animum admitteret. Nam præterquam quod Æneæ characterem non invenit, sed ab aliis jam traditum accepit, circumspiciendæ erant a poeta virtutes Æneæ ejusmodi, quæ in epico argumento vim et splendorem haberent, et factorum, quæ enarranda erant, caussas idoneas suppeditarent. Quod si ille studium suum ponere voluisset maxime in hoc, et Æneas Augusto assimularetur, quam multa et quam parum consentanea epicæ narrationi, argumento, operis characteri, temporum rationi, illaturus in carmen suum fuisset!

"Eadem fere via carmen πολιτικὸν conditum a poeta visum jam olim erat R. Patri le Bossu, ut Romanos partim ad amplectendum et probandum præsentem rerum statum adducere, partim Augustum ad moderationem ac clementiam adhortari, et a dominationis libidine et impotentia revocare voluerit. Sed nec huic consilio ulla ex parte respondet Æneidis sive argumentum sive tractatio: profugus ex urbe incensa Æneas novam sedem quærit, armis vim illatam propulsat, et sic porro; quid tandem his inest, quod ad imperandi artes ac virtutes spectet? Fabulæ tamen Virgilianæ universe inesse, et in singulis carminis partibus aut locis ac versibus occurrere talia, quæ principibus pro salubribus præceptis commendari possint, nemo neget; quin potius inter utilitates, quæ poetarum carminibus debentur, præcipue hoc commemorandum est. Verum non propterea dici potest ac debet, in condendo carmine et in fabula deligenda et ordinanda tale præceptum propositum poetæ fuisse, cujus explicandi, caussa narrationem institueret. Narrare ille voluit ac debuit rem magnam et arduam et mirabilem. Quod narratio illa, et delectatio quæ inde accipitur, cum utilitate ad omnes hominum ordines, inprimisque ad principum animos conjuncta est, hoc epicæ narrationi per se consentaneum est; ipsa enim rei natura ita fert, ut magnorum virorum facta magna et præclara sine summo ad hominum animos, mores ac virtutem, fructu exponi et narrari nequeant, multo magis si cum sententiarum splendore et orationis ornatu instituta sit narratio."—*Virg.* a C. G. Heyne, Disquisit. i. de Carm. Epico.

were celebrated in honour of Anchises. I insist not on their names; but am pleased to find the Memmii amongst them, derived from Mnestheus, because Lucretius dedicates to one of that family, a branch of which destroyed Corinth. I likewise either found or formed an image to myself of the contrary kind; that those, who lost the prizes, were such as had disobliged the poet, or were in disgrace with Augustus, or enemies to Mæcenas; and this was the poetical revenge he took: for *genus irritabile vatum*, as Horace says.* When a poet is thoroughly provoked, he will do himself justice, however dear it cost him; *animamque in vulnere ponit.* I think these are not bare imaginations of my own, though I find no trace of them in the commentators; but one poet may judge of another by himself. The vengeance we defer, is not forgotten. I hinted before that the whole Roman people were obliged by Virgil, in deriving them from Troy; an ancestry which they affected. We and the French are of the same humour: they would be thought to descend from a son, I think, of Hector; and we would have our Britain both named and planted by a descendant of Æneas. Spenser favours this opinion what he can. His Prince Arthur, or whoever he intends by him, is a Trojan. Thus the hero of Homer was a Grecian, of Virgil a Roman, of Tasso an Italian.

I have transgressed my bounds, and gone farther than the moral led me; but, if your lordship is not tired, I am safe enough.

Thus far, I think, my author is defended. But, as Augustus is still shadowed in the person of Æneas, (of which I shall say more, when I come to the manners which the poet gives his hero,) I must prepare that subject, by showing how dexterously he managed both the prince and people, so as to displease neither, and to do good to both; which is the part of a wise and an honest man, and proves, that it is possible for a courtier not to be a knave. I shall continue still to speak my thoughts like a free-born subject, as I am; though such things, perhaps, as no Dutch commentator could, and I am sure no Frenchman durst. I have already told your lordship my opinion of Virgil, that he was no arbitrary man. Obliged he was to his master for his bounty; and he repays him with good counsel, how to behave himself in his new monarchy, so as to gain the affections of his subjects, and deserve to be called the father of his country. From this consideration it is, that he chose, for the ground-work of his poem, one empire destroyed, and another raised from the ruins of it. This was just the parallel. Æneas could not pretend to be Priam's heir in a lineal succession; for Anchises, the hero's father, was only of the second branch of the royal family; and Helenus, a son of Priam, was yet surviving, and might lawfully claim before him. It may be, Virgil mentions him on that account. Neither has he forgotten Priamus, in the fifth of his Æneis, the son of Polites, youngest son to Priam, who was slain by Pyrrhus, in the Second Book. Æneas had only married Creüsa, Priam's daughter, and by her could have no title, while any of the male issue were remaining. In this case, the poet gave him the next title, which is that of an elective king. The remaining Trojans chose him to lead them forth, and settle them in some foreign country. Ilioneus, in his speech to Dido, calls him expressly by the name of king. Our poet, who all this while had Augustus in his eye, had no desire he should seem to succeed by any right of inheritance derived from Julius Cæsar, (such a title being but one degree removed from conquest,) for what was introduced by force, by force may be removed. It was better for the people that they should give, than he should take; since that gift was indeed no more at bottom than a trust. Virgil gives us an example of this in the person of Mezentius: he governed arbitrarily; he was expelled, and came to the deserved end of all tyrants. Our author shows us another sort of kingship in the person of Latinus: he was descended from Saturn, and, as I remember, in the third degree. He is described as a just and gracious prince, solicitous for the welfare of his people, always consulting with his senate to promote the common good. We find him at the head of them, when he enters into the council-hall, speaking first, but still demanding their advice, and steering by it, as far as the iniquity of the times would suffer him. And this is the proper character of a king by inheritance, who is born a father of his country. Æneas, though he married the heiress of the crown, yet claimed no title to it during the life of his father-in-law. *Pater arma Latinus habeto,* &c. are Virgil's words. As for himself, he was contented to take care of his country gods, who were not those of Latium: wherein our divine author seems to relate to the after-practice of the Romans, which was to adopt the gods of those they conquered, or received as members of their commonwealth. Yet, withal, he plainly touches at the office of the high priesthood, with which Augustus

* I suspect our author spoke from recollection of some of his own satirical strokes. Even in the "Hind and Panther," Sunderland, a convert to the religion defended by the poet, and Petre, the king's own chaplain and bosom counsellor, do not escape

was invested, and which made his person more sacred and inviolable, than even the tribunitial power. It was not therefore for nothing, that the most judicious of all poets made that office vacant by the death of Panthûs in the Second Book of the Æneis, for his hero to succeed in it, and consequently for Augustus to enjoy. I know not that any of the commentators have taken notice of that passage. If they have not, I am sure they ought; and if they have, I am not indebted to them for the observation. The words of Virgil are very plain:

Sacra, suosque tibi commendat Troja penates.

As for Augustus, or his uncle Julius, claiming by descent from Æneas, that title is already out of doors. Æneas succeeded not, but was elected. Troy was fore doomed to fall for ever.

Postquam res Asiæ Priamique evertere gentem
Immeritam visum superis.—*Æneis*, lib. iii. v. 1.

Augustus, it is true, had once resolved to rebuild that city, and there to make the seat of empire: but Horace writes an ode on purpose to deter him from that thought; declaring the place to be accursed, and that the gods would as often destroy it, as it should be raised.* Hereupon the emperor laid aside a project so ungrateful to the Roman people. But by this, my lord, we may conclude, that he had still his pedigree in his head, and had an itch of being thought a divine king, if his poets had not given him better counsel.

I will pass by many less material objections, for want of room to answer them; what follows next is of great importance, if the critics can make out their charge; for it is levelled at the manners which our poet gives his hero, and which are the same which were eminently seen in his Augustus. Those manners were, piety to the gods, and a dutiful affection to his father, love to his relations, care of his people, courage and conduct in the wars, gratitude to those who had obliged him, and justice in general to mankind.

Piety, as your lordship sees, takes place of all, as the chief part of his character; and the word in Latin is more full than it can possibly be expressed in any modern language; for there it comprehends not only devotion to the gods, but filial love, and tender affection to relations of all sorts. As instances of this, the deities of Troy, and his own Penates, are made the companions of his flight: they appear to him in his voyage, and advise him; and at last he replaces them in Italy, their native country. For his father, he takes him on his back: he leads his little son: his wife follows him; but, losing his footsteps through fear or ignorance, he goes back into the midst of his enemies to find her, and leaves not his pursuit until her ghost appears, to forbid his farther search. I will say nothing of his duty to his father while he lived, his sorrow for his death, of the games instituted in honour of his memory, or seeking him, by his command, even after his death, in the Elysian fields. I will not mention his tenderness for his son, which everywhere is visible—of his raising a tomb for Polydorus, the obsequies for Misenus, his pious remembrance of Deïphobus, the funerals of his nurse, his grief for Pallas, and his revenge taken on his murderer, whom otherwise, by his natural compassion, he had forgiven: and then the poem had been left imperfect; for we could have had no certain prospect of his happiness, while the last obstacle to it was unremoved. Of the other parts which compose his character, as a king, or as a general, I need say nothing; the whole Æneis is one continued instance of some one or other of them; and where I find any thing of them taxed, it shall suffice me, as briefly as I can, to vindicate my divine master to your lordship, and by you to the reader. But herein Ségrais, in his admirable preface to his translation of the Æneis, as the author of the Dauphin's Virgil justly calls it, has prevented me. Him I follow, and what I borrow from him, am ready to acknowledge to him. For, impartially speaking, the French are as much better critics than the English, as they are worse poets. Thus we generally allow, that they better understand the management of a war than our islanders; but we know we are superior to them in the day of battle. They value themselves on their generals, we on our soldiers. But this is not the proper place to decide that question, if they make it one. I shall perhaps say as much of other nations, and their poets, excepting only Tasso; and hope to make my assertion good, which is but doing justice to my country; part of which honour will reflect on your lordship, whose thoughts are always just, your numbers harmonious, your words chosen, your expressions strong and manly, your verse flowing, and your turns as happy as they are easy. If you would set us more copies, your examples would make all precepts needless. In the mean time, that little you have written is owned, and that particularly by the poets, (who are a nation not over lavish of praise to their contemporaries,) as a principal ornament of our language; but the sweetest essences are always confined in the smallest glasses.

When I speak of your lordship, it is never a digression, and therefore I need beg no pardon

* The prophecy of Juno in the Third Ode of the Third Book.

for it; but take up Segrais where I left him, and shall use him less often than I have occasion for him; for his preface is a perfect piece of criticism, full and clear, and digested into an exact method; mine is loose, and, as I intended it, epistolary. Yet I dwell on many things, which he durst not touch; for it is dangerous to offend an arbitrary master; and every patron, who has the power of Augustus, has not his clemency. In short, my lord, I would not translate him, because I would bring you somewhat of my own. His notes and observations on every book are of the same excellency; and, for the same reason, I omit the greater part.

He takes notice that Virgil is arraigned for placing piety before valour, and making that piety the chief character of his hero. I have said already from Bossu, that a poet is not obliged to make his hero a virtuous man; therefore, neither Homer nor Tasso are to be blamed, for giving what predominant quality they pleased to their first character. But Virgil, who designed to form a perfect prince, and would insinuate that Augustus, whom he calls Æneas in his poem, was truly such, found himself obliged to make him without blemish, thoroughly virtuous; and a thorough virtue both begins and ends in piety. Tasso, without question, observed this before me, and therefore split his hero in two: he gave Godfrey piety, and Rinaldo fortitude, for their chief qualities or manners. Homer, who had chosen another moral, makes both Agamemnon and Achilles vicious; for his design was to instruct in virtue, by showing the deformity of vice. I avoid repetition of what I have said above. What follows, is translated literally from Ségrais.

"Virgil had considered, that the greatest virtues of Augustus consisted in the perfect art of governing his people; which caused him to reign for more than forty years in great felicity. He considered, that his emperor was valiant, civil, popular, eloquent, politic, and religious; he has given all these qualities to Æneas. But, knowing that piety alone comprehends the whole duty of man towards the gods, towards his country, and towards his relations, he judged, that this ought to be his first character, whom he would set for a pattern of perfection. In reality, they who believed that the praises which arise from valour are superior to those which proceed from any other virtues, have not considered, (as they ought,) that valour, destitute of other virtues, cannot render a man worthy of any true esteem. That quality, which signifies no more than an intrepid courage, may be separated from many others which are good, and accompanied with many which are ill. A man may be very valiant, and yet impious and vicious. But the same cannot be said of piety, which excludes all ill qualities, and comprehends even valour itself, with all other qualities which are good. Can we, for example, give the praise of valour to a man, who should see his gods profaned, and should want the courage to defend them? to a man, who should abandon his father, or desert his king, in his last necessity?"

Thus far Ségrais, in giving the preference to piety before valour. I will now follow him, where he considers this valour, or intrepid courage, singly in itself; and this also Virgil gives to his Æneas, and that in a heroical degree.

Having first concluded, that our poet did for the best in taking the first character of his hero from that essential virtue on which the rest depend, he proceeds to tell us, that, in the ten years' war of Troy, he was considered as the second champion of his country, (allowing Hector the first place;) and this, even by the confession of Homer, who took all occasions of setting up his own countrymen, the Grecians, and of undervaluing the Trojan chiefs. But Virgil (whom Ségrais forgot to cite) makes Diomede give him a higher character for strength and courage. His testimony is this, in the Eleventh Book:

> Stetimus tela aspera contra,
> Contulimusque manus: experto credite, quantus
> In clypeum assurgat, quo turbine torqueat hastam.
> Si duo præterea tales Idæa tulisset
> Terra viros, ultro Inachias venisset ad urbes
> Dardanus, et versis lugeret Græcia fatis.
> Quidquid apud duræ cessatum est mœnia Trojæ,
> Hectoris Æneæque manu victoria Graiûm
> Hæsit, et in decimum vestigia retulit annum.
> Ambo animis, ambo insignes præstantibus armis:
> Hic pietate prior.

I give not here my translation of these verses, (though I think I have not ill succeeded in them,) because your lordship is so great a master of the original, that I have no reason to desire you should see Virgil and me so near together; but you may please, my lord, to take notice, that the Latin author refines upon the Greek, and insinuates, that Homer had done his hero wrong, in giving the advantage of the duel to his own countryman; though Diomede was manifestly the second champion of the Grecians; and Ulysses preferred him before Ajax, when he chose him for the companion of his nightly expedition; for he had a headpiece of his own, and wanted only the fortitude of another, to bring him off with safety, and that he might compass his design with honour.

The French translator thus proceeds: "They, who accuse Æneas for want of courage, either understand not Virgil, or have read him slightly; otherwise they would not raise an objection so easy to be answered." Hereupon he gives so many instances of the hero's valour, that to repeat them after him would tire your lordship, and put me to the unnecessary trouble of transcribing the greatest part of the last three Æneids. In short, more could not be expected from an Amadis, a Sir Lancelot, or the whole Round Table, than he performs. *Proxima quæque metit gladio*, is the perfect account of a knight-errant. "If it be replied," continues Ségrais, "that it was not difficult for him to undertake and achieve such hardy enterprises, because he wore enchanted arms; that accusation, in the first place, must fall on Homer, ere it can reach Virgil." Achilles was as well provided with them as Æneas, though he was invulnerable without them.* And Ariosto, the two Tassos, (Bernardo and Torquato,) even our own Spenser—in a word, all modern poets—have copied Homer as well as Virgil: he is neither the first nor last, but in the midst of them; and therefore is safe, if they are so. "Who knows," says Ségrais, "but that his fated armour was only an allegorical defence, and signified no more than that he was under the peculiar protection of the gods? born, as the astrologers will tell us out of Virgil, (who was well versed in the Chaldean mysteries,) under the favourable influence of Jupiter, Venus, and the Sun." But I insist not on this, because I know you believe not there is such an art; though not only Horace and Persius, but Augustus himself, thought otherwise. But, in defence of Virgil, I dare positively say, that he has been more cautious in this particular than either his predecessor or his descendants: for Æneas was actually wounded, in the Twelfth of the Æneis; though he had the same godsmith† to forge his arms as had Achilles. It seems he was no *warlock*,‡ as the Scots commonly call such men, who, they say, are iron-free, or lead-free. Yet, after this experiment, that his arms were not impenetrable—when he was cured indeed by his mother's help, because he was that day to conclude the war by the death of Turnus—the poet durst not carry the miracle too far, and restore him wholly to his former vigour; he was still too weak to overtake his enemy; yet we see with what courage he attacks Turnus, when he faces and renews the combat. I need say no more; for Virgil defends himself without needing my assistance, and proves his hero truly to deserve that name. He was not then a second-rate champion, as they would have him, who think fortitude the first virtue in a hero. But, being beaten from this hold, they will not yet allow him to be valiant, because he wept more often, as they think, than well becomes a man of courage.

In the first place, if tears are arguments of cowardice, what shall I say of Homer's hero? Shall Achilles pass for timorous, because he wept, and wept on less occasions than Æneas? Herein Virgil must be granted to have excelled his master. For once both heroes are described lamenting their lost loves: Briseïs was taken away by force from the Grecians; Creüsa was lost for ever to her husband. But Achilles went roaring along the salt-sea-shore, and, like a booby, was complaining to his mother, when he should have revenged his injury by arms. Æneas took a nobler course; for having secured his father and his son, he repeated all his former dangers, to have found his wife, if she had been above ground. And here your lordship may observe the address of Virgil; it was not for nothing that this passage was related with all these tender circumstances. Æneas told it: Dido heard it. That he had been so affectionate a husband, was no ill argument to the coming dowager, that he might prove as kind to her. Virgil has a thousand secret beauties, though I have not leisure to remark them.

Ségrais, on this subject of a hero shedding tears, observes, that historians commend Alexander for weeping when he read the mighty actions of Achilles; and Julius Cæsar is likewise praised, when, out of the same noble envy, he wept at the victories of Alexander. But, if we observe more closely, we shall find, that the tears of Æneas were always on a laudable occasion. Thus he weeps out of compassion and tenderness of nature, when, in the temple of Carthage, he beholds the pictures of his friends, who sacrificed their lives in defence of their country. He deplores the lamentable end of his pilot Palinurus, the untimely death of young Pallas his confederate, and the rest, which I omit. Yet, even for these tears his wretched critics dare condemn him. They make Æneas

* Dryden had forgot, what he must certainly have known, that the fiction of Achilles being invulnerable, bears date long posterior to the days of Homer. In the Iliad he is actually wounded.

† The same compound is used in "Absalom and Achitophel," as has been noticed by Mr. Malone.

> Gods they had tried of every shape and size,
> That godsmiths could produce, or priests devise.

‡ The Scots, about Dryden's time, had many superstitions concerning individuals, whom they supposed to be shot-proof, by virtue of a satanic charm. The famous Viscount of Dundee was supposed to be invulnerable to bullets of lead; and when Archbishop Sharpe was murdered, the assassins having missed him, although very near when they first discharged their pieces, imputed the scorched marks left by the powder on his skin to contusions received from their balls. But the word *warlock*, or *warlough*, means a male sorcerer in general; and has not, as Dryden seems to suppose, any reference to this particular charm. It seems rather to be derived from *wird* and *laere*, a compound which would imply "skilled in futurity."

little better than a kind of St. Swithin* hero, always raining. One of these censors is bold enough to argue him of cowardice, when, in the beginning of the first book, he not only weeps, but trembles, at an approaching storm—

> Extemplo Æneæ solvuntur frigore membra:
> Ingemit; et duplices tendens ad sidera palmas, &c.

But to this I have answered formerly, that his fear was not for himself, but for his people. And what can give a sovereign a better commendation, or recommend a hero more to the affection of the reader? They were threatened with a tempest, and he wept; he was promised Italy, and therefore he prayed for the accomplishment of that promise:—all this in the beginning of a storm; therefore he showed the more early piety, and the quicker sense of compassion. Thus much I have urged elsewhere in the defence of Virgil; and, since, I have been informed by Mr. Moyle,† a young gentleman whom I can never sufficiently commend, that the ancients accounted drowning an accursed death; so that, if we grant him to have been afraid, he had just occasion for that fear, both in relation to himself and his subjects. I think our adversaries can carry this argument no farther, unless they tell us, that he ought to have had more confidence in the promise of the gods; but how was he assured, that he had understood their oracles aright? Helenus might be mistaken; Phœbus might speak doubtfully; even his mother might flatter him, that he might prosecute his voyage, which, if it succeeded happily, he should be the founder of an empire; for, that she herself was doubtful of his fortune, is apparent by the address she made to Jupiter on his behalf; to which the god makes answer in these words:

> Parce metû, Cytherea: manent immota tuorum
> Fata tibi, &c.

Notwithstanding which, the goddess, though comforted, was not assured; for, even after this, through the course of the whole Æneis, she still apprehends the interest which Juno might make with Jupiter against her son. For it was a moot point in heaven, whether he could alter fate, or not. And indeed some passages in Virgil would make us suspect, that he was of opinion Jupiter might defer fate, though he could not alter it; for, in the latter end of the Tenth Book, he introduces Juno begging for the life of Turnus, and flattering her husband with the power of changing destiny: *Tua, qui potes, orsa reflectas!* To which he gracefully answers:

> Si mora præsentis leti, tempusque caduco
> Oratur juveni, meque hoc ita ponere sentis,
> Tolle fuga Turnum, atque instantibus eripe fatis.
> Hactenus indulsisse vacat. Sin altior istis
> Sub precibus venia ulla latet, totumque moveri
> Mutarive putas bellum, spes pascis inanes.

But, that he could not alter those decrees, the king of gods himself confesses, in the book above cited, when he comforts Hercules for the death of Pallas, who had invoked his aid, before he threw his lance at Turnus—

> Trojæ sub mœnibus altis.
> Tot nati cecidere deûm; quin occidit una
> Sarpedon, mea progenies. Etiam sua Turnum
> Fata manent, metasque dati pervenit ad ævi—

where he plainly acknowledges, that he could not save his own son, or prevent the death which he foresaw. Of his power to defer the blow, I once occasionally discoursed with that excellent person Sir Robert Howard,* who is better conversant than any man that I know, in the doctrine of the Stoics; and he set me right, from the concurrent testimony of philosophers and poets, that Jupiter could not retard the effects of fate, even for a moment. For, when I cited Virgil, as favouring the contrary opinion in that verse:

> Tolle fuga Turnum, atque instantibus eripe fatis—

he replied, and, I think, with exact judgment, that when Jupiter gave Juno leave to withdraw Turnus from the present danger, it was because he certainly foreknew that his fatal hour was not come; that it was in destiny for Juno at that time to save him; and that himself obeyed destiny, in giving her that leave.

I need say no more in justification of our hero's courage, and am much deceived, if he ever be attacked on this side of his character again. But he is arraigned with more show of reason by the ladies, who will make a numerous party against him, for being false to love, in forsaking Dido. And I cannot much blame them; for, to say the truth, it is an ill precedent for their gallants to follow. Yet, if I can bring him off with flying colours, they may learn experience at her cost, and, for her sake, avoid a cave, as the worst shelter they can choose from a shower of rain, especially when they have a lover in their company.

In the first place, Ségrais observes, with much acuteness, that they who blame Æneas for his

* The vulgar, to use Gay's account, believe,
How if on Swithin's feast the welkin lowers,
And every pent house streams with hasty showers;
Twice twenty days shall clouds their fleeces drain,
And wash the pavement with incessant rain.

† The son of Sir Walter Moyle, an accomplished scholar, whom Dryden elsewhere mentions with esteem. He died in 1621.

* It is agreeable to see, from this and other passages, that, notwithstanding an intervening rupture, our author, at the latter end of his life, was on good terms with his brother-in-law, to whom he was so much indebted at the commencement of his poetical career.

insensibility of love when he left Carthage, contradict their former accusation of him, for being always crying, compassionate, and effeminately sensible of those misfortunes which befell others. They give him two contrary characters; but Virgil makes him of a piece, always grateful, always tender-hearted. But they are impudent enough to discharge themselves of this blunder, by laying the contradiction at Virgil's door. He, say they, has shown his hero with these inconsistent characters, acknowledging and ungrateful, compassionate and hard-hearted, but, at the bottom, fickle and self-interested; for Dido had not only received his weather-beaten troops, before she saw him, and given them her protection, but had also offered them an equal share in her dominion—

> Vultis et his mecum pariter considere regnis?
> Urbem quam statuo, vestra est.

This was an obligement never to be forgotten; and the more to be considered, because antecedent to her love. That passion, it is true, produced the usual effects, of generosity, gallantry, and care to please; and thither we refer them. But, when she had made all these advances, it was still in his power to have refused them: after the intrigue of the cave, (call it marriage, or enjoyment only,) he was no longer free to take or leave; he had accepted the favour, and was obliged to be constant, if he would be grateful.

My lord, I have set this argument in the best light I can, that the ladies may not think I write booty; and perhaps it may happen to me, as it did to Doctor Cudworth,* who has raised such strong objections against the being of a God, and Providence, that many think he has not answered them. You may please at least to hear the adverse party. Ségrais pleads for Virgil, that no less than an absolute command from Jupiter could excuse this insensibility of the hero, and this abrupt departure, which looks so like extreme ingratitude. But, at the same time, he does wisely to remember you, that Virgil had made piety the first character of Æneas; and, this being allowed, (as I am afraid it must, he was obliged, antecedent to all other considerations, to search an asylum for his gods in Italy—for those very gods, I say, who had promised to his race the universal empire. Could a pious man dispense with the commands of Jupiter, to satisfy his passion, or (take it in the strongest sense) to comply with the obligations of his gratitude? Religion, it is true, must have moral honesty for its ground-work, or we shall be apt to suspect its truth; but an immediate revelation dispenses with all duties of morality. All casuists agree that theft is a breach of the moral law; yet, if I might presume to mingle things sacred with profane, the Israelites only spoiled the Egyptians, not robbed them, because the propriety was transferred by a revelation to their lawgiver. I confess, Dido was a very infidel in this point; for she would not believe, as Virgil makes her say, that ever Jupiter would send Mercury on such an immoral errand. But this needs no answer, at least no more than Virgil gives it—

> Fata obstant; placidasque viri Deus obstruit aures.

This notwithstanding, as Ségrais confesses, he might have shown a little more sensibility when he left her; for that had been according to his character.

But let Virgil answer for himself. He still loved her, and struggled with his inclinations, to obey the gods:

> Curam sub corde premebat,
> Multa gemens, magnoque animum labefactus amore.

Upon the whole matter, and humanly speaking, I doubt there was a fault somewhere; and Jupiter is better able to bear the blame, than either Virgil or Æneas. The poet, it seems, had found it out, and therefore brings the deserting hero and the forsaken lady to meet together in the lower regions, where he excuses himself when it is too late; and accordingly she will take no satisfaction, nor so much as hear him. Now Ségrais is forced to abandon his defence, and excuses his author, by saying, that the Æneis is an imperfect work, and that death prevented the divine poet from reviewing it; and for that reason he had condemned it to the fire;* though, at the same time, his two translators must acknowledge, that the Sixth Book is the most correct of the whole Æneis. Oh! how convenient is a machine sometimes in a heroic poem! This of Mercury is plainly one; and Virgil was constrained to use it here, or the honesty of his hero would be ill defended. And the fair sex, however, if they had the deserter in their power, would certainly have shown him no more mercy than the Bacchanals did Orpheus: for, if too much constancy may be a fault sometimes, then want of constancy, and ingratitude after the last favour, is a crime that never will be forgiven. But, of machines, more in their proper place; where I shall show with how much judgment they have been used by Virgil; and,

* Author of the "True Intellectual System of the Universe," folio, 1678.

* Milbourn is very severe on our author for crediting this story, of Virgil having condemned the Æneid to the flames. But it is sanctioned by the Elder Pliny. "*D. Augustus carmina Virgilii cremari contra testamenti ejus verecundiam, vetuit; majusque ita vati testimonium contigit, quam si ipse probasset.*"—*Hist. Nat.* viii. 30.

in the mean time, pass to another article of his defence, on the present subject; where, if I cannot clear the hero, I hope at least to bring off the poet; for here I must divide their causes. Let Æneas trust to his machine, which will only help to break his fall; but the address is incomparable. Plato, who borrowed so much from Homer, and yet concluded for the banishment of all poets, would at least have rewarded Virgil, before he sent him into exile. But I go farther, and say, that he ought to be acquitted, and deserved, besides, the bounty of Augustus, and the gratitude of the Roman people. If, after this, the ladies will stand out, let them remember, that the jury is not all agreed; for Octavia was of his party, and was of the first quality in Rome; she was also present at the reading of the Sixth Æneid; and we know not that she condemned Æneas; but we are sure she presented the poet, for his admirable elegy on her son Marcellus.

But let us consider the secret reasons which Virgil had, for thus framing this noble episode, wherein the whole passion of love is more exactly described than in any other poet. Love was the theme of his Fourth Book; and, though it is the shortest of the whole Æneis, yet there he has given its beginning, its progress, its traverses, and its conclusion; and had exhausted so entirely this subject, that he could resume it but very slightly in the eight ensuing books.

She was warmed with the graceful appearance of the hero; she smothered those sparkles out of decency; but conversation blew them up into a flame. Then she was forced to make a confidant of her whom she best might trust, her own sister, who approves the passion, and thereby augments it: then succeeds her public owning it; and, after that, the consummation. O Venus and Juno, Jupiter and Mercury, I say nothing; for they were all machining work; but, possession having cooled his love, as it increased hers, she soon perceived the change, or at least grew suspicious of a change; this suspicion soon turned to jealousy, and jealousy to rage; then she disdains and threatens, and again is humble, and entreats, and, nothing availing, despairs, curses, and at last becomes her own executioner. See here the whole process of that passion, to which nothing can be added. I dare go no farther, lest I should lose the connexion of my discourse.*

To love our native country, and to study its benefit and its glory, to be interested in its concerns, is natural to all men, and is indeed our common duty. A poet makes a farther step; for, endeavouring to do honour to it, it is allowable in him even to be partial in its cause; for he is not tied to truth, or fettered by the laws of history. Homer and Tasso are justly praised for choosing their heroes out of Greece and Italy. Virgil indeed made his a Trojan; but it was to derive the Romans and his own Augustus from him. But all the three poets are manifestly partial to their heroes, in favour of their country; for Dares Phrygius reports of Hector, that he was slain cowardly: Æneas, according to the best account, slew not Mezentius, but was slain by him; and the chronicles of Italy tell us little of that Rinaldo d'Estete, who conquers Jerusalem in Tasso. He might be a champion of the church; but we know not that he was so much as present at the siege. To apply this to Virgil, he thought himself engaged in honour to espouse the cause and quarrel of his country against Carthage. He knew he could not please the Romans better, or oblige them more to patronize his poem, than by disgracing the foundress of that city. He shows her ungrateful to the memory of her first husband; doting on a stranger; enjoyed, and afterwards forsaken by him. This was the original, says he, of the immortal hatred betwixt the two rival nations. It is true, he colours the falsehood of Æneas by an express command from Jupiter to forsake the queen, who had obliged him; but he knew the Romans were to be his readers; and them he bribed, perhaps at the expense of his hero's honesty; but he gained his cause, however, as pleading before corrupt judges. They were content to see their founder false to love; for still he had the advantage of the amour; it was their enemy whom he forsook; and she might have forsaken him, if he had not got the start of her; she had already forgotten her vows to her Sichæus; and *varium et mutabile semper femina*, is the sharpest satire, in the fewest words, that ever was made on woman-kind; for both the adjectives are neuter, and *animal* must be understood, to make them grammar. Virgil does well to put those words into the mouth of Mercury. If a god had not spoken them, neither durst he have written them, nor I translated them. Yet the deity was forced to come twice on the same errand; and the second time, as much a hero as Æneas was, he frighted him. It seems he feared not Jupiter so much as Dido; for your lordship may observe, that, as much intent as he was upon his voyage, yet he still delayed it, till the messenger was obliged to tell him plainly, that if he weighed not anchor in the night, the queen would be with him in the morning—*notumque, furens quid femina possit*—she was injured; she was re-

* I am afraid, this passage, given as a just description of love, serves to confirm what is elsewhere stated, that Dryden's ideas of the female sex, and of the passion, were very gross and malicious.

vengeful; she was powerful. The poet had likewise before hinted, that the people were naturally perfidious; for he gives their character in the queen, and makes a proverb of *Punica fides*, many ages before it was invented.

Thus, I hope, my lord, that I have made good my promise, and justified the poet, whatever becomes of the false knight. And sure a poet is as much privileged to lie as an ambassador, for the honour and interest of his country: at least as Sir Henry Wotton has defined.*

This naturally leads me to the defence of the famous anachronism, in making Æneas and Dido contemporaries; for it is certain, that the hero lived almost two hundred years before the building of Carthage. One who imitates Boccalini, says, that Virgil was accused before Apollo for this error. The god soon found, that he was not able to defend his favourite by reason; for the case was clear: he therefore gave this middle sentence, that any thing might be allowed to his son Virgil, on the account of his other merits; that, being a monarch, he had a dispensing power, and pardoned him. But, that this special act of grace might never be drawn into example, or pleaded by his puny successors in justification of their ignorance, he decreed for the future, no poet should presume to make a lady die for love two hundred years before her birth. To moralize this story, Virgil is the Apollo who has this dispensing power. His great judgment made the laws of poetry; but he never made himself a slave to them; chronology, at best, is but a cobweb-law, and he broke through it with his weight. They who will imitate him wisely, must choose, as he did, an obscure and remote era, where they may invent at pleasure, and not be easily contradicted. Neither he, nor the Romans, had ever read the Bible, by which only his false computation of times can be made out against him. This Segrais says in his defence, and proves it from his learned friend Bochartus, whose letter on this subject he has printed at the end of the Fourth Æneid, to which I refer your lordship and the reader. Yet the credit of Virgil was so great, that he made this fable of his own invention pass for an authentic history, or at least as credible as any thing in Homer. Ovid takes it up after him, even in the same age, and makes an ancient heroine of Virgil's new-created Dido; dictates a letter for her, just before her death, to the ungrateful fugitive; and, very unluckily for himself, is for measuring a sword with a man so much superior in force to him, on the same subject. I think I may be judge of this, because I have translated both. The famous author of the "Art of Love" has nothing of his own; he borrows all from a greater master in his own profession; and, which is worse, improves nothing which he finds. Nature fails him; and, being forced to his old shift, he has recourse to witticism. This passes indeed with his soft admirers, and gives him the preference to Virgil in their esteem. But let them like for themselves, and not prescribe to others; for our author needs not their admiration.

The motives that induced Virgil to coin this fable, I have showed already; and have also begun to show, that he might make this anachronism, by superseding the mechanic rules of poetry, for the same reason that a monarch may dispense with or suspend his own laws, when he finds it necessary so to do, especially if those laws are not altogether fundamental. Nothing is to be called a fault in poetry, says Aristotle, but what is against the art: therefore a man may be an admirable poet, without being an exact chronologer. Shall we dare, continues Segrais, to condemn Virgil for having made a fiction against the order of time, when we commend Ovid and other poets, who have made many of their fictions against the order of nature? For what else are the splendid miracles of the metamorphoses? Yet these are beautiful as they are related, and have also deep learning and instructive mythologies couched under them: but to give, as Virgil does in this episode, the original cause of the long wars betwixt Rome and Carthage, to draw truth out of fiction after so probable a manner, with so much beauty, and so much for the honour of his country, was proper only to the divine wit of Maro; and Tasso, in one of his discourses, admires him for this particularly. It is not lawful, indeed, to contradict a point of history which is known to all the world, as, for example, to make Hannibal and Scipio contemporaries with Alexander; but, in the dark recesses of antiquity, a great poet may and ought to feign such things as he finds not there, if they can be brought to embellish that subject which he treats. On the other side, the pains and diligence of ill poets is but

* "*Legatus est vir bonus, peregre missus ad mentiendum reipublicæ causa;*" a sentence which Sir Henry wrote in the *Album* of Christopher Flecamore, as he passed through Germany, when he went as ambassador to Venice. These words, says his biographer, Isaac Walton, "he could have been content should have been thus Englished: *An ambassador is an honest man, sent to* lie *abroad for the good of his country:* but the word *mentiendum* not admitting of a double meaning, like *lie*, (which at that time signified to *sojourn*, as well as to utter criminal falsehood,) this pleasantry brought my lord ambassador into some trouble; Jasper Scioppius, a Romanist, about eight years afterwards, asserting in one of his works, that this was an acknowledged principle of the religion professed by King James, and those whom he employed as his representatives in foreign countries." See the life of Sir Henry Wotton, p. 36. edit. 1670.—*Malone*, p. 486. *Note.*

thrown away, when they want the genius to invent and feign agreeably. But, if the fictions be delightful, (which they always are, if they be natural;) if they be of a piece; if the beginning, the middle, and the end, be in their due places, and artfully united to each other, such works can never fail of their deserved success. And such is Virgil's episode of Dido and Æneas, where the sourest critic must acknowledge, that if he had deprived his Æneis of so great an ornament because he found no traces of it in antiquity, he had avoided their unjust censure, but had wanted one of the greatest beauties of his poem. I shall say more of this in the next article of their charge against him, which is want of invention. In the mean time, I may affirm, in honour of this episode, that it is not only now esteemed the most pleasing entertainment of the Æneis, but was so accounted in his own age, and before it was mellowed into that reputation which time has given it; for which I need produce no other testimony, than that of Ovid, his contemporary—

> Nec pars ulla magis legitur de corpore toto,
> Quam non legitimo fœdere junctus amor—

where, by the way, you may observe, my lord, that Ovid, in those words, *Non legitimo fœdere junctus amor*, will by no means allow it to be a lawful marriage betwixt Dido and Æneas. He was in banishment when he wrote those verses, which I cite from his letter to Augustus: "You, sir," saith he, "have sent me into exile for writing my 'Art of Love,' and my wanton Elegies; yet your own poet was happy in your good graces, though he brought Dido and Æneas into a cave, and left them there not over-honestly together. May I be so bold to ask your majesty, is it a greater fault to teach the art of unlawful love, than to show it in the action?" But was Ovid, the court-poet, so bad a courtier, as to find no other plea to excuse himself, than by a plain accusation of his master? Virgil confessed it was a lawful marriage betwixt the lovers, that Juno the goddess of matrimony had ratified it by her presence; for it was her business to bring matters to that issue. That the ceremonies were short, we may believe: for Dido was not only amorous, but a widow. Mercury himself, though employed on a quite contrary errand, yet owns it a marriage by an innuendo—*pulchramque uxorius urbem extruis.* He calls Æneas not only a husband, but upbraids him for being a fond husband, as the word *uxorius* implies. Now mark a little, if your lordship pleases, why Virgil is so much concerned to make this marriage, (for he seems to be the father of the bride himself, and to give her to the bridegroom;) it was to make way for the divorce which he intended afterwards; for he was a finer flatterer than Ovid, and I more than conjecture, that he had in his eye the divorce which not long before had passed betwixt the emperor and Scribonia.* He drew this dimple in the cheek of Æneas, to prove Augustus of the same family, by so remarkable a feature in the same place. Thus, as we say in our home-spun English proverb, he killed two birds with one stone; pleased the emperor, by giving him the resemblance of his ancestor, and gave him such a resemblance as was not scandalous in that age. For, to leave one wife, and take another, was but a matter of gallantry at that time of day among the Romans. *Neque hæc in fœdera veni*, is the very excuse which Æneas makes, when he leaves his lady: "I made no such bargain with you at our marriage, to live always drudging on at Carthage: my business was Italy; and I never made a secret of it. If I took my pleasure, had not you your share of it? I leave you free, at my departure, to comfort yourself with the next stranger who happens to be shipwrecked on your coast. Be as kind a hostess as you have been to me; and you can never fail of another husband. In the mean time, I call the gods to witness, that I leave your shore unwillingly; for, though Juno made the marriage, yet Jupiter commands me to forsake you." This is the effect of what he saith, when it is dishonoured out of Latin verse, into English prose. If the poet argued not aright, we must pardon him for a poor blind heathen, who knew no better morals.

I have detained your lordship longer than I intended, on this objection, which would indeed weigh something in a spiritual court; but I am not to defend our poet there. The next, I think, is but a cavil, though the cry is great against him, and hath continued from the time of Macrobius to this present age. I hinted it before. They lay no less than want of invention to his charge—a capital crime, I must acknowledge; for a poet is a maker,† as the word signifies; and he who cannot make, that is, invent, hath his name for nothing. That which makes this accusation look so strange‡ at the first sight, is, that he has borrowed so many things from Homer, Apollonius Rhodius, and others who preceded him. But, in the first place, if invention is to be taken in so strict a sense, that the matter of a poem must be wholly new, and that in all its parts, then Scaliger hath made out, saith

* The Emperor Augustus divorced Scribonia, his second wife, in order to make room for his marriage with Livia. But the argument of our author from the Æneid seems far-fetched.

† This original and expressive word for a poet was long retained in Scotland.—See Dunbar's Lament for the Death of the Makyrs.

‡ Mr. Malone reads—*so strong*: but *strange* here seems to signify *alarming*, or *startling*.

Segrais, that the history of Troy was no more the invention of Homer than of Virgil. There was not an old woman, or almost a child, but had it in their mouths, before the Greek poet or his friends digested it into this admirable order in which we read it. At this rate, as Solomon hath told us, there is nothing new beneath the sun. Who then can pass for an inventor, if Homer, as well as Virgil, must be deprived of that glory? Is Versailles the less a new building, because the architect of that palace hath imitated others which were built before it? Walls, doors, and windows, apartments, offices, rooms of convenience and magnificence, are in all great houses. So descriptions, figures, fables, and the rest, must be in all heroic poems: they are the common materials of poetry, furnished from the magazine of nature; every poet hath as much right to them, as every man hath to air and water.

Quid prohibetis aquas? Usus communis aquarum est.

But the argument of the work, that is to say, its principal action, the economy and disposition of it; these are the things which distinguish copies from originals. The poet, who borrows nothing from others, is yet to be born; he and the Jews' Messias will come together. There are parts of the Æneis which resemble some parts both of the Ilias and of the Odysses; as, for example, Æneas descended into hell, and Ulysses had been there before him; Æneas loved Dido, and Ulysses loved Calypso; in few words, Virgil hath imitated Homer's Odysses in his first six books, and, in his last six, the Ilias. But from hence can we infer, that the two poets write the same history? Is there no invention in some other parts of Virgil's Æneis? The disposition of so many various matters, is not that his own? From what book of Homer had Virgil his episode of Nisus and Euryalus, of Mezentius and Lausus? From whence did he borrow his design of bringing Æneas into Italy? of establishing the Roman empire on the foundations of a Trojan colony? to say nothing of the honour he did his patron, not only in his descent from Venus, but in making him so like her in his best features, that the goddess might have mistaken Augustus for her son. He had indeed the story from common fame, as Homer had his from the Egyptian priestess. *Æneadûm genetrix* was no more unknown to Lucretius than to him. But Lucretius taught him not to form his hero, to give him piety or valour for his manners, and both in so eminent a degree, that, having done what was possible for man to save his king and country, his mother was forced to appear to him, and restrain his fury, which hurried him to death in their revenge. But the poet made his piety more successful; he brought off his father and his son; and his gods witnessed to his devotion, by putting themselves under his protection, to be replaced by him in their promised Italy. Neither the invention nor the conduct of this great action were owing to Homer, or any other poet. It is one thing to copy, and another thing to imitate from nature. The copier is that servile imitator, to whom Horace gives no better name than that of animal; he will not so much as allow him to be a man. Raphael imitated nature; they who copy one of Raphael's pieces, imitate but him; for his work is their original. They translate him as I do Virgil; and fall as short of him as I of Virgil. There is a kind of invention in the imitation of Raphael; for, though the thing was in nature, yet the idea of it was his own. Ulysses travelled; so did Æneas: but neither of them were the first travellers; for Cain went into the land of Nod before they were born; and neither of the poets ever heard of such a man. If Ulysses had been killed at Troy, yet Æneas must have gone to sea, or he could never have arrived in Italy. But the designs of the two poets were as different as the courses of their heroes; one went home, and the other sought a home. To return to my first similitude: suppose Apelles and Raphael had each of them painted a burning Troy, might not the modern painter have succeeded as well as the ancient, though neither of them had seen the town on fire? for the draughts of both were taken from the ideas which they had of nature. Cities had been burned, before either of them were in being. But, to close the simile as I began it; they would not have designed it after the same manner: Apelles would have distinguished Pyrrhus from the rest of all the Grecians, and showed him forcing his entrance into Priam's palace; there he had set him in the fairest light, and given him the chief place of all his figures; because he was a Grecian, and he would do honour to his country. Raphael, who was an Italian, and descended from the Trojans, would have made Æneas the hero of his piece; and perhaps not with his father on his back, his son in one hand, his bundle of gods in the other, and his wife following; for an act of piety is not half so graceful in a picture, as an act of courage: he would rather have drawn him killing Androgeos, or some other, hand to hand; and the blaze of the fires should have darted full upon his face, to make him conspicuous amongst his Trojans. This, I think, is a just comparison betwixt the two poets, in the conduct of their several designs. Virgil cannot be said to copy Homer; the Grecian had only the advantage of writing first. If it be urged, that I have granted a resemblance in some parts, yet therein Virgil has excelled him. For what are the tears of Calypso for being left, to the fury and death of Dido? Where is there the whole process of her passion, and all its violent effects to be found, in the languishing episode of the Odyssee? If this be to copy, let the critics show us the same dispositions, features, or colouring, in their original. The like may be said of the descent to hell, which was not of Homer's invention neither; he had it from the story of Orpheus and Eurydice. But to what end did Ulysses make that journey? Æneas undertook it by the express commandment of his father's ghost; there he was to show him all the succeeding heroes of his race, and, next to Romulus, (mark if you please, the address of Virgil,) his own patron, Augustus Cæsar. Anchises was likewise to instruct him how to manage the Italian war, and how to conclude it with his honour; that is, in other words, to lay the foundations of that empire which Augustus was to govern. This is the noble invention of our author; but it hath been copied by so many sign-post daubers, that now it has grown fulsome, rather by their want of skill, than by the commonness.

In the last place, I may safely grant, that, by reading Homer, Virgil was taught to imitate his invention—that is, to imitate like him; which is no more than if a painter studied Raphael, that he might learn to design after his manner. And thus I might imitate Virgil, if I were capable of writing a heroic poem, and yet the invention be my own: but I should endeavour to avoid a servile copying. I would not give the same story under other names, with the same characters, in the same order, and with the same sequel; for every common reader to find me out at the first sight for a plagiary, and cry,—This I read before in Virgil, in a better language, and in better verse. This is like Merry Andrew on the low rope, copying lubberly the same tricks which his master is so dexterously performing on the high.

I will trouble your lordship but with one objection more, which I know not whether I found in Le Fevre, or Valais; but I am sure I have read it in another French critic, whom I will not name, because I think it is not much for his reputation.* Virgil, in the heat of action—suppose, for example, in describing the fury of his hero in a battle, when he is endeavouring to raise our concernments to the highest pitch—turns short on the sudden into some similitude, which diverts, say they, your attention from the main subject, and mis-spends it on some trivial image. He pours cold water into the caldron, when his business is to make it boil.†

This accusation is general against all who would be thought heroic poets; but I think it touches Virgil less than any. He is too great a master of his art, to make a blot which may so easily be hit. Similitudes, as I have said, are not for tragedy, which is all violent, and where the passions are in a perpetual ferment; for there they deaden where they should animate; they are not of the nature of dialogue, unless in comedy: a metaphor is almost all the stage can suffer, which is a kind of similitude comprehended in a word. But this figure has a contrary effect in heroic poetry; there it is employed to raise the admiration, which is its proper business; and admiration is not of so violent a nature as fear or hope, compassion or horror, or any concernment we can have for such or such a person on the stage. Not but I confess, that similitudes and descriptions, when drawn into an unreasonable length, must needs nauseate the reader. Once, I remember, and but once, Virgil makes a similitude of fourteen lines; and his description of Fame is about the same number. He is blamed for both; and I doubt not but he would have contracted them, had he lived to have reviewed his work; but faults are no precedents. This I have observed of his similitudes in general, that they are not placed, as our unobserving critics tell us, in the heat of any action, but commonly in its declining. When he has warmed us in his description as much as possibly he can, then, lest that warmth should languish, he renews it by some apt similitude, which illustrates his subject, and yet palls not his audience. I need give your lordship but one example of this kind, and leave the rest to your observation, when next you review the whole Æneis in the original unblemished by my rude translation. It is in the first book, where the poet describes Neptune composing the ocean, on which Æolus had raised a tempest without his permission. He had already chidden the rebellious winds for obeying the commands of their usurping master; he had warned them from the seas; he had beaten down the billows with his mace, dispelled the clouds, restored the sunshine, while Triton and Cymothoë were heaving the ships

* Dacier.

† I fear there is something in this objection. Virgil, who lived in a peaceful court, does not draw his battles with the animation and reality of Homer, who, if he was not himself a warrior, was the poet of a rude and warlike age.

from off the quicksands, before the poet would offer at a similitude for illustration:

Ac, veluti magno in populo cum sæpe coörta est
Seditio, sævitque animis ignobile vulgus,
Jamque faces et saxa volant; furor arma ministrat;
Tum, pietate gravem ac meritis si forte virum quem
Conspexere, silent, arrectisque auribus adstant;
Ille regit dictis animos, et pectora mulcet:
Sic cunctus pelagi cecidit fragor, æquora postquam
Prospiciens genitor, cæloque invectus aperto,
Flectit equos, curruque volans dat lora secundo.

This is the first similitude which Virgil makes in this poem, and one of the longest in the whole; for which reason I the rather cite it. While the storm was in its fury, any allusion had been improper; for the poet could have compared it to nothing more impetuous than itself; consequently he could have made no illustration. If he could have illustrated, it had been an ambitious ornament out of season, and would have diverted our concernment: *nunc non erat his locus*; and therefore he deferred it to its proper place.*

These are the criticisms, of most moment which have been made against the Æneïs by the ancients or moderns. As for the particular exceptions against this or that passage, Macrobius and Pontanus have answered them already. If I desired to appear more learned than I am, it had been as easy for me to have taken their objections and solutions, as it is for a country parson to take the expositions of the fathers out of Junius and Tremellius,† and not to have named the authors from whence I had them; for so Ruæus, otherwise a most judicious commentator on Virgil's works, has used Pontanus, his greatest benefactor; of whom he is very silent; and I do not remember that he once cites him.

What follows next, is no objection; for that implies a fault; and it had been none in Virgil, if he had extended the time of his action beyond a year. At least Aristotle has set no precise limits to it. Homer's, we know, was within two months: Tasso, I am sure, exceeds not a summer; and, if I examined him, perhaps he might be reduced into a much less compass. Bossu leaves it doubtful whether Virgil's action were within the year, or took up some months beyond it. Indeed, the whole dispute is of no more concernment to the common reader, than it is to a ploughman, whether February this year had 28 or 29 days in it. But, for the satisfaction of the more curious, (of which number I am sure your lordship is one,) I will translate what I think convenient out of Ségrais, whom perhaps you have not read; for he has made it highly probable, that the action of the Æneïs began in the spring, and was not extended beyond the autumn And we have known campaigns that have begun sooner, and have ended later.

Ronsard, and the rest whom Ségrais names, who are of opinion, that the action of this poem takes up almost a year and half, ground their calculation thus. Anchises died in Sicily at the end of winter, or beginning of the spring. Æneas, immediately after the interment of his father, puts to sea for Italy. He is surprised by the tempest described in the beginning of the first book; and there it is that the scene of the poem opens, and where the action must commence. He is driven by this storm on the coasts of Afric; he stays at Carthage all that summer, and almost all the winter following, sets sail again for Italy just before the beginning of the spring, meets with contrary winds, and makes Sicily the second time. This part of the action completes the year. Then he celebrates the anniversary of his father's funeral; and shortly after arrives at Cumæ; and from thence his time is taken up in his first treaty with Latinus, the overture of the war, the siege of his camp by Turnus, his going for succours to relieve it, his return, the raising of the siege by the first battle, the twelve days' truce, the second battle, the assault of Laurentum, and the single fight with Turnus; all which, they say, cannot take up less than four or five months more; by which account, we cannot suppose the entire action to be contained in a much less compass than a year and half.

Ségrais reckons another way; and his computation is not condemned by the learned Ruæus, who compiled and published the commentaries on our poet, which we call the Dauphin's Virgil.

He allows the time of the year when Anchises died to be in the latter end of winter, or the beginning of the spring: he acknowledges, that, when Æneas is first seen at sea afterwards, and is driven by the tempest on the coast of Afric, is the time when the action is naturally to begin: he confesses, further, that Æneas left Carthage in the latter end of winter; for Dido tells him in express terms, as an argument for his longer stay,

Quinetiam hiberno moliris sidere classem.

But, whereas Ronsard's followers suppose, that, when Æneas had buried his father, he set sail immediately for Italy, (though the tempest

* Unquestionably the description, in the passage quoted, and the simile, aid each other with great mutual effect.

† Commentators on the Scripture, mentioned by our author in the "Religio Laici," where, speaking of Dickenson's translation of Pere Simon's "Critical History of the Old Testament," he calls it

A treasure, which, if country curates buy
They Junius and Tremellius may defy.

drove him on the coast of Carthage,) Ségrais will by no means allow that supposition, but thinks it much more probable, that he remained in Sicily till the midst of July, or the beginning of August; at which time he places the first appearance of his hero on the sea; and there opens the action of the poem. From which beginning, to the death of Turnus, which concludes the action, there need not be supposed above ten months of intermediate time: for, arriving at Carthage in the latter end of summer, staying there the winter following, departing thence in the very beginning of the spring, making a short abode in Sicily the second time, landing in Italy, and making the war, may be reasonably judged the business but of ten months. To this the Renardians reply, that, having been for seven years before in quest of Italy, and having no more to do in Sicily than to inter his father—after that office was performed, what remained for him, but, without delay, to pursue his first adventure? To which Ségrais answers, that the obsequies of his father, according to the rites of the Greeks and Romans, would detain him for many days; that a longer time must be taken up in the refitting of his ships after so tedious a voyage, and in refreshing his weather-beaten soldiers on a friendly coast. These indeed are but suppositions on both sides; yet those of Ségrais seem better grounded: for the feast of Dido, when she entertained Æneas first, has the appearance of a summer's night, which seems already almost ended, when he begins his story; therefore the love was made in autumn: the hunting followed properly when the heats of that scorching country were declining; the winter was passed in jollity, as the season and their love required; and he left her in the latter end of winter, as is already proved. This opinion is fortified by the arrival of Æneas at the mouth of the Tyber; which marks the season of the spring; that season being perfectly described by the singing of the birds saluting the dawn, and by the beauty of the place, which the poet seems to have painted expressly in the seventh Æneid:

> Aurora in roseis fulgebat lutea bigis,
> Cum venti posuere.——
> ——Variæ, circumque supraque,
> Assuetæ ripis volucres, et fluminis alveo,
> Æthera mulcebant cantu.——

The remainder of the action required but three months more: for, when Æneas went for succour to the Tuscans, he found their army in a readiness to march, and wanting only a commander: so that, according to this calculation, the Æneis takes not up above a year complete, and may be comprehended in less compass.

This, amongst other circumstances treated more at large by Ségrais, agrees with the rising of Orion, which caused the tempest described in the beginning of the First Book. By some passages in the "Pastorals," but more particularly in the "Georgics," our poet is found to be an exact astronomer, according to the knowledge of that age. Now Ilioneus (whom Virgil twice employs in embassies, as the best speaker of the Trojans) attributes that tempest to Orion, in his speech to Dido:

> Cum, subito assurgens fluctu, nimbosus Orion—

He must mean either the heliacal, or achronical rising of that sign. The heliacal rising of a constellation is, when it comes from under the rays of the sun, and begins to appear before day-light; the achronical rising, on the contrary, is when it appears at the close of day, and in opposition to the sun's diurnal course.

The heliacal rising of Orion is at present computed to be about the sixth of July; and about that time it is, that he either causes or presages tempests on the seas.

Ségrais has observed farther, that, when Anna counsels Dido to stay Æneas during the winter, she speaks also of Orion—

> Dum pelago desævit hiems, et aquosus Orion.

If, therefore, Ilioneus, according to our supposition, understand the heliacal rising of Orion, Anna must mean the achronical, which the different epithets given to that constellation seem to manifest. Ilioneus calls him *nimbosus*; Anna, *aquosus*. He is tempestuous in the summer, when he rises heliacally, and rainy in the winter, when he rises achronically. Your lordship will pardon me for the frequent repetition of these cant words, which I could not avoid in this abbreviation of Ségrais, who, I think, deserves no little commendation in this new criticism.*

I have yet a word or two to say of Virgil's machines, from my own observation of them. He has imitated those of Homer, but not copied them. It was established, long before this time, in the Roman religion as well as in the Greek, that there were gods; and both nations, for the most part, worshipped the same deities; as did also the Trojans, from whom the Romans, I

* This display of learning seems a little out of place. Undoubtedly it was important, if the accusation had been, that Virgil had misplaced his seasons. But, as to the mere length of time employed in his epic, there seems no better reason why it should be a year than a month, or two years than one so long as the interest is effectually maintained.

suppose, would rather be thought to derive the rites of their religion, than from the Grecians; because they thought themselves descended from them. Each of those gods had his proper office, and the chief of them their particular attendants. Thus Jupiter had in propriety Ganymede and Mercury, and Juno had Iris. It was not for Virgil then to create new ministers: he must take what he found in his religion. It cannot therefore be said, that he borrowed them from Homer, any more than Apollo, Diana, and the rest, whom he uses as he finds occasion for them, as the Grecian poet did; but he invents the occasions for which he uses them. Venus, after the destruction of Troy, had gained Neptune entirely to her party; therefore we find him busy, in the beginning of the Æneis, to calm the tempest raised by Æolus, and afterwards conducting the Trojan fleet to Cumæ in safety, with the loss only of their pilot, for whom he bargains. I name those two examples (amongst a hundred which I omit) to prove, that Virgil, generally speaking, employed his machines in performing those things which might possibly have been done without them. What more frequent than a storm at sea, upon the rising of Orion? What wonder, if, amongst so many ships, there should one be overset, which was commanded by Orontes, though half the winds had not been there which Æolus employed? Might not Palinurus, without a miracle, fall asleep, and drop into the sea, having been over-wearied with watching, and secure of a quiet passage, by his observation of the skies? At least Æneas, who knew nothing of the machine of Somnus, takes it plainly in this sense:

> O nimium cœlo et pelago confise sereno,
> Nudus in ignotâ, Palinure, jacebis arenâ.

But machines sometimes are specious things to amuse the reader, and give a colour of probability to things otherwise incredible. And besides, it soothed the vanity of the Romans, to find the gods so visibly concerned in all the actions of their predecessors. We, who are better taught by our religion, yet own every wonderful accident, which befalls us for the best, to be brought to pass by some special providence of Almighty God, and by the care of guardian angels: and from hence I might infer, that no heroic poem can be writ on the Epicurean principles, which I could easily demonstrate, if there were need to prove it, or I had leisure.*

* Our author seems always to have had a view to form the machinery of an epic poem, upon the principles of the Platonic philosophy, which he proposed to adapt to the guardian angels of kingdoms, mentioned by the prophet Daniel.

When Venus opens the eyes of her son Æneas, to behold the gods who combated against Troy in that fatal night when it was surprised, we share the pleasure of that glorious vision. (which Tasso has not ill copied in the sacking of Jerusalem.) But the Greeks had done their business, though neither Neptune, Juno, nor Pallas, had given them their divine assistance. The most crude machine which Virgil uses, is in the episode of Camilla, where Opis, by the command of her mistress, kills Aruns. The next is in the twelfth Æneid, where Venus cures her son Æneas. But, in the last of these, the poet was driven to a necessity; for Turnus was to be slain that very day; and Æneas, wounded as he was, could not have engaged him in single combat, unless his hurt had been miraculously healed. And the poet had considered, that the dittany which she brought from Crete, could not have wrought so speedy an effect, without the juice of ambrosia, which she mingled with it. After all, that his machine might not seem too violent, we see the hero limping after Turnus. The wound was skinned; but the strength of his thigh was not restored. But what reason had our author to wound Æneas at so critical a time? and how came the cuisses to be worse tempered than the rest of his armour, which was all wrought by Vulcan and his journeymen? These difficulties are not easily to be solved, without confessing that Virgil had not life enough to correct his work; though he had reviewed it, and found those errors, which he resolved to mend: but, being prevented by death, and not willing to leave an imperfect work behind him, he ordained, by his last testament, that his Æneis should be burned. As for the death of Aruns, who was shot by a goddess, the machine was not altogether so outrageous as the wounding Mars and Venus by the sword of Diomede. Two divinities, one would have thought, might have pleaded their prerogative of impassibility, or at least not have been wounded by any mortal hand; beside that the ιχωρ, which they shed, was so very like our common blood, that it was not to be distinguished from it, but only by the name and colour. As for what Horace says, in his Art of Poetry, that no machines are to be used, unless on some extraordinary occasion,

> Nec deus intersit, nisi dignus vindice nodus—

that rule is to be applied to the theatre, of which he is then speaking; and means no more than this, that, when the knot of the play is to be untied, and no other way is left for making the discovery; then, and not otherwise, let a god descend upon a rope, and clear the business to the audience: but this has no relation to the machines which are used in an epic poem.

In the last place, for the Dira, or flying pest, which flapping on the shield of Turnus, and fluttering about his head, disheartened him in the duel, and presaged to him his approaching death, I might have placed it more properly amongst the objections: for the critics, who lay want of courage to the charge of Virgil's hero, quote this passage as a main proof of their assertion. They say our author had not only secured him before the duel, but also, in the beginning of it, had given him the advantage in impenetrable arms, and in his sword; for that of Turnus was not his own, which was forged by Vulcan for his father, but a weapon which he had snatched in haste, and by mistake, belonging to his charioteer Metiscus; that, after all this, Jupiter, who was partial to the Trojan, and distrustful of the event, though he had hung the balance, and given it a jog of his hand to weigh down Turnus, thought convenient to give the Fates a collateral security, by sending the screech-owl to discourage him; for which they quote these words of Virgil,

> Non me tua turbida virtus
> Terret, ait: di me terrent, et Jupiter hostis.*

In answer to which, I say, that this machine is one of those which the poet uses only for ornament, and not out of necessity. Nothing can be more beautiful or more poetical than his description of the three Diræ, or the setting of the balance, which our Milton has borrowed from him, but employed to a different end; for, first, he makes God Almighty set the scales for St. Gabriel and Satan, when he knew no combat was to follow; then he makes the good angel's scale descend, and the Devil's mount, quite contrary to Virgil, if I have translated the three verses according to my author's sense:

> Jupiter ipse duas æquato examine lances
> Sustinet; et fata imponit diversa duorum;
> Quem damnet labor, et quo vergat pondere letum.

For I have taken these words, *quem damnet labor*, in the sense which Virgil gives them in another place, — *damnabis tu quoque votis*, — to signify a prosperous event. Yet I dare not condemn so great a genius as Milton: for I am much mistaken if he alludes not to the text in Daniel, where Belshazzar is put into the balance, and was found too light.—This is digression; and I return to my subject. I said above, that these two machines of the balance and the Diræ were only ornamental, and that the success of the duel had been the same without them: for, when Æneas and Turnus stood fronting each other before the altar, Turnus looked dejected, and his colour faded in his face, as if he desponded of the victory before the fight; and not only he, but all his party, when the strength of the two champions was judged by the proportion of their limbs, concluded it was *impar pugna*, and that their chief was overmatched: whereupon Juturna (who was of the same opinion) took this opportunity to break the treaty and renew the war. Juno herself had plainly told the nymph beforehand, that her brother was to fight

> Imparibus fatis, nec dis nec viribus æquis;

so that there was no need of an apparition to fright Turnus: he had the presage within himself of his impending destiny. The Dira only served to confirm him in his first opinion, that it was his destiny to die in the ensuing combat; and in this sense are those words of Virgil to be taken,

> Non me tua turbida virtus
> Terret, ait: di me terrent, et Jupiter hostis.*

I doubt not but the adverb *solum* is to be understood; "It is not your [valour] *only* that gives me this concernment; but I find also, by this portent, that Jupiter is my enemy:" for Turnus fled before, when his first sword was broken, till his sister supplied him with a better; which indeed he could not use, because Æneas kept him at a distance with his spear. I wonder Ruæus saw not this, where he charges his author so unjustly, for giving Turnus a second sword to no purpose. How could he fasten a blow, or make a thrust, when he was not suffered to approach? Besides, the chief errand of the Dira was to warn Juturna from the field; for she could have brought the chariot again, when she saw her brother worsted in the duel. I might farther add, that Æneas was so eager of the fight, that he left the city, now almost in his possession, to decide his quarrel with Turnus by the sword: whereas Turnus had manifestly declined the combat, and suffered his sister to convey him as far from the reach of his enemy as she could — I say, not only suffered her,

* These lines are inaccurately quoted, for

> Non me tua fervida terrent
> Dicta, ferox, &c.

Æneid, xii. l. 895.

* Misquoted again; for

> Non me tua fervida terrent
> Dicta, ferox.

I think the passage may easily be interpreted without disparagement of Æneas's valour, even without adopting Dryden's construction. Turnus, a brave and proud man, reduced to the humiliating situation of confessing his fears, naturally imputes them to the more honourable cause, a dread, namely, of supernatural interference. To confess his terror to arise from the force of his mortal adversary, would have been degrading to his character.

but consented to it; for it is plain, he knew her, by these words:

> O soror, et dudum agnovi, cum prima per artem
> Fœdera turbasti, teque hæc in bella dedisti;
> Et nunc necquidquam fallis dea.

I have dwelt so long on this subject, that I must contract what I have to say in reference to my translation, unless I would swell my preface into a volume, and make it formidable to your lordship, when you see so many pages yet behind. And indeed what I have already written, either in justification or praise of Virgil, is against myself, for presuming to copy, in my coarse English, the thoughts and beautiful expressions of this inimitable poet, who flourished in an age when his language was brought to its last perfection, for which it was particularly owing to him and Horace. I will give your lordship my opinion, that those two friends had consulted each other's judgment, wherein they should endeavour to excel; and they seem to have pitched on propriety of thought, elegance of words, and harmony of numbers. According to this model, Horace writ his Odes and Epodes: for his Satires and Epistles, being intended wholly for instruction, required another style—

> Ornari res ipsa negat, contenta doceri—

and therefore, as he himself professes, are *sermoni propiora*, nearer prose than verse. But Virgil, who never attempted the lyric verse, is everywhere elegant, sweet, and flowing in his hexameters. His words are not only chosen, but the places in which he ranks them for the sound. He who removes them from the station wherein their master set them, spoils the harmony. What he says of the Sibyl's prophecies, may be as properly applied to every word of his: they must be read in order as they lie; the least breath discomposes them; and somewhat of their divinity is lost. I cannot boast that I have been thus exact in my verses; but I have endeavoured to follow the example of my master, and am the first Englishman, perhaps, who made it his design to copy him in his numbers, his choice of words, and his placing them for the sweetness of the sound. On this last consideration, I have shunned the *cæsura* as much as possibly I could: for wherever that is used, it gives a roughness to the verse; of which we can have little need in a language which is overstocked with consonants.* Such is not the Latin, where the vowels and consonants are mixed in proportion to each other: yet Virgil judged the vowels to have somewhat of an overbalance, and therefore tempers their sweetness with *cæsuras*. Such difference there is in tongues, that the same figure, which roughens one, gives majesty to another: and that was it which Virgil studied in his verses. Ovid uses it but rarely; and hence it is that his versification cannot so properly be called sweet, as luscious. The Italians are forced upon it once or twice in every line, because they have a redundancy of vowels in their language. Their metal is so soft, that it will not coin without alloy to harden it. On the other side, for the reason already named, it is all we can do to give sufficient sweetness to our language: we must not only choose our words for elegance, but for sound; to perform which, a mastery in the language is required; the poet must have a magazine of words, and have the art to manage his few vowels to the best advantage, that they may go the farther. He must also know the nature of the vowels — which are more sonorous, and which more soft and sweet — and so dispose them as his present occasions require; all which, and a thousand secrets of versification beside, he may learn from Virgil, if he will take him for his guide. If he be above Virgil, and is resolved to follow his own *verve*, (as the French call it,) the proverb will fall heavily upon him:—"Who teaches himself, has a fool for his master."

Virgil employed eleven years upon his Æneis; yet he left it, as he thought himself, imperfect; which when I seriously consider, I wish, that, instead of three years which I have spent in the translation of his works, I had four years more allowed me to correct my errors, that I might make my version somewhat more tolerable than it is: for a poet cannot have too great a reverence for his readers, if he expects his labours should survive him. Yet I will neither plead my age nor sickness, in excuse of the faults which I have made: that I wanted time, is all that I have to say; for some of my subscribers grew so clamorous, that I could no longer defer the publication. I hope, from the candour of your lordship, and your often experienced goodness to me, that, if the faults are not too many, you will make allowances with Horace:

> ——— *si* plura nitent in carmine, non ego paucis
> Offendar maculis, quas aut incuria fudit,
> Aut humana parum cavit natura.—

You may please also to observe, that there is not, to the best of my remembrance, one vowel gaping on another for want of a *cæsura*, in this whole poem: but, where a vowel ends a word, the next begins either with a consonant, or what is its equivalent; for our *W* and *H* aspirate, and our

* It is singular, that, under this conviction, Dryden should have complied with the custom of his age, in striking out the vowel before the end of such words as *winged*.

diphthongs, are plainly such. The greatest latitude I take is in the letter *Y*, when it concludes a word, and the first syllable of the next begins with a vowel. Neither need I have called this a latitude, which is only an explanation of this general rule—that no vowel can be cut off before another, when we cannot sink the pronunciation of it; as *he, she, me, I*, &c. Virgil thinks it sometimes a beauty to imitate the license of the Greeks, and leave two vowels opening on each other, as in that verse of the Third Pastoral,

Et succus pecori, et lac subducitur agnis.

But, *nobis non licet esse tam disertis*, at least if we study to refine our numbers. I have long had by me the materials of an English *Prosodia*, containing all the mechanical rules of versification, wherein I have treated, with some exactness, of the feet, the quantities, and the pauses. The French and Italians know nothing of the two first; at least their best poets have not practised them. As for the pauses, Malherbe first brought them into France within this last century; and we see how they adorn their Alexandrines. But, as Virgil propounds a riddle, which he leaves unsolved—

Dic, quibus in terris, inscripti nomina regum
Nascantur flores; et Phyllida solus habeto—

so I will give your lordship another, and leave the exposition of it to your acute judgment. I am sure there are few who make verses, have not observed the sweetness of these two lines in Cooper's Hill:

Though deep, yet clear; though gentle, yet not dull;
Strong without rage; without o'erflowing, full—*

and there are yet fewer who can find the reason of that sweetness. I have given it to some of my friends in conversation; and they have allowed the criticism to be just. But, since the evil of false quantities is difficult to be cured in any modern language; since the French and the Italians, as well as we, are yet ignorant what feet are to be used in heroic poetry; since I have not strictly observed those rules myself, which I can teach others; since I pretend to no dictatorship among my fellow-poets; since, if I should instruct some of them to make well-running verses, they want genius to give them strength as well as sweetness; and, above all, since your lordship has advised me not to publish that little which I know, I look on your counsel as your command, which I shall observe inviolably, till you shall please to revoke it, and leave me at liberty to make my thoughts public. In the mean time, that I may arrogate nothing to myself, I must acknowledge that Virgil in Latin, and Spenser in English, have been my masters. Spenser has also given me the boldness to make use sometimes of his Alexandrine line, which we call, though improperly, the Pindaric, because Mr. Cowley has often employed it in his Odes. It adds a certain majesty to the verse, when it is used with judgment, and stops the sense from overflowing into another line. Formerly the French, like us, and the Italians, had but five feet, or ten syllables, in their heroic verse; but, since Ronsard's time, as I suppose, they found their tongue too weak to support their epic poetry, without the addition of another foot. That indeed has given it somewhat of the run and measure of a trimeter; but it runs with more activity than strength: their language is not strung with sinews, like our English; it has the nimbleness of a greyhound, but not the bulk and body of a mastiff. Our men and our verses overbear them by their weight; and *Pondere, non numero*, is the British motto. The French have set up purity for the standard of their language; and a masculine vigour is that of ours. Like their tongue, is the genius of their poets, light and trifling in comparison of the English; more proper for sonnets, madrigals, and elegies, than heroic poetry. The turn on thoughts and words is their chief talent; but the epic poem is too stately to receive those little ornaments. The painters draw their nymphs in thin and airy habits; but the weight of gold and of embroideries is reserved for queens and goddesses. Virgil is never frequent in those turns, like Ovid, but much more sparing of them in his Æneis, than in his Pastorals and Georgics.

Ignoscenda quidem, scirent si ignoscere manes.

That turn is beautiful indeed; but he employs it in the story of Orpheus and Eurydice, not in his great poem. I have used that license in his Æneis sometimes; but I own it as my fault. It was given to those who understand no better. It is like Ovid's

Semivirumque bovem, semibovemque virum.

The poet found it before his critics, but it was a darling sin, which he would not be persuaded to reform. The want of genius, of which I have accused the French, is laid to their charge by one of their own great authors, though I have forgotten his name, and where I read it. If rewards could make good poets, their great mas-

* This celebrated couplet occurs in Sir John Denham's "Cooper's Hill," a poem which was praised beyond its merit by the author's contemporaries. After allowing that the lines are smooth and sonorous, which indeed were infrequent qualities of the versification of the period, I fear much of their merit lies in the skilful antithesis of the attributes of the river.

ter* has not been wanting on his part in his bountiful encouragements; for he is wise enough to imitate Augustus, if he had a Maro. The triumvir and proscriber had descended to us in a more hideous form than they now appear, if the emperor had not taken care to make friends of him and Horace. I confess, the banishment of Ovid was a blot in his escutcheon: yet he was only banished; and who knows but his crime was capital, and then his exile was a favour? Ariosto, who, with all his faults, must be acknowledged a great poet, has put these words into the mouth of an evangelist:† but whether they will pass for gospel now I cannot tell.

> Non fu sì santo ni benigno Augusto,
> Come la tuba di Virgilio suona.
> L'haver havuto in poesia buon gusto,
> La proscrittione iniqua gli perdona.

But heroic poetry is not of the growth of France, as it might be of England, if it were cultivated. Spenser wanted only to have read the rules of Bossu; for no man was ever born with a greater genius, or had more knowledge to support it. But the performance of the French is not equal to their skill; and hitherto we have wanted skill to perform better. Ségrais, whose preface is so wonderfully good, yet is wholly destitute of elevation, though his version is much better than that of the two brothers, or any of the rest who have attempted Virgil. Hannibal Caro is a great name amongst the Italians; yet his translation of the Æneïs is most scandalously mean, though he has taken the advantage of writing in blank verse, and freed himself from the shackles of modern rhyme, if it be modern; for Le Clerc has told us lately, and I believe has made it out, that David's Psalms were written in as errant rhyme as they are translated. Now, if a Muse cannot run when she is unfettered, it is a sign she has but little speed. I will not make a digression here, though I am strangely tempted to it; but will only say, that he who can write well in rhyme, may write better in blank verse.‡ Rhyme is certainly a constraint even to the best poets, and those who make it with most ease; though perhaps I have as little reason to complain of that hardship as any man, excepting Quarles and Withers. What it adds to sweetness, it takes away from sense; and he who loses the least by it, may be called a gainer. It often makes us swerve from an author's meaning; as, if a mark be set up for an archer at a great distance, let him aim as exactly as he can, the least wind will take his arrow, and divert it from the white. I return to our Italian translator of the Æneïs. He is a footpoet, he lacqueys by the side of Virgil at the best, but never mounts behind him. Doctor Morelli,* who is no mean critic in our poetry, and therefore may be presumed to be a better in his own language, has confirmed me in this opinion by his judgment, and thinks, withal, that he has often mistaken his master's sense. I would say so, if I durst, but am afraid I have committed the same fault more often, and more grossly; for I have forsaken Ruæus, (whom generally I follow,) in many places, and made expositions of my own in some, quite contrary to him; of which I will give but two examples, because they are so near each other, in the Tenth Æneid—

> Sorti Pater æquus utrique.

Pallas says it to Turnus, just before they fight. Ruæus thinks that the word *Pater* is to be referred to Evander, the father of Pallas. But how could he imagine that it was the same thing to Evander, if his son were slain, or if he overcame? The poet certainly intended Jupiter, the common father of mankind; who, as Pallas hoped, would stand an impartial spectator of the combat, and not be more favourable to Turnus than to him. The second is not long after it, and both before the duel is begun. They are the words of Jupiter, who comforts Hercules for the death of Pallas, which was immediately to ensue, and which Hercules could not hinder, (though the young hero had addressed his prayers to him for his assistance,) because the gods cannot control destiny. The verse follows:

> Sic ait; atque oculos Rutulorum rejicit arvis,—

which the same Ruæus thus construes: Jupiter, after he had said this, immediately turns his eyes to the Rutulian fields, and beholds the duel. I have given this place another exposition, that he turned his eyes from the field of combat, that he might not behold a sight so unpleasing to him. The word *rejicit*, I know, will admit of both senses; but Jupiter having confessed that he could not alter fate, and being grieved he could not, in consideration of Hercules—it seems to me that

* Louis XIV., whom Dryden probably in his heart compared with disadvantage to the needy Charles, who loved literary merit without rewarding it; the saturnine James, who rewarded without loving it; and the phlegmatic William, who did neither the one nor the other.

† St. John, in his conversation with Astolfo, on the latter's arrival in the Moon.

‡ This is not expressed with sufficient precision. Undoubtedly one possessing those true poetic qualities, which consist in the thought and not in the mere arrangement of expression, will shine most in the easiest structure of versification. But there is a very inferior, yet not altogether contemptible kind of poet, whose merit consists more in melody of versification, and neatness or even felicity of expression, than in his powers of conception. Such bards will do well to avail themselves of the melody of rhyme.

* A learned physician of Dryden's time.

he should avert his eyes, rather than take pleasure in the spectacle. But of this I am not so confident as the other, though I think I have followed Virgil's sense.*

What I have said, though it has the face of arrogance, yet is intended for the honour of my country; and therefore I will boldly own, that this English translation has more of Virgil's spirit in it, than either the French or the Italian. Some of our countrymen have translated episodes and other parts of Virgil, with great success: as particularly your lordship, whose version of Orpheus and Eurydice is eminently good. Amongst the dead authors, the Silenus of my Lord Roscommon cannot be too much commended. I say nothing of Sir John Denham, Mr. Waller, and Mr. Cowley;† it is the utmost of my ambition to be thought their equal, or not to be much inferior to them, and some others of the living. But it is one thing to take pains on a fragment, and translate it perfectly; and another thing to have the weight of a whole author on my shoulders. They who believe the burden light, let them attempt the fourth, sixth, or eighth Pastoral; the first or fourth Georgic; and, amongst the Æneids, the fourth, the fifth, the seventh, the ninth, the tenth, the eleventh, or the twelfth; for in these I think I have succeeded best.

Long before I undertook this work, I was no stranger to the original. I had also studied Virgil's design, his disposition of it, his manners, his judicious management of the figures, the sober retrenchments of his sense, which always leave somewhat to gratify our imagination, on which it may enlarge at pleasure; but, above all, the elegance of his expressions, and the harmony of his numbers: for, as I have said in a former dissertation, the words are, in poetry, what the colours are in painting; if the design be good, and the draught be true, the colouring is the first beauty that strikes the eye.‡ Spenser and Milton are the nearest, in English, to Virgil and Horace in the Latin; and I have endeavoured to form my style by imitating these masters. I will further own to you, my lord, that my chief ambition is to please those readers who have discernment enough to prefer Virgil before any other poet in the Latin tongue. Such spirits as he desired to please, such would I choose for my judges, and would stand or fall by them alone. Ségrais has distinguished the readers of poetry, according to their capacity of judging, into three classes; (he might have said the same of writers too, if he had pleased.) In the lowest form he places those whom he calls *les petits esprits*—such things as are our upper gallery audience in a playhouse, who like nothing but the husk and rind of wit; prefer a quibble, a conceit, an epigram, before solid sense and elegant expression;—these are mob readers. If Virgil and Martial stood for parliament men, we know already who would carry it. But, though they make the greatest appearance in the field, and cry the loudest, the best on't is, they are but a sort of French Huguenots, or Dutch boors, brought over in herds, but not naturalized; who have not land of two pounds per annum in Parnassus, and therefore are not privileged to poll. Their authors are of the same level, fit to represent them on a mountebank's stage, or to be masters of the ceremonies in a bear garden. Yet these are they who have the most admirers. But it often happens, to their mortification, that, as their readers improve their stock of sense, (as they may by reading better books, and by conversation with men of judgment,) they soon forsake them: and when the torrent from the mountains falls no more, the swelling writer is reduced into his shallow bed, like the Mançanares at Madrid, with scarce water to moisten his own pebbles.* There are a middle sort of readers, (as we hold there is a middle state of souls,) such as have a farther insight than the former, yet have not the capacity of judging right; for I speak not of those who are bribed by a party, and know better, if they were not corrupted; but I mean a company of warm young men, who are not yet arrived so far as to discern the difference betwixt fustian, or ostentatious sentences, and the true sublime. These

* There can be, I think, little doubt, that in both these passages the poet has detected the true and poetical sense of the author, which has escaped the mere commentator.

† All of whom had made slight and partial attempts as translators from Virgil.

‡ This comparison our author has detailed in his preface to Fresnoy's "Art of Painting."

"I am now come, though with the omission of many likenesses, to the third part of Painting, which is called chromatic, or colouring. Expression, and all that belongs to words, is that in a poem which colouring is in a picture. The colours well chosen in their proper places, together with the lights and shadows which belong to them, lighten the design, and make it pleasant to the eye. The words, the expressions, the tropes and figures, the versification, and all the other elegancies of sound, as cadences, turns of words upon the thought, and many other things which are all parts of expression, perform exactly the same office, both in dramatic and epic poetry. Our author calls colouring *lena sororis*: in plain English, the bawd of her sister, the design or drawing: she clothes, she dresses her up, she paints her, she makes her appear more lovely than naturally she is, she procures for the design, and makes lovers for her; for the design of itself is only so many naked lines. Thus in poetry, the expression is that which charms the reader, and beautifies the design, which is only the outlines of the fables."

* This river, which flows past Madrid, is distinguished by the splendour of its bridge, and the scantiness of its waters.

are above liking Martial, or Owen's Epigrams, but they would certainly set Virgil below Statius or Lucan. I need not say their poets are of the same taste with their admirers. They affect greatness in all they write; but it is a bladdered greatness, like that of the vain man whom Seneca describes—an ill habit of body, full of humours, and swelled with dropsy. Even these too desert their authors, as their judgment ripens. The young gentlemen themselves are commonly misled by their pedagogue at school, their tutor at the university, or their governor in their travels: and many of those three sorts are the most positive blockheads in the world. How many of those flatulent writers have I known, who have sunk in their reputation, after seven or eight editions of their works; for indeed they are poets only for young men. They had great success at their first appearance; but not being of God, (as a wit said formerly,) they could not stand.

I have already named two sorts of judges; but Virgil wrote for neither of them: and, by his example, I am not ambitious of pleasing the lowest or the middle form of readers.

He chose to please the most judicious—souls of the highest rank, and truest understanding. These are few in number; but whoever is so happy as to gain their approbation, can never lose it, because they never give it blindly. Then they have a certain magnetism in their judgment, which attracts others to their sense. Every day they gain some new proselyte, and in time become the church. For this reason, a well weighed judicious poem, which at its first appearance gains no more upon the world than to be just received, and rather not blamed than much applauded, insinuates itself by insensible degrees into the liking of the reader: the more he studies it, the more it grows upon him; every time he takes it up, he discovers some new graces in it. And whereas poems, which are produced by the vigour of imagination only, have a gloss upon them at the first, which time wears off; the works of judgment are like the diamond; the more they are polished, the more lustre they receive. Such is the difference betwixt Virgil's Æneis and Marini's Adone. And, if I may be allowed to change the metaphor, I would say, that Virgil is like the Fame which he describes:

Mobilitate viget, viresque acquirit eundo.

Such a sort of reputation is my aim, though in a far inferior degree, according to my motto in the title-page—*Sequiturque patrem non passibus æquis:* and therefore I appeal to the highest court of judicature, like that of the peers, of which your lordship is so great an ornament.

Without this ambition, which I own, of desiring to please the *judices natos*, I could never have been able to have done any thing at this age, when the fire of poetry is commonly extinguished in other men. Yet Virgil has given me the example of Entellus for my encouragement: when he was well heated, the younger champion could not stand before him. And we find the elder contended not for the gift, but for the honour—*nec dona moror:* for Dampier has informed us, in his voyages, that the air of the country which produces gold, is never wholesome.

I had long since considered, that the way to please the best judges is not to translate a poet literally, and Virgil least of any other: for, his peculiar beauty lying in his choice of words, I am excluded from it by the narrow compass of our heroic verse, unless I would make use of monosyllables only, and those clogged with consonants, which are the dead weight of our mother-tongue. It is possible, I confess, though it rarely happens, that a verse of monosyllables may sound harmoniously; and some examples of it I have seen. My first line of the Æneis is not harsh—

Arms, and the man I sing, who, forced by fate, &c.

But a much better instance may be given from the last line of Manilius, made English, by our learned and judicious Mr. Creech—

Nor could the world have borne so fierce a flame—

where the many liquid consonants are placed so artfully, that they give a pleasing sound to the words, though they are all of one syllable.

It is true, I have been sometimes forced upon it in other places of this work: but I never did it out of choice; I was either in haste, or Virgil gave me no occasion for the ornament of words; for it seldom happens but a monosyllable line turns verse to prose; and even that prose is rugged and unharmonious. Philarchus, I remember, taxes Balzac for placing twenty monosyllables in file, without one dissyllable betwixt them. The way I have taken is not so strait as metaphrase, nor so loose as paraphrase: some things too I have omitted, and sometimes have added of my own. Yet the omissions, I hope, are but of circumstances, and such as would have no grace in English; and the additions, I also hope, are easily deduced from Virgil's sense. They will seem, (at least I have the vanity to think so,) not stuck into him, but growing out of him. He studies brevity more than any other poet: but he had the advantage of a language wherein much may be comprehended in a little space. We, and all the modern tongues, have more articles and pronouns, besides signs of tenses and cases, and other barbarities on which our speech is built by the faults of our forefathers. The Romans founded theirs upon the Greek: and the Greeks, we know, were labouring many hundred years upon their language, before they brought it to perfection. They rejected all those signs, and cut off as many articles as they could spare; comprehending in one word what we are constrained to express in two; which is one reason why we cannot write so concisely as they have done. The word *pater*, for example, signifies not only *a* father, but *your* father, *my* father, *his* or *her* father, all included in a word.

This inconvenience is common to all modern tongues; and this alone constrains us to employ more words than the ancients needed. But, having before observed, that Virgil endeavours to be short, and at the same time elegant, I pursue the excellence, and forsake the brevity: for there he is like ambergris, a rich perfume, but of so close and glutinous a body, that it must be opened with inferior scents of musk or civet, or the sweetness will not be drawn out into another language.

On the whole matter, I thought fit to steer betwixt the two extremes of paraphrase and literal translation; to keep as near my author as I could, without losing all his graces, the most eminent of which are in the beauty of his words; and those words, I must add, are always figurative. Such of these as would retain their elegance in our tongue, I have endeavoured to graff on it; but most of them are of necessity to be lost, because they will not shine in any but their own. Virgil has sometimes two of them in a line: but the scantiness of our heroic verse is not capable of receiving more than one; and that too must expiate for many others which have none. Such is the difference of the languages, or such my want of skill in choosing words. Yet I may presume to say, and I hope with as much reason as the French translator, that, taking all the materials of this divine author, I have endeavoured to make Virgil speak such English as he would himself have spoken, if he had been born in England, and in this present age. I acknowledge, with Ségrais, that I have not succeeded in this attempt according to my desire: yet I shall not be wholly without praise, if in some sort I may be allowed to have copied the clearness, the purity, the easiness, and the magnificence, of his style. But I shall have occasion to speak further on this subject before I end the Preface.

When I mentioned the Pindaric line, I should have added, that I take another license in my verses: for I frequently make use of triplet rhymes, and for the same reason, because they bound the sense. And therefore I generally join these two licenses together, and make the last verse of the triplet a Pindaric:* for, besides the majesty which it gives, it confines the sense within the barriers of three lines, which would languish if it were lengthened into four. Spenser is my example for both these privileges of English verses; and Chapman has followed him in his translation of Homer. Mr. Cowley has given into them after both; and all succeeding writers after him. I regard them now as the *Magna Charta* of heroic poetry, and am too much an Englishman to lose what my ancestors have gained for me. Let the French and Italians value themselves on their regularity; strength and elevation are our standard. I said before, and I repeat it, that the affected purity of the French has unsinewed their heroic verse. The language of an epic poem is almost wholly figurative: yet they are so fearful of a metaphor, that no example of Virgil can encourage them to be bold with safety. Sure they might warm themselves by that sprightly blaze, without approaching it so close as to singe their wings; they may come as near it as their master. Not that I would discourage that purity of diction in which he excels all other poets. But he knows how far to extend his franchises, and advances to the verge, without venturing a foot beyond it. On the other side, without being injurious to the memory of our English Pindar, I will presume to say, that his metaphors are sometimes too violent, and his language is not always pure. But, at the same time, I must excuse him; for, through the iniquity of the times, he was forced to travel, at an age when, instead of learning foreign languages, he should have studied the beauties of his mother-tongue, which, like all other speeches, is to be cultivated early, or we shall never write it with any kind of elegance.† Thus, by gaining abroad, he lost at home; like the painter in the "Arcadia," who, going to see a skirmish, had his arms lopped off, and returned, says Sir Philip Sidney, well instructed how to draw a battle, but without a hand to perform his work.

There is another thing in which I have presumed to deviate from him and Spenser. They both make hemistichs, (or half verses,) breaking

* Now more commonly called an Alexandrine. Pope had perhaps this passage in his memory, when he composed the famous triplet descriptive of Dryden's versification:

Waller was smooth; but Dryden taught to join
The varying verse, the full resounding line,
The long majestic march, and energy divine.

† He alludes to Cowley, who was forced abroad by the ill fate of the royal party in the civil wars.

off in the middle of a line. I confess there are not many such in the "Fairy Queen;" and even those few might be occasioned by his unhappy choice of so long a stanza. Mr. Cowley had found out, that no kind of staff is proper for a heroic poem, as being all too lyrical: yet, though he wrote in couplets, where rhyme is freer from constraint, he frequently affects half verses; of which we find not one in Homer, and I think not in any of the Greek poets, or the Latin, excepting only Virgil: and there is no question but he thought he had Virgil's authority for that license. But, I am confident, our poet never meant to leave him, or any other, such a precedent: and I ground my opinion on these two reasons: first, we find no example of a hemistich in any of his Pastorals or Georgics: for he had given the last finishing strokes to both these poems: but his Æneis he left so incorrect, at least so short of that perfection at which he aimed, that we know how hard a sentence he passed upon it: and, in the second place, I reasonably presume, that he intended to have filled up all those hemistichs, because in one of them we find the sense imperfect:

Quem tibi jam Troja———

which some foolish grammarian has ended for him with a half line of nonsense:

——— peperit fumante Creusa:

for Ascanius must have been born some years before the burning of that city; which I need not prove. On the other side, we find also, that he himself filled up one line in the Sixth Æneid, the enthusiasm seizing him, while he was reading to Augustus:

Misenum Æoliden, quo non præstantior alter
Ære ciere viros———

to which he added, in that transport, *Martemque accendere cantu:* and never was any line more nobly finished; for the reasons which I have given in the Book of Painting. On these considerations I have shunned hemistichs; not being willing to imitate Virgil to a fault, like Alexander's courtiers, who affected to hold their necks awry, because he could not help it.* I am confident your lordship is by this time of my opinion, and that you will look on those half lines hereafter, as the imperfect products of a hasty Muse: like the frogs and serpents in the Nile; part of them kindled into life, and part a lump of unformed unanimated mud.

I am sensible that many of my whole verses are as imperfect as those halves, for want of time to digest them better: but give me leave to make the excuse of Boccace, who, when he was upbraided that some of his novels had not the spirit of the rest, returned this answer, that Charlemagne, who made the paladins, was never able to raise an army of them. The leaders may be heroes, but the multitude must consist of common men.

I am also bound to tell your lordship, in my own defence, that, from the beginning of the First Georgic to the end of the last Æneid, I found the difficulty of translation growing on me in every succeeding book: for Virgil, above all poets, had a stock, which I may call almost inexhaustible, of figurative, elegant, and sounding words. I, who inherit but a small portion of his genius, and write in a language so much inferior to the Latin, have found it very painful to vary phrases, when the same sense returns upon me. Even he himself, whether out of necessity or choice, has often expressed the same thing in the same words, and often repeated two or three whole verses, which he had used before. Words are not so easily coined as money; and yet we see that the credit, not only of banks, but of exchequers, cracks, when little comes in, and much goes out. Virgil called upon me in every line for some new word: and I paid so long, that I was almost bankrupt; so that the latter end must needs be more burdensome than the beginning or the middle; and, consequently, the twelfth Æneid cost me double the time of the first and second. What had become of me, if Virgil had taxed me with another book? I had certainly been reduced to pay the public in hammered money, for want of milled; that is, in the same old words which I had used before and the receivers must have been forced to have taken any thing, where there was so little to be had.*

Besides this difficulty, (with which I have struggled, and made a shift to pass it over,) there is one remaining, which is insuperable to all translators. We are bound to our author's sense, though with the latitudes already mentioned; for I think it not so sacred, as that one *iota* must not be added or diminished, on pain of an *anathema*. But slaves we are, and labour on another man's plantation; we dress the vineyard, but the wine is the owner's: if the soil be sometimes barren, then we are sure of being scourged: if it be fruitful, and our care succeeds, we are not thanked; for the proud reader will only say, the poor drudge has done his duty. But this is nothing to what follows; for, being obliged to make his sense intelligible,

* Our author has, however, availed himself of this license in his earlier poetry.

* The confusion occasioned by the rules of the mint, then recently adopted, created great inconvenience and distress to individuals. It is often mentioned in the correspondence between Tonson and Dryden.

we are forced to untune our own verses, that we may give his meaning to the reader. He, who invents, is master of his thoughts and words: he can turn and vary them as he pleases, till he renders them harmonious; but the wretched translator has no such privilege: for, being tied to the thoughts, he must make what music he can in the expression; and, for this reason, it cannot always be so sweet as that of the original. There is a beauty of sound, as Ségrais has observed, in some Latin words, which is wholly lost in any modern language. He instances in that *mollis amaracus*, on which Venus lays Cupid, in the First Æneid. If I should translate it *sweet-marjoram*, as the word signifies, the reader would think I had mistaken Virgil: for those village words, as I may call them, give us a mean idea of the thing: but the sound of the Latin is so much more pleasing, by the just mixture of the vowels with the consonants, that it raises our fancies to conceive somewhat more noble than a common herb, and to spread roses under him, and strew lilies over him; a bed not unworthy the grandson of the goddess.

If I cannot copy his harmonious numbers, how shall I imitate his noble flights, where his thoughts and words are equally sublime? *Quem*

———quisquis studet æmulari
——— ceratis ope Dædalea
Nititur pennis, vitreo daturus
Nomina ponto.

What modern language, or what poet, can express the majestic beauty of this one verse, amongst a thousand others?

Aude, hospes, contemnere opes, et te quoque dignum
Finge deo.———

For my part, I am lost in the admiration of it: I contemn the world when I think on it, and myself when I translate it.*

Lay by Virgil, I beseech your lordship, and all my better sort of judges, when you take up my version; and it will appear a passable beauty when the original muse is absent. But, like Spenser's false Florimel made of snow, it melts and vanishes when the true one comes in sight. I will not excuse, but justify myself, for one pretended crime, with which I am liable to be charged by false critics, not only in this translation, but in many of my original poems—that I Latinise too much. It is true, that, when I find an English word significant and sounding, I neither borrow from the Latin, nor any other language; but, when I want at home, I must seek abroad.

If sounding words are not of our growth and manufacture, who shall hinder me to import them from a foreign country? I carry not out the treasure of the nation, which is never to return; but, what I bring from Italy, I spend in England: here it remains, and here it circulates; for, if the coin be good, it will pass from one hand to another. I trade both with the living and the dead, for the enrichment of our native language. We have enough in England to supply our necessity; but if we will have things of magnificence and splendour, we must get them by commerce. Poetry requires ornament; and that is not to be had from our old Teuton monosyllables: therefore, if I find any elegant word in a classic author, I propose it to be naturalized by using it myself; and, if the public approves of it, the bill passes. But every man cannot distinguish between pedantry and poetry: every man, therefore, is not fit to innovate. Upon the whole matter, a poet must first be certain that the word he would introduce is beautiful in the Latin, and is to consider, in the next place, whether it will agree with the English idiom: after this, he ought to take the opinion of judicious friends, such as are learned in both languages: and, lastly, since no man is infallible, let him use this license very sparingly; for, if too many foreign words are poured in upon us, it looks as if they were designed not to assist the natives, but to conquer them.

I am now drawing towards a conclusion, and suspect your lordship is very glad of it. But permit me first to own what helps I have had in this undertaking. The late Earl of Lauderdale* sent me over his new translation of the Æneis, which he had ended before I engaged in the same design. Neither did I then intend it: but, some proposals being afterwards made me by my bookseller, I desired his lordship's leave that I might accept them, which he freely granted; and I have his letter yet to show for that permission. He resolved to have printed his work, (which he might have done two years before I could publish mine,) and had performed it if death had not prevented him. But, having his manuscript in my hands, I consulted it as often as I doubted of my author's sense; for no man understood Virgil better than that learned nobleman. His friends, I hear, have

* Nevertheless our author, long before undertaking the translation of Virgil, had given a noble paraphrase of these lines in the Hind's address to the Panther:

This mean retreat did mighty Pan contain;
Be emulous of him, and pomp disdain,
And dare not to debase your soul to gain.

* Richard, fourth Earl of Lauderdale, nephew of that respectable minister the Duke of Lauderdale. "He had a fine genius for poetry," says Sir Robert Douglass, in his Peerage of Scotland; "witness his elegant translation of Virgil."

yet another and more correct copy of that translation by them, which, had they pleased to have given the public, the judges must have been convinced that I have not flattered him. Besides this help, which was not inconsiderable, Mr. Congreve has done me the favour to review the Æneis, and compare my version with the original. I shall never be ashamed to own, that this excellent young man has showed me many faults, which I have endeavoured to correct. It is true, he might have easily found more, and then my translation had been more perfect.

Two other worthy friends of mine, who desire to have their names concealed, seeing me straitened in my time, took pity on me, and gave me the "Life of Virgil," the two prefaces to the "Pastorals" and the "Georgics," and all the arguments in prose to the whole translation; which, perhaps, has caused a report, that the two first poems are not mine.* If it had been true, that I had taken their verses for my own, I might have gloried in their aid, and, like Terence, have fathered the opinion that Scipio and Lælius joined with me. But the same style being continued through the whole, and the same laws of versification observed, are proofs sufficient, that this is one man's work: and your lordship is too well acquainted with my manner, to doubt, that any part of it is another's.

That your lordship may see I was in earnest when I promised to hasten to an end, I will not give the reasons why I writ not always in the proper terms of navigation, land-service, or in the cant of any profession. I will only say, that Virgil has avoided those proprieties, because he writ not to mariners, soldiers, astronomers, gardeners, peasants, &c. but to all in general, and in particular to men and ladies of the first quality, who have been better bred than to be too nicely knowing in the terms. In such cases, it is enough for a poet to write so plainly, that he may be understood by his readers; to avoid impropriety, and not affect to be thought learned in all things.

I have omitted the four preliminary lines of the First Æneïd, because I think them inferior to any four others in the whole poem, and consequently believe they are not Virgil's.† There is too great a gap betwixt the adjective *vicina* in the second line, and the substantive *arva* in the latter end of the third, which keeps his meaning in obscurity too long, and is contrary to the clearness of his style.

Ut quamvis avido

is too ambitious an ornament to be his; and

Gratum opus agricolis,

are all words unnecessary, and independent of what he had said before.

———Horrentia Martis
Arma———

is worse than any of the rest. *Horrentia* is such a flat epithet, as Tully would have given us in his verses. It is a mere filler, to stop a vacancy in the hexameter, and connect the preface to the work of Virgil. Our author seems to sound a charge, and begins like the clangour of a trumpet:

Arma, virumque cano, Trojæ qui primus ab oris.

scarce a word without an *r*, and the vowels, for the greater part, sonorous. The prefacer began with *Ille ego*, which he was constrained to patch up in the fourth line with *at nunc*, to make the sense cohere; and, if both those words are not notorious botches, I am much deceived, though the French translator thinks otherwise. For my own part, I am rather of the opinion, that they were added by Tucca and Varius, than retrenched.

I know it may be answered, by such as think Virgil the author of the four lines, that he asserts his title to the Æneïs in the beginning of this work, as he did to the two former in the last lines of the Fourth Georgic. I will not reply otherwise to this, than by desiring them to compare these four lines with the four others, which we know are his, because no poet but he alone could write them. If they cannot distinguish creeping from flying, let them lay down Virgil, and take up Ovid, *de Ponto*, in his stead. My master needed not the assistance of that preliminary poet to prove his claim. His own majestic mien discovers him to be the king, amidst a thousand courtiers. It was a superfluous office; and, therefore, I would not set those verses in the front of Virgil, but have rejected them* to my own preface.

I, who before, with shepherds in the groves,
Sung, to my oaten pipe, their rural loves,
And, issuing thence, compelled the neighbouring field
A plenteous crop of rising corn to yield,
Manured the glebe, and stock'd the fruitful plain
(A poem grateful to the greedy swain, &c.)

If there be not a tolerable line in all these six, the most clumsy ... [continues]

*Dr. Knightly Chetwood and Mr. Addison. The former wrote the "Life of Virgil," and the "Preface to the Pastorals;" the latter, the "Essay on the Georgics." See introductory notes on these pieces.

† Ille ego, qui quondam gracili modulatus avena
Carmen, et, egressus silvis, vicina coegi
Ut quamvis avido parerent arva colono,
Gratum opus agricolis; at nunc horrentia Martis...

The characteristic modesty of our author, as well as the rugged and turgid structure of these lines, have authorized modern critics to conclude, that neither the sense nor expression of these four lines resembles the genuine productions of Virgil.

* A Latinism for "throwing back."

the prefacer gave me no occasion to write better. This is a just apology in this place; but I have done great wrong to Virgil in the whole translation: want of time, the inferiority of our language, the inconvenience of rhyme, and all the other excuses I have made, may alleviate my fault, but cannot justify the boldness of my undertaking. What avails it me to acknowledge freely, that I have not been able to do him right in any line? for even my own confession makes against me; and it will always be returned upon me, "Why then did you attempt it?" To which no other answer can be made, than that I have done him less injury than any of his former libellers.

What they called his picture, had been drawn at length so many times, by the daubers of almost all nations, and still so unlike him, that I snatched up the pencil with disdain; being satisfied beforehand, that I could make some small resemblance of him, though I must be content with a worse likeness. A Sixth Pastoral, a Pharmaceutria, a single Orpheus, and some other features, have been exactly taken: but those holyday-authors writ for pleasure; and only showed us what they could have done, if they would have taken pains to perform the whole.

Be pleased, my lord, to accept, with your wonted goodness, this unworthy present which I make you. I have taken off one trouble from you, of defending it, by acknowledging its imperfections; and, though some part of them are covered in the verse, (as Erichthonius rode always in a chariot, to hide his lameness,) such of them as cannot be concealed, you will please to connive at, though, in the strictness of your judgment, you cannot pardon. If Homer was allowed to nod sometimes in so long a work, it will be no wonder if I often fall asleep. You took my "Aureng-Zebe" into your protection, with all his faults: and I hope here cannot be so many, because I translate an author who gives me such examples of correctness. What my jury may be, I know not; but it is good for a criminal to plead before a favourable judge: if I had said partial, would your lordship have forgiven me? or will you give me leave to acquaint the world, that I have many times been obliged to your bounty since the Revolution? Though I never was reduced to beg a charity nor ever had the impudence to ask one, either of your lordship, or your noble kinsman the Earl of Dorset,* much less of any other; yet, when I least expected it, you have both remembered me. So inherent it is in your family not to forget an old servant. It looks rather like ingratitude on my part, that, where I have been so often obliged, I have appeared so seldom to return my thanks, and where I was also so sure of being well received. Somewhat of laziness was in the case, and somewhat too of modesty, but nothing of disrespect or of unthankfulness. I will not say that your lordship has encouraged me to this presumption, lest, if my labours meet with no success in public, I may expose your judgment to be censured. As for my own enemies, I shall never think them worth an answer; and, if your lordship has any, they will not dare to arraign you for want of knowledge in this art, till they can produce somewhat better of their own, than your "Essay on Poetry." It was on this consideration, that I have drawn out my preface to so great a length. Had I not addressed to a poet and a critic of the first magnitude, I had myself been taxed for want of judgment, and shamed my patron for want of understanding. But neither will you, my lord, so soon be tired as any other, because the discourse is on your art; neither will the learned reader think it tedious, because it is *Ad Clerum*.† At least, when he begins to be weary, the church-doors are open. That I may pursue the allegory with a short prayer after a long sermon—

May you live happily and long, for the service of your country, the encouragement of good letters, and the ornament of poetry; which cannot be wished more earnestly by any man, than by

Your Lordship's
Most humble,
Most obliged, and
Most obedient servant,
JOHN DRYDEN

* Their mothers were half sisters, being both daughters of Lionel Cranfield, Earl of Middlesex.

† *Concio ad Clerum*, a sermon preached before a learned body.

THE POEMS OF DRYDEN.

TRANSLATIONS FROM VIRGIL.

THE ÆNEIS.

BOOK I.

ARGUMENT.

The Trojans, after a seven years' voyage, set sail for Italy, but are overtaken by a dreadful storm, which Æolus raises at the request of Juno. The tempest sinks one, and scatters the rest. Neptune drives off the winds, and calms the sea. Æneas, with his own ship and six more, arrives safe at an African port. Venus complains to Jupiter of her son's misfortunes. Jupiter comforts her, and sends Mercury to procure him a kind reception among the Carthaginians. Æneas, going out to discover the country, meets his mother in the shape of a huntress, who conveys him in a cloud to Carthage, where he sees his friends whom he thought lost, and receives a kind entertainment from the queen. Dido, by a device of Venus, begins to have a passion for him, and, after some discourse with him, desires the history of his adventures since the siege of Troy, which is the subject of the two following books.

Arms, and the man I sing, who, forc'd by Fate
And haughty Juno's unrelenting hate,
Expell'd and exil'd, left the Trojan shore.
Long labours, both by sea and land, he bore,
And in the doubtful war, before he won
The Latin realm, and built the destin'd town,
His banish'd gods restor'd to rites divine,
And settled sure succession in his line,
From whence the race of Alban fathers come
And the long glories of majestic Rome.
O Muse! the causes and the crimes relate;
What goddess was provok'd, and whence her hate;
For what offence the queen of heav'n began
To persecute so brave, so just a man;
Involv'd his anxious life in endless cares,
Expos'd to wants, and hurried into wars!
Can heav'nly minds such high resentment show,
Or exercise their spite in human wo?
Against the Tyber's mouth, but far away,
An ancient town was seated on the sea—
A Tyrian colony—the people made
Stout for the war, and studious of their trade:
Carthage the name—belov'd by Juno more
Than her own Argos, or the Samian shore.
Here stood her chariot; here if heav'n were kind
The seat of awful empire she design'd.
Yet she had heard an ancient rumour fly,
(Long cited by the people of the sky,)
That times to come should see the Trojan race
Her Carthage ruin, and her tow'rs deface;
Nor thus confin'd, the yoke of sov'reign sway
Should on the necks of all the nations lay.
She ponder'd this, and fear'd it was in fate;
Nor could forget the war she wag'd of late,
For conqu'ring Greece, against the Trojan state.
Besides, long causes working in her mind,
And secret seeds of envy, lay behind:
Deep graven in her heart, the doom remain'd
Of partial Paris, and her form disdain'd;
The grace bestow'd on ravish'd Ganymed,
Electra's glories, and her injur'd bed.
Each was a cause alone; and all combin'd
To kindle vengeance in her haughty mind.
For this, far distant from the Latian coast,
She drove the remnants of the Trojan host:
And sev'n long years th' unhappy wand'ring train
Were toss'd by storms, and scatter'd through the main.
Such time, such toil, requir'd the Roman name,
Such length of labour for so vast a frame.
Now scarce the Trojan fleet, with sails and oars,
Had left behind the fair Sicilian shores,
Ent'ring with cheerful shouts the wat'ry reign,
And ploughing frothy furrows in the main;
When lab'ring still with endless discontent,
The queen of heav'n did thus her fury vent—
"Then am I vanquish'd? must I yield?" said she;
"And must the Trojans reign in Italy?
So fate will have it; and Jove adds his force;
Nor can my pow'r divert their happy course.
Could angry Pallas, with revengeful spleen,
The Grecian navy burn, and drown the men?
She, for the fault of one offending foe,
The bolts of Jove himself presum'd to throw:

With whirlwinds from beneath she toss'd the ship,
And bare expos d the bosom of the deep:
Then—as an eagle gripes the trembling game—
The wretch, yet hissing with her father's flame,
She strongly seiz'd, and, with a burning wound,
Transfix'd, and naked, on a rock she bound.
But I, who walk in awful state above,
The majesty of heav'n, the sister wife of Jove,
For length of years my fruitless force employ
Against the thin remains of ruin'd Troy!
What nations now to Juno's pow'r will pray?
Or offerings on my slighted altars lay?"
Thus rag'd the goddess; and with fury fraught,
The restless regions of the storms she sought,
Where, in a spacious cave of living stone,
The tyrant Æolus, from his airy throne,
With pow'r imperial curbs the struggling winds,
And sounding tempests in dark prisons binds.
This way, and that, th' impatient captives tend,
And, pressing for release, the mountains rend.
High in his hall th' undaunted monarch stands,
And shakes his sceptre, and their rage commands;
Which did he not, their unresisted sway
Would sweep the word before them in their way;
Earth, air, and seas, through empty space would roll,
And heav'n would fly before the driving soul.
In fear of this, the father of the gods
Confin'd their fury to those dark abodes,
And lock'd them safe within, oppress'd with mountain loads;
Impos'd a king with arbitrary sway,
To loose their fetters, or their force allay;
To whom the suppliant queen her pray'rs address'd,
And thus the tenor of her suit express'd,
"O, Æolus!—for to thee the king of heav'n
The pow'r of tempests and of winds has giv'n;
Thy force alone their fury can restrain,
And smooth the waves, or swell the troubled main—
A race of wand'ring slaves, abhorr'd by me,
With prosp'rous passage cut the Tuscan sea:
To fruitful Italy their course they steer,
And, for their vanquish'd gods, design new temples there.
Raise all thy winds, with night involve the skies;
Sink or disperse my fatal enemies.
Twice sev'n, the charming daughters of the main,
'Around my person wait, and bear my train:'
Succeed my wish, and second my design,
The fairest, Deiopeia, shall be thine,
And make thee father of a happy line."
To this the god—"'T is yours, O queen! to will
The work, which duty binds me to fulfil.
These airy kingdoms, and this wide command,
Are all the presents of your bounteous hand:
Yours is my sov'reign's grace; and, as your guest,
I sit with gods at their celestial feast.
Raise tempests at your pleasure, or subdue;
Dispose of empire, which I hold from you."
He said, and hurl'd against the mountain side
His quiv'ring spear, and all the god applied.
The raging winds rush through the hollow wound,
And dance aloft in air, and skim along the ground;
Then settling on the sea, the surges sweep,
Raise liquid mountains, and disclose the deep;
South, east, and west, with mix'd confusion roar,
And roll the foaming billows to the shore.
The cables crack; the sailors' fearful cries
Ascend; and sable night involves the skies;
And heav'n itself is ravish'd from their eyes.
Loud peals of thunder from the poles ensue;
Then flashing fires the transient light renew
The face of things a frightful image bears;
And present death in various forms appears.
Struck with unusual fright, the Trojan chief,
With lifted hands and eyes, invokes relief;
And "Thrice and four times happy those," he cried,
"That under Ilian walls, before their parents, died!
Tydides, bravest of the Grecian train!
Why could not I by that strong arm be slain,
And lie by noble Hector on the plain,
Or great Sarpedon, in those bloody fields,
Where Simois rolls the bodies and the shields
Of heroes, whose dismember'd hands yet bear
The dart aloft, and clench the pointed spear?"
Thus, while the pious prince his fate bewails,
Fierce Boreas drove against his flying sails,
And rent the sheets: the raging billows rise,
And mount the tossing vessel to the skies:
Nor can the shiv'ring oars sustain the blow;
The galley gives her side, and turns her prow;
While those astern, descending down the steep,
Through gaping waves behold the boiling deep.
Three ships were hurried by the southern blast,
And on the secret shelves with fury cast,
Those hidden rocks th' Ausonian sailors knew;
They call'd them altars, when they rose in view,
And show'd their spacious backs above the flood.
Three more fierce Eurus, in his angry mood,
Dash'd on the shallows of the moving sand,
And in mid ocean left them moor'd a-land.
Orontes' bark, that bore the Lycian crew
(A horrid sight,) e'en in the hero's view,

From stem to stern by waves was overborne:
The trembling pilot, from his rudder torn,
Was headlong hurl'd: thrice round the ship was toss'd,
Then bulg'd at once, and in the deep was lost;
And here and there above the waves were seen
Arms, pictures, precious goods, and floating men.
The stoutest vessel to the storm gave way,
And suck'd through loosen'd planks the rushing sea.
Ilioneus was her chief: Aletes old,
Achates faithful, Abas young and bold,
Endur'd not less: their ships, with gaping seams,
Admit the deluge of the briny streams.
Meantime imperial Neptune heard the sound
Of raging billows breaking on the ground.
Displeas'd, and fearing for his wat'ry reign,
He rear'd his awful head above the main
Serene in majesty,—then roll'd his eyes
Around the space of earth, and seas, and skies.
He saw the Trojan fleet dispers'd, distress'd,
By stormy winds and wint'ry heav'n oppress'd.
Full well the god his sister's envy knew,
And what her aims, and what her arts pursue.
He summon'd Eurus and the Western blast,
And first an angry glance on both he cast,
Then thus rebuk'd—"Audacious winds! from whence
This bold attempt, this rebel insolence!
Is it for you to ravage seas and land,
Unauthoriz'd by my supreme command?
To raise such mountains on the troubled main?
Whom I—but first 't is fit the billows to restrain:
And then you shall be taught obedience to my reign.
Hence, to your lord my royal mandate bear—
The realms of ocean and the fields of air
Are mine, not his. By fatal lot to me
The liquid empire fell, and trident of the sea.
His pow'r to hollow caverns is confin'd:
There let him reign, the jailor of the wind;
With hoarse commands his breathing subjects call,
And boast and bluster in his empty hall."
He spoke and while he spoke he smooth'd the sea,
Dispell'd the darkness and restor'd the day.
Cymothoe, Triton, and the sea-green train
Of beauteous nymphs, the daughters of the main,
Clear from the rocks the vessels with their hands:
The god himself with ready trident stands,
And opes the deep, and spreads the moving sands;
Then heaves them off the shoals.—Where'er he guides
His finny coursers, and in triumph rides,
The waves unruffle, and the sea subsides.
As when in tumults rise th' ignoble crowd,
Mad are their motions, and their tongues are loud;
And stones and brands in rattling volleys fly,
And all the rustic arms that fury can supply
If then some grave and pious man appear,
They hush their noise, and lend a list'ning ear:
He sooths with sober words their angry mood,
And quenches their innate desire of blood:
So, when the father of the flood appears,
And o'er the seas his sov'reign trident rears,
Their fury falls: he skims the liquid plains,
High on his chariot, and, with loosen'd reins,
Majestic moves along, and awful peace maintains.
The weary Trojans ply their shatter'd oars
To nearest land, and make the Libyan shores
Within a long recess there lies a bay:
An island shades it from the rolling sea,
And forms a port secure for ships to ride:
Broke by the jutting land on either side,
In double streams the briny waters glide
Betwixt two rows of rocks: a sylvan scene
Appears above, and groves for ever green:
A grot is form'd beneath, with mossy seats,
To rest the Nereids, and exclude the heats.
Down through the crannies of the living walls.
The crystal streams descend in murm'ring falls.
No halsers need to bind the vessels here,
Nor bearded anchors; for no streams they fear.
Sev'n ships within this happy harbour meet,
The thin remainders of the scatter'd fleet:
The Trojans, worn with toils, and spent with woes,
Leap on the welcom'd land, and seek their wish'd repose.
First, good Achates, with repeated strokes
Of clashing flints, their hidden fires provokes:
Short flame succeeds; a bed of wither'd leaves
The dying sparkles in their fall receives
Caught into life, in fiery fumes they rise,
And, fed with stronger food, invade the skies.
The Trojans, dropping wet, or stand around
The cheerful blaze, or lie along the ground:
Some dry their corn, infected with the brine,
Then grind with marbles, and prepare to dine.
Æneas climbs the mountain's airy brow,
And takes a prospect of the seas below,
If Capys thence, or Antheus, he could spy,
Or see the streamers of Caicus fly.
No vessels were in view, but on the plain,
Three beamy stags command a lordly train
Of branching heads: the more ignoble throng
Attend their stately steps, and slowly graze along.
He stood; and while secure they fed below,
He took the quiver and the trusty bow
Achates us'd to bear: the leaders first
He laid along, and then the vulgar pierc'd;

Nor ceas'd his arrows, till the shady plain
Sev'n mighty bodies with their blood distain.
For the sev'n ships, he made an equal share,
And to the port return'd triumphant from the war.
The jars of generous wine (Acestes' gift,
When his Trinacrian shores the navy left)
He set abroach, and for the feast prepar'd,
In equal portions with the ven'son shar'd.
Thus while he dealt it round, the pious chief
With cheerful words allay'd the common grief.
"Endure and conquer! Jove will soon dispose,
To future good, our past and present woes.
With me, the rocks of Scylla you have tried,
Th' inhuman Cyclops and his den defied.
What greater ills hereafter can you bear?
Resume your courage and dismiss your care.
An hour will come, with pleasure to relate
Your sorrows past, as benefits of Fate.
Through various hazards and events, we move
To Latium, and the realms foredoom'd by Jove:
Call'd to the seat (the promise of the skies)
Where Trojan kingdoms once again may rise,
Endure the hardships of your present state;
Live, and reserve yourselves for better fate."
These words he spoke, but spoke not from his heart;
His outward smiles conceal'd his inward smart.
The jolly crew, unmindful of the past,
The quarry share, their plenteous dinner haste.
Some strip the skin; some portion out the spoil;
The limbs, yet trembling, in the caldrons boil;
Some on the fire the reeking entrails broil.
Stretch'd on the grassy turf, at ease they dine,
Restore their strength with meat, and cheer their souls with wine.
Their hunger thus appeas'd, their care attends
The doubtful fortune of their absent friends:
Alternate hopes and fears their minds possess,
Whether to deem them dead or in distress
Above the rest, Æneas mourns the fate
Of brave Orontes, and th' uncertain state
Of Gyas, Lycus, and of Amycus.—
The day, but not their sorrows, ended thus;
When, from aloft, almighty Jove surveys
Earth, air, and shores, and navigable seas:
At length on Libyan realms he fix'd his eyes—
Whom, pond'ring thus on human miseries,
When Venus saw, she with a lowly look,
Not free from tears, her heav'nly sire bespoke:—
"O king of gods and men! whose awful hand
Disperses thunder on the seas and land
Disposes all with absolute command;
How could my pious son thy pow'r incense?
Or what, alas! is vanquish'd Troy's offence?
Our hope of Italy not only lost,
On various seas by various tempests toss'd,
But shut from ev'ry shore, and barr'd from ev'ry coast.
You promis'd once a progeny divine
Of Romans, rising from the Trojan line,
In after-times should hold the world in awe,
And to the land and ocean give the law.
How is your doom revers'd, which eas'd my care
When Troy was ruin'd in that cruel war?
Then fates to fates I could oppose: but now,
When Fortune still pursues her former blow,
What can I hope? What worse can still succeed?
What end of labours has your will decreed?
Antenor, from the midst of Grecian hosts,
Could pass secure, and pierce th' Illyrian coasts,
Where rolling down the steep, Timavus raves,
And through nine channels disembogues his waves.
At length he founded Padua's happy seat,
And gave his Trojans a secure retreat;
There fix'd their arms, and there renew'd their name,
And there in quiet rules, and crown'd with fame
But we, descended from your sacred line,
Entitled to your heav'n and rites divine,
Are banish'd earth, and, for the wrath of one,
Remov'd from Latium, and the promis'd throne.
Are these our sceptres? these our due rewards?
And is it thus that Jove his plighted faith regards?"
To whom the father of th' immortal race,
Smiling with that serene indulgent face,
With which he drives the clouds and clears the skies,
First gave a holy kiss; then thus replies—
"Daughter, dismiss thy fears: to thy desire,
The fates of thine are fix'd, and stand entire.
Thou shalt behold thy wish'd Lavinian walls;
And, ripe for heav'n, when Fate Æneas calls,
Then shalt thou bear him up, sublime, to me:
No counsels have revers'd my firm decree.
And, lest new fears disturb thy happy state,
Know, I have search'd the mystic rolls of Fate:
Thy son (nor is th' appointed season far)
In Italy shall wage successful war,
Shall tame fierce nations in the bloody field,
And sov'reign laws impose, and cities build,
Till, after ev'ry foe subdu'd, the sun
Thrice though the signs his annual race shall run:
This is his time prefix'd. Ascanius then,
Now call'd Iülus, shall begin his reign,
He thirty rolling years the crown shall wear,
Then from Lavinium shall the seat transfer,
And, with hard labour, Alba-longa build.—
The throne with his succession shall be fill'd
Three hundred circuits more: than shall be seen
Ilia, the fair, a priestess and a queen,

Who, full of Mars, in time, with kindly throes,
Shall at a birth two goodly boys disclose.
The royal babes a tawny wolf shall drain:
Then Romulus his grandsire's throne shall gain,
Of martial tow'rs the founder shall become,
The people Romans call, the city Rome.
To them no bounds of empire I assign,
Nor term of years to their immortal line.
E'en haughty Juno, who, with endless broils,
Earth, seas, and heav'n, and Jove himself, turmoils,
At length aton'd, her friendly pow'r shall join,
To cherish and advance the Trojan line.
The subject world shall Rome's dominion own,
And, prostrate, shall adore the nation of the gown.
An age is rip'ning in revolving fate,
When Troy shall overturn the Grecian state,
And sweet revenge her conqu'ring sons shall call,
To crush the people that conspir'd her fall.
Then Cæsar from the Julian stock shall rise,
Whose empire ocean, and whose fame the skies,
Alone shall bound; whom, fraught with eastern spoils,
Our heav'n, the just reward of human toils,
Securely shall repay with rites divine;
And incense shall ascend before his sacred shrine.
Then dire debate, and impious war, shall cease,
And the stern age be soften'd into peace:
Then banish'd faith shall once again return,
And vestal fires in hallow'd temples burn;
And Remus with Quirinus shall sustain
The righteous laws, and fraud and force restrain.
Janus himself before his fane shall wait,
And keep the dreadful issues of his gate,
With bolts and iron bars: within remains
Imprison'd Fury, bound in brazen chains:
High on a trophy rais'd, of useless arms,
He sits, and threats the world with vain alarms."
He said, and sent Cyllenius with command
To free the ports, and ope the Punic land
To Trojan guests; lest, ignorant of fate,
The queen might force them from her town and state.
Down from the steep of heav'n Cyllenius flies,
And cleaves with all his wings the yielding skies.
Soon on the Libyan shore descends the god,
Performs his message, and displays his rod.
The surly murmurs of the people cease;
And, as the Fates requir'd, they give the peace.
The queen herself suspends the rigid laws,
The Trojans pity, and protect their cause.
Meantime in shades of night Æneas lies:
Care seiz'd his soul, and sleep forsook his eyes.
But, when the sun restor'd the cheerful day,
He rose, the coast and country to survey,
Anxious and eager to discover more.—
It look'd a wild uncultivated shore:
But, whether human kind, or beasts alone,
Possess'd the new-found region, was unknown.
Beneath a ledge of rocks his fleets he hides:
Tall trees surround the mountain's shady sides:
The bending brow above a safe retreat provides.
Arm'd with two pointed darts, he leaves his friends;
And true Achates on his steps attends.
Lo! in the deep recesses of the wood,
Before his eye his goddess mother stood—
A huntress in her habit and her mien:
Her dress a maid, her air confess'd a queen.
Bare were her knees, and knots her garments bind;
Loose was her hair and wanton'd in the wind:
Her hand sustain'd a bow; her quiver hung behind.
She seem'd a virgin of the Spartan blood:
With such array Harpalyce bestrode
Her Tracian courser, and outstripp'd the rapid flood.
"Ho! strangers! have you lately seen," she said,
"One of my sisters, like myself array'd,
Who cross'd the lawn, or in the forest stray'd?
A painted quiver at her back she bore;
Varied with spots, a lynx's hide she wore;
And at full cry pursu'd the tusky boar."
Thus Venus: thus her son replied again:
"None of your sisters have we heard or seen,
O virgin! or what other name you bear
Above that style—O, more than mortal fair!
Your voice and mien celestial birth betray!
If, as you seem, the sister of the day,
Or one at least of chaste Diana's train,
Let not a humble suppliant sue in vain:
But tell a stranger long in tempests tost,
What earth we tread, and who commands the coast?
Then on your name shall wretched mortals call,
And offer'd victims at your altars fall."—
"I dare not," she replied, assume the name
Of goddess, or celestial honours claim:
For Tyrian virgins bows and quivers bear,
And purple buskins o'er their ankles wear.
Know, gentle youth, in Libyan lands you are—
A people rude in peace, and rough in war.
The rising city, which from far you see,
Is Carthage, and a Tyrian colony.
Phœnician Dido rules the growing state,
Who fled from Tyre to shun her brother's hate
Great were her wrongs, her story full of fate;
Which I will sum in short. Sichæus, known
For wealth, and brother to the Punic throne
Possess'd fair Dido's bed; and either heart
At once was wounded with an equal dart.
Her father gave her, yet a spotless maid;
Pygmalion then the Tyrian sceptre sway'd—

One who contemn'd divine and human laws:
Then strife ensu'd, and cursed gold the cause.
The monarch, blinded with desire of wealth,
With steel invades his brother's life by stealth
Before the sacred altar made him bleed,
And long from her conceal'd the cruel deed.
Some tale, some new pretence, he daily coin'd
To sooth his sister, and delude her mind.
At length, in dead of night, the ghost appears
Of her unhappy lord: the spectre stares,
And, with erected eyes, his bosom bares.
The cruel altars, and his fate, he tells,
And the dire secret of his house reveals;
Then warns the widow, and her household gods,
To seek a refuge in remote abodes.
Last, to support her, in so long a way,
He shows her where his hidden treasures lay.
Admonish'd thus, and seiz'd with mortal fright,
The queen provides companions of her flight.
They meet, and all combine to leave the state,
Who hate the tyrant, or who fear his hate.
They seize a fleet, which ready rigg'd they find;
Nor is Pygmalion's treasure left behind.
The vessels, heavy laden, put to sea
With prosp'rous winds: a woman leads the way.
I know not, if by stress of weather driv'n,
Or was their fatal course dispos'd by heav'n;
At last they landed, where from far your eyes
May view the turrets of new Carthage rise;
There bought a space of ground, which (Byrsa call'd
From the bull's hide) they first enclos'd, and wall'd.
But whence are you? what country claims your birth?
What seek you, strangers on our Libyan earth?"
To whom, with sorrow streaming from his eyes,
And deeply sighing, thus her son replies:
"Could you with patience hear, or I relate,
O nymph! the tedious annals of our fate,
Through such a train of woes if I should run,
The day would sooner than the tale be done.
From ancient Troy, by force expell'd, we came;
If you by chance have heard the Trojan name.
On various seas by various tempests toss'd,
At length we landed on your Libyan coast.
The good Æneas am I call'd—a name,
While Fortune favour'd, not unknown to fame.
My household gods, companions of my woes,
With pious care I rescu'd from our foes.
To fruitful Italy my course was bent;
And from the king of heav'n is my descent.
With twice ten sail I cross'd the Phrygian sea;
Fate and my mother goddess led my way.
Scarce sev'n, the thin remainders of my fleet,
From storms preserv'd, within your harbour meet.
Myself distress'd, an exile, and unknown,
Debarr'd from Europe, and from Asia thrown,
In Libyan deserts wander thus alone."
His tender parent could no longer bear,
But, interposing, sought to sooth his care.
"Whoe'er you are—not unbelov'd by heav'n,
Since on our friendly shore your ships are driv'n—
Have courage: to the gods permit the rest,
And to the queen expose your just request.
Now take this earnest of success for more;
Your scatter'd fleet is join'd upon the shore
The winds are chang'd, your friends from danger free;
Or I renounce my skill in augury.
Twelve swans behold in beauteous order move,
And stoop with closing pinions from above;
Whom late the bird of Jove had driv'n along,
And through the clouds pursu'd the scatt'ring throng.
Now all united in a goodly team,
They skim the ground, and seek the quiet stream:
As they, with joy returning, clap their wings,
And ride the circuit of the skies in rings;
Not otherwise your ships, and ev'ry friend,
Already hold the port, or with swift sails descend.
No more advice is needful, but pursue
The path before you, and the town in view."
Thus having said, she turn'd, and made appear
Her neck refulgent, and dishevell'd hair,
Which flowing from her shoulders reach'd the ground,
And widely spread ambrosial scents around.
In length of train descends her sweeping gown;
And, by her graceful walk, the queen of love is known.
The prince pursu'd the parting deity
With words like these: "Ah! whither do you fly?
Unkind and cruel! to deceive your son
In borrow'd shapes, and his embrace to shun;
Never to bless my sight, but thus unknown;
And still to speak in accents not your own."
Against the goddess these complaints he made,
But took the path, and her commands obey'd.
They march obscure; for Venus kindly shrouds,
With mists, their persons, and involves in clouds,
That, thus unseen, their passage none might stay,
Or force to tell the causes of their way.
This part perform'd, the goddess flies sublime,
To visit Paphos, and her native clime,
Where garlands, ever green and ever fair,
With vows are offer'd, and with solemn pray'r:
A hundred altars in her temple smoke:
A thousand bleeding hearts her pow'r invoke.

They climb the next ascent, and, looking down,
Now at a nearer distance view the town.
The prince with wonder sees the stately tow'rs,
(Which late were huts, and shepherds' homely bow'rs,)
The gates and streets; and hears, from ev'ry part,
The noise and busy concourse of the mart.
The toiling Tyrians on each other call,
To ply their labour; some extend the wall;
Some build the citadel; the brawny throng
Or dig, or push unwieldy stones along.
Some for their dwellings choose a spot of ground,
Which, first design'd, with ditches they surround;
Some laws ordain; and some attend the choice
Of holy senates, and elect by voice.
Here some design a mole, while others there
Lay deep foundations for a theatre,
From marble quarries mighty columns hew,
For ornaments of scenes, and future view.
Such is their toil, and such their busy pains,
As exercise the bees in flow'ry plains,
When winter past, and summer scarce begun,
Invites them forth to labour in the sun:
Some lead their youth abroad, while some condense
Their liquid store, and some in cells dispense:
Some at the gates stand ready to receive
The golden burden, and their friends relieve:
All, with united force, combine to drive
The lazy drones from the laborious hive:
With envy stung, they view each other's deeds
The fragrant work with diligence proceeds.
"Thrice happy you, whose walls already rise!"
Æneas said, and view'd, with lifted eyes,
Their lofty tow'rs: then ent'ring at the gate,
Conceal'd in clouds, (prodigious to relate,)
He mix'd, unmark'd, among the busy throng,
Borne by the tide, and pass'd unseen along.
Full in the centre of the town there stood,
Thick set with trees, a venerable wood:
The Tyrians, landing near this holy ground,
And digging here, a prosp'rous omen found:
From under earth a courser's head they drew,
Their growth and future fortune to foreshew:
This fated sign their foundress Juno gave,
Of a soil fruitful, and a people brave.
Sidonian Dido here with solemn state
Did Juno's temple build, and consecrate,
Enrich'd with gifts, and with a golden shrine
But more the goddess made the place divine.
On brazen steps the marble threshold rose,
And brazen plates the cedar beams enclose:
The rafters are with brazen cov'rings crown'd;
The lofty doors on brazen hinges sound.
What first Æneas in this place beheld,
Reviv'd his courage, and his fear expell'd.
For—while, expecting there the queen, he rais'd
His wondering eyes, and round the temple gaz'd,
Admir'd the fortune of the rising town,
The striving artists, and their arts' renown—
He saw, in order painted on the wall,
Whatever did unhappy Troy befall—
The wars that fame around the world had blown,
All to the life, and ev'ry leader known.
There Agamemnon, Priam here, he spies,
And fierce Achilles, who both kings defies.
He stopp'd, and weeping said, "O friend! e'en here
The monuments of Trojan woes appear!
Our known disasters fill e'en foreign lands:
See there, where old unhappy Priam stands!
E'en the mute walls relate the warrior's fame,
And Trojan griefs the Tyrians' pity claim."
He said—(his tears a ready passage find)
Devouring what he saw so well design'd,
And with an empty picture fed his mind:
For there he saw the fainting Grecians yield,
And here the trembling Trojans quit the field,
Pursu'd by fierce Achilles through the plain,
On his high chariot driving o'er the slain.
The tents of Rhesus next his grief renew,
By their white sails betray'd to nightly view;
And wakeful Diomede, whose cruel sword
The sentries slew; nor spar'd their slumb'ring lord.
Then took the fiery steeds, e're yet the food
Of Troy they taste, or drink the Xanthian flood.
Elsewhere he saw where Troilus defied
Achilles, and unequal combat tried;
Then, where the boy disarm'd, with loosen'd reins,
Was by his horses hurried o'er the plains
Hung by the neck and hair; and, dragg'd around,
The hostile spear yet sticking in his wound,
With tracks of blood inscrib'd the dusty ground.
Meantime the Trojan dames, oppress'd with wo,
To Pallas' fane in long procession go,
In hopes to reconcile their heavenly foe;
They weep; they beat their breasts; they rend their hair.
And rich embroider'd vests for presents bear:
But the stern goddess stands unmov'd with pray'r.
Thrice round the Trojan walls Achilles drew
The corpse of Hector, whom in fight he slew.
Here Priam sues; and there, for sums of gold,
The lifeless body of his son he sold.
So sad an object, and so well express'd,
Drew sighs and groans from the griev'd hero's breast,

To see the figure of his lifeless friend,
And his old sire his helpless hands extend.
Himself he saw amidst the Grecian train,
Mix'd in the bloody battle on the plain:
And swarthy Memnon in his arms he knew,
His pompous ensigns, and his Indian crew.
Penthesilea there, with haughty grace,
Leads to the wars an Amazonian race:
In their right hands a pointed dart they wield;
The left, for ward, sustains the lunar shield.
Athwart her breast a golden belt she throws,
Amidst the press alone provokes a thousand foes,
And dares her maiden arms to manly force oppose.
Thus while the Trojan prince employs his eyes,
Fix'd on the walls with wonder and surprise,
The beauteous Dido, with a num'rous train,
And pomp of guards, ascends the sacred fane.
Such on Eurotas' banks, or Cynthus' height,
Diana seems; and so she charms the sight,
When in the dance the graceful goddess leads
The choir of nymphs, and overtops their heads:
Known by her quiver, and her lofty mien,
She walks majestic, and she looks their queen:
Latonia sees her shine above the rest,
And feeds with sacred joy her silent breast.
Such Dido was; with such becoming state,
Amidst the crowd she walks serenely great.
Their labour to her future sway she speeds,
And passing with a gracious glance proceeds;
Then mounts the throne, high plac'd before the shrine:
In crowds around, the swarming people join.
She takes petitions, and dispenses laws,
Hears and determines ev'ry private cause:
Their task in equal portions she divides,
And where unequal, there by lot decides.
Another way by chance Æneas bends
His eyes, and unexpected sees his friends,
Antheus, Sergestus grave, Cloanthus strong,
And at their backs a mighty Trojan throng;
Whom late the tempest on the billows toss'd,
And widely scatter'd on another coast.
The prince, unseen, surpris'd with wonder stands,
And longs, with joyful haste, to join their hands:
But, doubtful of the wish'd event, he stays,
And from the hollow cloud his friends surveys;
Impatient till they told their present state,
And where they left their ships, and what their fate,
And why they came, and what was their request:
For these were sent, commission'd by the rest,
To sue for leave to land their sickly men,
And gain admission to the gracious queen.
Ent'ring, with cries they fill'd the holy fane;
Then thus, with lowly voice, Ilioneus began:

"O queen! indulg'd by favour of the gods
To found an empire in these new abodes;
To build a town; with statutes to restrain
The wild inhabitants beneath thy reign—
We wretched Trojans, toss'd on ev'ry shore,
From sea to sea, thy clemency implore.
Forbid the fires our shipping to deface;
Receive th' unhappy fugitives to grace,
And spare the remnant of a pious race!
We come not with design of wasteful prey,
To drive the country, force the swains away:
Nor such our strength, nor such is our desire;
The vanquish'd dare not to such thoughts aspire.
A land there is, Hesperia nam'd of old—
The soil is fruitful, and the men are bold—
Th' Œnotrians held it once—by common fame,
Now call'd Italia, from the leader's name.
To that sweet region was our voyage bent,
When winds, and every warring element,
Disturb'd our course, and, far from sight of land,
Cast our torn vessels on the moving sand:
The sea came on; the South, with mighty roar,
Dispers'd and dash'd the rest upon the rocky shore.
Those few you see escap'd the storm, and fear,
Unless you interpose, a shipwreck here.
What men, what monsters, what inhuman race,
What laws, what barbarous customs of the place,
Shut up a desert shore to drowning men,
And drive us to the cruel seas again?
If our hard fortune no compassion draws,
Nor hospitable rights, nor human laws,
The gods are just, and will revenge our cause.
Æneas was our prince—a juster lord,
Or nobler warrior, never drew a sword—
Observant of the right, religious of his word.
If yet he lives, and draws this vital air,
Nor we his friends of safety shall despair.
Nor you, great queen, these offices repent,
Which he will equal, and perhaps augment.
We want not cities, nor Sicilian coasts,
Where king Acestes Trojan lineage boasts.
Permit our ships a shelter on your shores,
Refitted from your woods with planks and oars,
That, if our prince be safe, we may renew
Our destin'd course, and Italy pursue.
But if, O best of men! the Fates ordain
That thou art swallow'd in the Libyan main,
And if our young Iülus be no more,
Dismiss our navy from your friendly shore,
That we to good Acestes may return,
And with our friends our common losses mourn."
Thus spoke Ilioneus: the Trojan crew
With cries and clamours his request renew.
The modest queen a while, with downcast eyes,
Ponder'd the speech, then briefly thus replies:

"Trojans! dismiss your fears: my cruel fate,
And doubts attending an unsettled state,
Force me to guard my coast from foreign foes.
Who has not heard the story of your woes,
The name and fortune of your native place,
The fame and valour of the Phrygian race?
We Tyrians are not so devoid of sense,
Nor so remote from Phœbus' influence.
Whether to Latian shores your course is bent,
Or, driv'n by tempests from your first intent,
You seek the good Ancestes' government,
Your men shall be receiv'd, your fleet repair'd,
And sail, with ships of convoy for your guard:
Or, would you stay, and join your friendly pow'rs
To raise and to defend the Tyrian tow'rs,
My wealth, my city, and myself are yours.
And would to heav'n, the storm you felt, would bring
On Carthaginian coasts your wand'ring king.
My people shall, by my command, explore
The ports and creeks of every winding shore,
And towns, and wilds, and shady woods, in quest
Of so renown'd, and so desir'd a guest."
Rais'd in his mind the Trojan hero stood,
And long'd to break from out his ambient cloud:
Achates found it, and thus urg'd his way:
"From whence, O goddess-born, this long delay?
What more can you desire, your welcome sure,
Your fleet in safety, and your friends secure?
One only wants! and him we saw in vain
Oppose the storm, and swallow'd in the main.
Orontes in his fate our forfeit paid:
The rest agrees with what your mother said."
Scarce had he spoken, when the cloud gave way,
The mist flew upward, and dissolv'd in day.
The Trojan chief appear'd in open sight,
August in visage, and serenely bright.
His mother goddess, with her hands divine,
Had form'd his curling locks and made his temples shine,
And giv'n his rolling eyes a sparkling grace,
And breath'd a youthful vigour on his face;
Like polish'd iv'ry beauteous to behold,
Or Parian marble, when enchas'd in gold.
Thus radiant from the circling cloud he broke
And thus with manly modesty he spoke:
"He whom you seek am I; by tempests toss'd
And sav'd from shipwreck on your Libyan coast;
Presenting, gracious queen, before your throne,
A prince that owes his life to you alone.
Fair majesty! the refuge and redress
Of those whom Fate pursues, and wants oppress!
You, who your pious offices employ
To save the relics of abandon'd Troy,
Receive the shipwreck'd on your friendly shore,
With hospitable rights relieve the poor;
Associate in your town a wand'ring train,
And strangers in your palace entertain.
What thanks can wretched fugitives return,
Who, scatter'd through the world, in exile mourn?
The gods, (if gods to goodness are inclin'd—
If acts of mercy touch their heavenly mind,)
And, more than all the gods, your gen'rous heart,
Conscious of worth, requites its own desert!
In you this age is happy, and this earth;
And parents more than mortal gave you birth.
While rolling rivers into seas shall run,
And round the space of heav'n the radiant sun;
While trees the mountain-tops with shades supply,
Your honour, name, and praise, shall never die.
Whate'er abode my fortune has assign'd,
Your image shall be present in my mind."
Thus having said, he turn'd with pious haste,
And joyful his expecting friends embrac'd:
With his right hand Ilioneus was grac'd,
Sergestes with the left; then to his breast
Cloanthus and the noble Gyas press'd;
And so by turns, descended to the rest.
The Tyrian queen stood fix'd upon his face,
Pleas'd with his motions, ravish'd with his grace;
Admir'd his fortunes, more admir'd the man,
Then recollected stood; and thus began:
"What fate, O goddess-born! what angry pow'rs
Have cast you shipwreck'd on our barren shores?
Are you the great Æneas, known to fame,
Who from celestial seed your lineage claim?
The same Æneas whom fair Venus bore
To fam'd Anchises on th' Idæan shore?
It calls into my mind, though then a child,
When Teucer came, from Salamis exil'd,
And sought my father's aid, to be restor'd:
My father Belus then with fire and sword
Invaded Cyprus, made the region bare,
And, conq'ring, finish'd the successful war.
From him the Trojan siege I understood,
The Grecian chiefs, and your illustrious blood
Your foe himself the Dardan valour prais'd,
And his own ancestry from Trojans rais'd.
Enter, my noble guest! and you shall find,
If not a costly welcome, yet a kind:
For I myself, like you, have been distress'd,
Till heav'n afforded me this place of rest;
Like you, an alien in a land unknown,
I learn to pity woes so like my own."
She said, and to the palace led her guest,
Then offer'd incense, and proclaim'd a feast.

Nor yet less careful for her absent friends,
Twice ten fat oxen to the ships she sends:
Besides a hundred boars, a hundred lambs,
With bleating cries, attend their milky dams:
And jars of gen'rous wine, and spacious bowls,
She gives to cheer the sailors' drooping souls.
Now purple hangings clothe the palace-walls
And sumptuous feasts are made in splendid halls.
On Tyrian carpets, richly wrought, they dine;
With loads of massy plate the sideboards shine,
And antique vases, all of gold emboss'd,
(The gold itself inferior to the cost
Of curious work,) where on the sides were seen,
The fights and figures of illustrious men,
From their first founder to the present queen.

The good Æneas, whose paternal care
Iülus' absence could no longer bear,
Despatch'd Achates to the ships in haste,
To give a glad relation of the past,
And fraught with precious gifts, to bring the boy,
Snatch'd from the ruins of unhappy Troy—
A robe of tissue, stiff with golden wire;
An upper vest, once Helen's rich attire,
From Argos by the fam'd adult'ress brought,
With golden flow'rs and winding foliage wrought—
Her mother Leda's present, when she came
To ruin Troy, and set the world on flame;
The sceptre Priam's eldest daughter bore,
Her orient necklace, and the crown she wore
Of double texture; glorious to behold;
One order set with gems, and one with gold.
Instructed thus, the wise Achates goes,
And in his diligence, his duty shows.

But Venus, anxious for her son's affairs,
New counsels tries, and new designs prepare
That Cupid should assume the shape and face
Of sweet Ascanius, and the sprightly grace;
Should bring the presents in her nephew's stead,
And in Eliza's veins the gentle poison shed:
For much she fear'd the Tyrians, double-tongu'd,
And knew the town to Juno's care belong'd.
These thoughts by night her golden slumbers broke;
And thus, alarm'd, to winged Love she spoke:
My son, my strength, whose mighty pow'r alone
Controls the thund'rer on his awful throne,
To thee thy much afflicted mother flies,
And on thy succour and thy faith relies.
Thou know'st, my son, how Jove's revengeful wife,
By force and fraud, attempts thy brother's life:
And often hast thou mourn'd with me his pains
Him Dido now with blandishment detains;
But I suspect the town where Juno reigns.
For this, 'tis needful to prevent her art,
And fire with love the proud Phœnician's heart—
A love so violent, so strong, so sure,
That neither age can change, nor art can cure.
How this may be perform'd, now take my mind:
Ascanius, by his father, is design'd
To come, with presents laden, from the port,
To gratify the queen, and gain the court.
I mean to plunge the boy in pleasing sleep,
And, ravish'd, in Idalian bow'rs to keep,
Or high Cythera, that the sweet deceit
May pass unseen, and none prevent the cheat.
Take thou his form and shape. I beg the grace,
But only for a night's revolving space,
Thyself a boy, assume a boy's dissembled face,
That when, amidst the fervour of the feast,
The Tyrian hugs and fonds thee on her breast,
And with sweet kisses in her arms constrains;
Thou mayst infuse thy venom in her veins."
The god of love obeys, and sets aside
His bow and quiver, and his plumy pride:
He walks Iülus in his mother's sight,
And in the sweet resemblance takes delight.

The goddess then to young Ascanius flies,
And in a pleasing slumber seals his eyes.
Lull'd in her lap amidst a train of Loves,
She gently bears him to her blissful groves,
Then with a wreath of myrtle crowns his head,
And softly lays him on a flow'ry bed.
Cupid meantime assum'd his form and face,
Following Achates with a shorter pace,
And brought the gifts. The queen already sate
Amidst the Trojan lords, in shining state,
High on a golden bed: her princely guest
Was next her side; in order sate the rest.
Then canisters with bread are heap'd on high:
Th' attendants water for their hands supply,
And, having wash'd, with silken towels dry.
Next fifty handmaids in long order bore
The censers, and with fumes the gods adore:
Then youths and virgins, twice as many, join
To place the dishes, and to serve the wine.
The Tyrian train admitted to the feast,
Approach, and on the painted couches rest.
All on the Trojan gifts with wonders gaze,
But view the beauteous boy with more amaze
His rosy colour'd cheeks, his radiant eyes,
His motions, voice, and shape, and all the god's disguise;
Nor pass unprais'd the vest and veil divine,
Which wan'dring foliage and rich flow'rs intwine.
But, far above the rest, the royal dame
(Already doom'd to love's disastrous flame,)
With eyes insatiate, and tumultuous joy,
Beholds the presents, and admires the boy.
The guileful god, about the hero, long,
With children's play, and false embraces, hung

Then sought the queen: she took him to her arms
With greedy pleasure, and devour'd his charms.
Unhappy Dido little thought what guest,
How dire a god, she drew so near her breast.
But he, not mindless of his mother's pray'r,
Works in the pliant bosom of the fair,
And moulds her heart anew, and blots her former care.
The dead is to the living love resign'd;
And all Æneas enters in her mind.
Now, when the rage of hunger was appeas'd,
The meat remov'd, and ev'ry guest was pleas'd,
The golden bowls with sparkling wine are crown'd,
And through the palace cheerful cries resound.
From gilded roofs depending lamps display
Nocturnal beams, that emulate the day.
A golden bowl, that shone with gems divine,
The queen commanded to be crown'd with wine—
The bowl that Belus us'd, and all the Tyrian line.
Then, silence through the hall proclaim'd, she spoke:
"O, hospitable Jove! we thus invoke,
With solemn rites, thy sacred name and pow'r:
Bless to both nations this auspicious hour!
So may the Trojan and the Tyrian line
In lasting concord from this day combine.
Thou, Bacchus, god of joys and friendly cheer,
And gracious Juno, both be present here!
And you, my lords of Tyre, your vows address
To heav'n, with mine, to ratify the peace."
The goblet then she took, with nectar crown'd,
(Sprinkling the first libations on the ground,)
And rais'd it to her mouth with sober grace,
Then, sipping, offer'd to the next in place.
'T was Bitias whom she call'd—a thirsty soul:
He took the challenge, and embrac'd the bowl,
With pleasure swill'd the gold, nor ceas'd to draw,
Till he the bottom of the brimmer saw.
The goblet goes around: Iöpas brought
His golden lyre, and sung what ancient Atlas taught—
The various labours of the wand'ring moon,
And whence proceed th' eclipses of the sun;
Th' original of men and beasts; and whence
The rains arise, and fires their warmth dispense,
And fix'd and erring stars dispose their influence;
What shakes the solid earth; what cause delays
The summer nights, and shortens winter days.
With peals of shouts the Tyrians praise the song;
Those peals are echo'd by the Trojan throng.
Th' unhappy queen with talk prolong'd the night,
And drank large draughts of love with vast delight;
Of Priam much inquir'd, of Hector more;
Then ask'd what arms the swarthy Memnon wore,
What troops he landed on the Trojan shore
(The steeds of Diomede varied the discourse,
And fierce Achilles, with his matchless force;)
At length, as Fate and her ill stars requir'd,
To hear the series of the war desir'd.
"Relate at large, my god-like guest," she said,
"The Grecian stratagems, the town betray'd:
The fatal issue of so long a war;
Your flight, your wand'rings, and your woes declare:
For, since on ev'ry sea, on ev'ry coast,
Your men have been distress'd, your navy toss'd,
Sev'n times the sun has either tropic view'd,
The winter banish'd, and the spring renew'd."

BOOK II.

ARGUMENT.

Æneas relates how the city of Troy was taken, after a ten year's siege, by the treachery of Sinon, and the stratagem of a wooden horse. He declares the fixed resolution he had taken not to survive the ruin of his country, and the various adventures he met with in defence of it. At last, having been before advised by Hector's ghost, and now by the appearance of his mother Venus, he is prevailed upon to leave the town, and settle his household gods in another country. In order to this, he carries off his father on his shoulders, and leads his little son by the hand, his wife following him behind. When he comes to the place appointed for the general rendezvous, he finds a great confluence of people, but misses his wife, whose ghost afterwards appears to him, and tells him the land which was designed for him.

All were attentive to the godlike man,
When from his lofty couch he thus began:
"Great queen, what you command me to relate
Renews the sad remembrance of our fate.
An empire from its old foundations rent,
And every wo the Trojans underwent;
A peopled city made a desert place;
All that I saw and part of which I was;
Not e'en the hardest of our foes could hear,
Nor stern Ulysses hear, without a tear.
And now the latter watch of wasting night,
And setting stars, to kindly rest invite.
But, since you take such int'rest in our wo,
And Troy's disastrous end desire to know,
I will restrain my tears, and briefly tell
What in our last and fatal night befell.
By destiny compell'd, and in despair,
The Greeks grew weary of the tedious war,
And, by Minerva's aid, a fabric rear'd,
Which like a steed of monstrous height appear'd:

The sides were plank'd with pine: they feign'd it made
For their return, and this the vow they paid.
Thus they pretend, but in the hollow side,
Selected numbers of their soldiers hide:
With inward arms the dire machine they load;
And iron bowels stuff the dark abode.
In sight of Troy lies Tenedos, an isle
(While Fortune did on Priam's empire smile)
Renown'd for wealth; but, since a faithless bay,
Where ships expos'd to wind and weather lay,
There was their fleet conceal'd. We thought for Greece
Their sails were hoisted, and our fears release.
The Trojans, coop'd within their walls so long,
Unbar their gates, and issue in a throng.
Like swarming bees, and with delight survey
The camp deserted, where the Grecians lay:
The quarters of the sev'ral chiefs they show'd—
Here Phœnix, here Achilles, made abode;
Here join'd the battles; there the navy rode.
Part on the pile their wand'ring eyes employ—
The pile by Pallas rais'd to ruin Troy.
Thymœtes first ('t is doubtful whether hir'd,
Or so the Trojan destiny requir'd)
Mov'd that the ramparts might be broken down,
To lodge the monster fabric in the town.
But Capys, and the rest, of sounder mind,
The fatal present to the flames design'd,
Or to the wat'ry deep; at least to bore
The hollow sides, and hidden frauds explore.
The giddy vulgar, as their fancies guide,
With noise say nothing, and in parts divide.
Laocoön, follow'd by a num'rous crowd,
Ran from the fort, and cried, from far, aloud:
"O wretched countrymen! what fury reigns?
What more than madness has possess'd your brains?
Think you the Grecians from your coasts are gone?
And are Ulysses' arts no better known?
This hollow fabric either must enclose,
Within its blind recess, our secret foes;
Or 't is an engine rais'd above the town
T' o'erlook the walls, and them to batter down.
Somewhat is sure design'd, by fraud or force—
Trust not their presents, nor admit the horse."
Thus having said, against the steed he threw
His forceful spear, which, hissing as it flew,
Pierc'd through the yielding planks of jointed wood,
And trembling in the hollow belly stood.
The sides transpierc'd, return a rattling sound;
And groans of Greeks enclos'd come issuing through the wound.
And had not heav'n the fall of Troy design'd,
Or had not men been fated to be blind,
Enough was said and done, t' inspire a better mind.
Then had our lances pierc'd the treach'rous wood,
And Ilian tow'rs and Priam's empire stood.
Meantime, with shouts, the Trojan shepherds bring
A captive Greek, in bands, before the king—
Taken, to take—who made himself their prey,
T' impose on their belief, and Troy betray;
Fix'd on his aim, and obstinately bent
To die undaunted, or to circumvent.
About the captive tides of Trojans flow;
All press to see, and some insult the foe.
Now hear how well the Greeks their wiles disguis'd:
Behold a nation in a man compris'd.
Trembling the miscreant stood: unarm'd and bound,
He star'd, and roll'd his haggard eyes around;
Then said, "Alas! what earth remains, what sea
Is open to receive unhappy me?
What fate a wretched fugitive attends,
Scorn'd by my foes, abandon'd by my friends?"
He said, and sigh'd, and cast a rueful eye;
Our pity kindles, and our passions die.
We cheer the youth to make his own defence,
And freely tell us what he was, and whence:
What news he could impart, we long to know,
And what to credit from a captive foe.
His fear at length dismiss'd, he said, "Whate'er
My fate ordains, my words shall be sincere:
I neither can, nor dare my birth disclaim;
Greece is my country, Sinon is my name,
Though plung'd by fortune's pow'r in misery,
'T is not in fortune's pow'r to make me lie.
If any chance has hither brought the name
Of Palamedes, not unknown to fame,
Who suffer'd from the malice of the times,
Accus'd and sentenc'd for pretended crimes,
Because the fatal wars he would prevent;
Whose death the wretched Greeks too late lament—
Me, then a boy, my father, poor and bare
Of other means, committed to his care,
His kinsman and companion in the war.
While Fortune favour'd, while his arms support
The cause, and rul'd the counsels of the court,
I made some figure there; nor was my name
Obscure, nor I without my share of fame.
But when Ulysses, with fallacious arts,
Had made impressions in the people's hearts,
And forg'd a treason in my patron's name,
(I speak of things too far divulg'd by fame,)
My kinsman fell. Then I, without support,
In private mourn'd his loss, and left the court.
Mad as I was, I could not bear his fate
With silent grief, but loudly blam'd the state,

And curs'd the direful author of my woes.—
'T was told again, and hence my ruin rose.
I threaten'd, if indulgent heaven once more
Would land me safely on my native shore,
His death with double vengeance to restore.
This mov'd the murd'rer's hate, and soon ensu'd
Th' effects of malice from a man so proud.
Ambiguous rumours through the camp he spread,
And sought, by treason, my devoted head;
New crimes invented; left unturn'd no stone,
To make my guilt appear, and hide his own;
Till Calchas was by force and threat'ning wrought—
But why—why dwell I on that anxious thought?
If on my nation just revenge you seek,
And 't is t' appear a foe t' appear a Greek;
Already you my name and country know:
Assuage your thirst of blood, and strike the blow:
My death will both the kingly brothers please
And set insatiate Ithacus at ease.
This fair unfinish'd tale, these broken starts,
Rais'd expectations in our longing hearts;
Unknowing as we were in Grecian arts.
His former trembling once again renew'd,
With acted fear, the villain thus pursu'd:
"Long had the Grecians (tir'd with fruitless care,
And wearied with an unsuccessful war)
Resolv'd to raise the siege and leave the town;
And, had the gods permitted, they had gone.
But oft the wintry seas, and southern winds,
Withstood their passage home, and chang'd their minds
Portents and prodigies their souls amaz'd;
But most, when this stupendous pile was rais'd:
Then flaming meteors, hung in air, were seen,
And thunders rattled through a sky serene.
Dismay'd and fearful of some dire event,
Eurypylus, t' inquire their fate, was sent.
He from the gods this dreadful answer brought:
'O Grecians! when the Trojan shores you sought,
Your passage with a virgin's blood was bought:
So must your safe return be bought again;
And Grecian blood once more atone the main.'
The spreading rumour round the people ran;
All fear'd, and each believ'd himself the man.
Ulysses took the advantage of their fright;
Call'd Calchas, and produc'd, in open sight,
Then bade him name the wretch, ordain'd by fate
The public victim to redeem the state.
Already some presag'd the dire event,
And saw what sacrifice Ulysses meant.
For twice five days the good old seer withstood
Th' intended treason, and was dumb to blood;
Till, tir'd with endless clamours and pursuit
Of Ithacus, he stood no longer mute,
But, as it was agreed, pronounc'd that I
Was destin'd by the wrathful gods to die.
All prais'd the sentence; pleas'd the storm should fall
On one alone, whose fury threaten'd all.
The dismal day was come, the priests prepare
Their leaven'd cakes, and fillets for my hair
I follow'd nature's laws, and must avow,
I broke my bonds, and fled the fatal blow.
Hid in a weedy lake, all night I lay,
Secure of safety when they sail'd away.
But now what further hopes for me remain,
To see my friends or native soil again;
My tender infants, or my careful sire,
Whom they returning will to death require;
Will perpetrate on them their first design,
And take the forfeit of their heads for mine
Which, O! if pity mortal minds can move,
If there be faith below, or gods above,
If innocence and truth can claim desert,
Ye Trojans, from an injur'd wretch avert."
False tears true pity move: the king commands
To loose his fetters, and unbind his hands,
Then adds these friendly words: "Dismiss thy fears:
Forget the Greeks: be mine as thou wert theirs:
But truly tell, was it for force or guile,
Or some religious end, you rais'd the pile?"
Thus said the king: He, full of fraudful arts,
This well-invented tale for truth imparts:
"Ye lamps of heav'n!" he said, and lifted high
His hands, now free—"thou venerable sky!
Inviolable pow'rs, ador'd with dread!
Ye fatal fillets that once bound this head;
Ye sacred altars from whose flames I fled!
Be all of you adjur'd; and grant I may,
Without a crime, th' ungrateful Greeks betray,
Reveal the secrets of the guilty state,
And justly punish whom I justly hate!
But you, O king, preserve the faith you gave,
If I, to save myself, your empire save.
The Grecian hopes, and all th' attempts they made,
Were only founded on Minerva's aid.
But from the time when impious Diomede
And false Ulysses, that inventive head,
Her fatal image from the temple drew,
The sleeping guardians of the castle slew,
Her virgin statue with their bloody hands
Polluted, and profan'd her holy bands;
From thence the tide of fortune left their shore,
And ebb'd much faster than it flow'd before:
Their courage languish'd, as their hopes decay'd;
And Pallas, now averse, refus'd her aid.
Nor did the goddess doubtfully declare
Her alter'd mind, and alienated care.

When first her fatal image touch'd the ground,
She sternly cast her glaring eyes around,
That sparkled as they roll'd, and seem'd to threat:
Her heav'nly limbs distill'd a briny sweat.
Thrice from the ground she leap'd, was seen to wield
Her brandish'd lance, and shake her horrid shield.
Then Calchas bade our host for flight prepare,
And hope no conquest from the tedious war,
Till first they sail'd for Greece: with pray'rs besought
Her injur'd pow'r, and better omens brought.
And, now their navy ploughs the wat'ry main;
Yet soon expect it on your shores again,
With Pallas pleas'd; as Calchas did ordain.
But first, to reconcile the blue-ey'd maid
For her stol'n statue and her tow'r betray'd,
Warn'd by the seer, to her offended name
We rais'd and dedicate this wond'rous frame,
So lofty, lest through your forbidden gates
It pass, and intercept our better fates:
For, once admitted there, our hopes are lost;
And Troy may then a new palladium boast:
For so religion and the gods ordain,
That, if you violate with hands profane
Minerva's gift, your town in flames shall burn,
(Which omen, O ye gods, on Græcia turn!)
But if it climb, with your assisting hands,
The Trojan walls, and in the city stands;
Then Troy shall Argos and Mycenæ burn,
And the reverse of fate on us return."
With such deceits he gain'd their easy hearts,
Too prone to credit his perfidious arts.
What Diomede nor Thetis, greater son,
A thousand ships, nor ten years' siege had done—
False tears and fawning words the city won.
A greater omen, and of worse portent
Did our unweary minds with fear torment,
Concurring to produce the dire event.
Laocoön, Neptune's priest by lot that year,
With solemn pomp then sacrific'd a steer;
When (dreadful to behold!) from sea we spied
Two serpents, rank'd abreast, the seas divide,
And smoothly sweep along the swelling tide.
Their flaming crests above the waves they show:
Their bellies seem to burn the seas below:
Their speckled tails advance to steer their course,
And on the sounding shore the flying billows force.
And now the strand, and now the plain, they held,
Their ardent eyes with bloody streaks were fill'd;
Their nimble tongues they brandish'd as they came, [flame.
And lick'd their hissing jaws, that sputter'd
We fled amaz'd: their destin'd way they take,
And to Laocoön and his children make:
And first around the tender boys they wind,
Then with their sharpen'd fangs their limbs and bodies grind.
The wretched father, running to their aid
With pious haste, but vain, they next invade;
Twice round his waist the winding volumes roll'd;
And twice about his gasping throat they told.
The priest thus doubly chok'd—their crests divide,
And tow'ring o'er his head in triumph ride.
With both his hands he labours at the knots;
His holy fillets the blue venom blots;
His roaring fills the flitting air around.
Thus, when an ox receives a glancing wound,
He breaks his bands, the fatal altar flies,
And with loud bellowings breaks the yielding skies [prey,
Their tasks perform'd, the serpents quit their
And to the tow'r of Pallas make their way:
Couch'd at her feet, they lie protected there,
By her large buckler, and pretended spear.
Amazement seizes all; the gen'ral cry
Proclaims Laocoön justly doom'd to die,
Whose hand the will of Pallas had withstood,
And dar'd to violate the sacred wood.
All vote t' admit the steed, that vows be paid,
And incense offer'd to th' offended maid.
A spacious breach is made: the town lies bare:
Some hoisting-levers, some the wheels prepare,
And fasten to the horse's feet: the rest
With cables haul along th' unwieldy beast.
Each on his fellow for assistance calls:
At length the fatal fabric mounts the walls,
Big with destruction. Boys with chaplets crown'd,
And choirs of virgins, sing and dance around.
Thus rais'd aloft, and then descending down,
It enters o'er our heads and threats the town.
A sacred city, built by hands divine!
O valiant heroes of the Trojan line!
Four times he struck: as oft the clashing sound
Of arms was heard, and inward groans rebound.
Yet, mad with zeal, and blinded with our fate,
We haul along the horse in solemn state;
Then place the dire portent within the tow'r.
Cassandra cried, and curs'd th' unhappy hour;
Foretold our fate: but, by the gods' decree
All heard, and none believ'd the prophecy.
With branches we the fanes adorn, and waste,
In jollity, the day ordain'd to be the last. [light,
Meantime the rapid heavens roll'd down the
And on the shaded ocean rush'd the night:

Our men secure, nor guards nor sentries held;
But easy sleep their weary limbs compell'd.
The Grecians had embark'd their naval pow'rs
From Tenedos, and sought our well-known shores.
Safe under covert of the silent night,
And guided by th' imperial galley's light;
When Sinon, favour'd by the partial gods,
Unlock'd the horse, and op'd his dark abodes;
Restor'd to vital air our hidden foes,
Who joyful from their long confinement rose,
Thessander bold, and Sthenelus their guide,
And dire Ulysses down the cable slide:
Then Thoas, Athamas, and Pyrrhus, haste;
Nor was the Podalirian hero last,
Nor injur'd Menelaüs, nor the fam'd
Epeus who the fatal engine fram'd.
A nameless crowd succeed; their forces join
T' invade the town, oppress'd with sleep and wine.
Those few they find awake first meet their fate;
Then to their fellows they unbar the gate.
'T was in the dead of night, when sleep repairs
Our bodies worn with toils, our minds with cares,
When Hector's ghost before my sight appears;
A bloody shroud he seem'd, and bath'd in tears;
Such as he was, when by Pelides slain
Thessalian coursers dragg'd him o'er the plain.
Swoln were his feet, as when the thongs were thrust
Through the bor'd holes; his body black with dust;
Unlike that Hector, who return'd from toils
Of war, triumphant in Æacian spoils,
Or him, who made the fainting Greeks retire,
And launch'd against their navy Phrygian fire.
His hair and beard stood stiffen'd with his gore;
And all the wounds he for his country bore
Now stream'd afresh, and with new purple ran.
I wept to see the visionary man,
And while my trance continu'd, thus began:
"O light of Trojans, and support of Troy,
Thy father's champion, and thy country's joy!
O, long expected by thy friends! from whence
Art thou so late return'd for our defence?
Do we behold thee, wearied as we are,
With length of labours, and with toils of war!
After so many fun'rals of thy own,
Art thou restor'd to thy declining town?
But say, what wounds are these? what new disgrace
Deforms the manly features of thy face?"
To this the spectre no reply did frame,
But answer'd to the cause for which he came,
And, groaning from the bottom of his breast,
This warning, in these mournful words express'd:
"O goddess born! escape, by timely flight,
The flames and horrors of this fatal night.
The foes already have possess'd the wall:
Troy nods from high, and totters to her fall.
Enough is paid to Priam's royal name,
More than enough to duty and to fame.
If by a mortal hand my father's throne
Could be defended, 't was by mine alone.
Now Troy to thee commends her future state,
And gives her gods companions of thy fate:
From their assistance happier walls expect,
Which, wand'ring long, at last thou shalt erect."
He said, and brought me from their blest abodes,
The venerable statues of the gods,
With ancient Vesta from the sacred choir,
The wreaths and relics of th' immortal fire.
Now peals of shouts come thund'ring from afar,
Cries, threats, and loud laments, and mingled war:
The noise approaches, though our palace stood
Aloof from streets, encompass'd with a wood.
Louder, and yet more loud, I hear th' alarms
Of human cries distinct, and clashing arms.
Fear broke my slumbers; I no longer stay,
But mount the terrace, thence the town survey,
And hearken what the frightful sounds convey.
Thus—when a flood of fire by wind is borne,
Crackling it rolls, and mows the standing corn,
Or deluges, descending on the plains,
Sweep o'er the yellow year, destroy the pains
Of labouring oxen and the peasant's gains;
Unroot the forest oaks, and bear away
Flocks, folds, and trees, an undistinguish'd prey;
The shepherd climbs the cliff, and sees from far
The wasteful ravage of the wat'ry war.
Then Hector's faith was manifestly clear'd
And Grecian frauds in open light appear'd.
The palace of Deiphobus ascends
In smoky flames, and catches on his friends.
Ucalegon burns next: the seas are bright
With splendour not their own, and shine with Trojan light.
New clamours and new clangours now arise,
The sound of trumpets mix'd with fighting cries.
With frenzy seiz'd, I run to meet th' alarms,
Resolv'd on death, resolv'd to die in arms.
But first to gather friends, with them to oppose
(If fortune favour'd) and repel the foes—
Spurr'd by my courage, by my country fir'd,
With sense of honour and revenge inspir'd.
Panthus, Apollo's priest, a sacred name,
Had 'scap'd the Grecian swords, and pass'd the flame:
With relics loaden, to my doors he fled,
And by the hand his tender grandson led.
"What hope, O Panthus! whither can we run?
Where make a stand? and what may yet be done?"

Scarce had I said, when Panthus, with a groan,
"Troy is no more, and Ilium was a town!
The fatal day, th' appointed hour, is come,
When wrathful Jove's irrevocable doom
Transfers the Trojan state to Grecian hands.
The fire consumes the town, the foe commands;
And armed hosts, and unexpected force,
Break from the bowels of the fatal horse.
Within the gates, proud Sinon throws about
The flames; and foes, for entrance, press without,
With thousand others, whom I fear to name,
More than from Argos or Mycenæ came.
To sev'ral posts their parties they divide:
Some block the narrow streets, some scour the wide;
The bold they kill, th' unwary they surprise:
Who fights finds death, and death finds him who flies.
The warders of the gates but scarce maintain
Th' unequal combat, and resist in vain."
I heard: and heav'n, that well-born souls inspires,
Prompts me, through lifted swords and rising fires,
To run where clashing arms and clamour calls,
And rush undaunted to defend the walls.
Ripheus and Iphitus by my side engage,
For valour one renown'd, and one for age:
Dymas and Hypanis by moonlight knew
My motions and my mien, and to my party drew;
With young Chorœbus, who by love was led
To win renown, and fair Cassandra's bed;
And lately brought his troops to Priam's aid,
Forewarn'd in vain by the prophetic maid:
Whom when I saw resolv'd in arms to fall,
And that one spirit animated all,
"Brave souls!" said I—"but brave, alas, in vain—
Come, finish what our cruel fates ordain.
You see the desp'rate state of our affairs;
And heav'n's protecting pow'rs are deaf to pray'rs.
The passive gods behold the Greeks defile
Their temples, and abandon to the spoil
Their own abodes: we, feeble few, conspire
To save a sinking town, involv'd in fire.
Then let us fall, but fall amidst our foes:
Despair of life the means of living shows."
So bold a speech encourag'd their desire
Of death, and added fuel to their fire.
As hungry wolves, with raging appetite,
Scour through the fields, nor fear the stormy night—
Their welps at home expect the promis'd food,
And long to temper their dry chaps in blood—
So rush'd we forth at once. Resolv'd to die,
Resolv'd in death the last extremes to try,
We leave the narrow lanes behind, and dare
Th' unequal combat in the public square:
Night was our friend; our leader was despair.
What tongue can tell the slaughter of that night?
What eyes can weep the sorrows and affright?
An ancient and imperial city falls:
The streets are fill'd with frequent funerals:
Houses and holy temples float in blood;
And hostile nations make a common flood.
Not only Trojans fall; but in their turn,
The vanquish'd triumph, and the victors mourn.
Ours take new courage from despair and night;
Confus'd the fortune is, confus'd the fight.
All parts resound with tumults, plaints, and fears;
And grisly Death in sundry shapes appears.
Androgeos fell among us, with his band,
Who thought us Grecians newly come to land.
"From whence," said he, "my friends, this long delay?
You loiter while the spoils are borne away:
Our ships are laden with the Trojan store;
And you, like truants, come too late ashore."
He said, but soon corrected his mistake,
Found, by the doubtful answers which we make.
Amaz'd, he would have shunn'd th' unequal fight;
But we, more num'rous, intercept his flight.
As when some peasant in a bushy brake,
Has with unwary footing press'd a snake;
He starts aside, astonish'd when he spies
His rising crest, blue neck, and rolling eyes;
So, from our arms, surpris'd Androgeos flies—
In vain: for him and his we compass round,
Possess'd with fear, unknowing of the ground;
And of their lives an easy conquest found.
Thus Fortune on our first endeavour smil'd.
Chorœbus then, with youthful hopes beguil'd,
Swoln with success, and of a daring mind,
This new invention fatally design'd.
"My friends," said he, "since Fortune shows the way,
'T is fit we should th' auspicious guide obey.
For what has she these Grecian arms bestow'd,
But their destruction, and the Trojans' good?
Then change we shields, and their devices bear
Let fraud supply the want of force in war.
They find us arms." This said, himself he dress'd.
In dead Androgeos' spoils, his upper vest,
His painted buckler and his plumy crest.
Thus Ripheus, Dymas, all the Trojan train,
Lay down their own attire and strip the slain
Mix'd with the Greeks, we go with ill presage
Flatter'd with hopes to glut our greedy rage.

Unknown assaulting whom we blindly meet,
And strew with Grecian carcasses the street.
Thus, while their straggling parties we defeat,
Some to the shore and safer ships retreat;
And some, oppress'd with more ignoble fear,
Remount the hollow horse, and pant in secret there.
But ah! what use of valour can be made,
When heav'n's propitious pow'rs refuse their aid?
Behold the royal prophetess, the fair
Cassandra, dragg'd by her dishevell'd hair,
Whom not Minerva's shrine, nor sacred bands,
In safety could protect from sacrilegious hands:
On heav'n she cast her eyes, she sigh'd, she cried—
'T was all she could—her tender arms' were [tied.
So sad a sight Chorœbus could not bear;
But fir'd with rage, distracted with despair,
Amid the barb'rous ravishers he flew.
Our leader's rash example we pursue:
But storms of stones, from the proud temple's height,
Pour down, and on our batter'd helms alight:
We from our friends receiv'd this fatal blow,
Who thought us Grecians, as we seem'd in show.
They aim at the mistaken crests, from high;
And ours beneath the pond'rous ruin lie.
Then mov'd with anger and disdain, to see
Their troops dispers'd, the royal virgin free,
The Grecians rally, and their pow'rs unite,
With fury charge us, and renew the fight.
The brother kings with Ajax join their force,
And the whole squadron of Thessalian horse.
Thus when the rival winds their quarrel try,
Contending for the kingdom of the sky,
South, East, and West, on airy coursers borne—
The whirlwind gathers, and the woods are [torn:
Then Nereus strikes the deep: the billows rise,
And, mix'd with ooze and sand, pollute the skies.
The troops we squander'd first again appear
From sev'ral quarters, and enclose the rear.
They first observe, and to the rest betray,
Our diff'rent speech; our borrow'd arms survey.
Oppress'd with odds, we fall; Chorœbus first,
At Pallas' altar, by Peneleus pierc'd,
Then Ripheus followed, in th' unequal fight
Just of his word, observant of the right:
Heav'n thought not so. Dymas their fate attends,
With Hypanis, mistaken by their friends,
Nor, Panthus, thee thy mitre nor the bands
Of awful Phœbus sav'd from impious hands.
Ye Trojan flames! your testimony bear,
What I perform'd and what I suffer'd there,
No sword avoiding in the fatal strife,
Expos'd to death, and prodigal of life.
Witness, ye heavens! I live not by my fault;
I strove to have deserv'd the death I sought.
But when I could not fight, and would have died,
Borne off to distance by the growing tide,
Old Iphitus and I were hurried thence,
With Pelias wounded, and without defence.
New clamours from th' invested palace ring:
We run to die, or disengage the king.
So hot th' assault, so high the tumult rose,
While ours defend, and while the Greeks op-
As all the Dardan and Argolic race [pose,
Had been contracted in that narrow space;
Or as all Ilium else were void of fear,
And tumult, war, and slaughter, only there.
Their targets in a tortoise cast, their foes,
Secure advancing, to the turrets rose: [bold,
Some mount the scaling ladders; some, more
Swerve upwards, and by posts and pillars hold:
Their left hand gripes their bucklers in th' ascent,
While with the right they seize the battlement.
From the demolish'd tow'rs the Trojans throw
Huge heaps of stones, that, falling, crush the foe:
And heavy beams and rafters from the sides,
(Such arms their last necessity provides!)
And gilded roofs come tumbling from on high,
The marks of state and ancient royalty.
The guards below, fix'd in the pass, attend
The charge undaunted, and the gate defend.
Renew'd in courage, with recover'd breath,
A second time we ran to tempt our death,
To clear the palace from the foe, succeed
The weary living, and revenge the dead.
A postern door yet unobserv'd, and free,
Join'd by the length of a blind gallery,
To the king's closet led—a way well known
To Hector's wife, while Priam held the throne—
Through which she brought Astyanax, unseen,
To cheer his grandshire, and his grandsire's queen.
Through this we pass, and mount the tow'r, from whence [fence.
With unavailing arms the Trojans make de-
From this the trembling king had oft descried
The Grecian camp, and saw their navy ride.
Beams from its lofty height with swords we hew,
Then, wrenching with our hands, th' assault renew;
And, where the rafters on the columns meet,
We push them headlong with our arms and feet.
The lightning flies not swifter than the fall;
Nor thunder louder than the ruin'd wall:

Down goes the top at once; the Greeks beneath
Are piecemeal torn, or pounded into death.
Yet more succeed, and more to death are sent:
We cease not from above, nor they below relent.
Before the gate stood Pyrrhus, threatening loud,
With glittering arms conspicuous in the crowd.
So shines, renew'd in youth, the crested snake,
Who slept the winter in a thorny brake,
And, casting off his slough when spring returns,
Now looks aloft, and with new glory burns,
Restor'd with pois'nous herbs: his ardent sides
Reflect the sun, and rais'd on spires, he rides
High o'er the grass: hissing he rolls along,
And brandishes by fits his forky tongue.
Proud Periphas, and fierce Automedon,
His father's charioteer, together run
To force the gate: the Syrian infantry
Rush on in crowds, and the barr'd passage free.
Ent'ring the court, with shouts the skies they rend;
And flaming firebrands to the roofs ascend.
Himself, among the foremost, deals his blows,
And with his axe repeated strokes bestows
On the strong doors: then all their shoulders ply,
Till from the posts the brazen hinges fly,
He hews apace: the double bars at length
Yield to his axe and unresisted strength.
A mighty breach is made: the rooms conceal'd
Appear, and all the palace is reveal'd—
The halls of audience, and of public state,
And where the lonely queen in secret sate.
Arm'd soldiers now by trembling maids are seen,
With not a door, and scarce a space, between.
The house is fill'd with loud laments and cries,
And shrieks of women rend the vaulted skies.
The fearful matrons run from place to place,
And kiss the thresholds, and the posts embrace.
The fatal work inhuman Pyrrhus plies;
And all his father sparkles in his eyes.
Nor bars nor fighting guards his force sustain:
The bars are broken and the guards are slain.
In rush the Greeks, and all th' apartments fill;
Those few defendants whom they find, they kill;
Not with so fierce a rage the foaming flood
Roars, when he finds his rapid course withstood;
Bears down the dams with unresisted sway,
And sweeps the cattle and the cots away.
These eyes beheld him, when he march'd between
The brother kings: I saw th' unhappy queen,
The hundred wives, and where old Priam stood,
To stain his hallow'd altar with his blood.
The fifty nuptial beds, (such hopes had he,
So large a promise, of a progeny,)
The posts of plated gold, and hung with spoils,
Fell the reward of the proud victor's toils.
Where'er the raging fire had left a space,
The Grecians enter and possess the place.
Perhaps you may of Priam's fate inquire.
He—when he saw his regal town on fire,
His ruin'd palace, and his ent'ring foes,
On ev'ry side inevitable woes—
In arms disus'd invests his limbs, decay'd,
Like them, with age; a late and useless aid.
His feeble shoulders scarce the weight sustain:
Loaded, not arm'd, he creeps along with pain,
Despairing of success, ambitious to be slain!
Uncover'd but by heav'n, there stood in view
An altar: near the hearth a laurel grew,
Dodder'd with age, whose boughs encompass round
The household gods, and shade the holy ground.
Here Hecuba, with all her helpless train
Of dames for shelter sought, but sought in vain.
Driv'n like a flock of doves along the sky,
Their images they hug, and to their altars fly.
The queen, when she beheld her trembling lord,
And hanging by his side a heavy sword,
"What rage," she cried, "has seiz'd my husband's mind?
What arms are these, and to what use design'd?
These times want other aids! were Hector here,
E'en Hector now in vain, like Priam, would appear.
With us, one common shelter thou shalt find,
Or in one common fate with us be join'd."
She said, and with a last salute embrac'd
The poor old man, and by the laurel plac'd.
Behold! Polites, one of Priam's sons,
Pursu'd by Pyrrhus, there for safety runs.
Through swords and foes, amaz'd and hurt, he flies
Through empty courts, and open galleries.
Him Pyrrhus, urging with his lance, pursues,
And often reaches, and his thrusts renews.
The youth transfix'd, with lamentable cries,
Expires before his wretched parents' eyes:
Whom gasping at his feet, when Priam saw,
The fear of death gave place to nature's law:
And, shaking more with anger than with age,
"The gods," said he, "requite thy brutal rage
As sure they will, barbarian, sure they must,
If there be gods in heaven, and gods be just—
Who tak'st in wrongs an insolent delight;
With a son's death t' infect a father's sight.
Not he whom thou and lying fame conspire
To call thee his—not he, thy vaunted sire,
Thus us'd my wretched age: the gods he fear'd,
The laws of nature and of nations heard.
He cheer'd my sorrows, and, for sums of gold,
The bloodless carcass of my Hector sold;
Pitied the woes a parent underwent,
And sent me back in safety from his tent."

This said, his feeble hand a javelin threw,
Which, flutt'ring, seem'd to loiter as it flew:
Just, and but barely, to the mark it held,
And faintly tinkled on the brazen shield.
Then Pyrrhus thus: "Go thou from me to fate,
And to my father my foul deeds relate.
Now die!"—With that he dragg'd the trembling sire,
Slidd'ring through clotter'd blood and holy mire,
(The mingled paste his murder'd son had made,)
Haul'd from beneath the violated shade,
And on the sacred pile the royal victim laid.
His right hand held his bloody falchion bare;
His left he twisted in his hoary hair:
Then, with a speeding thrust, his heart he found:
The lukewarm blood came rushing through the wound,
And sanguine streams distain'd the sacred ground.
Thus Priam fell, and shar'd one common fate,
With Troy in ashes, and his ruin'd state—
He who the sceptre of all Asia sway'd,
Whom monarchs like domestic slaves obey'd.
On the bleak shore now lies the abandon'd king,
A headless carcass, and a nameless thing.
Then, not before, I felt my curdled blood
Congeal with fear; my hair with horror stood:
My father's image fill'd my pious mind,
Lest equal years might equal fortune find.
Again I thought on my forsaken wife,
And trembled for my son's abandon'd life.
I look'd about, but found myself alone,
Deserted at my need! My friends were gone.
Some spent with toil, some with despair oppress'd,
Leap'd headlong from the heights; the flames consum'd the rest.
Thus wand'ring in my way without a guide,
The graceless Helen in the porch I spied
Of Vesta's temple: there she lurk'd alone:
Muffled she sate, and what she could, unknown:
But, by the flames that cast their blaze around,
That common bane of Greece and Troy I found.
For Ilium burnt, she dreads the Trojan sword;
More dreads the vengeance of her injur'd lord;
E'en by those gods, who refug'd her, abhorr'd.
Trembling with rage, the strumpet I regard,
Resolv'd to give her guilt the due reward.
"Shall she triumphant sail before the wind,
And leave in flames unhappy Troy behind?
Shall she her kingdom and her friends review,
In state attendedwith a captive crew,
While unreveng'd the good old Priam falls,
And Grecian fires consume the Trojan walls?
For this the Phrygian fields and Xanthian flood
Were swell'd with bodies, and were drunk with blood?
'T is true, a soldier can small honour gain,
And boast no conquest from a woman slain:
Yet shall the fact not pass without applause,
Of vengeance taken in so just a cause.
The punish'd crime shall set my soul at ease,
And murm'ring manes of my friends appease."
Thus while I rave, a gleam of pleasing light
Spread o'er the place; and, shining heav'nly bright,
My mother stood reveal'd before my sight—
(Never so radiant did her eyes appear;
Not her own star confess'd a light so clear)—
Great in her charms, as when on gods above
She looks, and breathes herself into their love.
She held my hand, the destin'd blow to break;
Then from her rosy lips began to speak:
"My son! from whence this madness, this neglect
Of my commands, and those whom I protect?
Why this unmanly rage? Recall to mind
Whom you forsake, what pledges leave behind.
Look if your helpless father yet survive,
Or if Ascanius or Creüsa live.
Around your house the greedy Grecians err;
And these had perish'd in the nightly war,
But for my presence and protecting care.
Not Helen's face, nor Paris, was in fault:
But by the gods was this destruction brought.
Now cast your eyes around, while I dissolve
The mists and films that mortal eyes involve,
Purge from your sight the dross, and make you see
The shape of each avenging deity.
Enlighten'd thus, my just commands fulfil,
Nor fear obedience to your mother's will.
Where yon disorder'd heap of ruin lies,
Stones rent from stones—where clouds of dust arise,
Amid that smother, Neptune holds his place,
Below the wall's foundation drives his mace,
And heaves the building from the solid base.
Look where, in arms, imperial Juno stands
Full in the Scæan gate, with loud commands,
Urging on shore the tardy Grecian bands.
See! Pallas, of her snaky buckler proud,
Bestrides the tow'r refulgent through the cloud:
See! Jove new courage to the foe supplies,
And arms against the town the partial deities.
Haste hence, my son! this fruitless labour end:
Haste where your trembling spouse and sire attend:
Haste! and a mother's care your passage shall befriend."
She said, and swiftly vanish'd from my sight,
Obscure in clouds, and gloomy shades of night.
I look'd; I listen'd: dreadful sounds I hear;
And the dire forms of hostile gods appear.
Troy sunk in flames I saw, (nor could prevent,)
And Ilium from its old foundations rent—

Rent like a mountain ash which dar'd the winds,
And stood the sturdy strokes of lab'ring hinds.
About the roots the cruel axe resounds;
The stumps are pierc'd with oft-repeated wounds:
The war is felt on high: the nodding crown
Now threats a fall, and throws the leafy honours down.
To their united force it yields, though late,
And mourns with mortal groans th' approaching fate:
The roots no more their upper load sustain;
But down she falls, and spreads a ruin through the plain.
Descending thence, I 'scap'd through foes and fire:
Before the goddess foes and flames retire.
Arriv'd at home, he, for whose only sake,
Or most for his, such toils I undertake—
The good Anchises—whom by timely flight,
I purpos'd to secure on Ida's height—
Refus'd the journey, resolute to die,
And add his fun'ral to the fate of Troy.
Rather than exile and old age sustain:
"Go you, whose blood runs warm in ev'ry vein.
Had Heav'n decreed that I should life enjoy,
Heav'n had decreed to save unhappy Troy.
'T is, sure, enough, if not too much, for one,
Twice to have seen our Ilium overthrown.
Make haste to save the poor remaining crew;
And give this useless corpse a long adieu.
These weak old hands suffice to stop my breath:
At least the pitying foes will aid my death.
To take my spoils and leave my body bare:
As for my sepulchre, let heav'n take care.
'T is long since I, for my celestial wife,
Loath'd by the gods, have dragg'd a ling'ring life;
Since ev'ry hour and moment I expire,
Blasted from heav'n by Jove's avenging fire."
This oft repeated, he stood fix'd to die:
Myself, my wife, my son, my family,
Entreat, pray, beg, and raise a doleful cry—
"What! will he still persist, on death resolve,
And in his ruin all his house involve."
He still persists his reason to maintain:
Our pray'rs our tears, our loud laments, are vain.
Urg'd by despair, again I go to try
The fate of arms, resolv'd in fight to die.
What hope remains but what my death must give?
"Can I without so dear a father live?
You term it prudence, what I baseness call:
Could such a word from such a parent fall?
If Fortune please, and so the gods ordain,
That nothing should of ruin'd Troy remain,
And you conspire with Fortune to be slain;
The way to death is wide, th' approaches near:
For soon relentless Pyrrhus will appear,
Reeking with Priam's blood—the wretch who slew
The son (inhuman) in the father's view,
And then the sire himself to the dire altar drew.
O goddess mother! give me back to Fate;
Your gift was undesir'd, and came too late.
Did you, for this, unhappy me convey
Through foes and fires to see my house a prey?
Shall I my father, wife, and son behold,
Welt'ring in blood, each other's arms infold?
Haste! gird my sword, though spent, and overcome:
'T is the last summons to receive our doom.
I hear thee, Fate! and I obey thy call!
Not unreveng'd the foe shall see my fall.
Restore me to the yet unfinish'd fight:
My death is wanting to conclude the night."
Arm'd once again, my glittering sword I wield,
While th' other hand sustains my weighty shield;
And forth I rush'd to seek the abandon'd field.
I went; but sad Creüsa stopp'd my way,
And 'cross the threshold in my passage lay,
Embrac'd my knees, and, when I would have gone
Show'd me my feeble sire, and tender son.
"If death be your design—at least," said she,
"Take us along to share your destiny
If any further hopes in arms remain,
This place, these pledges of your love, maintain.
To whom do you expose your father's life,
Your son's, and mine: your now forgotten wife?"
While thus she fills the house with clam'rous cries,
Our hearing is diverted by our eyes:
For, while I held my son, in the short space
Betwixt our kisses and our last embrace,
(Strange to relate!) from young Iulus' head,
A lambent flame arose, which gently spread
Around his brows, and on his temples fed.
Amaz'd, with running water we prepare
To quench the sacred fire, and slake his hair;
But old Anchises, vers'd in omens, rear'd
His hands to heav'n, and this request preferr'd:
"If any vows, almighty Jove, can bend
Thy will—if piety can pray'rs commend—
Confirm the glad presage which thou art pleas'd to send."
Scarce had he said, when on our left we hear
A peal of rattling thunder roll in air:
There shot a streaming lamp along the sky,
Which on the winged lightning seem'd to fly
From o'er the roof the blaze began to move,
And trailing, vanish'd in th' Idæan grove.
It swept a path in heav'n, and shone a guide,
Then in a steaming stench of sulphur died.

The good old man with suppliant hands implor'd
The gods' protection, and their star ador'd.
"Now, now," said he, "my son, no more delay!
I yield, I follow where heav'n shows the way.
Keep, (O my country gods!) our dwelling place,
And guard this relic of the Trojan race,
This tender child!—these omens are your own;
And you can yet restore the ruin'd town.
At least accomplish what your signs foreshow;
I stand resign'd, and am prepar'd to go."
He said. The crackling flames appear on high,
And driving sparkles dance along the sky.
With Vulcan's rage the rising winds conspire,
And near our palace rolls the flood of fire.
"Haste my dear father! ('t is no time to wait)
And load my shoulders with a willing freight.
Whate'er befalls, your life shall be my care:
One death, or one deliv'rance, we will share.
My hand shall lead our little son; and you,
My faithful consort, shall our steps pursue.
Next you, my servants, heed my strict commands:
Without the walls a ruin'd temple stands,
To Ceres hallow'd once: a cypress nigh,
Shoots up her venerable head on high,
By long religion kept: there bend your feet;
And in divided parties let us meet.
Our country gods, the relics, and the bands,
Hold you, my father, in your guiltless hands:
In me 't is impious holy things to bear,
Red as I am with slaughter, new from war
Till in some living stream I cleanse the guilt
Of dire debate, and blood in battle spilt.'
Thus ord'ring all that prudence could provide,
I clothe my shoulders with a lion's hide,
And yellow spoils; then on my bending back
The welcome load of my dear father take;
While on my better hand Ascanius hung,
And with unequal paces tript along.
Creüsa kept behind: by choice we stray
Through ev'ry dark and ev'ry devious way.
I, who, so bold and dauntless, just before,
The Grecian darts and shock of lances bore,
At ev'ry shadow now am seiz'd with fear,
Not, for myself, but for the charge I bear;
Till, near the ruin'd gate arriv'd at last,
Secure, and deeming all the danger past,
A frightful noise of trampling feet we hear.
My father, looking through the shades with fear,
Cried out, "Haste, haste my son! the foes are nigh!
Their swords and shining armour I descry."
Some hostile god, for some unknown offence,
Had sure bereft my mind of better sense
For, while through winding ways I took my flight,
And sought the shelter of the gloomy night,
Alas! I lost Creüsa; hard to tell
If by her fatal destiny she fell,
Or weary sate, or wander'd with affright;
But she was lost for ever to my sight.
I knew not, or reflected, till I meet
My friends at Ceres' now deserted seat.
We met: not one was wanting; only she
Deceiv'd her friends, her son, and wretched me.
What mad expressions did my tongue refuse?
Whom did I not of gods or men accuse?
This was the fatal blow, that pain'd me more
Than all I felt from ruin'd Troy before.
Stung with my loss, and raving with despair,
Abandoning my now forgotten care,
Of counsel, comfort, and of hope bereft,
My sire, my son, my country gods, I left.
In shining armour once again I sheathe
My limbs, not feeling wounds, nor fearing death,
Then headlong to the burning walls I run,
And seek the danger I was forc'd to shun.
I tread my former tracks, through night explore
Each passage, ev'ry street I cross'd before,
All things were full of horror and affright,
And dreadful e'en the silence of the night.
Then to my father's house I make repair,
With some small glimpse of hope to find her there.
Instead of her, the cruel Greeks I met:
The house was fill'd with foes, with flames beset.
Driv'n on the wings of winds, whole sheets of fire,
Through air transported, to the roofs aspire.
From thence to Priam's palace I resort,
And search the citadel, and desert court.
Then, unobserv'd, I pass by Juno's church:
A guard of Grecians had possess'd the porch;
There Phœnix and Ulysses watch the prey:
And thither all the wealth of Troy convey—
The spoils which they from ransack'd houses brought,
And golden bowls from burning altars caught,
The tables of the gods, the purple vests,
The people's treasure, and the pomp of priests.
A rank of wretched youths, with pinion'd hands,
And captive matrons, in long order stands.
Then, with ungovern'd madness, I proclaim,
Through all the silent streets Creüsa's name.
Creüsa still I call: at length she hears,
And sudden, through the shades of night, appears—
Appears, no more Creüsa, nor my wife,
But a pale spectre, larger than the life.
Aghast, astonish'd, and struck dumb with fear,
I stood: like bristles rose my stiffen'd hair.
Then thus the ghost began to sooth my grief:
"Nor tears, nor cries, can give the dead relief.

Desist, my much-lov'd lord, t' indulge your pain:
You bear no more than what the gods ordain.
My fates permit me not from hence to fly;
Nor he, the great controller of the sky.
Long wand'ring ways for you the pow'rs decree—
On land hard labours, and a length of sea.
Then, after many painful years are past,
On Latium's happy shore you shall be cast,
Where gentle Tyber from his bed beholds
The flow'ry meadows, and the feeding folds.
There end your toils; and there your fates provide
A quiet kingdom and a royal bride:
There fortune shall the Trojan line restore;
And you for lost Creüsa weep no more.
Fear not that I shall watch with servile shame,
Th' imperious looks of some proud Grecian dame,
Or, stooping to the victor's lust, disgrace
My goddess mother, or my royal race.
And now, farewell? the parent of the gods
Restrains my fleeting soul in her abodes,
I trust our common issue to your care."
She said, and gliding pass'd unseen in air.
I strove to speak: but horror tied my tongue:
And thrice about her neck my arms I flung,
And, thrice deceiv'd, on vain embraces hung.
Light as an empty dream at break of day,
Or as a blast of wind, she rush'd away.
Thus having pass'd the night in fruitless pain,
I to my longing friends return again—
Amaz'd th' augmented number to behold,
Of men and matrons mix'd, of young and old—
A wretched exil'd crew together brought,
With arms appointed, and with treasure fraught,
Resolv'd, and willing, under my command,
To run all hazards both of sea and land.
The Morn began, from Ida, to display
Her rosy cheeks; and Phosphor led the day;
Before the gates the Grecians took their post,
And all pretence of late relief was lost.
I yield to fate, unwillingly retire,
And, loaded, up the hill convey my sire.

BOOK III.

ARGUMENT.

Æneas proceeds in his relation; he gives an account of the fleet with which he sailed, and the success of his first voyage to Thrace. From thence he directs his course to Delos, and asks the oracle what place the gods had appointed for his habitation. By a mistake of the oracle's answer, he settles in Crete. His household gods give him the true sense of the oracle, in a dream. He follows their advice, and makes the best of his way for Italy. He is cast on several shores, and meets with very surprising adventures, till at length he lands on Sicily, where his father Anchises dies. This is the place which he was sailing from, when the tempest rose, and threw him upon the Carthaginian coast.

When heav'n had overturn'd the Trojan state,
And Priam's throne, by too severe a fate;
When ruin'd Troy became the Grecians' prey,
And Ilium's lofty tow'rs in ashes lay;
Warn'd by celestial omens, we retreat,
To seek in foreign lands a happier seat.
Near old Antandros, and at Ida's foot,
The timber of the sacred groves we cut,
And build our fleet—uncertain yet to find
What place the gods for our repose assign'd.
Friends daily flock; and scarce the kindly spring
Began to clothe the ground, and birds to sing
When old Anchises summon'd all to sea;
The crew my father and the Fates obey.
With sighs and tears I leave my native shore
And empty fields, where Ilium stood before.
My sire, my son, our less and greater gods,
All sail at once, and cleave the briny floods.
Against our coast appears a spacious land,
Which once the fierce Lycurgus did command
(Thracia the name—the people bold in war—
Vast are their fields, and tillage is their care,)
A hospitable realm, while Fate was kind,
With Troy in friendship and religion join'd.
I land, with luckless omens; then adore
Their gods, and draw a line along the shore:
I lay the deep foundations of a wall,
And Ænos, nam'd from me, the city call.
To Dionæan Venus vows are paid,
And all the pow'rs that rising labours aid;
A bull on Jove's imperial altar laid.
Not far, a rising hillock stood in view:
Sharp myrtles, on the sides, and cornels grew.
There, while I went to crop the sylvan scenes,
And shade our altar with their leafy greens,
I pull'd a plant—with horror I relate
A prodigy so strange and full of Fate—
The rooted fibres rose; and, from the wound,
Black bloody drops distill'd upon the ground.
Mute and amaz'd, my hair with terror stood,
Fear shrunk my sinews, and congeal'd my blood.
Mann'd once again, another plant I try:
That other gush'd with the same sanguine die.
Then, fearing guilt for some offence unknown,
With pray'rs and vows the dryads I atone,
With all the sisters of the woods, and most
The god of arms, who rules the Thracian coast—
That they, or he, these omens would avert,
Release our fears, and better signs impart.
Clear'd, as I thought, and fully fix'd at length
To learn the cause, I tugg'd with all my strength:

I bent my knees against the ground: once more
The violated myrtle ran with gore.
Scarce dare I tell the sequel: from the womb
Of wounded earth, and caverns of the tomb,
A groan, as of a troubled ghost, renew'd
My fright, and then these dreadful words ensu'd:
Why dost thou thus my bury'd body rend?
O spare the corpse of thy unhappy friend!
Spare to pollute thy pious hands with blood:
The tears distil not from the wounded wood:
But ev'ry drop this living tree contains,
Is kindred blood, and ran in Trojan veins.
O! fly from this unhospitable shore,
Warn'd by my fate, for I am Polydore!
Here loads of lances, in my blood imbru'd,
Again shoot upward, by my blood renew'd."
My faultering tongue and shivering limbs declare
My horror; and in bristles rose my hair.
When Troy with Grecian arms was closely pent,
Old Priam, fearful of the war's event,
This hapless Polydore to Thracia sent:
Loaded with gold, he sent his darling, far
From noise and tumults, and destructive war;
Committed to the faithless tyrant's care;
Who, when he saw the pow'r of Troy decline,
Forsook the weaker, with the strong to join—
Broke ev'ry bond of nature and of truth,
And murder'd, for his wealth, the royal youth.
O sacred hunger of pernicious gold!
What bands of faith can impious lucre hold?
Now, when my soul had shaken off her fears,
I call my father, and the Trojan peers—
Relate the prodigies of heav'n—require
What he commands, and their advice desire.
All vote to leave that execrable shore,
Polluted with the blood of Polydore;
But, ere we sail, his fun'ral rites prepare,
Then, to his ghost, a tomb and altars rear.
In mournful pomp the matrons walk the round,
With baleful cypress, and blue fillets bound,
With eyes dejected, and with hair unbound.
Then bowls of tepid milk and blood we pour,
And thrice invoke the soul of Polydore.
Now, when the raging storms no longer reign,
But southern gales invite us to the main,
We launch our vessels, with a prosp'rous wind,
And leave the cities and the shores behind.
An island in the Ægean main appears:
Neptune and watery Doris claim it theirs,
It floated once, till Phœbus fix'd the sides
To rooted earth; and now it braves the tides.
Here, borne by friendly winds, we come ashore,
With needful ease our weary limbs restore,
And the Sun's temple, and his town adore.
Anius, the priest and king, with laurel crown'd,
His hoary locks with purple fillets bound,
Who saw my sire the Delian shore ascend,
Came forth with eager haste to meet his friend,
Invites him to his palace; and, in sign
Of ancient love, their plighted hands they join.
Then to the temple of the god I went,
And thus before the shrine, my vows present:
"Give, O Thymbræus! give a resting place
To the sad relics of the Trojan race—
A seat secure, a region of their own,
A lasting empire, and a happier town.
Where shall we fix? where shall our labours end?
Whom shall we follow, and what fate attend?
Let not my pray'rs a doubtful answer find;
But in clear auguries unveil thy mind."
Scarce had I said: he shook the holy ground,
The laurels, and the lofty hills around;
And from the tripos rush'd a bellowing sound.
Prostrate we fell; confess'd the present god,
Who gave this answer from his dark abode:
"Undaunted youths! go, seek that nobler earth
From which our ancestors derive their birth.
The soil that sent you forth, her ancient race
In her old bosom shall again embrace.
Through the wide world th' Æneian house shall reign,
And children's children shall the crown sustain."
Thus Phœbus did our future fates disclose;
A mighty tumult, mix'd with joy, arose.
All are concern'd to know what place the god
Assign'd, and where determin'd our abode.
My father, long revolving in his mind
The race and lineage of the Trojan kind
Thus answer'd their demands; "Ye princes hear
Your pleasing fortune; and dispel your fear.
The fruitful isle of Crete, well known to fame
Sacred of old, to Jove's imperial name,
In the mid ocean lies, with large command;
And on its plains a hundred cities stand.
Another Ida rises there; and we
From thence derive our Trojan ancestry.
From thence, as 't is divulg'd by certain fame
To the Rhœtean shores old Teucer came;
There fix'd, and there the seat of empire chose,
Ere Ilium and the Trojan tow'rs arose.
In humble vales they built their soft abodes;
Till Cybele, the mother of the gods,
With tinkling cymbals charm'd th' Idæan woods.
She secret rights and ceremonies taught,
And to the yoke the savage lions brought.
Let us the land, which heav'n appoints, explore:
Appease the winds and seek the Gnossian shore.

If Jove assists the passage of our fleet,
The third propitious dawn discovers Crete."
Thus having said, the sacrifices laid
On smoking altars, to the gods he paid—
A bull, to Neptune an oblation due,
Another bull to bright Apollo slew—
A milk-white ewe, the western winds to please,
And one coal-black, to calm the stormy seas.
Ere this, a flying rumour had been spread,
That fierce Idomeneus from the Crete was fled,
Expell'd and exil'd; that the coast was free
From foreign or domestic enemy.
We leave the Delian ports, and put to sea;
By Naxos, fam'd for vintage, make our way;
Then green Donysa pass; and sail in sight
Of Paros' isle with marble quarries white.
We pass the scatter'd isles of Cyclades,
That, scarce distinguish'd, seem to stud the seas.
The shouts of sailors double near the shores;
They stretch their canvass, and they ply their oars.
"All hands aloft! for Crete! for Crete!" they cry,
And swiftly through the foamy billows fly.
Full on the promis'd land at length we bore,
With joy descending on the Cretan shore.
With eager haste a rising town I frame,
Which from the Trojan Pergamus I name:
The name itself was grateful: I exhort
To found their houses and erect a fort.
Our ships are haul'd upon the yellow strand:
The youth begin to till the labour'd land;
And I myself new marriages promote,
Give laws; and dwellings I divide by lot;
When rising vapours choke the wholesome air,
And blasts of noisome winds corrupt the year;
The trees devouring caterpillars burn;
Parch'd was the grass, and blighted was the corn:
Nor 'scape the beasts: for Sirius, from on high,
With pestilential heat infects the sky:
My men—some fall, the rest in fevers fry.
Again my father bids me seek the shore
Of sacred Delos, and the god implore,
To learn what end of woes we might expect,
And to what clime our weary course direct.
'T was night, when ev'ry creature, void of cares,
The common gift of balmy slumber shares:
The statues of my gods, (for such they seem'd)
Those gods whom I from flaming Troy redeem'd,
Before me stood, majestically bright,
Full in the beams of Phœbe's ent'ring light.
Then thus they spoke, and eas'd my troubled mind:
"What from the Delian god thou go'st to find,
He tells thee here, and sends us to relate,
Those pow'rs are we, companions of thy fate,
Who from the burning town by thee were brought,
Thy fortune follow'd, and thy safety wrought.
Through seas and lands as we thy steps attend,
So shall our care thy glorious race befriend.
An ample realm for thee thy fates ordain,
A town, that o'er the conquer'd world shall reign.
Thou mighty walls for mighty nations build;
Nor let thy weary mind to labours yield:
But change thy seat, for not the Delian god,
Nor we, have giv'n thee Crete for your abode.
A land there is, Hesperia call'd of old,
(The soil is fruitful, and the natives bold—
Th' Œnotrians held it once,) by later fame,
Now call'd Italia, from the leader's name.
Iasius there, and Dardanus, were born
From thence we came, and thither must return.
Rise, and thy sire with these glad tidings greet;
Search Italy; for Jove denies thee Crete."
Astonish'd at their voices and their sight,
(Nor were they dreams, but visions of the night;
I saw, I knew their faces, and descried,
In perfect view, their hair with fillets tied,)
I started from my couch; a clammy sweat
On all my limbs, and shiv'ring body, sate.
To heav'n I lift my hands with pious haste,
And sacred incense in the flames I cast.
Thus to the gods their perfect honours done
More cheerful to my good old sire I run,
And tell the pleasing news. In little space
He found his error of the double race,
Not, as before he deem'd, deriv'd from Crete;
No more deluded by the doubtful seat;
Then said, "O son, turmoil'd in Trojan fate!
Such things as these Cassandra did relate.
This day revives within my mind, what she
Foretold of Troy renew'd in Italy,
And Latian lands: but who could then have thought
That Phrygian gods to Latium should be brought;
Or who believ'd what mad Cassandra taught?
Now let us go where Phœbus leads the way."
He said; and we with glad consent obey;
Forsake the seat; and, leaving few behind,
We spread our sails before the willing wind.
Now from the sight of land our galleys move,
With only seas around and skies above;
When o'er our heads descends a burst of rain,
And night with sable clouds involves the main:
The ruffling winds the foamy billows raise:
The scatter'd fleet is forc'd to sev'ral ways:
The face of heav'n is ravish'd from our eyes;
And in redoubled peals the roaring thunder flies.
Cast from our course, we wander in the dark;
No stars to guide, no point of land to mark.

E'en Palinurus no distinction found
Betwixt the night and day; such darkness reign'd around.
Three starless nights the doubtful navy strays,
Without distinction, and three sunless days:
The fourth renews the light; and from our shrouds
We view a rising land, like distant clouds:
The mountain-tops confirm the pleasing sight,
And curling smoke ascending from their height.
The canvass falls; their oars the sailors ply;
From the rude strokes the whirling waters fly.
At length I land upon the Strophades,
Safe from the danger of the stormy seas.
Those isles are compass'd by th' Ionian main,
The dire abode where the foul Harpies reign;
Forc'd by the winged warriors to repair
To their old homes, and leave their costly fare.
Monsters more fierce offended heav'n ne'er sent
From hell's abyss for human punishment—
With virgin faces, but with wombs obscene,
Foul paunches, and with odour still unclean;
With claws for hands, and looks for ever lean.
We landed at the port, and soon beheld
Fat herds of oxen graze the flow'ry field:
And wanton goats without a keeper stray'd.
With weapons we the welcome prey invade,
Then call the gods for partners of our feast,
And Jove himself, the chief invited guest.
We spread the table on the greensward ground:
We feed with hunger; and the bowls go round;
When from the mountain-tops, with hideous cry,
And clatt'ring wings, the hungry Harpies fly:
They snatch the meat, defiling all they find,
And, parting, leave a loathsome stench behind.
Close by a hollow rock, again we sit
New dress the dinner, and the beds refit,
Secure from sight, beneath a pleasing shade,
Where tufted trees a native arbour made,
Again the holy fires on altars burn;
And once again the rav'nous birds return,
Or from the dark recesses where they lie,
Or from another quarter of the sky—
With filthy claws their odious meal repeat,
And mix their loathsome ordures with their meat.
I bid my friends for vengeance then prepare,
And with the hellish nation wage the war.
They, as commanded, for the fight provide,
And in the grass their glitt'ring weapons hide:
Then, when along the crooked shore we hear
Their clatt'ring wings, and saw the foes appear,
Misenus sounds the charge: we take th' alarm,
And our strong arms with swords and bucklers arm.
In this new kind of combat, all employ
Their utmost force, the monsters to destroy—
In vain: the fated skin is proof to wounds;
And from their plumes the shining sword rebounds.
At length rebuff'd, they leave their mangled prey,
And their stretch'd pinions to the skies display
Yet one remain'd—the messenger of Fate,
High on a craggy cliff Celæno sate,
And thus her dismal errand did relate:
"What? not contented with your oxen slain,
Dare you with heav'n an impious war maintain
And drive the Harpies from their native reign?
Heed, therefore, what I say; and keep in mind
What Jove decrees, what Phœbus has design'd,
And I, the Furies' queen from both relate—
You seek th' Italian shore, foredoom'd by Fate:
Th' Italian shores are granted you to find,
And a safe passage to the fort assign'd.
But know, that, ere your promis'd walls you build,
My curses shall severely be fulfill'd.
Fierce famine is your lot—for this misdeed,
Reduc'd to grind the plates on which you feed."
She said, and to the neighb'ring forest flew:
Our courage fails us, and our fears renew.
Hopeless to win by war, to pray'rs we fall,
And on the offended Harpies humbly call,
And (whether gods or birds obscene they were)
Our vows, for pardon and for peace, prefer.
But old Anchises, off'ring sacrifice,
And lifting up to heav'n his hands and eyes,
Ador'd the greater gods—"Avert," said he,
"These omens! render vain this prophecy,
And from th' impending curse a pious people free."
Thus having said, he bids us put to sea;
We loose from shore our halsers, and obey,
And soon with swelling sails pursue our wat'ry way.
Amidst our course, Zacynthian woods appear
And next by rocky Neritos we steer:
We fly from Ithaca's detested shore,
And curse the land which dire Ulysses bore.
At length Leucate's cloudy top appears,
And the Sun's temple, which the sailor fears.
Resolv'd to breathe awhile from labours past,
Our crooked anchors from the prow we cast,
And joyful to the little city haste.
Here, safe beyond our hopes, our vows we pay
To Jove, the guide and patron of our way.
The customs of our country we pursue,
And Trojan games and Actian shores renew.
Our youth their naked limbs besmear with oil,
And exercise the wrestlers' noble toil—
Pleas'd to have sail'd so long before the wind,
And left so many Grecian towns behind.

The sun had now fulfill'd his annual course,
And Boreas on the seas display'd his force:
I fix'd upon the temple's lofty door
The brazen shield which vanquish'd Abas bore:
The verse beneath my name and action speaks:
"These arms Æneas took from conqu'ring Greeks."
Then I command to weigh: the seamen ply
Their sweeping oars: the smoking billows fly.
The sight of high Phæacia soon we lost,
And skimm'd along Epirus' rocky coast.
Then to Chaonia's port our course we bend,
And, landed, to Buthrotus' heights ascend.
Here wond'rous things were loudly blaz'd by Fame—
How Helenus reviv'd the Trojan name,
And reign'd in Greece; that Priam's captive son
Succeeded Pyrrhus in his bed and throne;
And fair Andromache, restor'd by Fate,
Once more was happy in a Trojan mate.
I leave my galleys riding in the port,
And long to see the new Dardanian court.
By chance, the mournful queen, before the gate,
Then solemniz'd her former husband's fate.
Green altars, rais'd of turf, with gifts she crown'd;
And sacred priests in order stand around,
And thrice the name of hapless Hector sound.
The grove itself resembles Ida's woods;
And Simoïs seem'd the well-dissembled flood.
But when, at nearer distance, she beheld
My shining armour, and my Trojan shield,
Astonish'd at the sight, the vital heat
Forsook her limbs, her veins no longer beat:
She faints, she falls, and scarce recov'ring strength,
Thus, with a faultering tongue, she speaks at length:
"Are you alive, O goddess-born?" she said,
"Or, if a ghost, then where is Hector's shade?
At this she cast a loud and frightful cry.—
With broken words I made this brief reply:
"All of me that remains, appears in sight;
I live; if living be to loathe the light—
No phantom; but I drag a wretched life;
My fate resembling that of Hector's wife.
What have you suffer'd since you lost your lord?
By what strange blessing are you now restor'd?
Still are you Hector's? or is Hector fled,
And his remembrance lost in Pyrrhus' bed?"
With eyes dejected, in a lowly tone,
After a modest pause, she thus begun:
"Oh, only happy maid of Priam's race,
Whom death deliver'd from the foe's embrace!
Commanded on Achilles' tomb to die,
Nor forc'd, like us, to hard captivity,
Or in a haughty master's arms to lie.
In Grecian ships unhappy we were borne,
Endur'd the victor's lust, sustain'd the scorn:
Thus I submitted to the lawless pride
Of Pyrrhus, more a handmaid than a bride.
Cloy'd with possession, he forsook my bed,
And Helen's lovely daughter sought to wed;
Then me to Trojan Helenus resign'd,
And his two slaves in equal marriage join'd;
Till young Orestes, pierc'd with deep despair,
And longing to redeem the promis'd fair,
Before Apollo's altar slew the ravisher.
By Pyrrhus' death the kingdom we regain'd;
At least one half with Helenus remain'd.
Our part from Chaon, he Chaonia calls,
And names from Pergamus his rising walls,
But you what Fates have landed on our coast?
What gods have sent you, or what storms have toss'd?
Does young Ascanius life and health enjoy,
Sav'd from the ruins of unhappy Troy?
O! tell me how his mother's loss he bears,
What hopes are promis'd from his blooming years.
How much of Hector in his face appears?"
She spoke; and mix'd her speech with mournful cries;
And fruitless tears came trickling from her eyes.
At length her lord descends upon the plain,
In pomp, attended with a num'rous train,
Receives his friends, and to the city leads,
And tears of joy amidst his welcome sheds.
Proceeding on, another Troy I see,
Or, in less compass, Troy's epitome.
A riv'let by the name of Xanthus ran;
And I embrace the Scæan gate again:
My friends in porticoes were entertain'd;
And feasts and pleasures through the city reign'd.
The tables fill'd the spacious hall around;
And golden bowls with sparkling wine were crown'd.
Two days we pass'd in mirth, till friendly gales,
Blown from the south, supplied our swelling sails.
Then to the royal seer I thus began:
"O thou who know'st, beyond the reach of man,
The laws of heav'n and what the stars decree;
Whom Phœbus taught unerring prophecy,
From his own tripod, and his holy tree—
Skill'd in the wing'd inhabitants of air,
What auspices their notes and flights declare—
O say—for all religious rites portend
A happy voyage and a prosp'rous end;
And ev'ry pow'r and omen of the sky
Direct my course for destin'd Italy;
But only dire Celæno, from the gods,
A dismal famine fatally forebodes—

O! say, what dangers I am first to shun,
What toils to vanquish, and what course to run."
The prophet first with sacrifice adores
The greater gods; their pardon then implores;
Unbinds the fillet from his holy head;
To Phœbus, next, my trembling steps he led,
Full of religious doubts and awful dread.
Then, with his god possess'd, before the shrine,
These words proceeded from his mouth divine:
"O goddess born! (for heav'n's appointed will,
With greater auspices of good than ill,
Foreshows thy voyage, and thy course directs:
Thy fates conspire, and Jove himself protects,)
Of many things some few I shall explain,
Teach thee to shun the dangers of the main,
And how at length the promis'd shore to gain.
The rest the Fates from Helenus conceal,
And Juno's angry pow'r forbids to tell.
First, then, that happy shore, that seems so nigh,
Will far from your deluded wishes fly:
Long tracts of seas divide your hopes from Italy:
For you must cruise along Sicilian shores,
And stem the currents with your struggling oars;
Then round th' Italian coast your navy steer,
And, after this, to Circe's island veer;
And, last, before your new foundations rise,
Must pass the Stygian lake, and view the nether skies.
Now mark the signs of future ease and rest;
And bear them safely treasur'd in thy breast.
When, in the shady shelter of a wood,
And near the margin of a gentle flood,
Thou shalt behold a sow upon the ground,
With thirty sucking young encompass'd round:
The damn and offspring white as falling snow—
These on thy city shall their name bestow;
And there shall end thy labours and thy wo.
Nor let the threaten'd famine fright thy mind:
For Phœbus will assist; and Fate the way will find.
Let not thy course to that ill coast be bent,
Which fronts from far th' Epirian continent:
Those parts are all by Grecian foes possess'd.
The savage Locrians here the shores infest:
There fierce Idomeneus his city builds,
And guards with arms the Salentinian fields;
And on the mountain's brow Petilla stands,
Which Philoctetes with his troops commands.
E'en when thy fleet is landed on the shore,
And priests with holy vows the gods adore,
Then with a purple veil involve your eyes,
Lest hostile faces blast the sacrifice.
These rites and customs to the rest commend,
That to your pious race they may descend.
When parted, hence, the winds, that ready waits
For Sicily, shall bear you to the straits,
Where proud Pelorus opes a wider way,
Tack to the larboard, and stand off to sea;
Veer starbord sea and land. Th' Italian shore,
And fair Sicilia's coast, were one, before
An earthquake caus'd the flaw: the roaring tides
The passage broke, that land from land divides;
And, where the lands retir'd, the rushing ocean rides.
Distinguish'd by the straits, on either hand,
Now rising cities in long order stand
And fruitful fields: so much can time invade
The mould'ring work, that beauteous nature made.
Far on the right, her dogs fair Scylla hides:
Charybdis roaring on the left presides,
And in her greedy whirlpool sucks the tides:
Then spouts them from below: with fury driv'n,
The waves mount up, and wash the face of heav'n.
But Scylla from her den, with open jaws,
The sinking vessel in her eddy draws,
Then dashes on the rocks.—A human face,
And virgin bosom hides her tail's disgrace;
Her parts obscene below the waves descend,
With dogs enclos'd; and in a dolphin end.
'T is safer then to bear aloof to sea,
And coast Pachynus, though with more delay,
Than once to view misshapen Scylla near,
And the loud yells of wat'ry wolves to hear.
Besides, if faith to Helenus be due,
And if prophetic Phœbus tell me true,
Do not this precept of your friend forget,
Which therefore more than once I must repeat:
Above the rest, great Juno's name adore;
Pay vows to Juno; Juno's aid implore.
Let gifts be to the mighty queen design'd;
And mollify with pray'rs her haughty mind.
Thus, at the length, your passage shall be free,
And you shall safe descend on Italy.
Arriv'd at Cumæ, when you view the flood
Of black Avernus, and the sounding wood,
The mad prophetic Sibyl you shall find,
Dark in a cave, and on a rock reclin'd.
She sings the Fates, and, in her frantic fits,
The notes and names, inscrib'd, to leaves commits.
What she commits to leaves, in order laid,
Before the cavern's entrance are display'd:
Unmov'd they lie: but, if a blast of wind
Without, or vapours issue from behind,
The leaves are borne aloft in liquid air;
And she resumes no more her museful care,
Nor gathers from the rocks her scatter'd verse,
Nor sets in order what the winds disperse.
Thus many, not succeeding, must upbraid
The madness of the visionary maid,
And with loud curses leave the mystic shade.

Think it not loss of time a while to stay,
Though thy companions chide thy long delay;
Tho' summon'd to the seas, tho' pleasing gales
Invite thy course, and stretch thy swelling sails:
But beg the sacred priestess to relate
With willing words, and not to write thy fate.
The fierce Italian people she will show,
And all thy wars, and all thy future wo,
And what thou mayst avoid, and what must undergo.
She shall direct thy course, instruct thy mind,
And teach thee how the happy shores to find.
This is what heav'n allows me to relate:
Now part in peace; pursue thy better fate,
And raise, by strength of arms, the Trojan state."
This when the priest with friendly voice declar'd,
He gave me license, and rich gifts prepar'd;
Bounteous of treasure, he supplied my want
With heavy gold, and polish'd elephant,
Then Dodonæan caldrons put on board,
And ev'ry ship with sums of silver stor'd.
A trusty coat of mail to me he sent,
Thrice chain'd with gold, for use and ornament;
The helm of Pyrrhus added to the rest,
That flourish'd with a plume and waving crest.
Nor was my sire forgotten, nor my friends:
And large recruits he to my navy sends—
Men, horses, captains, arms, and warlike stores;
Supplies new pilots, and new sweeping oars.
Meantime, my sire commands to hoist our sails,
Lest we should lose the first auspicious gales.
The prophet bless'd the parting crew, and last,
With words like these, his ancient friend embrac'd:
"Old happy man, the care of gods above,
Whom heav'nly Venus honour'd with her love,
And twice preserv'd thy life when Troy was lost!
Behold from far the wish'd Ausonian coast:
There land; but take a larger compass round;
For that before is all forbidden ground.
The shore that Phœbus has design'd for you,
At further distance lies, conceal'd from view.
Go happy hence, and seek your new abodes,
Bless'd in a son, and favour'd by the gods:
For I with useless words prolong your stay
When southern gales have summon'd you away."
Nor less the queen our parting thence deplor'd,
Nor was less bounteous than her Trojan lord.
A noble present to my son she brought;
A robe with flow'rs on golden tissue wrought.
A Phrygian vest; and loads with gifts beside
Of precious texture, and of Asian pride.
"Accept," she said, "these monuments of love,
Which in my youth with happier hands I wove:
Regard these trifles for the giver's sake;
'T is the last present Hector's wife can make.
Thou call'st my lost Astyanax to mind:
In thee, his features and his form I find.
His eyes so sparkled with a lively flame;
Such were his motions; such was all his frame;
And ah! had heav'n so pleas'd, his years had been the same."
With tears I took my last adieu, and said,
"Your fortune, happy pair, already made,
Leaves you no further wish. My diff'rent state,
Avoiding one, incurs another fate.
To you a quiet seat the gods allow:
You have no shores to search, no seas to plough:
Nor fields of flying Italy to chase—
Deluding visions, and a vain embrace:
You see another Simois, and enjoy
The labour of your hands, another Troy,
With better auspice than her ancient tow'rs
And less obnoxious to the Grecian pow'rs.
If e'er the gods, whom I with vows adore,
Conduct my steps to Tyber's happy shore—
If ever I ascend the Latian throne,
And build a city I may call my own
As both of us our birth from Troy derive,
So let our kindred lines in concord live,
And both in acts of equal friendship strive.
Our fortunes, good or bad, shall be the same:
The double Troy shall differ but in name:
That what we now begin, may never end,
But long to late posterity descend."
Near the Ceraunian rocks our course we bore—
The shortest passage to th' Italian shore.
Now had the sun withdrawn his radiant light,
And hills were hid in dusky shades of night:
We land, and, on the bosom of the ground,
A safe retreat and a bare lodging found.
Close by the shore we lay; the sailors keep
Their watches, and the rest securely sleep.
The night, proceeding on with silent pace,
Stood in her noon, and view'd with equal face
Her steepy rise, and her declining race.
Then wakeful Palinurus rose, to spy
The face of heav'n, and the nocturnal sky;
And listen'd ev'ry breath of air to try;
Observes the stars, and notes their sliding course,
The Pleiads, Hyads, and their wat'ry force;
And both the Bears is careful to behold,
And bright Orion, arm'd with burnish'd gold.
Then, when he saw no threat'ning tempest nigh,
But a sure promise of a settled sky,
He gave the sign to weigh, we break our sleep,
Forsake the pleasing shore, and plough the deep.
And now the rising morn with rosy light
Adorns the skies, and puts the stars to flight

When we from far, like bluish mist, descry
The hills, and then the plains of Italy.
Achates first pronounc'd the joyful sound;
Then "Italy" the cheerful crew rebound;
My sire Anchises crown'd a cup with wine,
And off'ring, thus implor'd the pow'rs divine:
"Ye gods, presiding over lands and seas,
And you who raging winds and waves appease,
Breathe on our swelling sails a prosp'rous wind,
And smooth our passage to the port assign'd."
The gentle gales their flagging force renew;
And now the happy harbour is in view.
Minerva's temple then salutes our sight,
Plac'd, as a landmark, on the mountain's height.
We furl our sails, and turn the prows to shore;
The curling waters round the galleys roar.
The land lies open to the raging East;
Then, bending like a bow, with rocks compress'd,
Shuts out the storms; the winds and waves complain,
And vent their malice on the cliffs in vain.
The port lies hid within; on either side,
Two tow'ring rocks the narrow mouth divide.
The temple, which aloft we view'd before,
To distance flies, and seems to shun the shore.
Scarce landed, the first omens I beheld
Were four white steeds that cropp'd the flow'ry field.
"War, war, is threaten'd from this foreign ground,
(My father cried,) where warlike steeds are found.
Yet, since, reclaim'd, to chariots they submit,
And bend to stubborn yokes, and champ the bit,
Peace may succeed to war."—Our way we bend
To Pallas, and the sacred hill ascend;
There prostrate to the fierce virago pray,
Whose temple was the landmark of our way.
Each with a Phrygian mantle veil'd his head,
And all commands of Helenus obey'd,
And pious rites to Grecian Juno paid.
These dues perform'd, we stretch our sails, and stand
To sea, forsaking that suspected land.
From hence Tarentum's bay appears in view
For Hercules renown'd, if fame be true.
Just opposite, Licinian Juno stands;
Caulonian tow'rs and Scylacæan strands,
For shipwrecks fear'd. Mount Ætna thence we spy,
Known by the smoky flames which cloud the sky.
Far off we hear the waves with surly sound
Invade the rocks, the rocks their groans rebound.
The billows break upon the sounding strand,
And roll the rising tide, impure with sand.
Then thus Anchises, in experience old
"'T is that Charybdis which the seer foretold,
And those the promis'd rocks! Bear off to sea!"
With haste the frighted mariners obey.
First Palinurus to the larboard veer'd;
Then all the fleet by his example steer'd.
To heav'n aloft on ridgy waves we ride,
Then down to hell descend, when they divide:
And thrice our galleys knock'd the stony ground,
And thrice the hollow rocks return'd the sound,
And thrice we saw the stars that stood with dews around.
The flagging winds forsook us with the sun;
And, wearied, on Cyclopian shores we run.
The port, capacious and secure from wind,
Is to the foot of thund'ring Ætna join'd.
By turns a pitchy cloud she rolls on high;
By turns hot embers from her entrails fly,
And flakes of mountain flames that lick the sky.
Oft from her bowels massy rocks are thrown,
And, shiver'd by the force, come piecemeal down:
Oft liquid lakes of burning sulphur flow,
Fed from the fiery springs that boil below.
Enceladus, they say, transfix'd by Jove,
With blasted limbs came tumbling from above,
And, where he fell, th' avenging father drew
This flaming hill, and on his body threw.
As often as he turns his weary sides,
He shakes the solid isle, and smoke the heavens hides.
In shady woods we pass the tedious night,
Where bellowing sounds and groans our souls affright,
Of which no cause is offer'd to the sight.
For not one star was kindled in the sky,
Nor could the moon her borrow'd light supply
For misty clouds involv'd the firmament;
The stars were muffled, and the moon was pent.
Scarce had the rising sun the day reveal'd;
Scarce had his heat the pearly dews dispell'd;
When from the woods, their bolts before our sight,
Somewhat betwixt a mortal and a sprite,
So thin, so ghastly meager, and so wan,
So bare of flesh, he scarce resembled man.
This thing, all tatter'd, seem'd from far t' implore
Our pious aid, and pointed to the shore.
We look behind; then view his shaggy beard;
His clothes were tagg'd with thorns; and filth his limbs besmear'd.
The rest, in mien, in habit, and in face,
Appear'd a Greek; and such indeed he was.
He cast on us, from far, a frightful view,
Whom soon for Trojans and for foes he knew—

Stood still and paus'd; then all at once began
To stretch his limbs, and trembled as he ran.
Soon as approach'd, upon his knees he falls,
And thus with tears and sighs for pity calls:
" Now, by the powers above, and what we share
From nature's common gift, this vital air,
O Trojans, take me hence! I beg no more,
But bear me far from this unhappy shore.
'T is true, I am a Greek, and further own,
Among your foes besieg'd the imperial town.
For such demerits if my death be due,
No more for this abandon'd life I sue:
This only favour let my tears obtain,
To throw me headlong in the rapid main:
Since nothing more than death my crime demands
I die content, to die by human hands."
He said, and on his knees my knees embrac'd:
I bade him boldly tell his fortune past,
His present state, his lineage, and his name,
Th' occasion of his fears, and whence he came.
The good Anchises rais'd him with his hand,
Who, thus encourag'd, answer'd our demand:
" From Ithaca, my native soil, I came
To Troy; and Achæmenides my name.
Me my poor father with Ulysses sent;
(O! had I stay'd, with poverty content!)
But fearful for themselves, my countrymen
Left me forsaken in the Cyclop's den.
The cave, though large, was dark; the dismal floor
Was pav'd with mangled limbs and putrid gore.
Our monstrous host, of more than human size,
Erects his head, and stares within the skies.
Bellowing his voice, and horrid is his hue.
Ye gods, remove this plague from mortal view!
The joints of slaughter'd wretches are his food,
And for his wine he quaffs the streaming blood.
These eyes beheld, when with his spacious hand
He seiz'd two captives of our Grecian band;
Stretch'd on his back, he dash'd against the stones
Their broken bodies, and their crackling bones:
With spouting blood the purple pavement swims,
While the dire glutton grinds the trembling limbs.
Not unreveng'd Ulysses bore their fate,
Nor thoughtless of his own unhappy state;
For, gorg'd with flesh, and drunk with human wine,
While fast asleep the giant lay supine,
Snoring aloud, and belching from his maw
His indigested foam, and morsels raw—
We pray, we cast the lots, and then surround
The monstrous body, stretch'd along the ground:
Each, as he could approach him, lends a hand,
To bore his eyeball with a flaming brand.
Beneath his frowning forehead lay his eye;
For only one did the vast frame supply—
But that a globe so large, his front it fill'd,
Like the sun's disk, or like a Grecian shield.
The stroke succeeds; and down the pupil bends:
This vengeance follow'd for our slaughter'd friends.—
But haste, unhappy wretches! haste to fly!
Your cables cut, and on your oars rely!
Such and so vast as Polypheme appears,
A hundred more this hated island bears:
Like him, in caves, they shut their woolly sheep,
Like him, their herds on tops of mountains keep;
Like him, with mighty strides, they stalk from steep to steep.
And now three moons their sharpen'd horns renew,
Since thus in woods and wilds, obscure from view,
I drag my loathsome days with mortal fright,
And in deserted caverns lodge by night;
Oft from the rocks a dreadful prospect see,
Of the huge Cyclops, like a walking tree:
From far I hear his thund'ring voice resound,
And trampling feet that shake the solid ground.
Cornels, and savage berries of the wood,
And roots and herbs, have been my meager food.
While all around my longing eyes I cast,
I saw your happy ships appear at last.
On those I fix'd my hopes, to these I run:
'T is all I ask, this cruel race to shun.
What other death you please, yourselves bestow."
Scarce had he said, when on the mountain's brow
We saw the giant shepherd stalk before
His following flock, and leading to the shore—
A monstrous bulk, deform'd, depriv'd of sight;
His staff a trunk of pine, to guide his steps aright.
His pond'rous whistle from his neck descends.
His woolly care their pensive lord attends:
This only solace his hard fortune sends.
Soon as he reach'd the shore, and touch'd the waves
From his bor'd eye the glutt'ring blood he laves:
He gnash'd his teeth, and groan'd: through seas he strides;
And scarce the topmost billows touch'd his sides.
Seiz'd with a sudden fear, we run to sea,
The cables cut and silent haste away;
The well-deserving stranger entertain;
Then, buckling to the work, our oars divide the main.
The giant hearken'd to the dashing sound:
But, when our vessels out of reach he found,
He strided onward, and in vain essay'd
Th' Ionian deep, and durst no farther wade.
With that he roar'd aloud: the dreadful cry
Shakes earth and air and seas; the billows fly,
Before the bellowing noise, to distant Italy.

The neighb'ring Ætna trembling all around,
The winding caverns echo to the sound.
His brother Cyclops hear the yelling roar,
And rushing down the mountains, crowd the shore.
We saw their stern distorted looks from far,
And one-ey'd glance, that vainly threaten'd war—
A dreadful council! with their heads on high
(The misty clouds about their foreheads fly)
Not yielding to the tow'ring tree of Jove,
Or tallest cypress of Diana's grove.
New pangs of mortal fear our minds assail;
We tug at ev'ry oar, and hoist up ev'ry sail,
And take th' advantage of the friendly gale.
Forewarn'd by Helenus, we strive to shun
Charybdis' gulf, nor dare to Scylla run.
An equal fate on either side appears:
We, tacking to the left, are free from fears:
For, from Pelorus' point, the north arose,
And drove us back where swift Pantagias flows.
His rocky mouth we pass; and make our way
By Thapsus, and Megara's winding bay.
This passage Achæmenides had shown,
Tracing the course which he before had run.
Right o'er against Plemmyrium's wat'ry strand,
There lies an isle, once call'd th' Ortygian land.
Alpheüs, as old fame reports, has found
From Greece a secret passage under ground,
By love to beauteous Arethusa led;
And, mingling here, they roll in the same sacred bed.
As Helenus enjoin'd, we next adore
Diana's name, protectress of the shore.
With prosp'rous gales we pass the quiet sounds
Of still Helorus, and his fruitful bounds.
Then, doubling cape Pachynus, we survey
The rocky shore extended to the sea.
The town of Camarine from far we see,
And fenny lake, undrain'd by Fate's decree.
In sight of the Geloan fields we pass,
And the large walls, where mighty Gela was;
Then Agragas, with lofty summits crown'd,
Long for the race of warlike steeds renown'd.
We pass'd Selinus, and the palmy land,
And widely shun the Lilybæan strand,
Unsafe for secret rocks and moving sand.
At length on shore the weary fleet arriv'd,
Which Drepanum's unhappy port receiv'd.
Here, after endless labours, often toss'd
By raging storms, and driv'n on ev'ry coast,
My dear, dear father spent with age, I lost—
Ease of my cares, and solace of my pain,
Sav'd through a thousand toils, but sav'd in vain.
The prophet, who my future woes reveal'd,
Yet this, the greatest and the worst, conceal'd:
And dire Celæno, whose foreboding skill
Denounc'd all else, was silent of this ill.
This my last labour was. Some friendly god
From thence convey'd us to your blest abode.'
Thus to the list'ning queen, the royal guest
His wand'ring course and all his toils express'd,
And here concluding, he retir'd to rest.

BOOK IV.

ARGUMENT.

Dido discovers to her sister her passion for Æneas, and her thoughts of marrying him. She prepares a hunting match for his entertainment. Juno, by Venus's consent, raises a storm, which separates the hunters, and drives Æneas and Dido into the same cave, where their marriage is supposed to be completed. Jupiter despatches Mercury to Æneas, to warn him from Carthage. Æneas secretly prepares for his voyage. Dido finds out his design, and, to put a stop to it, makes use of her own and her sister's entreaties, and discovers all the variety of passions that are incident to a neglected lover. When nothing could prevail upon him, she contrives her own death, with which this book concludes.

But anxious cares already seiz'd the queen:
She fed within her veins a flame unseen;
The hero's valour, acts, and birth, inspire
Her soul with love, and fan the secret fire.
His words, his looks, imprinted in her heart,
Improve the passion, and increase the smart.
Now, when the purple morn had chas'd away
The dewy shadows, and restor'd the day,
Her sister first with early care she sought,
And thus in mournful accents eas'd her thought:
"My dearest Anna! what new dreams affright
My lab'ring soul! what visions of the night
Disturb my quiet, and distract my breast
With strange ideas of our Trojan guest!
His worth, his actions, and majestic air,
A man descended from the gods declare.
Fear ever argues a degen'rate kind:
His birth is well asserted by his mind.
Then, what he suffer'd when by Fate betray'd,
What brave attempts for falling Troy he made.
Such were his looks, so gracefully he spoke,
That, were I not resolv'd against the yoke
Of hapless marriage—never to be curs'd
With second love, so fatal was my first—
To this one error I might yield again:
For, since Sichæus was untimely slain,
This only man is able to subvert
The fix'd foundations of my stubborn heart.
And, to confess my frailty to my shame,
Somewhat I find within, if not the same,
Too like the sparkles of my former flame.
But first let yawning earth a passage rend,
And let me through the dark abyss descend—

First let avenging Jove, with flames from high,
Drive down this body to the nether sky,
Condemn'd with ghosts in endless night to lie—
Before I break the plighted faith I gave!
No! he who had my vows, shall ever have:
For, whom I lov'd on earth, I worship in the grave."
She said: the tears ran gushing from her eyes,
And stopp'd her speech. Her sister thus replies:
"O, dearer than the vital air I breathe!
Will you to grief your blooming years bequeath,
Condemn'd to waste in woes your lonely life,
Without the joys of mother, or of wife!
Think you these tears, this pompous train of wo,
Are known or valu'd by the ghosts below?
I grant that while your sorrows yet were green,
It well became a woman, and a queen,
The vows of Tyrian princes to neglect,
To scorn Iarbas, and his love reject.
With all the Libyan lords of mighty name:
But will you fight against a pleasing flame?
This little spot of land which heav'n bestows,
On ev'ry side is hemm'd with warlike foes:
Gætulian cities here are spread around,
And fierce Numidians there your frontiers bound:
Here lies a barren waste of thirsty land,
And there the Syrtes raise the moving sand:
Barcæan troops besiege the narrow shore,
And from the sea Pygmalion threatens more.
Propitious heav'n, and gacious Juno, lead
This wand'ring navy to your needful aid:
How will your empire spread, your city rise,
From such a union, and with such allies!
Implore the favour of the pow'rs above;
And leave the conduct of the rest of love.
Continue still your hospitable way,
And still invent occasions of their stay,
Till storms and winter winds thall cease to threat,
And planks and oars repair their shatter'd fleet."
These words, which from a friend and sister came,
With ease resolv'd the scruples of her fame,
And added fury to the kindled flame.
Inspir'd with hope, the project they pursue:
On ev'ry altar sacrifice renew;
A chosen ewe of two years old they pay
To Ceres, Bacchus, and the god of day.
Preferring Juno's pow'r (for Juno ties
The nuptial knot, and makes the marriage joys,)
The beauteous queen before her altar stands,
And holds the golden goblet in her hands,
A milk-white heifer she with flow'rs adorns,
And pours the ruddy wine betwixt her horns:
And, while the priests with pray'r the gods invoke,
She feeds their altars with Sabæan smoke,
With hourly care the sacrifice renews,
And anxiously the panting entrails views.
What priestly rites, alas! what pious art,
What vows avail to cure a bleeding heart?
A gentle fire she feeds within her veins,
Where the soft god secure in silence reigns.
Sick with desire, and seeking him she loves,
From street to street the raving Dido roves.
So, when the watchful shepherd, from the blind,
Wounds with a random shaft the careless hind,
Distracted with her pain she flies the woods,
Bounds o'er the lawn, and seeks the silent floods—
With fruitless care; for still the fatal dart
Sticks in her side, and rankles in her heart.
And now she leads the Trojan chief along
The lofty walls, amidst the busy throng;
Displays her Tyrian wealth, and rising town,
Which love, without his labour, makes his own.
This pomp she shows, to tempt her wand'ring guest;
Her fault'ring tongue forbids to speak the rest.
When day declines, and feasts renew the night,
Still on his face she feeds her famish'd sight;
She longs again to hear the prince relate
His own adventures, and the Trojan fate.
He tells it o'er and o'er; but still in vain,
For still she begs to hear it once again.
The hearer on the speaker's mouth depends:
And thus the tragic story never ends.
Then, when they part, when Phœbe's paler light
Withdraws, and falling stars to sleep invite
She last remains, when ev'ry guest is gone,
Sits on the bed he press'd, and sighs alone
Absent, her absent hero sees and hears;
Or in her bosom young Ascanius bears,
And seeks the father's image in the child,
If love by likeness might be so beguil'd.
Meantime the rising tow'rs are at a stand;
No labours exercise the youthful band,
Nor use of arts, nor toils of arms, they know;
The mole is left unfinish'd to the foe;
The mounds, the works, the walls, neglected lie,
Short of their promis'd height, that seem'd to threat the sky.
But when imperial Juno, from above,
Saw Dido fetter'd in the chains of love,
Hot with the venom which her veins inflam'd,
And by no sense of shame to be reclaim'd,
With soothing words to Venus she begun:
"High praises, endless honours, you have won,
And mighty trophies, with your worthy son!
Two gods a silly woman have undone!
Nor am I ignorant, you both suspect
This rising city, which my hands erect:

But shall celestial discord never cease?
'T is better ended in a lasting peace.
You stand possess'd of all your soul desir'd;
Poor Dido with consuming love is fir'd.
Your Trojan with my Tyrian let us join;
So Dido shall be yours, Æneas mine—
One common kingdom, one united line.
Eliza shall a Dardan lord obey,
And lofty Carthage for a dow'r convey."
Then Venus (who her hidden fraud descried,
Which would the sceptre of the world misguide
To Libyan shores) thus artfully replied:
"Who, but a fool, would wars with Juno choose,
And such alliance and such gifts refuse,
If fortune with our joint desires comply?
The doubt is all from Jove, and destiny;
Lest he forbid, with absolute command,
To mix the people in one common land—
Or will the Trojan and the Tyrian line,
In lasting leagues and sure succession, join.
But you, the partner of his bed and throne,
May move his mind: my wishes are your own."
"Mine," said imperial Juno, "be the care:—
Time urges now:—to perfect this affair,
Attend my counsel, and the secret share.
When next the Sun his rising light displays,
And gilds the world below with purple rays,
The queen, Æneas, and the Tyrian court,
Shall to the shady woods, for sylvan game, resort;
There, while the huntsmen pitch their toils around,
And cheerful horns, from side to side, resound,
A pitchy cloud shall cover all the plain
With hail, and thunder, and tempestuous rain:
The fearful train shall take their speedy flight,
Dispers'd and all involv'd in gloomy night:
One cave a grateful shelter shall afford
To the fair princess and the Trojan lord.
I will myself the bridal bed prepare,
If you, to bless the nuptials, will be there:
So shall their loves be crown'd with due delights,
And Hymen shall be present at the rites."
The queen of love consents, and closely smiles
At her vain project, and discover'd wiles.
The rosy morn was risen from the main,
And horns and hounds awake the princely train:
They issue early through the city gate,
Where the more wakeful huntsmen ready wait,
With nets, and toils, and darts, beside the force
Of Spartan dogs, and swift Massylian horse.
The Tyrian peers and officers of state,
For the slow queen, in antechambers wait:
Her lofty courser, in the court below,
(Who his majestic rider seems to know,)
Proud of his purple trapping, paws the ground,
And champs the golden bit, and spreads the foam around.
The queen at length appears: on either hand,
The brawny guards in martial order stand.
A flower'd cymar with golden fringe she wore,
And at her back a golden quiver bore.
Her flowing hair a golden caul restrains,
A golden clasp the Tyrian robe sustains.
Then young Ascanius, with a sprightly grace,
Leads on the Trojan youth to view the chase.
But far above the rest in beauty shines
The great Æneas, when the troop he joins;
Like fair Apollo, when he leaves the frost
Of wintry Xanthus, and the Lycian coast,
When to his native Delos he resorts,
Ordains the dances, and renews the sports;
Where painted Scythians, mix'd with Cretan bands,
Before the joyful altars join their hands:
Himself, on Cynthus walking, sees below
The merry madness of the sacred show.
Green wreaths of bays his length of hair enclose;
A golden fillet binds his awful brows:
His quiver sounds.—Not less the prince is seen
In manly presence, or in lofty mien.
Now had they reach'd the hills, and storm'd the seat
Of savage beasts, in dens, their last retreat.
The cry pursues the mountain-goats: they bound
From rock to rock, and keep the craggy ground:
Quite otherwise the stags, a trembling train,
In herds unsingled, scour the dusty plain,
And a long chase, in open view maintain.
The glad Ascanius, as his courser guides,
Spurs through the vale, and these and those outrides.
His horse's flanks and sides are forc'd to feel
The clanking lash, and goring of the steel.
Impatiently he views the feeble prey,
Wishing some nobler beast to cross his way;
And rather would the tusky boar attend,
Or see the tawny lion downward bend.
Meantime, the gath'ring clouds obscure the skies:
From pole to pole the forky lightning flies
The rattling thunders roll; and Juno pours
A wintry deluge down, and sounding show'rs.
The company dispers'd, to coverts ride,
And seek the homely cots, or mountain's hollow side.
The rapid rains, descending from the hills,
To rolling torrents raise the creeping rills.
The queen and prince, as Love or Fortune guides,
One common cavern in her bosom hides.
Then first the trembling earth the signal gave,
And flashing fires enlighten all the cave:

Hell from below, and Juno from above,
And howling nymphs, were conscious to their love.
From this ill-omen'd hour, in time arose
Debate and death, and all succeeding woes.
The queen, whom sense of honour could not move,
No longer made a secret of her love,
But call'd it marriage, by that specious name
To veil the crime, and sanctify the shame.
The loud report through Libyan cities goes:
Fame the great ill, from small beginnings grows—
Swift from the first; and ev'ry moment brings
New vigour to her flights, new pinions to her wings
Soon grows the pigmy to gigantic size;
Her feet on earth, her forehead in the skies.
Enrag'd against the gods, revengeful Earth
Produc'd her, last of the Titanian birth—
Swift is her walk, more swift her winged haste—
A monstrous phantom, horrible and vast.
As many plumes as raise her lofty flight,
So many piercing eyes enlarge her sight:
Millions of op'ning mouths to Fame belong;
And ev'ry mouth is furnish'd with a tongue;
And round with list'ning ears the flying plague is hung.
She fills the peaceful universe with cries:
No slumbers ever close her wakeful eyes:
By day, from lofty tow'rs her head she shows,
And spreads thro' trembling crowds disas'trous news,
With court informers haunts, and royal spies;
Things done relates; not done she feigns; and mingles truth with lies.
Talk is her bus'ness; and her chief delight
To tell of prodigies, and cause affright.
She fills the people's ears with Dido's name,
Who, "lost to honour and the sense of shame,
Admits into her throne and nuptial bed
A wand'ring guest, who from his country fled:
Whole days with him she passes in delights,
And wastes in luxury long winter nights,
Forgetful of her fame and royal trust,
Dissolv'd in ease, abandon'd to her lust."
The goddess widely spreads the loud report
And flies at length to king Iarbas' court.
When first possess'd with this unwelcome news,
Whom did he not of men and gods accuse?
This prince, from ravished Garmantis born,
A hundred temples did with spoils adorn,
In Ammon's honour, his celestial sire;
A hundred altars fed with wakeful fire;
And, through his vast dominions, priests ordain'd,
Whose watchful care these holy rites maintain'd.
The gates and columns were with garlands crown'd,
And blood of victim beasts enrich'd the ground.
He, when he heard a fugitive could move
The Tyrian princess, who disdain'd his love,
His breast with fury burn'd, his eyes with fire—
Mad with despair, impatient with desire—
Then on the sacred altars pouring wine,
He thus with pray'rs implor'd his sire divine.
"Great Jove, propitious to the Moorish race,
Who feast on painted beds, with off'rings grace
Thy temples, and adore thy pow'r divine,
With blood of victims, and with sparkling wine,
Seest thou not this? or do we fear in vain
Thy boasted thunder, and thy thoughtless reign?
Do thy broad hands the forky lightnings lance?
Thine are the bolts, or the blind work of chance?
A wand'ring woman builds, within our state,
A little town, bought at an easy rate;
She pays me homage, (and my grants allow
A narrow space of Libyan lands to plough,)
Yet, scorning me, by passion blindly led,
Admits a banish'd Trojan to her bed!
And now, this other Paris, with his train
Of conquer'd cowards, must in Afric reign!
(Whom, what they are, their looks and garb confess,
Their locks with oil perfum'd, their Lydian dress.)
He takes the spoil, enjoys the princely dame;
And I, rejected I, adore an empty name!
His vows, in haughty terms, he thus preferr'd,
And held his altar's horns: the mighty Thund'rer heard,
Then cast his eyes on Carthage, where he found
The lustful pair in lawless pleasure drown'd,
Lost in their loves, insensible of shame,
And both forgetful of their better fame.
He calls Cyllenius; and the god attends;
By whom this menacing command he sends:
"Go mount the western winds, and cleave the sky;
Then, with a swift descent, to Carthage fly;
There find the Trojan chief, who wastes his days
In slothful riot and inglorious ease,
Nor minds the future city, given by Fate.
To him this message from my mouth relate:
Not so fair Venus hop'd, when twice she won
Thy life with pray'rs; nor promis'd such a son.
Hers was a hero, destin'd to command
A martial race, and rule the Latian land;
Who should his ancient line from Teucer draw;
And on the conquer'd world impose the law.
If glory cannot move a mind so mean,
Nor future praise from fading pleasure wean,
Yet why should he defraud his son of fame
And grudge the Romans their immortal name

What are his vain designs? what hopes he more
From his long ling'ring on a hostile shore,
Regardless to redeem his honour lost,
And for his race to gain the Ausonian coast?
Bid him with speed the Tyrian court forsake:
With this command the slumb'ring warrior wake."
Hermes obeys: with golden pinions binds
His flying feet, and mounts the western winds:
And, whether o'er the seas or earth he flies,
With rapid force they bear him down the skies.
But first he grasps within his awful hand
The mark of sov'reign pow'r, his magic wand:
With this he draws the ghosts from hollow graves;
With this he drives them down the Stygian waves;
With this he seals in sleep the wakeful sight,
And eyes, though clos'd in death, restores to light.
Thus arm'd, the god begins his airy race,
And drives the racking clouds along the liquid space;
Now sees the top of Atlas, as he flies,
Whose brawny back supports the starry skies—
Atlas, whose head, with piny forests crown'd,
Is beaten by the winds—with foggy vapours bound.
Snows hide his shoulders: from beneath his chin
The founts of rolling streams their race begin:
A beard of ice on his large breast depends—
Here, pois'd upon his wings, the god descends:
Then, resting thus, he from the tow'ring height
Plung'd downward with precipitated flight,
Lights on the seas, and skims along the flood;
As water fowls, who seek their fishy food,
Less, and yet less, to distant prospect show;
By turns they dance aloft, and dive below;
Like these, the steerage of his wings he plies,
And near the surface of the water flies:
Till, having pass'd the seas, and cross'd the sands,
He clos'd his wings, and stoop'd on Libyan lands
Where shepherds once were hous'd in homely sheds,
Now tow'rs within the clouds advance their heads.
Arriving there, he found the Trojan prince
New ramparts raising for the town's defence,
A purple scarf, with gold embroider'd o'er,
(Queen Dido's gift,) about his waist he wore;
A sword, with glitt'ring gems diversified,
For ornament, not use, hung idly by his side.
Then thus, with winged words, the god began,
Resuming his own shape—"Degen'rate man!
Thou woman's property! what mak'st thou here,
These foreign walls and Tyrian tow'rs to rear,
Forgetful of thy own? All-powerful Jove,
Who sways the world below and heav'n above,
Has sent me down with this severe command:
What means thy ling'ring in the Libyan land?
If glory cannot move a mind so mean,
Nor future praise from flitting pleasure wean,
Regard the fortunes of thy rising heir:
The promis'd crown let young Ascanius wear,
To whom th' Ausonian sceptre, and the state
Of Rome's imperial name, is ow'd by Fate."
So spoke the god; and, speaking, took his flight,
Involv'd in clouds; and vanish'd out of sight.
The pious prince was seiz'd with sudden fear:
Mute was his tongue, and upright stood his hair:
Revolving in his mind the stern command,
He longs to fly, and loathes the charming land.
What should he say? or how should he begin?
What course, alas! remains, to steer between
Th' offended lover and the pow'rful queen?
This way, and that, he turns his anxious mind,
And all expedients tries, and none can find.
Fix'd on the deed, but doubtful of the means—
After long thought, to this advice he leans:
Three chiefs he calls, commands them to repair
The fleet, and ship their men, with silent care:
Some plausible pretence he bids them find,
To colour what in secret he design'd.
Himself, meantime, the softest hours would choose,
Before the love-sick lady heard the news;
And move her tender mind by slow degrees,
To suffer what the sov'reign power decrees;
Jove will inspire him, when, and what to say.—
They hear with pleasure, and with haste obey.
But soon the queen perceives the thin disguise:
(What arts can blind a jealous woman's eyes?)
She was the first to find the secret fraud,
Before the fatal news was blaz'd abroad.
Love the first motions of the lover hears,
Quick to presage, and e'en in safety fears.
Nor impious Fame was wanting to report
The ships repair'd, the Trojan's quick resort,
And purpose to forsake the Tyrian court.
Frantic with fear, impatient of the wound,
And impotent of mind, she roves the city round.
Less wild the Bacchanalian dames appear,
When, from afar, their nightly god they hear,
And howl about the hills, and shake the wreathy spear.
At length she finds the dear perfidious man,
Prevents his form'd excuse, and thus began:
"Base and ungrateful! could you hope to fly,
And, undiscover'd, 'scape a lover's eye?
Nor could my kindness your compassion move,
Nor plighted vows, nor dearer bands of love?

Or is the death of a despairing queen
Not worth preventing, though too well foreseen?
E'en when the wintry winds command your stay,
You dare the tempests, and defy the sea.
False as you are, suppose you were not bound
To lands unknown, and foreign coasts to sound;
Were Troy restor'd, and Priam's happy reign,
Now durst you tempt, for Troy, the raging main?
See, whom you fly! am I the foe you shun?
Now, by those holy vows, so late begun,
By this right hand (since I have nothing more
To challenge, but the faith you gave before)
I beg you by these tears too truly shed,
By the new pleasures of our nuptial bed;
If ever Dido, when you most were kind,
Were pleasing in your eyes, or touch'd your mind:
By these my pray'rs, if pray'rs may yet have place,
Pity the fortune of a falling race!
For you I have provok'd a tyrant's hate,
Incens'd the Libyan and the Tyrian state;
For you alone, I suffer in my fame,
Bereft of honour, and expos'd to shame!
Whom have I now to trust, ungrateful guest?
(That only name remains of all the rest!)
What have I left? or whither can I fly?
Must I attend Pygmalion's cruelty,
Or till Iarbas shall in triumph lead
A queen, that proudly scorn'd his proffer'd bed!
Had you deferr'd, at least, your hasty flight,
And left behind some pledge of our delight,
Some babe to bless the mother's mournful sight,
Some young Æneas to supply your place,
Whose features might express his father's face;
I should not then complain to live bereft
Of all my husband, or be wholly left."
Here paus'd the queen. Unmov'd he holds his eyes,
By Jove's command; nor suffer'd love to rise,
Tho' heaving in his heart; and thus at length replies:
"Fair queen, you never can enough repeat
Your boundless favours, or I own my debt;
Nor can my mind forget Eliza's name,
While vital breath inspires this mortal frame.
This only let me speak in my defence—
I never hop'd a secret flight from hence,
Much less pretended to the lawful claim
Of sacred nuptials, or a husband's name.
For, if indulgent heav'n would leave me free,
And not submit my life to Fate's decree,
My choice would lead me to the Trojan shore,
Those relics to review, their dust adore,
And Priam's ruin'd palace to restore.
And now the Delphian oracle commands,
And Fate invites me to the Latian lands.
That is the promis'd place to which I steer;
And all my vows are terminated there.
If you, a Tyrian and a stranger born,
With walls and tow'rs, a Libyan town adorn,
Why may not we—like you, a foreign race—
Like you, seek shelter in a foreign place?
As often as the night obscures the skies
With humid shades, or twinkling stars arise,
Anchises' angry ghost in dreams appears,
Chides my delay, and fills my soul with fears:
And young Ascanius justly may complain,
Defrauded of his fate, and destin'd reign.
E'en now the herald of the gods appear'd—
Waking I saw him, and his message heard.
From Jove he came commission'd, heavenly bright
With radiant beams, and manifest to sight
(The sender and the sent I both attest:)
These walls he enter'd, and these words express'd.
Fair queen, oppose not what the gods command:
Forc'd by my fate, I leave your happy land."
Thus while he spoke, already she began
With sparkling eyes to view the guilty man,
From head to foot, survey'd his person o'er,
Nor longer these outrageous threats forbore:
"False as thou art, and more than false, forsworn!
Not sprung from noble blood, nor goddess-born,
But hewn from harden'd entrails of a rock!
And rough Hyrcanian tigers gave thee suck!
Why should I fawn? what have I worse to fear?
Did he once look, or lend a list'ning ear,
Sigh'd when I sobb'd, or shed one kindly tear?
All symptoms of a base ungrateful mind,
So foul, that which is worse 't is hard to find.
Of man's injustice why should I complain?
The gods, and Jove himself, behold in vain
Triumphant treason; yet no thunder flies;
Nor Juno views my wrongs, with equal eyes:
Faithless is earth, and faithless are the skies!
Justice is fled, and truth is now no more!
I sav'd the shipwreck'd exile on my shore;
With needful food his hungry Trojans fed;
I took the traitor to my throne and bed:
Fool that I was—'t is little to repeat
The rest—I stor'd and rigg'd his ruin'd fleet.
I rave, I rave! a god's command he pleads,
And makes heav'n accessory to his deeds.
Now Lycian lots, and now the Delian god,
Now Hermes is employ'd from Jove's abode,
To warn him hence; as if the peaceful state
Of heav'nly pow'rs were touch'd with human fate.
But go! thy flight no longer I detain—
Go! seek thy promis'd kingdom through the main!
Yet, if the heav'ns will hear my pious vow,
The faithless waves, not half so false as thou,

Or secret sands, shall sepulchres afford
To the proud vessels, and their perjur'd lord.
Then shalt thou call on injur'd Dido's name:
Dido shall come in a black sulph'ry flame:
When death has once dissolv'd her mortal frame—
Shall smile to see the traitor vainly weep:
Her angry ghost arising from the deep,
Shall haunt thee waking, and disturb thy sleep.
At least my shade thy punishment shall know;
And Fame shall spread the pleasing news below."

Abruptly here she stops—then turns away
Her loathing eyes, and shuns the sight of day.
Amaz'd he stood, revolving in his mind
What speech to frame, and what excuse to find.
Her fearful maids their fearful mistress led,
And softly laid her on her iv'ry bed.

But good Æneas, though he much desir'd
To give that pity which her grief requir'd—
Though much he mourn'd and labour'd with his love—
Resolv'd at length, obeys the will of Jove;
Reviews his forces: they with early care
Unmoor their vessels, and for sea prepare.
The fleet is soon afloat, in all its pride;
And well-caulk'd galleys in the harbour ride.
Then oaks for oars they fell'd; or, as they stood,
Of its green arms despoil'd the growing wood,
Studious of flight. The beach is cover'd o'er
With Trojan bands that blacken all the shore:
On ev'ry side are seen, descending down,
Thick swarms of soldiers, loaden from the town.
Thus, in battalia, march imbodied ants,
Fearful of winter, and of future wants,
T' invade the corn, and to their cells convey
The plunder'd forage of their yellow prey.
The sable troops, along the narrow tracks,
Scarce bear the weighty burden on their backs:
Some set their shoulders to the pond'rous grain;
Some guard the spoil, some lash the lagging train;
All ply their sev'ral tasks, and equal toil sustain.
What pangs the tender breast of Dido tore,
When from the tow'r she saw the cover'd shore,
And heard the shouts of sailors, from afar,
Mix'd with the murmurs of the wat'ry war!
All-powerful Love! what changes canst thou cause
In human hearts, subjected to thy laws!
Once more her haughty soul the tyrant bends:
To pray'rs and mean submissions she descends.
No female arts or aids she left untried,
Nor counsels unexplor'd, before she died.
"Look, Anna! look! the Trojans crowd to sea;
They spread their canvass, and their anchors weigh.
The shouting crew their ships with garlands bind,
Invoke the sea-gods, and invite the wind.
Could I have thought this threat'ning blow so near,
My tender soul had been forewarn'd to bear.
But do not you my last request deny:
With yon perfidious man your int'rest try,
And bring me news, if I must live or die.
You are his fav'rite; you alone can find
The dark recesses of his inmost mind:
In all his trusted secrets you have part,
And know the soft approaches of his heart.
Haste then, and humbly seek my haughty foe
Tell him, I did not with the Grecians go,
Nor did my fleet against his friends employ,
Nor swore the ruin of unhappy Troy,
Nor mov'd with hands profane his father's dust:
Why should he then reject a suit so just?
Whom does he shun? and whither would he fly?
Can he this last, this only pray'r deny?
Let him at least his dangerous flight delay?
Wait better winds, and hope a calmer sea.
The nuptials, he disclaims, I urge no more:
Let him pursue the promis'd Latin shore.
A short delay is all I ask him now—
A pause of grief, an interval from wo,
Till my soft soul be temper'd to sustain
Accustom'd sorrows, and inur'd to pain.
If you in pity grant this one request,
My death shall glut the hatred of his breast."
This mournful message pious Anna bears,
And seconds, with her own, her sister's tears:
But all her arts are still employ'd in vain:
Again she comes, and is refus'd again.
His harden'd heart nor pray'rs nor threat'nings move;
Fate, and the god, had stopp'd his ears to love.

As when the winds their airy quarrel try,
Justling from ev'ry quarter of the sky,
This way and that the mountain oak they bend;
His boughs they shatter, and his branches rend;
With leaves and falling mast they spread the ground;
The hollow valleys echo to the sound:
Unmov'd, the royal plant their fury mocks,
Or, shaken, clings more closely to the rocks:
Far as he shoots his tow'ring head on high,
So deep in earth his fix'd foundations lie.
No less a storm the Trojan hero bears;
Thick messages and loud complaints he hears,
And bandied words, still beating on his ears.
Sighs, groans, and tears, proclaim his inward pains;
But the firm purpose of his heart remains.

The wretched queen, pursu'd by cruel Fate,
Begins at length the light of heav'n to hate,

And loathes to live. Then dire portents she sees,
To hasten on the death her soul decrees—
Strange to relate! for when before the shrine
She pours in sacrifice the purple wine,
The purple wine is turn'd to putrid blood;
And the white offer'd milk converts to mud
This dire presage, to her alone reveal'd,
From all, and e'en her sister, she conceal'd.
A marble temple stood within the grove,
Sacred to death, and to her murder'd love;
That honour'd chapel she had hung around
With snowy fleeces, and with garlands crown'd:
Oft, when she visited this lonely home,
Strange voices issued from her husband's tomb:
She thought she heard him summon her away,
Invite her to his grave, and chide her stay.
Hourly 't is heard, when with a boding note
The solitary screech-owl strains her throat,
And, on a chimney's top or turret's height,
With songs obscene disturbs the silence of the night.
Besides, old prophecies augment her fears;
And stern Æneas in her dreams appears,
Disdainful as by day: she seems alone,
To wander in her sleep, through ways unknown,
Guideless and dark; or, in a desert plain,
To seek her subjects, and to seek in vain—
Like Pentheus, when distracted with his fear,
He saw two suns and double Thebes appear;
Or mad Orestes, when his mother's ghost
Full in his face infernal torches toss'd,
And shook her snaky locks: he shuns the sight,
Flies o'er the stage, surpris'd with mortal fright;
The furies guard the door, and intercept his flight.
Now, sinking underneath a load of grief,
From death alone she seeks her last relief:
The time and means resolv'd within her breast,
She to her mournful sister thus address'd:
(Dissembling hope, her cloudy front she clears,
And a false vigour in her eyes appears.)
"Rejoice!" she said, "instructed from above,
My lover I shall gain, or lose my love.
Nigh rising Atlas, next the falling sun,
Long tracts of Æthiopian climates run:
There a Massylian priestess I have found,
Honour'd for age, for magic arts renown'd:
Th' Hesperian temple was her trusted care;
'T was she supplied the wakeful dragon's fare.
She poppy-seeds in honey taught to steep,
Reclaim'd his rage, and sooth'd him into sleep:
She watch'd the golden fruit. Her charms unbind
The chains of love, or fix them on the mind:
She stops the torrents, leaves the channel dry,
Repels the stars, and backward bears the sky.
The yawning earth rebellows to her call;
Pale ghosts ascend; and mountain ashes fall.
Witness, ye gods, and thou my better part,
How loath I am to try this impious art!
Within the secret court, with silent care,
Erect a lofty pile, expos'd in air;
Hang, on the topmost part, the Trojan vest,
Spoils, arms, and presents, of my faithless guest.
Next, under these, the bridal bed be plac'd,
Where I my ruin in his arms embrac'd.
All relics of the wretch are doom'd to fire;
For so the priestess and her charms require."
Thus far she said, and further speech forbears.
A mortal paleness in her face appears
Yet the mistrustless Anna could not find
The secret fun'ral in these rites design'd;
Nor thought so dire a rage possess'd her mind.
Unknowing of a train conceal'd so well,
She fear'd no worse than when Sichæus fell
Therefore obeys. The fatal pile they rear,
Within the secret court, expos'd in air.
The cloven holms and pines are heap'd on high,
And garlands on the hollow spaces lie.
Sad cypress, vervain, yew, compose the wreath;
And ev'ry baleful green denoting death.
The queen, determin'd to the fatal deed,
The spoils and sword he left, in order spread
And the man's image on the nuptial bed.
And now (the sacred altars plac'd around
The priestess enters with her hair unbound,
And thrice invokes the pow'rs below the ground.
Night, Erebus, and Chaos, she proclaims,
And threefold Hecat with her hundred names,
And three Dianas: next she sprinkles round,
With feign'd Avernian drops, the hallow'd ground;
Culls hoary simples, found by Phœbe's light,
With brazen sickles reap'd at noon of night;
Then mixes baleful juices in the bowl,
And cuts the forehead of a new-born foal,
Robbing the mother's love. The destin'd queen
Observes, assisting at the rites obscene:
A leaven'd cake in her devoted hands
She holds; and next the highest altar stands:
One tender foot was shod, her other bare;
Girt was her gather'd gown, and loose her hair.
Thus dress'd, she summon'd, with her dying breath,
The heavens and planets, conscious of her death,
And ev'ry pow'r, if any rules above,
Who minds or who revenges injur'd love.
'T was dead of night, when weary bodies close
Their eyes in balmy sleep, and soft repose:
The winds no longer whisper through the woods,
Nor murm'ring tides disturb the gentle floods.
The stars in silent order mov'd around;
And Peace, with downy wings, was brooding on the ground.

The flocks and herds, and partycolour'd fowl
Which haunt the woods or swim the weedy pool,
Stretch'd on the quiet earth, securely lay,
Forgetting the past labours of the day.
All else of nature's common gift partake;
Unhappy Dido was alone awake.
Nor sleep nor ease the furious queen can find:
Sleep fled her eyes, as quiet fled her mind.
Despair, and rage, and love, divide her heart;
Despair and rage had some, but love the greater part.
Then thus she said within her secret mind:
"What shall I do? what succour can I find?
Become a suppliant to Iarbas' pride,
And take my turn to court and be denied?
Shall I with this ungrateful Trojan go,
Forsake an empire, and attend a foe?
Himself I refug'd, and his train reliev'd—
'T is true—but am I sure to be receiv'd
Can gratitude in Trojan souls have place?
Laomedon still lives in all his race!
Then, shall I seek alone the churlish crew,
Or with my fleet, their flying sails pursue?
What force have I but those, who scarce before
I drew reluctant from their native shore?
Will they again embark at my desire,
Once more sustain the seas, and quit their second Tyre?
Rather with steel thy guilty breast invade,
And take the fortune thou thyself hast made.
Your pity, sister, first seduc'd my mind,
Or seconded too well what I design'd.
These dear-bought pleasures had I never known,
Had I continued free, and still my own—
Avoiding love, I had not found despair,
But shar'd with savage beasts the common air.
Like them, a lonely life I might have led,
Not mourn'd the living, nor disturb'd the dead."
These thoughts she brooded in her anxious breast.—
On board, the Trojan found more easy rest.
Resolv'd to sail, in sleep he pass'd the night;
And order'd all things for his early flight.
To whom once more the winged god appears
His former youthful mien and shape he wears,
And with this new alarm invades his ears:
"Sleep'st thou, O goddess-born? and canst thou drown
Thy needful cares, so near a hostile town,
Beset with foes; nor hear'st the western gales
Invite thy passage, and inspire thy sails?
She harbours in her heart a furious hate,
(And thou shalt find the dire effects too late,)
Fix'd on revenge, and obstinate to die.
Haste swiftly hence, while thou hast pow'r to fly.
The sea with ships will soon be cover'd o'er,
And blazing firebrands kindle all the shore.
Prevent her rage, while night obscures the skies;
And sail before the purple morn arise.
Who knows what hazards thy delay may bring?
Woman 's a various and a changeful thing."
Thus Hermes in the dream; then took his flight,
Aloft in air unseen, and mix'd in night.
Twice warn'd by the celestial messenger,
The pious prince arose with hasty fear;
Then rous'd his drowsy train without delay:
"Haste to your banks, your crooked anchors weigh,
And spreads your flying sails, and stand to sea!
A god commands: he stood before my sight,
And urg'd us once again to speedy flight.
O sacred pow'r! what pow'r soe'er thou art,
To thy blest orders I resign my heart.
Lead thou the way; protect thy Trojan bands
And prosper the design thy will commands."
He said; and, drawing forth his flaming sword,
His thund'ring arm divides the many-twisted cord.
An emulating zeal inspires his train:
They run; they snatch; they rush into the main.
With headlong haste they leave the desert shores,
And brush the liquid seas with lab'ring oars.
Aurora now had left her saffron bed,
And beams of early light the heav'ns o'erspread,
When from a tow'r, the queen, with wakeful eyes,
Saw day point upward from the rosy skies.
She look'd to seaward: but the sea was void,
And scarce in ken the sailing ships descried.
Stung with despite, and furious with despair,
She struck her trembling breast, and tore her hair.
'And shall th' ungrateful traitor go, (she said,)
My land forsaken, and my love betray'd?
Shall we not arm? not rush from ev'ry street?
To follow, sink, and burn his perjur'd fleet?
Haste! haul my galleys out! pursue the foe!
Bring flaming brands! set sail, and swiftly row!
What have I said! where am I? Fury turns
My brain; and my distemper'd bosom burns;
Then, when I gave my person and my throne
This hate, this rage, had been more timely shown.
See now the promis'd faith, the vaunted name,
The pious man, who rushing through the flame,
Preserv'd his gods, and to the Phrygian shore
The burden of his feeble father bore!
I should have torn him piece-meal—strew'd in floods
His scatter'd limbs, or left expos'd in woods—
Destroy'd his friends and son—and from the fire
Have sent the reeking boy before the sire.

Events are doubtful, which on battle wait!
Yet where's the doubt, to souls secure of fate?
My Tyrians, at their injur'd queen's command,
Had toss'd their fires amid the Trojan band;
At once extinguish'd all the faithless name;
And I myself, in vengeance of my shame,
Had fall'n upon the pile, to mend the fun'ral flame.
Thou sun, who view'st at once the world below!
Thou Juno, guardian of the nuptial vow!
Thou Hecat, hearken from thy dark abodes!
Ye Furies, fiends, and violated gods!
All pow'rs, invok'd with Dido's dying breath,
Attend her curses and avenge her death!
If so the Fates ordain, and Jove commands,
Th' ungrateful wretch should find the Latian lands,
Yet let a race untam'd, and haughty foes,
His peaceful entrance with dire arms oppose
Oppress'd with numbers in th' unequal field,
His men discourag'd, and himself expell'd,
Let him for succour sue from place to place,
Torn from his subjects, and his son's embrace.
First let him see his friends in battle slain,
And their untimely fate lament in vain:
And when at length the cruel war shall cease,
On hard conditions may he buy his peace:
Nor let him then enjoy supreme command;
But fall, untimely, by some hostile hand,
And lie unburied on the barren sand!
These are my pray'rs, and this my dying will:
And you, my Tyrians ev'ry curse fulfil.
Perpetual hate and mortal wars proclaim
Against the prince, the people, and the name.
These grateful off'rings on my grave bestow;
Nor league, nor love, the hostile nations know!
Now, and from hence, in ev'ry future age,
When rage excites your arms, and strength supplies the rage,
Rise some avenger of our Libyan blood,
With fire and sword pursue the perjur'd brood—
Our arms, our seas, our shores, oppos'd to theirs—
And the same hate descend on all our heirs!"
This said, within her anxious mind she weighs
The means of cutting short her odious days.
Then to Sichæus' nurse she briefly said,
(For, when she left her country, hers was dead)
"Go, Barce, call my sister. Let her care
The solemn rites of sacrifice prepare:
The sheep, and all th' atoning off'rings, bring,
Sprinkling her body from the crystal spring
With living drops; then let her come; and thou
With sacred fillets bind thy hoary brow.
Thus will I pay my vows to Stygian Jove,
And end the cares of my disastrous love;
Then cast the Trojan image on the fire;
And, as that burns, my passion shall expire."
The nurse moves onward with officious care
And all the speed her aged limbs can bear.
But furious Dido, with dark thoughts involv'd,
Shook at the mighty mischief she resolv'd.
With livid spots distinguish'd was her face;
Red were her rolling eyes, and discompos'd her pace:
Ghastly she gaz'd; with pain she drew her breath;
And nature shiver'd at approaching death.
Then swiftly to the fatal place she pass'd,
And mounts the fun'ral pile with furious haste;
Unsheaths the sword the Trojan left behind,
(Not for so dire an enterprise design'd.)
But when she view'd the garments loosely spread,
Which once he wore, and saw the conscious bed,
She paus'd, and with a sigh the robes embrac'd,
Then on the couch her trembling body cast,
Repress'd the ready tears, and spoke her last:
"Dear pledges of my love, while heav'n so pleas'd,
Receive a soul, of mortal anguish eas'd.
My fatal course is finish'd; and I go,
A glorious name, among the ghosts below.
A lofty city by my hands is rais'd;
Pygmalion punish'd and my lord appeas'd.
What could my fortune have afforded more,
Had the false Trojan never touch'd my shore?"
Then kiss the couch: and "Must I die," she said,
"And unreveng'd? 't is doubly to be dead;
Yet e'en this death with pleasure I receive:
On any terms, 't is better than to live.
These flames, from far, may the false Trojan view;
These boding omens his base flight pursue!"
She said, and struck: deep enter'd in her side
The piercing steel, with reeking purple dy'd:
Clogg'd in the wound the cruel weapon stands;
The spouting blood came streaming on her hands.
Her sad attendants saw the deadly stroke,
And with loud cries the sounding palace shook.
Distracted from the fatal sight they fled,
And through the town the dismal rumour spread.
First from the frighted court the yell began;
Redoubled, thence from house to house it ran:
The groans of men, with shrieks, laments, and cries
Of mixing women, mount the vaulted skies.
Not less the clamour, than if ancient Tyre,
Or the new Carthage, set by foes on fire—
The rolling ruin, with their lov'd abodes,
Involv'd the blazing temples of their gods.
Her sister hears, and, furious with despair,
She beats her breast, and rends her yellow hair

And, calling on Elisa's name aloud,
Runs breathless to the place, and breaks the crowd.
"Was all that pomp of wo for this prepar'd,
These fires, this fun'ral pile, these altars rear'd?
Was all this train of plots contriv'd, (said she,)
All only to deceive unhappy me?
Which is the worst? Didst thou in death pretend
To scorn thy sister, or delude thy friend?
Thy summon'd sister and thy friend had come:
One sword had serv'd us both, one common tomb:
Was I to raise the pile, the pow'rs invoke,
Not to be present at the fatal stroke?
At once thou hast destroy'd thyself and me,
Thy town, thy senate, and thy colony!
Bring water! bathe the wound; while I in death
Lay close my lips to hers, and catch the flying breath."
This said, she mounts the pile with eager haste,
And in her arms the gasping queen embrac'd,
Her temples chaf'd; and her own garments tore,
To stanch the streaming blood and cleanse the gore.
Thrice Dido tried to raise her drooping head,
And, fainting, thrice fell grov'ling on the bed;
Thrice op'd her heavy eyes, and saw the light,
But, having found it, sicken'd at the sight,
And clos'd her lids at last in endless night.
Then Juno, grieving that she should sustain
A death so ling'ring, and so full of pain,
Sent Iris down, to free her from the strife
Of lab'ring nature, and dissolve her life.
For, since she died, not doom'd by heav'n's decree,
Or her own crime, but human casualty,
And rage of love, that plung'd her in despair,
The sisters had not cut the topmost hair,
Which Proserpine and they can only know;
Nor made her sacred to the shades below.
Downward the various goddess took her flight,
And drew a thousand colours from the light;
Then stood above the dying lover's head,
And said, "I thus devote thee to the dead:
This off'ring to the infernal gods I bear."
Thus while she spoke, she cut the fatal hair:
The struggling soul was loos'd, and life dissolv'd in air.

BOOK V.

ARGUMENT.

Æneas, setting sail from Africa, is driven by a storm on the coast of Sicily, where he is hospitably receiv-ed, by his friend Acestes king of part of the island, and born of Trojan parentage. He applies himself to celebrate the memory of his father with divine honours, and accordingly institutes funeral games, and appoints prizes for those who should conquer in them. While the ceremonies are performing, Juno sends Iris to persuade the Trojan women to burn the ships, who, upon her instigation, set fire to them: which burned four, and would have consumed the rest, had not Jupiter, by a miraculous shower, extinguished it. Upon this, Æneas, by the advice of one of his generals, and a vision of his father, builds a city for the women, old men, and others, who were either unfit for war, or weary of the voyage, and sails for Italy. Venus procures of Neptune a safe voyage for him and all his men, excepting only his pilot Palinurus, who was unfortunately lost.

Meantime the Trojan cuts the wat'ry way
Fix'd on his voyage through the curling sea;
Then casting back his eyes, with dire amaze,
Sees on the Punic shore the mounting blaze.
The cause unknown; yet his presaging mind
The fate of Dido from the fire divin'd.
He knew the stormy souls of woman-kind;
What secret springs their eager passions move,
How capable of death for injur'd love.
Dire auguries from hence the Trojans draw;
Till neither fires nor shining shores they saw.
Now seas and skies their prospect only bound—
An empty space above, a floating field around.
But soon the heav'ns with shadows were o'erspread;
A swelling cloud hung hov'ring o'er their head;
Livid it look'd—the threat'ning of a storm
Then night and horror ocean's face deform.
The pilot, Palinurus, cried aloud,
"What gusts of weather from that gath'ring cloud
My thoughts presage! Ere yet the tempest roars,
Stand to your tackle, mates, and stretch your oars;
Contract your swelling sails, and luff to wind."
The frighted crew perfom the task assign'd.
Then, to his fearless chief, Not heav'n (said he)
Though Jove himself should promise Italy,
Can stem the torrent of this raging sea.
Mark, how the shifting winds from west arise,
And what collected night involves the skies!
Nor can our shaken vessels live at sea,
Much less against the tempest force their way.
'T is Fate diverts our course: and Fate we must obey.
Not far from hence, if I observ'd aright
The southing of the stars, and polar light
Sicilia lies, whose hospitable shores
In safety we may reach with strugg'ling oars."
Æneas then replied: "Too soon I find,
We strive in vain against the seas and wind:
Now shift your sails: what place can please me more
Than what you promise, the Sicilian shore,

Whose hallow'd earth Anchises' bones contains,
And where a prince of Trojan lineage reigns."
The course resolv'd, before the western wind
They scud amain, and make the port assign'd
Meantime Acestes, from a lofty stand,
Beheld the fleet descending on the land;
And, not unmindful of his ancient race,
Down from the cliff he ran with eager pace,
And held the hero in a strict embrace.
Of a rough Libyan bear the spoils he wore;
And either hand a pointed jav'lin bore.
His mother was a dame of Dardan blood;
His sire, Crinisus, a Sicilian flood.
He welcomes his returning friends ashore
With plenteous country cates, and homely store.
Now, when the following morn had chas'd away
The flying stars, and light restor'd the day,
Æneas call'd the Trojan troops around,
And thus bespoke them from the rising ground:
"Offspring of heav'n, divine Dardanian race!
The sun, revolving through th' etherial space,
The shining circle of the year has fill'd,
Since first this isle my father's ashes held:
And now the rising day renews the year—
A day for ever sad, for ever dear.
This would I celebrate with annual games,
With gifts on altars pil'd, and holy flames,
Though banish'd to Gætulia's barren sands,
Caught on the Grecian seas, or hostile lands:
But since this happy storm our fleet has driven
(Not, as I deem without the will of heaven)
Upon these friendly shores, and flow'ry plains,
Which hide Anchises and his blest remains;
Let us with joy perform his honours due,
And pray for prosp'rous winds, our voyage to renew—
Pray, that, in towns and temples of our own,
The name of great Anchises may be known;
And yearly games may spread the god's renown.
Our sports, Acestes, of the Trojan race,
With royal gifts ordain'd, is pleas'd to grace:
Two steers on every ship the king bestows:
His gods and ours shall share your equal vows.
Besides, if, nine days hence, the rosy morn
Shall, with unclouded light, the skies adorn,
That day with solemn sports I mean to grace:
Light galleys on the seas shall run a wat'ry race;
Some shall in swiftness for the goal contend,
And others try the twanging bow to bend:
The strong, with iron gauntlets arm'd, shall stand
Oppos'd in combat on the yellow sand.
Let all be present at the games prepar'd;
And joyful victors wait the just reward.
But now assist the rites, with garlands crown'd."
He said and first his brows with myrtle bound:
Then Helymus, by his example led,
And old Acestes, each adorn'd his head
Thus young Ascanius, with a sprightly grace,
His temples tied, and all the Trojan race.
Æneas then advanc'd amidst the train,
By thousands follow'd through the flow'ry plain,
To great Anchises' tomb; which when he found,
He pour'd to Bacchus, on the hallow'd ground,
Two bowls of sparkling wine, of milk two more,
And two (from offer'd bulls) of purple gore.
With roses then the sepulchre he strow'd,
And thus his father's ghost bespoke aloud:
"Hail, O ye holy manes! hail again,
Paternal ashes, now review'd in vain
The gods permitted not, that you, with me
Should reach the promis'd shores of Italy,
Or Tyber's flood, what flood soe'er it be."
Scarce had he finish'd, when, with speckled pride,
A serpent from the tomb began to glide
His hugy bulk on sev'n high volumes roll'd!
Blue was his breadth of back, but streak'd with scaly gold:
Thus riding on his curls, he seem'd to pass
A rolling fire along, and singe the grass.
More various colours through his body run,
Than Iris, when her bow imbibes the sun.
Betwixt the rising altars, and around,
The sacred monster shot along the ground
With harmless play amidst the bowls he pass'd,
And with his lolling tongue assay'd the taste?
Thus fed with holy food, the wondrous guest
Within the hollow tomb retir'd to rest.
The pious prince, surpris'd at what he view'd,
The fun'ral honours with more zeal renew'd,
Doubtful if this the place's genius were,
Or guardian of his father's sepulchre.
Five sheep, according to the rites, he slew;
As many swine, and steers of sable hue;
Now gen'rous wine he from the goblets pour'd,
And call'd his father's ghost, from hell restor'd.
The glad attendants in long order come,
Off'ring their gifts to great Anchises' tomb:
Some add more oxen; some divide the spoil,
Some place the chargers on the grassy soil;
Some blow the fires, and offer'd entrails broil.
Now came the day desir'd. The skies were bright
With rosy lustre of the rising light:
The bord'ring people, rous'd by sounding fame
Of Trojan feasts, and great Acestes' name,
The crowded shore with acclamations fill,
Part to behold, and part to prove their skill.

And first the gifts in public view they place,
Green laurel wreaths, and palm—the victor's grace.
Within the circle, arms and tripods lie,
Ingots of gold and silver heap'd on high,
And vests embroider'd, of the Tyrian die.
The trumpet's clangour then the feast proclaims,
And all prepare for their appointed games.
Four galleys first, which equal rowers bear,
Advancing, in the watery lists appear.
The speedy Dolphin that outstrips the wind,
Bore Mnestheus, author of the Memmian kind:
Gyas the vast Chimæra's bulk commands,
Which rising, like a towering city stands:
Three Trojans tug at ev'ry lab'ring oar;
Three banks, in three degrees, the sailors bore
Beneath their sturdy strokes the billows roar.
Sergestus, who began the Sergian race,
In the great Centaur took the leading place:
Cloanthus on the sea-green Scylla stood;
From whom Cluentius draws his Trojan blood.
Far in the sea, against the foaming shore,
There stands a rock: the raging billows roar
Above his head in storms: but, when 't is clear,
Uncurl their ridgy backs, and at his foot appear;
In peace below the gentle waters run;
The cormorants above lie basking in the sun.
On this the hero fix'd an oak in sight,
The mark to guide the mariners aright.
To bear with this, the seamen stretch their oars:
Then round the rock they steer, and seek the former shores.
The lots decide their place. Above the rest,
Each leader shining in his Tyrian vest;
The common crew, with wreaths of poplar boughs,
Their temples crown, and shade their sweaty brows;
Besmear'd with oil, their naked shoulders shine.
All take their seats, and wait the sounding sign:
They gripe their oars; and ev'ry panting breast
Is rais'd by turns with hope, by turns with fear depress'd.
The clangour of the trumpet gives the sign:
At once they start, advancing in a line:
With shouts the sailors rend the starry skies;
Lash'd with their oars, the smoky billows rise;
Sparkles the briny main, and the vex'd ocean fries.
Exact in time, with equal strokes they row:
At once the brushing oars and brazen prow
Dash up the sandy waves, and ope the depths below.
Not fiery coursers, in a chariot race,
Invade the field with half so swift a pace:
Not the fierce driver with more fury lends
The sounding lash, and, ere the stroke descends,
Low to the wheels his pliant body bends.
The partial crowd their hopes and fears divide,
And aid, with eager shouts, the favour'd side.
Cries, murmurs, clamours, with a mixing sound,
From woods to woods, from hills to hills rebound.
Amidst the loud applauses of the shore,
Gyas outstripp'd the rest, and sprung before:
Cloanthus, better mann'd, pursu'd him fast
But his o'er-masted galley check'd his haste
The Centaur and the Dolphin brush the brine
With equal oars, advancing in a line
And now the mighty Centaur seems to lead,
And now the speedy Dolphin gets ahead:
Now board to board the rival vessels row
The billows lave the skies, and ocean groans below.
They reach'd the mark. Proud Gyas and his train
In triumph rode, the victors of the main:
But, steering round, he charg'd his pilot—"Stand
More close to shore, and skim along the sand!
Let others bear to sea."—Menœtes heard;
But secret shelves too cautiously he fear'd,
And, fearing, sought the deep: and still aloof he steer'd.
With louder cries the captain call'd again:
"Bear to the rocky shore, and shun the main."
He spoke, and, speaking, at his stern he saw
The bold Cloanthus near the shelvings draw.
Betwixt the mark and him the Scylla stood,
And in a closer compass plough'd the flood.
He pass'd the mark; and, wheeling, got before:—
Gyas blasphem'd the gods, devoutly swore,
Cried out for anger, and his hair he tore.
Mindless of others' lives, (so high was grown
His rising rage,) and careless of his own,
The trembling dotard to the deck he drew,
And hoisted up, and overboard he threw:
This done, he seiz'd the helm; his fellows cheer'd;
Turn'd short upon the shelves, and madly steer'd.
Hardly his head the plunging pilot rears,
Clogg'd with his clothes, and cumber'd with his years;
Now dropping wet, he climbs the cliff with pain.
The crowd, that saw him fall, and float again,
Shout from the distant shore; and loudly laught,
To see his heaving breast disgorge the briny draught.
The following Centaur, and the Dolphin's crew,
Their vanish'd hopes of victory renew;
While Gyas lags they kindle in the race,
To reach the mark. Sergestus takes the place;

Mnestheus pursues; and, while around they wind,
Comes up not half his galley's length behind;
Then on the deck, amidst his mates, appear'd,
And thus their drooping courages he cheer'd;
"My friends, and Hector's followers heretofore,
Exert your vigour; tug the lab'ring oar;
Stretch to your strokes, my still unconquer'd crew,
Whom from the flaming walls of Troy I drew.
In this our common int'rest, let me find
That strength of hand, that courage of the mind,
As when you stemm'd the strong Malean flood,
And o'er the Syrtes' broken billows row'd.
I seek not now the foremost palm to gain;
Though yet—but, ah! that haughty wish is vain!
Let those enjoy it whom the gods ordain.
But to be last, the lags of all the race!—
Redeem yourselves and me from that disgrace."
Now, one and all, they tug amain; they row
At the full stretch, and shake the brazen prow.
The sea beneath them sinks; their lab'ring sides
Are swell'd, and sweat runs gutt'ring down in tides.
Chance aids their daring, with unhop'd success:—
Sergestus, eager with his beak to press
Betwixt the rival galley and the rock,
Shuts up the unwieldy Centaur in the lock,
The vessel struck; and, with the dreadful shock
Her oars she shiver'd and her head she broke.
The trembling rowers from their banks arise,
And anxious for themselves, renounce the prize.
With iron poles they heave her off the shores,
And gather from the sea the floating oars.
The crew of Mnestheus, with elated minds,
Urge their success, and call the willing winds;
Then ply their oars, and cut their liquid way
In larger compass on the roomy sea.
As when the dove her rocky hold forsakes,
Rous'd in a fright, her sounding wings she shakes;
The cavern rings with clatt'ring; out she flies,
And leaves her callow care, and cleaves the skies:
At first she flutters, but at length she springs
To smoother flight, and shoots upon her wings:
So Mnestheus in the Dolphin cuts the sea;
And flying with a force, that force assists his way.
Sergestus in the Centaur soon he pass'd,
Wedg'd in the rocky shoals, and sticking fast.
In vain the victor he with cries implores,
And practises to row with shatter'd oars.
Then Mnestheus bears with Gyas, and outflies;
The ship, without a pilot, yields the prize.
Unvanquish'd Scylla now alone remains:—
Her he persues; and all his vigour strains.
Shouts from the fav'ring multitude arise;
Applauding Echo to the shouts replies;
Shouts, wishes, and applause, run rattling through the skies.
These clamours with disdain the Scylla heard,
Much grudg'd the praise, but more the robb'd reward:
Resolv'd to hold their own, they mend their pace,
All obstinate to die, or gain the race.
Rais'd with success, the Dolphin swiftly ran—
For they can conquer who believe they can.—
Both urge their oars; and Fortune both supplies.
(And both perhaps had shar'd an equal prize;)
When to the seas Cloanthus holds his hands,
And succour from the wat'ry pow'rs demands:
"Gods of the liquid realms on which I row!
If, giv'n by you, the laurel bind my brow,
(Assist to make me guilty of my vow!)
A snow-white bull shall on your shore be slain;
His offer'd entrails cast into the main,
And ruddy wine from golden goblets thrown,
Your grateful gift, and my return shall own."
The choir of nymphs, and Phorcus from below,
With virgin Panopea, heard his vow;
And old Portunus with his breadth of hand,
Push'd on and sped the galley to the land.
Swift as a shaft, or winged wind, she flies,
And, darting to the port, obtains the prize.
The herald summons all, and then proclaims
Cloanthus conqueror of the naval games.
The prince with laurel crowns the victor's head;
And three fat steers are to his vessel led—
The ship's reward—with gen'rous wine beside,
And sums of silver, which the crew divide.
The leaders are distinguish'd from the rest;
The victor honour'd with a nobler vest,
Where gold and purple strive in equal rows,
And needlework its happy cost bestows.
There, Ganymede is wrought with living art,
Chasing through Ida's groves the trembling hart:
Breathless he seems, yet eager to pursue:
When from aloft descends, in open view,
The bird of Jove, and sousing on his prey,
With crooked talons bears the boy away.
In vain, with lifted hands and gazing eyes,
His guards behold him soaring through the skies,
And dogs pursue his flight, with imitated cries.
Mnestheus the second victor was declar'd
And, summon'd there, the second prize he shar'd—
A coat of mail, which brave Demoleus bore,
More brave Æneas from his shoulders tore,
In single combat on the Trojan shore;
This was ordain'd for Mnestheus to possess—
In war for his defence, for ornament in peace.
Rich was the gift, and glorious to behold,
And yet so pond'rous with its plates of gold,

That scarce two servants could the weight sustain:
Yet loaded thus, Demoleus o'er the plain
Pursu'd, and lightly seiz'd the Trojan train.
The third, succeeding to the last reward,
Two goodly bowls of massy silver shar'd,
With figures prominent, and richly wrought,
And two brass caldrons from Dodona brought.
Thus all rewarded by the hero's hands,
Their conqu'ring temples bound with purple bands.
And now Sergestus, clearing from the rock,
Brought back his galley, shatter'd with the shock.
Forlorn she look'd, without an aiding oar,
And, hooted by the vulgar, made to shore:
As when a snake, surpris'd upon the road,
Is crush'd athwart her body by the load
Of heavy wheels; or with a mortal wound
Her belly bruis'd, and trodden to the ground—
In vain, with loosen'd curls, she crawls along;
Yet, fierce above she brandishes her tongue,
Glares with her eyes, and bristles with her scales;
But, grov'ling in the dust, her parts unsound [she trails.
So slowly to the port the Centaur tends,
But, what she wants in oars, with sails amends.
Yet, for his galley sav'd, the grateful prince
Is pleas'd th' unhappy chief to recompense:
Pholoe, the Cretan slave, rewards his care,
Beauteous herself, with lovely twins as fair.
From thence his way the Trojan hero bent
Into the neighb'ring plain, with mountains pent,
Whose sides were shaded with surrounding wood.
Full in the midst of this fair valley stood
A native theatre, which, rising slow
By just degrees, o'erlook'd the ground below.
High on a sylvan throne the leader sate:
A num'rous train attend in solemn state.
Here those, that in the rapid course delight,
Desire of honour, and the prize, invite.
The rival runners without order stand;
The Trojans mix'd with the Sicilian band.
First, Nisus with Euryalus appears—
Euryalus, a boy of blooming years,
With sprightly grace and equal beauty crown'd—
Nisus, for friendship to the youth, renown'd.
Diores next, of Priam's royal race,
Then Salius, join'd with Patron, took their place;
(But Patron in Arcadia had his birth,
And Salius his from Acarnanian earth;)
Then two Sicilian youths—the names of these
Swift Helymus, and lovely Panopes,
(Both jolly huntsmen, both in forests bred,
And owning old Acestes for their head,)
With sev'ral others of ignobler name,
Whom time has not deliver'd o'er to fame.
To these the hero thus his thoughts explain'd
In words which gen'ral approbation gain'd;
"One common largess is for all design'd,
(The vanquish'd and the victor shall be join'd;)
Two darts of polish'd steel and Gnossian wood
A silver studded axe, alike bestow'd.
The foremost three have olive wreaths decreed:
The first of these obtains a stately steed
Adorn'd with trappings; and the next in fame
The quiver of an Amazonian dame,
With feather'd Thracian arrows well supplied:
A golden belt shall gird his manly side,
Which with a sparkling diamond shall be tied.
The third this Grecian helmet shall content."
He said. To their appointed base they went:
With beating hearts th' expected sign receive,
And, starting all at once, the barrier leave.
Spread out, as on the winged winds, they flew,
And seiz'd the distant goal with greedy view.
Shot from the crowd, swift Nisus all o'erpass'd,
Nor storms, nor thunder, equal half his haste.
The next, but, though the next, yet far disjoin'd,
Came Salius; and Euryalus behind;
Then Helymus, whom young Diores plied.
Step after step, and almost side by side,
His shoulders pressing—and, in longer space,
Had won, or left at least a dubious race.
Now spent, the goal they almost reach at last,
When eager Nisus, hapless in his haste,
Slipp'd, first, and, slipping, fell upon the plain.
Soak'd with the blood of oxen newly slain.
The careless victor had not mark'd his way;
But, treading where the treach'rous puddle lay,
His heels flew up; and on the grassy floor
He fell, besmear'd with filth and holy gore.
Not mindless then, Euryalus, of thee,
Nor of the sacred bonds of amity,
He strove th' immediate rival's hope to cross,
And caught the foot of Salius as he rose;
So Salius lay extended on the plain;
Euryalus springs out, the prize to gain,
And leaves the crowd;—applauding peals attend
The victor to the goal, who vanquish'd by his friend.
Next Helymus; and then Diores came,
By two misfortunes made the third in fame.
But Salius enters, and, exclaiming loud
For justice, deafens and disturbs the crowd;
Urges his cause may in the court be heard;
And pleads the prize is wrongfully conferr'd.
But favour for Euryalus appears;
His blooming beauty, with his tender years,
Had brib'd the judges for the promis'd prize;
Besides, Diores fills the court with cries,

Who vainly reaches at the last reward,
If the first palm on Salius be conferr'd.
Then thus the prince; "Let no disputes arise:
Where Fortune plac'd it, I award the prize.
But Fortune's errors give me leave to mend,
At least to pity my deserving friend."
He said, and, from among the spoils, he draws
(Pond'rous with shaggy mane and golden paws)
A lion's hide: to Salius this he gives:
Nisus with envy sees the gift, and grieves:
"If such rewards to vanquish'd men are due,
(He said,) and falling is to rise by you,
What prize may Nisus from your bounty claim,
Who merited the first rewards and fame?
In falling, both an equal fortune tried;
Would Fortune for my fall so well provide!"
With this he pointed to his face, and show'd
His hands and all his habit smear'd with blood.
Th' indulgent father of the people smil'd,
And caus'd to be produc'd an ample shield,
Of wondrous art, by Didymaon wrought,
Long since, from Neptune's bars, in triumph brought.
This giv'n to Nisus, he divides the rest,
And equal justice in his gifts express'd,
The race thus ended, and rewards bestow'd,
Once more the prince bespeaks th' attentive crowd:
"If there be here, whose dauntless courage dare
In gauntlet fight, with limbs and body bare,
His opposite sustain in open view,
Stand forth the champion, and the games renew.
Two prizes I propose, and thus divide—
A bull with gilded horns, and fillets tied,
Shall be the portion of the conqu'ring chief:
A sword and helm shall cheer the loser's grief."
Then haughty Dares in the lists appears:
Stalking he strides, his head erected bears:
His nervous arms the weighty gauntlet wield;
And loud applauses echo through the field.
Dares alone in combat us'd to stand
The match of mighty Paris, hand to hand;
The same, at Hector's fun'rals, undertook
Gigantic Butes, of th' Amycian stock,
And, by the stroke of his resistless hand,
Stretch'd the vast bulk upon the yellow sand.
Such Dares was; and such he strode along,
And drew the wonder of the gazing throng.
His brawny back and ample breast he shows;
His lifted arms around his head he throws,
And deals, in whistling air, his empty blows.
His match is sought; but, through the trembling band,
Not one dares answer to the proud demand.
Presuming of his force, with sparkling eyes
Already he devours the promis'd prize,
He claims the bull with awless insolence,
And, having seiz'd his horns, accosts the prince:
"If none my matchless valour dare oppose,
How long shall Dares wait his dastard foes?
Permit me, chief, permit without delay,
To lead this uncontended gift away."
The crowd assents, and, with redoubled cries,
For the proud challenger demands the prize.
Acestes, fir'd with just disdain to see
The palm usurp'd without a victory,
Reproach'd Entellus thus, who sate beside,
And heard, and saw, unmov'd, the Trojan's pride:
"Once, but in vain, a champion of renown,
So tamely can you bear the ravish'd crown,
A prize in triumph borne before your sight,
And shun for fear the danger of the fight?
Where is our Eryx now, the boasted name,
The god who taught your thund'ring arm the game?
Where now your baffled honour; where the spoil
That fill'd your house, any fame that fill'd our isle?"
Entellus thus: "My soul is still the same,
Unmov'd with fear, and mov'd with martial fame,
But my chill blood is curdled in my veins
And scarce the shadow of a man remains,
Oh! could I turn to that fair prime again,
That prime, of which this boaster is so vain!
The brave, who this decrepit age defies,
Should feel my force, without the promis'd prize."
He said, and rising at the word, he threw
Two pond'rous gauntlets down in open view—
Gauntlets, which Eryx wont in fight to wield,
And sheath his hands with, in the listed field.
With fear and wonder seiz'd, the crowd beholds
The gloves of death, with sev'n distinguish'd folds
Of tough bull-hides: the space within is spread
With iron, or with loads of heavy lead.
Dares himself was daunted at the sight
Renounc'd his challenge, and refus'd to fight.
Astonish'd at their weight, the hero stands,
And pois'd the pond'rous engines in his hands.
"What had your wonder (said Entellus) been,
Had you the gauntlets of Alcides seen
Or view'd the stern debate on this unhappy green:
These which I bear, your brother Eryx bore,
Still mark'd with batter'd brains, and mingled gore.
With these he long sustain'd the Herculean arm;
And these I wielded while my blood was warm,
This languish'd frame while better spirits fed,
Ere age unstrung my nerves, or time o'ersnow'd my head.

But, if the challenger these arms refuse,
And cannot wield their weight, or dare not use;
If great Æneas and Acestes join
In his request, these gauntlets I resign:
Let us with equal arms perform the fight;
And let him leave to fear, since I resign my right."
This said, Entellus for the strife prepares;
Stript of his quilted coat, his body bares;
Compos'd of mighty bones, and brawn he stands,
A goodly tow'ring object on the sands.
Then just Æneas equal arms supplied,
Which round their shoulders to their wrists they tied.
Both on the tiptoe stand, at full extent,
Their arms aloft, their bodies inly bent,
Their heads from aiming blows they bear afar;
With clashing gauntlets then provoke the war.
One on his youth and pliant limbs relies;
One on his sinews and his giant size.
The last is stiff with age, his motion slow;
He heaves for breath; he staggers to and fro;
And clouds of issuing smoke his nostrils loudly blow.
Yet equal in success, they ward, they strike;
Their ways are diff'rent, but their art alike.
Before, behind, the blows are dealt; around
Their hollow sides the rattling thumps resound.
A storm of strokes, well meant, with fury flies,
And errs about their temples, ears, and eyes—
Nor always errs; for oft the gauntlet draws
A sweeping stroke along the crackling jaws.
Heavy with age, Entellus stands his ground,
But with his warping body wards the wound.
His hand and watchful eye keep even pace;
While Dares traverses, and shifts his place,
And, like a captain who beleaguers round
Some strong-built castle on a rising ground,
Views all th' approaches with observing eyes:
This and that other part in vain he tries,
And more on industry than force relies.
With hands on high, Entellus threats the foe;
But Dares watch'd the motion from below,
And slipp'd aside, and shunn'd the long descending blow.
Entellus wastes his forces on the wind,
And, thus deluded of the stroke design'd,
Headlong and heavy fell: his ample breast
And weighty limbs his ancient mother press'd.
So falls a hollow pine, that long had stood
On Ida's height, or Erymanthus' wood,
Torn from the roots. The diff'ring nations rise;
And shouts and mingled murmurs rend the skies.
Acestes runs with eager haste, to raise
The fall'n companion of his youthful days.
Dauntless he rose, and to the fight return'd:
With shame his glowing cheeks, his eyes with fury burn'd.
Disdain and conscious virtue fir'd his breast,
And with redoubled force his foe he press'd;
He lays on load with either hand, amain,
And headlong drives the Trojan o'er the plain;
Nor stops, nor stays; nor rest, nor breath allows;
But storms of strokes descend about his brows,
A rattling tempest and a hail of blows.
But now the prince, who saw the wild increase
Of wounds, commands the combatants to cease,
And bounds Entellus' wrath, and bids the peace.
First to the Trojan, spent with toil, he came,
And sooth'd his sorrow for the suffer'd shame.
"What fury seiz'd my friend? The gods, (said he,)
To him propitious, and averse to thee,
Have giv'n his arms superior force to thine:
'T is madness to contend with strength divine."
The gauntlet-fight thus ended, from the shore
His faithful friends unhappy Dares bore:
His mouth and nostrils pour'd a purple flood
And pounded teeth came rushing with his blood
Faintly he stagger'd through the hissing throng,
And hung his head, and trail'd his legs along.
The sword and casques are carried by his train;
But with his foe the palm and ox remain.
The champion, then, before Æneas came,
Proud of his prize, but prouder of his fame;
"O goddess-born, and you, Dardanian host,
Mark with attention, and forgive my boast:
Learn what I was, by what remains; and know,
From what impending fate you sav'd my foe."
Sternly he spoke, and then confronts the bull;
And, on his ample forehead aiming full
The deadly stroke, descending, pierc'd the skull.
Down drops the beast, nor needs a second wound,
But sprawls in pangs of death, and spurns the ground.
Then thus: "In Dares' stead I offer this.
Eryx! accept a nobler sacrifice:
Take the last gift my wither'd arms can yield:
The gauntlets I resign, and here renounce the field."
This done, Æneas orders for the close,
The strife of archers, with contending bows.
The mast, Sergestus' shatter'd galley bore,
With his own hands he raises on the shore
A flutt'ring dove upon the top they tie,
The living mark at which their arrows fly.
The rival archers in a line advance,
Their turn of shooting to receive from chance.
A helmet holds their names: the lots were drawn;
On the first scroll was read Hippocoön:
The people shout. Upon the next was found
Young Mnestheus, late with naval honours crown'd.

The third contain'd Eurytion's noble name,
Thy brother, Pandarus, and next in fame,
Whom Pallas urg'd the treaty to confound,
And send among the Greeks a feather'd wound.
Acestes, in the bottom, last remain'd,
Whom not his age from youthful sports restrain'd.
Soon all with vigour bend their trusty bows;
And from the quiver each his arrow chose.
Hippocoön's was first: with forceful sway
It flew, and, whizzing, cut the liquid way,
Fix'd in the mast the feather'd weapon stands
The fearful pigeon flutters in her bands;
And the tree trembled; and the shouting cries
Of the pleas'd people rend the vaulted skies;
Then Mnestheus to the head his arrow drove,
With lifted eyes, and took his aim above,
But made a glancing shot, and miss'd the dove.
Yet miss'd so narrow that he cuts the cord,
Which fasten'd by the foot the flitting bird.
The captive thus releas'd, away she flies,
And beats with clapping wings the yielding skies.
His bow already bent, Eurytion stood;
And, having first invok'd his brother god,
His winged shaft with eager haste he sped.
The fatal message reach'd her as she fled:
She leaves her life aloft; she strikes the ground,
And renders back the weapon in the wound.
Acestes grudging at his lot, remains,
Without a prize to gratify his pains.
Yet shooting upward, sends his shaft, to show
An archer's art, and boast his twanging bow.
The feather'd arrow gave a dire portent:
And latter augurs judge from this event.
Chaf'd by the speed, it fir'd; and as it flew,
A trail of following flames, ascending, drew:
Kindling they mount, and mark the shiny way;
Across the sky as falling meteors play,
And vanish into wind, or in a blaze decay.
The Trojans and Sicilians wildly stare,
And, trembling, turn their wonder into pray'r
The Dardan prince put on a smiling face,
And strain'd Acestes with a close embrace;
Then hon'ring him with gifts above the rest,
Turn'd the bad omen, nor his fears confess'd,
"The gods (said he) this miracle have wrought,
And order'd you the prize without the lot.
Accept this goblet, rough with figur'd gold,
Which Thracian Cisseus gave my sire of old.
This pledge of ancient amity receive,
Which to my second sire I justly give."
He said, and with the trumpet's cheerful sound,
Proclaim'd him victor, and with laurel crown'd:
Nor good Eurytion envied him the prize,
Though he transfix'd the pigeon in the skies.
Who cut the line, with second gifts was grac'd;
The third was his, whose arrow pierc'd the mast.

The chief, before the games were wholly done,
Call'd Periphantes, tutor to his son,
And whisper'd thus: "With speed Ascanius find;
And, if his childish troop be ready join'd,
On horse back let him grace his grandsire's day,
And lead his equals arm'd in just array."
He said; and, calling out, the cirque he clears:
The crowd withdrawn, an open plain appears.
And now the noble youths, of form divine,
Advance before their fathers, in a line:
The riders grace the steeds; the steeds with glory shine.

Thus marching on in military pride,
Shouts of applause resound from side to side.
Their casques adorn'd with laurel wreaths they wear,
Each brandishing aloft a cornel spear.
Some at their backs their gilded quivers bore
Their chains of burnish'd gold hung down before.
Three graceful troops they form'd upon the green:
Three graceful leaders at their head were seen
Twelve follow'd ev'ry chief, and left a space between.
The first young Priam led—a lovely boy,
Whose grandsire was the unhappy king of Troy;
(His race in after-times was known to fame
New honours adding to the Latian name)
And well the royal boy his Thracian steed became.
White were the fetlocks of his feet before;
And on his front a snowy star he bore.
Then beauteous Atys, with Iülus bred
Of equal age, the second squadron led.
The last in order, but the first in place,
First in the lovely features of his face,
Rode fair Ascanius on a fiery steed,
Queen Dido's gift, and of the Tyrian breed.
Sure coursers for the rest the king ordains,
With golden bits adorn'd, and purple reins.

The pleas'd spectators peals of shouts renew
And all the parents in the children view;
Their make, their motions, and their sprightly grace,
And hopes and fears alternate in their face

Th' unfledg'd commanders, and their martial train,
First make the circuit of the sandy plain
Around their sires, and, at the appointed sign,
Drawn up in beauteous order form a line.
The second signal sounds: the troop divides
In three distinguish'd parts, with three distinguish'd guides.
Again they close, and once again disjoin:
In troop to troop oppos'd, and line to line,

They meet; they wheel; they throw their darts afar,
With harmless rage, and well-dissembled war.
Then in a round the mingled bodies run;
Flying they follow, and pursuing shun;
Broken, they break; and rallying, they renew
In other forms the military shew.
At last, in order undiscern'd they join,
And march together in a friendly line,
And as the Cretan labyrinth of old,
With wand'ring ways, and many a winding fold,
Involv'd the weary feet without redress,
In a round error, which denied recess;
So fought the Trojan boys in warlike play,
Turn'd and return'd, and still a diff'rent way.
Thus dolphins, in the deep, each other chase
In circles, when they swim around the wat'ry race.
This game, these carousals, Ascanius taught;
And building Alba, to the Latins brought;
Show'd what he learn'd: the Latin sires impart
To their succeeding sons the graceful art:
From these, imperial Rome receiv'd the game,
Which Troy, the youths the Trojan troop, they name.
Thus far the sacred sports they celebrate:
But Fortune soon resum'd her ancient hate:
For, while they pay the dead his annual dues,
Those envied rites Saturnian Juno views;
And sends the goddess of the various bow,
To try new methods of revenge below;
Supplies the winds to wing her airy way,
Where in the port secure the navy lay.
Swiftly fair Iris down her arch descends,
And, undiscern'd, her fatal voyage ends.
She saw the gath'ring crowd; and gliding thence,
The desert shore, and fleet without defence.
The Trojan matrons, on the sands alone,
With sighs and tears, Anchises' death bemoan:
Then, turning to the sea their weeping eyes,
Their pity to themselves, renew their cries.
"Alas!" said one, "what oceans yet remain
For us to sail! what labours to sustain!"
All take the word, and with a gen'ral groan,
Implore the gods for peace and places of their own.
The goddess, great in mischief, views their pains,
And in a woman's form her heavenly limbs restrains.
In face and shape, old Beroe she became,
Doryclus' wife, a venerable dame,
Once bless'd with riches and a mother's name.
Thus chang'd, amidst the crying crowd she ran,
Mix'd with the matrons, and these words began:
"O wretched we! whom not the Grecian pow'r,
Nor flames, destroy'd, in Troy's unhappy hour!
O wretched we! reserv'd by cruel Fate,
Beyond the ruins of the sinking state!
Now sev'n revolving years are wholly run,
Since this improsp'rous voyage we begun;
Since toss'd from shores to shores, from lands to lands,
Inhospitable rocks and barren sands,
Wand'ring in exile through the stormy sea,
We search in vain for flying Italy.
Now cast by Fortune on this kindred land,
What should our rest and rising walls withstand,
Or hinder here to fix our banish'd band?
O country lost, and gods redeem'd in vain,
If still in endless exile we remain!
Shall we no more the Trojan walls renew,
Or streams of some dissembled Simois view?
Haste! join with me! th' unhappy fleet consume!
Cassandra bids; and I declare her doom.
In sleep I saw her; she supplied my hands
(For this I more than dreamt) with flaming brands:
'With these (said she) these wand'ring ships destroy:
These are your fated seats, and this your Troy.
Time calls you now, the precious hour employ:
Slack not the good presage, while heav'n inspires
Our minds to dare, and gives the ready fires.
See! Neptune's altars minister their brands:
The god is pleas'd; the god supplies our hands."
Then from the pile a flaming fire she drew,
And, toss'd in air, amidst the galleys threw.
Rapt in amaze, the matrons wildly stare:
Then Pyrgo, reverenc'd for her hoary hair,
Pyrgo, the nurse of Priam's num'rous race,
"No Beroe this, though she belies her face
What terrors from her frowning front arise
Behold a goddess in her ardent eyes!
What rays around her heavenly face are seen!
Mark her majestic voice, and more than mortal mien!
Beroe but now I left, whom, pin'd with pain,
Her age and anguish from these rites detain."
She said. The matrons, seiz'd with new amaze,
Roll their malignant eyes, and on the navy gaze,
They fear, and hope, and neither part obey:
They hope the fated land, but fear the fatal way.
The goddess, having done her task below,
Mounts up on equal wings, and bends her painted bow.
Struck with the sight, and seiz'd with rage divine,
The matrons prosecute their mad design:
They shriek aloud; they snatch, with impious hands,
The food of altars, firs and flaming brands.

Green boughs and saplings, mingled in their haste,
And smoking torches, on the ships they cast.
The flame, unstopp'd at first, more fury gains;
And Vulcan rides at large with loosen'd reins:
Triumphant to the painted stern he soars,
And seizes, in his way, the banks, and crackling oars.
Eumelus was the first the news to bear,
While yet they crowd the rural theatre.
Then, what they hear, is witness'd by their eyes:
A storm of sparkles, and of flames, arise.
Ascanius took th' alarm, while yet he led,
His early warriors on his prancing steed,
And, spurring on, his equals soon o'erpass'd;
Nor could his frighted friends reclaim his haste.
Soon as the royal youth appear'd in view,
He sent his voice before him as he flew:
"What madness moves you, matrons! to destroy
The last remainders of unhappy Troy?
Not hostile fleets, but your own hopes you burn,
And on your friends your fatal fury turn.
Behold your own Ascanius!"—While he said,
He drew his glitt'ring helmet from his head,
In which the youths to sportful arms he led.
By this, Æneas and his train appear;
And now the women, seiz'd with shame and fear,
Dispers'd, to woods and caverns take their flight,
Abhor their actions, and avoid the light;
Their friends acknowledge, and their error find,
And shake the goddess from their alter'd mind.

Not so the raging fires their fury cease,
But, lurking in the seams, with seeming peace,
Work on their way amid the smould'ring tow,
Sure in destruction, but in motion slow.
The silent plague through the green timber eats,
And vomits out a tardy flame by fits,
Down to the keels, and upward to the sails,
The fire descends, or mounts, but still prevails;
Nor buckets pour'd, nor strength of human hand,
Can the victorious element withstand.

The pious hero rends his robe, and throws
To heav'n his hands, and with his hands, his vows.
"O Jove! (he cried,) if pray'rs can yet have place;
If thou abhor'st not all the Dardan race;
If any spark of pity still remain;
If gods are gods, and not invok'd in vain;
Yet spare the relics of the Trojan train!
Yet from the flames our burning vessels free!
Or let thy fury fall alone on me;
At this devoted head thy thunder throw,
And send the willing sacrifice below."

Scarce had he said, when southern storms arise:
From pole to pole, the forky lightning flies:
Loud rattling shakes the mountains and the plain:
Heav'n bellies downward, and descends in rain.
Whole sheets of water from the clouds are sent,
Which hissing through the planks the flames prevent,
And stop the fiery pest. Four ships alone
Burn to the waist, and four the fleet atone.

But doubtful thoughts the hero's heart divide,
If he should still in Sicily reside,
Forgetful of the fates,—or tempt the main,
In hope the promis'd Italy to gain.
When Nautes old and wise—to whom alone
The will of heav'n by Pallas was foreshown—
Vers'd in portents, experienc'd and inspir'd
To tell events, and what the Fates requir'd,
Thus while he stood, to neither part inclin'd,
With cheerful words reliev'd his lab'ring mind:
"O goddess-born! resign'd in ev'ry state,
With patience bear, with prudence push your fate.
By suff'ring well, our fortune we subdue;
Fly when she frowns; and when she calls pursue.
Your friend Acestes is of Trojan kind;
To him disclose the secrets of your mind;
Trust in his hands your old and useless train,
Too num'rous for the ships which yet remain—
The feeble, old, indulgent of their ease,
The dames who dread the dangers of the seas,
With all the dastard crew who dare not stand
The shock of battle with your foes by land.
Here you may build a common town for all,
And, from Acestes' name, Acesta call."
The reason, with his friend's experience join'd,
Encourag'd much, but more disturb'd his mind.
'T was dead of night; when to his slumb'ring eyes,
His father's shade descended from the skies;
And thus he spoke; "O, more than vital breath,
Lov'd while I liv'd, and dear ev'n after death!
O son, in various toils and troubles toss'd!
The king of heav'n employs my careful ghost
On his commands—the god who sav'd from fire
Your flaming fleet, and heard your just desire,
The wholesome counsel of your friend receive,
And here the coward train and women leave;
The chosen youth, and those who nobly dare,
Transport, to tempt the dangers of the war.
The stern Italians will their courage try;
Rough are their manners, and their minds are high.
But first to Pluto's palace you shall go,
And seek my shade among the blest below:

For not with impious ghosts my soul remains,
Nor suffers, with the damn'd, perpetual pains,
But breathes the living air of soft Elysian plains.
The chaste Sybilla shall your steps convey,
And blood of offer'd victims free the way.
There shall you know what realms the gods assign,
And learn the fates and fortunes of your line.
But now farewell! I vanish with the night,
And feel the blast of heav'n's approaching light."
He said, and mix'd with shades, and took his airy flight.
"Whither so fast?" the filial duty cried;
"Ah why, ah! why the wish'd embrace denied?"
He said, and rose: as holy zeal inspires,
He rakes hot embers, and renews the fires;
His country gods and Vesta then adores
With cakes and incense, and their aid implores.
Next, for his friends and royal host he sent,
Reveal'd his vision, and the god's intent,
With his own purpose.—All, without delay,
The will of Jove, and his desires, obey.
They list with women each degen'rate name,
Who dares not hazard life for future fame.
These they cashier. The brave remaining few,
Oars, banks, and cables, half consum'd, renew.
The prince designs a city with the plough:
The lots their sev'ral tenements allow.
This part is nam'd from Ilium, that from Troy;
And the new king ascends the throne with joy:
A chosen senate from the people draws;
Appoints the judges, and ordains the laws.
Then, on the top of Eryx, they begin
A rising temple to the Paphian queen,
Anchises, last, is honour'd as a god:
A priest is added, annual gifts bestow'd;
And groves are planted round his blest abode.
Nine days they pass in feasts, their temples crown'd;
And fumes of incense in the fanes abound,
Then from the south arose a gentle breeze,
That curl'd the smoothness of the glassy seas:
The rising winds a ruffling gale afford,
And call the merry mariners aboard.

Now loud laments along the shores resound,
Of parting friends in close embraces bound.
The trembling women, the degen'rate train
Who shunn'd the frightful dangers of the main,
E'en those desire to sail, and take their share
Of the rough passage, and the promis'd war;
Whom good Æneas cheers; and recommends
To their new master's care his fearful friends:
On Eryx' altars three fat calves he lays;
A lamb new-fallen to the stormy seas;
Then slips his halsers, and his anchors weighs.
High on the deck the godlike hero stands,
With olive crown'd, a charger in his hands,
Then cast the reeking entrails in the brine,
And pour'd the sacrifice of purple wine.
Fresh gales arise: with equal strokes they vie,
And brush the buxom seas, and o'er the billows fly.

Meantime the mother-goddess, full of fears,
To Neptune thus address'd, with tender tears:
"The pride of Jove's imperious queen, the rage,
The malice, which no suff'rings can assuage,
Compel me to these prayers; since neither fate,
Nor time, nor pity, can remove her hate.
E'en Jove is thwarted by his haughty wife
Still vanquish'd, yet she still renews the strife.
As if 't were little to consume the town
Which aw'd the world, and wore th' imperial crown,
She prosecutes the ghost of Troy with pains,
And gnaws, e'en to the bones, the last remains.
Let her the causes of her hatred tell;
But you can witness its effects too well.
You saw the storm she rais'd on Libyan floods,
That mix'd the mountain billows with the clouds;
When, bribing Æolus, she took the main,
And mov'd rebellion in your wat'ry reign.
With fury she possess'd the Dardan dames,
To burn their fleet with execrable flames,
And forc'd Æneas, when his ships were lost,
To leave his followers on a foreign coast.
For what remains, your godhead I implore,
And trust my son to your protecting pow'r.
If neither Jove's nor Fate's decree withstand,
Secure his passage to the Latian land."

Then thus the mighty ruler of the main:
"What may not Venus hope from Neptune's reign?
My kingdom claims your birth: my late defence
Of your endanger'd fleet may claim your confidence.
Nor less by land than sea my deeds declare,
How much your lov'd Æneas is my care.
Thee, Xanthus! and thee, Simois! I attest—
Your Trojan troops when proud Achilles press'd,
And drove before him headlong on the plain,
And dash'd against the walls the trembling train;
When floods were fill'd with bodies of the slain;
When crimson Xanthus, doubtful of his way,
Stood up on ridges to behold the sea;
(New heaps come tumbling in, and chok'd his way.)
When your Æneas fought, but fought with odds
Of force unequal, and unequal gods;

I spread a cloud before the victor's sight,
Sustain'd the vanquish'd, and secur'd his flight—
E'en then secur'd him, when I sought with joy
The vow'd destruction of ungrateful Troy.
My will's the same: fair goddess! fear no more,
Your fleet shall safely gain the Latian shore:
Their lives are giv'n: one destin'd head alone
Shall perish, and for multitudes atone." [mind;
Thus having arm'd with hopes her anxious
His finny team Saturnian Neptune join'd,
Then adds the foamy bridle to their jaws,
And to the loosen'd reins permits the laws.
High on the waves his azure car he guides:
Its axles thunder; and the sea subsides;
And the smooth ocean rolls her silent tides.
The tempests fly before their father's face;
Trains of inferior gods his triumph grace;
And monster whales before their master play,
And choirs of Tritons crowd the wat'ry way.
The marshall'd pow'rs in equal troops divide
To right and left: the gods his better side
Enclose; and, on the worse, the Nymphs and Nereids ride.
Now smiling hope, with sweet vicissitude,
Within the hero's mind his joys renew'd.
He calls to raise the masts, the sheets display:
The cheerful crew with diligence obey;
They scud before the wind, and sail in open sea
Ahead of all, the master pilot steers,
And, as he leads, the following navy veers.
The steeds of Night had travell'd half the sky
The drowsy rowers on their benches lie;
When the soft god of sleep, with easy flight,
Descends, and draws behind a trail of light.
Thou, Palinurus, art his destin'd prey;
To thee alone he takes his fatal way.
Dire dreams to thee, and iron sleep, he bears;
And, lighting on thy prow, the form of Phorbas wears.
Then thus the traitor god began his tale:
"The winds, my friend, inspire a pleasing gale;
The ships, without thy care, securely sail.
Now steal an hour of sweet repose; and I
Will take the rudder, and thy room supply."
To whom the yawning pilot, half asleep:
"Me dost thou bid to trust the treach'rous deep,
The harlot-smiles of her dissembling face,
And to her faith commit the Trojan race?
Shall I believe the Syren South again,
And, oft betray'd, not know the monster main?"
He said; his fasten'd hands the rudder keep;
And fix'd on heaven, his eyes repel invading sleep.
The god was wroth, and at his temples threw
A branch in Lethe dipp'd, and drunk with Stygian dew:
The pilot, vanquish'd by the pow'r divine,
Soon clos'd his swimming eyes, and lay supine.
Scarce were his limbs extended at their length;
The god, insulting with superior strength,
Fell heavy on him, plung'd him in the sea,
And, with the stern, the rudder tore away.
Headlong he fell, and struggling in the main,
Cried out for helping hands, but cried in vain.
The victor demon mounts obscur'd in air;
While the ship sails without the pilot's care.
On Neptune's faith the floating fleet relies:
But what the man forsook, the god supplies,
And o'er the dang'rous deep, secure the navy flies;
Glides by the Syren's cliffs, a shelfy coast,
Long infamous for ships and sailors lost,
And white with bones. Th' impetuous ocean roars,
And rocks rebellow from the sounding shores.
The watchful hero felt the knocks; and found
The tossing vessel sail'd on shoaly ground,
Sure of his pilot's loss, he takes himself
The helm, and steers aloof, and shuns the shelf.
Inly he griev'd, and, groaning from the breast,
Deplor'd his death; and thus his pain express'd:
"For faith repos'd on seas, and on the flatt'ring sky,
Thy naked corse is doom'd on shores unknown to lie."

BOOK VI.

ARGUMENT.

The Sibyl foretells Æneas the adventures he should meet with in Italy. She attends him to hell; describing to him the various scenes of that place, and conducting him to his father Anchises, who instructs him in those sublime mysteries, of the soul of the world, and the transmigration; and shows him that glorious race of heroes, which was to descend from him and his posterity

He said, and wept; then spread his sails before
The winds, and reach'd at length the Cuman shore:
Their anchors dropp'd, his crew the vessels moor;
They turn their heads to sea, their sterns to land,
And greet with greedy joy th' Italian strand.
Some strike from clashing flints their fiery seed
Some gather sticks, the kindled flames to feed,
Or search for hollow trees, and fell the wood,
Or trace through valleys the discover'd flood.
Thus while their sev'ral charges they fulfil,
The pious prince ascends the sacred hill
Where Phœbus is ador'd; and seeks the shade,
Which hides from sight his venerable maid.

Deep in a cave the Sibyl makes abode;
Thence full of fate returns, and of the god.
Through Trivia's grave they walk, and now behold,
And enter now, the temple roof'd with gold.
When Dædalus, to fly the Cretan shore,
His heavy limbs, on jointed pinions bore,
(The first who sail'd in air,) 't is sung by Fame,
To the Cumæan coast, at length he came,
And here alighting, built this costly frame.
Inscrib'd to Phœbus, here he hung on high
The steerage of his wings, that cut the sky:
Then o'er the lofty gate, his art emboss'd
Androgeos' death, and (off'rings to his ghost)
Sev'n youths from Athens, yearly sent to meet,
The fate appointed by revengeful Crete.
And next to these the dreadful urn was plac'd,
In which the destin'd names by lots were cast:
The mournful parents stand around in tears;
And rising Crete against their shore appears.
There too, in living sculpture, might be seen
The mad affection of the Cretan queen;
Then how she cheats her bellowing lover's eye;
The rushing leap, the doubtful progeny—
The lower part a beast, a man above—
The monument of their polluted love.
Nor far from thence he grav'd the wondrous maze,
A thousand doors, a thousand winding ways:
Here dwells the monster hid from human view,
Not to be found but by the faithful clue;
Till the kind artist, mov'd with pious grief,
Lent to the loving maid this last relief,
And all those erring paths describ'd so well
That Theseus conquer'd, and the monster fell.
Here hapless Icarus had found his part,
Had not the father's grief restrain'd his art.
He twice essay'd to cast his son in gold;
Twice from his hands he dropp'd the forming mould.
All this with wond'ring eyes Æneas view'd:
Each varying object his delight renew'd.
Eager to read the rest—Achates came,
And by his side the mad divining dame,
The priestess of the god, Deïphobe her name.
"Time suffers not," she said, "to feed your eyes
With empty pleasures: haste the sacrifice.
Sev'n bullocks, yet unyok'd, for Phœbus choose,
And for Diana sev'n unspotted ewes."
This said, the servants urge the sacred rites,
While to the temple she the prince invites.
A spacious cave, within its farmost part,
Was hew'd and fashion'd by laborious art,
Through the hill's hollow sides: before the place,
A hundred doors a hundred entries grace:
As many voices issue, and the sound
Of Sibyl's words as many times rebound.
Now to the mouth they come. Aloud she cries,
"This is the time! inquire your destinies!
He comes! behold the god!" Thus while she said,
(And shiv'ring at the sacred entry stay'd,)
Her colour chang'd; her face was not the same;
And hollow groans from her deep spirit came.
Her hair stood up; convulsive rage possess'd
Her trembling limbs, and heav'd her lab'ring breast.
Greater than human kind she seem'd to look,
And with an accent more than mortal spoke.
Her staring eyes with sparkling fury roll,
When all the god came rushing on her soul.
Swiftly she turn'd, and, foaming as she spoke,
"Why this delay?" she cried—"the pow'rs invoke.
Thy pray'rs alone can open this abode:
Else vain are my demands, and dumb the god."
She said no more. The trembling Trojans hear,
O'erspread with a damp sweat, and holy fear.
The prince himself, with awful dread possess'd,
His vows to great Apollo thus address'd:
"Indulgent god! propitious pow'r to Troy.
Swift to relieve, unwilling to destroy!
Directed by whose hand, the Dardan dart,
Pierc'd the proud Grecian's only mortal part!
Thus far, by Fate's decrees, and thy commands,
Through ambient seas, and through devouring sands,
Our exil'd crew has sought th' Ausonian ground:
And now, at length, the flying coast is found.
Thus far the fate of Troy, from place to place,
With fury has pursu'd her wand'ring race.
Here cease, ye pow'rs, and let your vengeance end:
Troy is no more, and can no more offend.
And thou, O sacred maid, inspir'd to see
The event of things in dark futurity;
Give me what heav'n has promis'd to my fate,
To conquer and command the Latian state;
To fix my wand'ring gods, and find a place
For the long exiles of the Trojan race:
Then shall my grateful hands a temple rear
To the twin gods, with vows and solemn pray'r;
And annual rites, and festivals, and games,
Shall be perform'd to their auspicious names.
Nor shalt thou want thy honours in my land:
For there thy faithful oracles shall stand,
Preserv'd in shrines: and ev'ry sacred lay
Which by thy mouth Apollo shall convey—
All shall be treasur'd by a chosen train
Of holy priests, and ever shall remain.

But oh! commit not thy prophetic mind
To flitting leaves, the sport of ev'ry wind,
Lest they disperse in air our empty fate.
Write not, but what the pow'rs ordain relate."
Struggling in vain, impatient of her load,
And lab'ring underneath the pond'rous god,
The more she strove to shake him from her breast,
With more and far superior force he press'd;
Commands his entrance, and without control,
Usurps her organs, and inspires her soul.
Now, with a furious blast, the hundred doors
Ope of themselves; a rushing whirlwind roars
Within the cave, and Sibyl's voice restores:
"Escap'd the dangers of the wat'ry reign,
Yet more and greater ills by land remain,
The coast, so long desir'd, (nor doubt th' event,)
Thy troops shall reach, but, having reach'd repent.
Wars, horrid wars, I view—a field of blood,
And Tyber rolling with a purple flood.
Simois nor Xanthus shall be wanting there:
A new Achilles shall in arms appear,
And he, too, goddess-born. Fierce Juno's hate,
Added to hostile force, shall urge thy fate.
To what strange nation shalt not thou resort,
Driv'n to solicit aid at every court!
The cause the same which Ilium once oppres'd—
A foreign mistress, and a foreign guest.
But thou, secure of soul, unbent with woes,
The more thy fortune frowns, the more oppose.
The dawnings of thy safety shall be shown,
From—whence thou least shalt hope—a Grecian town."
Thus, from the dark recess, the Sibyl spoke;
And the resisting air the thunder broke;
The cave rebellow'd, and the temple shook.
Th' ambiguous god, who rul'd her lab'ring breast,
In these mysterious words his mind express'd,
Some truths reveal'd, in terms involv'd the rest.
At length her fury fell; her foaming ceas'd,
And, ebbing in her soul, the god decreas'd.
Then thus the chief: "No terror to my view
No frightful face of danger can be new.
Inur'd to suffer, and resolv'd to dare,
The Fates, without my pow'r, shall be without my care.
This let me crave—since near your grove the road
To hell lies open, and the dark abode,
Which Acheron surrounds, th' innavigable flood—
Conduct me through the regions void of light,
And lead me longing to my father's sight.
For him, a thousand dangers I have sought,
And, rushing where the thickest Grecians fought,
Safe on my back the sacred burden brought.
He, for my sake, the raging ocean tried,
And wrath of heav'n, (my still auspicious guide,)
And bore, beyond the strength decrepit age supplied.
Oft since he breath'd his last, in dead of night,
His rev'rend image stood before my sight;
Enjoin'd to seek, below, his holy shade—
Conducted there by your unerring aid.
But you, if pious minds by pray'rs are won,
Oblige the father, and protect the son.
Yours is the pow'r; nor Proserpine in vain
Has made you priestess of her nightly reign.
If Orpheus, arm'd with his enchanting lyre,
The ruthless king with pity could inspire,
And from the shades below redeem his wife,
If Pollux, off'ring his alternate life,
Could free his brother, and can daily go
By turns aloft, by turns descend below;—
Why name I Theseus, or his greater friend,
Who trod the downward path, and upward could ascend?—
Not less than theirs, from Jove my lineage came;
My mother greater, my descent the same."
So pray'd the Trojan prince, and, while he pray'd,
His hand upon the holy altar laid.
Then thus replied the prophetess divine:
"O goddess-born, of great Anchises' line!
The gates of hell are open night and day;
Smooth the descent, and easy is the way
But, to return, and view the cheerful skies
In this the task and mighty labour lies.
To few great Jupiter imparts this grace,
And those of shining worth, and heav'nly race.
Betwixt those regions and our upper light,
Deep forests and impenetrable night
Possess the middle space: th' infernal bounds
Cocytus, with his sable waves, surrounds.
But, if so dire a love your soul invades,
As twice below to view the trembling shades,
If you so hard a toil will undertake,
As twice to pass th' innavigable lake;
Receive my counsel. In the neighb'ring grove
There stands a tree: the queen of Stygian Jove
Claims it her own: thick woods and gloomy night
Conceal the happy plant from human sight.
One bough it bears; but (wond'rous to behold)
The ductile rind and leaves of radiant gold:
This from the vulgar branches must be torn,
And to fair Proserpine the present borne,
Ere leave be giv'n to tempt the nether skies.
The first thus rent, a second will arise;
And the same metal the same room supplies.
Look round the wood with lifted eyes, to see
The lurking gold upon the fatal tree:
Then rend it off, as holy rites command
The willing metal will obey thy hand,

Following with ease, if, favoured by thy fate,
Thou art foredoom'd to view the Stygian state:
If not, no labour can the tree constrain;
And strength of stubborn arms, and steel, are vain.
Besides, you know not, while you here attend,
Th' unworthy fate of your unhappy friend:
Breathless he lies: and his unburied ghost,
Depriv'd of fun'ral rites, pollutes your host.
Pay first his pious dues; and, for the dead,
Two sable sheep around his hearse be led;
Then, living turfs upon his body lay:
This done, securely take the destin'd way,
To find the regions destitute of day."
She said, and held her peace.—Æneas went
Sad from the cave, and full of discontent,
Unknowing who the sacred Sibyl meant;
Achates, the companion of his breast,
Goes grieving by his side, with equal cares oppress'd.
Walking, they talk'd, and fruitlessly divin'd,
What friend the priestess by those words design'd.
But soon they found an object to deplore:
Misenus lay extended on the shore—
Son of the god of winds—none so renown'd,
The warrior trumpet in the field to sound,
With breathing brass, to kindle fierce alarms,
And rouse to dare their fate in honourable arms.
He serv'd great Hector, and was ever near,
Not with his trumpet only, but his spear.
But, by Pelides' arm when Hector fell,
He chose Æneas; and he chose as well.
Swoln with applause, and aiming still at more,
He now provokes the seagods from the shore.
With envy, Triton heard the martial sound,
And the bold champion, for his challenge, drown'd;
Then cast his mangled carcass on the strand.—
The gazing crowd around the body stand.
All weep: but most Æneas mourns his fate,
And hastens to perform the fun'ral state,
In altar-wise, a stately pile they rear;
The basis broad below, and top advanc'd in air.
An ancient wood, fit for the work design'd,
(The shady covert of the savage kind,)
The Trojans found: the sounding axe is plied:
Firs, pines, and pitch-trees, and the tow'ring pride
Of forest ashes, feel the fatal stroke;
And piercing wedges cleave the stubborn oak.
Huge trunks of trees, fell'd from the steepy crown
Of the bare mountains, roll with ruin down.
Arm'd like the rest the Trojan prince appears,
And by his pious labour, urges theirs.
Thus while he wrought, revolving in his mind
The ways to compass what his wish design'd,
He cast his eyes upon the gloomy grove,
And then with vows implor'd the queen of love:
"O may thy pow'r, propitious still to me,
Conduct my steps to find the fatal tree
In this deep forest, since the Sibyl's breath
Foretold, alas! too true, Misenus' death."
Scarce had he said, when, full before his sight,
Two doves descending from their airy flight,
Secure upon the grassy plain alight.
He knew his mother's birds, and thus he pray'd:
"Be you my guides with your auspicious aid;
And lead my footsteps till the branch be found,
Whose glitt'ring shadow gilds the sacred ground:
And thou, great parent! with celestial care,
In this distress, be present to my pray'r."
Thus having said, he stopp'd, with watchful sight
Observing still the motions of their flight,
What course they took, what happy signs they shew.
They fed, and fluttering by degrees, withdrew
Still farther from the place, but still in view:
Hopping and flying thus they led him on
To the slow lake, whose baleful stench to shun,
They wing'd their flight aloft, then stooping low,
Perch'd on the double tree, that bears the golden bough.
Through the green leaves the glitt'ring shadows glow,
As, on the sacred oak, the wintry misletoe,
Where the proud mother views her precious brood,
And happier branches which she never sow'd.
Such was the glitt'ring; such the ruddy rind,
And dancing leaves, that wanton'd in the wind.
He seiz'd the shining bough with griping hold,
And rent away, with ease, the ling'ring gold,
Then to the Sibyl's palace bore the prize
Meantime the Trojan troops, with weeping eyes,
To dead Misenus pay his obsequies.
First, from the ground, a lofty pile they rear,
Of pitch-trees, oaks, and pines, and unctuous fir;
The fabric's front with cypress twigs they strew,
And stick the sides with boughs of baleful yew.
The topmost part his glitt'ring arms adorn:
Warm waters, then, in brazen caldrons borne,
Are pour'd to wash his body, joint by joint;
And fragrant oils the stiffen'd limbs anoint.
With groans and cries, Misenus they deplore:
Then on a bier, with purple cover'd o'er,
The breathless body, thus bewail'd, they lay,
And fire the pile, their faces turn'd away:
(Such rev'rent rites their fathers us'd to pay.)

Pure oil and incense on the fire they throw,
And fat of victims which his friends bestow.
These gifts the greedy flames to dust devour;
Then on the living coals, red wine they pour;
And last the relics by themselves dispose,
Which in a brazen urn the priests enclose.
Old Corynæus compass'd thrice the crew,
And dipp'd an olive-branch in holy dew;
Which thrice he sprinkled round; and thrice aloud
Invok'd the dead, and then dismiss'd the crowd.
But good Æneas order'd on the shore
A stately tomb, whose top a trumpet bore,
A soldier's falchion, and a seaman's oar.
Thus was his friend interr'd: and deathless fame
Still to the lofty cape consigns his name.
These rites perform'd, the prince without delay,
Hastes to the nether world his destin'd way.
Deep was the cave; and, downward as it went
From the wide mouth, a rocky rough descent;
And here th' access a gloomy grove defends;
And here th' innavigable lake extends,
O'er whose unhappy waters, void of light,
No bird presumes to steer his airy flight:
And deadly stenches from the depth arise,
And streaming sulphur, that infects the skies.
From hence the Grecian bards their legends make,
And give the name Avernus to the lake.
Four sable bullocks, in the yoke untaught,
For sacrifice, the pious hero brought.
The priestess pours the wine betwixt their horns;
Then cuts the curling hair; that first oblation burns,
Invoking Hecat hither to repair—
A powerful name in hell, and upper air.
The sacred priests, with ready knives, bereave
The beasts of life, and in full bowls receive
The streaming blood: a lamb to Hell and Night
(The sable wool without a streak of white)
Æneas offers: and by Fate's decree,
A barren heifer, Proserpine to thee.
With holocausts he Pluto's altar fills;
Sev'n brawny bulls with his own hand he kills:
Then, on the broiling entrails, oil he pours:
Which, ointed thus, the raging flame devours.
Late the nocturnal sacrifice begun,
Nor ended, till the next returning sun.
Then earth began to bellow, trees to dance,
And howling dogs in glimm'ring light advance,
Ere Hecat came—"Far hence be souls profane!"
The Sibyl cried—"and from the grove abstain!
Now, Trojan, take the way thy fates afford:
Assume thy courage, and unsheath thy sword."
She said, and pass'd along the gloomy space:
The prince pursu'd her steps with equal pace.
Ye realms yet unreveal'd to human sight!
Ye gods, who rule the regions of the night!
Ye gliding ghosts! permit me to relate
The mystic wonders of your silent state.
Obscure they went thro' dreary shades, that led
Along the waste dominions of the dead.
Thus wander travellers in wood by night,
By the moon's doubtful and malignant light,
When Jove in dusky clouds involves the skies,
And the faint crescent shoots by fits before their eyes.
Just in the gate, and in the jaws of hell,
Revengeful Cares and sullen Sorrows dwell,
And pale Diseases, and repining Age,
Want, Fear, and Famine's unresisted rage;
Here, Toils, and Death, and Death's half-brother, Sleep,
(Forms terrible to view,) their sentry keep
With anxious Pleasure of a guilty mind,
Deep Frauds before, and open Force behind;
The furies' iron beds; and Strife, that shakes
Her hissing tresses, and unfolds her snakes:
Full in the midst of this infernal road,
An elm displays her dusky arms abroad;
The god of sleep there hides his heavy head:
And empty dreams on ev'ry leaf is spread.
Of various forms, unnumber'd spectres more,
Centaurs, and double shapes, besiege the door.
Before the passage horrid Hydra stands,
And Briareus with all his hundred hands;
Gorgons, Geryon with his triple frame;
And vain Chimæra vomits empty flame.
The chief unsheath'd his shining steel, prepar'd,
Though seiz'd with sudden fear, to force the guard,
Off'ring his brandish'd weapon, at their face,
Had not the Sibyl stopp'd his eager pace,
And told him what those empty phantoms were—
Forms without bodies, and impassive air.
Hence to deep Acheron they take their way,
Whose troubled eddies, thick with ooze and clay,
Are whirl'd aloft, and in Cocytus lost:
There Charon stands, who rules the dreary coast—
A sordid god: down from his hoary chin
A length of beard descends, uncomb'd, unclean:
His eyes like hollow furnaces on fire;
A girdle, foul with grease, binds his obscene attire.
He spreads his canvass; with his pole he steers;
The freights of flitting ghosts in his thin bottom bears.
He look'd in years; yet, in his years, were seen
A youthful vigour, and autumnal green.

An airy crowd came rushing where he stood,
Which fill'd the margin of the fatal flood—
Husbands and wives, boys and unmarried maids,
And mighty heroes' more majestic shades,
And youths, entomb'd before their fathers' eyes,
With hollow groans, and shrieks, and feeble cries.
Thick as the leaves in autumn strow the woods,
Or fowls, by winter forc'd, forsake the floods,
And wing their hasty flight to happier lands—
Such, and so thick, the shiv'ring army stands,
And press for passage with extended hands.
Now these, now those, the surly boatman bore:
The rest he drove to distance from the shore.
The hero, who beheld, with wond'ring eyes,
The tumult mix'd with shrieks, laments, and cries,
Ask'd of his guide, what the rude concourse meant?
Why to the shore the thronging people bent?
What forms of law among the ghosts were us'd?
Why some were ferried o'er, and some refus'd?
"Son of Anchises! offspring of the gods!
(The Sibyl said,) you see the Stygian floods,
The sacred streams, which heav'n's imperial state
Attests in oaths, and fears to violate.
The ghosts rejected are th' unhappy crew
Depriv'd of sepulchres and fun'ral due:
The boatman, Charon: those, the buried host,
He ferries over to the farther coast;
Nor dares his transport vessel cross the waves
With such whose bones are not compos'd in graves.
A hundred years they wander on the shore;
At length, their penance done, are wafted o'er."
The Trojan chief his forward pace repress'd,
Revolving anxious thoughts within his breast.
He saw his friends, who, whelm'd beneath the waves,
Their fun'ral honours claim'd, and ask'd their quiet graves.
The lost Leucaspis in the crowd he knew,
And the brave leader of the Lycian crew,
Whom, on the Tyrrhene seas, the tempest met;
The sailors master'd, and the ship o'erset.
Amidst the spirits, Palinurus press'd,
Yet fresh from life, a new-admitted guest,
Who, while he steering view'd the stars, and bore
His course from Afric to the Latian shore,
Fell headlong down. The Trojan fix'd his view,
And scarcely thro' the gloom the sullen shadow knew.
Then thus the prince: "What envious pow'r, O friend!
Brought your lov'd life to this disastrous end?
For Phœbus, ever true in all he said,
Has in your fate alone, my faith betray'd.
The god foretold you should not die, before
You reach'd secure from seas, th' Italian shore.
Is this th' unerring pow'r!"—The ghost replied:
"Nor Phœbus flatter'd, nor his answers lied;
Nor envious gods have sent me to the deep:
But, while the stars and course of heav'n I keep,
My wearied eyes were seiz'd with fatal sleep.
I fell; and, with my weight, the helm constrain'd,
Was drawn along, which yet my gripe retain'd.
Nor by the winds and raging waves I swear,
Your safety, more than mine, was then my care;
Lest, of the guide bereft, the rudder lost,
Your ship should run against the rocky coast.
Three blust'ring nights, borne by the southern blast,
I floated, and discover'd land at last;
High on a mounting wave, my head I bore,
Forcing my strength, and gath'ring to the shore.
Panting, but past the danger, now I seiz'd
The craggy cliffs, and my tir'd members eas'd.
While, cumber'd with my dropping clothes, I lay,
The cruel nation, covetous of prey,
Stain'd with my blood th' unhospitable coast:
And now by winds and waves, my lifeless limbs are toss'd:
Which, O! avert, by yon ethereal light,
Which I have lost for this eternal night!
Or, if by dearer ties you may be won,
By your dead sire, and by your living son,
Redeem from this reproach my wand'ring ghost,
Or with your navy seek the Velin coast,
And in a peaceful grave my corpse compose:
Or, if a nearer way your mother shows,
(Without whose aid, you durst not undertake
This frightful passage o'er the Stygian lake,)
Lend to this wretch your hand, and waft him o'er
To the sweet banks of yon forbidden shore."
Scarce had he said; the prophetess began:
"What hopes delude thee, miserable man
Think'st thou, thus unintomb'd, to cross the floods,
To view the Furies and infernal gods,
And visit, without leave, the dark abodes?
Attend the term of long revolving years:
Fate, and the dooming gods, are deaf to tears.
This comfort of thy dire misfortune take—
The wrath of heav'n, inflicted for thy sake,
With vengeance shall pursue th' inhuman coast,
Till they propitiate thy offended ghost,
And raise a tomb, with vows and solemn pray'r,
And Palinurus' name the place shall bear."

This calm'd his cares—sooth'd with his future fame,
And pleas'd to hear his propagated name.
Now nearer to the Stygian lake they draw;
Whom, from the shore, the surly boatman saw
Observ'd their passage through the shady wood,
And mark'd their near approaches to the flood:
Then thus he call'd aloud, inflam'd with wrath:
"Mortal, whate'er, who this forbidden path
In arms presum'st to tread! I charge thee, stand
And tell thy name, and bus'ness in the land.
Know this the realm of night—the Stygian shore:
My boat conveys no living bodies o'er:
Nor was I pleas'd, great Theseus once to bear,
(Who forc'd a passage with his pointed spear,)
Nor strong Alcides—men of mighty fame;
And from th' immortal gods their lineage came,
In fetters one the barking porter tied,
And took him trembling from his sov'reign's side:
Two sought by force to seize his beauteous bride."
To whom the Sibyl thus: "Compose thy mind:
Nor frauds are here contriv'd, nor force design'd.
Still may the dog the wand'ring troops constrain
Of airy ghosts, and vex the guilty train;
And with her grisly lord his lovely queen remain.
The Trojan chief, whose lineage is from Jove,
Much fam'd for arms, and more for filial love,
Is sent to seek his sire in your Elysian grove
If neither piety, nor heav'n's command,
Can gain his passage to the Stygian land,
This fatal present shall prevail, at least"—
Then show'd the shining bough, conceal'd within her vest.
No more was needful: for the gloomy god
Stood mute with awe, to see the golden rod;
Admir'd the destin'd off'ring to his queen—
A venerable gift, so rarely seen.
His fury thus appeas'd, he puts to land:
The ghosts forsake their seats at his command:
He clears the deck, receives the mighty freight;
The leaky vessel groans beneath the weight.
Slowly she sails, and scarcely stems the tides:
The pressing water pours within her sides.
His passengers at length are wafted o'er,
Expos'd, in muddy weeds, upon the miry shore
No sooner landed, in this den they found
The triple porter of the Stygian sound,
Grim Cerberus, who soon began to rear
His crested snakes, and arm'd his bristling hair.
The prudent Sibyl had before prepar'd
A sop, in honey steep'd to charm the guard;
Which, mix'd with powerful drugs, she cast before
His greedy grinning jaws, just op'd to roar.
With three enormous mouth he gapes; and straight,
With hunger press'd, devours the pleasing bait.
Long draughts of sleep his monstrous limbs enslave;
He reels, and falling, fills the spacious cave.
The keeper charm'd, the chief without delay
Pass'd on, and took th' irremeable way.
Before the gates, the cries of babes new-born,
Whom Fate had from their tender mothers torn,
Assault his ears: then those, whom form of laws
Condemn'd to die, when traitors judg'd their cause.
Nor want they lots, nor judges to review
The wrongful sentence, and award anew.
Minos, the strict inquisitor, appears;
And lives and crimes, with his assessors, hears.
Round in his urn, the blended balls he rolls,
Absolves the just, and dooms the guilty souls.
The next in place and punishment, are they
Who prodigally threw their souls away—
Fools, who, repining at their wretched state,
And loathing anxious life, suborn'd their fate.
With late repentance, now they would retrieve
The bodies they forsook, and wish to live;
Their pains and poverty desire to bear,
To view the light of heav'n, and breathe the vital air.
But fate forbids; the Stygian floods oppose,
And with nine circling streams, the captive souls enclose.

Not far from hence, the Mournful Fields appear,
So call'd from lovers that inhabit there.
The souls, whom that unhappy flame invades
In secret solitude and myrtle shades
Make endless moans, and, pining with desire,
Lament too late their unextinguish'd fire.
Here Procris, Eriphyle here he found
Baring her breast, yet bleeding with the wound
Made by her son. He saw Pasiphae there,
With Phædra's ghost, a foul incestuous pair.
There Laodamia, with Evadne, moves—
Unhappy both, but loyal in their loves
Cæneus, a woman once, and once a man,
But ending in the sex she first began.
Not far from these Phœnician Dido stood,
Fresh from her wound, her bosom bath'd in blood;
Whom when the Trojan hero hardly knew,
Obscure in shades, and with a doubtful view,
(Doubtful as he who sees, through dusky night,
Or thinks he sees, the moon's uncertain light;)
With tears he first approach'd the sullen shade;
And as his love inspir'd him, thus he said.

"Unhappy queen! then is the common breath
Of rumour true, in your reported death,
And I, alas! the cause?—By heav'n, I vow,
And all the pow'r's that rule the realms below,
Unwilling I forsook your friendly state,
Commanded by the gods, and forc'd by Fate—
Those gods, that Fate, whose unresisted might
Have sent me to those regions void of light
Through the vast empire of eternal night.
Nor dar'd I to presume, that, press'd with grief,
My flight should urge you to this dire relief.
Stay, stay your steps, and listen to my vows!
'T is the last interview that Fate allows!"
In vain he thus attempts her mind to move
With tears and pray'rs and late repenting love.
Disdainfully she look'd; then turning round,
She fix'd her eyes unmov'd upon the ground,
And, what he says and swears, regards no more,
Than the deaf rocks, when the loud billows roar;
But whirl'd away to shun his hateful sight,
Hid in the forest, and the shades of night;
Then sought Sichæus through the shady grove,
Who answer'd all her cares, and equall'd all her love.
Some pious tears the pitying hero paid,
And follow'd with his eyes the flitting shade,
Then took the forward way by Fate ordain'd,
And with his guide, the further fields attain'd,
Where, sever'd from the rest, the warrior souls remain'd.
Tydeus he met, with Meleager's race,
The pride of armies, and the soldier's grace;
And pale Adrastus with his ghastly face.
Of Trojan chiefs he view'd a numerous train,
All much lamented, all in battle slain—
Glaucus and Medon, high above the rest,
Antenor's sons, and Ceres' sacred priest,
And proud Idæus, Priam's charioteer,
Who shakes his empty reins, and aims his airy spear.
The gladsome ghosts, in circling troops, attend,
And with unwearied eyes behold their friend;
Delight to hover near, and long to know
What bus'ness brought him to the realms below.
But Argive chiefs, and Agamemnon's train,
When his refulgent arms flash'd through the shady plain,
Fled from his well-known face, with wonted fear,
As when his thund'ring sword and pointed spear
Drove headlong to their ships, and glean'd the routed rear.
They rais'd a feeble cry with trembling notes:
But the weak voice deceiv'd their gasping throats.
Here Priam's son, Deiphobus, he found,
Whose face and limbs were one continued wound.
Dishonest, with lopp'd arms, the youth appears,
Spoil'd of his nose, and shorten'd of his ears.
He scarcely knew him, striving to disown
His blotted form, and blushing to be known;
And therefore first began: "O Teucer's race
Who durst thy faultless figure thus deface?
What heart could wish, what hand inflict this dire disgrace?
'T was fam'd, that in our last and fatal night,
Your single prowess long sustain'd the fight,
Till tir'd, not forc'd, a glorious fate you chose
And fell upon a heap of slaughter'd foes.
But, in remembrance of so brave a deed,
A tomb and fun'ral honours I decreed;
Thrice call'd your manes on the Trojan plains:
The place your armour and your name retains.
Your body too I sought, and, had I found,
Design'd for burial in your native ground."
The ghost replied, "Your piety has paid
All needful rites, to rest my wand'ring shade:
But cruel Fate, and my more cruel wife,
To Grecian swords betray'd my sleeping life.
These are the monuments of Helen's love—
The shame I bear below, the marks I bore above.
You know in what deluding joys we past
The night, that was by heav'n decreed our last.
For, when the fatal horse, descending down,
Pregnant with arms, o'erwhelm'd th' unhappy town,
She feign'd nocturnal orgies: left my bed,
And, mix'd with Trojan dames, the dances led;
Then, waving high her torch, the signal made,
Which rous'd the Grecians from their ambuscade.
With watching overworn, with cares oppress'd,
Unhappy I had laid me down to rest;
And heavy sleep my weary limbs possess'd.
Meantime my worthy wife our arms mislaid,
And from beneath my head my sword convey'd:
The door unlatch'd, and, with repeated calls,
Invites her former lord within my walls.
Thus in her crime her confidence she plac'd,
And with new treasons would redeem the past.
What need I more? Into the room they ran,
And meanly murder'd a defenceless man.
Ulysses, basely born, first led the way.—
Avenging pow'rs! with justice if I pray,
That fortune be their own another day!
But answer you; and in your turn relate,
What brought you, living, to the Stygian state.
Driv'n by the winds and errors of the sea,
Or did you heav'n's superior doom obey?
Or tell what other chance conducts your way,
To view, with mortal eyes, our dark retreats,
Tumults and torments of th' infernal seats."
While thus, in talk, the flying hours they pass,
The sun had finish'd more than half his race:

And they perhaps in words and tears had spent
The little time of stay which heav'n had lent:
But thus the Sibyl chides their long delay:
"Night rushes down, and headlong drives the day
'T is here, in diff'rent paths, the way divides:
The right to Pluto's golden palace guides:
The left, to that unhappy region tends,
Which to the depth of Tartarus descends—
The seat of night profound, and punish'd fiends."
Then thus Deiphobus: "O sacred maid!
Forbear to chide; and be your will obey'd.
Lo! to the sacred shadows I retire,
To pay my penance till my years expire.
Proceed, auspicious prince, with glory crown'd,
And born to better fates than I have found."
He said: and, while he said, his steps he turn'd
To sacred shadows, and in silence mourn'd.
The hero, looking on the left, espied
A lofty tow'r, and strong on ev'ry side
With treble walls, which Phlegethon surrounds,
Whose fiery flood the burning empire bounds:
And, press'd betwixt the rocks, the bellowing noise resounds.
Wide is the fronting gate, and rais'd on high
With adamantine columns, threats the sky.
Vain is the force of man, and heav'n's as vain,
To crush the pillars which the pile sustain.
Sublime on these, a tow'r of steel is rear'd,
And dire Tisiphone there keeps the ward,
Girt in her sanguine gown, by night and day,
Observant of the souls that pass the downward way.
From hence are heard the groans of ghosts, the pains
Of sounding lashes and of dragging chains.
The Trojan stood astonish'd at their cries,
And ask'd his guide, from whence those yells arise;
And what the crimes, and what the tortures were,
And loud laments that rent the liquid air.
She thus replied: "The chaste and holy race
Are all forbidden this polluted place
But Hecat, when she gave to rule the woods,
Then led me trembling thro' these dire abodes,
And taught the tortures of th' avenging gods.
These are the realms of unrelenting Fate;
And awful Rhadamanthus rules the state.
He hears and judges each committed crime;
Inquires into the manner, place, and time.
The conscious wretch must all his acts reveal,
(Loath to confess, unable to conceal,)
From the first moment of his vital breath,
To his last hour of unrepenting death.
Straight o'er the guilty ghost, the Fury shakes
The sounding whip, and brandishes her snakes,
And the pale sinner, with her sisters, takes.
Then of itself, unfolds the eternal door:
With dreadful sounds, the brazen hinges roar.
You see, before the gate, what stalking ghost
Commands the guard, what sentries keep the post.
More formidable Hydra stands within,
Whose jaws with iron teeth severely grin.
The gaping gulf low to the centre lies,
And twice as deep as earth is distant from the skies.
The rivals of the gods, the Titan race,
Here sing'd with lightning, roll within th' unfathom'd space.
Here lie th' Aloean twins, (I saw them both,)
Enormous bodies of gigantic growth;
Who dar'd in fight the Thund'rer to defy,
Affect his heaven, and force him from the sky.
Salmoneus, suffering cruel pains, I found,
For emulating Jove; the rattling sound
Of mimic thunder, and the glitt'ring blaze
Of pointed lightnings, and their forky rays.
Through Elis, and the Grecian towns he flew:
The audacious wretch four fiery coursers drew:
He wav'd a torch aloft, and, madly vain,
Sought godlike worship from a servile train.
Ambitious fool! with horny hoofs to pass
O'er hollow arches of resounding brass,
To rival thunder in its rapid course,
And imitate inimitable force!
But he, the king of heav'n, obscure on high,
Bar'd his red arm, and launching from the sky
His writhen bolt, not shaking empty smoke,
Down to the deep abyss the flaming felon struck.
Where Tityus was to see, who took his birth
From heav'n, his nursing from the foodful earth.
Here his gigantic limbs, with large embrace,
Infold nine acres of infernal space.
A rav'nous vulture, in his open'd side,
Her crooked beak and cruel talons tried;
Still for the growing liver digg'd his breast:
The growing liver still supplied the feast;
Still are his entrails fruitful to their pains;
Th' immortal hunger lasts, th' immortal food remains.
Ixion and Pirithoüs I could name,
And more Thessalian chiefs of mighty fame.
High o'er their heads a mould'ring rock is plac'd,
That promises a fall, and shakes at ev'ry blast.
They lie below on golden beds display'd;
And genial feasts, with regal pomp are made.
The queen of Furies by their side is set,
And snatches from their mouths th' untasted meat,
Which if they touch, her hissing snakes she rears,
Tossing her torch and thund'ring in their ears

Then they, who brothers' better claim disown,
Expel their parents, and usurp the throne;
Defraud their clients, and, to lucre sold,
Sit brooding on unprofitable gold—
Who dare not give, and e'en refuse to lend
To their poor kindred, or a wanting friend—
Vast is the throng of these; nor less the train
Of lustful youths, for foul adult'ry slain—
Hosts of deserters, who their honour sold,
And basely broke their faith for bribes of gold.
All these within the dungeon's depth remain,
Despairing pardon, and expecting pain.
Ask not what pains; nor further seek to know
Their process, or the forms of law below:
Some roll a mighty stone; some, laid along,
And bound with burning wires, on spokes of
wheels are hung.
Unhappy Theseus, doom'd for ever there,
Is fix'd by Fate on his eternal chair:
And wretched Phlegyas warns the world with
cries, [wise,)
(Could warning make the world more just or
'Learn righteousness, and dread th' avenging
Deities.'
To tyrants others have their countries sold,
Imposing foreign lords, for foreign gold:
Some have old laws repeal'd, new statutes made,
Not as the people pleas'd, but as they paid.
With incest some their daughter's bed profan'd.
All dar'd the worst of ills, and, what they dar'd
attain'd.
Had I a hundred mouths, a hundred tongues,
And throats of brass, inspir'd with iron lungs,
I could not half those horrid crimes repeat,
Nor half the punishments those crimes have
met.
But let us haste, our voyage to pursue:
The walls of Pluto's palace are in view,
The gate, and iron arch above:—it stands—
On anvils labour'd by the Cyclops' hands.
Before our farther way the Fates allow,
Here must we fix on high the golden bough."
She said: and through the gloomy shades they
past,
And chose the middle path.—Arriv'd at last
The prince, with living water, sprinkled o'er
His limbs and body, then approach'd the door,
Possess'd the porch, and on the front above
He fix'd the fatal bough, requir'd by Pluto's love.
These holy rites perform'd, they took their way,
Where long extended plains of pleasure lay.
The verdant fields with those of heav'n may vie,
With ether vested, and a purple sky—
The blissful seats of happy souls below:
Stars of their own, and their own suns, they
know.
Their airy limbs in sports they exercise,
And, on the green, contend the wrestler's prize.
Some, in heroic verse, divinely sing:
Others in artful measures lead the ring.
The Thracian bard, surrounded by the rest,
There stands conspicuous in his flowing vest.
His flying fingers, and harmonious quill,
Strike seven distinguish'd notes, and seven at
once they fill.
Here found they Teucer's old heroic race,
Born, better times, and happier years to grace,
Assaracus and Ilus here enjoy
Perpetual fame, with him who founded Troy.
The chief beheld their chariots from afar,
Their shining arms and coursers train'd to war.
Their lances fix'd in earth—their steeds around,
Free from their harness, graze the flowery
ground.
The love of horses which they had alive,
And care of chariots, after death survive.
Some cheerful souls were feasting on the plain;
Some did the song and some the choir maintain,
Beneath a laurel shade, where mighty Po
Mounts up to woods above, and hides his head
below.
Here patriots live, who, for their country's good,
In fighting fields, were prodigal of blood:
Priests of unblemish'd lives here make abode,
And poets worthy their inspiring god;
And searching wits, of more mechanic parts,
Who grac'd their age with new-invented arts;
Those who to worth their bounty did extend,
And those who knew that bounty to commend.
The heads of these, with holy fillets bound,
And all their temples were with garlands
crown'd.
To these the Sibyl thus her speech address'd,
And first to him surrounded by the rest—
(Tow'ring his height, and ample was his
breast.)
"Say, happy souls! divine Musæus! say,
Where lives Anchises, and where lies our way
To find the hero, for whose only sake
We sought the dark abodes, and cross'd the
bitter lake."
To this the sacred poet thus replied:
"In no fix'd place the happy souls reside,
In groves we live, and lie on mossy beds,
By crystal streams, that murmur through the
meads:
But pass yon easy hill, and thence descend;
The path conducts you to your journey's end."
This said, he led them up the mountain's brow
And shows them all the shining fields below.
They wind the hill, and through the blissful
meadows go.
But old Anchises, in a flow'ry vale,
Review'd his muster'd race, and took the tale,—
Those happy spirits, which, ordain'd by Fate,
For future being and new bodies wait—

With studious thought, observ'd th' illustrious throng
In Nature's order, as they pass'd along—
Their names, their fates, their conduct, and their care,
In peaceful senates, and successful war
He, when Æneas on the plain appears,
Meets him with open arms and falling tears.
"Welcome," he said, "the gods' undoubted race!
O long expected to my dear embrace;
Once more 't is giv'n me to behold your face!
The love and pious duty which you pay,
Have pass'd the perils of so hard a way.
'T is true, computing times, I now believ'd
The happy day approach'd; nor are my hopes deceiv'd.
What length of lands, what oceans have you pass'd,
What storms sustain'd, and on what shores been cast!
How have I fear'd your fate, but fear'd it most,
When love assail'd you on the Lybian coast."
To this, the filial duty thus replies:
"Your sacred ghost, before my sleeping eyes,
Appear'd, and often urg'd this painful enterprise.
After long tossing on the Tyrrhene sea,
My navy rides at anchor in the bay.
But reach your hand, O parent shade! nor shun
The dear embraces of your longing son!"
He said; and falling tears his face bedew:
Then thrice around his neck his arms he threw;
And thrice the flitting shadow slipp'd away,
Like winds, or empty dreams that fly the day.
Now, in a secret vale, the Trojan sees
A sep'rate grove through which a gentle breeze
Plays with a passing breath, and whispers through the trees:
And, just before the confines of the wood,
The gliding Lethe leads her silent flood.
About the boughs an airy nation flew,
Thick as the humming bees, that hunt the golden dew,
In summer's heat; on tops of lilies feed,
And creep within their bells, to suck the balmy seed:
The winged army roams the field around;
The rivers and the rocks remurmur to the sound.
Æneas wond'ring stood, then ask'd the cause,
Which to the stream the crowding people draws.
Then thus the sire: "The souls that throng the flood
Are those, to whom by Fate are other bodies ow'd:
In Lethe's lake they long oblivion taste,
Of future life secure, forgetful of the past.
Long has my soul desir'd this time and place
To set before your sight your glorious race,
That this presaging joy may fire your mind,
To seek the shores by destiny design'd."—
"O father! can it be, that souls sublime
Return to visit our terrestrial clime,
And that the gen'rous mind, releas'd by death,
Can covet lazy limbs, and mortal breath?"
Anchises then, in order, thus begun
To clear those wonders to his godlike son:
"Know, first, that heav'n, and earth's compacted frame,
And flowing waters, and the starry flame,
And both the radiant lights, one common soul
Inspires and feeds—and animates the whole.
This active mind, infus'd through all the space,
Unites and mingles with the mighty mass.
Hence men and beasts the breath of life obtain,
And birds of air, and monsters of the main
Th' ethereal vigour is in all the same;
And ev'ry soul is fill'd with equal flame—
As much as earthly limbs and gross allay
Of mortal members, subject to decay,
Blunt not the beams of heav'n and edge of day.
From this coarse mixture of terrestrial parts,
Desire and fear by turns possess their hearts,
And grief, and joy: nor can the grov'ling mind,
In the dark dungeon of the limbs confin'd,
Assert the native skies, or own its heav'nly kind;
Nor death itself can wholly wash their stains.
But long-contracted filth e'en in the soul remains.
The relics of invet'rate vice they wear;
And spots of sin obscene in ev'ry face appear.
For this are various penances enjoin'd;
And some are hung to bleach upon the wind,
Some plung'd in waters, others purg'd in fires,
Till all the dregs are drain'd, and all the rust expires.
All have their manes, and those manes bear:
The few, so cleans'd, to these abodes repair,
And breath in ample fields the soft Elysian air.
Then are they happy, when by length of time
The scurf is worn away of each committed crime;
No speck is left to their habitual stains;
But the pure ether of the soul remains.
But, when a thousand rolling years are past,
(So long their punishments and penance last,)
Whole droves of minds are, by the driving god,
Compell'd to drink the deep Lethean flood,
In large forgetful draughts, to steep the cares
Of their past labours and their irksome years,
That, unrememb'ring of its former pain,
The soul may suffer mortal flesh again."

Thus having said, the father-spirit leads
The priestess and his son through swarms of shades,
And takes a rising ground, from thence to see
The long procession of his progeny.
"Survey (pursu'd the sire) this airy throng,
As, offer'd to the view, they pass along.
These are th' Italian names, which Fate will join
With ours, and graff upon the Trojan line.
Observe the youth who first appears in sight,
And holds the nearest station to the light,
Already seems to snuff the vital air,
And leans just forward on a shining spear;
Silvius is he, thy last begotten race,
But first in order sent, to fill thy place—
An Alban name, but mix'd with Dardan blood:
Born in the covert of a shady wood,
Him fair Lavinia, thy surviving wife,
Shall breed in groves, to lead a solitary life.
In Alba he shall fix his royal seat,
And, born a king, a race of kings beget;—
Then Procas, honour of the Trojan name,
Capys, and Numitor, of endless fame.
A second Silvius after these appears—
Silvius Æneas, for thy name he bears—
For arms and justice equally renown'd;
Who, late restor'd, in Alba shall be crown'd.
How great they look! how vigorously they wield
Their weighty lances, and sustain the shield!
But they, who crown'd with oaken wreaths appear,
Shall Gabian walls and strong Fidæne rear;
Nomentum, Bola, with Pometia, found:
And raise Collatian tow'rs on rocky ground.
All these shall then be towns of mighty fame,
Though now they lie obscure, and lands without a name.
See Romulus the great, born to restore
The crown that once his injur'd grandsire wore.
This prince a priestess of our blood shall bear;
And like his sire in arms he shall appear.
Two rising crests his royal head adorn:
Born from a god, himself to godhead born,
His sire already signs him for the skies,
And marks his seat amidst the deities.
Auspicious chief! thy race, in times to come,
Shall spread the conquests of imperial Rome—
Rome whose ascending tow'rs shall heav'n invade,
Involving earth and heav'n into her shade;
High as the mother of the gods in place,
And proud, like her, of an immortal race,
Then, when in pomp she makes the Phrygian round,
With golden turrets on her temples crown'd;
A hundred gods her sweeping train supply,
Her offspring all; and all command the sky
Now fix your sight, and stand intent to see
Your Roman race, and Julian progeny.
There mighty Cæsar waits his vital hour,
Impatient for the world, and grasps his promis'd pow'r.
But next behold the youth of form divine—
Cæsar himself, exalted in his line—
Augustus, promis'd oft, and long foretold,
Sent to the realm that Saturn rul'd of old;
Born to restore a better age of gold.
Afric and India shall his pow'r obey
He shall extend his propagated sway
Beyond the solar year, without the starry way.
Where Atlas turns the rolling heav'ns around,
And his broad shoulders with their lights are crown'd.
At his foreseen approach, already quake
The Caspian kingdoms and Mæotian lake.
Their seers behold the tempest from afar;
And threat'ning oracles denounce the war.
Nile hears him knocking at his sevenfold gates,
And seeks his hidden spring, and fears his nephew's fates.
No Hercules more lands or labours knew,
Not though the brazen-footed hind he slew
Freed Erymanthus from the foaming boar,
And dipp'd his arrows in Lernæan gore;
Nor Bacchus, turning from his Indian war,
By tigers drawn triumphant in his car,
From Nysa's top descending on the plains,
With curling vines around his purple reins.
And doubt we yet through dangers to pursue
The paths of honour, and a crown in view?—
But what 's the man, who from afar appears,
His head with olive crown'd, his hand a censer bears?
His hoary beard and holy vestments bring
His lost idea back. I know the Roman king.
He shall to peaceful Rome new laws ordain,
Call'd from his mean abode, a sceptre to sustain.
Him Tullus next in dignity succeeds,
An active prince, and prone to martial deeds.
He shall his troops for fighting fields prepare,
Disus'd to toils and triumphs of the war.
By dint of sword, his crown he shall increase,
And scour his armour from the rust of peace.
Whom Ancus follows with a fawning air,
But vain within, and proudly popular.
Next view the Tarquin kings, th' avenging sword
Of Brutus, justly drawn, and Rome restor'd.
He first renews the rods and axe severe,
And gives the consuls royal robes to wear.
His sons, who seek the tyrant to sustain,
And long for arbitrary lords again,

With ignominy scourg'd in open sight,
He dooms to death deserv'd, asserting public
right.
Unhappy man! to break the pious laws
Of nature, pleading in his children's cause!
Howe'er the doubtful fact is understood,
'T is love of honour, and his country's good:
The consul, not the father, sheds the blood.
Behold Tarquatus the same track pursue;
And next the two devoted Decii view—
The Drusian line, Camillus loaded home,
With standards wellredeem'd, and foreign foes,
shall come.
The pair, you see, in equal armour shine,
Now friends below, in close embraces join:
But, when they leave the shady realms of night,
And, cloth'd in bodies, breathe your upper light,
With mortal hate each other shall pursue:
What wars, what wounds, what slaughter, shall
ensue.
From Alpine heights the father first descends;
His daughter's husband in the plain attends:
His daughter's husband arms his eastern
friends.
Embrace again my sons! be foes no more;
Nor stain your country with her children's gore!
And thou, the first, lay down thy lawless claim,
Thou, of my blood, who bear'st the Julian
name!
Another comes, who shall in triumph ride,
And to the Capitol his chariot guide,
From conquer'd Corinth, rich with Grecian
spoils.
And yet another, fam'd for warlike toils
On Argus shall impose the Roman laws,
And on the Greeks revenge the Trojan cause;
Shall drag in chains their Achillean race;
Shall vindicate his ancestors' disgrace,
And Pallas, for her violated place.
Great Cato there, for gravity renown'd,
And conq'uering Cossus goes with laurels
crown'd.
Who can omit the Gracchi? who declare
The Scipio's worth, those thunderbolts of war,
The double bane of Carthage? Who can see
Without esteem for virtuous poverty,
Severe Fabricius, or can cease t' admire
The ploughman consul in his coarse attire?
Tir'd as I am, my praise the Fabii claim;
And thou, great hero, greatest of thy name,
Ordain'd in war to save the sinking state,
And by delays, to put a stop to Fate!
Let others better mould the running mass
Of metals, and inform the breathing brass,
And soften into flesh a marble face;
Plead better at the bar; describe the skies,
And when the stars descend, and when they
rise.
But Rome! 't is thine alone, with awful sway,
To rule mankind, and make the world obey,
Disposing peace and war thy own majestic
way:
To tame the proud, thy fetter'd slave to free:—
These are imperial arts and worthy thee."
He paus'd—and, while with wond'ring eyes
they view'd
The passing spirits, thus his speech renew'd:
"See great Marcellus! how, untir'd in toils,
He moves with manly grace, how rich with
regal spoils:
He, when his country (threaten'd with alarms)
Requires his courage, and his conq'ring arms,
Shall more than once the Punic bands affright;
Shall kill the Gaulish king in single fight;
Then to the Capitol in triumph move: [Jove."
And the third spoils shall grace Feretrian
Æneas here beheld, of form divine,
A godlike youth, in glitt'ring armour shine,
With great Marcellus keeping equal pace:
But gloomy were his eyes, dejected was his
face.
He saw, and wond'ring, ask'd his airy guide,
What and of whence was he, who press'd the
hero's side?
"His son, or one of his illustrious name?
How like the former, and almost the same?
Observe the crowds that compass him around,
All gaze, and all admire, and raise a shouting
sound:
But hovering mists around his brows are spread;
And night with sable shades involves his head."
"Seek not to know, (the ghost replied, with
tears,)
The sorrows of thy sons in future years.
This youth (the blissful vision of a day)
Shall just be shown on earth, then snatch'd
away.
The gods too high had rais'd the Roman state,
Were but their gifts as permanent as great.
What groans of men shall fill the Martian Field!
How fierce a blaze his flaming pile shall yield!
What fun'ral pomp shall floating Tyber see,
When, rising from his bed, he views the sad
solemnity!
No youth shall equal hopes of glory give,
No youth afford so great a cause to grieve.
The Trojan honour, and the Roman boast,
Admir'd when living, and ador'd when lost!
Mirror of ancient faith in early youth!
Undaunted worth, inviolable truth!
No foe, unpunish'd, in the fighting field
Shall dare thee, foot to foot, with sword and
shield,
Much less in arms oppose thy matchless force,
When thy sharp spurs shall urge thy foaming
horse.

Ah! couldst thou break through Fate's severe decree,
A new Marcellus shall arise in thee!
Full canisters of fragrant lilies bring,
Mix'd with the purple roses of the spring:
Let me with fun'ral flow'rs his body strow,
This gift, which parents to their children owe,
This unavailing gift, at least I may bestow!"
Thus having said, he led the hero round
The confines of the blest Elysian ground;
Which when Anchises to his son had shown,
And fir'd his mind to mount the promis'd throne,
He tells the future wars, ordain'd by Fate;
The strength and customs of the Latian state;
The prince, and people; and forearms his care
With rules, to push his fortune, or to bear.
Two gates the silent house of Sleep adorn;
Of polish'd iv'ry this, that of transparent horn:
True visions through transparent horn arise,
Through polish'd iv'ry pass deluding lies.
Of various things discoursing as he pass'd,
Anchises hither bends his steps at last.
Then, through the gate of iv'ry he dismiss'd
His valiant offspring, and divining guest.
Straight to the ships Æneas took his way,
Embark'd his men, and skimm'd along the sea,
Still coasting, till he gain'd Caieta's bay.
At length on oozy ground his galleys moor:
Their heads are turn'd to sea, their sterns to shore.

BOOK VII.

ARGUMENT.

King Latinus entertains Æneas, and promises him his only daughter, Lavinia, the heiress of his crown. Turnus, being in love with her, favoured by her mother, and by Juno and Alecto, breaks the treaty which was made, and engages in his quarrel Mezentius, Camilla, Messapus, and many other of the neighbouring princes; whose forces, and the names of their commanders, are particularly related.

And thou, O matron of immortal fame!
Here dying, to the shore hast left thy name:
Caieta still the place is call'd from thee,
The nurse of great Æneas' infancy.
Here rest thy bones in rich Hesperia's plains;
Thy name ('t is all a ghost can have) remains.
Now, when the prince her fun'ral rites had paid,
He plough'd the Tyrrhene seas with sails display'd.
From land a gentle breeze arose by night;
Serenely shone the stars; the moon was bright;
And the sea trembled with her silver light.
Now near the shelves of Circe's shores they run,
(Circe the rich, the daughter of the sun,)
A dang'rous coast!—the goddess wastes her days
In joyous songs; the rocks resound her lays.
In spinning, or the loom, she spends the night;
And cedar brands supply her father's light.
From hence were heard, rebellowing to the main,
The roars of lions that refuse the chain,
The grunts of bristled boars, and groans of bears,
And herds of howling wolves that stun the sailors' ears.
These from their caverns, at the close of night,
Fill the sad isle with horror and affright.
Darkling they mourn their fate, whom Circe's pow'r,
(That watch'd the moon, and planetary hour,)
With words and wicked herbs, from human-kind
Had alter'd, and in brutal shapes confin'd.
Which monsters lest the Trojan's pious host
Should bear, or touch upon th' enchanted coast,
Propitious Neptune steer'd their course by night,
With rising gales, that sped their happy flight.
Supplied with these, they skim the sounding shore,
And hear the swelling surges vainly roar.
Now, when the rosy morn began to rise,
And wav'd her saffron streamer through the skies,
When Thetis blush'd in purple, not her own,
And from her face the breathing winds were blown,
A sudden silence sate upon the sea,
And sweeping oars, with struggling urge their way.
The Trojan, from the main, beheld a wood,
Which, thick with shades, and a brown horror stood.
Betwixt the trees, the Tyber took his course,
With whirlpools dimpled; and with downward force
That drove the sand along, he took his way,
And roll'd his yellow billows to the sea.
About him, and above, and round the wood,
The birds that haunt the borders of his flood,
That bath'd within, or bask'd upon his side,
To tuneful songs their narrow throats applied.
The captive gives command: the joyful train
Glide through the gloomy shade, and leave the main.
Now, Erato! thy poet's mind inspire,
And fill his soul with thy celestial fire.
Relate what Latium was; her ancient kings;
Declare the past and present state of things,
When first the Trojan fleet Ausonia sought,
And how the rivals lov'd, and how they fought.

These are my theme, and how the war began,
And how concluded by the godlike man:
For I shall sing of battles, blood, and rage,
Which princes and their people did engage;
And haughty souls, that, mov'd with mutual hate,
In fighting fields pursu'd and found their fate;
That rous'd the Tyrrhene realm with loud alarms,
And peaceful Italy involv'd in arms.
A larger scene of action is display'd;
And, rising hence, a greater work is weigh'd.
Latinus, old and mild, had long possess'd
The Latian sceptre, and his people bless'd;
His father Faunus: a Laurentian dame
His mother; fair Marica was her name.
But Faunus came from Picus: Picus drew
His birth from Saturn, if records be true.
Thus king Latinus, in the third degree,
Had Saturn author of his family.
But this old peaceful prince, as heav'n decreed,
Was bless'd with no male issue to succeed:
His sons in blooming youth were snatch'd by fate:
One only daughter heir'd the royal state.
Fir'd with her love, and with ambition led,
The neighb'ring princes court her nuptial bed.
Among the crowd, but far above the rest,
Young Turnus to the beauteous maid address'd.
Turnus, for high descent and graceful mien,
Was first, and favour'd by the Latian queen:
With him she strove to join Lavinia's hand;
But dire portents the purpos'd match withstand.
Deep in the palace, of long growth, there stood
A laurel's trunk, a venerable wood;
Where rites divine were paid; whose holy hair
Was kept and cut with superstitious care.
This plant, Latinus, when his town he wall'd,
Then found, and from the tree Laurentium call'd:
And last, in honour of his new abode,
He vow'd the laurel to the laurel's god.
It happen'd once, (a boding prodigy!)
A swarm of bees, that cut the liquid sky,
(Unknown from whence they took their airy flight,)
Upon the topmost branch in clouds alight;
There, with their clasping feet, together clung,
And a long cluster from the laurel hung.
An ancient augur prophesied from hence:
"Behold on Latian shores a foreign prince!
From the same parts of heaven his navy stands,
To the same parts on earth: his army lands;
The town he conquers, and the tow'r commands."
Yet more, when fair Lavinia fed the fire
Before the gods, and stood beside her sire,
(Strange to relate!) the flames, involv'd in smoke
Of incense, from the sacred altar broke,
Caught her dishevell'd hair, and rich attire:
Her crown and jewels crackled in the fire:
From thence the fuming trail began to spread,
And lambent glories danc'd about her head.
This new portent the seer with wonder views,
Then pausing, thus his prophecy renews:
"The nymph, who scatters flaming fires around,
Shall shine with honour—shall herself be crown'd;
But, caus'd by her irrevocable fate,
War shall the country waste, and change the state."
Latinus, frighted at this dire ostent,
For counsel to his father Faunus went,
And sought the shades renown'd for prophecy,
Which near Albunea's sulph'rous fountain lie.
To those the Latian and the Sabine land
Fly, when distress'd: and thence relief demand.
The priest on skins of off'rings takes his ease,
And nightly visions in his slumber sees:
A swarm of thin aerial shapes appears,
And, flutt'ring round his temples, deafs his ears.
These he consults, the future fates to know,
From powers above, and from the fiends below.
Here for the god's advice Latinus flies,
Off'ring a hundred sheep for sacrifice;
Their woolly fleeces, as the rites requir'd,
He laid beneath him, and to rest retir'd.
No sooner were his eyes in slumber bound,
When from above, a more than mortal sound
Invades his ears; and thus the vision spoke:
"Seek not, my seed, in Latian bands to yoke
Our fair Lavinia, nor the gods provoke.
A foreign son upon the shore descends,
Whose martial fame from pole to pole extends.
His race, in arms and arts of peace renown'd,
Not Latium shall contain, nor Europe bound:
'T is theirs what'er the sun surveys around."
These answers, in the silent night receiv'd,
The king himself divulg'd, the land believ'd:
The fame through all the neighb'ring nations flew,
When now the Trojan navy was in view.
Beneath a shady tree, the hero spread
His table on the turf, with cakes of bread;
And, with his chiefs, on forest fruits he fed.
They sate; and, (not without the god's command,)
Their homely fare despatch'd, the hungry band
Invade their trenchers next, and soon devour,
To mend the scanty meal, their cakes of flour,
Ascanius this observ'd, and smiling said,
'See! we devour the plates on which we fed."

The speech had omen, that the Trojan race
Should find repose, and this the time and place.
Æneas took the word, and thus replies:—
(Confessing fate, with wonder in his eyes:)
"All hail, O earth! all hail, my household gods!
Behold the destin'd place of your abodes!
For thus Anchises prophesied of old,
And this our fatal place of rest foretold:
'When, on a foreign shore, instead of meat,
By famine forc'd, your trenchers you shall eat,
Then ease your weary Trojans will attend,
And the long labours of your voyage end.
Remember on that happy coast to build:
And with a trench enclose the fruitful field.'
This was that famine, this the fatal place,
Which ends the wand'ring of our exil'd race.
Then on to-morrow's dawn, your care employ,
To search the land, and where the cities lie,
And what the men; but give this day to joy.
Now pour to Jove; and, after Jove is blest,
Call great Anchises to the genial feast:
Crown high the goblets with a cheerful draught:
Enjoy the present hour; adjourn the future thought."

Thus having said, the hero bound his brows
With leafy branches, then perform'd his vows;
Adoring first the genius of the place,
Then Earth, the mother of the heav'nly race,
The nymphs, and native godheads yet unknown,
And Night, and all the stars that gild her sable throne,
And ancient Cybel, and Idæan Jove;
And last his sire below, and mother-queen above.

Then heaven's high monarch thunder'd thrice aloud
And thrice he shook aloft a golden cloud.
Soon through the joyful camp a rumour flew,
The time was come their city to renew.
Then ev'ry brow with cheerful green is crown'd;
The feasts are doubled, and the bowls go round.

When next the rosy morn disclos'd the day,
The scouts to sev'ral parts divide their way,
To learn the natives' names, their towns explore,
The coast, and tendings of the crooked shore:
Here Tyber flows, and here Numicus stands;
Here warlike Latians hold the happy lands.

The pious chief who sought by peaceful ways
To found his empire, and his town to raise,
A hundred youths from all his train selects,
And to the Latian court their course directs,
(The spacious palace where their prince resides,)
And all their heads with wreaths of olive hides,
To go commission'd to require a peace,
And carry presents to procure access.

Thus while they speed their pace, the prince designs
The new-elected seat, and draws the lines.
The Trojans round the place a rampire cast,
And palisades about the trenches plac'd.

Meantime the train, proceeding on their way,
From far the town and lofty tow'rs survey:
At length approach the walls. Without the gate,
They see the boys and Latian youth debate
The martial prizes on the dusty plain:
Some drive the cars, and some the coursers rein;
Some bend the stubborn bow for victory;
And some with darts their active sinews try.
A posting messenger, despatch'd from hence,
Of this fair troop advis'd their aged prince,
That foreign men, of mighty stature, came;
Uncouth their habit, and unknown their name.
The king ordains their entrance, and ascends
His regal seat, surrounded by his friends.
The palace built by Picus, vast and proud,
Supported by a hundred pillars stood,
And round encompass'd with a rising wood.
The pile o'erlook'd the town, and drew the sight,
Surpris'd at once with rev'rence and delight.
There kings receiv'd the marks of sov'reign pow'r:
In state the monarchs march'd; the lictors bore
Their awful axes and the rods before.
Here the tribunal stood, the house of pray'r;
And here the sacred senators repair;
All at large tables, in long order set,
A ram their off'ring, and a ram their meat.
Above the portal, carv'd in cedar wood,
Plac'd in their ranks, their godlike grandsire stood—
Old Saturn, with his crooked scythe, on high:
And Italus, that led the colony;
And ancient Janus, with his double face,
And bunch of keys, the porter of the place.
There stood Sabinus, planter of the vines:
On a short pruning-hook his head reclines,
And studiously surveys his gen'rous wines;
Then warlike kings, who for their country fought,
And honourable wounds from battle brought.
Around the posts hung helmets, darts, and spears,
And captive chariots, axes, shields, and bars
And broken beaks of ships, the trophies of their wars.
Above the rest, as chief of all the band,
Was Picus plac'd; a buckler in his hand;
His other wav'd a long divining wand.
Girt in his Gabine gown the hero sate,
Yet could not with his art avoid his fate:
For Circe long had lov'd the youth in vain,
Till love refus'd converted to disdain:

Then, mixing powerful herbs, with magic art
She chang'd his form, who could not change his heart;
Constrain'd him in a bird, and made him fly,
With party-colour'd plumes, a chatt'ring pie.
In this high temple, on a chair of state,
The seat of audience, old Latinus sate;
Then gave admission to the Trojan train;
And thus with pleasing accents he began:
"Tell me, ye Trojans—for that name you own;
Nor is your course upon our coasts unknown—
Say what you seek, and whither were your bound?
Were you by stress of weather cast aground?
(Such dangers of the sea are often seen,
And oft befall to miserable men;)
Or come your shipping in our ports to lay,
Spent and disabled in so long a way?
Say what you want: the Latians you shall find
Not forc'd to good-ness, but by will inclin'd.
For since the time of Saturn's holy reign,
His hospitable customs we retain:
I call to mind, (but time the tale has worn,)
Th' Aurunci told, that Dardanus, though born
On Latian plains, yet sought the Phrygian shore,
And Samothracia, Samos call'd before.
From Tuscan Corythum he claim'd his birth:
But after, when exempt from mortal earth,
From thence ascended to his kindred skies,
A god, and, as a god, augments their sacrifice."
He said.—Ilioneus made this reply;
O king, of Faunus' royal family!
Nor wintry winds to Latium forc'd our way,
Nor did the stars our wand'ring course betray.
Willing we sought your shores; and, hither bound,
The port, so long desir'd, at length we found;
From our sweet homes and ancient realms expell'd;
Great as the greatest that the sun beheld.
The god began our line, who rules above;
And, as our race, our king descends from Jove:
And hither are we come by his command,
To crave admission in your happy land.
How dire a tempest from Mycenæ pour'd,
Our plains, our temples, and our town, devour'd;
What was the waste of war, what fierce alarms
Shook Asia's crown with European arms;
E'en such have heard, if any such there be,
Whose earth is bounded by the frozen sea;
And such as, born beneath the burning sky
And sultry sun, betwixt the tropics lie.
From that dire deluge, through the wat'ry waste,
(Such length of years, such various perils past,)
At last escap'd, to Latium we repair,
To beg what you without your want may spare—
The common water, and the common air;
Sheds which ourselves will build, and mean abodes,
Fit to receive and serve our banish'd gods.
Nor our admission shall your realm disgrace,
Nor length of time our gratitude efface—
Besides what endless honour you shall gain,
To save and shelter Troy's unhappy train.
Now, by my sov'reign, and his fate, I swear—
Renown'd for faith in peace, for force in war—
Oft our alliance other lands desir'd,
And what we seek of you, of us requir'd.
Despise not then, that in our hands we bear
These holy boughs, and sue with words of pray'r.
Fate and the gods, by their supreme command,
Have doom'd our ships to seek the Latian land.
To these abodes, our fleet Apollo sends;
Here Dardanus was born, and hither tends;
Where Tuscan Tyber rolls with rapid force,
And where Numicus opes his holy source.
Besides, our prince presents, with his request,
Some small remains of what his sire possess'd.
This golden charger, snatch'd from burning Troy,
Anchises did in sacrifice employ:
This royal robe and this tiara wore
Old Priam, and this golden sceptre bore,
In full assemblies, and in solemn games:
These purple vests were weav'd by Dardan dames."

Thus while he spoke, Latinus roll'd around
His eyes, and fix'd a while upon the ground.
Intent he seem'd and anxious in his breast:
Not by the sceptre mov'd, or kingly vest,
But pond'ring future things, of wond'rous weight—
Succession, empire, and his daughter's fate.
On these he mus'd within his thoughtful mind;
And then revolv'd what Faunus had divin'd
This was the foreign prince, by fate decreed
To share his sceptre, and Lavinia's bed:
This was the race that sure portents foreshew
To sway the world, and land and sea subdue.
At length he rais'd his cheerful head, and spoke:
"The pow'rs," said he, "the pow'rs we both invoke,
To you, and yours, and mine, propitious be,
And firm our purpose with our augury!
Have what you ask: your presents I receive;
Land where and when you please, with ample leave:
Partake and use my kingdom as your own:
All shall be yours while I command the crown.
And, if my wish'd alliance please your king,
Tell him he should not send the peace, but bring:
Then let him not a friend's embraces fear:
The peace is made when I behold him here.

Besides this answer, tell my royal guest,
I add to his commands my own request:
One only daughter heirs my crown and state,
Whom not our oracles, nor heav'n, nor fate,
Nor frequent prodigies, permit to join
With any native of th' Ausonian line.
A foreign son-in-law shall come from far,
(Such is our doom,) a chief renown'd in war,
Whose race shall bear aloft the Latian name,
And through the conquer'd world diffuse our fame.
Himself to be the man the fates require,
I firmly judge, and, what I judge, desire."
He said, and then on each bestow'd a steed.
Three hundred horses, in high stables fed,
Stood ready, shining all, and smoothly dress'd:
Of these he chose the fairest and the best,
To mount the Trojan troop. At his command,
The steeds caparison'd with purple stand,
With golden trappings, glorious to behold,
And champ betwixt their teeth the foaming gold.
Then to his absent guest the king decreed
A pair of coursers born of heav'nly breed,
Who from their nostrils breath'd etherial fire,
Whom Circe stole from her celestial sire,
By substituting mares produc'd on earth,
Whose wombs conceiv'd a more than mortal birth.
These draw the chariot which Latinus sends;
And the rich present to the prince commends.
Sublime on stately steeds the Trojans borne,
To their expecting lord with peace return.
But jealous Juno, from Pachynus' height,
As she from Argos took her airy flight,
Beheld, with envious eyes, this hateful sight.
She saw the Trojan and his joyful train
Descend upon the shore, desert the main,
Design a town, and, with unhop'd success,
Th' ambassadors return with promis'd peace.
Then, pierc'd with pain, she shook her haughty head,
Sigh'd from her inward soul, and thus she said:
"O hated offspring of my Phrygian foes!
O fates of Troy, which Juno's fates oppose!
Could they not fall unpitied on the plain,
But, slain, revive, and taken, 'scape again?
When execrable Troy in ashes lay,
Through fires and swords and seas they forc'd their way.
Then vanquish'd Juno must in vain contend,
Her rage disarm'd, her empire at an end!
Breathless and tir'd, is all my fury spent?
Or does my glutted spleen at length relent?
As if 't were little from their town to chase,
I through the seas pursu'd their exil'd race:
Engag'd the heav'ns, oppos'd the stormy main:
But billows roar'd, and tempests rag'd in vain.
What have my Scyllas and my Syrtes done,
When these they overpass, and those they shun?
On Tyber's shores they land, secure of fate,
Triumphant o'er the storms of Juno's hate!
Mars could in mutual blood the Centaurs bathe;
And Jove himself gave way to Cynthia's wrath,
Who sent the tusky boar to Calydon?
(What great offence had either people done?)
But I, the consort of the Thunderer
Have wag'd a long and unsuccessful war,
With various arts and arms in vain have toil'd,
And by a mortal man at length am foil'd!
If native pow'r prevail not, shall I doubt
To seek for needful succour from without?
If Jove and heav'n my just desires deny,
Hell shall the pow'r of heav'n and Jove supply.
Grant that the Fates have firm'd, by their decree,
The Trojan race to reign in Italy:
At least I can defer the nuptial day,
And, with protracted wars, the peace delay:
With blood the dear alliance shall be bought,
And both the people near destruction brought,
So shall the son-in-law and father join,
With ruin, war, and waste of either line.
O fatal maid! thy marriage is endow'd
With Phrygian, Latian, and Rutulian blood!
Bellona leads thee to thy lover's hand:
Another queen brings forth another brand,
To burn with foreign fires another land!
A second Paris, diff'ring but in name,
Shall fire his country with a second flame."
Thus having said, she sinks beneath the ground,
With furious haste, and shoots the Stygian sound,
To rouse Alecto from th' infernal seat
Of her dire sisters, and their dark retreat.
This Fury, fit for her intent, she chose,
One who delights in wars and human woes.
E'en Pluto hates his own misshapen race;
Her sister Furies fly her hideous face;
So frightful are the forms the monster takes,
So fierce the hissings of her speckled snakes.
Her Juno finds, and thus inflames her spite:
"O virgin daughter of eternal Night,
Give me this once thy labour, to sustain
My right, and execute my just disdain.
Let not the Trojans, with a feign'd pretence,
Of proffer'd peace, delude the Latian prince.
Expel from Italy that odious name,
And let not Juno suffer in her fame.
'T is thine to ruin realms, o'erturn a state,
Betwixt the dearest friends to raise debate,
And kindle kindred blood to mutual hate.
Thy hand o'er towns the fun'ral torch displays,
And forms a thousand ills ten thousand ways.

Now shake, from out thy fruitful breast, the seeds
Of envy, discord, and of cruel deeds:
Confound the peace establish'd, and prepare
Their souls to hatred, and their hands to war."
Smear'd as she was with black Gorgonean blood,
The Fury sprang above the Stygian flood:
And on her wicker wings, sublime through night,
She to the Latian palace took her flight;
There sought the queen's apartment, stood before
The peaceful threshold, and besieg'd the door.
Restless Amata lay, her swelling breast
Fir'd with disdain for Turnus dispossess'd,
And the new nuptials of the Trojan guest.
From her black bloody locks the Fury shakes
Her darling plague, the fav'rite of her snakes;
With her full force she threw the pois'nous dart,
And fix'd it deep within Amata's heart,
That, thus envenom'd, she might kindle rage,
And sacrifice to strife her house and husband's age.
Unseen, unfelt, the fiery serpent skims
Betwixt her linen and her naked limbs,
His baneful breath, inspiring as he glides,
Now like a chain around her neck he rides,
Now like a fillet to her head repairs,
And with his circling volumes folds her hairs.
At first the silent venom slid with ease,
And seiz'd her cooler senses by degrees;
Then, ere th' infected mass was fir'd too far,
In plaintive accents she began the war,
And thus bespoke her husband: "Shall," she said,
"A wand'ring prince enjoy Lavinia's bed?
If nature pleads not in a parent's heart,
I dry my tears, and pity her desert.
I know my dearest lord, the time will come,
You would in vain reverse your cruel doom,
The faithless pirate soon will set to sea,
And bear the royal virgin far away!
A guest like him, a Trojan guest before,
In show of friendship sought the Spartan shore,
And ravish'd Helen from her husband bore.
Think on a king's inviolable word;
And think on Turnus, her once plighted lord.
To this false foreigner you give your throne,
And wrong a friend, a kinsman, and a son.
Resume your ancient care; and if the god,
Your sire, and you, resolve on foreign blood,
Know all are foreign, in a larger sense,
Not born your subjects or deriv'd from hence,
Then, if the line of Turnus you retrace,
He springs from Inacus of Argive race."
But, when she saw her reasons idly spent,
And could not move him from his fix'd intent,
She flew to rage; for now the snake possess'd
Her vital parts and poison'd all her breast.
She raves, she runs with a distracted pace,
And fills, with horrid howls, the public place.
And, as young striplings whip the top for sport,
On the smooth pavement of an empty court;
The wooden engine flies and whirls about,
Admir'd, with clamours, of the beardless rout;
They lash aloud; each other they provoke,
And lend their little souls at ev'ry stroke:
Thus fares the queen; and thus her fury blows
Amidst the crowd, and kindles as she goes.
Not yet content, she strains her malice more,
And adds new ills to those contriv'd before:
She flies the town, and, mixing with the throng
Of madding matrons, bears the bride along,
Wand'ring through woods and wilds and devious ways,
And with these arts the Trojan match delays.
She feign'd the rites of Bacchus; cried aloud,
And to the buxom god the virgin vow'd.
"Evoe! O Bacchus!" thus began the song;
And "Evoe!" answer'd all the female throng,
"O virgin, worthy thee alone!" she cried;
"O worthy thee alone!" the crew replied.
"For thee she feeds her hair, she leads thy dance,
And with thy winding ivy wreaths her lance."
Like fury seiz'd the rest: the progress known,
All seek the mountains, and forsake the town:
All clad in skins of beasts, the javelin bear,
Give to the wanton winds their flowing hair;
And shrieks and shoutings rend the suff'ring air.
The queen herself, inspir'd with rage divine,
Shook high above her head a flaming pine,
Then roll'd her haggard eyes around the throng,
And sung, in Turnus' name, the nuptial song:
"Iô! ye Latian dames, if any here
Hold your unhappy queen, Amata, dear;
If there be here," she said, "who dare maintain
My right, nor think the name of mother vain;
Unbind your fillets, loose your flowing hair,
And orgies and nocturnal rites prepare."
Amata's breast the Fury thus invades,
And fires with rage, amid the sylvan shades.
Then, when she found her venom spread so far,
The royal house embroil'd in civil war,
Rais'd on her dusky wings she cleaves the skies,
And seeks the palace where young Turnus lies.
His town as fame reports, was built of old
By Danae, pregnant with almighty gold,
Who fled her father's rage, and, with a train
Of following Argives, through the stormy main,
Driv'n by the southern blasts, was fated here to reign.
'Twas Ardua once: now Ardea's name it bears;
Once a fair city, now consum'd with years.

Here, in his lofty palace, Turnus lay,
Betwixt the confines of the night and day,
Secure in sleep.—The Fury laid aside
Her looks and limbs, and with new methods tried
The foulness of the infernal form to hide.
Propp'd on a staff, she takes a trembling mien:
Her face is furrow'd, and her front obscene;
Deep-dinted wrinkles on her cheeks she draws;
Sunk are her eyes, and toothless are her jaws;
Her hoary hair with holy fillets bound
Her temples with an olive wreath are crown'd.
Old Chalybe, who kept the sacred fane
Of Juno, now she seem'd, and thus began,
Appearing in a dream to rouse the careless man.
"Shall Turnus then such endless toils sustain
In fighting fields, and conquer towns in vain?
Win, for a Trojan head to wear the prize,
Usurp thy crown, enjoy thy victories?
The bride and sceptre, which thy blood has bought,
The king transfers; and foreign heirs are sought!
Go now, deluded man, and seek again
New toils, new dangers, on the dusty plain!
Repel the Tuscan foes; their city seize
Protect the Latians in luxurious ease!
This dream all-powerful Juno sends; I bear
Her mighty mandates; and her words you hear.
Haste! arm your Ardeans; issue to the plain;
With faith to friend, assault the Trojan train:
Their thoughtless chiefs, their painted ships that lie
In Tyber's mouth, with fire and sword destroy.
The Latian king, unless he shall submit,
Own his old promise, and his new forget—
Let him, in arms, the pow'r of Turnus prove,
And learn to fear whom he disdains to love.
For such is heaven's command."—The youthful prince
With scorn replied, and made this bold defence:
"You tell me, mother, what I knew before,
The Phrygian fleet is landed on the shore.
I neither fear nor will provoke the war:
My fate is Juno's most peculiar care.
But time has made you dote, and vainly tell
Of arms imagin'd in your lonely cell.
Go! be the temple and the gods your care:
Permit to men the thought of peace and war.
These haughty words Alecto's rage provoke;
And frighted Turnus trembled as she spoke.
Her eyes grow stiffen'd, and with sulphur burn;
Her hideous looks and hellish form return;
Her curling snakes with hissings fill the place
And open all the furies of her face:
Then, darting fire from her malignant eyes,
She cast him backwards as he strove to rise,
And, ling'ring sought to frame some new replies.
High on her head she rears two twisted snakes
Her chains she rattles, and her whip she shakes
And, churning bloody foam, thus loudly speaks:
"Behold whom time has made to dote, and tell
Of arms imagin'd in her lonely cell!
Behold the Fates' infernal minister!
War, death, destruction, in my hand I bear."
Thus having said, her smould'ring torch, impress'd
With her full force, she plung'd into his breast
Aghast he wak'd, and starting from his bed,
Cold sweat, in clammy drops, his limbs o'erspread.
"Arms! arms!" he cries: "my sword and shield prepare!"
He breathes defiance, blood, and mortal war.
So, when with crackling flames a caldron fries,
The bubbling waters from the bottom rise;
Above the brims they force their fiery way;
Black vapours climb aloft, and cloud the day,
The peace polluted thus, a chosen band
He first commissions to the Latian land,
In threat'ning embassy; then rais'd the rest,
To meet in arms th' intruding Trojan guest,
To force the foes from the Lavinian shore,
And Italy's endanger'd peace restore.
Himself alone an equal match he boasts,
To fight the Phrygian and Ausonian hosts.
The gods invok'd, the Rutuli prepare
Their arms, and warn each other to the war.
His beauty these, and those his blooming age,
The rest his house and his own fame engage.
While Turnus urges thus his enterprise,
The Stygian Fury to the Trojans flies;
New frauds invents, and takes a steepy stand,
Which overlooks the vale with wide command
Where fair Ascanius and his youthful train,
With horns and hounds, a hunting match ordain,
And pitch their toils around the shady plain.
The Fury fires the pack; they snuff, they vent,
And feed their hungry nostrils with the scent.
'T was of a well-grown stag, whose antlers rise
High o'er his front, his beams invade the skies.
From this light cause, th' infernal maid prepares
The country churls to mischief, hate, and wars.
The stately beast the two Tyrrhidæ bred,
Snatch'd from his dam, and the tame youngling fed.
Their father Tyrrheus did his fodder bring,
Tyrrheus, chief ranger to the Latian king:
Their sister Silvia cherish'd with her care
The little wanton, and did wreaths prepare
To hang his budding horns; with ribands tied
His tender neck, and comb'd his silken hide,
And bath'd his body. Patient of command
In time he grew, and growing, us'd to hand,

He waited at his master's board for food;
Then sought his savage kindred in the wood;
Where grazing all the day, at night he came
To his known lodgings, and his country dame.
This household beast, that us'd the woodland grounds,
Was view'd at first by the young hero's hounds,
As down the stream he swam, to seek retreat
In the cool waters, and to quench his heat.
Ascanius, young, and eager of his game,
Soon bent his bow, uncertain in his aim:
But the dire fiend the fatal arrow guides,
Which pierc'd his bowels through his panting sides.
The bleeding creature issues from the floods,
Possess'd with fear, and seeks his known abodes.
His old familiar hearth, and household gods.
He falls; he fills the house with heavy groans,
Implores their pity, and his pain bemoans.
Young Silvia beats her breast, and cries aloud
For succour from the clownish neighbourhood:
The churls assemble; for the fiend, who lay
In the close woody covert, urg'd their way.
One with a brand yet burning from the flame,
Arm'd with a knotty club another came;
What'er they catch or find, without their care,
Their fury makes an instrument of war.
Tyrrheus, the foster-father of the beast,
Then clench'd a hatchet in his horny fist,
But held his hand from the descending stroke,
And left his wedge within the cloven oak,
To whet their courage, and their rage provoke.
And now the goddess, exercis'd in ill,
Who watch'd an hour to work her impious will,
Ascends the roof, and to her crooked horn,
Such as was then by Latian shepherds borne,
Adds all her breath. The rocks and woods around,
And mountains, tremble at the infernal sound.
The sacred lake of Trivia from afar,
The Veline fountains, and sulphureous Nar,
Shake at the baleful blast, the signal of the war.
Young mothers wildly stare, with fear possess'd,
And strain their helpless infants to their breast.
The clowns, a boist'rous, rude, ungovern'd crew,
With furious haste to the loud summons flew.
The pow'rs of Troy, then issuing on the plain,
With fresh recruits their youthful chief sustain:
Not theirs a raw and unexperienc'd train,
But a firm body of embattled men.
At first, while fortune favour'd neither side,
The fight with clubs and burning brands was tried:
But now, both parties reinforc'd, the fields
Are bright with flaming swords and brazen shields.
A shining harvest either host displays,
And shoots against the sun with equal rays.
Thus when a black-brow'd gust begins to rise,
White foam at first on the curl'd ocean fries;
Then roars the main, the billows mount the skies;
Till, by the fury of the storm full blown,
The muddy bottom o'er the clouds is thrown.
First Almon falls, old Tyrrheus' eldest care,
Pierc'd with an arrow from the distant war:
Fix'd in his throat the flying weapon stood,
And stopp'd his breath, and drank his vital blood.
Huge heaps of slain around the body rise:
Among the rest, the rich Galesus lies,
A good old man, while peace he preach'd in vain,
Amidst the madness of th' unruly train:
Five herds, five bleating flocks, his pastures fill'd;
His lands a hundred yoke of oxen till'd.
Thus, while in equal scales their fortune stood,
The Fury bath'd them in each other's blood;
Then having fix'd the fight, exulting flies,
And bears fulfill'd her promise to the skies.
To Juno thus she speaks: "Behold! 'tis done,
The blood already drawn, the war begun;
The discord is complete; nor can they cease
The dire debate, nor you command the peace.
Now, since the Latian and the Trojan brood
Have tasted vengeance, and the sweets of blood;
Speak, and my power shall add this office more:
The neighb'ring nations of th' Ausonian shore
Shall hear the dreadful rumour, from afar,
Of arm'd invasion, and embrace the war."
Then Juno thus: "The grateful work is done,
The seeds of discord sow'd, the war begun:
Frauds, fears, and fury, have possess'd the state,
And fix'd the causes of a lasting hate.
A bloody Hymen shall th' alliance join
Betwixt the Trojan and Ausonian line:
But thou with speed to night and hell repair;
For not the gods, nor angry Jove, will bear
Thy lawless wand'ring walks in upper air.
Leave what remains to me." Saturnia said:
The sullen fiend her sounding wings display'd,
Unwilling left the light, and sought the nether shade.
In midst of Italy, well known to fame,
There lies a lake (Amsanctus is the name)
Below the lofty mounts: on either side
Thick forests the forbidden entrance hide
Full in the centre of the sacred wood
An arm arises of the Stygian flood,

Which, breaking from beneath with bellowing sound,
Whirls the black waves and rattling stones around.
Here Pluto pants for breath from out his cell,
And opens wide the grinning jaws of hell.
To this infernal lake the Fury flies;
Here hides her hated head, and frees the lab'ring skies.
Saturnian Juno now with double care
Attends the fatal process of the war.
The clowns, return'd from battle, bear the slain,
Implore the gods, and to their king complain.
The corpse of Almon, and the rest, are shown:
Shrieks, clamours, murmurs, fill the frighted town.
Ambitious Turnus in the press appears,
And, aggravating crimes, augments their fears;
Proclaims his private injuries aloud,
A solemn promise made, and disavow'd;
A foreign son is sought, and a mix'd mongrel brood.
Then they, whose mothers, frantic with their fear,
In woods and wilds the flags of Bacchus bear,
And lead his dances with dishevell'd hair,
Increase the clamour, and the war demand,
(Such was Amata's int'rest in the land,)
Against the public sanctions of the peace,
Against all omens of their ill success.
With fates averse, the rout in arms resort,
To force their monarch, and insult the court.
But, like a rock unmov'd, a rock that braves
The raging tempest and the rising waves—
Propp'd on himself he stands: his solid sides
Wash off the seaweeds, and the sounding tides—
So stood the pious prince unmov'd, and long
Sustain'd the madness of the noisy throng.
But, when he found that Juno's pow'r prevail'd,
And all the methods of cool council fail'd,
He calls the gods to witness their offence,
Disclaims the war, asserts his innocence.
"Hurried by fate," he cries, "and borne before
A furious wind, we leave the faithful shore!
O more than madmen! you yourselves shall bear
The guilt of blood and sacrilegious war:
Thou, Turnus, shalt atone it by thy fate,
And pray to heav'n for peace, but pray too late;
For me, my stormy voyage at an end,
I to the port of death securely tend.
The fun'ral pomp which to your kings you pay,
Is all I want, and all you take away."
He said no more, but, in his walls confin'd,
Shut out the woes which he too well divin'd:
Nor with the rising storm would vainly strive;
But left the helm, and let the vessel drive.
A solemn custom was observ'd of old,
Which Latium held, and now the Romans hold,
Their standard when in fighting fields they rear
Against the fierce Hyrcanians, or declare
The Scythian, Indian, or Arabian war—
Or from the boasting Parthians would regain
Their eagles lost, in Carræ's bloody plain.
Two gates of steel (the name of Mars they bear,
And still are worshipp'd with religious fear)
Before his temple stand, the dire abode,
And the fear'd issues of the furious god,
Are fenc'd with brazen bolts; without the gates,
The wary guardian Janus doubly waits.
Then, when the sacred senate votes the wars,
The Roman consul their decree declares,
And in his robes the sounding gates unbars.
The youth in military shouts arise,
And the loud trumpets break the yielding skies.
These rites, of old by sov'reign princes us'd,
Were the king's office: but the king refus'd,
Deaf to their cries, nor would the gates unbar
Of sacred peace, or loose th' imprison'd war;
But hid his head, and safe from loud alarms,
Abhorr'd the wicked ministry of arms.
Then heaven's imperious queen shot down from high;
At her approach the brazen hinges fly;
The gates are forc'd, and ev'ry falling bar;
And, like a tempest, issues out the war.
The peaceful cities of th' Ausonian shore,
Lull'd in their ease, and undisturb'd before,
Are all on fire; and some, with studious care,
Their restive steeds in sandy plains prepare;
Some their soft limbs in painful marches try,
And war is all their wish, and arms their general cry.
Part scour their rusty shields with seam; and part
New grind the blunted axe, and point the dart;
With joy they view the waving ensigns fly,
And hear the trumpets' clangour pierce the sky.
Five cities forge their arms—th' Atinian pow'rs
Antemnæ, Tiber with her lofty towers,
Ardea the proud, the Crustumerian town
All these of old were places of renown.

Some hammer helmets for the fighting field;
Some twine young sallows to support the shield,
The corslet some, and some the cuishes mould;
With silver plated, and with ductile gold.
The rustic honours of the scythe and share
Give place to swords and plumes, the pride of war.
Old falchions are new temper'd in the fires:
The sounding trumpet ev'ry soul inspires.
The word is giv'n; with eager speed they lace
The shining head-piece, and the shield embrace.
The neighing steeds are to the chariots tied;
The trusty weapon sits on ev'ry side.
And now the mighty labour is begun,
Ye muses open all your Helicon;
Sing you the chiefs that sway'd th' Ausonian land,
Their arms, and armies under their command;
What warriors in our ancient clime were bred;
What soldiers follow'd, and what heroes led.
For well you know, and can record alone,
What fame to future times conveys but darkly down.
Mezentius first appear'd upon the plain:
Scorn sate upon his brows, and sour disdain,
Defying earth and heav'n. Etruria lost,
He brings to Turnus' aid his baffled host.
The charming Lausus, full of youthful fire,
Rode in the ranks, and next his sullen sire;
To Turnus only second in the grace
Of manly mien, and features of the face:
A skilful horseman, and a huntsman bred,
With fates averse a thousand men he led:
His sire unworthy of so brave a son;
Himself well worthy of a happier throne.
Next Aventinus drives his chariot round
The Latian plains, with palms and laurels crown'd:
Proud of his steeds, he smokes along the field;
His father's hydra fills his ample shield:
A hundred serpents hiss about the brims;
The son of Hercules he justly seems,
By his broad shoulders and gigantic limbs—
Of heav'nly part, and part of earthly blood,
A mortal woman mixing with a god.
For strong Alcides, after he had slain
The triple Geryon, drove from conquer'd Spain
His captive herds: and, thence in triumph led,
On Tuscan Tyber's flow'ry banks they fed.
Then, on mount Aventine, the son of Jove
The priestess Rhea found, and forc'd to love.
For arms, his men long piles and javelins bore;
And poles with pointed steel their foes in battle gore.
Like Hercules himself, his son appears
In savage pomp: a lion's hide he wears:
About his shoulders hangs the shaggy skin;
The teeth and gaping jaws severely grin.
Thus like the god, his father, homely drest,
He strides into the hall, a horrid guest.
Then two twin-brothers from fair Tibur came,
(Which from their brother Tiburs took the name,)
Fierce Cornas and Catillus, void of fear:
Arm'd Argive horse they lead, and in the front appear,
Like cloud-born Centaurs, from the mountain's height,
With rapid course descending to the fight:
They rush along, the rattling woods give way;
The branches bend before their own sweepy sway.
Nor was Præneste's founder wanting there,
Whom fame reports the son of Mulciber:
Found in the fire, and foster'd in the plains.
A shepherd and a king at once he reigns,
And leads to Turnus' aid his country swains,
His own Præneste sends a chosen band,
With those who plough Saturnia's Gabine land;
Besides the succour which cold Anien yields,
The rocks of Hernicus, and dewy fields,
Anignia fat, and farther Amasene—
A num'rous rout, but all of naked men:
Nor arms they wear, nor swords and bucklers wield,
Nor drive the chariot through the dusty field,
But whirl from leathern slings huge balls of lead;
And spoils of yellow wolves adorn their head:
The left foot naked, when they march to fight;
But in a bull's raw hide they sheath the right.
Messapus next, (great Neptune was his sire,)
Secure of steel, and fated from the fire,
In pomp appears, and with his ardour warms
A heartless train, unexercis'd in arms:
The just Faliscans he to battle brings,
And those who live where late Ciminus springs,
And where Feronia's grove and temple stands,
Who till Fescennian or Flavinian lands:
All these in order march, and marching sing
The warlike actions of their sea-born king;

Like a long team of snowy swans on high,
Which clap their wings, and cleave the liquid sky,
When, homeward from their wat'ry pastures borne,
They sing, and Asia's lakes their notes return.
Not one, who heard their music from afar,
Would think these troops an army train'd to war,
But flocks of fowl, that, when the tempest roar,
With their hoarse gabbling seek the silent shore.

Then Clausus came, who led a num'rous band
Of troops imbodied from the Sabine land,
And, in himself alone, an army brought.
'T was he the noble Claudian race begot,
The Claudian race, ordain'd, in times to come,
To share the greatness of imperial Rome.
He led the Cures forth of old renown
Mutuscans from their olive-bearing town,
And all th' Eretrian pow'rs; besides a band
That follow'd from Velinum's dewy land,
And Amiternian troops, of mighty fame,
And mountaineers, that from Severus came,
And from the craggy cliffs of Tetrica,
And those where yellow Tyber takes his way,
And where Himella's wanton waters play.
Casperia sends her arms, with those that lie
By Fabaris, and fruitful Foruli:
The warlike aids of Horta next appear,
And the cold Nursians come to close the rear,
Mix'd with the natives borne of Latine blood
Whom Allia washes with her fatal flood.
Not thicker billows beat the Libyan main,
When pale Orion sets in wintry rain,
Nor thicker harvest on rich Hermus rise,
Or Lycian fields, when Phœbus burns the skies,
Than stand these troops: their bucklers ring around;
Their trampling turns the turf, and shakes the solid ground.

High in his chariot then Halesus came,
A foe by birth to Troy's unhappy name:
From Agamemnon born—to Turnus' aid,
A thousand men the youthful hero led,
Who till the Massic soil, for wine renown'd,
And fierce Auruncans from their hilly ground;
And those who live by Sidicinian shores,
And where with shoaly fords Vulturnus roars;
Cales' and Osca's old inhabitants,
And rough Saticulans, inur'd to wants.
Light demi-lances from afar they throw,
Fasten'd with leathern thongs, to gall the foe.
Short crooked swords in closer fight they wear
And on their warding arm light bucklers bear.

Nor Œbalus, shalt thou be left unsung
From nymph Se[illegible] and old Telon sprung.
Who then in Teleboan Capri reign'd;
But that short isle th' ambitious youth disdain'd,
And o'er Campania stretch'd his ample sway,
Where swelling Sarnus seeks the Tyrrhene sea—
O'er Batulum, and where Abella sees,
From her high tow'rs, the harvest of her trees.
And these (as was the Teuton use of old)
Wield brazen swords, and brazen bucklers hold;
Sling weighty stones when from afar they fight;
Their casques are cork, a cov'ring thick and light.

Next these in rank, the warlike Ufens went,
And led the mountain troops that Nursia sent.
The rude Æquiculæ his rule obey'd;
Hunting their sport, and plund'ring was their trade.
In arms they plough'd, to battle still prepar'd:
Their soil was barren, and their hearts were hard.

Umbro the priest, the proud Marrubians led,
By king Archippus sent to Turnus' aid;
And peaceful olives crown'd his hoary head.
His wand and holy words, the viper's rage,
And venom'd wounds of serpents could assuage.
He, when he pleas'd with powerful juice to steep
Their temples, shut their eyes in pleasing sleep.
But vain were Martian herbs, and magic art,
To cure the wound giv'n by the Dardan dart
Yet this untimely fate, th' Angitian woods
In sighs remurmur'd to the Fucine floods.

The son of fam'd Hippolytus was there,
Fam'd as his sire, and, as his mother fair;
Whom in Egerian groves Aricia bore,
And nurs'd his youth along the marshy shore,
Where great Diana's peaceful altars flame,
In fruitful fields; and Virbius was his name
Hippolytus, as old records have said,
Was by his stepdame sought to share her bed:
But, when no female arts his mind could move,
She turn'd to furious hate her impious love.
Torn by wild horses on the sandy shore,
Another's crime th' unhappy hunter bore;
Glutting his father's eyes with guiltless gore.
But Chaste Diana, who his death deplor'd,
With Æsculapian herbs his life restor'd:
When Jove, who saw from high, with just disdain,
The dead inspir'd with vital breath again,
Struck to the centre, with his flaming dart.
Th' unhappy founder of the godlike art.
But Trivia kept in secret shades alone,
Her care, Hippolytus, to fate unknown
And call'd him Verbius, in th' Egerian grove,
Where then he liv'd secure but safe from Jove.

For this, from Trivia's temple and her wood,
Are coursers driv'n, who shed their master's blood,
Affrighted by the monsters of the flood.
His son, the second Virbius, yet retain'd
His father's art, and warrior steeds he rein'd.
Amid the troops, and like the leading god,
High o'er the rest in arms, the graceful Turnus rode:
A triple pile of plumes his crest adorn'd,
On which, with belching flames, Chimæra burn'd:
The more the kindled combat rises higher,
The more with fury burns the blazing fire.
Fair Iö grac'd his shield; but Iö now
With horns exalted stands, and seems to low—
A noble charge! Her keeper by her side,
To watch her walks, her hundred eyes applied;
And on the brims, her sire, the wat'ry god,
Roll'd from his silver urn his crystal flood.
A cloud of foot succeeds, and fills the fields
With swords, and pointed spears, and clatt'ring shields;
Of Argive, and of old Sicanian bands,
And those who plough the rich Rutulian lands;
Auruncan youth, and those Sacrana yields,
And the proud Lubicans, with painted shields,
And those who near Numician streams reside,
And those whom Tibur's holy forests hide,
Or Circe's hills from the main land divide,
Where Ufens glides along the lowly lands,
Or the black water of Pomptina stands.
Last from the Volscians fair Camilla came,
And led her warlike troops, a warrior dame:
Unbred to spinning, in the loom unskill'd,
She chose the nobler Pallas of the field.
Mix'd with the first, the fierce virago fought,
Sustain'd the toils of arms, the dangers sought;
Outstripp'd the winds in speed upon the plain,
Flew o'er the field, nor hurt the bearded grain:
She swept the seas, and, as she skimm'd along,
Her flying feet, unbath'd, on billows hung.
Men, boys, and women, stupid with surprise,
Where'er she passes fix their wond'ring eyes:
Longing they look, and gaping at the sight,
Devour her o'er and o'er with vast delight;
Her purple habit sits with such a grace
On her smooth shoulders, and so suits her face:
Her head with ringlets of her hair is crown'd;
And in a golden caul the curls are bound.
She shakes her myrtle jav'lin; and, behind
Her Lycian quiver dances in the wind.

BOOK VIII.

ARGUMENT.

The war being now begun, both the generals make all possible preparations. Turnus sends to Diomedes. Æneas goes in person to beg succours from Evander and the Tuscans. Evander receives him kindly, furnishes him with men, and sends his son Pallas with him. Vulcan, at the request of Venus, makes arms for her son Æneas, and draws on his shield the most memorable actions of his posterity.

When Turnus had assembled all his pow'rs,
His standard planted on Laurentum's tow'rs,
When now the sprightly trumpet, from afar
Had giv'n the signal of approaching war,
Had rous'd the neighing steeds to scour the fields,
While the fierce riders clatter'd on their shields,
Trembling with rage, the Latian youth prepare
To join th' allies, and headlong rush to war.
Fierce Ufens, and Messapus led the crowd,
With bold Mezentius, who blasphem'd aloud.
These through the country took their wasteful course,
The fields to forage, and to gather force.
Then Venulus to Diomede they send,
To beg his aid, Ausonia to defend,
Declare the common danger, and inform
The Grecian leader of the growing storm:
"Æneas, landed on the Latian coast,
With banish'd gods, and with a baffled host,
Yet now aspir'd to conquest of the state,
And claim'd a title from the gods and fate;
What num'rous nations in his quarrel came,
And how they spread his formidable name,
What he design'd, what mischiefs might arise,
If fortune favour'd his first enterprise,
Was left for him to weigh, whose equal fears
And common int'rest was involv'd in theirs."
While Turnus and th' allies thus urge the war,
The Trojan, floating in a flood of care,
Beholds the tempest which his foes prepare.
This way and that he turns his anxious mind;
Thinks and rejects the counsels he design'd;
Explores himself in vain, in ev'ry part,
And gives no rest to his distracted heart.
So when the sun by day, or moon by night,
Stike on the polish'd brass their trembling light,
The glitt'ring species here and there divide,
And cast their dubious beams from side to side.
Now on the walls, now on the pavement play,
And to the ceiling flash the glaring day.
'T was night: and weary nature lull'd asleep
The birds of air, and fishes of the deep,
And beasts, and mortal men. The Trojan chief

Was laid on Tyber's banks, oppress'd with grief,
And found in silent slumber late relief.
Then, through the shadows of the poplar wood,
Arose the father of the Roman flood,
An azure robe was o'er his body spread,
A wreath of shady reeds adorn'd his head:
Thus, manifest to sight, the god appear'd,
And with these pleasing words his sorrow cheer'd:
"Undoubted offspring of ethereal race,
O long expected in this promis'd place! [gods,
Who, through the foes, hast borne thy banish'd
Restor'd them to their hearths, and old abodes—
This is thy happy home, the clime where fate
Ordains thee to restore the Trojan state.
Fear not! the war shall end in lasting peace,
And all the rage of haughty Juno cease.
And that this nightly vision may not seem
Th' effect of fancy, or an idle dream,
A sow beneath an oak shall lie along,
All white herself, and white her thirty young.
When thirty rolling years have run their race,
Thy son Ascanius, on this empty space,
Shall build a royal town, of lasting fame,
Which from this omen shall receive the name.
Time shall approve the truth.—For what remains,
And how with sure success to crown your pains,
With patience next attend. A banish'd band,
Driv'n with Evander from th' Arcadian land,
Have planted here, and plac'd on high their walls;
Their town the founder Pallenteum calls,
Deriv'd from Pallas, his great grandsire's name,
But the fierce Latians old possession claim,
With war infesting the new colony:
These make thy friends, and on their aid rely.
To thy free passage I submit my streams.
Wake, son of Venus, from thy pleasing dreams;
And, when the setting stars are lost in day,
To Juno's pow'r thy just devotion pay;
With sacrifice the wrathful queen appease:
Her pride at length shall fall, her fury cease.
When thou return'st victorious from the war,
Perform thy vows to me with grateful care.
The god am I, whose yellow water flows
Around these fields, and fattens as it goes:
Tyber my name—among the rolling floods,
Renown'd on earth, esteem'd among the gods.
This is my certain seat. In times to come,
My waves shall wash the walls of mighty Rome." [spoke,
He said; and plung'd below. While yet he
His dream Æneas and his sleep forsook.
He rose, and, looking up, beheld the skies
With purple blushing, and the day arise.
Then water in his hollow palm he took
From Tyber's flood, and thus the pow'rs bespoke:
"Laurentian nymphs, by whom the streams are fed,
And father Tyber, in thy sacred bed,
Receive Æneas, and from danger keep.
Whatever fount, whatever holy deep,
Conceals thy wat'ry stores—where'er they rise,
And, bubbling from below, salute the skies—
Thou, king of horned floods, whose plenteous urn
Suffices fatness to the fruitful corn,
For this thy kind compassion of our woes,
Shalt share my morning song, and ev'ning vows.
But oh! be present to thy people's aid,
And firm the gracious promise thou hast made."
Thus having said, two galleys, from his stores,
With care he chooses, mans, and fits with oars.
Now on the shore the fatal swine is found—
Wond'rous to tell!—She lay along the ground.
Her well-fed offspring at her udders hung;
She white herself, and white her thirty young.
Æneas takes the mother and her brood;
And all on Juno's altar are bestow'd.
The following night, and the succeeding day,
Propitious Tyber smooth'd his wat'ry way:
He roll'd his river back, and pois'd he stood,
A gentle swelling, and a peaceful flood.
The Trojans mount their ships; they put from shore,
Borne on the waves, and scarcely dip an oar.
Shouts from the land give omen to their course;
And the pitch'd vessels glide with easy force.
The woods and waters wonder at the gleam
Of shields, and painted ships that stem the stream.
One summer's night and one whole day they pass
Betwixt the green-wood shades, and cut the liquid glass.
The fiery sun had finish'd half his race,
Look'd back, and doubted in the middle space,
When they from far beheld the rising tow'rs,
The tops of sheds, and shepherds' lowly bow'rs,
Thin as they stood, which, then of homely clay,
Now rise in marble, from the Roman sway.
These cots (Evander's kingdom, mean and poor)
The Trojan saw, and turn'd his ships to shore.
'T was on a solemn day: th' Arcadian states,
The king and prince, without the city gates,
Then paid their off'rings in a sacred grove
To Hercules, the warrior son of Jove.
Thick clouds of rolling smoke involve the skies;
And fat of entrails on his altar fries.

But, when they saw the ships that stemm'd the flood,
And glitter'd through the covert of the wood,
They rose with fear, and left th' unfinish'd feast,
Till dauntless Pallas reassur'd the rest
To pay the rites. Himself without delay
A jav'lin seiz'd, and singly took his way.
Then gain'd a rising ground, and call'd from far:
"Resolve me, strangers, whence, and what you are;
Your bus'ness here; and bring you peace or war?"
High on the stern Æneas took his stand,
And held a branch of olive in his hand,
While thus he spoke: "The Phyrgians' arms you see,
Expell'd from Troy, provok'd in Italy
By Latian foes, with war unjustly made—
At first affianc'd, and at last betray'd,
This message bear: The Trojans and their chief
Bring holy peace, and beg the king's relief."
Struck with so great a name, and all on fire,
The youth replies: "Whatever you require,
Your fame exacts. Upon our shores descend,
A welcome guest, and, what you wish, a friend.
He said, and downward hasting to the strand,
Embrac'd the stranger prince, and join'd his hand.
Conducted to the grove, Æneas broke
The silence first, and thus the king bespoke:
"Best of the Greeks! to whom by fate's command,
I bear these peaceful branches in my hand—
Undaunted I approach you, though I know
Your birth is Grecian, and your land my foe:
From Atreus though your ancient lineage came,
And both the brother kings your kindred claim:
Yet my self-conscious worth, your high renown,
Your virtue, through the neighb'ring nations blown,
Our fathers' mingled blood, Apollo's voice,
Have led me hither, less by need than choice.
Our father Dardanus, as fame has sung,
And Greeks acknowledge, from Electra sprung:
Electra from the loins of Atlas came—
Atlas whose head sustains the starry frame.
Your sire is Mercury, whom long before
On cold Cyllene's top fair Maia bore.
Maia the fair, on fame if we rely,
Was Atlas' daughter, who sustains the sky.
Thus from one common source our streams divide:
Ours is the Trojan, yours th' Arcadian side.
Rais'd by these hopes, I sent no news before,
Nor ask'd your leave, nor did your faith implore;
But come, without a pledge, my own ambassador.
The same Rutulians, who with arms pursue
The Trojan race, are equal foes to you.
Our host expell'd, what further force can stay
The victor troops from universal sway?
Then will they stretch their pow'r athwart the land,
And either sea from side to side command.
Receive our offer'd faith, and give us thine:
Ours is a generous and experienc'd line:
We want not hearts nor bodies for the war:
In council cautious, and in fields we dare."
He said: and, while he spoke, with piercing eyes
Evander view'd the man with vast surprise—
Pleas'd with his action, ravish'd with his face;
Then answer'd briefly, with a royal grace:
"O valiant leader of the Trojan line,
In whom the features of thy father shine?
How I recall Anchises! how I see
His motion, mien, and all my friend, in thee!
Long though it be, 'tis fresh within my mind,
When Priam to his sister's court design'd
A welcome visit, with a friendly stay,
And through th' Arcadian kingdom took his way.
Then past a boy, the callow down began
To shade my chin, and call me first a man.
I saw the shining train with vast delight
And Priam's goodly person pleas'd my sight:
But great Anchises, far above the rest
With awful wonder fir'd my youthful breast.
I long'd to join, in friendship's holy bands,
Our mutual hearts, and plight our mutual hands.
I first accosted him: I sued, I sought,
And, with a loving force, to Pheneus brought.
He gave me, when at length constrain'd to go,
A Lycian quiver and a Gnossian bow,
A vest embroider'd, glorious to behold,
And two rich bridles, with their bits of gold,
Which my son's coursers in obedience hold.
The league you ask, I offer, as your right;
And when to-morrow's sun reveals the light,
With swift supplies you shall be sent away.
Now celebrate with us this solemn day,
Whose holy rites admit no long delay.
Honour our annual feast; and take your seat,
With friendly welcome, at a friendly treat."
Thus having said, the bowls remov'd (for fear)
The youth replac'd, and soon restor'd the cheer.
On sods of turf he set the soldiers round:
A maple throne, rais'd higher from the ground,
Receiv'd the Trojan chief; and o'er the bed
A lion's shaggy hide, for ornament they spread.
The loaves were serv'd in canisters: the wine
In bowls; the priest renew'd the rites divine:
Broil'd entrails are the food, and beefs continued chine.
But, when the rage of hunger was repress'd,
Thus spoke Evander to his royal guest

"These rites, these altars, and this feast, O king,
From no vain fears or superstition spring,
Or blind devotion, or from blinder chance,
Or heady zeal, or brutal ignorance:
But sav'd from danger, with a grateful sense,
The labours of a god we recompense.
See, from afar, yon rock that mates the sky;
About whose feet such heaps of rubbish lie;
Such undigested ruin; bleak and bare,
How desert now it stands, expos'd in air!
'T was once a robber's den, enclos'd around
With living stone, and deep beneath the ground.
The monster Cacus, more than half a beast,
This hold, impervious to the sun, possess'd.
The pavement ever foul with human gore;
Heads, and their mangled members, hung the door.
Vulcan this plague begot: and, like his sire,
Black clouds he belch'd and flakes of livid fire.
Time, long expected, eas'd us of our load,
And brought the needful presence of a god.
Th' avenging force of Hercules, from Spain,
Arriv'd in triumph, from Geryon slain:—
Thrice liv'd the giant, and thrice liv'd in vain.
His prize, the lowing herds, Alcides drove
Near Tyber's banks, to graze the shady grove.
Allur'd with hope of plunder, and intent
By force to rob, by fraud to circumvent,
The brutal Cacus, as by chance they stray'd,
Four oxen thence, and four fair kine, convey'd.
And, lest the printed footsteps might be seen,
He dragg'd them backwards to his rocky den.
The tracks averse a lying notice gave,
And led the searcher backward from the cave.
Meantime the herdsman hero shifts his place
To find fresh pasture and untrodden grass.
The beasts, who miss'd their mates, fill'd all around
With bellowings: and the rocks restor'd the sound.
One heifer, who had heard her love complain,
Roar'd from the cave, and made the project vain.
Alcides found the fraud: with rage he shook,
And toss'd about his head his knotted oak.
Swift as the winds, or Scythian arrow's flight,
He climb'd, with eager haste, the aerial height.
Then first we saw the monster mend his pace:
Fear in his eyes, and paleness in his face,
Confess'd the god's approach. Trembling he springs,
As terror had increas'd his feet with wings;
Nor stay'd for stairs: but down the depth he threw
His body: on his back the door he drew—
(The door a rib of living rock: with pains
His father hew'd it out, and bound with chains:)
He broke the heavy links, the mountain clos'd,
And bars and levers to his foe oppos'd.
The wretch had hardly made his dungeon fast,
The fierce avenger came with bounding haste;
Survey'd the mouth of the forbidden hold;
And here and there his raging eyes he roll'd.
He gnash'd his teeth; and thrice he compass'd round
With winged speed the circuit of the ground.
Thrice at the cavern's mouth he pull'd in vain;
And, panting, thrice desisted from his pain:
A pointed, flinty rock, all bare and black,
Grew gibbous from behind the mountain's back,
Owls, ravens, all ill omens of the night,
Here built their nests, and hither wing'd their flight.
The leaning head hung threat'ning o'er the flood,
And nodded to the left. The hero stood
Averse, with planted feet, and from the right,
Tugg'd at the solid stone with all his might.
Thus heav'd, the fix'd foundations of the rock
Gave way: heaven echo'd at the rattling shock.
Tumbling, it chok'd the flood: on either side
The banks leap backward, and the streams divide:
The sky shrunk upward with unusual dread;
And trembling Tyber div'd beneath his bed.
The court of Cacus stands reveal'd to sight:
The cavern glares with new-admitted light.
So the pent vapours, with a rumbling sound,
Heave from below, and rend the hollow ground;
A sounding flaw succeeds; and, from on high,
The gods with hate behold the nether sky:
The ghosts repine at violated night,
And curse th' invading sun, and sicken at the sight.
The graceless monster, caught in open day,
Enclos'd, and in despair to fly away,
Howls horrible from underneath, and fills
His hollow palace with unmanly yells.
The hero stands above, and from afar
Plies him with darts, and stones, and distant war.
He from his nostrils, and huge mouth, expires
Black clouds of smoke, amidst his father's fires;
Gath'ring, with each repeated blast, the night,
To make uncertain aim, and erring sight.
The watchful god then plunges from above,
And, where in thickest waves, the sparkles drove,
There lights; and wades through fumes, and gropes his way,
Half sing'd, half stifled, till he grasps his prey.
The monster spewing fruitless flames, he found;
He squeez'd his throat; he writh'd his neck around,
And in a knot his crippled members bound;

Then from their sockets tore his burning eyes:
Roll'd on a heap, the breathless robber lies.
The doors, unbarr'd, receive the rushing day;
And thorough lights disclose the ravish'd prey;
The bulls, redeem'd, breathe open air again.
Next, by the feet they drag him from his den.
The wond'ring neighbourhood, with glad surprise,
Beheld his shagged breast, his giant size,
His mouth that flames no more, and his extinguish'd eyes.
From that auspicious day, with rites divine,
We worship at the hero's holy shrine.
Portitius first ordain'd these annual vows:
As priests were added the Pinarian house,
Who rais'd this altar in the sacred shade,
Where honours, ever due, for ever shall be paid.
For these deserts, and this high virtue shown,
Ye warlike youths, your heads with garlands crown:
Fill high the goblets with a sparkling flood;
And with deep draughts invoke our common god."
This said, a double wreath Evander twin'd;
And poplars black and white his temples bind.
Then brims his ample bowl. With like design
The rest invoke the gods, with sprinkled wine.
Meantime the sun descended from the skies,
And the bright ev'ning star began to rise.
And now the priests, Portitius at their head,
In skins of beasts involv'd, the long procession led;
Held high the flaming tapers in their hands,
As custom had prescrib'd their holy bands;
Then with a second course the tables load,
And with full chargers offer to the god.
The Salii sing, and 'cense his altars round
With Saban smoke, their heads with poplar bound—
One choir of old, another of the young,
To dance, and bear the burden of the song.
The lay records the labours, and the praise,
And all th' immortal acts of Hercules:
First, how the mighty babe, when swath'd in bands,
The serpent strangled with his infant hands;
Then, as in years and matchless force he grew,
Th' Œchalian walls, and Trojan, overthew.
Besides a thousand hazards they relate,
Procur'd by Juno's and Eurystheus' hate.
"Thy hands, unconqur'd hero, could subdue
The cloud-born Centaurs, and the monster crew:
Nor thy resistless arm the bull withstood,
Nor he the roaring terror of the wood.
The triple porter of the Stygian seat,
With lolling tongue, lay fawning at thy feet,
And, seiz'd with fear, forgot his mangled meat
Th' infernal water trembled at thy sight;
Thee, god! no face of dangers could affright;
Not huge Typhœus, nor th' unnumber'd snake,
Increas'd with hissing heads, in Lerna's lake.
Hail, Jove's undoubted son! an added grace
To heaven and the great author of thy race;
Receive the grateful off'rings which we pay,
And smile propitious on the solemn day!"
In numbers thus they sung: above the rest,
The den and death of Cacus crown the feast.
The woods to hollow vales convey the sound;
The vales to hills; and hills the notes rebound.
The rites perform'd, the cheerful train retire.
Betwixt young Pallas and his aged sire,
The Trojan pass'd, the city to survey;
And pleasing talk beguil'd the tedious way.
The stranger cast around his curious eyes,
New objects viewing still with new surprise;
With greedy joy inquires of various things,
And acts and monuments of ancient kings.
Then thus the founder of the Roman tow'rs:
"These woods were first the seat of Sylvan pow'rs,
Of Nymphs and Fauns, and savage men who took
Their birth from trunks of trees and stubborn oak.
Nor laws they knew, nor manners, nor the care
Of lab'ring oxen, nor the shining share,
Nor arts of gain, nor what they gain'd to spare.
Their exercise the chase: the running flood
Supplied their thirst; the trees supplied their food.
Then Saturn came, who fled the pow'r of Jove,
Robb'd of his realms, and banish'd from above.
The men, dispers'd on hills, to towns he brought,
And laws ordain'd, and civil customs taught,
And Latium call'd the land where safe he lay
From his unduteous son, and his usurping sway.
With his mild empire, peace and plenty came,
And thence the golden times deriv'd their name.
A more degen'rate, and discolour'd age
Succeeded this, with avarice and rage.
Th' Ausonians then, and bold Sicanians, came
And Saturn's empire often chang'd the name.
Then kings—gigantic Tybris and the rest—
With arbitrary sway the land opprest;
For Tyber's flood was Albula before,
Till from the tyrant's fate, his name it bore.
I last arriv'd, driv'n from my native home,
By fortune's pow'r, and fate's resistless doom.
Long toss'd on seas, I sought this happy land,
Warn'd by my mother nymph, and call'd by heav'n's command."
Thus, walking on, he spoke and show'd the gate,
Since call'd Carmental by the Roman state;

Where stood an altar, sacred to the name
Of old Carmenta, the prophetic dame,
Who to her son foretold th' Ænean race,
Sublime in fame, and Rome's imperial place;—
Then shows the forest, which, in after-times,
Fierce Romulus, for perpetrated crimes,
A sacred refuge made;—with this, the shrine
Where Pan below the rock had rites divine;—
Then tells of Argus' death, his murder'd guest,
Whose grave and tomb his innocence attest.
Thence, to the steep Tarpeian rock he leads—
Now roof'd with gold, then thatch'd with homely reeds.
A rev'rent fear (such superstition reigns
Among the rude) ev'n then possess'd the swains. [not tell—
Some god, they knew—what god, they could
Did there amidst the sacred horror dwell. [saw
Th' Arcadians thought him Jove; and said they
The mighty Thund'rer with majestic awe,
Who shook his shield, and dealt his bolts around,
And scatter'd tempests on the teeming ground.
Then saw two heaps of ruins, (once they stood
Two stately towns, on either side the flood,)
Saturnia's and Janiculum's remains;
And either place the founder's name retains.
Discoursing thus together, they resort,
Where poor Evander kept his country court.
They view'd the ground of Rome's litigious hall;
(Once oxen low'd, where now the lawyers bawl;)
Then stooping, through the narrow gate they press'd,
When thus the king bespoke his Trojan guest:
"Mean as it is, this palace, and this door,
Receiv'd Alcides, then a conqueror.
Dare to be poor: accept our homely food,
Which feasted him; and emulate a god."
Then underneath a lowly roof he led
The weary prince, and laid him on a bed;
The stuffing, leaves, with hides of bears o'erspread.

Now night had shed her silver dews around,
And with her sable wings embrac'd the ground,
When love's fair goddess, anxious for her son,
(New tumults rising, and new wars begun,)
Couch'd with her husband in his golden bed,
With these alluring words invokes his aid—
And, that her pleasing speech his mind may move,
Inspires each accent with the charms of love.
"While cruel fate conspir'd with Grecian pow'rs
To level with the ground the Trojan tow'rs,
I ask'd not aid th' unhappy to restore,
Nor did the succour of thy skill implore,
Nor urg'd the labours of my lord in vain,
A sinking empire longer to sustain,
Though much I ow'd to Priam's house, and more
The danger of Æneas did deplore.
But now, by Jove's command, and Fate's decree,
His race is doom'd to reign in Italy;
With humble suit I beg thy needful art,
O still propitious pow'r, that rul'st my heart
A mother kneels a suppliant for her son.
By Thetis and Aurora thou wert won
To forge impenetrable shields, and grace
With fated arms a less illustrious race.
Behold what haughty nations are combin'd
Against the relics of the Phrygian kind,
With fire and sword my people to destroy,
And conquer Venus twice, in conq'ring Troy."
She said; and straight her arms, of snowy hue,
About her unresolving husband threw.
Her soft embraces soon infuse desire:
His bones and marrow sudden warmth inspire;
And all the godhead feels the wonted fire.
Not half so swift the rattling thunder flies,
Or forky lightnings flash along the skies.
The goddess, proud of her successful wiles,
And conscious of her form, in secret smiles.
Then thus the pow'r obnoxious to her charms,
Panting, and half dissolving in her arms:
"Why seek you reasons for a cause so just,
Or your own beauties or my love distrust?
Long since, had you requir'd my helpful hand,
Th' artificer and art you might command,
To labour arms for Troy: nor Jove, nor Fate,
Confin'd their empire to so short a date.
And, if you now desire new wars to wage,
My skill I promise, and my pains engage.
Whatever melting metal can conspire,
Or breathing bellows, or the forming fire,
Is freely yours: your anxious fears remove,
And think no task is difficult to love."
Trembling he spoke; and, eager of her charms,
He snatch'd the willing goddess to his arms;
Till, in her lap infus'd, he lay possess'd
Of full desire, and sunk to pleasing rest.
Now when the night her middle race had rode,
And his first slumber had refresh'd the god—
The time when early housewives leave the bed,
When living embers on the hearth are spread,
Supply the lamp, and call the maids to rise;—
With yawning mouths and with half open'd eyes
They ply the distaff by the winking light,
And to their daily labour add the night:
Thus frugally they earn their children's bread,
And uncorrupted keep their nuptial bed—
Not less concern'd, nor at a later hour,
Rose from his downy couch the forging pow'r.

Sacred to Vulcan's name, an isle there lay,
Betwixt Sicilia's coasts and Lipare,
Rais'd high on smoking rocks; and deep below
In hollow caves the fires of Ætna glow.

The Cyclops here their heavy hammers deal:
Loud strokes, and hissings of tormented steel,
Are heard around: the boiling waters roar;
And smoky flames through fuming tunnels soar.
Hither the father of the fire, by night,
Through the brown air precipitates his flight.
On their eternal anvils here he found
The brethren beating, and the blows go round:
A load of pointless thunder now there lies
Before their hands to ripen for the skies:
These darts, for angry Jove, they daily cast—
Consum'd on mortals with prodigious waste.
Three rays of writhen rain, of fire three more,
Of winged southern winds and cloudy store
As many parts, the dreadful mixture frame;
And fears are added, and avenging flame.
Inferior ministers, for Mars, repair
His broken axle-trees, and blunted war,
And send him forth again with furbish'd arms,
To wake the lazy war with trumpets' loud alarms.
The rest refresh the scaly snakes that fold
The shield of Pallas, and renew their gold.
Full on the crest the Gorgon's head they place,
With eyes that roll in death, and with distorted face.
"My sons!" said Vulcan, "set your tasks aside:
Your strength and master-skill must now be tried.
Arms for a hero forge,—arms that require
Your force, your speed, and all your forming fire."
He said. They set their former work aside,
And their new toils with eager haste divide.
A flood of molten silver, brass, and gold,
And deadly steel, in the large furnace roll'd:
Of this, their artful hands a shield prepare,
Alone sufficient to sustain the war.
Sev'n orbs within a spacious round they close.
One stirs the fire, and one the bellows blows.
The hissing steel is in the smithy drown'd;
The grot with beaten anvils groans around.
By turns, their arms advance in equal time:
By turns, their hands descend, and hammers chime.
They turn the glowing mass with crooked tongs:
The fiery work proceeds, with rustic songs.
While, at the Lemnian god's command, they urge
Their labours thus, and ply th' Æolian forge,
The cheerful morn salutes Evander's eyes,
And songs of chirping birds invite to rise.
He leaves his lowly bed: his buskins meet
Above his ankles; sandals sheath his feet:
He sets his trusty sword upon his side,
And o'er his shoulder throws a panther's hide.
Two menial dogs before their master press'd.
Thus clad, and gurded thus, he seeks his kingly guest.
Mindful of promis'd aid he mends his pace?
But meets Æneas in the middle space.
Young Pallas did his father's steps attend;
And true Achates waited on his friend.
They join their hands: a secret seat they choose:
Th' Arcadian first their former talk renews:
"Undaunted prince! I never can believe
The Trojan empire lost, while you survive.
Command th' assistance of a faithful friend:
But feeble are the succours I can send.
Our narrow kingdom here the Tyber bounds;
The other side the Latian state surrounds,
Insults our walls, and wastes our fruitful grounds.
But mighty nations I prepare to join
Their arms with yours, and aid your just design.
You come, as by your better genius sent;
And Fortune seems to favour your intent.
Not far from hence, there stands a hilly town,
Of ancient building, and of high renown,
Torn from the Tuscans by the Lydian race,
Who gave the name of Cære to the place,
Once Agyllina call'd. It flourish'd long,
In pride of wealth and warlike people strong,
Till curs'd Mezentius in a fatal hour,
Assum'd the crown, with arbitrary pow'r.
What words can paint those execrable times,
The subjects' suff'rings, and the tyrant's crimes?
That blood, those murders, O ye gods! replace
On his own head, and on his impious race!
The living and the dead, at his command,
Were coupled, face to face, and hand to hand,
Till, chok'd with stench, in loath'd embraces tied,
The ling'ring wretches pin'd away and died.
Thus plung'd in ills, and meditating more—
The people's patience tried, no longer bore
The raging monster; but with arms beset
His house, and vengeance and destruction threat.
They fire his palace: while the flame ascends,
They force his guards, and execute his friends.
He cleaves the crowd, and, favour'd by the night,
To Turnus' friendly court directs his flight.
By just revenge the Tuscans set on fire,
With arms, their king to punishment require:
Their num'rous troops, now muster'd on the strand,
My counsel shall submit to your command.
Their navy swarms upon the coasts: they cry
To hoist their anchors; but the gods deny,
An ancient augur, skill'd in future fate,
With these foreboding words, restrains their hate:

"Ye brave in arms, ye Lydian blood, the flow'r
Of Tuscan youth, and choice of all their pow'r,
Whom just revenge against Mezentius arms,
To seek your tyrant's death by lawful arms!
Know this: no native of our land may lead
This powerful people; seek a foreign head."
Aw'd with these words, in camps they still
abide, [guide.
And wait with longing looks their promis'd
Tarchon, the Tuscan chief, to me has sent
Their crown, and ev'ry regal ornament:
The people join their own with his desire;
And all my conduct, as their king, require.
But the chill blood, that creeps within my veins,
And age, and listless limbs unfit for pains,
And a soul, conscious of its own decay,
Have forc'd me to refuse imperial sway.
My Pallas were more fit to mount the throne,
And should, but he 's a Sabine mother's son,
And half a native; but in you, combine
A manly vigour and a foreign line. [way,
Where Fate and smiling Fortune show the
Pursue the ready path to sov'reign sway.
The staff of my declining days, my son,
Shall make your good or ill success his own;
In fighting fields, from you shall learn to dare,
And serve the hard apprenticeship of war;
Your matchless courage, and your conduct view:
And early shall begin t' admire and copy you.
Besides, two hundred horse he shall command—
Though few, a warlike and well chosen band.
These in my name are listed; and my son
As many more has added in his own."
Scarce had he said: Achates and his guest,
With downcast eyes, their silent grief express'd;
Who, short of succours, and in deep despair,
Shook at the dismal prospect of the war.
But his bright mother, from a breaking cloud,
To cheer her issue, thunder'd thrice aloud:
Thrice forky lightning flash'd along the sky;
And Tyrrhene trumpets thrice were heard on high
Then, gazing up, repeated peals they hear;
And, in a heav'n serene, refulgent arms appear:
Redd'ning the skies, and glitt'ring all around.
The temper'd metals clash, and yield a silver
sound: [vine.
The rest stood trembling; struck with awe di-
Æneas only, conscious to the sign,
Presag'd th' event, and joyful view'd, above,
The accomplish'd promise of the queen of love.
Then, to th' Arcadian king: "This prodigy
(Dismiss your fear) belongs alone to me.
Heav'n calls me to the war: th' expected sign
Is giv'n of promis'd aid, and arms divine.
My goddess mother, whose indulgent care
Foresaw the dangers of the growing war,
This omen gave, when bright Vulcanian arms
Fated from force of steel by Stygian charms,
Suspended, shone on high: she then foreshow'd
Approaching fights, and fields to float in blood.
Turnus shall dearly pay for faith forsworn:
And corpse, and swords, and shields, on Tyber
borne, [alarms;
Shall choke his flood: now sound the loud
And, Latian troops, prepare your perjur'd arms."
He said, and, rising from his homely throne,
The solemn rites of Hercules begun,
And on his altars wak'd the sleeping fires;
Then cheerful to his household gods retires:
There offers chosen sheep. Th' Arcadian king,
And Trojan youth, the same oblations bring.
Next, of his men and ships he makes review;
Draws out the best and ablest of the crew.
Down with the falling stream, the refuse run,
To raise with joyful news his drooping son.
Steeds are prepar'd to mount the Trojan band,
Who wait their leader to the Tyrrhene land.
A sprightly courser, fairer than the rest,
The king himself presents his royal guest:
A lion's hide his back and limbs infold,
Precious with studded work, and paws of gold.
Fame through the little city spreads aloud
Th' intended march; amid the fearful crowd,
The matrons beat their breasts, dissolve in tears,
And double their devotion in their fears.
The war at hand appears with more affright,
And rises ev'ry moment to the sight.
Then old Evander, with a close embrace,
Strain'd his departing friend, and tears o'erflow
his face. [youth recall,
"Would heav'n (said he) my strength and
Such as I was beneath Præneste's wall—
Then when I made the foremost foes retire,
And set whole heaps of conquer'd shields on fire;
When Herilus in single fight I slew,
Whom with three lives Feronia did endue;
And thrice I sent him to the Stygian shore,
Till the last ebbing soul return'd no more—
Such if I stood renew'd, not these alarms,
Nor death should rend me from my Pallas' arms;
Nor proud Mezentius, thus unpunish'd, boast
His rapes and murders on the Tuscan coast.
Ye gods! and mighty Jove! in pity bring
Relief, and hear a father and a king!
If Fate and you reserve these eyes to see
My son return'd with peace and victory:
If the lov'd boy shall bless his father's sight;
If we shall meet again with more delight;
Then draw my life in length; let me sustain,
In hopes of his embrace, the worst of pain.
But if your hard decrees—which O! I dread—
Have doom'd to death his undeserving head;
This, O! this very moment let me die,
While hopes and fears in equal balance lie;
While, yet possess'd of all his youthful charms,
I strain him close within these aged arms—

Before that fatal news my soul shall wound."
He said, and, swooning, sunk upon the ground.
His servants bore him off, and softly laid
His languish'd limbs upon his lonely bed.
The horsemen march; the gates are open'd wide;
Æneas at their head, Achates by his side.
Next these the Trojan leaders rode along:
Last follows in the rear th' Arcadian throng.
Young Pallas shone conspicuous o'er the rest;
Gilded his arms, embroider'd was his vest.
So from the seas, exerts his radiant head
The star, by whom the lights of heav'n are led;
Shakes from his rosy locks the pearly dews,
Dispels the darkness, and the day renews.
The trembling wives the walls and turrets crowd,
And follow, with their eyes, the dusty cloud,
Which winds disperse by fits, and show from far
The blaze of arms, and shields, and shining war.
The troops, drawn up in beautiful array,
O'er heathy plains pursue the ready way.
Repeated peals of shouts are heard around,
The neighing coursers answer to the sound,
And shake with horny hoofs the solid ground.
A greenwood shade, long for religion known,
Stands by the streams that wash the Tuscan town,
Encompass'd round the gloomy hills above,
Which add a holy horror to the grove.
The first inhabitants, of Grecian blood,
That sacred forest to Silvanus vow'd,
The guardian of their flocks and fields—and pay
Their due devotions on his annual day.
Not far from hence, along the river's side,
In tents secure, the Tuscan troops abide,
By Tarchon led. Now, from a rising ground,
Æneas cast his wond'ring eyes around,
And all the Tyrrhene army had in sight,
Stretch'd on the spacious plain from left to right.
Thither his warlike train the Trojan led,
Refresh'd his men, and wearied horses fed.
Meantime the mother-goddess, crown'd with charms,
Breaks throgh the clouds and brings the fated arms.
Within a winding vale she finds her son,
On the cool river's banks, retir'd alone.
She shows her heavenly form without disguise,
And gives herself to his desiring eyes.
"Behold (she said) perform'd, in every part,
My promise made, and Vulcan's labour'd art.
New seek, secure, the Latian enemy,
And haughty Turnus to the field defy."
She said: and, having first her son embrac'd,
The radiant arms beneath an oak she plac'd.
Proud of the gift, he roll'd his greedy sight
Around the work, and gaz'd with vast delight.
He lifts, he turns, he poises and admires,
The crested helm, that vomits radiant fires:
His hands the fatal sword and corslet hold,
One keen with temper'd steel, one stiff with gold:
Both ample, flaming both, and beamy bright,
So shines a cloud, when edg'd with adverse light.
He shakes the pointed spear, and longs to try
The plaited cuishes on his manly thigh;
But most admires the shield's mysterious mould,
And Roman triumphs rising on the gold:
For there, emboss'd, the heav'nly smith had wrought
(Not in the rolls of future fate untaught)
The wars in order, and the race divine
Of warriors issuing from the Julian line.
The cave of Mars was dress'd with mossy greens:
There, by the wolf, were laid the martial twins.
Intrepid on her swelling dugs they hung:
The foster dam loll'd out her fawning tongue:
They suck'd secure, while bending back her head,
She lick'd their tender limbs, and form'd them as they fed.
Not far from thence, new Rome appears, with games
Projected for the rape of Sabine dames.
The pit resounds with shrieks: a war succeeds,
For breach of public faith, and unexampled deeds
Here for revenge the Sabine troops contend:
The Romans there with arms the prey defend.
Wearied with tedious war, at length they cease;
And both the kings and kingdoms plight the peace.
The friendly chiefs before Jove's altar stand,
Both arm'd, with each a charger in his hand:
A fatted sow for sacrifice is led,
With imprecations on the perjur'd head.
Near this, the traitor Metius, stretch'd between
Four fiery steeds, is dragg'd along the green,
By Tullus' doom: the brambles drink his blood
And his torn limbs are left, the vulture's food.
There, Porsena to Rome proud Tarquin brings,
And would by force restore the banish'd kings.
One tyrant for his fellow-tyrant fights:
The Roman youth assert their native rights.
Before the town the Tuscan army lies,
To win by famine, or by fraud surprise.
Their king, half threat'ning, half disdaining stood,
While Cocles broke the bridge and stemm'd the flood.
The captive maids there tempt the raging tide,
'Scap'd from their chains, with Clœlia for their guide.
High on a rock heroic Manlius stood,
To guard the temple and the temple's god.

Then Rome was poor; and there you might behold
The palace, thatch'd with straw, now roof'd with gold.
The silver goose before the shining gate
There flew, and by her cackle, sav'd the state,
She told the Gauls' approach: th' approaching Gauls,
Obscure in night, ascend, and seize the walls.
The gold dissembled well their yellow hair:
And golden chains on their white necks they wear:
Gold are their vests: long Alpine spears they wield
And their left arm sustains a length of shield.
Hard by, the leaping Salian priests advance:
And naked through the streets the mad Luperci dance
In caps of wool; the targets dropt from heav'n.
Here modest matrons, in soft litters driv'n,
To pay their vows in solemn pomp appear:
And od'rous gums in their chaste hands they bear.
Far hence remov'd, the Stygian seats are seen;
Pains of the damn'd; and punish'd Catiline,
Hung on a rock—the traitor; and around,
The Furies hissing from the nether ground.
Apart from these, the happy souls he draws,
And Cato's holy ghost dispensing laws.
Betwixt the quarters flows a golden sea:
But foaming surges there in silver play.
The dancing dolphins with their tails divide
The glitt'ring waves, and cut the precious tide.
Amid the main, two mighty fleets engage—
Their brazen beaks oppos'd with equal rage.
Actium surveys the well-disputed prize:
Leucate's wat'ry plain with foaming billows fries.
Young Cæsar, on the stern, in armour bright,
Here leads the Romans and their gods to fight:
His beamy temples shoot their flames afar;
And o'er his head is hung the Julian star.
Agrippa seconds him, with prosp'rous gales,
And, with propitious gods, his foes assails.
A naval crown, that binds his manly brows,
The happy fortune of the fight foreshows.
Rang'd on the line oppos'd, Antonius brings
Barbarian aids, and troops of eastern kings,
Th' Arabians near, and Bactrians from afar,
Of tongues discordant, and a mingled war;
And, rich in gaudy robes, amidst the strife,
His ill fate follows him—th' Egyptian wife.
Moving they fight: with oars and forky prows
The froth is gather'd, and the water glows.
It seems, as if the Cyclades again
Were rooted up and justled in the main;
Or floating mountains floating mountains meet;
Such is the fierce encounter of the fleet.
Fire-balls are thrown, and pointed javelins fly;
The fields of Neptune take a purple dye.
The queen herself, amidst the loud alarms,
With cymbals toss'd, her fainting soldiers warms—
Fool as she was! who had not yet divin'd
Her cruel fate; nor saw the snakes behind.
Her country gods, the monsters of the sky,
Great Neptune, Pallas, and love's queen, defy.
The dog Anubis barks, but barks in vain,
Nor longer dares oppose th' ethereal train.
Mars in the middle of the shining shield,
Is grav'd, and strides along the liquid field.
The Diræ souse from heav'n with swift descent:
And Discord, dy'd in blood, with garments rent,
Divides the crowd: her steps Bellona treads,
And shakes her iron rod above their heads.
This seen, Apollo, from his Actian height,
Pours down his arrows; at whose winged flight
The trembling Indians and Egyptians yield,
And soft Sabæans quit the wat'ry field.
The fatal mistress hoists her silken sails,
And shrinking from the fight invokes the gales.
Aghast she looks, and heaves her breast for breath,
Panting, and pale with fear of future death.
The god had figur'd her, as driven along
By winds and waves, and scudding through the throng.
Just opposite, sad Nilus opens wide
His arms and ample bosom to the tide,
And spreads his mantle o'er the winding coast,
In which he wraps his queen, and hides the flying host.
The victor to the gods his thanks express'd,
And Rome triumphant with his presence bless'd.
Three hundred temples in the town he plac'd;
With spoils and altars every temple grac'd.
Three shining nights and three succeeding days
The fields resound with shouts, the streets with praise,
The domes with songs, the theatres with plays.
All altars flame: before each altar lies,
Drench'd in his gore, the destin'd sacrifice.
Great Cæsar sits sublime upon his throne,
Before Apollo's porch of Parian stone;
Accepts the presents vow'd for victory,
And hangs the monumental crowns on high.
Vast crowds of vanquish'd nations march along,
Various in arms, in habit, and in tongue,
Here, Mulciber assigns the proper place
For Carians, and th' ungirt Numidian race;
Then ranks the Thracians in the second row,
With Scythians, expert in the dart and bow.
And here the tam'd Euphrates humbly glides,
And there the Rhine submits her swelling tides,
And proud Araxes, whom no bridge could bind.

The Danes' unconquer'd offspring march behind;
And Morini, the last of human kind.
These figures on the shield divinely wrought,
By Vulcan labour'd, and by Venus brought,
With joy and wonder fill the hero's thought.
Unknown the names, he yet admires the grace,
And bears aloft the fame and fortune of his race.

BOOK IX.

ARGUMENT.

Turnus takes advantage of Æneas's absence, fires some of his ships (which are transformed into sea nymphs,) and assaults his camp. The Trojans, reduced to the last extremities, send Nisus and Euryalus to recall Æneas; which furnishes the poet with that admirable episode of their friendship, generosity, and the conclusion of their adventure.

While these affairs in distant places pass'd,
The various Iris Juno sends with haste,
To find bold Turnus, who, with anxious thought
The secret shade of his great grandsire sought.
Retir'd alone, she found the daring man,
And op'd her rosy lips, and thus began:
"What none of all the gods could grant thy vows—
That, Turnus, this auspicious day bestows!
Æneas, gone to seek th' Arcadian prince,
Has left the Trojan camp without defence:
And, short of succours there, employs his pains
In parts remote to raise the Tuscan swains.
Now snatch an hour that favours thy designs;
Unite your forces, and attack their lines."
This said, on equal wings she pois'd her weight,
And form'd a radiant rainbow in her flight.
The Daunian hero lifts his hands and eyes,
And thus invokes the goddess as she flies:
"Iris, the grace of heav'n! what pow'r divine
Has sent thee down, through dusky clouds to shine?
See, they divide: immortal day appears,
And glitt'ring planets dancing in their spheres!
With joy, these happy omens I obey,
And follow, to the war, the god that leads the way."
Thus having said, as by the brook he stood,
He scoop'd the water from the crystal flood;
Then, with his hands, the drops to heaven he throws,
And loads the pow'rs above with offer'd vows.
Now march the bold confed'rates through the plain,
Well hors'd, well clad—a rich and shining train.
Messapus leads the van; and, in the rear,
The sons of Tyrrheus in bright arms appear.
In the main battle, with his flaming crest,
The mighty Turnus tow'rs above the rest.
Silent they move, majestically slow,
Like ebbing Nile, or Ganges in his flow.
The Trojans view the dusty cloud from far,
And the dark menace of the distant war.
Caicus from the rampire saw it rise,
Black'ning the fields, and thick'ning through the skies;
Then to his fellows thus aloud he calls:
"What rolling clouds, my friends, approach the walls?
Arm! arm! and man the works! prepare your spears,
And pointed darts! the Latian host appears."
Thus warn'd, they shut their gates; with shouts ascend
The bulwarks, and, secure, their foes attend:
For their wise general, with foreseeing care,
Had charg'd them not to tempt the doubtful war:
Nor, though provok'd, in open fields advance,
But close within their lines attend their chance
Unwilling, yet they keep the strict command,
And sourly wait in arms the hostile band.
The fiery Turnus flew before the rest:
A piebald steed of Tracian strain he press'd;
His helm of massy gold; and crimson was his crest.
With twenty horse to second his designs,
An unexpected foe, he fac'd the lines.
"Is there (he said) in arms who bravely dare
His leader's honour and his danger share?"
Then spurring on, his brandish'd dart he threw,
In sign of war;—applauding shouts ensue.
Amaz'd to find a dastard race that run
Behind the rampires, and the battle shun,
He rides around the camp with rolling eyes,
And stops at ev'ry post, and ev'ry passage tries.
So roams the nightly wolf about the fold:
Wet with descending show'rs, and stiff with cold,
He howls for hunger, and he grins for pain,
(His gnashing teeth are exercis'd in vain,)
And, impotent of anger, finds no way
In his distended paws to grasp the prey.
The mothers listen; but the bleating lambs
Securely swig the dug, beneath the dams.
Thus ranges eager Turnus o'er the plain,
Sharp with desire, and furious with disdain;
Surveys each passage with a piercing sight,
To force his foes in equal field to fight.
Thus while he gazes round, at length he spies,
Where, fenc'd with strong redoubts, their navy lies,
Close underneath the walls: the washing tide
Secures from all approach this weaker side.
He takes the wish'd occasion, fills his hand
With ready fires, and shakes a flaming brand.

Urg'd by his presence, ev'ry soul is warm'd,
And ev'ry hand with kindled fires is arm'd.
From the fir'd pines, the scatt'ring sparkles fly;
Fat vapours, mix'd with flames, involve the sky.
What pow'r, O Muses, could avert the flame,
Which threaten'd, in the fleet, the Trojan name?
Tell: for, the fact, through length of time obscure,
Is hard to faith; yet shall the fame endure.
'T is said, that when the chief prepar'd his flight,
And fell'd his timber from mount Ida's height,
The grandame-goddess then approach'd her son,
And with a mother's majesty begun:
"Grant me (she said) the sole request I bring,
Since conquer'd heav'n has own'd you for its king.
On Ida's brows, for ages past, there stood,
With firs and maples fill'd, a shady wood;
And on the summit rose a sacred grove,
Where I was worshipp'd with religious love.
These woods, that holy grove, my long delight,
I gave the Trojan prince, to speed his flight.
Now, fill'd with fear, on their behalf I come;
Let neither winds o'erset, nor waves intomb,
The floating forest of the sacred pine;
But let it be their safety to be mine."
Then thus replied her awful son, who rolls
The radiant stars, and heav'n and earth controls:
"How dare you, mother, endless date demand,
For vessels moulded by a mortal hand?
What then is Fate? shall bold Æneas ride,
Of safety certain, on th' uncertain tide?
Yet, what I can, I grant: when, wafted o'er,
The chief is landed on the Latian shore,
Whatever ships escape the raging storms,
At my command shall change their fading forms
To nymphs divine, and plough the wat'ry way,
Like Doto and the Daughters of the sea."
To seal his sacred vow, by Styx he swore,
The lake of liquid pitch, the dreary shore,
And Phlegethon's innavigable flood,
And the black regions of his brother-god.
He said; and shook the skies with his imperial nod.
And now at length the number'd hours were [come,
Prefix'd by Fate's irrevocable doom,
When the great mother of the gods was free
To save her ships, and finish Jove's decree.
First from the quarter of the morn, there sprung
A light that sign'd the heav'ns, and shot along;
Then from a cloud, fring'd round with golden fires,
Were timbrels heard, and Berecynthian choirs;
And, last, a voice, with more than mortal sound,
Both hosts, in arms oppos'd, with equal horror wound:
"O Trojan race! your needless aid forbear:
And know, my ships are my peculiar care.
With greater ease, the bold Rutulian may
With hissing brands attempt to burn the sea,
Than singe my sacred pines. But you, my charge,
Loos'd from your crooked anchors, launch at [large,
Exalted each a nymph: forsake the sand,
And swim the seas, at Cybele's command.
No sooner had the goddess ceas'd to speak,
When, lo! th' obedient ships their halsers break;
And strange to tell, like dolphins, in the main
They plunge their prows, and dive, and spring again:
As many beauteous maids the billows sweep,
As rode before tall vessels on the deep.
The foes, surpris'd with wonder, stood aghast;
Messapus curb'd his fiery courser's haste:
Old Tyber roar'd, and raising up his head,
Call'd back his waters to their oozy bed.
Turnus alone, undaunted, bore the shock,
And with these words his trembling troops bespoke:
"These monsters for the Trojans' fate are meant,
And are by Jove for black presages sent.
He takes the cowards' last relief away;
For fly they cannot, and, constrain'd to stay,
Must yield unfought, a base inglorious prey.
The liquid half of all the globe is lost;
Heav'n shuts the seas; and we secure the coast.
Theirs is no more than that small spot of ground
Which myriads of our martial men surround.
Their fates I fear not, or vain oracles.
'T was giv'n to Venus, they should cross the seas,
And land secure upon the Latian plains:
Their promis'd hour is pass'd and mine remains.
'T is in the fate of Turnus, to destroy,
With sword and fire, the faithless race of Troy.
Shall such affronts as these, alone, inflame
The Grecian brothers, and the Grecian name?
My cause and theirs is one; a fatal strife,
And final ruin for a ravish'd wife.
Was't not enough, that punish'd for the crime,
They fell—but will they fall a second time?
One would have thought they paid enough before,
To curse the costly sex, and durst offend no more.

Can they securely trust their feeble wall,
A slight partition, a thin interval,
Betwixt their fate and them; when Troy, though built
By hands divine, yet perish'd by their guilt?
Lend me, for once, my friends, your valiant hands,
To force from out their lines these dastard bands.
Less than a thousand ships will end this war;
Nor Vulcan needs his fated arms prepare.
Let all the Tuscans, all th' Arcadians, join!
Nor these, nor those, shall frustrate my design.
Let them not fear the treasons of the night,
The robb'd Palladium, the pretended flight:
Our onset shall be made in open light.
No wooden engine shall their town betray:
Fires they shall have around, but fires by day.
No Grecian babes before their camp appear,
Whom Hector's arms detain'd to the tenth tardy year.
Now, since the sun is rolling to the west,
Give we the silent night to needful rest:
Refresh your bodies, and your arms prepare:
The morn shall end the small remains of war."
The post of honour to Messapus falls,
To keep the nightly guard; to watch the walls;
To pitch the fires at distances around,
And close the Trojans in their scanty ground.
Twice sev'n Rutulian captains ready stand;
And twice sev'n hundred horse these chiefs command:
All clad in shining arms the works invest;
Each with a radiant helm and waving crest.
Stretch'd at their length, they press the grassy ground;
They laugh; they sing; (the jolly bowls go round;)
With lights and cheerful fires renew the day,
And pass the wakeful night in feasts and play.
The Trojans from above their foes beheld,
And with arm'd legions all the rampires fill'd.
Seiz'd with affright, their gates they first explore;
Join works to works with bridges, tow'r to tow'r:
Thus all things needful for defence abound:
Mnestheus and brave Serestus walk the round,
Commission'd by their absent prince to share
The common danger, and divide the care.
The soldiers draw their lots, and, as they fall,
By turns relieve each other on the wall.
Nigh where the foes their utmost guards advance,
To watch the gate, was warlike Nisus' chance.
His father Hyrtacus of noble blood;
His mother was a huntress of the wood,
And sent him to the wars. Well could he bear
His lance in fight, and dart the flying spear;
But better skill'd unerring shafts to send.
Beside him stood Euryalus, his friend—
Euryalus, than whom the Trojan host
No fairer face, or sweeter air, could boast.
Scarce had the down to shade his cheeks begun,
One was their care, and their delight was one.
One common hazard in the war they shar'd;
And now were both by choice upon the guard.
Then Nisus thus: "Or do the gods inspire
This warmth, or make we gods of our desire?
A gen'rous ardour boils within my breast,
Eager of action, enemy to rest:
This urges me to fight, and fires my mind,
To leave a memorable name behind.
Thou seest the foe secure; how faintly shine
Their scatter'd fires! the most, in sleep supine,
Along the ground, an easy conquest lie.
The wakeful few the fuming flagon ply:
All hush'd around. Now hear what I revolve—
A thought unripe—and scarcely yet resolve.
Our absent prince both camp and council mourn;
By message both would hasten his return:
If they confer what I demand on thee,
(For fame is recompense enough for me,)
Methinks, beneath yon hill, I have espied
A way that safely will my passage guide."
Euryalus stood listening while he spoke;
With love of praise, and noble envy struck;
Then to his ardent friend expos'd his mind:
"All this alone, and leaving me behind!
Am I unworthy, Nisus, to be join'd?
Think'st thou I can my share of glory yield,
Or send thee unassisted to the field?
Not so my father taught my childhood arms—
Born in a siege, and bred among alarms
Nor is my youth unworthy of my friend,
Nor of the heaven-born hero I attend.
The thing call'd life, with ease I can disclaim,
And think it over-sold to purchase fame."
Then Nisus thus: "Alas! thy tender years
Would minister new matters to my fears:
So may the gods, who view this friendly strife,
Restore me to thy lov'd embrace with life,
Condemn'd to pay my vows, (as sure I trust,)
This thy request is cruel and unjust.
But if some chance—as many chances are,
And doubtful hazards, in the deeds of war—
If one should reach my head, there let it fall,
And spare thy life: I would not perish all,
Thy blooming youth deserves a longer date:
Live thou to mourn thy love's unhappy fate.
To bear my mangled body from the foe,
Or buy it back, and fun'ral rites bestow.
Or if hard fortune shall those dues deny,
Thou canst at least an empty tomb supply.
O! let not me the widow's tears renew;
Nor let a mother's curse my name pursue—

Thy pious parent, who, for love of thee,
Forsook the coasts of friendly Sicily,
Her age committing to the seas and wind,
When ev'ry weary matron stay'd behind."
To this, Euryalus: "You plead in vain,
And but protract the cause you cannot gain.
No more delays! but haste!" With that he wakes
The nodding watch: each to his office takes.
The guard reliev'd, the gen'rous couple went
To find the council at the royal tent.
All creatures else forgot their daily care,
And sleep, the common gift of nature, share;
Except the Trojan peers, who wakeful sate
In nightly council for the endanger'd state.
They vote a message to their absent chief,
Show their distress, and beg a swift relief.
Amid the camp a silent seat they chose,
Remote from clamour, and secure from foes.
On their left arms their ample shields they bear,
Their right inclin'd upon the bending spear.
Now Nisus and his friend approach'd the guard,
And beg admission, eager to be heard—
Th' affair important, not to be deferr'd.
Ascanius bids them be conducted in,
Ord'ring the more experienc'd to begin.
Then Nisus thus: "Ye fathers, lend your ears;
Nor judge our bold attempt beyond our years.
The foe, securely drench'd in sleep and wine,
Neglect their watch; the fires but thinly shine
And, where the smoke in cloudy vapours flies,
Cov'ring the plain, and curling to the skies,
Betwixt two paths which at the gate divide,
Close by the sea a passage we have spied,
Which will our way to great Æneas guide.
Expect each hour to see him safe again,
Loaded with spoils of foes in battle slain.
Snatch we the lucky minute while we may:
Nor can we be mistaken in the way;
For, hunting in the vales, we both have seen
The rising turrets, and the stream between;
And know the winding course, with ev'ry ford."
He ceas'd: and old Alethes took the word.
"Our country gods, in whom our trust we place,
Will yet from ruin save the Trojan race,
While we behold such dauntless worth appear
In dawning youth, and souls so void of fear."
Then into tears of joy the father broke;
Each in his longing arms by turns he took;
Panted and paus'd; and thus again he spoke:
"Ye brave young men, what equal gifts can we,
In recompense of such desert, decree?
The greatest sure, and best you can receive,
The gods and your own conscious worth will give.
The rest our grateful gen'ral will bestow,
And young Ascanius, till his manhood, owe."
"And I, whose welfare in my father lies,"
Ascanius adds, "by the great deities,
By my dear country, by my household gods,
By hoary Vesta's rites and dark abodes,
Adjure you both—(on you my fortune stands
That and my faith I plight into your hands)—
Make me but happy in his safe return,
Whose wanted presence I can only mourn;
Your common gift shall two large goblets be
Of silver, wrought with curious imagery,
And high emboss'd, which when old Priam reign'd,
My conqu'ring sire at sack'd Arisba gain'd:
And, more, two tripods cast in antique mould,
With two great talents of the finest gold;
Beside a costly bowl, engrav'd with art,
Which Dido gave, when first she gave her heart.
But, if in conquer'd Italy we reign,
When spoils by lot the victor shall obtain—
Thou saw'st the courser by proud Turnus press'd,
That, Nisus, and his arms, and nodding crest,
And shield, from chance exempt, shall be thy share;
Twelve lab'ring slaves, twelve handmaids young and fair,
All clad in rich attire, and train'd with care:
And, last, a Latian field with fruitful plains,
And a large portion of the King's domains.
But thou whose years are more to mine allied,
No fate my vow'd affection shall divide
From thee, heroic youth! Be wholly mine:
Take full possession: all my soul is thine.
One faith, one fame, and fate, shall both attend:
My life's companion, and my bosom friend—
My peace shall be committed to thy care;
And to thy conduct, my concerns in war."
Then thus the young Euryalus replied:
"Whatever fortune, good or bad, betide,
The same shall be my age, as now my youth:
No time shall find me wanting to my truth.
This only form your goodness let me gain—
(And, this ungranted, all rewards are vain;)
Of Priam's royal race my mother came—
And sure the best that ever bore the name—
Whom neither Troy nor Sicily could hold
From me departing, but, o'erspent and old,
My fate she follow'd. Ignorant of this
(Whatever) danger, neither parting kiss
Nor pious blessing taken, her I leave,
And in this only act of all my life deceive.
By this right hand, and conscious night I swear,
My soul so sad a farewell could not bear.
Be you her comfort; fill my vacant place;
(Permit me to presume so great a grace:)

Support her age, forsaken and distress'd.
That hope alone will fortify my breast
Against the worst of fortunes, and of fears."
He said. The mov'd assistants melt in tears.
Then thus Ascanius, wonder-struck to see
That image of his filial piety:
"So great beginnings, in so green an age,
Exact the faith which I again engage.
Thy mother all the dues shall justly claim
Creüsa had, and only want the name.
Whate'er event thy bold attempt shall have,
'T is merit to have borne a son so brave.
Now by my head, a sacred oath, I swear,
(My father us'd it,) what, returning here
Crown'd with success, I for thyself prepare,
That, if thou fail, shall thy lov'd mother share."
He said, and weeping while he spoke the word,
From his broad belt he drew a shining sword,
Magnificent with gold. Lycaon made,
And in an iv'ry scabbard sheath'd the blade.
This was his gift. Great Mnestheus gave his friend
A lion's hide, his body to defend;
And good Alethes furnish'd him beside,
With his own trusty helm, of temper tried.
Thus arm'd they went. The noble Trojans wait
Their issuing forth, and follow to the gate
With prayers and vows. Above the rest appears
Ascanius, manly far beyond his years;
And messages committed to their care,
Which all in winds were lost, and flitting air.
The trenches first they pass'd; then took their way
Where their proud foes in pitch'd pavilions lay;
To many fatal, ere themselves were slain.
They found the careless host dispers'd upon the plain,
Who gorg'd and drunk with wine, supinely snore.
Unharness'd chariots stand along the shore:
Amidst the wheels and reins, the goblet by,
A medley of debauch and war, they lie.
Observing Nisus show'd his friend the sight:
"Behold a conquest gain'd without a fight.
Occasion offers; and I stand prepar'd:
There lies our way: be thou upon the guard,
And look around, while I securely go,
And hew a passage through the sleeping foe."
Softly he spoke; then, striding, took his way,
With his drawn sword, where haughty Rhamnes lay;
His head rais'd high on tapestry beneath,
And heaving from his breast, he drew his breath—
A king and prophet, by king Turnus lov'd;
But fate by prescience cannot be remov'd
Him and his sleeping slaves he slew; then spies
Where Remus, with his rich retinue, lies.
His armour-bearer first, and next he kills
His charioteer, intrench'd betwixt the wheels
And his lov'd horses; last invades their lord:
Full on his neck he drives the fatal sword:
The gasping head flies off; a purple flood
Flows from the trunk, that welters in the blood,
Which, by the spurning heels dispers'd around,
The bed besprinkles, and bedews the ground.
Lamus the bold, and Lamyrus the strong,
He slew, and then Serranus fair and young.
From dice and wine the youth retir'd to rest,
And puff'd the fumy god from out his breast:
E'en then he dream'd of drink and lucky play—
More lucky, had it lasted till the day.
The famish'd lion thus, with hunger bold,
O'erleaps the fences of the nightly fold,
And tears the peaceful flocks: with silent awe
Trembling they lie, and pant beneath his paw.
Nor with less rage Euryalus employs
The wrathful sword, or fewer foes destroys:
But on th' ignoble crowd his fury flew:
He Fadus, Hebesus, and Rhœtus slew.
Oppress'd with heavy sleep the former fall,
But Rhœtus wakeful, and observing all:
Behind a spacious jar he slink'd for fear:
The fatal iron found and reach'd him there;
For, as he rose, it pierc'd his naked side,
And, reeking, thence return'd in crimson dy'd.
The wound pours out a stream of wine and blood:
The purple soul comes floating in the flood.
Now, where Messapus quarter'd, they arrive.
The fires were fainting there, and just alive:
The warrior-horses, tied in order, fed.
Nisus observ'd the discipline, and said:
"Our eager thirst of blood may both betray;
And see the scatter'd streaks of dawning day,
Foe to nocturnal thefts. No more, my friend:
Here let our glutted execution end.
A lane through slaughter'd bodies we have made."
The bold Euryalus, though loath, obey'd.
Of arms and arras, and of plate, they find
A precious load; but these they leave behind.
Yet, fond of gaudy spoils, the boy would stay
To make the rich caparison his prey,
Which on the steed of conquer'd Rhamnes lay.
Nor did his eyes less longingly behold
The girdle-belt, with nails of burnish'd gold.
This present Cœdicus the rich bestow'd
On Remulus, when friendship first they vow'd,
And, absent, join'd in hospitable ties:
He, dying, to his heir bequeath'd the prize;
Till by the conqu'ring Ardean troops oppress'd,
He fell; and they the glorious gift possess'd.

These glittering spoils (now made the victor's gain)
He to his body suits, but suits in vain.
Messapus' helm he finds among the rest.
And laces on, and wears the waving crest.
Proud of their conquest, prouder of their prey,
They leave the camp, and take the ready way.
But far they had not pass'd, before they spied
Three hundred horse, with Volscens for their guide.
The queen a legion to king Turnus sent:
But the swift horse the slower foot prevent,
And now, advancing, sought the leader's tent.
They saw the pair; for, through the doubtful shade,
His shining helm Euryalus betray'd.
On which the moon with full reflection play'd.
"'Tis not for naught," cried Volscens from the crowd,
"These men go there:" then rais'd his voice aloud:
"Stand! stand why thus in arms? and whither bent?
From whence, to whom, and on what errand sent?"
Silent they scud away, and haste their flight
To neighb'ring woods, and trust themselves to night.
The speedy horse all passages belay,
And spur their smoking steeds to cross their way;
And watch each entrance of the winding wood.
Black was the forest: thick with beech it stood,
Horrid with fern, and intricate with thorn:
Few paths of human feet, or tracks of beasts, were worn.
The darkness of the shades, his heavy prey,
And fear, misled the younger from his way.
But Nisus hit the turns with happier haste,
And thoughtless of his friend, the forest pass'd,
And Alban plains, (from Alba's name so call'd,)
Where king Latinus then his oxen stall'd;
Till turning at the length, he stood his ground,
And miss' his friend, and cast his eyes around.
"Ah wretch!" he cried—"where have I left behind
Th' unhappy youth? where shall I hope to find?
Or what way take?" Again he ventures back,
And treads the maze of his former track.
He winds the wood, and list'ning, hears the noise
Of trampling coursers, and the riders' voice.
The sound approach'd; and suddenly he view'd
The foes enclosing, and his friend pursu'd,
Forelaid and taken, while he strove in vain
The shelter of the friendly shades to gain.
What should he next attempt? what arms employ,
What fruitless force to free the captive boy?
Or desp'rate should he rush and lose his life,
With odds oppress'd, in such unequal strife!
Resolv'd at length, his pointed spear he shook
And casting on the moon a mournful look:
"Guardian of groves, and goddess of the night!
Fair queen!" he said, "direct my dart aright.
If e'er my pious father for my sake,
Did grateful off'rings on thy altars make,
Or I increas'd them with my sylvan toils,
And hung the holy roofs with savage spoils,
Give me to scatter these." Then from his ear
He pois'd, and aim'd, and launch'd the trembling spear.
The deadly weapon, hissing from the grove,
Impetuous on the back of Sulmo drove;
Pierc'd his thin armour, drank his vital blood,
And in his body left the broken wood.
He staggers round: his eyeballs roll in death;
And, with short sobs, he gasps away his breath.
All stand amaz'd:—a second jav'lin flies
With equal strength, and quivers through the skies.
This through thy temples, Tagus, forc'd the way,
And in the brain-pan warmly buried lay.
Fierce Volscens foams with rage, and, gazing round,
Descried not him who gave the fatal wound,
Nor knew to fix revenge: "but thou," he cries
"Shalt pay for both," and at the pris'ner flies
With his drawn sword. Then, struck with deep despair,
That cruel sight the lover could not bear;
But from his covert rush'd in open view,
And sent his voice before him as he flew:
"Me! me!" he cried—"turn all your swords alone
On me—the fact confess'd, the fault my own.
He neither could nor durst, the guiltless youth—
Ye moon and stars, bear witness to the truth!
His only crime (if friendship can offend)
Is too much love to his unhappy friend."
Too late he speaks:—the sword with fury guides,
Driv'n with full force, had pierc'd his tender sides.
Down fell the beauteous youth: the yawning wound
Gush'd out a purple stream, and stain'd the ground.
His snowy neck reclines upon his breast,
Like a fair flow'r by the keen share oppress'd—
Like a white poppy sinking on the plain,
Whose heavy head is overcharg'd with rain.
Despair and rage, and vengeance justly vow'd,
Drove Nisus headlong on the hostile crowd.
Volscens he seeks; on him alone he bends;
Born back and bor'd by his surrounding friends.

Onward he press'd, and kept him still in sight,
Then whirl'd aloft his sword with all his might:
Th' unerring steel descended while he spoke,
Pierc'd his wide mouth, and through his weazon broke.
Dying he slew; and stagg'ring on the plain,
With swimming eyes he sought his lover slain;
Then quiet on his bleeding bosom fell,
Content, in death, to be reveng'd so well.

O happy friends! for, if my verse can give
Immortal life, your fame shall ever live.
Fix'd as the Capitol's foundation lies,
And spread, where'er the Roman eagle flies?

The conq'ring party first divide the prey,
Then their slain leader to the camp convey.
With wonder, as they went, the troops were fill'd,
To see such numbers whom so few had kill'd.
Serranus, Rhamnes, and the rest they found:
Vast crowds the dying and the dead surround;
And the yet reeking blood o'erflows the ground.
All knew the helmet which Messapus lost,
But mourn'd a purchase that so dear had cost.
Now rose the ruddy morn from Tithon's bed,
And with the dawn of day the skies o'erspread:
Nor long the sun his daily course withheld,
But added colours to the world reveal'd;
When early Turnus, wak'ning with the light,
All clad in armour, calls his troops to fight;
His martial men with fierce harangues he fir'd,
And his own ardour in their souls inspir'd.
This done—to give new terror to his foes,
The head of Nisus and his friend he shows,
Rais'd high on pointed spears—a ghastly sight!
Loud peals of shouts ensue, and barbarous delight.

Meantime the Trojans run, where danger calls,
They line their trenches, and they man their walls:
In front extended to the left they stood:
Safe was the right, surrounded by the flood.
But, casting from their tow'rs a frightful view,
They saw the faces, which too well they knew,
Though then disguis'd in death, and smear'd all o'er
With filth obscene, and dropping putrid gore.
Soon hasty fame through the sad city bears
The mournful message to the mother's ears.
An icy cold benumbs her limbs: she shakes:
Her cheeks the blood, her hand the web forsakes.
She runs the rampires round amidst the war,
Nor fears the flying darts: she rends her hair,
And fills with loud laments the liquid air.
"Thus then my lov'd Euryalus appears!
Thus looks the prop of my declining years!
Was 't on this face my famish'd eyes I fed?
Ah! how unlike the living is the dead!
And couldst thou leave me, cruel, thus alone?
Not one kind kiss from a departing son!
No look, no last adieu before he went,
In an ill-boding hour to slaughter sent!
Cold on the ground, and pressing foreign clay,
To Latian dogs and fowls he lies a prey!
Nor was I near to close his dying eyes,
To wash his wounds, to weep his obsequies,
To call about his corpse his crying friends,
Or spread the mantle (made for other ends)
On his dear body, which I wove with care,
Nor did my daily pains or nightly labour spare.
Where shall I find his corpse? what earth sustains
His trunk dismember'd, and his cold remains?
For this, alas! I left my needful ease,
Expos'd my life to winds, and winter seas!
If any pity touch Rutulian hearts,
Here empty all your quivers, all your darts:
Or, if they fail, thou, Jove, conclude my wo,
And send me thunder-struck to shades below."

Her shrieks and clamours pierce the Trojans' ears,
Unman their courage, and augment their fears:
Nor young Ascanius could the sight sustain,
Nor old Ilioneus his tears restrain;
But Actor and Idæus jointly sent,
To bear the madding mother to her tent.
And now the trumpets terribly, from far,
With rattling clangour rouse the sleepy war.
The soldiers' shouts succeed the brazen sounds;
And heav'n from pole to pole the noise rebounds.
The Volscians bear their shields upon their head,
And, rushing forward, form a moving shed:
These fill the ditch; those pull the bulwarks down:
Some raise the ladders; others scale the town.
But, where void spaces on the walls appear,
Or thin defence, they pour their forces there.
With poles and missive weapons, from afar
The Trojans kept aloof the missive war;
Taught by their ten years' siege defensive fight,
And roll down ribs of rocks, an unresisted weight,
To break the penthouse with the pond'rous blow,
Which yet the patient Volscians undergo—
But could not bear th' unequal combat long;
For, where the Trojans find the thickest throng,
The ruin falls: their shatter'd shields give way,
And their crush'd heads become an easy prey.
They shrink for fear, abated of their rage,
Nor longer dare in a blind fight engage—
Contented now to gall them from below,
With darts and slings, and with the distant bow.

Elsewhere Mezentius, terrible to view,
A blazing pine within the trenches threw.

But brave Messapus, Neptune's warlike son,
Broke down the palisades, the trenches won,
And loud for ladders calls, to scale the town.
Calliope, begin! ye sacred Nine,
Inspire your poet in his high design,
To sing what slaughter manly Turnus made,
What souls he sent below the Stygian shade,
What fame the soldiers with their captain share,
And the vast circuit of the fatal war:
For you, in singing martial facts, excel;
You best remember, and alone can tell.
There stood a tower amazing to the sight,
Built up of beams, and of stupendous height:
Art, and the nature of the place, conspir'd,
To furnish all the strength that war requir'd.
To level this the bold Italians join;
The wary Trojans obviate their design;
With weighty stones o'erwhelm their troops below,
Shoot through the loopholes, and sharp jav'lins throw.
Turnus the chief toss'd from his thund'ring hand,
Against the wooden walls, a flaming brand:
It stuck, the fiery plague: the winds were high,
The planks were season'd and the timber dry.
Contagion caught the posts; it spread along,
Scorch'd, and to distance drove, the scatter'd throng.
The Trojans fled; the fire pursued amain,
Still gath'ring fast upon the trembling train;
Till, crowding to the corners of the wall,
Down the defence and the defenders fall.
The mighty flaw makes heav'n itself resound:
The dead and dying Trojans strew the ground.
The tow'r, that follow'd on the fallen crew,
Whelm'd o'er their heads, and buried whom it slew.
Some stuck upon the darts themselves had sent,
All the same equal ruin underwent.
Young Lycus and Helenor only 'scape;
Sav'd—how, they know not—from the steepy leap.
Helenor, elder of the two; by birth,
On one side royal, one a son of earth;
Whom to the Lydian king Lycimnia bare,
And sent her boasted bastard to the war:
(A privilege which none but freemen share.)
Slight were his arms, a sword and silver shield
No marks of honour charg'd its empty field.
Light as he fell, so light the youth arose,
And, rising, found himself amidst his foes;
Nor flight was left, nor hopes to force his way.
Imbolden'd by despair, he stood at bay;
And like a stag, whom all the troop surrounds
Of eager huntsmen and invading hounds—
Resolv'd on death, he dissipates his fears,
And bounds aloft against the pointed spears:
So dares the youth, secure of death; and throws
His dying body on his thickest foes.
But Lycus, swifter of his feet by far,
Runs, doubles, winds, and turns, amidst the war;
Springs to the walls, and leaves his foes behind,
And snatches at the beam he first can find;
Looks up, and leaps aloft at all the stretch,
In hopes the helping hand of some kind friend to reach.
But Turnus follow'd hard his hunted prey,
(His spear had almost reach'd him in the way,
Short of his reins, and scarce a span behind.)
"Fool!" said the chief, "though fleeter than the wind,
Couldst thou presume to 'scape, when I pursue?"
He said, and downward by the feet he drew
The trembling dastard: at the tug he falls:
Vast ruins come along, rent from the smoking walls.
Thus on some silver swan, or tim'rous hare,
Jove's bird comes sousing down from upper air;
Her crooked talons truss the fearful prey:
Then out of sight she soars, and wings her way.
So seizes the grim wolf the tender lamb,
In vain lamented by the bleating dam.
Then rushing onward with a barbarous cry,
The troops of Turnus to the combat fly.
The ditch with fagots fill'd, the daring foe
Toss'd firebrands to the steepy turrets throw.
Ilioneus, as bold Lucetius came
To force the gate, and feed the kindling flame,
Roll'd down the fragment of a rock so right,
It crush'd him double underneath the weight.
Two more young Liger and Asylas slew:
To bend the bow young Liger better knew;
Asylas best the pointed jav'lin threw.
Brave Cæneus laid Ortygius on the plain;
The victor Cæneus was by Turnus slain.
By the same hand, Clonius and Itys fall,
Sagar, and Idas standing on the wall.
From Capys' arms, his fate Privernus found:
Hurt by Themilla first—but slight the wound,—
His shield thrown by, to mitigate the smart,
He clapp'd his hand upon the wounded part:
The second shaft came swift and unespied,
And pierc'd his hand and nail'd it to his side,
Transfix'd his bleeding lungs, and beating heart;
The soul came issuing out, and hiss'd against the dart.
The son of Arcens shone amid the rest,
In glitt'ring armour and a purple vest,
(Fair was his face; his eyes inspiring love,)
Bred by his father in the Martian grove,
Where the fat altars of Pelicus flame,
And sent in arms to purchase early fame.
Him when he spied, from far, the Tuscan king
Laid by the lance, and took to him the sling,
Thrice whirl'd the thong around his head, and threw:
The heated lead half melted as it flew;

It pierc'd his hollow temples and his brain;
The youth came tumbling down, and spurn'd the plain.
Then young Ascanius, who, before this day,
Was wont in woods to shoot the savage prey,
First bent in martial strife the twanging bow,
And exercis'd against a human foe—
With this bereft Numanus of his life,
Who Turnus' younger sister took to wife.
Proud of his realm, and of his royal bride,
Vaunting before his troops, and lengthen'd with a stride,
In these insulting terms the Trojans he defied:
"Twice conquer'd cowards! now your shame is shown—
Coop'd up a second time within your town!
Who dare not issue forth in open field,
But hold your walls before you for a shield.
Thus treat you war? thus our alliance force?
What gods, what madness hither steer'd your course?
You shall not find the sons of Atreus here,
Nor need the frauds of sly Ulysses fear.
Strong from the cradle, of a sturdy brood,
We bear our new-born infants to the flood;
There bath'd amid the stream, our boys we hold,
With winter harden'd, and inur'd to cold.
They wake before the day to range the wood,
Kill ere they eat, nor taste unconquer'd food.
No sports, but what belong to war they know—
To break the stubborn colt, to bend the bow,
Our youth, of labour patient, earn their bread;
Hardly they work, with frugal diet fed.
From ploughs and harrows sent to seek renown,
They fight in fields, and storm the shaken town.
No part of life from toils of war is free,
No change in age or diff'rence in degree.
We plough and till in arms: our oxen feel,
Instead of goads, the spur and pointed steel:
The inverted lance makes furrows in the plain.
E'en time, that changes all, yet changes us in vain—
The body, not the mind—nor can control
Th' immortal vigour, or abate the soul.
Our helms defend the young, disguise the gray:
We live by plunder, and delight in prey.
Your vests embroider'd with rich purple shine;
In sloth you glory, and in dances join.
Your vests have sweeping sleeves; with female pride,
Your turbans underneath your chins are tied.
Go, Phrygians, to your Dindymus again!
Go, less than women, in the shapes of men!
Go! mix'd with eunuchs in the mother's rites,
(Where with unequal sound the flute invites,)
Sing, dance, and howl, by turns, in Ida's shade
Resign the war to men, who know the martial trade."
This foul reproach Ascanius could no bear
With patience, or a vow'd revenge forbear.
At the full stretch of both his hands, he drew
And almost join'd the horns of the tough yew.
But first before the throne of Jove he stood,
And thus with lifted hands invok'd the god:
"My first attempt, great Jupiter, succeed!
An annual offering in thy grove shall bleed,
A snow-white steer, before thy altar led,
Who, like his mother, bears aloft his head,
Butts with his threat'ning brows, and bellowing stands,
And dares the fight, and spurns the yellow sands."
Jove bow'd the heav'ns, and lent a gracious ear,
And thunder'd on the left, amidst the clear.
Sounded at once the bow; and swiftly flies
The feather'd death, and hisses through the skies.
The steel through both his temples forc'd the way:
Extended on the ground, Numanus lay.
"Go now, vain boaster! and true valour scorn!
The Phrygians, twice subdu'd, yet make this third return."
Ascanius said no more. The Trojans shake
The heav'ns, with shouting, and new vigour take,
Apollo then bestrode a golden cloud,
To view the feats of arms, and fighting crowd;
And thus the beardless victor he bespoke aloud:
"Advance, illustrious youth! increase in fame,
And wide from east to west, extend thy name—
Offspring of gods thyself; and Rome shall owe
To thee a race of demigods below.
This is the way to heav'n: the pow'rs divine
From this beginning date the Julian line.
To thee, to them, and their victorious heirs,
The conquer'd war is due; and the vast world is theirs.
Troy is too narrow for thy name." He said,
And plunging downward shot his radiant head;
Dispell'd the breathing air, that broke his flight:
Shorn of his beams, a man to mortal sight.
Old Butes' form he took, Anchises' squire,
Now left to rule Ascanius, by his sire;
His wrinkled visage, and his hoary hairs,
His mien, his habit, and his arms he wears,
And thus salutes the boy, too forward for his years:
"Suffice it thee, thy father's worthy son,
The warlike prize thou hast already won.
The god of archers gives thy youth a part
Of his own praise, nor envies equal art.

Now tempt the war no more." He said, and flew
Obscure in air, and vanish'd from their view.
The Trojans, by his arms, their patron know,
And hear the twanging of his heavenly bow.
Then duteous force they use, and Phœbus' name,
To keep from fight the youth too fond of fame.
Undaunted, they themselves no dangers shun:
From wall to wall, the shouts and clamours run:
They bend their bows; they whirl their slings around:
Heaps of spent arrows fall, and strew the ground;
And helms, and shields, and rattling arms resound.
The combat thickens, like the storm that flies
From westward, when the show'ry Kids arise;
Or patt'ring hail comes pouring on the main,
When Jupiter descends in harden'd rain,
Or bellowing clouds burst with a stormy sound,
And with an armed winter strew the ground.
Pand'rus and Bitias, thunder-bolts of war,
Whom Hiera to bold Alcanor bore,
On Ida's top—two youths of height and size
Like firs that on their mother-mountain rise—
Presuming on their force, the gates unbar,
And of their own accord invite the war,
With fates averse, against their king's command,
Arm'd, on the right and on the left, they stand,
And flank the passage: shining steel they wear,
And waving crests above their heads appear.
Thus two tall oaks, that Padus' banks adorn,
Lift up to heav'n their leafy heads unshorn,
And, over press'd with nature's heavy load,
Dance to the whistling winds, and at each other nod.
In flows a tide of Latians, when they see
The gates set open, and the passage free:
Bold Quercens, with rash Tmarus rushing on,
Equicolus, who in bright armour shone,
And Hæmon first: but soon repuls'd they fly,
Or in the well-defended pass they die.
These with success are fir'd, and those with rage;
And each on equal terms at length engage.
Drawn from their lines, and issuing on the plain,
The Trojans hand to hand the fight maintain.
Fierce Turnus in another quarter fought,
When suddenly th' unhop'd-for news was brought,
The foes had left the fastness of their place,
Prevail'd in fight, and had his men in chase.
He quits th' attack, and, to prevent their fate,
Runs, where the giant brothers guard the gate.
The first he met, Antiphates the brave,
But base begotten on a Theban slave—
Sarpedon's son) he slew: the deadly dart
Found passage through his breast, and pierc'd his heart.
Fix'd in the wound th' Italian cornel stood,
Warm'd in his lungs, and in his vital blood.
Aphidnus next, and Erymanthus dies,
And Meropes, and the gigantic size
Of Bitias, threat'ning with his ardent eyes;
Not by the feeble dart he fell oppress'd,
(A dart were lost within his roomy breast,)
But from a knotted lance, large, heavy, strong,
Which roar'd like thunder as it whirl'd along:
Not two bull-hides th' impetuous force withhold,
Nor coat of double mail, with scales of gold.
Down sunk the monster bulk, and press'd the ground,
(His arms and clatt'ring shield on the vast body sound.)
Not with less ruin than the Baian mole,
Rais'd on the seas, the surges to control—
At once comes tumbling down the rocky wall,
Prone to the deep; the stones disjointed fall
Of the vast pile; the scatter'd ocean flies;
Black sands, discolour'd froth, and mingled mud, arise,
The frighted billows roll, and seek the shores:
Then trembles Prochyta, then Ischia roars:
Typhœus, thrown beneath by Jove's command,
Astonish'd at the flaw that shakes the land,
Soon shifts his weary side, and, scarce awake,
With wonder feels the weight press lighter on his back.
The warrior god the Latian troops inspir'd,
And strung their sinews, and their courage fir'd,
But chills the Trojan hearts with cold affright:
Then black despair precipitates their flight.
When Pandarus beheld his brother kill'd,
The town with fear and wild confusion fill'd,
He turns the hinges of the heavy gate
With both his hands, and adds his shoulders to the weight;
Some happier friends within the walls enclos'd
The rest shut out, to certain death expos'd;
Fool as he was, and frantic in his care,
T' admit young Turnus, and include the war
He thrust amid the crowd, securely bold,
Like a fierce tiger pent amid the fold.
Too late his blazing buckler they descry,
And sparkling fires that shot from either eye,
His mighty members, and his ample breast,
His rattling armour, and his crimson crest.
Far from that hated face the Trojans fly,
All but the fool who sought his destiny.
Mad Pandarus steps forth, with vengeance vow'd
For Bitias' death, and threatens thus aloud:
"These are not Ardea's walls, nor this the town
Amata proffers with Lavinia's crown;

'T is hostile earth you tread. Of hope bereft,
No means of safe return by flight are left."
To whom, with count'nance calm, and soul sedate,
Thus Turnus: "Then begin; and try thy fate:
My message to the ghost of Priam bear;
Tell him a new Achilles sent thee there."
A lance of tough ground ash the Trojan threw,
Rough in the rind, and knotted as it grew:
With his full force he whirl'd it first around,
But the soft yielding air receiv'd the wound:
Imperial Juno turn'd the course before,
And fix'd the wand'ring weapon in the door.
"But hope not thou," said Turnus, "when I strike,
To shun thy fate: our force is not alike,
Nor thy steel temper'd by the Lemnian god."
Then rising, on his utmost stretch he stood,
And aim'd from high: the full descending blow
Cleaves the broad front, and beardless cheeks in two.
Down sinks the giant with a thund'ring sound:
His pond'rous limbs oppress the trembling ground; [wound.
Blood, brains, and foam, gush from the gaping
Scalp, face, and shoulders, the keen steel divides;
And the shar'd visage hangs on equal sides.
The Trojans fly from their approaching fate:
And, had the victor then secur'd the gate,
And to his troops without unclos'd the bars,
One lucky day had ended all his wars.
But boiling youth, and blind desire of blood,
Push on his fury, to pursue the crowd.
Hamstring'd behind, unhappy Gyges died:
Then Phalaris is added to his side.
The pointed jav'lins from the dead he drew,
And their friends' arms against their fellows threw.
Strong Halys stands in vain; weak Phegeus flies:
Saturnia, still at hand, new force and fire supplies.
Then Halius, Prytanis, Alcander fall—
Engag'd against the foes who scal'd the wall:
But whom they fear'd without, they found within.
At last, though late, by Lynceus he was seen.
He calls new succours, and assaults the prince:
But weak his force, and vain is their defence.
Turn'd to the right, his sword the hero drew,
And at one blow the bold aggressor slew.
He joints the neck: and with a stroke so strong,
The helm flies off, and bears the head along.
Next him, the huntsman, Amycus, he kill'd,
In darts envenom'd, and in poison skill'd.
Then Clytius fell beneath his fatal spear,
And Creteus, whom the Muses held so dear:
He fought with courage, and he sung the fight:
Arms were his bus'ness, verses his delight.
The Trojan chiefs behold, with rage and grief,
Their slaughter'd friends, and hasten their relief.
Bold Mnestheus rallies first the broken train,
Whom brave Serestus and his troops sustain.
To save the living and revenge the dead,
Against one warrior's arm all Troy they led.
"O, void of sense and courage!" Mnestheus cried,
"Where can you hope your coward heads to hide? [run?
Ah! where beyond these rampires can you
One man, and in your camp enclos'd, you shun!
Shall then a single sword such slaughter boast,
And pass unpunish'd from a num'rous host?
Forsaking honour, and renouncing fame,
Your gods, your country, and your king, you shame!"
This just reproach their virtue does excite:
They stand, they join, they thicken to the fight.
Now Turnus doubts, and yet disdains to yield,
But with slow paces measures back the field,
And inches to the walls, where Tyber's tide,
Washing the camp, defends the weaker side.
The more he loses, they advance the more,
And tread in every step he trod before.
They shout; they bear him back; and whom by might
They cannot conquer, they oppress with weight.
As, compass'd with a wood of spears around,
The lordly lion still maintains his ground;
Grins horrible, retires, and turns again;
Threats his distended paws, and shakes his mane:
He loses while in vain he presses on,
Nor will his courage let him dare to run:
So Turnus fares, and, unresolv'd of flight,
Moves tardy back, and just recedes from fight.
Yet twice enrag'd, the combat he renews,
Twice breaks, and twice his broken foes pursues.
But now they swarm, and with fresh troops supplied,
Come rolling on, and rush from every side:
Nor Juno, who sustain'd his arms before,
Dares with new strength suffice th' exhausted store;
For Jove, with sour commands, sent Iris down,
To force th' invader from the frighted town.
With labour spent, no longer can he wield
The heavy falchion, or sustain the shield,
O'erwhelm'd with darts, which from afar they fling
The weapons round his hollow temples ring;

His golden helm gives way, with stony blows
Batter'd and flat, and beaten to his brows.
His crest is rash'd away; his ample shield
Is falsified, and round with jav'lins fill'd.
The foe now faint, the Trojans overwhelm;
And Mnestheus lays hard load upon his helm.
Sick sweat succeeds, he drops at ev'ry pore;
With driving dust his cheeks are pasted o'er;
Shorter and shorter ev'ry gasp he takes;
And vain efforts and hurtless blows he makes.
Arm'd as he was, at length he leap'd from high,
Plung'd in the flood, and made the waters fly.
The yellow god the welcome burden bore,
And wip'd the sweat, and wash'd away the gore;
Then gently wafts him to the farther coast,
And sends him safe to cheer his anxious host.

BOOK X.

ARGUMENT.

Jupiter, calling a council of the gods, forbids them to engage in either party. At Æneas' return there is a bloody battle; Turnus killing Pallas; Æneas, Lausus and Mezentius. Mezentius is described as an atheist; Lausus as a pious and virtuous youth. The different actions and death of these two are the subject of a noble episode.

The gates of heav'n unfold: Jove summons all
The gods to council in the common hall.
Sublimely seated, he surveys from far
The fields, the camp, the fortune of the war,
And all th' inferior world. From first to last,
The sov'reign senate in degrees are plac'd.
Then thus the almighty sire began: "Ye gods,
Natives or denizens of blest abodes!
From whence these murmurs, and this change of mind,
This backward fate from what was first design'd?
Why this protracted war, when my commands
Pronounc'd a peace, and gave the Latian lands?
What fear or hope on either part divides
Our heav'ns, and arms our powers on diff'rent sides?
A lawful time of war at length will come,
(Nor need your haste anticipate the doom,)
When Carthage shall contend the world with Rome,
Shall force the rigid rocks and Alpine chains,
And, like a flood, come pouring on the plains.
Then is your time for faction and debate,
For partial favour, and permitted hate.
Let now your immature dissension cease:
Sit quiet, and compose your souls to peace."
Thus Jupiter in few unfolds the charge:
But lovely Venus thus replies at large:
"O pow'r immense! eternal energy!
(For to what else protection can we fly?)
See'st thou the proud Rutulians, how they dare
In fields, unpunish'd, and insult my care?
How lofty Turnus vaunts amidst his train,
In shining arms triumphant on the plain?
E'en in their lines and trenches they contend,
And scarce their walls the Trojan troops defend:
The town is fill'd with slaughter, and o'erfloats
With a red deluge, their increasing moats.
Æneas, ignorant, and far from thence,
Has left a camp expos'd, without defence.
This endless outrage shall they still sustain?
Shall Troy renew'd, be forc'd and fir'd again?
A second siege my banish'd issue fears;
And a new Diomede in arms appears.
One more audacious mortal will be found;
And I, thy daughter, wait another wound.
Yet, if, with fates averse, without thy leave,
The Latian lands my progeny receive,
Bear they the pains of violated law,
And thy protection from their aid withdraw.
But, if the gods their sure success foretell—
If those of heaven consent with those of hell,
To promise Italy; who dare debate
The pow'r of Jove, or fix another fate?
What should I tell of tempests on the main,
Of Æolus usurping Neptune's reign?
Of Iris sent, with Bacchanalian heat,
T' inspire the matrons, and destroy the fleet?
Now Juno to the Stygian sky descends,
Solicits hell for aid and arms the fiends.
That new example wanted yet above—
An act that well became the wife of Jove!
Alecto, rais'd by her, with rage inflames
The peaceful bosoms of the Latian dames.
Imperial sway no more exalts my mind;
(Such hopes I had indeed, while heav'n was kind;)
Now let my happier foes possess my place,
Whom Jove prefers before the Trojan race;
And conquer they whom you with conquest grace.
Since you can spare, from all your wide command,
No spot of earth, no hospitable land,
Which may my wand'ring fugitives receive,
(Since haughty Juno will not give you leave;)
Then, father, (if I still may use that name,)
By ruin'd Troy, yet smoking from the flame,
I beg you, let Ascanius, by my care,
Be freed from danger and dismiss'd the war:
Inglorious let him live, without a crown:
The father may be cast on coasts unknown,
Struggling with fate; but let me save the son.
Mine is Cythera, mine the Cyprian tow'rs:
In those recesses, and those sacred bow'rs,

Obscurely let him rest; his right resign
To promis'd empire, and his Julian line.
Then Carthage may th' Ausonian towns destroy,
Nor fear the race of a rejected boy.
What profits it my son to 'scape the fire,
Arm'd with his gods, and loaded with his sire;
To pass the perils of the seas and wind;
Evade the Greeks, and leave the war behind;
To reach th' Italian shores; if, after all,
Our second Pergamus is doom'd to fall?
Much better had he curb'd his high desires,
And hover'd o'er his ill-extinguish'd fires.
To Simoïs' banks the fugitive restore,
And give them back to war, and all the woes before.
Deep indignation swell'd Saturnia's heart:
"And must I own," she said, "my secret smart—
What with more decence were in silence kept,
And, but for this unjust reproach, had slept?
Did god or man your fav'rite son advise,
With war unhop'd the Latians to surprise.
By fate, you boast, and by the gods' decree,
He left his native land for Italy
Confess the truth; by mad Cassandra, more
Than heav'n, inspired, he sought a foreign shore.
Did I persuade to trust his second Troy
To the raw conduct of a beardless boy,
With walls unfinish'd, which himself forsakes,
And through the waves a wand'ring voyage takes?
When have I urg'd him meanly to demand
The Tuscan aid, and arm a quiet land?
Did I or Iris give this mad advice?
Or made the fool himself the fatal choice?
You think it hard, the Latians should destroy
With swords your Trojans, and with fires your Troy!
Hard and unjust indeed, for men to draw
Their native air, nor take a foreign law!
That Turnus is permitted still to live,
To whom his birth a god and goddess give.
But yet 't is just and lawful for your line [join;
To drive their fields, and force with fraud to
Realms, not your own, among your clans divide,
And from the bridegroom tear the promis'd bride.
Petition, while you public arms prepare;
Pretend a peace, and yet provoke a war:
'Twas giv'n to you, your darling son to shroud,
To draw the dastard from the fighting crowd,
And, for a man, obtend an empty cloud.
From flaming fleets you turn'd the fire away,
And chang'd the ships to daughters of the sea.
But 't is my crime—the queen of heav'n offends
If she presume to save her suff'ring friends!
Your son, not knowing what his foes decree,
You say, is absent: absent let him be.
Yours is Cythera, yours the Cyprian tow'rs
The soft recesses, and the sacred bow'rs.
Why do you then these needless arms prepare,
And thus provoke a people prone to war?
Did I with fire the Trojan town deface,
Or hinder from return your exil'd race?
Was I the cause of mischief, or the man,
Whose lawless lust the fatal war began?
Think on whose faith th' adult'rous youth relied,
Who promis'd, who procur'd the Spartan bride?
When all th' united states of Greece combin'd
To purge the world of the perfidious kind,
Then was your time to fear the Trojan fate:—
Your quarrels and complaints are now too late."
Thus Juno. Murmurs rise, with mix'd applause,
Just as they favour or dislike the cause.
So winds, when yet unfledg'd in woods they lie,
In whispers first their tender voices try;
Then issue on the main with bellowing rage,
And storms to trembling mariners presage.
Then thus to both replied th' imperial god,
(Who shakes heav'n's axles with his awful nod.
When he begins, the silent senate stand,
With rev'rence list'ning to the dread command:
The clouds dispel; the winds their breath restrain;
And the hush'd waves lie flatted on the main.)
"Celestials! your attentive ears incline!
Since (said the god) the Trojans must not join
In wish'd alliance with the Latian line—
Since endless jarrings and immortal hate
Tend but to discompose our happy state—
The war henceforward be resign'd to fate.
Each to his proper fortune stand or fall:
Equal and unconcern'd I look on all.
Rutulians, Trojans, are the same to me;
And both shall draw the lots their fates decree.
Let these assault, if Fortune be their friend;
And if she favours those, let those defend:—
The Fates will find their way." The Thund'rer said,
And shook the sacred honours of his head,
Attesting Styx, th' inviolable flood,
And the black regions of his brother god:
Trembled the poles of heav'n; and earth confess'd the nod.
This end the sessions had: the senate rise,
And to his palace wait their sov'reign through the skies.
Meantime, intent upon their siege, the foes
Within their walls the Trojan host enclose:
They wound, they kill, they watch at ev'ry gate
Renew the fires, and urge their happy fate.
Th' Æneans wish in vain their wonted chief,
Hopeless of flight, more hopeless of relief.

Thin on the tow'rs they stand; and ev'n those few,
A feeble, fainting, and dejected crew.
Yet in the face of danger some there stood:
The two bold brothers of Sarpedon's blood,
Asius, and Acmon: both th' Assaraci;
Young Hæmon, and, though young, resolv'd to die.
With these were Clarus and Thymœtes join'd;
Tybris and Castor, both of Lycian kind.
From Acmon's hands a rolling stone there came,
So large, it half deserv'd a mountain's name!
Strong-sinew'd was the youth, and big of bone:
His brother Mnestheus could not more have done,
Or the great father of th' intrepid son.
Some firebands throw, some flights of arrows send;
And some with darts, and some with stones, defend.
Amid the press appears the beauteous boy,
The care of Venus, and the hope of Troy.
His lovely face unarm'd, his head was bare;
In ringlets o'er his shoulders hung his hair.
His forehead circled with a diadem;
Distinguish'd from the crowd, he shines a gem,
Enchas'd in gold, or polish'd iv'ry set,
Amidst the meaner foil of sable jet.
Nor Ismarus was wanting to the war,
Directing ointed arrows from afar,
And death with poison arm'd—in Lydia born,
Where plenteous harvests the fat fields adorn;
Where proud Pactolus floats the fruitful lands,
And leaves a rich manure of golden sands.
There Capys, author of the Capuan name,
And there was Mnestheus too, increas'd in fame,
Since Turnus from the camp he cast with shame.
Thus mortal war was wag'd on either side.
Meantime the hero cuts the nightly tide.
For, anxious, from Evander when he went,
He sought the Tyrrhene camp, and Tarchon's tent;
Expos'd the cause of coming to the chief;
His name and country told, and ask'd relief;
Propos'd the terms; his own small strength declar'd;
What vengeance proud Mezentius had prepar'd;
What Turnus, bold and violent, design'd;
Then show'd the slipp'ry state of human-kind,
And fickle fortune; warn'd him to beware,
And to his wholesome counsel added pray'r.
Tarchon, without delay, the treaty signs,
And to the Trojan troops the Tuscan joins.
They soon set sail; nor now the Fates withstand;
Their forces trusted with a foreign hand.
Æneas leads; upon his stern appear
Two lions carv'd, which rising Ida bear—
Ida, to wand'ring Trojans ever dear.
Under their grateful shade Æneas sate,
Revolving war's events, and various fate,
His left young Pallas kept, fix'd to his side,
And oft of winds inquir'd, and of the tide:
Oft of the stars, and of their wat'ry way;
And what he suffer'd both by land and sea.
Now, sacred sisters, open all your spring!
The Tuscan leaders, and their army, sing,
Which follow'd great Æneas to the war:
Their arms, their numbers, and their names declare.
A thousand youths brave Massicus obey,
Borne in the Tiger through the foaming sea;
From Clusuim brought, and Cosa, by his care:
For arms, light quivers, bows, and shafts, they bear.
Fierce Abas next: his men bright armour wore:
His stern Apollo's golden statue bore.
Six hundred Populonia sent along,
All skill'd in martial exercise, and strong.
Three hundred more for battle Ilva joins,
An isle renown'd for steel, and unexhausted mines.
Asylas on his prow the third appears,
Who heav'n interprets, and the wand'ring stars;
From offer'd entrails, prodigies expounds,
And peals of thunder, with presaging sounds.
A thousand spears in warlike order stand;
Sent by the Pisans, under his command.
Fair Astur follows in the wat'ry field,
Proud of his manag'd horse, and painted shield
Gravisca, noisome from the neighb'ring fen,
And his own Cære, sent three hundred men,
With those which Minio's fields, and Pyrgi, gave;
All bred in arms, unanimous and brave.
Thou, Muse, the name of Cinyras renew,
And brave Cupavo follow'd but by few;
Whose helm confess'd the lineage of the man,
And bore, with wings display'd, a silver swan.
Love was the fault of his fam'd ancestry,
Whose forms and fortunes in his ensign fly.
For Cycnus lov'd unhappy Phaeton,
And sung his loss in poplar groves, alone,
Beneath the sister shades, to sooth his grief.
Heav'n heard his song, and hasten'b his relief,
And chang'd to snowy plumes his hoary hair,
And wing'd his flight, to chant aloft in air.
His son Cupavo brush'd the briny flood:
Upon his stern a brawny centaur stood,
Who heav'd a rock, and threat'ning stil to throw,
With lifted hands alarm'd the seas below;
They seem'd to fear the formidable sight,
And roll'd their billows on, to speed his flight.

Ocnus was next, who led his native train
Of hardy warriors through the wat'ry plain—
The son of Manto, by the Tuscan stream,
From whence the Mantuan town derives the name—
An ancient city, but of mix'd descent:
Three sev'ral tribes compose the government;
Four towns are under each; but all obey
The Mantuan laws, and own the Tuscan sway.
Hate to Mezentius arm'd five hundred more,
Whom Mincius from his sire Benacus bore—
Mincius, with wreaths of reeds his forehead cover'd o'er.
These grave Aulestes leads: a hundred sweep
With stretching oars at once the glassy deep.
Him, and his martial train, the Triton bears:
High on his poop the sea-green god appears:
Frowning he seems his crooked shell to sound;
And at the blast the billows dance around.
A hairy man above the waist he shows;
A porpoise-tail beneath his belly grows;
And ends a fish; his breast the waves divides;
And froth and foam augment the murm'ring tides.
Full thirty ships transport the chosen train,
For Troy's relief, and scour the briny main.
Now was the world forsaken by the sun,
And Phœbe half her nightly race had run.
The careful chief, who never clos'd his eyes,
Himself the rudder holds, the sails supplies.
A choir of Nereids meet him on the flood,
Once his own galleys, hewn from Ida's wood:
But now, as many nymphs, the sea they sweep,
As rode before tall vessels on the deep.
They know him from afar; and in a ring
Enclose the ship that bore the Trojan king.
Cymodoce, whose voice excell'd the rest,
Above the waves advanc'd her snowy breast;
Her right hand stops the stern, her left divides
The curling ocean, and corrects the tides.
She spoke for all the choir, and thus began
With pleasing words to warn th' unknowing man:
"Sleeps our lov'd lord? O goddess-born, awake!
Spread ev'ry sail, pursue your wat'ry track,
And haste your course. Your navy once were we,
From Ida's height descending to the sea;
Till Turnus, as at anchor fix'd we stood,
Presum'd to violate our holy wood.
Then, loos'd from shore, we fled his fires profane,
(Unwillingly we broke our master's chain,)
And since have sought you through the Tuscan main.
The mighty Mother chang'd our forms to these,
And gave us life immortal in the seas.
But young Ascanius, in his camp distress'd,
By your insulting foes is hardly press'd.
Th' Arcadian horsemen, and Etrurian host,
Advance in order on the Latian coast:
To cut their way the Daunian chief designs,
Before their troops can reach the Trojan lines.
Thou, when the rosy morn restores the light,
First arm thy soldiers for th' ensuing fight:
Thyself the fated sword of Vulcan wield,
And bear aloft th' impenetrable shield.
To-morrow's sun, unless my skill be vain,
Shall see huge heaps of foes in battle slain.
Parting she spoke; and with immortal force
Push'd on the vessel in the wat'ry course;
For well she knew the way. Impell'd behind,
The ship flew forward, and outstript the wind.
The rest make up. Unknowing of the cause,
The chief admires their speed, and happy omens draws.
Then thus he pray'd, and fix'd on heav'n his eyes:
"Hear thou, great Mother of the deities,
With turrets crown'd! (on Ida's holy hill,
Fierce tigers, rein'd and curb'd, obey thy will:)
Firm thy own omens; lead us on to fight;
And let thy Phrygians conquer in thy right."
He said no more. And now renewing day
Had chas'd the shadows of the night away.
He charg'd the soldiers, with preventing care,
Their flags to follow, and their arms prepare;
Warn'd of th' ensuing fight, and bade them hope the war.
Now, from his lofty poop, he view'd below
His camp encompass'd and th' enclosing foe.
His blazing shield embrac'd, he held on high:
The camp receive the sign, and with loud shouts reply.
Hope arms their courage: from their tow'rs they throw
Their darts with double force, and drive the foe.
Thus, at the signal giv'n, the cranes arise
Before the stormy south, and blacken all the skies.
King Turnus wonder'd at the fight renew'd,
Till, looking back, the Trojan fleet he view'd,
The seas with swelling canvass cover'd o'er,
And the swift ships descending on the shore.
The Latians saw from far, with dazzled eyes,
The radiant crest that seem'd in flames to rise,
And dart diffusive fires around the field;
And the keen glitt'ring of the golden shield.
Thus threat'ning comets, when by night they rise,
Shoot sanguine streams, and sadden all the skies:
So Sirius, flashing forth sinister lights,
Pale human-kind with plagues and with dry famine frights.

Yet Turnus with undaunted mind is bent
To man the shores and hinder the descent,
And thus awakes the courage of his friends:
"What you so long have wish'd, kind Fortune sends—
In ardent arms to meet th' invading foe:
You find, and find him at advantage now.
Yours is the day: you need but only dare;
Your swords will make you masters of the war:
Your sires, your sons, your houses, and your lands,
And dearest wives, are all within your hands.
Be mindful of the race from whence you came,
And emulate in arms your fathers' fame.
Now take the time, while stagg'ring yet they stand
With feet unfirm; and prepossess the strand:
Fortune befriends the bold." No more he said,
But balanc'd whom to leave, and whom to lead;
Then these elects, the landing to prevent;
And those he leaves to keep the city pent.
Meantime the Trojan sends his troops ashore:
Some are by boats expos'd, by bridges more,
With lab'ring oars they bear along the strand,
Where the tide languishes, and leap a-land.
Tarchon observes the coast with careful eyes,
And, while no ford he finds, no water fries,
Nor billows with unequal murmurs roar,
But mostly slide along, and swell the shore,
That course he steer'd, and thus he gave command:
"Here ply your oars, and at all hazard land
Force on the vessel, that her keel may wound
This hated soil, and furrow hostile ground.
Let me securely land—I ask no more;
Then sink my ships, or shatter on the shore."
This fiery speech inflames his fearful friends:
They tug at ev'ry oar, and ev'ry stretcher bends:
They run their ships aground: the vessels knock,
(Thus forc'd ashore,) and tremble with the shock.
Tarchon's alone was lost, and stranded stood:
Stuck on a bank, and beaten by the flood,
She breaks her back; the loosen'd sides gives way,
And plunge the Tuscan soldiers in the sea.
Their broken oars and floating planks withstand
Their passage, while they labour to the land;
And ebbing tides bear back upon th' uncertain sand.
Now Turnus leads his troops without delay,
Advancing to the margin of the sea.
The trumpets sound: Æneas first assail'd
The clowns new rais'd and raw; and soon prevail'd.
Great Theron fell, an omen of the fight—
Great Theron, large of limbs, of giant height.
He first in open fields defied the prince:
But armour scal'd with gold was no defence
Against the fated sword, which open'd wide
His plated shield, and pierc'd his naked side.
Next Lichas fell, who, not like others born,
Was from his wretched mother ripp'd and torn;
Sacred, O Phœbus! from his birth to thee
For his beginning life from biting steel was free.
Not far from him was Gyas laid along,
Of monstrous bulk; with Cissues fierce and strong:
Vain bulk and strength! for, when the chief assail'd,
Nor valour, nor Herculean arms avail'd,
Nor their fam'd father, wont in war to go
With great Alcides, while he toil'd below.
The noisy Pharos next receiv'd his death:
Æneas writh'd his dart, and stopp'd his bawling breath.
Then wretched Cydon had receiv'd his doom,
Who courted Clytius in his beardless bloom,
And sought with lust obscene polluted joys—
The Trojan sword had cur'd his love of boys,
Had not his seven bold brethren stopp'd the course
Of the fierce champion, with united force.
Sev'n darts were thrown at once; and some rebound
From his bright shield, some on his helmet sound:
The rest had reach'd him; but his mother's care
Prevented those, and turn'd aside in air.
The prince then call'd Achates, to supply
The spears, that knew the way to victory—
"Those fatal weapons, which, inur'd to blood,
In Grecian bodies under Ilium stood:
Not one of those my hand shall toss in vain
Against our foes on this contended plain."
He said: then seiz'd a mighty spear, and threw;
Which, wing'd with fate, through Mæon's buckler flew,
Pierc'd all the brazen plates, and reach'd his heart:
He stagger'd with intolerable smart.
Alcanor saw; and reach'd, but reach'd in vain,
His helping hand, his brother to sustain.
A second spear, which kept the former course,
From the same hand, and sent with equal force
His right arm pierc'd, and, holding on, bereft
His use of both, and pinion'd down his left.
Then Numitor from his dead brother drew
Th' ill-omen'd spear, and at the Trojan threw:
Preventing fate directs the lance awry,
Which, glancing, only mark'd Achates' thigh.
In pride of youth the Sabine Clausus came
And, from afar, at Dryops took his aim,

The spear flew hissing through the middle space,
And pierc'd his throat, directed at his face:
It stopp'd at once the passage of his wind,
And the free soul to flitting air resign'd:
His forehead was the first that struck the ground;
Life-blood and life rush'd mingled through the wound.
He slew three brothers of the Borean race,
And three, whom Ismarus, their native place,
Had sent to war, but all the sons of Thrace.
Halesus, next, the bold Aurunci leads:
The son of Neptune to his aid succeeds,
Conspicuous on his horse. On either hand,
These fight to keep, and those to win, the land.
With mutual blood th' Ausonian soil is dy'd,
While on its borders each their claim decide.
As wintry winds, contending in the sky,
With equal force of lungs their titles try;
They rage, they roar; the doubtful rack of heav'n
Stands without motion, and the tide undriv'n:
Each bent to conquer, neither side to yield,
They long suspend the fortune of the field.
Both armies thus perform what courage can;
Foot set to foot, and mingled man to man.
But in another part th' Arcadian horse
With ill success engage the Latian force:
For where the impetuous torrent rushing down,
Huge craggy stones and rooted trees had thrown,
They left their coursers, and, unus'd to fight
On foot, were scatter'd in a shameful flight.
Pallas, who, with disdain and grief, had view'd
His foes pursuing, and his friends pursu'd,
Us'd threat'nings mix'd with pray'rs, his last resource,
With these to move their minds, with those to fire their force.
"Which way, companions? whither would you run?
By you yourselves, and mighty battles won,
By my great sire, by his establish'd name,
An early promise of my future fame:
By my youth, emulous of equal right
To share his honours—shun ignoble flight!
Trust not your feet: your hands must hew your way
Through yon black body, and that thick array:
'T is through that forward path that we must come:
There lies a way, and there a passage home:
Nor pow'rs above, nor destinies below,
Oppress our arms, with equal strength we go,
With mortal hands to meet a mortal foe.
See on what foot we stand! a scanty shore—
The sea behind, our enemies before
No passage left, unless we swim the main;
Or, forcing these, the Trojan trenches gain."
This said, he strode with eager haste along,
And bore amidst the thickest of the throng.
Lagus, the first he met, with fate to foe,
Had heav'd a stone of mighty weight, to throw:
Stooping, the spear descended on his chine,
Just where the bone distinguish'd either loin:
It stuck so fast, so deeply buried lay,
That scarce the victor forc'd the steel away.
Hisbon came on: but, while he mov'd too slow
To wish'd revenge, the prince prevents his blow;
For, warding his at once, at once he press'd,
And plung'd the fatal weapon in his breast.
Then lewd Anchemolus he laid in dust,
Who stain'd his stepdame's bed with impious lust.
And, after him, the Daunian twins were slain,
Laris and Thymbrus, on the Latian plain;
So wond'rous like in feature, shape and size,
As caus'd an error in their parents' eyes—
Grateful mistake! but soon the sword decides
The nice distinction, and their fate divides:
For Thymbrus' head was lopp'd; and Laris' hand,
Dismember'd, sought its owner on the strand:
The trembling fingers yet the falchion strain,
And threaten still th' extended stroke in vain.
Now, to renew the charge, th' Arcadians came;
Sight of such acts, and sense of honest shame,
And grief, with anger mix'd, their minds inflame.
Then, with a casual blow was Rhœteus slain,
Who chanc'd, as Pallas threw, to cross the plain;
The flying spear was after Ilus sent;
But Rhœteus happen'd on a death unmeant:
From Theuthras and from Tyres, while he fled,
The lance, athwart his body, laid him dead:
Roll'd from his chariot with a mortal wound,
And intercepted fate, he spurn'd the ground.
As when in summer, welcome winds arise,
The watchful shepherd to the forest flies,
And fires the midmost plants; contagion spreads,
And catching flames infect the neighb'ring heads;
Around the forest flies the furious blast,
And all the leafy nation sinks at last;
And Vulcan rides in triumph o'er the waste.
The pastor, pleas'd with his dire victory,
Beholds the satiate flames in sheets ascend the sky;—
So Pallas' troops their scatter'd strength unite,
And pouring on their foes, their prince delight.
Halesus came, fierce with desire of blood;
But first collected in his arms he stood:
Advancing then, he plied the spear so well,
Ladon, Demodocus, and Pheres fell.

Around his head he toss'd his glitt'ring brand,
And from Strymonius hew'd his better hand,
Held up to guard his throat; then hurl'd a stone
At Thoas' ample front, and pierc'd the bone:
It struck beneath the space of either eye:
And blood, and mingled brains, together fly.
Deep skill'd in future fates, Halesus' sire
Did with the youth to lonely groves retire:
But, when the father's mortal race was run,
Dire destiny laid hold upon the son,
And haul'd him to the war, to find, beneath
Th' Evandrian spear, a memorable death.
Pallas th' encounter seeks, but, ere he throws,
To Tuscan Tyber, thus address'd his vows;
"O sacred stream! direct my flying dart,
And give to pass the proud Halesus' heart.
His arms and spoils thy holy oak shall bear."
Pleas'd with the bribe, the god receiv'd his pray'r;
For, while his shield protects a friend distress'd,
The dart came driving on and pierc'd his breast.
But Lausus, no small portion of the war,
Permits not panic fear to reign too far,
Caus'd by the death of so renown'd a knight;
But by his own example cheers the fight.
Fierce Abas first he slew—Abas, the stay
Of Trojan hopes, and hind'rance of the day.
The Phrygian troops escap'd the Greeks in vain:
They, and their mix'd allies, now load the plain.
To the rude shock of war both armies came:
Their leaders equal, and their strength the same.
The rear so press'd the front, they could not wield
Their angry weapons, to dispute the field.
Here Pallas urges on, and Lausus there:
Of equal youth and beauty both appear,
Both by fate forbid to breathe their native air.
Their congress in the field great Jove withstands—
Both doom'd to fall, and fall by greater hands.
Meantime Juturna warns the Daunian chief
Of Lausus' danger, urging swift relief.
With his driv'n chariot he divides the crowd
And making to his friends, thus calls aloud:
"Let none presume his needless aid to join:
Retire, and clear the field: the fight is mine:
To this right hand is Pallas only due:
O! were his father here, my just revenge to view!"
From the forbidden space his men retir'd.
Pallas their awe, and his stern words admir'd;
Survey'd him o'er and o'er with wond'ring sight,
Struck with his haughty mien, and tow'ring height:
Then to the king: "Your empty vaunts forbear:
Success I hope; and fate I cannot fear.
Alive, or dead, I shall deserve a name:
Jove is impartial, and to both the same,
He said, and to the void advanc'd his pace.
Pale horror sate on each Arcadian face.
Then Turnus, from his chariot, leaping light,
Address'd himself on foot to single fight.
And, as a lion—when he spies from far
A bull that seems to meditate the war,
Bending his neck, and spurning back the sand—
Runs roaring downward from his hilly stand;
Imagine eager Turnus not more slow,
To rush from high on his unequal foe.
Young Pallas, when he saw the chief advance
Within due distance of his flying lance,
Prepares to charge him first—resolv'd to try
If fortune would his want of force supply;
And thus to heav'n and Hercules address'd:
"Alcides, once on earth Evander's guest!
His son adjures thee, by those holy rites,
That hospitable board, those genial nights,
Assist my great attempt to gain this prize,
And let proud Turnus view, with dying eyes,
His ravish'd spoils." 'T was heard, the vain request;
Alcides mourn'd, and stifled sighs within his breast.
Then Jove, to sooth his sorrow, thus began:
"Short bounds of life are set to mortal man.
'T is virtue's work alone to stretch the narrow span.
So many sons of gods, in bloody fight
Around the walls of Troy, have lost the light:
My own Sarpedon fell beneath his foe;
Nor I, his mighty sire, could ward the blow.
E'en Turnus shortly shall resign his breath,
And stands already on the verge of death."
This said, the god permits the fatal fight,
But from the Latian fields averts his sight.
Now with full force his spear young Pallas threw;
And, having thrown, his shining falchion drew,
The steel just graz'd along the shoulder-joint,
And mark'd it slightly with the glancing point.
Fierce Turnus first to nearer distance drew,
And pois'd his pointed spear, before he threw:
Then as the winged weapon whizz'd along,
"See now," said he, "whose arm is better strung."
The spear kept on the fatal course, unstay'd
By plates of ir'n, which o'er the shield were laid:
Through folded brass, and tough bull-hides, it pass'd,
His corslet pierc'd, and reach'd his heart at last.
In vain the youth tugs at the broken wood:
The soul comes issuing with the vital blood:
He falls: his arms upon his body sound:
And with his bloody teeth he bites the ground.
Turnus bestrode the corpse: "Arcadians hear,"
Said he: "my message to your master bear:

Such as the sire deserv'd, the son I send:
It costs him dear to be the Phrygian's friend.
The lifeless body, tell him, I bestow
Unask'd, to rest his wand'ring ghost below."
He said, and trampled down, with all the force
Of his left foot, and spurn'd the wretched corse;
Then snatch'd the shining belt, with gold inlaid—
The belt Eurytion's artful hands had made;
Where fifty fatal brides, express'd to sight,
All in the compass of one mournful night,
Depriv'd their bridegrooms of returning light.
In an ill hour insulting Turnus tore
Those golden spoils, and in a worse he wore.
O mortals! blind in fate, who never know
To bear high fortunes, or endure the low!
The time shall come, when Turnus, but in vain,
Shall wish untouch'd the trophies of the slain—
Shall wish the fatal belt were far away,
And curse the dire remembrance of the day.
The sad Arcadians, from th' unhappy field,
Bear back the breathless body on a shield.
O grace and grief of war! at once restor'd,
With praises, to thy sire, at once deplor'd.
One day first sent thee to the fighting field,
Beheld whole heaps of foes in battle kill'd;
One day beheld thee dead, and borne upon thy shield.
This dismal news, not from uncertain fame,
But sad spectators, to the hero came:
His friends upon the brink of ruin stand,
Unless reliev'd by his victorious hand.
He whirls his sword around, without delay,
And hews through adverse foes an ample way,
To find fierce Turnus, of his conquest proud.
Evander, Pallas, all that friendship ow'd
To large deserts, are present to his eyes—
His plighted hand, and hospitable ties.
Four sons of Sulmo, four whom Ufens bred,
He took in fight, and living victims led,
To please the ghost of Pallas, and expire,
In sacrifice, before his fun'ral fire.
At Magus next he threw: he stoop'd below
The flying spear, and shunn'd the promis'd blow,
Then creeping, clasp'd the hero's knees, and pray'd:
"By young Iulus, by thy father's shade,
O! spare my life, and send me back to see
My longing sire, and tender progeny.
A lofty house I have, and wealth untold,
In silver ingots, and in bars of gold:
All these, and sums besides, which see no day,
The ransom of this one poor life shall pay.
If I survive, will Troy the less prevail?
A single soul's too light to turn the scale."
He said. The hero sternly thus replied:
"Thy bars and ingots, and the sums beside
Leave for thy children's lot. Thy Turnus broke
All rules of war by one relentless stroke,
When Pallas fell: so deems, nor deems alone,
My father's shadow, but my living son."
Thus having said, of kind remorse bereft,
He seiz'd his helm, and dragg'd him with his left;
Then with his right hand, while his neck he wreath'd,
Up to the hilt his shining falchion sheath'd.
Apollo's priest, Hæmonides was near:
His holy fillets on his front appear;
Glitt'ring in arms, he shone amidst the crowd,
Much of his god, more of his purple, proud.
Him the fierce Trojan follow'd through the field:
The holy coward fell; and, forc'd to yield,
The prince stood o'er the priest, and, at one blow,
Sent him an off'ring to the shades below.
His arms Serestus on his shoulders bears,
Design'd a trophy to the god of wars.
Vulcanian Cæculus renews the fight,
And Umbro, born upon the mountain's height.
The champion cheers his troops t' encounter those,
And seeks revenge himself on other foes.
At Anxur's shield he drove; and, at one blow
Both shield and arm to ground together go.
Anxur had boasted much of magic charms,
And thought he wore impenetrable arms,
So made by mutter'd spell; and, from the spheres,
Had life secur'd, in vain, for length of years.
Then Tarquitus the field in triumph trod;
A nymph his mother, and his sire a god.
Exulting in bright arms, he braves the prince:
With his protended lance he makes defence;
Bears back his feeble foe; then, pressing on
Arrests his better hand, and drags him down;
Stands o'er the prostrate wretch, and (as he lay,
Vain tales inventing, and prepar'd to pray)
Mows off his head: the trunk a moment stood,
Then sunk, and roll'd along the sand in blood.
The vengeful victor thus upbraids the slain:
"Lie there, proud man, unpity'd, on the plain;
Lie there, inglorious, and without a tomb,
Far from thy mother and thy native home,
Expos'd to savage beasts, and birds of prey,
Or thrown for food to monsters of the sea."
On Lycas and Antæus next he ran,
Two chiefs of Turnus, and who led his van.
They fled for fear; with these, he chas'd along
Camers the yellow-lock'd, and Numa strong,
Both great in arms; and both were fair and young.
Camers was son to Volscens, lately slain,
In wealth surpassing all the Latian train,
And in Amyclæ fix'd his silent easy reign

And as Ægæon, when with heav'n he strove,
Stood opposite in arms to mighty Jove;
Mov'd all his hundred hands, provok'd the war,
Defied the forky lightning from afar;
At fifty mouths his flaming breath expires,
And flash for flash returns, and fires for fires;
In his right hand as many swords he wields,
And takes the thunder on as many shields:
With strength like his, the Trojan hero stood;
And soon the fields with falling crops were strow'd,
When once his falchion found the taste of blood.
With fury scarce to be conceiv'd, he flew
Against Niphæus, whom four coursers drew.
They, when they see the fiery chief advance,
And pushing at their chests his pointed lance,
Wheel'd with so swift a motion, mad with fear,
They threw their master headlong from the chair.
They stare, they start, nor stop their course, before
They bear the bounding chariot to the shore.
Now Lucagus and Liger scour the plains,
With two white steeds; but Liger holds the reins,
And Lucagus the lofty seat maintains—
Bold brethren both. The former wav'd in air
His flaming sword: Æneas couch'd his spear,
Unus'd to threats, and more unus'd to fear.
Then Liger thus: "Thy confidence is vain
To 'scape from hence, as from the Trojan plain:
Nor these the steeds which Diomede bestrode,
Nor this the chariot where Achilles rode:
Nor Venus' veil is here, nor Neptune's shield:
Thy fatal hour is come; and this the field."
Thus Liger vainly vaunts: the Trojan peer
Return'd his answer with his flying spear.
As Lucagus, to lash his horses, bends
Prone to the wheels, and his left foot pretends
Prepar'd for fight—the fatal dart arrives,
And through the border of his buckler drives;
Pass'd through and pierc'd his groin. The deadly wound,
Cast from his chariot, roll'd him on the ground:
Whom thus the chief upbraids with scornful spite:
"Blame not the slowness of your steeds in flight:
Vain shadows did not force their swift retreat;
But you yourself forsake your empty seat."
He said and seiz'd at once the loosen'd rein:
For Liger lay already on the plain,
By the same shock: then, stretching out his hands,
The recreant thus his wretched life demands:
"Now, by thyself, O more than mortal man!
By her and him from whom thy breath began,
Who form'd thee thus divine, I beg thee, spare
This forfeit life, and hear thy suppliant's pray'r."
Thus much he spoke, and more he would have said,
But the stern hero turn'd aside his head,
And cut him short: "I hear another man:
You talk'd not thus before the fight began.
Now take your turn; and, as a brother should,
Attend your brother to the Stygian flood."
Then through his breast his fatal sword he sent;
And the soul issued at the gaping vent.
As storms the skies, and torrents tear the ground,
Thus rag'd the prince, and scatter'd deaths around.
At length Ascanius, and the Trojan train,
Broke from the camp, so long besieg'd in vain.
Meantime the king of gods, and mortal man,
Held conf'rence with his queen, and thus began:
"My sister goddess, and well pleasing wife,
Still think you Venus' aid supports the strife—
Sustains her Trojans—or themselves, alone,
With inborn valour force their fortune on?
How fierce in fight, with courage undecay'd!
Judge if such warriors want immortal aid."
To whom the goddess with the charming eyes,
Soft in her tone, submissively replies:
"Why, O my sov'reign lord, whose frown I fear,
And cannot, unconcern'd, your anger bear—
Why urge you thus my grief? when if I still
(As once I was) were mistress of your will,
From your almighty pow'r your pleasing wife
Might gain the grace of lengthening Turnus' life,
Securely snatch him from the fatal fight,
And give him to his aged father's sight.
Now let him perish, since you hold it good,
And glut the Trojans with his pious blood.
Yet from our lineage he derives his name,
And, in the fourth degree, from god Pilumnus came!
Yet he devoutly pays you rites divine,
And offers daily incense at your shrine."
Then shortly thus the sov'reign god replied:
"Since in my pow'r and goodness you confide,
If, for a little space, a lengthen'd span,
You beg reprieve for this expiring man,
I grant your leave to take your Turnus hence
From instant fate, and can so far dispense.
But, if some secret meaning lies beneath,
To save the short-liv'd youth from destin'd death,
Or, if a farther thought you entertain,
To change the fates; you feed your hopes in vain."
To whom the goddess thus, with weeping eyes:
"And what if that request, your tongue denies,

Your heart shall grant—and not a short reprieve,
But length of certain life, to Turnus give?
Now speedy death attends the guiltless youth,
If my presaging soul divines with truth;
Which, O! I wish might err, through causeless fears,
And you (for you have pow'r) prolong his years!"
Thus having said, involv'd in clouds, she flies,
And drives a storm before her through the skies.
Swift she descends, alighting on the plain,
Where the fierce foes a dubious fight maintain.
Of air condens'd, a spectre soon she made;
And, what Æneas was, such seem'd the shade.
Adorn'd with Dardan arms, the phantom bore
His head aloft; a plumy crest he wore;
This hand appear'd a shining sword to wield,
And that sustain'd an imitated shield.
With manly mien he stalk'd along the ground,
Nor wanted voice belied, nor vaunted sound.
(Thus haunting ghosts appear, to waking sight,
Or dreadful visions in our dreams by night.)
The spectre seems the Daunian chief to dare,
And flourishes his empty sword in air.
At this, advancing, Turnus hurl'd his spear:
The phantom wheel'd, and seem'd to fly for fear.
Deluded Turnus thought the Trojan fled,
And with vain hopes his haughty fancy fed.
"Whither, O coward?" (thus he calls aloud,
Nor found he spoke to wind, and chas'd a cloud,)
"Why thus forsake your bride? Receive from me
The fated land you sought so long by sea."
He said, and brandishing at once his blade,
With eager pace pursu'd the flying shade.
By chance, a ship was fasten'd to the shore,
Which from old Clusium king Osinius bore:
The plank was ready laid for safe ascent;
For shelter there the trembling shadow bent,
And skipp'd, and skulk'd, and under hatches went:
Exulting Turnus, with regardless haste,
Ascends the plank, and to the galley pass'd.
Scarce had he reach'd the prow, Saturnia's hand
The halsers cuts, and shoots the ship from land.
With wind in poop, the vessel ploughs the sea,
And measures back with speed her former way.
Meantime Æneas seeks his absent foe,
And sends his slaughter'd troops to shades below.
The guileful phantom now forsook the shroud,
And flew sublime, and vanish'd in a cloud.
Too late young Turnus the delusion found,
Far on the sea, still making from the ground.
Then thankless for a life redeem'd by shame,
With sense of honour stung, and forfeit fame,
Fearful besides of what in fight had pass'd,
His hands and haggard eyes to heav'n he cast
"O Jove!" he cried—"for what offence have I
Deserv'd to bear this endless infamy?
Whence am I forc'd, and whither am I borne?
How, and with what reproach shall I return?
Shall ever I behold the Latian plain,
Or see Laurentum's lofty tow'rs again?
What will they say of their deserting chief?
The war was mine: I fly from their relief!
I led to slaughter, and in slaughter leave;
And e'en from hence their dying groans receive:
Here, over-match'd in fight, in heaps they lie,
There, scatter'd o'er the fields, ignobly fly.
Gape wide, O earth, and draw me down alive!
Or, oh! ye pitying winds, a wretch relieve!
On sands or shelves, the splitting vessel drive;
Or set me shipwreck'd on some desert shore,
Where no Rutulian eyes may see me more—
Unknown to friends, or foes, or conscious fame,
Lest she should follow, and my flight proclaim."
Thus Turnus rav'd, and various fates revolv'd:
The choice was doubtful, but the death resolv'd.
And now the sword, and now the sea, took place—
That to revenge, and this to purge disgrace.
Sometimes he thought to swim the stormy main,
By stretch of arms the distant shore to gain.
Thrice he the sword essay'd, and thrice the flood:
But Juno, mov'd with pity, both withstood,
And thrice repress'd his rage; strong gales supplied,
And push'd the vessel o'er the swelling tide.
At length she lands him on his native shores,
And to his father's longing arms restores.
Meantime, by Jove's impulse, Mezentius arm'd,
Succeeding Turnus, with his ardour warm'd
His fainting friends, reproach'd their shameful flight,
Repell'd the victors, and renew'd the fight.
Against their king the Tuscan troops conspire;
Such is their hate, and such their fierce desire
Of wish'd revenge—on him, and him alone,
All hands employ'd, and all their darts are thrown.
He, like a solid rock by seas enclos'd,
To raging winds and roaring waves oppos'd,
From his proud summit looking down, disdains
Their empty menace, and unmov'd remains.
Beneath his feet fell haughty Hebrus dead,
Then Latagus, and Palmus, as he fled.
At Latagus a weighty stone he flung:
His face was flatted, and his helmet rung.

But Palmus from behind receives his wound:
Hamstring'd he falls, and grovels on the ground:
His crest and armour from his body torn,
Thy shoulders, Lausus, and thy head, adorn.
Evas and Mimas, both of Troy, he slew.
Mimas his birth from fair Pheano drew—
Born on that fatal night, when, big with fire,
The queen produc'd young Paris to his sire.
But Paris in the Phrygian fields was slain,
Unthinking Mimas on the Latian plain.
And as a savage boar, on mountains bred,
With forest mast and fatt'ning marshes fed,
When once he sees himself in toils enclos'd,
By huntsmen and their eager hounds oppos'd,
He whets his tusks, and turns, and dares the war,
Th' invaders dart their jav'lins from afar:
All keep aloof, and safely shout around;
But none presumes to give a nearer wound:
He frets and froths, erects his bristled hide,
And shakes a grove of lances from his side:
Not otherwise the troops, with hate inspir'd,
And just revenge against the tyrant fir'd,
Their darts with clamour at a distance drive,
And only keep the languish'd war alive.
From Corythus came Acron to the fight,
Who left his spouse betroth'd, and unconsummate night.
Mezentius sees him through the squadron ride,
Proud of the purple favours of his bride.
Then as a hungry lion, who beholds
A gamesome goat who frisks about the folds,
Or beamy stag that grazes on the plain—
He runs, he roars, he shakes his rising mane,
He grins, and opens wide his greedy jaws:
The prey lies panting underneath his paws:
He fills his famish'd maw; his mouth runs o'er
With unchew'd morsels, while he churns the gore:
So proud Mezentius rushes on his foes,
And first unhappy Acron overthrows;
Stretch'd at his length, he spurns the swarthy ground
The lance, besmear'd with blood, lies broken in the wound.
Then, with disdain, the haughty victor view'd
Orodes flying, nor the wretch pursu'd,
Nor thought the dastard's back deserv'd a wound,
But, running, gain'd th' advantage of the ground:
Then turning short, he met him face to face,
To give his victory the better grace.
Orodes falls, in equal fight oppress'd:
Mezentius fix'd his foot upon his breast,
And rested lance; and thus aloud he cries:
"Lo! here the champion of my rebels lies!"
The fields around with "Iō Pæan!" ring;
And peals of shouts applaud the conqu'ring king.
At this the vanquish'd, with his dying breath,
Thus faintly spoke, and prophesy'd in death:
"Nor thou, proud man, unpunish'd shalt remain,
Like death attends thee on this fatal plain."
Then, sourly smiling, thus the king replied:
"For what belongs to me, let Jove provide;
But die thou first, whatever chance ensue."
He said, and from the wound the weapon drew.
A hov'ring mist came swimming o'er his sight,
And seal'd his eyes in everlasting night.
By Cædicus, Alcathŏus was slain:
Sacrator laid Hydaspes on the plain:
Orses the strong to greater strength must yield;
He, with Parthenius, were by Rapo kill'd.
Then brave Messapus Ericetes slew,
Who from Lycaon's blood his lineage drew.
But from his headstrong horse his fate he found,
Who threw his master, as he made a bound:
The chief, alighting, struck him to the ground;
Then Clonius, hand to hand, on foot assails:
The Trojan sinks, and Neptune's son prevails.
Agis the Lycian, stepping forth with pride,
To single fight the boldest foe defied;
Whom Tuscan Valerus by force o'ercame,
And not belied his mighty father's fame.
Salius to death the great Authronius sent
But the same fate the victor underwent,
Slain by Nealces' hand, well skill'd to throw
The flying dart, and draw the far-deceiving bow.
Thus equal deaths are dealt with equal chance:
By turns they quit their ground, by turns advance,
Victors and vanquish'd in the various field,
Nor wholly overcome, nor wholly yield.
The gods from heav'n survey the fatal strife,
And mourn the miseries of human life.
Above the rest, two goddesses appear
Concern'd for each: here Venus, Juno there.
Amidst the crowd, infernal Ate shakes
Her scourge aloft, and crest of hissing snakes.
Once more the proud Mezentius, with disdain,
Brandish'd his spear, and rush'd into the plain
Where tow'ring in the midmost rank he stood,
Like tall Orion stalking o'er the flood,
(When with his brawny breast he cuts the waves,
His shoulders scarce the topmost billow laves;)
Or like a mountain-ash, whose roots are spread,
Deep fix'd in earth—in clouds he hides his head.
The Trojan prince beheld him from afar,
And dauntless undertook the doubtful war.
Collected in his strength, and like a rock
Pois'd on his base, Mezentius stood the shock.
He stood, and measuring first with careful eyes
The space his spear could reach, aloud he cries:

"My strong right hand and sword assist my stroke!
(Those only gods Mezentius will invoke,)
His armour, from the Trojan pirate torn,
By my triumphant Lausus shall be worn."
He said; and with his utmost force he threw
The massy spear, which hissing as it flew,
Reach'd the celestial shield: that stopp'd the course;
But glancing thence, the yet unbroken force
Took a new bent obliquely, and, betwixt
The side and bowels, fam'd Antoris fix'd.
Antoris had from Argos travelled far,
Alcides' friend, and brother of the war;
Till, tir'd with toils, fair Italy he chose;
And in Evander's palace sought repose.
Now falling by another's wound, his eyes
He cast to heav'n, on Argos thinks, and dies.
The pious Trojan then his jav'lin sent:
The shield gave way: through triple plates it went
Of solid brass, of linen triply toll'd,
And three bull-hides, which round the buckler roll'd,
All these it pass'd, resistless in the course,
Transpierc'd his thigh, and spent its dying force.
The gaping wound gush'd out a crimson flood.
The Trojan, glad with sight of hostile blood,
His falchion drew, to closer fight address'd,
And with new force his fainting foe oppress'd.
His father's peril Lausus view'd with grief:
He sigh'd, he wept, he ran to his relief.
And here heroic youth, 't is here I must
To thy immortal memory be just,
And sing an act so noble and so new,
Posterity will scarce believe 't is true.
Pain'd with the wound, and useless for the fight,
The father sought to save himself by flight:
Encumber'd, slow he dragg'd the spear along,
Which pierc'd his thigh and in his buckler hung.
The pious youth, resolv'd on death, below
The lifted sword springs forth to face the foe;
Protects his parent, and prevents the blow,
Shouts of applause ran ringing through the field.
To see the son the vanquish'd father shield.
All fir'd with gen'rous indignation, strive,
And, with a storm of darts, to distance drive
The Trojan chief, who, held at bay from far,
On his Vulcanian orb sustain'd the war.
As, when thick hail comes rattling in the wind,
The ploughman, passenger, and lab'ring hind
For shelter to the neighb'ring covert fly,
Or hous'd, or safe in hollow caverns, lie;
But, that o'erblown, when heav'n above them smiles,
Return to travail, and renew their toils:
Æneas, thus o'erwhelm'd on ev'ry side,
The storm of darts, undaunted, did abide,
And thus to Lausus loud with friendly threat'ning cried:
"Why wilt thou rush to certain death, and rage,
In rash attempts, beyond thy tender age,
Betray'd by pious love?"—Nor, thus forborne
The youth desists, but with insulting scorn
Provokes the ling'ring prince, whose patience tir'd,
Gave place; and all his breast with fury fir'd.
For now the Fates prepar'd their sharpen'd shears;
And lifted high the flaming sword appears,
Which full descending, with a frightful sway,
Through shield and corslet forc'd the impetuous way,
And buried deep in his fair bosom lay.
The purple streams through the thin armour strove,
And drench'd the embroider'd coat his mother wove;
And life at length forsook his heaving heart,
Loath from so sweet a mansion to depart.
But when, with blood and paleness all o'erspread,
The pious prince beheld young Lausus dead,
He griev'd, he wept; (the sight an image brought
Of his own filial love—a sadly pleasing thought;)
Then stretch'd his hand to hold him up, and said:
"Poor hapless youth! what praises can be paid
To love so great, to such transcendent store
Of early worth, and sure presage of more!
Accept whate'er Æneas can afford:
Untouch'd thy arms, untaken be thy sword;
And all that pleas'd the living, still remain
Inviolate, and sacred to the slain.
Thy body on thy parents I bestow,
To rest thy soul, at least, if shadows know,
Or have a sense of human things below.
There to thy fellow-ghosts with glory tell
'T was by the great Æneas' hand I fell."
With this his distant friends he beckons near,
Provokes their duty, and prevents their fear;
Himself assists to lift him from the ground,
With clotted locks and blood that well'd from out the wound.
Meantime, his father, now no father, stood,
And wash'd his wounds, by Tyber's yellow flood
Oppress'd with anguish, panting, and o'erspent,
His fainting limbs against an oak he leant.
A bough his brazen helmet did sustain,
His heavier arms lay scatter'd on the plain:
A chosen train of youth around him stand;
His drooping head was rested on his hand:

His grisly beard his pensive bosom sought;
And all on Lausus ran his restless thought.
Careful, concern'd, his danger to prevent,
He much inquir'd, and many a message sent
To warn him from the field—alas! in vain!
Behold his mournful followers bear him slain:
O'er his broad shield still gush'd the yawning wound,
And drew a bloody trail along the ground.
Far off he heard their cries, far off divin'd
The dire event with a foreboding mind.
With dust he sprinkled first his hoary head;
Then both his lifted hands to heaven he spread;
Last, the dear corpse embracing, thus he said:
"What joys, alas! could this frail being give,
That I have been so covetous to live?
To see my son, and such a son, resign
His life a ransom for preserving mine?
And am I then preserv'd, and art thou lost?
How much too dear has that redemption cost?
'T is now my bitter banishment I feel:
This is a wound too deep for time to heal.
My guilt thy growing virtues did defame;
My blackness blotted thy unblemish'd name.
Chas'd from a throne, abandon'd, and exil'd
For foul misdeeds, were punishments too mild:
I ow'd my people these, and, from their hate,
With less resentment could have borne my fate
And yet I live, and yet sustain the sight
Of hated men, and of more hated light—
But will not long." With that he rais'd from ground
His fainting limbs, that stagger'd with his wound;
Yet, with a mind resolv'd and unappall'd
With pains or perils, for his courser call'd—
Well mouth'd, well-manag'd, whom himself did dress
With daily care, and mounted with success—
His aid in arms, his ornament in peace.
Soothing his courage with a gentle stroke,
The steed seem'd sensible while thus he spoke:
"O Rhœbus! we have liv'd too long for me—
If life and long were terms that could agree.
This day thou either shalt bring back the head
And bloody trophies of the Trojan dead—
This day thou either shalt revenge my wo,
For murder'd Lausus, on his cruel foe;
Or, if inexorable Fate deny
Our conquest, with thy conquer'd master die;
For, after such a lord, I rest secure,
Thou wilt no foreign reins, or Trojan load, endure."
He said: and straight th' officious courser kneels,
To take his wonted weight. His hands he fills
With pointed jav'lins; on his head he lac'd
His glitt'ring helm, which terribly was grac'd
With waving horse-hair, nodding from afar;
Then spurr'd his thund'ring steed amidst the war.
Love, anguish, wrath, and grief, to madness wrought,
Despair, and secret shame, and conscious thought
Of inborn worth, his lab'ring soul oppress'd,
Roll'd in his eyes, and rag'd within his breast.
Then loud he call'd Æneas thrice by name:
The loud repeated voice to glad Æneas came.
"Great Jove," he said, "and the far-shooting god,
Inspire thy mind to make thy challenge good!"
He spoke no more, but hasten'd, void of fear,
And threaten'd with his long protended spear.
To whom Mezentius thus: "Thy vaunts are vain.
My Lausus lies extended on the plain:
He 's lost! thy conquest is already won:
The wretched sire is murder'd in the son.
Nor fate I fear, but all the gods defy.
Forbear thy threats: my bus'ness is to die.
But first receive this parting legacy."
He said: and straight a whirling dart he sent:
Another after, and another, went
Round in a spacious ring he rides the field,
And vainly plies th' impenetrable shield.
Thrice rode he round, and thrice Æneas wheel'd,
Turn'd as he turn'd: the golden orb withstood
The strokes and bore about an iron wood
Impatient of delay, and weary grown,
Still to defend, and to defend alone,
To wrench the darts which in his buckler light,
Urg'd and o'erlabour'd in unequal fight—
At length resolv'd, he throws, with all his force,
Full at the temples of the warrior horse.
Just were the stroke was aim'd, th' unerring spear
Made way, and stood transfix'd through either ear.
Seiz'd with unwonted pain, surpris'd with fright,
The wounded steed curvets, and, rais'd upright,
Lights on his feet before; his hoofs behind
Spring up in air aloft, and lash the wind
Down comes the rider headlong from his height;
His horse came after with unwieldy weight,
And, flound'ring forward, pitching on his head,
His lord's encumber'd shoulder overlaid.
From either host, the mingled shouts and cries
Of Trojans and Rutulians rend the skies:
Æneas, hast'ning, wav'd his fatal sword
High o'er his head, with this reproachful word:
"Now, where are now the taunts, the fierce disdain
Of proud Mezentius, and the lofty strain?"
Struggling, and wildly staring on the skies
With scarce recover'd sight, he thus replies:
"Why these insulting words, this waste of breath,
To souls undaunted, and secure of death?

'T is no dishonour for the brave to die;
Nor came I here with hope of victory:
Nor ask I life, nor fought with that design.
As I had us'd my fortune, use thou thine.
My dying son contracted no such band:
The gift is hateful from his murderer's hand.
For this, this only favour let me sue,
If pity can to conquer'd foes be due,
Refuse it not: but let my body have
The last retreat of human kind, a grave.
Too well I know the insulting people's hate.
Protect me from their vengeance after fate:
This refuge for my poor remains provide;
And lay my much-lov'd Lausus by my side."
He said, and to the sword his throat applied.
The crimson stream distain'd his arms around,
And the disdainful soul came rushing through
the wound.

BOOK XI.

ARGUMENT.

Æneas erects a trophy of the spoils of Mezentius, grants a truce for burying the dead, and sends home the body of Pallas with great solemnity. Latinus calls a council, to propose offers of peace to Æneas; which occasions great animosity betwixt Turnus and Drances. In the mean time there is a sharp engagement of the horse; wherein Camilla signalizes herself, is killed, and the Latine troops are entirely defeated.

Scarce had the rosy morning rais'd her head
Above the waves, and left her wat'ry bed:
The pious chief, whom double cares attend,
For his unburied soldiers and his friend,
Yet first to heav'n perform'd a victor's vows:
He bar'd an ancient oak of all her boughs;
Then on a rising ground the trunk he plac'd,
Which with the spoils of his dead foe he grac'd.
The coat of arms by proud Mezentius worn,
Now on a naked snag in triumph borne,
Was hung on high, and glitter'd from afar,
A trophy sacred to the god of war.
Above his arms, fix'd on the leafless wood,
Appear'd his plumy crest, besmear'd with blood.
His brazen buckler on the left was seen:
Truncheons of shiver'd lances hung between;
And on the right was plac'd his corslet, bor'd;
And to the neck was tied his unavailing sword.
A crowd of chiefs enclose the godlike man,
Who, thus, conspicuous in the midst, began:
"Our toils, my friends, are crown'd with sure
success;
The greater part perform'd, achieve the less.
Now follow cheerful to the trembling town:
Press but an entrance, and presume it won.
Fear is no more: for fierce Mezentius lies,
As the first fruits of war, a sacrifice.
Turnus shall fall extended on the plain,
And, in this omen, is already slain.
Prepar'd in arms, pursue your happy chance
That none unwarn'd may plead his ignorance;
And I, at heaven's appointed hour, may find
Your warlike ensigns waving in the wind.
Meantime the rites and fun'ral pomps prepare,
Due to your dead companions of the war—
The last respect the living can bestow,
To shield their shadows from contempt below.
That conquer'd earth be theirs, for which they
fought,
And which for us with their own blood they
bought.
But first the corpse of our unhappy friend
To the sad city of Evander send,
Who, not inglorious in his age's bloom,
Was hurried hence by too severe a doom."
Thus, weeping, while he spoke, he took his
way,
Where, new in death, lamented Pallas lay.
Acœtes watch'd the corpse, whose youth de-
serv'd
The father's trust; and now the son he serv'd
With equal faith, but less auspicious care:
Th' attendants of the slain his sorrow share.
A troop of Trojans mix'd with these appear,
And mourning matrons with dishevell'd hair.
Soon as the prince appears, they raise a cry;
All beat their breasts, and echoes rend the sky.
They rear his drooping forehead from the ground:
But, when Æneas view'd the grisly wound
Which Pallas in his manly bosom bore
And the fair flesh distain'd with purple gore;
First, melting into tears, the pious man
Deplor'd so sad a sight, then thus began:
"Unhappy youth! when fortune gave the rest
Of my full wishes, she refus'd the best!
She came; but brought not thee along, to bless
My longing eyes, and share in my success:
She grudg'd thy safe return, the triumphs due
To prosp'rous valour, in the public view.
Not thus I promis'd, when thy father lent
Thy needless succour with a sad consent;
Embrac'd me, parting for th' Etrurian land,
And sent me to possess a large command.
He warn'd, and from his own experience told,
Our foes were warlike, disciplin'd, and bold.
And now, perhaps, in hopes of thy return
Rich odours on his loaded altars burn,
While we, with vain officious pomp, prepare
To send him back his portion of the war,
A bloody breathless body, which can owe
No farther debt, but to the pow'rs below.
The wretched father, ere his race is run,
Shall view the fun'ral honours of his son!
These are my triumphs of the Latian war,
Fruits of my plighted faith and boasted care

And yet, unhappy sire, thou shalt not see
A son, whose death disgrac'd his ancestry:
Thou shalt not blush, old man, however griev'd:
Thy Pallas no dishonest wound receiv'd:
He died no death to make thee wish, too late,
Thou hadst not liv'd to see his shameful fate.
But what a champion has th' Ausonian coast,
And what a friend hast thou, Ascanius, lost!"
Thus having mourn'd, he gave the word around
To raise the breathless body from the ground;
And chose a thousand horse, the flow'r of all
His warlike troops, to wait the funeral,
To bear him back and share Evander's grief—
A well-becoming, but a weak relief.
Of oaken twigs they twist an easy bier,
Then on their shoulders the sad burden rear.
The body on his rural hearse is borne:
Strew'd leaves and fun'ral greens the bier adorn.
All pale he lies, and looks a lovely flow'r,
New cropt by virgin hands, to dress the bow'r:
Unfaded yet, but yet unfed below, [shall owe.
No more to mother-earth or the green stem
Then two fair vests, of wond'rous work and cost,
Of purple woven, and with gold emboss'd,
For ornament the Trojan hero brought,
Which with her hands Sidonian Dido wrought.
One vest array'd the corpse; and one they spread
O'er his clos'd eyes, and wrapt around his head.
That, when the yellow hair in flame should fall,
The catching fire might burn the golden caul.
Besides, the spoils of foes in battle slain,
When he descended on the Latian plain—
Arms, trappings, horses—by the hearse are led
In long array—th' achievements of the dead.
Then pinion'd with their hands behind, appear
Th' unhappy captives, marching in the rear,
Appointed off'rings in the victor's name,
To sprinkle with their blood the fun'ral flame.
Inferior trophies by the chiefs are borne:
Gauntlets and helms their loaded hands adorn;
And fair inscriptions fix'd, and titles read
Of Latian leaders conquer'd by the dead.
Acœtes on his pupil's corpse attends,
With feeble steps, supported by his friends.
Pausing at every pace, in sorrow drown'd,
Betwixt their arms he sinks upon the ground;
Where grov'ling while he lies in deep despair,
He beats his breast, and rends his hoary hair.
The champion's chariot next is seen to roll,
Besmear'd with hostile blood, and honourably foul.
To close the pomp, Æthon, the steed of state,
Is led, the fun'rals of his lord to wait.
Stripp'd of his trappings, with a sullen pace
He walks; and the big tears run rolling down his face.
The lance of Pallas, and the crimson crest,
Are borne behind:– the victor seiz'd the rest
The march begins; the trumpets hoarsely sound:
The pikes and lances trail along the ground.
Thus while the Trojan and Arcadian horse
To Palantean tow'rs direct their course,
In long procession rank'd; the pious chief
Stopp'd in the rear, and gave a vent to grief.
"The public care," he said, "which war attends,
Diverts our present woes, at least suspends.
Peace with the manes of great Pallas dwell!
Hail, holy relics! and a last farewell!"
He said no more, but, inly though he mourn'd,
Restrain'd his tears, and to the camp return'd.
Now suppliants, from Laurentum sent, demand
A truce, with olive-branches in their hand:
Obtest his clemency, and from the plain
Beg leave to draw the bodies of their slain.
They plead, that none those common rites deny
To conquer'd foes that in fair battle die.
All cause of hate was ended in their death;
Nor could he war with bodies void of breath.
A king, they hop'd, would hear a king's request,
Whose son he once was call'd, and once his guest.
Their suit, which was too just to be denied,
The hero grants, and farther thus replied:
"O Latian princes! how severe a fate
In causeless quarrels has involv'd your state,
And arm'd against an unoffending man,
Who sought your friendship ere the war began;
You beg a truce, which I would gladly give,
Not only for the slain, but those who live.
I came not hither but by heav'n's command,
And sent by fate to share the Latian land.
Nor wage I wars unjust: your king denied
My proffer'd friendship and my promis'd bride;
Left me for Turnus. Turnus then should try
His cause in arms, to conquer or to die.
My right and his are in dispute: the slain
Fell without fault, our quarrel to maintain.
In equal arms let us alone contend;
And let him vanquish, whom his fates befriend.
This is the way (so tell him) to possess
The royal virgin, and restore the peace.
Bear this my message back—with ample leave
That your slain friends may fun'ral rites receive."
Thus having said—the ambassadors, amaz'd,
Stood mute a while, and on each other gaz'd.
Drances, their chief, who harbour'd in his breast
Long hate to Turnus, as his foe profess'd

Broke silence first, and to the godlike man
With graceful action bowing, thus began:
"Auspicious prince, in arms a mighty name,
But yet whose actions far transcend your fame!
Would I your justice or your force express
Thoughts can but equal; and all words are less.
Your answer we shall thankfully relate,
And favours granted to the Latian state.
If wish'd success our labours shall attend,
Think peace concluded, and the king your friend:
Let Turnus leave the realm to your command;
And seek alliance in some other land:
Build you the city which your fates assign;
We shall be proud in the great work to join."
Thus Drances; and his words so well persuade,
The rest empower'd, that soon a truce is made.
Twelve days the term allow'd: and, during those,
Latians and Trojans, now no longer foes,
Mix'd in the woods, for fun'ral piles prepare
To fell the timber, and forget the war.
Loud axes through the groaning groves resound:
Oak, mountain-ash, and poplar, spread the ground;
Firs fall from high; and some the trunks receive
In loaden wains; with wedges some they cleave.
And now the fatal news by Fame is blown
Through the short circuit of th' Arcadian town,
Of Pallas slain—by Fame, which just before
His triumphs on distended pinions bore.
Rushing from out the gate, the people stand,
Each with a fun'ral flambeau in his hand.
Wildly they stare, distracted with amaze:
The fields are lighten'd with a fiery blaze,
That casts a sullen splendour on their friends—
The marching troop which their dead prince attends.
Both parties meet: they raise a doleful cry:
The matrons from the walls with shrieks reply;
And their mix'd mourning rends the vaulted sky.
The town is fill'd with tumult and with tears,
Till the loud clamours reach Evander's ears:
Forgetful of his state, he runs along,
With a disorder'd pace, and cleaves the throng;
Falls on the corpse; and groaning there he lies,
With silent grief, that speaks but at his eyes.
Short sighs and sobs succeed; till sorrow breaks
A passage, and at once he weeps and speaks:
"O Pallas! thou hast fail'd thy plighted word!
To fight with caution, not to tempt the sword.
I warn'd thee, but in vain! for well I knew
What perils youthful ardour would pursue—
That boiling blood would carry thee too far,
Young as thou wert in dangers, raw to war!
O curst essay of arms! disastrous doom!
Prelude of bloody fields, and fights to come!
Hard elements of inauspicious war!
Vain vows to heav'n, and unavailing care!
Thrice happy thou, dear partner of my bed,
Whose holy soul the stroke of Fortune fled—
Precious of ills, and leaving me behind,
To drink the dregs of life, by fate assign'd.
Beyond the goal of nature I have gone:
My Pallas late set out, but reach'd too soon.
If, for my league against th' Ausonian state,
Amidst their weapons I had found my fate,
(Deserv'd from them,) then I had been return'd
A breathless victor, and my son had mourn'd.
Yet will I not my Trojan friend upbraid,
Nor grudge th' alliance I so gladly made.
'T was not his fault my Pallas fell so young,
But my own crime for having liv'd too long.
Yet, since the gods had destin'd him to die,
At least, he led the way to victory:
First for his friends he won the fatal shore,
And sent whole herds of slaughter'd foes before—
A death too great, too glorious to deplore.
Nor will I add new honours to thy grave
Content with those the Trojan hero gave—
That funeral pomp thy Phrygian friends design'd,
In which the Tuscan chiefs and army join'd.
Great spoils and trophies, gain'd by thee they bear:
Then let thy own achievements be thy share.
E'en thou, O Turnus, hadst a trophy stood,
Whose mighty trunk had better grac'd the wood,
If Pallas had arriv'd, with equal length
Of years, to match thy bulk with equal strength.
But why, unhappy man! dost thou detain
These troops, to view the tears thou shedd'st in vain?
Go, friends! this message to your lord relate:
Tell him, that, if I bear my bitter fate,
And, after Pallas' death, live lingering on,
'T is to behold his vengeance for my son.
I stay for Turnus, whose devoted head
Is owing to the living and the dead.
My son and I expect it from his hand;
'T is all that he can give, or we demand.
Joy is no more: but I would gladly go,
To greet my Pallas with such news below."
The morn had now dispell'd the shades of night,
Restoring toils, when she restor'd the light.
The Trojan king, and Tuscan chief command
To raise the piles along the winding strand.
Their friends convey the dead to fun'ral fires;
Black smould'ring smoke from the green wood expires; [retires.
The light of heaven is chok'd, and the new day

Then thrice around the kindled piles they go,
(For ancient custom had ordain'd it so,)
Thrice horse and foot about the fires are led;
And thrice with loud laments they hail the dead.
Tears trickling down their breasts, bedew the ground;
And drums and trumpets mix their mournful sound.
Amid the blaze, their pious brethren throw
The spoils in battle taken from the foe—
Helms, bits emboss'd, and swords of shining steel:
One casts a target, one a chariot-wheel:
Some to their fellows their own arms restore—
The falchions which in luckless fight they bore,
Their bucklers pierc'd, their darts bestow'd in vain,
And shiver'd lances gather'd from the plain.
Whole herds of offer'd bulls, about the fire,
And bristled boars, and woolly sheep, expire.
Around the piles a careful troop attends,
To watch the wasting flames, and weep their burning friends—
Ling'ring along the shore, till dewy night
New decks the face of heav'n with starry light.
The conquer'd Latians, with like pious care,
Piles without number for their dead prepare.
Part, in the places where they fell, are laid;
And part are to the neighb'ring fields convey'd.
The corpse of kings, and captains of renown,
Borne off in state, are bury'd in the town;
The rest unhonour'd, and without a name,
Are cast a common heap to feed the flame.
Trojans and Latians vie with like desires
To make the field of battle shine with fires;
And the promiscuous blaze to heav'n aspires.
Now had the morning thrice renew'd the light,
And thrice dispell'd the shadows of the night,
When those who round the wasted fires remain,
Perform the last sad office to the slain.
They rake the yet warm ashes from below;
These, and the bones unburn'd, in earth bestow:
These relics with their country rites they grace,
And raise a mount of turf to mark the place.
But, in the palace of the king, appears
A scene more solemn, and a pomp of tears.
Maids, matrons, widows, mix their common moans
Orphans their sires, and sires lament their sons.
All in that universal sorrow share,
And curse the cause of this unhappy war—
A broken league, a bride unjustly sought,
A crown usurp'd, with which their blood is bought.
These are the crimes, with which they load the name
Of Turnus, and on him alone exclaim:
"Let him, who lords it o'er th' Ausonian land,
Engage the Trojan hero hand to hand;
His is the gain: our lot is but to serve:
'T is just the sway he seeks he should deserve."
This Drances aggravates; and adds, with spite.
His foe expects, and dares him to the fight.
Nor Turnus wants a party, to support
His cause and credit in the Latian court.
His former acts secure his present fame;
And the queen shades him with her mighty name.
While thus their factious minds with fury burn,
The legates from th' Ætolian prince return:
Sad news they bring, that, after all the cost
And care employ'd, their embassy is lost;
That Diomede refus'd his aid in war,
Unmov'd with presents, and as deaf to pray'r.
Some new alliance must elsewhere be sought,
Or peace with Troy on hard conditions bought.
Latinus, sunk in sorrow, finds too late,
A foreign son is pointed out by fate;
And, till Æneas shall Lavinia wed,
The wrath of heav'n is hov'ring o'er his head.
The gods, he saw, espous'd the juster side,
When late their titles in the field were tried:
Witness the fresh laments, and fun'ral tears undried.
Thus full of anxious thought, he summons all
The Latian senate to the council hall.
The princes come, commanded by their head,
And crowd the paths that to the palace lead.
Supreme in pow'r, and reverenc'd for his years,
He takes the throne, and in the midst appears.
Majestically sad, he sits in state,
And bids his envoys their success relate.
When Venulus began, the murm'ring sound
Was hush'd, and sacred silence reign'd around.
"We have," said he, "perform'd your high command,
And pass'd with peril a long tract of land:
We reach'd the place desir'd; with wonder fill'd,
The Grecian tents and rising tow'rs beheld.
Great Diomede has compass'd round with walls
The city, which Argyripa he calls,
From his own Argos nam'd: we touch'd with joy,
The royal hand that raz'd unhappy Troy.
When introduc'd, our presents first we bring,
Then crave an instant audience with the king.
His leave obtain'd, our native soil we name,
And tell th' important cause for which we came.
Attentively he heard us while we spoke;
Then with soft accents and a pleasing look,

Made this return: Ausonian race, of old
Renown'd for peace, and for an age of gold,
What madness has your alter'd minds possess'd,
To change for war hereditary rest,
Solicit arms unknown, and tempt the sword—
A needless ill your ancestors abhorr'd?
We—for myself I speak, and all the name
Of Grecians, who to Troy's destruction came—
(Omitting those who were in battle slain,
Or borne by rolling Simois to the main;)
Not one but suffer'd, and too dearly bought
The prize of honour which in arms he sought.
Some doom'd to death, and some in exile driv'n,
Outcasts, abandon'd by the care of heav'n—
So worn, so wretched, so despis'd a crew,
As e'en old Priam might with pity view,
Witness the vessels by Minerva toss'd
In storm—the vengeful Capharean coast—
Th' Eubœan rocks—the prince, whose brother led
Our armies to revenge his injur'd bed,
In Egypt lost. Ulysses, with his men,
Have seen Charybdis, and the Cyclops' den.
Why should I name Idomeneus, in vain
Restor'd to sceptres, and expell'd again?
Or young Achilles, by his rival slain?
E'en he, the king of men, the foremost name
Of all the Greeks, and most renown'd by fame,
The proud revenger of another's wife,
Yet by his own adult'ress lost his life—
Fell at his threshold; and the spoils of Troy
The foul polluters of his bed enjoy.
The gods have envied me the sweets of life,
My much-lov'd country and my more lov'd wife;
Banish'd from both, I mourn; while in the sky,
Transform'd to birds, my lost companions fly:
Hovering about the coasts, they make their moan,
And cuff the cliffs with pinions not their own.
What squalid spectres, in the dead of night,
Break my short sleep, and skim before my sight!
I might have promis'd to myself those harms,
Mad as I was, when I with mortal arms,
Presum'd against immortal pow'rs to move,
And violate with wounds the queen of love.
Such arms this hand shall never more employ;
No hate remains with me to ruin'd Troy.
I war not with its dust; nor am I glad
To think of past events, or good or bad.
Your presents I return: whate'er you bring
To buy my friendship, send the Trojan king.
We met in fight: I know him to my cost:
With what a whirling force his lance he toss'd!
Heav'ns! what a spring was in his arm, to throw!
How high he held his shield, and rose at ev'ry blow!
Had Troy produc'd two more his match in might
They would have chang'd the fortune of the fight:
The invasion of the Greeks had been return'd
Our empires wasted and our cities burn'd.
The long defence the Trojan people made,
The war protracted, and the siege delay'd,
Were due to Hector's and this hero's hand:
Both brave alike, and equal in command;
Æneas, not inferior in the field,
In pious rev'rence to the gods excell'd.
Make peace, ye Latians, and avoid with care
Th' impending dangers of a fatal war.'
He said no more; but with this cold excuse,
Refus'd th' alliance, and advis'd a truce."
Thus Venulus concluded his report.
A jarring murmur fill'd the factious court:
As when a torrent rolls with rapid force,
And dashes o'er the stones that stop their course,
The flood constrain'd within a scanty space,
Roars horrible along th' uneasy race;
White foam in gath'ring eddies floats around;
The rocky shores rebellow to the sound.
The murmur ceas'd: then from his lofty throne
The king invok'd the gods, and thus begun:
"I wish, ye Latians, what we now debate
Had been resolv'd before it was too late.
Much better had it been for you and me,
Unforc'd to this our last necessity,
To have been earlier wise than now to call
A council, when the foe surrounds the wall.
O citizens, we wage unequal war,
With men, not only heav'n's peculiar care,
But heav'n's own race—unconquer'd in the field,
Or conquer'd, yet unknowing how to yield.
What hopes you had in Diomede lay down:
Our hopes must centre on ourselves alone.
Yet those how feeble, and indeed how vain,
You see too well; nor need my words explain.
Vanquish'd without resource—laid flat by fate—
Factions within, a foe without the gate!
Not but I grant that all perform'd their parts
With manly force, and with undaunted hearts:
With our united strength the war we wag'd;
With equal numbers, equal arms, engag'd:
You see th' event.—Now hear what I propose,
To save our friends, and satisfy our foes.
A tract of land the Latians have possess'd
Along the Tyber, stretching to the west,
Which now Rutulians and Auruncans till;
And their mix'd cattle graze the fruitful hill.
Those mountains fill'd with firs, that lower land,
If you consent, the Trojans shall command,

Call'd into part of what is ours: and there,
On terms agreed, the common country share.
There let them build, and settle, if they please;
Unless they choose once more to cross the seas,
In search of seats remote from Italy,
And from unwelcome inmates set us free.
Then twice ten galleys let us build with speed,
Or twice as many more, if more they need.
Materials are at hand: a well grown wood
Runs equal with the margin of the flood:
Let them the number and the form assign;
The care and cost of all the stores be mine.
To treat the peace, a hundred senators
Shall be commission'd hence with ample pow'rs,
With olive crown'd: the presents they shall bear,
A purple robe, a royal iv'ry chair,
And all the marks of sway that Latian monarchs wear,
And sums of gold. Among yourselves debate
This great affair, and save the sinking state."
Then Drances took the word, who grudg'd, long since,
The rising glories of the Daunian prince,
Factious and rich, bold at the council board,
But cautious in the field, he shunn'd the sword—
A close caballer, and tongue-valiant lord.
Noble his mother was, and near the throne:
But, what his father's parentage, unknown.
He rose, and took th' advantage of the times,
To load young Turnus with invidious crimes.
"Such truths, O king," said he, "your words contain,
As strike the sense, and all replies are vain;
Nor are your loyal subjects now to seek
What common needs require; but fear to speak.
Let him give leave of speech, that haughty man,
Whose pride this inauspicious war began;
For whose ambition, (let me dare to say,
Fear set apart, though death is in my way,)
The plains of Latium run with blood around;
So many valiant heroes bite the ground;
Dejected grief in ev'ry face appears;
A town in mourning, and a land in tears;
While he, th' undoubted author of our harms,
The man who menaces the gods with arms,
Yet, after all his boasts, forsook the fight,
And sought his safety in ignoble flight.
Now, best of kings, since you propose to send
Such bounteous presents to your Trojan friend;
Add yet a greater, at our joint request,
One which he values more than all the rest:
Give him the fair Lavinia for his bride:
With that alliance let the league be tied,
And for the bleeding land a lasting peace provide.
Let insolence no longer awe the throne;
But, with a father's right bestow your own.
For this maligner of the general good,
If still we fear his force, he must be woo'd:
His haughty godhead we with pray'rs implore,
Your sceptre to release, and our just rights restore.
O cursed cause of all our ills! must we
Wage wars unjust, and fall in fight for thee!
What right hast thou to rule the Latian state,
And send us out to meet our certain fate?
'T is a destructive war: from Turnus' hand
Our peace and public safety we demand.
Let the fair bride to the brave chief remain;
If not, the peace, without the pledge, is vain.
Turnus, I know you think me not your friend,
Nor will I much with your belief contend:
I beg your greatness not to give the law
In other realms, but, beaten, to withdraw.
Pity your own, or pity our estate;
Nor twist our fortunes with your sinking fate.
Your int'rest is, the war should never cease;
But we have felt enough, to wish the peace—
A land exhausted to the last remains,
Depopulated towns, and driven plains.
Yet, if desire of fame, and thirst of pow'r,
A beauteous princess, with a crown in dow'r,
So fire your mind, in arms assert your right,
And meet your foe, who dares you to the fight.
Mankind, it seems, are made for you alone,
We, but the slaves who mount you to the throne—
A base ignoble crowd, without a name,
Unwept, unworthy of the fun'ral flame,
By duty bound to forfeit each his life,
That Turnus may possess a royal wife!
Permit not, mighty man, so mean a crew
Should share such triumphs, and detain from you
The post of honour, your undoubted due.
Rather alone your matchless force employ,
To merit what alone you must enjoy."
These words, so full of malice, mix'd with art,
Inflam'd with rage the youthful hero's heart.
Then groaning from the bottom of his breast,
He heav'd for wind, and thus his wrath express'd:
"You, Drances, never want a stream of words,
Then, when the public need requires our swords,
First, in the council-hall, to steer the state,
And ever foremost in a tongue debate,
While our strong walls secure us from the foe,
Ere yet with blood our ditches overflow;
But let the potent orator declaim,
And with the brand of coward blot my name;
Free leave is giv'n him, when his fatal hand
Has cover'd with more corpse the sanguine strand,
And high as mine his tow'ring trophies stand.
If any doubt remains who dares the most,
Let us decide it at the Trojan's cost,

And issue both a-breast, where honour calls—
(Foes are not far to seek without the walls;)
Unless his noisy tongue can only fight,
And feet were giv'n him but to speed his flight.
I beaten from the field? I forc'd away?
Who, but so known a dastard, dares to say?
Had he but ev'n beheld the fight, his eyes
Had witness'd for me, what his tongue denies—
What heaps of Trojans by this hand were slain,
And how the bloody Tyber swell'd the main.
All saw, but he, th' Arcadian troops retire
In scatter'd squadrons, and their prince expire.
The giant brothers, in their camp, have found,
I was not forc'd with ease to quit my ground.
Not such the Trojans tried me, when, enclos'd,
I singly their united arms oppos'd—
First forc'd an entrance through their thick array,
Then, glutted with their slaughter, freed my way.
'T is a destructive war! So let it be,
But to the Phrygian pirate, and to thee.
Meantime proceed to fill the people's ears
With false reports, their minds with panic fears:
Extol the strength of a twice-conquer'd race;
Our foes encourage, and our friends debase.
Believe thy fables, and the Trojan town
Triumphant stands; the Grecians are o'erthrown;
Suppliant at Hector's feet Achilles lies;
And Diomede from fierce Æneas flies.
Say, rapid Aufidus with awful dread
Runs backward from the sea, and hides his head,
When the great Trojan on his bank appears:
For that 's as true as thy dissembled fears:
Of my revenge: dismiss that vanity:
Thou Drances, art below a death from me.
Let that vile soul in that vile body rest;
The lodging is well worthy of the guest.
Now, royal father, to the present state
Of our affairs, and of this high debate—
If in your arms thus early you diffide,
And think your fortune is already tried;
If one defeat has brought us down so low,
As never more in fields to meet the foe;
Then I conclude for peace: 't is time to treat,
And lie like vassals at the victor's feet.
But oh! if any ancient blood remains,
One drop of all our fathers, in our veins,
That man would I prefer before the rest,
Who dar'd his death with an undaunted breast;
Who comely fell by no dishonest wound,
To shun that sight, and, dying, gnaw'd the ground.
But, if we still have fresh recruits in store,
If our confed'rates can afford us more;
If the contended field we bravely fought:
And not a bloodless victory was bought;
Their losses equal'd ours, and for their slain,
With equal fires they fill'd the shining plain;
Why thus, unforc'd, should we so tamely yield,
And, ere the trumpet sounds, resign the field;
Good unexpected, evils unforeseen,
Appear by turns, as fortune shifts the scene:
Some, rais'd aloft, come tumbling down amain;
Then fall so hard, they bound and rise again.
If Diomede refuse his aid to lend,
The great Messapus yet remains our friend:
Tolumnius, who foretells events, is ours:
Th' Italian chiefs, and princes, join their pow'rs:
Nor least in number, nor in name the last,
Your own brave subjects have our cause embrac'd.
Above the rest, the Volscian Amazon
Contains an army in herself alone,
And heads a squadron, terrible to sight,
With glitt'ring shields, in brazen armour bright.
Yet, if the foe a single fight demand,
And I alone the public peace withstand;
If you consent, he shall not be refus'd,
Nor find a hand to victory unus'd.
This new Achilles, let him take the field,
With fated armour, and Vulcanian shield!
For you, my royal father, and my fame,
"I, Turnus, not the least of all my name,
Devote my soul. He calls me hand to hand:
And I alone will answer his demand.
Drances shall rest secure, and neither share
The danger, nor divide the prize, of war."
While they debate, nor these nor those will yield,
Æneas draws his forces to the field,
And moves his camp. The scouts with flying speed
Return, and through the frighted city spread
Th' unpleasing news. "The Trojans are describ'd,
In battle marching by the river side,
And bending to the town." They take th' alarm:
Some tremble, some are bold, all in confusion arm.
Th' impetuous youth press'd forward to the field:
They clash the sword, and clatter on the shield:
The fearful matrons raise a screaming cry;
Old feeble men with fainter groans reply:
A jarring sound results, and mingles in the sky,
Like that of swans remurm'ring to the floods,
Or birds of diff'ring kinds in hollow woods.
Turnus th' occasion takes, and cries aloud:
"Talk on, ye quaint haranguers of the crowd:
Declaim in praise of peace, when danger calls,
And the fierce foes in arms approach the walls."
He said, and, turning short with speedy pace,
Casts back a scornful glance, and quits the place.

"Thou, Volusus, the Volscian troops command
To mount; and lead thyself our Ardean band.
Messapus, and Catillus, post your force
Along the fields, to charge the Trojan horse.
Some guard the passes; others man the wall;
Drawn up in arms, the rest attend my call."
They swarm from ev'ry quarter of the town,
And with disorder'd haste the rampires crown:
Good old Latinus, when he saw, too late,
The gath'ring storm just breaking on the state,
Dismiss'd the council till a fitter time,
And own'd his easy temper as his crime,
Who, forc'd against his reason, had complied
To break the treaty for the promis'd bride.
Some help to sink new trenches; others aid
To ram the stones, or raise the palisade.
Hoarse trumpets sound th' alarm: around the walls
Runs a distracted crew, whom their last labour calls.
A sad procession in the streets is seen,
Of matrons that attend the mother-queen.
High in her chair she sits, and, at her side,
With downcast eyes appears the fatal bride.
They mount the cliff, where Pallas' temple stands;
Pray'rs in their mouths, and presents in their hands:
With censers, first they fume the sacred shrine,
Then in this common supplication join:
"O patroness of arms! unspotted maid!
Propitious hear, and lend thy Latians aid!
Break short the pirate's lance: pronounce his fate;
And lay the Phrygian low before the gate."
Now Turnus arms for fight. His back and breast
Well-temper'd steel and scaly brass invest:
The cuishes, which his brawny thighs infold,
Are mingled metal, damask'd o'er with gold.
His faithful falchion sits upon his side;
Nor casque, nor crest, his manly features hide;
But, bare to view, amid surrounding friends,
With godlike grace, he from the tow'r descends.
Exulting in his strength, he seems to dare
His absent rival, and to promise war.
Freed from his keepers, thus, with broken reins,
The wanton courser prances o'er the plains,
Or in the pride of youth o'erleaps the bounds,
And snuffs the females in forbidden grounds,
Or seeks his wat'ring in the well-known flood,
To quench his thirst, and cool his fiery blood:
He swims luxuriant in the liquid plain,
And o'er his shoulder flows his waving mane:
He neighs, he snorts, he bears his head on high;
Before his ample chest the frothy waters fly.
Soon as the prince appears without the gate,
The Volscians, and their virgin leader, wait
His last commands. Then, with a graceful mien,
Lights from her lofty steed the warrior queen:
Her squadron imitates, and each descends;
Whose common suit Camilla thus commends:
"If sense of honour, if a soul secure
Of inborn worth that can all tests endure,
Can promise aught, or on itself rely,
Greatly to dare, to conquer or to die;
Then, I alone, sustain'd by these, will meet
The Tyrrhene troops, and promise their defeat.
Ours be the danger, ours the sole renown:
You, gen'ral, stay behind, and guard the town."
Turnus a while stood mute with glad surprise
And on the fierce virago fix'd his eyes;
Then thus return'd: "O grace of Italy,
With what becoming thanks can I reply?
Not only words lie lab'ring in my breast:
But thought itself is by thy praise oppress'd.
Yet rob me not of all; but let me join
My toils, my hazard, and my fame, with thine.
The Trojan, not in stratagem unskill'd,
Sends his light horse before to scour the field:
Himself, through steep ascents and thorny brakes,
A larger compass to the city takes.
This news my scouts confirm: and I prepare
To foil his cunning, and his force to dare;
With chosen foot his passage to forelay,
And place an ambush in the winding way.
Thou, with thy Volscians, face the Tuscan horse:
The brave Messapus shall thy troops enforce.
With those of Tibur, and the Latian band,
Subjected all to thy supreme command."
This said, he warns Messapus to the war,
Then ev'ry chief exhorts with equal care.
All thus encourag'd, his own troops he joins,
And hastes to prosecute his deep designs.
Enclos'd with hills a winding valley lies,
By nature form'd for fraud, and fitted for surprise:
A narrow track, by human steps untrod,
Leads, through perplexing thorns, to this obscure abode.
High o'er the vale, a steepy mountain stands,
Whence the surveying sight the nether ground commands.
The top is level—an offensive seat
Of war; and from the war a safe retreat:
For, on the right and left, is room to press
The foes at hand, or from afar distress;
To drive them headlong downward; and to pour,
On their descending backs, a stony show'r.
Thither young Turnus took the well-known way,
Possess'd the pass, and in blind ambush lay.
Meantime, Latonian Phœbe, from the skies,
Beheld th' approaching war with fearful eyes,

And call'd the light-foot Opis to her aid,
Her most belov'd and ever-trusty maid;
Then with a sigh began: "Camilla goes
To meet her death amidst her fatal foes—
The nymph I lov'd of all my mortal train,
Invested with Diana's arms in vain.
Nor is my kindness for the virgin new:
'T was born with her; and with her years it grew.
Her father Metabus, when forc'd away
From old Privernum, for tyrannic sway,
Snatch'd up, and sav'd from his prevailing foes,
This tender babe, companion of his woes.
Casmilla was her mother: but he drown'd,
One hissing letter in a softer sound,
And call'd Camilla. Through the woods he flies;
Wrapp'd in his robe, the royal infant lies.
His foes in sight, he mends his weary pace;
With shouts and clamours they pursue the chase.
The banks of Amasene at length he gains:
The raging flood his further flight restrains,
Rais'd o'er the borders with unusual rains.
Prepar'd to plunge into the stream, he fears,
Not for himself, but for the charge he bears.
Anxious, he stops a while, and thinks in haste,
Then, desp'rate in distress, resolves at last.
A knotty lance of well boil'd oak he bore:
The middle part with cork he cover'd o'er:
He clos'd the child within the hollow space;
With twigs of bending osier bound the case,
Then pois'd the spear, heavy with human weight,
And thus invok'd my favour for the freight:
'Accept, great goddess of the woods, (he said,)
Sent by her sire, this dedicated maid!
Through air she flies, a suppliant to the shrine;
And the first weapons that she knows, are thine.
He said; and with full force the spear he threw;
Above the sounding waves Camilla flew.
Then, press'd by foes, he stemm'd the stormy tide,
And gain'd, by stress of arms, the farther side.
His fasten'd spear he pull'd from out the ground,
And, victor of his vows, his infant nymph unbound;
Nor, after that, in towns which walls enclose,
Would trust his hunted life amidst his foes;
But, rough, in open air he chose to lie:
Earth was his couch; his covering was the sky.
On hills unshorn, or in a desert den,
He shunn'd the dire society of men.
A shepherd's solitary life he led:
His daughter with the milk of mares he fed.
The dugs of bears, and ev'ry savage beast,
He drew, and through her lips the liquor press'd.
The little Amazon could scarcely go—
He loads her with a quiver and a bow;
And, that she might her stagg'ring steps command,
He with a slender jav'lin fills her hand,
Her flowing hair no golden fillet bound;
Nor swept her trailing robe the dusty ground.
Instead of these, a tiger's hide o'erspread
Her back and shoulders, fasten'd to her head.
The flying dart she first attempts to fling,
And round her tender temples toss'd the sling
Then, as her strength with years increas'd began
To pierce aloft in air the soaring swan,
And from the clouds to fetch the heron and the crane.
The Tuscan matrons with each other vied
To bless their rival sons with such a bride;
But she disdains their love, to share with me
The sylvan shades, and vow'd virginity.
And, oh! I wish, contented with my cares
Of savage spoils, she had not sought the wars:
Then had she been of my celestial train,
And shunn'd the fate that dooms her to be slain.
But since, opposing heav'n's decree, she goes
To find her death among forbidden foes,
Haste with these arms and take thy steepy flight,
Where with the gods averse, the Latians fight.
This bow to thee, this quiver, I bequeath,
This chosen arrow to revenge her death:
By what'er hand Camilla shall be slain,
Or of the Trojan or Italian train,
Let him not pass unpunish'd from the plain.
Then, in a hollow cloud, myself will aid
To bear the breathless body of my maid.
Unspoil'd shall be her arms, and unprofan'd
Her holy limbs with any human hand,
And in a marble tomb laid in her native land.
She said. The faithful nymph descends from high
With rapid flight, and cuts the sounding sky:
Black clouds and stormy winds around her body fly.

By this, the Trojan and the Tuscan horse,
Drawn up in squadrons, with united force
Approach the walls: the sprightly coursers bound,
Press foward on their bits, and shift their ground,
Shields, arms, and spears, flash horribly from far;
And the fields glitter with a waving war.
Oppos'd to these, come on with furious force
Messapus, Coras, and the Latian horse;
These in a body plac'd on either hand,
Sustain'd and clos'd by fair Camilla's band.
Advancing in a line, they couch their spears
And less and less the middle space appears.

Thick smoke obscures the field, and scarce are seen
The neighing coursers, and the shouting men.
In distance of their darts they stop their course;
Then man to man they rush, and horse to horse.
The face of heav'n their flying jav'lins hide;
And deaths unseen are dealt on either side.
Tyrrhenus, and Aconteus, void of fear,
By mettled coursers borne in full career,
Meet first oppos'd; and, with a mighty shock,
Their horses' heads against each other knock.
Far from his steed is fierce Aconteus cast,
As with an engine's force, or lightning's blast:
He rolls along in blood, and breathes his last.
The Latin squadron take a sudden fright,
And sling their shields behind, to save their backs in flight.
Spurring at speed, to their own walls they drew;
Close in the rear the Tuscan troops pursue,
And urge their flight: Asylas leads the chase;
Till, seiz'd with shame, they wheel about and face,
Receive their foes, and raise a threat'ning cry.
The Tuscans take their turn to fear and fly.
So swelling surges with a thund'ring roar,
Driv'n on each other's backs, insult the shore,
Bound o'er the rocks, encroach upon the land,
And far upon the beach eject the sand;
Then backward, with a swing, they take their way
Repuls'd from upper ground, and seek their mother-sea;
With equal hurry quit th' invaded shore,
And swallow back the sand and stones they spew'd before.
Twice were the Tuscans masters of the field,
Twice by the Latins, in return repell'd.
Asham'd at length, to the third charge they ran—
Both hosts resolv'd, and mingled man to man.
Now dying groans are heard; the fields are strow'd
With falling bodies, and are drunk with blood.
Arms, horses, men, on heaps together lie:
Confus'd the fight, and more confus'd the cry.
Orsilochus, who durst not press too near,
Strong Remulus at distance drove his spear,
And struck the steel beneath his horse's ear.
The fiery steed, impatient of the wound,
Curvets, and, springing upwards with a bound,
His helpless lord, cast backward on the ground.
Catillus pierc'd Iolas first; then drew
His reeking lance, and at Herminius threw,
The mighty champion of the Tuscan crew.
His neck and throat unarm'd, his head was bare,
But shaded with a length of yellow hair:
Secure, he fought, expos'd on ev'ry part,
A spacious mark for swords, and for the flying dart.
Across the shoulders came the feather'd wound;
Transfix'd, he fell, and doubled to the ground.
The sands with streaming blood are sanguine dy'd,
And death, with honour sought on either side.
Resistless, through the war Camilla rode,
In danger unappall'd, and pleas'd with blood.
One side was bare for her exerted breast;
One shoulder with her painted quiver press'd.
Now from afar her fatal jav'lins play:
Now with her axe's edge she hews her way.
Diana's arms upon her shoulder sound;
And when too closely press'd, she quits the ground,
From her bent bow she sends a backward wound.
Her maids, in martial pomp, on either side,
Larina, Tulla, fierce Tarpeia, ride—
Italians all—in peace, their queen's delight;
In war, the bold companions of the fight.
So march'd the Thracian Amazons of old,
When Thermodon with bloody billows roll'd;
Such troops as these in shining arms were seen,
When Theseus met in fight their maiden queen:
Such to the field Penthesilea led,
From the fierce virgin when the Grecians fled;
With such return'd triumphant from the war,
Her maids with cries attend the lofty car;
They clash with manly force their moony shields;
With female shouts resound the Phrygian fields.
Who foremost, and who last, heroic maid,
On the cold earth were by thy courage laid?
Thy spear, of mountain-ash, Eumenius first,
With fury driv'n, from side to side transpierc'd:
A purple stream came spouting from the wound;
Bath'd in his blood he lies, and bites the ground.
Liris and Pagasus at once she slew:
The former, as the slacken'd reins he drew,
Of his faint steed—the latter, as he stretch'd
His arm to prop his friend—the jav'lin reach'd.
By the same weapon, sent from the same hand,
Both fall together, and both spurn the sand.
Amastrus next is added to the slain;
The rest in rout she follows o'er the plain:
Tereus, Harpalycus, Demophoon
And Chromis, at full speed her fury shun.
Of all her beauty's darts, not one she lost
Each was attended with a Trojan ghost.
Young Ornytus bestrode a hunter steed,
Swift for the chase, and of Apulian breed.
Him, from afar, she spied in arms unknown:
O'er his broad back an ox's hide was thrown;
His helm a wolf, whose gaping jaws were spread
A cov'ring for his cheeks, and grinn'd around [his head.

He clench'd within his hand an iron prong,
And tow'r'd above the rest, conspicuous in the throng,
Him soon she singled from the flying train,
And slew with ease; then thus insults the slain:
"Vain hunter! didst thou think through woods to chase
The savage herd, a vile and trembling race?
Here cease thy vaunts, and own my victory:
A woman warrior was too strong for thee.
Yet, if the ghosts demand the conqu'ror's name,
Confessing great Camilla, save thy shame."
Then Butes and Orsilochus she slew,
The bulkiest bodies of the Trojan crew—
But Butes breast to breast: the spear descends
Above the gorget, where his helmet ends,
And o'er the shield which his left side defends.
Orsilochus, and she, their coursers ply;
He seems to follow, and she seems to fly.
But in a narrower ring she makes the race;
And then he flies, and she pursues the chase.
Gath'ring at length on her deluded foe,
She swings her axe, and rises to the blow:
Full on the helm behind, with such a sway
The weapon falls, the riven steel gives way:
He groans, he roars, he sues in vain for grace;
Brains, mingled with his blood, besmear his face.
Astonish'd Aunus just arrives by chance,
To see his fall, nor further dares advance;
But, fixing on the horrid maid his eye,
He stares, and shakes, and finds it vain to fly;
Yet, like a true Ligurian, born to cheat,
(At least while Fortune favour'd his deceit)
Cries out aloud, "What courage have you shown,
Who trust your courser's strength, and not your own?
Forego the 'vantage of your horse; alight;
And then on equal terms begin the fight:
It shall be seen, weak woman, what you can,
When, foot to foot, you combat with a man."
He said. She glows with anger and disdain,
Dismounts with speed to dare him on the plain,
And leaves her horse at large among her train;
With her drawn sword defies him to the field,
And, marching, lifts aloft her maiden shield.
The youth, who thought his cunning did succeed,
Reins round his horse, and urges all his speed,
Adds the remembrance of the spur, and hides
The goring rowels in his bleeding sides.
"Vain fool, and coward!" said the lofty maid,
"Caught in the train, which thou thyself hast laid!
On others practice thy Ligurian arts:
Thin stratagems, and tricks of little hearts,
Are lost on me: nor shalt thou safe retire,
With vaunting lies to thy fallacious sire."
At this, so fast her flying feet she sped,
That soon she strain'd beyond his horse's head
Then turning short, at once she seiz'd the rein,
And laid the boaster grov'ling on the plain.
Not with more ease the falcon from above,
Trusses, in middle air, the trembling dove,
Then plumes the prey, in her strong pounces bound:
The feathers, foul with blood, come tumbling to the ground.
Now mighty Jove, from his superior height,
With his broad eye surveys th' unequal fight.
He fires the breast of Tarchon with disdain,
And sends him to redeem th' abandon'd plain.
Between the broken ranks the Tuscan rides,
And these encourages, and those he chides;
Recalls each leader, by his name, from flight;
Renews their ardour, and restores the fight.
"What panic fear has seiz'd your souls? O shame,
A brand perpetual of th' Etrurian name!
Cowards incurable! a woman's hand
Drives, breaks, and scatters your ignoble band!
Now cast away the sword, and quit the shield!
What use of weapons which you dare not wield?
Not thus you fly your female foes by night,
Nor shun the feast when the full bowls invite.
When to fat off'rings the glad augur calls,
And the shrill horn-pipe sounds to bacchanals.
These are your studied cares, your lewd delight—
Swift to debauch, but slow to manly fight."
Thus having said, he spurs amid the foes,
Not managing the life he meant to lose.
The first he found, he seiz'd, with headlong haste,
In his strong gripe, and clasp'd around the waist:
'Twas Venulus, whom from his horse he tore,
And, (laid athwart his own,) in triumph bore.
Loud shouts ensue: the Latins turn their eyes,
And view the unusual sight with vast surprise.
The fiery Tarchon, flying o'er the plains,
Press'd in his arms, the pond'rous prey sustains,
Then, with his shorten'd spear, explores around
His jointed arms, to fix a deadly wound.
Nor less the captive struggles for his life:
He writhes his body to prolong the strife,
And, fencing for his naked throat, exerts
His utmost vigour, and the point averts.
So stoops the yellow eagle from on high,
And bears a speckled serpent through the sky,
Fast'ning his crooked talons on the prey:
The pris'ner hisses through the liquid way;
Resists the royal hawk; and though oppress'd,
She fights in volumes, and erects her crest:
Turn'd to her foe, she stiffens ev'ry scale,
And shoots her forky tongue, and whisks her threat'ning tail.

Against the victor, all defence is weak:
Th' imperial bird still plies her with his beak;
He tears her bowels, and her breast he gores,
Then claps his pinions, and securely soars.
Thus, through the midst of circling enemies,
Strong Tarchon snatch'd and bore away his prize.
The Tyrrhene troops, that shrunk before, now press
The Latins, and presume the like success.
Then Aruns, doom'd to death, his arts essay'd,
To murder, unespied, the Volscian maid:
This way and that, his winding course he bends,
And, wheresoe'er she turns, her steps attends,
When she retires victorious from the chase,
He wheels about with care, and shifts his place;
When, rushing on, she seeks her foes in fight,
He keeps aloof, and keeps her still in sight:
He threats and trembles, trying ev'ry way,
Unseen to kill, and safely to betray.
Chloreus, the priest of Cybele, from far,
Glitt'ring in Phrygian arms amidst the war,
Was by the virgin view'd. The steed he press'd
Was proud with trappings; and his brawny chest
With scales of gilded brass was covered o'er:
A robe of Tyrian dye the rider wore.
With deadly wounds he gall'd the distant foe;
Gnossian his shafts, and Lycian was his bow:
A golden helm his front and head surrounds;
A gilded quiver from his shoulder sounds,
Gold weav'd with linen, on his thighs he wore,
With flow'rs of needle-work distinguish'd o'er,
With golden buckles bound, and gather'd up before,
Him the fierce maid beheld with ardent eyes,
Fond and ambitious of so rich a prize,
Or that the temple might his trophies hold,
Or else to shine herself in Trojan gold.
Blind in her haste, she chases him alone,
And seeks his life, regardless of her own.
This lucky moment the sly tailor chose;
Then, starting from his ambush, up he rose,
And threw, but first to heav'n address'd his vows:
"O patron of Soracte's high abodes!
Phœbus, the ruling pow'r among the gods!
Whom first we serve! whole woods of unctuous pine
Are fell'd for thee, and to thy glory shine;
By thee protected, with our naked soles,
Thro' flames unsing'd we march, and tread the kindled coals.
Give me, propitious pow'r, to wash away
The stains of this dishonourable day:
Nor spoils, nor triumph, from the fact I claim
But with my future actions trust my fame.
Let me, by stealth, this female plague o'ercome,
And from the field return inglorious home."
Apollo heard, and, granting half his pray'r,
Shuffled in winds the rest, and toss'd in empty air.
He gives the death desir'd: his safe return
By southern tempests to the seas is borne.
Now, when the jav'lin whizz'd along the skies,
Both armies on Camilla turn'd their eyes,
Directed by the sound. Of either host,
Th' unhappy virgin, though concern'd the most,
Was only deaf; so greedy was she bent
On golden spoils, and on her prey intent;
Till in her pap the winged weapon stood
Infix'd, and deeply drunk the purple blood.
Her sad attendants hasten to sustain
Their dying lady drooping on the plain.
Far from their sight the trembling Aruns flies,
With beating heart, and fear confus'd with joys;
Nor dares he further to pursue his blow,
Or e'en to bear the sight of his expiring foe.
As, when the wolf has torn a bullock's hide
At unawares, or ranch'd a shepherd's side,
Conscious of his audacious deed, he flies,
And claps his quivering tail between his thighs:
So, speeding once, the wretch no more attends,
But, spurring forward, herds among his friends.
She wrench'd the jav'lin with her dying hands:
But wedg'd within her breast the weapon stands:
The wood she draws, the steely point remains,
She staggers in her seat with agonizing pains,
(A gath'ring mist o'erclouds her cheerful eyes,
And from her cheeks the rosy colour flies)
Then turns to her, whom, of her female train,
She trusted most, and thus she speaks with pain:
"Acca 'tis past! he swims before my sight,
Inexorable Death: and claims his right.
Bear my last words to Turnus: fly with speed,
And bid him timely to my charge succeed,
Repel the Trojans, and the town relieve:—
Farewell! and in this kiss my parting breath receive."
She said, and, sliding, sunk upon the plain:
Dying, her open'd hand forsakes the rein;
Short and more short, she pants: by slow degrees
Her mind the passage from her body frees,
She drops her sword; she nods her plumy crest,
Her drooping head declining on her breast:
In the last sigh her struggling soul expires,
And, murm'ring with disdain, to Stygian sounds retires.
A shout, that struck the golden stars, ensu'd
Despair and rage, and languish'd fight renew'd
The Trojan troops and Tuscan, in a line,
Advance to charge; the mix'd Arcadians

But Cynthia's maid, high seated, from afar,
Surveys the field, and fortune of the war,
Unmov'd a while, till, prostrate on the plain,
Welt'ring in blood, she sees Camilla slain,
And, round her corpse, of friends and foes a fighting train.
Then, from the bottom of her breast, she drew
A mournful sigh, and these sad words ensue:
"Too dear a fine, ah, much lamented maid!
For warring with the Trojans, thou hast paid:
Nor aught avail'd, in this unhappy strife,
Diana's sacred arms to save thy life.
Yet unreveng'd the goddess will not leave
Her vot'ry's death, nor with vain sorrow grieve.
Branded the wretch, and be his name abhorr'd;
But after-ages shall thy praise record.
Th' inglorious coward soon shall press the plain:
Thus vows thy queen, and thus the Fates ordain. [mound—
High o'er the field, there stood a hilly
Sacred the place, and spread with oaks around—
Where, in a marble tomb, Dercenus, lay,
A king that once in Latium bore the sway.
The beauteous Opis thither bent her flight,
To mark the traitor Aruns, from the height.
Him in refulgent arms she soon espied,
Swoll'n with success; and loudly thus she cried:
"Thy backward steps, vain boaster, are too late:
Turn, like a man, at length, and meet thy fate.
Charg'd with my message to Camilla go,
And say I sent thee to the shades below—
An honour undeserv'd from Cynthia's bow."
She said, and from her quiver chose with speed
The winged shaft, predestin'd for the deed;
Then to the stubborn yew her strength applied
Till the far distant horns approach'd on either side. [she drew;
The bow-string touch'd her breast, so strong
Whizzing in air the fatal arrow flew.
At once the twanging bow and sounding dart
The traitor heard, and felt the point within his heart.
Him, beating with his heels in pangs of death,
His flying friends to foreign fields bequeath.
The conqu'ring damsel, with expanded wings,
The welcome message to her mistress brings.
Their leader lost, the Volscians quit the field;
And, unsustain'd, the chiefs of Turnus yield.
The frighted soldiers, when their captains fly,
More on their speed than on their strength rely.
Confus'd in flight, they bear each other down,
And spur their horses headlong to the town.
Driv'n by their foes, and to their fears resign'd,
Not once they turn, but take their wounds behind.
These drop the shield, and those the lance forego
Or on their shoulders bear the slacken'd bow.
The hoofs of horses with a rattling sound,
Beat short and thick, and shake the rotten ground.
Black clouds of dust come rolling in the sky,
And o'er the darken'd walls and rampires fly.
The trembling matrons, from their lofty stands,
Rend heav'n with female shrieks, and wring their hands.
All pressing on, pursuers and pursu'd,
Are crush'd in crowds, a mingled multitude.
Some happy few escape: the throng too late
Rush on for entrance, till they choke the gate.
E'en in the sight of home, the wretched sire
Looks on, and sees his helpless son expire.
Then, in a fright, the folding gates they close,
But leave their friends excluded with their foes.
The vanquish'd cry; the victors loudly shout;
'Tis terror all within, and slaughter all without.
Blind in their fear, they bounce against the wall,
Or, to the moats pursu'd, precipitate their fall.
The Latian virgins, valiant with despair,
Arm'd on the tow'rs, the common danger share:
So much of zeal their country's cause inspir'd:
So much Camilla's great example fir'd.
Poles, sharpen'd in the flames, from high they throw
With imitated darts to gall the foe.
Their lives, for godlike freedom they bequeath,
And crowd each other to be first in death.
Meantime to Turnus ambush'd in the shade,
With heavy tidings came th' unhappy maid:
"The Volscians overthrown—Camilla kill'd—
The foes, entirely masters of the field,
Like a resistless flood, come rolling on:
The cry goes off the plain, and thickens to the town."
Inflam'd with rage, (for so the Furies fire
The Daunian's breast, and so the Fates require)
He leaves the hilly pass, the woods in vain
Possess'd, and downward issues on the plain.
Scarce was he gone, when to the straits, now freed
From secret foes, the Trojan troops succeed.
Through the black forest and the ferny brake,
Unknowingly secure, their way they take,
From the rough mountains to the plain descend,
And there, in order drawn, their line extend.
Both armies now in open fields are seen;
Nor far the distance of the space between.
Both to the city bend, Æneas sees,
Through smoking fields, his hast'ning enemies
And Turnus views the Trojans in array,
And hears the approaching horses proudly neigh.

Soon had their hosts in bloody battle join'd;
But westward to the sea the sun declin'd.
Intrench'd before the town both armies lie,
While night with sable wings involves the sky.

BOOK XII.

ARGUMENT.

Turnus challenges Æneas to a single combat: articles are agreed on, but broken by the Rutuli, who wound Æneas. He is miraculously cured by Venus, forces Turnus to a duel, and concludes the poem with his death.

When Turnus saw the Latins leave the field,
Their armies broken, and their courage quell'd,
Himself become the mark of public spite,
His honour question'd for the promis'd fight—
The more he was with vulgar hate oppress'd
The more his fury boil'd within his breast:
He rous'd his vigour for the last debate,
And rais'd his haughty soul to meet his fate.
As, when the swains the Libyan lion chase,
He makes a sour retreat, nor mends his pace;
But, if the pointed jav'lin pierce his side,
The lordly beast returns with double pride:
He wrenches out the steel; he roars for pain;
His sides he lashes, and erects his mane:
So Turnus fares: his eye-balls flash with fire;
Through his wide nostrils clouds of smoke expire.
Trembling with rage, around the court he ran,
At length approach'd the king, and thus began:
"No more excuses or delays: I stand
In arms prepar'd to combat, hand to hand,
This base deserter of his native land.
The Trojan, by his word, is bound to take
The same conditions which himself did make.
Renew the truce; the solemn rites prepare,
And to my single virtue trust the war.
The Latians unconcern'd shall see the fight:
This arm unaided shall assert your right:
Then, if my prostrate body press the plain,
To him the crown and beauteous bride remain."
To whom the king sedately thus replied:
"Brave youth! the more your valour has been tried,
The more becomes it us, with due respect
To weigh the chance of war, which you neglect.
You want not wealth, or a successive throne,
Or cities which your arms have made your own:
My towns and treasures are at your command;
And stor'd with blooming beauties is my land:
Laurentum more than one Lavinia sees,
Unmarried, fair, of noble families.
Now let me speak, and you with patience hear,
Things which perhaps may grate a lover's ear,
But sound advice, proceeding from a heart
Sincerely yours, and free from fraudful art.
The gods, by signs have manifestly shown,
No prince, Italian born, shall heir my throne:
Oft have our augurs, in prediction skill'd,
And oft our priests, a foreign son reveal'd.
Yet, won by worth that cannot be withstood,
Brib'd by my kindness to my kindred blood,
Urg'd by my wife, who would not be denied,
I promis'd my Lavinia for your bride:
Her from her plighted lord by force I took:
All ties of treaties, and of honour, broke:
On your account I wag'd an impious war—
With what success, 'tis needless to declare;
I and my subjects feel; and you have had your share.
Twice vanquish'd while in bloody fields we strive
Scarce in our walls, we keep our hopes alive:
The rolling flood runs warm with human gore;
The bones of Latians blanch the neighb'ring shore.
Why put I not an end to this debate,
Still unresolv'd, and still a slave to fate?
If Turnus' death a lasting peace can give,
Why should I not procure it whilst you live?
Should I to doubtful arms your youth betray,
What would my kinsmen, the Rutulians, say?
And should you fall in fight, (which heav'n defend!)
How curse the cause, which hasten'd to his end
The daughter's lover, and the father's friend?
Weigh in your mind the various chance of war.
Pity your parent's age, and ease his care."
Such balmy words he pour'd, but all in vain:
The proffer'd med'cine but provok'd the pain,
The wrathful youth, disdaining the relief,
With intermitting sobs thus vents his grief:
"The care, O best of fathers! which you take
For my concerns, at my desire forsake.
Permit me not to languish out my days,
But make the best exchange of life for praise;
This arm, this lance, can well dispute the prize,
And the blood follows, where the weapon flies.
His goddess-mother is not near, to shroud
The flying coward with an empty cloud."
But now the queen, who fear'd for Turnus' life,
And loath'd the hard conditions of the strife,
Held him by force; and, dying in his death,
In these sad accents gave her sorrow breath:
"O Turnus! I adjure thee by these tears,
And whate'er price Amata's honour bears
Within thy breast, since thou art all my hope,
My sickly mind's repose, my sinking age's prop—

Since on the safety of thy life alone
Depends Latinus, and the Latian throne—
Refuse me not this one, this only pray'r,
To wave the combat, and pursue the war.
Whatever chance attends this fatal strife,
Think it includes, in thine, Amata's life.
I cannot live a slave, or see my throne
Usurp'd by strangers, or a Trojan son."
At this, a flood of tears Lavinia shed;
A crimson blush her beauteous face o'erspread,
Varying her cheeks by turns with white and red.
The driving colours, never at a stay,
Run here and there, and flush, and fade away.
Delightful change! thus Indian iv'ry shows,
Which with the bord'ring paint of purple glows;
Or lilies damask'd by the neighb'ring rose.
The lover gaz'd, and, burning with desire,
The more he look'd, the more he fed the fire:
Revenge, and jealous rage, and secret spite,
Roll in his breast, and rouse him to the fight.
Then fixing on the queen his ardent eyes,
Firm to his first intent, he thus replies:
"Oh mother! do not by your tears prepare
Such boding omens, and prejudge the war,
Resolv'd on fight, I am no longer free
To shun my death, if heav'n my death decree"—
Then turning to the herald, thus pursues:
"Go, greet the Trojan with ungrateful news:
Denounce from me, that, when to-morrow's light
Shall gild the heav'ns, he need not urge the fight:
The Trojan and Rutulian troops no more
Shall dye, with mutual blood, the Latian shore:
Our single swords the quarrel shall decide;
And to the victor be the beauteous bride."
He said, and, striding on with speedy pace,
He sought his coursers of the Thracian race.
At his approach, they toss their heads on high,
And, proudly neighing, promise victory.
The sires of these Orithyia sent from far,
To grace Pilumnus, when he went to war.
The drifts of Thracian snows were scarce so white,
Nor northern winds in fleetness match'd their flight.
Officious grooms stand ready by his side;
And some with combs their flowing manes divide,
And others stroke their chests, and gently sooth their pride.
He sheath'd his limbs in arms; a temper'd mass
Of golden metal those, and mountain-brass.
Then to his head his glitt'ring helm he tied,
And girt his faithful falchion to his side.
In his Ætnæan forge, the God of Fire
That falchion labour'd for the hero's sire,
Immortal keenness on the blade bestow'd,
And plung'd it hissing in the Stygian flood.
Propp'd on a pillar, which the ceiling bore,
Was plac'd the lance Auruncan Actor wore.
Which with such force he brandish'd in his hand,
The tough ash trembled like an osier wand:
Then cried, "O pond'rous spoil of Actor slain
And never yet by Turnus toss'd in vain!
Fail not this day thy wonted force: but go,
Sent by this hand, to pierce the Trojan foe:
Give me to tear his corslet from his breast,
And from that eunuch head to rend the crest;
Dragg'd in the dust, his frizzled hair to soil,
Hot from the vexing ir'n, and smear'd with fragrant oil."
Thus while he raves, from his wide nostrils flies
A fiery steam, and sparkles from his eyes.
So fares the bull in his lov'd female's sight.
Proudly he bellows, and preludes the fight:
He tries his goring horns against a tree,
And meditates his absent enemy;
He pushes at the winds; he digs the strand
With his black hoofs, and spurns the yellow sand,
Nor less the Trojan, in his Lemnian arms,
To future fight his manly courage warms:
He whets his fury, and with joy prepares
To terminate at once the ling'ring wars;
To cheer his chiefs and tender son, relates
What heav'n had promis'd, and expounds the fates.
Then to the Latian king he sends, to cease
The rage of arms, and ratify the peace.
The morn ensuing, from the mountain's height,
Had scarcely spread the skies with rosy light:
Th' etherial coursers, bounding from the sea,
From out their flaming nostrils breath'd the day;
When now the Trojan and Rutulian guard,
In friendly labour join'd, the list prepar'd.
Beneath the walls, they measure out the space;
Then sacred altars rear, on sods of grass,
Where with religious rites, their common gods they place.
In purest white, the priests their heads attire,
And living waters bear, and holy fire;
And o'er their linen hoods and shaded hair,
Long twisted wreaths of sacred vervain wear.
In order issuing from the town, appears
he Latin legion, arm'd with pointed spears:
And from the fields, advancing on a line,
The Trojan and the Tuscan forces join:
Their various arms afford a pleasing sight:
A peaceful train they seem, in peace prepar'd for fight.

Betwixt the ranks the proud commanders ride,
Glitt'ring with gold, and vests in purple died—
Here Mnestheus, author of the Memmian line,
And there Messapus, born of seed divine.
The sign is giv'n; and, round the listed space,
Each man in order fills his proper place.
Reclining on their ample shields, they stand,
And fix their pointed lances in the sand.
Now, studious of the sight, a num'rous throng
Of either sex promiscuous, old and young,
Swarm from the town: by those who rest behind,
The gates and walls, and houses' tops, are lin'd.
Meantime the queen of heav'n beheld the sight.
With eyes unpleas'd, from mount Albano's height:
(Since call'd Albano by succeeding fame,
But then an empty hill, without a name)
She thence survey'd the field, the Trojan pow'rs,
The Latian squadrons, and Laurentine tow'rs.
Then thus the goddess of the skies bespake,
With sighs and tears, the goddess of the lake;
King Turnus' sister, once a lovely maid,
Ere to the lust of lawless Jove betray'd—
Compress'd by force, but, by the grateful god,
Now made the Naïs of the neighb'ring flood.
"O nymph, the pride of living lakes! (said she)
O most renown'd, and most belov'd by me!
Long hast thou known, nor need I to record,
The wanton sallies of my wand'ring lord.
Of ev'ry Latian fair, whom Jove misled
To mount by stealth my violated bed,
To thee alone I grudg'd not his embrace,
But gave a part of heav'n, and an unenvied place.
Now learn from me thy near approaching grief,
Nor think my wishes want to thy relief.
While Fortune favour'd, nor heav'n's king denied
To lend my succour to the Latian side,
I sav'd thy brother, and the sinking state:
But now he struggles with unequal fate,
And goes, with gods averse, o'ermatch'd in might,
To meet inevitable death in fight;
Nor must I break the truce, nor can sustain the sight.
Thou, if thou dar'st, thy present aid supply:
It well becomes a sister's care to try."
At this the lovely nymph, with grief oppress'd,
Thrice tore her hair, and beat her comely breast.
To whom Saturnia thus: "Thy tears are late:
Haste, snatch him, if he can be snatch'd from fate:
New tumults kindle; violate the truce:
Who knows what changeful Fortune may produce?
'Tis not a crime t' attempt what I decree;
Or, if it were, discharge the crime on me."
She said, and, sailing on the winged wind,
Left the sad nymph suspended in her mind.

And now in pomp the peaceful kings appear:
Four steeds the chariot of Latinus bear:
Twelve golden beams around his temples play,
To mark his lineage from the god of day.
Two snowy coursers Turnus' chariot yoke,
And in his hand two massy spears he shook:
Then issu'd from the camp in arms divine,
Æneas, author of the Roman line;
And by his side Ascanius took his place,
The second hope of Rome's immortal race.
Adorn'd in white, a rev'rend priest appears,
And, off'rings to the flaming altars bears—
A porket, and a lamb that never suffer'd shears.
Then to the rising sun he turns his eyes,
And strews the beasts design'd for sacrifice,
With salt and meal: with like officious care
He marks their foreheads, and he clips their hair.
Betwixt their horns the purple wine he sheds,
With the same gen'rous juice the flame he feeds.
Æneas then unsheath'd his shining sword,
And thus with pious pray'rs the gods ador'd
"All-seeing sun! and thou, Ausonian soil,
For which I have sustain'd so long a toil;
Thou, king of heav'n! and thou, the queen of air,
Propitious now, and reconcil'd by pray'r!
Thou, god of war, whose unresisted sway
The labours and events of arms obey!
Ye living fountains, and ye running floods!
All powers of ocean, all ethereal gods!
Hear, and bear record: if I fall in field,
Or, recreant in the fight, to Turnus yield,
My Trojans shall increase Evander's town;
Ascanius shall renounce th' Ausonian crown:
All claims, all questions of debate shall cease,
Nor he, nor they, with force infringe the peace.
But, if my juster arms prevail in fight,
(As sure they shall, if I divine aright)
My Trojans shall not o'er th' Italians reign:
Both equal, both unconquer'd, shall remain,
Join'd in their laws, their lands, and their abodes;
I ask but altars for my weary gods.
The care of those religious rites be mine:
The crown to king Latinus I resign:
His be the sov'reign sway. Nor will I share
His pow'r in peace, or his command in war.
For me, my friends another town shall frame,
And bless the rising tow'rs with fair Lavinia's name."
Thus he. Then with erected eyes and hands,
The Latian king before his altar stands.
'By the same heav'n, (said he) and earth and main,
And all the pow'rs that all the three contain;
By hell below, and by that upper god,
Whose thunder signs the peace, who seals it with his nod;

So let Latonia's double offspring hear,
And double-fronted Janus, what I swear:
I touch the sacred altars, touch the flames,
And all those pow'rs attest, and all their names:
Whatever chance befall on either side,
No term of time this union shall divide:
No force, no fortune, shall my vows unbind,
Or shake the steadfast tenor of my mind;
Not tho' the circling seas should break their bound,
O'erflow the shores, or sap the solid ground;
Not tho' the lamps of heav'n their spheres forsake,
Hurl'd down, and hissing in the nether lake:
E'en as this royal sceptre (for he bore
A sceptre in his hand) shall never more
Shoot out in branches, or renew the birth—
An orphan now, cut from the mother-earth
By the keen axe, dishonour'd of its hair,
And cas'd in brass for Latian kings to bear."
When thus in public view the peace was tied
With solemn vows, and sworn on either side,
All dues perform'd which holy rites require,
The victim beasts, are slain before the fire,
The trembling entrails from their bodies torn,
And to the fatten'd flames in chargers borne.
Already the Rutulians deem'd their man
O'ermatch'd in arms, before the fight began.
First rising fears are whisper'd thro' the crowd;
Then, gath'ring round, they murmur more aloud.
Now, side to side, they measure with their eyes
The champions' bulk, their sinews, and their size:
The nearer they approach, the more is known
Th' apparent disadvantage of their own.
Turnus himself appears in public sight
Conscious of fate, desponding of the fight.
Slowly he moves, and at his altar stands
With eyes dejected, and with trembling hands:
And while he mutters undistinguish'd pray'rs,
A livid deadness in his cheeks appears.
With anxious pleasure when Juturna view'd
Th' increasing fright of the mad multitude,
When their short sighs and thick'ning sobs she heard
And found their ready minds for change prepar'd;
Dissembling her immortal form, she took
Camertes' mien, his habit, and his look—
A chief of ancient blood:—in arms well known
Was his great sire, and he his greater son.
His shape assum'd, amid the ranks she ran,
And, hum'ring their first motions, thus began:
"For shame, Rutulians! can you bear the sight
Of one expos'd for all, in single fight?
Can we, before the face of heav'n, confess
Our courage colder, or our numbers less?
View all the Trojan host, th' Arcadian band,
And Tuscan army; count them as they stand.
Undaunted to the battle if we go,
Scarce ev'ry second man will share a foe.
Turnus, 't is true, in this unequal strife,
Shall lose, with honour, his devoted life,
Or change it rather for immortal fame,
Succeeding to the gods, from whence he came:
But you, a servile and inglorious band,
For foreign lords shall sow your native land
Those fruitful fields, your fighting fathers gain'd,
Which have so long their lazy sons sustain'd."
With words like these, she carried her design.
A rising murmur runs along the line.
Then e'en the city troops, and Latians, tir'd
With tedious war, seem with new souls inspir'd:
Their champion's fate with pity they lament,
And of the league, so lately sworn, repent.
Nor fails the goddess to foment the rage
With lying wonders, and a false presage;
But adds a sign, which, present to their eyes,
Inspires new courage, and a glad surprise.
For, sudden, in the fiery tracts above,
Appears in pomp th' imperial bird of Jove:
A plump of fowl he spies, that swim the lakes,
And o'er their heads his sounding pinions shakes;
Then, stooping on the fairest of the train,
In his strong talons truss'd a silver swan.
Th' Italians wonder at th' unusual sight:
But, while he lags, and labours in his flight,
Behold, the dastard fowl return anew,
And with united force the foe pursue:
Clam'rous around the royal hawk they fly,
And, thick'ning in a cloud, o'ershade the sky.
They cuff, they scratch, they cross his airy course;
Nor can th' encumber'd bird sustain their force;
But, vex'd, not vanquish'd, drops the pond'rous prey,
And, lighten'd of his burden, wings his way.
Th' Ausonian bands with shouts salute the sight,
Eager of action, and demand the fight.
Then king Tolumnius, vers'd in augurs' arts,
Cries out, and thus his boasted skill imparts:
"At length 't is granted, what I long desir'd:
This, this is what my frequent vows requir'd.
Ye gods! I take your omen and obey.—
Advance, my friends, and charge! I lead the way.
These are the foreign foes, whose impious band,
Like that rapacious bird, infest our land:
But soon, like him, they shall be forc'd to sea
By strength united, and forego the prey.

Your timely succour to your country bring;
Hasten to rescue, and redeem your king."
He said: and pressing onward through the crew,
Pois'd in his lifted arm, his lance he threw.
The winged weapon, whistling in the wind,
Came driving on, nor miss'd the mark design'd.
At once the cornal rattled in the skies:
At once tumultuous shouts and clamours rise.
Nine brothers in a goodly band there stood,
Born of Arcadian, mix'd with Tuscan blood,
Gylippus' sons: the fatal jav'lin flew,
Aim'd at the midmost of the friendly crew.
A passage through the jointed arms it found,
Just where the belt was to the body bound,
And struck the gentle youth extended on the ground.
Then, fir'd with pious rage, the gen'rous train
Run madly forward to revenge the slain.
And some with eager haste their jav'lins throw;
And some with sword in hand assault the foe.
The wish'd insult the Latine troops embrace,
And meet their ardour in the middle space.
The Tuscans, Trojans, and Arcadian line,
With equal courage obviate their design.
Peace leaves the violated fields; and hate
Both armies urges to their mutual fate,
With impious haste their altars are o'erturn'd,
The sacrifice half broil'd, and half unburn'd.
Thick storms of steel from either army fly,
And clouds of clashing darts obscure the sky:
Brands from the fire are missive weapons made,
With chargers, bowls, and all the priestly trade.
Latinus, frighted, hastens from the fray,
And bears his unregarded gods away.
These on their horses vault; those yoke the car;
The rest, with swords on high, run headlong to the war.
Messapus, eager to confound the peace,
Spurr'd his hot courser through the fighting press,
At king Aulestes, by his purple known
A Tuscan prince, and by his regal crown;
And, with a shock encount'ring, bore him down.
Backward he fell; and, as his fate design'd,
The ruins of an altar were behind:
There pitching on his shoulders and his head,
Amid the scatt'ring fires he lay supinely spread.
The beamy spear, descending from above,
His cuirass pierc'd, and through his body drove.
Then, with a scornful smile, the victor cries
"The gods have found a fitter sacrifice."
Greedy of spoils, th' Italians strip the dead
Of his rich armour, and uncrown his head.
Priest Corynæus arm'd his better hand,
From his own altar, with a blazing brand;
And, as Ebusus with a thund'ring pace
Advanc'd to battle, dash'd it on his face:
His bristly beard shines out with sudden fires,
The crack'ling crop a noisome scent expires.
Following the blow, he seiz'd his curling crown
With his left hand; his other cast him down.
The prostrate body with his knees he press'd,
And plung'd his holy poniard in his breast.
While Podolirius, with his sword, pursued
The shepherd Alsus through the flying crowd,
Swiftly he turns, and aims a deadly blow
Full on the front of his unwary foe.
The broad axe enters with a crashing sound,
And cleaves the chin with one continu'd wound;
Warm blood, and mingled brains, besmear his arms around
An iron sleep his stupid eyes oppress'd
And seiz'd their heavy lids in endless rest,
But good Æneas rush'd amid the bands:
Bare was his head, and naked were his hands,
In sign of truce: then thus he cries aloud:
"What sudden rage, what new desire of blood,
Inflames your alter'd minds? O Trojans! cease
From impious arms, nor violate the peace.
By human sanctions, and by laws divine,
The terms are all agreed; the war is mine.
Dismiss your fears, and let the fight ensue;
This hand alone shall right the gods and you,
Our injur'd altars, and their broken vow,
To this avenging sword the faithless Turnus owe."
Thus while he spoke, unmindful of defence
A winged arrow struck the pious prince.
But, whether from some human hand it came,
Or hostile god, is left unknown by fame:
No human hand, or hostile god, was found,
To boast the triumph of so base a wound.
When Turnus saw the Trojan quit the plain,
His chiefs dismay'd, his troops a fainting train,
Th' unhop'd event his heighten'd soul inspires:
At once his arms and coursers he requires;
Then, with a leap, his lofty chariot gains,
And with a ready hand assumes the reins.
He drives impetuous, and, where'er he goes,
He leaves behind a lane of slaughter'd foes.
These his lance reaches; over those he rolls
His rapid car, and crushes out their souls.
In vain the vanquish'd fly: the victor sends
The dead men's weapons at their living friends.
Thus on the banks of Hebrus' freezing flood,
The god of battles, in his angry mood,
Clashing his sword against his brazen shield,
Lets loose the reins, and scours along the field;
Before the wind his fiery coursers fly:
Groans the sad earth, resounds the rattling sky.
Wrath, Terror, Treason, and Despair,
(Dire faces, and deform'd) surround the car—
Friends of the god, and followers of the war.

With fury not unlike, nor less disdain,
Exulting Turnus flies along the plain;
His smoking horses at their utmost speed,
He lashes on; and urges o'er the dead.
Their fetlocks run with blood, and when they bound,
The gore and gath'ring dust are dash'd around.
Thamyris and Pholus, masters of the war,
He kill'd at hand, but Sthenelus afar:
From far the sons of Imbrasus he slew,
Glaucus and Lades, of the Lycian crew—
Both taught to fight on foot, in battle join'd,
Or mount the courser that outstrips the wind.
Meantime Eumedes, vaunting in the field,
New fir'd the Trojans, and their foes repell'd.
This son of Dolon bore his grandsire's name,
But emulated more his father's fame—
His guileful father, sent a nightly spy,
The Grecian camp and order to descry—
Hard enterprise! and well he might require
Achilles' car and horses, for his hire:
But, met upon the scout, th' Ætolian prince
In death bestow'd a juster recompense.
Fierce Turnus view'd the Trojan from afar
And launch'd his jav'lin from his lofty car,
Then lightly leaping down, pursu'd the blow,
And, pressing with his foot his prostrate foe,
Wrench'd from his feeble hold the shining sword,
And plung'd it in the bosom of its lord.
"Possess," said he, "the fruit of all thy pains,
And measure at thy length, our Latian plains,
Thus are my foes rewarded by my hand:
Thus may they build their town, and thus enjoy the land!"
Then Dares, Butes, Sybaris he slew,
Whom o'er his neck the flound'ring courser threw.
As when loud Boreas, with his blust'ring train,
Stoops from above, incumbent on the main,
Where'er he flies, he drives the rack before,
And rolls the billows on the Ægean shore:
So, where resistless Turnus takes his course,
The scatter'd squadrons bend before his force.
His crest of horse's hair is blown behind
By adverse air, and rustles in the wind.
This haughty Phegeus saw with high disdain,
And, as the chariot roll'd along the plain,
Light from the ground he leap'd, and seiz'd the rein.
Thus hung in air, he still retain'd his hold,
The coursers frighted, and their course controll'd.
The lance of Turnus reach'd him as he hung,
And pierc'd his plated arms, but pass'd along,
And only rais'd the skin. He turn'd, and held
Against his threat'ning foe his ample shield,
Then call'd for aid: but, while he cried in vain,
The chariot bore him backward on the plain.
He lies revers'd: the victor king descends,
And strikes so justly where his helmet ends,
He lops the head. The Latian fields are drunk
With streams that issue from the bleeding trunk.
While he triumphs, and while the Trojans yield,
The wounded prince is forc'd to leave the field:
Strong Mnestheus, and Achates, often tried,
And young Ascanius, weeping by his side,
Conduct him to his tent. Scarce can he rear
His limbs from earth, supported on his spear.
Resolv'd in mind, regardless of the smart,
He tugs with both his hands, and breaks the dart.
The steel remains. No readier way he found
To draw the weapon, than t' enlarge the wound.
Eager of fight, impatient of delay,
He begs; and his unwilling friends obey.
Iapis was at hand to prove his art,
Whose blooming youth so fir'd Apollo's heart,
That, for his love, he proffer'd to bestow
His tuneful harp, and his unerring bow.
The pious youth, more studious how to save
His aged sire, now sinking to the grave,
Preferr'd the pow'r of plants and silent praise
Of healing arts, before Phœbean bays.
Propp'd on his lance, the pensive hero stood,
And heard and saw, unmov'd, the mourning crowd.
The fam'd physician tucks his robes around
With ready hands, and hastens to the wound.
With gentle touches he performs his part,
This way and that, soliciting the dart,
And exercises all his heav'nly art.
All soft'ning simples, known of sov'reign use,
He presses out, and pours their noble juice.
These first infus'd, to lenify the pain—
He tugs with pincers, but he tugs in vain.
Then to the patron of his art he pray'd:
The patron of his art refus'd his aid.
Meantime the war approaches to the tents:
Th' alarm grows hotter, and the noise augments:
The driving dust proclaims the danger near;
And first their friends, and then their foes appear:
Their friends retreat, their foes pursue the rear.
The camp is fill'd with terror and affright:
The hissing shafts within the trench alight:
An undistinguish'd noise ascends the sky—
The shouts of those who kill, and groans of those who die.
But now the goddess-mother, mov'd with grief,
And pierc'd with pity, hastens her relief.
A branch of healing dittany she brought,
Which in the Cretan fields with care she sought

Rough is the stem, which woolly leaves surround:
The leaves with flow'rs, the flow'rs with purple crown'd)
Well known to wounded goats; a sure relief
To draw the pointed steel, and ease the grief.
This Venus brings, in clouds involv'd, and brews
Th' extracted liquor with ambrosian dews,
And od'rous panacee. Unseen she stands,
Temp'ring the mixture with her heav'nly hands,
And pours it in a bowl, already crown'd
With juice of med'c'nal herbs prepar'd to bathe the wound.
The leech, unknowing of superior art
Which aids the cure, with this foments the part;
And in a moment ceas'd the raging smart.
Stanch'd is the blood, and in the bottom stands:
The steel, but scarcely touch'd with tender hands,
Moves up, and follows of its own accord;
And health and vigour are at once restor'd.
Iäpis first perceiv'd the closing wound;
And first the footsteps of a god he found.
"Arms! arms!" he cries: "the sword and shield prepare,
And send the willing chief renew'd to war,
This is no mortal work, no cure of mine,
Nor art's effect, but done by hands divine.
Some god our gen'ral to the battle sends;
Some god preserves his life for greater ends."
The hero arms in haste: his hands infold
His thighs with cuishes of refulgent gold:
Inflam'd to fight and rushing to the field,
That hand sustaining the celestial shield,
This gripes the lance, and with such vigour shakes,
That to the rest the beamy weapon quakes.
Then with a close embrace he strain'd his son,
And, kissing through his helmet thus begun:
"My son! from my example learn to war,
In camps to suffer, and in fields to dare:
But happier chance than mine attend thy care!
This day my hand thy tender age shall shield,
And crown with honours of the conquer'd field:
Thou, when thy riper years shall send thee forth
To toils of war, be mindful of my worth:
Assert thy birthright; and in arms be known
For Hector's nephew and Æneas' son."
He said; and, striding, issued on the plain.
Anteus and Mnestheus, and a num'rous train,
Attend his steps: the rest their weapons take,
And crowding to the field the camp forsake.
A cloud of blinding dust is rais'd around;
Labours beneath their feet the trembling ground.
Nor Turnus, posted on a hill, from far
Beheld the progress of the moving war:
With him the Latins view'd the cover'd plains
And the chill blood ran backward in their veins.
Juturna saw th' advancing troops appear,
And heard the hostile sound, and fled for fear,
Æneas leads; and draws a sweeping train,
Clos'd in their ranks, and pouring on the plain
As, when a whirlwind, rushing to the shore
From the mid ocean, drives the waves before;
The painful hind with heavy heart foresees
The flatted fields, and slaughter of the trees;
With such impetuous rage the prince appears,
Before his doubled front; nor less destruction bears.
And now both armies shock in open field;
Osiris is by strong Thymbræus kill'd.
Archetius, Ufens, Epulon, are slain
(All fam'd in arms, and of the Latian train)
By Gyas', Mnestheus', and Achates' band.
The fatal augur falls, by whose command
The truce was broken, and whose lance, embru'd
With Trojan blood, th' unhappy fight renew'd.
Loud shouts and clamours rend the liquid sky;
And o'er the fields the frighted Latins fly.
The prince disdains the dastards to pursue,
Nor moves to meet in arms the fighting few.
Turnus alone, amid the dusky plain,
He seeks, and to the combat calls in vain.
Juturna heard, and, seiz'd with mortal fear,
Forc'd from the beam her brother's chariot eer;
Assumes his shape, his armour, and his mien,
And, like Metiscus, in his seat is seen.
As the black swallow near the palace plies;
O'er empty courts, and under arches, flies;
Now hawks aloft, now skims along the flood,
To furnish her loquacious nest with food:
So drives the rapid goddess o'er the plains;
The smoking horses run with loosen'd reins.
She steers a various course among the foes:
Now here, now there, her conqu'ring brother shows;
Now with a straight, now with a wheeling flight.
She turns and bends, but shuns the single fight.
Æneas, fir'd with fury, breaks the crowd,
And seeks his foe, and calls by name aloud:
He runs within a narrower ring, and tries
To stop the chariot, but the chariot flies.
If he but gain a glimpse, Juturna fears,
And far away the Daunian hero bears.
What should he do? Nor arts nor arms avail;
And various cares in vain his mind assail.
The great Messapus, thund'ring through the field,
In his left hand two pointed jav'lins held:
Encount'ring on the prince, one dart he drew,
And with unerring aim, and utmost vigour, threw.

Æneas saw it come, and, stooping low
Beneath his buckler, shunn'd the threat'ning blow.
The weapon hiss'd above his head, and tore
The waving plume, which on his helm he wore,
Forc'd by this hostile act, and fir'd with spite,
That flying Turnus still declin'd the fight,
The prince, whose piety had long repell'd
His inborn ardour now invades the field;
Invokes the pow'rs of violated peace,
Their rites and injur'd altars to redress;
Then to his rage, abandoning the rein,
With blood and slaughter'd bodies fills the plain.
What god can tell, what numbers can display,
The various labours of that fatal day?
What chiefs and champions fell on either side,
In combat slain, or by what deaths they died?
Whom Turnus, whom the Trojan hero kill'd?
Who shar'd the fame and fortune of the field?
Jove! couldst thou view, and not avert thy sight,
Two jarring nations join'd in cruel fight,
Whom leagues of lasting love so shortly shall unite?
Æneas first, Rutulian Sucro found,
Whose valour made the Trojans quit their ground;
Betwixt his ribs the jav'lin drove so just,
It reach'd his heart, nor needs a second thrust.
Now Turnus, at two blows, two brethren slew;
First from his horse fierce Amycus he threw:
Then, leaping on the ground, on foot assail'd
Diores, and in equal fight prevail'd.
Their lifeless trunks he leaves upon the place
Their heads, distilling gore, his chariot grace.
Three cold on earth the Trojan hero threw,
Whom without respite at one charge he slew:
Cethegus, Tanais, Talus fell oppress'd,
And sad Onythes, added to the rest—
Of Theban blood, whom Peridia bore.
Turnus two brothers from the Lycian shore,
And from Apollo's fane to battle sent,
O'erthrew: nor Phœbus could their fate prevent.
Peaceful Menœtes after these he kill'd,
Who long had shunn'd the dangers of the field:
On Lerna's lake a silent life he led,
And with his nets and angle earn'd his bread.
Nor pompous cares, nor palaces, he knew,
But wisely from the infectious world withdrew.
Poor was his house: his father's painful hand
Discharg'd his rent, and plough'd another's land.
As flames among the lofty woods are thrown
On diff'rent sides, and both by winds are blown;
The laurels crackle in the sputt'ring fire;
The frighted sylvans from their shades retire;
Or as two neighb'ring torrents fall from high
Rapid they run: the foamy waters fry;
They roll to sea with unresisted force,
And down the rocks precipitate their course.
Not with less rage the rival heroes take
Their diff'rent ways; nor less destruction make
With spears afar, with swords at hand, they strike;
And zeal of slaughter fires their souls alike,
Like them, their dauntless men maintain the field!
And hearts are pierc'd, unknowing how to yield:
They blow for blow return, and wound for wound;
And heaps of bodies raise the level ground.
Murranus, boasting of his blood, that springs
From a long royal race of Latian kings,
Is by the Trojan from his chariot thrown;
Crush'd with the weight of an unwieldy stone:
Betwixt the wheels he fell; the wheels, that bore
His living load, his dying body tore.
His starting steeds, to shun the glitt'ring sword,
Paw down his trampled limbs, forgetful of their lord.
Fierce Hyllus threaten'd high, and, face to face,
Affronted Turnus in the middle space:
The prince encounter'd him in full career,
And at his temples aim'd the deadly spear:
So fatally the flying weapon sped,
That through his brazen helmet pierc'd his head.
Nor, Cisseus, couldst thou 'scape from Turnus' hand,
In vain the strongest of th' Arcadian band:
Nor to Cupentus could his gods afford
Availing aid against th' Ænean sword,
Which to his naked heart pursu'd the course;
Nor could his plated shield sustain the force.
Iōlus fell, whom not the Grecian pow'rs,
Nor great subverter of the Trojan tow'rs,
Were doom'd to kill, while heav'n prolong'd his date:
But who can pass the bounds prefix'd by Fate?
In high Lyrnessus, and in Troy, he held
Two palaces, and was from each expell'd:
Of all the mighty man, the last remains
A little spot of foreign earth contains.
And now both hosts their broken troops unite
In equal ranks, and mix in mortal fight.
Serestus and undaunted Mnestheus join
The Trojan, Tuscan, and Arcadian line;
Sea-born Messapus, with Atinas, heads
The Latin squadrons, and to battle leads.
They strike; they push; they throng the scanty space,
Resolv'd on death, impatient of disgrace;
And, where one falls, another fills his place.

The Cyprian goddess now inspires her son
To leave th' unfinish'd fight, and storm the town:
For, while he rolls his eyes around the plain
In quest of Turnus, whom he seeks in vain,
He views th' unguarded city from afar,
In careless quiet, and secure of war.
Occasion offers, and excites his mind
To dare beyond the task he first design'd.
Resolv'd he calls his chiefs: they leave the fight:
Attended thus, he takes a neighb'ring height:
The crowding troops about their gen'ral stand,
All under arms, and wait his high command.
Then thus the lofty prince: "Hear and obey
Ye Trojan bands, without the least delay.
Jove is with us; and what I have decreed,
Requires our utmost vigour, and our speed.
Your instant arms against the town prepare,
The source of mischief, and the seat of war
This day the Latian tow'rs, that mate the sky,
Shall, level with the plain, in ashes lie:
The people shall be slaves, unless in time
They kneel for pardon, and repent their crime.
Twice have our foes been vanquish'd on the plain:
Then shall I wait till Turnus will be slain?
Your force against the perjur'd city bend:
There it began, and there the war shall end.
The peace profan'd our rightful arms requires;
Cleanse the polluted place with purging fires."
He finish'd; and—one soul inspiring all—
Form'd in a wedge, the foot approach the wall.
Without the town, an unprovided train
Of gaping gazing citizens are slain.
Some firebrands, others scaling ladders, bear;
And those they toss aloft, and these they rear;
The flames now launch'd, the feather'd arrows fly;
And clouds of missive arms obscure the sky.
Advancing to the front, the hero stands,
And, stretching out to heav'n his pious hands,
Attests the gods, asserts his innocence,
Upbraids with breach of faith th' Ausonian prince,
Declares the royal honour doubly stain'd,
And twice the rites of holy peace profan'd.
Dissenting clamours in the town arise;
Each will be heard, and all at once advise.
One part for peace, and one for war, contends:
Some would exclude their foes, and some admit their friends.
The helpless king is hurried in the throng,
And (whate'er tide prevails) is borne along.
Thus, when the swain, within a hollow rock,
Invades the bees with suffocating smoke,
They run around, or labour on their wings,
Disus'd to flight, and shoot their sleepy stings;
To shun the bitter fumes, in vain they try;
Black vapours, issuing from the vent, involve the sky
But Fate and envious Fortune now prepare
To plunge the Latins in the last despair.
The queen, who saw the foes invade the town,
And brands on tops of burning houses thrown,
Cast round her eyes, distracted with her fear:—
No troops of Turnus in the field appear.
Once more she stares abroad, but still in vain;
And then concludes the royal youth is slain
Mad with her anguish, impotent to bear
The mighty grief, she loathes the vital air.
She calls herself the cause of all this ill,
And owns the dire effects of her ungovern'd will:
She raves against the gods; she beats her breast;
She tears with both her hands her purple vest:
Then round a beam a running noose she tied,
And fasten'd by the neck, obscenely died.
Soon as the fatal news by fame was blown,
And to her dames, and to her daughter known,
The sad Lavinia rends her yellow hair,
And rosy cheeks: the rest her sorrow share:
With shrieks the palace rings, and madness of despair.
The spreading rumour fills the public place:
Confusion, fear, distraction, and disgrace,
And silent shame, are seen in ev'ry face.
Latinus tears his garments as he goes,
Both for his public and his private woes:
With filth his venerable beard besmears;
And sordid dust deforms his silver hairs.
And much he blames the softness of his mind,
Obnoxious to the charms of womankind,
And soon reduc'd to change what he so well design'd—
To break the solemn league so long desir'd,
Nor finish'd what his fates, and those of Troy, requir'd.
Now Turnus rolls aloof o'er empty plains;
And here and there some straggling foes he gleans.
His flying coursers please him less and less,
Asham'd of easy fight, and cheap success.
Thus half contended, anxious in his mind,
The distant cries come driving in the wind—
Shouts from the walls, but shouts in murmurs drown'd;
A jarring mixture, and a boding sound.
"Alas!" said he, "what mean these dismal cries?
What doleful clamours from the town arise?"
Confus'd he stops, and backward pulls the reins
She, who the driver's office now sustains,
Replies: "Neglect, my lord, these new alarms;
Here fight, and urge the fortune of your arms;
There want not others to defend the wall.
If by your rival's hand th' Italians fall,

So shall your fatal sword his friends oppress
In honour equal, equal in success."
To this the prince: "O sister!—for I knew,
The peace infring'd proceeded first from you:
I knew you, when you mingled first in fight:
And now in vain you would deceive my sight—
Why, goddess, this unprofitable care?
Who sent you down from heav'n, involv'd in air,
Your share of mortal sorrows to sustain,
And see your brother bleeding on the plain?
For to what pow'r can Turnus have recourse,
Or how resist his fate's prevailing force?
These eyes beheld Murranus bite the ground.
Mighty the man, and mighty was the wound.
I heard my dearest friend, with dying breath,
My name invoking, to revenge his death.
Brave Ufens fell with honour on the place,
To shun the shameful sight of my disgrace.
On earth supine, a manly corpse he lies;
His vest and armour are the victor's prize.
Then shall I see Laurentum in a flame,
Which only wanted to complete my shame?
How will the Latins hoot their champion's flight!
How Drances will insult, and point them to the sight!
Is death so hard to bear?—Ye gods below!
(Since those above so small compassion show)
Receive a soul, unsullied yet with shame,
Which not belies my great forefather's name."
He said: and, while he spoke, with flying speed
Came Sages urging on his foamy steed:
Fix'd on his wounded face a shaft he bore,
And seeking Turnus, sent his voice before:
"Turnus! on you, on you alone, depends
Our last relief:—compassionate your friend;
Like light'ning, fierce Æneas, rolling on,
With arms invests, with flames invades the town:
The brands are toss'd on high: the winds conspire
To drive along the deluge of the fire.
All eyes are fixed on you: your foes rejoice;
E'en the king staggers, and suspends his choice—
Doubts to deliver or defend the town,
Whom to reject, or whom to call his son.
The queen, on whom your utmost hopes were plac'd,
Herself suborning death, has breath'd her last.
'Tis true, Messapus, fearless of his fate,
With fierce Atinas' aid, defends the gate:
On ev'ry side surrounded by the foe,
The more they kill, the greater numbers grow;
An iron harvest mounts, and still remains to mow.
You far aloof from your forsaken bands,
Your rolling chariot drive o'er empty sands."
Stupid he sate, his eyes on earth declin'd,
And various cares revolving in his mind:
Rage, boiling from the bottom of his breast,
And sorrow mix'd with shame, his soul oppress'd;
And conscious worth lay lab'ring in his thought,
And love by jealousy to madness wrought.
By slow degrees his reason drove away
The mists of passion, and resum'd her sway.
Then rising on his car, he turn'd his look,
And saw the town involv'd in fire and smoke.
A wooden tow'r with flames already blaz'd,
Which his own hands on beams and rafters rais'd,
And bridges laid above to join the space,
And wheels below to roll from place to place,
"Sister! the fates have vanquish'd; let us go
The way which heav'n and my hard fortune show.
The fight is fix'd: nor shall the branded name
Of a base coward blot your brother's fame,
Death is my choice: but suffer me to try
My force, and vent my rage before I die."
He said: and leaping down without delay,
Through crowds of scatter'd foes he freed his way
Striding he pass'd, impetuous as the wind,
And left the grieving goddess far behind.
As, when a fragment, from a mountain torn
By raging tempests, or by torrents borne,
Or sapp'd by time, or loosen'd from the roots—
Prone through the void the rocky ruin shoots,
Rolling from crag to crag, from steep to steep.
Down sink, at once, the shepherds and their sheep
Involv'd alike, they rush to nether ground;
Stunn'd with the shock they fall, and stunn'd from earth rebound:
So Turnus, hasting headlong to the town,
Should'ring and shoving, bore the squadrons down.
Still pressing onward, to the walls he drew,
Where shafts and spears and darts promiscuous flew,
And sanguine streams the slipp'ry ground embrue.
First stretching out his arm, in sign of peace,
He cries aloud, to make the combat cease:
"Rutulians, hold! and Latian troops, retire!
The fight is mine; and me the gods require.
'Tis just that I should vindicate alone
The broken truce, or for the breach atone.
This day shall free from wars th' Ausonian state,
Or finish my misfortunes in my fate."
Both armies from their bloody work desist,
And, bearing backward, from a spacious list.
The Trojan hero, who receiv'd from fame
The welcome sound, and heard the champion's name,
Soon leaves the taken works and mounted walls
Greedy of war where greater glory calls,

He springs to fight, exulting in his force;
His jointed armour rattles in the course.
Like Eryx, or like Athos, great he shows,
Or father Apennine, when, white with snows,
His head, divine, obscure in clouds he hides,
And shakes the sounding forest on his sides.
The nations, over-aw'd, surcease the fight:
Immoveable their bodies, fix'd their sight.
E'en Death stands still; nor from above they throw
Their darts, nor drive their batt'ring-rams below.
In silent order either army stands,
And drop their swords, unknowing, from their hands.
Th' Ausonian king beholds, with wond'ring sight,
Two mighty champions match'd in single fight,
Born under climes remote, and brought by fate,
With swords to try their titles to the state.
Now, in clos'd field, each other from afar
They view; and, rushing on, begin the war.
They launch their spears; then hand to hand they meet.
The trembling soil resounds beneath their feet:
Their bucklers clash; thick blows descend from high,
And flakes of fire from their hard helmets fly.
Courage conspires with chance; and both engage
With equal fortune yet, and mutual rage.
As, when two bulls for their fair female fight
In Sila's shades, or on Taburnus' height,
With horns adverse they meet: the keeper flies:
Mute stands the herd; the heifers roll their eyes,
And wait th' event—which victor they shall bear,
And who shall be the lord to rule the lusty year:
With rage of love, the jealous rivals burn,
And push for push, and wound for wound, return:
Their dewlaps gor'd, their sides are lav'd in blood:
Loud cries and roaring sounds rebellow thro' the wood:
Such was the combat in the listed ground;
So clash their swords, and so their shields resound.
Jove sets the beam: in either scale he lays
The champions' fate, and each exactly weighs.
On this side life and lucky chance ascends:
Loaded with death, that other scale descends.
Rais'd on the stretch, young Turnus aims a blow
Full on the helm of his unguarded foe:
Shrill shouts and clamours ring on either side,
As hopes and fears their panting hearts divide.
But all in pieces flies the traitor sword,
And in the middle stroke, deserts his lord.
Now 't is but death or flight: disarm'd he flies,
When in his hand an unknown hilt he spies.
Fame says that Turnus, when his steeds he join'd,
Hurrying to war, disorder'd in his mind,
Snatch'd the first weapon which his haste could find.
'T was not the fated sword his father bore,
But that his charioteer Metiscus wore.
This, while the Trojans fled, the toughness held:
But, vain against the great Vulcanian shield,
The mortal-temper'd steel deceiv'd his hand:
The shiver'd fragments shone amid the sand.
Surpris'd with fear, he fled along the field,
And now forthright, and now in orbits wheel'd:
For here the Trojan troops the list surround,
And there the pass is clos'd with pools and marshy ground.
Æneas hastens, though with heavier pace—
His wound, so newly knit, retards the chase,
And oft his trembling knees their aid refuse—
Yet, pressing foot by foot, his foe pursues.
Thus, when a fearful stag is clos'd around
With crimson toils, or in a river found,
High on the bank the deep-mouth'd hound appears,
Still op'ning, following still, where'er he steers:
The persecuted creature, to and fro,
Turns here and there, t' escape his Umbrian foe:
Steep is th' ascent, and, if he gains the land,
The purple death is pitch'd along the strand.
His eager foe, determin'd to the chase,
Stretch'd at his length, gains ground at ev'ry pace:
Now to his beamy head he makes his way,
And now he holds, or thinks he holds, his prey:
Just at the pinch, the stag springs out with fear:
He bites the wind, and fills his sounding jaws with air:
The rocks, the lakes, the meadows, ring with cries;
The mortal tumult mounts, and thunders in the skies:
Thus flies the Daunian prince, and, flying blames
His tardy troops, and, calling by their names,
Demands his trusty sword. The Trojan threats
Their realm with ruin, and their ancient seats
To lay in ashes, if they dare supply,
With arms or aid, his vanquish'd enemy;
Thus menacing, he still pursues his course,
With vigour, though diminish'd of his force.
Ten times already, round the listed place,
One chief had fled, and t' other giv'n the chase:
No trivial prize is play'd; for on the life
Or death of Turnus, now depends the strife.
Within the space, an olive-tree had stood,
A sacred shade, a venerable wood,
For vows to Faunus paid, the Latins' guardian god.

Here hung the vests, and tablets were engrav'd,
Of sinking mariners, from shipwreck sav'd.
With heedless hands the Trojans fell'd the tree,
To make the ground enclos'd for combat free.
Deep in the root, whether by fate or chance,
Or erring haste, the Trojan drove his lance;
Then stoop'd, and tugg'd with force immense, to free
Th' encumber'd spear from the tenacious tree
That whom his fainting limbs pursu'd in vain,
His flying weapon might from far attain.
Confus'd with fear, bereft of human aid,
Then Turnus to the gods, and first to Faunus pray'd:
"O Faunus! pity! and thou, mother Earth,
Where I thy foster-son receiv'd my birth,
Hold fast the steel! If my religious hand
Your plant has honour'd, which your foes profan'd,
Propitious hear my pious pray'r!" He said,
Nor with successless vows invok'd their aid.
Th' incumbent hero wrench'd, and pull'd, and strain'd;
But still the stubborn earth the steel detain'd.
Juturna took her time; and, while in vain
He strove, assum'd Metiscus' form again,
And, in that imitated shape, restor'd
To the despairing prince, his Daunian sword.
The queen of love—who, with disdain and grief,
Saw the bold nymph afford this prompt relief—
T' assert her offspring with a greater deed,
From the tough root the ling'ring weapon freed.
Once more erect, the rival chiefs advance:
One trusts the sword, and one the pointed lance;
And both resolv'd alike, to try their fatal chance.
Meantime imperial Jove to Juno spoke,
Who from a shining cloud beheld the shock:
"What new arrest, O queen of heav'n! is sent
To stop the Fates now lab'ring in th' event?
What further hopes are left thee to pursue?
Divine Æneas (and thou know'st it too)
Foredoom'd, to these celestial seats is due.
What more attempts for Turnus can be made,
That thus thou ling'rest in this lonely shade?
Is it becoming of the due respect
And awful honour of a god elect,
A wound unworthy of our state to feel,
Patient of human hands, and earthly steel?
Or seems it just the sister should restore
A second sword, when one was lost before,
And arm a conquer'd wretch against his conqueror?
For what, without thy knowledge and avow,
Nay more, thy dictate, durst Juturna do?
At last, in def'rence to my love, forbear
To lodge within thy soul this anxious care:
Reclin'd upon my breast, thy grief unload:—
Who should relieve the goddess, but the god?
Now all things to their utmost issue tend,
Push'd by the Fates to their appointed end.
While leave was giv'n thee, and a lawful hour
For vengeance, wrath, and unresisted pow'r,
Toss'd on the seas thou could'st thy foes distress,
And, driv'n ashore, with hostile arms oppress.
Deform the royal house; and from the side
Of the just bridegroom, tear the plighted pride:—
Now cease at my command." The Thund'rer said:
And, with dejected eyes, this answer Juno made:
"Because your dread decree too well I knew,
From Turnus and from earth, unwilling I withdrew.
Else should you not behold me here alone,
Involv'd in empty clouds, my friends bemoan,
But, girt with vengeful flames, in open sight,
Engag'd against my foes in mortal fight.
'Tis true, Juturna mingled in the strife
By my command, to save a brother's life,
At least to try; but (by the Stygian lake—
The most religious oath the gods can take)
With this restriction, not to bend the bow,
Or toss the spear, or trembling dart to throw.
And now, resign'd to your superior might,
And tir'd with fruitless toils, I loathe the fight.
This let me beg (and this no fates withstand)
Both for myself and for your father's land,
That, when the nuptial bed shall bind the peace
(Which I, since you ordain, consent to bless,)
The laws of either nation be the same;
But let the Latins still retain their name,
Speak the same language which they spoke before,
Wear the same habits which their grandsires wore.
Call them not Trojans: perish the renown
And name of Troy, with that detested town.
Latium be Latium still; let Alba reign,
And Rome's immortal majesty remain."
Then thus the founder of mankind replies
(Unruffled was his front, serene his eyes:)
"Can Saturn's issue, and heav'n's other heir,
Such endless anger in her bosom bear?
Be mistress, and your full desires obtain;
But quench the choler you foment in vain.
From ancient blood, th' Ausonian people sprung,
Shall keep their name, their habit, and their tongue:
The Trojans to their customs shall be tied:
I will, myself, their common rites provide:
The natives shall command, the foreigners subside.

All shall be Latium; Troy without a name
And her lost sons forget from whence they came.
From blood so mix'd, a pious race shall flow,
Equal to gods, excelling all below.
No nation more respect to you shall pay,
Or greater off'rings on your altars lay."
Juno consents, well pleas'd that her desires
Had found success, and from the cloud retires.
The peace thus made, the Thunderer next prepares
To force the wat'ry goddess from the wars.
Deep in the dismal regions void of light,
Three daughters, at a birth, were born to Night:
There their brown mother, brooding on her care,
Indu'd with windy wings, to flit in air,
With serpents girt alike, and crown'd with hissing hair.
In heav'n the Diræ call'd, and still at hand,
Before the throne of angry Jove they stand,
His ministers of wrath, and ready still
The minds of mortal men with fears to fill,
Whene'er the moody sire, to wreak his hate
On realms or towns deserving of their fate,
Hurls down diseases, death, and deadly care,
And terrifies the guilty world with war.
One sister-plague of these from heav'n he sent,
To fright Juturna with a dire portent.
The pest comes whirling down: by far more slow
Springs the swift arrow from the Parthian bow,
Or Cydon yew, when traversing the skies,
And drench'd in pois'nous juice, the sure destruction flies.
With such a sudden, and unseen a flight,
Shot through the clouds, the daughter of the Night.
Soon as the field inclos'd she had in view,
And from afar her destin'd quarry knew—
Contracted, to the boding bird she turns,
Which haunts the ruin'd piles and hallow'd urns,
And beats about the tombs with mighty wings,
Where songs obscene on sepulchres she sings.
Thus lessen'd in her form, with frightful cries
The Fury round unhappy Turnus flies,
Flaps on his shield, and flutters o'er his eyes.
A lazy chillness crept along his blood;
Chok'd was his voice; his hair with horror stood.
Juturna from afar beheld her fly,
And knew th' ill omen, by her screaming cry,
And stridor of her wing. Amaz'd with fear,
Her beauteous breast she beat, and rent her flowing hair.
"Ah me!" she cries, "in this unequal strife,
What can thy sister more to save thy life?
Weak as I am, can I, alas! contend
In arms with that inexorable fiend?
Now, now, I quit the field! forbear to fright
My tender soul, ye baleful birds of night!
The lashing of your wings I know too well,
The sounding flight, and fun'ral screams of hell!
These are the gifts you bring from haughty Jove,
The worthy recompense of ravish'd love:
Did he for this exempt my life from fate!
O hard conditions of immortal state!
Though born to death, not privileg'd to die,
But forc'd to bear impos'd eternity!
Take back your envious bribes, and let me go
Companion to my brother's ghost below!
The joys are vanish'd: nothing now remains
Of life immortal, but immortal pains.
What earth will open her devouring womb,
To rest a weary goddess in the tomb?"
She drew a length of sighs; nor more she said,
But in her azure mantle wrapp'd her head,
Then plung'd into her stream, with deep despair;
And her last sobs came bubbling up in air.
Now stern Æneas waves his weighty spear
Against his foe, and thus upbraids his fear:
"What further subterfuge can Turnus find?
What empty hopes are harbour'd in his mind?
'Tis not thy swiftness can secure thy flight:
Not with their feet, but hands, the valiant fight.
Vary thy shape in thousand forms, and dare
What skill and courage can attempt in war:
Wish for the wings of winds, to mount the sky
Or hid within the hollow earth to lie!"
The champion shook his head, and made this short reply:
"No threats of thine my manly mind can move
'Tis hostile heav'n I dread, and partial Jove."
He said no more, but, with a sigh, repress'd
The mighty sorrow in his swelling breast
Then, as he roll'd his troubled eyes around,
An antique stone he saw, the common bound
Of neighb'ring fields, and barrier of the ground—
So vast, that twelve strong men of modern days
Th' enormous weight from earth could hardly raise.
He heav'd it at a lift, and, pois'd on high,
Ran stagg'ring on against his enemy.
But so disorder'd, that he scarcely knew
His way, or what unwieldy weight he threw.
His knocking knees are bent beneath the load,
And shiv'ring cold congeals his vital blood.
The stone drops from his arms, and, falling short
For want of vigour, mocks his vain effort.
And as, when heavy sleep has clos'd the sight,
The sickly fancy labours in the night;
We seem to run; and, destitute of force,
Our sinking limbs forsake us in the course:
In vain we heave for breath; in vain we cry:
The nerves, unbrac'd, their usual strength deny;

And on the tongue th' falt'ring accents die:
So Turnus far'd: whatever means he tried
All force of arms, and points of art employ'd,
The Fury flew athwart, and made th' endeavour void.
A thousand various thoughts his soul confound:
He star'd about; nor aid, nor issue found:
His own men stop the pass; and his own walls surround.
Once more he pauses, and looks out again,
And seeks the goddess-charioteer in vain.
Trembling he views the thund'ring chief advance,
And brandishing aloft the deadly lance:
Amaz'd he cow'rs beneath his conqu'ring foe,
Forgets to ward, and waits the coming blow.
Astonish'd while he stands, and fix'd with fear,
Aim'd at his shield, he sees th' impending spear.
The hero measur'd first, with narrow view,
The destin'd mark; and, rising as he threw,
With its full swing, the fatal weapon flew.
Not with less rage the rattling thunder falls,
Or stones from batt'ring-engines break the walls
Swift as a whirlwind, from an arm so strong
The lance drove on, and bore the death along:
Naught could his seven-fold shield the prince avail,
Nor aught beneath his arms, the coat of mail:
It pierc'd through all, and with a grisly wound
Transfix'd his thigh, and doubled him to ground.
With groans the Latins rend the vaulted sky:
Woods, hills, and valleys, to the voice reply.
Now, low on earth, the lofty chief is laid,
With eyes cast upwards, and with arms display'd,
And, recreant, thus to the proud victor pray'd.
"I know my death deserv'd, nor hope to live
Use what the gods and thy good fortune give.
Yet think, oh! think, if mercy may be shown,
(Thou hadst a father once, and hast a son)—
Pity my sire, now sinking to the grave.
And for Anchises' sake, old Daunus save!
Or, if thy vow'd revenge pursue my death,
Give to my friends my body void of breath!
The Latian chiefs have seen me beg my life:
Thine is the conquest, thine the royal wife:
Against a yielded man, 'tis mean, ignoble strife."
In deep suspense, the Trojan seem'd to stand,
And, just prepar'd to strike, repress'd his hand.
He roll'd his eyes, and ev'ry moment felt
His manly soul with more compassion melt;
When, casting down a casual glance, he spied
The golden belt that glitter'd on his side,
The fatal spoil which haughty Turnus tore
From dying Pallas, and in triumph wore.
Then rous'd anew to wrath, he loudly cries,
(Flames while he spoke, came flashing from his eyes,)
"Traitor! dost thou, dost thou to grace pretend,
Glad as thou art, in trophies of my friend?
To his sad soul a grateful off'ring go!
'Tis Pallas, Pallas gives this deadly blow."
He rais'd his arm aloft, and at the word,
Deep in his bosom drove the shining sword.
The streaming blood distain'd his arms around;
And the disdainful soul came rushing through the wound.

ESSAY OF DRAMATIC POESY.

——— *Fungar vice cotis, acutum*
Reddere quæ ferrum valet, exors ipsa secandi.

This Essay contains the first detailed view of our author's opinions concerning the Drama. In many things, particularly in the main point of preference given to rhyme, he afterwards saw cause to retract some of the principles here laid down. We have endeavoured elsewhere to trace the progress and alteration of Dryden's sentiments upon these subjects.* But the reader's attention may be here called to the elegant form into which he has thrown his essay, and which has been so often in vain followed by clumsy imitators. The scene of the dialogue, and the striking incident by which it is introduced, have the happiest effect in arresting the attention; and infinite address is displayed in conducting the subject, from the distant noise of a bloody sea-fight, into the academic prolusions of dramatic criticism.

The speakers in the dialogue are four; three of whom are persons "whom their wit and quality have made known to all the town." The fourth, of whose properties the author speaks more modestly, is Neander, under which feigned appellation Dryden himself is figured. In corroboration of this, Mr. Malone produces two instances, in which Dryden is called Neander by the famous Corinna, or Eliza Thomas.† Moreover, the curious reader must be informed, that there is an anagram in the name of the second personage, Lisideius, which points him out to be Sir Charles Sedley, or Sidley, for his name was spelled both ways.‡ Crites, the advocate for blank verse, is Sir Robert Howard, our author's friend and brother-in-law; who, in the preface to his plays published in 1665, had censured rhyming tragedies as unnatural. Prior has assured us, that Eugenius means the witty Earl of Dorset, then Lord Buckhurst.* A very critical observer may remark an inaccuracy in introducing his lordship as listening to the sound of a sea-fight, in which he was himself actually engaged.† But Dryden did not mean to identify his speakers, and those shadowed out under them, otherwise than in their capacity of critics and authors.

Dryden has, with infinite address, avoided, or overcome, the obstacles which commonly attend an argumentative discussion, in form of a dialogue. The author of such disputations, in general, so obviously favours one of the combatants, that we as soon expect Hector to slay Achilles, or Turnus to defeat Æneas, as nourish the least hope of the unfriended champion

† In an elegy on his death, and in a poem addressed to Captain Gibbon.—*Malone*, Vol. i. p. [illegible]. For aught I know, an imperfect anagram may be intended; for the letters in the name of Dryden, with a very little aid, will make out the word *Neander*.

‡ For Dryden's connexion with this gay writer, see the dedication of the "Assignation," Lisideius is Sidleius, a little changed.

* "The most eminent masters in their several ways appealed to his determination. Waller thought it an honour to consult him in the softness and harmony of his verse, and Dr. Sprat in the delicacy and turn of his prose. Dryden determines by him, under the character of Eugenius, as to the laws of dramatic poetry." This occurs in Prior's dedication of his poems to Lionel, Earl of Dorset and Middlesex, in which he gives his father's character at length, 8vo. edit. 1709.

† The evening before the battle, he is said to have composed the lively song beginning,

To all you ladies now at land.

Prior gives the following account of the matter: "In the first Dutch war, he went a volunteer with the Duke of York; his behaviour during that campaign was such as distinguished the Sackvill, descended from that Hildebrand of the name, who was one of the greatest captains that came into England with the Conqueror. But his making a song the night before the engagement, and it is one of the prettiest that ever was made, carries with it so sedate a presence of mind, and such an unusual gallantry, that it deserves as much to be recorded as Alexander's jesting with his soldiers before he passed the Granicus, or William the First of Orange giving order over night for a battle, and desiring to be called in the morning, lest he should happen to sleep too long."

making any effectual resistance. Besides, in prepared arguments of this sort, as in prepared jests on the stage, there is an obvious opening left for those thrusts on which the author chiefly depends for success; so that, instead of admiring the victor, we are angry at the bad address of his antagonist. All these obstacles Dryden has contrived to surmount, by the number of his characters, and the variety of their dialogue; where not only the argument of Neander's antagonist is fairly stated, but the topics are so judiciously varied, that the reader is brought to the point which the author aims at, without stiffness or constraint, as if in the ordinary flow of literary conversation. Thus, as we never see the purpose which Dryden wishes to attain, we arrive at his conclusion without fatigue or prejudice.

The "Essay on Dramatic Poetry" was assailed by several critics. Martin Clifford, of the Charter-House, accused our author of pilfering from the French critics, in the second of four very abusive letters. The only existing edition of these diatribes is one in 1687; but, from their date and import, this may have been a reprint. Sir Robert Howard also attacked the Essay, in the preface to his "Duke of Lerma," which led Dryden to assert his preference of rhyming tragedies, in the Defence prefixed to the "Indian Emperor."

This Essay was first published in 1668, or perhaps in the December preceding. Sixteen years afterwards, Dryden bestowed on it a thorough revisal; and having, in many places, altered and amended the expression with unusual care, he published a second edition in 1684, with the following dedication to Lord Buckhurst, afterwards Earl of Dorset.

TO

THE RIGHT HONOURABLE

CHARLES,

EARL OF DORSET AND MIDDLESEX,

LORD CHAMBERLAIN OF THEIR MAJESTIES' HOUSEHOLD, KNIGHT OF THE MOST NOBLE ORDER OF THE GARTER, &c.

MY LORD,

As I was lately reviewing my loose papers, amongst the rest I found this Essay; the writing of which, in this rude and indigested manner, wherein your lordship now sees it, served as an amusement to me in the country, when the violence of the last plague had driven me from the town.* Seeing, then, our theatres shut up, I was engaged in these kind of thoughts with the same delight with which men think upon their absent mistresses. I confess I find many things in this discourse, which I do not now approve; my judgment being not a little altered since the writing of it, but whether for the better, or the worse, I know not: neither, indeed, is it much material in an Essay, where all I have said is problematical. For the way of writing plays in verse, which I have seemed to favour, I have, since that time, laid the practice of it aside, till I have more leisure, because I find it troublesome and slow: But I am no way altered from my opinion of it, at least with any reasons which have opposed it.† For your lordship may easily observe, that none are very violent against it, but those who either have not attempted it, or who have succeeded ill in their attempt. It is enough for me to have your lordship's example for my excuse in that little which I have done in it; and I am sure my adversaries can bring no such arguments against verse, as those with which the fourth act of "Pompey" will furnish me in its defence.‡ Yet, my lord, you must suffer me a little to complain of you, that you too soon withdraw from us a contentment, of which we expected the continuance, because you gave it us so early. It is a revolt, without occasion, from your party, where your merits had already raised you to the highest commands, and where you have not the excuse of other men, that you have been ill used, and therefore laid down arms. I know no other quarrel you can have to verse, than that which Spurina had to his beauty, when he tore and mangled the features of his

* The great pestilence in 1665.

† As early as 1676, Dryden confesses that he had grown weary of "his long-loved mistress, Rhyme." See the prologue to "Aureng-zebe," the last rhyming tragedy which he ever wrote. But although Dryden sometimes chose to abandon his own opinions, there is no instance of his owning conversion by the arguments of his adversaries.

‡ The tragedy of "Pompey the Great," 4to. 1664, translated out of French by certain persons of honour. Waller wrote the first act; Lord Buckhurst, it would seem, translated the fourth.

face, only because they pleased too well the sight.* It was an honour which seemed to wait for you, to lead out a new colony of writers from the mother-nation: and, upon the first spreading of your ensigns, there had been many in a readiness to have followed so fortunate a leader; if not all, yet the better part of poets:

> Pars, indocili melior grege; mollis et exspes
> Inominata perprimat cubilia.

I am almost of opinion, that we should force you to accept of the command, as sometimes the prætorian bands have compelled their captains to receive the empire. The court, which is the best and surest judge of writing, has generally allowed of verse; and, in the town, it has found favourers of wit and quality. As for your own particular, my lord, you have yet youth and time enough to give part of them to the divertisement of the public, before you enter into the serious and more unpleasant business of the world. That which the French poet said of the temple of Love, may be as well applied to the temple of the Muses. The words, as near as I can remember them, were these:

> Le jeune homme a mauvaise grace,
> N'ayant pas adoré dans le Temple d'Amour;
> Il faut qu'il entre; et pour le sage
> Si ce n'est pas son vrai sejour,
> C'est un gîte sur son passage.

I leave the words to work their effect upon your lordship in their own language, because no other can so well express the nobleness of the thought; and wish you may be soon called to bear a part in the affairs of the nation, where I know the world expects you, and wonders why you have been so long forgotten; there being no person amongst our young nobility, on whom the eyes of all men are so much bent. But, in the mean time, your lordship may imitate the course of nature, who gives us the flower before the fruit; that I may speak to you in the language of the Muses, which I have taken from an excellent poem to the king:

> As Nature, when she fruit designs, thinks fit
> By beauteous blossoms to proceed to it;
> And while she does accomplish all the spring,
> Birds to her secret operations sing.†

I confess I have no greater reason, in addressing this Essay to your lordship, than that it might awaken in you the desire of writing something, in whatever kind it be, which might be an honour to our age and country. And methinks it might have the same effect on you, which Homer tells us the fight of the Greeks and Trojans before the fleet, had on the spirit of Achilles; who, though he had resolved not to engage, yet found a martial warmth to steal upon him at the sight of blows, the sound of trumpets, and the cries of fighting men. For my own part, if, in treating of this subject, I sometimes dissent from the opinion of better wits, I declare it is not so much to combat their opinions, as to defend my own, which were first made public.* Sometimes, like a scholar in a fencing-school, I put forth myself, and show my own ill play, on purpose to be better taught. Sometimes I stand desperately to my arms, like the foot when deserted by their horse, not in hope to overcome, but only to yield on more honourable terms. And yet, my lord, this war of opinions, you well know, has fallen out among the writers of all ages, and sometimes betwixt friends. Only it has been prosecuted by some, like pedants, with violence of words; and managed by others, like gentleman, with candour and civility. Even Tully had a controversy with his dear Atticus; and in one of his dialogues makes him sustain the part of an enemy in philosophy, who, in his

* Valerius Maximus, lib. iv. cap. 5.
† "Poem to the King's most sacred Majesty."—*D'Avenant's Works*, folio, 1673, p. 263.
‡ See the dedication to the "Rival Ladies," which is elaborately written in the cause of Rhyme against Blank Verse.

letters, is his confidant of state, and made privy to the most weighty affairs of the Roman senate. And the same respect which was paid by Tully to Atticus, we find returned to him afterwards by Cæsar, on a like occasion, who, answering his book in praise of Cato, made it not so much his business to condemn Cato, as to praise Cicero.

But that I may decline some part of the encounter with my adversaries, whom I am neither willing to combat, nor well able to resist; I will give your lordship the relation of a dispute betwixt some of our wits on the same subject, in which they did not only speak of plays in verse, but mingled, in the freedom of discourse, some things of the ancient, many of the modern, ways of writing; comparing those with these, and the wits of our nation with those of others. It is true they differed in their opinions, as it is probable they would. neither do I take upon me to reconcile, but to relate them; and that, as Tacitus professes of himself, *Sine studio partium, aut irâ*, without passion, or interest; leaving your lordship to decide it in favour of which part you shall judge most reasonable, and withal, to pardon the many errors of

Your lordship's
Most obedient humble servant,
JOHN DRYDEN.

TO THE READER.

THE drift of the ensuing discourse was chiefly to vindicate the honour of our English writers, from the censure of those who unjustly prefer the French before them. This I intimate, lest any should think me so exceeding vain, as to teach others an art which they understand much better than myself. But if this incorrect Essay, written in the country, without the help of books, or advice of friends, shall find any acceptance in the world, I promise to myself a better success of the Second Part, wherein I shall more fully treat of the virtues and faults of the English poets, who have written either in this, the epic, or the lyric way.*

* This promise our author never fully performed, although the "Essay on Epic Poetry," and other parts of his critical works, exhibit the materials of the proposed Second Part.

AN ESSAY OF DRAMATIC POESY.

It was that memorable day, in the first summer of the late war, when our navy engaged the Dutch;* a day wherein the two most mighty and best-appointed fleets which any age had ever seen, disputed the command of the greater half of the globe, the commerce of nations, and the riches of the universe; while these vast floating bodies, on either side, moved against each other in parallel lines, and our countrymen, under the happy conduct of his Royal Highness,† went breaking, by little and little, into the line of the enemies; the noise of the cannon from both navies reached our ears about the city; so that all men being alarmed with it, and in a dreadful suspense of the event, which they knew was then deciding, every one went following the sound as his fancy led him; and leaving the town almost empty, some took towards the Park, some across the river, others down it; all seeking the noise in the depth of silence.

Amongst the rest, it was the fortune of Eugenius, Crites, Lisideius, and Neander, to be in company together; three of them persons whom their wit and quality have made known to all the town; and whom I have chose to hide under these borrowed names, that they may not suffer by so ill a relation as I am going to make of their discourse.

Taking then a barge, which a servant of Lisideius had provided for them, they made haste to shoot the bridge, and left behind them that great fall of waters which hindered them from hearing what they desired; after which, having disengaged themselves from many vessels which rode at anchor in the Thames, and almost blocked up the passage towards Greenwich, they ordered the watermen to let fall their oars more gently; and then every one favouring his own curiosity with a strict silence, it was not long ere they perceived the air to break about them like the noise of distant thunder, or of swallows in a chimney; those little undulations of sound, though almost vanishing before they reached them, yet still seeming to retain somewhat of their first horror which they had betwixt the fleets. After they had attentively listened till such time as the sound by little and little went from them,* Eugenius, lifting up his head, and taking notice of it, was the first who congratulated to the rest that happy omen of our nation's victory; adding, that we had but this to desire in confirmation of it, that we might hear no more of that noise which was now leaving the English coast. When the rest had concurred in the same opinion, Crites, a person of a sharp judgment, and somewhat too delicate a taste in wit, which the world hath mistaken in him for ill nature,† said, smiling to us, that if the concernment of this battle had not been so exceeding great, he could scarce have wished the victory at the price he knew he must pay for it, in being subject to the reading and hearing of so many ill verses as he was sure would be made on that subject. Adding, that no argument could 'scape some of those eternal rhymers, who watch a battle with more diligence than the ravens and birds of prey; and the worst of them surest to be first in upon the quarry; while the better able, either out of modesty writ not at all, or set that due value upon their poems, as to let them be often desired, and long expected. There are some of those impertinent people of whom you speak, answered Lisideius, who, to my knowledge, are already so provided, either way, that they can produce not only a panegyric upon the vic-

* The third of June 1665. See the "Annus Mirabilis." Our author, in his poem to the duchess, mentions the circumstance of the cannon being heard at London:

When from afar we heard the cannon play,
Like distant thunder on a shiny day.

† James Duke of York, afterwards James II.

* There is something very striking in this description, which was doubtless copied from reality.

† This is a favourable representation of the character of Sir Robert Howard, who is described by his contemporaries as very vain, obstinate, and opinionative, and as such was ridiculed by Shadwell under the Character of Sir Positive Atall, in the "Impertinents."

tory, but, if need be, a funeral elegy on the duke; wherein, after they have crowned his valour with many laurels, they will at last deplore the odds under which he fell, concluding, that his courage deserved a better destiny. All the company smiled at the conceit of Lisideius; but Crites, more eager than before, began to make particular exceptions against some writers, and said, the public magistrate ought to send betimes to forbid them; and that it concerned the peace and quiet of all honest people, that ill poets should be as well silenced as seditious preachers. In my opinion, replied Eugenius, you pursue your point too far; for as to my own particular, I am so great a lover of poesy, that I could wish them all rewarded, who attempt but to do well; at least, I would not have them worse used than one of their brethren was by Sylla the dictator: *Quem in concione vidimus*, (says Tully,) *cum ei libellum malus poeta de populo subjecisset, quod epigramma in eum fecisset tantummodo alternis versibus longiusculis, statim ex iis rebus quas tunc vendebat jubere ei præmium tribui, sub ea conditione ne quid postea scriberet.* I could wish with all my heart, replied Crites, that many whom we know were as bountifully thanked upon the same condition, that they would never trouble us again. For amongst others, I have a mortal apprehension of two poets, whom this victory, with the help of both her wings, will never be able to escape. 'Tis easy to guess whom you intend, said Lisideius; and without naming them, I ask you if one of them does not perpetually pay us with clenches upon words, and a certain clownish kind of raillery?* If now and then he does not offer at a *catachresis* or *Cleivelandism*,† wresting and torturing a word into another meaning; in fine, if he be not one of those whom the French would call *un mauvais buffon*; one who is so much a well-willer to the satire, that he intends at least to spare no man; and though he cannot strike a blow to hurt any, yet he ought to be punished for the malice of the action; as our witches are justly hanged, because they think themselves to be such; and suffer deservedly for believing they did mischief, because they meant it.* You have described him, said Crites, so exactly, that I am afraid to come after you with my other extremity of poetry; he is one of those, who, having had some advantage of education and converse, knows better than the other what a poet should be, but puts it into practice more unluckily than any man. His style and matter are every while alike; he is the most calm, peaceable writer you ever read; he never disquiets your passions with the least concernment, but still leaves you in as even a temper as he found you; he is a very leveller in poetry: he creeps along with ten little words in every line, and helps out his numbers with *For to*, and *Unto*, and all the pretty expletives he can find, till he drags them to the end of another line, while the sense is left tired half-way behind it; he doubly starves all his verses, first, for want of thought, and then of expression. His poetry neither has wit in it, nor seems to have it; like him in Martial:

Pauper videri *Cinna* vult, et est pauper.

He affects plainness, to cover his want of imagination; when he writes the serious way, the highest flight of his fancy is some miserable antithesis or seeming contradiction; and in the comic, he is still reaching at some thin conceit, the ghost of a jest, and that too flies before him, never to be caught. These swallows which we see before us on the Thames, are the just resemblance of his wit; you may observe how near the water they stoop, how many proffers they make to dip, and yet how seldom they touch it; and when they do, 'tis but the surface: they skim over it but to catch a gnat, and then mount into the air and leave it.—Well, gentlemen, said Eugenius, you may speak your pleasure of these authors; but though I and some few more about

* This was certainly Dr. Robert Wild; an allusion to whose "*Iter Boreale*" occurs a little below. It is written in a harsh and barbarous style, filled with "clenches and carwitchets," as the time called them; which having been in fashion in the reign of James I. and his unfortunate son, now revived after the Restoration. One of these poets would perhaps have told us, in rugged verse, that the Muse having been long in mourning, it was no wonder that her gayer dress should appear unfashionable when resumed. The other scribbler, Mr. Malone thinks, might be Flecnoe. Or it may have been Samuel Holland, a great scribbler on public occasions.

† Cleiveland, being a violent Cavalier, had a sort of claim to become a model after the Restoration. He has such notable conceits as the following comparison of a weeping mistress, to the angel in the scripture who moved the pool of Bethesda, the first passage which occurred at opening the book:

——————pious Julia, angel-wise,
Moves the Bethesda of her trickling eyes,
To cure the spirit'al world of maladies.
Cleiveland's Vindiciæ, 1677, p. 16.

* This was an absurd and cruel doctrine of the English lawyers of the time, who had begun to disbelieve in witchcraft, and were yet willing to justify the execution of witches. One of them says, that if a man firmly believes that, by whirling his hat round his head, and crying *bo*, he could occasion the death of an enemy, he becomes, by performing that ceremony, guilty of murder. Observe that, unless in virtue of special statute, he could not be capitally punished, if, instead of this whimsical device, he had actually fired a gun, and missed the person he aimed at.

the town may give you a peaceable hearing, yet assure yourselves, there are multitudes who would think you malicious, and them injured; especially him whom you first described. He is the very Withers of the city:* they have bought more editions of his works than would serve to lay under all their pies at the Lord Mayor's Christmas. When his famous poem first came out in the year 1660,† I have seen them reading it in the midst of change-time; nay, so vehement they were at it, that they lost their bargain by the candles' ends.‡ But what will you say if he has been received amongst great persons? I can assure you he is, this day, the envy of one, who is lord in the art of quibbling; and who does not take it well, that any man should intrude so far into his province. All I would wish, replied Crites, is, that they who love his writings, may still admire him, and his fellow poet: *Qui Bavium non odit*, &c. is curse sufficient. And farther, added Lisideius, I believe there is no man who writes well, but would think he had hard measure, if their admirers should praise any thing of his: *Nam quos contemnimus, eorum quoque laudes contemnimus.* There are so few who write well in this age, said Crites, that methinks any praises should be welcome; they neither rise to the dignity of the last age, nor to any of the ancients: and we may cry out of the writers of this time, with more reason than Petronius of his, *Pace vestrâ liceat dixisse, primi omnium eloquentiam perdidistis:* you have debauched the true old poetry so far, that nature, which is the soul of it, is not in any of your writings.

If your quarrel (said Eugenius) to those who now write, be grounded only on your reverence to antiquity, there is no man more ready to adore those great Greeks and Romans than I am; but, on the other side, I cannot think so contemptibly of the age in which I live, or so dishonourably of my own country, as not to judge we equal the ancients in most kinds of poesy, and in some surpass them; neither know I any reason why I may not be as zealous for the reputation of our age, as we find the ancients themselves were in reverence to those who lived before them. For you hear your Horace saying—

> Indignor quidquam reprehendi, non quia crasse
> Compositum, illepidave putetur, sed quia nuper.

And after,

> Si meliora dies, ut vina, poemata reddit,
> Scire velim, pretium chartis quotus arroget annus?

But I see I am engaging in a wide dispute, where the arguments are not like to reach close on either side; for poesy is of so large an extent, and so many, both of the ancients and moderns, have done well in all kinds of it, that in citing one against the other, we shall take up more time this evening, than each man's occasions will allow him: therefore I would ask Crites to what part of poesy he would confine his arguments, and whether he would defend the general cause of the ancients against the moderns, or oppose any age of the moderns against this of ours.

Crites, a little while considering upon this demand, told Eugenius, that if he pleased he would limit their dispute to Dramatic Poesy; in which he thought it not difficult to prove, either that the ancients were superior to the moderns, or the last age to this of ours.*

Eugenius was somewhat surprised when he heard Crites make choice of that subject. For aught I see, said he, I have undertaken a harder province than I imagined; for, though I never judged the plays of the Greek or Roman poets comparable to ours, yet, on the other side, those we now see acted come short of many which were written in the last age. But my comfort is, if we are overcome, it will be only by our own countrymen; and if we yield to them in this one part of poesy, we more than surpass them in all the other; for in the epic or lyric way, it will be hard for them to show us one such amongst them, as we have many now living, or who lately were. They can produce nothing so courtly writ, or which expresses so much the conversation of a gentleman, as Sir John Suckling; nothing so even, sweet, and flowing, as Mr. Waller; nothing so majestic, so correct, as Sir John Denham; nothing so elevated, so copious, and full of spirit, as Mr. Cowley. As for the Italian, French, and Spanish plays, I can make it evident, that those who now write, surpass them; and that the drama is wholly ours.

All of them were thus far of Eugenius his opinion, that the sweetness of English verse was never understood or practised by our fathers; even Crites himself did not much oppose it: and every one was willing to acknowledge how much our poesy is improved, by the happiness of some writers yet living; who first taught us to mould our thoughts into easy and signifi-

* A voluminous author of the reign of Charles I.
† The *Iter Boreale*.
‡ One mode of sale by auction

* If Crites be really Sir Robert Howard, as there is every reason to believe, Dryden here represents him as supporting a point which he gives up in his preface; for he censures both the plots and diction of the ancients, and concludes that, upon Horace's rules, "our English plays may justly challenge the pre-eminence." See preface to his Plays in folio, 1665.

cant words, to retrench the superfluities of expression, and to make our rhyme so properly a part of the verse, that it should never mislead the sense, but itself be led and governed by it.

Eugenius was going to continue this discourse, when Lisideius told him, that it was necessary, before they proceeded further, to take a standing measure of their controversy; for how was it possible to be decided, who wrote the best plays, before we know what a play should be? but, this once agreed on by both parties, each might have recourse to it, either to prove his own advantages, or to discover the failings of his adversary.

He had no sooner said this, but all desired the favour of him to give the definition of a play; and they were the more importunate, because neither Aristotle nor Horace, nor any other who had writ of that subject, had ever done it.

Lisideius, after some modest denials, at last confessed he had a rude notion of it; indeed rather a description than a definition; but which served to guide him in his private thoughts, when he was to make a judgment of what others writ: that he conceived a play ought to be, "A just and lively image of human nature, representing its passions and humours, and the changes of fortune to which it is subject, for the delight and instruction of mankind."

This definition (though Crites raised a logical objection against it—that it was only *à genere et fine*, and so not altogether perfect) was yet well received by the rest: and after they had given order to the watermen to turn their barge, and row softly, that they might take the cool of the evening in their return, Crites being desired by the company to begin, spoke on behalf of the ancients in this manner:

If confidence presage a victory, Eugenius, in his own opinion, has already triumphed over the ancients: nothing seems more easy to him, than to overcome those whom it is our greatest praise to have imitated well; for we do not only build upon their foundations, but by their models. Dramatic Poesy had time enough, reckoning from Thespis (who first invented it) to Aristophanes, to be born, to grow up, and to flourish in maturity. It has been observed of arts and sciences, that in one and the same century they have arrived to great perfection; and no wonder, since every age has a kind of universal genius, which inclines those that live in it to some particular studies: the work then being pushed on by many hands, must of necessity go forward.

Is it not evident, in these last hundred years, (when the study of philosophy has been the business of all the virtuosi in Christendom) that almost a new nature has been revealed to us? that more errors of the school have been detected, more useful experiments in philosophy have been made, more noble secrets in optics, medicine, anatomy, astronomy, discovered, than in all those credulous and doting ages from Aristotle to us?—so true it is, that nothing spreads more fast than science, when rightly and generally cultivated.

Add to this, the more than common emulation that was in those times of writing well; which, though it be found in all ages, and all persons that pretend to the same reputation, yet poesy being then in more esteem than now it is, had greater honours decreed to the professors of it, and consequently the rivalship was more high between them. They had judges ordained to decide their merit, and prizes to reward it: and historians have been diligent to record of Æschylus, Euripides, Sophocles, Lycophron, and the rest of them, both who they were that vanquished in these wars of the Theatre, and how often they were crowned; while the Asian kings and Grecian commonwealths scarce afforded them a nobler subject, than the unmanly luxuries of a debauched court, or giddy intrigues of a factious city:—*Alit æmulatio ingenia*, (says Paterculus,) *et nunc invidia, nunc admiratio incitationem accendit:* Emulation is the spur of wit; and sometimes envy, sometimes admiration, quickens our endeavours.

But now since the rewards of honour are taken away, that virtuous emulation is turned into direct malice; yet so slothful, that it contents itself to condemn and cry down others, without attempting to do better: 'tis a reputation too unprofitable, to take the necessary pains for it; yet wishing they had it, that desire is incitement enough to hinder others from it. And this, in short, Eugenius, is the reason, why you have now so few good poets, and so many severe judges. Certainly, to imitate the ancients well, much labour and long study is required; which pains, I have already shown, our poets would want encouragement to take, if yet they had ability to go through the work. Those ancients have been faithful imitators, and wise observers of that nature which is so torn and ill represented in our plays; they have handed down to us a perfect resemblance of her, which we, like ill copiers, neglecting to look on, have rendered monstrous and disfigured. But, that you may know how much you are indebted to those your masters, and be ashamed to have so ill requited them, I must remember you, that all the rules by which we practise the drama at this day, (either such as relate to the justness and symmetry of the plot, or the episodical ornaments, such as descriptions, narrations, and other beauties which are not essential to the play,) were delivered to us from the observations which Aristotle made, of those poets, who either lived before him, or were his contemporaries. We have added nothing of our own, except we have the confidence to say, our wit is better; of which none boast in this our age, but such as understand not theirs. Of that book which Aristotle has left us, περὶ τῆς Ποιητικῆς, Horace his "Art of Poetry" is an excellent comment, and, I believe, restores to us that Second Book of his concerning comedy, which is wanting in him.

Out of these two have been extracted the famous rules which the French call *Des Trois Unites*, or the Three Unities, which ought to be observed in every regular play; namely of time, place, and action.

The unity of time they comprehend in twenty-four hours, the compass of a natural day, or as near as it can be contrived; and the reason of it is obvious to every one,—that the time of the feigned action, or fable of the play, should be proportioned as near as can be to the duration of that time in which it is represented: since therefore all plays are acted on the theatre in a space of time much within the compass of twenty-four hours, that play is to be thought the nearest imitation of nature, whose plot or action is confined within that time. And, by the same rule which concludes this general proportion of time, it follows, that all the parts of it are (as near as may be) to be equally subdivided; namely, that one act take not up the supposed time of half a day, which is out of proportion to the rest; since the other four are then to be straitened within the compass of the remaining half: for it is unnatural that one act, which being spoke or written, is not longer than the rest, should be supposed longer by the audience; it is therefore the poet's duty to take care, that no act should be imagined to exceed the time in which it is represented on the stage; and that the intervals and inequalities of time be supposed to fall out between the acts.

This rule of time, how well it has been observed by the ancients, most of their plays will witness. You see them in their tragedies, (wherein to follow this rule is certainly most difficult,) from the very beginning of their plays, falling close into that part of the story which they intend for the action, or principal object of it, leaving the former part to be delivered by narration: so that they set the audience, as it were, at the post where the race is to be concluded; and saving them the tedious expectation of seeing the poet set out and ride the beginning of the course, they suffer you not to behold him, till he is in sight of the goal, and just upon you.

For the second unity, which is that of place, the ancients meant by it, that the scene ought to be continued through the play, in the same place where it was laid in the beginning: for the stage, on which it is represented, being but one and the same place, it is unnatural to conceive it many; and those far distant from one another. I will not deny, but by the variation of painted scenes, the fancy (which in these cases will contribute to its own deceit) may sometimes imagine it several places, with some appearance of probability; yet it still carries the greater likelihood of truth, if those places be supposed so near each other, as in the same town or city, which may all be comprehended under the larger denomination of one place: for a greater distance will bear no proportion to the shortness of time which is allotted, in the acting, to pass from one of them to another. For the observation of this, next to the ancients, the French are to be most commended. They tie themselves so strictly to the unity of place, that you never see, in any of their plays, a scene changed in the middle of an act: if the act begins in a garden, a street, or chamber, 'tis ended in the same place; and that you may know it to be the same, the stage is so supplied with persons, that it is never empty all the time: he who enters second, has business with him who was on before; and before the second quits the stage, a third appears who has business with him. This Corneille calls *la liaison des Scenes*, the continuity or joining of the scenes; and 'tis a good mark of a well-contrived play, when all the persons are known to each other, and every one of them has some affairs with all the rest.

As for the third unity, which is that of action, the ancients meant no other by it than what the logicians do by their *finis*, the end or scope of any action; that which is the first in intention, and last in execution. Now the poet is to aim at one great and complete action, to the carrying on of which all things in his play, even the very obstacles, are to be subservient; and the reason of this is as evident as any of the former.

For two actions equally laboured and driven on by the writer, would destroy the unity of the poem; it would be no longer one play, but two: not but that there may be many actions in the play, as Ben Jonson has observed in his "Discoveries;"* but they must be all subservient to

* Now, that it should be one, and entire. One is considerable two ways; either, as it is only separate, and by itself; or as being composed of many parts, it begins to be one, as those parts grow, or are wrought together. That it should be one the first way alone, and by itself, no man that hath

the great one, which our language happily expresses in the name of underplots; such as in Terence's *Eunuch* is the difference and reconcilement of Thais and Phædria, which is not the chief business of the play, but promotes the marriage of Chærea and Chremes's sister, principally intended by the poet. There ought to be but one action, says Corneille, that is, one complete action, which leaves the mind of the audience in a full repose; but this cannot be brought to pass, but by many other imperfect actions, which conduce to it, and hold the audience in a delightful suspense of what will be.

If by these rules (to omit many other drawn from the precepts and practice of the ancients) we should judge our modern plays, 'tis probable that few of them would endure the trial: that which should be the business of a day, takes up in some of them an age; instead of one action, they are the epitomes of a man's life; and for one spot of ground (which the stage should represent) we are sometimes in more countries than the map can show us.

But if we allow the ancients to have contrived well, we must acknowledge them to have written better. Questionless we are deprived of a great stock of wit in the loss of Menander among the Greek poets, and of Cæcilius, Afranius, and Varius, among the Romans. We may guess at Menander's excellency by the plays of Terence, who translated some of his; and yet wanted so much of him, that he was called by C. Cæsar the half-Menander; and may judge of Varius, by the testimonies of Horace, Martial, and Velleius Paterculus. 'Tis probable that these, could they be recovered, would decide the controversy; but so long as Aristophanes and Plautus are extant, while the tragedies of Euripides, Sophocles, and Seneca, are in our hands, I can never see one of those plays which are now written, but it increases my admiration of the ancients. And yet I must acknowledge further, that to admire them as we ought, we should understand them better than we do. Doubtless many things appear flat to us, the wit of which depended on some custom or story, which never came to our knowledge; or perhaps on some criticism in their language, which being so long dead, and only remaining in their books, 'tis not possible they should make us understand perfectly. To read Macrobius, explaining the propriety and elegance of many words in Virgil, which I had before passed over without consideration, as common things, is enough to assure me, that I ought to think the same of Terence; and that in the purity of his style, (which Tully so much valued, that he ever carried his works about him,) there is yet left in him great room for admiration, if I knew but where to place it. In the mean time, I must desire you to take notice, that the greatest man of the last age (Ben Jonson) was willing to give place to them in all things: he was not only a professed imitator of Horace, but a learned plagiary of all the others; you track him everywhere in their snow. If Horace, Lucan, Petronius Arbiter, Seneca, and Juvenal, had their own from him, there are few serious thoughts which are new in him: you will pardon me, therefore, if I presume he loved their fashion, when he wore their clothes.* But since I have otherwise a great veneration for him, and you, Eugenius, prefer him above all other poets,† I will use no farther argument to you than his example: I will produce before you father Ben, dressed in all the ornaments and colours of the ancients; you will need no other guide to our party, if you follow him; and whether you consider the bad plays of our age, or regard the good plays of the last, both the best and worst of the modern poets will equally instruct you to admire the ancients.

Crites had no sooner left speaking, but Eu-

tasted letters ever would say, especially having required, before, a just magnitude, and equal proportion of the parts in themselves. Neither of which can possibly be, if the action be single and separate, nor composed of parts, which laid together in themselves, with an equal and fitting proportion, tend to the same end, which thing, out of antiquity itself, hath deceived many; and more this day it doth deceive."—*Jonson's Discoveries.*

* Malone and Langbaine have both observed, that our author elsewhere uses the same image, applied indeed to the very same person:

Subtle was got by our Albumazar,
That Alchemist by this astrologer:
Here he was fashion'd; and we may suppose,
He liked the fashion well who wore the clothes.

† Dorset gave an instance of the honour in which he held Ben Jonson, by an excellent epilogue, upon the reviving of "Every Man in his Humour." When the speaker of the epilogue has proceeded a good way in the usual style of rallying the piece and author, he is interrupted by

Jonson's Ghost.

Hold, and give way, for I myself will speak:
Can you encourage so much insolence,
And add new faults still to the great offence
Your ancestors so rashly did commit
Against the mighty powers of art and wit,
When they condemn'd those noble works of mine,
Sejanus, and my best-loved Catiline?
Repent, or on your guilty heads shall fall
The curse of many a rhyming pastoral.
The three bold Beauchamps shall revive again,
And with the London-Prentice conquer Spain.
All the dull follies of the former age
Shall find applause on this corrupted stage.
But if you pay the great arrears of praise,
So long since due to my much injured plays,
From all past crimes I first will set you free,
And then inspire some one to write like me

genius, who had waited with some impatience for it, thus began:—

I have observed, in your speech, that the former part of it is convincing, as to what the moderns have profited by the rules of the ancients; but in the latter you are careful to conceal how much they have excelled them. We own all the helps we have from them, and want neither veneration nor gratitude, while we acknowledge, that to overcome them we must make use of the advantages we have received from them: but to these assistances we have joined our own industry; for, had we sat down with a dull imitation of them, we might then have lost somewhat of the old perfection, but never acquired any that was new. We draw not therefore after their lines, but those of Nature; and having the life before us, besides the experience of all they knew, it is no wonder if we hit some airs and features which they have missed. I deny not what you urge of arts and sciences, that they have flourished in some ages more than others; but your instance in philosophy makes for me: for if natural causes be more known now than in the time of Aristotle, because more studied, it follows, that poesy and other arts may, with the same pains, arrive still nearer to perfection; and, that granted, it will rest for you to prove, that they wrought more images of human life than we; which seeing in your discourse you have avoided to make good, it shall now be my task to show you some part of their defects, and some few excellencies of the moderns. And I think there is none among us can imagine I do it enviously, or with purpose to detract from them; for what interest of fame or profit can the living lose by the reputation of the dead? On the other side, it is a great truth which Velleius Paterculus affirms: *Audita visis libentius laudamus; et præsentia invidiâ, præterita admiratione prosequimur; et his nos obrui, illis instrui credimus:* that praise or censure is certainly the most sincere, which unbribed posterity shall give us.

Be pleased, then, in the first place, to take notice, that the Greek poesy, which Crites has affirmed to have arrived to perfection in the reign of the old comedy, was so far from it, that the distinction of it into acts was not known to them, or if it were, it is yet so darkly delivered to us, that we cannot make it out. All we know of it is, from the singing of their chorus; and that too is so uncertain, that in some of their plays we have reason to conjecture they sung more than five times. Aristotle indeed divides the integral parts of a play into four. First, the *Protasis*, or entrance, which gives light only to the characters of the persons, and proceeds very little into any part of the action. Secondly, the *Epitasis*, or working up of the plot; where the play grows warmer, the design or action of it is drawing on, and you see something promising that it will come to pass. Thirdly, the *Catastasis*, called by the Romans *Status*, the height and full growth of the play: we may call it properly the counter-turn, which destroys that expectation, imbroils the action in new difficulties, and leaves you far distant from that hope in which it found you; as you may have observed in a violent stream, resisted by a narrow passage,—it runs round to an eddy, and carries back the waters with more swiftness than it brought them on. Lastly, the *Catastrophe*, which the Grecians called λύσις, the French *le denouement*, and we the discovery, or unravelling of the plot: there you see all things settling again upon their first foundations, and, the obstacles which hindered the design or action of the play once removed, it ends with that resemblance of truth and nature, that the audience are satisfied with the conduct of it. Thus this great man delivered to us the image of a play; and I must confess it is so lively, that from thence much light has been derived to the forming it more perfectly into acts and scenes: but what poet first limited to five the number of the acts, I know not; only we see it so firmly established in the time of Horace, that he gives it for a rule in comedy,—*Neu brevior quinto, neu sit productior actu.* So that you see the Grecians cannot be said to have consummated this art; writing rather by entrances, than by acts, and having rather a general indigested notion of a play, than knowing how and where to bestow the particular graces of it.

But since the Spaniards at this day allow but three acts, which they call *Jornadas*, to a play, and the Italians in many of theirs follow them, when I condemn the ancients, I declare it is not altogether because they have not five acts to every play, but because they have not confined themselves to one certain number; it is building a house without a model; and when they succeeded in such undertakings, they ought to have sacrificed to Fortune, not to the Muses.

Next, for the plot, which Aristotle called τὸ μῦθος, and often τῶν πραγμάτων σύνθεσις, and from him the Romans *Fabula*, it has already been judiciously observed by a late writer, that in their tragedies it was only some tale derived from Thebes or Troy, or at least something that happened in those two ages; which was worn so thread bare by the pens of all the epic poets, and even by tradition itself of the talkative Greeklings, (as Ben Jonson calls them,) that before it came upon the stage, it was already known to all the audience; and the people, so soon as ever they heard the name of Œdipus, knew, as well as the poet, that he had killed his father by a mistake, and committed incest with his mother, before the play; that they were now to hear of a great plague, an oracle, and the ghost of Laius: so that they sate with a yawning kind of expectation, till he was to come with his eyes pulled out, and speak a hundred or more verses in a tragic tone, in complaint of his misfortunes. But one Œdipus, Hercules, or Medea, had been tolerable; poor people, they escaped not so good cheap; they had still the *chapon bouillé* set before them, till their appetites were cloyed with the same dish, and, the novelty being gone, the pleasure vanished; so that one main end of Dramatic Poesy in its definition, which was to cause delight, was of consequence destroyed.*

In their comedies, the Romans generally borrowed their plots from the Greek poets; and theirs was commonly a little girl stolen or wandered from her parents, brought back unknown to the city, there got with child by some lewd young fellow, who, by the help of his servant, cheats his father; and when her time comes, to cry, *Juno Lucina, fer opem*, one or other sees a little box or cabinet which was carried away with her, and so discovers her to her friends, if some god do not prevent it, by coming down in a machine, and taking the thanks of it to himself.

By the plot you may guess much of the characters of the persons. An old father, who would willingly, before he dies, see his son well married; his debauched son, kind in his nature to his mistress, but miserably in want of money; a servant or slave, who has so much wit to strike in with him, and help to dupe his father; a braggadocio captain, a parasite, and a lady of pleasure.

As for the poor honest maid, on whom the story is built, and who ought to be one of the principal actors in the play, she is commonly a mute in it: she has the breeding of the old Elizabeth way, which was for maids to be seen and not to be heard; and it is enough you know she is willing to be married, when the fifth act requires it.

These are plots built after the Italian mode of houses,—you see through them all at once: the characters are indeed the imitations of nature, but so narrow, as if they had imitated only an eye or a hand, and did not dare to venture on the lines of a face, or the proportion of a body.

But in how strait a compass soever they have bounded their plots and characters, we will pass it by, if they have regularly pursued them, and perfectly observed those three unities of time, place, and action; the knowledge of which you say is derived to us from them. But, in the first place, give me leave to tell you, that the unity of place, however it might be practised by them, was never any of their rules: we neither find it in Aristotle, Horace, or any who have written of it, till in our age the French poets first made it a precept of the stage. The unity of time, even Terence himself, who was the best and most regular of them, has neglected: his "*Heautontimorumenos*," or Self-punisher, takes up visibly two days, says Scaliger; the first two acts concluding the first day, the last three the day ensuing; and Euripides, in tying himself to one day, has committed an absurdity never to be forgiven him; for in one of his tragedies he has made Theseus go from Athens to Thebes, which was about forty English miles, under the walls of it to give battle, and appear victorious in the next act; and yet, from the time of his departure to the return of the Nuntius, who gives the relation of his victory, Æthra and the Chorus have but thirty-six verses; which is not for every mile a verse.

The like error is as evident in Terence his "Eunuch," when Laches, the old man, enters by mistake into the house of Thais; where, betwixt his exit, and the entrance of Pythias, who comes to give ample relation of the disorders he has raised within, Parmeno, who was left upon the stage, has not above five lines to speak. *C'est bien employer un temps si court*, says the French poet, who furnished me with one of the observations; and almost all their tragedies will afford us examples of the like nature.

It is true, they have kept the continuity, or, as you called it, *liaison des Scenes*, somewhat better; two do not perpetually come in together, talk, and go out together; and other two succeed them, and do the same throughout the act, which the English call by the name of single scenes; but the reason is, because they have seldom above two or three scenes, properly so

* This objection, although stated against Crites the prototype of Howard, occurs in Sir Robert's own preface, who points out an additional advantage attending it. He observes, that the subjects of the ancients were usually the most known stories and fables; a circumstance which led them to compose their plays rather of speeches and choruses, than of scenic action, and representation: Because, "Seneca making choice of Medea, Hippolytus, and Hercules Œtus, it was impossible to show Medea throwing the mangled limbs of Jason into her age-renewing kettle, or to present the scattered limbs of Hippolytus upon the stage, or show Hercules burning upon his own funeral pile."

called, in every act; for it is to be accounted a new scene, not only every time the stage is empty, but every person who enters, though to others, makes it so; because he introduces a new business. Now the plots of their plays being narrow, and the persons few, one of their acts was written in a less compass than one of our well-wrought scenes; and yet they are often deficient even in this. To go no farther than Terence, you find in the "Eunuch," Antipho entering single in the midst of the third act, after Chremes and Pythias were gone off; in the same play you have likewise Dorias beginning the fourth act alone; and after she has made a relation of what was done at the Soldier's entertainment, (which by the way was very inartificial, because she was presumed to speak directly to the audience, and to acquaint them with what was necessary to be known, but yet should have been so contrived by the poet, as to have been told by persons of the drama to one another, and so by them to have come to the knowledge of the people,) she quits the stage, and Phædria enters next, alone likewise: he also gives you an account of himself, and of his returning from the country, in monologue; to which unnatural way of narration Terence is subject in all his plays. In his "Adelphi, or Brothers," Syrus and Demea enter after the scene was broken by the departure of Sostrata, Geta, and Canthara; and indeed you can scarce look into any of his comedies, where you will not presently discover the same interruption.

But as they have failed both in the laying of their plots, and in the management, swerving from the rules of their own art, by misrepresenting nature to us, in which they have ill satisfied one intention of a play, which was delight; so in the instructive part they have erred worse: instead of punishing vice, and rewarding virtue, they have often shown a prosperous wickedness, and an unhappy piety: they have set before us a bloody image of revenge in Medea, and given her dragons to convey her safe from punishment: a Priam and Astyanax murdered, and Cassandra ravished, and the lust and murder ending in the victory of him who acted them. In short, there is no indecorum in any of our modern plays, which, if I would excuse, I could not shadow with some authority from the ancients.

And one farther note of them let me leave you: tragedies and comedies were not writ then as they are now, promiscuously, by the same person: but he who found his genius bending to the one, never attempted the other way. This is so plain, that I need not instance to you, that Aristophanes, Plautus, Terence, never any of them writ a tragedy; Æschylus, Euripides Sophocles, and Seneca, never meddled with comedy. the sock and buskin were not worn by the same poet. Having then so much care to excel in one kind, very little is to be pardoned them, if they miscarried in it; and this would lead me to the consideration of their wit, had not Crites given me sufficient warning not to be too bold in my judgment of it; because, the languages being dead, and many of the customs and little accidents on which it depended, lost to us, we are not competent judges of it. But though I grant, that here and there we may miss the application of a proverb or a custom, yet a thing well said will be wit in all languages; and though it may lose something in the translation, yet to him who reads it in the original, 'tis still the same; he has an idea of its excellency, though it cannot pass from his mind into any other expression or words than those in which he finds it. When Phædria in the "Eunuch" had a command from his mistress to be absent two days, and encouraging himself to go through with it, said, *Tandem ego non illâ caream, si sit opus, vel totum triduum?* Parmeno, to mock the softness of his master, lifting up his hands and eyes, cries out, as it were in admiration, *Hui! universum triduum!* the elegancy of which *universum*, though it cannot be rendered in our language, yet leaves an impression on our souls. But this happens seldom in him; in Plautus oftener, who is infinitely too bold in his metaphors and coining words, out of which many times his wit is nothing; which questionless was one reason why Horace falls upon him so severely in those verses:

> Sed proavi nostri Plautinos et numeros, et
> Laudavere sales, nimium patienter utrumque,
> Ne dicam stolide.*

For Horace himself was cautious to obtrude a new word on his readers, and makes custom and common use the best measure of receiving it into writings:

> Multa renascentur quæ nunc [jam] cecidere, cadentque
> Quæ nunc sunt in honore vocabula, si volet usus,
> Quem penes arbitrium est, et jus, et norma loquendi.

The not observing this rule, is that which the world has blamed in our satirist, Cleiveland; to express a thing hard and unnaturally, is his new way of elocution. It is true, no poet but may sometimes use a catachresis; Virgil does it,—

> Mistaque ridenti colocasia fundet acantho,—

* Our author has quoted from memory. The lines are—*At nostri proavi*, &c. and afterwards—*Ne dicam stulte mirati*.—*Malone*.

in his eclogue of Pollio; and in his seventh* Æneid,

——————mirantur et undæ,
Miratur nemus, insuetum fulgentia longe
Scuta virum fluvio, pictasque innare carinas.

And Ovid once so modestly, that he asks leave to do it:

——[quem] si verbo audacia detur,
Haud metuam summi dixisse Palatia cœli.

calling the court of Jupiter by the name of Augustus his palace; though in another place he is more bold, where he says, *Et longas visent Capitolia pompas.*† But to do this always, and never be able to write a line without it, though it may be admired by some few pedants, will not pass upon those who know that wit is best conveyed to us in the most easy language; and is most to be admired when a great thought comes dressed in words so commonly received, that it is understood by the meanest apprehensions, as the best meat is the most easily digested. But we cannot read a verse of Cleiveland's without making a face at it, as if every word were a pill to swallow: He gives us many times a hard nut to break our teeth, without a kernel for our pains. So that there is this difference betwixt his satires and Doctor Donne's, that the one gives us deep thoughts in common language, though rough cadence; the other gives us common thoughts in abstruse words. It is true, in some places his wit is independent of his words, as in that of the rebel Scot:

Had Cain been Scot, God would have changed his doom;
Not forced him wander, but confined him home.‡

Si sic omnia dixisset! This is wit in all languages; it is like mercury, never to be lost or killed:—and so that other,

For beauty, like white powder, makes no noise,
And yet the silent hypocrite destroys.

You see the last line is highly metaphorical, but it is so soft and gentle, that it does not shock us as we read it.

But, to return from whence I have digressed, to the consideration of the ancients' writing, and their wit; of which, by this time, you will grant us in some measure to be fit judges. Though I see many excellent thoughts in Seneca, yet he, of them who had a genius most proper for the stage, was Ovid; he had a way of writing so fit to stir up a pleasing admiration and concernment, which are the objects of a tragedy, and to show the various movements of a soul combating betwixt two different passions, that had he lived in our age, or in his own could have writ with our advantages, no man but must have yielded to him; and therefore I am confident the "Medea" is none of his; for though I esteem it for the gravity and sententiousness of it, which he himself concludes to be suitable to a tragedy,—*Omne genus scripti gravitate Tragœdia vincit,*—yet it moves not my soul enough to judge that he, who in the epic way wrote things so near the drama as the story of Myrrha, of Caunus and Biblis, and the rest, should stir up no more concernment where he most endeavoured it.* The masterpiece of Seneca I hold to be that scene in the "Troades," where Ulysses is seeking for Astyanax to kill him; there you see the tenderness of a mother, so represented in Andromache, that it raises compassion to a high degree in the reader, and bears the nearest resemblance of any thing in the tragedies of the ancients, to the excellent scenes of passion in Shakspeare, or in Fletcher.—For love scenes, you will find few among them; their tragic poets dealt not with that soft passion, but with lust, cruelty, revenge, ambition, and those bloody actions they produced; which were more capable of raising horror than compassion in an audience: leaving love untouched, whose gentleness would have tempered them, which is the most frequent of all the passions, and which, being the private concernment of every person, is soothed by viewing its own image in a public entertainment.

Among their comedies, we find a scene or two of tenderness, and that where you would least expect it, in Plautus; but to speak generally, their lovers say little, when they see each other, but *anima mea, vita mea; ζωὴ καὶ ψυχή,* as the women in Juvenal's time used to cry out in the fury of their kindness. Any sudden gust of passion (as an ecstasy of love in an unexpected meeting) cannot better be expressed than in a word, and a sigh, breaking one another. Nature is dumb on such occasions; and to make her speak, would be to represent her unlike herself. But there are a thousand other

* A mistake for eighth.

† This remark is unfounded; for the words are—*et longas visent Capitolia pompas.* Ovid. Met. l. i. In the preceding quotation, for *verbo,* we should read *verbis;* and for *metuam summi, timeam magni.*—*Malone.*

‡ The insurrection in Scotland, in Charles I.'s time, inflamed Cleiveland as much as the nation. We have often heard of poetic fire, but he is the only author who calls for a bucket of water to quench it:

Ring the bells backward, I am all on fire;
Not all the buckets in a country quire
Shall quench my rage—

* Our author (as Dr. Johnson has observed) "might have determined this question upon surer evidence; for it [Medea] is quoted by Quintilian as Seneca's, and the only line which remains of Ovid's play, (for one line is left us,) is not found there."

concernments of lovers, as jealousies, complaints, contrivances, and the like, where not to open their minds at large to each other, were to be wanting to their own love, and to the expectation of the audience; who watch the movements of their minds, as much as the changes of their fortunes. For the imagining of the first is properly the work of a poet; the latter he borrows from the historian.

Eugenius was proceeding in that part of his discourse, when Crites interrupted him. I see, said he, Eugenius and I are never like to have this question decided betwixt us; for he maintains, the moderns have acquired a new perfection in writing, I can only grant they have altered the mode of it. Homer described his heroes men of great appetites, lovers of beef broiled upon the coals, and good fellows; contrary to the practice of the French romances, whose heroes neither eat, nor drink, nor sleep, for love. Virgil makes Æneas a bold avower of his own virtues:

> Sum pius Æneas, fama super æthera notus;

which, in the civility of our poets, is the character of a fanfaron, or Hector; for with us the knight takes occasion to walk out, or sleep, to avoid the vanity of telling his own story, which the trusty squire is ever to perform for him. So in their love scenes, of which Eugenius spoke last, the ancients were more hearty, we more talkative; they writ love as it was then the mode to make it; and I will grant this much to Eugenius, that perhaps one of their poets, had he lived in our age,

> Si foret hoc nostrum fato delapsus in ævum,

as Horace says of Lucilius, he had altered many things; not that they were not natural before, but that he might accommodate himself to the age in which he lived. Yet in the mean time we are not to conclude any thing rashly against those great men, but preserve to them the dignity of masters, and give that honour to their memories,—*quos Libitina sacravit*,—part of which we expect may be paid to us in future times.

This moderation of Crites, as it was pleasing to all the company, so it put an end to that dispute; which Eugenius, who seemed to have the better of the argument, would urge no farther. But Lisideius, after he had acknowledged himself of Eugenius his opinion concerning the ancients, yet told him, he had forborne, till his discourse were ended, to ask him, why he preferred the English plays above those of other nations? and whether we ought not to submit our stage to the exactness of our next neighbours?

Though, said Eugenius, I am at all times ready to defend the honour of my country against the French, and to maintain, we are as well able to vanquish them with our pens, as our ancestors have been with their swords; yet, if you please, added he, looking upon Neander, I will commit this cause to my friend's management; his opinion of our plays is the same with mine: and besides, there is no reason that Crites and I, who have now left the stage, should re-enter so suddenly upon it; which is against the laws of comedy.

If the question had been stated, replied Lisideius, who had writ best, the French or English, forty years ago, I should have been of your opinion, and adjudged the honour to our own nation; but since that time, (said he, turning towards Neander,) we have been so long together bad Englishmen, that we had not leisure to be good poets. Beaumont, Fletcher, and Jonson, (who were only capable of bringing us to that degree of perfection which we have,) were just then leaving the world; as if, in an age of so much horror, wit, and those milder studies of humanity, they had no farther business among us. But the muses, who ever follow peace, went to plant in another country; it was then that the great Cardinal of Richelieu began to take them into his protection; and that, by his encouragement, Corneille, and some other Frenchmen, reformed their theatre, which before was as much below ours, as it now surpasses it and the rest of Europe. But because Crites, in his discourse for the ancients, has prevented me, by observing many rules of the stage which the moderns have borrowed from them, I shall only, in short, demand of you, whether you are not convinced, that of all nations the French have best observed them? In the unity of time you find them so scrupulous, that it yet remains a dispute among their poets, whether the artificial day of twelve hours, more or less, be not meant by Aristotle, rather than the natural one of twenty-four; and consequently, whether all plays ought not to be reduced into that compass. This I can testify, that in all their dramas writ within these last twenty years and upwards, I have not observed any that have extended the time to thirty hours. In the unity of place they are full as scrupulous; for many of their critics limit it to that very spot of ground where the play is supposed to begin; none of them exceed the compass of the same town or city.

The unity of action in all their plays is yet more conspicuous; for they do not burden them with under-plots, as the English do; which is the reason why many scenes of our tragi-come ther carry on a design that is nothing of kin to the main plot; and that we see two distinct webs in a play, like those in ill-wrought stuffs; and two actions, that is, two plays, carried on together, to the confounding of the audience; who, before they are warm in their concernments for one part, are diverted to another; and by that means espouse the interest of neither. From hence likewise it arises, that the one half of our actors are not known to the other. They keep their distances, as if they were Montagues and Capulets, and seldom begin an acquaintance till the last scene of the fifth act, when they are all to meet upon the stage. There is no theatre in the world has any thing so absurd as the English tragi-comedy; it is a drama of our own invention, and the fashion of it is enough to proclaim it so; here a course of mirth, there another of sadness and passion, and a third of honour and a duel: thus, in two hours and a half, we run through all the fits of Bedlam. The French affords you as much variety on the same day, but they do it not so unseasonably, or *mal à propos*, as we: our poets present you the play and the farce together; and our stages still retain somewhat of the original civility of the Red Bull:*

Atque ursum et pugiles media inter carmina poscunt

The end of tragedies or serious plays, says Aristotle, is to beget admiration, compassion, or concernment; but are not mirth and compassion things incompatible? and is it not evident, that the poet must of necessity destroy the former by intermingling of the latter? that is, he must ruin the sole end and object of his tragedy, to introduce somewhat that is forced into it, and is not of the body of it. Would you not think that physician mad, who, having prescribed a purge, should immediately order you to take restringents?

But to leave our plays, and return to theirs. I have noted one great advantage they have had in the plotting of their tragedies; that is, they are always grounded upon some known history: according to that of Horace, *Ex noto fictum carmen sequar:* and in that they have so imitated the ancients, that they have surpassed them. For the ancients, as was observed before, took for the foundation of their plays some poetical fiction, such as under that consideration could move but little concernment in the audience, because they already knew the event of it. But the French goes farther:

> Atque ita mentitur, sic veris falsa remiscet,
> Primo ne medium, medio ne discrepet imum.

He so interweaves truth with probable fiction, that he puts a pleasing fallacy upon us, mends the intrigues of fate, and dispenses with the severity of history, to reward that virtue which has been rendered to us there unfortunate. Sometimes the story has left the success so doubtful, that the writer is free, by the privilege of a poet, to take that which of two or more relations will best suit with his design; as for example, in the death of Cyrus, whom Justin and some others report to have perished in the Scythian war, but Xenophon affirms to have died in his bed of extreme old age. Nay more, when the event is past dispute, even then we are willing to be deceived, and the poet, if he contrives it with appearance of truth, has all the audience of his party; at least during the time his play is acting: so naturally we are kind to virtue, when our own interest is not in question, that we take it up as the general concernment of mankind. On the other side, if you consider the historical plays of Shakspeare, they are rather so many chronicles of kings, or the business many times of thirty or forty years, cramped into a representation of two hours and a half: which is not to imitate or paint nature, but rather to draw her in miniature; to take her in little; to look upon her through the wrong end of a perspective, and receive her images not only much less, but infinitely more imperfect than the life: this, instead of making a play delightful, renders it ridiculous:

Quodcunque ostendis mihi sic, incredulus odi.

For the spirit of man cannot be satisfied but with truth, or at least verisimility; and a poem is to contain, if not *τὰ ἔτυμα*, yet *ἐτύμοισιν ὁμοῖα*, as one of the Greek poets has expressed it.

Another thing in which the French differ from us and from the Spaniards, is, that they do not embarrass, or cumber themselves with too much plot: they only represent so much of a story as will constitute one whole and great action sufficient for a play: we, who undertake more, do but multiply adventures; which, not being produced from one another, as effects from causes, but barely following, constitute many actions in the drama, and consequently make it many plays.

But by pursuing closely one argument, which is not cloyed with many turns, the French have gained more liberty for verse, in which they write: they have leisure to dwell on a subject which deserves it; and to represent the passions, (which we have acknowledged to be the poet's work,) without being hurried from one thing to another, as we are in the plays of Calderon, which we have seen lately upon our thea-

* One of the old theatres and of the lowest order among them.

tres, under the name of Spanish plots. I have taken notice but of one tragedy of ours, whose plot has that uniformity and unity of design in it, which I have commended in the French; and that is "Rollo,"* or rather under the name of Rollo, the story of Bassianus and Geta in Herodian: there indeed the plot is neither large nor intricate, but just enough to fill the minds of the audience, not to cloy them. Besides, you see it founded upon the truth of history,—only the time of the action is not reducible to the strictness of the rules; and you see in some places a little farce mingled, which is below the dignity of the other parts: and in this all our poets are extremely peccant; even Ben Jonson himself, in "Sejanus" and "Catiline," has given us this olio of a play, this unnatural mixture of comedy and tragedy, which to me sounds just as ridiculously as the history of David with the merry humours of Goliah. In "Sejanus" you may take notice of the scene betwixt Livia and the physician, which is a pleasant satire upon the artificial helps of beauty: in "Catiline" you may see the parliament of women; the little envies of them to one another; and all that passes betwixt Curio and Fulvia: scenes admirable in their kind, but of an ill mingle with the rest.

But I return again to the French writers, who, as I have said, do not burden themselves too much with plot, which has been reproached to them by an ingenious person of our nation† as a fault; for he says, they commonly make but one person considerable in a play; they dwell on him, and his concernments, while the rest of the persons are only subservient to set him off. If he intends this by it,—that there is one person in the play who is of greater dignity than the rest, he must tax, not only theirs, but those of the ancients, and, which he would be loth to do, the best of ours; for it is impossible but that one person must be more conspicuous in it than any other, and consequently the greatest share in the action must devolve on him. We see it so in the management of all affairs: even in the most equal aristocracy, the balance cannot be so justly poised, but some one will be superior to the rest, either in parts, fortune, interest, or the consideration of some glorious exploit; which will reduce the greatest part of business into his hands.

But, if he would have us to imagine, that in exalting one character the rest of them are neglected, and that all of them have not some share or other in the action of the play, I desire him to produce any of Corneille's tragedies, wherein every person (like so many servants in a well-governed family) has not some employment, and who is not necessary to the carrying on of the plot, or at least to your understanding it.

There are indeed some protatic persons in the ancients, whom they make use of in their plays, either to hear, or give the relation: but the French avoid this with great address, making their narrations only to, or by such, who are some way interested in the main design. And now I am speaking of relations, I cannot take a fitter opportunity to add this in favour of the French, that they often use them with better judgment and more *à propos* than the English do. Not that I commend narrations in general, but there are two sorts of them; one, of those things which are antecedent to the play, and are related to make the conduct of it more clear to us; but it is a fault to choose such subjects for the stage as will force us on that rock, because we see they are seldom listened to by the audience, and that is many times the ruin of the play; for, being once let pass without attention, the audience can never recover themselves to understand the plot; and indeed it is somewhat unreasonable, that they should be put to so much trouble, as, that to comprehend what passes in their

* Although a zealous admirer of the author, I am at a loss to see much merit in the plot of "the Bloody Brother, or Rollo" of Fletcher. The hero is a Duke of Normandy, who first kills his brother in his mother's arms; then has his chancellor chopped to pieces, and thrown to the dogs; beheads his tutor, kills an officer of his guards for burying the reliques of his chancellor, and finally is stabbed by the captain of his guards, and succeeded in his dukedom by his cousin, a person of no note through the play, but who, being left alive when every other person is killed, is raised to the throne as a matter of necessity. This is the history of Geta and Caracalla, and a very disagreeable one it is, but certainly not the plot of a play. As for the farce mingled with it, there are three state criminals led to be hanged, who join in the old catch,

And three merry boys,
And three merry boys,
And three merry boys are we,
As ever did sing
Three parts in a string,
All under the triple tree.

† I thought I had discovered this ingenious person to be the honourable Edward Howard, author of the "British Princes," who, in the preface to the "Woman's Conquest," has this passage: "And here I cannot choose but reflect on our mean imitation of French plays, by introducing of servants and waiting-women to have parts, without being essential characters; an error well avoided by our former writers, who never admitted any otherwise than as messengers and attendants, except on the account of being characters, as is to be seen by Numphs in "Bartholomew Fair, and Face in the "Alchymist;" the latter of which (notwithstanding what can be objected against him) may deservedly be granted one of the best parts on our English stage." But the passage does not quite correspond with the sentiment in the text; besides, the "Woman's Conquest" did not appear till 1670–1, two years after the Essay. The preface contains some oblique attacks upon Dryden.

sight, they must have recourse to what was done, perhaps, ten or twenty years ago.

But there is another sort of relations, that is, of things happening in the action of the play, and supposed to be done behind the scenes; and this is many times both convenient and beautiful; for, by it the French avoid the tumult to which we are subject in England, by representing duels, battles, and the like; which renders our stage too like the theatres where they fight prizes. For what is more ridiculous than to represent an army with a drum and five men behind it; all which, the hero of the other side is to drive in before him? or to see a duel fought, and one slain with two or three thrusts of the foils, which we know are so blunted, that we might give a man an hour to kill another in good earnest with them?

I have observed, that in all our tragedies the audience cannot forbear laughing when the actors are to die; it is the most comic part of the whole play. All passions may be lively represented on the stage, if to the well writing of them the actor supplies a good commanded voice, and limbs that move easily and without stiffness; but there are many actions which can never be imitated to a just height: dying especially is a thing which none but a Roman gladiator could naturally perform on the stage, when he did not imitate, or represent, but do it; and therefore it is better to omit the representation of it.

The words of a good writer, which describe it lively, will make a deeper impression of belief in us, than all the actor can insinuate into us, when he seems to fall dead before us; as a poet, in the description of a beautiful garden, or a meadow, will please our imagination more than the place itself can please our sight. When we see death represented, we are convinced it is but fiction; but when we hear it related, our eyes (the strongest witnesses) are wanting, which might have undeceived us; and we are all willing to favour the slight when the poet does not too grossly impose on us. They, therefore, who imagine these relations would make no concernment in the audience, are deceived, by confounding them with the other, which are of things antecedent to the play: those are made often in cold blood, as I may say, to the audience; but these are warmed with our concernments, which were before awakened in the play. What the philosophers say of motion, that, when it is once begun, it continues of itself, and will do so to eternity, without some stop put to it, is clearly true on this occasion: the soul, being already moved with the characters and fortunes of those imaginary persons, continues going of its own accord; and we are no more weary to hear what becomes of them when they are not on the stage, that we are to listen to the news of an absent mistress. But it is objected, that if one part of the play may be related, then why not all? I answer, some parts of the action are more fit to be represented, some to be related. Corneille says, judiciously, that the poet is not obliged to expose to view all particular actions which conduce to the principal: he ought to select such of them to be seen, which will appear with the greatest beauty, either by the magnificence of the show, or the vehemence of passions which they produce, or some other charm which they have in them, and let the rest arrive to the audience by narration. 'Tis a great mistake in us to believe the French present no part of the action on the stage: every alteration or crossing of a design, every new-sprung passion, and turn of it, is a part of the action, and much the noblest, except we conceive nothing to be action till the players come to blows; as if the painting of the hero's mind were not more properly the poet's work, than the strength of his body. Nor does this any thing contradict the opinion of Horace, where he tells us,

> Segnius irritant animos demissa per aurem,
> Quam quæ sunt oculis subjecta fidelibus.

For he says immediately after,

> Non tamen intus
> Digna geri promes in scenam; *multaq*; tolles
> Ex oculis, quæ mox narret facundia præsens.

Among which many he recounts some:

> Nec pueros coram populo Medea trucidet,
> Aut in avem Progne mutetur, Cadmus in anguem, &c.

That is, those actions which by reason of their cruelty will cause aversion in us, or by reason of their impossibility, unbelief, ought either wholly to be avoided by a poet, or only delivered by narration. To which we may have leave to add such as, to avoid tumult, (as was before hinted,) or to reduce the plot into a more reasonable compass of time, or for defect of beauty in them, are rather to be related than presented to the eye. Examples of all these kinds are frequent, not only among all the ancients, but in the best received of our English poets. We find Ben Jonson using them in his "Magnetic Lady," where one comes out from dinner, and relates the quarrels and disorders of it to save the indecent appearance of them on the stage, and to abbreviate the story: and this in express imitation of Terence, who had done the same before him in his "Eunuch," where Pythias makes the like relation of what had happened within at the Soldier's entertainment. The relations, likewise, of Sejanus's death, and the prodigies before it, are remarkable; the one of which was hid from sight to avoid the horror and tumult of the representation; the other, to shun the introducing of things impossible to be believed. In that excellent play, "The King and no King," Fletcher goes yet farther; for the whole unravelling of the plot is done by narration in the fifth act, after the manner of the ancients; and it moves great concernment in the audience, though it be only a relation of what was done many years before the play. I could multiply other instances, but these are sufficient to prove, that there is no error in choosing a subject which requires this sort of narrations; in the ill management of them, there may.

But I find I have been too long in this discourse, since the French have many other excellencies not common to us; as that you never see any of their plays end with a conversion, or simple change of will, which is the ordinary way which our poets use to end theirs. It shows little art in the conclusion of a dramatic poem, when they who have hindered the felicity during the four acts, desist from it in the fifth, without some powerful cause to take them off their design; and though I deny not but such reasons may be found, yet it is a path that is cautiously to be trod, and the poet is to be sure he convinces the audience, that the motive is strong enough.* As, for example, the conversion of the Usurer in "The Scornful Lady," seems to me a little forced; for, being a usurer, which implies a lover of money to the highest degree of covetousness, (and such the poet has represented him,) the account he gives for the sudden change is, that he has been duped by the wild young fellow; which in reason might render him more wary another time, and make him punish himself with harder fare and coarser clothes to get up again what he had lost: but that he should look on it as a judgment, and so repent, we may expect to hear in a sermon, but I should never endure it in a play.

I pass by this; neither will I insist on the care they take, that no person after his first entrance shall ever appear, but the business which brings him upon the stage shall be evident; which rule, if observed, must needs render all the events in the play more natural; for there you see the probability of every accident, in the cause that produced it; and that which appears chance in the play, will seem so reasonable to you, that you will there find it almost necessary: so that in the exit of the actor you have a clear account of his purpose and design in the next entrance; (though, if the scene be well wrought, the event will commonly deceive you;) for there is nothing so absurd, says Corneille, as for an actor to leave the stage only because he has no more to say.

I should now speak of the beauty of their rhyme, and the just reason I have to prefer that way of writing in tragedies before ours in blank verse; but because it is partly received by us, and therefore not altogether peculiar to them, I will say no more of it in relation to their plays. For our own, I doubt not but it will exceedingly beautify them; and I can see but one reason why it should not generally obtain, that is, because our poets write so ill in it. This indeed may prove a more prevailing argument than all others which are used to destroy it, and therefore I am only troubled when great and judicious poets, and those who are acknowledged such, have writ or spoke against it: as for others, they are to be answered by that one sentence of an ancient author:† *Sed ut primo ad consequendos eos quos priores ducimus, accendimur, ita ubi aut præteriri, aut æquari eos posse desperavimus, studium cum spe senescit: quod, scilicet, assequi non potest, sequi desinit;—præteritoque eo in quo eminere non possumus, aliquid in quo nitamur, conquirimus.*

Lisideius concluded in this manner; and Neander, after a little pause, thus answered him:

I shall grant Lisideius, without much dispute, a great part of what he has urged against us; for I acknowledge, that the French contrive their plots more regularly, and observe the laws of comedy, and decorum of the stage, (to speak generally,) with more exactness than the English. Farther, I deny not but he has taxed us justly in some irregularities of ours, which he has mentioned; yet, after all, I am of opinion, that neither our faults, nor their virtues, are considerable enough to place them above us.

For the lively imitation of nature being in the definition of a play, those which best fulfil that law ought to be esteemed superior to the others. 'Tis true, those beauties of the French poesy are such as will raise perfection higher where it is, but are not sufficient to give it where it is not: they are indeed the beauties of a statue, but not of a man, because not animated with the soul of poesy, which is imitation of humour and passions: and this Lisideius himself, or any other, however biassed to their party, cannot but acknowledge, if he will either compare the humours of our comedies, or the characters of our serious plays, with theirs. He who will look upon theirs which have been written till

* Our author's last play of "Love Triumphant," is winded up in the last act by the mere change of will on the part of Veramond.

† Velleius Paterculus, l. 17.

these last ten years, or thereabouts, will find it a hard matter to pick out two or three passable humours amongst them. Corneille himself, their arch-poet, what has he produced except "The Liar?" and you know how it was cried up in France; but when it came upon the English stage, though well translated, and that part of Dorant acted* to so much advantage as I am confident it never received in its own country, the most favourable to it would not put it in competition with many of Fletcher's or Ben Jonson's. In the rest of Corneille's comedies you have little humour: he tells you himself, his way is, first to show two lovers in good intelligence with each other; in the working up of the play, to imbroil them by some mistake; and in the latter end to clear it, and reconcile them.

But of late years Molierè, the younger Corneille, Quinault, and some others, have been imitating afar off the quick turns and graces of the English stage. They have mixed their serious plays with mirth, like our tragi-comedies, since the death of Cardinal Richeliou,† which Lisideius, and many others, not observing, have commended that in them for a virtue, which they themselves no longer practise. Most of their new plays are, like some of ours, derived from the Spanish novels. There is scarce one of them without a veil, and a trusty Diego, who drolls much after the rate of the "Adventures."‡ But their humours, if I may grace them with that name, are so thin sown, that never above one of them comes up in any play. I dare take upon me to find more variety of them in some one play of Ben Jonson's, than in all theirs together: as he who has seen the "Alchemist," "The Silent Woman," or "Bartholomew Fair," cannot but acknowledge with me.

I grant the French have performed what was possible on the ground-work of the Spanish plays; what was pleasant before, they have made regular: but there is not above one good play to be writ on all those plots; they are too much alike to please often, which we need not the experience of our own stage to justify. As for their new way of mingling mirth with serious plot, I do not, with Lisideius, condemn the thing, though I cannot approve their manner of doing it. He tells us, we cannot so speedily recollect ourselves after a scene of great passion and concernment, as to pass to another of mirth and humour, and to enjoy it with any relish: but why should he imagine the soul of man more heavy than his senses? Does not the eye pass from an unpleasant object to a pleasant, in a much shorter time than is required to this? and does not the unpleasantness of the first commend the beauty of the latter? The old rule of logic might have convinced him, that contraries, when placed near, set off each other. A continued gravity keeps the spirit too much bent; we must refresh it sometimes, as we bait in a journey, that we may go on with greater ease. A scene of mirth, mixed with tragedy, has the same effect upon us which our music has betwixt the acts; which we find a relief to us from the best plots and language of the stage, if the discourses have been long. I must therefore have stronger arguments, ere I am convinced that compassion and mirth in the same subject destroy each other; and in the mean time, cannot but conclude, to the honour of our nation, that we have invented, increased, and perfected, a more pleasant way of writing for the stage, than was ever known to the ancients or moderns of any nation, which is tragi-comedy.

And this leads me to wonder why Lisideius and many others should cry up the barrenness of the French plots, above the variety and copiousness of the English. Their plots are single, they carry on one design, which is pushed forward by all the actors, every scene in the play contributing and moving towards it. Our plays, besides the main design, have under-plots, or by-concernments, of less considerable persons and intrigues, which are carried on with the motion of the main plot: as they say the orb of the fixed stars, and those of the planets, though they have motions of their own, are whirled about by the motion of the *primum mobile* in which they are contained. That similitude expresses much of the English stage; for if contrary motions may be found in nature to agree; if a planet can go east and west at the same time;—one way by virtue of its own motion, the other by the force of the first mover; it will not be difficult to imagine how the under-plot, which is only different, not contrary to the great design, may naturally be conducted along with it.

Eugenius has already shown us, from the

* Here the first edition has, "by Mr. Hart.' This play was first acted in 1661, under the title of "The Liar," and revived in 1685, under that of "The Mistaken Beauty."

† In 1642.

‡ "The Adventures of five Hours," is a comedy imitated from the Spanish of Calderon, by Sir Samuel Tuke, with some assistance from the Earl of Bristol. It was acted at court 1663, and received great applause. Cowley writes a laudatory poem, for which in the "Session of Poets" he is censured by Apollo; Diego is described, in the characters of the *dramatis personæ*, as "servant to Octavio, bred a scholar, a great coward, and a pleasant droll." It would seem from the preface, that this mode of affixing characters to the *dramatis personæ* was then a novelty.

confession of the French poets, that the unity of action is sufficiently preserved, if all the imperfect actions of the play are conducting to the main design; but when those petty intrigues of a play are so ill-ordered that they have no coherence with the other, I must grant that Lisideius has reason to tax that want of due connexion; for co-ordination in a play is as dangerous and unnatural as in a state. In the mean time he must acknowledge, our variety, if well ordered, will afford a greater pleasure to the audience.

As for his other argument, that by pursuing one single theme, they gain an advantage to express and work up the passions, I wish any example he could bring from them would make it good; for I confess their verses are to me the coldest I have ever read. Neither, indeed, is it possible for them, in the way they take, so to express passion, as that the effects of it should appear in the concernment of an audience, their speeches being so many declamations, which tire us with the length; so that, instead of persuading us to grieve for their imaginary heroes, we are concerned for our own trouble, as we are in tedious visits of bad company; we are in pain till they are gone. When the French stage came to be reformed by Cardinal Richelieu, those long harangues were introduced, to comply with the gravity of a churchman. Look upon the "Cinna" and the "Pompey;" they are not so properly to be called plays, as long discourses of reasons of state; and "Polieucte" in matters of religion is as solemn as the long stops upon our organs. Since that time it is grown into a custom, and their actors speak by the hour-glass, like our parsons;* nay, they account it the grace of their parts, and think themselves disparaged by the poet, if they may not twice or thrice in a play entertain the audience with a speech of a hundred lines. I deny not but this may suit well enough with the French; for as we, who are a more sullen people, come to be diverted at our plays, so they, who are of an airy and gay temper, come thither to make themselves more serious: and this I conceive to be one reason, why comedies are more pleasing to us, and tragedies to them. But to speak generally: It cannot be denied, that short speeches and replies are more apt to move the passions, and beget concernment in us, than the other; for it is unnatural for any one, in a gust of passion, to speak long together; or for another, in the same condition, to suffer him without interruption. Grief and passion are like floods raised in little brooks by a sudden rain; they are quickly up, and if the concernment be poured unexpectedly in upon us, it overflows us: But a long sober shower gives them leisure to run out as they came in, without troubling the ordinary current. As for comedy, repartee is one of its chiefest graces; the greatest pleasure of the audience is a chase of wit, kept up on both sides, and swiftly managed. And this our forefathers, if not we, have had in Fletcher's plays, to a much higher degree of perfection, than the French poets can reasonably hope to reach.

There is another part of Lisideius's discourse, in which he has rather excused our neighbours, than commended them; that is, for aiming only to make one person considerable in their plays. It is very true, what he has urged, that one character in all plays, even without the poet's care, will have advantage of all the others; and that the design of the whole drama will chiefly depend on it. But this hinders not that there may be more shining characters in the play; many persons of a second magnitude, nay, some so very near, so almost equal to the first, that greatness may be opposed to greatness, and all the persons be made considerable, not only by their quality, but their action. It is evident, that the more the persons are, the greater will be the variety of the plot. If then the parts are managed so regularly, that the beauty of the whole be kept entire, and that the variety become not a perplexed and confused mass of accidents, you will find it infinitely pleasing to be led in a labyrinth of design, where you see some of your way before you, yet discern not the end till you arrive at it. And that all this is practicable, I can produce for examples many of our English plays; as "The Maid's Tragedy," "The Alchemist," "The Silent Woman:" I was going to have named "The Fox," but that the unity of design seems not exactly observed in it; for there appear two actions in the play; the first naturally ending with the fourth act, the second forced from it in the fifth: which yet is the less to be condemned in him, because the disguise of Volpone, though it suited not with his character as a crafty or covetous person, agreed well enough with that of a voluptuary:* and by it the poet gained the end at which he aimed, the punishment of vice, and the reward of virtue, both which that disguise produced. So that to judge equally of it, it was an excellent fifth act, but not so naturally proceeding from the former.

* The custom of placing an hour-glass before the clergyman was then common in England. It is still the furniture of a country pulpit in Scotland. A facetious preacher used to press his audience to *take another glass with him.*

* Most modern readers revolt at the incident, as a monstrous improbability.

But to leave this, and pass to the latter part of Lisideius's discourse, which concerns relations, I must acknowledge with him, that the French have reason to hide that part of the action which would occasion too much tumult on the stage, and to choose rather to have it made known by narration to the audience. Farther, I think it very convenient, for the reasons he has given, that all incredible actions were removed; but, whether custom has so insinuated itself into our countrymen, or nature has so formed them to fierceness, I know not; but they will scarcely suffer combats and other objects of horror to be taken from them. And indeed, the indecency of tumults is all which can be objected against fighting: for why may not our imagination as well suffer itself to be deluded with the probability of it, as with any other thing in the play? For my part, I can with as great ease persuade myself that the blows are given in good earnest, as I can, that they who strike them are kings or princes, or those persons which they represent. For objects of incredibility,—I would be satisfied from Lisideius, whether we have any so removed from all appearance of truth, as are those of Corneille's "Andromede;" a play which has been frequented the most of any he has writ. If the Perseus, or the son of a heathen god, the Pegasus, and the Monster, were not capable to choke a strong belief, let him not blame any representation of ours hereafter. Those indeed were objects of delight, yet the reason is the same as to the probability; for he makes it not a ballet, or masque, but a play, which is to resemble truth. But for death, that it ought not to be represented, I have, besides the arguments alleged by Lisideius, the authority of Ben Jonson, who has forborne it in his tragedies: for both the death of Sejanus and Catiline are related; though, in the latter, I cannot but observe one irregularity of that great poet; he has removed the scene, in the same act, from Rome to Catiline's army, and from thence again to Rome; and besides, has allowed a very considerable time after Catiline's speech, for the striking of the battle, and the return of Petreius, who is to relate the event of it to the senate; which I should not animadvert on him, who was otherwise a painful observer of *τὸ πρέπον*, or the *decorum* of the stage, if he had not used extreme severity in his judgment on the incomparable Shakspeare for the same fault.* To conclude on this subject of relations, if we are to be blamed for showing too much of the action, the French are as faulty for discovering too little of it; a mean betwixt both should be observed by every judicious writer, so as the audience may neither be left unsatisfied by not seeing what is beautiful, or shocked by beholding what is either incredible or indecent.

I hope I have already proved in this discourse, that though we are not altogether so punctual as the French, in observing the laws of comedy, yet our errors are so few, and little, and those things wherein we excel them so considerable, that we ought of right to be preferred before them. But what will Lisideius say, if they themselves acknowledge they are too strictly bounded by those laws, for breaking which he has blamed the English? I will allege Corneille's words, as I find them in the end of his Discourse of the Three Unities: *Il est facile aux speculatifs d'estre severes*, &c. "It is easy for speculative persons to judge severely; but if they would produce to public view ten or twelve pieces of this nature, they would perhaps

* The insolence with which the dry and dogged Jonson used to carp at Shakspeare, is highly illustrative of that jealousy with which he is taxed by Drummond of Hawthornden. The most memorable attack on Shakspeare, on the score mentioned in the text, is the prologue to "Every man in his Humour."

Though need make many poets, and some such
As art and nature have not bettered much;
Yet ours, for want, hath not so loved the stage,
As he dare serve the ill customs of the age,
Or purchase your delight at such a rate,
As, for it, he himself must justly hate:
To make a child new swaddled, to proceed
Man, and then shoot up in one beard and weed
Past threescore years; or with three rusty swords
And help of some few foot, and half-foot words,
Fight over York and Lancaster's long jars,
And in the tyring-house bring wounds to scars.
He rather prays, you will be pleased to see
One such to-day, as other plays should be;
Where neither chorus wafts you o'er the seas,
Nor creaking throne comes down, the boys to please,
Nor nimble squib is seen, to make afeard
The gentlewomen; nor rolled bullet heard
To say, it thunders; nor tempestuous drum
Rumbles, to tell you when the storm doth come:
But deeds, and language, such as men do use,
And persons, such as comedy would choose,
When she would show an image of the times,
And sport with human follies, not with crimes;
Except we make them such, by loving still
Our popular errors, as you'll all confess,
By laughing at them, they deserve no less:
Which when you heartily do, there's hope left, then
You, that have so graced monsters, may like men.

"In 'Every Man Out of his Humour,' the same sneer is directed against the same quarter.

"*Mit.* He cannot alter the scene without crossing the seas.

"*Cor.* He need not, having a whole island to run through, I thinke.

"*Mit.* No! how comes it then that *in some one play we see so many seas, countries, and kingdomes passed over with such admirable dexteritie?*

"*Cor.* O, that but shows how well the authors can travaile in their vocation, and outrun the apprehension of their auditorie."

give more latitude to the rules than I have done, when, by experience, they had known how much we are limited and constrained by them, and how many beauties of the stage they banished from it." To illustrate a little what he has said:—by their servile observations of the unities of time and place, and integrity of scenes, they have brought on themselves that dearth of plot, and narrowness of imagination, which may be observed in all their plays. How many beautiful accidents might naturally happen in two or three days, which cannot arrive with any probability in the compass of twenty-four hours? There is time to be allowed also for maturity of design, which amongst great and prudent persons, such as are often represented in tragedy, cannot, with any likelihood of truth, be brought to pass at so short a warning. Farther, by tying themselves strictly to the unity of place, and unbroken scenes, they are forced many times to omit some beauties which cannot be shown where the act began; but might, if the scene were interrupted, and the stage cleared for the persons to enter in another place; and therefore the French poets are often forced upon absurdities: for if the act begins in a chamber, all the persons in the play must have some business or other to come thither, or else they are not to be shown that act; and sometimes their characters are very unfitting to appear there: as suppose it were the king's bed-chamber, yet the meanest man in the tragedy must come and despatch his business there, rather than in the lobby, or court-yard, (which is fitter for him,) for fear the stage should be cleared, and the scenes broken. Many times they fall by it into a greater inconvenience; for they keep their scenes unbroken, and yet change the place; as in one of their newest plays, where the act begins in the street. There a gentleman is to meet his friend; he sees him with his man, coming out from his father's house; they talk together, and the first goes out: the second, who is a lover, has made an appointment with his mistress; she appears at the window, and then we are to imagine the scene lies under it. This gentleman is called away, and leaves his servant with his mistress: presently her father is heard from within; the young lady is afraid the serving-man should be discovered, and thrusts him into a place of safety, which is supposed to be her closet. After this, the father enters to the daughter, and now the scene is in a house: for he is seeking from one room to another for this poor Philipin, or French Diego, who is heard from within, drolling and breaking many a miserable conceit on the subject of his sad condition. In this ridiculous manner the play goes forward, the stage being never empty all the while: so that the street, the window, the two houses, and the closet, are made to walk about, and the persons to stand still. Now, what, I beseech you, is more easy than to write a regular French play, or more difficult than to write an irregular English one, like those of Fletcher, or of Shakspeare?

If they content themselves, as Corneille did, with some flat design, which, like an ill riddle, is found out ere it be half proposed, such plots we can make every way regular as easily as they; but whenever they endeavour to rise to any quick turns and counter-turns of plot, as some of them have attempted, since Corneille's plays have been less in vogue, you see they write as irregularly as we, though they cover it more speciously. Hence the reason is perspicuous, why no French plays, when translated, have, or ever can succeed on the English stage. For, if you consider the plots, our own are fuller of variety; if the writing, ours are more quick and fuller of spirit; and therefore 'tis a strange mistake in those who decry the way of writing plays in verse, as if the English therein imitated the French. We have borrowed nothing from them; our plots are weaved in English looms: we endeavour therein to follow the variety and greatness of characters, which are derived to us from Shakspeare and Fletcher; the copiousness and well-knitting of the intrigues we have from Jonson; and for the verse itself we have English precedents of elder date than any of Corneille's plays. Not to name our old comedies before Shakspeare, which were all writ in verse of six feet, or Alexandrines, such as the French now use,* I can show in Shakspeare, many scenes of rhyme together, and the like in Ben Jonson's tragedies: in "Catiline" and "Sejanus" sometimes thirty or forty lines,—I mean besides the chorus, or the monologues; which, by the way, showed Ben no enemy to this way of writing, especially if you read his "Sad Shepherd," which goes sometimes on rhyme, sometimes on blank verse, like a horse

* Our old poets saw something peculiarly ludicrous in the anapæstic canter of these doggerel Alexandrines. The old comedy of "Gammer Gurton's Needle" is composed entirely of them. Shakspeare often uses them where the dialogue is carried on by his clowns, or comic characters; as in "Love's Labour's Lost," Act III.; in most of the quaint skirmishes of wit and punning, in the "Comedy of Errors;" and in the "Taming of the Shrew." Other examples from low comedy of that early age are given in Reed's edition of Shakspeare, vol. xx. p. 162. After all, this same Alexandrine is only the common ballad-stanza of "Chevy Chase," written in two lines at length, instead of being subdivided into four. Mr. Malone remarks that the assertion in the text is too general.

who eases himself on trot and amble. You find him likewise commending Fletcher's pastoral of "The Faithful Shepherdess," which is for the most part rhyme, though not refined to that purity to which it hath since been brought. And these examples are enough to clear us from a servile imitation of the French.

But to return whence I have digressed: I dare boldly affirm these two things of the English drama;—First, that we have many plays of ours as regular as any of theirs, and which, besides, have more variety of plot and characters; and, secondly, that in most of the irregular plays of Shakspeare or Fletcher, (for Ben Jonson's are for the most part regular,) there is a more masculine fancy, and greater spirit in the writing, than there is in any of the French. I could produce, even in Shakspeare's and Fletcher's works, some plays which are almost exactly formed; as the "Merry Wives of Windsor," and "The Scornful Lady:" but, because (generally speaking) Shakspeare, who writ first, did not perfectly observe the laws of comedy, and Fletcher, who came nearer to perfection, yet through carelessness made many faults; I will take the pattern of a perfect play from Ben Jonson, who was a careful and learned observer of the dramatic laws, and from all his comedies I shall select "The Silent Woman," of which I will make a short examen, according to those rules which the French observe.

As Neander was beginning to examine "The Silent Woman," Eugenius, earnestly regarding him; I beseech you, Neander, said he, gratify the company, and me in particular, so far as, before you speak of the play, to give us a character of the author; and tell us frankly your opinion, whether you do not think all writers, both French and English, ought to give place to him?

I fear, replied Neander, that, in obeying your commands, I shall draw some envy on myself. Besides, in performing them, it will be first necessary to speak somewhat of Shakspeare and Fletcher, his rivals in poesy; and one of them, in my opinion, at least his equal, perhaps his superior.*

To begin then with Shakspeare. He was the man who of all modern, and perhaps ancient poets, had the largest and most comprehensive soul. All the images of nature were still present to him, and he drew them not laboriously, but luckily: when he describes any thing, you more than see it, you feel it too. Those who accuse him to have wanted learning, give him the greater commendation: he was naturally learned; he needed not the spectacles of books to read nature; he looked inwards, and found her there. I cannot say he is every-where alike; were he so, I should do him injury to compare him with the greatest of mankind. He is many times flat, insipid; his comic wit degenerating into clenches, his serious swelling into bombast. But he is always great, when some great occasion is presented to him: no man can say, he ever had a fit subject for his wit, and did not then raise himself as high above the rest of poets,

> Quantum lenta solent inter viburna cupressi.

The consideration of this made Mr. Hales of Eton* say, that there was no subject of which any poet ever writ, but he would produce it much better done in Shakspeare; and however others are now generally preferred before him, yet the age wherein he lived, which had contemporaries with him, Fletcher and Jonson, never equalled them to him in their esteem: and in the last king's court, when Ben's reputation was at highest, Sir John Suckling, and with him the greater part of the courtiers, set our Shakspeare far above him.

Beaumont and Fletcher, of whom I am next to speak, had, with the advantage of Shakspeare's wit, which was their precedent, great natural gifts, improved by study; Beaumont especially being so accurate a judge of plays, that Ben Jonson, while he lived, submitted all his writings to his censure, and 'tis thought, used

* Mr. Malone justly observes, that the caution observed in this decision, proves the miserable taste of the age. In fact, Jonson, by dint of learning and arrogance, fairly bullied the age into receiving his own character of his merits; and he was not the only person of the name that has done so.

* The learned John Hales of Eton, whom Wood calls a *walking library*, and Clarendon pronounces the least man and greatest scholar of his time. Gildon tells the anecdote to which Dryden seems to allude, in an essay addressed to Dryden himself on the vindication of Shakspeare, and he quotes our author as his authority. "The matter of fact, if my memory fail me not, was this: Mr. Hales of Eton affirmed, that he would show all the poets of antiquity outdone by Shakspeare, in all the topics and common-places made use of in poetry. The enemies of Shakespear would by no means yield him so much excellence; so that it came to a resolution of a trial of skill upon that subject. The place agreed on for the dispute, was Mr. Hales' chamber at Eton. A great many books were sent down by the enemies of this poet; and on the appointed day, my Lord Falkland, Sir John Suckling, and all the persons of quality that had wit and learning, and interested themselves in the quarrel, met there; and upon a thorough disquisition of the point, the judges chosen by agreement out of this learned and ingenious assembly, unanimously gave the preference to Shakspeare, and the Greek and Roman poets were adjudged to veil at least their glory in that to the English hero."—*Gildon's Essays.*

Tate, in the preface to the "Loyal General," and Rowe, in his "Life of Shakspeare," quote the same anecdote.

his judgment in correcting, if not contriving, all his plots. What value he had for him, appears by the verses he writ to him; and therefore I need speak no farther of it. The first play that brought Fletcher and him in esteem, was their "Philaster;" for before that, they had written two or three very unsuccessfully: as the like is reported of Ben Jonson, before he writ "Every Man in his Humour." Their plots were generally more regular than Shakespeare's, especially those which were made before Beaumont's death; and they understood and imitated the conversation of gentlemen much better; whose wild debaucheries, and quickness of wit in repartees, no poet before them could paint as they have done. Humour,* which Ben Jonson derived from particular persons, they made it not their business to describe; they represented all the passions very lively, but above all, love. I am apt to believe the English language in them arrived to its highest perfection; what words have since been taken in, are rather superfluous than ornamental. Their plays are now the most pleasant and frequent entertainments of the stage; two of theirs being acted through the year for one of Shakspeare's or Jonson's: the reason is, because there is a certain gayety in their comedies, and pathos in their more serious plays, which suits generally with all men's humours. Shakspeare's language is likewise a little obsolete, and Ben Jonson's wit comes short of theirs.

As for Jonson, to whose character I am now arrived, if we look upon him while he was himself, (for his last plays were but his dotages,) I think him the most learned and judicious writer which any theatre ever had. He was a most severe judge of himself, as well as others. One cannot say he wanted wit, but rather that he was frugal of it. In his works you find little to retrench or alter. Wit and language, and humour also in some measure, we had before him; but something of art was wanting to the drama, till he came. He managed his strength to more advantage than any who preceded him. You seldom find him making love in any of his scenes, or endeavouring to move the passions; his genius was too sullen and saturnine to do it gracefully, especially when he knew he came after those who had performed both to such a height. Humour was his proper sphere; and in that he delighted most to represent mechanic people. He was deeply conversant in the ancients, both Greek and Latin, and he borrowed boldly from them: there is scarce a poet or historian among the Roman authors of those times, whom he has not translated in "Sejanus" and "Catiline." But he has done his robberies so openly, that one may see he fears not to be taxed by any law. He invades authors like a monarch; and what would be theft in other poets, is only victory in him. With the spoils of these writers he so represents old Rome to us, in its rites, ceremonies, and customs, that if one of their poets had written either of his tragedies, we had seen less of it than in him. If there was any fault in his language, it was, that he weaved it too closely and laboriously, in his comedies especially: perhaps, too, he did a little too much Romanize our tongue, leaving the words which he translated almost as much Latin as he found them: wherein, though he learnedly followed their language, he did not enough comply with the idiom of ours. If I would compare him with Shakspeare, I must acknowledge him the more correct poet, but Shakspeare the greater wit.* Shakspeare was the Homer, or father of our dramatic poets; Jonson was the Virgil, the pattern of elaborate writing: I admire him, but I love Shakspeare. To conclude of him; as he has given us the most correct plays, so in the precepts which he has laid down in his "Discoveries," we have as many and profitable rules for perfecting the stage, as any wherewith the French can furnish us.

Having thus spoken of the author, I proceed to the examination of his comedy, "The Silent Woman."

Examen of "The Silent Woman."

To begin first with the length of the action: it is so far from exceeding the compass of a natural day, that it takes not up an artificial one. It is all included in the limits of three hours and a half, which is no more than is required for the presentment of the stage; a beauty perhaps not much observed; if it had, we should not have looked on the Spanish translation of "Five Hours" with so much wonder. The scene of it is laid in London; the latitude of place is almost as little as you can imagine; for it lies all within the compass of two houses, and, after the first act, in one. The continuity of scenes is observed more than in any of our plays, except his own "Fox" and "Alchemist." They are not broken above twice, or thrice at most, in the whole comedy; and in the two best of Corneille's plays, the "Cid" and "Cinna," they are interrupted once. The action of the play is entirely one; the end or aim of which is the settling Morose's estate on Dauphine. The

* *Humour*, in the ancient dramatic language, signified some peculiar or fantastic bias, or habit of mind, in an individual.

* Dryden here understands *wit* in the enlarged sense of invention, or genius.

intrigue of it is the greatest and most noble of any pure unmixed comedy in any language: you see in it many persons of various characters and humours, and all delightful. As first, Morose, or an old man, to whom all noise, but his own talking, is offensive. Some, who would be thought critics, say this humour of his is forced: but to remove that objection, we may consider him first to be naturally of a delicate hearing, as many are to whom all sharp sounds are unpleasant; and secondly, we may attribute much of it to the peevishness of his age, or the wayward authority of an old man in his own house, where he may make himself obeyed; and to this the poet seems to allude in his name Morose. Beside this, I am assured from divers persons, that Ben Jonson was actually acquainted with such a man, one altogether as ridiculous as he is here represented. Others say, it is not enough to find one man of such a humour; it must be common to more, and the more common the more natural. To prove this, they instance in the best of comical characters, Falstaff. There are many men resembling him; old, fat, merry, cowardly, drunken, amorous, vain, and lying. But to convince these people, I need but tell them, that humour is the ridiculous extravagance of conversation, wherein one man differs from all others. If then it be common, or communicated to many, how differs it from other men's? or what indeed causes it to be ridiculous so much as the singularity of it? As for Falstaff, he is not properly one humour, but a miscellany of humours or images, drawn from so many several men: that wherein he is singular is his wit, or those things he says *præter expectatum*, unexpected by the audience; his quick evasions, when you imagine him surprised, which, as they are extremely diverting of themselves, so receive a great addition from his person; for the very sight of such an unwieldy old debauched fellow is a comedy alone. And here, having a place so proper for it, I cannot but enlarge somewhat upon this subject of humour into which I am fallen. The ancients had but little of it in their comedies; for the τὸ γελοῖον of the old comedy, of which Aristophanes was chief, was not so much to imitate a man, as to make the people laugh at some odd conceit, which had commonly somewhat of unnatural or obscene in it. Thus, when you see Socrates brought upon the stage, you are not to imagine him made ridiculous by the imitation of his actions, but rather by making him perform something very unlike himself: something so childish and absurd, as by comparing it with the gravity of the true Socrates, makes a ridiculous object for the spectators. In their new comedy which succeeded, the poets sought indeed to express the ἦθος, as in their tragedies the πάθος of mankind. But this ἦθος contained only the general characters of men and manners; as old men, lovers, serving-men, courtesans, parasites, and such other persons as we see in their comedies: all which they made alike: that is, one old man or father, one lover, one courtesan, so like another, as if the first of them had begot the rest of every sort: *Ex homine hunc natum dicas.* The same custom they observed likewise in their tragedies. As for the French, though they have the word *humeur* among them, yet they have small use of it in their comedies, or farces; they being but ill imitations of the *ridiculum*, or that which stirred up laughter in the old comedy. But among the English 'tis otherwise; where, by humour is meant some extravagant habit, passion, or affection, particular (as I said before) to some one person, by the oddness of which he is immediately distinguished from the rest of men; which being lively and naturally represented, most frequently begets that malicious pleasure in the audience which is testified by laughter; as all things which are deviations from custom are ever the aptest to produce it: though, by the way, this laughter is only accidental, as the person represented is fantastic or bizarre; but pleasure is essential to it, as the imitation of what is natural. The description of these humours, drawn from the knowledge and observation of particular persons, was the peculiar genius and talent of Ben Jonson; to whose play I now return.

Besides Morose, there are at least nine or ten different characters and humours in the "Silent Woman;" all which persons have several concernments of their own, yet are all used by the poet to the conducting of the main design to perfection. I shall not waste time in commending the writing of this play; but I will give you my opinion, that there is more wit and acuteness of fancy in it than in any of Ben Jonson's. Besides, that he has here described the conversation of gentlemen, in the persons of True-Wit and his friends, with more gayety, air, and freedom, than in the rest of his comedies.* For the contrivance of the plot, 'tis extreme, elaborate and yet withal easy; for the λύσις, or untying of it, 'tis so admirable, that when it is done, no one of the audience would think the poet could have missed it; and yet it was concealed so much before the last scene, that any other way would sooner have entered into your thoughts. But I dare not take upon me to commend the fabric of it, because it is altogether so full of

* This conversation, however, appears formidably stiff in the present age.

art, that I must unravel every scene in it to commend it as I ought. And this excellent contrivance is still the more to be admired, because 'tis comedy where the persons are only of common rank, and their business private, not elevated by passions or high concernments, as in serious plays. Here every one is a proper judge of all he sees; nothing is represented but that with which he daily converses: so that by consequence all faults lie open to discovery, and few are pardonable. 'Tis this which Horace has judiciously observed:

> Creditur, ex medio quia res arcessit, habere
> Sudoris minimum; sed habet Comedia tanto
> Plus oneris, quanto veniæ minus.

But our poet, who was not ignorant of these difficulties, has made use of all advantages; as he who designs a large leap, takes his rise from the highest ground. One of these advantages is that which Corneille has laid down as the greatest which can arrive to any poem, and which he himself could never compass above thrice in all his plays; viz. the making choice of some signal and long expected day, whereon the action of the play is to depend. This day was that designed by Dauphine for the settling of his uncle's estate upon him; which, to compass, he contrives to marry him. That the marriage had been plotted by him long beforehand, is made evident by what he tells True-Wit in the second act, that in one moment he had destroyed what he had been raising many months.

There is another artifice of the poet, which I cannot here omit, because by the frequent practice of it in his comedies, he has left it to us almost as a rule; that is, when he has any character or humour wherein he would show a *coup de maître*, or his highest skill, he recommends it to your observation, by a pleasant description of it before the person first appears. Thus, in "Bartholomew Fair," he gives you the pictures of Numps and Cokes, and in this, those of Daw, Lafoole, Morose, and the Collegiate Ladies; all which you hear described before you see them. So that before they come upon the stage, you have a longing expectation of them, which prepares you to receive them favourably; and when they are there, even from their first appearance you are so far acquainted with them, that nothing of their humour is lost to you.

I will observe yet one thing farther of this admirable plot; the business of it rises in every act. The second is greater than the first; the third than the second; and so forward to the fifth. There too you see, till the very last scene, new difficulties arising to obstruct the action of the play; and when the audience is brought into despair that the business can naturally be effected, then, and not before, the discovery is made. But that the poet might entertain you with more variety all this while, he reserves some new characters to show you, which he opens not till the second and third act. In the second, Morose, Daw, the Barber, and Otter; in the third, the Collegiate Ladies; all which he moves afterwards in by-walks, or under-plots, as diversions to the main design, lest it should grow tedious, though they are still naturally joined with it, and somewhere or other subservient to it. Thus, like a skilful chess-player, by little and little he draws out his men, and makes his pawns of use to his greater persons.

If this comedy, and some others of his, were translated into French prose, (which would now be no wonder to them, since Moliere has lately given them plays out of verse, which have not displeased them,) I believe the controversy would soon be decided betwixt the two nations, even making them the judges.* But we need not call our heroes to our aid; be it spoken to the honour of the English, our nation can never want in any age such, who are able to dispute the empire of wit with any people in the universe. And though the fury of a civil war, and power, for twenty years together, abandoned to a barbarous race of men, enemies of all good learning, had buried the muses under the ruins of monarchy; yet, with the restoration of our happiness, we see revived poesy lifting up its head, and already shaking off the rubbish which lay so heavy on it. We have seen, since his majesty's return, many dramatic poems which yield not to those of any foreign nation, and which deserve all laurels but the English. I will set aside flattery and envy; it cannot be denied but we have had some little blemish either in the plot or writing of all those plays which have been made within these seven years; and perhaps there is no nation in the world so quick to discern them, or so difficult to pardon them, as ours: yet if we can persuade ourselves to use the candour of that poet, who, though the most severe of critics, has left us this caution by which to moderate our censures—

> ——ubi plura nitent in carmine, non ego paucis
> Offendar maculis;—

if, in consideration of their many and great beauties, we can wink at some slight and little imperfections; if we, I say, can be thus equal

* I should be sorry to see the comparative merits of the stages tried upon that issue: Moliere, in natural comedy, is as far superior to Jonson, as Shakspeare is to both.

to ourselves, I ask no favour from the French. And if I do not venture upon any particular judgment of our late plays, 'tis out of the consideration which an ancient writer gives me: *vivorum, ut magna admiratio, ita censura difficilis:* betwixt the extremes of admiration and malice, 'tis hard to judge uprightly of the living. Only I think it may be permitted me to say, that as it is no lessening to us to yield to some plays, and those not many, of our own nation, in the last age, so can it be no addition to pronounce of our present poets, that they have far surpassed all the ancients, and the modern writers of other countries.

This was the substance of what was then spoke on that occasion; and Lisideius, I think, was going to reply, when he was prevented thus by Crites:—I am confident, said he, that the most material things that can be said, have been already urged on either side; if they have not, I must beg of Lisideius, that he will defer his answer till another time: for I confess I have a joint quarrel to you both, because you have concluded, without any reason given for it, that rhyme is proper for the stage. I will not dispute how ancient it hath been among us to write this way; perhaps our ancestors knew no better till Shakspeare's time. I will grant it was not altogether left by him, and that Fletcher and Ben Jonson used it frequently in their pastorals, and sometimes in other plays. Farther, I will not argue whether we received it originally from our own countrymen, or from the French; for that is an inquiry of as little benefit as theirs, who, in the midst of the late plague, were not so solicitous to provide against it, as to know whether we had it from the malignity of our own air, or by transportation from Holland. I have therefore only to affirm, that it is not allowable in serious plays; for comedies, I find you already concluding with me. To prove this, I might satisfy myself to tell you, how much in vain it is for you to strive against the stream of the people's inclination; the greatest part of which are prepossessed so much with those excellent plays of Shakspeare, Fletcher, and Ben Jonson, which have been written out of rhyme, that except you could bring them such as were written better in it, and those too by persons of equal reputation with them, it will be impossible for you to gain your cause with them, who still be judges. This it is to which, in fine, all your reasons must submit. The unanimous consent of an audience is so powerful, that even Julius Cæsar, (as Macrobius reports of him,) when he was perpetual dictator, was not able to balance it on the other side; but when Laberius, a Roman knight, at his request contended in the *Mime* with another poet, he was forced to cry out, *Etiam favente me victus es, Laberi.* But I will not, on this occasion, take the advantage of the greater number, but only urge such reasons against rhyme, as I find in the writings of those who have argued for the other way. First then, I am of opinion, that rhyme is unnatural in a play, because dialogue there is presented as the effect of sudden thought.* For a play is

* The reasons against rhyme,—and very weighty our author at last found them,—are taken from the Preface to Sir Robert Howard's plays, the Crites of the dialogue.

"Another way of the ancients, which the French follow, and our stage has now lately practised, is, to write in rhyme; and this is the dispute betwixt many ingenious persons, whether verse in rhyme, or verse without the sound, which may be called *blank* verse, (though a hard expression,) is to be preferred. But take the question largely, and it is never to be decided; but, by right application, I suppose it may; for in the general, they are both proper, that is, one for a play, the other for a poem or copy of verses; a blank verse being as much too low for one, as rhyme is unnatural for the other. A poem, being a premeditated form of thoughts upon designed occasions, ought not to be unfurnished of any harmony in words or sound; the other is presented as the present effect of accidents not thought of; so that it is impossible it should be equally proper to both these, unless it were possible that all persons were born so much more than poets, that verses were not to be composed by them, but already made in them. Some may object, that this argument is trivial, because, whatever is showed, it is known still to be but a play; but such may as well excuse an ill scene, that is not naturally painted, because they know it is only a scene, and not really a city or country.

"But there is yet another thing which makes verse upon the stage appear more unnatural; that is, when a piece of a verse is made up by one that knew not what the other meant to say, and the former verse answered as perfectly in sound as the last is supplied in measure; so that the smartness of a reply, which has its beauty by coming from sudden thoughts, seems lost by that which rather looks like a design of two, than the answer of one. It may be said, that rhyme is such a confinement to a quick and luxuriant fancy, that it gives a stop to its speed, till slow judgment comes in to assist it; but this is no argument for the question in hand; for the dispute is not, which way a man may write best in, but which is most proper for the subject he writes upon; and, if this were let pass, the argument is yet unsolved in itself; for he that wants judgment in the liberty of his fancy, may as well show the defect of it in its confinement; and, to say truth, he that has judgment will avoid the errors, and he that wants it will commit them both. It may be objected, it is improbable that any should speak *extempore* as well as Beaumont and Fletcher makes them, though in blank verse; I do not only acknowledge that, but that it is also imbrobable any will write so well that way. But if that may be allowed improbable, I believe it may be concluded impossible that any should speak as good verses in rhyme, as the best poets have writ; and therefore, that which seems nearest to what it intends, is ever to be preferred. Nor are great thoughts more adorned by verse, than verse unbeautified by mean ones; so that verse seems not only unfit in the best use of it, but much more in the worse, when a servant is called, or a door bid to be shut, in rhyme. Verses

the imitation of nature; and since no man, without premeditation, speaks in rhyme, neither ought he to do it on the stage. This hinders not but the fancy may be there elevated to a higher pitch of thought than it is in ordinary discourse; for there is a probability that men of excellent and quick parts may speak noble things *extempore*: but those thoughts are never fettered with numbers, or sound of verse, without study; and therefore it cannot be but unnatural to present the most free way of speaking in that which is the most constrained. For this reason, says Aristotle, 'tis best to write tragedy in that kind of verse which is the least such, or which is nearest prose: and this amongst the ancients was the iambic, and with us is blank verse, or the measure of verse kept exactly without rhyme. These numbers therefore are fittest for a play; the others, for a paper of verses, or a poem; blank verse being as much below them, as rhyme is improper for the drama. And if it be objected, that neither are blank verses made *extempore*, yet, as nearest nature, they are still to be preferred. But there are two particular exceptions, which many besides myself have had to verse, by which it will appear yet more plainly, how improper it is in plays. And the first of them is grounded on that very reason for which some have commended rhyme: they say, the quickness of repartees in argumentative scenes receives an ornament from verse. Now, what is more unreasonable than to imagine, that a man should not only light upon the wit, but the rhyme too, upon the sudden? This nicking of him who spoke before both in sound and measure, is so great a happiness, that you must at least suppose the persons of your play to be born poets: *Arcades omnes, et cantare pares, et respondere parati*: they must have arrived to the degree of *quicquid conabar dicere*, to make verses almost whether they will or no. If they are any thing below this, it will look rather like the design of two, than the answer of one: it will appear that your actors hold intelligence together; that they perform their tricks like fortune-tellers, by confederacy. The hand of art will be too visible in it, against that maxim of all professions—*Ars est celare artem*: that it is the greatest perfection of art to keep itself undiscovered. Nor will it serve you to object, that however you manage it, 'tis still known to be a play; and consequently, the dialogue of two persons understood to be the labour of one poet. For a play is still an imitation of nature; we know we are to be deceived, and we desire to be so; but no man ever was deceived but with a probability of truth; for who will suffer a gross lie to be fastened on him? Thus we sufficiently understand, that the scenes which represent cities and countries to us are not really such, but only painted on boards and canvass; but shall that excuse the ill painture or designment of them? Nay rather ought they not to be laboured with so much the more diligence and exactness, to help the imagination? since the mind of man does naturally tend to truth; and therefore the nearer any thing comes to the imitation of it, the more it pleases.

Thus, you see, your rhyme is incapable of expressing the greatest thoughts naturally, and the lowest it cannot with any grace: for what is more unbefitting the majesty of verse, than to call a servant, or bid a door be shut in rhyme? and yet you are often forced on this miserable necessity. But verse, you say, circumscribes a quick and luxuriant fancy, which would extend itself too far on every subject, did not the labour which is required to well-turned and polished rhyme set bounds to it. Yet this argument, if granted, would only prove, that we may write better in verse, but not more naturally. Neither is it able to evince that; for he who wants judgment to confine his fancy in blank verse, may want it as much in rhyme; and he who has it, will avoid errors in both kinds. Latin verse was as great a confinement to the imagination of those poets, as rhyme to ours: and yet you find Ovid saying too much on every subject. *Nescivit* (says Seneca) *quod bene cessit relinquere*: of which he gives you one famous instance in his description of the deluge:

> Omnia pontus erat, deerant quoque litora ponto
>
> Now all was sea nor had that sea a shore.

(I mean good ones) do in their height of fancy declare the labour that brought them forth, like majesty, that grows with care; and Nature, that made the poet capable, seems to retire, and leave its offers to be made perfect by pains and judgment. Against this I can raise no argument but my Lord of Orrery's writings, in whose verse the greatness of the majesty seems unsullied with the cares, and his inimitable fancy descends to us in such easy expressions, that they seem as if neither had ever been added to the other, but both together flowing from a height; like birds got so high, that use no labouring wings, but only with an easy care preserve a steadiness in motion. But this particular happiness, among those multitudes which that excellent person is owner of, does not convince my reason, but employ my wonder: yet I am glad such verse has been written for our stage, since it has so happily exceeded those whom we seemed to imitate. But while I give these arguments against verse, I may seem faulty that I have not only written ill ones, but written any: but, since it was the fashion, I was resolved, as in all indifferent things, not to appear singular, the danger of the vanity being greater than the error; and therefore I followed it as a fashion, though very far off."

Thus Ovid's fancy was not limited by verse, and Virgil needed not verse to have bounded his.

In our own language we see Ben Jonson confining himself to what ought to be said, even in the liberty of blank verse; and yet Corneille, the most judicious of the French poets, is still varying the same sense a hundred ways, and dwelling eternally on the same subject, though confined by rhyme. Some other exceptions I have to verse: but since these I have named are for the most part already public, I conceive it reasonable they should first be answered.

It concerns me less than any, said Neander, (seeing he had ended,) to reply to this discourse, because when I should have proved, that verse may be natural in plays, yet I should always be ready to confess, that those which I have written in this kind come short of that perfection which is required.* Yet since you are pleased I should undertake this province, I will do it, though with all imaginable respect and deference, both to that person from whom you have borrowed your strongest arguments, and to whose judgment, when I have said all, I finally submit. But before I proceed to answer your objections, I must first remember you, that I exclude all comedy from my defence; and next, that I deny not but blank verse may be also used; and content myself only to assert, that in serious plays, where the subject and characters are great, and the plot unmixed with mirth, which might allay or divert those concernments which are produced, rhyme is there as natural, and more effectual, than blank verse.

And now having laid down this as a foundation,—to begin with Crites,—I must crave leave to tell him, that some of his arguments against rhyme reach no farther than, from the faults or defects of ill rhyme, to conclude against the use of it in general. May not I conclude against blank verse by the same reason? If the words of some poets, who write in it, are either ill chosen, or ill placed, (which makes not only rhyme, but all kind of verse in any language unnatural,) shall I, for their vicious affectation, condemn those excellent lines of Fletcher, which are written in that kind? Is there any thing in rhyme more constrained than this line in blank verse?

I heaven invoke, and strong resistance make,

where you see both the clauses are placed unnaturally; that is, contrary to the common way of speaking, and that without the excuse of a rhyme to cause it: yet you would think me very ridiculous, if I should accuse the stubbornness of blank verse for this, and not rather the stiffness of the poet. Therefore, Crites, you must either prove, that words, though well chosen, and duly placed, yet render not rhyme natural in itself; or that, however natural and easy the rhyme may be, yet it is not proper for a play. If you insist on the former part, I would ask you, what other conditions are required to make rhyme natural in itself, besides an election of apt words, and a right disposition of them? For the due choice of your words expresses your sense naturally, and the due placing them adapts the rhyme to it. If you object, that one verse may be made for the sake of another, though both the words and rhyme be apt, I answer, it cannot possibly so fall out; for either there is a dependence of sense betwixt the first line and the second, or there is none: if there be that connexion, then in the natural position of the words the latter line must of necessity flow from the former; if there be no dependence, yet still the due ordering of words makes the last line as natural in itself as the other: so that the necessity of a rhyme never forces any but bad or lazy writers to say what they would not otherwise. 'Tis true, there is both care and art required to write in verse. A good poet never establishes the first line, till he has sought out such a rhyme as may fit the sense, already prepared to heighten the second: many times the close of the sense falls into the middle of the next verse, or farther off, and he may often avail himself of the same advantages in English which Virgil had in Latin,—he may break off in the hemistich, and begin another line. Indeed, the not observing these two last things, makes plays which are writ in verse so tedious: for though, most commonly, the sense is to be confined to the couplet, yet nothing that does *perpetuo tenore fluere*, run in the same channel, can please always. 'Tis like the murmuring of a stream, which, not varying in the fall, causes at first attention, at last drowsiness. Variety of cadences is the best rule; the greatest help to the actors, and refreshment to the audience.

If then verse may be made natural in itself, how becomes it unnatural in a play? You say the stage is the representation of nature, and no man in ordinary conversation speaks in rhyme. But you foresaw, when you said this, that it might be answered—neither does any man speak in blank verse, or in measure without rhyme. Therefore you concluded, that which is nearest nature is still to be preferred. But you took no notice, that rhyme might be made as natural as blank verse, by the well placing of the words, &c. All the difference between them, when they are both correct, is the sound

* This makes it obvious, that Neander is Dryden himself.

in one, which the other wants; and if so, the sweetness of it, and all the advantage resulting from it, which are handled in the preface to the "Rival Ladies," will yet stand good. As for that place of Aristotle, where he says plays should be writ in that kind of verse which is nearest prose, it makes little for you; blank verse being properly measured prose. Now measure alone, in any modern language, does not constitute verse; those of the ancients in Greek and Latin consisted in quantity of words, and a determinate number of feet. But when, by the inundation of the Goths and Vandals into Italy, new languages were introduced, and barbarously mingled with the Latin, of which the Italian, Spanish, French, and ours, (made out of them and the Teutonic,) are dialects, a new way of poesy was practised; new, I say, in those countries, for in all probability it was that of the conquerors in their own nations; at least we are able to prove, that the eastern people have used it from all antiquity.* This new way consisted in measure or number of feet, and rhyme. The sweetness of rhyme, and observation of accent, supplying the place of quantity in words, which could neither exactly be observed by those barbarians, who knew not the rules of it, neither was it suitable to their tongues as it had been to the Greek and Latin. No man is tied in modern poesy to observe any farther rule in the feet of his verse, but that they be dissyllables; whether Spondee, Trochee, or Iambic, it matters not; only he is obliged to rhyme: neither do the Spanish, French, Italians, or Germans, acknowledge at all, or very rarely, any such kind of poesy as blank verse amongst them. Therefore, at most 'tis but a poetic prose, a *sermo pedestris*; and, as such, most fit for comedies, where I acknowledge rhyme to be improper. Farther, as to that quotation of Aristotle, our couplet verses may be rendered as near prose as blank verse itself, by using those advantages I lately named, —as breaks in a hemistich, or running the sense into another line,—thereby making art and order appear as loose and free as nature: or, not tying ourselves to couplets strictly, we may use the benefit of the Pindaric way, practised in the "Siege of Rhodes;" where the numbers vary, and the rhyme is disposed carelessly, and far from often chiming. Neither is that other advantage of the ancients to be despised, of changing the kind of verse when they please, with the change of the scene, or some new entrance; for they confine not themselves always to iambics, but extend their liberty to all lyric numbers, and sometimes even to hexameter. But I need not go so far to prove, that rhyme, as it succeeds to all other offices of Greek and Latin verse, so especially to this of plays, since the custom of nations at this day confirms it; the French, Italian, and Spanish tragedies are generally writ in it; and sure the universal consent of the most civilized parts of the world, ought in this, as it doth in other customs, to include the rest.

But perhaps you may tell me, I have proposed such a way to make rhyme natural, and consequently proper to plays, as is impracticable; and that I shall scarce find six or eight lines together in any play, where the words are so placed and chosen as is required to make it natural. I answer, no poet need constrain himself at all times to it. It is enough he makes it his general rule; for I deny not but sometimes there may be a greatness in placing the words otherwise; and sometimes they may sound better; sometimes also the variety itself is excuse enough. But if, for the most part, the words be placed as they are in the negligence of prose, it is sufficient to denominate the way practicable; for we esteem that to be such, which in the trial oftener succeeds than misses. And thus far you may find the practice made good in many plays: where you do not, remember still, that if you cannot find six natural rhymes together, it will be as hard for you to produce as many lines in blank verse, even among the greatest of our poets, against which I cannot make some reasonable exception.

And this, sir, calls to my remembrance the beginning of your discourse, where you told us we should never find the audience favourable to this kind of writing, till we could produce as good plays in rhyme as Ben Jonson, Fletcher, and Shakspeare had writ out of it. But it is to raise envy to the living, to compare them with the dead. They are honoured, and almost adored by us, as they deserve; neither do I know any so presumptuous of themselves as to contend with them. Yet give me leave to say thus much, without injury to their ashes, that not only we shall never equal them, but they could never equal themselves, were they to rise and write again. We acknowledge them our fathers in wit, but they have ruined their estates themselves, before they came to their children's hands. There is scarce a humour, a character, or any kind of plot, which they have not used. All comes sullied or wasted to us; and were they to entertain this age, they could not now make so plenteous treatments out of such decayed fortunes. This therefore will be a good argument to us either not to write at

* Vide Daniel, his *Defence of Rhyme*. Dryden.

all, or to attempt some other way. There is no bays to be expected in their walks: *tentanda via est, quâ me quoque possum tollere humo.*

This way of writing in verse, they have only left free to us; our age is arrived to a perfection in it, which they never knew; and which (if we may guess by what of theirs we have seen in verse, as the "Faithful Shepherdess," and "Sad Shepherd") it is probable they never could have reached. For the genius of every age is different; and though ours excel in this, I deny not but that to imitate nature in that perfection which they did in prose, is a greater commendation than to write in verse exactly. As for what you have added,—that the people are not generally inclined to like this way,—if it were true, it would be no wonder, that betwixt the shaking off an old habit, and the introducing of a new, there should be difficulty. Do we not see them stick to Hopkins and Sternhold's Psalms, and forsake those of David, I mean Sandys his translation of them? If by the people you understand the multitude, the οἱ πολλοί, it is no matter what they think; they are sometimes in the right, sometimes in the wrong: their judgment is a mere lottery. *Est ubi plebs recté putat, est ubi peccat.** Horace says it of the vulgar, judging poesy. But if you mean the mixed audience of the populace and the noblesse, I dare confidently affirm, that a great part of the latter sort are already favourable to verse; and that no serious plays, written since the king's return, have been more kindly received by them, than "The Siege of Rhodes," the "Mustapha," "The Indian Queen," and "Indian Emperor."†

But I come now to the inference of your first argument. You said, that the dialogue of plays is presented as the effect of sudden thought, but no man speaks suddenly, or *extempore*, in rhyme; and you inferred from thence, that rhyme, which you acknowledge to be proper to epic poesy, cannot equally be proper to dramatic, unless we could suppose all men born so much more than poets, that verses should be made in them, not by them.

It has been formerly urged by you, and confessed by me, that since no man spoke any kind of verse *extempore*, that which was nearest nature was to be prefered. I answer you, therefore, by distinguishing betwixt what is nearest to the nature of comedy, which is the imitation of common persons and ordinary speaking, and what is nearest the nature of a serious play: this last is indeed the representation of nature, but 'tis nature wrought up to a higher pitch. The plot, the characters, the wit, the passions, the descriptions, are all exalted above the level of common converse, as high as the imagination of the poet can carry them, with proportion to verisimility. Tragedy, we know, is wont to image to us the minds and fortunes of noble persons, and to portray these exactly, heroic rhyme is nearest nature, as being the noblest kind of modern verse.

> Indignatur enim privatis, et probe socco
> Dignis, carminibus, narrari cœna Thyeste,

says Horace: and in another place,

> Effutire leves indigna tragœdia versus.

Blank verse is acknowledged to be too low for a poem, nay, more, for a paper of verses; but if too low for an ordinary sonnet, how much more for tragedy, which is, by Aristotle, in the dispute betwixt the epic poesy and the dramatic, for many reasons he there alleges, ranked above it?

But setting this defence aside, your argument is almost as strong against the use of rhyme in poems as in plays; for the epic way is every where interlaced with dialogue, or discoursive scenes; and therefore you must either grant rhyme to be improper there, which is contrary to your assertion, or admit it into plays by the same title which you have given it to poems. For though tragedy be justly preferred above the other, yet there is a great affinity between them, as may easily be discovered in that definition of a play which Lisideius gave us. The *genus* of them is the same,—a just and lively image of human nature, in its actions, passions, and traverses of fortune: so is the end,—namely for the delight and benefit of mankind. The characters and persons are still the same, viz. the greatest of both sorts; only the manner of acquainting us with those actions, passions, and fortunes, is different. Tragedy performs it *viva voce*, or by action in dialogue; wherein it excels the epic poem, which does it chiefly by narration, and therefore is not so lively an image of human nature. However, the agreement betwixt them is such, that if rhyme be proper for one, it must be for the other. Verse, 'tis true, is not the effect of sudden thought; but this hinders not that sudden thought may be represented in verse, since those thoughts are such as must be higher than nature can raise them without premeditation, especially to a continuance of them, even out of verse; and

* Accurately,

Interdum vulgus recte videt est ubi peccat.

† "The Siege of Rhodes," by Sir William D'Avenant; "Mustapha," by Lord Orrery; "The Indian Queen," by Sir Robert Howard and Dryden; and "The Indian Emperor," by Dryden alone.

consequently you cannot imagine them to have been sudden, either in the poet or the actors. A play, as I have said, to be like nature, is to be set above it; as statues which are placed on high are made greater than the life, that they may descend to the sight in their just proportion.

Perhaps I have insisted too long on this objection; but the clearing of it will make my stay shorter on the rest. You tell us, Crites, that rhyme appears most unnatural in repartees, or short replies; when he who answers, (it being presumed he knew not what the other would say, yet) makes up that part of the verse which was left incomplete, and supplies both the sound and measure of it. This, you say, looks rather like the confederacy of two, than the answer of one.

This, I confess, is an objection which is in every man's mouth, who loves not rhyme: but suppose, I beseech you, the repartee were made only in blank verse, might not part of the same argument be turned against you? for the measure is as often supplied there as it is in rhyme; the latter half of the hemistich as commonly made up, or a second line subjoined, as a reply to the former; which any one leaf in Jonson's plays will sufficiently clear to you. You will often find in the Greek tragedians, and in Seneca, that when a scene grows up into the warmth of repartees, (which is the close fighting of it,) the latter part of the trimeter is supplied by him who answers; and yet it was never observed as a fault in them by any of the ancient or modern critics.* The case is the same in our verse as it was in theirs; rhyme to us being in lieu of quantity to them. But if no latitude is to be allowed a poet, you take from him not only his license of *quidlibet audendi*, but you tie him up in a straiter compass than you would a philosopher. This is indeed *Musas colere severiores*. You would have him follow nature, but he must follow her on foot: you have dismounted him from his Pegasus. But you tell us, this supplying the last half of a verse, or adjoining a whole second to the former, looks more like the design of two, than the answer of one. Suppose we acknowledge it: How comes this confederacy to be more displeasing to you than in a dance which is well contrived? You see there the united design of many persons to make up one figure: after they have separated themselves in many petty divisions, they rejoin one by one into a gross: the confederacy is plain amongst them, for chance could never produce any thing so beautiful; and yet there is nothing in it that shocks your sight. I acknowledge the hand of art appears in repartees, as of necessity it must in all kind of verse. But there is also the quick and poignant brevity of it (which is a high imitation of nature in those sudden gusts of passion) to mingle with it; and this, joined with the cadency and sweetness of the rhyme, leaves nothing in the soul of the hearer to desire. It is an art which appears: but it appears only like the shadowings of painture, which being to cause the rounding of it, cannot be absent; but while that is considered, they are lost: so while we attend to the other beauties of the matter, the care and labour of the rhyme is carrried from us, or at least drowned in its own sweetness, as bees are sometimes buried in their honey. When a poet has found the repartee, the last perfection he can add to it is, to put it into verse. However good the thought may be, however apt the words in which it is couched, yet he finds himself at a little unrest, while rhyme is wanting. He cannot leave it till that comes naturally, and then is at ease, and sits down contented.

From replies, which are the most elevated thoughts of verse, you pass to those which are most mean, and which are common with the lowest of household conversation. In these, you say, the majesty of verse suffers. You instance in the calling of a servant, or commanding a door to be shut, in rhyme. This, Crites, is a good observation of yours, but no argument; for it proves no more but that such thoughts should be waived, as often as may be, by the address o. the poet. But suppose they are necessary in the places where he uses them, yet there is no need to put them into rhyme. He may place them in the beginning of a verse, and break it off, as unfit, when so debased, for any other use; or granting the worst,—that they require more room than the hemistich will allow, yet still there is a choice to be made of the best words, and least vulgar, provided they be apt to express such thoughts. Many have blamed rhyme in general for this fault, when the poet, with a little care, might have redressed it. But they do it with no more justice, than if English poesy should be made ridiculous for the sake of the Water-poet's rhymes.* Our language is

* There is this great difference, that, from the mode of pronouncing, the rhythm of the blank verse does not necessarily obtrude itself on the audience: that of the couplet indubitably must.

* John Taylor, the Water-poet, as he called himself from his profession of a waterman, was, according to Wood, a man who, having a prodigious genius to poetry, wrote eighty books, which not only made

noble, full, and significant; and I know not why he who is master of it may not clothe ordinary things in it as decently as the Latin, if he use the same diligence in his choice of words:

Delectus verborum origo est eloquentiæ.

It was the saying of Julius Cæsar, one so curious in his, that none of them can be changed but for a worse. One would think, *unlock the door*, was a thing as vulgar as could be spoken; and yet Seneca could make it sound high and lofty in his Latin:

Reserate clusos regii postes laris.*
Set wide the palace gates.

But I turn from this exception, both because it happens not above twice or thrice in any play that those vulgar thoughts are used; and then too, were there no other apology to be made, yet the necessity of them, which is alike in all kind of writing, may excuse them. For if they are little and mean in rhyme, they are of consequence such in blank verse. Besides that the great eagerness and precipitation with which they are spoken, makes us rather mind the substance than the dress; that for which they are spoken, rather than what is spoke. For they are always the effect of some hasty concernment, and something of consequence depends on them.

Thus, Crites, I have endeavoured to answer your objections: it remains only that I should vindicate an argument for verse, which you have gone about to overthrow. It had formerly been said, that the easiness of blank verse renders the poet too luxuriant; but that the labour of rhyme bounds and circumscribes an over-fruitful fancy; the sense there being commonly confined to the couplet, and the words so ordered, that the rhyme naturally follows them, not they the rhyme. To this you answered, that it was no argument to the question in hand; for the dispute was not, which way a man may write best, but which is most proper for the subject on which he writes.

First, give me leave, sir, to remember you, that the argument against which you raised this objection, was only secondary: it was built on this hypothesis,—that to write in verse was proper for serious plays. Which supposition being granted, (as it was briefly made out in that discourse, by showing how verse might be made natural,) it asserted, that this way of writing was a help to the poet's judgment, by putting bounds to a wild overflowing fancy. I think therefore it will not be hard for me to make good what it was to prove on that supposition. But you add, that were this let pass, yet he who wants judgment in the liberty of his fancy, may as well show the defect of it when he is confined to verse: for he who has judgment will avoid errors, and he who has it not, will commit them in all kinds of writing.

This argument, as you have taken it from a most acute person,* so, I confess, it carries much weight in it: but by using the word judgment here indefinitely, you seem to have put a fallacy upon us. I grant, he who has judgment, that is, so profound, so strong, or rather so infallible a judgment, that he needs no helps to keep it always poised and upright, will commit no faults either in rhyme or out of it. And on the other extreme, he who has a judgment so weak and crazed, that no helps can correct or amend it, shall write scurvily out of rhyme, and worse in it. But the first of these judgments is nowhere to be found, and the latter is not fit to write at all. To speak therefore of judgment as it is in the best poets; they who have the greatest proportion of it, want other helps than from it, within. As for example, you would be loth to say, that he who is endued with a sound judgment, has no need of history, geography, or moral philosophy, to write correctly. Judgment is indeed the master-workman in a play; but he requires many subordinate hands, many tools to his assistance. And verse I affirm to be one of these: it is a rule and line by which he keeps his building compact and even, which otherwise lawless imagination would raise either irregularly or loosely; at least, if the poet commits errors with this help, he would make greater and more without it:—it is, in short, a slow and painful, but the surest kind of working. Ovid, whom you accuse for luxuriancy in verse, had perhaps been farther guilty of it, had he writ in prose. And for your instance of Ben

much sport at the time, but were thought worthy of being remitted into a large folio. He was a stanch Cavalier, which might in some degree bribe Anthony's judgment of his poetry. His poetry is very like that which Skelton wrote a century before him. Among other pieces, there are some comical addresses to his subscribers, whom he divides into those who had received and paid their books; those who had done neither; and those who, having received, were unable to pay. To the first class he abounds in gratitude; the second he addresses as between hope and despair; the third he treats civilly, as they were defaulters from inability, and had always given him plenty of sack and fair promises; but, as was reason, he reserves the extremity of his displeasure for a fourth class of subscribers, who, having received his books, refused to pay the subscription.

* This Sir Robert Howard quoted, in his preface to the "Duke of Lerma," and unluckily translated it, "Shutting the palace gates," for which Dryden severely animadverts on him.

* Meaning Sir Robert Howard himself.

Jonson, who, you say, writ exactly without the help of rhyme; you are to remember, it is only an aid to a luxuriant fancy, which his was not: as he did not want imagination, so none ever said he had much to spare. Neither was verse then refined so much, to be a help to that age, as it is to ours. Thus then the second thoughts being usually the best, as receiving the maturest digestion from judgment, and the last and most mature product of those thoughts being artful and laboured verse, it may well be inferred, that verse is a great help to a luxuriant fancy; and that is what that argument which you opposed was to evince.

Neander was pursuing this discourse so eagerly, that Eugenius had called to him twice or thrice, ere he took notice that the barge stood still, and that they were at the foot of Somerset stairs where they had appointed it to land. The company were all sorry to separate so soon, though a great part of the evening was already spent; and stood a while looking back on the water, upon which the moonbeams played, and made it appear like floating quicksilver: at last they went up through a crowd of French people,* who were merrily dancing in the open air, and nothing concerned for the noise of guns, which had alarmed the town that afternoon. Walking thence together to the Piazze, they parted there; Eugenius and Lisideius to some pleasant appointment they had made, and Crites and Neander to their several lodgings.

*From the conduct of Louis XIV. who gradually retrenched until he altogether abolished the edict of Nantz, there was a constant emigration to England of his Huguenot subjects.

HEADS

OF

AN ANSWER TO RYMER'S REMARKS, &c.

Thomas Rymer, distinguished as the editor of the *Fœdera* of England, was in his earlier years ambitious of the fame of a critic. In 1678, he published a small duodecimo, entitled, "The Tragedies of the last Age considered and examined by the practice of the Ancients, and the common Sense of all Ages, in a letter to Fleetwood and Shepherd." The criticisms apply chiefly to the tragedies of the latter part of the reigns of Elizabeth and James I.; out of which he has singled, as the particular subjects of reprehension, those of "Rollo," "The Maid's Tragedy," and "King and no King." In this criticism, there was "much malice mingled with a little wit;" obvious faults and absurdities were censured as disgusting to common sense, on the one hand: on the other, licenses unpractised by the ancients were condemned as barbarous and unclassical.

A severe critic, if able but plausibly to support his remarks by learning and acumen, strikes terror through the whole world of literature. It is in vain to represent to such a person that he only examines the debtor side of the account, and omits to credit the unfortunate author with the merit that he has justly a title to claim. Instead of a fair accounting between the public and the poet, his cause is tried as in a criminal action, where, if he is convicted of a crime, all the merit of his work will not excuse him. There must be something in the mind of man favourable to a system which tends to the levelling of talents in the public estimation, or such critics as Rymer could never have risen into notice. Yet Dryden, in the following projected answer to his Remarks, has treated him with great respect: and Pope, according to Spence, pronounced him "one of the best critics we ever had."

That Dryden should have been desirous to conciliate the favour of an avowed critic, was natural enough; but that Pope should have so spoken of Rymer, only argues, either that he was prejudiced by the opinions which his youth had sucked in from Walsh, Wycherly, and Trumbull, or that his taste for the drama was far inferior to his powers in every other range of poetry.

If Dryden had arranged and extended the materials of his answer, it is possible that he would have treated Rymer with less deference than he showed while collecting them; for in the latter years of Dryden's life they were upon bad terms.

To a reader of the present day, when the cant of criticism has been in some degree abandoned, nothing can be more disgusting than the remarks of Rymer, who creeps over the most beautiful passages of the drama with eyes open only to their defects, or their departure from scholastic precept; who denies the name of poetry to the "Paradise Lost," and compares judging of "Rollo" by "Othello," to adjusting one crooked line by another. But I would be by no means understood to say, that there is not sometimes justice, though never mercy, in his criticism.

Dryden had intended to enter the lists with Rymer in defence of the ancient theatre, and with this view had wrote the following Heads of an Answer to the Remarks. They were jotted down on the blank leaves of a copy of the book presented to Dryden by Rymer. The volume falling into the hands of the publishers of Beaumont and Fletcher's works, in 1711, they prefixed Dryden's observations, as furnishing an apology for their authors. They were again published by Dr. Johnson, into whose hands they were put by Garrick, who had the original in his collection. The arrangement is different in the two copies; that of Dr. Johnson has been adopted, as preferred by Mr. Malone.

HEADS OF AN ANSWER

TO

RYMER'S REMARKS ON THE TRAGEDIES OF THE LAST AGE.

THAT we may the less wonder why pity and terror are not now the only spring on which our tragedies move,* and that Shakspeare may be more excused, Rapin confesses, that the French tragedies now all run on the *tendre*; and gives the reason, because love is the passion which most predominates in our souls; and that therefore the passions represented become insipid, unless they are conformable to the thoughts of the audience. But it is to be concluded, that this passion works not now amongst the French so strongly, as the other two did amongst the ancients. Amongst us, who have a stronger genius for writing, the operations from the writing are much stronger; for the raising of Shakspeare's passions is more from the excellency of the words and thoughts, than the justness of the occasion; and if he has been able to pick single occasions, he has never founded the whole reasonably; yet, by the genius of poetry in writing, he has succeeded.

Rapin attributes more to the *dictio*, that is, to the words and discourse of a tragedy, than Aristotle has done, who places them in the last rank of beauties; perhaps, only last in order, because they are the last product of the design, of the disposition or connexion of its parts, of the characters, of the manners of those characters, and of the thoughts proceeding from those manners. Rapin's words are remarkable:—It is not the admirable intrigue, the surprising events, and extraordinary incidents, that make the beauty of a tragedy; it is the discourses, when they are natural and passionate.—So are Shakspeare's.

The parts of a poem, tragic or heroic, are,

1. The fable itself.

2. The order or manner of its contrivance in relation of the parts to the whole.

3. The manners, or decency of the characters, in speaking or acting what is proper for them, and proper to be shown by the poet.

4. The thoughts, which express the manners.

5. The words, which express those thoughts.

In the last of these, Homer excels Virgil; Virgil all other ancient poets; and Shakspeare all modern poets.

For the second of these, the order: the meaning is, that a fable ought to have a beginning, a middle, and an end, all just and natural; so that that part, *e. g.* which is the middle, could not naturally be the beginning or end, and so of the rest; all depend on one another, like the links of a curious chain. If terror and pity are only to be raised, certainly this author follows Aristotle's rules, and Sophocles' and Euripides' example; but joy may be raised too, and that doubly, either by seeing a wicked man punished, or a good man at last fortunate; or perhaps indignation, to see wickedness prosperous, and goodness depressed: both these may be profitable to the end of tragedy, reformation of manners; but the last improperly, only as it begets pity in the audience; though Aristotle, I confess, places tragedies of this kind in the second form.

He who undertakes to answer this excellent critique of Mr. Rymer, in behalf of our English poets against the Greek, ought to do it in this manner: either by yielding to him the greatest part of what he contends for, which consists in this, that the μῦθος, *i. e.* the design and conduct of it, is more conducing in the Greeks to those ends of tragedy which Aristotle and he propose, namely, to cause terror and pity; yet the granting this does not set the Greeks above the English poets.

But the answerer ought to prove two things. First, That the fable is not the greatest masterpiece of a tragedy, though it be the foundation of it.

* Rymer sets out with the old dogma, that no source of tragedy was legitimate, except that springing from pity or terror.

Secondly, That other ends, as suitable to the nature of tragedy, may be found in the English, which were not in the Greek.

Aristotle places the fable first; not *quoad dignitatem, sed quoad fundamentum:* for a fable, never so movingly contrived to those ends of his, pity and terror, will operate nothing on our affections, except the characters, manners, thoughts, and words, are suitable.

So that it remains for Mr. Rymer to prove, that in all those, or the greatest part of them, we are inferior to Sophocles and Euripides; and this he has offered at, in some measure; but, I think, a little partially to the ancients.

For the fable itself: it is in the English more adorned with episodes, and larger than in the Greek poets; consequently more diverting. For if the action be but one, and that plain, without any counter-turn of design or episode, *i. e.* under-plot, how can it be so pleasing as the English, which have both under-plot and a turned design, which keeps the audience in expectation of the catastrophe? whereas in the Greek poets we see through the whole design at first.

For the characters, they are neither so many nor so various in Sophocles and Euripides, as in Shakspeare and Fletcher; only they are more adapted to those ends of tragedy which Aristotle commends to us, pity and terror.

The manners flow from the characters, and consequently must partake of their advantages and disadvantages.

The thoughts and words, which are the fourth and fifth beauties of tragedy, are certainly more noble and more poetical in the English than in the Greek, which must be proved by comparing them somewhat more equitably than Mr. Rymer has done.

After all, we need not yield, that the English way is less conducing to move pity and terror, because they often show virtue oppressed and vice punished; where they do not both, or either, they are not to be defended.

And if we should grant that the Greeks performed this better, perhaps it may admit of dispute, whether pity and terror are either the prime, or at least the only ends of tragedy.

It is not enough that Aristotle has said so, for Aristotle drew his models of tragedy from Sophocles and Euripides; and if he had seen ours, might have changed his mind. And chiefly we have to say, (what I hinted on pity and terror, in the last paragraph save one,) that the punishment of vice and reward of virtue are the most adequate ends of tragedy, because most conducing to good example of life. Now pity is not so easily raised for a criminal, (and the ancient tragedy always represents its chief person such,) as it is for an innocent man; and the suffering of innocence and punishment of the offender is of the nature of English tragedy: contrarily, in the Greek, innocence is unhappy often, and the offender escapes. Then we are not touched with the sufferings of any sort of men so much as of lovers, and this was almost unknown to the ancients: so that they neither administered poetical justice, of which Mr. Rymer boasts, so well as we, neither knew they the best common-place of pity, which is love.

He therefore unjustly blames us for not building on what the ancients left us; for it seems, upon consideration of the premises, that we have wholly finished what they began.

My judgment on this piece is this: that it is extremely learned, but that the author of it is better read in the Greek than in the English poets; that all writers ought to study this critique, as the best account I have ever seen of the ancients; that the model of tragedy he has here given is excellent, and extremely correct; but that it is not the only model of all tragedy, because it is too much circumscribed in plot, characters, &c.; and lastly, that we may be taught here justly to admire and imitate the ancients, without giving them the preference, with this author, in prejudice to our own country.

Want of method in this excellent treatise, makes the thoughts of the author sometimes obscure.

His meaning, that pity and terror are to be moved, is, that they are to be moved as the means conducing to the ends of tragedy, which are pleasure and instruction.

And these two ends may be thus distinguished. The chief end of the poet is to please; for his immediate reputation depends on it.

The great end of the poem is to instruct, which is performed by making pleasure the vehicle of that instruction; for poesy is an art, and all arts are made to profit.—*Rapin.*

The pity which the poet is to labour for, is for the criminal, not for those or him whom he has murdered, or who have been the occasion of the tragedy. The terror is likewise in the punishment of the same criminal, who, if he be represented too great an offender, will not be pitied; if altogether innocent, his punishment will be unjust.

Another obscurity is, where he says, Sophocles perfected tragedy by introducing the third actor;* that is, he meant, three kinds of action;

* "After much new modelling, many changes, and alterations, Æschylus came with a second actor on the stage, and lessened the business of the cho-

one company singing, or speaking; another playing on the music; a third dancing.

To make a true judgment in this competition betwixt the Greek poets and the English, in tragedy:

Consider, first, how Aristotle has defined a tragedy. Secondly, what he assigns the end of it to be. Thirdly, what he thinks the beauties of it. Fourthly, the means to attain the end proposed.

Compare the Greek and English tragic poets justly, and without partiality, according to those rules.

Then, secondly, consider whether Aristotle has made a just definition of tragedy; of its parts, of its ends, and of its beauties; and whether he, having not seen any others but those of Sophocles, Euripides, &c. had, or truly could determine what all the excellencies of tragedy are, and wherein they consist.

Next, show in what ancient tragedy was deficient; for example, in the narrowness of its plots, and fewness of persons; and try whether that be not a fault in the Greek poets, and whether their excellency was so great, when the variety was visibly so little; or whether what they did was not very easy to do.

Then make a judgment on what the English have added to their beauties; as, for example, not only more plot, but also new passions, as, namely, that of love, scarce touched on by the ancients, except in this one example of Phædra, cited by Mr. Rymer; and in that how short they were of Fletcher.

Prove also that love, being an heroic passion, is fit for tragedy, which cannot be denied, because of the example alleged of Phædra; and how far Shakspeare has outdone them in friendship, &c.

To return to the beginning of this inquiry; consider, if pity and terror be enough for tragedy to move; and I believe, upon a true definition of tragedy, it will be found that its work extends farther, and that is, to reform manners, by a delightful representation of human life in great persons, by way of dialogue. If this be true, then not only pity and terror are to be moved, as the only means to bring us to virtue, but generally love to virtue, and hatred to vice, by showing the rewards of one, and punishments of the other; at least, by rendering virtue always amiable, though it be shown unfortunate, and vice detestable, though it be shown triumphant.

If, then, the encouragement of virtue, and discouragement of vice, be the proper ends of poetry in tragedy, pity and terror, though good means, are not the only. For all the passions in their turns, are to be set in a ferment; as joy, anger, love, fear, are to be used as the poet's common-places, and a general concernment for the principal actors is to be raised, by making them appear such in their characters, their words, and actions, as will interest the audience in their fortunes.

And if, after all, in a larger sense, pity comprehends this concernment for the good, and terror includes detestation for the bad, then let us consider whether the English have not answered this end of tragedy, as well as the ancients, or perhaps better.

And here Mr. Rymer's objections against these plays are to be impartially weighed, that we may see whether they are of weight enough to turn the balance against our countrymen.

It is evident, those plays which he arraigns, have moved both those passions in a high degree upon the stage.

To give the glory of this away from the poet, and to place it upon the actors, seems unjust.*

One reason is, because whatever actors they have found, the event has been the same, that is, the same passions have been always moved; which shows, that there is something of force and merit in the plays themselves, conducing to the design of raising these two passions: and suppose them ever to have been excellently acted, yet action only adds grace, vigour, and

rus proportionably. But Sophocles adding a third actor and painted scenes, gave, in Aristotle's opinion, the utmost perfection to tragedy."—*Rymer's Remarks*, p. 13.

* Alluding to the following remarks of Rymer transferring the pleasing effect of the plays, which he censures, to the lively representation. "Amongst those who will be objecting against the doctrine I lay down, may peradventure appear a sort of men who have remembered so and so; and value themselves upon their experience. I may write by the book (say they) what I have a mind, but they know what will please. These are a kind of stage-quacks and empirics in poetry, who have got a receipt to please; and no collegiate like them for purging the passions.

"These say (for instance) a "King and no King" pleases. I say the comical part pleases.

"I say that Mr. Hart pleases; most of the business falls to his share, and what he delivers, every one takes upon content; their eyes are prepossessed and charmed by his action, before aught of the poet's can approach their ears; and to the most wretched of characters, he gives a lustre and brilliance, which dazzles the sight, that the deformities in the poetry cannot be perceived."—*Remarks*, p. 5.

He has a similar observation in page 138:—"We may remember, however we find this scene of Melantius and Amintor written in the book, that at the theatre we have a good scene acted. There is work cut out, and both our Æsopus and Roscius are on the stage together: whatever defect may be in Amintor and Melantius, Mr. Hart and Mr. Mohun are wanting in nothing. To these we owe for what is pleasing in the scene; and to this scene we may impute the success of the "Maid's Tragedy."

more life, upon the stage, but cannot give it wholly where it is not first. But secondly, I dare appeal to those who have never seen them acted, if they have not found these two passions moved within them; and if the general voice will carry it, Mr. Rymer's prejudice will take off his single testimony.

This, being matter of fact, is reasonably to be established by this appeal; as if one man says it is night, when the rest of the world conclude it to be day, there needs no farther argument against him, that it is so.

If he urge, that the general taste is depraved, his arguments to prove this can at best but evince, that our poets took not the best way to raise those passions; but experience proves against him, that those means which they have used have been successful, and have produced them.

And one reason of that success is, in my opinion, this, that Shakspeare and Fletcher have written to the genius of the age and nation in which they lived; for though nature, as he objects, is the same in all places, and reason too the same, yet the climate, the age, the disposition of the people, to whom a poet writes, may be so different, that what pleased the Greeks would not satisfy an English audience.

And if they proceeded upon a foundation of truer reason to please the Athenians, than Shakspeare and Fletcher to please the English, it only shows, that the Athenians were a more judicious people; but the poet's business is certainly to please the audience.

Whether our English audience have been pleased hitherto with acorns, as he calls it, or with bread, is the next question; that is, whether the means which Shakspeare and Fletcher have used in their plays to raise those passions before named, be better applied to the ends by the Greek poets than by them. And perhaps we shall not grant him this wholly: let it be yielded, that a writer is not to run down with the stream, or to please the people by their own usual methods, but rather to reform their judgments,—it still remains to prove, that our theatre needs this total reformation.

The faults which he has found in their designs, are rather wittily aggravated in many places, than reasonably urged; and as much may be returned on the Greeks by one who were as witty as himself.

2. They destroy not, if they are granted, the foundation of the fabric, only take away from the beauty of the symmetry: for example, the faults in the character of the "King and no King"* are not as he makes them, such as render him detestable, but only imperfections which accompany human nature, and are for the most part excused by the violence of his love; so that they destroy not our pity or concernment for him. This answer may be applied to most of his objections of that kind.

And Rollo† committing many murders, when he is answerable but for one, is too severely arraigned by him, for it adds to our horror and detestation of the criminal; and poetic justice is not neglected neither, for we stab him in our minds for every offence which he commits; and the point which the poet is to gain on the audience is not so much in the death of an offender, as the raising a horror of his crimes.

That the criminal should neither be wholly guilty, nor wholly innocent, but so participating of both as to move both pity and terror, is certainly a good rule, but not perpetually to be observed; for that were to make all tragedies too much alike; which objection he foresaw, but has not fully answered.

To conclude, therefore; if the plays of the ancients are more correctly plotted, ours are more beautifully written. And if we can raise passions as high on worse foundations, it shows our genius in tragedy is greater; for, in all other parts of it, the English have manifestly excelled them.

* After laying it down as a necessary rule, that a king in tragedy is, *ex jure*, a hero, Rymer proceeds to arraign the character of Arbaces, for his vain glory, presumption, incestuous passion for his sister, and extravagance of language. He sums his character up in the words of the Irish inscription:

> For fierceness and for furiousness,
> Men call me the queen's mortar-piece.

† "When Rollo has murdered his brother, he stands condemned by the laws of poetry; and nothing remains but that the poet see him executed, and the poet is to answer for all the mischief committed afterwards. But Rollo we find has made his escape, and wo be to the chancellor, to the schoolmaster, and to the chancellor's man; for those are to be men of this world no longer. Here is like to be poetical justice, so many lives taken away, and but the life of one guilty person to answer for all; and is not this a strange method of killing? If the planets had contrived him for a cock of thirteen, his first victory should not have been the most important; he should first have practised on his subjects, and have risen by degrees to the height of iniquity. His brother sovereign was his top-murder; nothing remained after that, unless it were his lady-mother."

THE LIFE OF PLUTARCH.

In 1683 appeared the first volume of a translation of Plutarch's Lives, executed by several hands. Among the persons engaged in this undertaking, Mr. Malone enumerates "Richard Duke, and Knightly Chetwood, Fellows of Trinity College, in Cambridge; Paul Rycaut, Esq.; Thomas Creech, of Wadham College, Oxford, the translator of Horace, &c.; Edward Brown, M. D. author of Travels in Germany, &c.; Dr. Adam Littleton, author of the Latin Dictionary; John Caryl, Esq. I believe the friend of Pope; Mr. Joseph Arrowsmith; Thomas Rymer, Esq.; Dr. William Oldys; John Evelyn, Esq.; and Mr. Somers, afterwards Lord Somers, who translated the Life of Alcibiades, though his name is not prefixed to it. Beside the persons here enumerated, twenty-nine others were engaged in this work; so that the total number of the translators was forty-one. Dryden translated none of the Lives."

Dryden was induced to honour this work, so creditable to those who had undertaken it, with a Dedication, and Life of Plutarch. The Dedication is addressed to the great Duke of Ormond, whom Dryden had celebrated, in "Absalom and Achitophel," under the name of Barzillai. It is doing no injustice to the other great qualities of Ormond, to say, that his generous and unwearied protection of Dryden will not be the soonest forgotten. The poet's feelings towards this noble family were expressed in the preface to the "Fables," his last great work.

The publication and translation of "Plutarch's Lives" was not completed until 1686, when the last volume appeared. The following remarkable advertisement was prefixed to the work; which, from internal evidence, Mr. Malone ascribes to our author, although bearing the name, and written in the character of Jacob Tonson, the publisher of the work.

"You have here the first volume of 'Plutarch's Lives' turned from Greek into English; and give me leave to say, the first attempt of doing it from the originals. You may expect the remainder in four more, one after another, as fast as they may conveniently be despatched from the press. It is not my business, or pretence, to judge of a work of this quality; neither do I take upon me to recommend it to the world, any farther than under the office of a fair and careful publisher, and in discharge of a trust deposited in my hands for the service of my country, and for a common good. I am not yet so insensible of the authority and reputation of so great a name, as not to consult the honour of the author, together with the benefit and satisfaction of the bookseller, as well as of the reader, in this undertaking. In order to which ends, I have, with all possible respect and industry, besought, solicited, and obtained, the assistance of persons equal to the enterprise, and not only critics in the tongue, but men of known fame and abilities for style and ornament; but I shall rather refer you to the learned and ingenious translators of this first part, (whose names you will find in the next page,) as a specimen of what you may promise yourself from the rest.

"After this right done to the Greek author, I shall not need to say what profit and delight will accrue to the English reader from this version, when he shall see this illustrious piece in his own mother tongue, and the very spirit of the original transfused into the traduction; and in one word, 'Plutarch's Worthies' made yet more famous, by a translation that gives a farther lustre even to Plutarch himself.

"Now as to the bookseller's part, I must justify myself, that I have done all that to me belonged; that is to say, I have been punctually faithful to all my commissions toward the correctness and decency of the work; and I have said to myself, that which I now say to the public,—It is impossible but a book that comes into the world with so many circumstances of dignity, usefulness, and esteem, must turn to account."

TO

HIS GRACE

THE

DUKE OF ORMOND, &c.

MY LORD,

LUCRETIUS, endeavouring to prove from the principles of his philosophy, that the world had a casual beginning from the concourse of atoms, and that men, as well as the rest of animals, were produced from the vital heat and moisture of their mother earth, from the same principles is bound to answer this objection,—why men are not daily formed after the same manner; which he tells us, is, because the kindly warmth and procreative faculty of the ground is now worn out; the sun is a disabled lover; and the earth is past her teeming time.

Though religion has informed us better of our origin, yet it appears plainly, that not only the bodies, but the souls of men, have decreased from the vigour of the first ages; that we are not more short of the stature and strength of those gigantic heroes, than we are of their understanding and their wit. To let pass those happy patriarchs, who were striplings at fourscore, and had afterwards seven or eight hundred years before them to beget sons and daughters, and to consider man in reference only to his mind, and that no higher than the age of Socrates, how vast a difference is there betwixt the productions of those souls, and these of ours? how much better Plato, Aristotle, and the rest of the philosophers understood nature; Thucydides and Herodotus adorned history; Sophocles, Euripides, and Menander advanced poetry, than those dwarfs of wit and learning who succeeded them in after times? That age was most famous amongst the Greeks which ended with the death of Alexander; amongst the Romans, learning seemed again to revive and flourish in the century which produced Cicero, Varro, Sallust, Livy, Lucretius, and Virgil: and after a short interval of years, wherein Nature seemed to take a breathing time for a second birth, there sprung up under the Vespasians, and those excellent princes who succeeded them, a race of memorable wits, such as were the two Plinies, Tacitus, and Suetonius; and, as if Greece was emulous of the Roman learning, under the same favourable constellation was born the famous philosopher and historian, Plutarch; than whom antiquity has never produced a man more generally knowing, or more virtuous; and no succeeding age has equalled him.

His Lives, both in his own esteem and that of others, accounted the noblest of his works, have been long since rendered into English; but as that translation was only from the French,* so it suffered this double disadvantage; first, that it was but a copy of a copy, and that too but lamely taken from the Greek original; secondly, that the English language was then unpolished, and far from the perfection which it has since attained; so that the first version is not only ungrammatical and ungraceful, but in many places almost unintelligible. For which reasons, and lest so useful a piece of history should lie oppressed under the rubbish of antiquated words, some ingenious and learned gentlemen have undertaken this task: and what would have been the labour of one man's life, will, by the several endeavours of many, be accomplished in the compass of a year. How far they have succeeded in this laudable attempt, to me it belongs not to determine, who am too much a party to be a judge. But I have the honour to be commissioned from the translators of this volume to inscribe their labours and my own, with all humility, to your grace's name and patronage; and never was any man more ambitious of an employment of which he was so little worthy. Fortune has at last gratified that earnest desire I have always had to show my devotion to your grace, though I despair of paying you my acknowledgments. And of all other opportunities, I have happened on the most favourable to myself, who, having never been able to produce any thing of my own which could be worthy of your view, am supplied by the assistance of my friends, and honoured with the presentation of their labours. The author they have translated has been long familiar to

* Sir Thomas North's translation, published in 1579, was executed through the medium of the French translation, by Jaques Amiot.

you, who have been conversant in all sorts of history both ancient and modern, and have formed the idea of your most noble life from the instructions and examples contained in them, both in the management of public affairs, and in the private offices of virtue; in the enjoyment of your better fortune, and sustaining of your worse; in habituating yourself to an easy greatness; in repelling your enemies, in succouring your friends; and in all traverses of fortune, in every colour of your life, maintaining an inviolable fidelity to your sovereign. It is long since that I have learned to forget the art of praising, but here the heart dictates to the pen; and I appeal to your enemies, (if so much generosity and good nature can have left you any,) whether they are not conscious to themselves that I have not flattered.

It is an age, indeed, which is only fit for satire, and the sharpest I have shall never be wanting to lance its villanies, and its ingratitude to the government. There are few men in it, who are capable of supporting the weight of a just and deserved commendation; but amongst those few there must always stand excepted the illustrious names of Ormond and of Ossory; a father and a son only worthy of each other. Never was one soul more fully infused into another's breast; never was so strong an impression made of virtue as that of your grace's into him; but though the stamp was deep, the subject which received it was of too fine a composition to be durable. Were not priority of time and nature in the case, it might have been doubted which of you had been most excellent; but Heaven snatched away the copy, to make the original more precious. I dare trust myself no farther on this subject; for after years of mourning, my sorrow is yet so green upon me, that I am ready to tax Providence for the loss of that heroic son: three nations had a general concernment in his death, but I had one so very particular, that all my hopes are almost dead with him; and I have lost so much, that I am past the danger of a second shipwreck. But he sleeps with an unenvied commendation; and has left your grace the sad legacy of all those glories which he derived from you: an accession which you wanted not, who were so rich before in your own virtues, and that high reputation which is the product of them.

A long descent of noble ancestors was not necessary to have made you great; but heaven threw it in as overplus when you were born. What you have done and suffered for two royal masters, has been enough to render you illustrious; so that you may safely waive the nobility of your birth, and rely on your actions for your fame. You have cancelled the debt which you owed to your progenitors, and reflect more brightness on their memory than you received from them.

Your native country, which Providence gave you not leave to preserve under one king, it has given you opportunity under another to restore. You could not save it from the chastisement which was due to its rebellion, but you raised it from ruin after its repentance; so that the trophies of war were the portion of the conqueror, but the triumphs of peace were reserved for the vanquished. The misfortunes of Ireland were owing to itself, but its happiness and restoration to your grace. The rebellion against a lawful prince was punished by an usurping tyrant, but the fruits of his victory were the rewards of a loyal subject. How much that noble kingdom has flourished under your grace's government, both the inhabitants and the crown are sensible: the riches of Ireland are increased by it, and the revenues of England are augmented. That which was a charge and burden of the government, is rendered an advantage and support; the trade and interest of both countries are united in a mutual benefit; they conspire to make each other happy; the dependence of the one is an improvement of its commerce, the pre-eminence of the other is not impaired by the intercourse, and common necessities are supplied by both. Ireland is no more a scion, to suck the nourishment from the mother tree; neither is it overtopped, or hindered from growth by the superior branches; but the roots of England diving, if I may dare to say it, underneath the seas, rise at a just distance on the neighboring shore, and there shoot up, and bear a product scarce inferior to the trunk from whence they sprung.

I may raise the commendation higher, and yet not fear to offend the truth; Ireland is a better penitent than England. The crime of rebellion was common to both countries, but the repentance of one island has been steady; that of the other, to its shame, has suffered a relapse; which shows the conversions of their rebels to have been real, that of ours to have been but counterfeit. The sons of guilty fathers there have made amends for the disloyalty of their families; but here the descendants of pardoned rebels have only waited their time to copy the wickedness of their parents, and, if possible, to outdo it. They disdain to hold their patrimonies by acts of grace and of indemnity; and by maintaining their old treasonable principles, make it apparent that they are still speculative traitors, for whether they are zealous sectaries, or profane republicans, (of which two sorts they are principally composed,) both our reformers o.

church and state pretend to a power superior to kingship. The fanatics derive their authority from the Bible, and plead religion to be antecedent to any secular obligation; by virtue of which argument, taking it for granted that their own worship is only true, they arrogate to themselves the right of disposing the temporal power according to their pleasure, — as that which is subordinate to the spiritual; so that the same reasons and scriptures which are urged by popes for the deposition of princes, are produced by sectaries for altering the succession. The episcopal reformation has manumized kings from the usurpation of Rome, for it preaches obedience and resignation to the lawful secular power; but the pretended reformation of our schismatics, is to set up themselves in the papal chair, and to make their princes only their trustees; so that, whether they or the Pope were uppermost in England, the royal authority were equally depressed: the prison of our kings would be the same; the gaolers only would be altered. The broad republicans are generally men of atheistic principles, nominal Christians, who are beholding to the font only that they are so called; otherwise Hobbists in their politics and morals. Every church is obliged to them that they own themselves of none, because their lives are too scandalous for any. Some of the sectaries are so proud, that they think they cannot sin; those commonwealth men are so wicked, that they conclude there is no sin. Lewdness, rioting, cheating, and debauchery, are their work-a-day practice; their more solemn crimes are unnatural lusts, and horrid murders.* Yet these are the patrons of the non-conformists; these are the swords and bucklers of God's cause, if his cause be that of separatists and rebels. It is not but these associates know each other at the bottom as well as Simeon knew Levi: the republicans are satisfied that the schismatics are hypocrites, and the schismatics are assured that the republicans are atheists; but their common principles of government are the chains that link them; for both hold kings to be creatures of their own making, and by inference to be at their own disposing; with this difference, notwithstanding, that the canting party face their pretences with a call from God, the debauched party with a commission from the people. So that if ever this ill-contrived and equivocal association should get uppermost, they would infallibly contend for the supreme right; and as it was formerly on their money, so now it would be in their interest; "God with us" would be set up on one side, and "the Commonwealth of England" on the other.* But I the less wonder at the mixture of these two natures, because two savage beasts of different species and sexes shut up together, will forget their enmity to satisfy their common lust; and it is no matter what kind of monster is produced betwixt them, so the brutal appetite be served. I more admire at a third party, who were loyal when rebellion was uppermost, and have turned rebels, (at least in principle,) since loyalty has been triumphant. Those of them whose services have not been rewarded, have some pretence for discontent; and yet they give the world to understand, that their honour was not their principle, but their interest. If they are old royalists, it is a sign their virtue is worn out and will bear no longer; if sons to royalists, they have probably been grafted on whig stocks, and grown out of kind, — like China oranges in Portugal: their mothers part has prevailed in them, and they are degenerated from the loyalty of their fathers.

But if they are such, as many of them evidently are, whose service has been not only fully but lavishly recompensed with honours and preferment, theirs is an ingratitude without parallel; they have destroyed their former merits, disowned the cause for which they fought, belied their youth, dishonoured their age; they have wrought themselves out of present enjoyments for imaginary hopes, and can never be trusted by their new friends, because they have betrayed their old. The greater and the stronger ties which some of them have had, are the deeper brands of their apostacy; for archangels were the first and most glorious of the whole creation; they were the morning work of God, and had the first impressions of his image, what creatures could be made; they were of kin to eternity itself, and wanting only that accession to be deities. Their fall was therefore more opprobrious than that of man, because they had no clay for their excuse; though I hope and wish the latter part of the allegory may not hold, and that repentance may be yet allowed them. But I delight not to dwell on so sad an object; let this part of the landscape be cast into shadows, that the heightenings of the other may appear more beautiful. For, as contraries, the nearer they are placed, are brighter, and the Venus is illustrated by the neighbourhood of the lazar, so the unblemished loyalty of your grace will shine more clearly, when set in competition with their stains.

* Lord Howard, Sir Thomas Armstrong, Ford Lord Grey, and others among the opposers of government, notorious for being libertines even beyond the license of that age, seem to be here pointed at.

* These devices were impressed on the coin struck by the commonwealth.

When the malady which had seized the nobler parts of Britain threw itself out into the limbs, and the first sores of it appeared in Scotland, yet no effects of it reached your province; Ireland stood untainted with that pest; the care of the physician prevented the disease, and preserved the country from infection. When that ulcer was rather stopped than cured, (for the causes of it still remained,) and that dangerous symptoms appeared in England; when the royal authority was here trodden under foot; when one plot was prosecuted openly, and another secretly fomented, yet even then was Ireland free from our contagion. And if some venomous creatures were produced in that nation, yet it appeared they could not live there; they shed their poison without effect; they despaired of being successfully wicked in their own country, and transported their evidence to another, where they knew it was vendible; where accusation was a trade, where forgeries were countenanced, where perjuries were rewarded, where swearing went for proof, and where the merchandise of death was gainful. That their testimony was at least discredited, proceeded not from its incoherence, for they were known by their own party when they first appeared; but their folly was then managed by the cunning of their tutors; they had still been believed had they still followed their instructors; but when their witness fell foul upon their friends, then they were proclaimed villains, discarded and disowned by those who sent for them; they seemed then first to be discovered for what they had been known too well before; they were decried as inventors of what only they betrayed; nay, their very wit was magnified, lest, being taken for fools, they might be thought too simple to forge an accusation.* Some of them still continue here detested by both sides, believed by neither, (for even their betters are at last uncased;) and some of them have received their hire in their own country. For perjury, which is malice to mankind, is always accompanied with other crimes; and though not punishable by our laws with death, yet draws a train of vices after it. The robber, the murderer, and the sodomite, have often hung up the forsworn villain; and what one sin took took on trust another sin has paid. These travelling locusts are at length swallowed up in their own Red Sea. Ireland, as well as England, is delivered from that flying plague; for the sword of justice in your grace's hand, like the rod of Moses, is stretched out against them; and the third part of his majesty's dominions is owing for its peace to your loyalty and vigilance.

But what Plutarch can this age produce to immortalize a life so noble? May some excellent historian at length be found, some writer not unworthy of his subject; but may his employment be long deferred! May many happy years continue you to this nation and your own; may your praises be celebrated late, that we may enjoy you living rather than adore you dead! And since yet there is not risen up amongst us any historian who is equal to so great an undertaking, let us hope that Providence has not assigned the workman, because his employment is to be long delayed; because it has reserved your grace for farther proofs of your unwearied duty, and a farther enjoyment of your fortune; in which, though no man has been less envied, because no other has more nobly used it, yet some droppings of the age's venom have been shed upon you. The supporters of the crown are placed too near it, to be exempted from the storm which was breaking over it. It is true, you stood involved in your own virtue, and the malice of your libellers could not sink through all those folds to reach you. Your innocence has defended you from their attacks, and your pen has so nobly vindicated that innocence, that it stands in need of no other second. The difference is as plainly seen betwixt sophistry and truth, as it is betwixt the style of a gentleman and the clumsy stiffness of a pedant. Of all historians, God deliver us from bigots; and of all bigots, from our sectaries! Truth is never to be expected from authors whose understandings are warped with enthusiasm; for they judge all actions, and their causes, by their own perverse principles, and a crooked line can never be the measure of a straight one. Mr. Hobbes was used to say,—that a man was always against reason, when reason was against a man:—so these authors are for obscuring truth, because truth would discover them. They are not historians of an action, but lawyers of a party; they are retained by their principles, and bribed by their interests; their narrations are an opening of their cause; and in the front of their histories there ought to be written the prologue of a pleading,—"I am for the plaintiff," or "I am for the defendant."

We have already seen large volumes of state collections, and church legends, stuffed with detected forgeries in some parts, and gaping with omissions of truth in others: not penned, I suppose, with so vain a hope as to cheat posterity but to advance some design in the present age· for these legerdemain authors are for telling sto-

* Alluding to the Irish witnesses in the time of the Popish Plot; one set of whom came over to England, on purpose to support by their evidence that supposed conspiracy, but afterwards turned against their employer Shaftesbury.

sies to keep their trick undiscovered, and to make their conveyance the more clean. What calumny your grace may expect from such writers, is already evident: but it will fare with them as it does with ill painters; a picture so unlike in all its features and proportions, reflects not on the original, but on the artist; for malice will make a piece more unresembling than ignorance; and he who studies the life, yet bungles, may draw some faint imitation of it, but he who purposely avoids nature, must fall into grotesque, and make no likeness. For my own part, I am of the former sort, and therefore presume not to offer my unskilfulness for so excellent a design as is your illustrious life. To pray for its prosperity and continuance is my duty, as it is my ambition to appear on all occasions,

Your grace's most obedient
and devoted servant,
JOHN DRYDEN.

THE

LIFE OF PLUTARCH.

I KNOW not by what fate it comes to pass, that historians, who give immortality to others, are so ill requited by posterity, that their actions and their fortunes are usually forgotten; neither themselves encouraged while they live, nor their memory preserved entire to future ages. It is the ingratitude of mankind to their greatest benefactors, that they who teach us wisdom by the surest ways, setting before us what we ought to shun or to pursue, by the examples of the most famous men whom they record, and by the experience of their faults and virtues, should generally live poor and unregarded; as if they were born only for the public, and had no interest in their own well-being, but were to be lighted up like tapers, and to waste themselves for the benefit of others. But this is a complaint too general, and the custom has been too long established to be remedied; neither does it wholly reach our author. He was born in an age which was sensible of his virtue, and found a Trajan to reward him, as Aristotle did an Alexander. But the historians who succeeded him have either been too envious or too careless of his reputation; none of them, not even his own countrymen, having given us any particular account of him; or if they have, yet their works are not transmitted to us; so that we are forced to glean from Plutarch what he has scattered in his writings concerning himself and his original; which (excepting that little memorial that Suidas, and some few others have left concerning him,) is all we cancollect relating to this great philosopher and historian.

He was born at Chæronea, a small city of Bœotia, in Greece, between Attica and Phocis, and reaching to both seas. The climate not much befriended by the heavens, for the air is thick and foggy; and consequently the inhabitants partaking of its influence, gross feeders and fat-witted, brawny and unthinking,—just the constitution of heroes, cut out for the executive and brutal business of war; but so stupid in the designing part, that in all the revolutions of Greece they were never masters, but only in those few years when they were led by Epaminondas, or Pelopidas. Yet this foggy air, this country of fat wethers, as Juvenal calls it, produced three wits, which were comparable to any three Athenians; Pindar, Epaminondas, and our Plutarch; to whom we may add a fourth, Sextus Chæronensis, the preceptor of the learned Emperor Marcus Aurelius, and the nephew of our author.

Chæronea, if we may give credit to Pausanias, in the ninth book of his description of Greece, was anciently called Arne, from Arne, the daughter of Æolus; but being situated to the west of Parnassus, in that lowland country, the natural unwholesomeness of the air was augmented by the evening vapours cast upon it from that mountain, which our late travellers describe to be full of moisture and marshy ground enclosed in the inequality of its ascents; and being also exposed to the winds which blew from that quarter, the town was perpetually unhealthful; for which reason, says my author, Chæron, the son of Apollo and Thero, made it be rebuilt, and turned it towards the rising sun, from whence the town became healthful, and consequently populous; in memory of which benefit it afterwards retained his name. But as etymologies are uncertain, and the Greeks, above all nations, given to fabulous derivations of names, especially when they tend to the honour of their country, I think we may be reasonably content to take the denomination of the town from its delightful or cheerful standing, as the word Chæron sufficiently implies.

But to lose no time in these grammatical etymologies, which are commonly uncertain guesses, it is agreed that Plutarch was here born; the year uncertain; but without dispute in the reign of Claudius.

Joh. Gerrard Vossius has assigned his birth in the latter end of that emperor; some other writers of his life have left it undecided whether then, or in the beginning of Nero's empire; but the most accurate Rualdus (as I find it in the Paris edition of Plutarch's Works) has mani-testy proved him to be born in the middle time of Claudius, or somewhat lower; for Plutarch, in the description at Delphos, (of which more hereafter,) remembers, that Ammonius, his master, disputed with him and his brother Lamprias concerning it, when Nero made his progress into Greece, which was in his twelfth year; and the question disputed could not be managed with so much learning as it was, by mere boys; therefore he was then sixteen, or rather eighteen years of age.

Xylander has observed, that Plutarch himself, in the Life of Pericles, and that of Antony, has mentioned both Nero and Domitian as his contemporaries. He has also left it on record in his Symposiacs, that his family was ancient in Chæronea, and that for many descents they had borne the most considerable offices in that petty commonwealth; the chiefest of which was known by the name of Archon amongst the Grecians, by that of Prætor Urbis among the Romans, and the dignity and power was not much different from that of our lord mayor of London. His great-grandfather, Nicarchus, perhaps enjoyed that office in the division of the empire betwixt Augustus Cæsar and Mark Antony; and when the civil wars ensued betwixt them, Chæronea was so hardly used by Antony's lieutenant or commissary there, that all the citizens, without exception, were servilely employed to carry on their shoulders a certain proportion of corn from Chæronea to the coast over against the island of Antycira, with the scourge held over them, if at any time they were remiss. Which duty, after once performing, being enjoined the second time with the same severity, just as they were preparing for their journey, the welcome news arrived that Mark Antony had lost the battle of Actium;* whereupon both the officers and soldiers belonging to him in Chæronea immediately fled for their own safety; and the provisions, thus collected, were distributed among the inhabitants of the city.

This Nicarchus, the great-grandfather of Plutarch, among other sons, had Lamprias, a man eminent for his learning, and a philosopher, of whom Plutarch has made frequent mention in his Symposiacs, or Table Conversations; and amongst the rest there is this observation of him,—that he disputed best, and unravelled the difficulties of philosophy with most success, when he was at supper, and well warmed with wine. These table entertainments were part of the education of those times, their discourses being commonly the canvassing and solution of some question, either philosophical or philological, always instructive, and usually pleasant; for the cups went round with the debate, and men were merry and wise together, according to the proverb. The father of Plutarch is also mentioned in those discourses, whom our author represents as arguing of several points in philosophy; but his name is nowhere to be found in any part of the works remaining to us. But yet he speaks of him as a man not ignorant in learning and poetry, as may appear by what he says, when he is introduced disputing in the Symposiacs; where also his prudence and humanity are commended in this following relation: "Being yet very young," says Plutarch, "I was joined in commission with another in an embassy to the proconsul, and my colleague falling sick, was forced to stay behind; so that the whole business was transacted by me alone. At my return, when I was to give account to the commonwealth of my proceedings, my father, rising from his seat, openly enjoined me not to name myself in the singular number,—*I did thus, or thus I said to the proconsul,*—but, *thus we did, and thus we said,* always associating my companion with me, though absent in the management." This was done to observe, as I suppose, the point of good manners with his colleague; that of respect to the government of the city, who had commissioned both, to avoid envy; and perhaps more especially to take off the forwardness of a pert young minister, commonly too apt to overvalue his own services, and to quote himself on every inconsiderable occasion.

The father of Plutarch had many children besides him; Timon and Lamprias, his brothers, were bred up with him, all three instructed in the liberal sciences, and in all parts of philosophy. It is manifest from our author, that they lived together in great friendliness, and in great veneration to their grandfather and father. What affection Plutarch bore in particular to his brother Timon, may be gathered from these words of his: "As for myself, though fortune on several occasions has been favourable to me, I have no obligation so great to her as the kindness and entire friendship which my brother Timon has always borne, and still bears me; and this is so evident, that it cannot but be noted by every one of our acquaintance." Lamprias, the youngest of the three, is introduced by him in his "Morals," as one of a sweet and pleasant conversation, inclined to mirth and raillery; or, as we say in English, a well-humoured man, and a good companion.

The whole family being thus addicted to philosophy, it is no wonder if our author was initiated betimes in study, to which he was natu-

* Fought A. U. C. 724.

ally inclined; in pursuit of which he was so happy to fall into good hands at first, being recommended to the care of Ammonius an Egyptian, who, having taught philosophy with great reputation at Alexandria, and from thence travelling into Greece, settled himself at last in Athens, where he was well received, and generally respected. At the end of Themistocles his life, Plutarch relates, that being young, he was a pensioner in the house of this Ammonius; and in his Symposiacs he brings him in disputing with his scholars, and giving them instruction: for the custom of those times was very much different from these of ours, where the greatest part of our youth is spent in learning the words of dead languages. The Grecians, who thought all barbarians but themselves, despised the use of foreign tongues; so that the first elements of their breeding was the knowledge of nature, and the accommodation of that knowledge, by moral precepts, to the service of the public, and the private offices of virtue: the masters employing one part of their time in reading to, and discoursing with, their scholars, and the rest in appointing them their several exercises either in oratory or philosophy, and setting them to declaim and to dispute amongst themselves. By this liberal sort of education, study was so far from being a burden to them, that in a short time it became a habit; and philosophical questions and criticisms of humanity were their usual recreations at their meals. Boys lived then as the better sort of men do now; and their conversation was so well-bred and manly, that they did not plunge out of their depth into the world, when they grew up, but slid easily into it, and found no alteration in their company. Amongst the rest, the reading and quotations of poets were not forgotten at their suppers, and in their walks; but Homer, Euripides, and Sophocles, were the entertainment of their hours of freedom. Rods and ferulas were not used by Ammonius, as being properly the punishment of slaves, and not the correction of ingenuous freeborn men; at least to be only exercised by parents, who had the power of life and death over their own children; as appears by the example of this Ammonius, thus related by our author:

"Our master," says he, "one time perceiving, at his afternoon lecture, that some of his scholars had eaten more largely than became the moderation of students, immediately commanded one of his freedmen to take his own son, and scourge him in our sight; because, said the philosopher, my young gentleman could not eat his dinner without poignant sauce, or vinegar; and at the same time he cast his eye on all of us; so that every criminal was given to understand, that he had a share in the reprehension, and that the punishment was as well deserved by all the rest, had the philosopher not known that it exceeded his commission to inflict it."

Plutarch, therefore, having the assistance of such a master, in a few years advanced to admiration in knowledge; and that without first travelling into foreign parts, or acquiring any foreign tongue; though the Roman language at that time was not only vulgar in Rome itself, but generally through the extent of that vast empire, and in Greece, which was a member of it, as our author has remarked towards the end of his Platonic Questions. For, like a true philosopher, who minded things, not words, he strove not even to cultivate his mother tongue with any great exactness; and himself confesses, in the beginning of Demosthenes his life, that during his abode in Italy, and at Rome, he had neither the leisure to study, nor so much as to exercise the Roman language, (I suppose he means to write in it, rather than to speak it,) as well by reason of the affairs he managed, as that he might acquit himself to those who were desirous to be instructed by him in philosophy: insomuch, that till the declination of his age, he began not to be conversant in Latin books; in reading of which it happened somewhat oddly to him, that he learned not the knowledge of things by words, but, by the understanding and use he had of things, attained to the knowledge of words which signified them: just as Adam (setting aside divine illumination) called the creatures by their proper names, by first understanding of their natures. But for the delicacies of the tongue, the turns of the expressions, the figures and connexions of words, in which consists the beauty of that language, he plainly tells us, that though he much admired them, yet they required too great labour for a man in age, and plunged in business, to attain perfectly; which compliment I should be willing to believe from a philosopher, if I did not consider that Dion Cassius, nay even Herodian and Appian after him, as well as Polybius before him, by writing the Roman History in the Greek language, had shown as manifest a contempt of Latin, in respect of the other, as Frenchmen now do of English, which they disdain to speak while they live among us; but, with great advantage to their trivial conceptions, drawing the discourse into their own language, have learned to despise our better thoughts, which must come deformed and lame in conversation to them, as being transmitted in a tongue of which we are not masters. This is to arrogate a superiority in nature over us, as undoubtedly the Grecians did over their conquerors, by establishing their language for a standard; it being become so much a mode to speak and write Greek in Tully's time, that with some indignation I have read his Epistles to Atticus, in which he desires to have his own consulship written by his friend in the Grecian language, which he afterwards performed himself; a vain attempt, in my opinion, for any man to endeavour to excel in a tongue which he was not born to speak. This, though it be digression, yet deserves to be considered at more leisure; for the honour of our wit and writings, which are of a more solid make than that of our neighbours, is concerned in it.

But to return to Plutarch. As it was his good fortune to be moulded first by masters the most excellent in their kind, so it was his own virtue to suck in with an incredible desire, and earnest application of mind, their wise instructions; and it was also his prudence so to manage his health by moderation of diet and bodily exercise, as to preserve his parts without decay to a great old age; to be lively and vigorous to the last, and to preserve himself to his own enjoyments, and to the profit of mankind: which was not difficult for him to perform, having received from nature a constitution capable of labour, and from the domestic example of his parents, a sparing sobriety of diet, a temperance in other pleasures, and, above all, a habitude of commanding his passions in order to his health. Thus principled and grounded, he considered with himself, that a larger communication with learned men was necessary for his accomplishment; and therefore, having a soul insatiable of knowledge, and being ambitious to excel in all kinds of science, he took up a resolution to travel. Egypt was at that time, as formerly it had been, famous for learning; and probably the mysteriousness of their doctrine might tempt him, as it had done Pythagoras and others, to converse with the priesthood of that country, which appears to have been particularly his business by the treatise of "Isis and Osiris," which he has left us; in which he shows himself not meanly versed in the ancient theology and philosophy of those wise men. From Egypt returning into Greece, he visited in his way all the academies or schools of the several philosophers, and gathered from them many of those observations with which he has enriched posterity.

Besides this, he applied himself with extreme diligence to collect not only all books which were excellent in their kind, and already published, but also all sayings and discourses of wise men, which he had heard in conversation, or which he had received from others by tradition; as likewise the records and public instruments preserved in cities which he had visited in his travels, and which he afterwards scattered through his works. To which purpose he took a particular journey to Sparta, to search the archives of that famous commonwealth, to understand thoroughly the model of their ancient government, their legislators, their kings, and their Ephori; digesting all their memorable deeds and sayings with so much care, that he has not omitted those even of their women, or their private soldiers; together with their customs, their decrees, their ceremonies, and the manner of their public and private living, both in peace and war. The same methods he also took in divers other commonwealths, as his Lives, and his Greek and Roman Questions, sufficiently testify. Without these helps, it had been impossible for him to leave in writing so many particular observations of men and manners, and as impossible to have gathered them without conversation and commerce with the learned antiquaries of his time. To these he added a curious collection of ancient statues, medals, inscriptions, and paintings, as also of proverbial sayings, epigrams, epitaphs, apophthegms, and other ornaments of history, that he might leave nothing unswept behind him. And as he was continually in company with men of learning, in all professions, so his memory was always on the stretch to receive and lodge their discourses; and his judgment perpetually employed in separating his notions, and distinguishing which were fit to be preserved, and which to be rejected.

By benefit of this, in little time he enlarged his knowledge to a great extent in every science. Himself, in the beginning of the treatise which he has composed of Content and Peace of Mind, makes mention of those collections, or commonplaces, which he had long since drawn together for his own particular occasions; and it is from this rich cabinet that he has taken out those excellent pieces which he has distributed to posterity, and which give us occasion to deplore the loss of the residue, which either the injury of time, or the negligence of copiers, have denied to us. On this account, though we need not doubt to give him this general commendation, that he was ignorant of no sort of learning, yet we may justly add this further,—that whoever will consider, through the whole body of his works, either the design, the method, or the contexture of his discourses, whether historical or moral, or questions of natural philosophy, or solutions of problems mathematical; whether he arraigns the opinions of other sects, or establishes the doctrines of his own; in all these kinds there will be found both the harmony of order, and the beauty of easiness: his reasons so solid and convincing, his inductions so pleasant and agreeable to all sorts of readers, that it must be acknowledged he was master of every subject which he treated, and treated none but what were improvable to the benefit of instruction. For we may perceive in his writings the desire he had to imprint his precepts in the souls of his readers, and to lodge morality in families, nay even to exalt it to the thrones of sovereign princes, and to make it the rule and measure of their government. Finding that there were many sects of philosophers then in vogue, he searched into the foundation of all their principles and opinions; and not content with this disquisition, he traced them to their several fountains; so that the Pythagorean, Epicurean, Stoic, and Peripatetic philosophy, were familiar to him. And though it may be easily observed, that he was chiefly inclined to follow Plato, whose memory he so much reverenced, that annually he celebrated his birth-day, and also that of Socrates; yet he modestly contained himself within the bounds of the latter academy, and was content, like Cicero, only to propound and weigh opinions, leaving the judgment of his readers free, without presuming to decide dogmatically. Yet it is to be confessed, that in the midst of this moderation he opposed the two extremes of the Epicurean and Stoic sects; both which he has judiciously combated in several of his treatises, and both upon the same account,—because they pretend too much to certainty in their dogmas, and to impose them with too great arrogance; which he, who, following the Academists, doubted more and pretended less, was no way able to support. The Pyrrhonians, or grosser sort of Skeptics, who bring all certainty in question, and startle even at the notions of common sense, appeared as absurd to him on the other side; for there is a kind of positiveness in granting nothing to be more likely on one part than on another, which his Academy avoided by inclining the balance to that hand where the most weighty reasons, and probability of truth, were visible. The moral philosophy, therefore, was his chiefest aim, because the principles of it admitted of less doubt; and because they were most conducing to the benefit of human life. For, after the example of Socrates, he had found, that the speculations of natural philosophy were more delightful than solid and profitable; that they were abstruse and thorny, and much of sophism in the solution of appearances:—that the mathematics, indeed, could reward his pains with many demonstrations, but though they made him wiser, they made him not more virtuous, and therefore attained not the end of happiness: for which reason, though he had far advanced in that study, yet he made it but his recreation, not his business. Some problem of it was his usual divertisement at supper, which he mingled also with pleasant and more light discourses; for he was no sour philosopher, but passed his time as merrily as he could, with reference to virtue. He forgot not to be pleasant while he instructed, and entertained his friends with so much cheerfulness and good humour, that his learning was not nauseous to them; neither were they afraid of his company another time. He was not so austere as to despise riches, but being in possession of a large fortune, he lived, though not splendidly, yet plentifully; and suffered not his friends to want that part of his estate which he thought superfluous to a philosopher.

The religion he professed, to speak the worst of it, was heathen. I say, the religion he *professed*; for it is no way probable that so great a philosopher, and so wise a man, should believe the superstitions and fopperies of Paganism; but that he accommodated himself to the use and received customs of his country. He was indeed a priest of Apollo, as himself acknowledges; but that proves him not to have been a Polytheist.

I have ever thought, that the wise men in all ages have not much differed in their opinions of religion; I mean, as it is grounded on human reason: for reason, as far as it is right, must be the same in all men; and truth being but one, they must consequently think in the same train. Thus it is not to be doubted but the religion of Socrates, Plato, and Plutarch, was not different in the main; who doubtless believed in the identity of one Supreme Intellectual Being, which we call God. But because they who have written the Life of Plutarch in other languages, are contented barely to assert that our author believed one God, without quoting those passages of his which would clear the point, I will give you two of them, amongst many, in his "Morals." The first is in his book of the Cessation of Oracles; where arguing against the Stoics, (in behalf of the Platonists,) who disputed against the plurality of worlds with this argument,—"That if there were many worlds, how then could it come to pass that there was one only Fate, and one Providence to guide them all? (for it was granted by the Platonists that there was but one;) and why should not many Jupiters or gods be necessary for government of many worlds?" To this Plutarch answers,—"That this their captious question was but trifling: for where is the necessity of supposing many Jupiters for this plurality of worlds, when one excellent Being, endued with mind and reason, such as he is whom we acknowledge *o* be the Father and Lord of all things, is sufficient to direct and rule these worlds; whereas if there were more Supreme Agents, their decrees must still be the more absurd and contradictious to one another." I pretend not this passage to be translated word for word, but it is the sense of the whole, though the order of the sentence be inverted. The other is more plain; it is in his comment on the word ΕΙ, or those two letters inscribed on the gates of the temple at Delphos; where, having given the several opinions concerning it, as first, that *εἰ* signifies *if*, because all the questions which were made to Apollo began with *If*: as suppose they asked,—*If* the Grecians should overcome the Persians,—*If* such a marriage should come to pass, &c.; and afterwards, that *εἶ* might signify *thou art*, as the second person of the present tense of *εἰμί*, intimating thereby the being or perpetuity of being belonging to Apollo, as a god (in the same sense that God expressed himself to Moses,—I AM *hath sent thee*:) Plutarch subjoins, (as inclining to this latter opinion,) these following words:—"*εἶ ἕν* (says he) signifies, *thou art one*, for there are not many deities, but only one:" Continues, "I mean not one in the aggregate sense, as we say—one army, or one body of men, constituted of many individuals, but that which is, must of necessity be one; and to be, implies to be one. One is that which is a simple being, uncompounded, or free from mixture; therefore to be one in this sense, is only consistent with a nature pure in itself, and not capable of alteration or decay."

That he was no Christian, is manifest; yet he is nowhere found to have spoken with contumely of our religion, like the other writers of his age and those who succeeded him. Theodoret says of him, "That he had heard of our holy gospel, and inserted many of our sacred mysteries in his works;" which we may easily believe, (because the Christian churches were then spread in Greece, and Pliny the younger was at the same time conversant amongst them in Asia,) though that part of our author's works is not now extant, from whence Theodoret might gather those passages. But we need not wonder that a philosopher was not easy to embrace the divine mysteries of our faith. A modern God, as our Saviour was to him, was of hard digestion to a man, who probably despised the vanities and fabulous relations of all the old. Besides, a crucified Saviour of mankind; a doctrine attested by illiterate disciples; the author of it a Jew, whose nation at that time was despicable, and his doctrine but an innovation among that despised people, to which the learned of his own country gave no credit, and which the magistrates of his nation punished with an ignominious death; the scene of his miracles acted in an obscure corner of the world; his being from eternity, yet born in time; his resurrection and ascension; these, and many more particulars, might easily choke the faith of a philosopher, who believed no more than what he could deduce from the principles of nature; and that too with a doubtful academical assent, or rather an inclination to assent to probability, which he judged was wanting in this new religion. These circumstances considered, though they plead not an absolute invincible ignorance in his behalf, yet they amount at least to a degree of it: for either he thought them not worth weighing, or rejected them when weighed; and in both cases he must of necessity be ignorant, because he could not know without revelation, and the revelation was not to him.

But leaving the soul of Plutarch, with our charitable wishes, to his Maker, we can only trace the rest of his opinions in religion from his philosophy, which we have said in the general to be Platonic; though it cannot also be denied, that there was a tincture in it of the Electic sect, which was begun by Potamon under the empire of Augustus, and which selected from all the other sects what seemed most probable in their opinions, not adhering singularly to any of them, nor rejecting every thing. I will only touch his belief of spirits. In his two Treatises of Oracles, the one concerning the reason of their cessation, the other inquiring why they were not given in verse, as in former times, he seems to assert the Pythagorean doctrine of transmigration of souls. We have formerly shown, that he owned the unity of a Godhead, whom, according to his attributes, he calls by several names; as Jupiter, from his almighty power; Apollo, from his wisdom; and so of the rest; but, under him, he places those beings whom he styles Genii, or Demons, of a middle nature betwixt divine and human: for he thinks it absurd, that there should be no mean betwixt the two extremes of an immortal and a mortal being; that there cannot be in nature so vast a flaw, without some intermedial kind of life, partaking of them both. As, therefore, we find the intercourse betwixt the soul and body to be made by the animal spirits, so, betwixt divinity and humanity, there is this species of demons, who, having first been men, and following the strict rules of virtue, had purged off the grossness and feculency of their earthly being, are exalted into these genii, and are from thence either raised higher into an ethereal life, if they still continue virtuous, or tumbled down again into mortal bodies, and sinking into flesh, after they have lost that purity which constituted their glorious being. And this sort of genii are those, who, as our author imagines, presided over oracles; spirits which have so much of their terrestrial principles remaining in them, as to be subject to passions and inclinations; usually beneficent, sometimes malevolent, to mankind, according as they refine themselves, or gather dross, and are declining into mortal bodies. The cessation, or rather the decrease of oracles, (for some of them were still remaining in Plutarch's time,) he attributes either to the death of those demons, (as appears by the story of the Egyptian Thamus, who was commanded to declare that the great god Pan was dead,) or to their forsaking of those places where they formerly gave out their oracles, from whence they were driven by stronger genii into banishment for a certain revolution of ages. Of this last nature was the war of the giants against the gods; the dispossession of Saturn by Jupiter: the banishment of Apollo from heaven; the fall of Vulcan, and many others; all which, according to our author, were the battles of these genii, or demons, amongst themselves. But supposing, as Plutarch evidently does, that these spirits administered, under the Supreme Being, the affairs of men, taking care of the virtuous, punishing the bad, and sometimes communicating with the best, (as particularly the genius of Socrates always warned him of approaching dangers, and taught him to avoid them,) I cannot but wonder, that every one who has hitherto written Plutarch's life, and particularly Rualdus, the most knowing of them all, should so confidently affirm, that these oracles were given by bad spirits according to Plutarch. As Christians, indeed, we may think them so; but that Plutarch so thought, is a most apparent falsehood. It is enough, to convince a reasonable man, that our author, in his old age, (and that then he doted not we may see by the Treatise he has written, that old men ought to have the management of public affairs,) I say, that then he initiated himself in the sacred rites of Delphos, and died, for aught we know, Apollo's priest. Now, it is not to be imagined that he thought the god he served a cacodemon, or, as we call him, a devil. Nothing could be farther from the opinion and practice of this holy philosopher than so gross an impiety. The story of the Pythias or Priestess of Apollo, which he relates immediately before the ending of that Treatise concerning the Cessation of Oracles, confirms my assertion, rather than shakes it; for it is there delivered, "That going with great reluctation into the sacred place to be inspired, she came out foaming at the mouth, her eyes goggling, her breast heaving, her voice undistinguishable and shrill, as if she had an earthquake within her, labouring for vent; and, in short, that thus tormented with the god, whom she was not able to support, she died distracted in a few days after." For he had said before, "that the divineress ought to have no perturbations of mind, or impure passions, at the time when she was to consult the oracle; and if she had, she was no more fit to be inspired, than an instrument untuned to render a harmonious sound." And he gives us to suspect, by what he says at the close of this relation "that this Pythias had not lived chastely for some time before it." So that her death appears more like a punishment inflicted for loose living by some holy power, than the mere malignancy of a spirit delighted naturally in mischief.—There is another observation, which indeed comes nearer to their purpose, which I will digress so far as to relate, because it somewhat appertains to our own country:—"There are many islands (says he) which lie scattered about Britain, after the manner of our Sporades. They are unpeopled, and some of them are called the islands of the Heroes, or the Genii. One Demetrius was sent by the emperor [who, by computation of the time, must either be Caligula or Claudius] to discover those parts; and arriving at one of the islands, next adjoining to the fore-mentioned, which was inhabited by some few Britons, (but those held sacred and inviolable by all their countrymen,) immediately after his arrival, the air grew black and troubled, strange apparitions were seen, the winds raised a tempest, and fiery spouts, or whirlwinds, appeared dancing towards the earth. When these prodigies were ceased, the islanders informed him, that some one of the aerial beings, superior to our nature, then ceased to live. For as a taper, while yet burning, affords a pleasant harmless light, but is noisome and offensive when extinguished, so those heroes shine benignly on us, and do us good; but at their death turn all things topsyturvy, raise up tempests, and infect the air with pestilential vapours." By those holy and inviolable men, there is no question but he means our Druids, who were nearest to the Pythagoreans of any sect; and this opinion of the genii might probably be one of theirs. Yet it proves not that all demons were thus malicious; only those who were to be condemned hereafter into human bodies, for their misdemeanours in their aerial being.

But it is time to leave a subject so very fanciful, and so little reasonable as this. I am apt to imagine the natural vapours arising in the cave where the temple afterwards was built, might work upon the spirits of those who entered the holy place, (as they did on the shepherd Coretas, who first found it out by accident,) and incline them to enthusiasm and prophetic madness: that, as the strength of those vapours diminished, (which were generally in caverns, as that of Mopsus, of Trophonius, and this of Delphos,) so the inspiration decreased by the same measures; that they happened to be stronger when they killed the Pythias, who being conscious of this, was so unwilling to enter; that the oracles ceased to be given in verse, when poets ceased to be the priests; and that the genius of Socrates (whom he confessed never to have seen, but only to have heard inwardly, and unperceived by others) was no more than the strength of his imagination; or to speak in the language of a Christian Platonist, his guardian angel.

I pretend not to an exactness of method in this Life, which I am forced to collect by patches from several authors, and therefore without much regard to the connexion of times, which are so uncertain.

I will in the next place, speak of his marriage. His wife's name, her parentage, and dowry, are nowhere mentioned by him, or any other, nor in what part of his age he married; though it is probable in the flower of it. But Rualdus has ingeniously gathered, from a convincing circumstance, that she was called Timoxena; because Plutarch, in a consolatory letter to her, occasioned by the death of their daughter, in her infancy, uses these words:—"Your Timoxena is deprived, by death, of small enjoyments; for the things she knew were of small moment, and she could be delighted only with trifles." Now, it appears by the letter, that the name of this daughter was the same with her mother's; therefore it could be no other than Timoxena. Her knowledge, her conjugal virtues, her abhorrency from the vanities of her sex, and from superstition, her gravity in behaviour, and her constancy in supporting the loss of children, are likewise celebrated by our author. No other wife of Plutarch is found mentioned, and therefore we may conclude he had no more, by the same reason for which we judge that he had no other master than Ammonius; because it is evident he was so grateful in his nature, that he would have preserved their memory.

The number of his children was at least five, so many being mentioned by him. Four of them were sons; of the other sex only Timoxena, who died at two years old, as is manifest from the epistle above mentioned. The French translator, Amiot, from whom our old English translation of the "Lives" was made, supposes him to have had another daughter, where he speaks of his son-in-law, Crato. But the word γαμβρὸς, which Plutarch there uses, is of a larger signification; for it may as well be expounded father-in-law, his wife's brother, or his sister's husband, as Budæus notes: this I the rather mention, because the same Amiot is tasked for an infinite number of mistakes by his own countrymen of the present age, which is enough to recommend this translation of our author into the English tongue, being not from any copy, but from the Greek original. Two other sons of Plutarch were already deceased before Timoxena; his eldest, Autobulus, mentioned in his Symposiacs, and another, whose name is not recorded. The youngest was called Charon, who also died in his infancy. The two remaining are supposed to have survived him: the name of one was Plutarch, after his own: and that of the other Lamprias, so called in memory of his grandfather. This was he, of all his children, who seems to have inherited his father's philosophy; and to him we owe the Table, or Catalogue, of Plutarch's writings, and perhaps also the Apophthegms. His nephew, but whether by his brother or sister remains uncertain, was Sextus Chæroneus, who was much honoured by that learned emperor, Marcus Aurelius, and who taught him the Greek tongue, and the principles of philosophy. This emperor professing Stoicism, (as appears by his writings,) inclines us to believe, that our Sextus Chæroneus was of the Stoic sect; and consequently, that the world has generally been mistaken in supposing him to have been the same man with Sextus Empiricus, the Skeptic, whom Suidas plainly tells us to have been an African. Now, Empiricus could not but be a Skeptic, for he opposes all dogmatists, and particularly them. But I heard it first observed by an ingenious and learned old gentleman, lately deceased, that many of Mr. Hobbes his seeming new opinions, are gathered from those which Sextus Empiricus exposed. The book is extant, and I refer the curious to it, not pretending to arraign or to excuse him.

Some think the famous critic, Longinus, was of Plutarch's family, descended from a sister of his; but the proofs are so weak, that I will not insert them: they may both of them rely on their proper merits, and stand not in want of a relation to each other.

It is needless to insist on his behaviour in his family. His love to his wife, his indulgence to his children, his care of their education, are all manifest in that part of his works, which is called his "Morals.' Other parts of his disposition have been touched already; as, that he was courteous and humane to all men, free from inconstancy, anger, and the desire of revenge; which qualities of his, as they have been praised by the authority of other writers, may also be recommended from his own testimony of himself:—"I had rather (says he) be forgotten in the memory of men, and that it should be said, there neither is, nor was, a man called Plutarch, than they should report,—This Plutarch was unconstant, changeable in his temper, prone to anger and revenge on the least occasions."—What he was to his slaves, you may believe from this; that, in general, he accuses those masters of extreme hardness and injustice, who use men like oxen, and sell them in their age when they can drudge no longer. "A man (says he) of a merciful disposition, ought not to retrench the fodder from his cattle, nor the provender from his horses, when they can work no longer, but to cherish them when worn out and old." Yet Plutarch, though he knew how to moderate his anger, was not, on the contrary, subject to an insensibility of wrongs; nor so remiss in exacting duty, or so tame in suffering the disobedience of his servants, that he could not correct, when they deserved it; as is manifest from the following story, which Aulus Gellius had from the mouth of Taurus the philosopher, concerning him: "Plutarch had a certain slave, a saucy, stubborn kind of fellow; in a word, one of those pragmatical servants, who never make a fault, but they give a reason for it. His justifications one time would not serve his turn, but his master commanded him to be stripped, and that the law should be laid on his backside. He no sooner felt the smart, but he muttered that he was unjustly punished, and that he had done nothing to deserve the scourge. At last he began to bawl out louder; and leaving off his groaning, his sighs, and his lamentations, to argue the matter with more show of reason; and, as under such a master he must needs have gained a smattering of learning, he cried out, that Plutarch was not the philosopher he pretended himself to be; that he had heard him waging war against all the passions, and maintaining, that anger was unbecoming a wise man; nay, that he had written a particular treatise in commendation of clemency: that therefore he contradicted his precepts by his practices, since, abandoning himself over to his choler, he exercised such inhuman cruelty on the body of his fellow-creature. "How is this, Mr. Varlet, (answered Plutarch,) by what signs and tokens can you prove I am in passion? Is it by my countenance, my voice, the colour of my face, by my words, or by my gestures, that you have discovered this my fury? I am not of opinion that my eyes sparkle, that I foam at mouth, that I gnash my teeth, or that my voice is more vehement, or that my colour is either more pale or more red than at other times; that I either shake or stamp with madness; that I say or do any thing unbecoming a philosopher. These, if you know them not, are the symptoms of a man in rage. In the mean, (turning to the officer who scourged him,) while he and I dispute this matter, mind you your business on his back."

His love to his friends, and his gratitude to his benefactors, are everywhere observable in his dedications of his several works; and the particular treatises he has written to them on several occasions, are all suitable either to the characters of the men, or to their present condition, and the circumstances under which they were. His love to his country is from hence conspicuous, that he professes to have written the life of Lucullus, and to have preserved the memory of his actions, because of the favours he conferred on the city of Chæronea; which, though his country received so long before, yet he thought it appertained to him to repay them, and took an interest in their acknowledgment: as also, that he vindicated the Bœotians from the calumnies of Herodotus, the historian, in his book concerning the malignity of that author. In which it is observable, that his zeal to his country transported him too far; for Herodotus had said no more of them than what was generally held to be true in all ages, concerning the grossness of their wits, their voracity, and those other national vices which we have already noted on this account; therefore, Petrarch has accused our author of the same malignity for which he taxed Herodotus. But they may both stand acquitted on different accounts: Herodotus for having given a true character of the Thebans, and Plutarch for endeavouring to palliate the vices of a people from whom he was descended. The rest of his manners, without entering into particulars, were unblamable, if we excuse a little proneness to superstition, and regulating his actions by his dreams. But how far this will bear an accusation, I determine not; though Tully has endeavoured to show the vanity of dreams in his "Treatise of Divinations," whither I refer the curious.

On what occasion he repaired to Rome, at what time of his age he came thither, how long he dwelt there, how often he was there, and in what year he returned to his own country, are all uncertain. This we know, that when Nero was in Greece, which was in his eleventh and twelfth years, our author was at Delphos, under Ammonius, his master, as appears by the disputation then managed, concerning the inscription of the two letters, Ε, Ι. Nero not living long afterwards, it is almost indisputable that he came not to Rome in all his reign. It is improbable that he would undertake the voyage during the troublesome times of Galba, Otho, and Vitellius: and we are not certain that he lived in Rome in the empire of Vespasian. Yet we may guess, that the mildness of this emperor's dominion, his fame, and the virtues of his son Titus, assumed into the empire afterwards by his father, might induce Plutarch, amongst other considerations, to take this journey in his time. It is argued from the following story, related by himself, that he was at Rome either in the joint reign of the two Vespasians, or at least in that of the survivor Titus. He says, then, in his last book concerning Curiosity,—"Reasoning, or rather reading once at Rome, Arulenus Rusticus, the same man whom afterwards Domitian put to death out of envy to his glory, stood hearkening to me amongst my auditors. It so happened, that a soldier, having letters for him from the emperor, [who was either Titus or his father Vespasian, as Rualdus thinks,] broke through the crowd, to deliver him those letters from the emperor. Observing this, I made a pause in my dissertation, that Rusticus might have the leisure to read the mandate which was sent him; but he absolutely refused to do it, neither would he be entreated to break the seals, till I had wholly made an end of my speech, and dismissed the company." Now I suppose the stress of the argument, to prove that this emperor was not Domitian, lies only in this clause, "whom Domitian afterwards put to death;" but I think it rather leaves it doubtful; for they might be Domitian's letters which he then received; and consequently he might not come to Rome till the reign of that emperor. This Rusticus was not only a learned but a good man. He had been tribune of the people under Nero, was prætor in the time of Vitellius, and sent ambassador to the forces raised under the name of Vespasian, to persuade them to a peace. What offices he bore afterwards, we know not; but the cause of his death, besides the envy of Domitian to his fame, was a certain book, or some Commentaries of his, wherein he had praised too much the sanctity of Thrasea Pætus, whom Nero had murdered; and the praise of a good citizen was insupportable to the tyrant; being, I suppose, exasperated further by some reflections of Rusticus, who could not commend Thrasea, but at the same time he must inveigh against the oppressor of the Roman liberty.

That Plutarch was married in his own country and that before he came to Rome, is probable. That the fame of him was come before him, by reason of some part of his works already published, is also credible, because he had so great resort of the Roman nobility to hear him read immediately, as we believe, upon his coming: that he was invited thither by the correspondence he had with Sossius Senecio, might be one reason of his undertaking that journey, is almost undeniable.* It likewise appears he was divers times at Rome; and perhaps, before he came to inhabit there, might make acquaintance with this worthy man, Senecio, to whom he dedicated almost all these Lives of Greeks and Romans. I say almost all, because one of them, namely, that of Aratus, is inscribed in most express words to Polycrates, the Sicyonian, the great-grandson of the said Aratus. This worthy patron and friend of Plutarch, Senecio, was four times consul: the first time in the short reign of Cocceius Nerva, a virtuous and a learned emperor; which opinion I rather follow than that of Aurelius Cassiodorus, who puts back his consulship into the last of Domitian, because it is not probable that vicious tyrant should exalt to that dignity a man of virtue. This year falls in with the year of Christ ninety-nine.

But the great inducement of our author to this journey was certainly the desire he had to lay in materials for his Roman Lives: that was the design which he had formed early, and on which he had resolved to build his fame. Accordingly, we have observed that he had travelled over Greece, to peruse the archives of every city, that he might be able to write properly not only the lives of his Grecian worthies, but the laws, the customs, the rites, and ceremonies of every place; which, that he might treat with the same mastery of skill, when he came to draw his PARALLELS of the Romans, he took the invitation of his friends, and particularly of our Sossius Senecio, to visit this mistress of the world, this imperial city of Rome; and, by the favour of many great and learned men then living, to search the records of the capitol, and the libraries, which might furnish him with instruments for so noble an undertaking. But that this may not seem to be my own bare opinion, or that of any modern author whom I follow, Plutarch himself has delivered it as his motive, in the Life of Demosthenes. The

* This sentence is ungrammatical, as has been observed by Mr. Malone. Perhaps we ought to read, "that he was invited thither; *and that*."

words are these: "Whosoever designs to write a history, (which it is impossible to form to any excellency from those materials that are ready at hand, or to take from common report while he sits lazily at home in his own study, but must of necessity be gathered from foreign observations, and the scattered writings of various authors,) it concerns him to take up his habitation in some renowned and populous city, where he may command all sorts of books, and be acquainted also with such particulars as have escaped the pens of writers, and are only extant in the memories of men. Let him inquire diligently, and weigh judiciously what he hears and reads, lest he publish a lame work, and be destitute of those helps which are required to its perfection." It is then most probable, that he passed his days at Rome in reading philosophy of all kinds to the Roman nobility, who frequented his house, and heard him as if there were somewhat more than human in his words; and his nights, which were his only hours of private study, in searching and examining records concerning Rome. Not but that he was intrusted also with the management of public affairs in the empire, during his residence in the metropolis; which may be made out by what Suidas relates of him:—"Plutarch," says he, "lived in the time of Trajan, and also before his reign. That emperor bestowed on him the dignity of consul; [though the Greek, I suppose, will bear, that he made him consul with himself, at least transferred that honour on him:] an edict was also made in favour of him, that the magistrates or officers of Illyria should do nothing in that province without the knowledge and approbation of Plutarch." Now, it is my particular guess, (for I have not read it anywhere,) that Plutarch had the affairs of Illyria, now called Sclavonia, recommended to him, because Trajan, we know, had wars on that side the empire with Decebalus, king of Dacia; after whose defeat and death, the province of Illyria might stand in need of Plutarch's wisdom to compose and civilize it. But this is only hinted as what possibly might be the reason of our philosopher's superintendency in those quarters, which the French author of his life seems to wonder at, as having no relation either to Chæronea or Greece.

When he was first made known to Trajan is like the rest uncertain; or by what means, whether by Senecio, or any other, he was introduced to his acquaintance; but it is most likely that Trajan, then a private man, was one of his auditors, amongst others of the nobility of Rome. It is also thought, this wise emperor made use of him in all his councils; and that the happiness which attended him in his undertakings, together with the administration of the government, which in all his reign was just and regular, proceeded from the instructions which were given him by Plutarch. Johannes Sarisberiensis, who lived above six hundred years ago, has transcribed a letter, written, as he supposed, by our author to that emperor. Whence he had it, is not known, nor the original in Greek to be produced; but it passed for genuine in that age, and if not Plutarch's, is at least worthy of him, and what might well be supposed a man of his character would write; for which reason I have here translated it.

PLUTARCH TO TRAJAN.

"I am satisfied that your modesty sought not the empire, which yet you have always studied to deserve by the excellency of your manners; and by so much the more are you esteemed worthy of this honour, by how much you are free from the ambition of desiring it. I therefore congratulate both your virtue and my own good fortune, if at least your future government shall prove answerable to your former merit; otherwise you have involved yourself in dangers, and I shall infallibly be subject to the censures of detracting tongues; because Rome will never support an emperor unworthy of her, and the faults of the scholar will be upbraided to the master. Thus Seneca is reproached, and his fame still suffers, for the vices of Nero. The miscarriages of Quintilian's scholars have been thrown on him; and even Socrates himself is not free from the imputation of remissness on the account of his pupil, Alcibiades. But you will certainly administer all things as becomes you, if you still continue what you are; if you recede not from yourself, if you begin at home, and lay the foundation of government on the command of your own passions; if you make virtue the scope of all your actions, they will all proceed in harmony and order. I have set before you the force of laws and civil constitutions of your predecessors, which if you imitate and obey, Plutarch is then your guide of living; if otherwise, let this present letter be my testimony against you, that you shall not ruin the Roman empire under the pretence of the counsel and authority of Plutarch."*

It may be conjectured, and with some show of probability, from hence, that our author not

* The authenticity of this letter has been doubted. Its dictatorial tone certainly rather resembles the forgery of some pedant, assuming the character of a great man, than that of a sage addressing a conquering emperor.

only collected his materials, but also made a rough draft of many of these parallel Lives at Rome; and that he read them to Trajan for his instruction in government: and so much the rather I believe it, because all historians agree that this emperor, though naturally prudent and inclined to virtue, had more of the soldier than the scholar in his education, before he had the happiness to know Plutarch; for which reason the Roman Lives, and the inspection into ancient laws, might be of necessary use to his direction.

And now for the time of our author's abode in the imperial city: if he came so early as Vespasian, and departed not till Trajan's death, as is generally thought, he might continue in Italy near forty years. This is more certain, because gathered from himself,—that his Lives were almost the latest of his works; and therefore we may well conclude, that having modelled but not finished them at Rome, he afterwards resumed the work in his own country; which perfecting in his old age, he dedicated to his friend Senecio, still living, as appears by what he has written in the proem to his Lives.

The desire of visiting his own country, so natural to all men, and the approaches of old age, (for he could not be much less than sixty,) and perhaps also the death of Trajan, prevailed with him at last to leave Italy; or, if you will have it in his own words, "he was not willing his little city should be one the less by his absence." After his return, he was, by the unanimous consent of his citizens, chosen Archon, or chief magistrate of Chæronea, and not long after admitted himself in the number of Apollo's priests; in both which employments he seems to have continued till his death, of which we have no particular account, either as to the manner of it, or the year; only it is evident that he lived to a great old age,* always continuing his studies. That he died a natural death, is only presumed, because any violent accident to so famous a man would have been recorded; and in whatsoever reign he deceased, the days of tyranny were overpassed, and there was then a golden series of emperors, every one emulating his predecessor's virtues.

Thus I have collected from Plutarch himself, and from the best authors, what was most remarkable concerning him; in performing which, I have laboured under so many uncertainties, that I have not been able to satisfy my own curiosity, any more than that of others. It is the life of a philosopher, not varied with accidents to divert the reader; more pleasant for himself to live, than for a historian to describe. Those works of his which are irrecoverably lost, are named in the catalogue made by his son, Lamprias, which you will find in the Paris edition, dedicated to King Louis the Thirteenth. But it is small comfort to a merchant to peruse his bill of freight, when he is certain his ship is cast away: moved by the like reason, I have omitted that ungrateful task. Yet that the reader may not be imposed on in those which yet remain, it is but reasonable to let him know, that the Lives of Hannibal and Scipio, though they pass with the ignorant for genuine, are only the forgery of Donato Acciaiolo, a Florentine. He pretends to have translated them from a Greek manuscript, which none of the learned have ever seen, either before or since. But the cheat is more manifest from this reason, which is undeniable; that Plutarch did indeed write the Life of Scipio, but he compared him not with Hannibal, but with Epaminondas; as appears by the catalogue or nomenclature of Plutarch's Lives, drawn up by his son Lamprias, and yet extant. But to make this out more clearly, we find the Florentine, in his Life of Hannibal, thus relating the famous conference betwixt Scipio and him:—"Scipio at that time being sent ambassador from the Romans to King Antiochus, with Publius Villius, it happened then that these two great captains met together at Ephesus; and amongst other discourses, it was demanded of Hannibal by Scipio,—whom he thought to have been the greatest captain? To whom he thus answered—In the first place, Alexander of Macedon; in the second, Pyrrhus of Epirus; and in the third, himself. To which Scipio, smiling, thus replied:—And what would you have thought had it been your fortune to have vanquished me? To whom Hannibal:—I should then have adjudged the first place to myself. Which answer was not a little pleasing to Scipio, because by it he found himself not disesteemed, nor put into comparison with the rest; but by the delicacy and gallantry of a well-turned compliment, set like a man divine above them all."

Now this relation is a mere compendium of the same conference, from Livy; but if we can conceive Plutarch to have written the Life of Hannibal, it is hard to believe that he should tell the same story after so different, or rather so contrary a manner, in another place. For, in the Life of Pyrrhus, he thus writes:—"Hannibal adjudged the pre-eminence to Pyrrhus above all captains, in conduct, and military skill; next to Pyrrhus he placed Scipio; and after Scipio himself; as we have declared in the Life of

* Plutarch is said to have died in the reign of Antoninus Pius, A. D. 140, aged ninety years.

Scipio." It is not that I would excuse Plutarch, as if he never related the same thing diversely; for it is evident, that, through want of advertency, he has been often guilty of that error, of which the reader will find too frequent examples in these Lives; but in this place he cannot be charged with want of memory or care, because what he says here is relating to what he had said formerly; so that he may mistake the story, as I believe he has done, (that other of Livy being much more probable,) but we must allow him to remember what he had before written.

From hence I might take occasion to note some other lapses of our author, which yet amount not to falsification of truth, much less to partiality, or envy, (both which are manifest in his countryman Dion Cassius, who writ not long after him,) but are only the frailties of human nature; mistakes not intentional, but accidental. He was not altogether so well versed either in the Roman language, or in their coins, or in the value of them; in some customs, rites, and ceremonies, he took passages on trust from others, relating both to them and the barbarians, which the reader may particularly find recited in the animadversions of the often-praised Rualdus on our author. I will name but one, to avoid tediousness, because I particularly observed it when I read Plutarch in the library of Trinity College, in Cambridge, to which foundation I gratefully acknowledge a great part of my education. It is, that Plutarch, in the life of Cicero, speaking of Verres, who was accused by him, and repeating a miserable jest of Tully's, says that Verres, in the Roman language, signifies a barrow-pig, that is, one which has been gelded. But we have a better account of the signification from Varro, whom we have more reason to believe; that the male of that kind, before he is cut, is called Verres: after cutting, Majalis, which is perhaps a diminutive of Mas, though generally the reason of the etymology is given from its being a sacrifice to the goddess Maja. Yet any man, who will candidly weigh this and the like errors, may excuse Plutarch, as he would a stranger mistaking the propriety of an English word; and besides the humanity of this excuse, it is impossible in nature, that a man of so various learning, and so covetous of engrossing all, should perfectly digest such an infinity of notions in many sciences; since to be excellent in one is so great a labour.

It may now be expected, that, having written the life of an historian, I should take occasion to write somewhat concerning history itself: but I think to commend it is unnecessary, for the profit and pleasure of that study are both so very obvious, that a quick reader will be beforehand with me, and imagine faster than I can write. Besides that the post is taken up already; and few authors have travelled this way, but who have strewed it with rhetoric as they passed.

For my own part, who must confess it to my shame, that I never read any thing but for pleasure, it has always been the most delightful entertainment of my life; but they who have employed the study of it as they ought, for their instruction, for the regulation of their private manners, and the management of public affairs, must agree with me, that it is the most pleasant school of wisdom. It is a familiarity with past ages, and an acquaintance with all the heroes of them; it is, if you will pardon the similitude, a prospective glass carrying your soul to a vast distance, and taking in the farthest objects of antiquity. It informs the understanding by the memory: it helps us to judge of what will happen, by showing us the like revolutions of former times. For mankind being the same in all ages, agitated by the same passions, and moved to action by the same interests, nothing can come to pass, but some precedent of the like nature has already been produced; so that having the causes before our eyes, we cannot easily be deceived in the effects, if we have judgment enough but to draw the parallel.

God, it is true, with his divine providence overrules and guides all actions to the secret end he has ordained them; but in the way of human causes, a wise man may easily discern that there is a natural connexion betwixt them; and though he cannot foresee accidents, or all things that possibly can come, he may apply examples, and by them foretell, that from the like counsels will probably succeed the like events; and thereby, in all concernments, and all offices of life, be instructed in the two main points on which depend our happiness; that, is what to avoid, and what to choose.

The laws of history, in general, are truth of matter, method, and clearness of expression. The first propriety is necessary, to keep our understanding from the impositions of falsehood; for history is an argument framed from many particular examples or inductions; if these examples are not true, then those measures of life which we take from them will be false, and deceive us in their consequence. The second is grounded on the former; for if the method be confused, if the words or expressions of thought are any way obscure, then the ideas which we receive must be imperfect; and if such, we are not taught by them what to elect or what to shun. Truth, therefore, is required as the foundation of history, to inform us; disposition and perspicuity, as the manner to inform us plainly; one is the being, the other the well-being of it.

History is principally divided into these three species; Commentaries, or Annals; History, properly so called; and Biographia, or the Lives of particular men.

Commentaries, or Annals, are (as I may so call them) naked history, or the plain relation of matter of fact, according to the succession of time, divested of all other ornaments. The springs and motives of actions are not here sought, unless they offer themselves, and are open to every man's discernment. The method is the most natural that can be imagined, depending only on the observation of months and years, and drawing, in the order of them, whatsoever happened worthy of relation. The style is easy, simple, unforced, and unadorned with the pomp of figures: councils, guesses, politic observations, sentences, and orations, are avoided; in few words, a bare narration is its business. Of this kind the "Commentaries of Cæsar" are certainly the most admirable, and after him the "Annals of Tacitus" may have place; nay, even the prince of Greek historians, Thucydides, may almost be adopted into the number. For, though he instructs everywhere by sentences, though he gives the causes of actions, the councils of both parties, and makes orations where they are necessary, yet it is certain that he first designed his work a Commentary; every year writing down, like an unconcerned spectator as he was, the particular occurrences of the time, in the order as they happened; and his eighth book is wholly written after the way of Annals; though, outliving the war, he inserted in his others those ornaments which render his work the most complete and most instructive now extant.

History, properly so called, may be described by the addition of those parts which are not required to Annals; and therefore there is little farther to be said concerning it; only, that the dignity and gravity of style is here necessary. That the guesses of secret causes inducing to the actions, be drawn at least from the most probable circumstances, not perverted by the malignity of the author to sinister interpretations, (of which Tacitus is accused,) but candidly laid down, and left to the judgment of the reader: That nothing of concernment be omitted; but things of trivial moment are still to be neglected, as debasing the majesty of the work: That neither partiality or prejudice appear, but that truth may everywhere be sacred: *Ne quid falsi dicere audeat, ne quid veri non audeat historicus:* That he neither incline to superstition, in giving too much credit to oracles, prophecies, divinations, and prodigies, nor to irreligion, in disclaiming the Almighty Providence; but where general opinion has prevailed of any miraculous accident or portent, he ought to relate it as such, without imposing his opinion on our belief. Next to Thucydides, in this kind, may be accounted Polybius, amongst the Grecians; Livy, though not free from superstition, nor Tacitus from ill nature, amongst the Romans; amongst the modern Italians, Guicciardini, and Davila, if not partial; but above all men, in my opinion, the plain, sincere, unaffected, and most instructive Philip de Comines, amongst the French, though he only gives his History the humble name of Commentaries. I am sorry I cannot find in our own nation, though it has produced some commendable historians, any proper to be ranked with these. Buchanan, indeed, for the purity of his Latin, and for his learning, and for all other endowments belonging to an historian, might be placed amongst the greatest, if he had not too much leaned to prejudice, and too manifestly declared himself a party of a cause, rather than an historian of it. Excepting only that, (which I desire not to urge too far on so great a man, but only to give caution to his readers concerning it,) our isle may justly boast in him a writer comparable to any of the moderns, and excelled by few of the ancients.

Biographia, or the history of particular men's lives, comes next to be considered; which in dignity is inferior to the other two, as being more confined in action, and treating of wars, and councils, and all other public affairs of nations, only as they relate to him whose life is written, or as his fortunes have a particular dependence on them, or connexion to them. All things here are circumscribed, and driven to a point, so as to terminate in one; consequently, if the action or counsel were managed by colleagues, some part of it must be either lame or wanting, except it be supplied by the excursion of the writer. Herein, likewise, must be less of variety, for the same reason; because the fortunes and actions of one man are related, not those of many. Thus the actions and achievements of Sylla, Lucullus, and Pompey, are all of them but the successive parts of the Mithridatic war; of which we could have no perfect image, if the same hand had not given us the whole, though at several views, in their particular lives.

Yet though we allow, for the reasons above alleged, that this kind of writing is in dignity inferior to History and Annals, in pleasure and instruction it equals, or even excels, both of them. It is not only commanded by ancient practice to celebrate the memory of great and worthy men, as the best thanks which posterity can pay them, but also the examples of virtue are of more vigour, when they are thus contracted into individuals. As the sunbeams, united in a burning glass to a point, have greater force than when they are darted from a plain superficies, so the virtues and actions of one man, drawn together into a single story, strike upon our minds a stronger and more lively impression, than the scattered relations of many men, and many actions; and, by the same means that they give us pleasure, they afford us profit too. For when the understanding is intent and fixed on a single thing, it carries closer to the mark; every part of the object sinks into it; and the soul receives it unmixed and whole. For this reason Aristotle commends the unity of action in a poem; because the mind is not capable of digesting many things at once, nor of conceiving fully any more than one idea at a time. Whatsoever distracts the pleasure, lessens it; and as the reader is more concerned at one man's fortune than those of many, so likewise the writer is more capable of making a perfect work if he confine himself to this narrow compass. The lineaments, features, and colourings of a single picture may be hit exactly; but in a history-piece of many figures, the general design, the ordonnance or disposition of it, the relation of one figure to another, the diversity of the posture, habits, shadowings, and all the other graces conspiring to an uniformity, are of so difficult performance, that neither is the resemblance of particular persons often perfect, nor the beauty of the piece complete; for any considerable error in the parts renders the whole disagreeable and lame. Thus then, the perfection of the work, and the benefit arising from it, are both more absolute in biography than in history. All history is only the precepts of moral philosophy reduced into examples. Moral philosophy is divided into two parts, ethics and politics; the first instructs us in our private offices of virtue, the second in those which relate to the management of the commonwealth. Both of these teach by argumentation and reasoning, which rush as it were into the mind, and possess it with violence; but history rather allures than forces us to virtue. There is nothing of the tyrant in example; but it gently glides into us, is easy and pleasant in its passage, and in one word reduces into practice our speculative notions; therefore the more powerful the examples are, they are the more useful also; and, by being more known, they are more powerful. Now unity, which is defined, is in its own nature more apt to be understood than multiplicity, which in some measure participates of infinity. The reason is Aristotle's.

Biographia, or the histories of particular lives, though circumscribed in the subject, is yet more extensive in the style than the other two; for it not only comprehends them both, but has somewhat superadded, which neither of them have. The style of it is various, according to the occasion. There are proper places in it for the plainness and nakedness of narration, which is ascribed to annals; there is also room reserved for the loftiness and gravity of general history, when the actions related shall require that manner of expression. But there is withal a descent into minute circumstances, and trivial passages of life, which are natural to this way of writing, and which the dignity of the other two will not admit. There you are conducted only into the rooms of state, here you are led into the private lodgings of the hero; you see him in his undress, and are made familiar with his most private actions and conversations. You may behold a Scipio and a Lælius gathering cockle-shells on the shore, Augustus playing at bounding-stones with boys, and Agesilaus riding on a hobby-horse among his children. The pageantry of life is taken away; you see the poor reasonable animal as naked as ever nature made him; are made acquainted with his passions and his follies, and find the demi-god a man. Plutarch himself has more than once defended this kind of relating little passages; for, in the Life of Alexander, he says thus: "In writing the lives of illustrious men, I am not tied to the laws of history; nor does it follow, that, because an action is great, it therefore manifests the greatness and virtue of him who did it; but, on the other side, sometimes a word, or a casual jest, betrays a man more to our knowledge of him, than a battle fought wherein ten thousand men were slain, or sacking of cities, or a course of victories." In another place he quotes Xenophon on the like occasion: "The sayings of great men in their familiar discourses, and amidst their wine, have somewhat in them which is worthy to be transmitted to posterity." Our author therefore needs no excuse, but rather deserves a commendation, when he relates, as pleasant, some sayings of his heroes, which appear (I must confess it) very cold and insipid mirth to us. For it is not his meaning to commend the jest, but to paint the man; besides, we may have lost somewhat of the idiom of that language in which it was spoken; and where the conceit is couched in a single word, if all the significations of it are not critically understood, the grace and the pleasantry are lost

But in all parts of biography, whether familiar or stately, whether sublime or low, whether serious or merry, Plutarch equally excelled. If we compare him to others, Dion Cassius is not so sincere; Herodian, a lover of truth, is oftentimes deceived himself with what he had falsely heard reported: then the time of his emperors exceeds not in all above sixty years; so that his whole history will scarce amount to three Lives of Plutarch. Suetonius and Tacitus may be called alike either authors of histories, or writers of lives; but the first of them runs too willingly into obscene descriptions, which he teaches, while he relates; the other, besides what has already been noted by him, often falls into obscurity; and both of them have made so unlucky a choice of times, that they are forced to describe rather monsters than men; and their emperors are either extravagant fools or tyrants, and most usually both. Our author, on the contrary, as he was more inclined to commend than to dispraise, has generally chosen such great men as were famous for their several virtues; at least such whose frailties or vices were overpoised by their excellencies; such from whose examples we may have more to follow than to shun. Yet, as he was impartial, he disguised not the faults of any man: an example of which is in the life of Lucullus; where, after he has told us that the double benefit which his countrymen, the Chæroneans, received from him, was the chiefest motive which he had to write his life, he afterwards rips up his luxury, and shows how he lost, through his mismanagement, his authority and his soldiers' love. Then he was more happy in his digressions than any we have named. I have always been pleased to see him, and his imitator, Montaigne, when they strike a little out of the common road; for we are sure to be the better for their wandering. The best quarry lies not always in the open field; and who would not be content to follow a good huntsman over hedges and ditches, when he knows the game will reward his pains? But if we mark him more narrowly, we may observe, that the great reason of his frequent starts is the variety of his learning; he knew so much of nature, was so vastly furnished with all the treasures of the mind, that he was uneasy to himself, and was forced, as I may say, to lay down some at every passage, and to scatter his riches as he went: like another Alexander or Adrian, he built a city, or planted a colony, in every part of his progress, and left behind him some memorial of his greatness. Sparta, and Thebes, and Athens, and Rome, the mistress of the world, he has discovered in their foundations, their institutions, their growth, their height; the decay of the three first, and the alteration of the last. You see those several people, in their different laws, and policies, and forms of government, in their warriors, and senators, and demagogues. Nor are the ornaments of poetry, and the illustrations of similitudes, forgotten by him; in both which he instructs, as well as pleases; or rather pleases, that he may instruct.

This last reflection leads me naturally to say somewhat in general of his style; though, after having justly praised him for copiousness of learning, integrity, perspicuity, and more than all this, for a certain air of goodness which appears through all his writings, it were unreasonable to be critical on his elocution. As on a tree which bears excellent fruit, we consider not the beauty of the blossoms,—for if they are not pleasant to the eye, or delightful to the scent, we know at the same time that they are not the prime intention of nature, but are thrust out in order to their product; so in Plutarch, whose business was not to please the ear, but to charm and to instruct the mind, we may easily forgive the cadences of words, and the roughness of expression. Yet, for manliness of eloquence, if it abounded not in our author, it was not wanting in him. He neither studied the sublime style, nor affected the flowery. The choice of words, the numbers of periods, the turns of sentences, and those other ornaments of speech, he neither sought nor shunned; but the depth of sense, the accuracy of judgment, the disposition of the parts, and contexture of the whole, in so admirable and vast a field of matter, and, lastly, the copiousness and variety of words, appear shining in our author. It is, indeed, observed of him, that he keeps not always to the style of prose, but if a poetical word, which carries in it more of emphasis or signification, offer itself at any time, he refuses it not because Homer or Euripides have used it; but if this be a fault, I know not how Xenophon will stand excused. Yet neither do I compare our author with him, or with Herodotus, in the sweetness and graces of his style, nor with Thucydides in the solidity and closeness of expression; for Herodotus is acknowledged the prince of the Ionic, the other two of the Attic eloquence. As for Plutarch, his style is so particular, that there is none of the ancients to whom we can properly resemble him. And the reason of this is obvious; for, being conversant in so great a variety of authors, and collecting from all of them what he thought most excellent, out of the confusion, or rather mixture, of all their styles, he formed his own, which, partaking of each, was yet none of them, but a compound of them all; like the Corinthian metal, which had in it gold, and brass, and silver, and yet was a species by itself. Add to this, that in Plutarch's time, and long before it, the purity of the Greek tongue was corrupted, and the native splendour of it had taken the tarnish of barbarism, and contracted the filth and spots of degenerating ages: for the fall of empires always draws after it the language and eloquence of the people; they, who labour under misfortunes or servitude, have little leisure to cultivate their mother tongue. To conclude; when Athens had lost her sovereignty to the Peloponnesians, and her liberty to Philip, neither a Thucydides nor a Demosthenes were afterwards produced by her.

I have formerly acknowledged many lapses of our author, occasioned through his inadvertency; but he is likewise taxed with faults which reflect on his judgment in matters of fact, and his candour in the comparisons of his Greeks and Romans; both which are so well vindicated by Montaigne, that I need but barely to translate him:—"First, then, he is accused of want of judgment, in reporting things incredible; for proof of which is alleged the story he tells of the Spartan boy, who suffered his bowels to be torn out by a young fox which he had stolen, choosing rather to hide him under his garment till he died, than to confess his robbery. In the first place, this example is ill chosen, because it is difficult to set a bound to the force of our internal faculties; it is not defined how far our resolution may carry us to suffer. The force of bodies may more easily be determined than that of souls. Then of all people, the Lacedemonians, by reason of their rigid institutions, were most hardened to undergo labours, and to suffer pains. Cicero, before our author's time, though then the Spartan virtue was degenerated, yet avows to have seen himself some Lacedemonian boys, who, to make trial of their patience, were placed before the altar of Diana, where they endured scourging till they were all over bloody, and that not only without crying, but even without a sigh or a groan; nay, and some of them so ambitious of this reputation, that they willingly resigned their lives under the hands of their tormentors.—The same may be said of another story, which Plutarch vouches with a hundred witnesses: that in the time of sacrifice, a burning coal by chance falling into the sleeve of a Spartan boy, who held the censer, he suffered his arm to be scorched so long without moving it, that the scent of it reeked up to the noses of the assistants.

"For my own [illegible] an idea of the [illegible], Plutarch's story is so far from seeming incredible to me, that I think it neither wonderful nor uncommon; for we ought not to measure possibilities or impossibilities by our own standard, that is, by what we ourselves could do or suffer. These, and some other slight examples, are made use of, to lessen the opinion of Plutarch's judgment.—But the common exception against his candour is, that in his parallels of Greeks and Romans, he has done too much honour to his countrymen, in matching them with heroes with whom they were not worthy to be compared. For instances of this, there are produced the comparisons of Demosthenes and Cicero, Aristides and Cato, Lysander and Sylla, Pelopidas and Marcellus, Agesilaus and Pompey. Now the ground of this accusation is most probably the lustre of those Roman names, which strikes on our imagination; for what proportion of glory is there betwixt a Roman consul or proconsul of so great a commonwealth, and a simple citizen of Athens? But he who considers the truth more nearly, and weighs not honours with honours, but men with men, which was Plutarch's main design, will find in the balance of their manners, their virtues, their endowments and abilities, that Cicero and the elder Cato were far from having the overweight against Demosthenes and Aristides. I might as well complain against him in behalf of his own countrymen; for neither was Camillus so famous as Themistocles, nor were Tiberius and Caius Gracchus comparable to Agis and Cleomenes, in regard of dignity; much less was the wisdom of Numa to be put in balance against that of Lycurgus, or the modesty and temperance of Scipio against the solid philosophy and perfect virtue of Epaminondas. Yet the disparity of victories, the reputation, the blaze of glory, in the two last, were evidently on the Roman side.—But, as I said before, to compare them this way was the least of Plutarch's aim; he openly declares against it; for, speaking of the course of Pompey's fortune, his exploits of war, the greatness of the armies which he commanded, the splendour and number of his triumphs, in his comparison betwixt him and Agesilaus,—I believe, says he, that if Xenophon were now alive, and would indulge himself the liberty to write all he could to the advantage of his hero, Agesilaus, he would be ashamed to put their acts in competition. In his comparison of Sylla and Lysander, there is, says he, no manner of equality either in the number of their victories, or in the danger of their battles; for Lysander only gained two naval fights, &c. Now this is far from partiality to the Grecians. He who must convict him of this vice, must show us in what particular judgment he has been too favourable to his countrymen; and make it out in general, where he has failed in matching such a Greek with such a Roman; which must be done by showing how he could have paired them better, and naming any other in whom the resemblance might have been more perfect. But an equitable judge, who takes things by the same handle which Plutarch did, will find there is no injury offered to either party, though there be some disparity betwixt the persons; for he weighs every circumstance by itself, and judges separately of it; not comparing men at a lump, nor endeavouring to prove they were alike in all things, but allowing for disproportion of quality or fortune, showing wherein they agreed or disagreed, and wherein one was to be preferred before the other."

I thought I had answered all that could reasonably be objected against our author's judgment; but casually casting my eye on the works of a French gentleman,* deservedly famous for wit and criticism, I wondered, amongst many commendations of Plutarch, to find this one reflection:—"As for his comparisons, they seem truly to me very great; but I think he might have carried them yet farther, and have penetrated more deeply into human nature. There are folds and recesses in our minds, which have escaped him; he judges man too much in gross, and thinks him not so different as he is often from himself; the same person being just, unjust, merciful, and cruel; which qualities seeming to belie each other in him, he attributes their inconsistencies to foreign causes. In fine, if he had described Catiline, he would have given him to us either prodigal or covetous: that *alieni appetens, sui profusus*, was above his reach. He could never have reconciled those contrarieties in the same subject, which Sallust had so well unfolded, and which Montaigne so much better understood."

This judgment could not have proceeded but from a man who has a nice taste in authors; and if it be not altogether just, it is at least delicate: but I am confident, that if he please to consider this following passage, taken out of the Life of Sylla, he will moderate, if not retract his censure:

"In the rest of his manners he was unequal, irregular, different from himself: *ἀνώμαλός τις ἔοικε, καὶ διάφορος πρὸς ἑαυτόν*. He took many things by rapine, he gave more; honoured men immoderately, and used them contumeliously; was submissive to those of whom he stood in need, insulting over those who stood in need of him; so that it was doubtful whether he were more formed by nature to arrogance or flattery. As to his uncertain way of punishing, he would sometimes put men to death on the least occasion; at other times, he would pardon the greatest crimes: so that judging him in the whole you may conclude him to have been naturally cruel, and prone to vengeance, but that he could remit of his severity, when his interests required it."

Here, methinks, our author seems to have sufficiently understood the folds and doubles of Sylla's disposition; for his character is full of variety and inconsistencies. Yet in the conclusion it is to be confessed, that Plutarch has assigned to him a bloody nature; the clemency was but artificial and assumed, the cruelty was inborn: but this cannot be said of his rapine, and his prodigality; for here the *alieni appetens, sui profusus*, is as plainly described, as if Plutarch had borrowed the sense from Sallust; and, as he was a great collector, perhaps he did. Nevertheless he judged rightly of Sylla, that naturally he was cruel, for that quality was predominant in him; and he was oftener revengeful than he was merciful. But this is sufficient to vindicate our author's judgment from being superficial, and I desire not to press the argument more strongly against this gentleman, who has honoured our country by his long residence amongst us.

It seems to me, I must confess, that our author has not been more hardly treated by his enemies, in his comparing other men, than he has been by his friends, in their comparing Seneca with him. And herein, even Montaigne himself is scarcely to be defended; for no man more esteemed Plutarch, no man was better acquainted with his excellencies; yet, this notwithstanding, he has done too great an honour to Seneca, by ranking him with our philosopher and historian; him, I say, who was so much less a philosopher, and no historian. It is a reputation to Seneca, that any one has offered at the comparison; the worth of his adversary makes his defeat advantageous to him; and Plutarch might cry out with justice,

Qui cum victus erit, mecum certasse feretur.

If I had been to find out a parallel for Plutarch, I should rather have pitched on Varro, the most learned of the Romans, if at least his works had yet remained; or Pomponius Atticus, if he had written. But the likeness of Seneca is so little, that except the one's being tutor to Nero, and the other to Trajan, both of them strangers to Rome, yet raised to the highest dignities in that city, and both philosophers, though of several sects; (for Seneca was a

* Mons. de St. Evremond.

Stoic, Plutarch a Platonician, at least an Academic, that is, half Platonist, half Skeptic;) besides some such faint resemblances as these, Seneca and Plutarch seem to have as little relation to one another as their native countries, Spain and Greece. If we consider them in their inclinations or humours, Plutarch was sociable and pleasant, Seneca morose and melancholy: Plutarch a lover of conversation, and sober feasts; Seneca reserved, uneasy to himself when alone, to others when in company. Compare them in their manners; Plutarch everywhere appears candid, Seneca often censorious. Plutarch, out of his natural humanity, is frequent in commending what he can; Seneca, out of the sourness of his temper, is prone to satire, and still searching for some occasion to vent his gall. Plutarch is pleased with an opportunity of praising virtue; and Seneca, to speak the best of him, is glad of a pretence to reprehend vice. Plutarch endeavours to teach others, but refuses not to be taught himself; for he is always doubtful and inquisitive; Seneca is altogether for teaching others, but so teaches them, that he imposes his opinions, for he was of a sect too imperious and dogmatical either to be taught or contradicted; and yet Plutarch writes like a man of a confirmed probity, Seneca like one of a weak and staggering virtue. Plutarch seems to have vanquished vice, and to have triumphed over it; Seneca seems only to be combating and resisting, and that too but in his own defence; therefore Plutarch is easy in his discourse, as one who has overcome the difficulty; Seneca is painful, as he who still labours under it. Plutarch's virtue is humble and civilized; Seneca's haughty and ill-bred: Plutarch allures you, Seneca commands you. One would make virtue your companion, the other your tyrant. The style of Plutarch is easy and flowing, that of Seneca precipitous and harsh: the first is even, the second broken. The arguments of the Grecian, drawn from reason, work themselves into your understanding, and make a deep and lasting impression in your mind; those of the Roman, drawn from wit, flash immediately on your imagination, but leave no durable effect: so this tickles you by starts with his arguteness, that pleases you for continuance with his propriety. The course of their fortunes seems also to have partaken of their styles; for Plutarch's was equal, smooth, and of the same tenor,—Seneca's was turbid, inconstant, and full of revolutions. The life of Plutarch was unblamable, as the reader cannot but have observed; and of all his writings, there is nothing to be noted as having the least tendency to vice, but only that little treatise which is entitled Ἐρωτικός, wherein he speaks too broadly of a sin to which the eastern and southern parts of the world are most obnoxious; but Seneca is said to have been more libertine than suited with the gravity of a philosopher, or with the austerity of a Stoic. An ingenious Frenchman esteems, as he tells us, his person rather than his works; and values him more as the preceptor of Nero, a man ambitious of the empire, and the gallant of Agrippina, than as a teacher of morality. For my part, I dare not push the commendation so far. His courage was perhaps praiseworthy, if he endeavoured to deliver Rome from such a monster of tyranny as Nero was then beginning to appear; his ambition too was the more excusable, if he found in himself an ability of governing the world, and a desire of doing good to human kind; but as to his good fortunes with the empress, I know not what value ought to be set on a wise man for them: except it be that women generally liking without judgment, it was a conquest for a philosopher, once in an age, to get the better of a fool. However, methinks there is something of awkward in the adventure: I cannot imagine, without laughter, a pedant, and a Stoic, making love in a long gown; for it puts me in mind of the civilities which are used by the cardinals and judges in the dance of "The Rehearsal." If Agrippina would needs be so lavish of her favours, since a sot grew nauseous to her, because he was her husband, and nothing under a wit could atone for Claudius, I am half sorry that Petronius was not the man. We could have borne it better from his character, than from one who professed the severity of virtue, to make a cuckold of his emperor and benefactor. But let the historian answer for his own relation; only, if true, it is so much the worse that Seneca, after having abused his bed, could not let him sleep quiet in his grave. The Apocolocynthisis, or mock deification of Claudius, was too sharp and insulting on his memory, and Seneca, though he could preach forgiveness to others, did not practise it himself in that satire. Where was the patience and insensibility of a Stoic, in revenging his banishment with a libel? Where was the morality of a philosopher, in defaming and exposing of a harmless fool? And where was common humanity, in railing against the dead? But the talent of his malice is visible in other places: he censures Mæcenas, and I believe justly, for the looseness of his manners, the voluptuousness of his life, and the effeminacy of his style; but it appears that he takes pleasure in so doing, and that he never forced his nature when he spoke ill of any man. For his own style, we see what it is; and if we may be as bold with him as he has been with our old patron, we may call it a shattered eloquence, not vigorous, not united, not imbodied, but broken into fragments; every part by itself pompous, but the whole confused and unharmonious. His Latin, as Monsieur St. Evremont has well observed, has nothing in it of the purity and elegance of Augustus his times; and it is of him and of his imitators that Petronius said—*pace vestrâ liceat dixisse, primi omnium eloquentiam perdidistis.* The *controversæ sententiæ vibrantibus pictæ*, and the *vanus sententiarum strepitus*, make it evident that Seneca was taxed under the person of the old Rhetorician. What quarrel he had to the uncle and the nephew, I mean Seneca and Lucan, is not known; but Petronius plainly points them out, one for a bad orator, the other for as bad a poet. His own Essay of the Civil War is an open defiance of the "Pharsalia;" and the first oration of Eumolpus as full an arraignment of Seneca's false eloquence. After all that has been said, he is certainly to be allowed a great wit, but not a good philosopher; not fit to be compared with Cicero, of whose reputation he was emulous, any more than Lucan is with Virgil. To sum up all in few words:—consider a philosopher declaiming against riches, yet vastly rich himself; against avarice, yet putting out his money at great extortion here in Britain; against honours, yet aiming to be emperor; against pleasure, yet enjoying Agrippina, and in his old age married to a beautiful young woman; and after this, let him be made a parallel to Plutarch.

And now with the usual vanity of Dutch prefacers, I could load our author with the praises and commemorations of writers; for both ancient and modern have made honourable mention of him: but to cumber pages with this kind of stuff, were to raise a distrust in common readers that Plutarch wants them. Rualdus indeed has collected ample testimonies of them: but I will only recite the names of some, and refer you to him for the particular quotations. He reckons Gellius, Eusebius, Himerius the Sophister, Eunapius, Cyrillus of Alexandria, Theodoret, Agathias, Photius and Xiphilin, patriarchs of Constantinople, Johannes Sarisberiensis, the famous Petrarch, Petrus Victorius, and Justus Lipsius.

But Theodorus Gaza, a man learned in the Latin tongue, and a great restorer of the Greek, who lived above two hundred years ago, deserves to have his suffrage set down in words at length; for the rest have only commended Plutarch more than any single author, but he has extolled him above all together.

It is said, that, having this extravagant question put to him by a friend,—that if learning must suffer a general shipwreck, and he had only his choice left him of preserving one author, who should be the man he would preserve? he answered Plutarch; and probably might give this reason, that, in saving him, he should secure the best collection of them all.

The Epigram of Agathias deserves also to be remembered. This author flourished about the year five hundred, in the reign of the Emperor Justinian; the verses are extant in the "Anthologia," and with the translation of them I will conclude the praises of our author; having first admonished you, that they are supposed to be written on a statue erected by the Romans to his memory:

Σεῖο πολυκλήεντα τύπον στήσαντο Χερωνεῦ
Πλούταρχε κρατερῶν υἷες Ἀυσονίων·
Ὅττι παραλλήλοισι βίοις Ἕλληνας ἀριστοὺς
Ῥώμης εὐπολέμοις ἥρμοσας ἐνναέταις·
Ἀλλὰ τεοῦ βιότοιο παράλληλον βίον ἄλλον
Οὐδὲ σύγ' ἂν γράψαις, οὐ γὰρ ὅμοιον ἔχεις.

Cheronean Plutarch, to thy deathless praise
Does martial Rome this grateful statue raise;
Because both Greece and she thy fame have shared,
(Their heroes written, and their lives compared;)
But thou thyself could'st never write thy own;
Their lives have parallels, but thine has none.

SPECIMEN OF THE TRANSLATION

OF THE

HISTORY OF THE LEAGUE.

HISTORY OF THE LEAGUE.

THE reader must recall to his mind the state of parties during the last years of Charles the Second's reign, to which so many allusions have been made in the notes upon "Absalom and Achitophel," and "The Medal." The flight of Shaftesbury, and the discovery of the Rye-house conspiracy, had been deep wounds to the credit of the Whigs. The wealthy part of the nation dreaded a party, whose chief support was in the riotous mob of London; and men of principle, while they felt the severity of a government which seemed approaching towards despotism, abhorred the assassination which a part at least of the popular leaders had meditated as a remedy. The king, meanwhile, was anxious to keep the advantage he had gained, and to stigmatize his adversaries as leagued together against him upon principles inimical to all kingly governments. For this purpose, Dryden was employed to translate from the French of the Jesuit Maimbourg, the "History of the League," a work undertaken in France under the auspices of Louis XIV. The evident intention of bringing out this translation at the time when it appeared, was to increase the unpopularity of the Whigs, by ascribing to the association which Shaftesbury had proposed, the same motives and principles which actuated the members of the League, and plunged France into the long and bloody civil war between their kings and the house of Guise. Dryden had already drawn such a parallel in the play called the "Duke of Guise," which he wrote in conjunction with Lee. The intended parallel between the faction of the League in France, and that of the Solemn League and Covenant, and afterwards of the Whigs in England, was avowed in the first lines of the prologue,* and more largely in the vindication of the play, which Dryden published shortly after its appearance.† Maimbourg, on the other hand, from whose work the translation was made, was not only a zealous royalist, but a professed enemy of the Huguenots, and had written a history of their religion calculated to place it in the most odious point of view. There was, therefore, to be found in his "History of the League," not only an accurate and terrifying account of that famous combination, but many hints towards completing the parallel to be deduced betwixt the principles of the Guisards and those of the Calvinists. With this intention, and under the immediate auspices of the king, the work was translated and published.

The title-page bears, that the translation was made according to his majesty's command; and the frontispiece represents Charles enthroned in state; Justice is seated upon one side, and upon the other is a view of a harbour, with two lighthouses, and a fleet in sail. A hand from heaven is about to place on the king's head an imperial crown, from which glances a ray of light, bearing the motto, *Per me reges regnant*. In front, are the lords temporal and spiritual, assembled before the throne, in a dutiful posture, and at their feet a scroll, on which is written, *Sibi et successoribus suis legitimis*, in allusion to the celebrated Exclusion Bill.

* Our play's a parallel; the Holy League
Begot our Covenant; Guisards got the Whig.

† Our intention, therefore, was to make a parallel betwixt the Holy League plotted by the house of Guise and its adherents, with the Covenant plotted by the rebels in the time of Charles I. and those of the New Association, which was the spawn of the Old Covenant."

TO THE KING.

SIR,

HAVING received the honour of your majesty's commands to translate the "History of the League," I have applied myself, with my utmost diligence, to obey them: First, by a thorough understanding of my author, in which I was assisted by my former knowledge of the French history in general, and, in particular, of those very transactions which he has so faithfully and judiciously related; then by giving his thoughts the same beauty in our language which they had in the original, and, which I most of all endeavoured, the same force and perspicuity: both of which, I hope, I have performed with some exactness, and without any considerable mistake. But of this your majesty is the truest judge, who are so great a master of the original; and who, having read this piece when it was first published, can easily find out my failings, but, to my comfort, can more easily forgive them. I confess, I could never have laid hold on that virtue of your royal clemency at a more unseasonable time; when your enemies have so far abused it, that pardons are grown dangerous to your safety, and consequently to the welfare of your loyal subjects. But frequent forgiveness is their encouragement; they have the sanctuary in their eye before they attempt the crime, and take all measures of security, either not to need a pardon, if they strike the blow, or to have it granted, if they fail. Upon the whole matter, your majesty is not upon equal terms with them; you are still forgiving, and they still designing against your sacred life; your principle is mercy, theirs inveterate malice; when one only wards, and the other strikes, the prospect is sad on the defensive side. Hercules, as the poet tells us, had no advantage on Antæus, by his often throwing him on the ground; for he laid him only in his mother's lap, which, in effect, was but doubling his strength to renew the combat. These sons of earth are never to be trusted in their mother-element; they must be hoisted into the air, and strangled.* If the experiment of clemency were new; if it had not been often tried without effect, or rather with effects quite contrary to the intentions of your goodness, your loyal subjects are generous enough to pity their countrymen, though offenders: but when that pity has been always found to draw into example of greater mischiefs; when they continually behold both your majesty and themselves exposed to dangers; the church, the government, the succession, still threatened; ingratitude, so far from being converted by gentle means, that it is turned at last into the nature of the damned, desirous of revenge, and hardened in impenitence,—it is time, at length, for self-preservation to cry out for justice, and to lay by mildness, when it ceases to be a virtue. Almighty God has hitherto miraculously preserved you; but who knows how long the miracle will continue? His ordinary operations are by second causes; and then reason will conclude, that to be preserved, we ought to use the lawful means of preservation. If, on the other side, it be thus argued, that, of many attempts, one may possibly take place, if preventing justice be not employed against offenders; what remains, but that we implore the divine assistance to avert that judgment; which is no more than to desire of God to work another and another, and, in conclusion, a whole series of miracles. This, sir, is the general voice of all true Englishmen; I might call it the loyal address of three nations infinitely solicitous of your safety, which includes their own prosperity. It is, indeed, a high presumption for a man so inconsiderable as I am

* I wish the fervour of Dryden's loyalty had left this exhortation to such writers as the author of "Justice Triumphant," an excellent new song, in commendation of Sir Thomas Jeffries, Lord Chief Justice of England. To a pleasant new tune, called, *Now the Tories that glories*.

Loyal Jeffries is judge again,
Let the Brimighams grudge amain,
Who to Tyburn must trudge amain.

to present it; but zeal and dutiful affection, in an affair of this importance, will make every good subject a counsellor. It is, in my opinion, the test of loyalty; and to be either a friend or foe to the government needs no other distinction, than to declare at this time either for remissness or justice. I said at this time, because I look not on the storm as overblown. It is still a gusty kind of weather; there is a kind of sickness in the air; it seems, indeed, to be cleared up for some few hours; but the wind still blowing from the same corner, and when new matter is gathered into a body, it will not fail to bring it round, and pour upon us a second tempest. I shall be glad to be found a false prophet; but he was certainly inspired, who, when he saw a little cloud arising from the sea, and that no bigger than a hand, gave immediate notice to the king, that he might mount the chariot, before he was overtaken by the storm.* If so much care was taken of an idolatrous king, a usurper, a persecutor, and a tyrant, how much more vigilant ought we to be in the concernments of a lawful prince, a father of his country, and a defender of the faith, who stands exposed by his too much mercy to the unwearied and endless conspiracies of parricides? He was a better prince than the former whom I mentioned out of the sacred history, and the allusion comes yet more close, who stopped his hand after the third arrow: Three victories were indeed obtained; but the effect of often shooting had been the total destruction of his enemies.† To come yet nearer: Henry the Fourth, your royal grandfather,* whose victories, and the subversion of the League, are the main argument of this history, was a prince most clement in his nature: he forgave his rebels, and received them all into mercy, and some of them into favour, but it was not till he had fully vanquished them: they were sensible of their impiety; they submitted, and his clemency was not extorted from him; it was his free gift, and it was seasonably given. I wish the case were here the same: I confess it was not much unlike it at your majesty's happy restoration; yet so much of the parallel was then wanting, that the amnesty you gave produced not all the desired effects. For our sects are of a more obstinate nature than were those leaguing Catholics, who were always for a king, and, yet more, the major part of them would have him of the royal stem; but our associates and sectaries are men of commonwealth principles; and though their first stroke was only aimed at the immediate succession, it was most manifest that it would not there have ended, for at the same time they were hewing at your royal prerogatives. So that the next successor, if there had been any, must have been a precarious prince, and depended on them for the necessaries of life. But of these and more outrageous proceedings, your majesty has already shown yourself justly sensible in your declaration, after the dissolution of the last parliament, which put an end to the arbitrary encroachments of a popular faction. Since which time it has pleased Almighty God so to prosper your affairs, that, without searching into the secrets of Divine Providence, it is evident your magnanimity and resolution, next under Him, have been the immediate cause of your safety and our present happiness. By weathering of which storm, may I presume to say it without flattery, you have performed a greater and more glorious work than all the conquests of your neighbours. For it is not difficult for a great monarchy, well united, and making use of advantages, to extend its limits; but to be pressed with wants, surrounded with dangers, your authority undermined in popular assemblies, your sacred life attempted by a conspiracy, your royal brother forced from your arms; in one word, to govern a kingdom, which was either possessed or turned into a bedlam, and yet in the midst of

* "And Elijah said unto Ahab, get thee up, eat and drink, for there is a sound of abundance of rain.

"So Ahab went up to eat and to drink; and Elijah went up to the top of Carmel, and cast himself down upon the earth, and put his head between his knees;

"And said to his servant, Go up now, look toward the sea; and he went up and looked, and said, There is nothing; and he said, Go again, seven times.

"And it came to pass at the seventh time, that he said, Behold there comes a little cloud out of the sea, like a man's hand: And he said, Go, say unto Ahab, prepare thy chariot, and get thee down, that the rain stop thee not.

"And it came to pass in the mean while, that the heaven was black with clouds and wind; and there was a great rain. And Ahab rode and went to Jezreel."—1 *Kings*, xviii 41—45.

† Joash, king of Israel, having visited the prophet Elisha while on his death bed, was desired, by the dying seer, to take a bow, and shoot an arrow towards the east, and he shot. "And he said, The arrow of the Lord's deliverance, and the arrow of deliverance from Syria; for thou shalt smite the Syrians in Aphek till thou have consumed them.

"And he said, Take the arrows, and he took them. And he said unto the king of Israel, Smite upon the ground; and he smote thrice, and stayed.

"And the man of God was wroth with him, and said, Thou shouldst have smitten five and six times; then hadst thou smitten Syria till thou hadst consumed it, whereas now thou shalt smite Syria but thrice.—2 *Kings*, xiii. 17—19.

* Our readers need hardly be reminded, that the League was a confederacy formed under pretence of maintaining the Catholic religion, and excluding Henry of Navarre, afterwards Henry IV., from the throne, on account of his being a Huguenot. It was only dispersed and subdued after the long and bloody war which was terminated by his ascending the throne in 1594.

ruin to stand firm, undaunted, and resolved, and at last to break through all these difficulties and dispel them,—this is indeed an action which is worthy the grandson of Henry the Great. During all this violence of your enemies, your majesty has contended with your natural clemency to make some examples of your justice; and they themselves will acknowledge, that you have not urged the law against them, but have been pressed and constrained by it to inflict punishments in your own defence, and in the mean time to watch every opportunity of showing mercy, when there was the least probability of repentance: so that they who have suffered, may be truly said to have forced the sword of justice out of your hand, and to have done execution on themselves. But by how much the more you have been willing to spare them, by so much has their impudence increased; and if by this mildness they recover from the great frost which has almost blasted them to the roots, if these venomous plants shoot out again, it will be a sad comfort to say they have been ungrateful, when it is evident to mankind that ingratitude is their nature. That sort of pity which is proper for them, and may be of use to their conversion, is to make them sensible of their errors; and this your majesty, out of your fatherly indulgence, amongst other experiments which you have made, is pleased to allow them in this book, which you have commanded to be translated for the public benefit; that at least all such as are not wilfully blind may view in it, as in a glass, their own deformities: for never was there a plainer parallel than of the troubles of France and of Great Britain; of their leagues, covenants, associations, and ours; of their Calvinists and our Presbyterians; they are all of the same family; and Titian's famous table of the Altar-piece, with the pictures of Venetian senators from great-grandfather to great-grandson, shows not more the resemblance of a race than this: for as there, so here, the features are alike in all; there is nothing but the age that makes the difference; otherwise the old man of a hundred, and the babe in swaddling clouts, that is to say, 1584 and 1684, have but a century and a sea betwixt them, to be the same. But I have presumed too much upon your majesty's time already, and this is not the place to show that resemblance, which is but too manifest in the whole history. It is enough to say, your majesty has allowed our rebels a greater favour than the law; you have given them the benefit of their clergy: if they can but read, and will be honest enough to apply it, they may be saved. God Almighty give an answerable success to this your royal act of grace; may they all repent, and be united as the body to their head! May that treasury of mercy which is within your royal breast have leave to be poured forth upon them, when they put themselves in a condition of receiving it! and, in the mean time, permit me to implore it humbly for myself, and let my presumption in this bold address be forgiven to the zeal which I have to your service and to the public good. To conclude: may you never have a worse-meaning offender at your feet, than him, who, besides his duty and his natural inclination, has all manner of obligations to be perpetually,

Sir,

Your majesty's most humble,

Most obedient, and most faithful

Subject and Servant,

John Dryden.

THE AUTHOR'S

DEDICATION TO THE FRENCH KING.*

SIR,

FRANCE, which being well united, as we now behold it, under the glorious reign of your majesty, might give law to all the world, was upon the point of self-destruction, by the division which was raised in it by two fatal leagues of rebels; the one in the middle, and the other towards the latter end, of the last age.

Heresy produced the first against the true religion;† ambition, under the mask of zeal, gave birth to the second, with pretence of maintaining what the other would have ruined: and both of them, though implacable enemies to each other, yet agreed in this, that each of them, at divers times, set up the standard of rebellion against our kings.

The crimes of the former I have set forth in the history of Calvinism, which made that impious League in France, against the Lord and his anointed; and I discover the wickedness of the latter in this work, which I present to your majesty, as the fruit of my exact obedience to those commands with which you have been pleased to honour me. I have endeavoured to perform them with so much the greater satisfaction to myself, because I believed that, in reading this history, the falsehood of some advantages which the Leaguers and Huguenots have ascribed to themselves may be easily discerned. These, by boasting, as they frequently do, even at this day, that they set the crown on the head of King Henry IV.; those, that their League was the cause of his conversion. I hope the world will soon be disabused of those mistakes; and that it will be clearly seen, that they were the Catholics of the royal party, who, next under God, produced those two effects, so advantageous to France. We are owing for neither of them to those two unhappy Leagues, which were the most dangerous enemies to the prosperity of the kingdom; and it is manifest at this present time, that the glory of triumphing over both of them was reserved, by the Divine Providence, to our kings of the imperial stem of Bourbon.

Henry IV. subdued and reduced the League of the false zealots, by the invincible force of his arms, and by the wonderful attractions of his clemency: Louis the Just disarmed that of the Calvinists, by the taking of Rochelle, and other places, which those heretics had moulded into a kind of commonwealth against their sovereign; and Louis the Great, without employing other arms than those of his ardent charity and incomparable zeal for the conversion of Protestants, accompanied by the justice of his laws,‡ has reduced it to that low condition, that we have reason to believe we shall behold its ruin, by the repentance of those, who, being deluded and held back by their ministers, continue still in their erroneous belief, rather through ignorance than malice. And this it is, which, when accomplished, will surpass even all those other wonders which daily are beheld, under your most auspicious government.

Undoubtedly, sir, your majesty has performed, by your victorious arms, your generous goodness, and your more than royal magnificence, all those great and heroic actions, which will ever be the admiration of the world, and infinitely above the commendations which future ages, in imitation of the present, will consecrate to your immortal memory. I presume not to undertake that subject, because it has already drained the praises of the noblest pens which yet have not been able to raise us to that idea of you, which we ought justly to conceive: I shall only say, that what you have done with so much prudence, justice, and glory, by extending the French monarchy to its ancient bounds, and rendering it, as it is at present, as flourishing, and as much respected by all the world, as it ever has been under the greatest and most renowned of all our monarchs, is not

* Louis XIV.

† The association of the Huguenots under the Prince of Conde, Coligni, and others.

‡ It would not have been decent to remind the Grand Monarque of such arguments as dragoons, banishment, and the galleys.

so great in the sight of God, as what your majesty performs daily, with so much piety, zeal, and good success, in augmenting the kingdom of Jesus Christ, and procuring the conversion of our Protestants, by those gentle and efficacious means which you have used.

This, sir, is, without exception, the most glorious of all your conquests; and while you continue to enjoy on earth that undisputed glory which your other actions have acquired you, is preparing an eternal triumph for you in the heavens.

It is what is continually implored of God, in his most ardent prayers, who, enjoying the abundant favours of your majesty, lives at this day the most happy of mankind, under your most powerful protection; and is most obliged to continue all his life, with all imaginable respect and zeal.

Sir,

Your majesty's most obedient

And most faithful subject and servant,

Louis Maimbourg.

THE AUTHOR'S

ADVERTISEMENT TO THE READER.

Since perhaps there are some, who may think themselves concerned in this history, because they are the grand-children or descendants of those who are here mentioned, I desire them to consider, that writing like a faithful historian, I am obliged sincerely to relate either the good or ill which they have done. If they find themselves offended, they must take their satisfaction on those who have prescribed the laws of history: let them give an account of their own rules; for historians are indispensably bound to follow them; and the sum of our reputation consists in a punctual execution of their orders.

Thus, as I pretend not to have deserved their thanks in speaking well of their relations, so I may reasonably conclude, that they ought not to wish me ill, when I say what is not much to their advantage. I faithfully relate what I find written in good authors, or in particular memoirs, which I take for good, after I have thoroughly examined them.

I do yet more; for, considering that no man is bound to believe, when I say in general that I have had the use of good manuscripts, on whose credit I give you what is not otherwise to be had; I sincerely and particularly point out the originals from whence I drew these truths; and am fully convinced, that every historian, who hopes to gain the belief of his reader, ought to transact in the same manner. For, if there were no more to be done, than barely to say, I have found such or such an extraordinary passage in an authentic manuscript, without giving a more particular account of it, under pretence of being bound to secrecy, there is no kind of fable which by this means might not be slurred upon the reader for a truth. An author might tell many a lusty lie, but a reader, who were not a very credulous fool, or a very complaisant gentleman, would have a care of believing him. It is for this reason that I have always marked in my margins, the books, relations, and memoirs, whether printed or manuscripts, from whence I take the substance of my relations.

One of those writers of whom I have made most use, is Monsieur Peter Victor Cayet, in his nine years' chronology, containing the history of the wars of Henry the Fourth.* Because he having always followed that prince, since he was placed in his service, together with Monsieur de la Gaucheric, who was his preceptor, it is exceeding probable that he was better informed of the passages of those times, of which he was an eye-witness, than others who had not that advantage.

For what else concerns him, he was one of the most learned and able ministers which our Protestants have ever had; and in that quality served Madam Catherine, the king's sister, till, about two years after the conversion of that great prince, he acknowledged the true Catholic religion, and made his solemn abjuration of heresy at Paris. He also published the motives of his conversion in a learned treatise, which was received with great applause both in France and in foreign countries; and his example, fortified with the strong reasons of a man so able as he was, to which no solid answer was ever given, was immediately followed by the conversion of a great number of Protestants, who by his means

* Peter Victor Palma Cayet studied at Geneva, and was a domestic in the house of Calvin. He afterwards became a reformed minister and chaplain to Catherine, sister to Henry IV. Being addicted to alchymy, and having written a work in defence of public stews, he was deposed by a synod from his ministerial functions, as a wizard and a libertine. Upon his disgrace he abjured the reformed doctrine, and was considered by the Catholics as a convert of such importance, that the Pope himself honoured his proselyte with a letter of congratulation. His historical works are, an Account of the War between the Turks and Hungarians, published in 1598; his "Septennary Chronology," comprising from 1598 to 1604; and his "Novennary Chronology," giving an account of the nine years' war, which broke out in 1589, and was terminated by the peace of Vervins. Cayet died in 1610

came to understand the falsehood of their religion pretendedly reformed.

This action so infinitely nettled his former brotherhood of ministers, that they grew outrageous against him. They ran down his reputation with full cry, and endeavoured to blacken it with a thousand horrible calumnies, with which they stuffed their libels; and, amongst others, that which they have inserted into the memoirs of the League, with the greatest villany imaginable, taking no notice of the solid and convincing answers he made them. Which proceeding of theirs is sufficient to discover the falsity of all they have written to defame him, according to the libelling genius of presbytery.

For, of all heretics, none have been more cruel, or more foul-mouthed, than the Calvinists; none have revenged themselves of their pretended enemies more barbarously, either by open arms, or private mischiefs, when the power was in their hands; or more impudently with their pens, and by their libels, when they had no other way to show their malice; murdering their reputations with all sorts of injuries and impostures, who have once declared themselves against their party.

In effect, what have they not said to defame the memory of Monsieur de Sponde, lieutenant-general in Rochelle; of Salette, counsellor to the king of Navarre; of Morlas, counsellor of state and superintendent of the magazines of France; as also of Du Fay, Clairville, Rehan, and a hundred others of their most celebrated ministers, who, after having been esteemed amongst them for good men, and looked on as the leaders of their consistory, are, by a strange sort of metamorphosis, become, on the sudden, profligate wretches, and the most infamous of mankind, only for renouncing Calvinism? By how many forgeries and calumnies have they endeavoured to ruin the repute of all such Catholics as have the most vigorously opposed their heresy, history will furnish us with abundant proofs; and we have but too many in the fragments which Monsieur le Laboreur has given us of their insolent satires, where they spare not the most inviolable and sacred things on earth, not even their anointed sovereigns.

For which reason, that writer, in a certain chapter of his book, wherein he mentions but a small parcel of those libels, after he has said, "that the most venomous satirists, and the greatest libertines, were those of the Huguenot party," adds these memorable words: "I should have been ashamed to have read all those libels, for the blasphemies and impieties with which they are filled, if that very consideration had not been aiding to confirm me in the belief, that there was more wickedness, than either error or blindness, in their doctrine; and that their morals were even more corrupt than their opinions."

He assures us in another place, that these new evangelists have made entire volumes of railing, of which he has seen above forty manuscripts; and that there needed no other arguments to decide the difference betwixt the two religions, and to elude the fair pretences of these reforming innovators.

So that all they have scribbled, with so much (I will not say violence, but) madness, against the Sieur Cayet, immediately upon his conversion, cannot do him the least manner of prejudice, no more than their ridiculous prediction, wherein they foretold, that it would not be long before he would be neither Huguenot nor Catholic, but that he would set up a third party betwixt the two religions. For he ever continued to live so well amongst the Catholics, that, after he had given on all occasions large proofs, both of his virtue and of his faith, he was thought worthy to receive the order of priesthood, and the degree of doctor in divinity, and was reader and professor royal of the oriental tongues.

Now seeing, in the year 1605, ten years after his conversion, he had published his "Septennary Chronology," of the peace which was made at Vervins in the year 1598; some of the greatest lords at court, who understood his merit, and had seen him with the king, (by whom he had the honour to be well known, and much esteemed,) obliged him to add to the history of the peace, that of the war, which that great prince made during nine years after his coming to the crown, till the peace of Vervins; which he performed in the three tomes of his "Nine Years' Chronology," printed at Paris in the year 1608; in which, before he proceeds to the reign of Henry the Fourth, he makes an abridgment of the most considerable passages in the League, to the death of Henry the Third. And it is partly from this author, and partly from such others as were eye-witnesses of what they wrote, whether in printed books, or particular memoirs, that I have drawn those things which are related by me in this history. I am not therefore myself the witness, nor as an historian do I take upon me to decide the merit of these actions, whether they are blamable or praiseworthy; I am only the relater of them; and since, in that quality, I pretend not to be believed on my own bare word, and that I quote my authors, who are my warrantees, as I have done in all my histories, I believe myself to stand exempted from any just reproaches, which can be fastened on me for my writing.

On which subject I think it may be truly said, that if instead of examining matters of fact, and inquiring whether they are truly or falsely represented, that consideration be laid aside, and the question taken up, whether such or such actions were good or bad, and matter of right pleaded, whether they deserve to be condemned or praised; it would be but loss of time in unprofitable discourses, in which an historian is no way concerned. For in conclusion, he is only answerable for such things as he reports, on the credit of those from whom he had them; taking from each of them some particulars, of which the rest are silent, and compiling out of all of them a new body of history, which is of a quite different mould and fashion from any of the authors who have written before him.

And it is this in which consists a great part of the delicacy and beauty of these kinds of works, and which produces this effect; that, keeping always in the most exact limits of truth, yet an author may lawfully pretend to the glory of the invention; having the satisfaction of setting forth a new history, though, writing only the passages of a former age, he can relate almost nothing but what has been written formerly, either in printed books or manuscripts; which, though kept up in private, and little known, are, notwithstanding, not the work of him who writes the history.

As to what remains, none ought to wonder that I make but one single volume on this subject, though the matter of it is of vast extent. I take not upon me to tell all that has been done, on occasion of the League, in all the provinces, nor to describe all the sieges; the taking and surprising of so many places which were sometimes for the king, and at other times for the League; or all those petty skirmishes, which have drawn (if I may have liberty so to express myself) such deluges of blood from the veins of France. All these particulars ought to be the ingredients of the general history of this nation, under the reigns of the two last Henries, which may be read in many famous historians; and principally in the last tome of the late Monsieur de Mezeray, who has surpassed himself in that part of his great work.

I confine my undertaking within the compass of what is most essential in the particular history of the League, and have only applied myself to the discovery of its true origin, to unriddle its intrigues and artifices, and find out the most secret motives, by which the heads of that conspiracy have acted, to which the magnificent title of the Holy Union has been given with so much injustice; and, in consequence of this, to make an exact description of the principal actions, and the greatest and most signal events, which decided the fortune of the League; and this, in short, is the model of my work.

As for the end which I proposed to myself in conceiving it, I may boldly say, that it was to give a plain understanding to all such as shall read this history, that all sorts of associations which are formed against lawful sovereigns, particularly when the conspirators endeavour to disguise them under the specious pretence of religion and piety, as did the Huguenots and Leaguers, are at all times most criminal in the sight of God, and most commonly of unhappy and fatal consequences to those who are either the authors or accomplices of the crime.

THE HISTORY OF THE LEAGUE

LIB. III.

If I intended to follow the example of Livy, the prince of Latin historians, who never suffers a prodigy to escape him, and describes it perhaps with as much superstition as exactness, I should here make long narrations how the sun was obscured on the sudden, without the interposition of any cloud appearing in the sky, with a flaming sword shooting out from the centre of the body; palpable darkness like that of the Egyptians at noon-day; extraordinary tempests, earthquakes, fiery phantasms in the air, and a hundred other prodigies, which are said to have been produced and seen in this unhappy year of one thousand five hundred and eighty-eight, and which were fancied to be so many ominous presages of those horrible disorders that ensued in it.

But because I am not of the opinion that much credit ought to be given to those sorts of signs, which are commonly the effects of natural causes, though very often unknown to us; nor to the predictions of astrologers, some of which verily believed they had found in the stars that this year should be the conclusion of the world, I will only say, that the most sure presage of so many misfortunes then impending, was the minds of men too much exasperated on both sides to live in peace with each other; and not rather to be searching out for means of making sure of those whom they suspected, and disposing of them according to their jealousies.

In order to this, the Duke of Guise, after he had made an end of ruining the county of Montbelliard, took his way to Nancy, whither he had invited all the princes of his house to assemble in the month of January, there to take their resolutions in reference to the present condition of affairs; and of that happy success which they had in the war against the Reyters. Some of them there were, as it is reported, so swollen with that victory, and so blinded with their prosperity, that they proposed, in this conference, the most dangerous and most violent expedients; to which the Duke of Lorraine, a moderate and wary prince, would by no means listen. Howsoever it were, (for I find nothing to confirm these relations, not even in the memoirs of their greatest enemies, who have written most exactly of that assembly,) it is most undoubted, that if they proceeded not so far as to those terrible extremities, yet what was then concluded, passed in the world for a most unjust and unlawful undertaking, and was condemned by all those who were not blindly devoted to the League.

It was, that a request should be presented to the king, containing articles, which, under the ordinary pretence of their desire to preserve in France the Catholic religion, tended manifestly to despoil him of his authority and power, and to invest the heads of the League in both. For those scandalous articles bore this substance in them, that, for the service of God, and the maintenance and security of religion, the king should not only be most humbly petitioned, but also summoned, to establish the Holy Inquisition in his realm; to cause the council of Trent to be there published, suspending nevertheless that article which revokes the exemption pretended by some chapters and abbeys against the bishops; to continue the war against the Huguenots and to cause the goods both of them and of their associates to be sold, with which to defray the charges of that war, and to pay the debts in which the heads of the League had been constrained to involve themselves for the prosecution of it; to refuse quarter to all prisoners who should be taken in that war, unless upon condition of paying the full value of their goods, and giving caution of living afterwards like good Catholics.

Behold here a most specious appearance of zeal for religion; but, in the next place, observe the venom which lies hidden under all these fair pretences: That the king shall unite himself more cordially, and more openly than before, to this holy League; thereby to keep exactly all its laws, to which men are obliged by this the most solemn and most inviolable of all oaths: That, besides the forces which he shall be obliged to set on foot to wage that war against the Huguenots, he shall maintain an army on the frontiers of Lorraine, to oppose the German Protestants, if they should determine once again to enter France: That, besides those places which the Leaguers already held for their security, there should be delivered to them other towns of more importance, which should be specified to him, where they might establish for governors those of their heads which they shall name, with power of introducing such garrisons, and making such fortifications, as they shall think fit, at the charges of the provinces in which they are situate: And, in conclusion, to secure them, that they shall be no more hindered, as till this present they have always been, in the executing of those things which have been promised them for the safety of religion, his majesty shall displace from his council, and from the court, and shall deprive of their governments and offices, those who shall be named to him as patrons of heretics, and enemies to religion and the state.

These were those extravagant demands which began to open the eyes of many good Catholics, who had suffered themselves to be innocently seduced by the appearances of true zeal, which being little illuminated, was not "according to knowledge," as the apostle speaks. For they now more clearly saw into some of those articles; that the League, to engage the Pope and the King of Spain in their interests, would be content to abandon those privileges and liberties which our ancestors have always maintained with so much vigour and resolution; and to subject to the yoke of a Spanish inquisition, the French, who have never been able to undergo it. And in others of them, that they designed to bereave the king of all the solid and essential parts of royalty, to leave him only the shadow and appearance of it, and afterwards to dispose even of his person, as the heads of their party should think fit.

And accordingly when the request was presented to the king on the part of the associated princes, and the Cardinal of Bourbon, whose simplicity and whose name they abused, and made it a cloak to their ambition, he conceived an extreme indignation against it, which immediately appeared in his eyes and countenance. Yet he thought it necessary at that time to dissemble, not finding himself then in a condition of returning such an answer to it, as was becoming a king justly provoked against his subjects, who stood on terms with him like lords and masters. For which reason, and withal to gain farther time, he contented himself to say, that he would examine these articles in his council, in order to his answer; which should be in such sort, that all good Catholics should have reason to be satisfied.

But in the mean time, the Duke of Guise, who took not fair words for payment, well understanding the king's design, and resolving not to give the Duke of Espernon the leisure to conjure down that tempest which was raised against him, and to infuse in his master those vigorous resolutions which were necessary for him to take, pressed the king continually to give a precise answer to every particular in those articles. For he doubted not, that, in case it proved favourable, he should engross all power to himself; and if it were otherwise, that it would be thought the king resolved to maintain the Huguenots, and that by consequence the Catholics would enter into a war against him.

On which considerations, being then retired into his government of Champaigne, to which place he went after the conference at Nancy, he plied the king incessantly with messages sent by gentlemen, one after another, to urge him to a speedy and punctual answer. And this he did with the more eagerness and importunity, because, on the one side, he found himself more powerful than ever, having a great part of the gentry, and almost all the people, and especially the Parisians, for him; and, on the other side, he observed the party of the Huguenots to be very low, and infinitely weakened, by the defeat of their great German succours, and by their late loss of the Prince of Conde, a person of all others the most strictly tied to their religion, and on whom they more relied than any man, not excepting the King of Navarre himself.

He deceased on the 5th of March, at St. Jean de Angely, of an exceeding violent distemper, with which he was suddenly seized one evening after supper and which carried him off in two days' time. The sixteen, with infamous baseness, made a great rejoicing for it; and their preachers failed not to roar out in their sermons, that it was the effect of the excommunication with which he had been thunderstruck by Pope Sixtus. But besides that the King of Navarre, who had been struck in the same manner by the bull, had his health never the worse for it, the king, to whom that poor creature the Cardinal of Bourbon had been telling the same story, and making wonderful exclamations in relating it, answered him with a smile, that it might very well be the occasion of his death, but withal there was something else which helped him on his journey. And truly the matter was put beyond all doubt, after the attestation of four physicians, and of two master chirurgeons, who deposed upon their oaths, that they had manifestly seen, in almost all the parts of his body, all the most evident signs and effects of a caustic poison, burning and ulcerating. A most execrable action, which could not be too rigorously punished; and yet the laws inflicted what was possible on the person of one of his domestic servants, who was drawn in pieces by four horses in the place of St. Jean de Angely.

As to the rest, he was a prince, who, excepting only his obstinate adhering to a religion in which he was born, and whose falsehood he might have known in time, if he had not been too much prepossessed, had, at the age of five-and-thirty years, at which he died, all the perfections which can meet together in one man, to render him one of the greatest and most accomplished persons in the world; if at least there might not possibly be discerned in his carriage and customs some of those little failings, from which the most wise are not exempted, and which may easily be pardoned, without lessening the esteem which we have for them. And if fortune, which is not always propitious to merit, was not favourable to him on some occasions, wherein he had need of her assistance, yet in this she was his friend, that she gave him the greater opportunity of showing his invincible courage in his adversities, in which he raised himself infinitely above her, by the vigour and greatness of his soul.

Accordingly, the death of this great prince was lamented, not only by those of his own party, who loved him passionately, but also by the Catholics, and even by the Duke of Guise himself; who, head as he was of an infamous and wicked faction, which he made subservient to his ends, had of his own stock, and the excellency of his nature, which was infinitely noble, all the generosity which is requisite to love and respect virtue, even in the person of his greatest and most formidable enemy.

All which notwithstanding, he was content to make what advantage he could of so lamentable an accident, towards the compassing of his designs: And as he observed, not only by this, but by a multitude of concomitant accidents and misfortunes, that the Huguenot party decreased in strength and reputation, and his own grew more bold and undertaking, he set himself more vigorously to push his fortune, and to demand an entire satisfaction to all the articles of his request: which had so puffed up the spirits of the sixteen, that they forgot all manner of moderation, and grew daily more and more insupportable. It happened also at the same time, that the king received several advertisements of the resolution which had been taken in their council to seize his person, and to enclose him in a monastery. And the same lieutenant of the provostship of the Isle of Paris, Nicholas Poulain, who had formerly discovered the like conspiracy, to which belief was not given, told him so many particular circumstances in relation to this, that though he was very diffident of that double-dealing man, whose integrity he much suspected, yet his evidence concurring with the extreme insolence of the sixteen, which rendered his report more credible, could not but leave a strong impression on his soul; insomuch, that at last following the counsel of those who had so long advised him to employ his power and justice against these mutineers, he took up a resolution, once for all, to take that thorn out of his side, to reduce Paris into that state of submission and obedience which belongs to subjects; and to extinguish the faction of the sixteen, by the exemplary chastisement of the most seditious amongst them.

The preparations which of necessity he was to make to secure the success of this undertaking; the three thousand Swissers, whom he caused to be quartered at Lagny; the companies of guards which were reinforced; the troops which were sent him from the Duke of Espernon, who was gone into his government of Normandy: and all the passages of the river, both above Paris and below it, being possessed by him,—were so many alarms to those mutineers, who, believing themselves already lost, implored the assistance of the Duke of Guise. That prince, who had advanced from Rheims as far as Soissons, in favour of the Duke of Aumale, his cousin, who met with trouble and resistance in his government of Picardy, satisfied himself at first with sending them some of his most experienced captains, to regulate and manage their militia in case of need. But some few days after, finding himself still pressed more eagerly by the solicitations of those people, who were now driven to despair, and believing this foundation of the League, on which he had built his hopes, being once shaken, he himself must perish under its ruins, (for that being destroyed, the next design was certainly to fall on him, who was the head and protector of it;) he gave immediate notice to his friends and creatures to get into Paris, one after another, at several gates, and ordered some to assure the sixteen in his name, that he would suddenly be there in person, to live and die with them.

The king, who was advertised of this resolution, and who was under great apprehensions of his coming, lest his presence might hinder the execution of his enterprise, and arm with a word speaking that great city, which was entirely a his devotion, sent the President de Bellievre, a man of great authority and known prudence, to tell the duke from him, that, in the present juncture of affairs, and just apprehension which he had that his coming would produce great troubles in Paris, he thought good he should not come till he received new orders from him, for otherwise he would render himself guilty of all those disorders which might thence ensue.

To this the duke, who was never to be beaten off from any resolution which he had once taken, answered calmly, but in doubtful terms, that he was ready to obey the king; that he had never intended to go to Paris, but in the condition of a private man, and without a train; that he desired to justify himself from those aspersions with which he knew his enemies had basely charged him in his absence; that he had reason to believe there was a design on foot to oppress the good Catholics, whose protector he had declared himself; and that he humbly besought his majesty to give him some security against so just an apprehension. Bellievre, who well knew that the king would stick at no manner of verbal satisfaction, in case that would prove sufficient to break his journey, promised he should have all the security he could possibly desire. In effect, the king was fully resolved to have given him all manner of assurances; but, as ill luck would have it, this was not done at the same time it was determined; insomuch that, without more delay, he got on horseback, and, crossing the country out of the common roads, that he might avoid the messengers, which he knew would be sent with new orders to him, entered Paris on Monday the 9th of May, with eight more in his company, just about noon, by the gate of St. Denis.

It may be said in one sort of meaning, that this day was the most unfortunate, and yet the most glorious, of all his life. For whether it were that the people, who were made to believe by the sixteen that the city was to be sacked, were advertised by them of his arrival, or that the report was spread at an instant, when he was first seen to approach the Fauxbourg, it is most certain that he had no sooner passed it, but the whole town running together from all parts of it, crowded up the street, and all the rest through which he passed; the windows were filled, and even the tiles of the houses; the air echoed with a thousand sorts of acclamations, and the loud cries of *Vive Guise!* were repeated with far higher peals than had been formerly of *Vive le Roy!* for those loyal shouts were grown out of date, and the League in a manner had abolished them.

There was a kind of madness in this transport, or rather in this furious torrent of their joy, which was so extravagant, that it passe even to idolatry. They haled and tore each other to get nearest to this prince; those who were borne off by the throng to a farther distance, stretched out their arms to him, with their hands clasped over their heads; they thought themselves happy, who could crowd so near as to touch any part of his cloak or boots. Some there were amongst them who kneeled to him, when he was passing by; and others who, when they could not reach him with their hands, endeavoured to touch him with their chaplets, which they kissed when they had received that honour, as the custom is in adoration at the shrines of saints. A thousand praises were given him, and a thousand blessings. He was called aloud the pillar of the church, the prop of faith, the protector of the Catholics, the saviour of Paris; and from all the windows there fell upon him a shower of flowers and of greens, with redoubled acclamations of *Vive Guise!*

To conclude, no imaginable demonstrations and testimonies of love, honour, and veneration, but were shown to the height at this tumultuous entry, by that sudden overflow of joy, and that wonderful dilatation of hearts and affections, which was to him a sort of triumph, more pleasing than any of the Cæsars'. Accordingly he enjoyed the full gust of it, with all the satisfaction of extreme pleasure; passing on horseback very leisurely through that infinite press of people, bare-headed, beholding them with a smiling countenance, and with that courteous and engaging air, which was so natural to him; saluting on the right and on the left, bowing to those below in the streets, and to those above in the windows, not neglecting the very meanest, holding out his hand to the nearest, and casting his obliging glances on the more remote, he passed in this manner to the queen-mother's palace, near St. Eustache, where he alighted, and from thence to the Louvre, following her on foot, who had taken her chair to conduct him to the king, and was witness to those incredible transports of public joy, and acclamations of that innumerable herd of people, which beat her ears incessantly with the name of Guise, bellowed from more than a hundred thousand mouths.

In the mean time, the king, who had heard, with infinite rage, of this sudden arrival of the duke, was shut up in his closet, where he was in consultation on that prince's life or death, who had been so blindly rash as to precipitate himself, in his single person, into inevitable danger, from whence only his good fortune (of which he was not master) could deliver him. Some there were, and amongst others the Abbot d'Elbene, and Colonel Alphonso d'Ornano, with the most resolute of those Gascons whom the Duke of Espernon had placed amongst the five-and-forty, to be always near the king's person, who counselled that irresolute and wavering prince to despatch him on the spot, having so fair a pretence, and the means so ready in his hand, to punish a rebellious subject; who, in opposition to his express orders, had audaciously presumed to come to Paris, as it were on purpose to let him know that he was absolute master of it.—The rest, more moderate, and amongst them the Chancellor de Chiverny, and the Sieurs de Bellievre, de la Guiche, and de Villequier, governor of Paris, dissuaded him from that attempt, laying before him, besides the dangerous consequences which this terrible action might produce in such a juncture, that it always concerned him, both for his reputation, and for the maintenance of the most inviolable laws of natural equity, before he passed to extremities, to hear a man who came to put himself so freely into the hands of his king, and to be answerable for all that was alleged against him

While these things were in debating, and the king in suspense betwixt his anger and his fear, uncertain which way to resolve, the duke (who had passed through the French guards commanded by Grillon, who loved him not, and through the Swissers, which stood ranked on both sides of the great staircase, and afterwards had traversed the hall and the antichamber filled with people, who made no very ceremonious returns to his salutations and civilities, entered into the presence-chamber, disguising a sudden fright which seized him, intrepid as he was, with the best face he could set upon the matter, which yet he could not act so well, but that it was easy to discern, through that affectation of bravery, that he could have been well contented to have been in some other place, and not to have engaged himself so far, especially when a certain princess whispered him in the ear to have a care of himself, and that his life and death were under consideration in the closet. Yet immediately after, as his courage was usually raised at the sight of the greatest dangers, he resumed his wonted boldness, and was not able to hinder himself, perhaps by a sudden motion purely natural, and arising from the magnanimity of his heart, from laying his hand on the pommel of his sword, without his own perceiving it, and from stepping hastily two or three paces forward, with a haughty walk, as if he were putting himself into a posture of selling his life as dear as he was able to his enemies. But the king at that instant coming out of the closet with Bellievre, he changed posture suddenly, made a low reverence, and threw himself almost at his feet; protesting to him, that not believing his presence ought to be displeasing to him, he was come to bring him his head, and fully to justify his carriage against the calumnies of his enemies; and withal to assure his majesty, that he had not a more faithful servant than himself. But the king demanding, in a grave and serious tone of voice, who had bid him come, and if he had not received an express prohibition from him? the business was then brought to a scanning, and some little contest there was betwixt him and Bellievre, the last maintaining that he had delivered him the king's commands, and the former, instead of answer, asking him if he had not engaged himself to return, with all possible speed, to Soissons, which he had not done, and protesting that he had never received those letters which Bellievre justified he had written to him.

Then the queen, who, though she seemed to be in much affliction for the duke's arrival, yet held a private correspondence with him, broke off the discourse, and, taking aside the king, her son, she managed his mind so dexterously, that, whether she made him apprehend a general revolt of Paris, which she had seen so openly to own the Duke of Guise, or whether he himself were mollified by the submissive humble way of speaking which that prince had used, he contented himself for that time to tell him, that his innocence, which he was so desirous to prove, would be more manifest if his presence should cause no stirs in Paris; and thereupon he sat down to table, remitting till the afternoon what he had farther to say to him, and appointing the queen's garden for the place. Then the duke bowing very low, retired, without being accompanied by any of the king's servants, but as well attended by all the town, to the Hotel de Guise, as he had been from the gate of St. Denis to the Louvre.

When he had made reflection on the danger into which he had so rashly thrown himself, and which now appeared more formidable, by considering it with cooler thoughts, than he could possibly in that agitation of spirits, and that anxiety wherein he was in spite of all his courage, when he found himself so far engaged; he resolved he would never hazard his life in that sort again, and took such order concerning it, that from the next day, and so onward, he had in his palace four hundred gentlemen, who, assembling there from all parts of Paris, according to his orders, never afterwards abandoned him. Neither would he adventure to go that afternoon to the queen's garden but well accompanied by the bravest of his officers, amongst whom Captain St. Paul, seeing that after his master was entered, he who kept the door was going to shut it on him, thrust him back roughly, and entered by force, followed by his companions, protesting and swearing, that if the game was there to be played, he was resolved to have his stake in it.

So that if the king had designed to have him murdered in that garden, which I believe not, though some have written it, it is easy to see that the presence of those brave men, who were fully resolved to defend their master, that of the queen, who made the third in this interview, the daring countenance of the duke, who from time to time was casting his eyes towards his sword, and to sum up all, that infinite multitude of Parisians which encompassed the queen's palace, and many of which were got upon the walls, had hindered the execution of such a purpose.

For that which passed betwixt them at this conference, since I find nothing of it in the most exact memoirs of those times, I shall not offer to relate it, as Davila has done by a certain poetical license which he and some other historians have used, to make men think and speak, without their leave, whatever they please to put into their thoughts and mouths. What I can deliver for undoubted truth is this, that there was nothing concluded at this interview; and that the king, who had resolved beforehand to chastise the most seditious of the sixteen, and to make himself master of Paris, after a long consultation taken by night, with those in whom he most confided, continued firm to the same resolution, and set up his rest to stand by it, in spite of the arrival of the duke.

With this determination, he sent the next morning for the provost of the merchants, and the sheriffs, and commanded them, in company of the lords De Villequier and Francis d'O. to make an exact search for all those strangers who were come to Paris some few days since, without any urgent occasion to call them thither, and to cause them forthwith to depart the town, without respect of persons. This was a manifest endeavour to weaken the Duke of Guise; to reduce him to those seven or eight gentlemen who attended him into Paris; and consequently to give him occasion of believing, that after they had rid themselves of the others, they would attack him. Perhaps the design was so laid, as some have conjectured with probability enough; but if this were really their intention, there are others who believe, that, according to the advice which was given by the abbot of Elbene, they had done more wisely to have begun with the Duke of Guise, when they had him single, and at their mercy, cooped up in the Louvre: and they ground this opinion on the meaning of that abbot's words, who quoted the scripture to this purpose, "It is written, I will strike the shepherd, and the flock shall be scattered." However it was intended, the Parisians immediately took the alarm, perceiving clearly that those strangers who were to be sent out of the city, were no others but those very men whom the Duke of Guise had conveyed into the town for their defence, and for his own. Insomuch that when they went about to execute that order, and to search their houses, every one opposed them; and the citizens set themselves with so much obstinacy to conceal their lodgers, that the deputies and commissaries, fearing a general insurrection through all the quarters, durst proceed no farther. And in the mean time, the Duke of Guise, who was the soul that actuated this great body, forbore not going to the Louvre, but well accompanied; and the very evening before the barricades he presented the napkin to the king.

But, as after the flashes of the lightning, and the rattling of the thunder, comes a furious tempest and lays waste the field; so after those mutual fears and jealousies, those nightly meetings, those murmurs and menaces, and those preparations which were made on both sides with so much tumult, either for assaulting or for defence, they came to the fatal day of the barricadoes, which was followed by that horrible deluge of misfortunes with which all France was overflowed.

For at last the king, more incensed than ever by the resistance which was made to his orders, and fully resolved to make himself be obeyed one way or other, caused the French guards to enter Paris, with some other companies, and the Swissers, which in all made up six thousand men: this was done on Thursday, the twelfth of May, just at day-break; he being present himself to receive them on horseback, at the gate of Saint Honoré. And after having given out his orders to their officers, to post them according to his direction, he enjoined them above all things, to be no ways injurious to the citizens, but only to repress the insolence of such who should go about to hinder the search for strangers: after which himself retiring to the Louvre, the marshals d'Aumont and Biron, who were at the head of the troops, went to post them with beat of drum, in the church-yard of St. Innocent, and the adjoining places, on the Pont Notre Dame, on that of St. Michael, on the Pont au Change, at the town-house, at the Greve, and at the avenues of the place Maubert.

It appeared immediately by what followed,

that this was in effect to give the signal of a mutiny and general revolt to all Paris. For a rumour being spread, that the king had determined to put to death a great number of the principal of the League, and a list being also forged of their names who were to be executed, and shown openly to the people, the citizens, according to the order of their captains and overseers of their wards, were in a readiness to put themselves into a posture of defence, at the least motion that was made. For which reason, so soon as they heard the drums and fifes, and that they beheld the Swissers and the guards advancing through the street of Saint Honorè, they doubted not but the report which was noised about by the sixteen was true; and further believed, (as they had been also assured,) that the town would be sacked, and exposed to pillage. The alarm therefore was given round the city: they began by shutting up their shops, and the church-doors on that side of the town; they rang the tocsin (or alarm-bell) first in one parish, and then in another; and immediately afterwards through all Paris, as if the whole city had been on fire.

Then the citizens came out in arms, under the overseers of their wards, and their captains, and other officers of the Duke of Guise, who had mingled themselves amongst them, to encourage and to marshal them. The Count of Brissac, who had placed himself at the quarter of the university towards the place Maubert, (where Crucé, one of the most hot-headed of the sixteen, caused the alarm to be sounded,) being himself encompassed with a multitude of students, a rabble of porters, watermen, and handicraftsmen, all armed, who waited only for the signal to assault the Swissers, was the first who gave orders to chain the streets, to unpave them, and erect the barricades, with great logs of timber, and barrels filled with earth and dung, at the avenues of the palace: and this word of barricades, passing in a moment from mouth to mouth, from the university into the city, and from the city into the town, the same was done everywhere, and that with such exceeding haste, that before noon, these barricades, which were continued from street to street, at the distance of thirty paces from each other, well flanked and manned with musketeers, were advanced within fifty paces of the Louvre; insomuch that the king's soldiers found themselves so encompassed on every side, that they could neither march forward nor retreat, nor make the least motion, without exposing themselves unprofitably to the inevitable danger of the musket-shot, (which the citizens could fire upon them, without missing, from behind their barricades,) or of being beaten down with a tempest of stones, which came pouring upon their heads from every window.

The marshals d'Aumont and Biron, and Villequier the governor of Paris, gained little by crying out to the citizens, that they intended them no harm, for they were too much enraged to give them the hearing; and were possessed with a belief of what Brissac, Bois Dauphin, and the other creatures of the Duke of Guise had told them; who roared out, on purpose to envenom them against the royalists, that those troops which were entered into Paris were sent for no other end, than to make a general massacre of all good Catholics, who were members of the Holy Union, and to give up to the soldiers their houses, their money, and their wives. Upon this the musket-shot, and the stones from above, were redoubled on those miserable men, and more especially upon the Swissers, to whom the citizens were most inexorable.

More than threescore were either slain or dangerously hurt, as well in St. Innocent's church-yard, as below on the place Maubert, without giving quarter, till Brissac (who with his sword in his hand was continually pushing forward the barricades) arriving there, and beholding those poor strangers, who cried out for mercy, with clasped hands, and both knees on the ground, and sometimes making the sign of the cross, in testimony of their being Catholics, stopped the fury of the citizens, and commanding them to cry out *Vive Guise!* which they did as loud as they could, for safeguard of their lives, he satisfied himself with leading them disarmed and prisoners into the Boucherie of the new market, by the bridge of St. Michael, which he had already mastered.

It cannot be denied, but that this count was he, amongst all the Leaguers, who acted with the most ardour against the royalists on that fatal day; as being infinitely exasperated because the king had refused him the admiralty, and refused it in a manner so disobliging as to say openly, he was a man that was good for nothing either by sea or land, accusing him at the same time, that he had not done his duty in the battle of the Azores, where the navy of Philippo Strozzi was defeated by the marquis of Santa Cruz, he burned inwardly with desire of revenge. And when he saw the soldiers enclosed on all sides by the barricades, which were of his raising, and the Swissers at his mercy, it is reported that he cried out, as insulting on the king, with a bitter scoff, and magnifying himself at the same time, "At least the king shall understand to-day, that I have found my element; and though I am good for nothing, either at sea or land, yet I am somebody in the streets."

In this manner it was, that the people, making use of their advantage, still pushed their fortune more and more, and seemed to be just upon the point of investing the Louvre; while the Duke of Guise, by whose secret orders all things were regularly managed amidst that horrible confusion, was walking almost unaccompanied in his own house, and coldly answering the queen, and those who came one on the neck of another, with messages to him from the king, entreating him to appease the tumult, that he was not master of those wild beasts which had escaped the toils; and that they were in the wrong to provoke them as they had done.

But at last, when he perceived that all things were absolutely at his command, he went himself from barricade to barricade, with only a riding switch in his hand, forbidding the people, who paid a blind obedience to him, from proceeding any farther; and desiring them to keep themselves only on the defensive. He spoke also very civilly to the French guards, who at that time were wholly in his power, to be disposed of as he thought good, for life or death. Only he complained to their officers, of the violent counsels which his enemies had given the king to oppress his innocence, and that of so many good Catholics, who had united themselves on no other consideration than the defence and support of the ancient religion. After which, he gave orders to Captain St. Paul to reconduct those soldiers to the Louvre; but their arms were first laid down, and their heads bare, in the posture of vanquished men, that he might give that satisfaction to the Parisians, who beheld the spectacle with joy, as the most pleasing effect of their present victory. He also caused the Swissers to be returned in the same manner by Brissac, and gave the king to understand, that, provided the Catholic religion were secured and maintained in France, in the condition it ought to be, and that himself and his friends were put in safety from the attempts of their enemies, they would pay him all manner of duty and service, which is owing from good subjects to their lord and sovereign.

This, in my opinion, makes it evident, that the duke had never any intention to seize the person of the king, and to enclose him in a monastery, as that Nicholas Poulain, who gave in so many false informations, and many writers, as well of the one religion as of the other, have endeavoured to make the world believe. For if that had been his purpose, what could have hindered him from causing the Louvre to be invested; as he might easily have done the same day, by carrying on the barricades close to it, while the tumult was at the height; and for what reason did he return the French guards and Swissers to the king, if his intention had been to have attacked him in the Louvre? This was not his business, nor his present aim, but to defend and protect his Leaguers with a high hand, and to avail himself of so favourable an opportunity, to obtain the thing which he demanded; and which, doubtless, had put him into a condition of mounting the throne after the king's decease, and becoming absolute master of all affairs even during his life.

In effect, the queen having undertaken to make the reconcilement, as believing that thereby she might re-enter into the management of business, from which the favourites had removed her, and having asked him what were his pretensions, he proposed such extravagant terms, and with so much haughtiness and resolvedness, speaking like a conqueror, who took upon him to dispose, at his pleasure, of the vanquished, that, as dexterous as she was in the art of managing men's minds, from the very beginning of the conference she despaired of her success. For, enhancing upon the articles of Nancy, he demanded, that, for the security of the Catholic religion in this realm, the king of Navarre, and all the princes of the house of Bourbon who had followed him in these last wars, should be declared to have forfeited for ever their right of succeeding to the crown: That the duke of Espernon, La Valette his brother, Francis d'O., the marshals of Retz and of Biron, colonel Alphonso d'Ornano, and all others who, like them, were favourers of the Huguenots, or were found to have held any correspondence with them, should be deprived of their governments and offices, and banished from the court, without hope of ever being restored again: That the spoils of all these should be given to the princes of his house, and to those lords who had engaged with him of whom he made a long list: That the king should cashier his guard of five-and-forty, as a thing unknown in the time of his predecessors; protesting that otherwise he could place no manner of confidence in him, nor ever dare to approach his person: That it would please his majesty to declare him his lieutenant-general through all his estates, with the same authority which the late Duke of Guise his father had, under the reign of Francis the Second; by virtue of which he hoped to give him so good an account of the Huguenots, that in a little time there should remain no other but the Catholic religion in all his kingdom. To conclude, That there should be called immediately an assembly of the three estates, to sit at Paris, where all this should be confirmed, and to hinder for the future, that the minions, who would dispose of all things at their pleasure, should not abuse their favour; that there should be established an unchangeable form of government, which it should not be in the power of the king to alter.

It is most evident, that demands so unreasonable, so arrogant, and so offensive, tended to put the government, and the power of it, into the duke's hands, who, being master of the armies, the offices, and the governments of the most principal provinces, in his own person, by his relations, his creatures, and the estates, where he doubted not of carrying all before him, especially at Paris, would be the absolute disposer of affairs; insomuch that there would be nothing wanting to him but the crown itself, to which it is very probable that at this time he pretended, in case he should survive the king, to the exclusion of the Bourbons, whom he would have declared incapable of succeeding to it.

For which reason, the queen, seeing that he would recede from no part of these articles, and beginning to fear that he would go farther than she desired, counselled the king to get out of Paris with all speed, while it was yet in his power so to do. And though some of his chief officers, as amongst others the Chancellor de Chiverny, and the Sieurs of Villeroy and Villequier, who were of opinion that more would be gained by the negotiation, and who foresaw that the Huguenots and the Duke of Espernon, whom they had no great cause to love, would make their advantage of this retreat so unworthy of a king, endeavoured to dissuade him from it, yet a thousand false advertisements, which came every moment, that they were going to invest the Louvre, and his accustomed fear, together with the diffidence he had of the Duke of Guise, whom he considered at that time as his greatest enemy, caused him at the last to resolve on his departure.

Accordingly, about noon the next day, while the queen-mother went to the duke with propositions only to amuse him, the king making show to take a turn or two in the Thuilleries, put on boots in the stables, and getting on horseback, attended by fifteen or sixteen gentlemen, and by ten or twelve lacqueys, having caused notice to be given to his guards to follow him, went out by the Pont Neuf, riding always on full gallop, for fear of being pursued by the Parisians, till, having gained the ascent above Chaliot, he stopped his horse to look back on Paris. It is said, that then reproaching that great city, which he had always honoured and enriched by his royal presence, and upbraiding its ingratitude, he swore he would not return into it but through a breach, and that he would lay it so low, that it should never more be in a condition of lifting up itself against the king. After this he went to lodge that night at Trappes, and the next morning arrived at Chartres; where his officers, those of his council, and the courtiers, came up to him, one after another, in great disorder; some on foot, others on horseback without boots, several on their mules, and in their robes, every man making his escape as he was best able, and in a great hurry, for fear of being stopped; in short, all of them in a condition not unlike the servants of David, at his departure from Jerusalem, travelling in a miserable equipage after their distressed master, when he fled before the rebel Absalom.

The Duke of Guise, who, on the one side, had been unwilling to push things to an extremity, to the end he might make his treaty with the king, and that it might not be said he was not at liberty; and, on the other side, not believing that he would have gone away in that manner, as if he fled from his subjects, who, stopping short of the Louvre by fifty paces, seemed unwilling to pursue their advantage any farther, was much surprised at this retreat, which broke the measures he had taken: but as he was endued with an admirable presence of mind, and that he could at a moment's warning accommodate his resolutions to any accident, how unexpected or troublesome soever, he immediately applied himself to put Paris in a condition of fearing nothing, to quiet all things there, and restore them to their former tranquillity, and withal to give notice to the whole kingdom how matters had passed at the barricades, as much to his own advantage as possibly he could.

To this effect he possessed himself of the strongest places in the city, of the Temple, of the Palace, of the town-house, of the two Chastelets, of the gates, where he set guards, of the arsenal, and of the Bastile, which was surrendered to him too easily by the governor Testu; the government of which he gave to Bussy Le Clerc, the most audacious of the sixteen. He obliged the magistrates to proceed in the courts of judicature as formerly; he made a new provost of merchants, and sheriffs, a lieutenant civil, colonels, and captains of the several wards, all devoted to the League, in the room of those whom he suspected: he retook, without much trouble, all the places both above and below on the river, that the passages for provisions might be free: he wrote at last to the king, to the towns, and to his particular friends, and drew up manifests (or declarations) in a style which had nothing in it but what was great and generous; while he endeavoured to justify his proceedings, and at the same time to preserve the respect which was owing to the king; protesting always, that he was most ready to pay him an entire obedience, and that he proposed nothing to himself, but that provision should be made for the safety of religion, and of good Catholics, which were designed to be oppressed through the pernicious counsels of such as held intelligence with heretics, and projected nothing but the ruin of religion and the state.

These letters, together with those which the Parisians wrote to the other towns, exhorting all men to combine with them for their common preservation in the Catholic faith, and those of the king, which on the contrary, were written in too soft a style, and where there appeared more of fear and of excuse than of resentment and just complaint for so sacrilegious an attempt, had this effect, that the greatest part of the people, far from being scandalized at the barricades, approved them, loudly praising the conduct of the Duke of Guise, whom they believed to be full of zeal for the Catholic faith, for the good of the kingdom, and for the service of the king. And as he desired nothing so much as to confirm them in that opinion, he was willing that the body of the city should send their deputies to the king, humbly to beseech his majesty that he would forget what was passed, and return to his good town of Paris, where his most loyal subjects were ready to give him all the highest demonstrations of their obedience and devotion to his service.

He permitted that even processions should be made in the habit of penitents, to desire of God that he would please to mollify the king's heart; and this was performed with so much ardour, that there was one which went from Paris as far as Chartres, in a most extraordinary equipage, under the conduct of the famous friar Ange. This honest father was Henry de Joyeuse, Count of Bouchage, and brother to the late duke. He had given up himself to be a capuchin about a year before this time; having such strong impressions made upon him by the death and good example of his wife, Catharine de Nogaret, sister to the Duke of Espernon, that he was inflamed with a desire of repentance; insomuch, that neither the tears of his brother, nor the entreaties and favours of the king, who loved him exceedingly, nor the ardent solicitations of all the court, were able to remove him from the resolution he had taken of leading so austere a life. This noble friar, having put a crown of thorns upon his head, and carrying an overgrown cross upon his shoulders, followed by his fraternity, and by a great number of penitents, and others who represented in their habits the several persons of the Passion, led on that procession, singing psalms and litanies. The march of these penitents was so well managed, that they entered the great church of Chartres just as the king was there at vespers. As they entered, they began to sing the *Miserere* in a very doleful tone; and at the same time, two swinging friars, armed with disciplines, laid lustily on poor friar Ange, whose back was naked. The application was not hard to make, nor very advantageous to the Parisians; for the charitable creature seemed evidently to desire the king, that he would please to pardon them, as Jesus Christ was willing to forgive the Jews for those horrible outrages which they had committed against him.

A spectacle so surprising produced different effects in the minds of the standers-by; according to the variety of their tempers, some of them were melted into compassion, others were moved to laughter, and some even to indignation; and more than all the rest, the Marshal de Biron, who, having no manner of relish for this sort of devotion, and fearing, besides, that some dangerous Leaguers might have crowded in amongst them, with intention to preach the people into a mutiny, counselled the king to clap them up in prison every mother's son. But that good prince, who, notwithstanding all his faults, had a stock of piety at the bottom, and much respect for all things that related to religion, rejected wholly this advice. He listened to them much more favourably than he had heard all the harangues of the former deputies; and promised to grant them the pardon they desired for the town which he had so much favoured, on condition they would return to their obedience. And truly, it is exceeding probable, that he had so done from that very time, if they had not afterwards given him fresh provocations, by proposing the terms on which they insisted for the peace which they desired.

For the Duke of Guise, to whom all these fair appearances were very serviceable, and could be no ways prejudicial, and who always pursued his designs in a direct line, knew so well to manage the disposition of the queen-mother, who had seemed at first to be much startled at his demands, that he recalled her with much dexterity into his interests, by working on these two passions which were rooted in her soul. She desired to raise to the throne, after the death of the king her son, her grandson Henry de Lorrain, Marquis du Pont; and believed that the Duke of Guise would contribute to it all that was in his power. But as cunning as she was, she saw not into the bottom of that prince, who fed her only with vain hopes of that succession for another, to which he personally aspired. She infinitely hated the Duke of Espernon; and believing he was the man who, having possessed himself of the king's soul, had rendered her suspected to him, longed to turn him out of court; promising herself, by that means, to be re-established in the management of affairs, from which the favourites had removed her. And the Duke of Guise, who had as little kindness as herself for the Duke of Espernon, concurred in the same design, with at least as much earnestness, but for a much different end, for he desired to be absolute himself. In this manner, this subtle prince, always dissembling, and artificially hiding the true motives by which he acted, drew the queen at last to consent to all that he desired; and, above all, to give her allowance, that a request should be presented to the king, in the name of the cardinals, the princes, the peers of France, the lords, the deputies of Paris, and the other towns, and of all the Catholics united for the defence of the Catholic, Apostolic, and Roman religion.

This request, which, in the manner of its expressions, was couched in most respectful terms, contained, notwithstanding, in the bottom of it, certain propositions, at least as hard as the Articles of Nancy; and even as those which, not long before, were proposed to the queen by the Duke of Guise. For after a protestation in the beginning of it, that in whatsoever had passed till that present time, there had been nothing done, but by a pure zeal for God's honour, and for the preservation of his church, they demand of the king, that he would make war with the Huguenots, and that he would conclude no peace till all heresies were rooted out: That it would please him to use the service of the Duke of Guise in so just and holy an undertaking: That he would drive out of the court, and despoil of all their offices, all those who held a secret correspondence with the Huguenots, and principally the Duke of Espernon, and his brother La Valette; against whom there are recited, in that request, all imaginable crimes that could be thought most capable of rendering them odious and insupportable to the whole kingdom: That he would deliver the nation from the just apprehensions it had, of falling one day under the power and dominion of heretics: And (that there might be given to the city of Paris a full assurance henceforth to enjoy a perfect tranquillity without fear of oppression,) he would not only please to confirm the new provosts and sheriffs, but that also the said city may have full and entire liberty for the future, to make choice of such as shall succeed in those places, and in those of city colonels and captains.

This request was extremely displeasing to the king, who saw but too clearly, that their intention was to give the law to him hereafter, whom they had first so haughtily affronted. He therefore caused it to be examined in his council, where there was but small agreement, because the members of it were divided in their interests. There were but two methods to be taken on that subject; either for the king to join with the League against the Huguenots, as the request demanded, or to make war against the League with all his power, in conjunction with the Huguenots; for unless he espoused one of those interests, it was impossible for him to succeed. Those of the council who loved not the Duke of Espernon, who were many, and who feared that the acting of the king's forces, in combination with the Huguenots, would prove of great prejudice to his reputation, and of greater to religion, were for the former proposition and counsel, that all differences should be accommodated in the best manner they could with the Duke of Guise,—which was also the desire of the queen-mother; but the rest, who, for the most part, consisted of those persons whose disgrace and banishment was demanded in the request, insisted strongly on the second, and gave their voice for a war to be made against the duke to the uttermost; fortifying their opinion by the number of forces which the king might raise promiscuously, both from Catholics and Protestants, because this was not a war of religion, but that the sovereign only armed himself to quell and chastise his rebellious subjects.

It would be a matter of much difficulty to tell precisely what was the true resolution which the king took betwixt the extremes of these different counsels; but it may be told for a certain truth, that having a long time deliberated, and that much more in his own breast than with his council, he seemed at length, all on a sudden, to pitch upon the first; whether it were, that being, as he was, a good Catholic, and hating the Huguenots, he could not yet come to a resolution of uniting himself to them; or were it, that he thought not himself at that time strong enough, even with the king of Navarre's assistance, to destroy the League, which was grown more powerful than ever since the barricades, and headed by a man so able, so bold, and so successful, as the Duke of Guise; or lastly, as many have believed, that being strongly persuaded he should never be in safety, nor be master in his kingdom, while that prince, whom he hated mortally, was living, he took up, from that very moment, a resolution within himself to despatch him out of the world: and that he might draw him into the net which he was spreading for him, was willing to grant in a manner whatsoever he desired, as if it were done in contemplation of a peace.

Whatsoever were his true motive, (for I desire not that random guesses should be taken for truths,) it is certain, that though the king was highly exasperated against the League, yet he answered their request with much gentleness and moderation. assuring them that he would assemble the three estates at Blois, in the month of September, there to advise of the means to give them satisfaction, and to deliver them from the jealousy they had of falling one day under the dominion of a Huguenot prince; that for what related to the Duke of Espernon, he would do them justice, like an equitable king, and would make it manifest that he preferred the public welfare before the consideration of any private person.

Accordingly, in the first place, that duke was despoiled of his government of Normandy, commanded to depart from court, and retire himself to Angouleme. Not long time afterwards, the king concluded a treaty with the lords of the League, to whom, besides the places which they had already in possession, the towns of Montreuil, Orleans, and Bourges, were given for six years. A publication of the Council of Trent was promised, with provision against that part of it which was contrary to the liberties of the Gallican church. There was given to the Duke of Guise, instead of the title of constable, that of head of the French gendarmerie, which signifies the same thing. Two armies were promised to be raised against the Huguenots; one in Dauphine, under the command of the Duke of Mayenne; and the other in Saintonge and Poitou, which should be commanded by a general of the king's own choice: For the new constable, under another name, would not be so far from court, lest his absence from thence might be of ill consequence to his party. In conclusion, the king caused to be published the famous edict of July, which he commanded to be called the Edict of the Reunion, where he did more in favour of the League than the League itself desired from him.

For, after having declared in that edict, that he would have all his subjects united to himself; that, in like manner as their souls are redeemed with the same price, by the blood of our Lord and Saviour Jesus Christ, so also they and their posterity should be one body with him,—he swears, that he will employ all his forces, without sparing his proper life, to exterminate from his realm all heresies condemned by councils, and principally by that of Trent, without ever making any peace or truce with heretics, or any edict in their favour. He wills, that all princes, lords, gentlemen, and inhabitants of towns, and, generally, all his subjects, as well ecclesiastical as secular, should take the same oath: That farther, they should swear and promise, for the time present, and for ever, after it shall have pleased God to dispose of his life, without having given him issue male, not to receive for king, any prince whatsoever who shall be a heretic, or a promoter of heresy. He declares rebels, and guilty of high treason, and to have forfeited all privileges which have formerly been granted to them, all persons and all towns which shall refuse to take this oath, and sign this union. He promises never to bestow any military employment, but on such as shall make a signal profession of the Roman Catholic religion; and prohibits, in express terms, that any man whosoever shall be admitted to the exercise of any office of judicature, or any employment belonging to the treasury, whose profession of the Roman Catholic religion appears not under the attestation of the bishop, or his substitutes, or at least of the curates or their vicars, together with the deposition of ten witnesses, all qualified and unsuspected persons. He also swears to hold for his good and loyal subjects, and to protect and defend, as well those who have always followed the League, as those others who have formerly united and associated themselves against the heretics; and that at this present he unites them to himself, to the end they may all act together in order to one common end: And that he holds for null, and as never done, that which seems to have been done against him, as well in the town of Paris as elsewhere; particularly since the twelfth of May to the day of the publication of this edict; without future molestation, or bringing into trouble any person whomsoever, for any thing relating to the premises. But he also wills, that all his subjects, of what quality soever, swear, that they will and do renounce all leagues and confederations, as well without as within the realm, which are contrary to this union, on pain of being punished as infringers of their oath, and guilty of high treason.

This edict was verified in parliament the one-and-twentieth of July, and published immediately after; being received with extraordinary transports of joy by the Leaguers, who believed that by it they had obtained a clear victory against the king, whom they beheld entirely subjected to the will and good pleasure of their heads. He himself also, as it is reported, with profound dissimulation, endeavoured all he was able to confirm them in that opinion, by making public demonstrations of his joy and satisfaction for the peace. He was very solicitous to cause his edict to be signed by all the princes and lords who were then at court: He proclaimed the convention of the three estates at Blois, which was to be at the beginning of October following: He procured the letters patent for the Duke of Guise's commission of intendant-general over all his armies, with the same power which is annexed to that of constable, to be verified in parliament: He received him at Chartres, with such particular tokens of esteem, affection, and trust, that it was believed the tender friendship which was betwixt them, when the king was then but Duke of Anjou, was once more renewed: He favoured all his creatures, on whom he bestowed considerable employments; and, at last, to satisfy him in that point which of all others was most nice, he caused the Cardinal of Bourbon to be solemnly declared the next of blood to him, by allowing him all the privileges and prerogatives which belong to the heir-presumptive of the crown. After all, as it is almost impossible that a violent passion in the soul, what care soever be taken to conceal it, should not discover itself by its consequences, and by some indications which break out even from the closest men; so this prince, as great a master as he was in the art of dissimulation, could not act his part so well, but that he gave occasion to those who were more clear-sighted to believe, or at leastwise to suspect, that all which at that time was done by him to testify his joy, was only to cover his indignation and his hatred, which urged him incessantly to revenge himself on those from whom he had received such unworthy usage. For, being departed from Chartres, and going thence to Rouen, where he made the edict of reunion, he would never be persuaded to go to Paris at his return, what instance soever the deputies of the parliament, and those of the town, could make to him; always alleging faint excuses, which he grounded only on the preparations which he was to make in order to his meeting the estates at Blois. He still retained near his person his guard of the five-and forty, which the Duke of Guise had requested him to dismiss. He gave the command of the army designed for Poitou to the Duke of Nevers, whom the Duke of Guise, his brother-in-law, could never endure since his renunciation of the League. He admitted none to his private friendship but the Marshal d'Aumont, the Lord Nicholas d'Angennes de Rambouillet, Colonel Alphonso d'Ornano, and some few others, who were no friends to the Duke of Guise.

In fine, that which made the greatest noise was, that the Chancellor de Chiverny, the Presidents Bellievre and Brulart, and the Sieurs de Villeroy and Pinart, (the two secretaries of state, who had given him advice to accommodate matters with the Duke of Guise,) were absolutely disgraced. The queen-mother, who had managed that accommodation, had little or no part in business, and was wholly excluded from the cabinet council. The seals were given to Francis de Monthelon, a famous advocate, a man of rare integrity, and of inviolable fidelity to the king's service, who raised him to that high employment, without his own seeking, at the recommendation of the Duke of Nevers, who was known to be on very ill terms with the Duke of Guise.

All this was sufficient, without doubt, to alarm that prince, and give him caution to look about him, or at least to suspect the king's intentions towards him; but the flourishing condition wherein he was placed, the applauses which were given him both by the people and by the court itself, which admired both his conduct and his perpetual felicity, and regarded him as arbitrator and master of affairs, and the certain opinion which he had that all things would go for him in the estates, had so far blinded him, that he believed it was not in the power of fortune to do him any prejudice, not so much as to shake him, or to give the smallest stop to the full career of his success. Thus he entered as it were in triumph into Blois at the end of September; and the king came thither about the same time, to order the preparations for the estates. He commanded, that all future proceedings should be as it were sanctified by two solemn and conspicuous acts of piety; which were a most devout and magnificent procession made on the first Sunday of October, the second day of that month, and by a general communion, taken by all the deputies on the Sunday following, the ninth of the same month; on which the king, in token of a perfect reconcilement, received, with the Duke of Guise, the precious body of Jesus Christ from the hands of the Cardinal de Bourbon, in the church of Saint Saviour. After which, all those who were expected being at length arrived, the assembly of the states was opened on Sunday the sixteenth of that month, in the great hall of the castle of Blois.

As it is not my business to say any thing of this assembly, which relates not precisely to the history of the League, I shall not trouble myself with every particular which passed in it. I shall only say, that the king, who was naturally eloquent, opened the assembly with an excellent oration; wherein, after he had, in a most majestic manner, and with most pathetic words, exhorted the deputies to their duty, he either could not, or would not, conceal from them, that he had not so far forgotten the past actions, but that he had taken up a firm resolution to inflict an exemplary punishment on such who should persist in acting against his authority, and continue to be still possessed with that spirit of leaguing and caballing which was upon the point of ruining the state; neither would he henceforth spare those who should have any other union than that which the members ought to have with their head, and subjects with their sovereign.

This touched so sensibly the Leaguers of that assembly, and principally their head, who looked on this speech as particularly addressed to himself, that they proceeded even to threatening that they would break off the estates by their departure, if the king, who had commanded his speech to be printed, would not give order to suppress it, or at least correct that passage. There are some who affirm, that, after a rough dispute concerning it, the king permitted at last that something should be altered, and the harshness of his expressions a little mollified; but there are others, and even of their number who heard it spoken, who assure us, that it came out in public in the same terms it was pronounced. However it were, it is certain that this complaint of theirs much exasperated the king's mind, who saw clearly by this proceeding, that the League, notwithstanding its reunion with him, had still a separate interest of its own, and extremely opposite to his.

I will adventure to say farther, that he was then fully persuaded of it, when he perceived that the Duke of Guise, who was the true head of it, was evidently more powerful than himself in those estates. For, besides that the greatest part of the deputies had been elected by the factious intrigues of his dependants in the provinces, those who were chosen to preside over the several orders, that is to say, the Cardinals of Bourbon and of Guise for the clergy; the Count of Brissac and the Baron of Magnac for the nobility; and the provost of merchants, La Chapelle Martau, for the third order, were all of them entirely at the duke's devotion.

Insomuch, that at the second session, after the edict of reunion had been solemnly confirmed, sworn to again, and passed into a fundamental law of the state, when the petitions of the three orders were read, he saw, that, under pretence of desiring to reform some abuses which were crept into the state, they were filled with an infinite number of propositions, which tended to the manifest diminution, or rather the annihilation, of the royal autherity; and to reduce the government to that pass, that there should remain to the king no more than the empty name and vain appearance of a sovereign monarch; and that all the real and essential part of sovereignty should be in the League, which absolutely depended on the Duke of Guise.

Yet, further, they were not satisfied barely to propose these things; leaving to the king, according to the ancient laws and constitution of the monarchy, the power of either passing or refusing them, according to his pleasure, after they had been well examined in his council; but they pretended, that after they had been received by the consent of the three orders, they should become laws of course, and be inviolable, so that the king should not have the power either to change or abrogate them in his council. Then they would have an abatement of taxes and imposts; but so much out of measure, that they took away from the king the means of making that war in which themselves had engaged him. They would also, that the Council of Trent should be received absolutely, and without modification. And the famous attorney-general Jaques de Faye d'Espesses, who, in a great assembly held on that occasion, maintained, with strength of reason, against some decrees of that council, the prerogatives of the king, (or regalia) and the immunities of the Gallican church, was so ill treated there, though he had baffled the archbishop of Lyons, who undertook to destroy those privileges, that the king, who was affronted in the person of his attorney, was not a little displeased at their proceedings.

But above all things they were urgent with him, and pressed it with incredible obstinacy, that the King of Navarre, who at the same time had assembled the estates of his party at Rochelle, and from thence had sent to those at Blois, intimating his desire of a general council to be summoned, where all things might be accommodated, should from that time forward be declared incapable of ever succeeding to the crown. They had made a decree concerning this, by consent of the three orders, at the particualr instance of the order of the clergy. And the king, who clearly foresaw the terrible consequences of this unparalleled injustice, and who was plied incessantly to subscribe it, was not able to defend himself otherwise, than by amusing them with delays, and rubs which he dexterously caused to be thrown in their way, on sundry pretences. It was not doubted but that the Duke of Guise (who, having two-thirds of the estates for him, was consequently the master there,) was author of all these propositions, so contrary to the true interests and authority of the king, especially when it was evident, that he employed all his managers to cause himself to be declared, in the estates, lieutenant-general through the whole kingdom, as if he would possess himself of that supreme command, without dependence on the king, and that he pretended his prince to be no more his master, as not having power to deprive him of a dignity which he was to hold from a commission given him by others.

All these things, so unworthy of the majesty of a great king, at the length quite wearied out his patience; which, after so long dissembling his injuries, on the sudden broke out into the extremity of rage; insomuch that those among his confidants, who ardently desired the destruction of the duke for their own advantage, found not the least trouble in passing on the king for truths many reports, and oftentimes very groundless rumours, which ran of the duke: adding to them, that it was he who underhand had drawn the Duke of Savoy to possess himself of the marquisate of Saluces, as he had lately done. And this they confidently affirmed, though the duke, by his own interest in the estates, had procured them to vote a war against the Savoyard. Thus, whether it were that the king had long since resolved to rid his hands of the Duke of Guise, in revenge of some ancient grudge and sense of the affronts he had received from him, particularly on that fatal day of the barricades; or were it, that, being sincerely reconciled to him, he had taken, or perhaps resumed, that resolution when he saw him act against him in the estates, of which he had made himself the master, and believing his own condition desperate if he made not haste to prevent it; most certain it is, that he deliberated no more, but only concerning the manner of executing what he had determined.

He had only two ways to choose; the one by justice, first committing him, and afterwards making his process; the other by fact, which was to have him slain. He managed this consultation with exceeding secrecy, admitting only four or five of his confidants, on whom he most relied. One of these was Beauvais Nangis, who, having served the king well in his army against the Reyters, was restored so fully in his favour, that in recompense of the command of colonel of the French infantry which the Duke of Espernon had got over his head, he made him afterwards admiral of France, though he never enjoyed that great dignity, which he had only under the signet.

This lord, who was as prudent and temperate in council, as prompt and daring in execution, concluded for the methods of justice, maintaining that they were not only the more honest, but also the more safe, because the fear alone which would possess the duke's party, lest they should kill him, in case they attempted to deliver him by force, and by that means hinder the course of justice, would stop all manner of such proceeding, and restrain them within the terms of duty: That after all, if he were once made prisoner, which might be done without noise or tumult, it would be easy to give him such judges as should soon despatch his trial, and that afterwards he might be executed in prison, according to the laws. But if, on the contrary, they should enter crudely on so bloody an execution, there was danger lest that action, which was never to be well justified, and which the Leaguers would certainly cause to pass in the world for tyrannical and perfidious, might raise a rebellion in the greatest part of France, which had already declared so loudly for that prince, whom they regarded as the pillar of religion, and would afterwards look on as the martyr of it. But the rest, who believed it impossible on that occasion to observe the ordinary forms of law and justice, and thought that, the head being once cut off, the body of the League would immediately fall like a dead body, were of opinion, that he should be despatched with all possible speed, which was easy to perform, especially in the castle, where the duke was almost hourly in the king's power, whom he had in no manner of distrust, as sufficiently appeared by his lodging there.

In the mean time, it is most certain that this secret was not kept so close, but that he received advertisement from more than one of his imminent danger, and that his death already was resolved. And he slighted not so much these observations, as intrepid as he was, or as he affected to appear, by replying continually, They dare not, but that, two or three days before his death, he consulted on this affair, which so nearly concerned him, with the cardinal of Guise his brother, the archbishop of Lyons, the president de Neuilly, the provost of the merchants, and the Sieur de Mandrevile, governor of St. Menehoud, on whom he principally relied. In weighing those proofs which in a manner were indubitable that a design was laid against him, they were unanimously of opinion, that the safest course was to be taken, and that under some pretence or other he should instantly retire; excepting only the archbishop, who continued obstinate to the contrary, fortifying his opinion with this argument, that since he was upon the point of carrying all things in the estates according to his wish, he ran the hazard of losing all by leaving them; and that, for the test, it was not credible that the king should be so ill advised, as to incur the manifest danger of ruining himself, by striking that unhappy blow. To which Mandrevile replied, swearing, that for a man of sense, as he was, he was the worst arguer he ever knew. "For," said he, "you talk of the king as if he were a wary and cool-headed prince, looking before him at every step; and will not understand that he is only a hot-brained fool, who thinks no farther than how to execute what his two base passions, fear and hatred, which possess him, have once made sink into his imagination, and never considers what a wise man ought to do on this occasion. It were a folly, therefore, for the duke to hazard himself in such a manner, and to be moved by so weak a reason, to lose all in a moment."

It is wonderful to observe, that the most clear-sighted men, who have it in their power, if they will use the means before them, to avoid that which is called their destiny, after the misfortune is happened, should suffer themselves to be dragged and hurried to it as it were by force, in spite of their understanding and their foresight, which their own rashness, and not a pretended fatality, renders unprofitable to them. It is reported, that the Duke of Guise confessed that this discourse of Mandrevile carried the greater force of reason; yet nevertheless, he added, that having gone so far forward as he then was, if he should see death coming in at the windows upon him, he would not give one step backward to the door, though by so doing, he were certain to avoid it. Nevertheless, it is very probable, that the encouragement he had to speak with so much loftiness and resolution, was the assurance, which he thought he had, that the king, whose genius he knew, particularly since the day when he entered into the Louvre, where the duke gave himself for lost, would never afterwards dare to take up so bold a resolution as to kill him.

It is certain, that when the Sieur de Vins, one of his greatest confidants, had written to him from Provence, that he should beware of keeping so near the king, and not rely on those large testimonies of his affection which he said he had received; the duke answered him, that he reposed not the hopes of his own safety on the king's virtue, whom he knew to be ill-natured, and a hypocrite, but on his judgment and on his fear; because it was not credible, but he must needs understand, that he himself was ruined in case he made any attempt against his person. But he learned, at his own cost, by the unhappy experiment which he made, that it had been better for him to have followed the wise advice which was given him, and which he himself had approved, than a bare conjecture, and the impulse of his inborn generosity, which his bloody and lamentable death, as things are commonly judged by their event, has caused to pass in the world for an effect of the greatest rashness.

It ought not here to be expected, that I should dwell on an exact and long description of all the circumstances of that tragical action, which has been so unfortunate to France, and so ill received in the world. Besides that they are recounted, in very different manners, by the historians of one and the other religion, according to their different passions, and that the greatest part of them are either false, or have little in them worth observation; the thing was done with so great facility and precipitation, and withal in so brutal a manner, that it cannot be too hastily passed over: this then is the plain and succinct relation of it.

After that the brave Grillon, Maitre de Camp of the regiment of guards, had generously refused to kill the Duke of Guise, unless in single duel, and in an honourable way, the king had recourse to Lognac, the first gentleman of his chamber, and captain of the forty-five, who promised him eighteen or twenty of the most resolute amongst them, and for whom he durst be answerable. They were of the number of those whom the Duke of Guise, who had always a distrust of those Gascons, as creatures of the duke of Espernon, had formerly demanded that they might be dismissed, from which request he had afterwards desisted; insomuch that it may be said he foresaw the misfortune that attended him, without being able to avoid it. For, on Friday the twenty-third of December, being entered about eight of the clock in the morning into the great hall, where the king had intimated on Thursday night that he intended to hold the council very early, that he might afterwards go to *Nostre Dame de Clery*; some came to tell him that his majesty expected him in the old closet, yet he was not there, but in the other which looks into the garden. Upon this, he arose from the fireside, where, finding himself somewhat indisposed, he had been seated; and passed through a narrow entry, which was on one side the hall, into the chamber, where he found Lognac, with seven or eight of the forty-five; the king himself having caused them to enter into that room very secretly before daybreak: the rest of them were posted in the old closet, and all of them had great poniards hid under their cloaks, expecting only the coming of the Duke of Guise, to make sure work with him, whether it were in the chamber or in the closet, in case he should retire thither for his defence.

There needed not so great a preparation for

the killing of a single man, who came thither without distrust of any thing that was designed against him; and who, holding his hat in one hand, and with the other the lappet of his cloak, which he had wrapped under his left arm, was in no condition of defence. In this posture he advanced to the old closet, saluting very civilly, as his custom was, those gentlemen who made show of attending him out of respect, as far as the door. And as in lifting up the hangings, with the help of one of them, he stooped to enter, he was suddenly seized by the arms, and by the legs; and at the same instant struck into the body before, with five or six poniards, and from behind, into the nape of the neck. and the throat; which hindered him from speaking one single word of all that he is made to say, or so much as drawing out his sword. All that he could do, was to drag along his murderers, with the last and strongest effort that he could make, struggling and striving till he fell down at the bed's feet, where, some while after, with a deep groan, he yielded up his breath.

The cardinal of Guise, and archbishop of Lyons, who were in the council-hall, rising up at the noise, with intention of running to his aid, were made prisoners by the marshals D'Aumon and De Retz; at the same time, the cardinal of Bourbon was also seized in the castle, together with Anne d'Este, Duchess of Nemours, and mother of the Guises, and the Prince of Joinville, the Dukes of Elbeuf, and Nemours, Brissac, and Boisdauphin, with many other lords who were confidants of the duke, and Pericard, his secretary. And in the mean time the grand provost of the king's house went with his archers to the chamber of the third estate, in the town-house, and there arrested the president Neuilly, the provost of merchants, the sheriffs Compan and Cotte-Blanch, who were deputies for Paris, and some other notorious Leaguers.

This being done, the king himself brought the news of it to the queen-mother; telling her that now he was a real king, since he had cut off the Duke of Guise. At which that princess being much surprised and moved, asking him if he had made provision against future accidents, he answered her in an angry kind of tone, much differing from his accustomed manner of speaking to her, that she might set her heart at rest, for he had taken order for what might happen, and so went out surlily to go to mass; yet before he went, he sent particularly to cardinal Gondi, and to the cardinal Legat Morosini, and informed them both of what had passed, with his reasons to justify his proceedings.

POSTSCRIPT OF THE TRANSLATOR.

That government, generally considered, is of divine authority, will admit of no dispute: for whoever will seriously consider, that no man has naturally a right over his own life, so as to murder himself, will find, by consequence, that he has no right to take away another's life; and that no pact betwixt man and man, or of corporations and individuals, or of sovereigns and subjects, can entitle them to this right; so that no offender can lawfully, and without sin, be punished, unless that power be derived from God. It is He who has commissioned magistrates, and authorized them to prevent future crimes, by punishing offenders, and to redress the injured by distributive justice; subjects therefore are accountable to superiors, and the superior to Him alone. For, the sovereign being once invested with lawful authority, the subject has irrevocably given up his power, and the dependence of a monarch is alone on God. A king, at his coronation, swears to govern his subjects by the laws of the land, and to maintain the several orders of men under him, in their lawful privileges; and those orders swear allegiance and fidelity to him, but with this distinction, that the failure of the people is punishable by the king, that of the king is only punishable by the King of kings. The people then are not judges of good or ill administration in their king; for it is inconsistent with the nature of sovereignty that they should be so; and if at some times they suffer, through the irregularities of a bad prince, they enjoy more often the benefits and advantages of a good one, as God in his providence shall dispose, either for their blessing or their punishment. The advantages and disadvantages of such subjection, are supposed to have been first considered, and upon this balance they have given up their power without a capacity of resumption; so that it is in vain for a commonwealth party to plead, that men, for example, now in being, cannot bind their posterity, or give up their power; for if subjects can swear only for themselves, when the father dies the subjection ends, and the son, who has not sworn, can be no traitor or offender, either to the king or to the laws. And at this rate, a long-lived prince may outlive his sovereignty, and be no longer lawfully a king, but in the mean time it is evident, that the son enjoys the benefit of the laws and government, which is an implicit acknowledgment of subjection. It is endless to run through all the extravagances of these men, and it is enough for us that we are settled under a lawful government of a most gracious prince; that our monarchy is hereditary; that it is naturally poised by our municipal laws, with equal benefit of prince and people; that he governs, as he has promised, by explicit laws; and what the laws are silent in, I think I may conclude to be part of his prerogative; for what the king has not granted away, is inherent in him. The point of succession has sufficiently been discussed, both as to the right of it, and to the interest of the people: one main argument of the other side is, how often it has been removed from the right line? as in the case of King Stephen, and of Henry the Fourth, and his descendants of the house of Lancaster. But it is easy to answer them, that matter of fact, and matter of right, are different considerations: both those kings were but usurpers in effect, and the providence of God restored the posterities of those who were dispossessed. By the same argument, they might as well justify the rebellion and murder of the late king; for there was not only a prince inhumanly put to death, but a government overturned; and first an arbitrary commonwealth, then two usurpers set up against the lawful sovereign; but, to our happiness, the same providence has miraculously restored the right heir, and, to their confusion, as miraculously preserved him. In this present history, to go no farther, we see Henry the Third, by a decree of the Sorbonne, divested, what in them lay, of his imperial rights; a parliament of Paris, such another as our first long parliament, confirming their decree; a pope authorizing all this by his excommunication; and a Holy League and Covenant prosecuting this deposition by arms: yet an untimely death only hindered him from reseating himself in glory on the throne, after he was in manifest possession of the victory.* We see also the same Sorbonnists, the same pope, parliament, and league, with greater force opposing the undoubted right of King Henry the Fourth; and we see him in the end surmounting all these difficulties, and triumphing over all these dangers. God Almighty taking care of his own anointed, and the true succession; neither the Papist nor Presbyterian Association prevailing at the last in their attempts, but both baffled and ruined, and the whole rebellion ending either in the submission or destruction of the conspirators.

It is true, as my author has observed in the beginning of his history, that before the Catholic League, or Holy Union, which is the subject of this book, there was a league or combination of Huguenots against the government of France, which produced the conspiracy of Ambois; and the Calvinist preachers (as Mezeray, a most impartial historian, informs us) gave their opinion, that they might take up arms in their own defence, and make way for a free access to the king, to present their remonstrances. But it was ordered at the same time, that they should seize on the Duke of Guise, and the Cardinal of Lorraine, his brother, who were then chief ministers, that they might be brought to trial by process before the States; but he adds immediately, who could answer for them, that the prisoners should not have been killed out of hand, and that they would not have made themselves masters of the queen-mother's person, and of the young king's, which was laid afterwards to their charge? The concealed heads of this conspiracy were Lewis, Prince of Conde, and the famous Admiral de Coligny; who being discontented at court, because their enemies, the Guises, had the management of affairs under the queen regent, to their exclusion, and being before turned Calvinists, made use of that rebellious sect, and the pretence of religion, to cover their ambition and revenge. The same Mezeray tells us in one of the next pages, that the name of Huguenots or Fidnos, (from whence it was corrupted,) signifies League or Association, in the Swiss language; and was brought, together with the sect, from Geneva into France. But from whencesoever they had their name, it is most certain that pestilent race of people cannot, by their principles, be good subjects; for whatever enforced obedience they pay to authority, they believe their class above the king; and how they would order him if they had him in their power, our most gracious sovereign has sufficiently experienced when he was in Scotland.* As for their boasts that they brought him in, it is as much as true that of the Calvinists, who pretended, as my author tells you in his preface, that they seated his grandfather, Henry IV. upon the throne. For both French and English Presbyterians were fundamentally and practically rebels; and the French have this advantage over ours, that they came in to the aid of Henry III. at his greatest need, or rather were brought over by the king of Navarre, their declared head, on a prospect of great advantage to their religion; whereas ours never inclined to the king's restoration, till themselves had been trodden under foot by the independent party, and till the voice of three nations called aloud for him; that is to say, when they had no possibility of keeping him any longer out of England. But the beginning of leagues, unions, and associations, by those who called themselves God's people, for reformation of religious worship, and for the redress of pretended grievances in the state, is of a higher rise, and is justly to be dated from Luther's time; and the private spirit, or the gift of interpreting scriptures by private persons without learning, was certainly the original cause of such cabals in the reformed churches; so dangerous an instrument of rebellion is the holy scriptures in the hands of ignorant and bigoted men.

The Anabaptists of Germany led up the dance, who had always in their mouths, faith, charity, the fear of God, and mortifications of the flesh: prayers, fastings, meditations, contempt of riches and honours, were their first specious practices. From thence they grew up, by little and little, to a separation from other men, who, according to their pharisaical account, were less holy than themselves; and decency, civility, neatness of attire, good furniture, and order in their houses, were the brands of carnal-minded men. Then they proceeded to nickname the days of the weeks, and Sunday, Monday, Tuesday, &c. as heathen names, must be rejected for the first, second, and third days, distinguishing only by their numbers. Thus they began to play, as it were, at cross-purposes with mankind; and to do every thing by contraries, that they might be esteemed more godly and more illuminated. It had been

* He was assassinated, by Jaques Clement, on the 2d August. 1589, when he had besieged Paris with every prospect of success.

* To which kingdom Charles repaired upon the invitation of the Presbyterians, whose clergy, however, treated him with an indecent rigour, which he never forgave to the sect.

a wonder, considering their fanciful perfections, if they had stopped here. They were now knowing and pure enough to extend their private reformation to the church and state; for God's people love always to be dealing as well in temporals as spirituals; or rather, they love to be fingering spirituals, in order to their grasping temporals. Therefore they had the impudence to pretend to inspiration in the exposition of scriptures; a trick which since that time has been familiarly used by every sect in its turn, to advance their interests. Not content with this, they assumed to themselves a more particular intimacy with God's holy spirit; as if it guided them, even beyond the power of the scriptures, to know more of him than was therein taught. For now the Bible began to be a dead letter of itself; and no virtue was attributed to the reading of it, but all to the inward man, the call of the Holy Ghost, and the ingrafting of the word, opening their understanding to hidden mysteries by faith. And here the mountebank way of canting words came first in use; as if there were something more in religion than could be expressed in intelligible terms, or nonsense were the way to heaven. This of necessity must breed divisions amongst them; for every man's inspiration being particular to himself, must clash with another's, who set up for the same qualification; the Holy Ghost being infallible in all alike, though he spoke contradictions in several mouths. But they had a way of licking one another whole; mistakes were to be forgiven to weak brethren; the failing was excused for the right intention; he who was more illuminated, would allow some light to be in the less, and degrees were made in contradictory propositions. But godfathers and godmothers, by common consent, were already set aside, together with the observation of festivals, which they said were of antichristian institution. They began at last to preach openly, that they had no other king but Christ, and by consequence earthly magistrates were out of doors. All the gracious promises in scripture they applied to themselves, as God's chosen, and all the judgments were the portion of their enemies. These impieties were at first unregarded, and afterwards tolerated by their sovereigns; and Luther himself made request to the Duke of Saxony, to deal favourably with them, as honest-meaning men, who were misled. But in the end, when, by these specious pretences, they had gathered strength, they who had before concluded that Christ was the only king on earth, and at the same time assumed to themselves that Christ was theirs, inferred by good consequence, that they were to maintain their king, and not only so, but to propagate that belief in others; for what God wills, man must obey; and for that reason, they entered into a league of association amongst themselves, to deliver their Israel out of Egypt; to seize Canaan, and to turn the idolaters out of possession. Thus you see by what degrees of saintship they grew up into rebellion, under their successive heads, Muncer, Phifer, John of Leyden, and Knipperdolling, where what violences, impieties, and sacrileges they committed, those who are not satisfied may read in Sleidan. The general tradition is, that after they had been besieged in Munster, and were forced by assault, their ringleaders being punished, and they dispersed, two ship's-lading of these precious saints was disembogued in Scotland, where they set up again, and broached anew their pernicious principles. If this be true, we may easily perceive on what a noble stock presbytery was grafted. From Scotland they had a blessed passage into England; or at least arriving here from other parts, they soon came to a considerable increase. Calvin, to do him right, wrote to King Edward VI. a sharp letter against these people; but our Presbyterians after him have been content to make use of them in the late civil wars, where they and all the rest of the sectaries were joined in the good old cause of rebellion against his late majesty; though they could not agree about dividing the spoils, when they had obtained the victory: and it is impossible they ever should, for all claiming to the spirit, no party will suffer another to be uppermost, nor indeed will they tolerate each other; because the scriptures, interpreted by each to their own purpose, is always the best weapon in the strongest hand: observe them all along, and Providence is still the prevailing argument. They who happen to be in power, will ever urge it against those who are undermost; as they who are depressed, will never fail to call it persecution. They are never united but in adversity, for cold gathers together bodies of contrary natures, and warmth divides them.

How Presbytery was transplanted into England, I have formerly related out of good authors. The persecution arising in Queen Mary's reign, forced many Protestants out of their native country into foreign parts, where Calvinism having already taken root (as at Frankfort, Strasburg, and Geneva,) those exiles grew tainted with that new discipline; and returning in the beginning of Queen Elizabeth's reign, spread the contagion of it both amongst the clergy and laity of this nation.

Any man who will look into the tenets of the

first sectaries, will find these to be more or less imbued with them: Here they were supported underhand by great men for private interests. What trouble they gave that queen, and how she curbed them, is notoriously known to all who are conversant in the histories of those times. How King James was plagued with them, is known as well to any man who has read the reverend and sincere Spottiswoode:* And how they were baffled by the Church of England, in a disputation which he allowed them at Hampton-Court,† even to the conversion of Dr. Sparks, who was one of the two disputants of their party, and afterwards writ against them, any one who pleases may be satisfied.

The agreement of their principles with the fiercest Jesuits, is as easy to be demonstrated, and has already been done, by several hands. I will only mention some few of them, to show how well prepared they came to that solemn covenant of theirs, which they borrowed first from the Holy League of France, and have lately copied out again in their intended association against his present majesty.

Bellarmine,‡ as the author of this history has told you, was himself a preacher for the League in Paris during the rebellion there, in the reign of King Henry the Fourth. Some of his principles are these following:

"In the kingdoms of men, the power of the king is from the people, because the people make the king." Observing that he says, "In the kingdoms of men," there is no doubt but he restrains this principle to the subordination of the pope; for his Holiness, in that rebellion, as you have read, was declared Protector of the League: So that the pope first excommunicates, (which is the outlawry of the church,) and, by virtue of this excommunication, the people are left to their own natural liberty, and may, without farther process from Rome, depose him.

Accordingly, you see it practised in the same instance: Pope Sixtus first thunderstruck King Henry the Third and the King of Navarre; then the Sorbonne make decrees, that they have successively forfeited the crown; the parliament verifies these decrees, and the pope is petitioned to confirm the sense of the nation, that is of the rebels.

But I have related this too favourably for Bellarmine; for we hear him, in another place, positively affirming it as matter of faith, "If any Christian prince shall depart from the Catholic religion, and shall withdraw others from it, he immediately forfeits all power and dignity, even before the pope has pronounced sentence on him; and his subjects, in case they have power to do it, may and ought to cast out such a heretic from his sovereignty over Christians."

Now, consonant to this is Buchanan's principle, "That the people may confer the government on whom they please;" and the maxim of Knox, "That if princes be tyrants against God and his truth, their subjects are released from their oath of obedience." And Goodman's, "That when magistrates cease to do their duties, God gives the sword into the people's hands: evil princes ought to be deposed by inferior magistrates; and a private man, having an inward call, may kill a tyrant."*

It is the work of a scavenger to rake together and carry off all these dunghills: they

* John Spottiswoode, archbishop of St. Andrews, who wrote a valuable, and, the times considered, a moderate history of the Church of Scotland, with a bias, as was natural, to the interests of episcopacy. It is a valuable record of Scottish history. James's harassing disputes with the Presbyterian clergymen, of course make a great figure in his annals. Spottiswoode was born in 1565, and died in 1639, just about the breaking out of those troubles which ruined the Scottish episcopal church.

† In 1603, when the king heard, at Hampton-Court, the bishops dispute against Dr. Reynolds, Dr. Sparks, Mr. Knewstubs, and Mr. Chadderton, James, infinitely better skilled in the subtleties of polemical divinity, than in the arts of ruling a great kingdom, threw his influence into the scale of episcopacy with such ingenuity, that even the pious Whitegift, then primate of England, did not hesitate to avow his persuasion, that "the king spoke by the very spirit of God." It was therefore no wonder, that Dr. Thomas Sparks, although so learned as to be called the Pillar of Puritanism, and so zealous a despiser of forms, as to appear in a Turkey merchant's gown at the conference, instead of canonicals, should be so melted and overcome by the king's eloquence and argument, as to become in future a strict conformist. He died in 1616, after having experienced the favour of James, which indeed was due to a proselyte of his own making. Sparks wrote several tracts in favour of the establishment; as, "A Brotherly Persuasion to Unity and Uniformity," &c.

‡ Robert Bellarmine, one of the most able controversialists whom the church of Rome has produced, and whose very name became a sort of war-cry of polemical divinity. He was born at Monte Pulciano, in 1542, and entered, in 1560, the order of Jesuits, of which he soon became a distinguished ornament. In the year 1599 he was honoured with a cardinal's hat, but not till he had carried the principle of "Nolo Episcopari" so far, that the pope was obliged to threaten an anathema should he persist in declining the proffered honour. Bellarmine died 17th September, 1621, leaving behind him sundry huge volumes of polemical divinity.

* Queen Elizabeth was very much startled by these and other similar reasons which John Knox assigned to persuade the nobility to depose the queen-regent, Mary of Lorraine; and the reformer was obliged to humble himself before he could obtain her forgiveness for broaching doctrines so deeply fraught with danger to monarchy.

are easy to be found at the doors of all our sects, and all our atheistical commonwealth's men. And, besides, it is a needless labour; they are so far from disowning such positions, that they glory in them; and wear them like marks of honour, as an Indian does a ring in his nose, or a Soldanian a belt of garbage. In the mean time, I appeal to any impartial man, whether men of such principles can reasonably expect any favour from the government in which they live, and which, viper-like, they would devour.

What I have remarked of them is no more than necessary to show how aptly their principles are suited to their practices: the history itself has sufficiently discovered to the unbiassed reader, that both the last rebellion, and this present conspiracy, (which is the mystery of iniquity still working in the three nations,) were originally founded on the French League: that was their model, according to which they built their Babel. You have seen how warily the first association in Picardy was worded; nothing was to be attempted but for the king's service; and an acknowledgment was formally made, that both the right and power of the government was in him: but it was pretended, that, by occasion of the true Protestant rebels, the crown was not any longer in condition, either of maintaining itself, or protecting them; and that therefore, in the name of God, and by the power of the Holy Ghost, they joined together in their own defence, and that of their religion. But all this while, though they would seem to act by the king's authority, and under him, the combination was kept as secret as possibly they could, and even without the participation of the sovereign; a sure sign that they intended him no good at the bottom. Nay, they had an evasion ready too against his authority; for it is plain they joined Humieres, the governor of the province, in commission with him, and only named the king for show; but engaged themselves at the same time to his lieutenant, to be obedient to all his commands; levying men and money, without the king's knowledge, or any law, but what they made amongst themselves. So that, in effect, the rebellion and combination of the Huguenots* was only a leading card, and an example to the Papists to rebel on their side. And there was only this difference in the cause, that the Calvinists set up for their reformation, by the superior power of religion, and inherent right of the people, against the king and pope. The Papists pretended the same popular right for their rebellion against the king, and for the same end of reformation, only they faced it with church and pope.

Our sectaries, and long parliament of forty-one, had certainly these French precedents in their eye. They copied their methods of rebellion, at first with great professions of duty and affection to the king: all they did was in order to make him glorious; all that was done against him was pretended to be under his authority, and in his name; and even the war they raised was pretended for the king and parliament. But those proceedings are so notoriously known, and have employed so many pens, that it would be a nauseous work for me to dwell on them. To draw the likeness of the French transactions and ours, were, in effect, to transcribe the history I have translated; every page is full of it; every man has seen the parallel of the Holy League and our Covenant; and cannot but observe, that, besides the names of the countries, France and England, and the names of religions, Protestant and Papist, there is scarcely to be found the least difference in the project of the whole, and in the substance of the articles. In the mean time I cannot but take notice, that our rebels have left this eternal brand upon their memories, that, while all their pretence was for the setting up the Protestant religion, and pulling down of popery, they have borrowed from Papists both the model of their design, and their arguments to defend it; and not from loyal, well-principled Papists, but from the worst, the most bigoted, and most violent of that religion; from some of the Jesuits, an order founded on purpose to combat Lutheranism and Calvinism. The matter of fact is so palpably true, and so notorious, that they cannot have the impudence to deny it. But some of the Jesuits are the shame of the Roman church, as the sectaries are of ours. Their tenets in politics are the same; both of them hate monarchy, and love democracy; both of them are superlatively violent; they are inveterate haters of each other in religion, and yet agree in the principles of government. And if, after so many advices to a painter, I might advise a Dutch maker of emblems,* he should draw a Presbyterian in arms on one side, a Jesuit on

* Dryden alludes to the conspiracy of Amboise, in 1559, by which the Huguenots, under direction of the Prince of Condé, and Coligni, meditated to surprise the court, possess themselves of the person of the king, and drive from his councils the family of Guise. It was dissipated by the policy of Catherine of Medicis and the bravery of the Duke of Guise.

* This passage affords Tom Brown grounds for a flat sneer at our author. The "Advices to a Painter," to which Dryden alludes, were a series of satires upon Charles II. and his court, published under the name of Denham, but which, in reality, were written by Andrew Marvell. They are printed in the State Poems.

the other, and a crowned head betwixt them; for it is perfectly a battle-royal. Each of them is endeavouring the destruction of his adversary; but the monarch is sure to get blows on both sides. But for those sectaries and commonwealth's men of forty-one, before I leave them, I must crave leave to observe of them, that, generally, they were a sour sort of thinking men, grim, and surly hypocrites; such as could cover their vices with an appearance of great devotion and austerity of manners; neither profaneness nor luxury were encouraged by them, nor practised publicly, which gave them a great opinion of sanctity amongst the multitude; and by that opinion, principally, they did their business. Though their politics were taken from the Catholic League, yet their Christianity much resembled those Anabaptists who were their original in doctrine; and these, indeed, were formidable instruments of a religious rebellion. But our new conspirators of these last seven years are men of quite another make: I speak not of their non-conformist preachers, who pretend to enthusiasm, and are as morose in their worship as were those first sectaries, but of their leading men, the heads of their faction, and the principal members of it; what greater looseness of life, more atheistical discourse, more open lewdness, was ever seen, than generally was and is to be observed in those men? I am neither making a satire nor a sermon here; but I would remark a little the ridiculousness of their management. The strictness of religion is their pretence: and the men who are to set it up, have theirs to choose. The long-parliament rebels frequented sermons, and observed prayers and fastings with all solemnity; but these new reformers, who ought, in prudence, to have trodden in their steps, because their end was the same, to gull the people by an outside of devotion, never used the means of insinuating themselves into the opinion of the multitude. Swearing, drunkenness, blasphemies, and worse sins than adultery, are the badges of the party: nothing but liberty in their mouths, nothing but license in their practice.

For which reason, they were never esteemed by the zealots of their faction but as their tools; and had they got uppermost, after the royalists had been crushed, they would have been blown off as too light for their society. For my own part, when I had once observed this fundamental error in their politics, I was no longer afraid of their success. No government was ever ruined by the open scandal of its opposers. This was just a Catiline's conspiracy, of profligate, debauched, and bankrupt men: The wealthy amongst them were the fools of the party, drawn in by the rest, whose fortunes were desperate; and the wits of the cabal sought only their private advantages. They had either lost their preferments, and consequently were piqued, or were in hope to raise themselves by the general disturbance; upon which account, they never could be true to one another. There was neither honour nor conscience in the foundation of their league, but every man, having an eye to his own particular advancement, was no longer a friend than while his interest was carrying on: So that treachery was at the bottom of their design, first against the monarchy, and, if that failed, against each other; in which, be it spoken to the honour of our nation, the English are not behind any other country. In few words, just as much fidelity might be expected from them in a common cause, as there is amongst a troop of honest murdering and ravishing bandits: while the booty is in prospect, they combine heartily and faithfully; but when a proclamation of pardon comes out, and a good reward into the bargain, for any one who brings in another's head, the scene is changed, and they are in more danger of being betrayed, every man by his companion, than they were formerly by the joint forces of their enemies. It is true, they are still to be accounted dangerous, because, though they are dispersed at present, and without a head, yet time and lenity may furnish them again with a commander; and all men are satisfied, that the debauched party of them have no principle of godliness to restrain them from violence and murders; nor the pretended saints any principle of charity,—for it is an action of piety in them to destroy their enemies, having first pronounced them enemies of God. What my author says, in general, of the Huguenots, may justly be applied to all our sectaries: They are a malicious and bloody generation; they bespatter honest men with their pens when they are not in power; and when they are uppermost, they hang them up like dogs. To such kind of people, all means of reclaiming, but only severity, are useless, while they continue obstinate in their designs against church and government; for though now their claws are pared, they may grow again to be more sharp. They are still lions in their nature, and may profit so much by their own errors in late managements, that they may become more sanctified traitors another time.

In the former part of our history, we see what Henry III. gained from them by his remissness and concessions. Though our last king was not only incomparably more pious than that prince, but also was far from being taxed with any of his vices, yet in this they may be compared, without the least manner of reflection, that extreme indulgence, and too great concessions, were the ruin of them both. And by how much the more a king is subject, by his nature, to this frailty of too much mildness, which is so near resembling the godlike attribute of mercy, by so much is he the more liable to be taxed with tyranny. A strange paradox, but which was sadly verified in the persons of those two princes. For a faction, appearing zealous for the public liberty, counts him a tyrant who yields not up whatever they demand, even his most undoubted and just prerogatives; all that distinguishes a sovereign from a subject; and the yielding up, or taking away of which, is the very subversion of the government.

Every point which a monarch loses or relinquishes, but renders him weaker to maintain the rest; and, besides, they so construe it, as if what he gave up were the natural right of the people, which he, or his ancestors, had usurped from them; which makes it the more dangerous for him to quit his hold, and is truly the reason why so many mild princes have been branded with the names of tyrants by their encroaching subjects. I have not room to enlarge upon this matter as I would, neither dare I presume to press the argument more closely; but passing by, as I promised, all the remarkable passages in the late king's reign, which resemble the transactions of the League, I will briefly take notice of some few particulars, wherein our late associators and conspirators have made a third copy of the League; for the original of their first politics was certainly no other than the French. This was first copied by the rebels in forty-one, and since recopied within these late years by some of those who are lately dead, and by too many others yet alive, and still drawing after the same design; in which, for want of time, many a fair blot shall be left unhit; neither do I promise to observe any method of times, or to take things in order as they happened.

As for the persons who managed the two associations, theirs and ours, it is most certain that in them is found the least resemblance: And it is well for us they were not like; for they had men of subtlety and valour to design, and then to carry on their conspiracy. Ours were but bunglers in comparison of them, who, having a faction not made by them, but ready formed and fashioned to their hands, (thanks to their fathers,) yet failed in every one of their projections, and managed their business with much less dexterity, though far more wickedness, than the French. They had, indeed, at their head an old conspirator, witty and turbulent, like the Cardinal of Lorraine,* and for courage in execution much such another. But the good sense and conduct was clearly wanting on the English side; so that, if we will allow him the contrivance of the plot, or at least of the conspiracy, which is an honour that no man will be willing to take from him, in all other circumstances he more resembled the old decrepit Cardinal of Bourbon, who fed himself with imaginary hopes of power, dreamed of outliving a king and his successor, much more young and vigorous than himself, and of governing the world after their decease. To die in prison, or in banishment, I think, will make no mighty difference; but this is a main one, that the one was the dupe of all his party, the other led after him, and made fools of all his faction. As for a Duke of Guise, or even so much as a Duke of Mayenne, I can find none in their whole cabal. I cannot believe that any man now living could have the vanity to pretend to it. It is not every age that can produce a Duke of Guise,—a man who, without the least shadow of a title, (unless we will believe the memoirs of the crack-brained advocate David, who gave him one from Charlemagne,) durst make himself head of a party, and was not only so in his own conceit, but really; presumed to beard a king, and was upon the point of being declared his lieutenant-general and his successor. None of these instances will hold in the comparison; and therefore I leave it to be boasted, it may be, by one party, but I am sure to be laughed at by another. Many hot-headed Chevaliers d'Aumale, and ambitious bravoes, like Captain St. Paul,* may be found amongst them; intriguing ladies and gallants of the times, such as are described in the army of the League, at the battle of Yvry;† and besides them, many underling knaves, pimps, and fools; but these are not worthy to be drawn into resemblance.

Therefore, to pass by their persons, and consider their design, it is evident, that on both sides they began with a League, and ended

* The Cardinal of Lorraine, brother to the Duke of Guise, and the political head of the Leaguers. He was assassinated at the same time with his brother. Dryden compares him to Shaftesbury.

* A fiery and gallant adherent of the Duke of Guise. He distinguished himself by his bravery in the battles, and his forwardness in the councils of the League; on the famous day of the barricades, he entered the queen's garden by force, supposing his patron's life in danger, and swearing, if the game was to be played, he would have his stake in it. He was created Marshal of France in 1598, by the Duke Mayenne, and afterwards governor of Champagne. These honours cost him his life; for the young Duke of Guise having requested him to withdraw some troops from Rheims, and receiving an insolent refusal, drew his sword and killed him on the spot.

† "There was scarcely any thing to be seen in the army of the League but gold and silver embroideries, upon costly and magnificent coats of velvet, of all sorts of colours, and an infinite number of banderolles fluttering about their thick forest of lances."—*Dryden's Translation of the History of the League.*

with a conspiracy. In this they have copied, even to the word Association, which you may observe was used by Humieres, in the first wary League which was formed in Picardy; and we see to what it tended in the event: For when Henry III. by the assistance of the king of Navarre, had in a manner vanquished his rebels, and was just upon the point of mastering Paris, a Jacobin, set on by the preachers of the League, most barbarously murdered him; and, by the way, take notice, that he pretended enthusiasm, or inspiration of God's Holy Spirit, for the commission of this parricide. I leave my superiors to conclude from thence, the danger of tolerating non-conformists, who, (be it said with reverence,) under pretence of a whisper from the Holy Ghost, think themselves obliged to perpetrate the most enormous crimes against the person of their sovereign, when they have first voted him a tyrant and an enemy to God's people. This, indeed, was not so impudent a method as what was used in the formal process of a pretended high court of justice, in the murder of King Charles I., and therefore I do not compare those actions; but it is much resembling the intended murder of our gracious king at the Rye, and other places: And, that the head of a college might not be wanting to urge the performance of this horrible attempt, instead of Father Edm. Bourgoing,* let Father Ferguson† appear, who was not wanting in his spiritual exhortations to our conspirators, and to make them believe, that to assassinate the king was only to take away another Holofernes. It is true, the Jacobin was but one; and there were many joined in our conspiracy, and more perhaps than Rumsey or West‡ have ever named; but this, though it takes from the justness of the comparison, adds incomparably more to the guilt of it, and makes it fouler on our side of the water.

My author makes mention of another conspiracy against Henry IV., for the seizing of his person at Mante, by the young Cardinal of Bourbon, who was head of the third party, called at that time the Politics, that is to say, in modern English, Trimmers. This, too, was a limb of our conspiracy; and the more moderate party of our traitors were engaged in it.* But had it taken effect, the least it could have produced, was to have overthrown the succession; and no reasonable man would believe, but they who could forget their duty so much as to have seized the king, might afterwards have been induced to have him made away, especially when so fair a provision was made by the House of Commons, that the Papists were to suffer for it.

But they have not only rummaged the French histories of the League for conspiracies and parricides of kings; I shall make it apparent, that they have studied those execrable times, for precedents of undermining the lawful authority of their sovereigns. Our English are not generally commended for invention; but these were merchants of small wares, very pedlers in policy; they must, like our tailors, have all their fashions from the French, and study the French League for every alteration, as our snippers go over once a year into France, to bring back the newest mode, and to learn to cut and shape it.

For example: The first estates convened at Blois by Henry III. (the League being then on foot, and most of the three orders dipped in it,) demanded of that king, that the articles which should be approved by the three orders should pass for inviolable laws, without leaving to the king the power of changing any thing in them. That the same was designed here by the leading men of their faction, is obvious to every one: for they had it commonly in their mouths in ordinary discourse; and it was offered in print by Plato Redivivus† as a good expedient for the nation, in case his majesty would have consented to it.

Both in the first and last estates at Blois, the bill of exclusion against the King of Navarre was pressed; and in the last carried by all the three orders, though the king would never pass it. The end of that bill was very evident; it was to have introduced the Duke of Guise into the throne, after the king's decease: to which he had no manner of title, or at least a very cracked one, of which his own party were ashamed. Our bill of exclusion was copied from hence; but thrown out by the House of

* Father Edmund Bourgoing, prior of the convent in which Jaques Clement, who assassinated Henry III., was a Jacobin monk. As he vindicated the action when committed, and compared the murderer, in his sermons, to Judith, it was not doubted, that he had prompted, or at least confirmed, his execrable resolution.

† Robert Ferguson, called the Plotter, who told the conspirators, that if they took off Charles on a Sunday, the day would sanctify the deed, and proposed to consecrate the blunderbuss with which he was to be shot.

‡ Evidences for the king on the trial of the conspirators for the Rye-house plot.

* This is apparently an allusion to the designs of Lord Russell and others, who meditated a change of councils, not of government, by the schemes which they agitated.

† A tract in octavo, published in October 1680, shortly after the sitting of the short parliament. The author was Henry Neville, second son of Sir Henry Neville, knight, who made some figure among the speculative commonwealth's men, yet was not so much attached to their doctrines, as to prevent his submitting to be one of Cromwell's council of state. He died 20th September 1694

Peers, before it came to the king's turn to have wholly quashed it.

After the Duke of Guise had forced the king to fly from Paris by the barricades, the queen-mother being then in the traitor's interests, when he had outwitted her so far, as to persuade her to join in the banishment of the Duke of Espernon, his enemy, and to make her believe, that if the King of Navarre, whom she hated, were excluded, he would assist her in bringing her beloved grandchild of Lorraine to the possession of the crown; it was proposed by him for the Parisians, that the lieutenantcy of the city might be wholly put into their hands; that the new provost of merchants, and present sheriffs of the faction, might be confirmed by the king; and for the future, they should not only elect their sheriffs, but the colonels and captains of the several wards.

How nearly this was copied in the tumultuous meetings of the city for their sheriffs, both we and they have cause to remember; and Mr. Hunt's book, concerning their rights in the city charter, mingled with infamous aspersions of the government, confirms the notions to have been the same.* And I could produce some very probable instances out of another libel, (considering the time at which it was written, which was just before the detection of the conspiracy,) that the author of it, as well as the supervisor, was engaged in it, or at least privy to it; but let villany and ingratitude be safe and flourish.

By the way, an observation of Philip de Comines comes into my mind: That when the Dukes of Burgundy, who were Lords of Ghent, had the choice of the sheriffs of that city, in that year all was quiet and well governed; but when they were elected by the people, nothing but tumults and seditions followed.†

I might carry this resemblance a little farther: for in the heat of the plot, when the Spanish pilgrims were coming over,‡ nay more, were reported to be landed; when the representatives of the Commons were either mortally afraid, or pretended to be so, of this airy invasion, a request was actually made to the king, that he would put the militia into their hands, which how prudently he refused, the example of his father has informed the nation.

To show how the heads of their party had conned over their lesson of the barricades of Paris, in the midst of Oates his Popish plot, when they had fermented the city with the leaven of their sedition, and they were all prepared for a rising against the government: let it be remembered, that as the Duke of Guise and the council of sixteen forged a list of names, which they pretended to be of such as the king had set down for destruction; so a certain earl of blessed memory caused a false report to be spread of his own danger, and some of his accomplices, who were to be murdered by the Papists and the royal party; which was a design to endear themselves to the multitude, as the martyrs of their cause; and at the same time, to cast an odious reflection on the king and ministers, as if they sought their blood with unchristian cruelty, without the ordinary forms of justice. To which may be added, as an appendix, their pretended fear, when they went to the parliament at Oxford; before which some of them made their wills, and showed them publicly; others sent to search about the places where the two houses were to sit, as if another gunpowder plot was contriving against them; and almost every man of them, according to his quality, went attended with his guard of Janizaries, like Titus:* so that what with their followers, and the seditious townsmen of the city, they made the formidable appearance of an army; at least sufficient to have swallowed up the guards, and to have seized the person of the king, in case he had not prevented it by a speedy removal, as soon as he had dissolved that parliament.

I begin already to be tired with drawing after their deformities, as a painter would be, who had nothing before him in his table but lazars, cripples, and hideous faces, which he was obliged to represent: yet I must not omit some few of their most notorious copyings. Take for example their Council of Six, which was an imitation of the League, who set up their famous council, commonly called "Of the Sixteen:" And take notice, that on both sides they picked out the most heady and violent men of the whole party; nay, they considered not so much as their natural parts, but heavy blockheads were thrown in for lumber, to make up the

* Mr. Hunt's book was entitled, a "Defence of the Charter and Municipal Rights of the City of London." Our author was fiercely attacked in that work, and defended himself in the Vindication of the Duke of Guise.

† The author alludes to the exertions made by the crown to secure the election of sheriffs.

‡ Among the absurdities sworn to and believed at the time of the Popish plot, Bedloe's assertion, that 40,000 pilgrims, assembled in Spain to pay their devotion at Saint James's, were to be employed in the invasion of England, was not the less terrifying because so eminently incredible. A false report that the pilgrims had actually landed, obtained general credit, and one nobleman gallopped to London with the news.

* Many of the opposition members, particularly those for the city of London, went armed and escorted to the parliament of Oxford, so that they resembled Titus Oates, who in his days of splendour was always attended by a guard.

weight. Their zeal for the party, and their ambition, atoned for their want of judgment, especially if they were thought to have any interest in the people. Loud roarers of *ay* and *no* in the parliament, without common sense in ordinary discourses, if they were favourites of the multitude, were made privy-counsellors of their cabal; and fools, who only wanted a party-coloured coat, a cap, and a bawble, to pass for such amongst reasonable men, were to redress the imaginary grievances of a nation, by murdering, or at least seizing of the king. Men of scandalous lives, cheats, and murderers, were to reform the nation, and propagate the Protestant religion: and the rich ideots to hazard their estates and expectations, to forsake their ease, honour, and preferments, for an empty name of heading a party; the wittiest man amongst them to encumber and vex his decrepit age, for a silly pique of revenge, and to maintain his character to the last, of never being satisfied with any government, in which he was not more a king than the present master. To give the last stroke to this resemblance, fortune did her part; and the same fate, of division amongst themselves, ruined both those councils which were contriving their king's destruction. The Duke of Mayenne and his adherents, who were much the most honest of the Leaguers, were not only for a king, but for a king of the royal line, in case that duke could not cause the election to fall on himself, which was impossible, because he was already married. The rest were, some for this man, some for another, and all in a lump for the daughter of Spain: this disunited them, and in the end ruined their conspiracy. In our Council of Six, some were for murdering, and some for securing of the king; some for a rising in the west, and some for an insurrection of the Brisk Boys of Wapping: in short, some were for a mongrel kind of kingship, to the exclusion of the royal line, but the greater part for a bare-faced commonwealth. This raised a division in their council; that division was fomented into a mutual hatred of each other; and the conclusion was, that instead of one conspiracy, the machines played double, and produced two, which were carried on at the same time. A kind of spread-eagle plot was hatched, with two heads growing out of the same body: such twin treasons are apt to struggle like Esau and Jacob in the womb, and both endeavouring to be first born, the younger pulls back the elder by the heel.

I promised to observe no order, and am performing my word before I was aware. After the barricades, and at many other times, the Duke of Guise, and Council of Sixteen, amongst the rest of the articles, demanded of the king to cashier his guards of the forty-five gentlemen, as unknown in the times of his predecessors, and unlawful; as also, to remove his surest friends from about his person, and from their places, both military and civil. I leave any man to judge, whether our conspirators did not play the second part to the same tune; whether his majesty's guards were not alleged to be unlawful, and a grievance to the subjects; and whether frequent votes did not pass in the House of Commons at several times, for removing and turning out of office those, who, on all occasions, behaved themselves most loyally to the king, without so much as giving any other reason of their misdemeanors than public fame; that is to say, reports forged and spread by their own faction, or without allowing them the common justice of vindicating themselves from those calumnies and aspersions.

I omit the many illegal imprisonments of freeborn men, by their own representatives, who, from a jury, erected themselves into judges; because I find nothing resembling it in the worst and most seditious times of France. But let the history be searched, and I believe Bussy Le Clerc never committed more outrages in pillaging of houses, than Waller in pretending to search for Popish relics:* Neither do I remember that the French Leaguers ever took the evidence of a Jew, as ours did of Faria.† But this I wonder at the less, considering what Christian witnesses have been used, if at least the chief of them was ever christened. Bussy Le Clerc, it is true, turned out a whole parliament together, and brought them prisoners to the Bastile; and Bussy Oates was for garbling

* Jean Le Clerc, otherwise called Bussy, once a *procureur* before the parliament of Paris: being a bold, active, and ferocious man, he was created governor of the Bastile by the Duke of Guise, and employed in seizing the persons of the President Harlai, and other counsellors of parliament, and exercising severities on all those suspected of disaffection to the cause of the League. Dryden compares him to Waller, whom the Catholics accused of pillaging their houses, under pretence of searching for relics during the times of the plot.

† Francisco de Faria, who designed himself interpreter and secretary of languages to Gasper de Abreu de Freitas, ambassador from the crown of Portugal, was one of the witnesses concerning the popish plot. He pretended he had been employed by the Portuguese ambassador to assassinate Oates, Bedlow, and Shaftesbury. His narrative was licensed for publication on 19th November, 1680; and concludes with an impudent affectation of admiring the Divine Providence, which had brought him "from almost the utmost parts of the far distant habitable world, to be an instrument, in England, to detect, or at least more convincingly to prove the truth of these horrid treasons and conspiracies." Faria was a native of Pernambuco, in Brasil and apparently a Portuguese Jew

too, when he informed against a worthy and loyal member, whom he caused to be expelled the House, and sent prisoner to the Tower:* But that which was then accounted a disgrace to him, will make him be remembered with honour to posterity.

I will trouble the reader but with one observation more, and that shall be to show how dully and pedantically they have copied even the false steps of the League in politics, and those very maxims which ruined the heads of it. The Duke of Guise was always ostentatious of his power in the states, where he carried all things in opposition to the king; but, by relying too much on the power he had there, and not using arms when he had them in his hand, I mean by not prosecuting his victory to the uttermost, when he had the king enclosed in the Louvre, he missed his opportunity, and fortune never gave it him again.

The late Earl of Shaftesbury, who was the undoubted head and soul of that party, went upon the same maxims; being (as we may reasonably conclude) fearful of hazarding his fortunes, and observing, that the late rebellion, under the former king, though successful in war, yet ended in the restoration of his present majesty, his aim was to have excluded his royal highness by an act of parliament; and to have forced such concessions from the king, by pressing the chimerical dangers of a popish plot, as would not only have destroyed the succession, but have subverted the monarchy; for he presumed he ventured nothing, if he could have executed his designs by form of law, and in a parliamentary way. In the mean time, he made notorious mistakes; first, in imagining that his pretensions would have passed in the House of Peers, and afterwards by the king. When the death of Sir Edmondbury Godfrey had fermented the people; when the city had taken the alarm of a popish plot, and the government of it was in fanatic hands; when a body of White Boys was already appearing in the west,† and many other counties waited but the word to rise—then was the time to have pushed his business: but Almighty God, who had otherwise disposed of the event, infatuated his counsels, and made him slip his opportunity; which he himself observed too late, and would have redressed by an insurrection, which was to have begun at Wapping, after the king had been murdered at the Rye.

And now, it will be but justice, before I conclude, to say a word or two of my author.* He was formerly a Jesuit. He has, amongst others of his works, written the history of Arianism, of Lutheranism, of Calvinism, the Holy War, and the Fall of the Western Empire. In all his writings, he has supported the temporal power of sovereigns, and especially of his master the French King, against the usurpations and encroachments of the papacy. For which reason, being in disgrace at Rome, he was in a manner forced to quit his order, and, from Father Maimbourg, is now become Monsieur Maimbourg. The great king, his patron, has provided plentifully for him by a large salary, and indeed he has deserved it from him. As for his style, it is rather Ciceronian, copious, florid, and figurative, than succinct: He is esteemed in the French court equal to their best writers, which has procured him the envy of some who set up for critics. Being a professed enemy of the Calvinists, he is particularly hated by them; so that their testimonies against him stand suspected of prejudice. This history of the League is generally allowed to be one of his best pieces.† He has quoted everywhere his authors in the margin, to show his impartiality; in which, if I have not followed him, it is because the chiefest of them are unknown to us, as not being hitherto translated into English. His particular commendations of men and families, is all which I think superfluous in his book; but that, too, is pardonable in a man, who, having created himself many enemies, has need of the support of friends. This particular work was written by express order of the French King, and is now translated by our king's command. I hope the effect of it in this nation will be, to make the well-meaning men of the other party sensible of their past errors, the worst of them ashamed, and prevent posterity from the like unlawful and impious design.

* Sir Robert Peyton was expelled the House, and committed to the Tower, on account of expressing some hesitation as to the credibility of Oates.

† White was the dress affected by those who crowded to see Monmouth in his western tour. Mr. Trenchard undertook to raise 1500 men in and about Taunton alone. See *Lord Grey's Account of the Rye-house Plot*, p. 18; where the plan of the city insurrection is also distinctly detailed, Pp. 32–46.

* Louis Maimbourg was born at Nanci in 1610, and became a Jesuit in 1626. But he was degraded from that order by the general, because he espoused, in some of his writings, the cause of the Gallican church against the claims of the Roman see. He retired to the Abbey of St. Victor, where he died in 1686. His historical writings, which are numerous, are now held in little esteem, being all composed in the spirit of a partisan, and without even the affectation of impartiality. They are, however, lively and interesting during the perusal; which led an Italian to say, that Maimbourg was among the historians, what Momus was among the deities.

† Maimbourg's History of the League was first published at Paris in 1683.

THE ART OF PAINTING

BY C. A. DU FRESNOY.

WITH REMARKS.

TRANSLATED INTO ENGLISH; WITH AN ORIGINAL PREFACE, CONTAINING A PARALLEL BETWEEN PAINTING AND POETRY. FIRST PRINTED IN QUARTO IN 1695.

CHARLES ALPHONSE DU FRESNOY, as we learn from his life by Mason, was born in Paris in the year 1611. He studied the art of painting in Rome and Venice, and afterwards practised it in France with great reputation. Meanwhile, he did not neglect the sister pursuit of poetry: and combining it with the studies of an artist, he composed his poem on the Art of Painting. It did not appear till after the author's death, in 1658, when it was published with the French version, and remarks of De Piles. The first edition was printed in 1661. This poem, as containing, in elegant and perspicuous language, the most just rules for artists and amateurs, has been always held in esteem by the admirers of the art which it professes to teach.

The version of Dryden first appeared in 4to, in 1695, and was republished by Richard Graham in 1716, by whom it is inscribed to Lord Burlington. The editor of 1716 informs us, that Mr. Jervas had undertaken to correct such passages of the translation as Dryden had erred in, by following too closely the French version of De Piles. To Graham's edition is prefixed the epistle from Pope to Jervas, with Dryden's version; an honourable and beautiful testimony from the living to the dead poet, which I have retained with pleasure, as also the epistle from Mason to Sir Joshua Reynolds, which contains some remarks on Dryden's version.

The late Mr. Mason, as a juvenile exercise, executed a poetical version of Fresnoy's poem, which has had the honour to be admitted into the works of Sir Joshua Reynolds, vol. iii. and might have superseded the necessity of here reprinting the prose of Dryden. But there is something so singular in a great poet undertaking to render into prose the admired poem of a foreign bard, that, as a specimen of such an uncommon task, as well as on account of its brevity, I have retained this translation.

Being no judge of the art to which the poem refers, I follow the readings of Jervas, as published by Graham in 1716.

Mason has retained the Parallel between Painting and Poetry, in his edition of Fresnoy, with the following note:

"It was thought proper to insert in this place the pleasing preface, which Mr. Dryden printed before his translation of M. Du Fresnoy's poem. There is a charm in that great writer's prose, peculiar to itself; and though, perhaps, the parallel between the two arts, which he has here drawn, be too superficial to stand the test of strict criticism, yet it will always give pleasure to readers of taste, even when it fails to satisfy their judgment."

P

TO MR. JARVIS,

WITH FRESNOY'S ART OF PAINTING.

TRANSLATED BY MR. DRYDEN.

THIS verse be thine, my friend; nor thou refuse
This from no venal or ungrateful muse.
Whether thy hand strike out some free design,
Where life awakes, and dawns at every line;
Or blend in beauteous tints the colour'd mass,
And from the canvass call the mimic face;
Read these instructive leaves, in which conspire
Fresnoy's close art, and Dryden's native fire;
And reading wish, like theirs, our fate and fame,
So mix'd our studies, and so join'd our name;
Like them to shine through long succeeding age,
So just thy skill, so regular my rage.
Smit with the love of sister-arts we came,
And met congenial, mingling flame with flame;
Like friendly colours found our arts unite,
And each from each contract new strength and light.
How oft in pleasing tasks we wear the day,
While summer suns roll unperceived away?
How oft our slowly growing works impart,
While images reflect from art to art?
How oft review; each finding, like a friend,
Something to blame, and something to commend?
What flattering scenes our wandering fancy wrought,
Rome's pompous glories rising to our thought!
Together o'er the Alps methinks we fly,
Fired with ideas of fair Italy.
With thee, on Raphael's monument I mourn,
Or wait inspiring dreams at Maro's urn;
With thee repose where Tully once was laid,
Or seek some ruin's formidable shade;
While fancy brings the vanish'd piles to view,
And builds imaginary Rome anew.
Here thy well-studied marbles fix our eye;
A fading Fresco here demands a sigh;
Each heavenly piece unwearied we compare,
Match Raphael's grace, with thy loved Guido's air,
Caracci's strength, Correggio's softer line,
Paulo's free stroke, and Titian's warmth divine.
How finish'd with illustrious toil appears,
This small well-polish'd gem, the work of years! *
Yet still how faint by precept is exprest,
The living image in the painter's breast?
Thence endless streams of fair ideas flow,
Strike in the sketch, or in the picture glow;
Thence beauty, waking all her forms, supplies
An angel's sweetness, or Bridgewater's eyes.
Muse! at that name thy sacred sorrows shed
Those tears eternal that embalm the dead;
Call round her tomb each object of desire,
Each purer frame inform'd with purer fire;
Bid her be all that cheers or softens life,
The tender sister, daughter, friend, and wife.
Bid her be all that makes mankind adore;
Then view this marble, and be vain no more!
Yet still her charms in breathing paint engage;
Her modest cheek shall warm a future age.
Beauty, frail flower, that every season fears,
Blooms in thy colours for a thousand years.
Thus Churchil's race shall other hearts surprise,
And other beauties envy Wortley's eyes;
Each pleasing Blount shall endless smiles bestow,
And soft Belinda's blush for ever glow.
Oh! lasting as those colours may they shine,
Free as thy stroke, yet faultless as thy line!
New graces yearly, like thy works, display;
Soft without weakness, without glaring gay;
Led by some rule, that guides, but not constrains;
And finish'd more through happiness than pains.
The kindred arts shall in their praise conspire,
One dip the pencil, and one string the lyre.
Yet should the Graces all thy figures place,
And breathe an air divine on every face;
Yet should the Muses bid my numbers roll,
Strong as their charms, and gentle as their soul;
With Zeuxis' Helen thy Bridgewater vie,
And these be sung till Granville's Myra die;
Alas! how little from the grave we claim!
Thou but preserv'st a Form, and I a Name.

A. POPE.

* Fresnoy employed above twenty years in finishing this poem.

TO SIR JOSHUA REYNOLDS.

When Dryden, worn with sickness, bow'd with years,
Was doom'd (my friend, let pity warm thy tears)
The galling pang of penury to feel,
For ill-placed loyalty, and courtly zeal;
To see that laurel which his brows o'erspread,
Transplanted droop on Shadwell's barren head,
The bard oppress'd, yet not subdued by fate,
For very bread descended to translate;
And he, whose fancy, copious as his phrase,
Could light at will expression's brightest blaze,
On Fresnoy's lay employ'd his studious hour;
But niggard there of that melodious power,
His pen in haste the hireling task to close,
Transform'd the studied strain to careless prose,
Which, fondly lending faith to French pretence,
Mistook its meaning, or obscured its sense.
Yet still he pleased, for Dryden still must please,
Whether with artless elegance and ease
He glides in prose or from its tinkling chime,
By varied pauses, purifies his rhyme,
And mounts on Maro's plumes, and soars his heights sublime.
This artless elegance, this native fire,
Provoked his tuneful heir to strike the lyre,
Who proud his numbers with that prose to join,
Wove an illustrious wreath for friendship's shrine.
How oft, on that fair shrine when poets bind
The flowers of song, does partial passion blind
Their judgment's eye! How oft does truth disclaim
The deed, and scorn to call it genuine fame!
How did she here, when Jervas was the theme,
Waft through the ivory gate the poet's dream!
How view, indignant, error's base alloy
The sterling lustre of his praise destroy,
Which now if praise like his my muse could coin,
Current through ages, she would stamp for thine!
Let friendship, as she caused, excuse the deed·
With thee, and such as thee, she must succeed.
But what if fashion tempted Pope astray?
The witch has spells, and Jervas knew a day,
When mode-struck belles and beaux were proud to come,
And buy of him a thousand years of bloom.
Even then I deem it but a venal crime;
Perish alone that selfish sordid rhyme,
Which flatters lawless sway, or tinsel pride;
Let black oblivion plunge it in her tide.
From fate like this my truth-supported lays,
Even if aspiring to thy pencil's praise,
Would flow secure; but humbler aims are mine:
Know, when to thee I consecrate the line,
'Tis but to thank thy genius for the ray,
Which pours on Fresnoy's rules a fuller day,
Those candid strictures, those reflections new,
Refined by taste, yet still as nature true,
Which, blended here with his instructive strains,
Shall bid thy art inherit new domains;
Give her in Albion as in Greece to rule,
And guide (what thou hast form'd) a British school.
And oh, if aught thy poet can pretend
Beyond his favourite wish to call thee friend,
Be it that here his tuneful toil has drest
The muse of Fresnoy in a modern vest;
And, with that skill his fancy could bestow,
Taught the close folds to take an easier flow,
Be it, that here thy partial smile approved
The pains he lavish'd on the art he loved.

W. Mason.

A PARALLEL OF POETRY AND PAINTING.

It may be reasonably expected that I should say something on my own behalf, in respect to my present undertaking. First, then, the reader may be pleased to know, that it was not of my own choice that I undertook this work. Many of our most skilful painters, and other artists, were pleased to recommend this author to me, as one who perfectly understood the rules of painting; who gave the best and most concise instructions for performance, and the surest to inform the judgment of all who loved this noble art; that they who, before, were rather fond of it than knowingly admired it, might defend their inclination by their reason; that they might understand those excellencies which they blindly valued, so as not to be farther imposed on by bad pieces, and to know when nature was well imitated by the most able masters. It is true indeed, and they acknowledge it, that beside the rules which are given in this treatise, or which can be given in any other, to make a perfect judgment of good pictures, and to value them more or less, when compared with one another, there is farther required a long conversation with the best pieces, which are not very frequent either in France or England; yet some we have, not only from the hands of Holbein, Rubens, and Vandyck, (one of them admirable for history painting, and the other two for portraits,) but of many Flemish masters, and those not inconsiderable, though for design not equal to the Italians. And of these latter also, we are not unfurnished with some pieces of Raphael, Titian, Correggio, Michael Angelo, and others.

But to return to my own undertaking of this translation. I freely own that I thought myself incapable of performing it, either to their satisfaction or my own credit. Not but that I understood the original Latin, and the French author, perhaps as well as most Englishmen; but I was not sufficiently versed in the terms of art; and therefore thought that many of those persons who put this honourable task on me, were more able to perform it themselves,—as undoubtedly they were. But they, assuring me of their assistance in correcting my faults where I spoke improperly, I was encouraged to attempt it, that I might not be wanting in what I could, to satisfy the desires of so many gentlemen, who were willing to give the world this useful work. They have effectually performed their promise to me, and I have been as careful, on my side, to take their advice in all things; so that the reader may assure himself of a tolerable translation,—not elegant, for I proposed not that to myself, but familiar, clear, and instructive: in any of which parts if I have failed, the fault lies wholly at my door. In this one particular only, I must beg the reader's pardon. The prose translation of this poem is not free from poetical expressions, and I dare not promise that some of them are not fustian, or at least highly metaphorical; but this being a fault in the first digestion, (that is, the original Latin,) was not to be remedied in the second, viz. the translation. And I may confidently say, that whoever had attempted it must have fallen into the same inconvenience, or a much greater, that of a false version.

When I undertook this work, I was already engaged in the translation of Virgil,* from whom I have borrowed only two months; and am now returning to that which I ought to understand better. In the mean time, I beg the reader's pardon for entertaining him so long with myself: it is a usual part of ill manners in all authors, and almost in all mankind, to trouble others with their business; and I was so sensible of it beforehand, that I had not now committed it, unless some concernments of the reader's had been interwoven with my own. But I know not, while I am atoning for one error, if I am not falling into another; for I have been importuned to say something farther of this art; and to make some observations on it, in relation to the likeness and agreement which it has with poetry, its sister. But before I proceed, it will not be amiss, if I copy from Bellori, (a most ingenious author yet

* Our author began his translation of Virgil in the preceding year, 1694.—*Malone.*

living,) some part of his idea of a painter,* which cannot be unpleasing, at least to such who are conversant in the philosophy of Plato; and, to avoid tediousness, I will not translate the whole discourse, but take and leave as I find occasion.

"God Almighty, in the fabric of the universe, first contemplated himself, and reflected on his own excellencies; from which he drew and constituted those first forms which are called ideas; so that every species which was afterwards expressed, was produced from that first idea, forming that wonderful contexture of all created beings. But the celestial bodies above the moon being incorruptible, and not subject to change, remained for ever fair and in perpetual order. On the contrary, all things which are sublunary, are subject to change, to deformity, and to decay. And though nature always intends a consummate beauty in her productions, yet through the inequality of the matter, the forms are altered; and in particular, human beauty suffers alteration for the worse, as we see to our mortification, in the deformities and disproportions which are in us. For which reason, the artful painter and the sculptor, imitating the Divine Maker, form to themselves, as well as they are able, a model of the superior beauties; and reflecting on them, endeavour to correct and amend the common nature, and to represent it as it was at first created, without fault, either in colour or in lineament.

"This idea, which we may call the goddess of painting and of sculpture, descends upon the marble and the cloth, and becomes the original of those arts; and being measured by the compass of the intellect, is itself the measure of the performing hand; and being animated by the imagination, infuses life into the image. The idea of the painter and the sculptor is undoubtedly that perfect and excellent example of the mind, by imitation of which imagined form all things are represented which fall under human sight: such is the definition which is made by Cicero in his book of the "Orator" to Brutus:—'As therefore in forms and figures there is somewhat which is excellent and perfect, to which imagined species all things are referred by imitation, which are the objects of sight, in like manner we behold the species of eloquence in our minds, the *effigies* or actual image of which we seek in the organs of our hearing. This is likewise confirmed by Proclus in the dialogue of Plato, called "Timæus." If, says he, you take a man as he is made by nature, and compare him with another, who is the effect of art, the work of nature will always appear the less beautiful, because art is more accurate than nature.' But Zeuxis, who, from the choice which he made of five virgins, drew that wonderful picture of Helena, which Cicero in his "Orator" before mentioned, sets before us as the most perfect example of beauty, at the same time admonishes a painter, to contemplate the ideas of the most natural forms, and to make a judicious choice of several bodies, all of them the most elegant which he can find; by which we may plainly understand, that he thought it impossible to find in any one body all those perfections which he sought for the accomplishment of a Helena, because nature in any individual person makes nothing that is perfect in all its parts. For this reason, Maximus Tyrius also says, that the image which is taken by a painter from several bodies, produces a beauty which it is impossible to find in any single natural body, approaching to the perfection of the fairest statues. Thus nature on this account is so much inferior to art, that those artists who propose to themselves only the imitation and likeness of such or such a particular person, without election of those ideas before mentioned, have often been reproached for that omission. Demetrius was taxed for being too natural; Dionysius was also blamed for drawing men like us, and was commonly called ἀνθρωπόγραφος, that is, a painter of men. In our times, Michael Angelo da Caravaggio was esteemed too natural. He drew persons as they were; and Bamboccio, and most of the Dutch painters, have drawn the worst likeness. Lysippus of old upbraided the common sort of sculptors, for making men such as they were found in nature; and boasted of himself, that he made them as they ought to be: which is a precept of Aristotle, given as well to poets as to painters. Phidias raised an admiration, even to astonishment, in those who beheld his statues, with the forms which he gave to his gods and heroes, by imitating the idea, rather than nature. And Cicero, speaking of him, affirms, that figuring Jupiter and Pallas, he did not contemplate any object from whence he took the likeness, but considered in his own mind a great and admirable form of beauty; and according to that image in his soul, he directed the operation of his hand. Seneca also seems to wonder, that Phidias, having never beheld either Jove, or Pallas, yet could conceive their divine images in his mind.

* In May, 1664, Gio. Pietro Bellori read a discourse in the Academy of St. Luke at Rome, (Carlo Maratti being then president,) entitled—*L'Idea del Pittore, dello Scultore, e dell' Architetto, scelta dalle bellezze naturali superiore alla Natura*. This discourse, from which the following extract is taken, was afterwards prefixed to *Le Vite de Pittore*, &c. by the same author, printed at Rome in 4to. 1672.—*Malone*.

Apollonius Tyanæus says the same in other words,—that the fancy more instructs the painter, than the imitation; for the last makes only the things which it sees, but the first makes also the things which it never sees.

"Leon Battista Alberti tells us, that we ought not so much to love the likeness as the beauty, and to choose from the fairest bodies severally the fairest parts. Leonardo da Vinci instructs the painter to form this idea to himself; and Raffaelle, the greatest of all modern masters, writes thus to Castiglione, concerning his Galatea: 'To paint a fair one, it is necessary for me to see many fair ones; but because there is so great a scarcity of lovely women, I am constrained to make use of one certain idea, which I have formed to myself in my own fancy.' Guido Rheni sending to Rome his St. Michael, which he had painted for the church of the Capuchins, at the same time wrote to Monsignor Massano, who was *Maestro di Casa*, (or Steward of the House,) to Pope Urban the Eighth, in this manner: I wish I had the wings of an angel, to have ascended into Paradise, and there to have beheld the forms of those beautiful spirits, from which I might have copied my archangel. But not being able to mount so high, it was in vain for me to search his resemblance here below; so that I was forced to make an introspection into my own mind, and into that idea of beauty which I have formed in my own imagination. I have likewise created there the contrary idea of deformity and ugliness; but I leave the consideration of it, till I paint the devil; and in the mean time shun the very thought of it as much as possibly I can, and am even endeavouring to blot it wholly out of my remembrance.'

"There was not any lady in all antiquity, who was mistress of so much beauty as was to be found in the Venus of Gnidus, made by Praxiteles, or the Minerva of Athens, by Phidias; which was therefore called the *beautiful form*. Neither is there any man of the present age equal in the strength, proportion, and knitting of his limbs, to the Hercules of Farnese, made by Glycon: or any woman, who can justly be compared with the Medicean Venus of Cleomenes. And upon this account, the noblest poets and the best orators, when they desire to celebrate any extraordinary beauty, are forced to have recourse to statues and pictures, and to draw their persons and faces into comparison. Ovid, endeavouring to express the beauty of Cyllarus, the fairest of the Centaurs, celebrates him as next in perfection to the most admirable statues:

Gratus in ore vigor, cervix, humerique, manusque,
Pectoraque artificum laudatis proxima signis.

A pleasing vigour his fair face express'd;
His neck, his hands, his shoulders, and his breast,
Did next in gracefulness and beauty, stand
To breathing figures of the sculptor's hand.

In another place he sets Apelles above Venus:

Si Venerem Cous nunquam pinxisset Apelles,
Mersa sub æquoreis illa lateret aquis.

Thus varied:

One birth to seas the Cyprian goddess owed,
A second birth the painter's art bestow'd:
Less by the seas than by his power was given,
They made her live, but he advanced to heaven.

"The idea of this beauty is indeed various, according to the several forms which the painter or sculptor would describe; as one in strength, another in magnanimity: and sometimes it consists in cheerfulness, and sometimes in delicacy, and is always diversified by the sex and age.

"The beauty of Jove is one, and that of Juno another; Hercules and Cupid are perfect beauties, though of different kinds; for beauty is only that which makes all things as they are in their proper and perfect nature, which the best painters always choose by contemplating the forms of each. We ought farther to consider, that a picture being the representation of a human action, the painter ought to retain in his mind the examples of all affections and passions, as a poet preserves the idea of an angry man, of one who is fearful, sad, or merry, and so of all the rest; for it is impossible to express that with the hand which never entered into the imagination. In this manner, as I have rudely and briefly shown you, painters and sculptors, choosing the most elegant natural beauties, perfectionate the idea, and advance their art even above nature itself in her individual productions; which is the utmost mastery of human performance.

"From hence arises that astonishment, and almost adoration, which is paid by the knowing to those divine remainders of antiquity. From hence Phidias, Lysippus, and other noble sculptors, are still held in veneration; and Apelles, Zeuxis, Protogenes, and other admirable painters, though their works are perished, are and will be eternally admired; who all of them drew after the ideas of perfection, which are the miracles of nature, the providence of the understanding, the exemplars of the mind, the light of the fancy; the sun, which from its rising, inspired the statue of Memnon and the fire which warmed into life the image of Prometheus. It is this which causes the Graces and the Loves to take up their habitations in the hardest marble, and to subsist in the emptiness of light and shadows. But since the idea of eloquence is as far inferior to that of painting, as the force of words is to the sight, I must here break off abruptly, and having conducted the reader, as it were, to a secret walk, there leave him in the midst of silence, to contemplate those ideas which I have only sketched, and which every man must finish for himself.

In these pompous expressions, or such as these, the Italian has given you his idea of a painter; and though I cannot much commend the style, I must needs say, there is somewhat in the matter. Plato himself is accustomed to write loftily, imitating, as the critics tell us, the manner of Homer; but surely that inimitable poet had not so much of smoke in his writing, though not less of fire. But, in short, this is the present genius of Italy. What Philostratus tells us in the proem of his figures,* is somewhat plainer; and therefore I will translate it almost word for word:—"He who will rightly govern the art of painting, ought of necessity first to understand human nature. He ought likewise to be endued with a genius to express the signs of their passions, whom he represents; and to make the dumb, as it were, to speak. He must yet further understand what is contained in the constitution of the cheeks, in the temperament of the eyes, in the naturalness (if I may so call it) of the eyebrows; and in short, whatsoever belongs to the mind and thought. He, who thoroughly possesses all these things, will obtain the whole; and the hand will exquisitely represent the action of every particular person. If it happen that he be either mad or angry, melancholic or cheerful, a sprightly youth or a languishing lover; in one word, he will be able to paint whatsoever is proportionable to any one. And even in all this there is a sweet error, without causing any shame; for the eyes and minds of the beholders being fastened on objects which have no real being, as if they were truly existent, and being induced by them to believe them so, what pleasure is it not capable of giving? The ancients, and other wise men, have written many things concerning the symmetry which is in the art of painting,—constituting, as it were, some certain laws for the proportion of every member; not thinking it possible for a painter to undertake the expression of those motions which are in the mind, without a concurrent harmony in the natural measure; for that which is out of its own kind and measure, is not received from nature, whose motion is always right. On a serious consideration of this matter, it will be found, that the art of painting has a wonderful affinity with that of poetry; and that there is betwixt them a certain common imagination. For, as the poets introduce the gods and heroes, and all those things which are either majestical, honest, or delightful, in like manner the painters, by the virtue of their outlines, colours, lights, and shadows, represent the same things and persons in their pictures."

Thus, as convoy ships either accompany or should accompany their merchants,* till they may prosecute the rest of their voyage without danger; so Philostratus has brought me thus far on my way, and I can now sail on without him. He has begun to speak of the great relation betwixt painting and poetry, and thither the greatest part of this discourse, by my promise, was directed. I have not engaged myself to any perfect method, neither am I loaded with a full cargo; it is sufficient if I bring a sample of some goods in this voyage. It will be easy for others to add more, when the commerce is settled; for a treatise twice as large as this of painting, could not contain all that might be said on the parallel of these two sister arts. I will take my rise from Bellori, before I proceed to the author of this book.

The business of his preface is to prove, that a learned painter should form to himself an idea of perfect nature. This image he is to set before his mind in all his undertakings, and to draw from thence, as from a storehouse, the beauties which are to enter into his work; thereby correcting nature from what actually she is in individuals, to what she ought to be, and what she was created. Now, as this idea of perfection is of little use in portraits, or the resemblances of particular persons, so neither is it in the characters of comedy and tragedy, which are never to be made perfect, but always to be drawn with some specks of frailty and deficience; such as they have been described to us in history, if they were real characters, or such as the poet began to show them at their first appearance, if they were only fictitious or imaginary. The perfection of such stage-characters consists chiefly in their likeness to the deficient faulty nature, which is their original; only, as it is observed more at large hereafter, in such cases there will always be found a better likeness and a worse, and the better is constantly to be chosen; I mean in tragedy, which represents the figures of the highest form amongst mankind. Thus in portraits, the

* The ΕΙΚΟΝΕΣ of Flavius Philostratus, who flourished in the beginning of the third century, was first printed by Aldus in 1502.—*Malone.*

* *i. e.* Merchant vessels. The passage seems to be so worded, as to contain a sneer at the negligence of King William's government in protecting the trade. Perhaps Dryden alluded to the misfortune of Sir Francis Wheeler in 1693, who, being sent with a convoy into the Mediterranean, was wrecked in the Bay of Gibraltar.

painter will not take that side of the face, which has some notorious blemish in it; but either draw it in profile, (as Apelles did Antigonus, who had lost one of his eyes,) or else shadow the more imperfect side; for an ingenious flattery is to be allowed to the professors of both arts, so long as the likeness is not destroyed. It is true, that all manner of imperfections must not be taken away from the characters; and the reason is, that there may be left some grounds of pity for their misfortunes. We can never be grieved for their miseries, who are thoroughly wicked, and have thereby justly called their calamities on themselves. Such men are the natural objects of our hatred, not of our commiseration. If, on the other side, their characters were wholly perfect, (such as, for example, the character of a saint or martyr in a play,) his or her misfortunes would produce impious thoughts in the beholders; they would accuse the heavens of injustice, and think of leaving a religion where piety was so ill requited. I say, the greater part would be tempted so to do, I say not that they ought; and the consequence is too dangerous for the practice. In this I have accused myself for my own St. Catherine;* but let truth prevail. Sophocles has taken the just medium in his "Œdipus." He is somewhat arrogant at his first entrance, and is too inquisitive through the whole tragedy; yet these imperfections being balanced by great virtues, they hinder not our compassion for his miseries; neither yet can they destroy that horror, which the nature of his crimes has excited in us. Such in painting are the warts and moles, which, adding a likeness to the face, are not therefore to be omitted; but these produce no loathing in us; but how far to proceed, and where to stop, is left to the judgment of the poet and the painter. In comedy there is somewhat more of the worse likeness to be taken, because that is often to produce laughter, which is occasioned by the sight of some deformity; but for this I refer the reader to Aristotle. It is a sharp manner of instruction for the vulgar, who are never well amended, till they are more than sufficiently exposed.

That I may return to the beginning of this remark concerning perfect ideas, I have only this to say,—that the parallel is often true in epic poetry. The heroes of the poets are to be drawn according to this rule. There is scarce a frailty to be left in the best of them, any more than is to be found in a divine nature; and if Æneas sometimes weeps, it is not in bemoaning his own miseries, but those which his people undergo. If this be an imperfection, the Son of God, when he was incarnate, shed tears of compassion over Jerusalem; and Lentulus* describes him often weeping, but never laughing; so that Virgil is justified even from the holy scriptures. I have but one word more, which for once I will anticipate from the author of this book. Though it must be an idea of perfection, from which both the epic poet and the history painter draws, yet all perfections are not suitable to all subjects; but every one must be designed according to that perfect beauty which is proper to him. An Apollo must be distinguished from a Jupiter, a Pallas from a Venus; and so, in poetry, an Æneas from any other hero; for piety is his chief perfection. Homer's Achilles is a kind of exception to this rule; but then he is not a perfect hero, nor so intended by the poet. All his gods had somewhat of human imperfection, for which he has been taxed by Plato as an imitator of what was bad; but Virgil observed his fault, and mended it. Yet Achilles was perfect in the strength of his body, and the vigour of his mind. Had he been less passionate, or less revengeful, the poet well foresaw that Hector had been killed, and Troy taken, at the first assault; which had destroyed the beautiful contrivance of his Iliads, and the moral of preventing discord amongst confederate princes, which was his principal intention. For the moral (as Bossu observes,†) is the first business of the poet, as being the groundwork of his instruction. This being formed, he contrives such a design, or fable, as may be most suitable to the moral; after this he begins to think of the persons whom he is to employ in carrying on his design; and gives them the manners which are most proper to the several characters. The thoughts and words are the last parts, which give beauty and colouring to the piece.

When I say that the manners of the hero ought to be good in perfection, I contradict not the Marquis of Normanby's opinion, in that admirable verse,‡ where speaking of a perfect character, he calls it

"A faultless monster, which the world ne'er knew;"

for that excellent critic intended only to speak of dramatic characters, and not of epic.

* The principal female character in "Tyrannic Love, or the Royal M[arty]r."

* In the epistle in which he describes our Saviour's person and manners.

† In his treatise on Epic Poetry.

‡ This line is a little misquoted. The couplets run

Reject that vulgar error, which appears
So fair, of making perfect characters;
There's no such thing in nature, and you'll draw
A faultless monster which the world ne'er saw.
Essay on Poetry

Thus at least I have shown, that in the most perfect poem, which is that of Virgil, a perfect idea was required and followed; and consequently that all succeeding poets ought rather to imitate him, than even Homer. I will now proceed, as I promised, to the author of this book.

He tells you almost in the first lines of it, that "the chief end of painting is, to please the eyes; and it is one great end of poetry to please the mind." Thus far the parallel of the arts holds true; with this difference, that the principal end of painting is to please, and the chief design of poetry is to instruct. In this the latter seems to have the advantage of the former; but if we consider the artists themselves on both sides, certainly their aims are the very same; they would both make sure of pleasing, and that in preference to instruction. Next, the means of this pleasure is by deceit; one imposes on the sight, and the other on the understanding. Fiction is of the essence of poetry, as well as of painting; there is a resemblance in one, of human bodies, things, and actions, which are not real; and in the other, of a true story by a fiction; and as all stories are not proper subjects for an epic poem or a tragedy, so neither are they for a noble picture. The subjects, both of the one and of the other, ought to have nothing of immoral, low, or filthy in them; but this being treated at large in the book itself, I waive it, to avoid repetition. Only I must add, that though Catullus,* Ovid, and others, were of another opinion,—that the subject of poets, and even their thoughts and expressions, might be loose, provided their lives were chaste and holy, yet there are no such licenses permitted in that art, any more than, in painting, to design and colour obscene nudities. *Vita proba est*, is no excuse; for it will scarcely be admitted, that either a poet or a painter can be chaste, who give us the contrary examples in their writings and their pictures. We see nothing of this kind in Virgil; that which comes the nearest to it, is the Adventure of the Cave, where Dido and Æneas were driven by the storm; yet even there the poet pretends a marriage before the consummation, and Juno herself was present at it. Neither is there any expression in that story, which a Roman matron might not read without a blush. Besides, the poet passes it over as hastily as he can, as if he were afraid of staying in the cave with the two lovers, and of being a witness to their actions. Now I suppose that a painter would not be much commended, who should pick out this cavern from the whole Æneids, when there is not another in the work. He had better leave them in their obscurity, than let in a flash of lightning to clear the natural darkness of the place, by which he must discover himself, as much as them. The altar-pieces, and holy decorations of painting, show, *that* art may be applied to better uses, as well as poetry; and amongst many other instances, the Farnesian gallery, painted by Annibale Caracci, is a sufficient witness yet remaining; the whole work being morally instructive, and particularly the *Herculis Bivium*, which is a perfect triumph of virtue over vice; as it is wonderfully well described by the ingenious Bellori.

Hitherto I have only told the reader, what ought not to be the subject of a picture or of a poem. What it ought to be on either side, our author tells us: it must in general be great and noble; and in this the parallel is exactly true. The subject of a poet, either in tragedy or in an epic poem, is a great action of some illustrious hero. It is the same in painting; not every action, nor every person, is considerable enough to enter into the cloth. It must be the anger of an Achilles, the piety of an Æneas, the sacrifice of an Iphigenia, for heroines as well as heroes are comprehended in the rule; but the parallel is more complete in tragedy, than in an epic poem. For as a tragedy may be made out of many particular episodes of Homer or of Virgil, so may a noble picture be designed out of this or that particular story in either author. History is also fruitful of designs both for the painter and the tragic poet: Curtius throwing himself into a gulf, and the two Decii sacrificing themselves for the safety of their country, are subjects for tragedy and picture. Such is Scipio restoring the Spanish bride,* whom he either loved, or may be supposed to love; by which he gained the hearts of a great nation to interest themselves for Rome against Carthage. These are all but particular pieces in Livy's History; and yet are full complete subjects for the pen and pencil. Now the reason of this is evident. Tragedy and Picture are more narrowly circumscribed by the mechanic rules of time and place, than the epic poem. The time

* Our author had previously quoted the lines here alluded to, in defence of the indecencies of one of his comedies.

> ——— castum esse decet pium poetam
> Ipsum. Versiculos nihil necesse est;
> Qui tum denique habent salem ac leporem
> Si sunt molliculi et parum pudici

* The celebrity of that action, which is generally called the continence of Scipio, gives us a woful idea of the gross barbarity of the age in which he lived. What would now be said of a general, who did not act as Scipio is said to have done? Assuredly, his refusing the ransom would be thought more wonderful, than his dismissing, uninjured the betrothed princess.

of this last is left indefinite. It is true, Homer took up only the space of eight-and-forty days for his Iliads; but whether Virgil's action was comprehended in a year, or somewhat more, is not determined by Bossu. Homer made the place of his action Troy, and the Grecian camp besieging it. Virgil introduces his Æneas sometimes in Sicily, sometimes in Carthage, and other times at Cumæ, before he brings him to Laurentum; and even after that, he wanders again to the kingdom of Evander, and some parts of Tuscany, before he returns to finish the war by the death of Turnus. But tragedy, according to the practice of the ancients, was always confined within the compass of twenty-four hours, and seldom takes up so much time. As for the place of it, it was always one, and that not in a larger sense, (as for example, a whole city, or two or three several houses in it,) but the market, or some other public place, common to the chorus and all the actors; which established law of theirs I have not an opportunity to examine in this place, because I cannot do it without digression from my subject: though it seems too strict at the first appearance, because it excludes all secret intrigues, which are the beauties of the modern stage; for nothing can be carried on with privacy, when the chorus is supposed to be always present.—But to proceed; I must say this to the advantage of painting, even above tragedy, that what this last represents in the space of many hours, the former shows us in one moment.* The action, the passion, and the manners of so many persons as are contained in a picture, are to be discerned at once, in the twinkling of an eye; at least they would be so, if the sight could travel over so many different objects all at once, or the mind could digest them all at the same instant, or point of time. Thus, in the famous picture of Poussin, which represents the Institution of the Blessed Sacrament, you see our Saviour and his twelve disciples, all concurring in the same action, after different manners, and in different postures; only the manners of Judas are distinguished from the rest. Here is but one indivisible point of time observed; but one action performed by so many persons, in one room, and at the same table; yet the eye cannot comprehend at once the whole object, nor the mind follow it so fast; it is considered at leisure, and seen by intervals. Such are the subjects of noble pictures; and such are only to be undertaken by noble hands.

There are other parts of nature, which are meaner, and yet are the subjects both of painters and of poets. For, to proceed in the parallel; as comedy is a representation of human life in inferior persons, and low subjects, and by that means creeps into the nature of poetry, and is a kind of juniper, a shrub belonging to the species of cedar; so is the painting of clowns, the representations of a Dutch kermis,† the brutal sport of snick-or-snee, and a thousand other things of this mean invention; a kind of picture which belongs to nature, but of the lowest form. Such is a lazar in comparison to a Venus: both are drawn in human figures; they have faces alike, though not like faces. There is yet a lower sort of poetry and painting, which is out of nature; for a farce is that in poetry, which grotesque is in a picture. The persons and action of a farce are all unnatural, and the manners false, that is, inconsisting with the characters of mankind. Grotesque painting is the just resemblance of this; and Horace begins his "Art of Poetry" by describing such a figure, with a man's head, a horse's neck, the wings of a bird, and a fish's tail; parts of different species jumbled together, according to the mad imagination of the dauber; and the end of all this, as he tells you afterward, is to cause laughter; a very monster in a Bartholomew-fair, for the mob to gape at for their twopence. Laughter is indeed the propriety of a man, but just enough to distinguish him from his elder brother with four legs. It is a kind of bastard pleasure too, taken in at the eyes of the vulgar gazers, and at the ears of the beastly audience. Church painters use it to divert the honest countryman at public prayers, and keep his eyes open at a heavy sermon; and farce scribblers make use of the same noble invention, to entertain citizens, country gentlemen, and Covent Garden fops. If they are merry, all goes well on the poet's side. The better sort go thither too, but in despair of sense and the just images of nature, which are the adequate pleasures of the mind; but the author can give the stage no better than what was given him by nature; and the actors must represent such things as they are capable to perform and by which both they and the scribbler may get their living. After all, it is a good thing to laugh a-

* There is a fallacy in this, which a moment's consideration may detect. Painting does not present in one moment what tragedy shows in many hours, and cannot, on the contrary, show more than one scene, at one minute and point of time. Doubtless, by presenting to us one striking situation, the painting recalls, if we know the story, all that has preceded and is to follow; but this arises from association, and happens equally if we come suddenly into a theatre where a well-known tragedy is performing.

† A Dutch fair. Dryden probably recollected the pieces of Teniers.

any rate; and if a straw can tickle a man, it is an instrument of happiness. Beasts can weep when they suffer, but they cannot laugh. And as Sir William D'Avenant observes in his Preface to "Gondibert," "It is the wisdom of a government to permit plays, (he might have added—farces,) as it is the prudence of a carter to put bells upon his horses, to make them carry their burdens cheerfully.

I have already shown, that one main end of poetry and painting is to please, and have said something of the kinds of both, and of their subjects, in which they bear a great resemblance to each other. I must now consider them as they are great and noble arts; and as they are arts, they must have rules, which may direct them to their common end.

To all arts and sciences, but more particularly to these, may be applied what Hippocrates says of physic, as I find him cited by an eminent French critic: "Medicine has long subsisted in the world. The principles of it are certain, and it has a certain way; by both which there has been found, in the course of many ages, an infinite number of things, the experience of which has confirmed its usefulness and goodness. All that is wanting to the perfection of this art will undoubtedly be found, if able men, and such as are instructed in the ancient rules, will make a farther inquiry into it; and endeavour to arrive at that which is hitherto unknown, by that which is already known. But all who, having rejected the ancient rules, and taken the opposite ways, yet boast themselves to be masters of this art, do but deceive others, and are themselves deceived; for that is absolutely impossible."

This is notoriously true in these two arts; for the way to please being to imitate nature, both the poets and the painters in ancient times, and in the best ages, have studied her; and from the practice of both these arts the rules have been drawn, by which we are instructed how to please, and to compass that end which they obtained, by following their example; for nature is still the same in all ages, and can never be contrary to herself. Thus, from the practice of Æschylus, Sophocles, and Euripides, Aristotle drew his rules for tragedy, and Philostratus for painting. Thus, amongst the moderns, the Italian and French critics, by studying the precepts of Aristotle and Horace, and having the example of the Grecian poets before their eyes, have given us the rules of modern tragedy; and thus the critics of the same countries in the art of painting, have given the precepts of perfecting that art.

It is true that poetry has one advantage over painting in these last ages, that we have still the remaining examples both of the Greek and Latin poets; whereas the painters have nothing left them from Apelles, Protogenes, Parrhasius, Zeuxis, and the rest, but only the testimonies which are given of their incomparable works. But instead of this they have some of their best statues, bass-relievos, columns, obelisks, &c. which were saved out of the common ruin, and are still preserved in Italy; and by well distinguishing what is proper to sculpture, and what to painting, and what is common to them both, they have judiciously repaired that loss. And the great genius of Raffaelle, and others, having succeeded to the times of barbarism and ignorance, the knowledge of painting is now arrived to a supreme perfection, though the performance of it is much declined in the present age. The greatest age for poetry amongst the Romans was certainly that of Augustus Cæsar: and yet we are told that painting was then at its lowest ebb; and perhaps sculpture was also declining at the same time. In the reign of Domitian, and some who succeeded him, poetry was but meanly cultivated, but painting eminently flourished. I am not here to give the history of the two arts; how they were both in a manner extinguished by the irruption of the barbarous nations, and both restored about the times of Leo the Tenth, Charles the Fifth, and Francis the First; though I might observe, that neither Ariosto, nor any of his contemporary poets, ever arrived at the excellency of Raffaelle, Titian, and the rest, in painting. But in revenge, at this time, or lately, in many countries, poetry is better practised than her sister art. To what height the magnificence and encouragement of the present king of France may carry painting and sculpture, is uncertain; but by what he has done before the war in which he is engaged, we may expect what he will do after the happy conclusion of a peace, which is the prayer and wish of all those who have not an interest to prolong the miseries of Europe. For it is most certain, as our author, amongst others, has observed, that reward is the spur of virtue, as well in all good arts as in all laudable attempts; and emulation, which is the other spur, will never be wanting, either amongst poets or painters, when particular rewards and prizes are proposed to the best deservers.

But to return from this digression, though it was almost necessary. All the rules of painting are methodically, concisely, and yet clearly delivered in this present treatise, which I have translated. Bossu has not given more exact rules for the epic poem, nor Dacier for tragedy, in his late excellent translation of Aristotle, and his notes upon him, than our Fresnoy has made for painting; with the parallel of which I must resume my discourse, following my author's text, though with more brevity than I intended, because Virgil calls me.

The principal and most important part of painting is, to know what is most beautiful in nature, and most proper for that art. That which is the most beautiful is the most noble subject: so in poetry, tragedy is more beautiful than comedy; because, as I said, the persons are greater whom the poet instructs, and consequently the instructions of more benefit to mankind: the action is likewise greater and more noble, and thence is derived the greater and more noble pleasure.

To imitate nature well in whatsoever subject, is the perfection of both arts; and that picture, and that poem, which comes nearest to the resemblance of nature, is the best. But it follows not, that what pleases most in either kind is therefore good, but what ought to please. Our depraved appetites, and ignorance of the arts, mislead our judgments, and cause us often to take that for true imitation of nature, which has no resemblance of nature in it. To inform our judgments, and to reform our tastes, rules were invented, that by them we might discern when nature was imitated, and how nearly. I have been forced to recapitulate these things, because mankind is not more liable to deceit, than it is willing to continue in a pleasing error, strengthened by a long habitude. The imitation of nature is therefore justly constituted as the general, and indeed the only rule of pleasing, both in poetry and painting. Aristotle tells us, that imitation pleases, because it affords matter for a reasoner to inquire into the truth or falsehood of imitation,* by comparing its likeness, or unlikeness, with the original; but by this rule every speculation in nature, whose truth falls under the inquiry of a philosopher, must produce the same delight, which is not true. I should rather assign another reason. Truth is the object of our understanding, as good is of our will; and the understanding can no more be delighted with a lie, than the will can choose an apparent evil. As truth is the end of all our speculations, so the discovery of it is the pleasure of them; and since a true knowledge of nature gives us pleasure, a lively imitation of it, either in poetry or painting, must of necessity produce a much greater: for both these arts, as I said before, are not only true imitations of nature, but of the best nature, of that which is wrought up to a nobler pitch. They present us with images more perfect than the life in any individual; and we have the pleasure to see all the scattered beauties of nature united by a happy chymistry, without its deformities or faults. They are imitations of the passions, which always move, and therefore consequently please; for without motion there can be no delight, which cannot be considered but as an active passion. When we view these elevated ideas of nature, the result of that view is admiration, which is always the cause of pleasure.

This foregoing remark, which gives the reason why imitation pleases, was sent me by Mr. Walter Moyle, a most ingenious young gentleman, conversant in all the studies of humanity much above his years. He had also furnished me, according to my request, with all the particular passages in Aristotle and Horace, which are used by them to explain the art of poetry by that of painting; which, if ever I have time to retouch this Essay, shall be inserted in their places.

Having thus shown that imitation pleases,

* The passage alluded to is in Aristotle's "Treatise on Poetry," in which he accounts for the pleasure afforded by the imitative arts, by observing, that "to *learn* is a natural pleasure." "To the same purpose (says Mr. Twining,) in his 'Rhetoric,' lib. i. cap. xi. p. 637, edit. Duval. Επει δε το μανθανειν, κ. τ. λ. 'And as it is by nature delightful to *learn*, to *admire*, and the like, hence we necessarily receive pleasure from imitative arts, as *Painting*, *Sculpture*, and *Poetry*, and from whatever is well imitated, even though the original may be disagreeable; but our pleasure does not arise from the beauty of the thing itself, but from the *inference*, the *discovery* that *this is that*, &c. so that we seem to learn something.'

"Μανθανειν—to *learn*, to *know*, i. e. merely to *recognize*, *discover*," &c. See Harris, On Music, Painting, &c. ch. iv. note (*b*). The meaning is sufficiently explained by what follows.

"Dryden, who scarce ever mentions Aristotle without discovering that he had looked only at the wrong side of the tapestry, (a translation,) says, 'Aristotle tells us, that imitation pleases, because it affords matter for a reasoner to inquire into the truth or falsehood of imitation,' &c. But Aristotle is not here speaking of *reasoners*, or *inquiry*, but, on the contrary, of the vulgar, the generality of mankind, whom he expressly opposes to philosophers, or reasoners. and his συλλογιζεσθαι is no more than that rapid, habitual, and imperceptible act of the mind that '*raisonnement aussi prompt que le coup d'œil*,' (as it is well paraphrased by M. Batteaux,) by which we *collect* or infer, from a comparison of the picture with the image of the original in our minds, that it was intended to represent that original.

"The fullest illustration of this passage is to be found in another work of Aristotle, his 'Rhetoric, lib. iii. cap. x., where he applies the same principle to metaphorical language, and resolves the pleasure we receive from such language, into that which arises from the μαθησις ΤΑΧΕΙΑ, the exercise of our understandings in *discovering* the meaning by a *quick* and *easy* perception of some quality, or qualities, common to the thing expressed, and the thing intended; to a mirror, for example, and to the theatre, when the latter is called metaphorically, *the mirror of human life*.

and why it pleases in both these arts, it follows, that some rules of imitation are necessary to obtain the end; for without rules there can be no art, any more than there can be a house without a door to conduct you into it.

The principal parts of painting and poetry next follow. Invention is the first part, and absolutely necessary to them both; yet no rule ever was or ever can be given, how to compass it. A happy genius is the gift of nature: it depends on the influence of the stars, say the astrologers; on the organs of the body, say the naturalists; it is the particular gift of heaven, say the divines, both Christians and heathens. How to improve it, many books can teach us; how to obtain it, none; that nothing can be done without it, all agree:

> Tu nihil invita dices facierve Minerva.

Without invention, a painter is but a copier, and a poet but a plagiary of others. Both are allowed sometimes to copy and translate; but, as our author tells you, that is not the best part of their reputation. "Imitators are but a servile kind of cattle," says the poet; or at best the keepers of cattle for other men; they have nothing which is properly their own: that is a sufficient mortification for me, while I am translating Virgil. But to copy the best author, is a kind of praise, if I perform it as I ought; as a copy after Raffaelle is more to be commended than an original of any indifferent painter.

Under this head of *Invention* is placed the disposition of the work,—to put all things in a beautiful order and harmony, that the whole may be of a piece. The compositions of the painter should be conformable to the text of ancient authors, to the customs, and the times. And this is exactly the same in poetry: Homer and Virgil are to be our guides in the epic; Sophocles and Euripides in tragedy: in all things we are to imitate the customs and the times of those persons and things which we represent; not to make new rules of the drama, as Lopez de Vega has attempted unsuccessfully to do,* but to be content to follow our masters, who understood nature better than we. But if the story which we treat be modern, we are to vary the customs, according to the time and the country where the scene of action lies; for this is still to imitate nature, which is always the same, though in a different dress.

As in the composition of a picture the painter is to take care that nothing enter into it which is not proper or convenient to the subject, so likewise is the poet to reject all incidents which are foreign to his poem, and are naturally no parts of it; they are wens, and other excrescences, which belong not to the body, but deform it. No person, no incident, in the piece, or in the play, but must be of use to carry on the main design. All things else are like six fingers to the hand, when nature, which is superfluous in nothing, can do her work with five. A painter must reject all trifling ornaments; so must a poet refuse all tedious and unnecessary descriptions. A robe which is too heavy is less an ornament than a burden.

In poetry Horace calls these things—*versus inopes rerum, nugæque canoræ*, there are also the *lucus et ara Dianæ*, which he mentions in the same "Art of Poetry." But since there must be ornaments both in painting and poetry, if they are not necessary, they must at least be decent; that is, in their due place, and but moderately used. The painter is not to take so much pains about the drapery, as about the face, where the principal resemblance lies; neither is the poet, who is working up a passion, to make similes, which will certainly make it languish. My Montezuma dies with a fine one in his mouth;* but it is ambitious, and out of season. When there are more figures in a picture than are necessary, or at least ornamental, our author calls them "figures to be let;" because the picture has no use of them. So I have seen in some modern plays about twenty actors, when the action has not required half the number.† In the principal figures of a pic-

"Dryden (Mr. Twining further observes) seems to have taken his idea from Dacier's note on this place, (in the 'Treatise on Poetry,') which is extremely confused, and so expressed, as to leave it doubtful whether he misunderstood the original, or only explained himself awkwardly. The use that Dryden made of French critics and translators is well known." *Aristotle's Treatise on Poetry, translated, with Notes, &c. by Thomas Twining*, A. M. 8vo, 1789, p. 186.—*Malone.*

* This is hardly accurate, Lopez de Vega did twised despise the rules laid down by others, but he made no new regulations.

* —————— O Powers divine,
Take my last thanks! no longer I repine.
I might have lived my own mishaps to mourn,
While some would pity me, but more would scorn;
For pity only on fresh objects stays,
But with the tedious sight of woes decays.
Still less and less my boiling spirits flow,
And I grow stiff, as cooling metals do.—
Farewell, Almeria.

† Nothing can be more hazardous for a dramatist than the introduction of many inferior characters. In proportion to the numbers of the *Dramatis Personæ*, the difficulty of *getting* up a piece is increased in a tremendous ratio; since even the awkwardness of a domestic, or the ridiculous gait of a guard, may throw the audience into a tone of feeling very inconsistent with tragic effect. Undoubtedly, could the expense be supported, something might be gained by drilling underlings to such inferior characters, and teaching even the mutes to look, as if they took some interest in what is going forward; but, at present, the entrance and exit of a hero, *cum suis*, has

ture, the painter is to employ the sinews of his art; for in them consists the principal beauty of his work. Our author saves me the comparison with tragedy; for he says, that herein he is to imitate the tragic poet, who employs his utmost force in those places, wherein consists the height and beauty of the action.

Du Fresnoy, whom I follow, makes *design*, or *drawing*, the second part of painting; but the rules which he gives concerning the posture of the figures, are almost wholly proper to that art, and admit not any comparison, that I know, with poetry. The posture of a poetic figure is, as I conceive, the description of his heroes in the performance of such or such an action; as of Achilles, just in the act of killing Hector, or of Æneas, who has Turnus under him. Both the poet and the painter vary the posture, according to the action or passion which they represent, of the same person; but all must be great and graceful in them. The same Æneas must be drawn a suppliant to Dido, with respect in his gestures, and humility in his eyes; but when he is forced, in his own defence, to kill Lausus, the poet shows him compassionate, and tempering the severity of his looks with a reluctance to the action which he is going to perform. He has pity on his beauty and his youth, and is loth to destroy such a masterpiece of nature. He considers Lausus rescuing his father at the hazard of his own life, as an image of himself, when he took Anchises on his shoulders, and bore him safe through the rage of the fire, and the opposition of his enemies; and therefore, in the posture of a retiring man, who avoids the combat, he stretches out his arm in sign of peace, with his right foot drawn a little back, and his breast bending inward, more like an orator than a soldier; and seems to dissuade the young man from pulling on his destiny, by attempting more than he was able to perform. Take the passage as I have thus translated it:

> Shouts of applause ran ringing through the field,
> To see the son the vanquish'd father shield:
> All, fired with noble emulation, strive,
> And with a shower of darts to distance drive
> The Trojan chief; who, held at bay, from far
> On his Vulcanian orb sustain'd the war.
> Æneas, thus o'erwhelm'd on every side,
> Their first assault undaunted did abide,
> And thus to Lausus, loud with friendly threat'ning cried:
> Why wilt thou rush to certain death, and rage,
> In rash attempts, beyond thy tender age,
> Betray'd by pious love?——

And afterwards:

> He grieved, he wept; the sight an image brought
> Of his own filial love; a sadly pleasing thought.

But beside the outlines of the posture, the design of the picture comprehends, in the next place, the forms of faces, which are to be different; and so in a poem or a play must the several characters of the persons be distinguished from each other. I knew a poet, whom out of respect I will not name, who, being too witty himself, could draw nothing but wits in a comedy of his; even his fools were infected with the disease of their author. They overflowed with smart repartees, and were only distinguished from the intended wits by being called coxcombs,* though they deserved not so scandalous a name. Another, who had a great genius for tragedy,† following the fury of his natural temper, made every man, and woman too, in his plays, stark raging mad; there was not a sober person to be had for love or money. All was tempestuous and blustering; heaven and earth were coming together at every word; a mere hurricane from the beginning to the end, —and every actor seemed to be hastening on the day of judgment.‡

"Let every member be made for its own head," says our author; not a withered hand to a young face. So, in the persons of a play, whatsoever is said or done by any of them, must be consistent with the manners which the poet has given them distinctly; and even the habits must be proper to the degrees and humours of

something in it irresistibly ludicrous. Here the painter has a decisive advantage over the dramatist, since it costs him nothing to finish his inferior personages in a style as correspondent to truth as the principal.

* I retain Mr. Malone's excellent note. "This description seems at the first view to be intended for Congreve, to whom it is certainly sufficiently applicable, and who had produced his 'Double Dealer' in the preceding year, and his 'Love for Love' in 1695. But beside that Dryden's high admiration of Congreve, which he had so strongly manifested in the admirable verses addressed to that poet on the former play, will not admit of such an application, the words—'I *knew*,' clearly denote a *dead* poet, and consequently will exclude Wycherley also. The person meant therefore, I think, was Sir George Etherege, who died a few years before. In Dryden's Epilogue to that author's 'Man of Mode,' he says,

> "Sir Fopling is a *fool* so nicely writ,
> Most ladies would mistake him for a *wit*."

† Nat. Lee.

‡ Dryden probably recollected, particularly Lee's famous rant at the conclusion of the fourth act of Œdipus:

> Fall darkness then, and everlasting night
> Shadow the globe; may the sun never dawn,
> The silver moon be blotted from her orb!
> And for an universal rout of nature,
> Through all the inmost chambers of the sky,
> May there not be a glimpse, one starry spark,
> But gods meet gods, and jostle in the dark;
> That jars may rise, and wrath divine be hurl'd,
> Which may to atoms shake the solid world!

the persons, as well as in a picture. He who entered in the first act a young man, like Pericles, Prince of Tyre,* must not be in danger, in the fifth act, of committing incest with his daughter; nor an usurer, without great probability and causes of repentance, be turned into a *cutting* Morecraft.†

I am not satisfied, that the comparison betwixt the two arts in the last paragraph is altogether so just as it might have been; but I am sure of this which follows:

"The principal figure of the subject must appear in the midst of the picture, under the principal light, to distinguish it from the rest, which are only its attendants." Thus, in a tragedy, or an epic poem, the hero of the piece must be advanced foremost to the view of the reader or spectator: he must outshine the rest of all the characters; he must appear the prince of them, like the sun in the Copernican system, encompassed with the less noble planets: because the hero is the centre of the main action; all the lines from the circumference tend to him alone: he is the chief object of pity in the drama, and of admiration in the epic poem.

As in a picture, besides the principal figures which compose it, and are placed in the midst of it, there are less groups or knots of figures disposed at proper distances, which are parts of the piece, and seem to carry on the same design in a more inferior manner; so, in epic poetry there are episodes, and a chorus in tragedy, which are members of the action, as growing out of it, not inserted into it. Such in the ninth book of the "Æneids" is the episode of Nisus and Euryalus. The adventure belongs to them alone; they alone are the objects of compassion and admiration; but their business which they carry on, is the general concernment of the Trojan camp, then beleagured by Turnus and the Latins, as the Christians were lately by the Turks. They were to advertise the chief here of the distresses of his subjects occasioned by his absence, to crave his succour, and solicit him to hasten his return.

The Grecian tragedy was at first nothing but a chorus of singers; afterwards one actor was introduced, which was the poet himself, who entertained the people with a discourse in verse, betwixt the pauses of the singing. This succeeding with the people, more actors were added, to make the variety the greater; and, in process of time, the chorus only sung betwixt the acts, and the Coryphæus, or chief of them, spoke for the rest, as an actor concerned in the business of the play.

Thus tragedy was perfected by degrees; and being arrived at that perfection, the painters might probably take the hint from thence of adding groups to their pictures. But as a good picture may be without a group, so a good tragedy may subsist without a chorus, notwithstanding any reasons which have been given by Dacier to the contrary.

Monsieur Racine has, indeed, used it in his "Esther;" but not that he found any necessity of it, as the French critic would insinuate. The chorus at St. Cyr was only to give the young ladies an occasion of entertaining the king with vocal music, and of commending their own voices. The play itself was never intended for the public stage, nor, without disparagement to the learned author, could possibly have succeeded there; and much less the translation of it here. Mr. Wycherley, when we read it together, was of my opinion in this, or rather I of his; for it becomes me so to speak of so excellent a poet, and so great a judge. But since I am in this place, as Virgil says, *spatiis exclusus iniquis*, that is, shortened in my time, I will give no other reason, than that it is impracticable on our stage. A new theatre, much more ample and much deeper, must be made for that purpose, besides the cost of sometimes forty or fifty habits, which is an expense too large to be supplied by a company of actors. It is true, I should not be sorry to see a chorus on a theatre more than as large and as deep again as ours, built and adorned at a king's charges; and on that condition, and another, which is, that my hands were not bound behind me, as now they are,* I should not despair of making

* "Pericles, Prince of Tyre," which has been generally imputed to Shakspeare, though the internal evidence is not in favour of the supposition. Dryden believed it to be one of his earliest pieces:

> Shakspeare's own muse his Pericles first bore,
> The Prince of Tyre was elder than the Moor.

This order was probably assigned from the confessed inferiority of Pericles to Shakspeare's later plays. But that apology cannot be received; for if Shakspeare had any hand in Pericles at all, it was at a late period of his dramatic career.—See the remarks on Pericles in Mr. Malone's Shakspeare.

† Morecraft is an usurer in Beaumont and Fletcher's comedy of the "Scornful Lady," who, having been cheated and discomfited, as usurers commonly are in the drama, (I suppose to compensate their success in real life,) at the end of the play suddenly changes his character for that of an extravagant gallant, and assumes the denomination of *cutting*, or as we would now say *dashing*, Morecraft.

* Mr. Malone thinks this alludes to the translation of Virgil, in which Dryden was now engaged. But I conceive it has a general reference to his situation as a suspected and discountenanced person; restrained from free exertion of his genius, by the necessity of considering that he was exposed to misconstruction. He must have recollected the suppression of "Cleomenes," and the offence taken by government at the prologue to the "Prophetess."

such a tragedy as might be both instructive and delightful, according to the manners of the Grecians.

To make a sketch, or a more perfect model of a picture, is, in the language of poets, to draw up the scenery of a play; and the reason is the same for both; to guide the undertaking, and to preserve the remembrance of such things, whose natures are difficult to retain.

To avoid absurdities and incongruities, is the same law established for both arts. The painter is not to paint a cloud at the bottom of a picture, but in the uppermost parts; nor the poet to place what is proper to the end or middle, in the beginning of a poem. I might enlarge on this; but there are few poets or painters, who can be supposed to sin so grossly against the laws of nature and of art. I remember only one play, and for once I will call it by its name, "The Slighted Maid,"* where there is nothing in the first act, but what might have been said or done in the fifth; nor any thing in the midst, which might not have been placed as well in the beginning, or the end. To express the passions which are seated in the heart, by outward signs, is one great precept of the painters, and very difficult to perform. In poetry, the same passions and motions of the mind are to be expressed; and in this consists the principal difficulty, as well as the excellency of that art. This, says my author, is the gift of Jupiter; and, to speak in the same heathen language, we call it the gift of our Apollo,—not to be obtained by pains or study, if we are not born to it; for the motions which are studied, are never so natural as those which break out in the height of a real passion. Mr. Otway possessed this art as thoroughly as any of the ancients or moderns. I will not defend every thing in his "Venice Preserved;" but I must bear this testimony to his memory,—that the passions are truly touched in it,* though perhaps there is somewhat to be desired, both in the grounds of them, and in the height and elegance of expression; but nature is there, which is the greatest beauty.

"In the passions," says our author, "we must have a very great regard to the quality of the persons who are actually possessed with them." The joy of a monarch for the news of a victory, must not be expressed like the ecstacy of a Harlequin on the receipt of a letter from his mistress:—this is so much the same in both the arts, that it is no longer a comparison. What he says of face-painting, or the portrait of any one particular person, concerning the likeness, is also as applicable to poetry. In the character of a hero, as well as in an inferior figure, there is a better or worse likeness to be taken: the better is a panegyric, if it be not false, and the worse is a libel. Sophocles, says Aristotle, always drew men as they ought to be, that is, better than they were; another, whose name I have forgotten,† drew them worse than naturally they were: Euripides altered nothing in the character, but made them such as they were represented by history, epic poetry, or tradition. Of the three, the draught of Sophocles is most commended by Aristotle. I have followed it in that part of "Œdipus" which I writ,‡ though perhaps I have made him too good a man. But my characters of Antony and Cleopatra, though they are favourable to them, have nothing of outrageous panegyric. Their passions were their own, and such as were given them by history; only the deformities of them were cast into shadows, that they might be objects of compassion: whereas if I had chosen a noon-day light for them, somewhat must have been discovered, which would rather have moved our hatred than our pity.

In truth, the very expression in the text is elsewhere hitched into rhyme:

> The labouring bee, when his sharp sting is gone,
> Forgets his golden work, and turns a drone;
> Such is a satire when you take away
> That rage in which his noble vigour lay.
>
> * * * * * *
>
> How can he show his manhood if you bind him,
> To box like boys with one hand tied behind him.
>
> *Prologue to Amphitryon.*

* A comedy written by Sir Robert Stapylton, and acted by the Duke of York's servants, at their theatre in Lincoln's-Inn Fields, in 1663. Dryden has elsewhere undervalued this play:

> Your Ben and Fletcher, in their first young flight,
> Did no Volpone, nor no Arbaces write;
> But hopp'd about, and short excursions made
> From bough to bough, as if they were afraid;
> And each was guilty of some "Slighted Maid."

Sir Robert Stapylton, the author of the "Slighted Maid," translated Juvenal and Musæus, and wrote other two plays, called "The Step-Mother," and Hero and Leander."

* "Otway," says Pope, "has written but two tragedies, out of six, that are pathetic. I believe he did it without much design, as Lillo has done in his 'Barnwell.' It is a talent of nature, rather than an effect of judgment, to write so movingly."—*Spence's Anecdotes*, quoted by Malone. Dryden, at an early period, is said to have set no high value upon Otway in other respects, while he allowed he excelled him in the art of affecting the passions.

† "Aristotle, in the place referred to, (περὶ ποιητ. κ. κε.) does not mention any third dramatic poet by name. He does indeed put the case of a third poet, who might pursue a method different from the practice either of Sophocles or Euripides, and represent things *as they are said and believed to be*. In the same passage, (which is manifestly corrupt,) he mentions an observation of Xenophanes, who, I believe, was the person here in our author's thoughts."—*Malone*.

‡ The first and third Acts.

The Gothic manner, and the barbarous ornaments, which are to be avoided in a picture, are just the same with those in an ill-ordered play. For example, our English tragi-comedy must be confessed to be wholly Gothic, notwithstanding the success which it has found upon our theatre, and in the "Pastor Fido" of Guarini; even though Corisca and the Satyr contribute somewhat to the main action. Neither can I defend my "Spanish Friar," as fond as otherwise I am of it, from this imputation: for though the comical parts are diverting, and the serious moving, yet they are of an unnatural mingle: for mirth and gravity destroy each other, and are no more to be allowed for decent, than a gay widow laughing in a mourning habit.

I had almost forgotten one considerable resemblance. Du Fresnoy tells us, "That the figures of the groups must not be all on a side, that is, with their face and bodies all turned the same way; but must contrast each other by their several positions." Thus in a play, some characters must be raised, to oppose others, and to set them off the better; according to the old maxim, *Contraria juxta se posita, magis elucescunt*. Thus, in "The Scornful Lady," the usurer is set to confront the prodigal: thus, in my "Tyrannic Love," the atheist Maximin is opposed to the character of St. Catherine.

I am now come, though with the omission of many likenesses, to the Third Part of Painting, which is called the Chromatic, or Colouring Expression, and all that belongs to words, is that in a poem which colouring is in a picture. The colours well chosen in their proper places, together with the lights and shadows which belong to them, lighten the design, and make it pleasing to the eye. The words, the expressions, the tropes and figures, the versification, and all the other elegancies of sound, as cadences, turns of words upon the thought, and many other things, which are all parts of expression, perform exactly the same office both in dramatic and epic poetry. Our author calls Colouring, *lena sororis*: in plain English, the bawd of her sister, the design or drawing: she clothes, she dresses her up, she paints her, she makes her appear more lovely than naturally she is; she *procures* for the design, and makes lovers for her: for the design of itself is only so many naked lines. Thus in poetry, the expression is that which charms the reader, and beautifies the design, which is only the outlines of the fable. It is true, the design must of itself be good; if it be vicious, or, in one word, unpleasing, the cost of colouring is thrown away upon it: it is an ugly woman in a rich habit set out with jewels;—nothing can become her; but granting the design to be moderately good, it is like an excellent complexion with indifferent features: the white and red well mingled on the face, make what was before but passable appear beautiful. *Operum colores* is the very word which Horace uses to signify words and elegant expressions, of which he himself was so great a master, in his Odes. Amongst the ancients Zeuxis was most famous for his colouring: amongst the moderns, Titian and Correggio. Of the two ancient epic poets, who have so far excelled all the moderns, the invention and design were the particular talents of Homer. Virgil must yield to him in both; for the design of the Latin was borrowed from the Grecian: but the *dictio Virgiliana*, the expression of Virgil, his colouring, was incomparably the better; and in that I have always endeavoured to copy him. Most of the pedants, I know, maintain the contrary, and will have Homer excel even in this part. But of all people, as they are the most ill-mannered, so they are the worse judges. Even of words, which are their province, they seldom know more than the grammatical construction, unless they are born with a poetical genius, which is a rare portion amongst them. Yet some I know may stand excepted; and such I honour. Virgil is so exact in every word, that none can be changed but for a worse; nor any one removed from its place, but the harmony will be altered. He pretends sometimes to trip; but it is only to make you think him in danger of a fall, when he is most secure: like a skilful dancer on the ropes, (if you will pardon the meanness of the similitude,) who slips willingly, and makes a seeming stumble, that you may think him in great hazard of breaking his neck, while at the same time he is only giving you a proof of his dexterity. My late Lord Roscommon was often pleased with this reflection, and with the examples of it in this admirable author.

I have not leisure to run through the whole comparison of lights and shadows with tropes and figures; yet I cannot but take notice of metaphors, which like them have power to lessen or greaten any thing. Strong and glowing colours are the just resemblances of bold metaphors: but both must be judiciously applied; for there is a difference betwixt daring and foolhardiness. Lucan and Statius often ventured them too far; our Virgil never. But the great defect of the "Pharsalia" and the "Thebais" was in the design: if that had been more perfect, we might have forgiven many of their bold strokes in the colouring, or at least excused them; yet some of them are such as Demosthenes or Cicero could not have defended. Virgil, if he could have seen the first verses of the "Sylvæ,"* would have thought Statius mad, in his fustian description of the statue on the brazen horse. But that poet was always in a foam at his setting out, even before the motion of the race had warmed him. The soberness of Virgil, whom he read, it seems to little purpose might have shown him the difference betwixt

Arma virumque cano

and

Magnanimum Æacidem, formidatamque tonanti
Progeniem.

But Virgil knew how to rise by degrees in his expressions: Statius was in his towering heights at the first stretch of his opinions. The description of his running horse, just starting in the Funeral Games for Archemorus, though the verses are wonderfully fine, are the true image of their author:

Stare adeò nescit, pereunt vestigia mille
Ante fugam; absentemque ferit gravis ungula campum;†

which would cost me an hour, if I had the leisure to translate them, there is so much of beauty in the original.

Virgil, as he better knew his colours, so he knew better how and where to place them. In as much haste as I am, I cannot forbear giving one example. It is said of him that he read the Second, Fourth, and Sixth Books of his Æneids to Augustus Cæsar. In the Sixth, (which we are sure he read, because we know Octavia was present, who rewarded him so bountifully for the twenty verses which were made in honour of her deceased son Marcellus,)—in his Sixth Book, I say, the poet, speaking of Misenus, the trumpeter, says,

——— quo non præstantior alter
Ære ciere viros, ———

and broke off in the hemistich, or midst of the verse; but in the very reading, seized as it were with a divine fury, he made up the latter part of the hemistich with these following words,

martemque accendere cantu.

How warm, nay, how glowing a colouring is this! In the beginning of his verse, the word *æs*, or brass was taken for a trumpet, because the instrument was made of the metal,—which of itself was fine; but in the latter end, which was made extempore, you see three metaphors, *martemque;—accendere,—cantu.* Good heavens! how the plain sense is raised by the beauty of the words! But this was happiness, the former might be only judgment: this was the *curiosa felicitas*, which Petronius attributes to Horace; it is the pencil thrown luckily full upon the horse's mouth, to express the foam which the painter with all his skill could not perform without it. These hits of words a true poet often finds, as I may say, without seeking; but he knows their value when he finds them, and is infinitely pleased. A bad poet may sometimes light on them, but he discerns not a diamond from a Bristol-stone; and would have been of the cock's mind in Æsop,—a grain of barley would have pleased him better than the jewel.

The lights and shadows which belong to colouring, put me in mind of that verse of Horace,

Hoc amat obscurum, vult hoc sub luce videri.

Some parts of a poem require to be amply written, and with all the force and elegance of words; others must be cast into shadows, that is, passed over in silence, or but faintly touched. This belongs wholly to the judgment of the poet and the painter. The most beautiful parts of the picture, and the poem, must be the most finished, the colours and words most chosen; many things in both, which are not deserving of this care, must be shifted off, content with vulgar expressions, and those very short, and left, as in a shadow, to the imagination of the reader.

We have the proverb *manum de tabulâ* from the painters; which signifies to know when to give over, and lay by the pencil. Both Homer and Virgil practised this precept wonderfully well, but Virgil the better of the two. Homer knew, that when Hector was slain, Troy was as good as already taken; therefore he concludes his action there: for what follows in the funerals of Patroclus, and the redemption of Hector's body, is not, properly speaking, a part of the main action. But Virgil concludes with the death of Turnus; for after that difficulty was removed, Æneas might marry, and establish the

* Our author has already compared the first of the lines alluded to—

Quæ superimposito moles geminata Colosso—

with the first line of Virgil's Eclogues.

† Theb. vi. 400, 401.

Our author's confession of the difficulty of translating these lines, probably induced Pope to transplant them into his "Windsor Forest," where they are thus beautifully paraphrased:

The impatient courser pants in every vein,
And pawing seems to beat the distant plain;
Hills, vales, and floods, appear already crost,
And, ere he starts, a thousand steps are lost.

Our author trusted, as usual, to memory; for the first of the lines, quoted from Statius, runs differently:

Stare adeò *miserum est*———

but he was thinking on a passage in the Third Georgic.

——— tum, si qua sonum procul arma dedere,
Stare loco *nescit*: micat auribus, et tremit artus;
Collectumque premens volvit sub naribus ignem.
Malone.

Trojans, when he pleased. This rule I had before my eyes in the conclusion of the "Spanish Friar," when the discovery was made that the king was living, which was the knot of the play untied; the rest is shut up in the compass of some few lines, because nothing then hindered the happiness of Torrismond and Leonora. The faults of that drama are in the kind of it, which is tragi-comedy. But it was given to the people; and I never writ any thing for myself but "Antony and Cleopatra."

This remark, I must acknowledge, is not so proper for the colouring as the design; but it will hold for both. As the words, &c. are evidently shown to be the clothing of the thought, in the same sense as colours are the clothing of the design, so the painter and the poet ought to judge exactly when the colouring and expressions are perfect, and then to think their work is truly finished. Apelles said of Protogenes, —that he knew not when to give over. A work may be over-wrought, as well as under-wrought; too much labour often takes away the spirit by adding to the polishing, so that there remains nothing but a dull correctness, a piece without any considerable faults, but with few beauties; for when the spirits are drawn off, there is nothing but a *caput mortuum*. Statius never thought an expression could be bold enough; and if a bolder could be found, he rejected the first. Virgil had judgment enough to know daring was necessary; but he knew the difference betwixt a glowing colour and a glaring. As, when he compared the shocking of the fleets at Actium to the jostling of islands rent from their foundations, and meeting in the ocean, he knew the comparison was forced beyond nature, and raised too high; he therefore softens the metaphor with a *credas*: "you would *almost believe* —that mountains or islands rushed against each other:"

——pelago credas innare revulsas
Cycladas, aut montes concurrere montibus altos.

But here I must break off without finishing the discourse.

Cynthius, aurem vellit, et admonuit, &c. The things which are behind are of too nice a consideration for an essay, begun and ended in twelve mornings; and perhaps the judges of painting and poetry, when I tell them how short a time it cost me, may make me the same answer which my late Lord Rochester made to one, who, to commend a tragedy, said it was written in three weeks: "How the devil could he be so long about it?" For that poem was infamously bad; and I doubt this Parallel is little better; and then the shortness of the time is so far from being a commendation, that it is scarcely an excuse. But if I have really drawn a portrait to the knees, or a half-length, with a tolerable likeness, then I may plead, with some justice, for myself, that the rest is left to the imagination. Let some better artist provide himself of a deeper canvass, and, taking these hints which I have given, set the figure on its legs, and finish it in the invention, design, and colouring.

THE

PREFACE

OF

MONSIEUR DE PILES, THE FRENCH TRANSLATOR.

Among all the beautiful and delightful arts, that of painting has always found the most lovers; the number of them almost including all mankind. Of whom great multitudes are daily found, who value themselves on the knowledge of it: either because they keep company with painters; or that they have seen good pieces; or, lastly, because their gusto is naturally good. Which notwithstanding that knowledge of theirs (if we may so call it) is so very superficial, and so ill grounded, that it is impossible for them to describe in what consists the beauty of those works which they admire, or the faults, which are in the greatest part of those which they condemn. And truly it is not hard to find, that this proceeds from no other cause, than that they are not furnished with rules by which to judge; nor have any solid foundations, which are as so many lights set up to clear their understanding, and lead them to an entire and certain knowledge. I think it superfluous to prove, that this is necessary to the knowledge of painting. It is sufficient, that painting be acknowledged for an art; for that being granted, it follows, without dispute, that no arts are without their precepts. I shall satisfy myself with telling you, that this little treatise will furnish you with infallible rules of judging truly; since they are not only founded upon right reason, but upon the best pieces of the best masters, which our author hath carefully examined, during the space of more than thirty years; and on which he has made all the reflections which are necessary, to render this treatise worthy of prosperity; which, though little in bulk, yet contains most judicious remarks, and suffers nothing to escape that is essential to the subject which it handles. If you will please to read it with attention, you will find it capable of giving the most nice and delicate sort of knowledge, not only to the lovers, but even to the professors of that art.

It would be too long to tell you the particular advantages, which it has above all the books that have appeared before it, in this kind; you need only read it, and that will convince you of this truth. All that I will allow myself to say, is only this, that there is not a word in it which carries not its weight; whereas in all others, there are two considerable faults, which lie open to the sight, viz. that saying too much, they always say too little. I assure myself, that the reader will own it is a work of general profit: to the lovers of painting, for their instruction how to judge knowingly, from the reason of the thing; and to the painters themselves, by removing their difficulties, that they may work with pleasure; because they may be in some manner certain, that their productions are good. It is to be used like spirits, and precious liquors: the less you drink of it at a time, it is with the greater pleasure. Read it often, and but little at once, that you may digest it better; and dwell particularly on those passages which you find marked with an asterism, *. For the observations which follow such a note will give you a clearer light on the matter which is there treated. You will find them by the numbers which are of on the side of the translation, from five to five verses, by searching for the like number in the remarks which are at the end of it, and which are distinguished from each other by this note, †. You will find, in the latter pages of this book the judgment of the author on those painters who have acquired the greatest reputation in the world; amongst whom he was not willing to comprehend those who are now living. They are undoubtedly his, as being found among his papers, written in his own hand.

As for the prose translation, which you will find on the other side of the Latin poem, I must inform you on what occasion, and in what manner, it was performed. The love which I had for painting, and the pleasure which I found in the exercise of that noble art, at my leisure hours, gave me the desire of being acquainted with the late Monsieur du Fresnoy, who was generally reputed to have a thorough knowledge of it. Our acquaintance at length proceeded to that degree of intimacy, that he intrusted me with his poem, which he believed me capable both of understanding and translating, and accordingly desired me to undertake it. The truth is, we had conversed so often on that subject, and he had communicated his thoughts of it so fully to me, that I had not the least remaining difficulty concerning it. I undertook therefore to translate it, and employed myself in it with pleasure, care, and assiduity; after which, I put it into his hands, and he altered in it what he pleased, till at last it was wholly to his mind. And then he gave his consent that it should be published; but his death preventing that design, I thought it a wrong to his memory to deprive mankind any longer of this translation, which I may safely affirm to be done according to the true sense of the author, and to his liking: since he himself has given great testimonies of his approbation to many of his friends. And they, who are acquainted with him, know his humour to be such, that he would never constrain himself so far, as to commend what he did not really approve. I thought myself obliged to say thus much, in vindication of the faithfulness of my work, to those who understand not the Latin; for as to those who are conversant in both the tongues, I leave them to make their own judgment of it.

The remarks which I have added to his work, are also wholly conformable to his opinions; and I am certain that he would not have disapproved them. I have endeavoured in them to explain some of the most obscure passages, and those which are most necessary to be understood: and I have done this according to the manner wherein he used to express himself, in many conversations which we had together. I have confined them also to the narrowest compass I was able, that I might not tire the patience of the reader, and that they might be read by all persons. But if it happens that they are not to the taste of some readers, (as doubtless it will so fall out,) I leave them entirely to their own discretion, and shall not be displeased that another hand should succeed better. I shall only beg this favour from them, that in reading what I have written, they will bring no particular gusto along with them, or any prevention of mind; and that whatsoever judgment they make, it may be purely their own, whether it be in my favour, or in my condemnation.

DE

ARTE GRAPHICA.

LIBER.

Ut pictura poesis erit; similisque poesi
Sit pictura; refert par æmula quæque sororem,
Alternantque vices et nomina; muta poesis
Dicitur hæc, pictura loquens solet illa vocari.
Quod fuit auditu gratum cecinere poetæ;
Quod pulchrum aspectu pictores pingere curant:
Quæque poetarum numeris indigna fuêre,
Non eadem pictorum operam studiumque merentur:
Ambæ quippe sacros ad religionis honores
Sydereos superant ignes, aulamque tonantis
Ingressæ divûm aspectu, alloquioque fruuntur;
Oraque magna deûm, et dicta observata reportant,
Cœlestemque suorum operum mortalibus ignem.
Inde per hunc orbem studiis coeuntibus errant,
Carpentes quæ digna sui, revolutaque lustrant
Tempora, quærendis consortibus argumentis.
Denique quæcunque in cœlo, terraque, marique
Longius in tempus durare, ut pulchra, merentur,
Nobilitate sua, claroque insignia casu,
Dives et ampla manet pictores atque poetas
Materies; inde alta sonant per sæcula mundo
Nomina, magnanimis heroibus inde superstites
Gloria, perpetuoque operum miracula restant.
Tantus inest divis honor artibus atque potestas.
Non mihi Pieridum chorus hic, nec Apollo vocandus,
Majus ut eloquium numeris, aut gratia fandi
Dogmaticis illustret opus rationibus horrens:

THE

ART OF PAINTING.†

Painting and Poesy are two sisters, which are so like in all things, that they mutually lend to each other both their name and office. One is called a dumb poesy, and the other a speaking picture. The poets have never said any thing, but what they believed would please the ears. And it has been the constant endeavour of the painters to give pleasure to the eyes. In short, those things which the poets have thought unworthy of their pens, the painters have judged to be unworthy of their pencils. * For both "those arts, that they might advance the sacred honours of religion," have raised themselves to heaven; and, having found a free admission into the palace of Jove himself, have enjoyed the sight and conversation of the gods; whose "awful majesty they observe, and whose dictates they communicate to mankind; whom at the same time they inspire with those celestial flames, which shine so gloriously in their works. From heaven they take their passage through the world; and "with concurring studies" collect whatsoever they find worthy of them. * They dive (as I may say) into all past ages; and search the histories, for subjects which are proper for their use: with care, avoiding to treat of any but those which, by their nobleness, or by some remarkable accident, have deserved to be consecrated to eternity; whether on the seas, or earth, or in the heavens. And by this their care and study, it comes to pass, that the glory of heroes is not extinguished with their lives; and that those admirable works, those prodigies of skill, which even yet are the objects of our admiration, are still preserved. * So much these divine arts have been almost honoured; and such authority they preserve amongst mankind. It will not here be necessary to implore the succour of Apollo, and the muses, for the grace-

† The passages which you see marked with an asterism, *, are more amply explained in the remarks.

Cum nitidâ tantum et facili digesta loquelâ,
Ornari præcepta negent, contenta doceri.
Nec mihi mens animusve fuit constringere nodos
Artificum manibus, quos tantùm dirigit usus;
Indolis ut vigor inde potens obstrictus hebescat,
Normarum numero immani, geniumque moretur:
Sed rerum ut pollens ars cognitione, gradatim
Naturæ sese insinuet, verique, capacem
Transeat in genium, geniusque usu induat artem.

Primum præceptum. De pulchro.

Præcipua imprimis artisque potissima pars est,
Nôsse quid in rebus natura creârit ad artem
Pulchrius, idque modum juxta, mentemque vetustam:
Quæ sine barbaries cæca et temeraria pulchrum
Negligit, insultans ignotæ audacior arti,
Ut curare nequit, quæ non modo noverit esse;
Illud aput veteres fuit unde notabile dictum,
Nil pictore malo securius atque poeta.

Cognita amas, et amata cupis, sequerisque cupita;
Passibus assequeris tandem quæ fervidus urges:
Illa tamen quæ pulchra decent; non omnia casus
Qualiacumque dabunt, etiamve simillima veris:
Nam quamcumque modo servili haud sufficit ipsam
Naturam exprimere ad vivum; sed ut arbiter artis,

fulness of the discourse, or for the cadence of the verses; which, containing only precepts, have not so much need of ornament as of perspicuity.

I pretend not in this treatise to tie the hands of artists, "whom practice only directs;" neither would I stifle the genius, by a jumbled heap of rules; nor extinguish the fire of a vein which is lively and abundant. But rather to make this my business, that art being strengthened by the knowledge of things, may at length pass into nature by slow degrees; and so, in process of time, may be sublimed into a pure genius, which is capable of choosing judiciously what is true; and of distinguishing betwixt the beauties of nature, and that which is low and mean in her; and that this original genius, by long exercise and custom, may perfectly possess all the rules and secrets of that art.

Precept I. Of what is beautiful.

* The principal and most important part of painting, is to find out, and thoroughly to understand, what nature has made most beautiful, and most proper to this art; * and that a choice of it may be made according to the taste and manner of the ancients; * without which, all is nothing but a blind and rash barbarity; which rejects what is most beautiful, and seems, with an audacious insolence, to despise an art, of which it is wholly ignorant; which has occasioned these words of the ancients: "That no man is so bold, so rash, and so overweening of his own works, as an ill painter, and a bad poet, who are not conscious to themselves of their own ignorance."

We love what we understand; we desire what we love; we pursue the enjoyment of those things which we desire; and arrive at last to the possession of what we have pursued, if we warmly persist in our design. In the mean time, we ought not to expect, that blind fortune should infallibly throw into our hands those beauties; for though we may light by chance on some which are true and natural, yet they may prove either not to be decent, or not to be ornamental. Because it is not sufficient to imitate nature in every circumstance, dully, and as it were literally, and minutely; but it becomes a painter to take

Seliget ex illa tantùm pulcherrima pictor.
Quodque minus pulchrum, aut mendosum, corriget ipse
Marte suo, formæ veneres captando fugaces.

what is most beautiful, * as being the sovereign judge of his own art; "what is less beautiful, or is faulty, he shall freely correct by the dint of his own genius," * and permit no transient beauties to escape his observation.

II. De speculatione et praxi.

Utque manus grandi nil nomine practica dignum
Assequitur, purum arcanæ quam deficit artis
Lumen, et in præceps abitura ut cæca vagatur;
Sic nihil ars operâ manuum privata supremum
Exequitur, sed languet iners uti vincta lacertos;
Dispositumque typum non linguâ pinxit Apelles.

Ergo licèt totâ normam haud possimus in arte
Ponere (cùm nequeant quæ sunt pulcherrima dici)
Nitimur hæc paucis, scrutati summa magistræ
Dogmata naturæ, artisque exemplaria prima
Altiùs intuiti; sic mens, habilisque facultas
Indolis excolitur, geniumque scientia complet;
Luxuriansque in monstra furor compescitur arte:
Est modus in rebus, sunt certi denique fines,
Quos ultra citraque nequit consistere rectum.

II. Of theory and practice.

* In the same manner, that bare practice, destitute of the lights of art, is always subject to fall into a precipice, like a blind traveller, without being able to produce any thing which contributes to a solid reputation; so the speculative part of painting, without the assistance of manual operation, can never attain to that perfection which is its object, but slothfully languishes as in a prison; for it was not with his tongue that Apelles performed his noble works. Therefore, though there are many things in painting, of which no precise rules are to be given, * (because the greatest beauties cannot always be expressed for want of terms,) yet I shall not omit to give some precepts, which I have selected from among the most considerable which we have received from nature, that exact school-mistress, after having examined her most secret recesses, as well as * those master-pieces of antiquity, which were the chief examples of this art; and it is by this means, that the mind and the natural disposition are to be cultivated, and that science perfects genius; * and also moderates that fury of the fancy which cannot contain itself within the bounds of reason, but often carries a man into dangerous extremes. For there is a mean in all things; and certain limits or bounds, wherein the good and the beautiful consists, and out of which they never can depart.

III. De argumento.

His positis, erit optandum thema nobile, pulchrum,
Quodque venustatum circa formam atque colorem
Sponte capax, amplam emeritæ mox præbeat arti
Materiam, retegens aliquid salis et documenti.

III. Concerning the subject.

This being premised, the next thing is to make choice of * a subject beautiful and noble; which being of itself capable of all the charms and graces that colours, and the elegance of design, can possibly give, shall afterwards afford, to a perfect and consummate art, an ample field of matter wherein to expatiate itself; to exert all its power, and to produce somewhat to the sight, which is excellent, judicious, * and ingenious; and at the same time proper to instruct, and to enlighten the understanding.

Tandem opus aggredior; primoque occurrit in albo
Disponenda typi, concepta potente Minervâ,
Machina, quæ nostris *Inventio* dicitur oris.

Inventio prima picturæ pars.

Illa quidem priùs ingenuis instructa sororum
Artibus Aonidum, et Phœbi sublimior æstu.

IV. Dispositio, sive operis totius œconomia.

Quærendasque inter posituras, luminis, umbræ,
Atque futurorum jam præsentire colorum
Par erit harmoniam, captando ab utrisque venustum.

V. Fidelitas argumenti.

Sit thematis genuina ac viva expressio, juxtà
Textum antiquorum, propriis cum tempore formis.

VI. Inane rejiciendum.

Nec quod inane, nihil facit ad rem, sive videtur
Improprium, miniméque urgens, potiora tenebit
Ornamenta operis; tragicæ sed lege sororis,
Summa ubi res agitur, vis summa requiritur artis.
Ista labore gravi, studio, monitisque magistri
Ardua pars nequit addisci rarissima: namque,
Ni priùs æthereo rapuit quod ab axe Prometheus
Sit jubar infusum menti cum flamine vitæ,
Mortali haud cuivis divina hæc munera dantur;
Non uti Dædaleam licet omnibus ire Corinthum.
Ægypto informis quondam pictura reperta,
Græcorum studiis, et mentis acumine crevit:
Egregiis tandem illustrata, et adulta magistris,
Naturam visa est miro superare labore.
Quos inter, graphidos gymnasia prima fuêre
Portus Athenarum, Sicyon, Rhodos, atque Corinthus,
Disparia inter se, modicùm ratione laboris;
Ut patet ex veterum statuis, formæ atque decoris

"At length I come to the work itself, and at first find only a bare strained canvass, on which the sketch is to be disposed by the strength of a happy imagination;" * which is what we properly call invention.

Invention the first part of painting.

* Invention is a kind of muse, which, being possessed of the other advantages common to her sisters, and being warmed by the fire of Apollo, is raised higher than the rest, and shines with a more glorious and brighter flame.

IV. The disposition, or economy of the whole work.

* It is the business of a painter, in his choice of attitudes, to foresee the effect and harmony of the lights and shadows, with the colours which are to enter into the whole; taking from each of them that which will most conduce to the production of a beautiful effect.

V. The faithfulness of the subject.

* Let "there be a genuine and lively expression of the subject," conformable to the text of ancient authors, to customs, and to times.

VI. Whatsoever palls the subject to be rejected.

"Whatever is trivial, foreign, or improper, ought by no means to take up the principal part of the picture." But herein imitate the sister of painting, Tragedy; which employs the whole forces of her art in the main action.

* This part of painting, so rarely met with, is neither to be acquired by pains or study, nor by the precepts or dictates of any master. For they alone who have been inspired at their birth with some portion of that heavenly fire, * which was stolen by Prometheus, are capable of receiving so divine a present.

Painting in Egypt was at first rude and imperfect, till being brought into Greece, and being cultivated by the study and sublime genius of that nation, * it arrived at length to that height of perfection, that it seemed to surpass even original nature.

Amongst the academies, which were composed by the rare genius of those great men, these four are reckoned as the principal: namely, the Athenian school, that of Sicyon, that of Rhodes, and that of Corinth. These were little different from each other, only in the manner of their work; as it may be seen by the an-

Achetypis; queis posterior nil protulit ætas
Condignum, et non inferius longè, arte, modoque.

VII. Graphis, seu positura, secunda picturæ pars.

Horum igitur vera ad normam Positura legetur:
Grandia, inæqualis, formosaque partibus amplis
Anteriora dabit membra, in contraria motu
Diverso variata, suo librataque centro.
Membrorumque sinus ignis flammantis ad instar,
Serpenti undantes flexu; sed lævia, plana,
Magnaque signa, quasi sine tubere subdita tactu,
Ex longo deducta fluant, non secta minutim.
Insertisque toris sint nota ligamina, juxta
Compagem anatomes, et membrificatio Græco
Deformata modo, paucisque expressa lacertis,
Qualis apud veteres; totoque Eurythmia partes
Componat; genitumque suo generante sequenti
Sit minus, et puncto videantur cuncta sub uno.
Regula certa licet nequeat prospectica dici,
Aut complementum graphidos; sed in arte juvamen,
Et modus accelerans operandi: at corpora falso
Sub visu in multis referens, mendosa labascit:
Nam geometralem nunquam sunt corpora juxtà
Mensuram depicta oculis, sed qualia visa.

VIII. Varietas in figuris.

Non eadem formæ species, non omnibus ætas
Æqualis, similisque color, crinesque figuris:
Nam variis velut orta plagis gens dispare vultu est.

IX. Figura sit una cum membris et vestibus.

Singula membra, suo capiti conformia, fiant
Unum idemque simul corpus cum vestibus ipsis;

X. Mutorum actiones imitandæ.

Mutorumque silens positura imitabitur actus.

cient statues, which are the rule of beauty and gracefulness; and to which succeeding ages have produced nothing that is equal; "or indeed that is not very much inferior, both in science, and in the manner of its execution."

VII. Design, the second part of painting.

* An attitude therefore must be chosen, according to their taste: * the parts of it must be great * and large, * "contrasted by contrary motions; the most noble parts foremost in sight, and each figure carefully poised on its own centre.

* "The parts must be drawn with flowing, gliding outlines, large and smooth, rising gradually, not swelling suddenly, but which may be just felt in the statues, or cause a little relievo in painting. Let the muscles have their origin and insertion, * according to the rules of anatomy; let them not be subdivided into small sections, but kept as entire as possible, * in imitation of the Greek forms, and expressing only the principal muscles." In fine, * let there be a perfect relation betwixt the parts and the whole, that they may be entirely of a piece.

Let the part which produces another part, be more strong than that which it produces; and let the whole be seen by one point of sight. * Though perspective cannot be called a perfect ruler "for designing," yet it is a great succour to art, and facilitates the "despatch of the work:" though frequently falling into error, it makes us behold things under a false aspect; for bodies are not always represented according to the geometrical plane, but such as they appear to the sight.

VIII. Variety in the figures.

Neither the shape of faces, nor the age, nor the colour, ought to be alike in all figures, any more than the hair; because men are as different from each other, as the regions in which they are born are different.

IX. The members and drapery of every figure to be suitable to it.

* Let every member be made for its own head, and agree with it; and let all together compose but one body, with the draperies which are proper and suitable to it. And, above all, * let the figures to which art cannot give a voice, imitate the mutes in their actions.

X. The action of mutes to be imitated.

XI. *Figura princeps.*

Prima figurarum, seu princeps dramatis, ultrò
Prosiliat media in tabula, sub lumine primo
Pulchrior ante alias, reliquis nec operta figuris.

XI. *Of the principal figure of the subject.*

* Let the principal figure of the subject appear in the middle of the piece, under the strongest light, that it may have somewhat to make it more remarkable than the rest; and that the figures which accompany it may not steal it from our sight.

XII. *Figurarum globi, seu cumuli.*

Agglomerata simul sint membra, ipsæque figuræ
Stipentur, circumque globos locus usque vacabit;
Nè, malè dispersis dum visus ubique figuris
Dividitur, cunctisque operis fervente tumultu
Partibus implicitis, crepitans confusio surgat.

XII. *Groups of figures.*

* Let the "parts be brought together, and the figures disposed in groups:" and let those groups be separated by a void space, to avoid a confused heap; which proceeding from parts that are dispersed without any regularity, and entangled one within another, divides the sight into many rays, and causes a disagreeable confusion.

XIII. *Positurarum diversitas in cumulis.*

Inque figurarum cumulis non omnibus idem
Corporis inflexus, motusque; vel artubus omnes
Conversis pariter non connitantur eodem;
Sed quædam in diversa trahant contraria membra,
Transversèque aliis pugnent, et cætera frangant.
Pluribus adversis aversam oppone figuram,
Pectoribusque humeros, et dextera membra sinistris.
Seu multis constabit opus, paucisve figuris.

XIII. *The diversity of attitudes in the groups.*

* The figures in the groups ought not to "have the same inflections of the body, nor the same motions; nor should they lean all one way, but break the symmetry, by proper oppositions and contrasts.

"To several figures seen in front, oppose others with the back toward the spectator; that is, the shoulders of some opposed to the breast of others, and right limbs to left, whether the piece consists of many figures, or but of few."

XIV. *Tabulæ libramentum.*

Altera pars tabulæ vacuo ne frigida campo,
Aut deserta fiet, dum pluribus altera formis
Fervida mole sua supremam exurgit ad oram.
Sed tibi sic positis respondeat utraque rebus,
Ut si aliquid sursum se parte attollat in unâ,
Sic aliquid parte ex aliâ consurgat, et ambas
Æquiparet, geminas cumulando æqualiter oras.

XIV. *Equality of the piece.*

* One side of the picture must not be void, while the other is filled to the borders; but let matters be so well disposed, that if "any thing rises high on one side of the piece, you may raise something to answer it on the other," so that they shall appear in some sort equal.

XV. *Numerus figurarum.*

Pluribus implicitum personis drama supremo
In genere ut rarum est; multis ita densa figuris
Rarior est tabula excellens; vel adhuc ferè nulla
Præstitit in multis, quod vix bene præstat in unâ;

XV. *Of the number of figures.*

* As a play is seldom very good in which there are too many actors, so it is very seldom seen, and almost impossible to perform, that a picture should be perfect in which there are too great a number of figures together, who can scarce excel in a single one?

Quippe solet rerum nimio dispersa tumultu,
Majestate carere gravi, requieque decora;
Nec speciosa nitet vacuo nisi libera campo.
Sed, si opere in magno, plures thema grande requirat
Esse figurarum cumulos, spectabitur unà
Machina tota rei; non singula quæque seorsim.

"Many dispersed objects breed confusion, and take away from the picture that solemn majesty, and agreeable repose, which give beauty to the piece, and satisfaction to the sight. But if you are constrained by the subject to admit of many figures, you must then make the whole to be seen together, and the effect of the work at one view; and not every thing separately, and in particular."

XVI. Internodia et pedes exhibendi.

Præcipua extremis raro internodia membris
Abdita sint: sed summa pedum vestigia nunquam.

XVI. Of the joints and feet.

* The extremities of the joints must be seldom hidden; and the extremities or end of the feet never.

XVII. Motus manuum motui capitis jungendus.

Gratia nulla manet, motusque, vigorque figuras
Retro aliis subter majori ex parte latentes,
Ni capitis motum manibus comitentur agendo.

XVII. The motions of the hands and head must agree.

The figures which are behind others, have neither grace nor vigour, unless the motions of the hands accompany those of the head.

XVIII. Quæ fugienda in distributione et compositione.

Difficiles fugito aspectus, contractaque visu
Membra sub ingrato, motusque, actusque coactos;
Quodque refert signis, rectos quodammodo tractus,
Sive parallelos plures simul, et vel acutas,
Vel geometrales, (ut quadra, triangula,) formas:
Ingratamque pari signorum ex ordine quandam
Symmetriam: sed præcipua in contraria semper
Signa volunt duci transversa, ut diximus antè.
Summa igitur ratio signorum habeatur in omni
Composito; dat enim reliquis pretium, atque vigorem.

XVIII. What must be avoided in the distribution of the figures.

Avoid "all odd aspects or positions, and all ungraceful or forced actions and motions." Show no parts which are unpleasing to the sight, as all foreshortenings usually are.

* Avoid all those lines and outlines which are equal; which make parallels, or other sharp-pointed and geometrical figures; such as are squares and triangles: all which, by being too exact, give to the eye a certain displeasing symmetry, which produces no good effect. But, as I have already told you, the principal lines ought to contrast each other: for which reason, in these outlines, you ought to have a special regard to the whole together: for it is from thence that the beauty and force of the parts proceed.

XIX. Natura genio accommodanda.

Non ita naturæ astrictè sis cuique revinctus,
Hanc præter nihil ut genio studioque relinquas;
Nec sine teste rei natura, artisque magistra,
Quidlibet ingenio, memor ut tantummodo rerum,
Pingere posse putes; errorum est plurima sylva,

XIX. That we must not tie ourselves to nature; but accommodate her to our genius.

* Be not so strictly tied to nature, that you allow nothing to study, and the bent of your own genius. But on the other side, believe not that your genius alone, and the remembrance of those things which you have seen, can afford you wherewithal to furnish out a beautiful piece, without the succour of that incomparable schoolmistress, Nature; * whom you must have always present as a witness to the truth. "Errors are infinite" and amongst many ways

Multiplicesque viæ, bene agendi terminus unus;
Linea recta velut sola est, et mille recurvæ.

Sed juxta antiquos naturam imitabere pulchram,
Qualem forma rei propria, objectumque requirit.

XX. Signa antiqua naturæ modum constituunt.

Non te igitur lateant antiqua numismata, gemmæ,
Vasa, typi, statuæ, cælataque marmora signis,
Quodque refert specie veterum post secula mentem;
Splendidior quippe ex illis assurgit imago,
Magnaque se rerum facies aperit meditanti;
Tunc nostri tenuem sæcli miserebere sortem,
Cùm spes nulla siet rediture æqualis in ævum.

XXI. Sola figura, quomodo tractanda.

Exquisita siet formâ, dum sola figura
Pingitur; et multis variata coloribus esto.

XXII. Quid in pannis observandum.

Lati, amplique sinus pannorum, et nobilis ordo
Membra sequens, subter latitantia, lumine et umbrâ
Exprimat; ille licet transversus sæpe feratur,
Et circumfusos pannorum porrigat extra
Membra sinus; non contiguos, ipsisque figuræ
Partibus impressos, quasi pannus adhæreat illis;
Sed modicè expressos cum lumine servet et umbris.
Quæque intermissis passim sunt dissita vanis,
Copulet, inductis subtérve, supérve lacernis,
Et membra, ut magnis, paucisque expressa lacertis,
Majestate aliis præstant, forma, atque decore:
Haud secus in pannis, quos supra optavimus amplos,
Perpaucos sinuum flexus, rugasque, striasque,
Membra super, versu faciles, inducere præstat.

which mislead a traveller, there is but one true one, which conducts him surely to his journey's end; as also there are many several sorts of crooked lines, but there is one only which is straight.

Our business is to imitate the beauties of nature, as the ancients have done before us, and as the object and nature of the thing require from us.

XX. Ancient figures the rules of imitating nature.

And for this reason, we must be careful in the search of ancient medals, statues, gems, vases, paintings, and basso relievos; * and of all other things which discover to us the thoughts and inventions of the Grecians; because they furnish us with great ideas, and make our productions wholly beautiful. And in truth, after having well examined them, we shall therein find so many charms, that we shall pity the destiny of our present age, without hope of ever arriving at so high a point of perfection.

XXI. A single figure how to be treated.

* If you have but one single figure to work upon, you ought to make it perfectly finished, and diversified with many colours.

XXII. Of the draperies.

* Let the draperies be nobly spread upon the body; let the folds be large, * and let them follow the order of the parts, that they may be seen underneath, by means of the lights and shadows; notwithstanding that the parts should be often traversed (or crossed) by the flowing of the folds, which loosely encompass them, * without sitting too straight upon them; but let them mark the parts which are under them, so as in some manner to distinguish them, by the judicious ordering of the lights and shadows. * And if the parts be too much distant from each other, so that there be void spaces, which are deeply shadowed, we are then to take occasion to place in those voids some fold to make a joining of the parts. "* And as those limbs and members which are expressed by few and large muscles, excel in majesty and beauty," in the same manner the beauty of the draperies consists not in the multitude of the folds, but in their natural order, and plain simplicity. The quality of the persons is also to

Naturæque rei proprius sit pannus, abundans
Patriciis; succinctus erit, crassus, que bubulcis,
Mancipiisque; levis, teneris, gracilisque puellis.
Inque cavis maculisque umbrarum aliquando tumescet,
Lumen ut excipiens, operis quà massa requirit,
Latius extendat, sublatisque aggreget umbris.

XXIII. *Quid multum conferat ad tabulæ ornamentum.*

Nobilia arma juvant virtutum, ornantque figuras,
Qualia musarum, belli, cultusque deorum.

XXIV. *Ornamentum auri et gemmarum.*

Nec sit opus nimium gemmis auroque refertum;
Rara etenim magno in pretio, sed plurima vili.

XXV. *Prototypus.*

Quæ deinde ex vero nequeunt præsente videri,
Prototypum prius illorum formare juvabit.

XXVI. *Convenientia rerum cum scena.*

XXVII. *Charites et nobilitas.*

Conveniat locus, atque habitus; ritusque decusque
Servetur: sit nobilitas, charitumque venustas,
(Rarum homini munus, cœlo, non arte petendum.)

XXVIII. *Res quæque locum suum teneat.*

Naturæ sit ubique tenor, ratioque sequenda.
Non vicina pedum tabulato excelso tonantis
Astra domus depicta gerent, nubesque notosque;
Nec mare depressum laquearia summa, vel orcum:
Marmoreamque feret cannis vaga pergula molem:
Congrua sed propriâ semper statione locentur.

be considered in the drapery. * As supposing them to be magistrates, their draperies ought to be large and sample; if country clowns, or slaves, they ought to be coarse and short; * if ladies, or damsels, light and soft It is sometimes requisite to draw out, as it were from the hollows and deep shadows, some fold, and give it a swelling, that so receiving the light, it may contribute to extend the clearness to those places where the body requires it; and by this means we shall disburden the piece of those hard shadowings, which are always ungraceful.

XXIII. *What things contribute to adorn the picture.*

* The marks or ensigns of virtues contribute not a little, by their nobleness, to the ornament of the figures. Such, for example, as are the decorations belonging to the liberal arts, to war, or sacrifices.

XXIV. *Of precious stones and pearl for ornaments.*

* But let not the work be too much enriched with gold or jewels; "for the abundance or them makes them look cheap, their value arising from the scarcity."

XXV. *The model*

* It is very expedient to make a model of those things, which we have not in our sight, and whose nature is difficult to be retained in the memory.

XXVI *The scene of the picture.*

* We are to consider the places where we lay the scene of the picture; the countries where they were born, whom we represent; the manner of their actions, their laws, and customs, and all that is properly belonging to them.

XXVII. *The graces and the nobleness.*

* Let a nobleness and grace be remarkable through all your work. But, to confess the truth, this is a most difficult undertaking, and a very rare present, which the artist receives rather from the hand of Heaven, than from his own industry and studies.

XXVIII. *Let every thing be set in its proper place*

In all things you are to follow the order of nature; for which reason you must beware of drawing or painting clouds, winds, and thunder, towards the bottom of your piece, and hell, and waters, in the uppermost parts of it; you are not to place a stone column on a foundation of reeds, but let every thing be set in its proper place.

XXIX. Affectus.

Hæc præter, motus animorum, et corde repostos
Exprimere affectus, paucisque coloribus ipsam
Pingere posse animam, atque oculis præbere videndam,
Hoc opus, hic labor est. Pauci, quos æquus amavit
Jupiter, aut ardens evexit ad æthera virtus,
Dis similes, potuere manu miracula tanta.
Hos ego rhetoribus tractandos desero; tantùm
Egregii antiquam memorabo sophisma magistri,
Verius affectus animi vigor exprimit ardens,
Solliciti nimiùm quam sedula cura laboris.

XXIX. Of the passions.

Besides all this, you are to express the motions of the spirits, and the affections or passions, whose centre is the heart; in a word, to make the soul visible, by the means of some few colours; * this is that in which the greatest difficulty consists. Few there are, whom Jupiter regards with a favourable eye in this undertaking; so that it appertains only to those few, who participate somewhat of divinity itself, to work these mighty wonders. It is the business of rhetoricians, to treat the characters of the passions; and I shall content myself with repeating what an excellent master has formerly said on this subject, that a "true and lively expression of the passions, is rather the work of genius, than of labour and study."

XXX. Gothorum ornamenta fugienda.

Denique nil sapiat Gothorum barbara trito
Ornamenta modo, sæclorum et monstra malorum:
Queis ubi bella, famem, et pestem, discordia, luxus,
Et Romanorum res grandior intulit orbi,
Ingenuæ periere artes, periere superbæ
Artificum moles; sua tunc miracula vidit
Ignibus absumi pictura; latere coacta
Fornicibus, sortem et reliquam confidere cryptis;
Marmoribusque diu sculptura jacere sepultis.

Imperium interea, scelerum gravitate fatiscens,
Horrida nox totum invasit, donoque superni
Luminis indignum, errorum caligine mersit,
Impiaque ignaris damnavit sæcla tenebris.

Unde coloratum graiis huc usque magistris
Nil superest tantorum hominum, quod mente modoque

XXX. Gothic ornaments are to be avoided.

We are to have no manner of relish for Gothic ornaments, as being in effect so many monsters, which barbarous ages have produced; during which, when discord and ambition, caused by the too large extent of the Roman empire, had produced wars, plagues, and famine, through the world, then I say the stately buildings and colosses fell to ruin, and the nobleness of all beautiful arts was totally extinguished. Then it was that the admirable, and almost supernatural, works of painting were made fuel for the fire; but that this wonderful art might not wholly perish, * some relics of it took sanctuary under ground, "in sepulchres and catacombs," and thereby escaped the common destiny. And in the same profane age, sculpture was for a long time buried under the same ruins, with all its beautiful productions and admirable statues. The empire, in the mean time, under the weight of its proper crimes, and undeserving to enjoy the day, was enveloped with a hideous night, which plunged it into an abyss of errors, and covered with a thick darkness of ignorance those unhappy ages, in just revenge of their impieties. From hence it comes to pass, that the works of those great Grecians are wanting to us; nothing of their painting and colouring now remains to assist our modern artists either in the invention, or the manner

Nostrates juvet artifices, doceatque laborem ;

Chromatice tertia pars picturæ.

Nec qui chromatices nobis, hoc tempore, partes
Restituat, quales Zeuxis tractaverat olim,
Hujus quando magâ velut arte æquavit Apellem
Pictorum Archigraphum, meruitque coloribus altam
Nominis æterni famam, toto orbe sonantem.
Hæc quidem ut in tabulis fallax, sed grata venustas,
Et complementum graphidos (mirabile visu)
Pulchra vocabatur, sed subdola, lena sororis:
Non tamen hoc lenocinium, fucusque, dolusque
Dedecori fuit unquam ; illi sed semper honori,
Laudibus et meritis ; hanc ergo nosse juvabit.

Lux varium, vivumque dabit, nullum umbra, colorem.
Quo magis adversum est corpus, lucique propinquum,
Clarius est lumen ; nam debilitatur eundo.

Quo magis est corpus directum, oculisque propinquum,
Conspicitur melius ; nam visus hebescit eundo.

XXXI. *Tonorum luminum et umbrarum ratio.*

Ergo in corporibus, quæ visa adversa, rotundis,
Integra sint, extrema abscedant perdita signis
Confusis, non præcipiti labantur in umbram
Clara gradu, nec adumbrata in clara alta repentè
Prorumpant ; sed erit sensim hinc atque inde meatus
Lucis et umbrarum ; capitisque unius ad instar,
Totum opus, ex multis quamquam sit partibus, unus
Luminis umbrarumque globus tantummodo fiet,

of these ancients. Neither is there any man who is able to restore * the chromatic part, or colouring, or to renew it to that point of excellency to which it had been carried by Zeuxis ; who by this part, which is so charming, so magical, and which so admirably deceives the sight, made himself equal to the great Apelles, that prince of painters ; and deserved that height of reputation, which he still possesses in the world.

Colouring the third part of painting.

And as this part, which we may call the utmost perfection of painting, is a deceiving beauty, but withal soothing and pleasing ; so she has been accused of procuring lovers for * her sister, and artfully engaging us to admire her. But so little have this prostitution, these false colours, and this deceit, dishonoured painting, that, on the contrary, they have only served to set forth her praise, and to make her merit farther known ; and therefore it will be profitable to us, to have a more clear understanding of what we call colouring.

* The light produces all kinds of colours, and the shadow gives us none. The more a body is nearer to the eyes, and the more directly it is opposed to them, the more it is enlightened : Because the light languishes and lessens, the farther it removes from its proper source.

The nearer the object is to the eyes, and the more directly it is opposed to them, the better it is seen ; because the sight is weakened by distance.

XXX. *The conduct of the tints of light and shadows.*

It is therefore necessary, "that those parts of round bodies which are seen directly opposite to the spectator, should have the light entire ;" and that the extremities turn, in losing themselves insensibly and confusedly, without precipitating the light all on the sudden into the shadow, or the shadow into the light. But the passage of one into the other must be common and imperceptible, that is, by degrees of lights into shadows, and of shadows into lights. And it is in conformity to these principles, that you ought to treat a whole group of figures, though it be composed of several parts, in the same manner as

Sive duas, vel tres ad summum, ubi grandius esset
Divisum pegma in partes statione remotas.
Sintque ita discreti inter se, ratione colorum,
Luminis, umbrarumque, antrorsum ut corpora clara
Obscura umbrarum requies spectanda relinquat;
Claroque exiliant umbrata atque aspera campo.

Ac veluti in speculis convexis, eminet ante
Asperior reipsâ vigor, et vis aucta colorum
Partibus adversis; magis et fuga rupta retrorsum
Illorum est (ut visa minùs vergentibus oris)
Corporibus dabimus formas hoc more rotundas.
Mente modoque igitur plastes, et pictor, eodem
Dispositum tractabit opus: quæ sculptor in orbem
Atterit, hæc rupto procul abscedente colore
Assequitur pictor, fugientiaque illa retrorsum
Jam signata minùs confusa coloribus aufert:
Anteriora quidem directè adversa, colore
Integra vivaci, summo cum lumine et umbra
Antrorsum distincta refert, velut aspera visu.
Sicque super planum inducit leucoma colores.
Hos velut ex ipsâ naturâ immotus eodem
Intuiti circum statuas daret inde rotundas.

XXXII. Corpora densa et opaca cum translucentibus.

Densa figurarum solidis quæ corpora formis
Subdita sunt tactu, non translucent, sed opaca
In translucendi spacio ut super aera, nubes,
Lympida stagna undarum, et inania cætera debent
Asperiora illis prope circumstantibus esse;

you would do a single head: "or if the wideness of the space, or largeness of the composition, requires that you should have two groups or three, (which should be the most,) let the lights and shadows be so discreetly managed, that light bodies may have a sufficient mass or breadth of shadow to sustain them, and that dark bodies may have a sudden light behind to detach them from the ground.

"As in a convex mirror, the collected rays strike stronger and brighter in the middle than upon the natural object, and the vivacity of the colours is increased in the parts full in your sight; while the goings off are more and more broken and faint as they approach to the extremities, in the same manner bodies are to be raised and rounded."

Thus the painter and the sculptor are to work with one and the same intention, and with one and the same conduct. For what the sculptor strikes off, and makes round with his tool, the painter performs with his pencil, casting behind that which he makes less visible, by the dimunition and breaking of his colours: "That which is foremost and nearest to the eye, must be so distinctly expressed, as to be sharp, or almost cutting to the sight. Thus shall the colours be disposed upon a plane, which from a proper place and distance will seem so natural and round, as to make the figures appear so many statues.

XXXII. Of dark bodies on light grounds.

"Solid bodies subject to the touch, are not to be painted transparent; and even when such bodies are placed upon transparent grounds, as upon clouds, waters, air, and the like vacuities, they must be preserved opaque,† that their solidity be not destroyed among those light, aerial, transparent species; and must therefore be expressed sharper and rougher than what is next to them, more dis-

† The French translator here, as well as Mr. Dryden, is unintelligible; which happened by their mistaking the meaning of the word *opaca*, which is not put for *dark*, but *opaque* in opposition to *transparent*; for a white garment may be *opaque*, &c.

Ut distincta magis firmo cum lumine et umbra,
Et gravioribus ut sustenta coloribus, inter
Aerias species subsistant semper opaca:
Sed contra, procul abscedant perlucida, densis
Corporibus leviora; uti nubes, aer, et undæ.

XXXIII. Non duo ex æquo lumina in tabulam æqualia.

Non poterunt diversa locis duo lumina eâdem
In tabulâ paria admitti, aut æqualia pingi:
Majus at in mediam lumen cadet usque tabellam
Latius infusum, primis qua summa figuris
Res agitur, circumque oras minuetur eundo:
Utque in progressu jubar attenuatur ab ortu
Solis, ad occasum paulatim, et cessat eundo;
Sic tabulis lumen, tota in compage colorum,
Primo à fonte, minus sensim declinat eundo.
Majus ut in statuis, per compita stantibus urbis,
Lumen habent partes superæ, minus inferiores;
Idem erit in tabulis: majorque nec umbra, vel ater
Membra figurarum intrabit color, atque secabit:
Corpora sed circum umbra cavis latitabit oberrans:
Atquè ita quæretur lux opportuna figuris,
Ut late infusum lumen lata umbra sequatur.
Unde, nec immeritò, fertur Titianus ubique
Lucis et umbrarum Normam appellâsse Racemum.

XXXIV. Album et nigrum.

Purum album esse potest propiusque magisque remotum:
Cum nigro antevenit propiùs; fugit absque remotum.
Purum autem nigrum antrorsum venit usque propinquum.

Lux fucata suo tingit, miscetque colore
Corpora, sicque suo, per quem lux funditur, aer.

tinct by a firm light and shadow, and with more solid and substantial colours; that, on the contrary, the smoother and more transparent may be thrown off to a farther distance."

XXXIII. That there must not be two equal lights in a picture

We are never to admit two equal lights in the same picture, but the greater light must strike forcibly on the middle; and there extend its greatest clearness on those places of the picture, where the principal figures of it are, and where the strength of the action is performed; diminishing by degrees as it comes nearer and nearer to the borders: and after the same manner that the light of the sun languishes insensibly, in its spreading from the east, from whence it begins, towards the west, where it decays and vanishes; so the light of the picture being distributed over all the colours, will become less sensible the farther it is removed from its original.

The experience of this is evident in those statues which we see set up in the midst of public places, whose upper parts are more enlightened than the lower; and therefore you are to imitate them in the distribution of your lights.

Avoid strong shadows on the middle of the limbs, lest the great quantity of black which composes those shadows should seem to enter into them, and to cut them: rather take care to place those shadowings round about them, thereby to heighten the parts; and take such advantageous lights, that after great lights great shadows may succeed. And therefore Titian said, with reason, that he knew no better rule for the distribution of the lights and shadows, than his observations drawn from a * bunch of grapes.

XXXIV. Of white and black.

* Pure, or unmixed white, either draws an object nearer, or carries it off to a farther distance; it draws it nearer with black, and throws it backward without it. * But as for pure black, there is nothing which brings the object nearer to the sight.

The light being altered by some colour, never fails to communicate somewhat of that colour to the bodies on which it strikes; and the same

XXXV. Colorum reflectio.

Corpora juncta simul, circumfusosque colores
Excipiunt, propriumque aliis radiosa reflectunt.

XXXVI. Unio colorum.

Pluribus in solidis liquida sub luce propinquis,
Participes, mixtosque simul decet esse colores.
Hanc Normam Veneti pictores ritè sequuti,
(Quæ fuit antiquis corruptio dicta colorum)
Cùm plures opere in magno posuêre figuras;
Nè conjuncta simul variorum inimica colorum
Congeries formam implicitam, et concisa minutis
Membra daret pannis, totam unamquamque figuram
Affini, aut uno tantùm vestire colore,
Sunt soliti; variando tonis tunicamque togamque
Carbaseosque sinus, vel amicum in lumine et umbra
Contiguis circum rebus sociando colorem.

XXXVII. Aer interpositus.

Qua minus est spacii aerii, aut quâ purior aer,
Cuncta magis distincta patent, speciesque reservant:
Quâque magis densus nebulis, aut plurimus aer
Amplum inter fuerit spatium porrectus, in auras
Confundet rerum species, et perdet inanes.

XXXVIII. Distantiarum relatio.

Anteriora magis semper finita, remotis
Incertis dominentur et abscedentibus, idque
More relativo, ut majura minoribus extent.

XXXIX. Corpora procul distantia.

Cuncta minuta procul massam densantur in unam;
Ut folia arboribus sylvarum, et in æquore fluctus.

XL. Contigua et dissita.

Contigua inter se coëant, sed dissita distent,
Distabuntque tamen grato, et discrimine parvo.

effect is performed by the medium of air, through which it passes.

XXXV. The reflection of colours.

The bodies which are close together receive from each other that colour which is opposite to them; and reflect on each other that which is naturally and properly their own.

XXXVI. Union of colours.

It is also consonant to reason, that the greatest part of those bodies which are under a light, which is extended, and distributed equally through all, should participate of each other's colours. The Venetian school having a great regard for that maxim, (which the ancients called the breaking of colours,) in the quantity of figures with which they fill their pictures, have always endeavoured the union of colours; for fear, that, being too different, they should come to encumber the sight: "therefore they painted each figure with one colour, or with colours of near affinity, though the habit were of different kinds, distinguishing the upper garment from the under, or from the loose and flowing mantle, by the tints, or degrees, harmonizing and uniting the colours, with whatever was next to them."

XXXVII. Of the interposition of air.

The less aerial space which there is betwixt us and the object, and the more pure the air is, by so much the more the species are preserved and distinguished; and, on the contrary, the more space of air there is, and the less pure it is, so much the more the object is confused and embroiled.

XXXVIII. The relation of distances.

Those objects which are placed foremost to the view, ought always to be more finished than those which are cast behind; and ought to have dominion over those things which are confused and transient. * But let this be done relatively, viz. one thing greater and stronger, casting the less behind, and rendering it less sensible by its opposition.

XXXIX. Of bodies which are distanced.

Those things which are removed to a distant view, though they are many, yet ought to make but one mass; as for example, the leaves on the trees, and the billows in the sea.

XL. Of bodies which are contiguous, and of those

Let not the objects which ought to be contiguous be separated; and let those which ought to be separated, be apparently so to us; but let this

XLI. Contraria extrema fugienda.

Extrema extremus contraria jungere noli;
Sed medio sint usque gradu sociata coloris.

XLII. Tonus et color varii.

Corporum erit tonus atque color variatus ubique;
Quærat amicitiam retro; ferus emicet ante.

XLIII. Luminis delectus.

Supremum in tabulis lumen captare diei.
Insanus labor artificum; cùm attingere tantùm
Non pigmenta queant: auream sed vespere lucem;
Seu modicùm mane albentem; sive ætheris actam
Post hyemem nimbis transfuso sole caducam;
Seu nebulis fultam accipient, tonitruque rubentem.

XLIV. Quædam circa praxim.

Lævia quæ lucent, veluti crystalla, metalla,
Ligna, ossa, et lapides; villosa, ut vellera, pelles,
Barbæ, aqueique oculi, crines, holoserica, plumæ;
Et liquida, ut stagnans aqua, reflexæque sub undis
Corporeæ species, et aquis contermina cuncta,
Subter ad extremum liquidè sint picta, superque
Luminibus percussa suis, signisque repostis.

XLV. Campus tabulæ.

Area, vel campus tabulæ vagus esto, levisque
Abscedat latus, liquidèque bene unctus amicis
Tota ex mole coloribus, unâ sive patellâ;
Quæque cadunt retrò in campum, confinia campo.

be done by a small and pleasing difference. *which are separated*

XLI. Contrary extremities to be avoided.

* Let two contrary extremities never touch each other, either in colour or in light; but let there always be a medium partaking both of the one and of the other.

XLII. Diversity of tints and colours.

Let the bodies everywhere be of different tints and colours; that those which are behind may be tied in friendship together; and that those which are foremost may be strong and lively.

XLIII. The choice of light.

* It is labour in vain to paint a high-noon, or mid-day light, in your picture; because we have no colours which can sufficiently express it: but it is better counsel to choose a weaker light; such as is that of the evening, with which the fields are gilded by the sun; or a morning light, whose whiteness is allayed; or that which appears after a shower of rain, which the sun gives us through the breaking of a cloud; or during thunder, when the clouds hide him from our view, and make the light of a fiery colour.

XLIV. Of certain things relating to the practical part.

Smooth bodies, such as crystals, polished metals, wood, bones, and stones; those which are covered with hair, as skins, the beard, or the hair of the head; as also feathers, silks, and the eyes, which are of a watery nature; and those which are liquid, as waters, and those corporeal species, which we see reflected by them; and in fine, all that which touches them, or is near them, ought to be "carefully painted flat, in flowing colours; then touched up with sprightly lights, and the true lines of the drawing restored, which were lost, or confused, in working the colours together.

XLV. The field or ground of the picture.

* Let the field, or ground of the picture, be pleasant, free, transient, light, and well united with colours, which are of a friendly nature to each other: and of such a mixture, as there may be something in it of every colour that composes your work, as it were the contents of your palette. "And let those bodies that are back in the ground be painted with colours allied to those of the ground itself."

XLVI. Color vividus, non tamen pallidus.

Vividus esto color, nimio non pallidus albo;
Adversisque locis ingestus plurimus ardens:
Sed levitèr parcèque datus vergentibus oris.

XLVI. Of the vivacity of colours.

* Let your colours be lively, and yet not look (according to the painters' proverb) as if they had been rubbed or sprinkled with meal; that is to say, let them not be pale.

* Let the parts which are nearest to us, and most raised, be strongly coloured, and as it were sparkling; and let those parts which are more remote from sight, and towards the borders, be more faintly touched.

XLVII. Umbra.

Cuncta labore simul coeant, velut umbrâ in eâdem.

XLVII. Of shadows.

* Let there be so much harmony, or consent, in the masses of the picture, that all the shadowings may appear as if they were but one.

XLVIII. Ex una patella sit tabula.

Tota sit tabula ex unâ depicta patellâ.

XLVIII. The picture to be of one piece.

"Let the whole picture be of one piece, as if it were painted from one palette."

XLIX. Speculum pictorum magister.

Multa ex naturâ speculum præclara docebit;
Quæque procul sero spatiis spectantur in amplis.

XLIX. The looking-glass the painter's best master.

* The looking-glass will instruct you in many beauties, which you may observe from nature; so will also those objects which are seen in an evening in a large prospect.

L. Dimidia figura, vel integra ante alias.

Dimidia effigies, quæ sola, vel integra plures
Ante alias posita ad lucem, stat proxima visu,
Et latis spectanda locis, oculisque remota,
Luminis umbrarumque gradu sit picta supremo.

L. A half figure, or a whole one, before others.

If there be a half figure, or a whole one, to be set before the other figures, and placed nearer to the view, and next the light; or if it is to be painted in a great place, though at a distance from the eye; be sure on these occasions not to be sparing of great lights, the most lively colours, nor the strongest shadows.

LI. Effigies.

Partibus in minimis imitatio justa juvabit
Effigiem, alternas referendo tempore eodem
Consimiles partes; cum luminis atque coloris
Compositis, justisque tonis; tunc parta labore
Si facili et vegeto micat ardens, vivâ videtur.

LI. A portrait.

* As for a portrait, or pictures by the life, you are to work precisely after nature, and to express what she shows you, working at the same time on those parts which are resembling to each other: as for example, the eyes, the cheeks, the nostrils, and the lips; so that you are to touch the one, as soon as you have given a stroke of the pencil to the other, lest the interruption of time cause you to lose the idea of one part, which nature has produced to resemble the other; and thus imitating feature for feature, with a just and harmonious composition of the lights and shadows, and of the colours; and giving to the picture that liveliness, which the freedom and force of the pencil make appear, it may seem, the living hand of nature.

LII. Locus tabulæ.

Visa loco angusto tenerè pingantur, amico
Juncta colore, graduque; procul quæ picta, feroci

LII. The place of the picture.

The works which are painted to be seen near, in little or narrow places, must be very tender and well united with tints and colours; "let

Sint et in æquali variata colore, tonoque.
Grandia signa volunt spacia ampla, ferosque colores.

LIII. *Lumina lata.*

Lumina lata, unctas simul undique copulet umbras

LIV. *Quantitas luminis loci in quo tabula est exponenda.*

Extremus labor. In tabulas demissa fenestris
Si fuerit lux parva, color clarissimus esto:
Vividus at contra, obscurusque, in lumine aperto.

LV. *Errores et vitia picturæ.*

Quæ vacuis divisa cavis, vitare memento;
Trita, minuta, simul quæ non stipata dehiscunt;
Barbara, cruda oculis, rugis fucata colorum,
Luminis umbrarumque tonis æqualia cuncta;
Fœda, cruenta, cruces, obscœna, ingrata, chimeras,
Sordidaque et misera, et vel acuta, vel aspera tactu;
Quæque dabunt formæ, temerè congesta, ruinam,
Implicitas aliis confundent mixtaque partes.

LVI. *Prudentia in pictore.*

Dumque fugis vitiosa, cave in contraria labi
Damna mali; vitium extremis nam semper inhæret.

LVII. *Elegantium idea tabularum.*

Pulchra gradu summo, graphidos stabilita vetustæ
Nobilibus signis, sunt grandia, dissita, pura,
Tersa, velut minimè confusa, labore ligata,
Partibus ex magnis paucisque efficta, colorum
Corporibus distincta feris, sed semper amicis.

LVIII. *Pictor tyro.*

Qui bene cœpit, uti facti jam fertur habere
Dimidium; picturam ita nil, sub limine primo
Ingrediens, puer, offendit damnosius arti,
Quàm varia errorum genera, ignorante magistro,

those which are to be seen at a distance, be varied with fiercer colours and stronger tints.

"Very large figures must have room enough, and strong, or rather fierce colouring."

LIII. *Large lights.*

* You are to "take the utmost care, that broad lights may be joined to a like breadth of shadows."

LIV. *What lights are requisite.*

If the picture be set in a place which receives but little light, the colours must be very clear; as, on the contrary, very brown, if the place be strongly enlightened, or in the open air.

LV. *Things which are vicious in painting to be avoided.*

Remember to avoid objects which are full of hollows, broken in pieces, little, and which are separated, or in parcels; shun also those things which are barbarous, shocking to the eye, and party-coloured, and which are all of an equal force of light and shadow; as also all things which are obscene, impudent, filthy, unseemly, cruel, fantastical, poor, and wretched; and those things which are sharp to the feeling; in short, all things which corrupt their natural forms, by a confusion of their parts which are entangled in each other: "For the eyes have a horror for those things, which the hands will not condescend to touch."

LVI. *The prudential part of a painter.*

But while you endeavour to avoid one vice, be cautious lest you fall into another; for "extremes are always vicious."

LVII. *The idea of a beautiful piece.*

Those things which are beautiful in the utmost degree of perfection, according to the axiom of ancient painters, * ought to have somewhat of greatness in them, and their outlines to be noble; they must be disentangled, pure, and without alteration, clean, and knit together; composed of great parts, yet those but few in number. In fine, distinguished by bold colours; but of such as are related and friendly to each other.

LVIII. *Advice to a young painter.*

And as it is a common saying, that "he who has begun well, has already performed half his work;" * so there is nothing more pernicious to a youth who is yet in the elements of painting, than to engage himself under the discipline of an ignorant master; who depraves his taste by

Ex pravis libare *Typis*, mentemque veneno
Inficere in toto quod non abstergitur ævo.

Nec graphidos rudis artis adhuc citò qualiacunque
Corpora viva super, studium meditabitur, ante
Illorum quam symmetriam, internodia, formam
Noverit, inspectis, docto evolvente magistro,
Archetypis; dulcesque dolos præsenserit artis.
Plusque manu ante oculos quam voce docebitur usus.

an infinite number of mistakes, of which his wretched works are full, and thereby makes him drink the poison which infects him through all his future life.

Let him who is yet but a beginner, not make so much haste to study after nature every thing which he intends to imitate, as not in the mean time to learn proportions, the connexion of the joints, and their outlines: and let him first have well examined the excellent originals, and have thoroughly studied all the pleasing deceptions of his art; which he must be rather taught by a knowing master, than by practice; and by seeing him perform, without being contented only to hear him speak.

LIX.
Ars debet servire pictori, non pictor arti.

Quære artem quæcumque juvant; fuge quæque repugnant.

LIX.
Art must be subservient to the painter.

* Search whatsoever is aiding to your art, and convenient; and avoid those things which are repugnant to it.

LX.
Oculos recreant diversitas et operis facilitas, quæ speciatim ars dicitur.

Corpora diversæ naturæ juncta placebunt;
Sic ea quæ facili contempta labore videntur;
Æthereus quippe ignis inest et spiritus illis;
Mente diu versata, manu celeranda repenti.
Arsque laborque operis grata sic fraude latebit:
Maxima deinde erit ars, nihil artis inesse videri.

LX.
Diversity and facility are pleasing.

* Bodies of divers natures, which are aggrouped (or combined) together, are agreeable and pleasant to the sight; * as also those things which seem to be slightly touched, and performed with ease; because they are ever full of spirit, and appear to be animated with a kind of celestial fire. But we are not able to compass these things with facility, till we have for a long time weighed them in our judgment, and thoroughly considered them: by this means the painter shall be enabled to conceal the pains and study which his art and work have cost him, under a pleasing sort of deceit; for the greatest secret which belongs to art, is to hide it from the discovery of spectators.

LXI.
Archetypus in mente, apographum in tela.

Nec prius inducas tabulæ pigmenta colorum,
Expensi quàm signa typi stabilita nitescant,
Et menti præsens operis sit pegma futuri.

LXII.
Circinus in oculis.

Prævaleat sensus rationi, quæ officit arti
Conspicuæ; inque oculis tantummodo circinus esto.

LXI.
The original must be in the head, and the copy on the cloth.

Never give the least touch with your pencil, till you have well examined your design, and have settled your outlines; * nor till you have present in your mind a perfect idea of your work.

LXII.
The compass to be in the eyes.

* Let the eye be satisfied in the first place, even against and above all other reasons, which beget difficulties in your art, which of itself suffers none; and let the compass be rather in your eyes, than in your hands.

LXIII. Superbia pictori nocet plurimum.

Utere doctorum monitis, nec sperne superbus
Discere, quæ de te fuerit sententia vulgi.
Est cæcus nam quisque suis in rebus, et expers
Judicii, prolemque suam miratur amatque.
Ast ubi consilium deerit sapientis amici,
Id tempus dabit, atque mora intermissa labori.
Non facilis tamen ad nutus, et inania vulgi
Dicta, levis mutabis opus, geniumque relinques:
Nam qui parte sua sperat bene posse mereri
Multivaga de plebe, nocet sibi, nec placet ulli.

LXIII. Pride an enemy to good painting.

* Profit yourself by the counsels of the knowing; and do not arrogantly disdain to learn the opinion of every man concerning your work. All men are blind as to their own productions, and no man is capable of judging in his own cause. * But if you have no knowing friend to assist you with his advice, yet length of time will never fail; it is but letting some weeks pass over your head, or at least some days, without looking on your work; and that intermission will faithfully discover to you the faults and beauties. Yet suffer not yourself to be carried away by the opinions of the vulgar, who often speak without knowledge; neither give up yourself altogether to them, and abandon wholly your own genius, so as lightly to change that which you have made; for he who has a windy head, and flatters himself with the empty hope of deserving the praise of the common people, (whose opinions are inconsiderate and changeable,) does but injure himself, and pleases no man.

LXIV. Γνῶθι σεαυτόν

Cumque opere in proprio soleat se pingere pictor,
(Prolem adeo sibi ferre parem natura suevit,)
Proderit imprimis pictori γνῶθι σεαυτόν,
Ut data quæ genio colat, abstineatque negatis.
Fructibus utque suus nunquam est sapor, atque venustas
Floribus, insueto in fundo, præcoce sub anni
Tempore, quos cultus violentus et ignis adegit:
Sic nunquam, nimio quæ sunt extorta labore,
Et picta invito genio, nunquam illa placebunt.

LXIV. Know yourself.

Since every painter paints himself in his own works, (so much is nature accustomed to produce her own likeness,) it is advantageous to him to know himself, * to the end that he may cultivate those talents which make his genius, and not unprofitably lose his time, in endeavouring to gain that which she has refused him. As neither fruits have the taste, nor flowers the beauty which is natural to them, when they are transplanted into an unkindly or foreign soil, and are forced to bear before their season, by an artificial heat; so it is in vain for the painter to sweat over his works, in spite of nature and of genius; for without them it is impossible for him to succeed.

LXV. Quod mente conceperis manu comproba.

Vera super meditando, manûs labor improbus adsit.
Nec tamen obtundat genium, mentisque vigorem.

LXV. Perpetually practise, and do easily what you have conceived.

* While you meditate on these truths, and observe them diligently, by making necessary reflections on them, let the labour of the hand accompany the study of the brain; let the former second and support the latter; yet without blunting the sharpness of your genius, and abating of its vigour by too much assiduity.

LXVI. Matutinum tempus labori aptum.

Optima nostrorum pars matutina dierum,

LXVI. The morning most proper for work.

* The morning is the best and most proper part of the day for your

Difficili hanc igitur potiorem impende labori.

LXVII. Singulis diebus aliquid faciendum.

Nulla dies abeat, quin linea ducta supersit.

LXVIII. Affectus inobservati et naturales.

Perque vias, vultus hominum, motusque notabis
Libertate sua proprios, positasque figuras
Ex sese faciles, ut inobservatus, habebis.

LXIX. Non desint pugillares.

Mox quodcumque mari, terris, et in aere pulchrum
Contigerit, chartis propera mandare paratis,
Dum præsens animo species tibi fervet hianti.
Non epulis nimis indulget pictura, meroque
Parcit: amicorum nisi cum sermone benigno
Exhaustam reparet mentem recreata; sed inde
Litibus, et curis, in cœlebe libre vita,
Secessus, procul à turba, strepituque remotos,
Villarum, rurisque beata silentia quærit.
Namque recollecto, totâ incumbente Minervâ,
Ingenio, rerum species præsentior extat;
Commodiusque operis compagem amplectitur omnem.

Infami tibi non potior sit avara peculî
Cura, aurique fames, modicâ quam sorte beato,
Nominis æterni, et laudis pruritus habendæ,
Condignæ pulchrorum operum mercedis in ævum.

Judicium, docile ingenium, cor nobile, sensus

business; employ it therefore in the study and exercise of those things which require the greatest pains and application.

LXVII. Every day do something.

* Let no day pass over you without a line.

LXVIII. The passions which are true and natural.

Observe as you walk the streets, the airs of heads; the natural postures and expressions; which are always the most free, the less they seem to be observed.

LXIX. Of table-books.

* Be ready to put into your table-book (which you must always carry about you) whatsoever you judge worthy of it; whether it be upon the earth, or in the air, or upon the waters, while the species of them is yet fresh in your imagination.

* Wine and good cheer are no great friends to painting; they serve only to recreate the mind, when it is oppressed and spent with labour; then indeed it is proper to renew your vigour by the conversation of your friends. Neither is a true painter naturally pleased with the fatigue of business, and particularly of the law, but delights in the liberty which belongs to the bachelor's estate. * Painting naturally withdraws from noise and tumult, and pleases itself in the enjoyment of a country retirement; because silence and solitude set an edge upon the genius, and cause a greater application to work and study; and also serve to produce the ideas, which, so conceived, will be always present in the mind, even to the finishing of the work; the whole compass of which the painter can at that time more commodiously form to himself, than at any other.

* Let not the covetous design of growing rich, induce you to ruin your reputation, but rather satisfy yourself with a moderate fortune; and let your thoughts be wholly taken up with acquiring to yourself a glorious name, which can never perish, but with the world; and make that the recompense of your worthy labours.

* The qualities requisite to form an excellent painter, are a true discerning judgment, a mind which is docible, a noble heart, and a sublime

Sublimes, firmum corpus, florensque juventa
Commoda res, labor, artis amor, doctusque magister.

sense of things and fervour of soul; after which follow, health of body, a convenient share of fortune, the flower of youth, diligence, an affection for the art, and to be bred under the discipline of a knowing master.

Et quamcumque voles occasio porrigat ansam,
Ni genius quidam adfuerit, sydusque benignum,
Dotibus his tantis, nec adhuc ars tanta paratur.

And remember, that whatsoever your subject be, whether of your own choice, or what chance or good fortune shall put into your hand, if you have not that genius or natural inclination, which your art requires, you shall never arrive to perfection in it, even with all those great advantages which I have mentioned. For the wit and the manual operation are things vastly distant from each other. It is the influence of your stars, and the happiness of your genius, to which you must be obliged for the greatest beauties of your art.

Distat ab ingenio longè manus. Optima doctis
Censentur, quæ parva minus; latet omnibus error:
Vitaque tam longæ brevior non sufficit arti.
Desinimus nam posse senes, cùm scire periti
Incipimus, doctamque manum gravat ægra senectus;
Néc gelidis fervet juvenilis in artubus ardor.

Nay, even your excellencies sometimes will not pass for such in the opinion of the learned, but only as things which have less of error in them; for no man sees his own failings; * and life is so short, that it is not sufficient for so long an art. Our strength fails us in our old age, when we begin to know somewhat; age oppresses us by the same degrees that it instructs us; and permits not, that our mortal members, which are frozen with our years, should retain the vigour and spirits of our youth.

Quare agite, O juvenes, placido quos sydere natos
Paciferæ studia allectant tranquilla Minervæ;
Quosque suo fovet igne, sibique optavit alumnos!
Eja agite, atque animis ingentem ingentibus artem
Exercete alacres, dum strenua corda juventus
Viribus extimulat vegetis, patiensque laborum est;
Dum vacua errorum, nulloque imbuta sapore
Pura nitet mens, et rerum sitibunda novarum,
Præsentes haurit species, atque humida servat.

* Take courage therefore, O ye noble youths! you legitimate offspring of Minerva, who are born under the influence of a happy planet, and warmed with a celestial fire, which attracts you to the love of science! Exercise, while you are young, your whole forces, and employ them with delight in an art, which requires a whole painter. Exercise them, I say, while your boiling youth supplies you with strength, and furnishes you with quickness and with vigour; while your mind, yet pure, and void of error, has not taken any ill habitude to vice; while yet your spirits are inflamed with the thirst of novelties, and your mind is filled with the first species of things which present themselves to a young imagination, which it gives in keeping to your memory, and which your memory retains for length of time, be

LXX. Ordo studiorum.

In geometrali prius arte parumpèr adulti,
Signa antiqua super Graiorum addiscite formam;
Nec mora, nec requies, noctuque diuque labori,
Illorum menti atque modo, vos donec agendi
Praxis ab assiduo faciles assueverit usu.

Mox, ubi judicium emensis adoleverit annis,
Singula quæ celebrant primæ exemplaria classis,
Romani, Veneti, Parmenses, atque Bononi,
Partibus in cunctis pedetentìm, atque ordine recto,
Ut monitum suprà est, vos expendisse juvabit.

Hos apud invenit Raphael miracula summo
Ducta modo, veneresque habuit quas nemo deinceps.
Quidquid erat formæ scivit Bonarota potenter.

Julius à puero musarum eductus in antris,
Aonias reseravit opes, graphicâque poesi
Quæ non visa prius, sed tantùm audita poetis,
Ante oculos spectanda dedit sacraria Phœbi:
Quæque coronatis complevit bella triumphis
Heroum fortuna potens, casusque decoros,
Nobilius reipsâ antiqua pinxisse videtur.

Clarior ante alios Corregius extitit, ampla
Luce superfusa, circum coeuntibus umbris,
Pingendique modo grandi, et tractando colore

LXX. The method of studies for a young painter.

reason of the moisture wherewith at that age the brain abounds. * You will do well * to begin with geometry, and after having made some progress in it, * set yourself on designing after the ancient Greeks: * and cease not day or night from labour, till, by your continual practice, you have gained an easy habitude of imitating them in their invention, and in their manner. * And when afterwards your judgment shall grow stronger, and come to its maturity with years, it will be very necessary to see and examine one after the other, and part by part, those works which have given so great a reputation to the masters of the first form in pursuit of that method, which we have taught you here above, and according to the rules which we have given you; such are the Romans, the Venetians, the Parmesans, and the Bolognese. Amongst those excellent persons, Raphael had the talent of invention for his share, by which he made as many miracles as he made pictures. In which is observed * a certain grace, which was wholly natural and peculiar to him, and which none since him have been able to appropriate to themselves. Michael Angelo possessed powerfully the part of design, above all others. * Julio Romano (educated from his childhood among the muses) has opened to us the treasures of Parnassus; and in the poetry of painting has discovered to our eyes the most sacred mysteries of Apollo, and all the rarest ornaments which that god is capable of communicating to those works that he inspires which we knew not before, but only by the recital that the poets made of them. He seems to have painted those famous wars "in which fortune has crowned her triumphant heroes;" and those other glorious events which she has caused in all ages, even with more magnificence and nobleness, than when they were acted in the world.

"The shining eminence of Correggio consists in his laying on ample broad lights encompassed with friendly shadows and in a grand style of painting, with a delicacy in the

Corpora. Amicitiamque, gradusque, dolosque colorum,
Compagemque ita disposuit Titianus, ut inde
Divus appellatus, magnis sit honoribus auctus,
Fortunæque bonis: quos sedulus Hannibal omnes
In propriam mentem, atque modum mirâ arte coegit.

management of colours." And Titian understood so well the union of the masses, and the bodies of colours, the harmony of the tints and the disposition of the whole together, that he has deserved those honours and that wealth which were heaped upon him, together with that attribute of being sirnamed the divine painter. The laborious and diligent Annibal Caracci has taken from all these great persons already mentioned whatsoever excellencies he found in them, and, as it were, converted their nourishment into his own substance.

LXXI. Natura et experientia artem perficiunt.

Plurimus inde labor *Tabulas* imitando juvabit
Egregias, operumque *Typos*; sed plura docebit
Natura ante oculis præsens; nam firmat et auget
Vim genii, ex illâque artem experientia complet.
Multa supercilio quæ *Commentaria* dicent.

LXXI. Nature and experience perfect art.

It is a great means of profiting yourself, to copy diligently those excellent pieces, and those beautiful designs: but Nature, which is present before your eyes, is yet a better mistress; for she augments the force and vigour of the genius, and she it is from whom art derives her ultimate perfection, by the means of sure experience. * I pass in silence many things which will be more amply treated in the ensuing commentary.

Hæc ego, dum memoror subitura volubilis ævi
Cuncta vices, variisque olim peritura ruinis,
Pauca sophismata sum graphica immortalibus ausus
Credere pieriis, Romæ meditatus: ad Alpes,
Dum super insanas moles, inimicaque castra
Borbonidum decus et vindex Lodoicus avorum,
Fulminat ardenti dextrâ, patriæque resurgens
Gallicus Alcides premit Hispani ora Leonis.

And now, considering that all things are subject to the vicissitudes of time, and that they are liable to destruction by several ways, I thought I might reasonably take the boldness * to intrust to the muses (those lovely and immortal sisters of painting) these few precepts, which I have here made and collected of that art.

I employed my time in the study of this work at Rome, while the glory of the Bourbon family, and the just avenger of his injured ancestors, the victorious Louis XIII. was darting his thunder on the Alps, and causing his enemies to feel the force of his unconquerable arms; while he, like another Gallic Hercules, born for the benefit and honour of his country, was griping the Spanish Geryon by the throat, and at the point of strangling him.

OBSERVATIONS

ON

THE ART OF PAINTING.

OF

CHARLES ALPHONSE DU FRESNOY.

1.* PAINTING and Poesy are two sisters, &c.

It is a received truth, that the arts have a certain relation to each other. "There is no art, (said Tertullian, in his Treatise of Idolatry,) which is not either the father, or the near relation of another." And Cicero, in his oration for Archias the poet, says, "That the arts, which have respect to human life, have a kind of alliance among themselves, and hold each other (as we may say) by the hand." But those arts, which are the nearest related, and claim the most ancient kindred with each other, are painting and poetry; and whosoever shall thoroughly examine them, will find them so much resembling one another, that he cannot take them for less than sisters.

They both follow the same bent, and suffer themselves to be rather carried away, than led by their secret inclinations, which are so many seeds of the Divinity. "There is a god within us, (says Ovid, in the beginning of his sixth book *De Fastis*, there speaking of the poets,) who by his agitation warms us." And Suidas says, "That the famous sculptor Phidias, and Zeuxis that incomparable painter, were both of them transported by the same enthusiasm which gave life to all their works." They both of them aim at the same end, which is imitation. Both of them excite our passions, and we suffer ourselves willingly to be deceived, both by the one and by the other: our eyes and souls are so fixed to them, that we are ready to persuade ourselves, that the painted bodies breathe, and that the fictions are truths. Both of them are set on fire by the great actions of heroes; and both endeavour to eternize them. Both of them, in short, are supported by the strength of their imagination, and avail themselves of those licenses, which Apollo has equally bestowed on them, and with which their genius has inspired them.

> "Pictoribus atque poetis
> Quidlibet audendi, semper fuit æqua potestas."

> "Painters and poets, free from servile awe,
> May treat their subjects, and their objects draw."

As Horace tells us in his "Art of Poetry."

The advantage which painting possesses above poesy is this; that amongst so great a diversity of languages, she makes herself understood by all the nations of the world; and that she is necessary to all other arts, because of the need which they have of demonstrative figures, which often give more light to the understanding than the clearest discourses we can make:

> "Segnius irritant animos demissa per aurem,
> Quam quæ sunt oculis commissa fidelibus."

> "Hearing excites the mind by slow degrees:
> The man is warmed at once by what he sees."

Horace in the same "Art of Poetry."

"For both those arts, that they might advance," &c. Poetry, by its hymns and anthems; and Painting, by its statues, altar-pieces, and by all those decorations which inspire respect and reverence for our sacred mysteries, have been serviceable to religion. Gregory of Nice, after having made a long and beautiful description of Abraham sacrificing his son Isaac, says these words:—"I have often cast my eyes upon a picture, which represents this moving † 9.

* The number at the head of every observation serves to find in the text the particular passage on which the observation was made.

object, and could never withdraw them without tears. So well did the picture represent the thing itself, even as if the action were then passing before my sight."

24. "So much these divine arts have been always honoured," &c. "The greatest lords, whole cities, and their magistrates of old, (says Pliny, lib. xxxv.) took it for an honour to obtain a picture from the hands of those great ancient painters." But this honour is much fallen late amongst the French nobility: and if you will understand the cause of it, Vitruvius will tell you, that it comes from their ignorance of the charming arts, "*Propter ignorantiam artis, virtutes obscurantur;*" (in the Preface to his Fifth Book.) Nay more, we should see this admirable art fall into the last degree of contempt, if our mighty monarch, who yields in nothing to the magnanimity of Alexander the Great, had not shown as much love for painting as for valour in the wars: we daily see him encouraging this noble art, by the considerable presents, which he makes to his chief painter.* And he has also founded an academy for the progress and perfectionating of painting, which his first minister† honours with his protection, his care, and frequent visits; insomuch that we might shortly see the age of Apelles reviving in our country, together with all the beauteous arts, if our generous nobility, who follow our incomparable king with so much ardour and courage in those dangers to which he exposes his sacred person, for the greatness and glory of his kingdom, would imitate him in that wonderful affection which he bears to all who are excellent in this kind. Those persons who were the most considerable in ancient Greece, either for birth or merit, took a most particular care, for many ages, to be instructed in the art of painting; following that laudable and profitable custom, begun and established by the great Alexander, which was to learn how to design. And Pliny, who gives testimony to this, in the tenth chapter of his thirty-fifth book, tells us farther, (speaking of Pamphilius, the master of Apelles,) "That it was by the authority of Alexander, that, first at Sicyon, and afterwards through all Greece, the young gentlemen learned, before all other things, to design upon tablets of boxen-wood; and that the first place, among all the liberal arts, was given to painting." And that which makes it evident that they were very knowing in this art, is the love and esteem which they had for painters. Demetrius gave high testimonies of this, when he besieged the city of Rhodes; for he was pleased to employ some part of that time which he owed to the care of his arms, in visiting Protogenes, who was then drawing the picture of Ialysus.

"This Ialysus (says Pliny) hindered King Demetrius from taking Rhodes, out of fear lest he should burn the pictures; and not being able to fire the town on any other side, he was pleased rather to spare the painting, than to take the victory, which was already in his hands." Protogenes, at that time, had his painting-room in a garden out of the town, and very near the camp of the enemies, where he was daily finishing those pieces which he had already begun, the noise of soldiers not being capable of interrupting his studies. But Demetrius causing him to be brought into his presence, and asking him, what made him so bold as to work in the midst of enemies? he answered the king, "That he understood the war which he made was against the Rhodians, and not against the arts." This obliged Demetrius to appoint him guards for his security, being infinitely pleased that he could preserve that hand, which by this means he saved from the barbarity and insolence of soldiers. Alexander had no greater pleasure than when he was in the painting-room of Apelles, where he commonly was found. And that painter once received from him a sensible testimony of love and esteem which that monarch had for him; for, having caused him to paint naked (by reason of her admirable beauty) one of his concubines, called Campaspe, who had the greatest share in his affections, and perceiving that Apelles was wounded with the same fatal dart of beauty, he made a present of her to him. In that age, so great a deference was paid to painting, that they, who had any mastery in that art, never painted on any thing but what was portable from one place to another, and what could be secured from burning. "They took a particular care (says Pliny, in the place above cited,) not to paint any thing against a wall, which could only belong to one master, and must always remain in the same place, and for that reason could not be removed in case of an accidental fire. Men were not suffered to keep a picture, as it were in prison, on the walls. It dwelt in common in all cities, and the painter himself was respected as a common good to all the world." See this excellent author, and you shall find, that the tenth chapter of his thirty-fifth book is filled with the praises of this art, and with the honours which were ascribed to it. You will there find, that it was not permitted to any but those of noble blood to profess it. Francis the First (as Vasari tells us) was in love with painting to that degree, that he allured out of Italy all the best masters, that this art might flourish in his own kingdom; and amongst oth-

* M. Le Brun. † M. Colbert.

ers Leonardo da Vinci, who, after having continued for some time in France, died at Fontainbleau in the arms of that great king, who could not behold his death without shedding tears over him. Charles the Fifth has adorned Spain with the noblest pictures which are now remaining in the world. Ridolphi, in his Life of Titian, says, "That emperor one day took up a pencil which fell from the hand of that artist, who was then drawing his picture; and upon the compliment which Titian made him on this occasion, he said these words:—'Titian has deserved to be served by Cæsar.'" And in the same Life it is remarkable, "That the emperor valued himself not so much in subjecting kingdoms and provinces, as that he had been thrice made immortal by the hand of Titian." If you will but take the pains to read this famous Life in Ridolphi, you will there see the relation of all those honours which he received from Charles the Fifth. It would take up too much time here to recount all the particulars; I will only observe, that the greatest lords who composed the court of that emperor, not being able to refrain from some marks of jealousy, upon the preference which he made of the person and conversation of Titian, to that of all his other courtiers, he freely told them, "That he could never want a court, or courtiers; but he could not have Titian always with him." Accordingly, he heaped riches on him; and whensoever he sent him money, which, ordinarily speaking, was a great sum, he always did it with this obliging testimony, "That his design was not to pay him the value of his pictures, because they were above any price." After the example of the worthies of antiquity, who bought the rarest pictures with bushels of gold, without counting the weight or the number of the pieces. "*In summo auro, mensurâ accepit, non numero,*" says Pliny, speaking of Apelles. Quinctilian infers from hence, "that there is nothing more noble than the art of painting; because other things, for the most part, are merchandise, and bought at certain rates: "Most things for this very reason (says he) are vile, because they have a price;" "*Pleraque hoc ipso possunt videri vilia, quod pretium habent.*" (See the 34th, 35th, and 36th Books of Pliny.) Many great persons have loved it with an extreme passion, and have exercised themselves in it with delight. Amongst others, Lælius Fabius, one of those famous Romans, who, (as Cicero relates,) after he had tasted painting, and had practised it, would be called Fabius Pictor; as also Turpilius, a Roman knight; Labeo, prætor and consul; Quintus Pedius; the poets Ennius and Pacuvius; Socrates, Plato, Metrodorus, Pyrrho, Commodus, Nero, Vespasian, Alexander Severus, Antoninus, and many other kings and emperors, who thought it not below their majesty to employ some part of their time in this honourable art.

"The principal and most important part of painting, is to find out, and thoroughly to understand, what nature hath made most beautiful, and most proper to this art," &c. Observe here the rock on which the greatest part of the Flemish painters have split: Most of that nation know how to imitate nature, at least as well as the painters of other countries; but they make a bad choice in nature itself; whether it be, that they have not seen the ancient pieces, to find those beauties; or that a happy genius, and the beautiful nature, is not of the growth of their country. And to confess the truth, that which is naturally beautiful is so very rare, that it is discovered by few persons; it is difficult to make a choice of it, and to form to ourselves such an idea of it, as may serve us for a model.

"And that a choice of it may be made † 39. according to the gust and manner of the ancients," &c. That is to say, according to the statues, the basso-relievos, and the other ancient pieces, as well of the Grecians as of the Romans. Ancient (or antic) is that which has been made from the time of Alexander the Great, till that of Phocas; during whose empire the arts were ruined by war. These ancient works from their beginning have been the rule of beauty: and in effect, the authors of them have been so careful to give them that perfection, which is still to be observed in them, that they made use not only of one single body, whereby they formed them, but of many, from which they took the most regular parts to compose from them a beautiful whole. "The sculptors," says Maximus Tyrius, in his 7th dissertation, "with admirable artifice, chose out of many bodies those parts which appeared to them the most beautiful; and out of that diversity made but one statue: but this mixture is made with so much prudence and propriety, that they seem to have taken but one only perfect beauty. And let us not imagine that we can ever find one natural beauty, which can dispute with statues that art, which has always somewhat more perfect than nature." It is also to be presumed, that in the choice which they made of those parts, they followed the opinions of the physicians, who at that time were very capable of instructing them in the rules of beauty; since beauty and health ordinarily follow each other. "For beauty," says Galen, "is nothing else but a just accord, and mutual harmony of the members, animated by a healthful constitution. And men," says the same author, "commend a certain statue of Polycletus, which they call the rule, and which deserves that name, for having so perfect an agreement in all its parts, and a proportion so exact, that it is not possible to find a fault in it." From what I have quoted we may conclude, that the ancient pieces are truly beautiful, because they resemble the beauties of nature; and that nature will ever be beautiful which resembles those beauties of antiquity. It is now evident upon what account none have presumed to contest the proportion of those ancient pieces; and that, on the contrary, they have always been quoted as models of the most perfect beauty. Ovid, in the twelfth book of his "Metamorphoses," where he describes Cyllarus, the most beautiful of all the Centaurs, says, "That he had so great a vivacity in his countenance, his neck, his shoulders, his hands, and stomach, were so fair, that it is certain the manly part of him was as beautiful as the most celebrated statues." And Philostratus, in his "Heroics," speaking of Protesilaus, and praising the beauty of his face, says, "That the form of his nose was square, as if it had been of a statue." And in another place, speaking of Euphorbus, he says, "That his beauty had gained the affections of all the Greeks; and that it resembled so nearly the beauty of a statue, that one might have taken him for Apollo." Afterwards also, speaking of the beauty of Neoptolemus, and of his likeness to his father Achilles, he says, "That, in beauty, his father had the same advantage over him, as statues have over the beauty of living men."

This ought to be understood of the fairest statues; for amongst the multitude of sculptors which were in Greece and Italy, it is impossible but some of them must have been bad workmen, or rather less good; for though their works were much inferior to the artists of the first form, yet somewhat of greatness is to be seen in them, and somewhat of harmonious in the distribution of their parts, which makes it evident, that, at that time, they wrought on common principles; and that every one of them availed himself of those principles, according to his capacity and genius. Those statues were the greatest ornaments of Greece. We need only open the book of Pausanias to find the prodigious quantity of them, whether within or without their temples, or in the crossing of streets, or in the squares and public places, or even the fields, or on the tombs. Statues were erected to the muses, to the nymphs, to heroes, to great captains, to magistrates, philosophers, and poets; in short, they were set up to all those who had made themselves eminent, either in defence of their country, or for any noble action which deserved a recompense; for it was the most ordinary and most authentic way, both amongst the Greeks and Romans, thus to testify their gratitude. The Romans, when they had conquered Græcia, transported from thence not only their most admirable statues, but also brought along with them the most excellent of their sculptors, who instructed others in their art, and have left to posterity the immortal examples of their knowledge, which we see confirmed by those curious statues, those vases, those basso-relievos, and those beautiful columns called by the names of Trajan and Antonine. These are those beauties which our author proposes to us for our models, and the true fountains of science, out of which both painters and statuaries are bound to draw for their own use, without amusing themselves with dipping in streams which are often muddy, at least troubled; I mean the manner of their masters, after whom they creep, and from whom they are unwilling to depart, either through negligence, or through the meanness of their genius. "It belongs only to heavy minds," says Cicero, "to spend their time on streams, without searching for the springs, from whence their materials flow in all manner of abundance."

"Without which, all is nothing but a † 40.
blind and rash barbarity," &c. All that
has nothing of the ancient gusto, is called a barbarous or Gothic manner, which is not conducted by any rule, but only follows a wretched fancy, which has nothing in it that is noble. We are here to observe, that painters are not obliged to follow the antique as exactly as the sculptors; for then the picture would savour too strongly of the statue, and would seem to be without motion. Many painters, and some of the ablest amongst them, believing they do well, and taking that precept in too literal a sense, have fallen thereby into great inconveniences. It therefore becomes the painters to make use of those ancient patterns with discretion, and to accommodate the nature to them in such a manner, that their figures, which must seem to live, may rather appear to be models for the antique, than the antique a model for their figures.

It appears, that Raphael made a perfect use of this conduct; and that the Lombard school have not precisely searched into this precept any farther, than to learn from thence how to make a good choice of the nature, and to give a certain grace and nobleness to all their works, by the general and confused idea which they had of what is beautiful. As for the rest, they are sufficiently licentious, excepting only Titian, who, of all the Lombards, has preserved the greatest purity in his works. This barbarous manner, of which I spoke, has been in great vogue from the year 611 to 1450. They who have restored painting in Germany (not having seen any of those fair relics of antiquity,) have retained much of that barbarous manner. Amongst others, Lucas van Leyden, a very laborious man, who, with his scholars, has infected almost all Europe with his designs for tapestry, which, by the ignorant, are called ancient hangings, (a greater honour than they deserve;) these, I say, are esteemed beautiful by the greatest part of the world. I must acknowledge, that I am amazed at so gross a stupidity, and that we of the French nation should have so barbarous a taste as to take for beautiful those flat, childish, and insipid tapestries. Albert Durer, that famous German, who was contemporary to that Lucas, has had the like misfortune to fall into that absurd manner, because he had never seen any thing that was beautiful. Observe what Vasari tells us, in the Life of Marc Antonio, (Raphael's graver,) having first commended Albert for his skill in graving, and his other talents:—"And in truth," says he, "if this so excellent, so exact, and so universal a man, had been born in Tuscany, as he was in Germany, and had formed his studies according to those beautiful pieces which are seen at Rome, as the rest of us have done, he had proved the best painter of all Italy, as he was the greatest genius, and the most accomplished which Germany ever bore."

† 45. "We love what we understand," &c. This period informs us, that though our inventions are never so good, though we are furnished by nature with a noble genius, and though we follow the impulse of it, yet this is not enough, if we learn not to understand what is perfect and beautiful in nature; to the end, that, having found it, we may be able to imitate it, and by this instruction we may be capacitated to observe those errors which she herself has made, and to avoid them, so as not to copy her in all sorts of subjects, such as she appears to us, without choice or distinction.

† 50. "As being the sovereign judge of his own art," &c. This word, sovereign judge, or arbiter of his own art, presupposes a painter to be fully instructed in all the parts of painting; so that being set as it were above his art, he may be the master and sovereign of it, which is no easy matter. Those of that profession are so seldom endowed with that supreme capacity, that few of them arrive to be good judges of painting; and I should many times make more account of their judgment, who are men of sense, and yet have never touched a pencil, than of the opinion which is given by the greatest part of painters. All painters, therefore, may be called arbiters of their own art; but to be sovereign arbiters, belongs only to knowing painters.

"And permit not transient beauties to escape his observation," &c. Those fugitive or transient beauties, are no other than such as we observe in nature, with a short and transient view, and which remain not long in their subjects. Such are the passions of the soul. There are of this sort of beauties which last but for a moment; as the different airs of an assembly upon the sight of an unexpected and uncommon object, some particularity of a violent passion, some graceful action, a smile, a glance of an eye, a disdainful look, a look of gravity, and a thousand other such-like things; we may also place in the catalogue of these flying beauties, fine clouds, such as ordinarily follow thunder, or a shower of rain. † 52.

"In the same manner that bare practice, destitute of the lights of art," &c. † 54.
We find in Quinctilian, that Pythagoras said, "The theory is nothing without the practice." "And what means," says the younger Pliny, "have we to retain what has been taught us, if we put it not in practice?" We would not allow that man to be an orator who had the best thoughts imaginable, and who knew all the rules of rhetoric, if he had not acquired by exercise the art of using them, and of composing an excellent discourse. Painting is a long pilgrimage; what avails it to make all the necessary preparatives for our voyage, or to inform ourselves of all the difficulties in the road? If we do not actually begin the journey, and travel at a round rate, we shall never arrive at the end of it. And as it would be ridiculous to grow old in the study of every necessary thing in an art, which comprehends so many several parts; so, on the other hand, to begin the practice without knowing the rules, or at least with a light tincture of them, is to expose ourselves to the scorn of those who can judge of painting, and to make it apparent to the world that we have no care of our reputation. Many are of opinion, that we need only work, and mind the practical part, to become skilful and able painters; and that the theory only encumbers the mind, and ties the hand. Such men do just like the squirrel, who is perpetually turning the wheel in her cage; she runs apace, and wearies herself with her continual motion, and yet gets no ground. "It is not enough for doing well to

walk apace," says Quinctilian, "but it is enough for walking apace to do well." It is a bad excuse to say, I was but a little while about it. That graceful easiness, that celestial fire, which animates the work, proceeds not so much from having often done the like, as from having well understood what we have done. See what I shall farther say, on the 60th rule, which concerns easiness. Others there are who believe precepts and speculation to be of absolute necessity; but as they were ill instructed, and what they knew rather entangled than cleared their understanding, so they oftentimes turn short; and if they perform a work, it is not without anxiety and pain. And in truth, they are so much the more worthy of compassion, because their intentions are right; and if they advance not in knowledge as far as others, and are sometimes cast behind, yet they are grounded upon some sort of reason; for it is belonging to good sense not to go over fast, when we apprehend ourselves to be out of the way, or even where we doubt which way we ought to take. Others, on the contrary, being well instructed in good maxims, and in the rules of art, after having done fine things, yet spoil them all, by endeavouring to make them better, which is a kind of overdoing; and they are so intoxicated with their work, and with an earnest desire of being above all others, that they suffer themselves to be deceived with the appearance of an imaginary good. "Apelles, one day, admiring the prodigious labour which he saw in a picture of Protogenes, and knowing how much sweat it must have cost him, said, that Protogenes and himself were of equal strength; nay, that he yielded to him, in some parts of painting; but in this he surpassed him, that Protogenes never knew when he had done well, and could never hold his hand. He also added, in the nature of a precept, that he wished all painters would imprint this lesson deeply in their memory, that with overstraining and earnestness of finishing their pieces, they often did them more harm than good."* "There are some," says Quinctilian, "who never satisfy themselves, never are contented with their first notions and expressions, but are continually changing all, till nothing remains of their first ideas. Others there are," continues he, "who dare never trust themselves, nor resolve on any thing; and who being, as it were, entangled in their own genius, imagine it to be a laudable correctness, when they form difficulties to themselves in their own work. And, to speak the truth, it is hard to discern whether of the two is in the greatest error; he, who is enamoured of all he does; or he, whom nothing of his own can please. For it has happened to young men, and often even to those of the greatest wit, to waste their spirits, and to consume themselves with anxiety and pain of their own giving, so far as even to doze upon their work with too much eagerness of doing well. I will now tell you how a reasonable man ought to carry himself on this occasion. It is certain, that we ought to use our best endeavour to give the last perfection to our works; yet it is always to be understood, that we attempt no more than what is in the compass of our genius, and according to our vein. For, to make a true progress, I grant that diligence and study are both requisite; but this study ought to have no mixture, either of self-opinion, obstinacy, or anxiety; for which reason if it blows a happy gale, we must set up all our sails, though in so doing it sometimes happens, that we follow those motions where our natural heat is more powerful than our care and our correctness, provided we abuse not this license, and suffer not ourselves to be deceived by it; for all our productions cannot fail to please us at the moment of their birth, as being new to us."*

"Because the greatest beauties cannot always be expressed for want of terms," &c. I have learned from the mouth of Monsieur du Fresnoy, that he had oftentimes heard Guidò say, "that no man could give a rule of the greatest beauties; and that the knowledge of them was so abstruse, that there was no manner of speaking which could express them." This comes just to what Quinctilian says,† "That things incredible wanted words to express them; for some of them are too great, and too much elevated, to be comprehended by human discourse." From hence it proceeds, that the best judges, when they admire a noble picture, seem to be fastened to it; and when they come to themselves, you would say, they had lost the use of speech. † 61.

"*Pausiacâ torpes, insane, tabellâ,*" says Horace;‡ and Symmachus says,§ "that the greatness of astonishment hinders men from giving a just applause." The Italians say, *Opera da stupire*," when a thing is wonderfully good.

"Those masterpieces of antiquity, which were the chief examples of this art," &c. He means the most knowing and best painters of antiquity: that is to say, from the last two ages to our times. † 53.

* Pliny xxxv. 10.

* Quinc. x. 3.
† Declam. xix
‡ Lib. ii. Sat. 7.
§ Lib. x. Ep. 22.

† 66. "And also moderates that fury of the fancy," &c. There is in the Latin Text 'which produces only monsters," that is to say, things out of all probable resemblance. Such things as are often found in the works of Pietro Testa. "It often happens," says Dionysius Longius, a grave author, "that some men, imagining themselves to be possessed with a divine fury, far from being carried into the rage of Bacchanalians, often fall into toys and trifles, which are only puerilities."

† 69. "A subject beautiful and noble," &c. Painting is not only pleasing and divertising, but is also a kind of memorial of those things which antiquity has had the most beautiful and noble in their kinds, replacing the history before our eyes; as if the thing were at this very time effectually in action; even so far, that, beholding the pictures wherein those noble deeds are represented, we find ourselves stung with a desire of endeavouring somewhat, which is like that action, there expressed, as if we were reading it in the history. The beauty of the subject inspires us with love and admiration for the pictures, as the fair mixture causes us to enter into the subject which it imitates, and imprints it the more deeply into our imagination, and our memory. These are two chains which are interlinked, which contain, and are at the same time contained, and whose matter is equally precious and estimable.

† 72. "And ingenious," &c. *Aliquid salis*, somewhat that is well seasoned, fine, and piquant, extraordinary, of a high relish, proper to instruct, and to clear the understanding. "The painters ought to do like the orators," says Cicero;* "let them instruct, let them divertise, let them move us;" this is what is properly meant by the word *salt*.

† 74. "On which the sketch, as it may be called, of the picture is to be disposed," &c. It is not without reason, nor by chance, that our author uses the word *machina*. A machine is a just assembling or combination of many pieces, to produce one and the same effect. And the disposition in a picture is nothing else but an assembling of many parts, of which we are to foresee the agreement with each other, and the justness to produce a beautiful effect, as you shall see in the 4th precept, which is concerning the economy. This is also called the composition, by which is meant the distribution and orderly placing of things, both in general, and in particular.

† 75. "Which is what we properly call invention," &c. Our author establishes three parts of painting; the *invention*; the *design*, or *drawing*; and the *colouring*, which in some places he calls the *chromatic*. Many authors who have written of painting, multiply the parts according to their pleasure; and without giving you, or myself, the trouble of discussing this matter, I will only tell you, that all the parts of painting which others have named, are reducible into these three which are mentioned by our author.

For which reason, I esteem this division to be the justest: and as three parts are essential to painting, so no man can be truly called a painter, who does not possess them altogether: in the same manner that we cannot give the name of man to any creature which is not composed of body, soul, and reason, which are the three parts necessarily constituent of a man. How therefore can they pretend to the quality of painters, who can only copy and purloin the works of others, who therein employ their whole industry, and with that only talent would pass for able painters? And, do not tell me, that many great artists have done this; for I can easily answer you, that it had been their better course to have abstained from so doing; that they have not thereby done themselves much honour, and that copying was not the best part of their reputation. Let us then conclude, that all painters ought to acquire this part of excellence; not to do it, is to want courage, and not dare to show themselves. It is to creep and grovel on the ground; it is to deserve this just reproach, *O imitatores, servum pecus!* It is with painters, in reference to their productions, as it is with orators; a good beginning is always costly to both; much sweat and labour is required, but it is better to expose our works, and leave them liable to censure for fifteen years, than to blush for them at the end of fifty. On this account, it is necessary for a painter to begin early to do somewhat of his own, and to accustom himself to it by continual exercise; for so long as, endeavouring to raise himself, he fears falling, he shall be always on the ground. See the following observation:

"Invention is a kind of Muse, which being possessed of the other advantages common to her sisters," &c. † 76.
The attributes of the Muses are often taken for the Muses themselves; and it is in this sense, that invention is here called a Muse. Authors ascribe to each of them in particular, the sciences which they have, say they, invented; and in general the Belles Lettres, because they contain almost all the others. These sciences are those advantages of which our author speaks, and with which he would have a painter furnish himself sufficiently: and in truth, there is no man, though his un-

* De Opt. Gen. Orat.

oerstanding be very mean, who knows not, and who finds not of himself, how much learning is necessary to animate his genius, and to complete it. And the reason of this is, that they who have studied, have not only seen and learned many excellent things, in their course of studies; but also they have acquired, by that exercise, a great facility of profiting themselves, by reading good authors. They who will make profession of painting, must heap up treasures out of their reading: and there they will find many wonderful means of raising themselves above others, who can only creep upon the ground; or if they elevate themselves, it is only to fall from a higher place, because they serve themselves of other men's wings, neither understanding their use, nor their virtue. It is true, that it is not the present mode for a painter to be so knowing: and, if any of them, in these times, be found to have either a great wit, or much learning, the multitude would not fail to say, that it was great pity; and that the youth might have come to somewhat in the practical part of the law, or it may be in the treasury, or in the families of some noblemen. So wretched is the destiny of painting in these latter ages. By learning, it is not so much the knowledge of the Greek and Latin tongue which is here to be understood, as the reading of good authors, and understanding those things of which they treat: for translations being made of the best authors, there is not any painter who is not capable, in some sort, of understanding those books of humanity, which are comprehended under the name of the Belles Lettres. In my opinion, the books which are of the most advantage to those of the profession, are these which follow:

The Bible.

The History of Josephus.

The Roman History of Coffeteau, for those who understand the French; and that of Titus Livius, in Latin.

Homer, whom Pliny calls the fountain-head of invention and noble thoughts.

Virgil, and in him particularly his Æneis.

The ecclesiastical History of Godeau, or the abridgment of Baronius.

Ovid's Metamorphoses.

The pictures of Philostratus.*

Plutarch's Lives.

Pausanias, who is wonderful for giving of great ideas; and chiefly for such as are to be placed at a distance, or cast behind, and for the combining of figures. This author, in conjunction with Homer, makes a good mingle of what is pleasing, and what is perfect.

The Religion of the Ancient Romans, by Du Choul; and in English, Godwin's Roman Antiquities.

Trajan's Pillar, with the discourse which explains the figures on it, and instructs a painter in those things with which he is indispensably to be acquainted. This is one of the most principal and most learned books, which we have for the modes, the customs, the arms, and the religion of the Romans. Julio Romano made his chief studies on the marble itself.

The books of medals.

The Bass-Reliefs of Perrier, and others, with their explanations at the bottom of the pages, which give a perfect understanding of them.

Horace's Art of Poetry, because of the relation which there is betwixt the rules of poetry, and those of painting.

And other books of the like nature, the reading of which are profitable to warm the imagination; such as in English, are Spenser's Fairy Queen; the Paradise Lost of Milton; Tasso, translated by Fairfax; and the history of Polybius, by Sir Henry Shere.

Some romances also are very capable of entertaining the genius, and of strengthening it, by the noble ideas which they give of things: but there is this danger in them, that they almost always corrupt the truth of history.

There are also other books which a painter may use upon some particular occasions, and only when he wants them: Such are, The Mythology of the Gods; The Images of the Gods; The Iconology; The Tables of Hyginus; The Practical Perspective; and some others not here mentioned.

Thus it is necessary, that they who are desirous of a name in painting, should read at leisure times these books with diligence; and make their observations of such things as they find for their purpose in them, and of which they believe they may some time or other have occasion. Let the imagination be employed in this reading, and let them make sketches and light touches of those ideas which that reading forms in their imagination. Quinctilian, Tacitus, or whoever was the author of that dialogue which is called in Latin *De Causis corruptæ Eloquentiæ*, says, "That painting resembles fire, which is fed by the fuel, inflamed by motion, and gathers strength by burning; for the power of the genius is only augmented by the abundance of matter to supply it; and it is impossible to make a great and magnificent work, if that matter be wanting, or not disposed rightly." And therefore a painter, who has a genius, gets nothing by long thinking, and taking all imaginable care to make a noble composition, if he be not as-

* Tableaux.

sisted by those studies which I have mentioned. All that he can gain by it is only to weary his imagination, and to travel over many vast countries, without dwelling on any one thing which can give him satisfaction.

All the books which I have named may be serviceable to all sorts of persons, as well as to painters. As for those books which were of particular use to them, they were unfortunately lost in those ages which were before the invention of printing,—the copiers neglecting (probably out of ignorance) to transcribe them, as not finding themselves capable of making the demonstrative figures.* In the mean time, it is evidently known, by the relation of authors, that we have lost fifty volumes of them at the least. See Pliny in his 35th book; and Franc Junius, in his 3d chapter of the 2d book of the "Painting of the Ancients." Many moderns have written of it with small success, taking a large compass, without coming directly to the point; and talking much, without saying any thing; yet some of them have acquitted themselves successfully enough. Amongst others, Leonardo da Vinci, (though without method;) Paulo Lomazzo, whose book is good for the greatest part, but whose discourse is too diffusive and very tiresome; John Baptist Armenini, Franciscus Junius, and Monsieur de Cambray, to whose preface I rather invite you, than to his book. We are not to forget what Monsieur Felebien has written of the historical piece of Alexander, by the hand of Monsieur Le Brun: besides that the work itself is very eloquent, the foundations which he establishes for the making of a good picture are wonderfully solid. Thus I have given you very near the library of a painter, and a catalogue of such books as he ought either to read himself, or have read to him; at least if he will not satisfy himself with possessing painting as the most sordid of all trades, and not as the noblest of all arts.

† 77. "It is the business of a painter, in his choice of attitudes," &c. See here the most important precept of all those which relate to painting. It belongs properly to a painter alone, and all the rest are borrowed either from learning, or from physic, or from the mathematics, or, in short, from other arts; for it is sufficient to have a natural wit and learning, to make that which we call in painting a good invention: for the design, we must have some insight into anatomy: to make buildings, and other things in perspective, we must have knowledge in the mathematics: and other arts will bring in their quotas, to furnish out the matter of a good picture. But for the economy, or ordering of the whole together, none but only the painter can understand it; because the end of the artist is pleasingly to deceive the eyes, which he can never accomplish if this part be wanting to him. A picture may have an ill effect, though the invention of it be truly understood, the design of it correct, and the colours of it the most beautiful and fine that can be employed in it. And, on the contrary, we may behold other pictures ill invented, ill designed, and painted with the most common colours, which shall have a very good effect, and which shall more pleasingly deceive. "Nothing pleases a man so much as order," says Xenophon;* and Horace, in his "Art of Poetry," lays it down as a rule,

Singula quæque locum teneant sortita decenter.

Set all things in their own peculiar place;
And know that order is the greatest grace.

This precept is properly the use and application of all the rest; for which reason it requires much judgment. You are therefore in such manner to foresee things, that your picture may be painted in your head, before it comes upon the canvass. "When Menander," says a celebrated author,† "had ordered the scenes of his comedy, he held it to be, in a manner, already made; though he had not begun the first verse of it." It is an undoubted truth, that they who are endued with this foresight, work with incredible pleasure and facility; others, on the contrary, are perpetually changing and rechanging their work, which, when it is ended, leaves them but anxiety for all their pains. It seems to me, that these sorts of pictures remind us of those old Gothic castles, made at several times and which hold together only as it were by rags and patches.

It may be inferred from that which I have said, that the invention and the disposition are two several and distinct parts. In effect, though the last of them depends upon the first, and is commonly comprehended under it; yet we are to take great care, that we do not confound them. The invention simply finds out the subjects, and makes a choice of them suitable to the history which we treat; and the disposition distributes those things which are thus found, each to its proper place, and accommodates the figures and the groups in particular, and the *tout ensemble* (or whole together) of the picture in general; so that this economy produces the same effect in relation to the eyes, as a concert of music to the ears.

* That is to the eye, by diagrams and sketches, &c.

* In Œconomico.

† Comm. Vetus.

the greatest parts of the body ought to appear

There is one thing of great consequence to be observed in the economy of the whole work, which is, that at the first sight we may be given to understand the quality of the subject; and that the picture, at the first glance of the eye, may inspire us with the principal passion of it; for example, if the subject which you have undertaken to treat be of joy, it is necessary that every thing which enters into your picture should contribute to that passion, so that the beholders shall immediately be moved with it. If the subject be mournful, let every thing in it have a stroke of sadness; and so of the other passions and qualities of the subjects.

† 81. "Let there be a genuine and lively expression of the subject, conformable to the text of ancient authors," &c. Take care that the licenses of painters be rather to adorn the history, than to corrupt it. And though Horace gives permission to painters and poets* to dare every thing, yet he encourages neither of them to make things out of nature or verisimility; for he adds immediately after,

But let the bounds of licenses be fix'd;
Not things of disagreeing natures mix'd:
Not sweet with sour, nor birds with serpents join'd:
Nor the fierce lion with the fearful hind.

The thoughts of a man endued with good sense, are not of kin to visionary madness; men in fevers are only capable of such dreams. Treat then the subjects of your pictures with all possible faithfulness, and use your licenses with a becoming boldness; provided they be ingenious, and not immoderate and extravagant.

† 83. "Take care that whatsoever makes nothing to your subject," &c. Nothing deadens so much the composition of a picture, as figures which are not appertaining to the subject; we may call them pleasantly enough, *figures to be let*.

† 87. "This part of painting so rarely met with," &c. That is to say, *invention*.

† 89. "Which was stolen by Prometheus," &c. The poets feign, that Prometheus formed out of clay so fair a statue, that Minerva one day, having long admired it, said to the workman, that if he thought there was any thing in heaven, which could add to its perfection, he might ask it of her; but he being ignorant of what might be most beautiful in the habitation of the gods, desired leave that he might be carried thither, and being there, to make his choice. The goddess bore him thither upon her shield, and so soon as he had perceived that all celestial things were animated with fire, he stole a parcel of it, which he carried down to earth, and applying it to the stomach of his statue, enlivened the whole body.

"That it happens not to every one to † 92. see Corinth," &c. This is an ancient proverb, which signifies, that every man has not the genius, nor the disposition, that is necessary for the sciences; neither yet a capacity fit for the undertaking of things which are great and difficult. Corinth was heretofore the centre of all arts, and the place whither they sent all those whom they would render capable of any thing. Cicero calls it the light of all Græcia.*

"It arrived at length to that height of † 95. perfection," &c. This was in the time of Alexander the Great, and lasted even to Augustus, under whose reign painting fell to great decay. But under the emperors Domitian, Nerva, and Trajan, it appeared in its primitive lustre; which lasted to the time of Phocas the emperor, when vices prevailing over the arts, and war being kindled through all Europe, and especially in Lombardy, (occasioned by the eruption of the Huns,) painting was totally extinguished. And if some few, in the succeeding ages, strained themselves to revive it, it was rather in finding out the most glaring, gaudy, and costly colours, than in imitating the harmonious simplicity of those illustrious painters who preceded them. At length, in the fourteenth century, some there were who began to set it again on foot. And it may truly be said, that about the end of the fifteenth age, and the beginning of our sixteenth, it appeared in much splendour, by means of many knowing men in all parts of Italy who were in perfect possession of it. Since those happy times, which were so fruitful of the noble arts, we have also had some knowing painters, but very few in number, because of the little inclination which sovereign princes have had for painting: but thanks to the zeal of our great monarch, and to the care of his first minister, Monsieur Colbert, we may shortly behold it more flourishing than ever.

"An attitude therefore must be chosen, † 103. according to their taste," &c. This is the second part of painting, which is called design, or drawing. As the ancients have sought as much as possible whatsoever contributes to the making of a perfect body; so they have diligently examined in what consists the beauty of good attitudes, as their works sufficiently inform us.

"The parts of it must be great," &c. † 104. Yet not so great as to exceed a just proportion. But he means, that in a noble attitude

* Art of Poetry.

* Pro lege Man.

most, rather than the less; for which reason, in another passage, he vehemently forbids the fore-shortenings, because they make the parts appear little, though of themselves they are great.

†104. "And large," &c. To avoid the dry manner, such as is most commonly the nature which Lucas van Leyden and Albert Durer have imitated.

†105. "Contrasted by contrary motions, the most noble parts foremost in sight, and each figure carefully poised on its own centre," &c. The motions are never natural, when the members are not equally balanced on their centre; and these members cannot be balanced on their centre in an equality of weight, but they must contrast each other. A man who dances on the rope, makes a manifest demonstration of this truth. The body is a weight balanced on its feet, as upon two pivots. And though one of the feet most commonly bears the weight, yet we see that the whole weight rests centrally upon it. In so much, that if, for example, one arm is stretched out, it must of necessity be, either that the other arm, or the leg, be cast backward, or the body somewhat bowed on the opposite side, so as to make an equilibrium, and be in a situation which is unforced. It may be, though seldom, if it be not in old men, that the feet bear equally; and for that time half the weight is equally distributed on each foot. You ought to make use of the same prudence, if one foot bears three parts in four of the burden, and that the other foot bears the remaining part. This, in general, is what may be said of the balance, and the libration of the body. In particular, there may many things be said which are very useful and curious, of which you may satisfy yourselves in Leonardo da Vinci. He has done wonderfully well on that subject; and one may truly say, that the ponderation is the best and soundest part of all his book of painting. It begins at the 181st chapter, and concludes at the 273d. I would also advise you to read Paulo Lomazzo, in his 6th book, chapter 4th, *Del moto del corpo humano*, that is, the motion of a human body. You will there find many things of great profit. For what concerns the contrast, I will only say, in general, that nothing gives so much grace and life to figures. See the 19th precept, and what I say upon it in the remarks.

†107. "The parts must be drawn with flowing, gliding outlines," &c. The reason of this proceeds from the action of the muscles, which are so many well-buckets: when one of them acts and draws, it is necessary that the other must obey; so that the muscles which act, drawing always towards their principal, and those which obey stretching in length, and on the side of their insertion, it must needs follow, that the parts must be designed in waves; but beware, lest in giving this form to the parts, you do not break the bones which sustain them, and which always must make them appear firm.

This maxim is not altogether so general, but that actions may be found, where the masses of the muscles are situate one over against another; but that is not very common. The outlines, which are in waves, give not only a grace to the parts, but also to the whole body, when it is only supported on one leg. As we see in the figures of Antinous, Meleager, the Venus of Medicis, that of the Vatican, the two others of Borghese, and that of Flora, of the goddess Vesta, the two Bacchus's of Borghese, and that of Ludovisio, and in fine, of the greatest number of the ancient figures, which are standing, and which always rest more upon one foot than the other. Besides, that the figures and their parts ought almost always to have a serpentine and flaming form naturally; these sorts of outlines have, I know not what of life and seeming motion in them, which very much resembles the activity of the flame, and of the serpent.

"According to the rules of anatomy," †112.
&c. This part is nothing known at present amongst our modern painters. I have shown the profit, and even the necessity of it, in the preface of a little epitome which I have made, and which Monsieur Torrebat has published. I know there are some who think this science a kind of monster, and believe it to be of no advantage, either because they are mean-spirited, or that they have not considered the want which they have of it, nor reflected, as they ought, on its importance; contenting themselves with a certain tract, to which they have been used. But certain it is, that whoever is capable of such a thought, will never be capable of becoming a great designer.

"In imitation of the Greek forms," &c. †113.
That is to say, according to the ancient statues, which for the most part come from Greece.

"Let there be a perfect relation be- †114.
twixt the parts and the whole," &c. or let them agree well together, which is the same thing. His meaning in this place is, to speak of the justness of proportions, and the harmony which they make with one another. Many famous authors have thoroughly treated this matter. Amongst others, Paulo Lomazzo, whose first book speaks of nothing else; but there are so many subdivisions, that a reader must have a good brain not to be turned with them. See those which our author has remarked in general

on the most beautiful statues of the ancients. I believe them to be so much the better, as they are more conformable to those which Vitruvius gives us in the first chapter of his third book; and which he tells us, that he learned from the artists themselves; because in the preface to his seventh book, he makes his boast to have had them from others, and particularly from architects and painters.

The Measures of a Human Body.

The ancients have commonly allowed eight heads to their figures, though some of them have but seven. But we ordinarily divide the figures into ten faces;* that is to say, from the crown of the head to the sole of the foot; in the following manner:

From the crown of the head to the forehead, is the third part of a face.

The face begins at the root of the lowest hairs which are upon the forehead, and ends at the bottom of the chin.

The face is divided into three proportionable parts; the first contains the forehead, the second the nose, and the third the mouth and the chin.

From the chin to the pit betwixt the collar-bones, are two lengths of a nose.

From the pit betwixt the collar-bones to the bottom of the breast, one face.

* From the bottom of the breasts to the navel, one face.

† From the navel to the genitories, one face.

From the genitories to the upper part of the knee, two faces.

The knee contains half a face.

From the lower part of the knee to the ankle, two faces.

From the ankle to the sole of the foot, half a face.

A man, when his arms are stretched out, is, from the longest finger of his right hand, to the longest of his left, as broad as he is long.

From one side of the breasts to the other, two faces.

The bone of the arm, called humerus, is the length of two faces from the shoulder to the elbow.

From the end of the elbow to the root of the little finger, the bone called cubitus, with part of the hand, contains two faces.

From the box of the shoulder-blade to the pit betwixt the collar-bones, one face.

If you would be satisfied in the measures of breadth, from the extremity of one finger to the other, so that this breadth should be equal to the length of the body, you must observe, that the bones of the elbows with the humerus, and of the humerus with the shoulder-blade, bear the proportion of half a face, when the arms are stretched out.

The sole of the foot is the sixth part of the figure.

The hand is the length of a face.

The thumb contains a nose.

The inside of the arm, from the place where the muscle disappears, which makes the breast, (called the pectoral muscle,) to the middle of the arm, four noses.

From the middle of the arm to the beginning of the hand, five noses.

The longest toe is a nose long.

The two utmost parts of the teats, and the pit betwixt the collar-bones of a woman, make an equilateral triangle.

For the breadth of the limbs, no precise measures can be given; because the measures themselves are changeable, according to the quality of the persons, and according to the movement of the muscles.

If you would know the proportions more particularly, you may see them in Paulo Lomazzo: it is good to read them, once at least, and to make remarks on them; every man according to his own judgment, and according to the occasion which he has for them.

"Though perspective cannot be called † 117. a perfect rule," &c. That is to say, purely of itself, without prudence and discretion. The greatest part of those who understand it, desiring to practise it too regularly, often make such things as shock the sight, though they are within the rules. If all those great painters, who have left us such fair platforms, had rigorously observed it in their figures, they had not wholly found their account in it. They had indeed made things more regularly true, but withal very unpleasing. There is great appearance, that the architects and statuaries of former times have not found it to their purpose always; nor have followed the geometrical part so exactly as perspective ordains. For he who would imitate the frontispiece of the Rotunda according to perspective, would be grossly deceived; since the columns which are at the extremities have more diameter than those which are in the middle. The cornice of the Palazzo Farnese, which makes so beautiful an effect below, when viewed more nearly, will be found not to have its just measures. In the pillar of Trajan, we see that the highest figures are greater than those below; and make an effect quite contrary to perspective, increasing according to the measure of their distance. I know there is a rule which teaches a way of making them in that manner, and which, though it is to be found in some books

* This depends on the age and quality of the persons. The Apollo and Venus of Medicis have more than ten faces.

† The Apollo has a nose more.

‡ The Apollo has half a nose more; and the upper half of the Venus de Medicis, is to the lower part of the belly, and not to the privy parts.

of perspective, yet notwithstanding is no rule of perspective; because it is never made use of, but only when we find it for our purpose: for if, for example, the figures which are at the top of Trajan's pillar were but as great as those which are at the bottom, they would not be for all that against perspective: and thus we may say, with more reason, that it is a rule of decorum in perspective, to ease the sight, and to render objects more agreeable. It is on this general observation, that we may establish in perspective the rules of decorum, or convenience, whensoever occasion shall offer. We may also see another example in the base of the Farnesian Hercules; which is not upon the level, but on an easy declivity on the advanced part, that the feet of the figure may not be hidden from the sight, to the end that it may appear more pleasing; which the noble authors of these things have done, not in contempt of geometry and perspective, but for the satisfaction of the eyes, which was the end they proposed to themselves in all their works.

We must therefore understand perspective as a science which is absolutely necessary, and which a painter must not want; yet without subjecting ourselves so wholly to it as to become slaves of it. We are to follow it when it leads us in a pleasing way, and shows us pleasing things; but for some time to forsake it, if it leads us through mire, or to a precipice. Endeavour after that which is aiding to your art, and convenient, but avoid whatsoever is repugnant to it, as the 59th rule teaches.

† 126. "Let every member be made for its own head," &c. That is to say, you ought not to set the head of a young man on the body of an old one; nor make a white hand for a withered body. Not to habit a Hercules in taffeta, nor an Apollo in coarse stuff. Queens, and persons of the first quality, whom you would make appear majestical, are not to be too negligently dressed, or *en dishabillée*, no more than old men; the nymphs are not to be overcharged with drapery. In fine, let all that which accompanies your figures, make them known for what effectively they are.

† 128. "Let the figures to which art cannot give a voice, imitate the mutes in their actions," &c. Mutes having no other way of speaking, or expressing their thoughts, but only by their gestures, and their actions, it is certain that they do it in a manner more expressive than those who have the use of speech; for which reason, the picture which is mute, ought to imitate them, so as to make itself understood.

† 129. "Let the principal figure of the subject," &c. It is one of the greatest blemishes of a picture, not to give knowledge, at the first sight, of the subject which it represents. And truly nothing is more perplexing, than to extinguish, as it were, the principal figure, by the opposition of some others, which present themselves to us at the first view, and which carry a greater lustre. An orator, who had undertaken to make a panegyric on Alexander the Great, and who had employed the strongest figures of his rhetoric in the praise of Bucephalus, would do quite the contrary to that which was expected from him; because it would be believed, that he rather took the horse for his subject, than the master. A painter is like an orator in this. He must dispose his matter in such sort, that all things may give place to his principal subject. And if the other figures, which accompany it, and are only as accessories there, take up the chief place, and make themselves most remarkable, either by the beauty of their colours, or by the splendour of the light which strikes upon them, they will catch the sight, they will stop it short, and not suffer it to go farther than themselves, till after some considerable space of time, to find out that which was not discerned at first. The principal figure in a picture is like a king among his courtiers, whom we ought to know at the first glance, and who ought to dim the lustre of all his attendants. Those painters who proceed otherwise, do just like those, who, in the relation of a story, engage themselves so foolishly in long digressions, that they are forced to conclude quite another way than they began.

"Let the parts be brought together, † 132. and the figures disposed in groups," &c. I cannot better compare a group of figures, than to a concert of voices, which, supporting themselves altogether by their different parts, make a harmony, which pleasingly fills the ears, and flatters them; but if you come to separate them, and that all the parts are equally heard as loud as one another, they will stun you to that degree, that you would fancy your ears were torn in pieces. It is the same of figures: if you so assemble them, that some of them sustain the others, and make them appear, and that altogether they make but one entire whole, then your eyes will be fully satisfied; but if, on the contrary, you divide them, your eyes will suffer by seeing them altogether dispersed, or each of them in particular. Altogether, because the visual rays are multiplied by the multiplicity of objects. Each of them in particular; because, if you fix your sight on one, those which are about it will strike you, and attract your eyes to them, which extremely pains them in this sort of separation and diversity of objects. The eye, for example, is satisfied with the sight of one single grape; and is distracted, if it carries itself at one view to look upon many several grapes, which lie scattered on a table. We must have the same regard for the members; they aggroup, and contrast each other in the same manner as the figures do. Few painters have observed this precept as they ought, which is a most solid foundation for the harmony of a picture.

† 137. "The figures in the groups ought not to have the same inflections of the body," &c. Take heed, in this contrast, to do nothing that is extravagant; and let your postures be always natural. The draperies, and all things that accompany the figures, may enter into the contrast with the members, and with the figures themselves; and this is what our poet means in these words of his verses, *cætera frangant*.

† 145. "One side of the picture must not be void, while the other is filled," &c. This sort of symmetry, when it appears not affected, fills the picture pleasingly, keeps it in a kind of balance, and infinitely delights the eyes, which thereby contemplate the work with more repose.

† 152. "As a play is seldom good, in which there are too many actors," &c. Annibal Caracci did not believe that a picture could be good, in which there were above twelve figures. It was Albano who told our author this, and from his mouth I had it. The reasons which he gave were, first, that he believed there ought not to be above three great groups of figures in any picture; and secondly, that silence and majesty were of necessity to be there, to render it beautiful; and neither the one nor the other could possibly be in a multitude and crowd of figures. But nevertheless, if you are constrained by the subject, (as, for example, if you painted the day of judgment, the massacre of the innocents, a battle, &c.) on such occasions, you are to dispose things by great masses of lights and shadows, and union of colours, without troubling yourself to finish every thing in particular, independently one of the other, as is usual with painters of a little genius, and whose souls are incapable of embracing a great design, or a great composition.

Æmilium circa ludum, faber imus et ungues
Exprimet, et molles imitabitur ære capillos;
Infelix operis summa: quia ponere totum
Nesciet.

The meanest sculptor in the Æmilian square,
Can imitate in brass the nails and hair;
Expert in trifles, and a cunning fool,
Able to express the parts, but not dispose the whole.

Says Horace in his "Art of Poetry."

† 162. "The extremities of the joints must be seldom hidden, and the extremities or end of the feet never," &c. These extremities of the joints are as it were the hafts, or handles of the members. For example, the shoulders, the elbows, the thighs, and the knees. And if a drapery should be found on these ends of the joints, it is the duty of science, and of decorum, to mark them by folds, but with great discretion, for what concerns the feet, though they should be hidden by some part of the drapery, nevertheless, if they are marked by folds, and their shape be distinguished, they are supposed to be seen. The word *never* is not here to be taken in the strictest sense; he means but this,—so rarely, that it may seem we should avoid all occasions of dispensing with the rule.

"The figures which are behind others, † 161. have neither grace nor vigour," &c. Raphael and Julio Romano have perfectly observed this maxim; and Raphael especially in his last works.

"Avoid also those lines and outlines † 169. which are equal, which make parallels," &c. He means principally to speak of the postures so ordered, that they make together those geometrical figures which he condemns.

"Be not so strictly tied to nature," &c. † 176. This precept is against two sorts of painters; first, against those who are so scrupulously tied to nature, that they can do nothing without her; who copy her, just as they believe they see her, without adding or retrenching any thing, though never so little, either for the nudities, or for the draperies. And secondly, against those who paint every thing by practice, without being able to subject themselves to retouch any thing, or to examine by the nature. These last, properly speaking, are the libertines of painting, as there are libertines of religion, who have no other law but the vehemence of their inclinations, which they are resolved not to overcome; and in the same manner the libertines of painting have no other model but a rhodomontado genius, and very irregular, which violently hurries them away. Though these two sorts of painters are both of them in vicious extremes, yet nevertheless the former sort seems to be the more supportable; because though they do not imitate nature, as she is accompanied by all her beauties and her graces, yet at least they imitate that nature which we know, and daily see. Instead of which, the others show us a wild or savage nature, which is not of our acquaintance, and which seems to be of a quite new creation.

"Whom you must have always present, † 178. as a witness to the truth," &c. This passage seems to be wonderfully well said. The nearer a picture approaches to the truth, the better it is; and though the painter, who is its author, be the first judge of the beauties which are in it, he is nevertheless obliged not to pronounce it till he has first consulted Nature, who is an irreproachable evidence, and who will frankly, but withal truly, tell you its defects and beauties, if you compare it with her work.

† 183. "And of all other things which discover to us the thoughts and inventions of the Grecians," &c. As good books, such as are Homer and Pausanias. The prints which we see of the antiquities may also extremely contribute to form our genius, and to give us great ideas; in the same manner as the writings of good authors are capable of forming a good style, in those who are desirous of writing well.

† 193. "If you have but one single figure to work upon," &c. The reason of this is, that there being nothing to attract the sight but this only figure, the visual rays will not be too much divided by the diversity of colours and draperies; but only take heed to put in nothing which shall appear too sharp, or too hard; and be mindful of the 41st precept, which says, that two extremities are never to touch each other, either in colour or in light; but that there must be a mean partaking of the one and of the other.

† 195. "Let the draperies be nobly spread upon the body; let the folds be large," &c. As Raphael practised, after he had forsaken the manner of Pietro Perugino, and principally in his latter works.

† 196. "And let them follow the order of the parts," &c. As the fairest pieces of antiquity will show us. And take heed that the folds do not only follow the order of the parts, but that they also mark the most considerable muscles; because that those figures, where the drapery and the naked part are seen both together, are much more graceful than the other.

† 200. "Without sitting too straight upon them," &c. Painters ought not to imitate the ancients in this circumstance. The ancient statuaries made their draperies of wet linen, on purpose to make them sit close and straight to the parts of their figures; for doing which they had great reason, and in following which the painters would be much in the wrong; and you shall see upon what grounds. Those great geniuses of antiquity, finding that it was impossible to imitate with marble the fineness of stuffs or garments, which is not to be discerned but by the colours, the reflexes, and more especially by the lights and shadows; finding it, I say, out of their power to dispose of those things, thought they could not do better, nor more prudentially, than to make use of such draperies, as hindered not from seeing, through their folds, the delicacy of the flesh, and the purity of the outlines; things which, truly speaking, they possessed in the last perfection, and which in all appearance were the subject of their chief study. But painters, on the contrary, who are to deceive the sight, quite otherwise than statuaries, are bound to imitate the different sorts of garments, such as they naturally seem; and such as colours, reflexes, lights, and shadows, (of all which they are masters,) can make them appear. Thus we see, that those who have made the nearest imitations of nature, have made use of such stuffs or garments which are familiar to our sight; and these they have imitated with so much art, that in beholding them we are pleased that they deceive us: such were Titian, Paul Veronese, Tintoret, Rubens, Van Dyck, and the rest of the good colourists, who have come nearest to the truth of nature. Instead of which, others, who have scrupulously tied themselves to the practice of the ancients, in their draperies, have made their works crude and dry; and by this means have found out the lamentable secret, how to make their figures harder than even the marble itself; as Andrea Mantegna, and Pietro Perugino have done; and Raphael also had much of that way in his first works, in which we behold many small foldings often repeated, which look like so many whipcords. It is true these repetitions are seen in the ancient statues, and they are very proper there; because they who made use of wet linen, and close draperies, to make their figures look more tender, reasonably foresaw, that the members would be too naked, if they left not more than two or three folds, such as those sorts of draperies afford them, and therefore have used those repetitions of many folds; yet in such a manner, that the figures are always soft and tender, and thereby seem opposite to the hardness of marble. Add to this, that in sculpture, it is almost impossible that a figure, clothed with coarse draperies, can make a good effect on all the sides; and that in painting, the draperies, of what kind soever they be, are of great advantage, either to unite the colours and the groups, or to give such a ground, as one would wish to unite, or to separate; or farther to produce such reflections as set off; or for filling void spaces; or, in short, for many other advantages, which help to deceive the sight, and which are noways necessary to sculptors, since their work is always of relievo.

Three things may be inferred from what I have said, concerning the rule of draperies. First, that the ancient sculptors had reason to clothe their figures as we see them. Secondly that painters ought to imitate them in the c of their folds, but not in their quality, nor in their number. Thirdly, that sculptors are obliged to follow them as much as they can, without desiring to imitate unprofitably, or improperly, the manner of the painters, by making many ample folds, which are insufferable hardnesses, and look more like a rock than a natural garment.—See the 211th remark, about the middle of it.

†203. "And if the parts be too much distant from each other," &c. It is with intent to hinder (as we have said in the rule of groups) the visual rays from being too much divided; and that the eyes may not suffer, by looking on so many objects, which are separated. Guido was very exact in this observation. See, in the text, the end of the rule which relates to draperies.

†204. "And as those limbs and members which are expressed by few and large muscles," &c. Raphael, in the beginning of his painting, has somewhat too much multiplied the folds; because, being with reason charmed with the graces of the ancients, he imitated their beauties somewhat too regularly; but having afterwards found, that this quantity of folds glittered too much upon the limbs, and took off that repose and silence, which in painting are so friendly to the eyes, he made use of a contrary conduct in the works which he painted afterwards, which was at that time when he began to understand the effect of lights, of groups, and the oppositions of the lights and shadows; so that he wholly changed his manner, (this was about eight years before his death,) and though he always gave a grace to whatsoever he painted, yet he made appear, in his latter works, a greatness, a majesty, and a harmony, quite other than what we see in his first manner: and this he did by lessening the number of his folds, making them more large, and more opposing them, and by making the masses of the lights and shadows greater, and more disentangled. Take the pains to examine these his different manners in the prints which we see of that great man.

†210. "As, supposing them to be magistrates, their draperies ought to be large," &c. Yet make not your draperies so large, that they may be big enough to clothe four or five figures, as some there are who follow that method. And take heed, that the foldings be natural, and so disposed, that the eye may be directed to discover the folds, from the beginning of them to the end. By magistrates he means all great and grave persons, and such as are advanced in age.

†211. "If ladies or damsels, light and soft," &c. By this name of ladies, maids, or damsels, he means all young persons, slender, finely shaped, airy, and delicate. Such as are Nymphs and Naiades, and Fountains. Angels are also comprehended under this head, whose drapery should be of pleasing colours, and resembling those which are seen in the heavens, and chiefly when they are suspended in the air. They are only such sorts of light habits as are subject to be ruffled by the winds, which can bear many folds; yet so, that they may be freed from any hardnesses. It is easy for every one to judge, that betwixt the draperies of magistrates, and those of young maids, there must be some mediocrity of folds, such as are most commonly seen and observed; as in the draperies of a Christ, of a Madonna, of a king, a queen, or a duchess, and of other persons of consideration and majesty; and those also who are of a middle age; with this distinction, that the habits must be made more or less rich, according to the dignity of the persons; and that cloth garments may be distinguished from those of silk, satin from velvets, brocard from embroidery, and that, in one word, the eye may be deceived by the truth, and the difference of the stuffs. Take notice, if you please, that the light and tender draperies having been only given to the female sex, the ancient sculptors have avoided, as much as they could, to clothe the figures of men, because they thought (as we have formerly said) that in sculpture garments could not be well imitated, and that great folds made a very bad effect. There are almost as many examples of this truth, as amongst the ancients there are statues of naked men. I will name only that of Laocoon, which, according to all probability, ought to have been clothed: And in effect, what likelihood can there be, that the son of a king, and the priest of Apollo, should appear naked in the actual ceremony of sacrifice? for the serpents passed from the Isle of Tenedos to the Trojan shore, and surprised Laocoon, and his sons, while they were sacrificing to Neptune on the sea-shore, as Virgil witnesses in the second of his Æneids. Notwithstanding which, the sculptors,* who were authors of this noble work, had well considered, that they could not give vestments suitable to the quality of the persons represented, without making as it were a heap of stones, whose mass would rather be like a rock, than those three admirable figures, which will ever be the admiration of all ages. And for this reason, of two inconveniences, they judged that of draperies to be greater than that which was against the truth itself.

This observation well confirms what I have said in the 200th remark. It seems to me, that

* Polydorus, Athenodorus, and Agesander, all Rhodians.

it deserves you should make some reflection on it; and to establish it the better in your mind, I will tell you, that Michael Angelo, following this maxim, has given the prophets which he painted in the chapel of the pope, such draperies, whose folds are large, and whose garments are coarse; instead of which, the Moses, which he has made in sculpture, is habited with a drapery much more close to the parts, and holding more of the ancients. Nevertheless, he is a prophet, as well as those in the chapel, a man of the same quality, and to whom Michael Angelo ought to have given the same draperies, if he had not been hindered by those very reasons which have been given you.

†215. "The marks or ensigns of virtues," &c. That is, to say, of the sciences and arts. The Italians call a man a *virtuoso*, who loves the noble arts, and is a critic in them. And amongst our French painters, the word *vertueux* is understood in the same signification.

†217. "But let not the work be too much enriched with gold or jewels," &c. Clemens Alexandrinus relates,* "That Apelles having seen a Helena, which a young scholar of his had made, and adorned with a great quantity of golden ornaments and jewels, said to him, My good friend, though thou couldst not make her beautiful, at least thou hast made her rich." Besides that these glittering things in painting, as precious stones prodigally strewed over the habits, are destructive to each other, because they draw the sight to several places at the same time, and hinder round bodies from turning, and making their due effect; it is the very quantity which often makes us judge that they are false. And besides, it is to be presumed, that precious things are always rare. Corinna, that learned Theban lady, reproached Pindar, whom she had five times overcome in poetry, that he scattered through all his works the flowers of Parnassus too prodigally: saying to him, "That men sowed with the hand, and not with the sack;"† for which reason, a painter ought to adorn his vestments with great discretion. And precious stones look exceedingly well, when they are set in those places which we would make to come out of the picture; as for example, on a shoulder, or an arm, to tie some drapery, which of itself is of no strong colouring. They do also perfectly well with white, and other light colours, which are used in bringing the parts or bodies forward; because jewels make a show, and glitter through the opposition of the great lights, in the deep brown, which meet together.

"It is very expedient, to make a model of †220 those things which we have not in our sight, and whose nature is difficult to be retained in the memory," &c. As, for example, the groups of many figures, the postures difficult to be long kept, the figures in the air, in cielings, or much raised above the sight; and even of animals, which are not easily to be disposed.

By this rule we plainly see, how necessary it is for a painter to know how to model, and to have many models of soft wax. Paul Veronese had so good store of them, with so great a quantity of different sorts, that he would paint a whole historical composition on a perspective plan, how great and how diversified soever it were. Tintoret practised the same; and Michael Angelo (as Gioyan. Bapt. Armenini relates) made use of it for all the figures of his Day of Judgment. It is not that I would advise any one, who would make any very considerable work, to finish after these sorts of models; but they will be of vast use and advantage to see the masses of great lights and great shadows, and the effect of the whole together. For what remains, you are to have a layman* almost as big as the life, for every figure in particular, besides the natural figure before you, on which you must also look, and call it for a witness, which must first confirm the thing to you, and afterwards to the spectators, as it is in reality.

You may make use of these models with delight, if you set them on a perspective plan, which will be in the manner of a table made on purpose. You may either raise or let it down, according to your convenience; and if you look on your figures, through a hole, so contrived that it may be moved up and down, it will serve you for a point of sight, and a point of distance when you have once fixed it.

The same hole will farther serve you, to set your figures in the ceiling, and disposed upon a grate of iron wire, or supported in the air, by little strings raised at discretion, or by both ways together.

You may join to your figures what you see fitting, provided that the whole be proportioned to them; and, in short, what you yourself may judge to be of no greater bigness than theirs. Thus, in whatsoever you do, there will be more of truth seen, your work itself will give you infinite delight, and you will avoid many doubts and difficulties, which often hinder you; and chiefly for what relates to lineal perspective, which you will there infallibly find, provided that you remember to proportion all things to the greatness of your figures, and especially the points of

* Lib. ii. Pædag. cap 12. † Plutarch.

* A figure of wood, or cork, turning upon joints

sight and of distance; but for what belongs to aerial perspective, that not being found, the judgment must supply it. Tintoret (as Ridolphi tells us in his life) had made chambers of board and pasteboard, proportioned to his models, with doors and windows, through which he distributed on his figures artificial lights, as much as he thought reasonable, and often passed some part of the night, to consider and observe the effect of his compositions. His models were two feet high.

†221. "We are to consider the places where we lay the scene of the picture," &c. This is what Monsieur de Chambray calls, to do things according to *decorum.* See what he says of it, in the interpretation of that word, in his book of the Perfection of Painting. It is not sufficient, that in the picture there be nothing found which is contrary to the place where the action which is represented passes; but we ought, besides, to mark out the place, and make it known to the spectator by some particular address, that his mind may not be put to the pains of discovering it; as whether it be Italy, or Spain, or Greece, or France; whether it be near the sea-shore, or the banks of some river; whether it be the Rhine, or the Loire; the Po, or the Tyber; and so of other things, if they are essential to the history. "Nealces, a man of wit, and an ingenious painter," as Pliny tells us,* "being to paint a naval fight betwixt the Egyptians and the Persians, and being willing to make it known that the battle was given upon the Nile, whose waters are of the same colour with the sea, drew an ass drinking on the banks of the river, and a crocodile endeavouring to surprise him."

†222. "Let a nobleness and grace," &c. It is difficult enough to say what this grace of painting is; it is to be conceived and understood much more easily than to be explained by words. It proceeds from the illuminations of an excellent mind, (not to be acquired,) by which we give a certain turn to things, which makes them pleasing. A figure may be designed with all its proportions, and have all its parts regular, which, notwithstanding all this, shall not be pleasing, if all those parts are not put together in a certain manner, which attracts the eye to them, and holds it fixed upon them; for which reason there is a difference to be made betwixt grace and beauty. And it seems that Ovid had a mind to distinguish them, when he said, speaking of Venus,

Multaque cum forma gratia mixta fuit.

A matchless grace was with her beauty mix'd.

* Lib. xxv. 12.

And Suetonius, speaking of Nero, says, he was rather beautiful than graceful: *Vultu pulchro, magis quam venusto.* How many fair women do we see, who please us much less than others who have not such beautiful features? It is by this grace that Raphael has made himself the most renowned of all the Italians, as Apelles by the same means carried it above all the Greeks.

"This is that in which the greatest †223. difficulty consists," &c. For two reasons; first, because great study is to be made, as well upon the ancient beauties and noble pictures, as upon nature itself; and, secondly, because that part depends entirely on the genius, and seems to be purely the gift of heaven, which we have received at our birth: upon which account our author adds, "Undoubtedly we see but few whom in this particular Jupiter has regarded with a gracious eye; so that it belongs only to those elevated souls, who partake somewhat of divinity, to work such mighty wonders. Though they, who have not altogether received from heaven this precious gift, cannot acquire it without great labour; nevertheless, it is needful, in my opinion, that both the one and the other should perfectly learn the character of every passion.

All the actions of the sensitive appetite are in painting called passions, because the soul is agitated by them, and because the body suffers through them, and is sensibly altered. They are those divers agitations and different motions of the body in general, and of every one of its parts in particular, that our excellent painter ought to understand; on which he ought to make his study, and to form to himself a perfect idea of them. But it will be proper for us to know, in the first place, that the philosophers admit eleven—love, hatred, desire, shunning, joy, sadness, hope, despair, boldness, fear, and anger. The painters have multiplied them not only by their different degrees, but also by their different species; for they will make, for example, six persons in the same degree of fear, who shall express that passion all of them differently. And it is that diversity of species which distinguishes those painters who are able artists, from those whom we may call mannerists, and who repeat five or six times over in the same picture the same airs of a head. There are a vast number of other passions, which are as the branches of those which we have named; we might, for example, under the notion of love, comprehend grace, gentleness, civility, caresses, embraces, kisses, tranquillity, sweetness, &c.; and without examining whether all these things which painters comprise under the name of passions, can be reduced to those of the philosophers, I am of opinion, that every one may use them at his pleasure, and that he may study them after his own manner; the name makes nothing. One may even make passions of majesty, fierceness, dissatisfaction, care, avarice, slothfulness, envy, and many other things like these. These passions (as I have said) ought to be learned from the life itself, or to be studied on the ancient statues, and excellent pictures: we ought to see, for example, all things which belong to sadness, or serve to express it; to design them carefully, and to imprint them in our memories, after such a manner, as we may distinctly understand seven or eight kinds of them more or less, and immediately after draw them upon paper, without any other original than the image which we have conceived of them. We must be perfect masters of them, but above all, we must make sure of possessing them thoroughly. We are to know, that it is such or such a stroke, or such a shadow, stronger or weaker, which makes such or such a passion, in this or that degree. And thus if any one should ask you, what makes, in painting, the majesty of a king, the gravity of a hero, the love of a Christ, the grief of a Madonna, the hope of the good thief, the despair of the bad one, the grace and beauty of Venus, and, in fine, the character of any passion whatsoever; you may answer positively, on the spot, and with assurance, that it is such a posture, or such lines in the parts of the face, formed of such or such a passion, or even the one and the other both together; for the parts of the body, separately, make known the passions of the soul, or else conjointly one with the other. But of all the parts, the head is that which gives the most of life and the most of grace to the passion, and which alone contributes more to it than all the rest together. The others separately can only express some certain passions, but the head expresses all of them. Nevertheless, there are some which are more particular to it; as, for example, humility, which it expresses by the stooping or bending of the head; arrogance, when it is lifted, or, as we say, tossed up; languishment, when we hang it on one side, or lean it upon one shoulder; obstinacy, (or, as the French call it, *opiniâtreté*,) with a certain stubborn, unruly, barbarous humour, when it is held upright, stiff, and poised betwixt the shoulders. And of the rest, there are many marks, more easily conceived than they can be expressed, as bashfulness, admiration, indignation, and doubt. It is by the head that we make known more visibly our supplications, our threatenings, our mildness, our haughtiness, our love, our hatred, our joy, our sadness, our humility; in fine, it is enough to see the face, and to understand the mind at half a word. Blushing and paleness speak to us, as also the mixture of them both.

The parts of the face do all of them contribute to expose the thoughts of our hearts; but above the rest, the eyes, which are as it were the two windows, through which the soul looks out and shows itself. The passions which they more particularly express, are pleasure, languishment, disdain, severity, sweetness, admiration, and anger. Joy and sadness may bear their parts, if they did not more especially proceed from the eyebrows and the mouth. And the two parts last named agree more particularly in the expression of those two passions; nevertheless, if you join the eyes as a third, you will have the product of a wonderful harmony for all the passions of the soul.

The nose has no passion which is particular to it; it only lends its assistance to the other before named, by the stretching of the nostrils, which is as much marked in joy as it is in sadness. And yet it seems, that scorn makes us wrinkle up the nose, and stretch the nostrils also, at the same time drawing up the upper lip to the place which is near the corners of the mouth. The ancients made the nose the seat of derision; *eum subdolæ irrisioni, di caverunt*, says Pliny; that is, they dedicated the nose to a cunning sort of mockery. We read in the 3d satire of Persius,

> Disce, sed ira cadat naso, rugosaque sanna

Learn, but let your anger fall from your nose, and the sneering wrinkles be dismounted. And Philostratus, in the picture of Pan, whom the Nymphs had bound, and scornfully insulted over, says of that god, "That, before this, he was accustomed to sleep with a peaceable nose, softening in his slumbers the wrinkles of it, and the anger which commonly mounted to that part; but now his nostrils were widened to the last degree of fury." For my own part, I should rather believe that the nose was the seat of wrath in beasts than in mankind; and that it was unbecoming of any god but only Pan, who had very much of the beast in him, to wrinkle up his nose in anger, like other animals. The moving of the lips ought to be but moderate, if it be in conversation, because we speak much more by the tongue than by the lips; and if you make the mouth very open, it is only when you are to express the violence of passion, and more properly of anger.

For what concerns the hands, they are the servants of the head, they are his weapons and his auxiliaries; without them the action is weak, languishing, and half dead. Their motions which are almost infinite, make innumerable expressions. Is it not by them, that we desire, that we hope, that we promise, that we call towards us, and that we reject? Besides, they are the instruments of our threats, of our petitions, of the horror which we show for things, and of the praises which we give them. By them we fear, we ask questions, we approve, and we refuse, we show our joy and our sadness, our doubts and our lamentations, our concernments of pity, and our admirations. In short, it may be said, that they are the language of the dumb, that they contribute not a little to the speaking of the universal tongue common to all the world, which is that of painting.

Now, to tell you how these parts are to be disposed, so as to express the different passions, is impossible; no precise rules can be given of it, both because the task itself is infinite, and also because every one is left to the conduct of his own genius, and to the fruit of his former studies; only remember to be careful, that all the actions of your figures must be natural. "It seems to me," says Quinctilian, speaking of the passions, "that this part, which is so noble, and so great, is not altogether inaccessible, and that an easy way may be found to it; it is to consider nature, and to copy her; for the spectators are satisfied, when in artificial things they can discern that nature, which they are accustomed to behold." This passage of Quinctilian is perfectly explained by the words of an excellent master, which our author proposes to us for a rule. They are these which follow: "That the studied motions of the soul are never so natural, as those which we see in the transport of a true passion." These motions will better be expressed, and be much more natural, if we enter into the same thoughts, become of the same piece, and imagine ourselves to be in the same circumstances with those whom we would represent. "For nature," says Horace, in his Art of Poetry, "disposes the inside of mankind to all sorts of fortunes; sometimes she makes us contented, sometimes she drives us into choler, and sometimes she so oppresses us with grief, that she seems to tread us down, and plunge us into mortal anxieties; and on all these occasions, she drives outward the motions of the heart by the tongue, which is her interpreter." Now, instead of the tongue, let the painter say by the actions, which are her interpreters. "What means have we," says Quinctilian, "to give a colour to a thing, if we have not the same colour? It is necessary that we ourselves should first be touched with a passion, before we endeavour to move others with it. And how," continues he, "can we be touched, since the passions are not in our power? This is the way, in my opinion: we must form to ourselves the visions and images of absent things, as if they were in reality before our eyes; and he who conceives these images with the greatest strength of imagination, shall possess that part of the passions with the most advantage, and the greatest ease." But we must take care, (as I have already said,) that in these visions the motions may be natural; for there are some who imagine they have given abundance of light to their figures, when they have made them do violent and extravagant actions; which we may more reasonably call the convulsions, or contortions of the body, than the passions of the mind; and by this means they often put themselves to much pains, to find a strong passion, where no passion is required. Add to all that I have said concerning the passions, that we are to have a very serious regard to the quality of the persons who are to be expressed in passions. The joy of a king ought not to resemble that of a serving-man, and the fierceness of a private soldier must not be like that of an officer. In these differences consists all the fineness and delicacy of the passions. Paulo Lomazzo has written at large on every passion in particular, in his second book; but beware you dwell not too long upon it, and endeavour not to force your genius.

"Some relics of it took sanctuary under ground," &c. † 247. All the ancient painting that was in Italy perished in the invasion of the Huns and Goths, excepting those works which were hidden under ground, or there painted; which by reason they had not been much exposed to view, were preserved from the insolence of those barbarians.

"The chromatic part, or colouring," † 256. &c. The third and last part of painting, is called the chromatic, or colouring. Its object is colour; for which reason lights and shadows are therein also comprehended, which are nothing else but white and brown, (or dark,) and by consequence have their place among the colours. Philostratus says, in his life of Apollonius, "That that may be truly called painting, which is made only with two colours, provided the lights and shadows be observed in it; for there we behold the true resemblance of things with their beauties; we also see the passions, though without other colours; so much of life may be also expressed in it, that we may perceive even the very blood; the colour of the hair, and of the beard, are likewise to be discerned; and we can distinguish, without confusion, the fair from the black, and the young from the old, the differences betwixt the white and the flaxen hair; we distinguish with ease betwixt the

Moors and the Indians, not only by the Camus noses of the blacks, their woolly hair, and their high jaws, but also by that black colour which is natural to them." We may add to what Philostratus has said, that with two colours only, (the light and the dark,) there is no sort of stuff, or habit, but may be imitated. We say, then, that the colouring makes its observations on the masses or bodies of the colours, accompanied with lights and shadows, more or less evident by degrees of diminution, according to the accidents. First, of a luminous body; as, for example, the sun, or a torch. Secondly, of a diaphanous or transparent body, which is betwixt us and the object, as the air, either pure or thick, or a red glass, &c. Thirdly, of a solid body illuminated, as a statue of white marble, a green tree, a black horse, &c. Fourthly, from his part, who regards the body illuminated, as beholding it either near, or at a distance, directly in a right angle, or aside in an obtuse angle, from the top to the bottom, or from the bottom to the top. This part, in the knowledge which it has of the virtue of colours, and the friendship which they have with each other, and also their antipathies, comprehends the strength, the relievo, the briskness, and the delicacy, which are observed in good pictures. The management of colours, and the labour, depend also on this last part.

† 263. "Her sister," &c. That is to say, the design or drawing, which is the second part of painting; which, consisting only of lines, stands altogether in need of the colouring to appear. It is for this reason, that our author calls this part her sister's procurer, that is, the colouring shows us the design, and makes us fall in love with it.

† 267. "The light produces all kinds of colours," &c. Here are three theorems successively following, which our author proposes to us, that from thence we may draw some conclusions. You may likewise find others, which are in the nature of so many propositions, to which we ought to agree, that from thence we may draw the precepts contained in the following part of this treatise: they are all founded on the sense of seeing.

† 280. "Which should be the most," &c. See the remark of number 152.

† 283. "That light bodies may have a sufficient mass, or breadth of shadow, to sustain them," &c. That is properly to say, that after the great lights, there must be great shadows, which we call reposes; because, in reality, the sight would be tired, if it were attracted by a continuity of glittering objects. The lights may serve for a repose to the darks, and the darks to the lights. I have said in another place, that a group of figures ought to be considered as a choir of music, in which the basses support the trebles, and make them to be heard with greater pleasure. These reposes are made two several ways, one of which is natural, the other artificial. The natural is made by an extent of lights or of shadows, which naturally and necessarily follow solid bodies; or the masses of solid bodies aggrouped, when the light strikes upon them. And the artificial consists in the bodies of colours, which the painter gives to certain things, such as pleases him; and composes them in such a manner, that they do no injury to the objects which are near them. A drapery, for example, which is made yellow, or red, on some certain place, in another place may be brown, and will be more suitable to it, to produce the effect required. We are to take occasion, as much as possibly we can, to make use of the first manner, and to find the repose of which we speak, by the light and by the shadow which naturally accompany solid bodies. But since the subjects on which we work are not always favourable to dispose the bodies as we desire, a painter in such a case may take his advantage by the bodies of colours, and put into such places as ought to be darkened, draperies, or other things, which we may suppose to be naturally brown and sullied, which will produce the same effect, and give him the same reposes as the shadows would do, which could not be caused by the disposition of the objects.

Thus an understanding painter will make his advantages both of the one manner and the other. And if he makes a design to be graved, he is to remember, that the gravers dispose not their colours as the painters do; and that, by consequence, he must take occasion to find the reason of his design in the natural shadows of the figures, which he has disposed to cause the effect. Rubens has given us a full information of this in those prints of his which he caused to be engraved; and I believe that nothing was ever seen more beautiful in that kind; the whole knowledge of groups, of the lights and shadows, and of those masses which Titian calls a bunch of grapes, is there exposed so clearly to the sight, that the view of those prints, and the careful observation of them, might very much contribute to the forming of an able painter. The best and fairest of them are graven by Vosterman, Pontius, and Bolsvert, all of them admirable gravers, whose works Rubens himself took care to oversee; and which, without doubt, you will find to be excellent, if you examine them. But expect not there the elegance of design, nor the correctness of the outlines.

It is not but the gravers can, and ought to imitate the bodies of the colours by the degrees of the lights and shadows, as much as they shall judge that this imitation may produce a good effect. On the contrary, it is impossible, in my opinion, to give much strength to what they grave, after the works of the school of Venice, and of all those who have had the knowledge of colours, and of the contrast of the lights and shadows, without imitating in some sort the colour of the objects, according to the relation which they have to the degrees of white and black. We see certain prints of good gravers different in their kinds, where these things are observed, and which have a wonderful strength. And there appears in public, of late years, a gallery of archduke Leopold, which, though very ill graven, yet shows some part of the beauty of its originals, because the gravers who have executed it, though otherwise they were sufficiently ignorant, have observed, in almost the greatest parts of their prints, the bodies of colours, in the relation which they have to the degrees of the lights and shadows. I could wish the gravers would make some reflection upon this whole remark: it is of wonderful consequence to them; for when they have attained to the knowledge of these reposes, they will easily resolve those difficulties which many times perplex them; and then chiefly, when they are to engrave after a picture, where neither the lights and shadows, nor the bodies of the colours, are skilfully observed, though in its other parts the picture may be well performed.

† 286. "As in a convex mirror the collected rays strike stronger," &c. A convex mirror alters the objects which are in the middle, so that it seems to make them come out from the superficies. The painter must do in the same manner, in respect of the lights and shadows of his figures, to give them more relievo and more strength.

† 290. "While the goings off are more and more broken and faint, as they approach to the extremities," &c. It is the duty of a painter, even in this also, to imitate the convex mirror, and to place nothing which glares either in colour or in light, at the borders of his picture: for which there are two reasons; the first is, that the eye at the first view directs itself to the midst of the object which is presented to it, and by consequence must there necessarily find the principal object, in order to its satisfaction; and the other reason is, that the sides or borders being overcharged with a strong and glittering work, attract the eyes thither, which are in a kind of pain not to behold a continuity of that work, which is on the sudden interrupted by the borders of the picture; instead of which, the borders being lightened, and eased of so much work, the eye continues fixed on the centre of the picture, and beholds it with greater pleasure. It is for the same reason, that, in a great composition of figures, those which, coming most forward, are cut off by the bottom of the picture, will always make an ill effect.

"A bunch of grapes," &c. It is sufficiently manifest, that Titian, by this judicious and familiar comparison, means, that a painter ought to collect the objects, and to dispose them in such a manner as to compose one whole; the several contiguous parts of which may be enlightened, many shadowed, and others of broken colours to be in the turnings; as on a bunch of grapes, many grapes, which are the parts of it, are in the light, many in the shadow, and the rest faintly coloured to make them go farther back. Titian once told Tintoret, that in his greatest works, a bunch of grapes had been his principal rule, and his surest guide. † 329.

"Pure, or unmixed white, either draws an object nearer, or carries it off to farther distance. It draws it nearer with black, and throws it backward without it," &c. All agree, that white can subsist on the fore-ground of the picture, and there be used without mixture; the question therefore is to know, if it can equally subsist, and be placed in the same manner, upon that which is backward, the light being universal, and the figures supposed in a champaigne and open field. † 330.

Our author concludes affirmatively; and the reason on which he establishes his rule is this; that there being nothing which partakes more of the light than whiteness, and the light being capable of subsisting well in remoteness, or at a long distance, as we daily see in the rising and setting of the sun, it follows, that white may subsist in the same manner. In painting, the light and a white colour are but one and the same thing. Add to this, that we have no colour which more resembles the air than white, and by consequence no colour which is lighter; from whence it comes, that we commonly say the air is heavy, when we see the heavens covered with black clouds, or when a thick fog takes from us that clearness which makes the lightness or serenity of the air. Titian, Tintoret, Paul Veronese, and all those who best understood lights, have observed it in this manner, and no man can go against this precept, at least without renouncing any skill in landscape, which is an undoubted confirmation of this truth. And we see, that all the great masters of landscape have followed Titian in this, who has always employed brown and earthy colours upon the fore-part, and has reserved his greatest lights for remotenesses, and the back parts of his landscapes.

It may be objected against this opinion, that white cannot maintain itself in remotenesses, because it is ordinarily used to bring the objects nearer on the advanced part. It is true that so it is used, and that to very good purpose, to render the objects more sensible, by the opposition of the dark, which must accompany it, and which retains it, as it were, by force, whether the dark serves it for a ground, or whether it be combined to it. For example, if you would make a white horse on the fore-ground of your picture, it is of absolute necessity, that the ground must be of a mixed brown, and large enough, or that the furniture must be of very sensible colours; or lastly, that some figure must be set upon it, whose shadows and the colour may bring it forward.

But it seems, say you, that blue is the most flying or transient colour, because the heavens and mountains, which are at the greatest distance, are of that colour. It is very true that blue is one of the lightest and sweetest colours; but it is also true, that it possesses these qualities so much the more, because the white is mingled in it, as the example of the distances demonstrate to us. But if the light of your picture be not universal, and that you suppose your figures in a chamber, then recall to your memory that theorem which tells you, that the nearer a body is to the light, and the more directly it is opposed to us, so much the more it is enlightened, because the light grows languishing the farther it removes from its original.

You may also extinguish your white, if you suppose the air to be somewhat thicker, and if you foresee that this supposition will make a good effect in the economy of the whole work; but let not this proceed so far, as to make your figures so brown, that they may seem as if were in a filthy fog, or that they may appear to be part of the ground. See the following remark.

† 332. "But as for pure black, there is nothing that brings the object nearer to the sight," &c. Because black is the heaviest of all colours, the most earthy, and the most sensible. This is clearly understood by the qualities of white, which is opposed to it, and which is, as we have said, the lightest of all colours. There are few who are not of this opinion; and yet I have known some, who have told me, that the black being on the advanced part, makes nothing but holes. To this there is little else to be answered, but that black always makes a good effect, being set forward, provided it be placed there with prudence. You are therefore so to dispose the bodies of your pictures which you intend to be on the fore-ground, that those sorts of holes may not be perceived, and that the blacks may be there by masses, and insensibly confused. See the 47th rule.

That which gives the relievo to a bowl, (may some say to me,) is the quick light, or the white, which appears to be on the side which is nearest to us, and the black, by consequence, distances the object. We are here to beware, not to confound the turnings with the distances: the question is only in respect of bodies, which are separated by some distance of a backward position; and not of round bodies, which are of the same continuity: the brown, which is mingled in the turnings of the bowl, makes them go off rather in confounding them (as we may say) than in blackening them. And do you not see, that the reflects are an artifice of the painter, to make the turnings seem more light, and that by this means the greatest blackness remains towards the middle of the bowl, to sustain the white, and make it deceive us with more pleasure?

This rule of white and black is of so great consequence, that unless it be exactly practised, it is impossible for a picture to make any great effect, that the masses can be disentangled, and the different distances may be observed at the first glance of the eye, without trouble.

It may be inferred from this precept, that the masses of other colours will be so much the more sensible, and approach so much the nearer to the sight, the more brown they bear; provided this be amongst other colours which are of the same species. For example, a yellow brown shall draw nearer to the sight than another which is less yellow. I said, provided it be amongst other colours which are of the same species; because there are simple colours, which naturally are strong and sensible, though they are clear as vermilion; there are others also, which, notwithstanding that they are brown, yet cease not to be soft and faint, as the blue of ultramarine. The effect of a picture comes not only therefore from the lights and shadows, but also from the nature of the colours. I thought it was not from the purpose in this place to give you the qualities of those colours which are most in use, and which are called capital, because they serve to make the composition of all the rest, whose number is almost infinite.

Red ochre is one of the most heavy colours.

Yellow ochre is not so heavy, because it is clearer.

And the masticot is very light, because it is a very clear yellow, and very near to white.

Ultramarine, or azure, is very light, and a very sweet colour.

Vermilion is wholly opposite to ultramarine.

Lake is a middle colour betwixt ultramarine and vermilion, yet it is rather more sweet than harsh.

Brown red is one of the most earthy and most sensible colours.

Pink is in its nature an indifferent colour, that is very susceptible of the other colours by the mixture: if you mix brown red with it, you will make it a very earthy colour; but, on the contrary, if you join it with white or blue, you shall have one of the most faint and tender colours.

Terra verte (or green earth) is light; it is a mean betwixt yellow ochre and ultramarine.

Umbre is very sensible and earthy; there is nothing but pure black which can dispute with it.

Of all blacks, that is the most earthy which is most remote from blue. According to the principle which we have established of white and black, you will make every one of these colours before named more earthy and more heavy, the more black you mingle with them; and they will be lighter, the more white you join with them.

For what concerns broken or compound colours, we are to make a judgment of their strength by the force of those colours which compose them. All who have thoroughly understood the agreement of colours, have not employed them wholly pure and simple in their draperies, unless in some figure upon the fore-ground of the picture; but they have used broken and compound colours, of which they made a harmony for the eyes, by mixing those which have some kind of sympathy with each other, to make a whole, which has an union with the colours which are neighbouring to it. The painter who perfectly understands the force and power of his colours, will use them most suitably to his present purpose, and according to his own discretion.

† 355. "But let this be done relatively," &c. One body must make another body fly off, in such a manner that itself may be chased by those bodies which are advanced before it. "We are to take care, and use great attention," says Quinctilian, "not only of one separate thing, but of many which follow each other, and, by a certain relation which they have with each other, are as it were continued. In the same manner as if, in a straight street, we cast our eyes from one end of it to the other, we discover at once those different things which are presented to the sight, so that we not only see the last, but whatsoever is relating to the last.

† 361. "Let two contrary extremities never touch each other," &c. The sense of seeing has this in common with all the rest of the senses, that it abhors the contrary extremities. And in the same manner as our hands, when they are very cold, feel a grievous pain when on the sudden we hold them near the fire: so the eyes, which find an extreme white next to an extreme black, or a fair cool azure next to a hot vermilion, cannot behold these extremities without pain, though they are always attracted by the glaring of two contraries.

This rule obliges us to know those colours which have a friendship with each other, and those which are incompatible; which we may easily discover in mixing together those colours of which we would make trial.

And if by this mixture they make a gracious and sweet colour, which is pleasing to the sight, it is a sign that there is an union and a sympathy betwixt them; but if, on the contrary, that colour which is produced by the mixture of the two be harsh to the sight, we are to conclude, that there is a contrariety and antipathy betwixt these two colours. Green, for example, is a pleasing colour, which may come from a blue and a yellow mixed together; and, by consequence, blue and yellow are two colours which sympathize: and, on the contrary, the mixture of blue with vermilion produces a sharp, harsh, and unpleasant colour; conclude then, that blue and vermilion are of a contrary nature. And the same may be said of other colours, of which you may make experiment, and clear that matter once for all. (See the conclusion of the 332d remark, where I have taken occasion to speak of the force and quality of every capital colour.) Yet you may neglect this precept, when your piece consists but of one or two figures, and when amongst a great number you would make some one figure more remarkable than the rest; one, I say, which is one of the most considerable of the subject, and which otherwise you cannot distinguish from the rest. Titian, in his Triumph of Bacchus, having placed Ariadne on one of the borders of the picture, and not being able (for that reason) to make her remarkable by the brightness of light, which he was to keep in the middle of his picture, gave her a scarf of a vermilion colour, upon a blue drapery, as well to loosen her from his ground, which was a blue sea, as because she is one of the principal figures of his subject, upon which he desired to attract the eye. Paul Veronese, in his Marriage of Cana, because Christ, who is the principal figure of the subject, is carried somewhat into the depth of the picture, and that he could not make him distinguishable by the strength of the lights and shadows, has clothed him with vermilion and blue, thereby to conduct the sight to that figure.

The hostile colours may be so much the more allied to each other, the more you mix them with other colours which mutually sympathize, and which agree with those colours which you desire to reconcile.

† 365. "It is labour in vain to paint a high-noon," &c. He said in another place, "endeavour after that which aids your art, and is suitable to it, and shun whatsoever is repugnant:" it is the 59th precept. If the painter would arrive to the end he has proposed, which is to deceive the sight, he must make choice of such a nature as agrees with the weakness of his colours; because his colours cannot accommodate themselves to every sort of nature. This rule is particularly to be observed, and well considered, by those who paint landscapes.

† 382. "Let the field or ground of the picture," &c. The reason of it is, that we are to avoid the meeting of those colours which have an antipathy to each other, because they offend the sight; so that this rule is proved sufficiently by the 41st, which tells us, that two contrary extremities are never to touch each other, whether it be in colour or in light; but that there ought to be a mean betwixt them, which partakes of both.

† 312. "Let your colours be lively, and yet not look (according to the painters' proverb) as if they had been rubbed or sprinkled with meal," &c. *Donner dans la farine*, is a phrase amongst painters, which perfectly expresses what it means; which is to paint with clear or bright colours and dull colours together; for being so mingled, they give no more life to the figures, than if they had been rubbed with meal. They who make their flesh-colours very white, and their shadows gray, or inclining to green, fall into this inconvenience. Red colours in the shadows of the most delicate or finest flesh, contribute wonderfully to make them lively, shining, and natural; but they are to be used with the same discretion, that Titian, Paul Veronese, Rubens, and Van Dyck have taught us, by their example.

To preserve the colours fresh, we must paint by putting in more colours, and not by rubbing them in after they are once laid; and (if it could be done) they should be laid just in their proper places, and not be any more touched, when they are once so placed; because the freshness of the colours is tarnished and lost, by vexing them with the continual drudgery of daubing.

All they who have coloured well have had yet another maxim to maintain their colours fresh and flourishing, which was to make use of white grounds upon which they painted, and oftentimes at the first stroke, without retouching any thing, and without employing new colours. Rubens always used this way; and I have seen pictures from the hand of that great person, painted up at once, which were of a wonderful vivacity.

The reason why they made use of those kinds of grounds is, because white as well preserves a brightness under the transparency of colours, which hinders the air from altering the whiteness of the ground, as that it likewise repairs the injuries which they receive from the air, so that the ground and the colours assist and preserve each other. It is for this reason, that glazed colours have a vivacity which can never be imitated by the most lively and most brilliant colours; because, according to the common way, the different tints are simply laid on, each in its place, one after another. So true it is, that white with other strong colours, with which we paint at once that which we intend to glaze, are, as it were, the life, the spirit, and the lustre of it. The ancients most certainly have found, that white grounds were much the best, because, notwithstanding that inconvenience which their eyes received from that colour, yet they did not forbear the use of it; as Galen testifies, in his Tenth Book of the Use of the Parts. "Painters," says he, "when they work upon their white grounds, place before them dark colours, and others mixed with blue and green, to recreate their eyes; because white is a glaring colour, which wearies and pains the sight more than any other." I know not the reason why the use of it is left off at present, if it be not that in our days there are few painters who are curious in their colouring, or that the first strokes which are begun upon white are not seen soon enough, and that a more than French patience is required to wait till it be accomplished; and the ground, which by its whiteness tarnishes the lustre of the other colours, must be entirely covered, to make the whole work appear pleasingly.

"Let the parts which are nearest to us, and most raised," &c. The reason of this is, that upon a flat superficies, and as much united as a cloth can be, when it is strained, the least body is very appearing, and gives a heightening to the place which it possesses: do not therefore load those places with colours, which you would make to turn; but let those be well loaded, which you would have come out of the canvass. † 383.

"Let there be so much harmony or consent in the masses of the picture, that all the shadowings may appear as if they were but one," &c. He has said in another place, that after great lights, great shadows are necessary, which he calls reposes. What he means by the present rule is this, that whatsoever is found in † 385.

those great shadows, should partake of the colours of one another; so that the different colours which are well distinguished in the lights, seem to be but one in the shadows, by their great union.

† 386. "Let the whole picture be of one piece," &c. That is to say, of one and the same continuity of work, and as if the picture had been painted up all at once: the Latin says, all of one palette.

† 387. "The looking-glass will instruct you," &c. The painter must have a principal respect to the masses, and to the effect of the whole together. The looking-glass distances the objects, and, by consequence, gives us only to see the masses, in which all the little parts are confounded. The evening, when the night approaches, will make you better understand this observation, but not so commodiously; for the proper time to make it lasts but a quarter of an hour, and the looking-glass may be useful all the day.

Since the mirror is the rule and master of all painters, as showing them their faults by distancing the objects, we may conclude, that the picture which makes not a good effect at a distance, cannot be well done: and a painter must never finish his picture, before he has examined it at some reasonable distance, or with a looking-glass, whether the masses of the lights and shadows, and the bodies of the colours, be well distributed. Giorgione and Correggio have made use of this method.

† 393. "As for a portrait, or picture by the life," &c. The end of portraits is not so precisely, as some have imagined, to give a smiling and pleasing air, together with the resemblance; this is indeed somewhat, but not enough. It consists in expressing the true temper of those persons which it represents, and to make known their physiognomy. If the person whom you draw, for example, be naturally sad, you are to beware of giving him any gayety, which would always be a thing which is foreign to his countenance. If he or she be merry, you are to make that good humour appear, by the expressing of those parts where it acts, and where it shows itself. If the person be grave and majestical, the smiles, or laughing, which is too sensible, will take off from that majesty, and make it look childish and indecent. In short, the painter who has a good genius, must make a true discernment of all these things; and if he understands physiognomy, it will be more easy to him, and he will succeed better than another. Pliny tells us, "That Apelles made his pictures so very like, that a certain physiognomist and fortuneteller (as it is related by Appion the grammarian) foretold, by looking on them, the very time of their deaths, whom those pictures represented; or at what time their death happened, if such persons were already dead.

"You are to take the utmost care, that † 403. broad lights may be joined," &c. This must be done tenderly, yet not so as to make our colours die, by force of tormenting them; but that you should mix them as hastily as you can, and not retouch the same place, if conveniently you can avoid it.

"Broad lights," &c. It is in vain to † 403. take pains if you cannot preserve large lights; because without them your work will never make a good effect at a distance, and also because little lights are confused, and effaced proportionably as you are at a distance from the picture. This was the perpetual maxim of Correggio.

"Ought to have somewhat of great- † 417. ness in them, and their outlines to be noble," &c. As the pieces of antiquity will evidently show us.

"There is nothing more pernicious to † 422. a youth," &c. It is common to place ourselves under the discipline of a master, of whom we have a good opinion, and whose manner we are apt to embrace with ease; which takes root more deeply in us, and augments, the more we see him work, and the more we copy after him. This happens oftentimes to that degree, and makes so great an impression in the mind of the scholar, that he cannot give his approbation to any other manner whatsoever, and believes there is no man under the cope of heaven who is so knowing as his master.

But what is most remarkable in this point is, that nature appears to us always like that manner which we love, and in which we have been taught; which is just like a glass through which we behold objects, and which communicates its colour to them, without our perceiving it. After I have said this, you may see of what consequence is the choice of a good master, and of following in our beginning the manner of those who have come nearest to nature. And how much injury, do you think, have the ill manners which have been in France done to the painters of that nation, and what hinderance have they been to the knowledge of what is well done, or of arriving to what is so, when once we know it? The Italians say to those whom they see infected with an ill manner, which they are not able to forsake, "If you knew just nothing, you would soon learn something."

"Search whatsoever is aiding to your † 433. art, and convenient; and avoid those things which are repugnant to it," &c. This is an admirable rule; a painter ought to have it perpetually present in his mind and memory. It resolves those difficulties which the rules beget; it loosens his hands, and assists his understanding; in short, this is the rule which sets the painter at liberty; because it teaches him, that he ought not to subject himself servilely, and be bound, like an apprentice, to the rules of his art; but that the rules of his art ought to be subject to him, and not hinder him from following the dictates of his genius, which is superior to them.

† 434. "Bodies of diverse natures, which are aggrouped, or combined together, are agreeable and pleasant to the sight," &c. As flowers, fruits, animals, skins, satins, velvets, beautiful flesh, works of silver, armours, instruments of music, ornaments of ancient sacrifices, and many other pleasing diversities which may present themselves to the painter's imagination. It is most certain, that the diversity of objects recreates the sight, when they are without confusion, and when they diminish nothing of the subject on which we work. Experience teaches us, that the eye grows weary with poring perpetually on the same thing; not only on pictures, but even on nature itself: for who is he, who would not be tired in the walks of a long forest, or with beholding a large plain which is naked of trees, or in the sight of a ridge of mountains, which, instead of pleasure, give us only the view of heights and bottoms? Thus to content and fill the eye of the understanding, the best authors have had the address to sprinkle their works with pleasing digressions, with which they recreate the minds of readers. Discretion in this, as in all other things, is the surest guide; and as tedious digressions, which wander from their subject, are impertinent; so the painter who, under pretence of diverting the eyes, would fill his picture with such varieties as alter the truth of the history, would make a ridiculous piece of painting, and a mere gallimaufry of his work.

† 435. "As also those things which seem to be slightly touched, and performed with ease," &c. This ease attracts our eyes and spirits so much the more, because it is to be presumed, that a noble work, which appears so easy to us, is the product of a skilful hand, which is master of its art. It was in this part that Apelles found himself superior to Protogenes, when he blamed him for not knowing when to lay down his pencil, and, as I may almost say, to make an end of finishing his piece. And it was on this account he plainly said, "That nothing was more prejudicial to painters, than too much exactness; and that the greatest part of them knew not when they had done enough:" as we have likewise a proverb, which says, "An Englishman never knows when he is well." It is true, that the word *enough* is very difficult to understand. What you have to do, is to consider your subject thoroughly, and in what manner you intend to treat it, according to your rules, and the force of your genius; after this, you are to work with all the ease, and all the speed you can, without breaking your head so very much, and being so very industrious in starting scruples to yourself, and creating difficulties in your work. But it is impossible to have this facility without possessing perfectly all the precepts of the art, and to have made it habitual to you: for ease consists in making precisely that work which you ought to make, and to set every thing in its proper place with speed and readiness, which cannot be done without the rules; for they are the assured means of conducting you to the end that you design, with pleasure. It is then most certain, (though against the opinion of many,) that the rules give facility, quiet of mind, and readiness of hand to the slowest genius; and that the same rules increase and guide that ease in those who have already received it at their birth, from the happy influence of their stars.

From whence it follows, that we may consider facility two several ways; either simply, as diligence, and a readiness of mind, and of the hand; or, as a disposition in the mind to remove readily all those difficulties which can arise in the work. The first proceeds from an active temper full of fire; and the second from a true knowledge and full possession of infallible rules: the first is pleasing, but it is not always without anxiety, because it often leads us astray; and, on the contrary, the last makes us act with a repose of mind and wonderful tranquillity, because it ascertains us of the goodness of our work. It is a great advantage to possess the first; but it is the height of perfection to have both in that manner which Rubens and Van Dyck possessed them, excepting the part of design, or drawing, which both of them too much neglected.

Those who say, that the rules are so far from giving us this facility, that, on the contrary, they puzzle and perplex the mind, and tie the hand, are generally such people who have passed half their lives in an ill practice of painting, the habit of which is grown so inveterate in them, that to change it by the rules, is to take, as it were, their pencils out of their hands, and to put them out of condition of doing any thing in the same manner as we make a countryman dumb, whom we will not allow to speak, but by the rules of grammar.

Observe, if you please, that the facility and diligence of which I spoke, consists not in that which we call bold strokes, and a free handling of the pencil, if it makes not a great effect at a distance: that sort of freedom belongs rather to a writing-master than a painter. I say yet farther, that it is almost impossible, that things which are painted should appear true and natural, where we observe these sorts of bold strokes. And all those who have come nearest to nature, have never used that manner of painting. Those tender hairs, and those hatching strokes of the pencil, which make a kind of minced meat in painting, are very fine, I must confess, but they are never able to deceive the sight.

† 442. "Nor till you have present in your mind a perfect idea of your work," &c. If you will have pleasure in painting, you ought to have so well considered the economy of your work, that it may be entirely made and disposed in your head, before it be begun upon the cloth. You must, I say, foresee the effect of the groups, the ground, and the lights and shadows of every thing, the harmony of the colours, and the intelligence of all the subject, in such a manner, that whatsoever you shall put upon the cloth, may be only a copy of what is in your mind. If you make use of this conduct, you will not be put to the trouble of so often changing and rechanging.

† 443. "Let the eye be satisfied, in the first place, even against and above all other reasons," &c. This passage has a respect to some particular licenses which a painter ought to take; and, as I despair not to treat this matter more at large, I adjourn the reader to the first opportunity which I can get for his farther satisfaction on this point, to the best of my ability. But in general, he may hold for certain, that those licenses are good which contribute to deceive the sight, without corrupting the truth of the subject on which the painter is to work.

† 445. "Profit yourself by the counsels of the knowing," &c. Parrhasius and Cliton thought themselves much obliged to Socrates for the knowledge which he gave them of the passions. (See their dialogue in Xenophon, towards the end of the third book of Memoirs.) "They who the most willingly bear reproof," says Pliny* the Younger, "are the very men in whom we find more to commend than in other people." Lysippus was extremely pleased when Apelles told him his opinion; and Apelles as much when Lysippus told him his. That which Praxiteles said of Nicias, in Pliny,* shows the soul of an accomplished and an humble man. "Praxiteles being asked, which of all his works he valued most? "Those," says he, "which Nicias has retouched." So much account he made of his criticisms and his opinions. You know the common practice of Apelles: when he had finished any work, he exposed it to the sight of all passengers, and concealed himself to hear the censure of his faults, with the prospect of making his advantage of the informations which unknowingly they gave him; being sensible that the people would examine his works more rigorously than himself, and would not forgive the least mistake.

The opinions and counsels of many together are always preferable to the advice of one single person. And Cicero wonders, that any are besotted on their own productions, and say to one another, "Very good, if your works please you, mine are not unpleasing to me.'† In effect, there are many who, through presumption, or out of shame to be reprehended, never let their works be seen. But there is nothing can be of worse consequence; "for the disease is nourished and increases," says Virgil,‡ "while it is concealed." "There are none but fools," says Horace, "who, out of shamefacedness, hide their ulcers, which, if shown, might easily be healed:

Stultorum incurata malus pudor ulcera celat."§

There are others, who have not altogether so much of this foolish bashfulness, and who ask every one's opinion with prayers and earnestness; but if you freely and ingenuously give them notice of their faults, they never fail to make some pitiful excuse for them; or, which is worse, they take in ill part the service which you thought you did them, which they but seemingly desired of you, and out of an established custom amongst the greatest part of painters. If you desire to get yourself any honour, and acquire a reputation by your works, there is no surer way than to show them to persons of good sense, and chiefly to those who are critics in the art; and to take their counsel with the same mildness, and the same sincerity, as you desired them to give it you. You must also be industrious to discover the opinion of your enemies, which is commonly the truest; for you may be assured, that they will give you no quarter, and allow nothing to complaisance.

* Lib. viii. 20.

* Lib. v. 8.
† Tuscul. lib. v.
‡ Georg. iii. l. 5
§ Ep. xvi.

† 449. "But if you have no knowing friend," &c. Quinctilian gives the reason of this, when he says, "that the best means to correct our faults is doubtless this, to remove our designs out of sight, for some space of time, and not to look upon our pictures; to the end, that after this interval we may look on them as it were with other eyes, and as a new work, which was of another hand, and not our own." Our own productions do but too much flatter us; they are always too pleasing, and it is impossible not to be fond of them at the moment of their conception. They are children of a tender age, which are not capable of drawing our hatred on them. It is said, that apes, as soon as they have brought their young into the world, keep their eyes continually fastened on them, and are never weary of admiring their beauty; so amorous is nature of whatsoever she produces.

† 458. "To the end that he may cultivate those talents which make his genius," &c.

Qui sua metitur pondera, ferre potest.

"That we may undertake nothing beyond our forces, we must endeavour to know them." On this prudence our reputation depends. Cicero calls it "a good grace," because it makes a man seen in his greatest lustre. "It is," says he,* "a becoming grace, which we shall easily make appear, if we are careful to cultivate that which nature has given us in propriety, and made our own; provided it be no vice or imperfection. We ought to undertake nothing which is repugnant to nature in general; and when we have paid her this duty, we are bound so religiously to follow our own nature, that though many things which are more serious and more important present themselves to us, yet we are always to conform our studies and our exercises to our natural inclinations. It avails nothing to dispute against nature, and think to obtain what she refuses; for then we eternally follow what we can never reach; for, as the proverb says, there is nothing can please, nothing can be graceful, which we enterprise in spite of Minerva; that is to say, in spite of nature. When we have considered all these things attentively, it will then be necessary that every man should regard that in particular which nature has made his portion, and that he should cultivate it with care. It is not his business to give himself the trouble of trying whether it will become him to put on the nature of another man, or, as one would say, to act the person of another; there is nothing which can more become us, than what is properly the gift of nature. Let every one therefore endeavour to understand his own talent, and, without flattering himself, let him make a true judgment of his own virtues, and his own defects and vices, that he may not appear to have less judgment than the comedians, who do not always choose the best plays, but those which are best for them; that is, those which are most in the compass of their acting. Thus we are to fix on those things for which we have the strongest inclination. And if it sometimes happens, that we are forced by necessity to apply ourselves to such other things, to which we are no ways inclined, we must bring it so about, by our care and industry, that if we perform them not very well, at least we may not do them so very ill, as to be shamed by them: we are not so much to strain ourselves, to make those virtues appear in us which really we have not, as to avoid those imperfections which may dishonour us." These are the thoughts and the words of Cicero, which I have translated, retrenching only such things as were of no concernment to my subject: I was not of opinion to add any thing, and the reader, I doubt not, will find his satisfaction in them.

"While you meditate on these truths, and observe them diligently," &c. There is a great connexion betwixt this precept and that other, which tells you, "That you are to pass no day without a line." It is impossible to become an able artist, without making your art habitual to you; and it is impossible to gain an exact habitude, without an infinite number of acts, and without perpetual practice. In all arts the rules of them are learned in little time; but the perfection is not acquired without a long practice and a severe diligence. "We never saw, that laziness produced any thing which was excellent," says Maximus Tyrius;* and Quinctilian tells us, "That the arts draw their beginning from nature;" the want we often have of them causes us to search the means of becoming able in them, and exercise makes us entirely masters of them. † 464.

"The morning is the best and most proper part of the day," &c. Because then the imagination is not clouded with the vapours of meat, nor distracted by visits, which are not usually made in the morning; and the mind, by the sleep of the foregoing night, is refreshed and recreated from the toils of former studies. Malherbe says well to this purpose, † 466.

Le plus beau de nos jours, est dans leur matinee.

The sprightly morn is the best part of the day.

* 1 Off.

* Diss. 24.

†468. "Let no day pass over you, without a line, &c. That is to say, without working, without giving some strokes of the pencil or the crayon. This was the precept of Apelles; and it is of so much the more necessity, because painting is an art of much length and time, and is not to be learned without great practice. Michael Angelo, at the age of fourscore years, said, "That he learned something every day."

†473. "Be ready to put into your table-book," &c. As it was the custom of Titian and the Carraches. There are yet remaining in the hands of some who are curious in painting, many thoughts and observations which those great men have made on paper, and in their table-books, which they carried continually about them.

†475. "Wine and good cheer are no great friends to painting; they serve only to recreate the mind, when it is oppressed and spent with labour," &c. "During the time," says Pliny,* "that Protogenes was drawing the picture of Jalysus, which was the best of all his works, he took no other nourishment than Lupines, mixed with a little water, which served him both for meat and drink, for fear of clogging his imagination, by the luxury of his food." Michael Angelo, while he was drawing his Day of Judgment, fed only on bread and wine at dinner; and Vasari observes in his life, that he was so sober, that he slept but little, and that he often rose in the night to work, as being not disturbed by the vapours of his thin repasts.

†478. "But delights in the liberty which belongs to the bachelor's estate," &c. We never see large, beautiful, and well-tasted fruits proceeding from a tree which is encompassed round, and choked with thorns and briars. Marriage draws a world of business on our hands, subjects us to law-suits, and loads us with multitudes of domestic cares, which are as so many thorns that encompass a painter, and hinder him from producing his works in that perfection of which otherwise he is capable. Raphael, Michael Angelo, and Hannibal Carrache, were never married: and amongst the ancient painters we find none recorded for being married, but only Apelles, to whom Alexander the Great made a present of his own mistress Campaspe; which yet I would have understood, without offence to the institution of marriage; for that calls down many blessings upon families, by the carefulness of a virtuous wife. If marriage be in general a remedy against concupiscence, it is doubly so in respect of painters, who are more frequently under the occasions of such than other men, because they are under a frequent necessity of seeing nature bare-faced. Let every one examine his own strength upon this point; but let him prefer the interest of his soul, to that of his art, and of his fortune.

"Painting naturally withdraws from noise and tumult," &c. I have said at the end of the first remark, that both poetry and painting were upheld by the strength of imagination. Now there is nothing which warms it more than repose and solitude; because, in that estate, the mind being freed from all sorts of business, and in a kind of sanctuary, undisturbed by vexatious visits, is more capable of forming noble thoughts, and of application to its studies: †480.

Carmina secessum scribentis, et otia quærunt.

Good verse recess and solitude requires,
And ease from cares, and undisturbed desires.

We may properly say the same of painting, by reason of its conformity with poetry, as I have shown in the first remark.

"Let not the covetous design of growing rich," &c. We read in Pliny, that Nicias refused sixty talents from King Attalus, and rather chose to make a free gift of his picture to his country. "I inquired of a prudent man," says a grave author,* "in what times those noble pictures were made, which now we see; and desired him to explain to me some of their subjects, which I did not well understand. I asked him likewise the reason of that great negligence, which is now visible amongst painters; and from whence it proceeded, that the most beautiful arts were now buried in oblivion; and principally painting, a faint shadow of which is at present remaining to us? To which he thus replied, that the immoderate desire of riches had produced this change: for of old, when naked virtue had her charms, the noble arts then flourished in their vigour; and if there was any contest amongst men, it was only who should be the first discoverer of what might be of advantage to posterity. Lysippus and Myron, those renowned sculptors, who could give a soul to brass, left no heirs, no inheritance, behind them; because they were more careful of acquiring fame than riches. But as for us of this present age, it seems, by the manner of our conduct, that we upbraid antiquity for being as covetous of virtue as we are of vice: wonder not so much, therefore, if painting has lost its strength and vigour, because many are now of opinion, that a heap of gold is much more beautiful than all the pictures and statues of Apelles and Phidias, and all the noble performances of Greece." †484.

* Lib. xxxv. 10.

* Petron. Arbiter.

I would not exact so great an act of abstinence from our modern painters; for I am not ignorant, that the hope of gain is a wonderful sharp spur in arts, and that it gives industry to the artist; from whence it was that Juvenal said, even of the Greeks themselves, who were the inventors of painting, and who first understood all the graces of it, and its whole perfection,

> Græculus esuriens, in Cœlum, jusseris, ibit.
> A hungry Greek, if bidden, scales the skies.

But I could heartily wish, that the same hope which flatters them, did not also corrupt them; and did not snatch out of their hands a lame imperfect piece, rudely daubed over with too little reflection, and too much haste.

† 487. "The qualities requisite to form an excellent painter," &c. It is to be confessed, that very few painters have those qualities which are required by our author, because there are very few who are able painters. There was a time, when only they who were of noble blood were permitted to exercise this art; because it is to be presumed, that all these ingredients of a good painter are not ordinarily found in men of vulgar birth. And, in all appearance, we may hope, that though there be no edict in France which takes away the liberty of painting from those to whom nature has refused the honour of being born gentlemen, yet at least that the Royal Academy will admit henceforward only such, who being endued with all the good qualities, and the talents which are required for painting, those endowments may be to them instead of an honourable birth. It is certain, that which debases painting, and makes it descend to the vilest and most despicable kind of trade, is the great multitude of painters, who have neither noble souls, nor any talent for the art, nor even so much as common sense. The origin of this great evil is, that there have always been admitted into the schools of painting, all sorts of children promiscuously, without examination of them, and without observing (for some convenient space of time) if they were conducted to this art by their inward disposition, and all necessary talents, rather than by a foolish inclination of their own, or by the avarice of their relations, who put them to painting, as a trade which they believe to be somewhat more gainful than another. The qualities properly required are these following:—

A good judgment, that they may do nothing against reason and verisimility.

A docile mind, that they may profit by instructions, and receive, without arrogance, the opinion of every one, and principally of knowing men.

A noble heart, that they may propose glory to themselves, and reputation rather than riches.

A sublimity and reach of thought, to conceive readily, to produce beautiful ideas, and to work on their subjects nobly, and after a lofty manner, wherein we may observe somewhat that is delicate, ingenious, and uncommon.

A warm and vigorous fancy, to arrive at least to some degree of perfection, without being tired with the pains and study which are required in painting.

Health, to resist the dissipation of spirits, which are apt to be consumed by pains-taking.

Youth, because painting requires a great experience, and a long practice.

Beauty, or handsomeness, because a painter paints himself in all his pictures; and nature loves to produce her own likeness.

A convenient fortune, that he may give his whole time to study, and may work cheerfully, without being haunted with the dreadful image of poverty, ever present to his mind.

Labour, because the speculation is nothing without the practice.

A love for his art: we suffer nothing in the labour which is pleasing to us; or if it happen that we suffer, we are pleased with the pain.

And to be under the discipline of a knowing master, &c. Because all depends on the beginnings; and because commonly they take the manner of their master, and are formed according to his gusto. See verse 422, and the remark upon it. All these good qualities are insignificant, and unprofitable to the painter, if some outward dispositions are wanting to him. By which I mean favourable times, such as are times of peace, which is the nurse of all noble arts: there must also some fair occasion offer to make their skill manifest, by the performance of some considerable work within their power; and a protector, who must be a person of authority, one who takes upon himself the care of their fortune, at least in some measure, and knows how to speak well of them in time and place convenient. "It is of much importance," says the younger Pliny, "in what times virtue appears. And there is no wit, howsoever excellent it may be, which can make itself immediately known; time and opportunity are necessary to it, and a person who can assist us with his favour and be a Mecænas to us."

"And life is so short, that it is not sufficient for so long an art," &c. † 496. Not only painting, but all other arts, considered in themselves, require almost an infinite time to possess them perfectly. It is in this sense, that Hippocrates begins his Aphorisms with this saying, "That art is long, and life is short. But if we consider arts as they are in us, and according to a certain degree of perfection, sufficient enough to make it known that we possess them above the common sort, and are comparatively better than most others, we shall not find that life is too short on that account, provided our time be well employed. It is true, that painting is an art which is difficult, and a great undertaking; but they who are endued with the qualities that are necessary to it, have no reason to be discouraged by that apprehension. "Labour always appears difficult before it is tried."* The passages by sea, and the knowledge of the stars, have been thought impossible, which notwithstanding have been found and compassed, and that with ease, by those who endeavoured after them. "It is a shameful thing," says Cicero,† "to be weary of inquiry, when what we search is excellent." That which causes us to lose most of our time, is the repugnance which we naturally have to labour, and the ignorance, the malice, and the negligence of our masters: we waste much of our time in walking, and talking to no manner of purpose, in making and receiving idle visits; in play, and other pleasures which we indulge; without reckoning those hours which we lose in the too great care of our bodies; and in sleep, which we often lengthen out till the day is far advanced; and thus we pass that life which we reckon to be short, because we count by the years which we have lived rather than by those which we have employed in study. It is evident, that they who lived before us have passed through all those difficulties, to arrive at that perfection which we discover in their works; though they wanted some of the advantages which we possess, and none had laboured for them as they have done for us. For it is certain, that those ancient masters, and those of the last preceding ages, have left such beautiful patterns to us, that a better and more happy age can never be than ours; and chiefly under the reign of our present king, who encourages all the noble arts, and spares nothing, to give them the share of that felicity of which he is so bountiful to his kingdom; and to conduct them with all manner of advantages to that supreme degree of excellence, which may be worthy of such a master, and of that sovereign love which he has for them. Let us therefore put our hands to the work, without being discouraged by the length of time which is requisite for our studies; but let us seriously contrive how to proceed with the best order, and to follow a ready, diligent, and well-understood method.

† 500. "Take courage, therefore, O ye noble youths! ye legitimate offspring of Minerva, who are born under the influence of a happy planet," &c. Our author intends not here to sow in a barren, ungrateful ground, where his precepts can bear no fruit: he speaks to young painters, but to such only who are born under the influence of a happy star; that is to say, those who have received from nature the necessary dispositions of becoming great in the art of painting; and not to those who follow that study through caprice, or by a sottish inclination, or for lucre, who are either incapable of receiving the precepts, or will make a bad use of them when received.

"You will do well," &c. Our author † 508. speaks not here of the first rudiments of design; as, for example, the management of the pencil, the just relation which the copy ought to have to the original, &c. He supposes, that before he begins his studies, one ought to have a facility of hand, to imitate the best designs, and the noblest pictures and statues; that, in few words, he should have made himself a key, wherewith to open the closet of Minerva, and to enter into that sacred place, where those fair treasures are to be found in all abundance, and even offer themselves to us, to make our advantage of them, by our care and genius.

"To begin with geometry," &c. Because that is the ground of perspective, † 509. without which, nothing is to be done in painting. Besides, geometry is of great use in architecture, and in all things which are of its dependence; it is particularly necessary for sculptors.

"Set yourself on designing, after the ancient Greeks," &c. Because they are † 510. the rule of beauty, and give us a good gusto; for which reason it is very proper to tie ourselves to them, I mean generally speaking; but the particular fruit which we gather from them, is what follows: To learn by heart four several airs of heads, of a man, a woman, a child, and an old man. I mean those which have the most general appprobation; for example, those of the Apollo, of the Venus de Medicis, of the little Nero, (that is, when he was a child,) and of the god Tiber. It would be a good means of learning them, if when you have designed one after the statue itself, you design it immediately after from your own imagination, without seeing it; and afterwards examine, if your own work be conformable to the first design; thus exercising yourself on the same head, and turning it on ten or twelve sides. You must do the same to the feet, to the hands, to the whole figure. But to understand the beauty of these figures, and the justness of their outlines, it will be necessary to learn anatomy. When I speak of four heads,

* Veget. de Re Milit. lib. 2. † Lib. 1. de fin.

and four figures, I pretend not to hinder any one from designing many others, after this first study; but my meaning is only to show by this, that a great variety of things undertaken at the same time, dissipates the imagination, and hinders all the profit; in the same manner, as too many sorts of meat are not easily digested, but corrupt in the stomach, instead of nourishing the parts.

† 511. "And cease not day or night from labour, till by your continual practice," &c. In the first principles, the students have not so much need of precepts as of practice; and the antique statues being the rule of beauty, you may exercise yourselves in imitating them, without apprehending any consequence of ill habits and bad ideas, which can be formed in the soul of a young beginner. It is not as in the school of a master, whose manner and whose gusto are ill, and under whose discipline the scholar spoils himself the more he exercises.

† 514. "And when afterwards your judgment shall grow stronger," &c. It is necessary to have the soul well formed, and to have a right judgment to make the application of his rules upon good pictures, and to take nothing but the good. For there are some who imagine, that whatsoever they find in the picture of a master who has acquired reputation, must of necessity be excellent: and these kind of people never fail, when they copy, to follow the bad as well as the good things, and to observe them so much the more, because they seem to be extraordinary, and out of the common road of others, so that at last they come to make a law and precept of them. You ought not also to imitate what is truly good in a crude and gross manner, so that it may be found out in your works, that whatsoever beauties there are in them, come from such or such a master. But, in this, imitate the bees, who pick from every flower that which they find most proper in it to make honey. In the same manner, a young painter should collect from many pictures what he finds to be the most beautiful; and from his several collections form that manner which thereby he makes his own.

† 520. "A certain grace which was wholly natural and peculiar to him," &c. Raphael in this may be compared to Apelles, who, in praising the works of other painters, said, "That gracefulness was wanting to them; and that, without vanity, he might say, it was his own peculiar portion." See the remark on the 218th verse.

"Julio Romano, educated from his † 522.
childhood in the country of the Muses," &c. He means in the studies of the *belles lettres*, and above all in poesy, which he infinitely loved. It appears, that he formed his ideas, and made his gusto, from reading Homer; and in that imitated Zeuxis and Polygnotus, who, as Maximus Tyrius relates, treated their subjects in their pictures as Homer did in his poetry.

To these remarks I have annexed the opinions of our author, upon the best and chiefest painters of the two foregoing ages. He tells you candidly, and briefly, what were their excellencies, and what their failings.

"I pass in silence many things which † 541.
will be more amply treated in the ensuing Commentary." It is evident by this, how much we lose, and what damage we have sustained by our author's death, since those commentaries had undoubtedly contained things of high value and of great instruction.

"To intrust with the Muses," &c. † 544.
That is to say, to write in verse; poetry being under their protection, and consecrated to them.

THE JUDGMENT

OF CHARLES ALPHONSE DU FRESNOY,

ON THE WORKS OF THE PRINCIPAL AND BEST PAINTERS OF THE TWO LAST AGES.

PAINTING was in its perfection amongst the Greeks. The principal schools were at Sicyon, afterwards at Rhodes, at Athens, and at Corinth, and at last in Rome. Wars and luxury having overthrown the Roman empire, it was totally extinguished, together with all the noble arts, the studies of humanity, and the other sciences.

It began to appear again, in the year 1450, amongst some painters of Florence, of which Domenico Chirlandaio was one, who was master to Michael Angelo, and had some kind of reputation, though his manner was Gothic, and very dry.

Michael Angelo, his disciple, flourished in the times of Julius the Second, Leo the Tenth, and of seven successive popes. He was a painter, a sculptor, and an architect, both civil and military. The choice which he made of his attitudes was not always beautiful or pleasing; his gusto of design was not the finest, nor his outlines the most elegant; the folds of his draperies, and the ornaments of his habits, were neither noble nor graceful. He was not a little fantastical and extravagant in his compositions; he was bold, even to rashness, in taking liberties against the rules of perspective. His colouring is not over true, or very pleasant. He knew not the artifice of the lights and shadows; but he designed more learnedly, and better understood all the knittings of the bones, with the office and situation of the muscles, than any of the modern painters. There appears a certain air of greatness and severity in his figures; in both which he has oftentimes succeeded. But above the rest of his excellencies, was his wonderful skill in architecture, wherein he has not only surpassed all the moderns, but even the ancients also. The St. Peter's of Rome, the St. John's of Florence, the Capitol, the Palazzo Farnese, and his own house, are sufficient testimonies of it. His disciples were Marcello Venusti, Il Rosso, Georgio Vasari, Fra. Bastiano, who commonly painted for him, and many other Florentines.

Pietro Perugino designed with sufficient knowledge of nature; but he is dry, and his manner little. His disciple was

Raphael Santio, who was born on Good Friday, in the year 1483, and died on Good Friday, in the year 1520, so that he lived only thirty-seven years complete. He surpassed all modern painters, because he possessed more of the excellent parts of painting than any other; and it is believed that he equalled the ancients, excepting only that he designed not naked bodies with so much learning as Michael Angelo; but his gusto of design is purer, and much better. He painted not with so good, so full, and so graceful a manner as Correggio; nor has he any thing of the contrast of the lights and shadows, or so strong and free a colouring as Titian; but he had a better disposition in his pieces, without comparison, than either Titian, Correggio, Michael Angelo, or all the rest of the succeeding painters to our days. His choice of attitudes, of heads, of ornaments; the suitableness of his drapery, his manner of designing, his varieties, his contrasts, his expressions, were beautiful in perfection; but above all, he possessed the graces in so advantageous a manner, that he has never since been equalled by any other. There are portraits, or single figures, of his, which are finished pieces. He was an admirable architect. He was handsome, well-made, and tall of stature, civil and well-natured, never refusing to teach another what he knew himself. He had many scholars, amongst others, Julio Romano, Polydore, Gaudenzio, Giovanni d'Udine, and Michael Coxis.

his graver was Marc Antonio, whose prints are admirable for the correctness of their outlines.

Julio Romano was the most excellent of all Raphael's disciples. He had conceptions which were more extraordinary, more profound, and more elevated, than even his master himself. He was also a great architect; his gusto was pure and exquisite. He was a great imitator of the ancients; giving a clear testimony in all his productions, that he was desirous to restore to practice the same forms and fabrics which were ancient. He had the good fortune to find great persons, who committed to him the care of edifices, vestibules, and porticoes, all tetrastyles, xistes, theatres, and such other places as are not now in use. He was wonderful in his choice of attitudes. His manner was drier and harder than any of Raphael's school. He did not exactly understand the lights and shadows, or the colours. He is frequently harsh and ungraceful. The folds of his draperies are neither beautiful nor great, easy nor natural; but all extravagant, and too like the habits of fantastical comedians. He was very knowing in human learning. His disciples were, Pirro Ligorio, (who was admirable for ancient buildings, as for towns, temples, tombs, and trophies, and the situation of ancient edifices,) Æneas Vico, Bonasone, Georgio Mantuano, and others.

Polydore, a disciple of Raphael, designed admirably well, as to the practical part, having a particular genius for friezes, as we may see by those of white and black which he has painted at Rome. He imitated the ancients; but his manner was greater than that of Julio Romano; nevertheless, Julio seems to be the truer. Some admirable groups are seen in his works, and such as are not elsewhere to be found. He coloured very seldom, and made landscapes of a reasonable good gusto.

Gio. Bellino, one of the first who was of any consideration at Venice, painted very drily, according to the manner of his time. He was very knowing, both in architecture and perspective. He was Titian's first master, which may easily be observed in the first painting of that noble disciple; in which we may remark, that propriety of colours which his master has observed.

About this time, Georgione, the contemporary of Titian, came to excel in portraits, or face-painting, and also in great works. He first began to make choice of glowing and agreeable colours, the perfection and entire harmony of which were afterwards to be found in Titian's pictures. He dressed his figures wonderfully well; and it may be truly said, that, but for him, Titian had never arrived to that height of perfection, which proceeded from the rivalship and jealousy of honour betwixt those two.

Titian was one of the greatest colourists who was ever known. He designed with much more ease and practice than Georgione. There are to be seen women and children of his hand, which are admirable, both for the design and colouring. The gusto of them is delicate, charming, and noble, with a certain pleasing negligence of the head-dresses, the draperies, and ornaments of habits, which are wholly peculiar to him. As for the figures of men, he has designed them but moderately well. There are even some of his draperies which are mean, and savour of a little gusto. His painting is wonderfully glowing, sweet, and delicate. He made portraits, which were extremely noble; the attitudes of them being very graceful, grave, diversified, and adorned after a very becoming fashion. No man ever painted landscape with so great a manner, so good a colouring, and with such a resemblance of nature. For eight or ten years' space, he copied with great labour and exactness whatsoever he undertook; thereby to make himself an easy way, and to establish some general maxims for his future conduct. Besides the excellent gusto which he had of colours, in which he excelled all mortal men, he perfectly understood how to give every thing the touches which were most suitable and proper to them; such as distinguished them from each other, and which gave the greatest spirit, and the most of truth. The pictures which he made in his beginning and in the declension of his age, are of a dry and mean manner. He lived ninety-nine years. His disciples were Paulo Veronese, Giacomo Tintoret, Giacomo da Ponte Bassano, and his sons.

Paulo Veronese was wonderfully graceful in his airs of women, with great variety of shining draperies, and incredible vivacity and ease. Nevertheless, his composition is sometimes improper, and his design is incorrect; but his colouring, and whatsoever depends on it, is so very charming in his pictures, that it surprises at the first sight, and make us totally forget those other qualities which are wanting in him.

Tintoret was the disciple of Titian, great in the practical part of design, but sometimes also sufficiently extravagant. He had an admirable genius for painting, if he had had as great an affection to his art, and as much patience in undergoing the difficulties of it, as he had fire and vivacity of nature. He has made pictures not inferior in beauty to those of Titian. His composition, and his dresses, are, for the most part, improper, and his outlines are not correct; but his colouring, and the dependencies of it, like that of his master, are most admirable.

The Bassans had a more mean and poor gusto in painting than Tintoret, and their designs were also less correct than his: they had, indeed, an excellent gusto of colours, and have touched all kinds of animals with an admirable manner, but were notoriously imperfect in the composition and design.

Correggio painted at Parma two large cupolas in fresco, and some altar-pieces. This artist found out certain natural and unaffected graces, for his Madonnas, his Saints, and Little Children, which were peculiar to him. His manner is exceeding great, both for the design and for the work, but withal is very incorrect. His pencil was both easy and delightful; and it is to be acknowledged, that he painted with great strength, great heightening, great sweetness, and liveliness of colours, in which none surpassed him.

He understood how to distribute his lights in such a manner as was wholly peculiar to himself; which gave a great force and great roundness to his figures. This manner consists in extending a larger light, and then making it lose itself insensibly in the dark shadowings which he placed out of the masses; and those give them this great roundness, without our being able to perceive from whence proceeds so much of force, and so vast a pleasure to the sight. It is probable, that, in this part, the rest of the Lombard school copied him. He had no great choice of graceful attitudes, nor of distribution for beautiful groups; his design oftentimes appears lame, and the positions are not much observed in them. The aspects of his figures are many times unpleasing; but his manner of designing heads, hands, feet, and other parts, is very great, and well deserves our imitation. In the conduct and finishing of a picture, he has done wonders; for he painted with so much union, that his greatest works seemed to have been finished in the compass of one day, and appear as if we saw them from a looking-glass. His landscape is equally beautiful with his figures.

At the same time with Correggio lived and flourished Parmegiano; who, besides his great manner of well colouring, excelled also both in invention and design, with a genius full of gentleness and of spirit, having nothing that was ungraceful in his choice of attitudes, and in the dresses of his figures, which we cannot say of Correggio. There are pieces of his to be seen, which are both beautiful and correct.

These two painters last mentioned had very good disciples, but they are known only to those of their own province; and besides, there is little to be credited of what his countrymen say; for painting is wholly extinguished amongst them.

I say nothing of Leonardo da Vinci, because I have seen but little of his, though he restored the arts at Milan, and had many disciples there.

Ludovico Carrache, cousin of Hannibal and Augustine, studied at Parma after Correggio; and excelled in design and colouring with such a gracefulness, and so much candour, that Guido, the scholar of Hannibal, did afterwards imitate him with great success. There are some of his pictures to be seen, which are very beautiful, and well understood. He made his ordinary residence at Bologna; and it was he who put the pencil into the hands of Hannibal his cousin.

Hannibal in a little time, excelled his master in all parts of painting. He imitated Correggio, Titian, and Raphael, in their different manners as he pleased; excepting only, that you see not in his pictures the nobleness, the graces, and the charms of Raphael; and his outlines are neither so pure nor so elegant as his. In all other things he is wonderfully accomplished, and of an universal genius.

Augustine, brother to Hannibal, was also a very good painter, and an admirable graver. He had a natural son, called Antonio, who died at the age of thirty-five, and who, (according to the general opinion) would have surpassed his uncle Hannibal; for by what he left behind him, it appears that he was of a more lofty genius.

Guido chiefly imitated Ludovico Carrache, yet retained always somewhat of the manner which his master, Denis Calvert, the Fleming, taught him. This Calvert lived at Bologna, and was competitor and rival to Ludovico Carrache. Guido made the same use of Albert Durer as Virgil did of old Ennius; borrowed what pleased him, and made it afterwards his own; that is, he accommodated what was good in Albert to his own manner; which he executed with so much gracefulness and beauty, that he alone got more money and more reputation in his time than his own masters and all the scholars of the Carraches, though they were of greater capacity than himself. His heads yield no manner of precedence to those of Raphael.

Sisto Badolocchi designed the best of all his disciples, but he died young.

Domenichino was a very knowing painter, and very laborious, but otherwise of no great natural endowments. It is true, he was profoundly skilled in all the parts of painting, but wanting genius, (as I said,) he had less of nobleness in his works than all the rest who studied in the school of the Carraches.

Albani was excellent in all that belonged to painting, and adorned with variety of learning.

Lanfranc, a man of great and sprightly wit, supported his reputation for a long time with an extraordinary gusto of design and colouring. But his foundation being only on the practical part, he at length lost ground in point of correctness; so that many of his pieces appear extravagant and fantastical. And after his decease the school of the Carraches went daily to decay in all the parts of painting.

Gio. Viola was very old before he learned landscape; the knowledge of which was imparted to him by Hannibal Carrache, who took pleasure to instruct him, so that he painted many of that kind, which are wonderfully fine, and well coloured.

If we cast our eyes towards Germany and the Low Countries, we may there behold Albert Durer, Lucas Van Leyden, Holbein, Aldegrave, &c., who were all contemporaries. Amongst these, Albert Durer and Holbein were both of them wonderfully knowing, and had certainly been of the first form of painters, had they travelled into Italy; for nothing can be laid to their charge, but only that they had a Gothic gusto. As for Holbein, he performed yet better than Raphael; and I have seen a portrait of his painting, with which one of Titian's could not come in competition.

Amongst the Flemings, we had Rubens, who derived from his birth, a lively, free, noble, and universal genius; a genius which was capable not only of raising him to the rank of the ancient painters, but also to the highest employment in the service of his country; so that he was chosen for one of the most important embassies of our age. His gusto of design savours somewhat more of the Fleming than of the beauty of the antique, because he stayed not long at Rome. And though we cannot but observe in all his paintings somewhat of great and noble, yet, it must be confessed, that, generally speaking, he designed not correctly; but, for all the other parts of painting, he was as absolute a master of them, and possessed them all as thoroughly, as any of his predecessors in that noble art. His principal studies were made in Lombardy, after the works of Titian, Paul Veronese, and Tintoret; whose cream he has skimmed, (if you will allow the phrase,) and extracted from their several beauties many general maxims and infallible rules, which he always followed, and by which he has acquired in his works a greater facility than that of Titian; more of purity, truth, and science, than Paul Veronese; and more of majesty, repose, and moderation, than Tintoret. To conclude; his manner is so solid, so knowing, and so ready, that it may seem this rare accomplished genius was sent from heaven to instruct mankind in the art of painting.

His school was full of admirable disciples, amongst whom Van Dyck was he who best comprehended all the rules and general maxims of his master; and who has even excelled him in the delicacy of his colouring, and in his cabinet pieces; but his gusto, in the designing part, was nothing better than that of Rubens.

PREFACE

TO

A DIALOGUE CONCERNING WOMEN.

The author of this Dialogue, as Dr. Johnson has observed, was more remarkable for his familiarity with men of genius, than for any productions of his own. He was the son of Joseph Walsh of Abberley, in Worcestershire, and was born to an easy fortune. This last circumstance may have contributed something to the extreme respect in which he seems to have been held by the most accomplished of his age. Dryden, in the Postscript to "Virgil," calls Walsh the best critic of the English nation; and, in the following Preface, he is profuse in his commendation. But though these praises may have exceeded the measure of Walsh's desert, posterity owe a grateful remembrance to him, who, though a stanch Whig, respected and befriended Dryden in age and adversity, and who encouraged the juvenile essays of Pope, by foretelling his future eminence. Walsh's own Poems and Essays entitle him to respectable rank among the minor poets.

The "Dialogue concerning Women," contains a critical disquisition upon the virtues and foibles of the sex. But though the pleasantry be stale, and the learning pedantic, it seems to have excited some attention when published; perhaps because, as an angry defender of the ladies observes,

> ———" To begin with Dryden's dreadful name,
> Should mark out something of no common fame."

I cannot omit remarking, that the Dialogue concludes with a profuse panegyric, upon a theme not very congenial to Dryden's political feelings, the character of Queen Mary.

PREFACE

TO WALSH'S DIALOGUE CONCERNING WOMEN.

The perusal of this Dialogue, in defence of the fair sex, written by a gentleman of my acquaintance, much surprised me; for it was not easy for me to imagine, that one so young* could have treated so nice a subject with so much judgment. It is true, I was not ignorant that he was naturally ingenious, and that he had improved himself by travelling; and from thence I might reasonably have expected that air of gallantry, which is so visibly diffused through the body of the work, and is indeed the soul that animates all things of this nature; but so much variety of reading, both in ancient and modern authors, such digestion of that reading, so much justness of thought, that it leaves no room for affectation or pedantry, I may venture to say, are not over-common amongst practised writers, and very rarely to be found amongst beginners. It puts me in mind of what was said of Mr. Waller, the father of our English numbers, upon the sight of his first verses, by the wits of the last age; that he came out into the world forty thousand strong, before they heard of him.* Here, in imitation

* Mr. Walsh was born in 1663, and in 1691 must have been twenty-eight years old. Still he was but a youth in the eyes of Dryden, who was now advanced in life.

* Mr. Malone observes, that, according to Antony Wood, (*Ath. Oxon.* ii. 423,) this was not said *of* Waller, but *by* that poet, of Sir John Denham.—"In the latter end of the year 1641, Sir John published the tragedy called the 'Sophy,' which took extremely much, and was admired by all ingenious men, particularly by Edmund Waller of Beaconsfield, who then said of the author, that he broke out, like the Irish rebellion, threescore thousand strong, before any body was aware, or the least suspected it." Mr. Malone adds, that the observation is more applicable to Denham than to Waller; for Denham, from the age of sixteen, when he went to Trinity College, in Oxford, November 18, 1631, to the time of his father's death, January 6, 1638-9, was considered as a dull and dissipated young man; whereas Waller distinguished himself, as a poet, before he was eighteen. Besides, the "Sophy" was published just when the Irish rebellion broke out

of my friend's apostrophes, I hope the reader need not be told, that Mr. Waller is only mentioned for honour's sake; that I am desirous of laying hold on his memory on all occasions, and thereby acknowledging to the world, that unless he had written, none of us could write.

I know, my friend will forgive me this digression; for it is not only a copy of his style, but of his candour. The reader will observe, that he is ready for all hints of commending merit, and the writers of this age and country are particularly obliged to him, for his pointing out those passages which the French call *beaux endroits*, wherein they have most excelled. And though I may seem in this to have my own interest in my eyes, because he has more than once mentioned me* so much to my advantage, yet I hope the reader will take it only for a parenthesis, because the piece would have been very perfect without it. I may be suffered to please myself with the kindness of my friend, without valuing myself upon his parti lity: he had not confidence enough to send it out into the world, without my opinion of it, that it might pass securely, at least amongst the fair readers, for whose service it was principally designed. I am not so presuming to think my opinion can either be his touchstone, or his passport; but I thought I might send him back to Ariosto, who has made it the business of almost thirty stanzas, in the beginning of the thirty-seventh book of his "Orlando Furioso," not only to praise that beautiful part of the creation, but also to make a sharp satire on their enemies, to give mankind their own, and to tell them plainly, that from their envy it proceeds, that the virtue and great actions of women are purposely concealed, and the failings of some few amongst them exposed with all the aggravating circumstances of malice. For my own part, who have always been their servant, and have never drawn my pen against them, I had rather see some of them praised extraordinarily, than any of them suffer by detraction; and that in this age, and at this time particularly, wherein I find more heroines than heroes. Let me therefore give them joy of their new champion. If any will think me more partial to him than really I am, they can only say, I have returned his bribe; and the worst I wish him is, that he may receive justice from the men, and favour only from the ladies.

* In one passage of the Dialogue, our author's version of the sixth satire of Juvenal is mentioned with commendation; and in another, the tragedy of "Aureng-Zebe" is quoted.

CHARACTER OF ST. EVREMONT.

Charles de St. Denis, Seigneur de St. Evremont, was born in 1613, of a noble Norman family, and was early distinguished by the vivacity of his wit, as well as by his gallantry; for, like all the French noblesse, he followed the profession of arms. The Duke D'Enghien, afterwards Prince of Conde, was particularly attached to him, and gave him an appointment in his household. This he lost by ill-timed raillery on his patron. He was committed to the Bastile for a joke on Cardinal Mazarine: and afterwards forced to fly to Holland for writing a satirical history of the peace of the Pyrenees. From Holland St. Evremont retreated to England, where, at the witty court of Charles, his raillery was better understood than in Holland, and less likely to incur unpleasant consequences than in France. St. Evremont naturally addressed himself to his fair countrywoman Louise de Querouaille Duchess of Portsmouth, and the Duchess of Mazarine; and though they were rivals in Charles' affections, they united in protecting the Norman *bel-esprit*. The king conferred on him a thousand caresses, and a small pension; on which he lived, amusing himself by the composition of lighter pieces of literature, and despising the country, which afforded him refuge, so very thoroughly, that he did not even deign to learn English. The people of England did not, however, consider the labours of their foreign guest with similar apathy. After several surreptitious editions of his various tracts had appeared, there was published, in 1692, a collection entitled, "Miscellaneous Essays, by Monsieur St. Evremont, translated out of French; with his character, by a person of honour here in England, continued by Mr. Dryden." Desmaiseaux, by whom a complete edition of St. Evremont's works was edited in 1705, mentions it as well known, that Dr. Knightly Chetwood, who died dean of Gloucester, was the person of honour in the title-page of 1692. His connexion with Dryden makes this highly probable; although there is reason to believe, that the title of "person of honour" was not strictly applicable, and was probably assumed for the purpose of disguising the real translator.

CHARACTER OF M. ST. EVREMONT.

I know how nice an undertaking it is to write of a living author; yet the example of Father Bouhours has somewhat encouraged me in this attempt. Had not Monsieur St. Evremont been very considerable in his own country, that famous jesuit would not have ventured to praise a person in disgrace with the government of France, and living here in banishment. Yet, in his "*Pensees Ingenieuses*," he has often cited our author's thoughts and his expressions, as the standard of judicious thinking and graceful speaking; an undoubted sign that his merit was sufficiently established, when the disfavour of the court could not prevail against it. There is not only a justness in his conceptions, which is the foundation of good writing, but also a purity of language, and a beautiful turn of words, so little understood by modern writers; and which, indeed, was found at Rome but at the latter end of the commonwealth, and ended with Petronius, under the monarchy. If I durst extend my judgment to particulars, I would say, that our author has determined very nicely in his opinion of Epicurus; and that what he has said of his morals, is according to nature and reason.

It is true, that as I am a religious admirer of Virgil, I could wish that he had not discovered our father's nakedness.* But, after all, we must confess, that Æneas was none of the greatest heroes, and that Virgil was sensible of it himself. But what could he do? the Trojan on whom he was to build the Roman empire, had been already vanquished; he had lost his country, and was a fugitive. Nay, more, he had fought unsuccessfully with Diomedes, and was only preserved from death by his mother-goddess, who received a wound in his defence. So that Virgil, bound as he was to follow the footsteps of Homer, who had thus described him, could not reasonably have altered his character, and raised him in Italy to a much greater height of prowess than he found him formerly in Troy. Since, therefore, he could make no more of him in valour, he resolved not to give him that virtue as his principal; but chose another, which was piety. It is true, this latter, in the composition of a hero, was not altogether so shining as the former; but it entitled him more to the favour of the gods, and their protection, in all

* St. Evremont wrote "Observations on Segrais's Translation of Virgil."

his undertakings; and, which was the poet's chiefest aim, made a nearer resemblance betwixt Æneas and his patron Augustus Cæsar, who, above all things, loved to be flattered for being pious, both to the gods and his relations. And that very piety, or gratitude, (call it which you please,) to the memory of his uncle Julius, gave him the preference, amongst the soldiers, to Mark Antony; and, consequently raised him to the empire. As for personal courage, that of Augustus was not pushing;* and the poet, who was not ignorant of that defect, for that reason durst not ascribe it, in the supreme degree, to him who was to represent his emperor under another name: which was managed by him with the most imaginable fineness; for had valour been set uppermost, Augustus must have yielded to Agrippa. After all, this is rather to defend the courtier than the poet; and to make his hero escape again, under the covert of a cloud. Only we may add, what I think Bossu says, that the Roman commonwealth being now changed into a monarchy, Virgil was helping to that design; by insinuating into the people the piety of their new conqueror, to make them the better brook this innovation, which was brought on them by a man who was favoured by the gods. Yet we may observe, that Virgil forgot not, upon occasion, to speak honourably of Æneas, in point of courage, and that particularly in the person of him by whom he was overcome. For Diomedes compares him with Hector, and even with advantage:

> Quicquid apud duræ cessatum est mœnia Trojæ
> Hectoris Æneæque manu victoria Graiûm
> Hæsit, et in decimum vestigia retulit annum:
> Ambo animis, ambo insignes præstantibus armis;
> Hic pietate prior.

As for that particular passage, cited by Monsieur St. Evremont, where Æneas shows the utmost fear, in the beginning of a tempest,

> Extemplo Æneæ solvuntur frigore membra, &c.

why may it not be supposed, that, having been long at sea, he might be well acquainted with the nature of a storm; and, by the rough beginning, foresee the increase and danger of it? at least, as a father of his people, his concernment might be greater for them than for himself; and if so, what the poet takes from the merit of his courage, is added to the prime virtue of his character, which was his piety. Be this said with all manner of respect and deference to the opinion of Monsieur St. Evremont; amongst whose admirable talents, that of penetration is not the least. He generally dives into the very bottom of his authors; searches into the inmost recesses of their souls, and brings up with him those hidden treasures which had escaped the diligence of others. His examination of the "*Grand Alexandre*,"* in my opinion, is an admirable piece of criticism; and I doubt not, but that his observations on the English theatre had been as absolute in their kind, had he seen with his own eyes, and not with those of other men. But conversing in a manner wholly with the court, which is not always the truest judge, he has been unavoidably led into mistakes, and given to some of our coarsest poets a reputation abroad, which they never had at home. Had his conversation in the town been more general, he had certainly received other ideas on that subject, and not transmitted those names into his own country, which will be forgotten by posterity in ours.

Thus I have contracted my thoughts on a large subject; for whatever has been said, falls short of the true character of Monsieur St. Evremont, and his writings: and if the translation you are about to read does not everywhere come up to the original, the translator desires you to believe, that it is only because that he has failed in his undertaking.

* ——"He at Philippi kept
His sword even like a dancer;——
——he alone
Dealt on lieutenancy, and no practice had
In the brave squares of war."
Antony and Cleopatra.

* A tragedy by Racine. St. Evremont, in a dissertation on this play, addressed to Madame Borneau severely reprobates the fault so common in French tragedy, of making a play, though the scene is laid in ancient Rome or India, centre and turn upon Parisian manners. He concludes, that Corneille is the only author of the nation that displays a true taste for antiquity.

CHARACTER OF POLYBIUS.

The character of Polybius was prefixed to a translation executed by Sir Henry Shere, or Sheers;* the same gentleman whom Dryden has elsewhere classed among the "finer spirits of the age."† Our author had announced this work to the public in the preface to "Cleomenes." It was probably at that time under the press, or at least subjected to Dryden for his correction. The translation itself is of little value. Sir Henry disclaims all extent of erudition, and frankly confesses, he "has no warrant from his depth of learning whereof to make ostentation; wherein, indeed, he who most abounds ever finds least cause of boasting." Accordingly, his preface is employed in an attempt to convince the world, that mere scholars, or book-learned men, have rather traduced than translated Polybius and most authors of his class; such being totally at a loss to discover the sense of many passages in history, wherein matters military and naval are handled. He therefore takes up the pen as a man of the world, of business, science, and conversation, long intimate with such matters as are principally treated of by the historian. Finally, he describes his undertaking as an "employment, wherein he who performs best, traffics for small gain, and it would be unfair and unconscionable to make the loss more than the adventure; and, at the worst, it having been rather a diversion than a task, helping me to while away a few winter hours, which is some recreation to one who has led a life of action and business; and whose humour and fortune suit not with the pleasures of the town. Wherefore I shall have little cause of complaint, if my well-meaning in consenting to its publication be not so well received; I have been worse treated by the world, to which I am as little indebted as most men, who have spent near thirty years in public trusts, wherein I laboured, and wasted my youth and the vigour of my days, more to the service of my country, and the impairment of my health, than the improvement of my fortune; having stood the mark of envy, slander, and hard usage, without gleaning the least of those advantages, which use to be the anchor-hold and refuge of such as wrongfully or otherwise suffer the stroke of censure."

Our author, who seems to have had an especial regard for Sir Henry Shere, contributed this preliminary discourse.

Mr. Malone has fixed Sir Henry Shere's death to the year 1713, when his library was exposed to sale by advertisement in "The Guardian."

THE CHARACTER OF POLYBIUS,

AND HIS WRITINGS.

The worthy author of this translation, who is very much my friend, was pleased to intrust it in my hands for many months together, before he published it, desiring me to review the English, and to correct what I found amiss; which he needed not have done, if his modesty would have given him leave to have relied on his own abilities, who is so great a master of our style and language, as the world will acknowledge him to be, after the reading of this excellent version.

It is true, that Polybius has formerly appeared in an English dress,‡ but under such a cloud of errors in his first translation, that his native beauty was not only hidden, but his sense perverted in many places; so that he appeared unlike himself, and unworthy of that esteem which has always been paid him by antiquity, as the most sincere, the clearest, and most instructive, of all historians. He is now not only redeemed from those mistakes, but also restored to the first purity of his conceptions; and the style in which he now speaks is as plain and unaffected as that he wrote. I had only the pleasure of reading him in a fair manuscript, without the toil of alteration; at least it was so very inconsiderable, that it only cost me the dash of a pen in some few places, and those of very small importance. So much had the care, the diligence, and exactness of my friend prevented my trouble, that he

* The full title is, "The History of Polybius, the Megalopolitan; containing a general Account of the Transactions of the World, and principally of the Roman People during the first and Second Punic wars. Translated by Sir H. S. To which is added a Character of Polybius and his Writings, by Mr. Dryden, 1693.

† Where he enumerates the Translators of Lucian in the Supplement to his Life.

‡ "History of Polybius, the five first bookes entire, with all the parcels of subsequent bookes unto the eighteenth, according to the Greeke original. Also, the manner of the Roman encamping. Translated into English, by Edward Grimestone, sergeant at arms." London, 1634. Folio.

left me not the occasion of serving him, in a work which was already finished to my hands. I doubt not but the reader will approve my judgment. So happy it is for a good author to fall into the hands of a translator, who is of a genius like his own; who has added experience to his natural abilities; who has been educated in business of several kinds; has travelled, like his author, into many parts of the world, and some of them the same with the present scene of history; has been employed in business of the like nature with Polybius, and, like him, is perfectly acquainted not only with the terms of the mathematics, but has searched into the bottom of that admirable science, and reduced into practice the most useful rules of it, to his own honour, and the benefit of his native country; who, besides these advantages, possesses the knowledge of shipping and navigation; and, in few words, is not ignorant of any thing that concerns the tactics; so that here, from the beginning, we are sure of finding nothing that is not thoroughly understood."* The expression is clear, and the words adequate to the subject. Nothing in the matter will be mistaken; nothing of the terms will be misapplied; all is natural and proper; and he who understands good sense and English, will be profited by the first, and delighted with the latter. This is what may be justly said in commendation of the translator, and without the note of flattery to a friend.

As for his author, I shall not be ashamed to copy from the learned Casaubon, who has translated him into Latin,† many things which I had not from my own small reading, and which I could not, without great difficulty, have drawn, but from his fountain; not omitting some which came casually in my way, by reading the preface of the Abbot Pichon to the Dauphin's "Tacitus," an admirable and most useful work; which helps I ingenuously profess to have received from them, both to clear myself from being a plagiary of their writings, and to give authority, by their names, to the weakness of my own performance.

The taking of Constantinople, by Mahomet the Great, fell into the latter times of Pope Nicholas the Fifth,* a pope not only studious of good letters, and particularly of history, but also a great encourager of it in others. From the dreadful overthrow of that city, and final subversion of the Greek empire, many learned men escaped, and brought over with them into

* From these expressions, one would suppose Sir Henry Shere to have been a seaman, which may also be conjectured from his writing an "Essay on the Certainty and Causes of the Earth's motion on its Axis;" and a "Discourse concerning the Mediterranean Sea and the Straits of Gibraltar;" the one published in 1698, the other in 1705. The naval and military professions were, however, formerly accounted less absolutely distinct branches of service than at present. Many officers distinguished themselves in both. Mr. Malone may therefore be right in conjecturing Sir Henry Shere to have been a soldier, though his studies would argue him a seaman or engineer.

† Polybii Lycortæ F. Megalopolites Historiarum Libri, qui supersunt Gr. Lat. Isaacus Casaubonus, ex antiquis libris emendavit, Lat. vertit et commentariis illustravit. Accessit Æneæ vetustissimi, Tactici commentarius de toleranda obsidione. Isaacus Casaubonus primus vulgavit, Latinam interpretationem ac notas adjecit.—*Parisiis*, 1609, *Folio*.

* "The fame of Nicholas the Fifth, (who sat in the papal chair from 1447 to 1455,) has not," says Mr. Gibbon,—(*Decline and Fall of the Roman Empire*, vi. 429, 4to.) "been adequate to his merits. From a plebeian origin, he raised himself, by his virtue and learning. The character of the man prevailed over the interests of the pope; and he sharpened those weapons, which were soon pointed against the Roman church. He had been the friend of the most eminent scholars of the age; he became their patron; and such was the humility of his manners, that the change was scarcely discernible, either to them or to himself. If he pressed the acceptance of a liberal gift, it was not as the measure of desert, but as the proof of benevolence; and when modest merit declined his bounty, 'Accept it,' would he say, with a consciousness of his own worth; 'you will not always have a Nicholas among ye.' The influence of the holy see pervaded Christendom; and he exerted that influence in the search, not of benefices, but of books. From the ruins of the Byzantine libraries, from the darkest monasteries of Germany and Britain, he collected the dusty manuscripts of the writers of antiquity; and wherever the original could not be removed, a faithful copy was transcribed, and transmitted for his use. The Vatican, the old repository for bulls and legends, for superstition and forgery, was daily replenished with more precious furniture; and such was the industry of Nicholas, that, in a reign of eight years, he formed a library of five thousand volumes. To his munificence, the Latin world was indebted for the versions of Xenophon, Diodorus, Polybius, Thucydides, Herodotus, and Appian; of Strabo's Geography; of the Iliad; of the most valuable works of Plato and Aristotle; of Ptolemy and Theophrastus; and of the fathers of the Greek church. The example of the Roman pontiff was preceded, or imitated, by a Florentine merchant, who governed the republic without arms, and without a title. Cosmo, of Medicis, was the father of a line of princes, whose name and age are almost synonymous with the restoration of learning. His credit was ennobled into fame; his riches were dedicated to the service of mankind; he corresponded at once with Cairo and London, and a cargo of Indian spices and Greek books was imported in the same vessel. The genius and education of his grandson, Lorenzo, rendered him not only a patron, but a judge and candidate in the literary race. In his palace, distress was entitled to relief, and merit to reward. His leisure hours were delightfully spent in the Platonic academy; he encouraged the emulation of Demetrius Chalcocondyles and Angelo Politian; and his active missionary, Janus Lascaris, returned from the East with a treasure of two hundred manuscripts, fourscore of which were as yet unknown in the libraries of Europe. The rest of Italy was animated by a similar spirit, and the progress of the nation repaid the liberality of the princes. The Latins held the exclusive property of their own literature; and these disciples of Greece were soon capable of trans-

Italy that treasure of ancient authors,* which, by their unhappiness, we now possess; and, amongst the rest, some of these remaining fragments of Polybius. The body of this his tory, as he left it finished, was consisting of forty books, of which the eighth part† is only remaining to us entire. As for his negotiations, when he was sent ambassador either from his own countrymen,‡ the commonwealth of the Achaians, or afterwards was employed by the Romans on their business with other nations, we are obliged to Constantine the Great for their preservation; for that emperor was so much in love with the dexterous management and wisdom of our author, that he caused them all to be faithfully transcribed, and made frequent use of them in his own despatches and affairs with foreign princes, as his best guides in his concernments with them.

Polybius, as you will find in reading of him, though he principally intended the history of the Romans, and the establishment of their empire over the greatest part of the world which was then known, yet had in his eye the general history of the times in which he lived, not forgetting either the wars of his own country with their neighbours of Etolia, or the concurrent affairs of Macedonia and the provinces of Greece, which is properly so called; nor the monarchies of Asia and Egypt; nor the republic of the Carthaginians, with the several traverses of their fortunes, either in relation to the Romans, or independent to the wars which they waged with them; besides what happened in Spain and Sicily, and other European countries. The time, which is taken up in this history, consists of three-and-fifty years; and the greatest part of it is employed in the description of those events, of which the author was an eye-witness, or bore a considerable part in the conduct of them. But in what particular time or age it was, when mankind received that irrecoverable loss of this noble history, is not certainly delivered to us. It appears to have been perfect in the reign of Constantine, by what I have already noted; and neither Casaubon, nor any other, can give us any farther account concerning it.

The first attempt towards a translation of him, was by command of the same Pope Nicholas the Fifth, already mentioned, who esteemed him the prince of Greek historians; would have him continually in his hands; and used to make this judgment of him,—that, if he yielded to one or two, in the praise of eloquence, yet, in wisdom, and all other accomplishments belonging to a perfect historian, he was at least equal to any other writer, Greek or Roman, and perhaps excelled them all. This is the author, who is now offered to us in our mother-tongue, recommended by the nobility of his birth, by his institution in art and sciences, by his knowledge in natural and moral philosophy, and particularly the politics; by his being conversant both in the arts of peace and war; by his education under his father Lycortas, who voluntarily deposed himself from his sovereignty of Megalopolis to become a principal member of the Achaian commonwealth, which then flourished under the management of Aratus; by his friendship with Scipio Africanus, who subdued Carthage, to whom he was both a companion and a counsellor; and by the good-will, esteem, and intimacy, which he had with several princes of Asia, Greece, and Egypt, during his life; and after his decease, by deserving the applause and approbation of all succeeding ages

mitting and improving the lessons which they had imbibed. After a short succession of foreign teachers, the tide of emigration subsided; but the language of Constantinople was spread beyond the Alps: and the natives of France, Germany, and England, imparted to their country the sacred fire which they had kindled in the schools of Florence and Rome."

* Our author recollected the following panegyric on Pope Nicholas, in the Dedication of Casaubon's edition of Polybius, to Henry IV. of France:

"Qum enim a pluribus retro sæculis, in principum animis, toto Occidente, amor politioris literaturæ et Græci sermonis excoluisset; accidit non sine numine profecto, ut circa illa ipsa tempora Byzantinæ cladis, et paullo ante, summi in Europa viri et principes generossissimi hunc veternum seu virgula divina tacti, opportune excuterent, et ad bene merendum de studiis politioribus et de linguis, ardore incredibili accenderentur. Prima terrarum Italia ad hanc palmam occupandam, à diuturno torpore tunc demum expergefacta, sese, concitavit, et nationibus aliis per Europam, exemplum quod imitarentur præbuit. In ipsa vero Italia, ad certamen adeo gloriosum, Nicolaus Quintus Pontifex Maximus, in cujus extrema tempora Byzantini imperii eversio incidit, princeps, quod equidem sciam signum sustulit. Nam et literarum dicitur fuisse intelligentissimus; et, quod res arguit earum amore erat flagrantissimus. Primus hic, illa ætate, libros antiquorum scriptorum sedulo conquirere curæ habuit; magnamque earum copiam in Vaticanam intulit; primus cum assiduis hortatibus, tum ingentibus etiam propositis præmiis, ad meliorem literaturam à tenebris oblivionis in lucem revocandam, homines Italos stimulavit: primus, Græcæ linguæ auctores omnis sincerioris doctrine esse promos condos qui non ignoraret, ut Latino sermone exprimerentur, vehementissime optavit, et efficere contendit."

† That is, the first five books.

‡ Polybius, the historian, was born at Megalopolis, in Arcadia, in the fourth year of the 143d Olympiad, about 205 years before the Christian æra. Being carried to Rome as an hostage, he became the companion and friend of the younger Scipio Africanus; accompanied him in his campaigns; and is said to have witnessed the destruction of Carthage, in the 158th Olympiad. Having returned to his native country, he died in the 164th Olympiad, 124 years before Christ, in consequence of a fall from his horse.

The history of Polybius embraced the space from the first year of the 140th to the first of the 153d Olympiad, being fifty-three years.

This author, so long neglected in the barbarous times of Christianity, and so little known in Europe, (according to the fate which commonly follows the best of writers,) was pulled from under the rubbish which covered him, by the learned bishop, Nicholas the Fifth; and some parts of his history (for with all his diligence he was not able to recover the whole) were by him recommended to a person knowing both in the Greek and Roman tongues, and learned for the times in which he lived, to be translated into Latin; and, to the honour of our Polybius, he was amongst the first of the Greek writers, who deserved to have this care betowed on him; which notwithstanding, so many hindrances occurred in this attempt, that the work was not perfected in his popedom, neither was any more than a third part of what is now recovered in his hands; neither did that learned Italian,* who had undertaken him, succeed very happily in that endeavour; for the perfect knowledge of the Greek language was not yet restored, and that translator was but as a one-eyed man amongst the nation of the blind; only suffered till a better could be found to do right to an author, whose excellence required a more just interpreter than the ignorance of that age afforded. And this gives me occasion to admire, (says Casaubon,) that in following times, when eloquence was redeemed, and the knowledge of the Greek language flourished, yet no man thought of pursuing that design, which was so worthily begun in those first rudiments of learning. Some, indeed, of almost every nation in Europe, have been instrumental in the recovery of several lost parts of our Polybius, and commented on them with good success; but no man, before Casaubon, had reviewed the first translation, corrected its errors, and put the last hand to its accomplishment. The world is therefore beholden to him for this great work; for he has collected into one their scattered fragments, has pieced them together according to the natural order in which they were written, made them intelligible to scholars, and rendered the French translator's task more easy to his hands.

Our author is particularly mentioned with great honour by Cicero, Strabo, Josephus, and Plutarch; and in what rank of writers they are placed, none of the learned need to be informed. He is copied in whole books together, by Livy, commonly esteemed the prince of the Roman history, and translated word for word, though the Latin historian is not to be excused, for not mentioning the man to whom he had been so much obliged, nor for taking, as his own, the worthy labours of another. Marcus Brutus, who preferred the freedom of his country to the obligations which he had to Julius Cæsar, so prized Polybius, that he made a compendium of his works; and read him not only for his instruction, but for the diversion of his grief, when his noble enterprize for the restoration of the commonwealth had not found the success which it deserved. And this is not the least commendation of our author, that he who was not wholly satisfied with the eloquence of Tully, should epitomise Polybius with his own hand.* It was on the consideration of Brutus, and the veneration which he paid him, that Constantine the Great took so great a pleasure in reading our author, and collecting the several treaties of his embassies; of which, though many are now lost, yet those which remain are a sufficient testimony of his abilities; and I congratulate my country, that a prince of our extraction (as was Constantine) has the honour of obliging the Christian world by these remainders of our great historian.

It is now time to enter into the particular praises of Polybius, which I have given you before in gross; and the first of them, (following the method of Casaubon,) is his wonderful skill in political affairs. I had read him, in English, with the pleasure of a boy, before I was ten years of age; and yet, even then, had some dark notions of the prudence with which he conducted his design, particularly in making me know, and almost see, the places where such and such actions were performed. This was the first distinction which I was then capable of making betwixt him and other historians which I read early. But when, being of a riper age, I took him again into my hands, I must needs say that I have profited more by reading him than by Thucydides, Appian, Dion Cassius, and all the rest of the Greek historians together; and amongst all the Romans, none have reached him in this particular, but Tacitus, who is equal with him. It is wonderful to consider with how much

* Nicolo Paretti published a Latin version of the first five books of Polybius, at Rome, in 1473, folio. The first Greek edition appeared in 1530; the second at Basle, in 1549. The last is most esteemed.

* "Plutarch tells us, that Brutus was thus employed the day before the battle of Pharsalia. 'It was the middle of summer; the heats were intense, the marshy situation of the camp disagreeable, and his tent-bearers were long in coming. Nevertheless, though extremely harassed and fatigued, he did not anoint himself till noon; and then taking a morsel of bread, while others were at rest, or musing on the event of the ensuing day, he employed himself till the evening in writing an epitome of Polybius.'"—*Malone.*

care and application he instructs, counsels, warns, admonishes, and advises, whensoever he can find a fit occasion. He performs all these sometimes in the nature of a common parent of mankind; and sometimes also limits his instructions to particular nations, by a friendly reproach of those failings and errors to which they were most obnoxious. In this last manner, he gives instructions to the Mantinæans, the Elæans, and several other provinces of Greece, by informing them of such things as were conducing to their welfare. Thus he likewise warns the Romans of their obstinacy and wilfulness, vices which have often brought them to the brink of ruin. And thus he frequently exhorts the Greeks, in general, not to depart from their dependence on the Romans; nor to take false measures, by embroiling themselves in wars with that victorious people, in whose fate it was to be masters of the universe. But as his peculiar concernment was for the safety of his own countrymen, the Achaians, he more than once insinuates to them the care of their preservation, which consisted in submitting to the yoke of the Roman people, which they could not possibly avoid; and to make it easy to them, by a cheerful compliance with their commands, rather than unprofitably to oppose them with the hazard of those remaining privileges which the clemency of the conquerors had left them. For this reason, in the whole course of his history he makes it his chiefest business to persuade the Grecians in general, that the growing greatness and fortune of the Roman empire was not owing to mere chance, but to the conduct and invincible courage of that people, to whom their own virtue gave the dominion of the world. And yet this counsellor of patience and submission, as long as there was any probability of hope remaining to withstand the progress of the Roman fortune, was not wanting to the utmost of his power to resist them, at least to defer the bondage of his country, which he had long foreseen. But the fates inevitably drawing all things into subjection to Rome, this well-deserving citizen was commanded to appear in that city,* where he suffered the imprisonment of many years; yet even then his virtue was beneficial to him, the knowledge of his learning and his wisdom procuring him the friendship of the most potent in the senate; so that it may be said with Casaubon, that the same virtue which had brought him into distress, was the very means of his relief, and of his exaltation to greater dignities than those which he lost; for by the intercession of Cato the Censor, Scipio Æmilianus, who afterwards destroyed Carthage, and some other principal noblemen, our Polybius was restored to liberty. After which, having set it down as a maxim, that the welfare of the Achaians consisted, as I have said, in breaking their own stubborn inclinations, and yielding up that freedom which they no longer could maintain, he made it the utmost aim of his endeavours to bring over his countrymen to that persuasion; in which, though, to their misfortunes, his counsels were not prevalent, yet thereby he not only proved himself a good patriot, but also made his fortunes with the Romans. For his countrymen, by their own unpardonable fault, not long afterwards drew on themselves their own destruction; for when Mummius, in the Achaian war, made a final conquest of that country, he dissolved the great council of their commonwealth.* But, in the mean time, Polybius enjoyed that tranquillity of fortune which he had purchased by his wisdom, in that private state, being particularly dear to Scipio and Lælius, and some of the rest, who were then in the administration of the Roman government. And that favour which he had gained amongst them, he employed not in heaping riches to himself, but as a means of performing many considerable actions; as particularly when Scipio was sent to demolish Carthage,† he went along with him in the nature of a counsellor and companion of his enterprize. At which time, receiving the command of a fleet from him, he made discoveries in many parts of the Atlantic Ocean, and especially on the shores of Africa; and‡ doing many good offices to all sorts of people whom he had power to oblige, especially to the Grecians, who, in honour of their benefactor, caused many statues of him to be erected, as Pausanias has written. The particular gratitude of the Locrians in Italy is also an undeniable witness of this truth; who, by his mediation, being discharged from the burden of taxes which oppressed them, through the hardship of those conditions which the Romans had imposed on them in the treaty of peace, professed themselves to be owing for their lives and fortunes, to the interest only and good nature of Polybius, which they took care to express by all manner of acknowledgment.

Yet, as beneficent as he was, the greatest obligement which he could lay on human kind, was the writing of this present history, wherein he has left a perpetual monument of his

* With a thousand of his countrymen, whom the Romans ordered thither as hostages, after the conquest of Macedonia.

* A.U. C. 608. † A. U. C. 607.

‡ The word *and* renders this passage ungrammatical.—*Malone.*

public love to all the world in every succeeding age of it, by giving us such precepts as are most conducing to our common safety and our benefit. This philanthropy (which we have not a proper word in English to express) is everywhere manifest in our author; and from hence proceeded that divine rule which he gave to Scipio,—that whensoever he went abroad, he should take care not to return to his own house, before he had acquired a friend by some new obligement. To this excellency of nature we owe the treasure which is contained in this most useful work: this is the standard by which all good and prudent princes ought to regulate their actions. None have more need of friends than monarchs; and though ingratitude is too frequent in the most of those who are obliged, yet encouragement will work on generous minds; and if the experiment be lost on thousands, yet it never fails on all: and one virtuous man in a whole nation is worth the buying, as one diamond is worth the search in a heap of rubbish. But a narrow-hearted prince, who thinks that mankind is made for him alone, puts his subjects in a way of deserting him on the first occasion;* and teaches them to be as sparing of their duty, as he is of his bounty. He is sure of making enemies, who will not be at the cost of rewarding his friends and servants; and, by letting his people see he loves them not, instructs them to live upon the square with him, and to make him sensible in his turn, that prerogatives are given, but privileges are inherent. As for tricking, cunning, and that which in sovereigns they call king-craft, and reason of state in commonwealths, to them and their proceedings Polybius is an open enemy. He severely reproves all faithless practices, and that κακοπραγμοσυνη, or vicious policy, which is too frequent in the management of the public. He commends nothing but plainness, sincerity, and the common good, undisguised, and set in a true light before the people. Not but that there may be a necessity of saving a nation, by going beyond the letter of the law, or even sometimes by superseding it; but then that necessity must not be artificial,—it must be visible, it must be strong enough to make the remedy not only pardoned, but desired, to the major part of the people; not for the interest only of some few men, but for the public safety; for otherwise, one infringement of a law draws after it the practice of subverting all the liberties of a nation, which are only intrusted with any government, but can never be given up to it. The best way to distinguish betwixt a pretended necessity and a true, is to observe if the remedy be rarely applied, or frequently; in times of peace, or times of war and public distractions, which are the most usual causes of sudden necessities. From hence Casaubon infers, that this our author, who preaches virtue, and probity, and plain-dealing, ought to be studied principally by kings and ministers of state; and those youth, who are bred up to succeed in the management of business, should read him carefully, and imbibe him thoroughly, detesting the maxims that are given by Machiavel and others, which are only the instruments of tyranny. Furthermore, (continues he,) the study of truth is perpetually joined with the love of virtue; for there is no virtue which derives not its original from truth; as, on the contrary, there is no vice which has not its beginning from a lie. Truth is the foundation of all knowledge, and the cement of all societies; and this is one of the most shining qualities in our author.

I was so strongly persuaded of this myself, in the perusal of the present history, that I confess, amongst all the ancients I never found any who had the air of it so much; and amongst the moderns, none but Philip de Commines.* They had this common to them, that they both changed their masters. But Polybius changed not his side, as Philip did: he was not bought off to another party, but pursued the true interest of his country, even when he served the Romans. Yet since truth, as one of the philosophers has told me, lies in the bottom of a well, so it is hard to draw it up; much pains, much diligence, much judgment is necessary to hand it us; even cost is oftentimes required; and Polybius was wanting in none of these.

We find but few historians of all ages, who have been diligent enough in their search for truth: it is their common method to take on trust what they distribute to the public; by which means a falsehood once received from a famed writer becomes traditional to posterity. But Polybius weighed the authors from whom he was forced to borrow the history of the times immediately preceding his, and often-

* Mr. Malone justly conjectures, that Dryden here thought of his old master James II., whose economy bordered on penury, and whose claims of prerogative approached to tyranny.

* Philip de Commines, author of the excellent Memoirs of his own time. He was born in Flanders, and was for several years a distinguished ornament of the court of Charles the Bold, Duke of Burgundy, his native sovereign; but was tempted to desert his service for that of Louis XI., by whom he was employed in several negotiations. After the death of that monarch, Commines fell into disgrace with his successor, and was long detained in prison: he died in 1509. It was of this historian Catherine de Medicis was wont to say, "that he made as many heretics in the state, as Luther in the church."

times corrected them, either by comparing them each with other, or by the lights which he had received from ancient men of known integrity amongst the Romans, who had been conversant in those affairs which were then managed, and were yet living to instruct him. He also learned the Roman tongue; and attained to that knowledge of their laws, their rites, their customs, and antiquities, that few of their own citizens understood them better: having gained permission from the senate to search the Capitol, he made himself familiar with their records, and afterwards translated them into his mother tongue. So that he taught the noblemen of Rome their own municipal laws, and was accounted more skilful in them than Fabius Pictor, a man of the senatorian order, who wrote the transactions of the Punic wars. He who neglected none of the laws of history, was so careful of truth, (which is the principal,) that he made it his whole business to deliver nothing to posterity which might deceive them; and by that diligence and exactness, may easily be known to be studious of truth, and a lover of it. What therefore Brutus thought worthy to transcribe with his own hand out of him, I need not be ashamed to copy after him:—"I believe," says Polybius, "that Nature herself has constituted truth as the supreme deity, which is to be adored by mankind, and that she has given it greater force than any of the rest; for being opposed, as she is on all sides, and appearances of truth so often passing for the thing itself, in behalf of plausible falsehoods, yet by her wonderful operation she insinuates herself into the minds of men; sometimes exerting her strength immediately, and sometimes lying hid in darkness for length of time; but at last she struggles through it, and appears triumphant over falsehood." This sincerity Polybius preferred to all his friends, and even to his father: "in all other offices of life," says he, "praise a lover of his friends, and of his native country; but in writing history, I am obliged to divest myself of all other obligations, and sacrifice them all to truth."

Aratus, the Sicyonian, in the childhood of our author, was the chief of the Achaian commonwealth; a man in principal esteem, both in his own country and all the provinces of Greece; admired universally for his probity, his wisdom, his just administration, and his conduct: in remembrance of all which, his grateful countrymen, after his decease, ordained him those honours which are only due to heroes. Him our Polybius had in veneration, and formed himself by imitation of his virtues; and is never wanting in his commendations through the course of his history. Yet even this man, when the cause of truth required it, is many times reproved by him for his slowness in counsel, his tardiness in the beginning of his enterprizes, his tedious and more than Spanish deliberations; and his heavy and cowardly proceedings are as freely blamed by our Polybius, as they were afterwards by Plutarch, who questionless drew his character from this history. In plain terms, that wise general scarce ever performed any great action but by night; the glittering of a sword before his face was offensive to his eyes; our author therefore boldly accuses him of his faint-heartedness; attributes the defeat at Caphiæ wholly to him; and is not sparing to affirm, that all Peloponnesus was filled with trophies, which were set up as the monuments of his losses. He sometimes praises, and at other times condemns, the proceedings of Philip, King of Macedon, the son of Demetrius, according to the occasions which he gave him by the variety and inequality of his conduct; and this most exquisite on either side. He more than once arraigns him for the inconstancy of his judgment, and chaptors even his own Aratus on the same head; showing, by many examples, produced from their actions, how many miseries they had both occasioned to the Grecians; and attributing it to the weakness of human nature, which can make nothing perfect. But some men are brave in battle, who are weak in counsel, which daily experience sets before our eyes; others deliberate wisely, but are weak in the performing part; and even no man is the same to-day, which he was yesterday, or may be to-morrow. On this account, says our author, "a good man is sometimes liable to blame, and a bad man, though not often, may possibly deserve to be commended." And for this very reason he severely taxes Timæus, a malicious historian, who will allow no kind of virtue to Agathocles, the tyrant of Sicily, but detracts from all his actions, even the most glorious, because in general he was a vicious man. "Is it to be thought," says Casaubon, "that Polybius loved the memory of Agathocles, the tyrant, or hated that of the virtuous Aratus?" But it is one thing to commend a tyrant, and another thing to overpass in silence those laudable actions which are performed by him; because it argues an author of the same falsehood, to pretermit what has actually been done, as to feign those actions which have never been.

It will not be unprofitable, in this place, to give another famous instance of the candour and integrity of our historian. There had been an ancient league betwixt the republic of Achaia and the kings of Egypt, which was entertained by both parties sometimes on the same conditions, and sometimes also the confederacy was renewed on other terms. It happened, in the 148th Olympiad,* that Ptolomy Epiphanes, on this occasion, sent one Demetrius, his ambassador, to the commonwealth of Achaia. That republic was then ruinously divided into two factions; whereof the heads on one side were Philopœmen, and Lycortas, the father of our author: of the adverse party, the chief was Aristænus, with some other principal Achaians. The faction of Philopœmen was prevalent in the council, for renewing the confederacy with the king of Egypt; in order to which, Lycortas received a commission to go to that court, and treat the articles of alliance. Accordingly, he goes, and afterwards returns, and gives account to his superiors, that the treaty was concluded. Aristænus, hearing nothing but a bare relation of a league that was made, without any thing belonging to the conditions of it, and well knowing that several forms of those alliances had been used in the former negotiations, asked Lycortas, in the council, according to which of them this present confederacy was made? To this question of his enemy, Lycortas had not a word to answer; for it had so happened by the wonderful neglect of Philopœmen, and his own, and also that of Ptolomy's counsellors, (or, as I rather believe, by their craft contrived,) that the whole transaction had been loosely and confusedly managed, which, in a matter of so great importance, redounded to the scandal and ignominy of Philopœmen and Lycortas, in the face of that grave assembly. Now these proceedings our author so relates, as if he had been speaking of persons to whom he had no manner of relation, though one of them was his own father, and the other always esteemed by him in the place of a better father. But being mindful of the law which himself had instituted, concerning the indispensable duty of an historian, (which is truth,) he chose rather to be thought a lover of it, than of either of his parents. It is true, Lycortas, in all probability, was dead when Polybius wrote this history; but, had he been then living, we may safely think, that his son would have assumed the same liberty, and not feared to have offended him in behalf of truth.

Another part of this veracity is also deserving the notice of the reader, though at the same time we must conclude, that it was also an effect of a sound judgment, that he perpetually explodes the legends of prodigies and miracles, and, instead of them, most accurately searches into the natural causes of those actions which he describes; for, from the first of these, the latter follows of direct consequence. And for this reason he professes an immortal enmity to those tricks and jugglings, which the common people believe as real miracles; because they are ignorant of the causes which produced them. But he had made a diligent search into them, and found out, that they proceeded either from the fond credulity of the people, or were imposed on them by the craft of those whose interest it was that they should be believed. You hear not in Polybius, that it rained blood or stones; that a bull had spoken; or a thousand such impossibilities, with which Livy perpetually crowds the calends of almost every consulship.* His new years could no more begin without them, during his description of the Punic wars, than our prognosticating almanacks without the effects of the present oppositions betwixt Saturn and Jupiter, the foretelling of comets and coruscations in the air, which seldom happen at the times assigned by our astrologers, and almost always fail in their events. If you will give credit to some other authors, some god was always present with Hannibal or Scipio, to direct their actions; that a visible deity wrought journey-work under Hannibal, to conduct him through the difficult passages of the Alps; and another did the same office of drudgery for Scipio when he besieged New Carthage, by draining the water, which otherwise would have drowned his army in their rash approaches; which Polybius observing, says wittily and truly, that the authors of such fabulous kind of stuff write tragedies, not histories; for, as the poets, when they are at a loss for the solution of a plot, bungle up their catastrophe with a god descending in a machine, so these inconsiderate historians, when they have brought their heroes into a plunge by some rash and headlong undertaking, having no human way remaining to disengage them with honour, are forced to have recourse to miracle, and introduce a god for their deliverance. It is a common frenzy of the ignorant multitude, says Casaubon, to be always engaging heaven on their side; and indeed it is a successful stratagem of any general to gain authority among his soldiers, if he can persuade them, that he is the man by fate appointed for such or such an action, though most impracticable. To be favoured of God, and command (if it may be

* In the year of Rome, 862.

* I believe the most enthusiastic admirers of Livy must tire of these unrivalled prodigies. *Bos locutus* occurs as often, and is mentioned with as much indifference, as a nomination of sheriffs in Hall, Stowe, or Speed.

permitted so to say,) the extraordinary concourse of Providence, sets off a hero, and makes more specious the cause for which he fights, without any consideration of morality, which ought to be the beginning and end of all our actions; for, where that is violated, God is only present in permission; and suffers a wrong to be done, but not commands it. Light historians, and such as are superstitious in their natures, by the artifice of feigned miracles captivate the gross understandings of their readers, and please their fancies by relations of things which are rather wonderful than true; but such as are of a more profound and solid judgment, (which is the character of our Polybius,) have recourse only to their own natural lights, and by them pursue the methods at least of probability, if they cannot arrive to a settled certainty. He was satisfied that Hannibal was not the first who had made a passage through the Alps, but that the Gauls had been before him in their descent on Italy; and also knew, that this most prudent general, when he laid his design of invading that country, had made an alliance with the Gauls, and prepossessed them in his favour; and before he stirred a foot from Spain, had provided against all those difficulties which he foresaw in his attempt, and compassed his undertaking, which indeed was void of miracles, but full of conduct, and military experience. In the same manner, Scipio, before he departed from Rome, to take his voyage into Spain, had carefully considered every particular circumstance which might cross his purpose, and made his enterprise as easy to him as human prudence could provide; so that he was victorious over that nation, not by virtue of any miracle, but by his admirable forecast, and wise conduct in the execution of his design. Of which, though Polybius was not an eye-witness, he yet had it from the best testimony, which was that of Lælius, the friend of Scipio, who accompanied him in that expedition; of whom our author, with great diligence, inquired concerning every thing of moment which happened in that war, and whom he commends for his sincerity in that relation.

Whensoever he gives us the account of any considerable action, he never fails to tell us why it succeeded, or for what reason it miscarried; together with all the antecedent causes of its undertaking, and the manner of its performance; all which he accurately explains; of which I will select but some few instances, because I want leisure to expatiate on many. In the fragments of the seventeenth book he makes a learned dissertation concerning the Macedonian phalanx, or gross body of foot, which was formerly believed to be invincible, till experience taught the contrary by the success of the battle which Philip lost to the commonwealth of Rome; and the manifest and most certain causes are therein related, which prove it to be inferior to the Roman legions. When also he had told us in his former books, of the three great battles wherein Hannibal had overthrown the Romans, and the last at Cannæ, wherein he had in a manner conquered that republic, he gives the reasons of every defeat, either from the choice of ground, or the strength of the foreign horse in Hannibal's army, or the ill-timing of the fight on the vanquished side. After this, when he describes the turn of fortune on the part of the Romans, you are visibly conducted upwards to the causes of that change, and the reasonableness of the method which was afterwards pursued by that commonwealth, which raised it to the empire of the world. In these and many other examples, which for brevity are omitted, there is nothing more plain than that Polybius denies all power to fortune, and places the sum of success in Providence; *συμβαίνειν τὴν τύχην αἰτιᾶσθαι φαῦλον* indeed, are his words. It is a madness to make fortune the mistress of events; because in herself she is nothing, can rule nothing, but is ruled by prudence. So that whenever our author seems to attribute any thing to chance, he speaks only with the vulgar, and desires so to be understood.

But here I must make bold to part company with Casaubon for a moment. He is a vehement friend to any author with whom he has taken any pains; and his partiality to *Persius*, in opposition to Juvenal, is too fresh in my memory to be forgotten. Because Polybius will allow nothing to the power of chance, he takes an occasion to infer, that he believed a providence; sharply inveighing against those who have accused him of atheism. He makes Suidas his second in this quarrel; and produces his single evidence, and that but a bare assertion, without proof, that Polybius believed, with us Christians, God administered all human actions and affairs. But our author will not be defended in this case; his whole history reclaims to that opinion. When he speaks of Providence, or of any divine admonition, he is as much in jest, as when he speaks of fortune; it is all to the capacity of the vulgar. Prudence was the only divinity which he worshipped, and the possession of virtue the only end which he proposed. If I would have disguised this to the reader, it was not in my power. The passages which manifestly prove his irreligion are so obvious, that I need not quote them. Neither do I know any reason why Casaubon should enlarge so much in his justification; since to believe false gods, and to believe none, are errors of the same importance. He who knew not our God, saw now through the ridiculous opinions of the heathens concerning theirs; and not being able without revelation to go farther, stopped at home in his own breast, and made prudence his goddess, truth his search, and virtue his reward. If Casaubon, like him, had followed truth, he would have saved me the ungrateful pains of contradicting him; but even the reputation of Polybius, if there were occasion, is to be sacrificed to truth, according to his own maxim.

As for the wisdom of our author, whereby he wonderfully foresaw the decay of the Roman empire, and those civil wars which turned it down from a commonwealth to an absolute monarchy, he who will take the pains to review this history will easily perceive, that Polybius was of the best sort of prophets, who predict from natural causes those events which must naturally proceed from them. And these things were not to succeed even in the compass of the next century to that wherein he lived, but the person was then living who was the first mover towards them; and that was that great Scipio Africanus, who, by cajoling the people to break the fundamental constitutions of the government in his favour, by bringing him too early to the consulship,* and afterwards by making their discipline of war precarious, first taught them to devolve the power and authority of the senate into the hands of one, and then to make that one to be at the disposition of the soldiery; which though he practised at a time when it was necessary for the safety of the commonwealth, yet it drew after it those fatal consequences, which not only ruined the republic, but also, in process of time, the monarchy itself. But the author was too much in the interests of that family, to name Scipio; and therefore he gives other reasons, to which I refer the reader, that I may avoid prolixity.

By what degrees Polybius arrived to this height of knowledge, and consummate judgment in affairs, it will not be hard to make the reader comprehend; for, presupposing in him all that birth or nature could give a man, who was formed for the management of great affairs, and capable of recording them, he was likewise entered from his youth into those employments which add experience to natural endowments; being joined in commission with his father Lycortas, and the younger Aratus, before the age of twenty, in an embassy to Egypt: after which he was perpetually in the business of his own commonwealth, or that of Rome. So that it seems to be one part of the Roman felicity, that he was born in an age when their commonwealth was growing to the height; that he might be the historian of those great actions, which were performed not only in his lifetime, but the chief of them even in his sight. I must confess, that the preparations to his history, or the Prolegomena, as they are called, are very large, and the digressions in it are exceeding frequent. But as to his preparatives, they were but necessary to make the reader comprehend the drift and design of his undertaking: and the digressions are also so instructive, that we may truly say, they transcend the profit which we receive from the matter of fact. Upon the whole, we may conclude him to be a great talker; but we must grant him to be a prudent man. We can spare nothing of all he says, it is so much to our improvement; and if the rest of his history had remained to us, in all probability it would have been more close: for we can scarce conceive what was left in nature for him to add, he has so emptied almost all the common-places of digressions already; or if he could have added any thing, those observations might have been as useful and as necessary as the rest which he has given us, and that are descended to our hands.

I will say nothing farther of the "Excerpta," which (as Casaubon thinks) are part of that epitome which was begun to be made by Marcus Brutus, but never finished; nor of those embassies which are collected and compiled by the command of Constantine the Great; because neither of them are translated in this work. And whether or no they will be added in another impression, I am not certain; the translator of these five books having carried his work no farther than it was perfect. He, I suppose will acquaint you with his own purpose, in the preface which I hear he intends to prefix before Polybius.

Let us now hear Polybius himself describing an accomplished historian, wherein we shall see his own picture, as in a glass, reflected to him, and given us afterwards to behold in the writing of this history.

Plato said of old, that it would be happy for mankind, if either philosophers administered the government, or that governors applied themselves to the study of philosophy. I may also say, that it would be happy for history, if those who undertake to write it, were men conversant in political affairs, who applied themselves seriously to their undertaking, not negligently, but as such who were fully persuaded that they undertook a work of the greatest moment, of the greatest excellency, and the most necessary for

* In his thirty-eighth year, forty-three being the legal age.

mankind; establishing this as the foundation whereon they are to build, that they can never be capable of performing their duty as they ought, unless they have formed themselves beforehand to their undertaking, by prudence, and long experience of affairs; without which endowments and advantages, if they attempt to write a history, they will fall into a various and endless labyrinth of errors.

When we hear this author speaking, we are ready to think ourselves engaged in a conversation with Cato the Censor, with Lælius, with Massinissa, and with the two Scipios; that is, with the greatest heroes and most prudent men of the greatest age in the Roman commonwealth. This sets me so on fire, when I am reading, either here, or in any ancient author, their lives and actions, that I cannot hold from breaking out with Montagne into this expression: "It is just," says he, "for every honest man to be content with the government and laws of his native country, without endeavouring to alter or subvert them; but if I were to choose where I would have been born, it should have been in a commonwealth." He indeed names Venice, which, for many reasons, should not be my wish; but rather Rome, in such an age, if it were possible, as that wherein Polybius lived; or that of Sparta, whose constitution for a republic is by our author compared with Rome, to which he justly gives the preference.

I will not undertake to compare Polybius and Tacitus; though, if I should attempt it upon the whole merits of the cause, I must allow to Polybius the greater comprehension, and the larger soul; to Tacitus the greater eloquence, and the more close connexion of his thoughts. The manner of Tacitus in writing is more like the force and gravity of Demosthenes; that of Polybius more like the copiousness and diffusive character of Cicero. Amongst historians, Tacitus imitated Thucydides, and Polybius, Herodotus. Polybius foresaw the ruin of the Roman commonwealth, by luxury, lust, and cruelty; Tacitus foresaw in the causes those events which would destroy the monarchy. They are both of them, without dispute, the best historians in their several kinds. In this they are alike, that both of them suffered under the iniquity of the times in which they lived: both their histories are dismembered, the greater part of them lost, and they are interpolated in many places. Had their works been perfect, we might have had longer histories, but not better. Casaubon, according to his usual partiality, condemns Tacitus that he may raise Polybius; who needs not any sinister artifice to make him appear equal to the best. Tacitus described the times of tyranny; but he always writes with some kind of indignation against them. It is not his fault that Tiberius, Caligula, Nero, and Domitian, were bad princes. He is accused of malevolence, and of taking actions in the worst sense; but we are still to remember, that those were the actions of tyrants. Had the rest of his history remained to us, we had certainly found a better account of Vespasian, Titus, Nerva, and Trajan, who were virtuous emperors; and he would have given the principles of their actions a contrary turn. But it is not my business to defend Tacitus; neither dare I decide the preference betwixt him and our Polybius. They are equally profitable and instructive to the reader; but Tacitus more useful to those who are born under a monarchy, Polybius to those who live in a republic.

What may farther be added concerning the history of this author, I leave to be performed by the elegant translator of his work.*

* The elegant translator, however, gives us no information on that subject; his preface being principally a panegyric upon good discipline, which, without much risk of contradiction, he affirms to be the "substance and sum total of military science."

THE LIFE OF LUCIAN.

The Dialogues of Lucian were translated by Walter Moyle, Sir Henry Shere, Charles Blount, and others, and seem to have been intended for publication about 1696, when our author supplied the following prefatory life. The design was, however, for a time laid aside, and the work did not appear until 1711, several years after Dryden's death. Hence the preface wants those last corrections, which, I suspect, Dryden contented himself with bestowing upon the proof-sheets, as they came from press. I have followed several of Mr. Malone's judicious, and indeed indispensable, corrections of the printed copy.

The writing a life is at all times, and in all circumstances, the most difficult task of an historian; and, notwithstanding the numerous tribe of biographers, we can scarce find one, except Plutarch, who deserves our perusal, or can invite a second view. But if the difficulty be so great where the materials are plentiful, and the incidents extraordinary, what must it be when the person, that affords the subject, denies matter enough for a page? The learned seldom abound with action, and it is action only that furnishes the historian with things agreeable and instructive. It is true, that Diogenes Laertius, and our learned countryman, Mr. Stanley,* have both written the "Lives of the Philosophers;" but we are more obliged to the various principles of their several sects, than to any thing remarkable that they did, for our entertainment.

But Lucian, as pleasing and useful as he was in his writings, in the opinion of the most candid judges, has left so little of his own affairs on record, that there is scarce sufficient to fill a page, from his birth to his death.

There were many of the name of Lucian among the ancients, eminent in several ways, and whose names have reached posterity with honour and applause. Suidas mentions one, as a man of singular probity, who, having discharged the administration of the chief Prefect of the Oriental empire,† under Arcadius, with extraordinary justice and praise of the people, drew on himself the envy and hate of the courtiers, (the constant attendant of eminent virtue and merit,) and the anger of the emperor himself; and was at last murdered by Rufinus.*

Among those who were eminent for their learning, were some divines and philosophers. Of the former, we find one in St. Cyprian, to whom the fourth and seventeenth epistles are inscribed. There was another priest of the church of Antioch, who, as Suidas assures us, reviewed, corrected, and restored to its primi-

* Thomas Stanley's "History of Philosophy," &c. was published in folio, in detached parts, between 1655 and 1660; and reprinted entire in 1687.

† A. D. 375. Rufinus was chief prefect of the East. The person here alluded to was only count of fifteen provinces. Dryden, writing from memory, confounded the offices of the murderer and murdered. See the next note.

* Gibbon thus narrates the catastrophe:—"The extreme parsimony of Rufinus left him only the reproach and envy of ill-gotten wealth. His dependants served him without attachments; the universal hatred of mankind was repressed only by the influence of servile fear. The fate of Lucian proclaimed to the East, that the prefect, whose industry was much abated in the despatch of ordinary business, was active and indefatigable in the pursuit of revenge. Lucian, (the son of the prefect Florentius, the oppressor of Gaul, and the enemy of Julian,) had employed a considerable part of his inheritance, the fruit of rapine and corruption, to purchase the friendship of Rufinus, and the high office of Count of the East. But the new magistrate imprudently departed from the maxims of the Court and of the times; disgraced his benefactor, by the contrast of a virtuous and temperate administration; and presumed to refuse an act of injustice, which might have tended to the profit of the emperor's uncle. Arcadius was easily persuaded to resent the supposed insult; and the prefect of the East resolved to execute in person the cruel vengeance which he meditated against this ungrateful delegate of his power. He performed, with incessant speed, the journey of seven or eight hundred miles, from Constantinople to Antioch, entered the capital of Syria at the dead of night, and spread universal consternation among a people ignorant of his design, but not ignorant of his character. The count of the fifteen provinces of the East was dragged, like the vilest malefactor, before the arbitrary tribunal of Rufinus. Notwithstanding the clearest evidence of his integrity, which was not impeached even by the voice of an accuser, Lucian was condemned, almost without a trial, to suffer a cruel and ignominious punishment. The ministers of the tyrant, by the order, and in the presence, of their master, beat him on the neck with leather thongs, armed at the extremities with lead; and when he fainted under the violence of the pain, he was removed in a close litter, to conceal his dying agonies from the eyes of the indignant city. No sooner had Rufinus perpetrated this inhuman act, the sole object of his expedition, than he returned amidst the deep and

tive purity, the Hebrew Bible, and afterwards suffered martyrdom, at Nicomedia, under Maximinian.* A third was a priest of Jerusalem, who not only made a figure among the learned of his own age,† but, as Gesnerus observes, conveyed his reputation to posterity by the remains of his writings.

But none of this name has met with the general applause of so many ages, as Lucian the philosopher and eminent sophist, who was author of the following Dialogues, of whose birth, life, and death, I shall give you all I could collect of any certain and historical credit.

He had not the good fortune to be born of illustrious or wealthy parents, which give a man a very advantageous rise on his first appearance in the world; but the father of our Lucian laboured under so great a straitness of estate, that he was fain to put his son apprentice to a statuary, whose genius for the finer studies was so extraordinary and so rare; because he hoped from that business, not only a speedy supply to his own wants, but was secure that his education in that art would be much less expensive to him.

He was born in Samosata, a city of Syria, not far from the river Euphrates; and for this reason, he calls himself more than once an Assyrian, and a Syrian; but he was derived from a Greek original, his forefathers having been citizens of Patras in Achaia.

We have nothing certain as to the exact time of his birth. Suidas confirms his flourishing under the Emperor Trajan; but then he was likewise before him. Some mention the reign of Adrian; but it cannot be fixed to any year or consulate.‡

The person he was bound to was his uncle, a man of a severe and morose temper, of whom he was to learn the statuary's and stone-cutter's art; for his father observing our Lucian, now a boy, of his own head, and without any instructor, make various figures in wax, he persuaded himself, that if he had a good master, he could not but arrive to an uncommon excellence in it.

But it happened, in the very beginning of his time, he broke a model, and was very severely called to account for it by his master. He, not liking this treatment, and having a soul and genius above any mechanic trade, ran away home.

After which, in his sleep, there appeared to him two young women, or rather the tutelar goddesses of the statuary art, and of the liberal sciences, hotly disputing of their preference to each other; and on a full hearing of both sides, he bids adieu to statuary, and entirely surrenders himself to the conduct of virtue and learning. And as his desires of improvement were great, and the instructions he had very good, the progress he made was as considerable, till, by the maturity of his age and his study, he made his appearance in the world.

Though it is not to be supposed, that there is any thing of reality in this dream, or vision, of Lucian, which he treats of in his works, yet this may be gathered from it,—that Lucian himself, having consulted his genius, and the nature of the study his father had allotted him, and that to which he found a propensity in himself, he quitted the former, and pursued the latter, choosing rather to form the minds of men than their statues.

In his youth, he taught rhetoric in Gaul, and in several other places. He pleaded likewise at the bar in Antioch, the capital of Syria; but the noise of the bar disgusting, and his ill success in causes disheartening him, he quitted the practice of rhetoric and the law, and applied himself to writing.

He was forty years old, when he first took to philosophy. Having a mind to make himself known in Macedon, he took the opportunity of speaking in the public assembly of all that region. In his old age, he was received in the imperial family, and had the place of intendant of Egypt,* after he had travelled through almost all the known countries of that age to improve his knowledge in men, manners, and arts; for some writers make this particular observation on his travel into Gaul, and residence in that country, that he gained there the greatest part of his knowledge in rhetoric, that region being in his age, and also before it, a nursery of eloquence and oratory, as Juvenal, Martial, and others, sufficiently witness.†

silent curses of a trembling people, from Antioch to Constantinople; and his diligence was accelerated by the hope of accomplishing, without delay, the nuptials of his daughter with the emperor of the East."—*Gibbon's Decline and Fall of the Roman Empire*, vol. iii. p. 209.

The punctuation throughout this piece is so inaccurate, and the paragraphs so strangely divided, that it must have been printed from a copy very carelessly written. In the present passage, we find *Rafany*, instead of *Rufinus*.—*Malone.*

* A. D. 312. He suffered for favouring the Arians. —*Malone.*

† A. D. 415. He was minister of Caphargamala, and pretended to have been instructed by a dream of the burial place of the proto-martyr Stephen, Gamaliel, and other saints. See *Gibbon's History*, vol. iii. p. 97.

Several other persons of this name, besides those here mentioned, are enumerated by Fabricius.—*Bibl. Græc.* iv. 568.

‡ Dr. Franklin seems disposed to fix on the year 90.

* *Procurator principis.* Under Marcus Arelius.

† See *Juv.* Sat. i. 44; vii. 148; xv. 111. *Quinctil.* lib. x. cap. 3.

The manner of his death is obscure to us, though it is most probable he died of the gout. Suidas alone tells a story of his being worried to death, and devoured by dogs, returning from a feast; which being so uncommon a death, so very improbable, and attested only by one author, has found little credit with posterity. If it be true, that he was once a Christian, and afterwards became a renegade to our belief, perhaps some zealots may have invented this tale of his death, as a just and signal punishment for his apostacy. All men are willing to have the miracle, or at least the wonderful providence, go on their side, and will be teaching God Almighty what he ought to do in this world, as well as in the next; as if they were proper judges of his decrees, and for what end he prospers some, or punishes others, in this life. Ablancourt, and our learned countryman Dr. Mayne,* look on the story as a fiction: and, for my part, I can see no reason either to believe he ever professed Christianity, or, if he did, why he might† not more probably die in his bed at so great an age as fourscore and ten, than be torn in pieces and devoured by dogs, when he was too feeble to defend himself. So early began the want of charity, the presumption of meddling with God's government, and the spirit of calumny, amongst the primitive believers.

Of his posterity we know nothing more, than that he left a son behind him, who was as much in favour with the Emperor Julian, as his father had been with Aurelius the philosopher. This son became in time a famous sophist; and among the works of Julian we find an epistle of that great person to him.‡

I find that I have mingled, before I was aware, some things which are doubtful with some which are certain; forced indeed by the narrowness of the subject, which affords very little of undisputed truth. Yet I find myself obliged to do right to Monsieur d'Ablancourt,§ who is not positively of opinion, that Suidas was the author of this fable; but rather that it descended to him by the tradition of former times, yet without any certain ground of truth. He concludes it, however, to be a calumny, perhaps a charitable kind of lie, to deter others from satirizing the new dogmas of Christianity, by the judgment shown in Lucian. We find nothing in his writings, which gives any hint of his professing our belief; but being naturally curious, and living not only amongst Christians, but in the neighbourhood of Judea, he might reasonably be supposed to be knowing in our points of faith, without believing them. He ran a muck, and laid about him on all sides with more fury on the heathens, whose religion he professed; he struck at ours but casually, as it came in his way, rather than as he sought it; he contemned it too much to write in earnest against it.

We have indeed the highest probabilities for our revealed religion; arguments which will preponderate with a reasonable man, upon a long and careful disquisition; but I have always been of opinion, that we can demonstrate nothing, because the subject-matter is not capable of a demonstration. It is the particular grace of God, that any man believes the mysteries of our faith; which I think a conclusive argument against the doctrine of persecution in any church. And though I am absolutely convinced, as I heartily thank God I am, not only of the general principles of Christianity, but of all truths necessary to salvation in the Roman church, yet I cannot but detest our inquisition, as it is practised in some foreign parts, particularly in Spain and in the Indies.

Those reasons, which are cogent to me, may not prevail with others, who bear the denomination of Christians; and those which are prevalent with all Christians, in regard of their birth and education, may find no force, when they are used against Mahometans or heathens. To instruct is a charitable duty; to compel, by threatenings and punishment, is the office of a hangman, and the principle of a tyrant.

But my zeal in a good cause, as I believe, has transported me beyond the limits of my subject. I was endeavouring to prove, that Lucian had never been a member of the Christian church; and methinks it makes for my opinion, that, in relating the death of Peregrinus, who, being born a Pagan, pretended afterwards to turn Christian, and turned himself publicly at the Olympic games, at his death professing himself a cynic philosopher, it seems, I say, to me, that Lucian would not have so severely declaimed against this Proteus, (which was another of Peregrinus his names,) if he himself had been guilty of that apostacy.

I know not that this passage has been observed by any man before me;* and yet in this

* Dr. Jasper Mayne, who published a translation of some select dialogues of Lucian, in folio, in 1664.

† I follow Mr. Malone in reading *might;* the printed copy has *must.*

‡ This is a gross mistake, 180 years intervening between the death of Aurelius and the reign of Julian.

§ Nicolas Perrot, Sieur d'Ablancourt, whose translation of the Dialogues of Lucian into French was first published at Paris in 1654. His continuation of the True History of Lucian is very much in the tone of the original.

* This observation had been made by Gilbertus Cognatus, and by Thomas Hicks, in his life of Lucian, printed in 1634.—*Malone.*

very place it is, that this author has more severely handled our belief, and more at large, than in any other part of all his writings, excepting only the Dialogue of Triephon and Critias,* wherein he lashes his own false gods with more severity than the true; and where the first Christians, with their cropped hair, their whining voices, melancholy faces, mournful discourses, and nasty habits, are described with a greater air of Calvinists or Quakers, than of Roman Catholics or Church-of-England men.

After all, what if this discourse last mentioned, and the rest of the dialogues wherein the Christians are satirized, were none of Lucian's? The learned and ingenious Dr. Mayne, whom I have before cited, is of this opinion, and confirms it by the attestation of Philander, Obsobœus, Mycillus, and Cognatus, whom since I have not read, or two of them but very superficially, I refer you for the faith of his quotation to the authors themselves.†

The next supposition concerning Lucian's religion is, that he was of none at all. I doubt not but the same people, who broached the story of his being once a Christian, followed their blow upon him in this second accusation.

There are several sorts of Christians at this day reigning in the world, who will not allow any man to believe in the Son of God, whose other articles of faith are not in all things conformable to theirs. Some of these exercise this rigid and severe kind of charity, with a good intent of reducing several sects into one common church; but the spirit of others is evidently seen by their detraction, their malice, their spitting venom, their raising false reports of those who are not of their communion. I wish the ancientness of these censorious principles may be proved by better arguments, than by any near resemblance they have with the primitive believers. But till I am convinced that Lucian has been charged with atheism of old, I shall be apt to think that this accusation is very modern.

One of Lucian's translators pleads in his defence, that it was very improbable a man, who has laughed paganism out of doors, should believe no God; that he, who could point to the sepulchre of Jupiter in Crete, as well as our Tertullian, should be an atheist. But this argument, I confess, is of little weight to prove him a deist, only because he was no polytheist. He might as well believe in none as in many gods: and on the other side, he might believe in many, as Julian did, and not in one. For my own part, I think it is not proved that either of them were apostates, though one of them, in hopes of an empire, might temporize, while Christianity was the mode at court. Neither is our author cleared any thing the more, because his writings have served, in the times of the heathens, to destroy that vain, unreasonable, and impious religion; *that* was an oblique service, which Lucian never intended us; for his business, like that of some modern polemics, was rather to pull down every thing, than to set up any thing. With what show of probability can I urge in his defence, that one of the greatest among the fathers has drawn whole homilies from our author's dialogues, since I know that Lucian made them not for that purpose? The occasional good which he has done, is not to be imputed to him. St. Chrysostom, St. Augustin, and many others, have applied his arguments on better motives than their author proposed to himself in framing them.

These reasons, therefore, as they make nothing against his being an atheist, so they prove nothing of his believing one God; but only leave him as they found him, and leave us in as great an obscurity concerning his religion as before. I may be as much mistaken in my opinion as these great men have been before me; and this is very probable, because I know less of him than they; yet I have read him over more than once, and therefore will presume to say, that I think him either one of the Electic school,* or else a Skeptic: I mean, that he either formed a body of philosophy for his own use, out of the opinions and dogmas of several heathen philosophers disagreeing amongst themselves, or that he doubted of every thing; weighed all opinions, and adhered to none of them; only used them as they served his occasion for the present dialogue, and perhaps rejected them in the next. And indeed this last opinion is the more probable of the two, if we consider the genius of the man, whose image we may clearly see in the glass which he holds before us of his writings, which reflects him to our sight.

Not to dwell on examples, with which his works are amply furnished, I will only mention two. In one, Socrates convinces his friend Chærephon of the power of the gods in transformations, and of a supreme Providence which accompanies that power in the administration of the world. In another, he confutes Jupiter, and pulls him down from heaven to earth, by his own Homerical chain; and makes him only a subser-

* Entitled "Philopatris." The Christian religion, and its mysteries, are ridiculed in this piece with very little ceremony.

† Gesner has written a long Latin essay upon this point, which is subjoined to the third volume of Lucian's works, in the quarto edition of Hemsterhusius.

* I follow Mr. Malone in reading *electic* for *elective*

vient slave to blind eternal Fate. I might add, that he is, in one half of his book, a Stoic, in the other an Epicurean; never constant to himself in any scheme of divinity, unless it be in despising his gentile gods. And this derision, as it shows the man himself, so it gives us an idea of the age in which he lived; for if that had been devout or ignorant, his scoffing humour would either have been restrained, or had not passed unpunished; all knowing ages being naturally skeptic, and not at all bigoted; which, if I am not much deceived, is the proper character of our own.

To conclude this article: He was too fantastical, too giddy, too irresolute, either to be any thing at all, or any thing long; and in this view I cannot think he was either a steady atheist, or a deist, but a doubter, a skeptic, as he plainly declares himself to be, when he puts himself under the name of Hermotimus, the Stoic, in the dialogue called the "Dialogue of the Sects."

As for his morals, they are spoken of as variously as his opinions. Some are for decrying him more than he deserves; his defenders themselves dare not set him up for a pattern of severe virtue. No man is so profligate, as openly to profess vice; and therefore it is no wonder, if under the reign of Nerva, Trajan, Hadrian, and the two Antonines, of which the last was his patron and benefactor, he lived not so much a libertine as he had it to be in his nature. He is more accused for his love of boys than of women. Not that we have any particular story to convince us of this detestable passion in him; but his own writings bear this record against him, that he speaks often of it, and I know not that ever he condemns it. Repeated expressions, as well as repeated actions, witness some secret pleasure in the deed, or at least some secret inclination to it. He seems to insinuate, in his "Dialogue of Loves," that Socrates was given to this vice; but we find not that he blames him for it, which, if he had been wholly innocent himself, it became a philosopher to have done. But as we pass over a foul way as hastily as we can, so I will leave this abominable subject, which strikes me with horror when I name it.

If there be any who are guilty of this sin, we may assure ourselves they will never stop at any other; for when they have overleaped the bounds of nature, they run so fast to all other immoralities, that the grace of God, without a miracle, can never overtake them.

Lucian is accused likewise for his writing so lusciously in his "Dialogues of the Harlots."* It has been the common fault of all satirists, to make vice too amiable, while they expose it; but of all men living, I am the most unfit to accuse Lucian, who am so little able to defend myself from the same objection. We find not, however, that Lucian was charged with the wantonness of his "Dialogues" in his own life-time. If he had been, he would certainly have answered for himself; as he did to those who accused him for exposing Socrates, Plato, Diogenes, and other great philosophers, to the laughter of the people, when Jupiter sold them by any inch of candle. But, to confess the truth, [as] I am of their opinion, who think that answer of his not over-ingenuous, viz. that he only attacked the false philosophers of their sects, in their persons whom he honoured; so I am persuaded, that he could not have alleged more in his excuse for these "Dialogues," than that, as he taught harlots to deceive, so, at the same time, he discovered their deceits to the knowledge of young men, and thereby warned them to avoid the snare.

I find him not charged with any other faults, than what I have already mentioned. He was otherwise of a life as unblameable as any man, for aught we find to the contrary; and I have this probable inducement to believe it, because he had so honourable an employment under Marcus Aurelius, an emperor as clear-sighted as he was truly virtuous; for both which qualities we need not quote Lucian, who was so much obliged to him, but may securely appeal to Herodian, and to all the historians who have written of him,—besides the testimony of his own admirable works, which are yet in the hands of all the learned.

As for those who condemn our author for the too much gall and virulency of his satires, it is to be suspected, says Dr. Mayne, that they themselves are guilty of those hypocrisies, crimes, and follies, which he so sharply exposes, and at the same time endeavours to reform. I may add, that, for the most part, he rather laughs like Horace, than bites like Juvenal. Indeed his genius was of kin to both, but more nearly related to the former. Some diseases are curable by lenitives; to others corrosives are necessary. Can a man inveigh too sharply against the cruelty of tyrants, the pride and vanity of the great, the covetousness of the rich, the baseness of the Sophists, and particularly of the Cynics, (who, while they preach poverty to

* The best judges have condemned Etairikoi Dialogoi, or, "Dialogues of the Harlots," as not being genuine. They are at any rate gross and devoid of humour

others, are heaping up riches, and living in gluttony,) besides the wrangling of the sects amongst themselves about supreme happiness, which he describes at a drunken feast, and calls it the battle of the Lapithæ.

Excepting what already is excepted, he seems to me to be an enemy to nothing but to vice and folly. The pictures which he draws of Nigrinus and of Demonax are as fair as that of virtue herself, if, as the philosopher said, she could wear a body. And if we oppose to them the lives of Alexander the false prophet, and of Peregrinus, how pleasingly, and with how much profit, does the deformity of the last set off the beauty of the first.

Some of his censurers accuse him of flatness and want of wit in many places. These I suppose have read him in some Latin translations, which, I confess, are generally dull; and this is the only excuse I can make for them. Otherwise they accuse themselves too manifestly for want of taste or understanding. Of this number is the wretched author of the *Lucien en Belle Humeur*, who being himself as insipid as a Dutch poet, yet arraigns Lucian for his own fault; introduces the ghost of Ablancourt, confessing his coldness in many places, the poorness of his thoughts, and his want of humour; represents his readers tired and yawning at his ill buffoonery and false mirth, and sleeping over his melancholic stories, which are everywhere stuffed with improbabilities. He could have said no worse of a Leyden slip.*

The best on it is, the jaundice is only in his own eyes, which makes Lucian look yellow to him. All mankind will exclaim against him for preaching this doctrine; and be of opinion when they read his Lucian, that he looked in a glass when he drew his picture. I wish I had the liberty to lash this frog-land wit as he deserves, but when a speech is not seconded in Parliament, it falls of course; and this author has the whole senate of the learned to pull him down: *incipient omnes pro Cicerone loqui.*

It is to be acknowledged, that his best translator, Ablancourt, thinks him not a profound master in any sort of philosophy; but only that he skimmed enough from every sect, to serve his turn in rhetoric, which was his profession. This he gathers from his superficial way of arguing. But why may not another man reply in his defence, that he made choice of those kinds of reasons which were most capable of being made to shine in his facetious way of arguing; and these undoubtedly were not the most knotty, nor the deepest, but the most diverting by the sharpness of the raillery. Dr. Mayne, so often praised, has another opinion of Lucian's learning, and the strength of his witty arguments, concluding on that subject in these words, or near them: "For my part, I know not to whose writings we owe more our Christianity, where the true God has succeeded to a multitude of false,—whether to the grave confutation of Clemens Alexandrinus, Arnobius, Justin Martyr, St. Augustin, Lactantius, &c. or the facetious wit of Lucian." I cannot doubt but the treacherous translator would have given his hand to what the Englishman has said of their common author. The success has justified his opinion in the sight of all the world. Lucian's manner of convincing, was certainly more pleasant than that of the Christian writers, and we know the effect was full as powerful; so easily can the Eternal Wisdom draw good out of evil, and make his enemy subservient to the establishment of his faith.

I will not enlarge on the praises of his oratory. If we compare his style with the Greek historians, his contemporaries, or near his time, we shall find it much more pure than that of Plutarch, Dion, or Appian, though not so grave; because his subjects and theirs required to be treated after a different manner. It was not of an uniform web, says Mayne, like Thucydides, Polybius, and some others whom he names, but was somewhat peculiar to himself; his words well chosen, his periods round, the parts of his sentences harmoniously divided, a full flood or even a torrent of persuasion, without inequalities or swellings; such as might be put in equal comparison with the best orations of Demosthenes or Isocrates; not so dry as the first, nor so flowery as the last. His wit, says Ablancourt, was full of urbanity, that Attic salt, which the French call fine raillery; not obscene, not gross, not rude, but facetious, well-mannered, and well-bred: only he will not allow his love the quality last mentioned, but thinks it rustical, and according either to his own genius, or that of the age in which he lived.

If wit consists in the propriety of thoughts and words, (which I imagined I had first found out, but since am pleasingly convinced that Aristotle has made the same definition in other terms,) then Lucian's thoughts and words are always proper to his characters and his subject. If the pleasure arising from comedy and satire be either laughter, or some nobler sort of delight, which is above it, no man is so great a master of irony as our author. That figure is not only a keen, but a shining weapon in his hand; it glitters in the eyes of those it kills; his own gods, his greatest enemies, are not butchered

* I presume, a cant phrase for a graft from that garden of knowledge.

by him, but fairly slain: they must acknowledge the hero in the stroke, and take the comfort which Virgil gives to a dying captain:—

Æneæ magni dextra cadis.

I know not whom Lucian imitated, unless it might be Aristophanes; (for you never find him mentioning any Roman wit, so much the Grecians thought themselves superior to their conquerors;) but he, who has best imitated him in Latin, is Erasmus; and in French, Fontenelle, in his "Dialogues of the Dead," which I never read but with a new pleasure.

Any one may see, that our author's chief design was to dis-nest heaven of so many immoral and debauched deities; his next, to expose the mock philosophers; and his last, to give us examples of a good life in the persons of the true.

The rest of his discourses are on mixed subjects, less for profit than delight; and some of them too libertine.

The way which Lucian chose of delivering these profitable and pleasing truths, was that of dialogue: a choice worthy of the author; happily followed, as I said above, by Erasmus and Fontenelle particularly, to whom I may justly add a triumvir of our own,—the reverend, ingenious, and learned Dr. Eachard,* who, by using the same method, and the same ingredients of raillery and reason, has more baffled the philosopher of Malmesbury, than those who assaulted him with blunt heavy arguments, drawn from orthodox divinity; for Hobbes foresaw where those strokes would fall, and leaped aside before they could descend; but he could not avoid those nimble passes, which were made on him by a wit more active than his own, and which were within his body, before he could provide for his defence.

I will not here take notice of the several kinds of dialogue, and the whole art of it, which would ask an entire volume to perform. This has been a work long wanted, and much desired, of which the ancients have not sufficiently informed us; and I question whether any man now living can treat it accurately. Lucian, it seems, was very sensible of the difficult task, which he undertook in writing dialogues, as appears in his discourse against one who had called him Prometheus. He owns himself, in this particular, to be like to him, to whom he was resembled, to be the inventor of a new work, attempted in a new manner,—the model of which he had from none before him; but adds withal, that if he could not give it the graces which belong to so happy an invention, he deserves to be torn by twelve vultures, instead of one, which preys upon the heart of that first man-potter. For, to quit the beaten road of the ancients, and take a path of his own choosing, he acknowledges to be a bold and ridiculous attempt, if it succeed not. "The mirth of dialogue and comedy in my work," says he, "is not enough to make it pleasing, because the union of two contraries may as well produce a monster as a miracle; as a centaur results from the joint natures of a horse and man. It is not but that from two excellent beings a third may arise of perfect beauty; but it is what I dare not promise to myself; for dialogue being a solemn entertainment of grave discourse, and comedy the wit and fooling of a theatre, I fear that through the corruption of two good things, I have made one bad. But whatever the child be, it is my own at least; I beg not with another's brat upon my back. From which of the ancients should I have stolen or borrowed it? My chimeras have no other being, than my own imagination; let every man produce who can; and whether this be a lawful birth, or a misshapen mass, is left for the present age, and for posterity, to judge.

This is the sense of my author's words contracted in a narrow compass; for, if you will believe Ablancourt, and others, his greatest fault is, that he exhausts his argument,—like Ovid, knows not when to give over, but is perpetually gallopping beyond his stage.

But though I cannot pursue our author any farther, I find myself obliged to say something of those translators of the following Dialogues, whom I have the honour to know, as well as of some other translations of this author, and a word or two of the translation itself.

As for the translators, all of them, that I know, are men of established reputation, both for wit and learning, at least sufficiently known to be so among all the finer spirits of the age. Sir Henry Sheers has given many proofs of his excellence in this kind; for while we, by his admirable address, enjoy Polybius in our mother tongue, we can never forget the hand that bestowed the benefit. The learning and judgment above his age, which every one discovers in Mr. Moyle,* are proofs of those abilities he has shown in his country's service, when he was

* The work alluded to, which was written by the Rev. Dr. John Eachard, (Master of Catharine Hall, in Cambridge, and author of the "Grounds of the Contempt of the Clergy,") was published in 1671, and was entitled "Mr. Hobbe's State of Nature considered; in a Dialogue between Philautos and Timothy."—*Malone.*

* This gentleman, whom our author has again mentioned with esteem, in the "Parallel of Poetry and Painting," (p. 338,) was the son of Sir Walter Moyle, and was born in the year 1672. He was educated to the study of law, and became a

chose to serve it in the senate, as his father had done. The wit of Mr. Blount,* and his other performances, need no recommendation from me; they have made too much noise in the world to need a herald. There are some other persons concerned in this work, whose names deserve a place among the foremost, but that they have not thought fit to be known, either out of a bashful diffidence of their own performance, or out of apprehension of the censure of an ill-natured and ill-judging age; for criticism is now become mere hangman's work, and meddles only with the faults of authors; nay, the critic is disgusted less with their absurdities than excellence; and you cannot displease him more than in leaving him little room for his malice, in your correctness and perfection; though that indeed is what he never allows any man; for like the bed of Procrustes, they stretch or cut off an author to its length. These spoilers of Parnassus are a just excuse for concealing the name, since most of their malice is levelled more at the person than the thing; and as a sure mark of their judgment, they will extol to the skies the anonymous work of a person they will not allow to write common sense.

But this consideration of our modern critics has led me astray, and made me insensibly deviate from the subject before me; the modesty or caution of the anonymous translators of the following work. Whatever the motive of concealing their names may be, I shall not determine; but it is certain, nothing could more contribute to make a perfect version of Lucian, than a confederacy of many men of parts and learning to do him justice. It seems a task too hard for any one to undertake; the burden would indeed be insupportable, unless we did what the French have done in some of their translations, allow twenty years to perfect the work, and bestow all the brightest intervals, the most sprightly hours, to polish and finish the work.*

But this has not been the fate of our author hitherto; for Lucian, that is the sincere example of Attic eloquence, as Grævius says of him, is only a mass of solecism and mere vulgarisms in Mr. Spence.† I do not think it worth my while to rake into the filth of so scandalous a version; nor had I vouchsafed so much as to take notice of it, had it not been so gross an affront to the memory of Lucian, and so great a scandal to our nation. D'Ablancourt has taken a great deal of pains to furnish this intruder into print, with Lucian, in a language more known to him than Greek; nay, he has left him not one crabbed idiom to study for, since he has admirably clothed him in a garb more familiar to the moderns, still keeping the sense of his author in view. But in spite of all these helps, these leading-strings were not sufficient to keep Mr. Spence from falling to the ground every step he made; while he makes him speak in the style and language of a jack-pudding, not a master of eloquence, admired for it through all the ages since he wrote. But too much of this trifler.

I have said enough already of the version of the learned Dr. Mayne, to show my approbation of it; but it is only a select parcel of Lucian's Dialogues which pleased him most, but far from the whole. As for any other translation, if there be any such in our language, it is what I never saw,‡ and suppose it must be antiquated, or of so inferior a degree, as not even to rival Spence.

The present translation, as far as I can judge by what I have seen, is no way inferior to Ablancourt's, and in many things is superior. It has indeed the advantage of appearing in a language more strong and expressive than French, and by the hands of gentlemen who perfectly understand him and their own language.

This has brought me to say a word or two about translation in general; in which no nation might more excel than the English, though, as matters are now managed, we come so far short of the French. There may indeed be a reason assigned, which bears a very great

member of Parliament in 1695. He composed a variety of treatises, on various subjects, which are comprised in a collection of three volumes 8vo, the last being posthumous. Mr. Moyle died in 1721.

* Charles Blount, the son of Sir Henry, and brother to Sir Edward Pope Blount. He early appeared as a defender and admirer of Dryden, by publishing an answer to Leigh's "Censure of the Rota on the Conquest of Granada." It was entitled, "Mr. Dryden Vindicated, in Reply to the Friendly Vindication of Mr. Dryden, with Reflections on the Rota." Mr. Blunt distinguished himself as a friend to civil liberty during the crisis preceding the Revolution; but was still better known by the deistical tracts entitled, "*Anima Mundi*," "Life of Appollonius Tyaneus," "Diana of the Ephesians," and the "*Religio Laici*," which last he published anonymously in 1683, and inscribed to our author.

The death of Blount was voluntary. Having lost his wife, the daughter of Sir Timothy Tyrrel of Shotover, he fell in love with her sister, and being unable to remove her scruples upon the lawfulness of their union, shot himself in a fit of despair, in August, 1693. His miscellaneous works were published by Galden in 1695.

He was a man of deep and extensive reading, and probably better qualified, in point of learning, to translate Lucian, than most of his coadjutors.

* This, and two or three other passages, show that this life was written hastily, and that it had not been carefully revised by the author.—*Malone.*

† Ferrand Spence, who published a translation of Lucian's Dialogues in four volumes, 8vo., in 1684.

‡ Francis Hickes published a translation of Select Dialogues from Lucian, 4to. 1634.

probability; and that is, that here the booksellers are the undertakers of works of this nature, and they are persons more devoted to their own gain than the public honour. They are very parsimonious in rewarding the wretched scribblers they employ; and care not how the business is done, so that it be but done. They live by selling titles, not books; and if that carry off one impression, they have their ends, and value not the curses they and their authors meet with from the bubbled chapmen. While translations are thus at the disposal of the booksellers, and have no better judges or rewarders of the performance, it is impossible that we should make any progress in an art so very useful to an inquiring people and for the improvement and spreading of knowledge, which is none of the worst preservatives against slavery.

It must be confessed, that when the bookseller has interest with gentlemen of genius and quality, above the mercenary prospects of little writers, as in that of Plutarch's lives,* and this of Lucian, the reader may satisfy himself that he shall have the author's spirit and soul in the traduction. These gentlemen know very well, that they are not to creep after the words of their author, in so servile a manner as some have done; for that must infallibly throw them on a necessity of introducing a new mode of diction and phraseology with which we are not at all acquainted, and would incur that censure which my Lord Dorset made formerly on those of Mr. Spence, viz. that he was so cunning a translator, that a man must consult the original to understand the version. For every language has a propriety and idiom peculiar to itself, which cannot be conveyed to another without perpetual absurdities.

The qualification of a translator, worth reading, must be, a mastery of the language he translates out of, and that he translates into; but if a deficience be to be allowed in either, it is in the original; since if he be but master enough of the tongue of his author, as to be master of his sense, it is possible for him to express that sense with eloquence in his own, if he have a thorough command of that. But without the latter, he can never arrive at the useful and the delightful; without which reading is a penance and fatigue.

It is true that there will be a great many beauties, which in every tongue depend on the diction, that will be lost* in the version of a man not skilled in the original language of the author; but then on the other side, first it is impossible to render all those little ornaments of speech in any two languages; and if he have a mastery in the sense and spirit of his author, and in his own language have a style and happiness of expression, he will easily supply all that is lost by that defect.

A translator that would write with any force or spirit of an original, must never dwell on the words of his author. He ought to possess himself entirely, and perfectly comprehend the genius and sense of his author, the nature of the subject, and the terms of the art or subject treated of; and then he will express himself as justly, and with as much life, as if he wrote an original; whereas, he who copies word for word, loses all the spirit in the tedious transfusion.

I would not be understood that he should be at liberty to give such a turn as Mr. Spence has in some of his; where for the fine raillery and attic salt of Lucian, we find the gross expressions of Billingsgate, or Moorfields and Bartholomew Fair. For I write not to such translators, but to men capacious of the soul and genius of their authors, without which all their labour will be of no use but to disgrace themselves, and injure the author that falls into their slaughter-house.

I believe I need give no other rules to the reader than the following version, where example will be stronger than precept, to which I now refer them; in which a man justly qualified for a translator will discover many rules extremely useful to that end. But [to] a man who wants these natural qualifications which are necessary for such an undertaking, all particular precepts are of no other use, than to make him a more remarkable coxcomb.

LETTERS OF DRYDEN.

The Letters of Dryden, so far as hitherto given to the public, are, with a few exceptions, singularly uninteresting. To the publication of some, which are known to exist, there were found to occur still stronger objections. I have been only able to add one to those collected by Mr. Malone; and I was strongly tempted to omit several. There is, however, a satisfaction in seeing how such a man expresses himself, even upon the most trivial occasions; and I have therefore retained those complimentary acknowledgments of turkeys, marrow-puddings, and bacon, which have nothing but such a consideration to recommend them.

DRYDEN'S LETTERS.

LETTER I.

TO THE FAIRE HANDS OF MADAME HONOR DRYDEN, THESE CRAVE ADMITTANCE.*

MADAME, Camb. May 23, 16[55.]

IF you have received the lines I sent by the reverend Levite, I doubt not but they have exceedingly wrought upon you; for beeing so longe in a clergyman's pocket, assuredly they have acquired more sanctity than theire authour meant them. Alasse, Madame! for ought I know, they may become a sermon ere they could arrive at you; and believe it, haveing you for the text, it could scarcely proove bad, if it light upon one that could handle it indifferently. But I am so miserable a preacher, that though I have so sweet and copious a subject, I still fall short in my expressions; and, instead of an use of thanksgiving, I am allways makeing one of comfort, that I may one day againe have the happinesse to kisse your faire hand; but that is a message I would not so willingly do by letter, as by word of mouth.

This is a point, I must confesse, I could willingly dwell longer on; and, in this case, what ever I say you may confidently take for gospell. But I must hasten. And indeed, Madame, (*beloved* I had almost sayd,) hee had need hasten who treats of you; for to speake fully to every part of your excellencyes, requires a longer houre than most persons* have allotted them. But, in a word, your selfe hath been the best expositor upon the text of your own worth, in that admirable comment you wrote upon it; I meane your incomparable letter. By all that's good, (and you, Madame, are a great part of my oath,) it hath put mee so farre besides my selfe, that I have scarce patience to write prose, and my pen is stealing into verse every time I kisse your letter. I am sure, the poor paper smarts for my idolatry, which, by wearing it continually neere my brest, will, at last, be burnt and martyrd in those flames of adoration, which it hath kindled in mee. But I forgett, Madame, what rarityes your letter came fraught with, besides words. You are such a deity that commands worship by provideing the sacrifice. You are pleasd, Madame, to force me to write, by sending me materialls, and compell me to my greatest happinesse. Yet, though I highly value your magnificent presents, pardon mee, if I must tell the world, they are imperfect emblems of your beauty; for the white and red of waxe and paper are but shaddowes of that vermillion and snow in your lips and forehead; and the silver

* The lady to whom this letter is addressed was our author's first cousin, one of the daughters of his uncle, Sir John Dryden. She probably was born, (says Mr. Malone,) about the year 1637, and died unmarried, some time after 1707.

The seal, (he adds,) under which runs a piece of blue riband, is a crest of a demi-lion, on a wreath, holding in his paws an armillary sphere at the end of a stand. The letter seems in reply to one from the fair lady, with a present of writing materials. It is a woful sample of the gallantry of the time, alternately coarse and pedantic.

* Person *quasi* parson, which word was originally so spelled. The custom of preaching by an hour-glass has been before noticed.

of the inksherne, if it presume to vye in whitenesse with your purer skinne, must confesse itselfe blacker then the liquor it containes. What then do I more then retrieve your own guifts, and present you with that paper adulterated with blotts, which you gave spotlesse?

For, since, 'twas mine, the white hath lost its hiew,
To show 'twas n'ere it selfe, but whilst in you:
The virgin waxe hath blusht it selfe to red,
Since it with mee hath lost its maydenhead.
You, fairest nymph, are waxe. Oh! may you be
As well in softnesse, as in purity!
Till fate, and your own happy choice, reveale,
Whom you so farre shall blesse, to make your seale.

Fairest Valentine, the unfeigned wishe of your humble votary.

Jo. Dryden.

LETTER II.*

TO [JOHN WILMOT,] EARL OF ROCHESTER.

MY LORD, Tuesday, [July, 1673.]

I have accused my selfe this month together, for not writing to you. I have called my selfe by the names I deserved, of unmannerly and ungratefull. I have been uneasy, and taken up the resolutions of a man, who is betwixt sin and repentance, convinc'd of what he ought to do, and yet unable to do better. At the last I deferred it so long, that I almost grew hardened in the neglect; and thought I had suffered so much in your good opinion, that it was in vain to hope I could redeem it. So dangerous a thing it is to be inclin'd to sloath, that I must confess, once for all, I was ready to quit all manner of obligations, and to receive, as if it were my due, the most handsome compliment, couch'd in the best language I have read, and this too from my Lord of Rochester, without shewing myself sensible of the favour. If your Lordship could condescend so far to say all those things to me, which I ought to have say'd to you, it might reasonably be concluded, that you had enchanted me to believe those praises, and that I owned them in my silence. 'Twas this consideration that moved me at last to put off my idleness. And now the shame of seeing my selfe overpay'd so much for an ill Dedication, has made me almost repent of my address. I find, it is not for me to contend any way with your Lordship, who can write better on the meanest subject, then I can on the best. I have only engaged my selfe in a new debt, when I had hoped to cancell a part of the old one; and should either have chosen some other patron, whom it was in my power to have obliged by speaking better of him then he deserv'd, or have made your Lordship only a hearty Dedication of the respect and honour I had for you, without giving you the occasion to conquer me, as you have done, at my own weapon.

My only relief is, that what I have written is publique, and I am so much my own friend as to conceal your Lordship's letter; for that which would have given vanity to any other poet, has only given me confusion.

You see, my Lord, how far you have push'd me; I dare not own the honour you have done me, for fear of shewing it to my own disadvantage. You are that *rerum natura* of your own Lucretius;

Ipsa suis pollens opibus, nihil indiga nostri.*

You are above any incense I can give you, and have all the happiness of an idle life, join'd with the good nature of an active. Your friends in town are ready to envy the leisure you have given your selfe in the country, though they know you are only their steward, and that you treasure up but so much health as you intend to spend on them in winter. In the mean time, you have withdrawn your selfe from attendance, the curse of courts; you may think on what you please, and that as little as you please; for, in my opinion, thinking it selfe is a kind of pain to a witty man; he finds so much more in it to disquiet than to please him. But I hope your Lordship will not omitt the occasion of laughing at the great Duke of B[uckingham,] who is so uneasy to himselfe by pursuing the honour of lieutenant-general, which flyes him, that he can enjoy nothing he possesses,† though, at the same time, he is so unfit to command an army, that he is the only man in the three na-

* A copy of this letter is in the Museum, MSS. Harl. 7003. The Dedication alluded to, must have been that of "Marriage A-la-Mode," to which Rochester had replied by a letter of thanks; and we have here Dryden's reply. The date is supplied by Mr. Malone from internal evidence.

* Lord Rochester translated some part of Lucretius.

† In the year 1672, Monsieur Schomberg was invited into England to command the army raised for the Dutch war, then encamped on Blackheath. He was to be joined in this command with Villiers, Duke of Buckingham, who held a commission of lieutenant-general only. But when Schomberg arrived, he refused to serve equally with Buckingham, and was made general; on which the other resigned his commission in disgust. (See Sheffield, Duke of Buckingham's *Memoirs*, p. 5.) Dryden, still smarting under the "Rehearsal," just then come out, was probably not sorry to take this opportunity to turn the author's pretensions into ridicule.

tions, who does not know it; yet he still picques himself, like his father, to find another Isle of Rhe in Zealand;* thinking this disappointment an injury to him, which is indeed a favour, and will not be satisfied but with his own ruin and with ours. 'Tis a strange quality in a man to love idleness so well as to destroy his estate by it; and yet, at the same time, to pursue so violently the most toilsome and most unpleasant part of business. These observations would soon run into lampoon, if I had not forsworn that dangerous part of wit; not so much out of good nature, but lest from the inborn vanity of poets I should show it to others, and betray my selfe to a worse mischief than what I do to my enemy. This has been lately the case of Etherege, who, translating a satyr of Boileau's, and changing the French names for English, read it so often, that it came to their ears who were concerned, and forced him to leave off the design, ere it were half finished. Two of the verses I remember:

I call a spade, a spade; Eaton,† a bully;
Frampton,‡ a pimp; and brother John, a cully.

But one of his friends imagin'd those names not enough for the dignity of a satyr, and chang'd them thus:

I call a spade, a spade; Dunbar,§ a bully:
Brounckard, a pimp; and Aubrey Vere, a cully.

Because I deal not in satyr, I have sent your Lordship a prologue and epilogue, which I made for our players when they went down to Oxford. I hear they have succeeded; and by the event your Lordship will judge how easy 'tis to pass any thing upon an university, and how gross flattery the learned will endure.* If your lordship had been in town, and I in the country, I durst not have entertained you with three pages of a letter; but I know they are very ill things which can be tedious to a man who is fourscore miles from Covent Garden. 'Tis upon this confidence, that I dare almost promise to entertain you with a thousand *bagatelles* every week, and not to be serious in any part of my letter, but that wherein I take leave to call myself your lordship's

Most obedient servant,

JOHN DRYDEN.

* Eight thousand land-forces were embarked on board the English fleet, to make a descent in Zealand.

† Sir John Eaton was a noted writer of songs at the time.

‡ Mr. Malone conjectures Tregonwell Frampton, keeper of the royal stud at Newmarket: who was born in 1641, and died in 1727. Brother John must remain in obscurity.

§ Probably the grandson of Sir George Hume, created Earl of Dunbar by James the First, in 1605.

Henry Brouncker, younger brother of William, Viscount Brouncker. He was a gentleman of the Duke of York's bed-chamber, and carried the false order to slacken sail, after the great battle in 1665, when the Duke was asleep, by which the advantage gained in the victory was entirely lost. There is a great cloud over the story; but that Brouncker was an infamous character, must be concluded on all hands. He was expelled the House of Commons; and countenanced by the king more than he deserved, being "never notorious for any thing but the highest degree of impudence, and stooping to the most infamous offices."—*Continuation of Clarendon's Life, quoted by Malone.*

Aubrey de Vere, the twentieth and last Earl of Oxford, of that family. This nobleman seduced an eminent actress (said, by some authorities, to be Mrs. Marshall, but conjectured, by Mr. Malone, to have been Mrs. Davenport) to exchange her profession for his protection. The epithet, applied to him in the lines, renders it improbable that he imposed on her by a mock-marriage, though the story is told by Count Hamilton, and others.

* The Prologue and Epilogue in question may have been those spoken by Mr. Hart, and Mrs. Marshall.

LETTER III.

[The following note and letter contain the determination of a dispute, and probably of a wager which had been referred to our author by the parties. It concerns a passage in Creech's "Lucretius," and probably was written soon after the publication of that translation in 1682, when it was a recent subject of conversation. The full passage in "Lucretius" runs thus:

Præterea quæcunque vetustate amovet ætas,
Si penitus perimit, consumens materiam omnem,
Unde animale genus generatim in lumina vitæ
Redducit Venus?

Which Creech thus renders:

Besides, if o'er whatever years prevail,
Should wholly perish, and its matter fail,
How could the powers of all kind Venus breed
A constant race of animals to succeed?

The translation of Creech is at least complicated and unintelligible; and I am uncertain whether even Dryden's explanation renders it grammatical. Dryden speaks elsewhere with great applause of Creech's translation.

The original of this decision (in Dryden's handwriting) is in the possession of Mrs. White of Bownham-hall, Gloucestershire, and was most obligingly communicated to the editor by that lady through the medium of Mr. Constable of Edinburgh.]

THE two verses, concerning which the dispute is raised, are these:

Besides, if o're whatever yeares prevaile
Shou'd wholly perish, and its matter faile.

The question arising from them is, whether any true grammaticall construction can be made of them? The objection is, that there is no nominative case appearing to the word *perish*, or that can be understood to belong to it.

I have considered the verses, and find the author of them to have notoriously bungled; that he has plac'd the words as confus'dly as if he had studied to do so. This notwithstanding, the very words, without adding or diminishing in theire proper sence, (or at least what the authour meanes,) may run thus:—*Besides, if what ever yeares prevaile over, should wholly perish, and its matter faile.*

I pronounce therefore, as impartially as I can upon the whole, that there *is* a nominative case, and that figurative, so as Terence and Virgil, amongst others, use it; that is, the whole clause precedent is the nominative case to *perish*. My reason is this, and I think it obvious; let the question be ask'd, what it is that shou'd wholly perish, or that perishes? The answer will be, That which yeares prevaile over. If you will not admit a clause to be in construction a nominative case, the word *thing*, *illud*, or *quodcunque*, is to be understood, either of which words, in the feminine gender, agree with *res*, so that he meanes what ever *thing* time prevails over shou'd wholly perish, and its matter faile.

Lucretius his Latine runs thus:

> Præterea, quæcunque vetustate amovet ætas,
> Si penitus perimit, consumens materiam omnem,
> Unde animale genus, generatim in lumina vitæ
> Reiducit Venus? &c.

which ought to have been translated thus:

> Besides, what ever time removes from view,
> If he destroys the stock of matter too,
> From whence can kindly propagation spring,
> Of every creature, and of every thing?

I translated it *whatever* purposely, to shew, that *thing* is to be understood; which, as the words are heere plac'd, is so very perspicuous, that the nominative case cannot be doubted.

The word *perish*, used by Mr. Creech, is a verb neuter; where Lucretius puts *perimit*, which is active; a licence which, in translating a philosophical poet, ought not to be taken; for some reason, which I have not room to give. But to comfort the loser, I am apt to believe, that the cross-grain confused verse put him so much out of patience, that he wou'd not suspect it of any sence.

SIR,

The company having done me so great an honour as to make me their judge, I desire from you the favour of presenting my acknowledgments to them; and shou'd be proud to heere from you, whether they rest satisfyed in my opinion, who am,

Sir,
Your most humble servant,
JOHN DRYDEN.*

But, in this case, the date of their being delivered has been placed too late. Exact accuracy is of little consequence; but I fear the hint in the letter gives some reason for Tom Brown's alleging that Dryden flattered alternately the wits of the town at the cost of the university, and the university scholars at the expense of the London audience. I cry that facetious person mercy, for having said there was no proof of his accusation.

LETTER IV.

THE REV. DR. BUSBY.

Wednesday Morning, [1682.]

HONOUR'D SIR,

We have, with much ado, recover'd my younger sonn,† who came home extreamly sick of a violent cold, and, as he thinks him selfe, a chine-cough. The truth is, his constitution is very tender; yet his desire of learning, I hope, will inable him to brush through the college. He is allwayes gratefully acknowledging your fatherly kindnesse to him; and very willing, to his poore power, to do all things which may continue it. I have no more to add, but only to wish the eldest may also deserve some part of your good opinion; for I believe him to be of vertuous and pious inclinations; and for both, I dare assure you, that they can promise to themselves no farther share of my indulgence, then while they carry them selves with that reverence to you, and that honesty to all others, as becomes them. I am, honour'd Sir,

Your most obedient servant and scholar,
JOHN DRYDEN.‡

LETTER V.

TO THE REV. DR. BUSBY.

SIR, [1682.]

If I could have found in my selfe a fitting temper to have waited upon you, I had done it

* There is no address or superscription.

† John Dryden, admitted a king's scholar in 1682.

‡ This letter from Lady Elizabeth Dryden seems to have been written at the same time, and on the same subject:

Honoured Sir, Ascension Day, [1682.]

I hope I need use noe other argument to you in excuse of my sonn for not coming to church to Westminster then this, that he now lies at home, and thearfore cannot esilly goe soe far backwards and forwards. His father and I will take care that he shall duely goe to church heare, both on holydayes and Sundays, till he comes to be more nearly under your care in the college. In the mean time, will you please to give me leave to accuse you of forget-the day you dismissed my sonn* from the colledge: for he did the message; and by what I find from Mr. Meredith, as it was delivered by you to him; namely, that you desired to see me, and had somewhat to say to me concerning him. I observed likewise somewhat of kindnesse in it, that you sent him away, that you might not have occasion to correct him. I examined the business, and found, it concern'd his having been *custos*† foure or five dayes together. But if he admonished, and was not believed, because other boyes combined to discredit him with false witnesseing, and to save them selves, perhaps his crime is not so great. Another fault it seems, he made, which was going into one Hawkes his house, with some others; which you haпning to see, sent your servant to know who they were, and he onely returned you my sonn's name; so the rest escaped.

I have no fault to find with my sonn's punishment; for that is, and ought to be, reserv'd to any master, much more to you, who have been his father's. But your man was certainly to blame to name him onely; and 'tis onely my respect to you, that I do not take notice of it to him. My first rash resolutions were, to have brought things past any composure, by immediately sending for my sonn's things out of colledge; but upon reflection, I find, I have a double tye upon me not to do it: one, my obligations to you for my education; another, my great tendernesse of doeing any thing offensive to my Lord Bishop of Rochester,‡ as cheife governour of the college. It does not consist with the honour I beare him and you to go so precipitately to worke; no, not so much as to have any difference with you, if it can possibly be avoyded. Yet, as my sonn stands now, I cannot see with what credit he can be elected; for, being but sixth, and (as you are pleased to judge,) not deserving that neither, I know not whether he may not go immediately to Cambridge, as well as one of his own election went to Oxford this yeare* by your consent. I will say nothing of my second sonn, but that, after you had been pleased to advise me to waite on my Lord Bishop for his favour, I found he might have had the first place if you had not opposed it; and I likewise found at the election, that, by the pains you had taken with him, he in some sort deserved it.

I hope, sir, when you have given your selfe the trouble to read thus farr, you, who are a prudent man, will consider, that none complaine, but they desire to be reconciled at the same time: there is no mild expostulation, at least, which does not intimate a kindness and respect in him who makes it. Be pleas'd, if there be no merit on my side, to make it your own act of grace to be what you were formerly to my sonn. I have done something, so far to conquer my own spirit as to ask it; and, indeed, I know not with what face to go to my Lord Bishop, and to tell him I am takeing away both my sonns; for though I shall tell him no occasion, it will looke like a disrespect to my old master, of which I will not be guilty, if it be possible. I shall add no more, but hope I shall be so satisfyed with a favourable answer from you, which I promise to my selfe from your goodnesse and moderation, that I shall still have occasion to continue,

Sir,

Your most obliged humble servant,

JOHN DRYDEN.†

ting your prommis conserning my eldest sonn, who, as you once assured me, was to have one night in a weeke alowed him to be at home, in considirasion both of his health and cleanliness. You know, Sir, that promises mayd to women, and espiceally mothers, will never faille to be be cald upon; and thearfore I will add noe more, but that I am, at this time, your remembrancer, and allwayes, honnord Sir,

Your humble servant,

E. DRYDEN.

* His eldest son Charles, as Mr. Malone supposes.

† In the hall of the college of Westminster, when the boys are at dinner, it is, *ex officio*, the place of the second boy, in the second election, to keep order among the two under elections; and if any word, after he has ordered silence, be spoken, except in Latin, he says to the speaker, *Tu es Custos*; and this term passes from the second speaker to the third, or more, till dinner is over. Whoever is then *custos*, has an imposition.

It is highly probable, (adds the very respectable gentleman, to whom I am indebted for this information,) that there had formerly been a *tessera* or *symbolum*, delivered from boy to boy, as at some French schools now, and that *custos* meant *custos tesseræ*, *symboli*, &c.; but at Westminster, the symbol is totally unknown at present.—*Malone.*

‡ Dr. John Dolben, then Bishop of Rochester, afterwards of York.

* Mr. Malone says, "The person meant was Robert Morgan, who was elected with Charles Dryden into the college of Westminster, in 1680, and is the only one of those then admitted, who was elected to Oxford in 1682. That circumstance, therefore, ascertains the year when this letter was written."

† The two last letters are printed from Mr. Malone's copy, to whom the originals were communicated by Mr. John Nichols, author of the History of Leicestershire.

‡ To this curious and valuable letter, Mr. Malone has added the address to Rochester and the date

LETTER VI.

TO LAURENCE HYDE, EARL OF ROCHESTER.‡

MY LORD, [Perhaps August 1683.]

I KNOW not whether my Lord Sunderland has interceded with your Lordship for half a yeare in my salary; but I have two other advocates, my extreme wants, even almost to arresting, and my ill health, which cannot be repaired without immediate retireing into the country. A quarter's allowance is but the Jesuit's powder to my disease; the fit will return a fortnight hence. If I durst, I would plead a little merit, and some hazards of my life from the common enemyes; my refuseing advantages offered by them, and neglecting my beneficiall studyes, for the King's service: but I only thinke I merit not to sterve. I never apply'd myselfe to any interest contrary to your Lordship's; and on some occasions, perhaps not known to you, have not been unserviceable to the memory and reputation of my Lord, your father.* After this, my Lord, my conscience assures me, I may write boldly, though I cannot speake to you. I have three sonns growing to man's estate; I breed them all up to learning, beyond my fortune; but they are too hopefull to be neglected, though I want. Be pleased to looke on me with an eye of compassion. Some small employment would render my condition easy. The King is not unsatisfied of me; the Duke has often promised me his assistance; and your Lordship is the conduit through which they passe, either in the Customes, or the Appeals of the Excise,† or some other way, meanes cannot be wanting, if you please to have the will. 'Tis enough for one age to have neglected Mr. Cowley, and sterv'd Mr. Butler; but neither of them had the happiness to live till your Lordship's ministry. In the meane time, be pleased to give me a gracious and speedy answer to my present request of halfe a yeare's pention for my necessityes. I am going to write somewhat by his Majesty's command,‡ and cannot stir, into the country for my health and studies, till I secure my family from want. You have many petitions of this nature, and cannot satisfy all; but I hope, from your goodness, to be made an exception to your general rules,* because I am, with all sincerity,

Your Lordship's

Most obedient humble servant,

JOHN DRYDEN.

both of which are conjectural. Hyde, Earl of Rochester, was made first commissioner of the treasury in 1679, and continued prime minister till September 1684. Let it be remembered by those men of talents, who may be tempted to engage in the sea of politics, that Dryden thus sued for what was his unquestionable due, within two years after having written "Absalom and Achitophel," and "The Medal," in defence of the government, to whom he was suppliant for so small a boon.

* Edward, Earl of Clarendon. It is uncertain in what manner our author undertook his defence.

† The place which our author here solicits, (worth only 200*l.* a-year,) was the first office that Addison obtained, which he used to call "the *little thing* given me by Lord Halifax." Locke also, after the Revolution, was a commissioner of appeals.—*Malone.*

‡ The "History of the League," entered on the Stationers' books early in 1684, and "Englished by his Majestie's express command."

* This application was successful; and Dryden elsewhere expresses his gratitude, that his wants were attended to and relieved during the penury of an exhausted Exchequer; Cowley's simile, he observed, was reversed, and Gideon's fleece was watered, while all around remained parched and arid.

LETTER VII.

TO MR. JACOB TONSON.

[The letters to Tonson are without dates. I have retained those which Mr. Malone has attached to them, from circumstances of internal evidence which it seems unnecessary to detail, but which appear in general satisfactory, though not given as absolutely conclusive.]

MR. TONSON, Monday Morning, [1684.]

THE two melons you sent I received before your letter, which came foure houres after: I tasted one of them, which was too good to need an excuse; the other is yet untouched. You have written diverse things which give me great satisfaction; particularly that the History of the League is commended: and I hope the onely thing I feared in it is not found out.† Take it all together, and I dare say without vanity, 'tis the best translation of any history in English, though I cannot say 'tis the best history; but that is no fault of mine. I am glad my Lord Duke of Ormond has one; I did not forget him; but I thought his sorrows were too fresh upon him to receive a present of that nature.‡ For my Lord Roscommon's Essay,§ I am of your opinion, that you should reprint it, and that you may safely venture on a thousand more. In my verses before it, pray let the printer mend his errour, and let the line stand thus:

That heer his conqu'ring ancestors were nurs'd;—‖

Charles his copy¶ is all true. The other faults my Lord Roscommon will mend in the booke,

† What this circumstance was cannot now be discovered.

‡ The Duchess of Ormond died July 1684.

§ The first edition of Lord Roscommon's "Essay on Translated Verse" appeared in 1684, and a second edition was published by Jacob Tonson in 4to, early in 1685.

‖ In the first edition it stood,

"That here his conqu'ring ancestors *was* nursed,"

¶ Latin verses by Charles Dryden, prefixed to Lord Roscommon's Essay.

or Mr. Chetwood* for him, if my Lord be gone for Ireland: of which pray send me word.

Your opinion of the Miscellanyes† is likewise mine: I will for once lay by the "*Religio Laici*," till another time. But I must also add, that since we are to have nothing but new, I am resolved we will have nothing but good, whomever we disoblige. You will have of mine, four Odes of Horace, which I have already translated; another small translation of forty lines from Lucretius; the whole story of Nisus and Eurialus, both in the fifth and the ninth of Virgil's Æneids: and I care not who translates them beside me; for let him be friend or foe, I will please myself, and not give off in consideration of any man. There will be forty lines more of Virgil in another place, to answer those of Lucretius: I meane those very lines which Montagne has compared in those two poets; and Homer shall sleep on for me,—I will not now meddle with him. And for the Act which remains of the Opera,‡ I believe I shall have no leysure to mind it, after I have done what I proposed; for my business here is to unweary my selfe after my studyes, not to drudge.

I am very glad you have pay'd Mr. Jones, because he has carryed him selfe so gentlemanlike to me; and, if ever it lyes in my power, I will requite it. I desire to know whether the Duke's House are makeing cloaths, and putting things in a readiness for the singing Opera, to be played immediately after Michaelmasse.§ For the actors in the two playes‖ which are to be acted of mine this winter, I had spoken with Mr. Betterton by chance at the Coffee-house the afternoon before I came away; and I believe that the persons were all agreed on, to be just the same you mentioned; only Octavia was to be Mrs. Butler, in case Mrs. Cooke were not on the stage; and I know not whether Mrs. Percival, who is a comedian, will do well for Benzayda.

I came hither for health, and had a kind of hectique feavour for a fortnight of the time: I am now much better. Poore Jacke¶ is not yet recovered of an intermitting feavour, of which this is the twelfth day; but he mends, and now begins to eat flesh: to add to this, my man, with over care of him, is fallen ill too, of the same distemper; so that I am deep in doctors, 'pothecaries, and nurses; but though many in this country fall sick of feavours, few or none dye. Your friend, Charles,* continues well. If you have any extraordinary newes, I should be glad to heare it. I will answer Mr. Butler's letter next week for it requires no hast.

I am yours,
JOHN DRYDEN.

* Knightly Chetwood. He wrote Lord Roscommon's life.

† Dryden was now about to publish the second volume of the Miscellanies; in which it would appear to have been settled, that nothing should be inserted but what was new. "*Religio Laici*," therefore, as having been formerly published, was laid aside for the present.

‡ Probably "Albion and Albanius," which was afterwards completed and ready to be performed in February 1684-5.

§ The singing Opera was probably that of "King Arthur," to which "Albion and Albanius" was originally designed as a prelude. But it was not acted till after the Revolution.

‖ "All for Love," and "The Conquest of Granada."

¶ His second son.

* His eldest son.

LETTER VIII.

FROM JACOB TONSON TO JOHN DRYDEN, ESQ.

[Probably written in Jan. or Feb. 1692-3.]†

SIR,

I HAVE here returned ye Ovid, wch I read wth a great deal of pleasure, and think nothing can be more entertaining; but by this letter you find I am not soe well satisfied as perhaps you might think. I hope at ye same time the matter of fact I lay down in this letter will appear grounds for it, and wch I beg you wou'd concider of; and then I believe I shall at least bee excused.

You may please, Sr, to remember, that upon my first proposal about ye 3d Miscellany, I offer'd fifty pounds, and talk'd of several authours, without naming Ovid. You ask'd if it shou'd not be guynneas, and said I shou'd not repent it; upon wch I immediately comply'd, and left it wholy to you what, and for ye quantity too: and I declare it was the farthest in ye world from my thoughts that by leaving it to you I should have the less. Thus the case stood when you went into Essex. After I came out of Northamptonshire I wrote to you, and received a letter dated Monday Oct. 3d, 92, from wch letter I now write word for word what followes:

"I am translating about six hundred lines, or somewhat less, of ye first book of the Metamorphoses. If I cannot get my price, wch shall be twenty guyneas, I will translate the whole book; wch coming out before the whole translation, will spoyl Tate's undertakings. 'Tis one of the best I have ever made, and very pleasant. This, wth Heroe and Leander, and the piece of Homer, (or, if it be not enough, I will add more,) will make a good part of a Miscellany."

† The Third Miscellany was published in July 1693

Those, Sr, and ye very words, and ye onely ones in that letter relating to that affair; and ye Monday following you came to town.—After your arrivall you shew'd Mr. Motteaux what you had done, (wch he told me was to ye end of ye story of Daphnis,) [Daphne,] and demanded, as you mention'd in your letter, twenty guyneas, wch that bookseller refus'd. Now, Sr, I the rather believe there was just soe much done, by reason ye number of lines you mention in yor letter agrees wth ye quantity of lines that soe much of ye first book makes; wch upon counting ye Ovid, I finde to be in ye Lattin 566, in ye English 759; and ye bookseller told me there was noe more demanded of him for it.—Now, Sr, what I entreat you wou'd please to consider of is this: that it is reasonable for me to expect at least as much favour from you as a strange bookseller; and I will never believe yt it can be in yr nature to use one ye worse for leaveing it to you; and if the matter of fact as I state it be true, (and upon my word what I mention I can shew you in yor letter,) then pray, Sr, consider how much dearer I pay then you offered it to ye other bookseller; for he might have had to ye end of ye story of Daphnis for 20 guynneas, wch is in yor translation 759 lines;

And then suppose 20 guynneas
more for the same number . . . 759 lines,

that makes for 40 guynneas . . . 1518 lines; and all that I have for fifty guynneas are but 1446; soe that, if I have noe more, I pay 10 guyneas above 40, and have 72 lines less for fifty, in proportion, than the other bookseller shou'd have had for 40, at ye rate you offered him ye first part. This is, Sir, what I shall take as a great favour if you please to think of. I had intentions of letting you know this before; but till I had paid ye money, I would not ask to see the book, nor count the lines, least it shou'd look like a design of not keeping my word. When you have looked over ye rest of what you have already translated, I desire you would send it; and I own yt if you don't think fit to add something more, I must submit: 'tis wholly at yor choice, for I left it entirely to you; but I believe you cannot imagine I expected so little; for you were pleased to use me much kindlyer in Juvenall, which is not recon'd soe easy to translate as Ovid. Sr, I humbly beg yor pardon for this long letter, and upon my word I had rather have yor good will than any man's alive; and, whatever you are pleased to doe, will alway acknowledge my self, Sr,

Yor most obliged humble Servt,

J. Tonson.

LETTER IX.

TO MR. JACOB TONSON.*

MR. TONSON, August 30. [1693.]

I am much asham'd of my self, that I am so much behind-hand with you in kindness. Above all things I am sensible of your good nature, in bearing me company to this place, wherein, besides the cost, you must needs neglect your own business; but I will endeavour to make you some amends; and therefore I desire you to command me something for your service. I am sure you thought my Lord Radclyffe† wou'd have done something: I ghess'd more truly, that he cou'd not; but I was too far ingag'd to desist, though I was tempted to it by the melancholique prospect I had of it. I have translated six hundred lines of Ovid; but I believe I shall not compasse his 772 lines under nine hundred or more of mine.—This time I cannot write to my wife, because he who is to carry my letter to Oundle, will not stay till I can write another. Pray, sir, let her know that I am well; and for feare the few damsins shou'd be all gone, desire her to buy me a sieve-full, to preserve whole, and not in mash.‡

I intend to come up at least a week before Michaelmass; for Sir Matthew§ is gone abroad, I suspect a wooeing, and his caleche is gone with him: so that I have been but thrice at Tichmarsh, of which you were with me once. This disappointment makes the place wearysome to me, which otherwise wou'd be pleasant.

About a fortnight ago I had an intimation from a friend by letter, that one of the secretaryes, I suppose Trenchard,‖ had informed the

* The author was at this time in Northamptonshire. The original has no date but August 30th; but the year is ascertained by the reference to the Third Miscellany, which was published in July 1693.—*Malone.*

† To whom the Third Miscellany is dedicated. I fear this alludes to some disappointment in the pecuniary compliment usual on such occasions.

‡ This commission will probably remind the reader of the poetic diet recommended by Bayes.—"If I am to write familiar things, as sonnets to Armida, and the like, I make use of *stewed prunes* only; but, when I have a grand design in hand, I ever take physic, and let blood; for, when you would have pure swiftness of thought, and fiery flights of fancy, you must have a care of the pensive part. In fine, you must purge the belly.

Smith. By my troth, sir, this is a most admirable receipt for writing.

Bayes. Ay, 'tis my secret; and, in good earnest, I think one of the best I have."—*Rehearsal*, Act I.

This is an instance of the minute and malicious diligence, with which the most trivial habits and tastes of our author were ridiculed in the "Rehearsal."

§ Sir Matthew, with whom Dryden appears to have resided at this time, is unknown.

‖ Sir John Trenchard, who was made one of the

queen, that I had abus'd her government (those were the words) in my epistle to my Lord Radcliffe; and that thereupon she had commanded her historiographer, Rymer, to fall upon my playes; which he assures me is now doeing. I doubt not his malice, from a former hint you gave me; and if he be employ'd, I am confident 'tis of his own seeking; who, you know, has spoken slightly of me in his last critique:* and that gave me occasion to snarl againe. In your next, let me know what you can learn of this matter. I am Mr. Congreve's true lover, and desire you to tell him, how kindly I take his often remembrances of me; I wish him all prosperity, and hope I shall never loose his affection; nor yours, sir, as being

Your most faithfull,

And much obliged Servant,

JOHN DRYDEN.

I had all your letters.

Sir Matthew had your book when he came home last; and desir'd me to give you his acknowledgements.

LETTER X.

MR. JOHN DENNIS† TO MR. DRYDEN.

DEAR SIR,

You may see already by this presumptuous greeting, that encouragement gives as much assurance to friendship, as it imparts to love. You may see too, that a friend may sometimes proceed to acknowledge affection, by the very same degrees by which a lover declares his passion. This last at first confesses esteem, yet owns no passion but admiration. But as soon as he is animated by one kind expression, his look, his style, and his very soul are altered. But as sovereign beauties know very well, that he who confesses he esteems and admires them, implies that he loves them, or is inclined to love them: a person of Mr. Dryden's exalted genius, can discern very well, that when we esteem him highly, 'tis respect restrains us, if we say no more. For where great esteem is without affection, 'tis often attended with envy, if not with hate; which passions detract even when they commend, and silence is their highest panegyrick. 'Tis indeed impossible, that I should refuse to love a man, who has so often given me all the pleasure that the most insatiable mind can desire: when at any time I have been dejected by disappointments, or tormented by cruel passions, the recourse to your verses has calmed my soul, or raised it to transports which made it contemn tranquility. But though you have so often given me all the pleasure I was able to bear, I have reason to complain of you on this account, that you have confined my delight to a narrower compass. Suckling, Cowley, and Denham, who formerly ravished me in every part of them, now appear tasteless to me in most; and Waller himself, with all his gallantry, and all that admirable art of his turns, appears three quarters prose to me. Thus, 'tis plain, that your Muse has done me an injury; but she has made me amends for it. For she is like those extraordinary women, who, besides the regularity of their charming features, besides their engaging wit, have secret, unaccountable, enchanting graces; which though they have been long and often enjoyed, make them always new and always desirable.—I return you my hearty thanks for your most obliging letter. I had been very unreasonable if I had repined that the favour arrived no sooner. 'Tis allowable to grumble at the delaying a payment; but to murmur at the deferring a benefit, is to be impudently ungrateful beforehand. The commendations which you give me, exceedingly sooth my vanity. For you with a breath can bestow or confirm reputation; a whole numberless people proclaims the praise which you give, and the judgments of three mighty kingdoms appear to depend upon yours. The people gave me some little applause before; but to whom, when they are in the humour, will they not give it? and to whom, when they were froward, will they not refuse it? Reputation with them depends upon chance, unless they are guided by those above them. They are but the keepers, as it were of the lottery which Fortune sets up for renown; upon which Fame is bound to attend with her trumpet, and sound when men draw the prizes. Thus I had rather have your approbation than the applause of Fame. Her commendation argues good luck, but Mr. Dryden's implies desert. Whatever low opinion I have hitherto had of myself, I have so great a value for your judgment, that for the sake of that, I shall be willing henceforward to believe that I am not wholly desertless; but that you may find me still more supportable, I shall endeavour to compensate whatever I want in those glittering qualities, by which the world

Secretaries of State, March 23, 1691-2, died in office in April 1695.

*"A short view of tragedy," published (as appears from the Gentleman's Journal, by P. Motteux,) in December 1692. The date in the title-page is 1693.

†Dennis, the critic, afterwards so unfortunately distinguished by the satire of Pope. Like Rymer, and others, he retained considerable reputation for critical acumen, until he attempted to illustrate his precepts by his own compositions.

so dazzled, with truth, with faith, and with zeal to serve you; qualities which for their rarity might be objects of wonder, but that men dare not appear to admire them, because their admiration would manifestly declare their want of them. Thus, Sir, let me assure you, that though you are acquainted with several gentlemen, whose eloquence and wit may capacitate them to offer their services with more address to you, yet no one can declare himself, with greater chearfulness, or with greater fidelity, or with more profound respect, than myself,

Sir,

Your most, &c.

March 3, [1693-4.] JOHN DENNIS.

LETTER XI.

TO MR. JOHN DENNIS.

In answer to the foregoing.

[Probably March, 1693-4.]

MY DEAR MR. DENNIS,

WHEN I read a letter so full of my commendations as your last, I cannot but consider you as the master of a vast treasure, who having more than enough for yourself, are forced to ebb out upon your friends. You have indeed the best right to give them, since you have them in propriety; but they are no more mine when I receive them than the light of the moon can be allowed to be her own, who shines but by the reflexion of her brother. Your own poetry is a more powerful example, to prove that the modern writers may enter into comparison with the ancients, than any which Perrault could produce in France: yet neither he, nor you, who are a better critick, can persuade me, that there is any room left for a solid commendation at this time of day, at least for me.

If I undertake the translation of Virgil, the little which I can perform will shew at least, that no man is fit to write after him, in a barbarous modern tongue. Neither will his machines be of any service to a Christian poet. We see now ineffectually they have been tryed by Tasso, and by Ariosto. It is using them too dully, if we only make devils of his gods: as if, for example, I would raise a storm, and make use of Æolus, with this only difference of calling him Prince of the Air; what invention of mine would there be in this? or who would not see Virgil through me; only the same trick played over again by a bungling juggler? Boileau has well observed, that it is an easy matter in a Christian poem, for God to bring the Devil to reason. I think I have given a better hint for new machines in my preface to Juvenal; where I have particularly recommended two subjects, one of King Arthur's conquest of the Saxons, and the other of the Black Prince in his conquest of Spain. But the guardian angels of monarchys and kingdoms are not to be touched by every hand: a man must be deeply conversant in the Platonic philosophy, to deal with them; and therefore I may reasonably expect, that no poet of our age will presume to handle those machines, for fear of discovering his own ignorance; or if he should, he might perhaps be ingrateful enough not to own me for his benefactour.*

After I have confessed thus much of our modern heroic poetry, I cannot but conclude with Mr. Rymer, that our English comedy is far beyond any thing of the ancients: and notwithstanding our irregularities, so is our tragedy. Shakspeare had a genius for it; and we know, in spite of Mr. Rymer, that genius alone is a greater virtue (if I may so call it) than all other qualifications put together. You see what success this learned critick has found in the world, after his blaspheming Shakspeare.† Almost all the faults which he has discovered are truly there; yet who will read Mr. Rymer, or not read Shakspeare? For my own part, I reverence Mr. Rymer's learning, but I detest his ill nature and his arrogance. I indeed, and such as I, have reason to be afraid of him, but Shakspeare has not.‡

There is another part of poetry, in which the English stand almost upon an equal foot with the ancients; and it is that which we call Pindarique; introduced, but not perfected, by our famous Mr. Cowley; and of this, Sir, you are one of the greatest masters. You have the sublimity of sense as well as sound, and know how far the boldness of a poet may lawfully extend. I could wish you would cultivate this kind of Ode; and reduce it either to the same measures which Pindar used, or give new measures of your own. For, as it is, it looks like a vast tract of land newly discovered; the soil is wonderfully fruitful, but unmanured; overstocked with inhabitants, but almost all savages, without laws, arts, arms, or policy.

I remember poor Nat. Lee, who was then upon the verge of madness, yet made a sober

*Sir Richard Blackmore was doomed to accomplish this prophecy.

†In his Short View of Tragedy.

‡This lesson was thrown away upon poor Dennis, who, by his rash and riotous attacks upon Pope, afterwards procured an immortality of a kind very different from that to which he aspired.

and a witty answer to a bad poet, who told him, "It was an easie thing to write like a madman:" "No," said he, "it is very difficult to write like a madman, but it is a very easie matter to write like a fool." Otway and he are safe by death from all attacks, but we poor poets militant (to use Mr. Cowley's expression) are at the mercy of wretched scribblers: and when they cannot fasten upon our verses, they fall upon our morals, our principles of state, and religion. For my principles of religion, I will not justifie them to you: I know yours are far different. For the same reason, I shall say nothing of my principles of state. I believe you in yours follow the dictates of your reason, as I in mine do those of my conscience. If I thought myself in an errour, I would retract it. I am sure that I suffer for them; and Milton makes even the Devil say that no creature is in love with pain. For my morals betwixt man and man, I am not to be my own judge. I appeal to the world, if I have deceived or defrauded any man: and for my private conversation, they who see me every day can be the best witnesses, whether or no it be blameless and inoffensive. Hitherto I have no reason to complain that men of either party shun my company. I have never been an impudent beggar at the doors of noblemen: my visits have indeed been too rare to be unacceptable; and but just enough to testifie my gratitude for their bounty, which I have frequently received, but always unasked, as themselves will witness.

I have written more than I needed to you on this subject; for I dare say you justifie me to yourself. As for that which I first intended for the principal subject of this letter, which is my friend's passion and his design of marriage, on better consideration I have changed my mind; for having had the honour to see my dear friend Wycherly's letter to him on that occasion, I find nothing to be added or amended. But as well as I love Mr. Wycherly, I confess I love myself so well, that I will not shew how much I am inferiour to him in wit and judgment, by undertaking any thing after him. There is Moses and the Prophets in his council. Jupiter and Juno, as the poets tell us, made Tiresias their umpire in a certain merry dispute, which fell out in heaven betwixt them. Tiresias, you know, had been of both sexes, and therefore was a proper judge; our friend Mr. Wycherly is full as competent an arbitrator; he has been a bachelor, and marryed man, and is now a widower. Virgil says of Ceneus,

——Nunc vir, nunc fœmina, Ceneus,
Rursus et in veterem fato revoluta figuram.

Yet I suppose he will not give any large commendations to his middle state: nor, as the sailer said, will be fond after a shipwrack to put to sea again.* If my friend will adventure after this, I can but wish him a good wind, as being his, and

My dear Mr. Dennis,
Your most affectionate
and most faithful Servant,
JOHN DRYDEN.

LETTER XII.

TO MR. JACOB TONSON.

[The copy money for translating the Æneid was fifty pounds for each book. The rising of the second subscription seems to allude to the practice of fixing a day, after which no subscriptions were to be received except on payment of an advanced price. The first subscribers to Dryden's Virgil paid five guineas; a plate was dedicated to each of them, and ornamented with his arms. A second class paid two guineas only, and were not so honoured. In the subsequent letters there occur several allusions to these arrangements, and to the transference of names from the higher to the lower class.]

Probably written in April 1695.
MR. TONSON, Wednesday morning.

IT is now three dayes since I have ended the fourth Eneid; and I am this morning beginning to transcribe it, as you may do afterwards; for I am willing some few of my friends may see it, and shall give leave to you, to shew your transcription to some others, whose names I will tell you. The paying Ned Sheldon the fifty pounds put me upon this speed; but I intend not so much to overtoil myself, after the sixth book is ended. If the second subscriptions rise, I will take so much the more time, because the profit will incourage me the more; if not, I must make the more haste; yet always with as much care as I am able. But however, I will not fail in my paines of translating the sixth Eneid with the same exactness as I have performed the fourth: because that book is my greatest favourite. You know money is now very scrupulously receiv'd: in the last which you did me the favour to change for my wife, besides the clip'd money, there were at least forty shillings brass. You may, if you please, come to me at the Coffee-house this afternoon, or at farthest to-morrow, that we may take care together, where and when I may receive the

* Dryden's evil opinion of the state of matrimony never fails to glance forth upon such occasions as the present.

fifty pounds and the guinneys; which must be some time this week.

I am your servant,
JOHN DRYDEN.

I have written to my Lord Lawderdail, for his decorations.*

LETTER XIII.

TO MR. JACOB TONSON.

Saturday, June the 8th, (f. 1695.)

MR. TONSON,

'TIS now high time for me to think of my second subscriptions; for the more time I have for collecting them, the larger they are like to be. I have now been idle just a fortnight; and therefore might have called sooner on you, for the remainder of the first subscriptions. And besides, Mr. Aston will be goeing into Cheshire a week hence, who is my onely help, and to whom you are onely beholding for makeing the bargain betwixt us, which is so much to my loss; but I repent nothing of it that is passed, but that I do not find myself capable of translating so great an author, and therefore feare to lose my own credit, and to hazard your profit, which it wou'd grieve me if you should loose, by your too good opinion of my abilities. I expected to have heard of you this week, according to the intimation you gave me of it; but that failing, I must defer it no longer than till the ensueing week, because Mr. Aston will afterwards be gone, if not sooner.

Be pleased to send me word what day will be most convenient to you; and be ready with the price of paper, and of the books. No matter for any dinner; for that is a charge to you, and I care not for it.† Mr. Congreve may be with us, as a common friend; for as you know him for yours, I make not the least doubt, but that he is much more mine; send an immediate answer, and you shall find me ready to do all things wch become

Your Servant,
JOHN DRYDEN.

* One of the subscribers of the higher class. The decorations were probably his armorial bearings.

† It was an ancient British custom, and prevailed in Scotland within these forty years, to finish all bargains, contracts, and even consultations, at a tavern, that the parties might not, according to the ancient Caledonian phrase, part *dry-lipp'd*. The custom between authors and booksellers seems to have been universal; and the reader may recollect, that the supposed poisoning of the celebrated Edmund Curl took place at a meeting of this kind.

LETTER XIV

TO MR. JACOB TONSON.

[Wednesday the 18th of 7ber. f. 1695.]

MY GOOD FRIEND,

THIS is onely to acquaint you, that I have taken my place in the Oundel coach for Tuesday next; and hope to be at London on Wednesday night. I had not confidence enough to hope Mr. Southern and Mr. Congreve would have given me the favour of their company for the last foure miles; but since they will be so kind to a friend of theirs, who so truely loves both them and you, I will please myself with expecting it, if the weather be not so bad as to hinder them.

I assure you I lay up your last kindnesses to me in my heart: and the less I say of them, I charge them to account so much the more; being very sensible that I have not hitherto deserved them. Having been obliged to sit up all last night almost out of civility to strangers who were benighted, and to resign my bed to them, I am sleepy all this day; and if I had not taken a very lusty pike that day, they must have gone supperless to bed, foure ladyes and two gentlemen; for Mr. Dudley and I were alone, with but one man and no mayd in the house.—This time I cannot write to my wife; do me the favour to let her know I received her letter, am well, and hope to be with her on Wednesday next, at night. No more but that

I am very much
Your Friend and Servant,
JOHN DRYDEN.

LETTER XV.

TO MR. JACOB TONSON.

MR. TONSON, October the 29th, [f. 1695.]

SOME kind of intercourse must be carryed on betwixt us, while I am translating Virgil. Therefore I give you notice that I have done the seaventh Eneid in the country;* and intend some few days hence to go upon the eight: when that is finished, I expect fifty pounds in good silver; not such as I have have had formerly. I am not obliged to take gold,† neither

* At Burleigh, the seat of John, the fifth Earl of Essex.

† Both the gold and silver coin were at this time much depreciated; and remained in a fluctuating state till a new coinage took place.

will I; nor stay for it beyond four-and-twenty houres after it is due. I thank you for the civility of your last letter in the country; but the thirty shillings upon every book remains with me. You always intended I should get nothing by the second subscriptions, as I found from first to last. And your promise to Mr. Congreve, that you had found a way for my benefit, which was an encouragement to my paines, came at last, for me to desire Sir Godfrey Kneller and Mr. Closterman to gather for me. I then told Mr. Congreve, that I knew you too well to believe you meant me any kindness: and he promised me to believe accordingly of you, if you did not. But this is past; and you shall have your bargain, if I live and have my health. You may send me word what you have done in my business with the Earl of Derby, and I must have a place for the Duke of Devonshire. Some of your friends will be glad to take back their three guinneys. The Countess of Macclesfield gave her money to Will Plowden before Christmas; but he remembered it not, and payd it not in. Mr. Aston tells me, my Lord Derby expects but one book. I find, my Lord Chesterfield and my Lord Petre are both left out; but my Lady Macclesfield must have a place, if I can possibly: and Will Plowden shall pay you in three guinneys if I can obtain so much favour from you.* I desire neither excuses nor reasons from you: for I am but too well satisfyed already. The Notes and Prefaces shall be short; because you shall get the more by saving paper.†

John Dryden.

LETTER XVI.

TO MR. JACOB TONSON.

MR. TONSON, Friday night. [f. Dec. 1695.]

Meeting Sir Robert Howard at the playhouse this morning, and asking him how he lik'd my seaventh Eneid, he told me you had not brought it. He goes out of town to-morrow, being Satturday, after dinner. I desire you not to fail of carrying my manuscript for him to read in the country; and desire him to bring it up with him, when he comes next to town. I doubt you have not yet been with my Lord Chesterfield, and am in pain about it.

Yours,

John Dryden.

When you have leysure, I shou'd be glad to see how Mr. Congreve and you have worded my propositions for Virgil.* When my sonne's play† is acted, I intend to translate again, if my health continue. Some time next week let me heare from you concerning the propositions.

LETTER XVII.

TO MR. JACOB TONSON.

SIR, Friday forenoon. [f. Feb. 1695-6.]

I receiv'd your letter very kindly,‡ because indeed I expected none; but thought you as very a tradesman as Bentley,§ who has cursed our Virgil so heartily. I shall loose enough by your bill upon Mr. Knight;‖ for after having taken it all in silver, and not in half-crowns neither, but shillings and sixpences, none of the money will go; for which reason I have sent it all back again, and as the less loss will receive it in guinneys at 29 shillings each. 'Tis troublesome to be a looser, but it was my own fault to accept it this way, which I did to avoyd more trouble.

I am not sorry that you will not allow any thing towards the notes; for to make them good, would have cost me half a yeare's time at least. Those I write shall be only marginall, to help the unlearned, who understand not the poeticall fables. The prefaces, as I intend them, will be somewhat more learned. It wou'd require seaven yeares to translate Virgil exactly. But I promise you once more to do my best in the four remaining books, as I have hitherto done in the foregoing. Upon triall I find all of your trade are sharpers, and you not more than others; therefore I have not wholly left you. Mr. Aston does not blame you for getting as good a

* From inspecting the plates of Dryden's Virgil, it appears, that the Earl of Derby had one inscribed to him, as had Lord Chesterfield. But this wrathful letter made no farther impression on the mercantile obstinacy of Tonson; and neither the Duke of Devonshire, Lord Petre, nor Lady Macclesfield, obtained the place among the first subscribers, which Dryden so peremptorily demands for them.

† This seems to be a bitter jibe at Jacob's parsimony.

* Perhaps the proposals for the second subscription. See Letter XI.

† "The Husband his own Cuckold," written by our author's second son, John, and published in July 1696.

‡ Tonson's answer to the foregoing letter, seems to have been pacific and apologetical, yet peremptory as to his terms.

§ Richard Bentley, a bookseller and printer, who lived in Russel Street, Covent Garden

‖ A banker or goldsmith, afterwards notorious for his share in the South-Sea scheme, to which company he was cashier.

bargain as you cou'd, though I cou'd have gott an hundred pounds more; and you might have spared almost all your trouble if you had thought fit to publish the proposalls for the first subscriptions; for I have guynneas offered me every day, if there had been room; I believe, modestly speaking, I have refused already 25. I mislike nothing in your letter therefore, but onely your upbraiding me with the publique encouragement, and my own reputation concerned in the notes; when I assure you I cou'd not make them to my mind in less than half a year's time. Get the first half of Virgil transcribed as soon as possibly you can, that I may put the notes to it; and you may have the other four books which lye ready for you when you bring the former; that the press may stay as little as possibly it can. My Lord Chesterfield has been to visite me, but I durst say nothing of Virgil to him, for feare there should be no void place for him; if there be, let me know; and tell me whether you have made room for the Duke of Devonshire. Haveing no silver by me, I desire my Lord Derby's money, deducting your own. And let it be good, if you desire to oblige me, who am not your enemy, and may be your friend,

JOHN DRYDEN.

Let me heare from you as speedily as you can.

LETTER XVIII.

TO MR. JACOB TONSON.

May 26th, 1696.

SEND word, if you please, Sir, what is the most you will give for my sonn's play, that I may take the fairest chapman, as I am bound to do for his benefit; and if you have any silver which will go, my wife will be glad of it. I lost thirty shillings or more by the last payment of fifty pounds, wch you made at Mr. Knights.

Yours,

JOHN DRYDEN.

Sir Ro: Howard* writt me word, that if I cou'd make any advantage by being paid in clipp'd money, he would change it in the Exchequer.

* Sir Robert Howard had been appointed auditor of the Exchequer in 1673, and held that office till his death.

LETTER XIX.

TO MR. JACOB TONSON.

Thursday morning, [f. Aug. 1696.]

MR. TONSON,

I HAD yesterday morning two watches sent me by Mr. Tompion,* which I am to send my sonnes this week.† I cou'd not persuade him to take gold at any rate; but he will take a goldsmith's bill for two and twenty pounds, which is their price. I desire you wou'd give him such a bill, and abate it out of the next fifty pounds which you are to pay me when Virgil is finish'd. Ten Eneids are finish'd, and the ninth and tenth written out in my own hand. You may have them with the eight, which is in a foul copy, when you please to call for them, and to bring those which are transcrib'd. Mr. Tompion's man will be with me at four o'clock in the afternoon, and bring the watches, and must be paid at sight. I desire you therefore to procure a goldsmith's bill, and let me have it before that houre, and send an answer by my boy.

Yours,

JOHN DRYDEN.

LETTER XX.

TO MR. JACOB TONSON.

From the Coffee House. Nov. 25th.
Wednesday afternoon.

MR. TONSON,

I HAVE the remainder of my Northamptonshyre rents come up this weeke, and desire the favour of you to receive them for me, from the carrier of Tocester, who lodges at the Castle in Smithfield. I suppose it is the same man from whom you lately receiv'd them for my wife. Any time before ten o'clock to-morrow morning will serve the turne. If I were not deeply ingaged in my studyes, which will be finished in a day or two, I would not put you to this trouble. I have inclosed my tenant's letter to me, for you to shew the carrier, and to testify the summ, which is sixteen pounds and about tenn shillings; which the letter sets down. Pray, Sir, give in an acquittance for so much receiv'd, as I suppose you did last time.

I am,

Your very faithful Servant,

JOHN DRYDEN.

* The celebrated watchmaker, who was originally a jacksmith.—*Malone.*

† They were at this time at Rome.

LETTER XXI.

TO MR. JACOB TONSON.

SIR, [I. Jan. 1696-7.]

According to my promise, I have sent you all that is properly yours of my translation. I desire, as you offer'd, that it should be transcrib'd in a legible hand, and then sent back to me for the last review. As for some notes on the margins, they are not every where, and when they are, are imperfect; so that you ought not to transcribe them, till I make them compleat. I feare you can scarcely make any thing of my foul copy; but it is the best I have. You see, my hand fails me, and therefore I write so short a letter. What I wrote yesterday was too sharp; but I doubt it is all true. Your boy's coming upon so unseasonable a visit, as if you were frighted for yourself, discomposed me.

Transcribe on very large paper, and leave a very large margin.

Send your boy for the foul copies, and he shall have them; for it will not satisfy me to send them by my own servant.

I cannot yet find the first sheet of the first Eneid. If it be lost; I will translate it over againe: but perhaps it may be amongst the loose papers. The fourth and ninth Eclogues, which I have sent, are corrected in my wife's printed Miscellany.*

LETTER XXII.

TO MR. JACOB TONSON.

Tuesday Morning, July the 6th, 1697.

MR. TONSON,

I desire you wou'd let Mr. Pate† know, I can print no more names of his subscribers than I have money for, before I print their names. He has my acknowledgment of ten guineas receiv'd from him; and, as I told you, I owe him for above three yards of fine cloath: let him reckon for it; and then there will remain the rest for me, out of the ten more names wch he has given in. If he has not money by him, let him blott out as many of his names as he thinks good; and print onely those for which he pays or strikes off, in adjusting the accounts betwixt me and him. This is so reasonable on both sides, that he cannot refuse it; but I wou'd have things ended now, because I am to deal with a draper, who is of my own perswasion,* and to whom I have promis'd my custome.

Yours,

John Dryden.

I have sent to my tailour, and he sends me word, that I had three yards and half elle of cloath from Mr. Pate: I desire he would make his price, and deduct so much as it comes to, and make even for the rest with ready money; as also that he would send word what the name was, for whom Sam Atkins left him to make account for.

LETTER XXIII.

TO HIS SONS AT ROME.

Sept. the 3d, our Style, [1697.]

DEAR SONS,

Being now at Sir William Bowyer's† in the country, I cannot write at large, because I find myself somewhat indisposed with a cold, and am thick of hearing, rather worse than I was in town. I am glad to find by your letter of July 26th, your style, that you are both in health, but wonder you should think me so negligent as to forget to give you an account of the ship in which your parcel is to come. I have written to you two or three letters concerning it, which I have sent by safe hands, as I told you; and doubt not but you have them before this can arrive to you. Being out of town, I have for-

* The Eclogues of Virgil had been published in the first Miscellany. Dryden probably corrected them with a pen in Lady Elizabeth's copy of the printed book, and sent it to the bookseller as what is technically termed *copy*.

† This person, in the last age, was frequently called "the learned tradesman." "Sir Andrew Fountaine (says Swift in his *Journal*, October 6, 1710,) came this morning, and caught me writing in bed. I went into the city with him, and we dined at the Chop-house, with Will Pate, *the learned woollen-draper*; then we sauntered at china shops and booksellers; went to the tavern, and drank two pints of white wine," &c. Mr. William Pate was educated at Trinity Hall in Cambridge, where he took the degree of B. C. L. He died in 1746, and was buried at Lee, in Kent.

Mr. Malone, who mentions these particulars, transcribes Mr. Pate's epitaph, the moral of which is:—

Nervos atque artus esse sapientiæ,
Non temere credere.

It would seem from Dryden's letter, that this learned tradesman understood the mercantile, as well as the literary use of the apothegm.

* A Roman Catholic.

† At Denham Court, in Buckinghamshire. Sir William Bowyer married a kinswoman of Lady Elizabeth Dryden, Frances, daughter of Charles, Lord Cranbourne, eldest son of William, the second Earl of Salisbury.—*Malone.*

gotten the ship's name, which your mother will enquire, and put it into her letter, which is joined with mine. But the master's name I remember; he is called Mr. Ralph Thorp; the ship is bound to Leghorn, consigned to Mr. Peter and Mr. Tho. Ball, merchants. I am of your opinion, that, by Tonson's means, almost all our letters have miscarried for this last year.* But, however, he has missed of his design in the dedication, though he had prepared the book for it;† for, in every figure of Æneas he has caused him to be drawn like King William, with a hooked nose.‡

After my return to town, I intend to alter a play of Sir Robert Howard's, written long since, and lately put by him into my hands; 'tis called the "Conquest of China by the Tartars."§ It will cost me six weeks study, with the probable benefit of an hundred pounds. In the mean time, I am writing a song for St. Cecilia's Feast, who, you know, is the patroness of music. This is troublesome, and no way beneficial; but I could not deny the stewards of the feast, who came in a body to me to desire that kindness, one of them being Mr. Bridgman, whose parents are your mother's friends. I hope to send you thirty guineas between Michaelmass and Christmass, of which I will give you an account when I come to town. I remember the counsel you give me in your letter; but dissembling, though lawful in some cases, is not my talent; yet, for your sake, I will struggle with the plain openness of my nature, and keep in my just resentments against that degenerate order.‖ In the mean time, I flatter not myself with any manner of hopes, but do my duty, and suffer for God's sake; being assured, beforehand, never to be rewarded, though the times should alter. Towards the latter end of this month, September, Charles will begin to recover his perfect health, according to his nativity, which, casting it myself, I am sure is true; and all things hitherto have happened accordingly to the very time that I predicted them. I hope, at the same time, to recover more health, according to my age. Remember me to poor Harry, whose prayers I earnestly desire. My Virgil succeeds in the world beyond its desert, or my expectation. You know, the profits might have been more; but neither my conscience nor my honour would suffer me to take them;* but I never can repent of my constancy, since I am thoroughly persuaded of the justice of the cause for which I suffer. It has pleased God to raise up many friends to me amongst my enemies, though they, who ought to have been my friends, are negligent of me. I am called to dinner, and cannot go on with this letter, which I desire you to excuse; and am

Your most affectionate father,

JOHN DRYDEN.

Superscribed,

Al illustrissimo Sigre.

Carlo Dryden,

Camariere d'Honore A. S. S.

Franca per Mantoua. In Roma.

[To this Letter, Lady Elizabeth Dryden subjoined, on the same paper, the following Postscript.]

MY dear sons, I sent your letter emediately to your father, after I had read it, as you will find by his. I have not room to say much, having writ former letters to you, datted the 27 of August, your father being then out of town; he writes me word—he is much at woon as to his health, and his defnese is not wosce, but much as he was when he was heare. He expresses a great desire to see my deare Charlles; and trully I see noe reason why you should not both come together, to be a comfort to woon another, and to us both, if the King of France includ Ingland in the peace;† for you doe but gust make shift to live wheare you are, and soe I hope you may doe heare; for I will leaf noe sten untturn'd to help my belov'd sonns. If I cane, I will send this letter by the same way it came;‡ that is,

* This seems to imply a suspicion, though an odd one, that Jacob, being bent to convert Dryden to his own views of politics, intercepted his sons' letters from Rome, as proceeding from an interest hostile to his views. (See p. .) His earnest wish was, that the Æneid should be inscribed to King William.

† The translation of Virgil.

‡ In MS. Harl. p. 95, in the Museum, are the following verses, occasioned by this circumstance:

"To be published in the next edition of Dryden's Virgil.

Old Jacob, by deep judgment sway'd,
To please the wise beholders,
Has placed old Nassau's hook-nosed head
On poor Æneas' shoulders.

'To make the parallel hold tack,
Methinks there's little lacking;
One took his father pick-a-pack,
And t'other sent his packing.'

In a copy I have seen of this epigram, "poor" Æneas is improved into "young" Æneas.

§ This Dryden never effected, nor was Howard's play ever printed.

‖ Probably the clergy of England.

* This probably alludes to the proposition which appears to have been made to him, concerning the dedication of his Virgil to King William; for which a valuable pecuniary reward might have been expected.—*Malone.*

† The peace of Ryswick, which was proclaimed at London in the following month, October 19, 1697, O. S.

‡ She *means*, I suppose,—by the same way her son's letter came to her.

it was brought me from woon Mr. Galowway, who corresponds with Rozie; I payd woon and sixpence for it, and do offer to pay him what he demandes, so that he would take ceare the [packet] might come safe to your handes. I long tell I heare my deare Charlles is better. I have only room to tell you the names of the merchantes your parcell went in; you are to demmand them of Mr. Robert Ball and Thommas Ball in Lindovino in Livorno. You are not to pay any charges for the box, for the port of London. If the have demanded any of you, send word to me what it is; for otherwayes wee shall pay twice for them; and this Mr. Walkeson telles me with his service to you both. Farwell, my deare children: God Almighty keep you in his protection, for that is the wishes and prayers of your most affec: mother, that sends her blessinge to you all; not forgetting my sonn Harry, whose prayers I desire for a comfortable meetinge. I hope I may have some better thinges against you come, than what is sent you in that box; there being nothing considurabell but my deare Jackes play, who I desire in his next to me to give me a true account how my deare sonn Charlles is head dus; for I cane be at noe rest tell I heare he is better or rather thourely well, which I dally pray for.,*

LETTER XXIV.

TO MR. JACOB TONSON.

MR. TONSON, [f. Dec. 1697.]

I THANK you heartily for the sherry; it was, as you sayd, the best of the kind I ever dranke. I have found the catalogue you desire, of the subscriber's names you left with me; and have sent them to you inclosed. Remember, in the copy of verses for St. Cecilia, to alter the name of *Lais*, which is twice there, for *Thais*; those two ladyes were contemporaryes, which caused that small mistake. I wish you cou'd tell me how to send my sonns our Virgil, which you gave me; and should be glad if you cou'd put me in a way of remitting thirty guineas to Rome, which I woud pay heer, for my sonns to have the vallue there, according as the exchange goes. Any time this fortnight will be soon enough to send the money: the book, I know, will require a longer space, because ships go not for Italy every day.

I am
Your humble servant,
JOHN DRYDEN.

I hear Tom Brown is comeing out upon me.*

LETTER XXV.

TO MR. JACOB TONSON.

MR. TONSON, Wednesday. [f. Dec. 1697.]

I HAVE broken off my studies from the "Conquest of China,"† to review Virgil, and bestowed nine entire days upon him. You may have the printed copy you sent me to-morrow morning, if you will come for it yourself; for the printer is a beast, and understands nothing I can say to him of correcting the press. Dr. Chetwood‡ claims my promise of the Ode on St. Cecilia's Day, which I desire you to send to him (according to the Parliament phrase) forthwith. My wife says you have broken your promise about the picture, and desires it speedily; the rest I will tell you when you come.

Yours,
JOHN DRYDEN.

LETTER XXVI.

TO MR. JACOB TONSON

MR. TONSON, [f. Dec. 1697.]

YOU were no sooner gone, but I felt in my pocket, and found my Lady Chudleigh's § verses; which this afternoon I gave Mr. Walsh to read in the coffee-house. His opinion is the same with mine, that they are better than any

*To account for the difference between the exquisite orthography of Lady Elizabeth's present epistle, and that to Dr. Busby, Mr. Malone suggests, that Dryden probably revised the latter before it was sent.

* Tom Brown had, in the year of the Revolution, published "The Reasons of Mr. Bayes changing his Religion;" and in 1690, a second Part, called the "Late Converts Exposed." What this small wit now had in hand is difficult to guess; none of his direct attacks against Dryden appear in his works; but his insignificant enmity survived Dryden, for he wrote a burlesque account of the poet's funeral in verse, and libelled his memory in prose, in his "Letters from the Dead to the Living."

† This labour he never resumed.

‡ The Rev. Dr. Knightly Chetwood, an intimate friend of our author.

§ Mary Leigh, the wife of Sir George Chudleigh of Ashton, in the same county, bart. She died in the year 1710. Her life is among those of Ballard's "Learned Ladies." The verses mentioned in the text are not prefixed to the "Virgil," but printed in Lady Chudleigh's Poems.

which are printed before the book: so thinks also Mr. Wycherly. I have them by me; but do not send them till I heare from my Lord Clifford, whether my lady will put her name to them or not: therefore I desire they may be printed last of all the copyes, and of all the book. I have also written this day to Mr. Chetwood, and let him know, that the book is immediately goeing to the press again. My opinion is, that the printer shou'd begin with the first Pastoral, and print on to the end of the Georgiques; or farther, if occasion be, till Dr. Chetwood corrects his preface,* which he writes me word is printed very false. You cannot take too great care of the printing this edition exactly after my amendments; for a fault of that nature will disoblige me eternally.

I am glad to heare from all hands, that my Ode† is esteemed the best of all my poetry, by all the town: I thought so myself when I writ it; but, being old, I mistrusted my own judgment. I hope it has done you service, and will do more. You told me not, but the town says you are printing Ovid *de Arte Amandi*. I know my translation‡ is very uncorrect; but at the same time I know, nobody else can do it better, with all their paines. If there be any loose papers left in the Virgil I gave you this morning, look for them, and send them back by my man; I miss not any yet; but 'tis possible some may be left, because I gave you the book in a hurry. I vow to God, if Everingham takes not care of this impression, he shall never print any thing of mine heerafter: for I will write on, since I find I can.

I desire you to make sure of the three pounds of snuff, the same of which I had one pound from you. When you send it any morning, I will pay for it all together. But this is not the business of this letter.—When you were heer, I intended to have sent an answer to poor Charles his letter; but I had not then the letter which my chirurgeon promised me, of his advice, to prevent a rupture, which he fears.§ Now I have the surgeon's answer, which I have inclosed in my letter to my sonn. This is a business of the greatest consequence in the world; for you know how I love Charles: and therefore I write you with all the earnestness of a father, that you will procure Mr. Francia* to inclose it in his packet this week: for a week lost may be my sonn's ruine; whom I intend to send for next summer, without his brother, as I have written him word: and if it please God that I must dye of over-study, I cannot spend my life better than in saving his. I vallue not any price for a double letter; let me know it, and it shall be payd; for I dare not trust it by the post; being satisfy'd by experience, that Ferrand will do by this, as he did by two letters which I sent my sonns, about my dedicating to the king;† of which they received neither. If you cannot go yourself, then send a note to Signior Francia, as earnestly as you can write it, to beg that it may go this day, I meane Friday. I need not tell you, how much herein you will oblige

Your friend and servant,

J. D.

* The preface to the "Pastorals."

† The "Ode for St. Cecilia's Day." It is pleasing to be assured, that the best of English lyrics was received with due honour on its first appearance.

‡ Our author only translated the First Book.

§ His son Charles had probably been much hurt by a dangerous fall at Rome; probably that mentioned by Mrs. Thomas, in her exaggerated account of his accident at the Vatican. In a former letter, his mother inquires particularly about his *head*.

* Probably the Genoese resident at that time.

† See page 439.

LETTER XXVII.

TO MRS. STEWARD.‡

MADAM, Saturday, Octob. 1st —98.

You have done me the honour to invite so often, that it would look like want of respect to refuse it any longer. How can you be so good

‡ Of Mrs. Steward Mr. Malone gives the following account:—"This lady, who was not less distinguished for her talents and accomplishments than her beauty and virtues, having been both a painter and a poetess, was the eldest surviving daughter of John Creed of Oundle, Esq. (secretary to Charles II. for the affairs of Tangier,) by Elizabeth Pickering, his wife, who was the only daughter of Sir Gilbert Pickering, Baronet, our author's cousin-german. Her eldest son, Richard Creed, as we have seen, fell in the battle of Blenheim, and was honoured with a monument in Westminster Abbey. Her eldest daughter, Elizabeth, was born in the year 1672, and, in 1692, married Elmes Steward of Cotterstock, in the county of Northampton, Esq.; where they principally resided. By this gentleman, who is said to have preferred field-sports to any productions of the Muses, she had three children; Elizabeth, who became the wife of Thomas Gwillim, Esq. of Old Court, in the parish of Whitchurch, near Ross in Herefordshire; Anne, who died unmarried; and Jemima, who married Elmes Spinckes of Aldwinkle, Esq. Mrs. Steward, who survived her husband above thirty years, in the latter part of her life became blind, in which melancholy state she died in the house of her son-in-law Mr. Gwillim, at the age of seventy-one, Jan. 17, 1742-3; and a monument was erected to her memory in the church of Whitchurch. The hall of Cotterstock-house was painted in fresco by her, in a very masterly style, and she drew several portraits of her friends in Northamptonshire. Her own portrait, painted by herself, is in the possession of her kinswoman, Mrs. Ord of Queen Anne Street."

to an old decrepid man, who can entertain you with no discours which is worthy of your good sense, and who can onely be a trouble to you in all the time he stays at Cotterstock. Yet I will obey your commands as far as possibly I can, and give you the inconvenience you are pleas'd to desire; at least for the few days which I can spare from other necessary business, which requires me at Tichmarsh. Therefore, if you please to send your coach on Tuesday next by eleven o'clock in the morning, I hope to wait on you before dinner. There is onely one more trouble, which I am almost ashamed to name. I am obliged to visit my cousin, Driden of Chesterton, some time next week, who is nine miles from hence, and only five from you. If it be with your convenience to spare me your coach thether for a day, the rest of my time till Monday is at your service; and I am sorry for my own sake it cannot be any longer this year, because I have some visits after my return hether, which I cannot avoyd. But if it please God to give me life and health, I may give you occasion another time to repent of your kindness, by makeing you weary of my company. My sonn kisses your hand. Be pleas'd to give his humble service to my cousin Steward, and mine, who am,

Madam,

Your most obedient oblig'd servant,

John Dryden.

For my Honour'd Cousine,
Mrs. Steward, att Cotterstock,
These.

LETTER XXVIII.

TO ELMES STEWARD, ESQ.

[Probably, Nov. 20, 1698.]

MY HONOUR'D COUSIN,

I shou'd have received your letter with too much satisfaction, if it had not been allay'd with the bad news of my cousin your wife's indisposition; which yet I hope will not continue. I am sure, if care and love will contribute to her health, she will want neither from so tender a husband as you are; and indeed you are both worthy of each other. You have been pleased, each of you, to be kind to my sonn* and me, your poor relations, without any merit on our side, unless you will let our gratitude pass for our desert. And now you are pleas'd to invite another trouble on your self, which our sad company may possibly draw upon you next year, if I have life and health to come into Northamptonshire; and that you will please not to make so much a stranger of me another time.—I intend my wife shall tast the plover you did me the favour to send me. If either your lady or you shall at any time honour me with a letter, my house is in Gerard-street, the fifth door on the left hand, comeing from Newport-street. I pray God I may hear better news of both your healths, and of my good cousin Creed's,* and my cousin Dorothy,† than I have had while I was in this country. I shall languish till you send me word; and I assure you I write this without poetry, who am, from the bottome of my heart,

My honour'd cousin's most obliged

Humble servant,

John Dryden.

My sonn and I kiss my cousin Steward's hand; and give our service to your sister, and pretty Miss Betty.

For my Honour'd Cousin,
Elmes Steward, Esq. Att Cotterstock.

* His eldest son Charles, who returned from Italy to England about the middle of the year 1698.

LETTER XXIX.

TO MRS. STEWARD.

MADAM, Nov. 23d, 1698.

To take acknowledgments of favours for favours done you, is onely yours. I am always on the receiving hand; and you, who have been pleas'd to be troubled so long with my bad company, in stead of forgiveing, which is all I could expect, will turn it to a kindness on my side. If your house be often so molested, you will have reason to be weary of it, before the ending of the year: and wish Cotterstock were planted in a desart, an hundred miles off from any poet.—After I had lost the happiness of your company, I could expect no other than the loss of my health, which followed, according to the proverb, that misfortunes seldome come alone. I had no woman to visite‡ but the parson's wife; and she, who was intended by nature as a help meet for a deaf husband, was somewhat of the loudest for my conversation; and for other things, I will say no more then that she is just your contrary, and

* Mrs. Steward's father, Mr. John Creed.
† Miss, or, in the language of that day, *Mistress* Dorothy Creed, second daughter of John Creed, Esq.
‡ At Tichmarsh, after his return from Cotterstock.

an epitome of her own country. My journey to London was yet more unpleasant than my abode at Tichmarsh; for the coach was crowded up with an old woman fatter than any of my hostesses on the rode. Her weight made the horses travel very heavily; but, to give them a breathing time, she would often stop us, and plead some necessity of nature, and tell us, we were all flesh and blood: but she did this so frequently, that at last we conspired against her; and that she might not be inconvenienced by staying in the coach, turned her out in a very dirty place, where she was to wade up to the ankles, before she cou'd reach the next hedge. When I was ridd of her, I came sick home, and kept my house for three weeks together; but, by advice of my doctour, takeing twice the bitter draught, with sena in it, and looseing at least twelve ounces of blood, by cupping on my neck, I am just well enough to go abroad in the afternoon; but am much afflicted that I have you a companion of my sickness: though I 'scap'd with one cold fit of an aguo, and yours, I feare, is an intermitting feavour. Since I heard nothing of your father, whom I left ill, I hope he is recovered of his real sickness, and that your sister is well of hers, which was onely in imagination. My wife and sonn return you their most humble service, and I give mine to my cousin Steward.—Madam,

Your most obliged and
most obedient servant,
JOHN DRYDEN.

[The Superscription has not been preserved.]

LETTER XXX.

TO MRS. STEWARD.

MADAM, Dec. 12th.—98.

ALL my letters being nothing but acknowledgments of your favours to me, 'tis no wonder if they are all alike: for they can but express the same thing, I being eternally the receiver, and you the giver. I wish it were in my power to turn the skale on the other hand, that I might see how you, who have so excellent a wit, cou'd thank on your side. Not to name my selfe or my wife, my sonn Charles is the great commender of your last receiv'd present; who being of late somewhat indispos'd, uses to send for some of the same sort, which we call heer marrow-puddings, for his suppers; but the tast of yours has so spoyl'd his markets heer, that there is not the least comparison betwixt them. You are not of an age to be a Sybill, and yet I think you are a prophetess; for the direction on your basket was for him; and he is likely to enjoy the greatest part of them: for I always think the young are more worthy than the old; especially since you are one of the former sort, and that he meads upon your medicine.—I am very glad to hear my cousin, your father, is comeing or come to town; perhaps this ayr may be as beneficiall to him as it has been to me: but you tell me nothing of your own health, and I fear Cotterstock is too agueish for this season.—My wife and sonn give you their most humble thanks and service; as I do mine to my cousin Steward; and am, Madam,

Your most oblig'd obedient servant,
JOHN DRYDEN.

For Mrs. Steward,
Att Cotterstock, near Oundle,
in the county of Northampton, These.
To be left with the Postmaster of Oundle.

LETTER XXXI.

TO MRS. STEWARD.

MADAM, Candlemas-Day, 1698 [-9.]

OLD men are not so insensible of beauty as, it may be, you young ladies think. For my own part, I must needs acknowledge, that your fair eyes had made me your slave before I received your fine presents. Your letter puts me out of doubt that they have lost nothing of their lustre, because it was written with your own hand; and not heareing of a feavour or an ague, I will please my self with the thoughts that they have wholly left you. I wou'd also flatter my self with the hopes of waiting on you at Cotterstock some time next summer; but my want of health may perhaps hinder me. But if I am well enough to travell as farr northward as Northamptonshyre, you are sure of a guest, who has been too well us'd not to trouble you again.

My sonn, of whom you have done me the favour to enquire, mends of his indisposition very slowly; the ayr of England not agreeing with him hetherto so well as that of Italy. The Bath is proposed by the doctours, both to him and me: but we have not yet resolved absolutely on that journey; for that city is so close and so ill situated, that perhaps the ayr may do us more harm than the waters can do us good: for which reason we intend to try them heer first; and, if we find not the good effect which is promis'd of them, we will save our selves the pains of goeing thether. In the mean time, betwixt my intervalls of physique, and other remedies which I am useing for my gravel, I am still drudgeing on: always a poet, and never a good one. I pass my time sometimes with Ovid, and sometimes with our old English poet Chaucer; translateing such stories as best please my fancy; and intend, besides them, to add somewhat of my own; so that it is not impossible, but ere the summer be pass'd, I may come down to you with a volume in my hand, like a dog out of the water, with a duck in his mouth. As for the rarities you promise, if beggars might be choosers, a part of a chine of honest bacon wou'd please my appetite more than all the marrow puddings; for I like them better plain, having a very vulgar stomach. My wife, and your cousin, Charles, give you their most humble service, and thanks for your remembrance of them. I present my own to my worthy cousin, your husband, and am with all respect,

Madam,

Your most obliged servant,

JOHN DRYDEN.

For

Mrs. Stewart, att Cotterstock

near Oundle, in Northamptonshire,

These.

To be left with the Postmaster of Oundle.

LETTER XXXII.

TO MRS. STEWAR.

MADAM, Thursday, Feb. 9th. —98 [-9.]

FOR this time I must follow a bad example, and send you a shorter letter than your short one: you were hindered by dancers, and I am forced to dance attendance all this afternoon after a troublesome business, so soon as I have written this and seal'd it. Onely I can assure you, that your father and mother, and all your relations, are in health, or were yesterday, when I sent to enquire of their welfare. On Tuesday night we had a violent wind, which blew down three of my chimneys, and dismantled all one side of my house, by throwing down the tiles. My neighbours, and indeed all the town, suffered more or less; and some were kill'd. The great trees in St. James's Park are many of them torn up from the roots; as they were before Oliver Cromwell's death,* and the late queen's: but your father had no damage. I sent my man for the present you designed me; but he return'd empty-handed; for there was no such man as *Carter*, a carrier, inning at the Bear and Ragged Staff in Smith field, nor any one there ever heard of such a person; by which I ghess that some body has deceiv'd you with a counterfeited name. Yet my obligations are the same; and the favour shall be always own'd by,

Madam,

Your most humble servant,

and kinsman,

JOHN DRYDEN.

For Mrs. Stewart,

Att Cotterstocke neare Oundle, &c.

* Our author commemorated this circumstance in his "Elegy on the Protector:"—

——The isle, when her protecting genius went,
Upon his obsequies loud sighs conferr'd.

LETTER XXXIII.

TO MRS. STEWARD.

MADAM, March the 4th, 1698 [-9.]

I HAVE reason to be pleas'd with writeing to you, because you are daily giveing me occasions to be pleas'd. The present which you made me this week, I have receiv'd; and it will be part of the treat I am to make to three of my friends about Tuesday next: my cousin Driden, of Chesterton, having been also pleas'd to add to it a turkey hen with eggs, and a good young goose; besides a very kind letter, and the news of his own good health, which I value more than all the rest; he being so noble a benefactor to a poor and so undeserving a kinsman, and one of another persuasion in matters of religion. Your enquiry of his welfare, and sending also mine, have at once oblig'd both him and me. I hope my good cousin Stewart will often visite him, especially before hunting goes out,* to be a comfort to him in his sorrow for the loss of his deare brother,† who was a most extraordinary well-natured man, and much my friend. Exercise, I know, is my cousin Dryden's life, and the oftner he goes out will be the better for his health. We poor Catholics daily expect a most severe proclamation to come out against us;‡ and at the same time are

* Driden, of Chesterton, who, as appears from our author's Epistle addressed to him, was a keen sportsman.

† Probably Bevil Driden.

‡ This severe proclamation appeared in the London Gazette, No. 3476, Monday, March 6, 1698-9. It enjoined all Popish recusants to remove to their respective places of abode; or if they had none, to the dwellings of their fathers or mothers; and not to remove five miles from thence: and it charged the lord mayor of London, and all other justices of

satisfyed that the King is very unwilling to persecute us, considering us to be but an handfull, and those disarmed; but the archbishop of Canterbury is our heavy enemy, and heavy indeed he is in all respects.*

This day was played a revived comedy of Mr. Congreve's, called, "The Double Dealer," which was never very takeing. In the play-bill was printed—"Written by Mr. Congreve; with severall expressions omitted." What kind of expressions those were, you may easily ghess, if you have seen the Monday's Gazette, wherein is the king's order for the reformation of the stage:† but the printing an author's name in a play-bill is a new manner of proceeding, at least in England. When any papers of verses in manuscript, which are worth your reading, come abroad, you shall be sure of them; because being a poetess yourself, you like those entertaiaments. I am still drudging at a book of Miscellanyes,* which I hope will be well enough; if otherwise, threescore and seven will be pardon'd. Charles is not yet so well recover'd as I wish him; but I may say, without vanity, that his virtue and sobriety have made him much belov'd in all companies. Both he and his mother give you their most humble acknowledgments of your remembring them. Be pleas'd to give mine to my cousin Stewart, who am both his and your

Most obliged obedient servant,

JOHN DRYDEN.

You may see I was in hast, by writeing on the wrong side of the paper.

For Mrs. Steward, etc. ut supra.

peace, to put the statute 1st William and Mary, c. 9. for amoving Papists ten miles from London and Westminster, into execution, by tendering them the declaration therein mentioned; and also another act of William and Mary, for disarming Papists.

* Dr. Thomas Tennison, who succeeded to the see of Canterbury in 1694, on the death of Tillotson. He is thus sarcastically described by William Shippen, in "Faction Displayed," a poem written a few years afterwards:

"A pause ensued, till Patriarcho's grace
Was pleased to rear his huge unwieldy mass;
A mass unanimated with a soul,
Or else he'd ne'er be made so vile a tool;
He'd ne'er his apostolic charge profane,
And atheists' and fanaticks' cause maintain.
At length, as from the hollow of an oak,
The bulky primate yawn'd, and silence broke:
I much approve," &c.

So also Edmund Smith, in his elegant ode, *Charlettus Percivallo suo:*

"*Scribe securus, quid agit Senatus,*
Quid caput stertit grave Lembethanum,
Quid comes Guilford, quid habent novorum
Dawksque Dyerque."—*Malone.*

† The London Gazette, No. 3474, Monday, Feb. 27 1698 9, contains the order alluded to:

"His majesty has been pleased to command, that the following order should be sent to both Play-houses:

"His majesty being informed, that, notwithstanding an order made the fifth of June, 1697, by the Earl of Sunderland, then lord chamberlain of his majesty's household, to prevent the profaneness and immorality of the stage, several plays have lately been acted, containing expressions contrary to religion and good manners: And whereas the master of the revels has represented, that, in contempt of the said order, the actors do often neglect to leave out such profane and indecent expressions as he has thought proper to be omitted: These are therefore to signify his majesty's pleasure, that you do not hereafter presume to act any thing in any play, contrary to religion and good manners, as you shall answer it at your utmost peril. Given under my hand this 18th of February, 1698, in the eleventh year of his majesty's reign. "*Pere Bertie.*

"An order has been likewise sent, by his majesty's command, to the master of the revels, not to license any plays containing expressions contrary to religion and good manners; and to give notice to the lord chamberlain of his majesty's household, or, in his absence, to the vice-chamberlain, if the players presume to act any thing which he has struck out."

LETTER XXXIV

TO MRS. STEWARD.

MADAM, Tuesday, July the 11th, [1699.]

As I cannot accuse my self to have receiv'd any letters from you without answer, so, on the other side, I am oblig'd to believe it, because you say it. 'Tis true, I have had so many fitts of sickness, and so much other unpleasant business, that I may possibly have receiv'd those favours, and deferr'd my acknowledgment till I forgot to thank you for them. However it be, I cannot but confess, that never was any unanswering man so civilly reproach'd by a fair lady. I presum'd to send you word by your sisters† of the trouble I intended you this summer; and added a petition, that you would order some small beer to be brew'd for me without hops, or with a very inconsiderable quantity; because I lost my health last year by drinking bitter beer at Tichmarsh. It may perhaps be sour, but I like it not the worse, if it be small enough. What els I have to request, is onely the favour of your coach, to meet me at Oundle, and to convey me to you: of which I shall not fail to give you timely notice. My humble service attends my cousin Stewart and your relations at Oundle. My wife and sonn desire the same favour; and I am particularly, Madam,

Your most obedient servant,

JOHN DRYDEN.

For Mrs. Stewart, etc.

* The beautiful fables.

† Dorothy and Jemima Creed; the latter of whom died Feb. 28, 1765-6, and was buried at Tichmarsh.

LETTER XXXV.

TO SAMUEL PEPYS, ESQ.*

ADRON MIO, July the 14th, 1699.

I REMEMBER, last year, when I had the honour of dineing with you, you were pleased to recommend to me the character of Chaucer's "Good Parson." Any desire of yours is a command to me; and accordingly I have put it into my English, with such additions and alterations as I thought fit. Having translated as many Fables from Ovid, and as many Novills from Boccace and Tales from Chaucer, as will make an indifferent large volume in folio, I intend them for the press in Michaelmas term next. In the mean time, my parson desires the favour of being known to you, and promises, if you find any fault in his character, he will reform it. Whenever you please, he will wait on you, and for the safer conveyance, I will carry him in my pocket; who am

My *Padrons* most obedient servant,
JOHN DRYDEN.

For Samuel Pepys, Esq.
Att his house in York-street, These.

LETTER XXXVI.

Answer to the foregoing, by Mr. Pepys.

SIR, Friday, July 14, 1699.

YOU truly have obliged mee; and possibly, in saying so, I am more in earnest then you can readily think; as verily hopeing, from this your copy of one "Good Parson," to fancy some amends made mee for the hourly offence I beare with from the sight of so many lewd originalls.

I shall with great pleasure attend you on this occasion, when ere you'l permit it; unless you would have the kindness to double it to mee, by suffering my coach to wayte on you (and who you can gayne mee ye same favour from) hither, to a cold chicken and a sallade, any noone after Sunday, as being just stepping into the ayre for 2 days.

I am, most respectfully,
Your honord and obednt servant,
S. P.

LETTER XXXVII.

TO MRS. STEWARD.

MADAM, Saturday, Aug. 5th, 1699.

THIS is only a word, to threaten you with a troublesome guest, next week: I have taken places for my self and my sonn in the Oundle coach, which setts out on Thursday next the tenth of this present August; and hope to wait on a fair lady at Cotterstock on Friday the eleventh. If you please to let your coach come to Oundle, I shall save my cousin Creed the trouble of hers. All heer are your most humble servants, and particularly an old cripple, who calls him self

Your most obliged kinsman,
And admirer,
JOHN DRYDEN.

For Mrs. Stewart, Att
Cotterstock, near Oundle,
in Northamptonshire. These.
To be left with the Postmaster of Oundle.

LETTER XXXVIII.

TO MRS. STEWARD.

MADAM, Sept. 28th, 1699.

YOUR goodness to me will make you sollicitous of my welfare since I left Cotterstock. My journey has in general been as happy as it cou'd be, without the satisfaction and honour of your company. 'Tis true, the master of the stage-coach has not been over civill to me; for he turned us out of the road at the first step, and made us go to Pilton; there we took in a fair young lady of eighteen, and her brother, a young gentleman; they are related to the Treshams, but not of that name: thence we drove to Higham, where we had an old serving-woman, and a young fine mayd: we dined at Bletso, and lay at Silso, six miles beyond Bedford. There we put out the old woman, and took in Councellour Jennings his daughter; her father goeing along

* The founder of the Pepysian library, Magdalen College, Cambridge. He was secretary to the Admiralty in the reign of Charles II. and James II. "He first (says Granger, *Biogr. Hist.* iv. 322.) reduced the affairs of the Admiralty to order and method; and that method was so just, as to have been a standing model to his successors in that important office. His 'Memoirs' relating to the Navy is a well-written piece; and his copious collection of manuscripts, now remaining with the rest of his library at Magdalen College in Cambridge, is an invaluable treasure of naval knowledge. He was far from being a mere man of business: his conversation and address had been greatly refined by travel. He thoroughly understood and practised music; was a judge of painting, sculpture, and architecture; and had more than a superficial knowledge in history and philosophy. His fame among the virtuosi was such, that he was thought to be a very proper person to be placed at the head of the Royal Society, of which he was some time [1685, 1686,] president. His prints have been already mentioned. His collection of English Ballads, in five large folio volumes, begun by Mr. Selden, and carried down to 1700, is one of his singular curiosities. —*Ob.* 26 May 1703.'

in the Kittering coach, or rideing by it, with other company. We all dined at Hatfield together, and came to town safe at seaven in the evening. We had a young doctour, who rode by our coach, and seemed to have a smickering* to our young lady of Pilton, and ever rode before to get dinner in a readiness. My sonn, Charles, knew him formerly a Jacobite; and now going over to Antigoo, with Colonel Codrington,† haveing been formerly in the West Indies.—Which of our two young ladies was the handsomer, I know not. My son liked the Councellour's daughter best: I thought they were both equall. But not goeing to Tichmarsh Grove, and afterwards by Catworth, I missed my two couple of rabbets, which my cousin, your father, had given me to carry with me, and cou'd not see my sister by the way; I was likewise disappointed of Mr. Cole's Ribadavia wine: but I am almost resolved to sue the stage-coach, for putting me six or seaven miles out of the way, which he cannot justify.

Be pleased to accept my acknowledgment of all your favours, and my Cousin Stuart's; and by employing my sonn and me in any thing you desire to have done, give us occasion to take our revenge on our kind relations both at Oundle and Cotterstock. Be pleas'd, your father, your mother, your two fair sisters, and your brother,‡ may find my sonn's service and mine made acceptable to them by your delivery; and believe me to be with all manner of gratitude, give me leave to add, all manner of adoration, Madam,

Your most obliged obedient servant,

John Dryden.

For Mrs. Stewart, Att
Cotterstock near Oundle,
In Northamptonshire, These.
To be left with the Postmaster of Oundle.

LETTER XXXIX.

TO THE RIGHT HON. CHARLES MONTAGUE.§

SIR, [Octob. 1699.]

These verses had waited on you with the former, but that, they wanted that correction which I have given them,* that they may the better endure the sight of so great a judge and poet. I am now in feare that I purged them out of their spirit; as our Master Bushby us'd to whip a boy so long, till he made him a confirm'd blockhead. My cousin Driden saw them in the country; and the greatest exception he made to them was a satire against the Dutch valour in the last war. He desir'd me to omit it, (to use his own words,) "out of the respect he had to his Sovereign." I obeyed his commands, and left onely the praises, which I think are due to the gallantry of my own countrymen. In the description which I have made of a parliament-man,† I think that I have not only drawn the features of my worthy kinsman, but have also given my own opinion of what an Englishman in Parliament ought to be; and deliver it as a memorial of my own principles to all posterity. I have consulted the judgment of my unbyass'd friends, who have some of them the honour to be known to you: and they think there is nothing which can justly give offence in that part of the poem. I say not this to cast a blind on your judgment, (which I could not do, if I endeavoured it,) but to assure you, that nothing relateing to the publique shall stand without your permission; for it were to want common sense to desire your patronage, and resolve to disoblige you. And as I will not hazard my hopes of your protection, by refusing to obey you in any thing which I can perform with my conscience or my honour, so I am

* To *smicker*, though omitted by Dr. Johnson, is found, says Mr. Malone, in Kersey's Dictionary, 1708; where it is interpreted—"To look amorously, or wantonly."

† Christopher Codrington, Governor of the Caribbee Islands.

‡ Colonel John Creed, a gallant soldier. He died at Oundle, Nov. 21, 1751, aged 78, and was buried in the church of Tichmarsh.

§ The superscription of this letter is wanting; but that it was addressed to Mr. Montague, is ascertained by the words—"From Mr. Dryden," being indorsed on it, in that gentleman's handwriting. Charles Montague, (afterwards Earl of Hallifax,) was at this time First Lord of the Treasury, and Chancellor of the Exchequer; the latter of which offices he had held from the year 1694.—The date is supplied by the subsequent letter.—*Malone.*

* The verses addressed to his kinsman, John Driden, of Chesterton, Esq.—The former poem which had been submitted to Mr. Montague, was that addressed to Mary, Duchess of Ormond. They were both inserted in the volume of Fables which was then printing. See the next letter.—*Malone.*

† The lines alluded to occur in the Epistle to Driden of Chesterton. They are very cautiously worded; yet obviously imply that opposition to government was one quality of a good patriot. Dryden, sensible of the suspicion arising from his politics and religion, seems, in this letter, to deprecate Montague's displeasure, and to prepossess him in favour of the poem, as inoffensive toward the government. I am afraid that indemnity was all he had to hope for from the protection of this famed Mæcenas; at least, he returns no thanks for benefits hitherto received; and of these he was no niggard where there was room for them. Pope's bitter verses on Halifax are well known:

"Dryden alone what wonder came not nigh,
Dryden alone escaped his judging eye;
Yet still the great have kindness in reserve,—
He help'd to bury, whom he help'd to starve."

very confident you will never impose any other terms on me. My thoughts at present are fix'd on Homer; and by my translation of the first Iliad, I find him a poet more according to my genius than Virgil, and consequently hope I may do him more justice in his fiery way of writeing; which, as it is liable to more faults, so it is capable of more beauties, than the exactness and sobriety of Virgil. Since 'tis for my country's honour, as well as for my own, that I am willing to undertake this task, I despair not of being encourag'd in it by your favour, who am,

Sir,
Your most obedient servant,
JOHN DRYDEN.

LETTER XL.

TO MRS. STEWARD.

MADAM, Nov. 7th, [1699.]

EVEN your expostulations are pleasing to me; for though they shew you angry, yet they are not without many expressions of your kindness; and therefore I am proud to be so chidden. Yet I cannot so farr abandon my own defence, as to confess any idleness or forgetfulness on my part. What has hind'red me from writeing to you, was neither ill health, nor, a worse thing, ingratitude; but a flood of little businesses, which yet are necessary to my subsistance, and of which I hop'd to have given you a good account before this time: but the court rather speaks kindly of me, than does any thing for me, though they promise largely; and perhaps they think I will advance as they go backward, in which they will be much deceived; for I can never go an inch beyond my conscience and my honour.* If they will consider me as a man who has done my best to improve the language, and especially the poetry, and will be content with my acquiescence under the present government, and forbearing satire on it, that I can promise, because I can perform it; but I can neither take the oaths, nor forsake my religion; because I know not what church to go to, if I leave the Catholique; they are all so divided amongst them selves in matters of faith necessary to salvation, and yet all assumeing the name of Protestants. May God be pleas'd to open your eyes, as he has open'd mine! Truth is but one; and they who have once heard of it, can plead no excuse, if they do not embrace it. But these are things too serious for a trifling letter.

If you desire to hear any thing more of my affairs, the Earl of Dorsett, and your cousin Montague, have both seen the two poems, to the Duchess of Ormond, and my worthy cousin Driden; and are of opinion, that I never writt better. My other friends are divided in their judgments, which to preferr; but the greater part are for those to my dear kinsman; which I have corrected with so much care, that they will now be worthy of his sight, and do neither of us any dishonour after our death.

There is this day to be acted a new tragedy, made by Mr. Hopkins,† and, as I believe, in rhime. He has formerly written a play in verse, call'd "Boadicea," which you fair ladyes lik'd; and is a poet who writes good verses without knowing how or why; I mean, he writes naturally well, without art, or learning, or good sence. Congreve is ill of the gout at Barnet Wells. I have had the honour of a visite from the Earl of Dorsett, and din'd with him.—Matters in Scotland are in a high ferment,† and next door to a breach betwixt the two nations; but they say from court, that France and we are hand and glove. 'Tis thought, the king will endeavour to keep up a standing army, and make the stirr in Scotland his pretence for it; my cousin Driden,‡ and the country party, I suppose, will be against it; for when a spirit is raised, 'tis hard conjuring him down again.—You see I am dull by my writeing news; but it may be my cousin Creed§ may be glad to

* Dryden probably alludes to some expectations through the interest of Halifax. They were never realized; whether from inattention, or on account of his politics and religion, cannot now be known.

* Charles Hopkins, son of Hopkins, Bishop of Derry, in Ireland. He was educated at Cambridge, and became Bachelor of Arts in 1688; he afterwards bore arms for King William in the Irish wars. In 1694, he published a collection of epistolary poems and translations; and in 1695, "The History of Love," which last gained him some reputation. Dorset honoured Hopkins with his notice; and Dryden himself is said to have distinguished him from the undergrowth of authors. He was careless both of his health and reputation, and fell a martyr to excess in 1700, aged only thirty-six years. Hopkins wrote three plays, 1. "Pyrrhus, King of Epirus," 1695; 2. 'Boadicea, Queen of Britain," 1697; 3. "Friendship Improved." This last is mentioned in the text as to be acted on 7th November.

† The fate of the Scottish colony at Darien, accelerated by the inhuman proclamations of William, who prohibited his American subjects to afford them assistance, was now nearly decided, and the nation was almost frantic between rage and disappointment. "The most inflammatory publications had been dispersed among the nation, the most violent addresses were presented from the towns and counties, and whosoever ventured to dispute or doubt the utility of Darien, was reputed a public enemy, devoted to a hostile and corrupt court."—*Laing's History*, Book x.

‡ Mr. John Driden of Chesterton, member for the county of Huntingdon.

§ Mrs. Steward's father, Mr. John Creed, of Oundle.

hear what I believe is true, though not very pleasing. I hope he recovers health in the country, by his staying so long in it. My service to my cousin Stuart, and all at Oundle. I am, faire Cousine,

Your most obedient servant,

JOHN DRYDEN.

For Mrs. Stuart, Att
Cotterstock, near Oundle,
In Northamptonshyre,
These.
To be left at the Posthouse
in Oundle.

LETTER XLI.

TO MRS. ELIZABETH THOMAS, JUN.*

MADAM, Nov. 12, 1699.

THE letter you were pleas'd to direct for me, to be left at the coffee-house last summer, was a great honour; and your verses† were, I thought, too good to be a woman's; some of my friends, to whom I read them, were of the same opinion. 'Tis not over-gallant, I must confess, to say this of the fair sex; but most certain it is, that they generally write with more softness than strength. On the contrary, you want neither vigour in your thoughts, nor force in your expressions, nor harmony in your numbers; and methinks I find much of Orinda‡ in your manner; to whom I had the honour to be related, and also to be known. But I continued not a day in the ignorance of the person to whom I was oblig'd; for, if you remember, you brought the verses to a bookseller's shop, and enquir'd there, how they might be sent to me. There happen'd to be in the same shop a gentleman, who hearing you speak of me, and seeing a paper in your hand, imagin'd it was a libel against me, and had you watch'd by his servant, till he knew both your name, and where you liv'd, of which he sent me word immediately. Though I have lost his letter, yet I remember you live some where about St. Giles's,* and are an only daughter. You must have pass'd your time in reading much better books than mine; or otherwise you cou'd not have arriv'd to so much knowledge as I find you have. But whether Sylph or Nymph, I know not: those fine creatures, as your author, Count Gabalis, assures us,† have a mind to be christen'd, and since you do me the favour to desire a name from me, take that of Corinna, if you please; I mean not the lady with whom Ovid was in Love, but the famous Theban poetess, who overcame Pindar five times, as historians tell us. I would have call'd you Sapho, but that I hear you are handsomer. Since you find I am not altogether a stranger to you, be pleas'd to make me happier by a better knowledge of you; and in stead of so many unjust praises which you give me, think me only worthy of being,

Madam,

Your most humble servant,

and admirer,

JOHN DRYDEN.

* Mrs. Thomas, "Curll's Corinna," well known as a hack authoress some years after this period, was now commencing her career. She was daughter of Emanuel Thomas, of the Inner Temple, barrister. Her person, as well as her writings, seems to have been dedicated to the service of the public. The story of her having obtained a parrel of Pope's letters, written in youth, from Henry Cromwell, to whom they were addressed, and selling them to Curll the bookseller, is well known. In that celebrated collection, 2d vol. 8vo. 1736, the following letters from Dryden also appear. It would seem Corinna had contrived to hook an acquaintance upon the good-natured poet, by the old pretext of sending him two poems for his opinion. She afterwards kept up some communication with his family, which she made the ground of two marvellous stories, one concerning the astrological predictions of the poet, the other respecting the mode of his funeral.

† "A Pastoral Elegy to the Memory of the Hon. Cecilia Bew," published afterwards in the Poems of Mrs. Thomas, 8vo. 1727.

‡ Mrs. Catharine Philips, a poetess of the last age.

* She lived with her mother, Mrs. Elizabeth Thomas, (as we learn from Curll,) in Dyot street, St. Giles; but in the first edition of the letter, for the greater honour, she represents it as addressed to herself at Great Russel-street, Bloomsbury.

† In this lively romance, written to ridicule the doctrines of the Rosicrucian philosophy, we are informed, that the Nymphs of water, air, earth, and fire, are anxious to connect themselves with the sages of the human race. I remember nothing about their wish to be baptized; but that desire was extremely strong among the fays, or female genii, of the North, who were anxious to demand it for the children they had by human fathers, as the means of securing to them that immortality which they themselves wanted. Einar Godmund, an ancient priest, informed the learned Torfæus, that they often solicited this favour, (usually in vain,) and were exceedingly incensed at the refusal. He gave an instance of Siward Fostre, who had promised to one of these fays, that if she bore him a child, he would cause it to be christened. In due time she appeared, and laid the child on the wall of the church-yard, with a chalice of gold and a rich cope, as an offering at the ceremony. But Siward, ashamed of this extraordinary intrigue, refused to acknowledge the child, which, therefore, remained unbaptized. The incensed mother reappeared and carried off the infant and the chalice, leaving behind the cope, fragments of which are still preserved. But she failed not to inflict upon Siward and his descendants, to the ninth generation, a peculiar disorder, with which they were long afflicted. Other stories to the same purpose are told by Torfæus in his preface to the "History of Hrolf Kraka," 12mo. 1715. I suppose, however, that Dryden only recollected the practice of magicians, who, on invoking

LETTER XLII.

TO MRS. ELIZABETH THOMAS, JUN.*

MADAM, [Nov. 1699.]

THE great desire which I observe in you to write well, and those good parts which God Almighty and nature have bestow'd on you, make me not to doubt, that, by application to study, and the reading of the best authors, you may be absolute mistress of poetry. 'Tis an unprofitable art to those who profess it; but you, who write only for your diversion, may pass your hours with pleasure in it, and without prejudice; always avoiding (as I know you will,) the licence which Mrs. Behn† allowed her self, of writeing loosely, and giveing, if I may have leave to say so, some scandall to the modesty of her sex. I confess, I am the last man who ought, in justice, to arraign her, who have been my self too much a libertine in most of my poems; which I shou'd be well contented I had time either to purge, or to see them fairly burn'd. But this I need not say to you, who are too well born, and too well principled, to fall into that mire.

In the mean time, I would advise you not to trust too much to Virgil's Pastorals; for as excellent as they are, yet Theocritus is far before him, both in softness of thought, and simplicity of expression. Mr. Creech has translated that Greek poet, which I have not read in English. If you have any considerable faults, they consist chiefly in the choice of words, and the placeing them so as to make the verse run smoothly; but I am at present so taken up with my own studies, that I have not leisure to descend to particulars; being, in the mean time, the fair Corinna's

Most humble and most
faithful Servant,
JOHN DRYDEN.

P. S. I keep your two copies* till you want them, and are pleas'd to send for them.

LETTER XLIII.

TO MRS. STEWARD.

Saturday, Nov. 8th, [1699.]

AFTER a long expectation, Madam, at length your happy letter came to your servant, who almost despair'd of it. The onely comfort I had, was, my hopes of seeing you, and that you defer'd writeing, because you wou'd surprise me with your presence, and beare your relations company to town. Your neighbour, Mr. Price, has given me an apprehension, that my cousin, your father, is in danger of being made sheriff the following yeare; but I hope 'tis a jealousy without ground, and that the warm season only keeps him in the country.—If you come up next week, you will be entertain'd with a new tragedy, which the author of it, one Mr. Dennis, cries up at an excessive rate; and Colonel Codrington, who has seen it, prepares the world to give it loud applauses. 'Tis called "Iphigenia," and imitated from Euripides, an old Greek poet.† This is to be acted at Betterton's house; and another play of the same name is very shortly to come on the stage at Drury-Lane.—I was lately to visite the Duchess of Norfolk;‡ and she speaks of you with much affection and respect. Your cousin Montague,§ after the present session of parliament, will be created Earl of Bristoll,‖ and I hope is much my friend; but I doubt I am in no condition of having a kindness done, having the Chancellour¶ my enemy; and not being capable of renounceing the cause for which I have so long suffer'd.—My cousin Driden of Chesterton is

astral spirits, and binding them to their service, usually imposed on them some distinguishing name. It is possible Paracelsus says something to the purpose in his Magna Philosophia.

* In printing this letter, Mr. Malone says, he "followed a transcript which he made some years ago from the original. It is preserved in a small volume in the Bodleian Library, consisting chiefly of Pope's original Letters to Henry Cromwell, which Mrs. Thomas sold to Curll, the bookseller, who published them unfaithfully. It afterwards fell into the hands of Dr. Richard Rawlinson, by whom it was bequeathed to that Library."

† Afra Behn, whose plays, poems, and novels are very indecent; yet an aged lady, a relation of the editor, assured him, that, in the polite society of her youth, in which she held a distinguished place, these books were accounted proper reading; and added, with some humour, it was not till after a long interval, when she looked into them, at the age of seventy, that she was shocked at their indecorum.

* The Pastoral Elegy on Mrs. Bew, and the Triple League.

† Colonel Codrington wrote an epilogue to Dennis's "Iphigenia." Dryden here talks rather slightingly of his acquaintance; but "Iphigenia" is a most miserable piece.

‡ Mary, the daughter of Henry Mordaunt, the second Earl of Peterborough, and wife of Thomas, the seventh Duke of Norfolk, afterwards divorced for criminal conversation with Sir John Germaine. See the proceedings in the *State Trials*.

§ The Right Hon. Charles Montague.

‖ He was about a year after created Lord Halifax.

¶ Lord Somers.—Mr. Malone is of opinion, that this passage adds some support to what has been suggested in our author's Life, that a part of Dryden's "Satire to his Muse" was written in his younger days by this great man. Yet I cannot think, that great man would be concerned in so libellous a piece: and in the same breath Dryden tells us, that he hoped Montague, who had really written against him, was much his friend.

in town, and lodges with my brother in Westminster.* My sonn has seen him, and was very kindly received by him. Let this letter stand for nothing, because it has nothing but news in it, and has so little of the main business, which is to assure my fair cousine how much I am her admirer, and her

Most devoted Servant,

JOHN DRYDEN.

I write no recommendation of service to our friends at Oundle, because I suppose they are leaveing that place; but I wish my Cousin Stuart a boy, as like Miss Jem:† as he and you can make him. My wife and sonn are never forgetfull of their acknowledgments to you both.

For Mrs. Stuart, Att
Cotterstock near Oundle,
in the County of Northampton, These.
To be left at the Posthouse
in Oundle.

LETTER XLIV.

TO MRS. STEWARD.

MADAM, Thursday, Dec. the 14th, 1699.

WHEN I have either too much business or want of health, to write to you, I count my time is lost, or at least my conscience accuses me that I spend it ill. At this time my head is full of cares, and my body ill at ease. My book is printing,‡ and my bookseller makes no hast. I had last night at bed-time an unwelcome fit of vomiting; and my sonn, Charles, lyes sick upon his bed with the colique, which has been violent upon him for almost a week. With all this, I cannot but remember that you accus'd me of barbarity, I hope in jeast onely, for mistaking one sheriff for another, which proceeded from my want of heareing well. I am heartily sorry that a chargeable office is fallen on my cousin Stuart.§ But my cousin Dryden comforts me, that it must have come one time or other, like the small-pox; and better have it young than old. I hope it will leave no great marks behind it, and that your fortune will no more feel it than your beauty, by the addition of a year's wearing. My cousine, your mother, was heer yesterday, to see my wife, though I had not the happiness to be at home.—Both the "Iphigenias" have been played with bad success;* and being both acted one against the other in the same week, clash'd together, like two rotten ships which could not endure the shock, and sunk to rights. The King's proclamation against vice and profaneness is issued out in print;† but a deep disease is not to be cur'd with a slight medicine. The parsons, who must read it, will find as little effect from it, as from their dull sermons: 'tis a scare-crow, which will not fright many birds from preying on the fields and orchards. The best news I heare is, that the land will not be charg'd very deep this yeare: let that comfort you for your shrievalty, and continue me in your good graces, who am, fair cousin,

Your most faithfull oblig'd servant,

JO. DRYDEN.

For Mrs. Stuart,
Att Cotterstock, near Oundle,
in Northamptonshyre,
These.
To be left with the Postmaster
of Oundle.

LETTER XLV.

TO MRS. ELIZABETH THOMAS, JUN.

MADAM, Friday, Dec. 29, 1699.

I HAVE sent your poems back again, after having kept them so long from you; by which you see I am like the rest of the world, an impudent borrower, and a bad pay-master. You take more care of my health than it deserves; that of an old man is always crazy, and, at present mine is worse than usual, by a St. Anthony's fire in one of my legs; though the swelling is much abated, yet the pain is not wholly gone, and I am too weak to stand upon it. If I re-

* Erasmus Dryden, who lived in King's-street, Westminster, and was a grocer. In Dec. 1710, he succeeded to the title of Baronet.

† Jemima, Mrs. Steward's youngest daughter, probably then four or five years old.

‡ "Fables Ancient and Modern."

§ Elmes Steward, Esq., was appointed sheriff of the county of Northampton in Nov. 1699.

* Dennis's "Iphigenia" was performed at the theatre in Little Lincoln's Fields; and "Achilles, or Iphigenia in Aulis," written by Abel Boyer, and, if we are to believe the author, corrected by Dryden, was acted at the theatre in Drury-Lane. Dennis says in his Preface, that the success of his play was "neither despicable, nor extraordinary;" but Gildon, in his "Comparison between the two Stages," 8vo. 1702, informs us, that it was acted but six times; and that the other tragedy, after four representations, was laid aside.—*Malone.*

† In the London Gazette, No. 3557, Thursday, December 14, 1699, it is mentioned, that a proclamation for preventing and *punishing* immorality and profaneness, had been issued out on the 11th instant. We know, by the experience of our own time, the justice of Dryden's observation.

cover, it is possible I may attempt Homer's Iliad. A specimen of it (the first book) is now in the press, among other poems of mine, which will make a volume in folio, of twelve shillings' price; and will be published within this month. I desire, fair author, that you will be pleas'd to continue me in your good graces, who am, with all sincerity and gratitude,

Your most humble servant,
and admirer,
JOHN DRYDEN.

LETTER XLVI.

TO MRS. STEWARD.

MADAM, Feb. 23d. 1699 [1700.]

THOUGH I have not leisure to thank you for the last trouble I gave you, yet haveing by me two lampoons lately made, I know not but they may be worth your reading; and therefore have presum'd to send them. I know not the authours; but the town will be ghessing. The "Ballad of the Pews," which are lately rais'd higher at St. James's church,* is by some sayd to be Mr. Manwareing, or my Lord Peterborough. The poem of the "Confederates" some think to be Mr. Walsh; the copies are both lik'd.† And there are really two factions of ladyes, for the two playhouses. If you do not understand the names of some persons mention'd, I can help you to the knowledge of them. You know Sir Tho. Skipwith is master of the

* Not at St. James's Church, but at the Chapel Royal. The pews, it seems, were raised to prevent the devotions of the maids of honour from any distractions in time of service. But the ballad maliciously supposes, that the intention was to confine the sun-beams of their eyes to the preacher, Bishop Burnet.

† This poem is a banter upon the interest which the nobility took in the disputes between the Drury-Lane theatre, where Skipwith was manager, and that in Lincoln's Inn Fields, of which Betterton was sovereign. The "Island Princess" of Fletcher had been converted into a sort of opera, by Peter Motteux, and acted at Drury-Lane in 1699. The peculiar taste of Rich for every thing that respected show and machinery is well known.

The Confederates, or the First Happy Day of the Island Princess.

Ye vile traducers of the female kind,
Who think the fair to cruelty inclin'd,
Recant your error, and with shame confess
Their tender care of Skipwith in distress:
For now to vindicate this monarch's right,
The Scotch and English equal charms unite;
In solemn leagues contending nations join,
And Britain labours with the vast design.
An opera with loud applause is play'd,
Which famed Motteux in soft heroics made;
And all the sworn Confederates resort,
To view the triumph of their sovereign's court.

In bright array the well-train'd host appears;
Supreme command brave Derwentwater bears;*
And next in front George Howard's† bride does
shine,
The living honour of that ancient line.
The wings are led by chiefs of matchless worth;
Great Hamilton,‡ the glory of the North,
Commands the left; and England's dear delight,
The bold Fitzwalter§ charges on the right.
The Prince, to welcome his propitious friends,
A throne erected on the stage ascends.
He said:—Blest angels! for great ends design'd,
The best, and sure the fairest, of your kind,
How shall I praise, or in what numbers sing
Your just compassion of an injured king?
Till you appeared, no prospect did remain,
My crown and falling sceptre to maintain;
No noisy beaus in all my realm were found;
No beauteous nymphs my empty boxes crown'd;
But still I saw, O dire heart-breaking wo!
My own sad consort‖ in the foremost row.
But this auspicious day new empire gives;
And if by your support my nation lives,
For you my bards shall tune the sweetest lays,
Norton¶ and Henley** shall resound your praise;
And I, not last of the harmonious train,
Will give a loose to my poetic vein.—
To him great Derwentwater thus replied:
Thou mighty prince, in many dangers tried
Born to dispute severe decrees of fate,
The nursing-father of a sickly state;
Behold the pillars of thy lawful reign!
Thy legal rights we promise to maintain;
Our brightest nymphs shall thy dominions grace,
With all the beauties of the Highland race;
The beaus shall make thee their peculiar care,
For beaus will always wait upon the fair:
For thee kind Beereton and bold Webbe shall
fight;††
Lord Scott‡‡ shall ogle, and my spouse shall
write.§§
Thus shall thy court our English youth engross,
And all the Scotch, from Drummond down to Ross.

* Sir Thomas Skipwith, joint patentee and manager with Charles Rich of the Drury-Lane theatre.

* Mary Tudor, natural daughter of Charles the Second, and lady of Lord Ratcliff, (now Earl of Derwentwater,) to whom Dryden dedicated his Third Miscellany.

† Arabella, daughter of Sir Edward Allen, Bart. She first married Francis Thompson, Esq., and was at this time the wife of Lord George Howard, (eldest son of Henry, the sixth Duke of Norfolk, by his second wife,) who died in March 1720-21.—Malone.

‡ Elizabeth, daughter of Digby, Lord Gerard, and second wife of James, Duke of Hamilton, who was killed in a duel by Lord Mohun, in November, 1712.—Malone.

§ Elizabeth, daughter of Charles Bertie of Uffington, in the county of Lincoln, Esq. a younger son of Montague, the second Earl of Lindsey. She was at this time the wife of Charles Mildmay, the second Lord Fitzwalter of that family.—Malone.

‖ Margaret, daughter of George, Lord Chandos, and relict of William Brownlow of Humby, in Lincolnshire.

¶ Richard Norton of Southwick, in Hampshire, Esq. Cibber's comedy, entitled, "Love's last Shift," was dedicated to this gentleman, in February 1696-7. Mr. Norton died December 10, 1732, in his sixty-ninth year.

** Anthony Henley, of the Grange, in Hampshire, Esq., a man of parts and learning, and a correspondent of Swift, who died in 1711.

†† Perhaps General Webbe, whose "firm platoon" was afterwards celebrated by Tickell. Of the prowess of Mr. Beereton no memorials have been discovered.—Malone.

‡‡ Lord Henry Scott, second surviving son of James, Duke of Monmouth, who was born in 1676. In 1706 he was created Earl of Deloraine; and died about 1730.

§§ The Earl of Derwentwater's poetry, which, according to Dryden, was none of the best.

playhouse in Drury-Lane; and my Lord Scarsdale is the patron of Betterton's house, being in love with somebody there. The Lord Scott is second sonn to the Duchess of Monmouth. I need not tell you who my Lady Darentwater is; but it may be you know not her Lord is a poet, and none of the best. Forgive this hasty billet from

Your most obliged servant,
JOHN DRYDEN.

For Mrs. Stewart,
Att Cotterstock, near Oundle,
in Northamptonshire, These.
To be left with the Postmaster of Oundle.

LETTER XLVII.

TO MRS. STEWARD.

MADAM, Tuesday, March 12th, 1699 [-1700.]

'TIS a week since I receiv'd the favour of a letter, which I have not yet acknowledg'd to you. About that time, my new poems were publish'd, which are not come till this day into my hands. They are a debt to you, I must confess; and I am glad, because they are so unworthy to be made a present. Your sisters, I hope, will be so kind to have them convey'd to you; that my writeings may have the honour of waiting on you, which is deny'd to me. The town encourages them with more applause than any thing of mine deserves; and particularly, my cousin Driden accepted one from me so very indulgently, that it makes me more and more in love with him. But all our hopes of the House of Commons are wholly dash'd. Our properties are destroy'd; and rather than we shou'd not perish, they have made a breach in the Magna Charta;* for which God forgive them! Congreve's new play has had but moderate success, though it deserves much better.† I am neither in health, nor do I want afflictions of any kind; but I am, in all conditions, Madam,

Your most oblig'd obedient servant,
JOHN DRYDEN.

For Mrs. Stuart, att Cotterstock,
near Oundle, These.
By the Oundle Carrier, with
a book directed to her, These.
Northamptonshyre.

LETTER XLVIII.

TO MRS. STEWARD.

MADAM, Thursday, April the 11th, 1700.

THE ladies of the town have infected you at a distance; they are all of your opinion, and like my last book of Poems‡ better than any thing they have formerly seen of mine. I always thought my verses to my cousin Driden were the best of the whole; and to my comfort, the town thinks them so; and he, which pleases me most, is of the same judgment, as appears by a noble present he has sent me, which surprised me, because I did not in the least expect it. I doubt not, but he receiv'd what you were pleas'd to send him; because he sent me the letter, which you did me the favour to write me. At this very instant I heare the guns, which, goeing off, give me to understand, that the King is goeing to the Parliament to pass acts, and consequently to prorogue them; for yesterday I heard, that both he and the Lords have given

Now in his throne the king securely sat;
But O! this change alarm'd the rival state;
Besides, he lately bribed, in breach of laws,
The fair deserter of her uncle's cause.
This roused the monarch of the neighbouring crown,
A drowsy prince, too careless of renown.*
Yet prompt to vengeance, and untaught to yield,
Great Scarsdale† challenged Skipwith to the field.
Whole shoals of poets for this chief declare,
And vassal players attend him to the war.
Skipwith with joy the dreadful summons took,
And brought an equal force; then Scarsdale spoke:—
Thou bane of empire, foe to human kind,
Whom neither leagues nor laws of nations bind;
For cares of high poetic sway unfit,
Thou shame of learning, and reproach of wit;
Restore bright Helen to my longing sight,
Or now my signal shall begin the fight.
Hold, said the foe, thy warlike host remove,
Nor let our bards the chance of battle prove:
Should death deprive us of their shining parts,
What would become of all the liberal arts?
Should Dennis fall, whose high majestic wit,
And awful judgment, like two tallies, fit,
Adieu, strong odes, and every lofty strain,
The tragic rant, and proud Pindaric vein.
Should tuneful D'Urfey now resign his breath,
The lyric Muse would scarce survive his death;
But should divine Motteux untimely die,
The gasping Nine would in convulsions lie;
For these bold champions safer arms provide,
And let their pens the double strife decide.
The king consents; and urged by public good,
Wisely retreats to save his people's blood;
The moving legions leave the dusty plain,
And safe at home poetic wars maintain.

* The famous Betterton, who, in 1695, again divided the two companies, and headed that in Lincoln's inn Fields.

† Robert, third Earl of Scarsdale, a protector of Betterton's company.

* Alluding to the statutes imposing the oath of allegiance and supremacy on all Catholics, under the penalty of incapacity to hold landed property, 11 and 12 William III. cap. 4.

† The excellent comedy entitled the "Way of the World." It had cost Congreve much pains, and he was so much disgusted with the cold reception alluded to in the text, that he never again wrote for the stage.

‡ His Fables.

up the cause, and the House of Commons have gained an entire victory.* Though under the rose, I am of opinion, that much of the confidence is abated on either side, and that whensoever they meet next, it will give that House a farther occasion of encroaching on the prerogative and the Lords: for they, who beare the purse, will rule. The Parliament being risen, my cousin Driden will immediately be with you, and, I believe, return his thanks in person. All this while I am lame at home, and have not stirr'd abroad this moneth at least. Neither my wife nor Charles are well; but have intrusted their service in my hand. I humbly add my own to the unwilling High Sheriff,* and wish him fairly at an end of his trouble.

The latter end of last week, I had the honour of a visite from my cousine, your mother, and my cousine Dorothy, with which I was much comforted. Within this moneth there will be play'd for my profit, an old play of Fletcher's, call'd the "Pilgrim," corrected by my good friend Mr. Vanbrook;† to which I have added a new masque; and am to write a new prologue and epilogue. Southern's tragedy, call'd the "Revolt of Capua, will be play'd at Betterton's house within this fortnight. I am out with that Company, and therefore, if I can help it, will not read it before 'tis acted, though the authour much desires I shou'd. Do not think I will refuse a present from fair hands; for I am resolved to save my bacon. I beg your pardon for this slovenly letter; but I have not health to transcribe it.‡ My service to my cousin, your brother, who, I heare, is happy in your company, which he is not who most desires it, and who is, Madam,

Your most obliged obedient

Servant,

John Dryden.

For Mrs. Stuart,

Att Cotterstock, near Oundle,

in Northamptonshyre, These.

To be left with the Postmaster of Oundle.

* King William had made large grants of lands out of the forfeited estates in Ireland, to his foreign servants, Portland, Albemarle, Rochford, Galway, and Athlone, and to his favourite, Lady Orkney. The Commons, who now watched every step of their deliverer with bitter jealousy, appointed a commission to inquire into the value of these grants; and followed it with a bill for resuming and applying them to the payment of public debt; "and, in order to prevent the bill from being defeated in the House of Lords, they, by a form seldom used, and which very seldom should be used, tacked it to their bill of supply, so that the Lords could not refuse the one, without disappointing the other. The Lords, to secure themselves from that insignificancy, to which the form of the bill tended to reduce them, disputed, in some conferences with the Commons, the form of it with warmth; but the resumption which it contained with indifference. And in both houses, even the servants of the crown gave themselves little trouble to defeat it; partly to gain popularity, but more from national antipathy to foreigners, and envy at gifts in which themselves were no sharers. The King, making allowances for national weaknesses, and for those of human nature, passed the bill without any complaint in public, but with a generous indignation in private, which perhaps made the blow fall more heavy on his friends, when, in order to soften it, he said to them, that it was for his sake, and not for their own, they were suffering." —*Dalrymple's Annals.* William felt so deeply the unkindness offered to him, that he, prorogued the Parliament without the usual ceremony of a speech from the throne

* Mr. Steward.

† More commonly called Vanbrugh. In Dryden's age, the spelling of proper names was not punctiliously adhered to.

‡ Dryden died on the 1st of May, and this letter was written on the 11th of the preceding month. The prologue and epilogue were therefore composed within less than a month of his death.

END OF VOL. II.

CPSIA information can be obtained
at www.ICGtesting.com
Printed in the USA
LVHW112042130123
737132LV00003B/232

9 783375 134037